SO LITTLE TIME
and
POINT OF NO RETURN
[Two Complete Novels]

JOHN P. MARQUAND

So Little Time and Point of No Return

TWO COMPLETE NOVELS

LITTLE, BROWN AND COMPANY · BOSTON

The lines from "Easter Parade" by Irving Berlin are quoted by permission of Irving Berlin Music Corporation. Copyright 1933 Irving Berlin.

The lines from "School Days," words by Will D. Cobb, music by Gus Edwards. Copyright 1906 and 1907 by Gus Edwards Pub. Co. Copyright renewed. By permission Mills Music, Inc., and Shapiro Bernstein and Co., Inc.

The quotation on page 561 is from "The Boston Evening Transcript" from *Collected Poems 1909–1935* by T. S. Eliot, copyright, 1936, by Harcourt, Brace and Company, Inc.

The lines beginning "When I was one-and-twenty" are from *A Shropshire Lad* by A. E. Housman. Reproduced by permission of Henry Holt and Company, Inc.

The lines from Rudyard Kipling's "If" are quoted by permission of Doubleday & Company, Inc.

LIBRARY OF CONGRESS CATALOG CARD NUMBER 61–14546

PRINTED IN THE UNITED STATES OF AMERICA

SO LITTLE TIME

To
ALFRED McINTYRE

In memory of all the trips we have taken together over the rough roads of fiction

For the Reader Who Takes His Fiction Seriously

This novel is an attempt to depict certain phases of contemporary life, and it is hoped that these will be realistic enough to appear familiar to the reader. To create this illusion the names of certain widely known persons have been mentioned, particularly in the dialogue, although none of these persons actually appear in any scene. The active characters, and the backgrounds against which they move are drawn, as these always must be, from a reservoir of experience derived from what an author has seen, heard and read. If these characters are successful, they should exhibit traits which will arouse the reader's own recollection and should seem like persons of his own acquaintance. This, it must be emphasized, is only a trick of illusion observable in all presentable fiction. The persons in these pages are known to the author only in his creative mind. He has never known a world correspondent, for example, like Walter Newcombe. Individuals who have worked for him have been honest and faithful and have in no wise resembled the transient couples in these pages, or the busy Mr. Gorman. If these characters bear the names of real persons, this is a purely unintentional and unavoidable coincidence, considering the large population of the world. In short, no one here is intended to represent, however remotely, either accurately or in caricature, any actual person, whether living or dead.

A device, shopworn perhaps, but still effective, for evoking in a reader's mind the spirit of some period in the recent past is the quoting of a snatch of some popular song representative of that time. The author is most grateful to the music publishers for permission to quote occasional lines from their copyrighted works, and detailed acknowledgment appears at the end of this foreword. In this connection, the careful reader will note that a song about "looking for a happy land where everything is bright" has been used frequently and is seldom quoted in exactly the same way, since it was a parody fashioned in the first World War and still, as far as can be discovered, is word-of-mouth. It was parodied from a song, "The Dying Hobo," which appears in the anthology by Sigmund Spaeth, *Weep Some More, My Lady*.

For courteous permission to use the lines from various songs quoted, grateful acknowledgment is made to the following:—

To Leo Feist, Inc. for the line from "Give Me a Kiss by the Numbers" by Lieutenant Joseph F. Trounstine. Copyright 1918 Leo Feist, Inc. Used by special permission of the Copyright Proprietor.

To Mrs. Reginald DeKoven, for the line "It's half past kissing time, and time to kiss again," from the song by Reginald DeKoven.

To Edward B. Marks Music Corporation, for the line from the song

"Manhattan" from the "Garrick Gaieties," and the chorus from the song "Everybody Works but Father," Copyright Edward B. Marks Music Corporation, RCA Building, Radio City, New York; used by permission.

To Music Publishers Holding Corporation, for lines from the song "Who Are You With Tonight?" appearing on pages 108, 110 and 327, by permission of Remick Music Corp., Copyright Owners.

To Music Publishers Holding Corporation, for the lines from the song from "The Red Mill," appearing on pages 47, 190, 191 and 194, by permission of M. Witmark & Sons, Copyright Owners.

To Paull-Pioneer Music Corp., Copyright Owners, for the lines from "The Sidewalks of New York."

To Charles Scribner's Sons, for several lines from the poem "America for Me," from *Collected Poems of Henry van Dyke*, published 1930.

JOHN P. MARQUAND

KENT'S ISLAND
NEWBURY, MASSACHUSETTS
1943

Contents

SO LITTLE TIME

1

Why Didn't You Ever Tell Me?

In the mornings when they were in the city, they had breakfast on a card table in Jeffrey's study. The table was placed in front of a window which looked south over the chimneys and skylights of old brownstone houses. The geometric bulk of apartment houses rose up among them and the pointed top of the Chrysler Building and hazy large buildings stood beyond. In the morning those buildings seemed to have an organic life of their own, and their texture changed with the changing light.

Madge always had orange juice and Melba toast and black coffee without any sugar in it, although Jeffrey could not understand why. Madge had always been too thin and Jeffrey often told her that she would feel much better if she had a boiled egg or a little bacon in the morning, or perhaps oatmeal and cream. He could never understand why the mention of oatmeal and cream seemed to Madge revolting.

"The only thing I have left is my figure," Madge used to say. "And I'm not going to lose my figure."

Jeffrey always told her that she looked fine except when she looked tired, and how could she help looking tired if she didn't eat anything?

"I don't want to look like a contented cow," Madge used to say. "Besides you'd feel a great deal better if you just had orange juice and coffee. Breakfast always makes you lazy."

Jeffrey would tell her that breakfast was the only meal that ever pulled him together—that he had never been accustomed to working before eleven in the morning. And then Madge always said that it was because he was Bohemian—a word which always annoyed Jeffrey. She used to tell him that if he would get up at a quarter to eight in the morning like other people's husbands, he would get his work done with and not have it hanging over him until the last minute. Other people's husbands were out of the house and on their way downtown by eight-thirty, but Jeffrey was deliberately different because he wanted to be Bohemian. Jeffrey never could tell exactly what she meant by the term except that it embraced all those traits of his against which Madge never could stop struggling.

"Try to find another word for it," he used to tell her. "Call me a congenital loafer if you want, but whatever else we are, you've fixed it so we aren't Bohemian."

Sometimes Madge would laugh, because time had made it one of those controversies which had no rancor left in it.

"Darling," she would say, "you might get to be Bohemian almost any time."

Breakfast was always like that, but still it was a pleasant meal at which you could talk about plans without anything's worrying you too much. Madge wore her blue satin slippers that morning, and she wore her blue kimono with the white bamboo design on it. Jeffrey liked to see her in it because it seemed to add to the tilt of her nose and to the curve of her lips. She never looked serious in the morning. Jeffrey wore a Burgundy silk dressing gown and slippers that pinched his feet. He had to wear both the dressing gown and the slippers because the children had given them to him for Christmas and because Madge had picked them out herself.

"What's in the paper?" Madge asked.

"Just about the same as yesterday," he said. "Here, do you want to read it?"

She always asked him what was in the paper, but she never wanted to read it.

"I can't," she said. "You always leave it all twisted-up. When you get through with it all I can find is the obituaries."

Jeffrey picked up the paper again. In all the thousands of mornings they had spent together, she had always hated to have him read.

"Darling," Madge said, "if you want me to pay the bills, you'll have to put some more money in the account."

"All right," Jeffrey said.

"I can't pay the bills," Madge said, "until you put some more in the account."

"Where's Jim?" Jeffrey asked.

"He's still asleep," Madge said. "Don't wake him up, please don't, Jeffrey."

"It's time he got up," Jeffrey said, "all he does is sleep whenever he comes home. Where's Gwen?"

"Where she is every weekday," Madge said, "at school, of course. Other people's families get up in the morning. . . ." She began to open letters from the pile beside her plate. "Jeffrey, they want us to be patrons for the Finnish Relief Dinner. It's on the twenty-third."

Jeffrey lighted a cigarette and sipped his coffee. It was like every other morning. He always felt better when he drank his coffee. Madge picked up her silver pencil and a block of paper.

"Twenty-five dollars for the Finnish Relief," she said. "You'll have to have lunch on a tray today. Some of the girls are coming to lunch."

"That's all right," Jeffrey told her, "I'm going out."

"Where?" Madge asked.

"You can get me at the Astor," Jeff said, "and after the Astor I'll be at the theater. They're going to start rehearsing right after lunch. They may be going all night." Jeffrey was feeling better now that he was drinking his coffee. "This show is very lousy, darling."

"Can't you ever tell me your plans sooner, dear?" Madge asked. "They won't want you tomorrow, will they? Tomorrow's Saturday."

"What's happening Saturday?" Jeffrey asked.

"Darling," Madge said, "I wrote it down myself on your engagement pad.

What good does it do if you don't ever read it? We're going to Fred's and Beckie's for a nice October week end, and you know what happened last time. You can't keep putting it off. Fred and Beckie don't understand it, and I can't keep explaining to them."

"Oh God," Jeffrey said. "All right, all right."

"I know the way you feel about them, dear," Madge said, "but you know the way I feel about Beckie. Other people don't let old friends down."

"All right," Jeffrey said, "don't try to explain it. There's nothing to explain."

"Beckie keeps being afraid you don't like them," Madge said, "and I have to keep telling her that it's only the way you are. You know how hard they try to get people for you to talk to."

"I can talk to anybody," Jeffrey said, "as long as they don't play pencil and paper games."

"Darling," Madge said, "it's only because she wants you to do something you're used to and they don't play bridge."

"All right, all right," Jeffrey said, "as long as it isn't the names of rivers, and as long as I don't have to be tongue-tied and go out somewhere into the hall."

Madge reached across the table and patted the back of his hand.

"When you go anywhere," she said, "if you ever do go, you know you really do have a good time when you get there. Why, I can't ever get you to go home to bed." Madge frowned, and then she smiled. "It's just your act. Who do you think they're having for the week end?"

"Who?" Jeffrey asked.

"They're having Walter Newcombe," Madge said, "the foreign correspondent who wrote *World Assignment*. He's just back. He was at the evacuation of Dunkirk."

"What?" Jeffrey said.

"It's true," Madge told him. "You may think Fred and Beckie are dull, but interesting people like to come to their house. We never have anyone around like Walter Newcombe."

"My God," Jeffrey said, "Walter Newcombe? Is he back again? Why, he was here in April." And he saw that Madge was looking at him.

"You don't know him, do you?"

"Yes," Jeffrey said, "of course I know him."

The little perpendicular lines above her nose grew deeper. She was looking at him curiously as she still did sometimes.

"Jeff," she asked, "why do you keep things from me, as though you led a double life, as though I were your mistress? Where did you ever know him?"

Jeffrey began to laugh. "Why, he was one of the Newcombes who lived on West Street. The old man ran the trolley to Holden, and Walter was on the paper in Boston. He started out in the telegraph room just before I left, and he used to be on the old sheet down here too."

"Darling," she said, "I wish you'd tell me—why is it you never bring friends like that around here?"

"He isn't a friend," Jeffrey said. "I just know him. Besides you wouldn't like him much."

She lighted a cigarette, still looking at him, and the lines above her nose were deeper.

"It's like a wall," she said, "a wall."

"What's like a wall?" he asked.

"You never tell me things," she said, and she put her elbows on the table and rested her chin on the palms of her hands. "Even now, these little things come out. It makes you like a stranger; it's like waking up and finding a strange man in the bedroom; it isn't fair. I've told you again and again I want to know everything about you."

"When I try to tell you, you're always thinking about something else," Jeffrey said, and then he began to laugh again.

"What is it," she asked, "that's so funny?"

"I was thinking," Jeffrey said, "about a man I met once on the train when I was going into Boston to the old telegraph room. I used to commute, you know. That was the day Walter got his job there. He was a prize fighter."

"Who was a prize fighter?" Madge asked.

"Not Walter," Jeffrey told her, "the man on the train. It's funny—I haven't thought about it for years. It was in the smoking car of the old 8:12 and it hasn't got anything to do with anything at all, but it's just the sort of thing I don't tell you because you'd be bored. You ought to get dressed and order the meals, but I'll tell you."

When he told her things like that it always amused him to watch her, because she never understood—neither she nor anybody like her. It was in the summer of 1919, just after he got back from the war, and the smoking car of the old 8:12 hadn't changed. Just as many cinders blew through the open windows in the summertime and the seats had the same black leather and the same crowd got on at Norton and the same group turned the seats back to play pitch, when old Mr. Fownes, the conductor, brought out the pitchboard. They all took their coats off and sat in their shirt sleeves. It must have been at one of those stations before you got to Lynn that a stranger slumped into the seat beside him.

"Is this seat taken, Bud?" the stranger asked. It was obvious from the new occupant's breath that he had been drinking. He was a small wiry young man with a short nose and a red face and light blue eyes. He wore a purple suit with padded shoulders and a silk shirt with green stripes on it and a celluloid collar with a bright red necktie.

"Bud," the stranger said, "do you take anything?"

"Take any what?" Jeffrey asked.

"Any whisky, for Christ's sake," the stranger said, and he pulled a black pint bottle from his back hip pocket, extracted the cork and wiped the neck with his sleeve. "Here," he said, "for Christ's sake."

There was something appealing in the other's bid for friendship.

"Why, thanks," Jeffrey said. It was very bad whisky.

"Bud," the other asked him, "was you overseas?"

Jeffrey said he had been and he asked if the other had been there too, and he wiped the neck of the bottle and handed it back.

"They t'rew me out," the other said, and he beat his chest with his fist. "T.b.; they t'rew me out."

Jeffrey told himself that whisky was antiseptic.

"I'm in the game," the stranger said, and he looked proud and took another drink.

"What game?" Jeffrey asked him.

"The fight game," the stranger said, and his voice was louder.

"Oh," Jeffrey said, "you're a fighter, are you?"

"That's what I've been telling you, Bud," the stranger said. "They t'rew me out because I have t.b., and I can lick any son-of-a-bitch my weight."

The man's voice rose higher. He was disturbing the concentration of the pitch players.

"It must be nice to know you can," Jeffrey told him.

The stranger scowled at him. "You think I'm kidding, don't you, Bud?" he said. "You don't think I'm a fighter, do you, Bud?" and suddenly he thrust his fist under Jeffrey's nose. "All right, bite my thumb."

"Why should biting your thumb prove anything?" Jeffrey asked.

The stranger's voice grew belligerent.

"Go on," he shouted, "I tol' you, didn't I? Bite my thumb."

The little man had risen and was holding his thumb under Jeffrey's nose. The scene had caused a flurry, and nearly everyone else in the car was standing up.

"Sit down," Jeffrey said, "and have a drink."

"Go on," the stranger shouted, "like I tol' you, and bite my thumb."

There was a novelty in the invitation which appealed to the smoking car.

"Go ahead and bite it, fella," someone called, "if he wants you to."

There was only one thing to do under the circumstances. Jeffrey took the stranger's thumb and placed it between his back teeth and bit it hard. The little man did not wince. On the contrary, he seemed pleased.

"You get me, do you?" he inquired. "No sensation; I bust it, see? On Attell's jaw, seventh round at the Arena. Now you know me, don't you, Bud?"

"I ought to," Jeffrey said, "but I've been away for quite a while."

The stranger held out his hand, which was marked by the indentations of Jeffrey's teeth.

"I can lick any son-of-a-bitch my weight," he said. "My name's Kid Regan—get me, Kid Regan, Bud, and if you don't believe it, look at this."

With a quick gesture, he unbuttoned the front of his green striped shirt and displayed a blue spread eagle tattooed upon his chest.

"Now," he asked, "you believe I'm Kid Regan, don't you, Bud?"

"Yes," Jeffrey said, "that certainly ties it all together."

The stranger sank back in his seat.

"Well, for Christ sake, let's take something—" he said, and he pulled out his bottle.

Jeffrey stopped and poured himself another cup of coffee while his wife sat looking at him. He could still hear the sounds of the smoking car, and he could still feel it sway.

"Jeffrey," Madge asked, "did you make that up?"

"No, I didn't make it up," he said. "It's the sort of thing that happens. People act that way sometimes."

There was another silence; he could still hear the rattle of the car.

"Well," Madge asked, "go on, what else?"

"There wasn't anything else," Jeffrey told her. "When I got to the telegraph room, there was Walter Newcombe. Old Fernald had hired him that day. I just happened to remember it—there isn't anything else."

There was another silence while Jeffrey stirred his coffee.

"Darling," Madge said, "why didn't you ever tell me about that little man before? I love it when you tell me things, and it's quite a funny story."

Jeffrey shook his head. "It isn't really funny. Basically, it's sad. Maybe that's why I never told you."

"Sad?" his wife repeated. It was exactly what Jeffrey had meant. It was not her fault, but you could not tell her things like that.

"Yes," he said, "he was a sad little man. You see, he knew that he was through. He knew that he couldn't lick any son-of-a-bitch his weight in the world, darling." And Jeffrey looked out of the window at the buildings stretching beneath them, and there wasn't anything more to say.

"Tell me some more about Walter Newcombe," Madge asked him.

"There isn't any more to tell, darling," Jeffrey said, "he was just in the old telegraph room."

"But you haven't told me anything," she said, "not anything at all."

Jeffrey picked up his own mail beside the coffee cup.

"Maybe I'll think of something later," he said, "but it's getting late now." And Madge sat looking at him.

"Darling," she said, "I love it when you tell me things. That little man—maybe he was sad."

Jeffrey's mind was not where he wanted it, at all. He did not seem to be in New York; he did not seem to be anywhere. That was the trouble with getting mixed up in reminiscence which had nothing to do with Madge and the children. When he looked at the walls of his study and at the pictures, and at the books which he and Madge had bought and had arranged together, he had a most uncomfortable sensation. He could not believe that he owned such things as the red-backed Aldine Poets and the green Smith and Elder Thackeray and the Currier and Ives print of the "Country Home in Winter." He and Madge had bought them because they had both liked and wanted them, but he did not seem to own them.

"It's funny how people pop up when you least expect it," he said. "As a matter of fact, I saw Walter last April. He spoke at the Bulldog Club lunch."

"What's the Bulldog Club?" Madge asked.

"Oh, nothing much," he said. "Just one of those newspaper clubs."

"You never told me," she said. "Jeffrey, why don't you ever tell me anything?"

It made him feel wretched, because he could not think of any convincing reason.

"I don't know why," he said. "It didn't have anything to do with you and me."

She sat there silently in her blue kimono. Her brown eyes looked wide and hurt.

"Other people," she began, "other people–"

Jeffrey reached across the table and took her hand.

"Never mind about other people," he said, "I love you, Madge."

He had not realized he was going to say it, and when he did, it sounded like a complete answer to everything. She was looking back at him, still puzzled.

"I wish you'd say that more often," she said, and she sighed. "You're awfully hard to understand."

He never could see what there was in him that was puzzling, because to himself he seemed extraordinarily uncomplex. It was only that you could not share your whole life with anyone else in the world, although this was what women seemed to want. No two people, whether they were married or not, could possibly look at any subject in exactly the same way. Everyone's vision was warped by individual astigmatism. He picked up one of his letters and opened it and began to read before he heard her voice again.

"Jeff, is that from Alf?" She must have seen the writing. "You just sent him five hundred dollars, didn't you?"

"It looks as though he's broke again," he answered. "You know Alf."

But she did not know Alf the way he knew him. You could not share everything with anybody in the world.

"If you'd just put him on a definite allowance," she began. "Other people's brothers–" She stopped, and Jeffrey looked back at the letter. It was Air Mail from California. Soon there would be a telegram and then there would be a telephone call, charges reversed. He knew Alf.

"Jeffrey," he heard her say, "Jim's overdrawn. There's a letter from the Cambridge Trust Company."

Jeffrey folded his letter.

"When he tells me about it, I'll take it up with him," he said. Breakfast was over, and it was time that he was going.

"Don't forget," she told him, "to put some money into the housekeeping account this morning, and then there's the country–"

"What's wrong in the country?" Jeffrey asked.

"Closing the house," she told him. "Mr. Gorman had the Martinelli boy wrapping up the rosebushes. You know how much you like the garden."

"Oh yes," he said, "the garden."

"Jeff." A change in her voice made him look at her quickly. "You're not sorry, are you?"

"Sorry?" he repeated after her. "Sorry about what?"

"I mean," she said, "you've liked it, haven't you? The children and the country and being here in the winter. You *have* liked it, haven't you?"

You would think that everything was settled, and then when you least expected it, a question like that would come out of nowhere. He could not imagine why she had selected such a time to ask him.

"Why, of course I like it," he said. "Why, Madge, if you hadn't married me, I'd have been Bohemian."

"I just wonder sometimes," she said.

"If I've said anything," he began, "to make you think—"

"No," she said, "I just wonder sometimes, if it's what you really wanted. Jeff, we *have* had a good time, haven't we?"

"Look here," Jeffrey told her, "we're just having breakfast, aren't we? We're just beginning another day, aren't we? Don't talk as though you were going to die."

"All our friends," Madge said, "and the house in the country—I wouldn't have bought it if you hadn't wanted it—and the children. They are nice children."

"Look here," Jeffrey said, "why do we have to go into this the first thing in the morning? I didn't say the children weren't nice—they're swell. Everything is swell. The house in the country is swell, even the garage."

"You wanted the garage," Madge said.

"I didn't say I didn't want it," Jeffrey told her, "I just told you everything is swell."

"I just wonder sometimes," Madge said, "I just wonder what you'd have been like if we hadn't got married."

"Look here," Jeffrey told her, "I don't see why you bring this up. It's pretty late in the game to wonder—we'll be married twenty-one years December."

"Well, here we are," Madge said; "I didn't think you were going to remember."

"That's exactly the point," Jeffrey told her. "Here we are, and I'm not going to stay here any longer because I've got to get dressed and get out. Just remember everything is swell, that is, unless you're tired of it."

"No," she said, "of course I'm not. It's everything I've wanted."

Jeffrey walked around the card table and kissed her, and she clung to him for a moment.

"Jeffrey."

"What?" he asked her.

"Don't worry about the war. You can't do anything about it."

Sometimes when he thought she did not know anything about him, suddenly he found she knew just what he was thinking.

"It hasn't been on my mind at all," he said, but he knew she did not believe him. "Nothing's on my mind. Wait a minute, if we're going to Fred's and Beckie's, have you read *World Assignment?* Wait a minute." He crossed the room to one of the shelves and pulled out a book. "I haven't read it, either, but maybe you'd better look at it. Here it is. Walter gave it to me," and he opened the cover and showed her the flyleaf. "See, he wrote in it.

'Cheerio, to my old friend Jeff, with very sincere regards, Walter Newcombe.'"

Jeffrey stood leaning over her shoulder, and she looked up at him.

"Why, Jeff," she said, "you never told me that he gave you that book. I thought it had come from the Book-of-the-Month Club. You never tell me anything at all."

The elevator boy wore white cotton gloves that wrinkled above his knuckles.

"Good morning, Mr. Wilson," he said, "it's a fine morning."

"Yes," Jeffrey said, "it is a nice morning, isn't it?"

"It's always good weather in October," the elevator boy said.

"Yes," Jeffrey said, "October is always a fine month."

"October is the best month of the year," the elevator boy said.

"Yes," Jeffrey said, "that's so. October is always a good month."

The doorman held open the door for him. "Good morning, Mr. Wilson," the doorman said.

"Good morning," Jeffrey answered.

"It's a fine morning, Mr. Wilson," the doorman said.

"Yes," Jeffrey said, "it's a nice October morning."

"October, I always say," the doorman told him, "is the best month of the year."

Jeffrey was out in the street in the best month of the year, but he was not thinking about it.

"I wonder sometimes . . ." he heard Madge saying, but then, perhaps everyone occasionally wondered. He could hear her voice again. The background of sound made by the elevated and by the trucks and taxicabs had the same quality of rushing water which sometimes seems to reproduce a voice.

"Don't worry about the war."

You had to admire that ability of hers to turn her back upon anything unpleasant.

"Let's not talk about it now," she used to say.

You could get away from the war for a little while, but not for long, because it was everywhere, even in the sunlight. It lay behind everything you said or did. You could taste it in your food, you could hear it in music. And she was right, there was nothing you could do about it.

2

Portrait of the Artist as a Young Man

If you had known someone well long ago, it was hard to break the habit of thinking of him as he looked and behaved in what we sometimes call "those days." Back in those days Walter Newcombe had looked like a young clerk in a general store from the interior of Massachusetts. This was not peculiar because Walter did come from there and his uncle did keep a general store, although Walter's father was a motorman. After graduating from High School Walter attended Dartmouth. It was too far away now for Jeffrey to recall exactly how Walter got a newspaper job. After all, how is anyone ever taken on a paper? At any rate, Walter used to sit at the telegraph desk and when the Associated Press dispatches popped out of the tube, falling like light explosive bombs into a wire basket, Walter would pull them out of their leather projectiles, unfold and smooth the sheets, and hand them over to Mr. Fernald.

He was a thin blond boy with irregular teeth and incorrect posture. His nose always had a red, shiny look, and he wore steel-rimmed glasses. He also wore those elastic bands around his shirt sleeves—pink, crinkly elastic bands, to keep his cuffs from getting soiled. No one seemed to wear those things any more and even then they were a badge of crude unworldliness. Someone told Jeffrey later—because he had left the paper in Boston very shortly after Walter had been taken on—that Walter bought a pair because Mr. Fernald wore them. Old Mr. Jenks wore them too—Mr. Jenks who clipped the bits out of the foreign exchanges for Miscellany, and did the column called "What's New in Europe's Capitals" for the Saturday paper. His arm bands, however, were not conspicuous because Mr. Jenks always wore an old frock coat, except in midsummer, when he used to hang it up on the hook beside the water cooler. Mr. Jenks must have been close to seventy then, and he was a newspaper man of the old school. Years earlier, before he came to that safe port in the old telegraph room, Mr. Jenks had been the Paris correspondent for the old *New York Herald*—years earlier, and he brought with him a faint continental atmosphere and a bland sophistication that Jeffrey never forgot.

When the page for the last edition closed at ten minutes to four each afternoon, Edgar, the office boy, would bring out the dominoes, and Mr. Jenks and Mr. Fernald would play for a while to see who would pay for the five-cent cigars. Walter was the one who went to buy them at the United Cigar Store on the corner of Washington Street, just as Jeffrey had when he had started there. On the occasions when Mr. Jenks won, he would lapse into gay reminiscence concerning those bright lands across the Atlantic, for they were as fresh in his memory as though he had been there yesterday. He would usually tell of the time when he met Prince Henry of Prussia, or perhaps about his interview with that intrepid aviator, Santos-Dumont. His stories sounded somewhat like Du Maurier, and they went well with the fresh smell of ink from the composing room that blew down the dusty stairs from the floor above. Once when he was examining the photographs in the *Manchester Guardian* Mr. Jenks contributed an interesting sidelight on his private life.

"By thunder," Mr. Jenks said. He was looking at the photograph of a fountain in Stuttgart. The fountain consisted of a thinly draped girl holding a conch shell from which came a jet of water that descended into a basin held up by sea horses. "By thunder," Mr. Jenks said, pointing to the photograph of that marble figure, "I slept with that girl once, in Berlin, in 1885—" At least this was what his old friends on the paper told Jeffrey.

"What?" Walter said. "How could you? She's a statue, Mr. Jenks."

Walter was always a little slow on the uptake then, and when everybody began to laugh, he turned beet-red. He was a shy boy, and he knew that he had spoken out of turn, but Mr. Jenks was always kind to the young men. He never barked at them the way Mr. Fernald did.

"Yes, yes," Mr. Jenks said, "she's a statue now, but she wasn't a statue then. Her name was Tinka."

"Oh, God," Mr. Fernald said, "excuse me just a minute," and he pushed back his swivel chair and ran out front to the editorial room to tell Mr. Eldridge and Mr. Nichols, who did the columns called "The Listener" and "Books and Authors." And then Mr. Fernald went in back to the City Desk and then he told old Frank Sims, who was the foreman of the composing room. That is the sort of thing that sticks in a journalist's memory. Whenever any of the old crowd spoke of Walter afterwards, in spite of all the years between, they would somehow get back to the statue.

They would say, "But she's a statue, Mr. Jenks," and then although their ways had not crossed in years, and though Mr. Jenks was moldering in his grave, and though a lot of them were also dead or dead-broke, and though the old paper had folded up, somehow those bright days would come back and they would all be drawn together. Outsiders could never see why it was as funny as it really was. You had to be a part of the mystic brotherhood in that old telegraph room. You had to have the feel of it and the smell of it.

"My God," Walter said once, "can't anybody ever forget it? Why, they even told it at an informal little dinner that the Governor General gave for me in Hong Kong—and back in London, even Winston knows about it."

"Winston who?" someone asked, and Walter blushed slightly. He never seemed able to tell whether or not people were serious.

"Churchill," he said, "Mr. Churchill."

"How about the Duke of Windsor?" someone asked.

"Who? David?" Walter asked, and he brightened. Clearly he wished to get away from his salad days. "Did I ever tell you boys about that swim we took together at Deauville?"

Once, during the September that marked the second year of World War II, when Jeffrey had been in Boston, he had looked up Mr. Fernald in Woburn. It was years since he had "got through," as the saying was, and there was no longer any paper and he even had a sickening uncertainty as to whether Mr. Fernald might be alive or dead or in a poorhouse. But Mr. Fernald was there in Woburn in the house that he had bought out of his sixty-five a week. He was sitting on his front piazza with his feet up on the railing watching his boy Earl, who was a clerk in Kresge's, mow the patch of lawn out front. Mr. Fernald looked very frail and old, older than Mr. Jenks had ever looked. Mr. Fernald's coat was off, his vest unbuttoned, and sprinkled as it had always been with cigar ash, and he still wore those pink garters around his arms. It was hard to find anything to talk about until the telegraph room came into the conversation.

"Jesus," Mr. Fernald said, "do you remember Walter Newcombe? That was just before you went to New York." And Walter's face came back, with its shiny nose and the shock of yellow hair.

"I wonder," Mr. Fernald said, "what the hell ever happened. He was always a damned fool. How the hell did he ever do it?"

If you had ever known anyone in his early budding years, living through those chapters which a biographer might entitle "Boyhood Portents," it was hard to imagine that he ever could amount to much. Sitting there with Mr. Fernald seemed to Jeffrey a little like sitting in a projection room and running a picture backward just for fun. In both their minds, Walter Newcombe was running backward to the time that must have pleased him least; and after all, how had he ever done it? What hidden springs had there been within him that had pushed him out ahead? It was a little like those marathon runs, where some scrawny, hollow-chested boy, the last one who you would think could do it, would cough and wheeze his way out front.

"Why, hell," Mr. Fernald said, "I had to fire him because he couldn't write a twelve head—not to save his life he couldn't. He used to cry when he tried to write one. Hell's fire, all he could do right was to pull A.P. papers out of those leather tubes, and sometimes at that he used to tear them."

Jeffrey had almost forgotten about the type of headline on the old paper that was known in the composing room as "number twelve." It was one column wide and went down about six lines, a line and a word, each word growing shorter. The result was as monumental and beautiful as an old bookkeeper's penmanship, and you had to be versatile to have it fill the space and still make sense.

"I don't know," Mr. Fernald said, "maybe it was luck."

Luck might have been a contributing factor, but you couldn't get away with everything indefinitely just because you were lucky.

"Maybe it's because he never got married," Mr. Fernald said, and perhaps Mr. Fernald was thinking of himself as he watched the picture go backwards. "He didn't have to dress a lot of kids and buy them an education."

But this was not strictly true, because actually Walter had been married twice. His first wife was a trained nurse named Nancy something, who had taken care of him the time he had his tonsils and adenoids removed at the Presbyterian Hospital, shortly after Walter had also "got through" and had also arrived in New York. It may have been the removal of those obstructions which had changed Walter, but that was long ago, and Nancy had faded out of the picture during some European tour of duty. His second wife was Mildred Hughes—Mildred Hughes the writer—who used to do articles for *Good Housekeeping* and the *Companion* and the *Journal*, sometimes about factory conditions and sometimes about washed-out farmers' wives and stump farms and sometimes about society figures. Mildred had white hair and used a jade cigarette holder, but there was no use telling Mr. Fernald about Mildred, or that Walter had a daughter named Edwina, who had gold bands on her teeth and went to one of the big boarding schools, tuition free, because she was her father's daughter. There was no use telling Mr. Fernald that Walter had encumbrances.

Mr. Fernald snorted through his nose and chewed the end of his cigar.

"Why, he wasn't even a second-rate newspaper man," Mr. Fernald said. "He never had the makings. Yes, how the hell did he do it?—*World Assignment—Beware Those Honeyed Words—I Call the Turn.*"

As Mr. Fernald mentioned those works of Walter Newcombe's, the Literary Guild and Book-of-the-Month Club selections which fixed it so that Walter was good for five hundred dollars a night on any lecture platform, Mr. Fernald spat over the piazza rail.

"I'm not sour," he said. "I like to think of the boys in the old shop getting on, but Walter—how could he call the turn on anything? And every turn he's ever called is wrong because he isn't a newspaper man. Now you tell me, because I want to hear, how does he get away with it?"

There was no answer. There was nothing you could say. Walter had never sent Mr. Fernald one of those books, but that may have been out of delicacy because he had been fired, yet the old man would have liked to have one very much indeed.

"I wonder . . ." Mr. Fernald said. "Sometimes I think old Jenksy had something to do with it. 'All about Europe's Capitals.' Say, do you remember 'But she's a statue, Mr. Jenks'?"

3

Really Simple Fellows, Just like You or Me

Readers of *I Call the Turn* may recall perusing, perhaps with dubious pleasure, the human and warm thumbnail biography of Walter Newcombe that appeared on the rear of what is known in the publishing trade as the "dust jacket." This was prefaced by an informal snapshot of Walter taken when Walter was spending a week end at Happy Rocks, his publisher's country home. Thus it gave a mistaken idea of the luxury of Walter's surroundings, for only a few cynics realized that Walter was not comfortably at home. Walter was standing in front of the great fieldstone fireplace surrounded by shelves, ceiling high, of books which had been purchased from an English gentleman's library. This gave the impression that Walter was versed in the classics, which was not true, because Walter had stopped with Dickens' *Dombey and Son*, had let the Russians go with a hundred pages of *Crime and Punishment*, had read *Julius Caesar* and *The Mill on the Floss* in school English, and had done limited work on *The House of the Seven Gables* while at Dartmouth. In this photograph the camera had caught Walter swaying slightly, like the Tower of Pisa, a defect which was only partially corrected by the retouch artist of the Publicity Department. Walter was dressed informally in a gabardine coat, white flannels and tennis shoes. His eyes, without his glasses, looked innocent and startled, but his lips were compressed in a thin, determined line. The thumb of his right hand was thrust into the side pocket of his jacket and his other four fingers hung limply downward.

When you saw the photograph, the opening sentence of the biography—"Walter Newcombe, no relation to Thackeray's Colonel Newcombe, if you please"—seemed on the whole superfluous. It might be better if publishers did not assign bright boys and girls from Yale and Vassar to write about their authors with glowing human interest.

> In those all too rare moments [the sketch concluded] when Walter Newcombe is not on the plane to Lisbon, perchance on his way to see his old friend General Wavell in Cairo or may it be to hobnob for a while with some other world figure, say the Generalissimo or Madam Chiang Kai-shek in their bungalow at Chungking—he lives a quietly harassed life trying to finish another of his commentaries on this changing world. (The sooner the better, say his readers!) As this is written, Mr. and Mrs. Newcombe and their daughter Edwina are safely tucked away in the gardener's cottage of his publisher's country estate, where Mr. Newcombe complains that his portable typewriter is continually getting mixed up with two dachshund puppies and his daughter's roller skates. Someday, Mr. Newcombe says, he is going to write a book about Edwina.

Most of this was an imaginary half-truth, for Walter was never fond of dogs, and he did all his writing in an office in New York; but there was one bit of that "blurb" which was illuminating—a single sentence which must have come from something which Walter had said himself.

> Newcombe's career as a journalist, which saw its inception in Boston, really began when he joined those distinguished ranks of young men—and young women too—who first spread their creative wings in New York's old Newspaper Row, who hobnobbed with Heywood Broun and F.P.A. of the old *Tribune*, with Cobb of the *World*, and with Don Marquis of the *Sun*. . . .

It is doubtful whether Walter ever hobnobbed, except in the vaguest sense, with any of these individuals, but this was only a detail. All that was interesting was that Walter had thrust behind him those awkward days and all that kindly environment of the old telegraph desk. He always said that he only began to find himself when he walked into the City Room one morning and got himself a job on what he ever afterwards loyally called "the Paper"—or "the Old Sheet," in New York.

Walter appeared there in one of those critical journalistic periods when many New York dailies could not adjust to the changing styles and tastes of the Twenties. The Paper was like a little country in the throes of a social revolution. There were the same frantic changes of policy and format. In desperation the owner of the Paper had moved to town, completely abandoning his previous pursuits, and appeared at his office every day. There was a continual transfusion of new blood. Correspondents were snapped back from Europe and put on the slot, or were set to running the Morgue or taking wrappers off exchanges. New cartoonists came and went with new managing editors, city editors, promotion experts, dramatic editors, and feature writers for the new women's page. They all appeared like Kerenski as possible saviors of the Paper, but they were gone like a summer shower. Later, when people who worked there tried to remember Walter, it was very difficult, but then at this time you never knew who your boss would be the next morning, or whether you might be looking for a new job yourself in the afternoon. Besides, Walter had only been there for a little while before he was sent to the London Office.

In the past twenty years, the United States has been most fickle in its selection of types for hero-worship. It is difficult to realize, in the light of the present, that Bankers and Business Executives once were heroes, in the Twenties. Jeffrey Wilson could remember when the circulation of periodicals such as the *American Magazine* was built largely on the heroic backlog of Big Business. Pages were filled with photographs of bankers at play, and with inspiring interviews with men like the late Messrs. Schwab and Vanderlip, telling the youth of America how they, too, could succeed. This, of course, was before Bankers and Executives were swept away into the Limbo of disrepute when the dam of the depression broke, and before some wag at the Senate hearing placed that midget on the knee of Mr. Morgan.

After the Bankers came a new type of hero. He was the Man in White; he was that quiet, nerveless soldier fighting his lonely battle on the murky frontier of Science, strangling microbes, manufacturing artificial hearts, so that America might live. This era brought us *The Microbe Hunters* and *The Hunger Fighters* and young Dr. Kildare and hospital nurses and horse-and-buggy doctors and *Arrowsmith* and doctors' Odysseys; but by the middle of the Thirties the Doctor too began to lose his dramatic punch. That was when the Foreign Correspondent at last came into his own.

We discovered that the Foreign Correspondent was not a disreputable, disillusioned journalistic wastrel. The Foreign Correspondent, it all at once appeared, was not a stoop-shouldered man, bending over a typewriter or bickering with the cable office or living amid the smell of cabbage in some dingy apartment on the Boulevard Saint-Germain. The Correspondent, we suddenly realized, was a debonair man of the world, a streamlined troubadour who hobnobbed, as they said on Walter's jacket, with nearly everyone. The doors of the Chancelleries were open to him. Brüning, Hitler, Mussolini, Dollfuss, Simon, Churchill, King George and Léon Blum, Trotsky, Lenin, Stalin, the Shah of Persia, the Duke of Windsor, Gandhi, the Old Marshal, the Young Marshal, Sun Yat-sen, Kemal Ataturk, Konoye, Beneš, Tojo, and Prince Chichibu—all these gentlemen were familiar and rather amusingly uncomplex figures to Your Foreign Correspondent. There seemed to be no barrier of language, no shyness, no secret repressions when Your Correspondent tapped upon their doors. They might be in their palaces or in a political dungeon or devoting their attention to an attack of gallstones or international anarchy, but they still had lots and lots of time to see Your Correspondent; and they were genial, ordinary fellows, too, not stand-offish or stuck up, but very much like you or me. It seemed that they enjoyed ping-pong, or cattle raising, or a good laugh, or some quaint American gadget like an automatic cigarette lighter, or the latest volume of Edgar Wallace, just like you or me. It seemed that they all had all sorts of personal habits, just like you or me. They picked their teeth and they put their bridgework in a glass of water every night. They smoked cigarettes or drank warm milk. They loved dogs and rolypoly children. They were tousle-headed, florid-faced, tranquil, clear-eyed, filmy-eyed, lethargic, dynamos of nervous energy, and they put you at ease at once, just like you or me.

They were always in a disarming mood when they saw Your Correspondent, just a little tired, just a little wistful as they gazed back upon their achievements—when they saw Your Correspondent. Taken off their guard that way—something in Your Correspondent's personality must have done it, although really he was an ordinary fellow, too, just like you or me—they were trapped into being amazingly revealing. It is true that they were tactful and only too aware of the weight of state secrets, so that often they told Your Correspondent confidences off the record which may be revealed fifty or sixty years from now, confidences a bit too heady for you or me at present. Yet even so, subconsciously they gave still more. They gave by a lift of the eyebrow, by a nervous tic of the larynx, by an involuntary fidgeting in their padded chairs, by a far-off look out of the window at the chimney pots of London, at the majesty of the Dolomites, at the minarets of Istanbul, at the miniature quaintness of the Nippon countryside—but Your Correspondent understood those hidden meanings. There was an invariable communion of souls between Your Correspondent and his subject which resulted in a mutual perfection of comprehension and a wholesome and mutual respect each for the other —Your Correspondent went away from there feeling that he had made another friend. Although he could never tell you or me quite all about it (because not the greatest writer in the world could wholly express the essence of that communion), still Your Correspondent brought away something that he would always remember—the sad lilt of a voice, the brave self-confidence of a laugh, the silence of that austere little room in the palace, or perchance the snap of a coal in the grate while outside yellow fog billowed through the streets of London. Your Correspondent saw it all. He felt, as he never had before, the gathering of great imponderable forces in the making, the tramp of peoples inexorably on the march, the gathering of the clouds signifying what?

It didn't matter what. Your Correspondent saw it; he sensed it; he vibrated with it. It turned out that Correspondents were not the humdrum lads whom we used to know. The *apéritifs* of Europe's capitals, the rice wine of Japan, had done a lot to change them in the middle 1930's. The world knew it when suddenly they broke away from their newspaper columns and began to give a jaded, worried nation the benefit of their personal confessions. There were *Personal History* and *The Way of a Transgressor* and *I Write as I Please*; but there is no need to call the roll of those volumes—*Inside Europe*—*Assignment in Utopia*—*Inside Asia*—those men had seen everything.

When *World Assignment* by Walter Newcombe was published it is said that his publisher, Sinclair Merriwell, was somewhat dubious. In fact, Mr. Merriwell admitted as much himself with rueful humor that made the tables rock with sympathetic laughter at one of those Book and Author Luncheons at the Hotel Astor. He actually thought—publishers, you know, never do know a good thing, even when it is right under their noses—that Mr. Newcombe's manuscript, which he had brought timidly to the office himself, believe it or not, all done up in a cardboard hot-water bottle carton, was just another of those books. But the Book-of-the-Month Club had taught him better and so also had the public, the most intelligent public in the world. Mr. Merriwell wanted right here and now to apologize to the public, and to tell them that they knew more about books than he did. They had given *World Assignment* the accolade. They had seen its inner quality, that literary essence which raised it above mere adventure, mere personal chronology, mere journalistic analysis.

Yet, what was that quality? Once, in a confidential mood and very much off the record, Walter's publisher had said that he was everlastingly damned if he could say.

"Don't quote me," he said, "but I took it to balance the list. There was too much whimsy-whamsy and we needed something heavy, but who ever heard of Newcombe? But that's the beauty of publishing. I had never heard of him, and now he's a great friend of mine—one of my best friends, and we have him tied up for his next two books as long as they aren't fiction."

It was easy enough to say that the works of Walter Newcombe possessed a plus quality of literary essence, as his publisher put it in that speech at the Astor, but it was more difficult to define what that essence was. When the Stanhope Agency added Walter to its literary stable, George Stanhope expressed it differently.

"Walter Newcombe," Stanhope said, "certainly has a whole lot on the ball."

Yet, when pressed to be more specific, George Stanhope could not tell what it was that Walter had on the ball. *World Assignment* was on the whole quiet and unoriginal compared with the efforts of his competitors. To Walter, Paris was not "a jewel encircled by the loving but avaricious arms of the silver Seine." What impressed him more than the width of the boulevards was the stone buildings. "They have a spaciousness," Walter wrote, "which somehow always reminds me of the steps of the New York Public Library." He did not react like Napoleon when he beheld the pyramids. He was mainly amazed that you could walk right up the sides. Rome, Walter observed, had been disfigured by Mussolini, much more than by King Victor Emmanuel, because Mussolini had uncovered a great many more pagan ruins than were necessary. Teheran, in Persia, Walter found, was a conglomeration of French-looking villas, hardly worth a visitor's time. What had interested him most was the sight of some crabs by a drain in one of the Shah's palace gardens—crabs, although Teheran was exactly so-many miles away from the Caspian Sea. Somehow Peking was not what he had thought it would be in the least. All the buildings were the same height except the Pekin and the Wagon Lits Hotels. And China did not smell as badly as he had expected it to. In Tokyo he had trouble with the sunken bathtubs made of mosaic blocks in Mr. Frank Lloyd Wright's earthquake-proof hotel. Walter confided to his readers that he had scraped himself severely in one an hour previous to his being received by Prince Chichibu.

His reactions to the great figures in his world gallery of portraits were equally unexciting. If it had not been for the background of the Quirinal Palace, Mussolini would have reminded him of a friend of his who had been in the engineering company which had built the George Washington Bridge. When Herr Hitler lost his self-consciousness, as he did after the first few moments of their meeting, Walter observed that he was "quite a lot of fun." (This remark was deleted from the annotated and revised war edition of *World Assignment.*) If Stalin's hair had been a little shorter and he had been minus a mustache, Walter would have thought that he was entering the room of his old High School principal.

Jeffrey thought it was hardly fair to take these extreme examples from *World Assignment* and set them all together, as they gave an exaggerated impression of stupidity and gaucheness. The truth was that there was a dullness in Walter's work which lent it the authenticity of Daniel Defoe. An innocence about his paragraphs and periods, a completely gullible acceptance of everything he saw, were exasperating until they became almost subtle. Walter saw everything, and he put down everything. This may have been the "plus quality" of Walter's work. Every reader of *World Assignment* felt that he knew exactly what Walter meant, and yet each reader closed the book with a different impression. If you did not like Mr. Léon Blum, you were sure that Walter did not. If you did like Léon Blum, you could grasp the conviction of Walter's enthusiasm.

In his later works his world stood a little more breathless, waiting for the turn of fate, its drama moving forward with the inexorable sweep of Greek tragedy. He began to write of shepherd's pipes ushering in the spring above the anemone-incrusted hills of Greece, their brave notes rising above the rumble of approaching forces. Yet even through these picturesque periods, Walter still remained simple. And that perhaps was the whole answer to Walter Newcombe—the guileless simplicity that had made him say, "But she's a statue, Mr. Jenks." He was still walking down the path of life saying that she was only a statue, in a great many different ways.

4

Just a Report from London

Sometimes it seemed tragic to Jeffrey Wilson that his past, and perhaps the past of anyone else, divided itself into compartments each completely separate from the other and without communicating doors. He would live for a while in one of those compartments among familiar faces, familiar scenes, and then, without ever knowing quite the basic reason for it, some inner force of growth or of decay would move him out of there. Once, at one of those week-end parties out in Connecticut, when it had been raining and when some people named the Hoadleys had come in with some of their guests, and when the Jessups had come in with some more guests, and when everybody began putting ice cubes into glasses, trying to think of something to say when there was nothing to talk about at all, Jeffrey had brought up the subject of compartments. He had not intended for a single minute to hold the whole room spellbound; he had simply found himself sitting in a corner with a pale blond girl, who wore a canary-yellow sweater and whose name he had not caught. They had talked first about the rising price of gin, and then for no particular reason about electric refrigerators, and then about the use of bone meal as a fertilizer for suburban gardens. At this point Jeffrey found it simpler to do what he had done before, to carry on a monologue, rather than cope with an extraneous personality who would never mean anything to him in the present or the future. After the bone meal, he began to talk about compartments. It did not matter to him that the blond girl looked confused—it was easier to do the talking all himself. It occurred to him that the senior Oliver Wendell Holmes had once presented a similar idea in his familiar schoolroom poem "The Chambered Nautilus." The shellfish of Dr. Holmes—and Jeffrey had never seen one—kept building pearly rooms and then moving out of them.

"In other words," Jeffrey said, "it was a Victorian shellfish, rather Late than Middle."

"I don't see how a shellfish can be Victorian," the blond girl said, and she tittered. "What are we talking about, and why is it Victorian?"

Jeffrey had not intended to speak loudly. He would have stopped if he had known that other people were listening.

"Because the compartments were lined with pearl," he said. "Now, most of my compartments aren't lined with pearl, and I don't believe yours are either."

"I don't know what you're talking about," the blond girl said, but it did not bother Jeffrey.

"It's about the phases through which you pass in living," Jeffrey told her. "You know a lot of people, and then you meet a lot of other people and forget the first people, and then you meet a lot more and forget again. I only mean you can't keep them all together."

Then Madge heard him across the room.

"Don't mind Jeff," she called, "think nothing of it. Jeff's only sounding off again."

"You frightened her," Madge told him afterwards. "She didn't know what you were leading up to, and now she will tell everyone you were drunk."

"I was only trying to talk to her," Jeffrey said. "I had to, didn't I?"

"You know you were doing it on purpose," Madge said. "You know just as well as I do that most people don't like ideas. They don't expect them from you—only from a celebrity, and you're not a celebrity."

Jeffrey told Madge that he did not have the slightest desire to be a celebrity—but it was true about compartments.

Jeffrey could divide his life into them, and there were some about which Madge knew nothing, and he could not explain them to her clearly any more than she could explain to him what had happened to her the year she had come out.

"I wish you would tell me more about that," Madge had asked him sometimes, but he was never able to tell her, because the walls were sealed.

"Why don't you ever bring any of those people around?" Madge would say sometimes, but it never worked—bringing those people around—any more than explaining them ever worked. They were the shadowy dwellers in the forgotten mansions of the soul.

It was hard even for Jeffrey to recall what he had ever seen in some of those acquaintances or how they had ever fitted into the pattern of his life. Occasionally it shocked him to hear his name called and to see someone suddenly who remembered all sorts of things which he had forgotten, someone in whose mind he still lived vividly—younger, gayer, still moving about in performances which he had left forever. Waldo Berg was just like that.

Back in the days when Jeffrey had first come to New York, Waldo Berg was one of the Sports Writers on the paper where Jeffrey had worked down on Park Row. Waldo Berg could not have been more than three or four years older than Jeffrey, but he seemed to Jeffrey a man of the world—a leader in his profession. He had a two-room apartment in the Village off Sheridan Square. He knew bartenders and policemen by their first names, and he had been generous to Jeffrey.

When Jeffrey was standing on the corner of 43d Street and Fifth Avenue waiting for the lights to change, someone called to him, and there was Waldo Berg. It was early April, in the spring of 1940, six months before Jeffrey and Madge had sat that morning discussing Fred and Beckie, and the crowd on Fifth Avenue looked shabby, and Waldo Berg looked shabby, too. The ends of the sleeves of his black overcoat were shiny, the band of his gray felt hat, perched on the back of his round bald head, was greasy. Waldo himself appeared pale and bloated, a weary projection of the way he used to look. He made Jeffrey conscious of his own custom-tailored suit, of the shine on his brown low shoes and of the crease in his trousers.

"Why don't you ever ask him around?" Madge would have said. "You know I love to see your old friends."

Madge would not have loved to see Waldo Berg, and Waldo would surely not have loved to see Madge, but Madge would have been nice about it.

"He was interesting," Madge would have said, "if he hadn't kept dropping ashes on the rug. And I was perfectly cordial to him, wasn't I? I didn't high-hat him at all, did I? I always like your old friends, and I always get on very well with them, but you never bring them around."

That was what Madge would have said, and there would not have been a word to answer. There would only have been inadequacy and embarrassment. There was nothing so dangerous or so impossible as to try to mix divergent worlds.

"Hey," Waldo called. "Hey there, Jeffie. How are you, you big bastard?"

Jeffrey recalled that no one had called him "Jeffie" except back in the past.

"Why," Jeffrey said, "hello, Waldo." He was thinking that they had been great friends once. Waldo had been kind to Jeffrey back there, and now it was all gone. It was the sort of kindness you could never repay, the sort of friendship that could only last back there.

"Cripes," Waldo said. "Where are you eating? Come on to the Bulldog meeting, or can't you stand the food?"

There was something elaborate about it, and something sad. Waldo was asking him to lunch, and at the same time he was telling him to go to hell if he did not want to come. There were plenty of things Jeffrey should have done, but Waldo had fixed it so that he had to go to lunch.

"I can take it if you can," Jeffrey said. "Where are they eating now?"

"Up on top of the Hotchkiss," Waldo said, "over by Lexington Avenue. Poops is talking to us—off the record, just to his old pals. Poops was in the newspaper game once himself."

"Who's Poops?" Jeffrey asked, and Waldo was silent for a moment while they both tried to turn the clock back.

"He may be Walter Newcombe, the news ace, to you," Waldo said, "but we used to call him 'Poops' in the sports department, and he's Poops to me—Poops." And Waldo made a vulgar noise.

Jeffrey had never been a member of the Bulldog Club, a name connected, of course, with the early edition of a morning newspaper, but in the past he had occasionally been present at the luncheon meetings. The Bulldog Club was one of those organizations of reporters and editors and its beginnings were shrouded in doubt, because successive careless secretaries had lost the early records, just as its treasurers were apt to lose the account books. There was no documentary way of disputing the rumor that the Bulldog Club had been founded either by Horace Greeley of the *Tribune* or by Bennett of the *Herald*. It was even said that it was older than the Gridiron Club at Washington, which meant that its members thought highly of it. It was important enough to cause those national figures known to the trade as "big names" genuine pleasure when they were asked to speak for fifteen or twenty minutes on any subject they pleased, entirely off the record, at the

Club's bimonthly luncheons. Certain hotels were happy to receive the Club, even though many of its members spilled, broke glasses, tried to run up bills for the Martinis at the bar, and drew diagrams on the tablecloths. The Club had a definite publicity value, what with the radio commentators and the guests of honor who appeared in the hotel lobby, and besides, it was always well to be in right with those people whom hotel managers affectionately called "newspaper boys and girls." Siegfried Carter, who wrote a column called "Gotham's Snacks and Napery," was a member, and so was Ellen Burton Kinsley, whose "Mr. Doakes Surveys the Menu" had a wide popular following. At any moment they might write some laudatory line:—

> By-the-by, if you and Someone Else are starved both for swing and for canapés, glide down the red velvet carpet to the air-conditioned Bijou Room at the Hotchkiss and bask in the gracious magic of André, who rules that tiny but uncrowded bit of Shangri-la.

The Hotchkiss told you that it was "your New York home, small enough to find your way around in, tucked away from the wear and tear of the metropolis, yet a mere stone's throw from shop, train or theater." Also, every room had been redecorated and it had a sun deck and a big bar and a "Bijou Bar." The bellboys wore white duck trousers and horizon-blue mess jackets.

"Bulldog Club on the fifteenth floor," they were calling in the lobby. "Fifteenth floor, please. Bulldog Club, please, on the fifteenth floor, please."

The elevator was jammed with loud-voiced members of the Bulldog Club. Up on the fifteenth floor the corridor and the cocktail lounge were jammed with more members, many of whom were furtively hiding their coats and hats in odd corners where they could get them in a hurry.

"Put it behind the palm pot," Waldo said. "Why stand in line and pay a dime?"

The formality of the Hotchkiss lobby had evaporated on the fifteenth floor. The Hotchkiss staff, although used to handling conventions, had a harassed and hunted look. The mess jackets of the bar boys were moist from mixed drinks and perspiration, but they still said "please."

"Watch it, please," they said, as they carried the trays. "Gangway, please."

They were being treated with an undue familiarity by the Bulldog Club. The members were addressing them by the names of motion picture stars and pugilists.

"Snap into it, Chaplin," the members were calling to them. "Six more Martinis, Ronald. I said old-fashioneds, Banjo-Eyes."

The members blew clouds of cigarette smoke into each other's eyes. They were all ages, through youth to middle age, but their mouths looked alike, and their eyes. They all had the same good-natured cynicism, the same tinge of disillusioned bitterness. They had been everywhere and seen everything. They had seen charity dinners at the Waldorf and Spanish street-fighting and executions at Sing Sing, and they still were ready for more. Even if they hadn't seen all this, they could look as though they had. They were neither proud of themselves nor sorry for themselves. They all knew each other, and they didn't care how they looked, and they were not going to throw their cigarette butts into those Chinese vases filled with white sand—they were going to throw them anywhere they damn pleased.

"Hey, Toots," Waldo said, "Jeffie, here's Toots Flannigan, you know Toots Flannigan." Jeffrey did not know her, but it did not matter. He was glad to be there, and to watch all the faces and listen to the noise. He was no longer a part of it, but he had been once.

"Hey, big boy," Waldo called to the waiter.

"Let me order," Jeffrey said, "this is on me." But Waldo would not let him.

There was no social effort, no make-believe. It seemed that a lot of them had been in the reporters' car on the train which had carried King George and Queen Elizabeth across Canada and back, and one of them named Shorty was telling how he had asked the King to sit in on a crap game.

There was a sound of a gong booming through the cocktail lounge, the same sort of gong that used to tell visitors to leave the ship and go ashore.

"Please take your seats in the dining room, please. Table numbers on the tickets, please."

"Say it in French," someone called.

"Jeffrey here knows Newcombe," Waldo said.

Everybody looked at Jeffrey.

"Yes," Jeffrey said, "I used to know him. We worked in the same telegraph room in Boston, and we came to New York about the same time."

"Jeffrey used to be a newspaper man once himself," Waldo said.

Everyone looked at him suspiciously. It had been a long while ago. Jeffrey had never felt so lonely.

The food and the Sky View Dining Room of the Hotchkiss added a poignant sort of disappointment to Jeffrey's loneliness. It did not help him to realize that perhaps he would have enjoyed it ten years before. It did no good to tell himself that he was in a group of exceptional and interesting people. They were stamped with the same bourgeois sort of unreality as the Hotchkiss Sky View Dining Room itself.

The pillars of the dining room and the beams along the ceiling were festooned with artificial ivy, and from the ivy were suspended paper New Year's bells, although it was the seventh day of April. The food had the flat unwholesome flavor of a standardized caterer's selection. The clear and lukewarm consommé, the pallid and heavily creamed chicken, the tough-skinned green peas and the accompanying plate of vegetable salad, and then the half-melted brick of green, white and orange ice cream, sat heavily on Jeffrey's stomach. Everyone that he could see consumed it happily, and why? They were the actors in an endlessly repeated national gastronomic drama. He thought of all the other festooned dining rooms that stretched in belts across the continent, tended by other waiters in other mess jackets. At that very moment, thousands of other groups were in those other dining rooms eating their creamed chicken and green peas. Rotary Clubs were in that bond of fellowship, and Lions, and Elks, and Brotherhoods of Redmen, and American

Legion Posts, and Daughters of the Revolution, and Daughters of Rebecca. They were all eating their creamed chicken at that moment, and there was not much time, because speakers everywhere were among them, waiting to say a few words.

It gave Jeffrey a cold sensation in the pit of his stomach. Why were they all together? Was there comfort in doing the same thing? There must have been some comfort. They must have felt vaguely what he was feeling, a need for companionship, because they were moving into a grim, uncharted future without their own volition, and because together there was some futile hope that they might find some solution. They would not find it, but they would meet and try again.

The air was smoky and stuffy. The waiters were bringing small cups of coffee. "Sugar, please," they were saying.

"Hey," Waldo asked him, "what's on your mind?"

Waldo had lighted a cigar; he had chewed the end of it; he had dipped the end of it into his coffee.

"I was just wondering what it's all about," Jeffrey said.

There was a flicker in Waldo's eyes, a momentary glimmer of interest. Waldo's face was fat and impassive, but Waldo understood him. It brought them closer together, just as though he had said something profound.

"Yeh," Waldo said, and his voice was gentle. "I know—I know." And he pushed back his chair to get a better view of the long speakers' table, and folded his hands across his stomach.

The president of the Bulldog Club, a florid-faced man with gray temples, was pounding the table with a small black mallet and adjusting a microphone in front of him. First the microphone stuck; then it collapsed and his neighbors to right and left snatched for it and someone tipped over a glass of water. Then the speaker's voice sounded simultaneously through horns fixed at each corner of the banquet hall. The volume of sound, and the supernatural illusion that his voice came from everywhere at once, demanded a solemn and world-shaking pronouncement.

"Will the waiters kindly refrain from clearing off plates from the tables during the speaking period?"

That was all he said, and then he paused as though he expected some reaction. Then he picked up a card and adjusted his glasses.

Before the speaking, he continued, he would like to call attention to some distinguished guests who were with us this afternoon. When he read their names, would they please stand up and take a bow so that everyone could see them? First there was a lovely lady known to all of us, Goya Ayres, just in from Hollywood, and we're certainly glad to have you with us, Goya. After Miss Ayres, the celebrities began to fade. They were Leo Fish, editor of that well-known trade paper, the *Something World*, and Hal Ryan, ace Washington correspondent, and last but not least, an ace commentator, Will Sykes (everyone knows Will). And now, our fellow member, Mr. H. J. Jacoby, would say a few words about the speaker.

A chair fell over as Mr. Jacoby stepped to the microphone. Mr. Jacoby was lantern-jawed, and had plainly taken his assignment seriously, for he held a typewritten sheet before him, which quivered in his hand. First Mr. Jacoby cleared his throat. It sounded like tearing cloth over the public address system.

"Walter Duranty," Mr. Jacoby said, "has defined a successful foreign correspondent as one who is under the bed when the assignation takes place. That, I believe, is where Walter Newcombe has been always. Born in the best newspaper tradition, indefatigable in his search for fact . . ."

Mr. Jacoby's face grew frozen. It was clear that he had not intended to be amusing and the President banged the table with his hammer, and the rest of Mr. Jacoby's address, neither in content nor in delivery, was amusing. It rolled out in awkward sentences: "An inveterate traveler, he . . . An artist in word pictures, he . . ." The words droned on, and no one listened until the conclusion came.

"But it is superfluous for me to continue, when Mr. Walter Newcombe can speak for himself better than I can for him."

It was the first time in years that Jeffrey Wilson had seen him. Walter Newcombe stood in front of the microphone waiting while the applause died down. The pointed lapels of his coat and the pleated, high-waisted trousers showed that his clothes had come from across the ocean. Jeffrey respected Walter as he stood without fidgeting, not afraid to wait. Walter had developed a personality that now was gathering the room's attention. His hair, which had once been corn-colored, had grown darker and was more closely cut, but his nose was still thin and shiny, and his eyes had their same near-sighted intensity, and his voice, when he finally spoke, was nasal. All attributes which Jeffrey had remembered as awkward were now a part of character and stamped Walter with authenticity.

It was needless, Walter said, to tell the members of the Bulldog Club how glad he was to be there. It was like getting home to be with people who were all doing the same sort of work, and he hoped to see a lot of old friends afterwards, and he did not want to make a set speech. The Bulldog Club was no place for that. He just wanted to give a report of what he had seen and of what he had heard in London before he sailed. If any other members had been there in that early spring of 1940, they could give the report better than he could, and they would have to put up with his mistakes, because everyone made mistakes. Afterwards, he hoped that they would ask him questions because he needed their ideas, and their reactions. He wanted to feel that he was home again.

First, Walter said, he wanted to tell a story, and he told it. It was about a cockney cab driver in the blackout off Piccadilly. Even in the spring of 1940 the reporters from overseas were using the cockney as the mouthpiece for the British Empire. The cockney cab driver had talked to Walter about the "old woman." The old woman had been grousing (indeed she 'ad, sir) about the shortage of various commodities, and that little ill-nourished cockney cab driver had told her off. (I gave the old woman wot-for, sir.) He had told her that she might be pinched a bit, but it was nothing to how old Chamberlain with his umbrella was pinching that monkey Hitler and his 'Uns. That, Walter said, was his report from England in a nutshell.

He wished that he might have a map to bring home his points more accurately. He wished to make it clear that these ideas were not his own. They were the result of conversations with persons who naturally could not be named or quoted. He could say in brief that Germany was surrounded by a ring of steel, which was ever being tightened by the dominance of sea power. It was what the General Staff of France called the *cordon sanitaire*, and Walter used the phrase carelessly, with a conscious accent. He pictured a harassed Germany, surrounded by the crushing economic forces of the French and British Empires, which were slowly being mobilized. The mills of the gods grind slowly, Walter said, but they grind exceeding small, and over in London you had the exciting, thrilling sense of grinding mills. As a man high in the British Government had told him: "To use one of your jolly American expressions, we have old Hitler in the bag." Bag, Walter pointed out, was not quite the word for it. The grand strategy of England and France might better be compared to a tube of toothpaste or shaving cream. Walter paused, and the room was watchfully silent.

If they would permit him, Walter went on, he might take the liberty of mixing metaphors since no one on the desk was blue-penciling his copy. Walter paused and waited for the laugh, and sure enough, it came, but not too loud, because everyone was listening. If he might mix his metaphors, when France and Great Britain piped, Herr Hitler now must dance their tune. They could squeeze the German Reich as you might squeeze the shaving cream. As that cockney in the Piccadilly blackout had said in his simple way, they were squeezing Hitler. They only had to continue this process to make Hitler burst out where they wanted against that ring of steel. And why was this? It was because, for some unfathomable reason, during an entire winter Herr Hitler had not struck. Now he had thrown away his one chance. Now it was too late. There had been gaps in the line, but those gaps had been repaired during those dull months of the "sitzkrieg," the months that the cynics had called the phony war. The noose was drawing tighter. It was significant, he thought, that the British were mining the Norwegian coast. It was all part of the plan. That was Walter's report from England. But before he finished, he would like to tell one more story, which in some way rounded it off, because it showed the spirit of democracy. It was about the simple old charlady who used to do his hotel room in London. He fell to talking with her one morning. . . .

Jeffrey Wilson never heard the story of the charlady for he was thinking that if things had been a little different, if the chains of circumstances had changed, he too might have been like Walter Newcombe, picking up ideas.

"And now," Walter said, "that's about all. I'm not saying these ideas are mine, but I should love to know what you think of them. I don't need to say that a lot of you know more than I do, or that I should love to answer any questions." There was a moment's silence as he stood there and then there was applause. Chairs were being pushed back. The April 7th luncheon of the Bulldog Club was ending. A man in the back of the room had risen.

"I've got a question," he called. "I want to know if Mr. Newcombe believes any of this." The President rapped upon the table with his hammer, and Walter, smiling, spoke across the room.

"It's just a report from London," Walter said, "I didn't say I believed it. I was only repeating what I heard."

"Well," someone called, "how can you win a war without fighting?" Walter smiled and shrugged his shoulders.

"I'm only repeating a point of view," he said, and then he added the truest remark that he had made that afternoon. "With things the way they are over there, it's dangerous to make predictions. I only try to give a picture. That's all, a picture."

The President pounded his hammer again upon the table.

"And I'm sure that Mr. Newcombe has given us a very definite picture," he said. "One which we will carry away with us until the next meeting. Thank you, Walter Newcombe. Thank you for being with us."

"Thank *you*, sir," Walter said. "Thank you for listening to me."

They were pushing out of the room, and voices were rising. If you shut your eyes it brought you back to the end of a High School assembly. Everyone was going back to what he had been doing before, not any wiser, for in the end the talk had been like other talks. Walter Newcombe had said nothing which you could not have read in the morning *Times*, but then, perhaps no one had expected him to say anything. The only question may have been whether he knew anything that he did not say. It all made Walter Newcombe an enigma to Jeffrey Wilson. What right had he to be in that position? There were other injustices in the world beside the injustices caused by the accident of birth. There were the injustices caused by luck which no New Deal could rectify. Yet Walter must have had ability and experience must have changed him. He could not have been as simple as he had seemed, or as provincial—and yet there had been that story about the cockney and the blackout, and the quality of Walter Newcombe's voice. "*Cordon sanitaire*," he had said, and somehow his voice as he mouthed the phrase had left a sour note.

"Well," Waldo said, "so what?"

A little knot of people had penned Walter Newcombe into a corner of the room. The waiters were clearing off the dishes.

"I don't know what," Jeffrey said, "but it was funny."

"Funny?" Waldo answered. "It was nuts."

Jeffrey stood gazing at the corner of the room.

"Let's go and speak to him," he said.

"Baby," Waldo answered, "no pleated-pants is going to high-hat me. All those boys are pansies."

"Well, I'm going to speak to him," Jeffrey said.

"What the hell for?" Waldo asked.

Walter knew Jeffrey right away. There was no fumbling in his memory.

Walter knew him right away, but Jeffrey could not tell whether Walter was expressing pleasure or relief when he saw him. Whatever it was, the recognition pleased Jeffrey secretly.

"Why, Jeff," Walter called. "Hello there, Jeff. Wait, I'm going out with you." And he turned to the crowd around him. "I've got to be going," he said. "Jeff, don't go away."

The elevator was filled with a sickly perfume from the beauty parlor on the second floor. Walter stole a glance at himself in the elevator mirror. His hat was an olive-green featherweight felt.

"Old man," Walter said, "how about a drink in a quiet corner somewhere?"

There were a lot of other things Jeffrey should have done, but he put them from his mind.

"Let's get a taxi," Walter said, "and go up to my place."

"Where's your place?" Jeffrey asked.

"Just a couple of rooms," Walter said, "in the Waldorf Tower." He glanced at Jeffrey sideways. "I had to have some place to stay after the book came out. It's funny, isn't it?"

They were getting into a yellow taxicab by then with a skyview top.

"You can press the button, and the top goes right back, doesn't it?" Walter said. "It's funny, isn't it? All buttons. Everything over here is that way." And he glanced at Jeffrey again.

"What do you mean?" Jeffrey asked. "I don't quite follow you, Walter."

"I mean, I don't know where I am," Walter said. "Did you ever get that way, so you didn't know where you were? I mean that's why when I saw you it gave me sort of a kick. It pulled me all together."

There was no basis for friendship between them, absolutely none, but Walter was still speaking.

"Now, don't ask me questions," Walter said. "Don't ask me what I know."

Jeffrey felt better, and he began to laugh.

"Relax, Walter," Jeffrey said. "I know you don't know anything. You never did."

Instead of being annoyed, Walter laughed.

"Good old Jeff," he said, "that's what I wanted. Good old Jeff." And still Walter went on talking. "I don't want you to think this Waldorf Tower was my idea," he said. "I don't care for it myself, Jeff. You know I don't want to show off, don't you? I'm just the same as I ever was."

"Relax, Walter," Jeffrey said.

"When I got home," Walter said, "I didn't know anything about the book's going so big—I don't want you to think for a minute it's made any difference with me, Jeff. That's why I mean it's nice to see someone—like you."

"All right, Walter," Jeffrey said.

"I'm not showing off," Walter said. "That's what I know you're thinking, and it isn't so."

"That's great, Walter," Jeffrey said.

"Well, I've just been thinking out loud," Walter answered. "Just out loud without fanfare. Here's the Waldorf." Walter paused and snapped his fingers. "Mildred won't be there. You know Mildred, don't you, Jeff?"

"No, Walter," Jeffrey said, "I don't know Mildred."

"I thought everyone knew Mildred," Walter said, and he snapped his fingers again, and shot back his cuff and looked at a gold wrist watch. "She won't be there, not for quite a while. Perhaps it's just as well." He glanced hastily at Jeffrey. "Not that I don't want you to meet her, but I'd like you to meet her without any fanfare."

"What do you mean by 'fanfare'?" Jeffrey asked.

"Let's skip it," Walter said. "It's just a working phrase. Everything is 'fanfare.' Too God-damn' much fanfare, Jeff. Let's skip it, here we are."

The suite in the Waldorf Tower had the same impermanence as Walter Newcombe. There were no possessions of Walter's in the sitting room except six copies of *World Assignment* piled upon a secretary desk, and a portable typewriter on a table near the window, and these did nothing to alter the room's impersonal perfection. It had been done in colonial reproduction mahogany by some wholesale decorator. The two overstuffed armchairs, the pearl-gray carpet, and the sofa upholstered in old rose—all were devoid of character. It made you feel that within five minutes Walter Newcombe could pack up and go. It made you think of Walter Newcombe always packing up, and going, and never leaving behind him the slightest trace of himself.

"Well," Walter said again, "this is it." And then a little girl opened a door.

She must have been twelve or thirteen, the most unattractive age for little girls. She had on a brown woolen dress. Her tow hair was done in two tight braids. Her feet and hands were too large. Her features were irregular and sprinkled with freckles and she had gold bands on her teeth. It seemed to Jeffrey that Walter had looked startled when she appeared, as though something in his past had been revealed. She was like a bill collector, or like a letter that he had not burned.

"Sweetie-pie," Walter said, "why, sweetie-pie!"

Jeffrey looked away, because it seemed indecent for him to watch. It was the way he often felt when he saw the children of friends, for they revealed all sorts of intimacies and maladjustments which a casual observer should not see. Walter hesitated, and then he put his hands on her shoulders and kissed her.

"Umm, umm, *umm*, sweetie-pie," Walter said. "I thought you were out with Belle Mère."

"No," the little girl answered. She was looking hard at Jeffrey.

"Well," Walter said, "have you got anything to do? This is Mr. Wilson, dear."

The little girl held out her hand. It was cold and moist and completely limp. She bobbed in a quick curtsy with her eyes fixed on the floor.

"Hello," Jeffrey said, "well, well. I've got a little girl myself. She's about three years older than you. Well, well."

There was one of those shy silences.

"Well, well," Walter said, "think of that." And he snapped his fingers.

"Would you ask Room Service to send up a bowl of ice and some White Rock, dear? And then how about working on your picture puzzle? What is this one about?"

The little girl swallowed as though her mouth were dry.

"It's the one called 'Two Pals,'" she said. "It has a horse and a hen in it, I think."

"Well, well," Walter said, "you'd better go and finish it now, dear, but give Daddy another kiss before you go."

Jeffrey wanted to look away, but he could not.

"Sweetie-pie," Walter said, "umm, umm, *umm*."

5

Don't Get Me Started on That

Then the door closed, and Walter opened a lower drawer of the secretary desk and pulled out a bottle of whisky and held it to the light.

"That was Edwina," Walter said. "We brought her over with us. I don't know where her mother is."

"Oh," Jeffrey said, "Edwina."

"She was a trained nurse," Walter said. "You know how women get in Paris. They can't handle it."

"Who was a trained nurse?" Jeffrey asked.

"Edwina's mother," Walter said. "You remember Nancy, don't you?"

"Oh," Jeffrey said, "oh yes."

Walter cleared his throat.

"When Nancy got to Paris, she took a stray," he said. "He was a Greek." Walter set the bottle carefully on the table.

There was another awkward silence as the scroll of Walter Newcombe's life lay open. There was something disconcerting in his complete belief that anyone would understand, that everyone must have faced a similar marital problem in his own life.

"Well," Walter said, "let's skip it. It's great to see you, Jeff. You pull me all together."

Walter sat down in one of the armchairs, but almost immediately he got up and pulled a tortoise-shell cigarette case from his pocket.

"Excuse me for not thinking," he said. "I wonder where the devil that Room Service is." And he snapped the case open. "Naples," he said. "They can do anything in Naples with tortoise-shell." He paused and reconsidered his statement. "That is, almost anything."

"Are the Italians going to get into the war?" Jeffrey asked.

Walter sat down and tapped the cigarette case.

"Yes," he said, "and no, perhaps, but don't get me started on that."

"Have you met Gamelin?" Jeffrey asked.

"Gamelin?" Walter's forehead puckered. "Oh, Gamelin. Everyone meets Gamelin, but don't get me started on that."

Walter Newcombe sat there. Whatever it was that Walter knew, it was safely shrouded in silence.

"Not that I want to be snotty," Walter said. "It's just—oh, hell."

A buzzer sounded, and Walter jumped up. It was the Room Service waiter with the ice and White Rock. Walter signed the check with a streamlined fountain pen, and began fumbling through his pockets until he produced a quarter.

"Here," Walter said to the waiter, "keep this for yourself." And he poured out the whisky and reached for the bottle opener. "Hell's fire," he said. The charged mineral water from the White Rock bottle had cascaded over his vest. "Never mind it, that's just life, isn't it? Well, cheerio."

"Cheerio," Jeffrey said.

"Jeff," Walter said, "I just want you to understand none of this—this fanfare makes any difference. I'm just the same as I always was."

"Don't say that again," Jeffrey said. "No one's the same as he always was."

Walter Newcombe was grasping for something, and Jeffrey sat there waiting.

"Never mind about me," Walter said. "Tell me about yourself."

Jeffrey felt uncomfortable.

"Why do you want to know?" he asked. He picked up his glass and stared at it. He had nothing to conceal and nothing to be ashamed of. "There isn't very much to tell."

Walter Newcombe sat watching him, and Jeffrey wondered whether Walter looked like that when he talked to usually well-informed sources. It was professional, but it was kindly.

"There isn't much to tell," Jeffrey said again. "I've got a wife and three kids, two boys and a girl. They're pretty well grown-up now."

"Jesus," Walter said. His profanity indicated that he had never associated himself with family groups. There was an incredulous sort of interrogation in it, as though he were asking whether Jeffrey had done it on purpose or otherwise.

"Edwina was a mistake," Walter said, and he looked uncomfortable. His face grew redder. "Well, what else have you been doing?"

"Oh, this and that," Jeffrey said.

"Someone over in London—" Walter said—"I've forgotten who—told me you had written a play."

"Yes," Jeffrey said, "I've done a little bit of everything. It ran for two weeks."

"Oh," Walter said. He looked as though he had mentioned the name of a mutual friend only to discover that the friend was dead. "No one told me, Jeff, excuse my mentioning it."

Jeffrey felt a faint glow of triumph.

"But the pictures bought it," he said, "for sixty-five thousand dollars. So that's all right. Never mind about having mentioned it."

"Jesus," Walter said. "Why didn't you write another?"

Jeffrey looked at Walter in much the same way that he might have contemplated a public monument. He was feeling better.

"I doctor them now," he said. "They call me in to bail out someone else. A producer has a play that's sour and I try to fix it. Then sometimes I go out to the Coast."

"Jesus," Walter said, "that's real money."

Jeffrey still examined him thoughtfully. "Three kids," he said gently, "take quite a lot of money."

Walter was sitting on the edge of his chair.

"I've got an idea for a play myself," Walter said, "the last days of Vienna. I was there. I knew Dollfuss personally."

Jeffrey hesitated and spoke gently.

"A play?" he said. "Well, don't get me started on that. I don't mean to be snotty, Walter, but I have to work on plays for a living. I'd give it all up if I'd written *World Assignment*."

"Oh, no, you wouldn't," Walter said. "When did you read it, Jeff?"

Jeffrey hesitated again before he answered.

"I haven't read it yet, but I'm going to. You see all the boys are writing books now, and it's hard to read them all."

He had Walter there, but he could not tell whether Walter knew it. Walter had risen. He hurried to the secretary.

"If you haven't read it," he said, "it's time you did. Let me give you a copy, Jeff."

"No," Jeffrey said, "that isn't fair. I always buy friends' books."

"Oh, no," Walter said. "What's thirty cents in royalties? Here, take one, Jeff." He paused. "Actually, it's thirty-seven-and-a-half cents now." He pulled out his fountain pen. "I'll sign it," he said.

"Why, thanks," Jeffrey said. "That's nice of you, Walter."

Walter looked up quickly from the flyleaf of *World Assignment*.

"Say," Walter said, "you know your way around, don't you?"

"Yes," Jeffrey answered, "yes—slightly, Walter."

"Jeff—" Walter's voice had a different note—"are you in *Who's Who?*"

Jeffrey leaned back and reached very slowly for his glass as though some sudden movement might break the spell.

"Yes," Jeffrey said, "I'm in *Who's Who*, Walter."

"They sent me the form last week," Walter said. "Jeff, do you know what I'm thinking?"

"No," Jeffrey answered. "What, Walter?"

"I was thinking—" there was a new ring in Walter's voice—"you and I are the only ones from back home who are in *Who's Who in America!*"

It had been a long while since Jeffrey had considered anything of such proportion. It reminded him of one spring night when he had turned the corner into 57th Street and had seen a row of elephants walking westward apparently by themselves, each holding another's tail.

"My God," Jeffrey said, "so that's it."

From Walter there came an aura, a warm triumphant glow that made Jeffrey wonder whether all triumphs were not the same and whether the solace which anyone derived from them might not be based upon some half-forgotten slight. When you thought of it in those terms, Walter Newcombe might be egregious, but not preposterous. You could imagine him carrying his past with him through every change of scene seeking blindly for some personal sort of vindication.

"Jeff," Walter asked, "how's everything back there?"

It was unnecessary to ask Walter what he meant—it was like looking at blurred shapes on a picture screen, just as someone adjusted the lens, snapping every image into instantaneous focus.

"I haven't been in Bragg for quite a long while," Jeffrey said.

"Pa and Ma are still there," Walter said. Momentarily his veneer had cracked. His hair seemed yellower and longer and his nose more shiny.

"Your father—" Walter hesitated. "Is he still there?"

"No," Jeffrey said, "he's dead." It was uncomfortable, not suitable, wandering through the past with Walter Newcombe.

"He was a lovely person," Walter said, "very lovely."

The characterization made Jeffrey wince, and he did not answer.

"What happened to the house on Lime Street?" Walter asked.

"We sold it," Jeffrey said.

"Who bought it?" Walter asked.

"Jimmy Ryan," Jeffrey said.

"Jesus," Walter said, "Jimmy Ryan."

His exclamation was not profanity, but rather a tribute to decline.

"What happened to Ethel?" Walter asked. "Did she get married?"

"Ethel?" Jeffrey said. "Yes, she's married. They're living in West Springfield."

He did not know why he added where they were living, except that his mind was running that way.

"She was a very lovely girl," Walter said. "She must still be a very lovely person. What became of Alf?"

"In California, the last I heard of him," Jeffrey said. "San Bernardino, California."

"Alf always struck me," Walter said, "as being kind of wild. Is Alf still that way?"

"Yes," Jeffrey said, "he's still that way." Walter was still exploring the past. Jeffrey wished that he would stop, but there was no way to stop him.

"Jeff," he said, "what happened to that girl you used to go with? Of course, I was just a kid, but we used to see you out walking."

"What girl?" Jeffrey asked, but he did not need to ask. He was thinking of the hideous indelicacy of the way Walter put it.

"You know," Walter said, "Louella Barnes, the one with the big bow on the back of her head. You know."

"Oh," Jeffrey said, "Louella Barnes. She's married."

"Who'd she marry?" Walter asked.

"Milt Rolfe."

"Jesus," Walter said, "Milt Rolfe." And there was another silence. "I always thought," Walter added, "she was a very lovely person."

Jeffrey pushed himself out of his chair. Walter was like a book which contained everything in the first chapter—there might be more pages, but the first chapter was all you needed.

"Don't go," Walter said, "please don't."

"I've got to," Jeffrey answered, "it's getting close to five o'clock."

"I wish you wouldn't," Walter said. "This has pulled me all together. Say, Jeff—"

"What?" Jeffrey asked him.

"I wish you'd stick around," Walter said. "Mildred will be coming back. Say, Jeff, I've been reading the damnedest book. I wonder if you've read it."

"What book?" Jeffrey asked. He was putting on his coat.

"*War and Peace*," Walter said. "Have you ever read it?"

"Yes," Jeffrey said, "I've read it."

Walter looked disappointed, but he went right on.

"I just happened to run into it," he said, "at Liggett's Drug Store—just before I was hopping the train to lecture at Rochester. You know the way you run into things. That book weighs about a ton, but I couldn't put it down. I read it all night at the hotel."

"Well," Jeffrey said, "that's fine, Walter."

"More people ought to know about that book," Walter said, and he gave his pleated trousers a gentle hitch. "Where's it been all these years?—That's what I told them at Rochester. Every thoughtful American ought to read it."

"Walter," Jeffrey said, "just before I go, I wish you would tell me something."

"Sure," Walter said, "anything, anything at all."

Then Jeffrey was asking the question he had come there to ask.

"Walter," he said, "you've been everywhere. You've seen everything. You have a right to an opinion, and for God's sake, don't say, 'Let's skip it.' What's going on over there in Europe? What the hell is the matter with the Allies, and don't tell me to read *War and Peace*."

He spoke more urgently than he had intended. Walter was standing almost motionless and a strange cloak of dignity seemed to have fallen on him. He was not a clown any longer, and things that he had seen were reflected on his face.

"Jeff," Walter said, and a break in his voice made his words sound very kind, "you know better than to ask me that. You know I'm just a fool, Jeff, but there's one thing I thank God for. It looks as though we're out of the mess, this time. Thank God we're here in America."

He did not spoil it by going on. Jeffrey held out his hand.

"Yes," he said, "thank God for that. You see—I've got a son—"

When he thought of it afterwards, it sounded a little like Irving Berlin.

When Jeffrey stood on the corner of Park Avenue, he felt as though he had been on an ocean voyage. He could see the city in the detached way one sometimes sees it after finishing with the customs. He had that same feeling of gratitude that he was permitted to see it again. He had the same impression of its vitality, the same astonishment at its beauty. The air was soft with spring and a clean west breeze was blowing and the sun was dropping low. The sun made the façades of the buildings near him warm and glowing, and it made the Grand Central tower shadowy. They were selling gardenias and violets at the street corner. The traffic lights had turned red, so that the avenue was choked with yellow and orange taxicabs, and with blue and gray private cars, all absolutely motionless, shining in the sun. Then the lights turned and they all moved by him like a stream. There was nothing in the world just like it. The whole Avenue was gay in the sunlight.

The dogwood blossoms in the florists' windows were too big. They were as artificially cultivated as the dogs themselves that paraded down the Avenue: cinnamon poodles, waddling dachshunds, and freshly plucked wire-haired terriers, moving like mechanical toys. The taxi starter at the Waldorf was too big and he had too many buttons. There were too many apartment houses on the avenue and there were too many taxicabs. Westward on Broadway when dusk came, there would be too many people at Times Square and too many lights and too many tropical fishes on the electric signs. There would be too many people trying to be like Hedy Lamarr and Ronald Colman and too many girls trying to look like debutantes and too many debutantes trying not to look that way. In the windows of the steak houses there would be too many steaks. There would be too many orange drinks and too many copies of *Life* magazine and too many hamburgers and too many people who did not have the price of a hamburger. There was too much of everything, and he certainly could not tell what it added up to and no one else could either, but it was the greatest city in the world.

It was time he was getting home, and he took a taxicab when he came to St. Bartholomew's Church, which resembled a model in the Metropolitan Museum, now that so many high buildings rose around it. The driver of the cab had been reading a tabloid and listening to his radio, but when Jeffrey approached he gave a galvanic jerk, and reached to open the door, like a fisherman who feels a bite.

Nearly everyone Jeffrey knew had interesting experiences with taxi drivers. There were always stories at dinner parties that revealed their wit and salty wisdom. Taxi drivers left other people with a glow of democratic comfort because they had talked to them confidentially through the window just as though they were like anybody else. Jeffrey wondered whether there might be something wrong with him, for taxi drivers never gave him any new ideas, and this one was no exception. His collar was frayed and the back of his neck was dirty. As he crossed Lexington Avenue, he swore softly at the traffic cop.

"You see that cop?" he asked. "Smile at him, and he gives you a ticket. That's the kind he is."

"Yes," Jeffrey said, "cops are all like that."

"Yes," the driver said, "cops are all like that."

The conversation ended. It was nothing you could talk about at a dinner party. It would be impossible to say that you saw the funniest taxi driver today, and what do you think he said? "Cops are all like that." Yet the driver must have had a life of his own. He must have possessed ambitions and some sort of ideology.

"It takes all kinds to make a world," he said. "That's the truth, isn't it?"

"Yes," Jeffrey said, "I guess you're right."

"I know I'm right," the driver said, "it takes all kinds to make a world."

The trouble was that there were too many kinds making up the world in New York. The weight of their numbers made it impossible for you to think of them as individuals; the man was a taxi driver, and Jeffrey was a fare, and the chances were about a thousand to one that they would never meet again, yet back there where he and Walter had come from you knew everything about everybody. Perhaps it was just as well not to know too much.

"Good evening, Mr. Wilson," the doorman said.

"Good evening," Jeffrey answered.

"It's been a nice day for April," the doorman said, and then the elevator boy was saying that it was a nice day for April.

They had said it all a number of times before, the only difference was that Jeffrey was more conscious of it.

"Tell me about yourself," Walter Newcombe had asked him.

If he had told about himself he would have described ten thousand such rides in taxicabs and elevators. The starter would snap his button or whatever it was that starters snapped; the doors would close. Floors please. Fifth floor out. Going up. Floors please. Watch your step getting out. Floors please.

6

There's Everything in New York

When the elevator stopped, Jeffrey felt in his pocket for his key. Inside, he put his hat on the table beneath the mirror. Then he took off his overcoat and tossed it on one of the chairs in the hall that you never sat on, and then he saw that there was another overcoat and another hat. As he looked at it, he heard voices from the kitchen beyond the dining room. It was the new couple, Albert and Effie, arguing. You could ask that man until you were blue in the face, and still he would never close the pantry door, and when you rang the bell or called, he would never hear because he was either scolding Effie or Effie was scolding him. . . . There was always something wrong with couples, but as Madge had said, these two were willing to go to the country.

The hat and coat were familiar, but he could not place them. It was obviously someone waiting to see him, because he knew that Madge was out. It would be someone who wanted to sell something or talk seriously about something or else he wouldn't have waited. Then a voice called:—

"Hello, Pops, is that you?"

It was the voice of his eldest boy, Jim. Jeffrey hurried past the staircase and into the living room. The armchairs and the sofas had on their chintz slipcovers and there were daffodils in the bowl on the table by the wall, but in spite of those signs of spring the living room still looked very much as it had in winter. There were the same ornaments on the mantelpiece above the fireplace and the same birch logs behind the brass andirons and the same low coffee table in front of the sofa, and the piano, with its piece of damask, and the silver cigarette boxes and the eighteenth-century armchairs which Madge had bought at the Anderson Galleries. The walls and the window curtains, in fact the room itself, seemed temporary, but the furniture was different because it had been in so many other of their rooms that every piece of it was a sort of accepted fact. They had bought the piano when they had lived on Eighteenth Street. The dark refectory table, which stood between the windows, they had bought in an antique shop on the Left Bank in Paris once. It was a fake but they did not know it at the time. The Jacobean chair on one side of it had come from Madge's family's house, and so had the sofa. The second time he had ever kissed Madge was when they had been sitting on that sofa, but since then it had adjusted itself to the other furniture. The drum table near it had belonged to his mother, one of the few things he owned that had come from the house on Lime Street, and the two pink Staffordshire dogs on the mantelpiece had come from Lime Street also.

He remembered the occasions when all that furniture had stood in the street, suddenly naked and insignificant on its passage in and out of moving vans, but when it was arranged in some new place, it all came alive again, expanding like those Japanese sticks which swelled up and turned into flowers when you dropped them into water. Jim had crawled on that sofa when he was a baby and once he had soiled it so that the whole thing had to be reupholstered. Once Jim had pulled the drum table on top of himself and there was still a slight scar on his forehead where it had struck him. Jim had also smashed one of the pink dogs and you could still see the marks where it had been mended, but there was no danger of Jim's being destructive any longer. You did not have to watch him and tell him not to pull the cigarettes off the table, and not to tip over the flowers because the flowers were meant to be looked at and not to be torn to pieces. You did not need any longer to tell him to go upstairs for a minute and then he could come right down after he had been upstairs for a minute, because Jim was entirely grown-up, although the chairs and tables were just the same. Jim was standing in front of the fireplace between the two pink dogs, looking almost like a stranger, not even adolescent. He had his mother's brown eyes, but his nose and hands and the set of his shoulders were like the pictures which Jeffrey remembered of himself, and something like Jeffrey's mental image of his own father.

Jim stood there, a combination of complex circumstances dressed in a tweed suit made by J. Press, that ubiquitous school and college tailor. His brown hair, which used to be rumpled, was now held in place by some sort of lotion which Jim always spilled all over the bathroom. His soft collar was held in place by a clip and his trousers were held in place by a belt with a monogram buckle, but nothing held up his blue wool socks, which cascaded toward the uppers of his crepe-soled low shoes, one of which was untied.

"Hello, Pops," Jim said. "Where's everybody?"

"What's the matter?" Jeffrey asked. "What's the trouble, Jim?"

"Why is it," Jim asked him, "when I drop in you always ask me that? I just came down on the one o'clock. I'm going back tomorrow."

"You just came down on the one o'clock," Jeffrey said. "What are you doing, commuting?"

"Listen," Jim answered, "don't be sarcastic, Pops."

"Don't call me 'Pops,'" Jeffrey said.

"What else can I call you?" Jim asked him. "I always think of you as 'Pops.'"

"Well, think of something else," Jeffrey said, and he stood and looked at Jim. If it wasn't Jim at college it was Charley at school, and if it wasn't Charley it was Gwen.

"It's all right," Jim said, "relax, Pops. I'm not here for anything you think. I just came down on the one o'clock. Didn't you ever come down on the one o'clock?"

"No," Jeffrey answered, "I never used to have money to travel on Pullmans. I used to stay there and like it." But he was not sure that this was true.

Jim shifted his weight from one foot to the other while Jeffrey watched him. He could not understand what boys did with their time at college now. He could remember vaguely what he had done, but everything had been different then.

"Jim," he asked, "what good is a day in New York?"

Jim's eyes grew wide. His whole face was incredulous.

"That's a hot question," Jim said. "'What good is a day in New York?' Why, a day in New York is everything."

When Jeffrey considered his own day he could sympathize with Jim, though only academically. It was like reading a book of travel about some distant country where one had been once and which one would never see again. Talking with Jim was becoming very much like that. Jeffrey was always striving to remember what things had been like when he had been Jim's age. They must have been as new as they were to Jim; the values and the impulses and the wishes must have been essentially the same. Yet, though they used the same language and the same words, for each of them the words had a different meaning and a different value.

"How do you mean 'everything'?" Jeffrey asked.

"What I say," Jim answered: "New York has everything. Everything's in New York."

"'New York has everything,'" Jeffrey repeated. "'Everything's in New York.'" He spoke the words with a cadence that made them sound like a song. They sounded as tinny and at the same time as poignant. They sounded like "The Red Mill" and all the others . . . "In old New York, in old New York" . . . "Tell me what street compares with Mott Street in July" . . . "Me and Mamie Rorke, tripped the light fantastic on the Sidewalks of New York."

"What are you laughing at?" Jim asked him. "What's so funny about it?"

"I'm laughing," Jeffrey said, "but it isn't very funny . . ."

Out of the window he could see the East River. The sky above Queens was hazy and the buildings along the waterfront were fading into dusk. The tide was ebbing and three sand barges were being pulled against the current and the cars on the bridge upstream looked like little drugstore toys. Even with the windows closed, he heard the sound of a plane and the faint droning of the motors made him turn again and look at Jim.

"Just try to remember," Jim said, "just remember you were young once yourself."

"Thanks for reminding me," Jeffrey said, "but when you're my age, don't be your age. Suppose you remember that."

"Okay," Jim answered, "but I'm not your age. What's so funny now?"

"Nothing," Jeffrey said. "Have you told Albert you're here? Are you going to be in to dinner?"

Jim moved from one foot to the other.

"Stay in here to dinner?" he said. "When I have only one day in New York? I don't mean I don't want to see the family, but I called up Sally and we're going out some place."

"Sally," Jeffrey repeated the name, "Sally who?"

Jim's face assumed a patient, pained expression.

"She says her father knows you," Jim said. "He knew you back in the war or somewhere. Sally Sales."

"Oh," Jeffrey said, "well, that was a pretty big war and there were a lot of people in it."

"Well, he remembers you," Jim said. "Listen, just remember you were in love once yourself."

"What?" Jeffrey said.

"Just remember you were in love once yourself."

Jeffrey sat down on the sofa and opened the cigarette box on the coffee table.

"Yes," he said, "it happens sometimes."

"Then don't be so hard-boiled," Jim said.

"I'm not hard-boiled," Jeffrey answered, "I'm just trying to adjust myself. This spring you're in love with a girl named Sally Sales. All right. I didn't know."

"In love with her?" Jim's voice made him look up. "Why, I'm practically engaged to her."

It was nice of Jim to tell him. It made Jeffrey feel that they were friends in spite of all the difficulties that stood in the way of friendship between a father and a son, but he should probably have reminded Jim that he was in his second year of college and that he would have to earn his living.

"I mean," Jim said, "we're not really engaged. You know the way it is, I'm just telling you because it's different this time and I know you'll keep it under your hat. There are a lot of things I want to talk to you about sometime, you know—you were young once yourself."

There were a lot of things Jeffrey knew he should have said, but instead he felt proud and grateful because Jim had told him and had not told anyone else.

"I'd like to meet her sometime," he said.

"You'd like her," Jim said, "she's swell." And Jeffrey found it hard to think of anything further to say.

"Well," he said, "I've got to get dressed. I'm going out. Ring the bell for Albert."

He was smiling when Jim turned back to him.

"What's so funny now?" Jim asked. "Don't you believe me?"

"Yes," Jeffrey said, "I believe you. New York has everything, there's everything in New York."

He watched Jim searching for the bell and it afforded him a moment's amusement because he always had a hard time remembering about the bell himself.

"It's behind that thing on the wall," he said. "It's a bell pull, only don't pull it."

The antique belt of petit point from England which Madge had bought at the Anderson Galleries was, like so many decorative ideas, self-conscious and only remotely functional.

"No, no, no," Jeffrey said, "don't pull it." He became nervous just as though Jim were in the destructive age of childhood. "There's an electric button just behind it. Push the button."

"Say," Jim said, "pretty trick, isn't it?"

"All right," Jeffrey said, "ring it."

After all, he paid the bills and he might as well get something out of Albert, but Albert was like Jim, something with which Jeffrey was not entirely familiar. Albert appeared, wearing a black alpaca housecoat which was too short in the sleeves and a trifle tight around the shoulders, since it had been purchased for Ferdinand, the male half of the previous couple. Ferdinand had left with six bottles of Scotch and half a dozen neckties, but he had left the coat. Albert's wrists dangled from the sleeves when he stood up straight.

"Did you ring, sir?" Albert asked.

Everything that Albert said was vaguely annoying. It was all correct, but it did not seem to belong to Albert.

"Yes," Jeffrey said, "would you put out my evening clothes, please, Albert?"

And somehow Jeffrey himself did not sound exactly natural. It was a little as though he and Albert were both playing a game which neither of them particularly liked.

"White tie or black tie, sir?" Albert asked. At any rate, Albert did not use the expression "Formal or informal, sir?" which Ferdinand had used.

"Black tie."

"Thank you, sir, anything further, sir?"

"No," Jeffrey said, "nothing further, Albert," and he and Jim were silent while Albert walked away.

"Pretty trick, isn't he?" Jim said.

"Yes," Jeffrey answered, "he's trick."

"Where did you get him?" Jim asked.

"I don't know," Jeffrey answered, "they come and go."

"Where are you going?" Jim asked.

Jeffrey sat looking at the ancient bell pull with the electric wiring behind it.

"We have a dinner once a year," he said. "The Contact Club–the old Air Squadron I was with in France."

He spoke self-consciously, because it made him sound unnatural, like a retired army officer, and somehow it did not fit in with Jim or with anything that he and Jim had known together.

"Say," Jim said, "does that racket still go on?"

Jeffrey's common sense told him that it was ridiculous to be annoyed. He could even see what the boy meant, but it did not help.

"I mean," Jim said quickly, "I should think you would want to forget about it. I wouldn't want to remember."

Jeffrey was trying to do the impossible and put himself in the position of his son.

"I mean," Jim said, "I'm not blaming you, or any of your generation. It was a matter of mass hysteria wasn't it, and the old British propaganda? It just doesn't work with my generation. Personally, my generation thinks that war stinks."

"You mean," Jeffrey said slowly, "that we all made a big mistake–is that your point of view?"

"Sure," Jim said, "it's obvious isn't it? The best minds of your generation have been saying it. You're not sore, are you? I mean, you're not so dumb–I mean, it's perfectly obvious."

Then the apartment door was opening and Jeffrey stood up.

"Here's your mother and Gwen," he said.

"You're not sore, are you?" Jim asked again. He looked anxious, almost hurt.

Jeffrey stood looking at him, and he had to answer something.

"You see, some of us were killed," he said, "not so many, but quite a lot."

Jim looked surprised, as though he had never thought of it in that way.

"Maybe it wasn't such a bad way to die," Jeffrey went on, but it sounded old and dusty, and he seemed to be speaking from a great distance. He was sorry that he had brought it up.

"Well," he said again, "here's your mother and Gwen."

Madge and Gwen came into the room together and Jeffrey found himself trying to remember what it was they had said they were going to do together that afternoon. It always left him confused because it was never clear to him exactly what it was that women did do in New York. They were always out somewhere on meaningless errands of their own. They filled the busses and Schrafft's and all the teashops and the Museum of Modern Art and the Plaza and all the department stores. Madge was dressed in her light brown broadcloth suit with her hat that looked too small and her gloves that always fitted her without a wrinkle and with a little sable scarf tight about her neck. She was one of those timeless people who sometimes looked younger as they grew older. When she saw Jim her face lighted up and she might have been a girl whom he had asked to a college dance.

"Why, Jim!" she cried and she ran to him and threw her arms around him and Jim bent down and kissed her forehead.

"Hello, Mom," Jim said, "you've got a new hair-do, haven't you?"

Jeffrey wished that he had not read the works of Sigmund Freud, for they made even the most normal family relationship, when you stopped to think of it, seem slightly clinical.

"Daddy," Gwen said, "Daddy, darling."

Jeffrey had noticed lately that Gwen's whole manner toward him had changed. Gwen was now making him into a romantic character, a quaint old lovable gaffer who bumbled about, making mistakes because of growing senility.

"Where do you think we've been, Daddy darling?" Gwen asked. "We've been out shopping."

She seemed to expect him to express incredulity that such a slip of a girl could ever have been shopping. In spite of himself, Jeffrey discovered that he was doing what Gwen wanted, speaking just like a dear old gentleman.

"Well," he said, "shopping, eh?" If he had let himself go, he would have pinched her cheek playfully. It was the subconscious again, for the time had passed when he could be natural with Gwen. He would never spank Gwen again, and he would never wash her face.

"And what do you think we bought, Daddy?" Gwen asked. Jeffrey pulled himself together.

"My God, Gwen," he said, "I don't know." But Gwen's mind had already leapt to something else.

"Why, Daddy," she said, "oh, Daddy." Her voice was reproachful, and her eyes were wide. "Hasn't anyone brought you your pipe and your tobacco?" And then she turned on Jim before Jeffrey had time to answer.

"Jim," she said, "at least you might see that Daddy has his pipe when he comes home tired."

Jim gazed at her critically.

"We all see you," he said; "we're right in there with you, Gwen. Where did you buy the lipstick?"

But she was living a life of her own and no brother of hers was going to spoil it.

"Well, Daddy likes it," she said, "don't you, Daddy dear? It's Orange-Tan."

"All right," Jim said, "if you want to look like a hostess, that's all right with me."

"Jim," Madge cried, "what a thing to say to Gwen. What do you mean by a hostess, dear?"

Jeffrey pulled himself together. The atmosphere was heavy with a new sort of emotional tumult.

"I've got to get dressed," he said. "I know I'm missing a lot, but you'll excuse Daddy dear, won't you?"

"Why, Jeff," Madge said, "are you going out? Jeff, you never told me."

"Madge," Jeffrey said, "I told you yesterday. It's the Air Squadron dinner. Minot's coming here to pick me up at seven."

"You never told me," Madge said again. "Have you ordered cocktails? Minot always likes one. Jim, ask Albert to get the cocktail things."

Jeffrey was tying his tie when Madge came upstairs. He was sure he had told her that he was going out. He could remember it distinctly.

"Jeff," she said, "I'm awfully glad you're going to have a good time. You always do at the Contact Club dinner, don't you?"

Jeffrey examined his tie in the mirror.

"What's the matter with Gwen?" he asked. "Where did she get that 'Daddy darling' stuff?"

"Darling," Madge told him, "it's just a phase. I used to be that way with Father. Don't you remember?"

Jeffrey shook his head. He did not remember.

"Jeff, what were you and Jim talking about when we came in?"

"Oh, this and that," Jeffrey told her. "About the war."

"Jeff," she said, "he's going out somewhere. Do you know where he's going?"

"Oh, out with a girl, I guess," Jeffrey answered.

"What girl?"

"It doesn't matter much what girl at his time of life," Jeffrey said. "Just a girl. Her name is Sally Sales."

"Oh, dear," Madge said, "Sally Sales."

Jeffrey had picked up his coat, and now he held it by the collar.

"Do you know her?" he asked. "What's wrong with her?"

"There's nothing wrong with her," Madge answered, "I've only heard Beckie speak about her. She just isn't the type of girl for Jim. She's—Oh, I don't know, I just wish it weren't Sally Sales."

"Madge," Jeffrey told her, "you can't have Jim to yourself all the time. You mustn't be jealous of his girls."

"Of course I'm jealous," Madge said, "and I'm not ashamed of it. Darling, any mother is."

Jeffrey put on his dinner coat. If it was not one thing, it was another. When you were in love you had a feeling that all problems would be automatically settled once you had married the girl you loved. When the children were born and the house became filled with screams and diapers, you were certain that the problem would solve itself when the children were able to walk and button themselves. The future kept holding a bundle of hay in front of you, and you plodded after it, but you never got the hay. Now that Jim was grown up, there was a new kind of emotion, and a whole new tangle of jealousies and values, far more complicated than any that had gone before. Motherhood was more intense than fatherhood, a force with which it was impossible to argue.

"Well," Jeffrey said, "there must be some girl who is almost good enough for Jim."

"I wish you wouldn't joke about it," Madge said. "I was thinking the other day, whenever I come to you with a problem, you try to pass it over. It doesn't help when I'm worried, Jeffrey."

"Everybody's worried," Jeffrey said. "You are, I am, everybody is."

"Jeff," she said, "you don't know what boys and girls are like now. He might marry her."

"Who?" Jeffrey asked. "Who might?"

"Sally Sales. Aren't you listening, Jeffrey?"

It had a sort of universal value. When he answered he could almost hear the same thing being said by a million other people.

"Every time Jim speaks to a girl, you think he's going to marry her," Jeffrey said. "Why don't you put your mind on Gwen? Now almost any minute Gwen might marry—one of the elevator boys or the man who fixes the telephone or someone."

"Oh, Gwen," Madge said, and she laughed. "I don't see how you can help noticing—Gwen isn't the type that attracts men at all."

"There's the bell," Jeffrey said. "That must be Minot, now."

There was one good thing about middle age. There might be new worries, but a lot of old ones were gone. There were a lot of things which you finally knew you could not do, so that it was logical to give up trying to do them. Jeffrey knew that he would never read all the books in the library, for example —that it was impossible, simply because of the cold mathematics of time. He knew that he would never succeed completely in doing much that he had wished. There was a pack trip, for instance, which he had always wanted to take in the Rockies. He could think about it still, but he would never have the time. Among other things that he would never do or be, he knew finally that he would never be the sort of person that Minot Roberts was. He was not even sure that he cared much now for those attributes in his friend which he had admired for so long. His manner and his composure would never be like Minot's and he would never have Minot's sportsmanship or his code of honor or his generosity. Now, he was not sure that he wanted to be as far removed from the world as Minot.

Yet, when he saw Minot, he felt a great warmth of friendship for him and a certain wonder at how much that friendship had changed his life. If he had not met Minot Roberts years before in France, he would not have been where he was at all, but there was no use trying to be like Minot any longer.

Minot's hair was gray, but his figure looked extraordinarily lithe. He looked as though he could ride as well as he ever could, and his gray eyes were just as keen and the set of his jaw was just as firm as in the past. The trouble was that he looked too young. Time should have changed him in some way, and he seemed impervious to change. As Minot stood near the cocktail shaker and the glasses, he reminded Jeffrey of one of those portraits that you see in advertisements of some rare old blended whisky. You could almost make up a caption to put beneath him as you saw him standing there. You might have called it "The Portrait of a Gentleman Meeting His Old Friend," the old friend being a bottle. You might have called it "Aristocrats, Both" or "Fifty Years in the Wood, but as Sound as Ever." It was not right to think of Minot in that way. It was not loyal, but there it was.

"Minot," Madge said, "it's been ages."

"Madge, dear," Minot said.

That was all. It was uncomplicated, but if Jeffrey had said it, he knew he would have sounded like a fool. Minot and Madge were speaking a language which he would never speak, but he felt no resentment. Madge had had her chance once and she had wanted him, not Minot. There had been times when Jeffrey had been amazed at that effort of Madge's at natural selection, and times when he was certain that Madge had made a mistake in not marrying a man with a background like her own, but now he was not so sure. It may have been that Madge had been endowed with a flash of intuition, an instinct for survival in that desire she once had possessed for change. There was something about Minot which was static, a little like the face of a clock which no longer ticked. It did not change Jeffrey's affection for him, but there it was. He had never thought before of Minot as a type, but that was what he was; and now—it may have been because the world was shaking with the new war—the type was a little outmoded, a little dry and sterile: beautiful, but of no present use. It was so exactly like the portrait beside the whisky bottle of distinction that Jeffrey wished he had not thought of it. It was not right. It was disturbing to think that the world might no longer have time for what Minot Roberts represented, and it was not because Minot was old. It was because he looked so young.

Minot looked at him as he always did whenever they met.

"Hi, boy," Minot said.

"Hi," Jeffrey answered.

It meant that they were very old friends, but Jeffrey could never convey in that monosyllable all that Minot could.

Jeffrey poured three of gin and one of vermouth into the cocktail shaker and stirred it carefully because Minot was always particular about Martinis.

"It's better to have one here before we go," Jeffrey said; "they always have bad cocktails at the dinner."

Minot smiled at him and the little wrinkles narrowed about the corners of his eyes. "Boy," he said, "that's a good idea. We'll have one with Madge."

Jeffrey looked up from the shaker.

"Here, you'd better do it."

"It's all in the lemon," Minot said. "Just the outside peel–That batman cuts the peel too thick, Jeff, but don't let it bother you, here we are."

None of it ever spilled when Minot poured Martinis. His lean bronzed hand was as steady as a surgeon's.

"Here you are, darling," he said to Madge, as he handed her a glass. "Down the hatch and happy days."

That speech was not trite when Minot spoke it; it glowed with kindly hospitality, and it made Madge laugh.

"Minot," she said, "why is it you always give me a sense of security?"

"That isn't kind," Minot said. "Whenever I show up, dear, the Romans always hide their wives. You know, I've just thought of something."

"Don't keep it to yourself," Jeffrey said, "be sure to tell us, Minot." But he said it affectionately as one would to one's best friend.

"It's a poem," Minot said, "it's been running through my head all day. It goes something like this: 'Four things greater than all things are, Women and horses and power and war.' We've got them all now, haven't we?"

It was exactly what Minot should have said, being what he was.

"Maybe we'd better be pushing on," Jeffrey said.

"Why, Jeffrey," Madge said, "don't be so rude. Minot's only just come."

"He knows what I mean," Jeffrey answered. "We've got to be going, to the war, at the Contact Club."

"That's right," Minot said. "It's time we were up and over the lines. I've got the car downstairs, but I'll tell you what we'll do first."

"We'll have another drink," Jeffrey said.

"Naturally," Minot answered, "we'll have another drink, but first let's give Madge the old song, shall we?"

"What old song?" Jeffrey asked.

"Come on," Minot said, "one, two, three–"

"Oh, I'm looking for a happy land where everything is bright,
Where the hangouts grow on bushes and we stay out every night . . ."

While they were singing it Jeffrey forgot about the strange, chaotic day–Waldo Berg and the Bulldog Club and Walter Newcombe and Madge and Gwen and Jim and the apartment–and he forgot what he had been thinking about Minot because Minot gave him too that sense of security of which Madge had been speaking.

"You'll take care of him, won't you, Minot?" Madge asked. "And Jeff, dear, you'd better sleep in the study in case you fall over things. . . . Oh, Jim, here's Uncle Minot, dear."

Jim came into the living room, ready to go out, too. His dinner coat made him stand up straighter.

"How about a lift," he asked, "if you're going as far as Park Avenue and 52d Street?"

"We're going to a happy land where everything is bright," Minot said, "and 52d Street is on the way. Well, well, look at him."

"What about him?" Jeffrey asked.

Minot Roberts was smiling at Jim, and the wrinkles at the corners of his eyes were deeper.

"Jeff," Minot said, "he looks about ready to take a crack at the Boches."

Somehow the term put them back to where they really were, two old men looking at a boy. It gave Jeffrey a curious twinge of something that was almost anger. Jim was his son, not Minot Roberts', and what had bothered him all day came nearer until it gripped him with cold fingers.

"We're not in this show," he said, but Minot only laughed. His reactions were definite and undeviating, never changed by doubt.

"That's what they said in '16," he answered. "Remember, Wilson kept us out of war? It's always an open season on the Boches. If I were Jim's age, I'd be over there right now. Let's go, Jeff."

The doorman scurried out to the sidewalk and blew his whistle. "Mr. Roberts' car, Mr. Roberts' car, coming up."

Minot's black town car rolled out of the dusk and stopped at the curb by the apartment awning. It was an addition to the picture that Jeffrey's mind was making—Minot Roberts, sportsman and man about town, master of hounds, member of the stock exchange, clubman, World War ace. It was everything that the writers of light fiction were always looking for. It was a paragraph in a gossip column or a bit of a true confession. It was not Henry James, but it was Robert W. Chambers, and Richard Harding Davis' Van Bibber, and Mr. Gray's Gallops I and Gallops II. The frustrations of the doorman vanished and his job achieved a dignity and a sublimation when Minot's car stopped at the curb.

Minot's chauffeur, trig and lean, with iron-gray hair, had sprung to the sidewalk. He was smiling because Pierre was an old friend of the family who knew all of Mr. Minot's friends and who understood their values. Pierre, too, fitted into the picture. He might have been the confidential servant who had grown gray as a rat in the service of the Robertses, who had been with his master through many a scrape, who had doubtless followed just behind him when he went over the top in the Great War. Actually, Pierre was none of those things. He was just a good chauffeur with good references, but he looked them, and perhaps he thought them, too.

"Good evening, sir," he said to Jeffrey. "Good evening, Mr. Jim."

The instant that the door was opened, the interior of the car glowed with a soft, warm light, showing the fawn-colored upholstery and the mirror and the ash tray and the neatly folded rug.

"I'm looking for a happy land," Minot was humming, "where everything is bright."

Jeffrey wished that Minot would stop humming that tune. It was one of Minot's worst habits; and now that he was started, that tune would keep on with him all the evening. When they had walked across the fields near

Bar-le-Duc to the planes waiting on the line, Minot had always been humming. It may have been what was the matter with all of them—looking for a happy land where everything was bright. Jeffrey could imagine Minot looking for it in the sky when he dove at Richthofen's Circus, looking for it later when he rode point to point and when he got his Kodiak bear. That happy land must be somewhere, and you must search for it until you died, and the larger the gesture of the search, the better. Madge was looking for the happy land and now Jim was starting.

Jeffrey leaned back in the seat.

"I never get used to town cars," he said.

He thought a slight shadow crossed Minot's face, and he realized that his remark had the quality of a small boy's derisive whistle.

"It's a temporary luxury," Minot answered. "I won't have it long, come the Revolution."

That was what they always said, "come the Revolution," and you were meant to laugh, come the Revolution. But come hell or high water, Minot must have believed that he would always have his car.

"Not that I'm conservative," Minot said. "It's been a great show. This is a great time to live. Jim here's the boy who's going to see the fun." Minot picked up a mechanism that looked like a miniature broadcasting instrument, which came out of a little pocket on the side of the seat. "Pierre, stop on the corner of Park and 52d. Mr. Jim is leaving us."

Then Minot thought of something else. He pulled a wallet from his pocket.

"How's the money situation, Jim?" he asked. "Jeff, you'll let me do this, won't you?" He pulled a bill from his wallet. "Take this, and go to Twenty-One, Jim. Tell Jack or Charlie that I sent you, and spend it all tonight. Don't save it. Spend it all tonight."

Jeffrey glanced at the bill. It was fifty dollars.

"Jim," Jeffrey said, "say thank you to the nice gentleman."

"Gosh," Jim said, "well, gosh, Uncle Minot, thanks a lot."

Minot laughed. The car was stopping at the corner of 52d and Park.

"I'm your godfather, you know," he said. "Have a good time while you can, and spend it all tonight."

"Gosh, Uncle Minot," Jim said again. "Well, gosh, thanks a lot."

Then the door closed and Jim was gone.

"You shouldn't have done that," Jeffrey said. "Fifty dollars is a lot of money." And Minot laughed again.

"That's what money's for." And he slapped Jeffrey's knee. "It's great to see you, boy. You're looking fine."

"It's great to see you, Minot," Jeffrey said. "You're always looking fine." Then they did not speak for a minute, and the lights of Park Avenue moved past them.

It was inconceivable to Jeffrey to think of Minot Roberts in a patronizing way, but now all at once it came over him that Minot had been everywhere, but he had never been around. As he sat beside him, Jeffrey felt older and wearier than Minot Roberts. He had seen too many worlds; he had been around too much.

"Jeff," Minot said, "have you heard about the solicitor for the Crown from Bermuda who met the little streetwalker in the London blackout? Stop me if you've heard it."

Jeffrey did not stop him. There was Minot Roberts in the London blackout just like Walter Newcombe.

"Well it seems," Minot said, "as his Majesty's solicitor was crossing Piccadilly—" There it was, the blackout stories were always in Piccadilly— "he was accosted by a little streetwalker. 'My dear girl, you don't know who I am,' he said. 'I'm a solicitor for the Crown.' And what do you think the little girl said?"

"What?" Jeffrey asked.

"She said, 'Then you must come along with me, sir, for we 'ave a great deal in common, though I only solicit for 'alf a crown.'"

Jeffrey laughed—he wanted to do his best to make Minot think he hadn't heard it.

"Jeff," Minot said, "you didn't think that I was too impulsive giving Jim that cash—that I stepped on your toes, or anything?"

"No," Jeffrey answered. "I was thinking of what I'd have done if anybody had given me fifty dollars when I was Jim's age."

"It just came over me," Minot said. "It's just possible that Jim won't have much time."

"What?" Jeffrey asked him. "What do you mean, 'much time'?"

"You know what I mean," Minot answered. His accent was clipped and precise, but his tone was gentle and casual. "Now there was Stan—he always knew his number was up. He didn't have much time."

Jeffrey looked out of the window. He did not want to answer, and when he did, every word hurt him.

"Yes," he said, "that's so."

"Jeff," Minot went on. "You know how a moment strikes you, sometimes, as being more valuable than another moment. Now up there in the apartment when I saw you and Madge and then when Jim came in, I thought it was particularly swell. You all looked so darned happy. There isn't any trouble any more. Madge has everything she wants."

Jeffrey did not answer. He saw that Minot was watching him through the dark of the car.

"Jeff," Minot asked him, "you've got what you want, haven't you?"

"Yes," Jeffrey answered, "yes, I guess so." And Minot Roberts laughed.

"Well, that's swell," he said. "Well, here we are." And he began to sing that tune again.

> "We're looking for a happy land, where everything is bright."

"Minot," Jeffrey told him, "if it's all the same to you, would you get your mind on something else?"

"Why, Jeff, you old sourpuss," Minot said.

His own waspishness gave Jeffrey a twinge of shame. He could not explain that he had seen too many people in too many happy lands.

"Besides," Jeffrey said, "you haven't got the words right. We're not 'looking for' it—you're 'going to' it."

Minot put a firm hand on his shoulder. Pierre had opened the door and the little overhead light was glowing so that Jeffrey could see every line of Minot's face. His lips were curved and his eyes were hard and merry.

"Boy," Minot answered, "we're both of us right. We've been looking for it and now we've found it. Here we are, let's go."

That was what Jeffrey used to hear them call.

"All right, let's go," a second lieutenant was calling.

"Come on, you," he could hear a sergeant calling, "take a reef in your pants. Let's go."

"All right, fellows." It was what Captain Strike used to say when he pushed back his chair before they went to the line, when everything was cold in the dusk of early morning. "Let's go."

7

It Completely Lacks Validity

Jeffrey took a cold shower and a glass of Bromo-Seltzer. Madge was in the study when he got there and breakfast was already on the table, and Madge smiled at him as though he had been a naughty little boy.

"What time did you get in?" Madge asked, but there was no sharpness in the question. It was approving because he had been to the right sort of dinner. She was intimating that boys had to be boys sometimes and that anything practised by the boys he was with last night was absolutely all right.

"Did you have a good time, dear? Who was there?"

"Everybody was there," Jeffrey said.

"What did you do?"

"What they always do," Jeffrey said, "made speeches and sang songs."

"You needn't pretend you didn't like it," Madge said. "Every year you say you're not going to go, and then you always do."

"Yes," Jeffrey said, "I know." And he picked up the paper.

As he stood there, staring incredulously at the headlines, he could not entirely absorb their meaning. The Nazis had already overrun Denmark. They were in Norway. Their transports already were crowding into the harbors. They were landing troops on the airfields, and they were in Trondheim and even in Narvik.

"What is it, dear?" Madge asked. "Is there something new in the paper?"

He thought of Walter Newcombe at the Bulldog Club only yesterday, giving his report from England, speaking of squeezing Hitler and of the *cordon sanitaire*. He could see Walter in his coat with its sharp lapels and his pleated trousers, talking about the ring of steel and the tube of toothpaste. As he heard himself reading Madge snatches from the paper, he recalled every inflection of Walter's voice.

"Well," he said, "there it is. I've got to be going, Madge."

In a way it was like going to the Bulldog Club again for Jeffrey was moving into another of those worlds of his which had nothing much to do with the apartment or with Madge, yet it was surely as important, for he earned his living in it. He had to be at the theater that morning at half past ten o'clock to attend a rehearsal and there was one good thing about the theater—no matter what happened, whether it was personal grief or war or disaster, once he was involved with all its personalities, he and everyone else would have to put their minds on work. He would forget the shock of the war news, once he was there, but as he rode across town in a taxicab he still was deeply concerned with it.

The audacity and perfection of that German move still bewildered him. All the plans must surely have been known for some time by the intelligence of the French and British staffs. There would be a reaction by afternoon, very definite and violent, now that a new blow had been struck in the European War. It might even be that Walter Newcombe was right and that it was a part of grand French and British strategy to force Germany into Norway to a field of battle already selected by the Allied staff. The Germans were shooting the works now, and now the show was on. The British Navy would be in the game already. There would be light stuff in the Skagerrak, already, shooting up the German transports and cutting off the supply lines. The carriers and the heavy ships would be charging down on the Norwegian coast bombarding Oslo and Trondheim, and the transports would be with them and the French and British shock troops would be landing on the coast. He could feel the same sort of excitement which he had felt years ago when a big push was starting on the western front. Trondheim would be the place to hit. He wished that he were there, or at any rate in some place where the news was coming in, but he was not. Norway and the war were leaving him already, because the taxi was stopping before the theater west of Broadway.

The orchestra was a deserted dark space filled with the peculiar sort of loneliness which he always associated with theaters in the morning. He was taking off his hat and coat, walking down the empty aisle. The glare of the stage lights added to the emptiness and he could see his old friend, Jesse Fineman, the producer, and Hazel Harris, Jesse Fineman's secretary, down in the front row. There was no make-believe or illusion about that vacant theater with all its mechanics pitilessly bared before him. The stage was stripped of scenery so that he could see all the wires and ropes and the brick back wall. Sidney Coles, the leading man, in light gray flannels, was standing in the center of the stage facing Marianna Miller, for whom Jesse had bought the play. She was wearing a very severely tailored suit, and her yellow hair was pushed tightly under her hat—an unmistakable effort to look plain, because Jeffrey had told her once that actresses were always self-conscious and always overdressed.

He had known Marianna for a good many years and Jesse Fineman a great deal longer, but it was business which brought them together that morning, and not friendship. His attitude toward Marianna, as she stood on the stage, was entirely professional. He knew from Marianna's worried look the exact part of the play on which they were working. It was where the husband surprised his wife in the midst of a telephone conversation with her lover, and Marianna and Sidney had never been able to do it naturally. At the moment Sidney and Marianna were themselves, probably quarreling, because they did not like each other, while the rest of the cast sat on wooden chairs or benches looking like a group of people who had just walked in from anywhere.

"Oh," Jesse Fineman said, "there you are, Jeffrey."

"Yes," Jeffrey said, "I'm sorry I'm late." He was sorry because it made Jesse Fineman very, very nervous when people weren't on time.

"They're at the telephone," Jesse said, "and Jeff, it completely lacks validity. Give Mr. Wilson a script, Hazel, dear."

You always called everyone "dear." You were always sweet, whether you felt that way or not. In a little while Jeffrey would be calling Marianna "dear," whether he felt that way or not.

"It's between here and here, Mr. Wilson," Hazel said.

"I think," Jesse said, "she'll have to throw him another line. See what you think, Jeff."

Jeffrey sat down with the script on his knee and looked up at the stage. He was watching Marianna Miller impersonally but with a sort of creative pride. At such a time he could think of her as a piece of property and not as a person. He was thinking that she was looking very well that morning, rested and not too nervous. He was pleased with the way she stood, even on that dismantled stage. He had begun talking to her years ago about the importance of detail, and now she appreciated it more than he did, because Marianna was an artist now.

"We're ready now, Sidney," Jesse Fineman called. "She's just talking as you come in. We'll start right there, Marianna darling."

Marianna looked at Jeffrey through the glare of light and her face lighted up in a quick smile. Her smile had an artless quality and was one of her greatest assets; it came slowly and lighted up her entire face, and Jeffrey had taught her not to use it too often.

"Hello, Jeff dear," Marianna called. "Thank God you're here! You've simply got to give me something else to say."

"Try it the way it was," Jeffrey said. "Pretend it isn't a line."

"Yes, dear," Marianna said.

"Keep your voice like that," Jeffrey said, "just like that."

"All right. . . . Marianna, darling, perhaps if you take it just a little more slowly . . ." Jesse Fineman called. ". . . It's merely a suggestion."

"Jesse," Marianna called back, "don't say that again, please. Jeffrey, ask him not to say that again."

"No, no," Jesse Fineman said, "it was merely a suggestion, darling." And then Jesse held his head in both his hands, his fingers writhed through his black hair. "Oh God," he whispered, "oh God."

"Don't," Jeffrey whispered back. "Just let her go, Jesse."

"Jeff," Sidney called, "may I interrupt for just a moment? Not that I wish in any way to inject my personality, but my interpretation is that I should not be surprised, but whimsical, cynically whimsical."

"You're always your old whimsical self, Sidney, dear," Marianna said, "and you don't have to try."

Sidney gave his head a gentle shake.

"All right, sweetheart," he said.

"Sidney, dear," Marianna said, and she turned towards Sidney slowly. Jeffrey was more conscious of her motion than of what she was saying. He had known the first day he had ever watched her that timing could become her greatest gift. "I've never mentioned this before, but since we have to play together I would really much rather, if you don't mind, not be called 'sweetheart.' You don't mind, do you, dear?"

"Mercy, no," Sidney said, "please don't think it was a term of endearment."

"I know it wasn't, Sidney dear," Marianna said.

"Oh God," Mr. Fineman whispered, "God."

"Marianna," Jeffrey called; their eyes met. "How about getting on with it?"

"Jeff, dear," Marianna called back, "I love you, I always have."

"That's fine," Jeffrey said, "and I'm right here just loving you. Let's get on with it."

Mr. Fineman raised his head from his hands.

"And now," he said, "if we're all ready, Marianna darling, the telephone."

He always felt anxious for her when she started. There was a pause, and she had changed into another person. She was holding an imaginary telephone and her voice had choked into a low, seductive laugh. Her voice range was magnificent. Jeffrey had often lectured her on the importance of control.

"Hugh," she was saying. "How can we, Hugh? It's like wildfire. I know, dear, but I can't tonight. Yes, I remember. Oh darling . . . oh darling . . ."

Then she turned, and he loved to watch her because she always did the right thing by instinct. It was not her fault, if the lines were bad. She was aware for the first time of Sidney standing near her.

"Why," she gasped, "why, Reggie!" It was not her fault if the lines were bad.

"Perhaps I'm interrupting, my dear," Sidney said, and she gave a gasping, throaty laugh.

"No, no," she said, "it's nothing, Reggie, darling. It . . . why, it was just . . ."

"Cecily," and Sidney's voice rose, "let's be frank for once. Let's not go on living forever in a tissue of lies. Look at me, Cecily darling."

Mr. Fineman clapped his hands, and the illusion was over.

Marianna shrugged her shoulders in an ugly way, one of her few bad gestures.

"Stop a minute," Mr. Fineman called. "That was marvelous, Marianna, darling. Marvelous."

"Jeff," Marianna called, "you've got to do something with those damn lines."

Jeffrey looked up from the script.

"Where's the author?" he asked. "The author ought to be here."

"What would you be here for," Jesse Fineman said, "if the author was not utterly hopeless, Jeffrey? It actually doesn't sound real, does it? Although Marianna was marvelous."

"Jeff," Marianna called, "you've got to do something."

"All right," Jeffrey called. "It was lousy."

"Jeff . . ." Marianna began.

"Not you," Jeffrey said, "I wasn't talking about you."

Then she smiled at him again.

"Jeff . . ." she began.

"Please," Mr. Fineman called, "will you give us just a little minute, darling?"

Marianna walked to the footlights.

"You leave Jeff alone," she said. "You don't have to tell him what you think. He can fix it. Just leave Jeff alone."

She stopped and no one spoke for a moment. Marianna was always temperamental at rehearsals, but in a way it pleased Jeffrey.

"That's it," he said. "You tell him, darling. Maybe we'd better go through the whole thing, Jesse." And Mr. Fineman clapped his hands.

"Act One," he called, "all ready for Act One."

Jeffrey was watching Marianna again as though she were not a friend. He was trying to be both an appreciative unit of an audience, and an artisan who would eventually take that play apart. It was never wholly possible to be both at once, but he knew that he was better at it than most; it was all that he was really good at—making a bad play better, giving it technical precision and making it run more smoothly. His skill was derived from a sort of dramatic instinct, a sense of theater if you wished, but no term could entirely define it. You had to be born with it. The gift of rebuilding someone else's work might be a small one, but still it was a gift which called for an accurate appraisal of dramatic values and a sensitive ear for dialogue.

As he sat there listening he could see why Jesse had bought the play and also why Jesse had hesitated for a long while to produce it. The inexpertness of its structure was dangerous and at the same time refreshing. It had been written by a professor of economics at Columbia, which was not strange, since Columbia professors seemed to do almost everything except teach there. It was what Jesse called a "comedy of manners." Jesse felt it would come to the theater like a clean breath of spring, and perhaps it might if it were fixed. The acts, as they were outlined in the manuscript, told the story without his listening: Act One—Cecily and Reggie's penthouse apartment overlooking Central Park. Act Two—Hugh's bachelor apartment, three hours later. Act Three—Cecily and Reggie's penthouse apartment overlooking Central Park the next morning. They would be through with their infidelities the next morning and would be reconciled as man and wife again, as they looked out over Central Park. It had the quality of what was known as a vehicle, and nothing else.

When it was time for lunch he was absorbed in it as a problem. The dialogue needed cutting and the opening of the first act was not right. It very seldom was in a beginner's play. Given some hours of intensive work he could smooth it and change the emphasis and take out the vagueness. He wished that Jesse had not put it into rehearsal first, although he admitted there was an advantage in hearing the lines spoken.

"Jeff," Marianna said, "will you take me out to lunch?"

The actors had finished and they were in the orchestra putting on their hats and coats. There was no use having them go on with it until he had completed the revisions. Jeffrey stood up and put the manuscript in his pocket.

"Yes," he said, "where do you want to go?"

"I don't know," Marianna answered. "Anywhere. I'm tired."

"Well, make up your mind," Jeffrey said. "Everybody's tired."

"Let's go to the Echelon," she said, and then she raised her eyebrows. "Who let you out with that tie?" she asked.

"Don't be possessive, Marianna," Jeffrey said.

"I always am," she said. "You always are with me."

"Not any more," he answered. "You're quite a big girl now."

"Jeff," she said, "please don't say that. You're the only one who tells me anything that makes sense."

Now that the rehearsal was over they were friends with a mutual sort of respect for each other's abilities. It was pleasant to think that Marianna still admired him. He thought of all the times that they had sat at tables in hotels when they were trying out other plays. Once she had been a wide-eyed and rather awkward girl who was delighted to have lunch with anyone like him, but it was different now. He could see people watching her and he could hear them speaking her name in undertones. The Echelon was a small place, so that he was particularly aware of the patrons watching him, wondering who he was, simply because he was with her.

"God," Marianna said, "I'm tired, dear."

"Then you'd better have a drink," Jeffrey said.

"I don't usually," Marianna answered. "Do you think I ought to? What do you think I ought to have?"

"Make up your mind," Jeffrey said. "You're a big girl now."

"Don't start that again," Marianna said. "Do you think you can fix it?"

"Fix what?" Jeffrey asked.

"The play," Marianna answered, "that lousy play."

"Yes," Jeffrey said, "I guess so. It's going to be all right."

Marianna sighed, and rested her elbow on the table.

"Do you mind if I say something, dear?" she asked.

"No," Jeffrey answered, "of course not." He did not mind exactly, but he wished that everyone in the Echelon did not know who Marianna was as she leaned toward him across the little table.

"Jeff," she said, "why do you waste your time fixing up those rotten plays? You could write better ones with the same effort—so much better."

He smiled at her, although he did not want to smile.

"Let's not start on that either," he said. "It's one thing writing a play, it's another thing fixing someone else's."

She leaned farther across the table.

"It's only that you don't believe in yourself," Marianna said, "and I don't see why."

"Marianna," Jeffrey said, "don't talk lines."

"It isn't a line," Marianna said, "I wish you wouldn't keep saying that about me. I believe in you, I believe—"

"Marianna," Jeffrey said, "stop and think and you'll see that it doesn't make sense. You're a nice girl, and we're just having lunch. Don't talk lines."

"I wish—" Marianna began.

"Listen, sweet," Jeffrey said, "let's talk about something else. This doesn't get us anywhere. I'm not as good as you think I am."

"All right," Marianna said, "you talk about something else. When did I see you last?"

"At Jesse's office," Jeffrey said, "the day before yesterday. You wore a gardenia, and you never look well with gardenias."

"All right," Marianna said, "then tell me what you did yesterday."

Then everything was pleasant and he forgot that everyone in the Echelon knew who Marianna was. It was always easy to talk to her because he knew that she liked to listen to him and would not be thinking of something else. She was interested in all sorts of things which would never have interested Madge. He found himself telling her about Walter Newcombe and the Bulldog Club and it made an amusing story, considering the news in the morning paper.

"You know," he said, "I wonder what Walter is thinking. Do you know what I'm going to do? I'm going to call him up and ask him. You don't mind, do you?" And she said she did not mind.

She smiled at him as he stood up.

"Just don't be too long," she said.

The telephone booth was in a stuffy little corner near the cloakroom. Its interior smelled of face powder when he closed the door and dialed the number of the Waldorf.

"Mr. Newcombe's apartment," he said. "Mr. Walter Newcombe."

There was a moment's silence, and then he heard a thin childish voice answering, and it sounded surprisingly domestic after Marianna's.

"Is that you, Edwina?" Jeffrey asked. "This is Mr. Wilson. I saw you yesterday afternoon. Is your father there?"

"No," he heard her answer. "No, he isn't here."

"Where is he?" Jeffrey asked.

"He's gone."

"Gone where?" Jeffrey said.

"To London," he heard her say. "He took the Clipper this morning, but Belle Mère's here, if you want to speak to Belle Mère."

"No thanks," Jeffrey said. "Good-by, Edwina."

It was just as though a telephone connection had been broken. There was the same dead sound in his ears and the same sense of frustration.

"How the devil does he do it?" Jeffrey said. He wished that he were going to London. He wanted to be anywhere but where he was.

8

That Old Town by the Sea

It was very hard for Jeffrey to remember what he had been thinking that previous spring, now that it was October. So many of the days of that spring and summer were like the parts of one of those dreams, which you know are dreams even when you are asleep and the worst parts of which, your sleeping logic tells you, are not true. He was still not able to understand how the city, in October of 1940, could look as it always had, beautiful and indifferent, or how there could be new model cars, or how there could still be antiques and silver and flowers and saddles and bridles and tweeds for sale on Madison Avenue. Everyone was back in town again and there was the same feeling of anticipation in the air. You could not tell from externals that isolationists and interventionists were quarreling. There was no way of knowing whether aid to Britain would keep us out or get us into war that October morning. The voice of Wendell Willkie and the Willkie Campaign Kits made no impression on the weather. It was easy to forget that "A VOTE FOR WILLKIE IS A VOTE FOR HITLER," and, "IT'S MOVING DAY ELEANOR, THE WILLKIES ARE COMING." It was easy to forget the speeches and the fireside chats. It was another October morning, and he and Madge were going to Fred and Beckie's for that week end in the country.

The bags were in the elevator. The garage had delivered the coupé at the door and Madge had given Albert and Effie the telephone number where they were staying in case anything should happen, and now Madge was wondering whether there might still be anything important that she had forgotten and Jeffrey was telling her not to worry, that it was easy enough to telephone. It was possible to think of German bombers sweeping over London and at the same time it was possible to think about the suitcases. Madge had said that they could put all their clothes together in one suitcase. For years she had been suggesting this, because it was easier to have one piece of luggage than two. She could never understand that it was undignified and that her boxes of powder might get open and spill on Jeffrey's evening clothes and that Jeffrey could never possibly find anything in a woman's suitcase.

"Jeffrey," she asked, "did you pack your sport clothes? Have you got the keys to the car? Have you set your watch, Jeffrey?"

"Yes," Jeffrey answered, "everything's all right."

"Jeffrey, I'll drive," she said.

"No, that's all right," he answered, "I'll drive."

"Then keep your mind on it," Madge said, "and don't start thinking about the war."

Madge was looking in her bag to be sure that she had her lipstick and her compact, and then she asked if he had any money with him, and he told her that of course he had money, and she said that he never carried enough with him in case the car broke down or something, and the last time they were at Fred's and Beckie's he might remember that he had to borrow something from Fred so that he could leave something for the servants. Jeffrey said that he had enough money and he looked at his watch. It seemed to him that they were starting early. It was true that they were to stop on the way at Madge's Uncle Judson's for lunch, but there would be nothing to do if they got there early.

"And remember this, Madge," he said, "let's get away from there as soon as we can. It—you know the way it is."

Madge smiled her brightest smile.

"It won't be any problem," she said. "Uncle Judson always has his nap right after lunch, and we'll just say we can't wait until he wakes up. And Jeffrey dear, remember . . ."

"Remember what?" Jeffrey asked.

"Remember not to say you have any doubts about Wendell Willkie, and don't say you think it's funny that Mr. Ickes called him a 'barefoot boy from Wall Street' the way you did last night. Uncle Judson might think you weren't going to vote for him."

"Maybe I'm not," Jeffrey said, and he started the car. "Maybe that's just what he is—a 'barefoot boy from Wall Street.'"

And then she made an unexpected suggestion.

"Let's go out on the Post Road, the way we used to," she said. "We haven't been there for years."

"The Post Road?" Jeffrey repeated after her.

The Post Road had become an ugly highway of oil-spattered concrete, choked with trucks and bordered by hamburger heavens and filling stations. You could avoid it now and save twenty-five minutes by cutting across town to the West Side Highway and then taking the new Parkway and cutting back to the Sound, but all at once he felt the way Madge must have. He wanted to see the Post Road again.

It was hard to find the landmarks on it, and even the towns had changed, except for their names. The road seemed to have sucked a part of the city out with it, making the highway a little like a river full of driftwood. Mt. Vernon and New Rochelle were full of apartment houses and so were Pelham

Manor, Larchmont and Mamaroneck. There had been fine country residences once along the Post Road, and now they had been turned into convalescent homes, or tourist homes, or roadhouses. They stood sadly behind gasoline pumps and roadside booths with their grounds and shrubbery uncouth.

The farther Madge and Jeffrey got from the city along the road the more familiar the sights became. Jeffrey had the sensation of having been dead for a hundred years, and of now being back and trying to orient himself in the land of the living, and of looking vainly for stone walls, close-cropped lawns and tree-shaded driveways. Of course everyone had left the Post Road years before, because of the roar of traffic which continued day and night along it, and because the houses were too old, or too ugly, and the city was crowding outwards.

The town where he had first met Madge was a place now where commuters lived. The lawns and meadows which had once surrounded it were cut by little roads that led into real estate developments made up of small houses, each with a garage attached. These stood now among the red of small maple trees and among the gold-yellow of poplars. The Willis place was gone and so was the Henderson place. As they started down the hill to what used to be the village, he could see the fieldstone Episcopal Church, but he could not recognize a single house near it. The Roberts place was as completely gone as though it had never been there. There was no sign of the driveway or of the gray granite house or of the garage-stable or of the greenhouses. He was sure that this was just where it had stood beside the Post Road, but now he could not recognize a single tree.

"Jeff," Madge said, "go a little slowly. Here—do you remember this?"

An oil truck roared by them clanging a chain behind it on the concrete. To the right was a white house with two fir trees in front of it, and beneath the trees were wire cages filled with cocker spaniel pups for sale.

"Jeff," Madge said, "don't you remember? This was where you kissed me."

"What?" Jeffrey asked. "Where?"

"Right here," Madge said. "Jeff, can't you remember? It was the first time you ever kissed me—when we came back from the Golf Club dance. I had to drive you. It was the family's old Cadillac. You didn't know how to drive anything except a plane."

Then he remembered the white house and the fir trees. There had not been a sound, for it had been very late. There had not been another car on the Post Road that night, and all the houses had been sound asleep, but no one would ever select it again as a propitious spot in which to kiss a girl. It made him feel sad, exactly like a ghost.

"We're early," Madge said. "Let's drive through the village to the railroad station. Do you remember the first time I met you there when you came down to stay with us? I've thought about it all day. I didn't think you were glad to see me."

She was wrong there. He had not wanted her to know how glad he was to see her.

There was no past tense about that town, only a pushing present and a doubtful future. It was just a suburb now where commuters spent the night, where houses were leased and sublet as casually as apartments in New York. There was no permanence and no very tangible evidence that it was a town at all. One's children would not live there. The store names had changed on Purchase Street and all the façades were new, glittering with plate glass and neon lights and plastics, but the railroad station had not been touched. It was painted the same sickly buff yellow; and as they looked, an express train hurtled by it on its way to Boston.

"Well, we'd better turn around now," Madge said. "Jeffrey, it's queer, isn't it? It was so lovely once."

It was not exactly queer because it was a concrete fact to which one might as well adjust oneself. You thought things would remain the same, and somehow nothing did. It was a picture of one generation giving way to another, and the new one never wanted any longer what the old one had to offer.

"You can't tell," Jeffrey said. "Maybe the people here think it's lovely now."

He wished they had not come up the Post Road, and Madge must have been thinking the same thing. As they drove toward the Sound there were fewer small houses, but no one was living in the large ones any longer. They stood ugly and unwanted on their uncut lawns, their windows unwashed and blank. The weeds were growing on their drives, but there were signs of hopeful real estate agents staked in front of them. There was an amusement park on the old beach by the Sound and no one wanted to live near an amusement park, and the water of the Sound, which he always thought of as clear and bluish green, was too polluted for bathing any longer. He wondered if it all struck Madge in the same way. As a stranger, he had once thought the places along the Sound were impregnable. It must have been more of a shock to him than it was to her to see them now.

"No," Madge said, suddenly, "don't take Willow Road. Take Rock Point Road, it's only a little longer."

He knew she did not want to see the house where she had lived on Willow Road, and she did not want to see what had happened to the privet hedge or to the wall garden or to the cutting garden, and he did not want to either.

A few miles back in the country from the Massachusetts town where Jeffrey had been born there had been plenty of deserted farms with their barn roofs falling and with the saplings growing up in the hayfields, but these had been peaceful in their utter loneliness because there had been no life around them. It was different here because there was too much life. It all made him think of the place which he and Madge owned in Connecticut, and of all the trees he had planted, and it filled him with a sense of futility. There was no use thinking any longer that someone who belonged to you might live in your house after you were through with it. The rows of trees which he and Madge had planted on the hill in the country would not look like much for another forty years because elm trees seldom did, but Madge had said that they would be nice for the children and their children. She must have known, if she had faced it, that even if the children wanted it, they would never be able to afford it, but still you went on hoping in that archaic way. Madge's father and mother must have had some sort of belief that the house on Willow Road would surely be owned by Madge, just as surely as the coupons would be good on a gilt-edged bond. He wondered what her uncle thought about it, for he was the only one who had not sold and moved away, but then, perhaps the old gentleman was too old to think at all. Jeffrey heard Madge sigh.

"Jeff," he heard her ask, "do you remember when I took you to see him?"

He knew that she meant the time when she took him there to tell her Uncle Judson and her Aunt Clara, who was living then, that they were engaged.

Somehow it was discordant after all the rest of it that her uncle's house and grounds should still be exactly as he first remembered them. The lawn had been freshly mowed, although it was October. The crimson woodbine around the gateposts had been pruned back, and the turf along the edges of the drive was freshly trimmed. There was the same dark bank of rhododendrons, with the oak trees just behind them. The leaves of the copper beech in the center of the lawn had not turned yet. Two gardeners were cutting back the shrubbery and a third was mulching the rosebed. The sun was striking the roof of the greenhouse that held the hothouse grapes. The stable door was open and the blue gravel of the whole drive was raked smooth. The flower boxes on the edge of the porte-cochère contained their familiar red geraniums and nasturtiums. The sun struck on the veranda with its green rocking chairs and there was a smell of smoke in the air from burning autumn leaves.

"Do not leave anything to be done in the spring," Madge's uncle had always said, "that can possibly be done in the autumn."

The house itself glistened with a fresh coat of gray paint and there was not a slate missing on the mansard roof. As the coupé stopped beneath the shadow of the porte-cochère, the screen door at the top of the granite steps was opened by old Lizzie who had been Madge's aunt's maid. Lizzie's face was firmly set and her apron was freshly starched and her hair, though it was sparser and whiter, was done up in the same tight knot that Jeffrey remembered.

"Lizzie, dear," Madge said, "we're not late, are we?"

"No, Miss Madge," Lizzie answered, "he's just coming down the stairs." And when she looked at Jeffrey he felt as he had that time when he had first come to call. Lizzie must still be thinking of all the young gentlemen whom Miss Madge might have married.

"Hello, Lizzie," he said.

"Good afternoon," she answered, "Mr. Wilson."

The hall seemed dark after the bright October sunlight, but he could distinguish the long Kermanshah carpet, the seat that opened for rubbers with the mirror above it and racks for canes and umbrellas on either side, the wide gaping arch of the fireplace with the head of a moose over it and the oil painting of a grass-grown Roman ruin. He could see the cool, waxed yellow-oak staircase curving upward two ways from the landing—the design sometimes used on ocean liners. There was a tart, clean smell of chrysanthemums from the vases just below the landing window, and sure enough, just as Lizzie had said, Madge's Uncle Judson, clean and brushed for lunch, was walking down the stairs.

He walked deliberately but not feebly, resting his hand lightly on the golden-oak bannister. His face was long and thin and paler than it had been. His starched collar and his dark suit looked too large for him.

"Well, well," he said to Madge, when he kissed her, "if you want to tidy up, everything is ready in your Aunt Clara's room."

"No, no, Uncle Judson," Madge said, "I don't want to keep you waiting."

He moved his head sharply sideways when she spoke, toward the tall clock which was ticking beside the umbrella stand.

"You have time," he said, "you're early. There is everything in your Aunt Clara's room."

Then he moved another step down the hall, and Jeffrey moved toward him.

"How do you do, Jeffrey?" he said.

"How do you do, sir?" Jeffrey answered.

Uncle Judson cleared his throat.

"Do you want to wash your hands?"

"No thanks, sir," Jeffrey said.

From the way Uncle Judson looked at him, Jeffrey could not tell whether he was suspected of exhibiting exceptional strength or weakness. Time had nothing to do with it. Jeffrey felt the way he always had with Madge's uncle, that he was being dealt with according to the best rules of hospitality, but that it had all been a whim of Madge's—an accident.

"There's sherry in the library," Uncle Judson said.

The French doors of the library opened to a piazza, and from outside there was the same smell of chrysanthemums.

"Thank you, sir," Jeffrey said when the old man handed him a glass.

"Well," Uncle Judson said, and sipped his sherry, "well—"

It seemed to Jeffrey that there was nothing much more to say. Through an open window he could hear the metallic ring of a rake on the driveway.

"The place is looking very well, sir," Jeffrey said.

"They're busy now," Uncle Judson answered. "Never leave anything to be done in the spring that can possibly be done in the autumn."

"It's always one long fight," Jeffrey said, "to keep a garden going."

"You think so?" Uncle Judson asked. "Not if one is systematic. It's a matter of routine."

"I don't suppose I'm systematic," Jeffrey said.

"No," Uncle Judson answered, "I suppose you're not. Let me see, I haven't seen you for some time."

"No," Jeffrey answered, "not for quite a while."

"I hope," Uncle Judson said, "that everything has been going well with you. Have Madge and the children been well?"

"Yes, they've been all right, thanks," Jeffrey said.

"Jim is quite a boy," Uncle Judson said, "but it always strikes me queer—he looks like you."

"Well," Jeffrey said, "of course he can't help that."

"Let me see," Uncle Judson said, "you were an aviator in the last war, weren't you?"

"Yes, sir," Jeffrey answered.

"They seem to be driving the British back," Uncle Judson said, "in the air, I mean."

"That's true, the forward fields are too hot for the fighters now," Jeffrey answered.

"I see that they've bombed St. Paul's," Uncle Judson said.

"Yes," Jeffrey answered, "London's getting it."

"I'm glad that I won't have to see it later." The old man waved to the decanter. "Another glass of sherry?"

"No, thank you, sir," Jeffrey said.

The old man clasped his hands behind his back.

"I wonder what's keeping Madgie," he said. "Well, we must always wait as patiently as we can for the ladies. This morning—do you know what I've been thinking?"

"No, sir," Jeffrey answered.

"I've been thinking that I'm very pleased to be my age with the way the world's been going."

As far as Jeffrey could recall in all their meetings, that was the only remark that old Judson Mapes had ever made to him that was intentionally informal.

"I think you're right, sir," Jeffrey said, "but my age is the worst. Right now I'd rather be old or young."

Uncle Judson clasped his hands behind his back. His pale blue eyes met Jeffrey's squarely.

"Everything is changing—for the worse," he said, "for the worse. The lavatory's right here—are you sure you don't want to wash your hands?"

"Thanks, quite sure," Jeffrey said.

"Well," Uncle Judson said, "here comes Madge. Madge is like her mother. She always kept us waiting, but her Aunt Clara was punctual. Madge, will you lead the way?"

Jeffrey had always heard that one became set in one's opinions as time went on, but he could never see this working in himself. It seemed to him that his attitude toward people whom he had known for long was always undergoing alterations, so that personal relationships were nearly as impermanent as real estate values and liking kept changing to indifference and dislike merged into tolerance simply because of living. Nevertheless, he had always been sure that his attitude toward Madge's uncle would never undergo much change. He would always call him "Mr. Mapes" rather than "Uncle Judson," but now as they entered the dining room, he knew that they shared the experience of observing the passing of time.

Lizzie, assisted by another maid about her age, was waiting on the table.

The ceiling of the room was high. The walls were done in a greenish artificial leather. The curtains which framed the tall windows were heavy blackish-green velvet bordered by tarnished gold tapes. The table was round, made of black fumed oak like the sideboard, and its legs had the same heavy ornate carving. The chairs were black oak too, upholstered in dark green leather that was held in place by elaborate brass-capped tacks. Lizzie was removing the place plates, which were gold-embossed and dark purple, each with a different flower in its center. The silver was a variation of the Crown pattern, a heavy elaborate contortion of motifs such as you saw sold by weight in those strange New York shops that collected bric-a-brac from liquidating estates. Lizzie was bringing in the clear pale consommé, and Mr. Mapes was picking up his spoon. There was nothing in that room that anyone in his right senses would want any more.

"You never come to see us, Uncle Judson," he heard Madge saying.

"I do not like New York now," he said, "and I am very busy here."

There was no way at all of telling what went on behind that pale façade. Jeffrey had never thought of him except as a pompous old stuffed shirt and a snob, but now he felt a faint glow of admiration for him. He was like a ship sinking with its guns still firing.

"You ought to see more people, Uncle Judson," Jeffrey heard Madge saying, and he wondered how her Uncle Judson liked it when she tried to run his life.

"There is no one I wish to see," Uncle Judson said. "No one lives here any longer."

"But you must be lonely, Uncle Judson."

"Lonely?" he answered. "No, not lonely."

He was running his own show, and perhaps that was all that anyone could do. Jeffrey was wondering what he would be like himself if he reached that age, and he hoped he would not reach it. The hothouse grapes with their silver scissors had scarcely been passed before the old man was pushing back his chair.

"It is time for my nap," he said, "if you'll excuse me. Shall I find you here when I come down?"

Jeffrey thought that Madge was going to say they would wait, and if she had, he was not sure that he could have stood it.

"I wish we could wait," Madge said, "but we can't. We're driving to Connecticut."

"Then good-by," Uncle Judson said. "It was kind of you to come. Gregory has put some chrysanthemums in your car." His pale eyes met Jeffrey's for a moment. "It was kind of you to come. There are cigars on my desk in the library, and the door to the right—in case you want to wash your hands."

The car now had that same clean acrid smell of chrysanthemums.

"Darling," Madge said, "thanks for going. I know it was an awful beating for you."

"Oh," Jeffrey said, "it wasn't bad."

"Well, it wasn't fun," Madge said.

"It wasn't fun," Jeffrey answered, "but he puts on quite a show."

"Jeffrey," Madge said, "drive a little faster, please let's hurry."

He knew what she wanted, because he wanted the same thing. Now that it was over, she wanted to get away. She wanted to get away from the Sound and the Post Road and memory, and she thought that she could do it by driving faster.

"Jeffrey," she said, "it's such a clear day, isn't it?" And then he saw that she was crying, but there was nothing that anyone could do about it.

"I'll be all right in a minute," she said, "I'm sorry."

"That's all right," Jeffrey answered, "go ahead and cry."

"I'm all right now," she said, "and Jeff, all week end we'll have fun."

He was not so sure of that. They would be moving up the Merritt Parkway to adjust themselves to something else, and at any rate he had never liked the word. He supposed it was an Anglo-Saxon monosyllable—"fun."

9

And Fred Too, of Course

"It seems ages since I've seen Beckie," Madge said. "I'll be awfully glad to see her."

Beckie, as Madge always said, was her oldest, dearest friend. Their families had both owned houses on Willow Road, for one thing, and then they had both gone to Farmington for years, and years, and years. Madge always said that Beckie was the most intelligent girl she knew—that was one of Madge's favorite words, "intelligent," and it always brought a picture to Jeffrey's mind of a bright little dog walking on its hind legs and wearing a soldier cap. Madge was always sure that Jeffrey would like to see Beckie because Beckie was so intelligent about books. Each Sunday she saved the *New York Times Book Review* so that she could read it bit by bit through the week and could form her own judgment as to what was really worth while. She did not want to have books picked out for her beforehand by anyone like Henry Canby and his crowd at the Book-of-the-Month Club. Beckie was not sure, for instance, that she agreed entirely with Dr. Canby's taste, at least as far as she could gather it from his writings in the *Saturday Review of Literature*, which she also read carefully every week. At any rate, good or bad, it was not her taste, and she did not want that of someone else imposed upon her. It was all well enough, she said, for someone to publish a book of reading that *he* liked, but Beckie wanted her mind to be full of reading that *she* liked. That was why Madge said that Beckie was intelligent about books. They had a fight once when Jeffrey said that he didn't believe that Beckie had read all the books she talked about—but Beckie always said she never talked about a book she hadn't read; she never cheated that way.

"She would be better," Jeffrey said, "if she cheated in any sort of way."

"Jeffrey," Madge said, "you know Beckie is intelligent."

"Nothing she reads does her any good," Jeffrey said.

"You're being mean about her," Madge told him. "I only wish that we could be as happy as Fred and Beckie."

There was no use telling her that he hoped to heaven that he would never have to be happy the way Fred and Beckie were, because it was the sort of happiness that went with charcoal briquettes and grills on wheels and eating steaks outdoors and drinking out of glasses with "Whoops" written on them and using towels marked "His" and "Hers" and cocktail napkins embroidered with "Freddie and Beckie." There was at least one thing you could do, Madge always said, and that was to be loyal to your friends, even if they did use those napkins.

"You do like Fred and Beckie," Madge said as they drove out the Merritt Parkway, "you just pretend you don't to be contrary. Do you know what Beckie used to do at school?"

Jeffrey said he did not, but he did know that Beckie and Madge had passed the most glorious years of their lives at Farmington.

"She used to memorize ten lines of Shakespeare every morning while she brushed her teeth," Madge said, "and she still does."

"If she did it in the evening, too," Jeffrey said, "she'd memorize it twice as fast."

"Well, I wish I could do anything like that," Madge said.

"Thank God you can't, dearie," Jeffrey told her.

"No matter how I try," Madge said, "I can't ever be such a good wife and such a good mother as Beckie, so there."

"Dearie," Jeffrey told her, "just give up trying. It's time you settled down."

"I like it when you call me 'dearie,'" Madge said, "it means you're in a good mood. I wish I knew what gets you into one. I can't ever seem to tell."

Then they began talking about the children, about the boys who were beginning to call on Gwen, and Jeffrey said he could not see what she saw in any of them, and Madge said she liked the little one named Norman Phelps, and Jeffrey could not remember Norman Phelps at all. Then they talked about Charley at school and they both agreed they ought to go sometime to see Charley there, but Jeffrey said a boy Charley's age was always ashamed of his parents. Charley was always afraid that they would behave abnormally. Then they talked about Jim and what Jim was going to do when he got through College. Madge had wanted him to be a doctor because doctors lived such full, useful lives, or if they didn't they should, and speaking of doctors, Madge wondered why obstetricians were always so happy, and Jeffrey told her it was because they brought babies into the world and didn't have to support them. He was in a good mood. Then they talked about Jim and Sally Sales, and Jeffrey told her not to keep worrying about Sally Sales. He admitted that he had never seen the girl and it might very well be that she was gauche and a little ordinary, as Madge had heard her friend Beckie say. But there was no use worrying about Jim or wondering what he was doing because when it came to a boy Jim's age, maybe what you didn't know didn't hurt you. Besides, Jeffrey told her, it was normal for a boy to have a love object that wasn't his mother and Madge told him not to put it in such a horrid way.

"When I was Jim's age I was in love myself," Jeffrey said.

"Who?" Madge asked. "You never told me."

"Back at home," Jeffrey said. "You know, I've often told you about her—Louella—Louella Barnes."

"Oh, yes," Madge said. "That one. You must have been awfully cunning."

"If it's just the same to you," Jeffrey told her, "would you find another word for it?"

"Darling," Madge said, "you'd be happier if you didn't worry about words." Jeffrey was in a good mood that afternoon. She leaned her head against his shoulder.

"Jeffrey, are you in love with anyone now?" she asked. "And don't put it off by saying you're in love with me. Married people can't always be in love."

"They can be according to sex manuals," Jeffrey said.

"Jeffrey," Madge asked, "are you in love with Marianna Miller?"

"Marianna?" Jeffrey said. "Good God, no!"

"Well, when I see her with you—" Madge began.

"You don't understand that sort of person," Jeffrey told her. "She—she's a great artist and all great artists go on that way."

"She's going to be at Fred's and Beckie's."

"Dearie," Jeffrey told her, "it's beginning to sound like the queer people at the circus at Fred's and Beckie's. We'll lock our bedroom door. We won't let Marianna in."

It was just the way things had been in '39. He was not thinking about the war news. They were going along the Merritt Parkway at fifty miles an hour and soon they would turn off on Route 7.

The leaves of the newly planted trees between the concrete lanes were turning like the larger trees on either side. He was always vaguely disturbed by the Merritt Parkway and all the other parkways because once you were on them you had no way of telling that you were getting anywhere. There were no houses, just trees and bridges, trees and bridges, and no grades that were too steep. The whole thing must have cost the taxpayers a great deal more money than was necessary, but no one cared about money any more. The parkway was like a part of the new national thought, and it was all too easy. There were no towns, only shrubs and bushes from some nursery, and you never knew where you were until you got to Route 7.

"I wish," Madge said, "we could think of all the things to do to our house that Fred and Beckie think of doing to theirs. This time I'm going to make a list."

That was one of the things that always worried him about going to Fred and Beckie's, because Madge inevitably came back with ideas that she wanted to apply to their own house, and he never wanted any of them. Fred and Beckie were always reading catalogues and going to architects' sample rooms and getting new ideas such as paddock fences and outdoor fireplaces. He didn't want any of those things.

"We can never seem to think of anything," Madge said. "I wish our place were half so cunning."

"Don't," Jeffrey said, "please, don't say 'cunning.'"

It annoyed Jeffrey particularly when Madge wanted her life to be more like Fred and Beckie's, and wanted their children to be more like Fred and Beckie's. It never did any good to explain to her that nothing was ever like that unless you had a large and regular income derived from inherited securities. Madge always said that they could be more like Fred and Beckie if they would only budget. Beckie had three large account books all ruled off for Laundry, Dentist, Entertainment and Miscellaneous, and she put everything down in those books. She was able to do this because Fred could remember where the money went, and he was always doing little things for Beckie, always. Jeffrey had said something once which Madge had asked him never to repeat again as long as they lived, and if he did, she would walk right out of the house and leave him. Jeffrey had said that Fred and Beckie's life that Madge liked so much was like playing dolls. He never repeated the remark again, though in his own thoughts, he often elaborated on it.

After Yale, Fred had gone into his father's business—which involved chiefly the selling of safe municipal bonds to investors able to afford to live on the low yield of these securities and thus avoid the burden of state and federal income taxes. Thus Fred knew a great deal about tax exempts, though Jeffrey could never see why there was much to know, but Fred once said that it was tax exempts that kept him young.

It had never seemed to Jeffrey remarkable that Fred should have married Beckie, but to Madge that courtship and its subsequent culmination was invested with a sort of deathless beauty. It seemed that, for some reason which Madge always took for granted, all the girls wanted to marry Fred, but after Fred met Beckie at one of the Met dances—and Madge remembered everything about it because she and Beckie had been there together, just little girls from Farmington, and neither of them had hoped to have a good time—there had been no one else for Fred. Beckie had on a red dress and red slippers and she had that beautiful hair—it looked more like fresh taffy then than it did now—and she was so intelligent. Fred and Beckie had danced five dances and then they had gone away somewhere, and when Madge had asked Beckie afterwards how in the world they had found so much to talk about, Beckie had said they had talked about life and Omar Khayyám. Jeffrey imagined that the scene must have been a little like a page of F. Scott Fitzgerald and once considerably later, Fred had actually met Fitzgerald at the Ivy Club or somewhere, after one of the games with Princeton, and Fred had always had a suspicion, one which Jeffrey himself had heard him mention once, that because of that meeting he could see himself as one of the characters in the Fitzgerald novel, *The Beautiful and Damned*.

When they went to bed that night, Madge and Beckie had talked about Fred for three hours. Fred had not tried to paw her as some of those drunken boys from Groton and Harvard had. He was a very real person. And the next day, what do you think happened? Fred sent her at the Plaza where she had spent the night an enormous box of snow-white orchids all pinned separately on a card so that the bottom of the box was just a field of white and green and with the orchids a card without his name or anything, just these words: "Do you remember? I do." And Beckie would never tell Madge, although they were best friends, what it was that she remembered because it was something that she could never tell anyone, not ever. But that very next Sunday, although she had never told him where she lived—when he asked her she had just told him to find out—Fred came up the drive of Beckie's house on Willow Road in the big red Cadillac runabout that the family had given him for Christmas, and they had played tennis all afternoon, and then when Beckie was afraid he might be bored seeing too much of her, he stayed all evening and didn't go home until half-past one in the morning. . . . And Madge had been the maid of honor at the wedding. There was only one touch more which had tied it into a sort of unity to which Jeffrey could scarcely give credence because it seemed so remote from human behavior as he knew it. Beckie had shown Madge the inner surface of her wedding ring —not platinum but a plain gold band like Beckie's mother's—and in it was engraved in tiny letters these words: "Do you remember? I do."

Jeffrey often wished that Madge had never told him, for the honesty and enthusiasm and paucity of thought embarrassed him whenever he saw the ring on Beckie's finger, and it did no good to tell himself that he was a cynic. No man should have had such a thing engraved inside a wedding ring, and yet perhaps millions of other people had. And that was all there was to it, except that Madge loved them. They were like the characters of those magazine stories of the Twenties where everyone had been gay at the Country Club and where no one took to drink or ran off with someone else's wife or talked about working conditions in the steel mills, or about the uneven distribution of wealth, because the advertisers would not have liked it. Madge said they had everything, and they deserved everything, Fred and Beckie.

Madge said they had such luck, and their old farm in Connecticut was just another example of it. It had simply been an old ramshackle tumbledown place occupied by an Italian family named Leveroni, although the house was one of the dearest old salt-boxes that Beckie had ever seen, whatever a salt-box might be, and it dated back easily to the Revolutionary War. Beckie was the one who saw its possibilities. Before those Italians moved in, when all the farms in that soft blue valley were going to seed, the place had been owned by good Yankee stock. It had been called "the Higgins farm," and after Beckie and Fred had bought it they rode around the country calling on the last of the old natives who were left in the valley to ask for details about the Higgins farm, because Beckie wanted it to have tradition; and Beckie had written the story of it and had collected all those anecdotes in a tooled Florentine leather book which Fred had given her. The book lay on the maple drop-front desk in the little formal parlor, a desk which Fred and Beckie had found in the kitchen of one of the natives. The little cabinetmaker in the little village had been surprised at how well the little desk came out, but Beckie had seen its possibilities right away. Now the book lay on the desk, and the book was called "Higgins Farm—1770"—and that was what the place was called, just "Higgins Farm."

It seemed that one of the main characters of this Higgins family, or at least the one who lived most vividly within the memories of the natives whom Fred and Beckie had visited, was a man named Joel Higgins. This "old bird," as Fred called him, although he sometimes referred to him as "Beckie's real boy friend," must have been what Fred called "quite a salty character." He used to go down at six in the morning to the cellar in back of the summer basement kitchen, where the Rumpus Room now was, and draw off a gallon of hard cider; and at four o'clock in the afternoon he would go down cellar again, his jug empty, and replenish it. That was why Beckie always kept a barrel of cider in the Rumpus Room, and called it "Uncle Joel's barrel." Jeffrey often wondered what Uncle Joel would have said if he could have seen what Fred and Beckie had done to the Old House and to the Springhouse and to the old barn of the Higgins Farm.

"They must have put a hundred thousand dollars into it," Jeffrey said once. Madge had told him that that didn't represent the thought they had put into it, and that she wished that he would not always think about how much people put into things, and besides, it was perfectly darling.

Beckie used to say that she hated to think of those beautiful farms in Connecticut with their big elms and maples and rolling meadows that had been simply ruined by the people who had bought them, some of them dear friends of hers and Fred's, too, although she was not going to mention names. The things they had done in polishing up and landscaping those old New England farms hurt Beckie almost physically and she simply had not allowed anything like that to happen to their place. She wanted it to have personality: hers, and Fred's too, of course; but she wanted it also to have primarily the atmosphere of those dear old people who had lived on it and who had made things with their hands, such as pail yokes and wooden scoops and sap buckets, and those dear little cobblers' benches that you could stand in front of the fireplace to put things on, such as cigarettes and cocktail glasses and what have you. She wanted the barn to be full of the things that those dear old people used, an old pung, perhaps, some sleighbells on a hook, a wooden rake and a part of a hay rigging and what have you—not in the way, of course, but still there to give the atmosphere. Someday, perhaps, they would really have cows and chickens and some fluffy white ducks in the brook and all those other things that go with a farm, and what have you, but you couldn't very well have them all in the barn so near the house with a manure pile right by the clothesyard. Someday when Freddie made a lot of money selling some of those City of Detroits at one-and-a-half, or whatever it was that Freddie did, they were going to build a little house on a corner of the place for a real farm, and it was going to be surrounded by sheep barns and cow barns and pig barns, and what have you, and everybody could go down and look at it, and really learn about life in a barnyard—but that was going to be someday.

In the meanwhile, Beckie knew that they must start on everything very carefully. She and Fred weren't idiots enough to think that they could do it all themselves as the Waldrons down the road had tried to do, and other people whom she would not mention. She had tried and tried to get Madge to employ an architect when Madge had bought her place, and not one of those little country contractors who had no imagination and who didn't really know anything about plumbing or about gracious living. Beckie knew that the selection of an architect was a very crucial problem and one which had made many of her friends, whose names she wouldn't mention either, fall perfectly flat on their faces at the start. She wanted an architect who of course would have ideas about vistas and stairs and halls and sinks and things like that, but she wanted one who would be receptive to her ideas, and Fred's too, since after all, it was going to be their house and not the architect's, wasn't it? In short, she wanted an architect who would work both with her, as she said, and for her. And that was how they had found Simpson Bolling. They had just met quite by accident at a cocktail party after she had been listening to "Tristan," and Simpson had been wonderful.

Simpson had built those stone wings on either side of the old house, one for the children and one for the guests, exactly the way she and Fred, too, had wanted them. Simpson and Beckie had both been quite passionate about Norman-French architecture and at almost the same time they had thought of a turret, not for a staircase, but for a little hide-a-way study, and when it was all finished, it had proved what Beckie had always said—that Norman-French and New England were really the same thing, basically, and she and Simpson had not done a single thing, either, to spoil the spirit of the old house. They had simply made it the central motif of a little old Norman courtyard where peaches and plums were espaliered against the walls.

Beckie was never tired of telling about the fun that she and Simpson and Fred, too, had had with that old house, and if they had to start and do it all over again, they would not have done a thing differently, not even Fred. She was the one who had discovered, when they started to scrape away the wallpaper in the little parlor, that there had been layers and layers, but underneath them was the original paper of all, made to look like gray-stone blocks with little flowers growing in the cracks. One of the little men from the village had been scraping the wall, and he had scraped off most of it, but Beckie had caught him in time to save enough of it, which only went to show that you had to be there every *minute* when you were doing an old house, even if you were working with someone who had Simpson Bolling's reverence. No one had seen anything like that paper, and Fred had known how wild she was about it. It had been perfectly mad of him, and he never would tell her how much it cost, but he had had that paper copied, printed from wood blocks and everything, and now the blocks were right upstairs in the attic and no one else could ever have any paper like that, ever.

That was only one of the discoveries lying in wait for them in the old house. There was the Dutch oven in the Rumpus Room, for instance, which had been all covered up with plaster, and the hand-hewn oak beams in the living room—Simpson knew they would be there if you ripped off the ceiling

—and then the enormous fireplace. First there had only been a hole for a stovepipe, made, Beckie supposed, by those Leveroni people; but when you took the plaster away, there was a tiny little bit of a fireplace, and when you took the bricks away from that, there was a bigger one. It was the size of the fluted pine mantel that had shown that there must have been a bigger one still sometime, although you couldn't hope that it existed. Yet, when they tore out that second fireplace, there was the great big one, and the old crane was hanging right inside it with the old pothooks on it, just as you could see it now, and Fred could warm a toddy from it when they came down there in winter.

There had been only one real disagreement with Simpson, but Fred had stood right behind her, and Beckie and Fred had been perfectly right. Simpson had wanted to tear down the old barn, because he said it was leaky and full of rats, but when she, and Fred too, saw the old rafters, all pegged together by hand-cut pegs, they simply could not do it, and so you had the barn as it was now—a sort of a museum and a sort of a secondary playroom when the Rumpus Room grew too crowded on rainy days, but it was still a barn. Even the hay was still on the lofts on either side, and you did not need to worry about cigarettes because the hay had been fire-proofed by something that had been squirted all over it. It no longer smelled like hay, but Beckie said perhaps this was just as well because couples never wanted to get lost long in the hayloft. The rest of it was simple, once you had the groundwork. It was then only a question of moving old trees and grouping them, and Fred had seen to that. Fred used to call it a rodeo, when they rounded up old trees. You just herded them together and fed them, and there you were.

10

Just Don't Say We're Dead

"It's the next road to the right," Madge said. "We've passed the big signboard with the cigarette advertisement, and there's the filling station."

There had not been a cloud in the sky all day, and now the shadows were growing long, and the leaves of the maple trees glowed red and yellow in the sunlight. Now they had turned off the concrete of Route 7, there were no more roadside stands or signboards; they were in the real country. The only day that was ever as good as you thought it was going to be was an October day. There was a sweetish smell of falling leaves and of fresh earth then that always turned Jeffrey's thoughts backwards to where he had lived as a boy, although the air was not cold enough, and there was not quite the same autumn haze. He and Madge were driving in the country, but the aura of the city was still over it because there were too many city people there. Too many writers, too many illustrators, too many advertising men and motion-picture executives and actors and radio-script men, and frustrated women who did houses over, and business men who wanted to get away somewhere—come the Revolution—and nice young couples and ones that weren't so nice, and retired colonels, were all buying Connecticut farms and setting up roadhouses and tearooms and antique shops and camps and schools. It was the vanguard of the city moving out through those stony fields and old orchards. You could hop in a car and be at 42d Street in an hour and a half, using the Merritt Parkway, and yet it reminded Jeffrey of what he still thought of as home. It was the air and the smell of leaves and that dank musty smell from the alders and the brown grass that were the same. For some reason, it made Jeffrey think of Halloween, of stealing garden gates and of tying strings to knockers.

They were approaching what Beckie called the "little" village where she tried to buy as much as she could from the "little" grocery store and the "little" hardware store. The village had the wide, elm-shaded street characteristic of all Connecticut towns, the white church with its double-arched window with small uneven glass panes that glittered crookedly in the sunset, the white houses with green blinds, and the general store with its wide front stoop and its placards advertising soft drinks and tobacco. The store looked as though it had always been there, but the old house beside it had been turned into an antique shop with a cradle, a rocking-horse, and four huge green glass bottles on its lawn. The old inn had been renovated, all fitted out with a taproom. It was called the Coach and Kettle, and a sign hanging from it, new and fresh, depicted a coach and a kettle. The village green had never been intended to be quite so neat. There should have been a cow grazing on it and a milk pail sunning on a hook by a kitchen door and boys playing ball or tag. Now there was nothing except the clear October sun and a boy in a white coat brushing the steps of the Coach and Kettle. Jeffrey could see that nearly all the houses on the green had been bought by people from New York, interesting, sensitive people, and that the villagers lived on a back street somewhere else. Beckie had said that they were getting just the kind of people who would appreciate the charm of that little village. Phil Rheingold lived on the green—the Rheingold who did the etchings of wild ducks. Then there was a Mr. Tevis of the firm of Tevis and Waddley, insurance brokers in New York, who collected locks and door latches as a hobby. Then, too, there was Mrs. Leland Hanscom who sold the antiques, a very gallant person from New York whose husband never could seem to get anywhere but now she had him in back somewhere regluing chairs—and there were more people like this who were coming all the time. Fred and Beckie's place was still a mile beyond the village.

"Jeffrey," Madge said, "please drive past the graveyard very slowly."

Madge was always interested in graveyards, and there it was beside the road, an acre or so of tilting stones surrounded by sapling-choked fields. Some of the stones, you could see, were very old slate, and there were some flat tombs of red sandstone that were disintegrating with the weather, and others were newer, of white marble, and some still newer of purplish polished granite. The little flags from Decoration Day, bleached and sodden by the rain, still stood above the graves of those who had been soldiers.

"It's like 'Our Town,'" Madge said.

He knew that she was not referring to her town, or his, but to the play by Thornton Wilder.

"Well," Jeffrey said, "you can't hurt a graveyard."

"But Jeff," Madge said, "you said you liked 'Our Town.'"

"It was all right," Jeffrey said, "but—never mind."

It was not the memory of the play so much as the actors that bothered him, and it was not the actors so much as the critics who had written of it, for they had been dealing only with what they thought a town should be. It was like one of those sweet potatoes which used to stand on the kitchen windowsill immersed in a glass of water. Sprouts would come from the top of it, and roots would drop down from below, dangling nakedly in that slightly turbid water, seeking vainly for the earth. He might be wrong, but he thought that the play had lacked earth, except for the graveyard scene, and you couldn't do much to a graveyard. The village green had been like that, an artistic conception more than a place.

"We're nearly there," Madge said. "There are Fred's new hurdle fences." Then they saw the Norman tower and the barn roof of Higgins Farm, and they turned up the driveway.

"Look," Madge said, "they're on the lawn, sitting on the Joggle Board."

"What?" Jeffrey said. "What in hell is that?"

"Oh, Jeff," Madge said, "Fred brought one from Carolina. They used to have them on plantations. It's just a big long board bench, and when you sit in the middle of it, it joggles."

"Oh me, oh my!" Jeffrey said.

"Oh, Jeff," Madge told him, "please be nice. Fred sees us. He's going to ring the bell."

"Oh me, oh my," Jeffrey said. "Since when did he start bell ringing?"

"Oh, Jeff," Madge said, "*please* be nice. He just bought the bell."

Sure enough, you could see the front of the house now with the fanlight over the doorway and the terrace and a long board bench with people sitting on it; and sure enough, Fred was running to the side of the driveway ringing a large dinner bell. Fred was dressed in something light blue from Brooks Brothers called a "Frontier Suit," and with it he wore a red-checked shirt.

"Hi," Fred was yelling, "hi." The car was suddenly stuffy as it always was after a long trip. There were stray packages of cigarettes on the seats and petals from the chrysanthemums, and extra overcoats, and powder had spilled from Madge's compact. Beckie was running toward them. Beckie was wearing a full pleated gingham dress, brownish purple with little roses on it. Her skirt was billowing and her legs were bare; she was wearing sandals and horn-rimmed glasses. Then Jeffrey was shaking hands with Fred while Madge and Beckie kissed. Then Fred dropped the bell and threw his arms around

Madge and kissed her, and then Jeffrey kissed Beckie. Years ago Madge had told him always to kiss Beckie, because she expected it. Your best friend, Madge had told him, always expected to be kissed by your husband.

"Jeff," Beckie said, "you oaf, you, I was worried you weren't coming." Jeffrey started to answer, but there was no time.

"We've been working all day," Beckie said, "and you've missed it. We've had weeding teams, but now Adam is going to make us juleps."

"Maybe that's why I was late," Jeffrey said.

"You oaf," Beckie told him, "you'll work tomorrow, even if it's Sunday. You'll be on my team tomorrow."

"Leave the car right here," Fred called. "Adam will put it away, and he'll rustle up the bags. Come and meet everybody. They're great people."

"Fred, dear," Beckie said, "perhaps they'd like to see their room, first, and wash up a little. You're going to be in the Old House, in Uncle Joel's room."

Jeffrey looked across the lawn. The old well was still there with a brand-new well sweep on it.

"All day long," Jeffrey said, "someone has been asking me if I don't want to wash my hands."

"Jeff," Madge said, and looked at him hard, "Jeff." But Beckie had begun to laugh.

"Don't scold him, dear," she said, and she linked her arm through his.

"Come on," Fred said, "stop necking, and meet the company."

"Fred," Beckie said, "perhaps some of the others will begin to think you always talk this way—just like a local yokel."

"That's what a farm's for, ain't it, by heck?" Fred said. "Come out and see my new turning lathe, Jeff. I've got a real woodworking shop here now."

"A woodworking shop," Jeffrey said, "by heck!"

"Jeff," Madge said, "you don't have to be a local yokel, too."

Then her voice dropped, and she raised her hand to brush a wisp of hair behind her ear, and Beckie and Fred, too, stopped being funny. Fred gave his light blue coat a little pull, because they were approaching all the rest of the company, and there was that familiar indecisive moment of wondering what may come of it, when you meet people at someone else's house on a week end.

The others had risen from the Joggle Board, and from iron chairs which surrounded two white round iron tables, each table shaded by a deep blue canvas umbrella on the top of a pole plunged through the table's vitals. There were lots of other chairs on the terrace—those canvas sun-bathing chairs that were difficult to disentangle when they were folded, rattan chairs from China, and chairs with bunches of grapes on their backs, and long reclining chairs with small canopies over them and with wheels instead of legs. All the people standing up looked as if they belonged in those chairs. The women wore gingham dresses like Beckie's and the men wore coats with large checks and squares on them. Everyone looked very sunburned and happy with the possible exception of Walter Newcombe. Walter was wearing white flannels and the same gabardine coat which had appeared on the dust jacket of *I Call the Turn.* Walter's nose was peeling.

"Everybody here knows everybody else, don't they?" Beckie asked, and Jeffrey knew everyone vaguely, and if he did not, the faces were like others which he knew. There were Mr. and Mrs. Newcombe, Beckie was saying, right over there. It interested Jeffrey to learn that the Newcombes, who must have been there all day, had not achieved a first-name basis yet.

"Hello, Walter," Jeffrey said.

"Why, I didn't know you knew Mr. Newcombe," Beckie said. Next there was a couple named Dorothy and Dick Sales, who came, Beckie said, from Scarsdale. The names seemed familiar to Jeffrey and then he remembered Sally Sales, of whom Jim had spoken, but he could not remember ever having seen either of them before. When Mr. Sales called him "Jeff," Jeffrey must have assumed that vague look of incomprehension which you try to hide but never can.

"It's Dick Sales, Jeff," he said, "Paris 1918. July. We were both on leave. Café de la Paix, and elsewhere."

"Oh," Jeffrey said, "oh, yes."

"Do you remember how you put that girl on roller skates and pushed her out on the floor and ran away and left her?" Mr. Sales asked.

"What girl?" Jeffrey asked. "Where was that?"

And then he heard Madge saying, "Why, Jeff, you never told me about that," but there was only a flutter of interest because Beckie was introducing them to a bald-headed youngish man, tall and hollow-chested, wearing a russet-brown tweed coat cut into squares by crimson lines.

"This is Buchanan Greene," Beckie said, and there was a change in her voice, indicating that this time she had produced something. Jeffrey thought that she was going to add, "the poet, and of course you have read him," but she did not.

"And here," Beckie went on, "I didn't mean to leave you until last, darling, but you know them both."

It was Marianna Miller with a Quaker girl's sunbonnet pushed back from her bright gold hair, and with a dress that reminded him of one of those nice little girls in *Pride and Prejudice* or *Barchester Towers*—and obviously Marianna was trying to be a nice little girl who loved dogs and cows and flowers and possibly croquet.

"Darling," Marianna said to Madge, "how windswept you look." Then she turned to Jeffrey and kissed him. It was one of those swift embraces which was partly Broadway and partly Hollywood, and Jeffrey had often explained to Madge that it was perfectly all right. It was just the way stage people behaved.

"Hello, darling," Marianna said, and she smelled of Cuir de Russie, the way she always did.

"Hello," Jeffrey said, "you look like an Anthony Trollope this afternoon."

The line struck Marianna as funny and she laughed and Jeffrey was sorry that he had said it, because he saw Madge looking at him. Madge always told him that she could not understand how it was, when he had such good manners everywhere else, that he was always a little bawdy and off-color whenever they went to Fred's and Beckie's, but Beckie was laughing too.

"Naughty," she said, "naughty Jeff. And here, I nearly forgot—here's Godfrey."

She was referring to her oldest son. Godfrey must have been about twenty. The shoulders of his coat were padded so that his head looked too small, and yet though his head was too small, his features looked too large for his head.

"Hi ya, Aunt Madge. Hi ya, Uncle Jeffrey," Godfrey said.

Everyone was looking at Godfrey politely, for of course there was nothing you could do about your friends' children. Jeffrey had never asked the boy to call him "Uncle Jeffrey" and it was the last thing he wanted, but Beckie always wanted her children to be perfectly at home with her friends.

"Jeffrey, dear," Beckie said, "I hope you and Godfrey can have a good long talk together tomorrow, and perhaps with Miss Miller too, if Marianna doesn't mind. What do you think? Godfrey is thinking of going on the stage."

There was another pause, but it was broken by Buchanan Greene, who spoke in the sonorous voice he used when he read from his own works.

"Life's but a walking shadow, a poor player—"

Jeffrey looked up at the pointed Norman dovecote and wriggled his toes inside his shoes.

"Oh, darling," Marianna said, "go on, I love it so."

It looked for a moment as though Buchanan might go on, and he would have if it had not been for Fred.

"Never mind it now," Fred said. "Here comes Adam with the drinks."

"Fred," Jeffrey heard Beckie whisper, "*Fred.*" The front door with the fanlight above it had opened and Adam, the Negro houseman from Harlem, appeared in his white coat carrying a tray of frosted glasses.

"Buchanan wants a drink, too," Fred said. "His tongue is hanging out."

"Parched," Buchanan answered, "swollen and blackened by the desert heat."

"Jeffrey," Beckie whispered, "it's an experience."

Jeffrey's eye was on Adam with the glasses. It seemed to him that Adam was moving more slowly than was necessary.

"Yes," Jeffrey said, "it always is to be here, Beckie."

"To have a poet," Beckie said, "and no mean poet."

Holding his glass and occasionally sipping his drink through the little silver tube that went with it, Jeffrey crossed the grass toward Walter Newcombe. Walter and his wife were standing a little distance away from the rest, wearing the set smiles of people in a gathering where everyone knows everyone else well except themselves. Walter's clothes were not quite right, and he looked tired, and that wife of his looked about the way Jeffrey thought she would. She wore a white knitted dress and her hair was prematurely white and her eyebrows made a straight and rather bushy line across her forehead. She was older than Walter, and Jeffrey wondered what whim of natural selection had brought those two together.

"Hello, Walter," Jeffrey said.

Walter blinked and cleared his throat.

"Hi, old man," he said, "let's see, you met Mildred didn't you?"

Jeffrey looked at Mrs. Newcombe, and Mrs. Newcombe stared at him hard.

"Walt," she said, "my cigarettes and my holder, please." Walter plunged his right hand quickly into the side pocket of his gabardine coat.

"Yes, sweet," Walter said, "coming right up."

"Here," Jeffrey said, and reached for his own cigarette case. "Let me, please."

Mrs. Newcombe still looked at him searchingly.

"Thank you," she said slowly, "I only smoke those London fags. Walt brought me some over." She paused a moment. "On the Clipper. Thank you, Walt." Walter had handed her a white jade cigarette holder with a cigarette inserted in it, and whipped out his lighter. She exhaled a cloud of smoke gracefully and deliberately.

"Yes," she said, and her voice had grown more gracious, "Mr. Wilson and I might as well have met. I've heard so much about him."

Jeffrey understood her. She was not having a happy time and she wanted to make it plain that she was Mildred Hughes who wrote for the *Pictorial* and the *Cosmopolitan* and it didn't matter if her husband had written *World Assignment*. She was Mildred Hughes.

"I've always wanted to meet you," Jeffrey said, "I've seen your name so often."

"Oh," she said, "have you read my stuff? I hate to write. It's like childbirth, do you feel so?"

"I wouldn't know," Jeffrey said, "the barrier of sex intervenes."

Walter began to laugh. He raised his right leg and slapped his thigh.

"Oh, baby," he said, "oh, baby."

Mrs. Newcombe exhaled another cloud of smoke from the British fag. "Walter," she said, "don't make a God-damned monkey of yourself."

"Well," Jeffrey said, "how's everything? It was last April I saw you, wasn't it? When did you get back, Walter?"

Walter's features smoothed out quickly.

"Ten days ago on the Clipper," he said, "or was it eleven, sweet?"

"How the hell should I know?" Mrs. Newcombe said. "You just came batting at my bedroom one morning at the Waldorf." She looked again at Jeffrey. "What is your first name, Mr. Wilson?"

"It's 'Jeff,' sweet," Walter said. "You remember, I told you how Jeff came to the Waldorf and was so sweet to Edwina, sweet."

"All right," Mrs. Newcombe said, "I'll call you 'Jeff' and you call me 'Mildred'! Artists should call each other by their first names."

"I'd love it," Jeffrey said, "but I'm not an artist."

"Neither am I," Mrs. Newcombe said, "and by God, neither is Walter."

"But sweet," Walter said, and he cleared his throat again, "I never said I was."

Mrs. Newcombe glanced quickly across the lawn and back at them.

"Why didn't you tell me about Jeff?" she asked. "I wish we three could get off somewhere under a bush with a bottle."

"Now sweet," Walter said, "it's almost dinnertime. Jeff, I never expected to see you here. They're very lovely people, aren't they, and they have a very lovely home."

"They certainly have," Jeffrey said. "When did you meet them, Walter?"

"It was after a lecture at the Colony Club last March," Walter said. "She came up to me afterwards—"

"They all come up to him afterwards," Mrs. Newcombe said, "these brittle—"

"Now, sweet," Walter said, "it's very lovely to be here. I've never been in an American—*galère* like this. I've been to châteaux near Tours and I've been entertained in English country homes, but I don't think I've seen anything quite like this, and Mildred hasn't either."

"The hell I haven't," Mildred said, "I've been in lots and lots of homes, and in lots and lots of beds, and now don't start saying how you knew the Duke of Windsor at Cannes. God knows why I married you over there except that I was lonely."

"Now, sweet," Walter said, "I only meant it's new to me—this whole sort of home." He looked at the trees along the driveway and sighed, and then he said just what Jeffrey thought he would. "Someday," Walter said, "when I settle down, I should like a home like this."

Jeffrey knew it was not the time or the place to ask a question, but still he asked it. It was growing cooler and darker. The figures of the others sitting in the chairs were growing dim.

"Walter," he asked, "what did you see over there this time? I tried to call you up when they jumped Norway, and you'd gone."

Walter Newcombe sighed.

"Jeff," he said, "don't get me started on that. I've been across Belgium with the British. I was in Gorty's headquarters."

"Gorty?" Jeffrey asked. "Who's Gorty?"

"Lord Gort, you know, the Commanding General," Walter said. "And then there was the Dunkirk show, and then London, but don't get me started on that."

"No, don't," Mrs. Newcombe said. "Wait till after supper." She lowered her voice into a horrid parody. "Do *pulease* tell us, Mr. Newcombe. We're all so dying to know. Do please tell us what you've been through, and a little of what has happened to the dear old lovely things in London. Don't draw him out now on an empty stomach."

"Now, sweet," Walter began, "it isn't that way at all."

"What the hell do you think they asked you for?" Mrs. Newcombe said. "Your face?"

"It must be great to be back," Jeffrey said.

"Wait," Mrs. Newcombe said, "don't ask Walt. I know the answer to that one, and all the other answers. 'Don't quote me, but, yes, it *is* great to be back. I don't think that any of you over here know quite how great it is to be back

—how lucky you are to have an abundance of food and clothing and roofs over your heads. I don't think that any of you quite realize the suffering over there. If I could take you there for five minutes—'"

Walter's face had grown brick-red.

"Sweet," he said, and his voice had changed. "Please. It isn't funny."

And all at once there was a dull sort of soundproof silence—and Walter cleared his throat.

"Because it's true," he said. "My God, it's true."

Jeffrey looked over at the parasols and the chairs with wheels and the house, and Fred and his tailored dungarees and the bell and the Joggle Board.

"Yes," he said, "of course it is."

Mrs. Newcombe stood dead still.

"All right, Walt, you win," she said. And then they heard Fred calling.

"One more drink," he called, "and dress for dinner."

The lights of Higgins Farm had been turned on and shafts of light from the small-paned windows cut across the dusky lawn.

"Jeff," Walter asked, "does that mean we just wash, or do we dress?"

"You dress," Jeffrey said, "but you wear a soft shirt because we're in the country."

"You know damn well we dress," Mrs. Newcombe said. "Don't act as though you haven't been to houses."

"I was only asking, sweet," Walter said, "sometimes they do and sometimes they don't."

"Afterwards," Mrs. Newcombe said, "let's go up to our room and get fried. Walter has a bottle."

"Now, sweet," Walter said, "Jeffrey's wife is here. We'll see you later, Jeff. It's like old times."

He understood what Walter meant, but it wasn't like old times.

The stairway of the old Higgins house, built around the old chimney, was steep and narrow, but Beckie had left it just that way. The paint had been scraped off the old pine railing and risers and one of the old pine doors still had an original butterfly hinge on it which had been carefully copied so that now all the doors had them. Uncle Joel's room was done in blue-and-pink-checked glazed chintz. The only new things in it, Beckie always said, were the box spring mattresses on the twin beds. The beds themselves were old spool bedsteads cut down and waxed and oiled. The room had a fireplace with Hessian andirons and a tavern table with a mirror over it decorated with a picture of a tombstone and a weeping willow. There was also an old maple chest of drawers which Beckie and Fred had scraped down themselves and there were some of those comical old framed mottoes on the wall, such as "God Bless Our Home," and several more tombstone memorials of weeping willows with the names of the deceased written in with pen and ink. On the mantel was an arrangement of wax flowers under glass. There were also two very early bannister-back chairs and a Boston rocker with an embroidered picture of a cat on its cushion. Then there were the rugs. Beckie and Fred had been everywhere to find them. There was an old braided rug in front of the fireplace made by a little old country woman whom Beckie had found, and several hooked rugs with cats and horses on them. The plumbing connected with Uncle Joel's room was modern, of course. It had been installed in a closet, called by connoisseurs of old houses the "prayer room," and perhaps it had been better for prayers than bathing. The checked chintz spreads were still over the beds, and Madge's suitcase rested on one baggage rack, and Jeffrey's on another. There were some autumn leaves on the bedside table and a copy of Peter Arno's *Stag at Eve,* and two copies of *House and Garden.* Jeffrey took off his coat and opened his suitcase. It was empty.

"Madge," Jeffrey said, "they've unpacked everything. It's going to be like 'Button, button, find the button.'"

It was one of those houses where the maids unpacked and hid everything and you tipped them for it, but they never packed you up again.

"Don't shout so," Madge said. "Fred and Beckie are right across the hall."

Those oiled pine doors were not meant for privacy—he could hear Fred singing in his shower. Jeffrey began opening the drawers of the maple chest. All of them squeaked and stuck.

"These damn drawers—" Jeffrey began.

"Don't bang around so," Madge said. "You can't expect an old bureau to be perfect. That's half the fun of it." She was beginning to sound like Beckie, as she always did when she was there. She was examining enviously the details of that room. "You know it's all awfully cunning."

"Only guests sleep in it," Jeffrey told her, "and the toilet paper is connected with a music box—"

"Jeff," Madge said, "they'll hear you. It's just a joke of Fred's."

Jeffrey did not answer; he was still struggling with the bureau drawers.

"Jeff," Madge said, "Mr. Newcombe looks very intelligent. What were you and his wife talking about?"

Jeffrey did not answer. His socks were not in the bureau. They were on a shelf in a little cupboard beside the fireplace with his shirts.

"Jeff, what is Mrs. Newcombe like?"

"Like?" Jeffrey repeated. "Not what you'd think from looking at her."

"Jeff, you're having a good time, you know you are."

"Damnation!" Jeffrey said. "Button, button, button?"

"But Jeff, they're the sort of people you always say you like."

Jeffrey was looking for his brushes, and he found them, for no conceivable reason, in the drawer of the bedside table, together with a bottle of aspirin, but her voice made him look up. She wanted him to say he liked it all.

"They're all right," he said. "Maybe it's this room that gets me down. Madge, I have the damnedest sort of feeling."

"Jeff," Madge said, "you should have let me drive. You're tired."

"It's just a sort of feeling," Jeffrey said, "like the end of the world. None of us belong here."

They stood staring at each other across the room. He could see the vertical lines deepen in her forehead, and he noticed that they both were holding hairbrushes. He had the ivory-backed ones which she had given him, and she had the gold-backed one which he had given her. They had nothing to do with the subject, but there they were.

"How do you mean," she asked, "that we don't belong here?"

"It's just a feeling," Jeffrey said, "it came over me out there on the lawn, when I saw all of us—It was a little—" He walked over to the mirror. "Maybe it's these pictures of tombstones. It was a little as though we all were dead, and didn't know it."

He heard her catch her breath, but he could not see her face.

"Jeff," she said, "please—" Then he saw that she was smiling at him. "I know what you mean," she said, "but don't be so gloomy. Just don't say we're dead."

He had not thought that she would have felt it too, but she must have felt it. He wished that he had Madge's resilience. Madge could toss away any thought that was uncomfortable as you might toss off a coat when the weather was too hot.

11

This—Is London

Fred was downstairs waiting for them, wearing a velvet dinner jacket the color of old Burgundy and a tie and cummerbund to match.

"Come on, everybody," he called, "cocktails in the Rumpus Room."

The Rumpus Room in the basement had been the summer kitchen. Its floors were paved with bricks and its walls were finished in old pine paneling which Beckie had picked up here and there, and Fred had found a bar in an antique store in New York—a real old tap bar such as had existed in taverns at the time of the midnight ride of Paul Revere. There was a ping-pong table in the Rumpus Room and all sorts of indoor games such as slot machines.

"Here," Beckie called, "here are nickels for anyone who wants to play the slot machines."

Fred was behind the bar taking ice cubes from a small electric refrigerator and arranging bottles and glasses and maraschino cherries and slices of orange and bitters.

"Anybody who doesn't want an old-fashioned yell," Fred said, but no one yelled.

"Dotty," Beckie said to Mrs. Sales, "help Fred, will you dear? Before he drops something."

Mr. Sales and Marianna were playing the slot machine. Marianna had a red-and-white-striped camellia in her gold hair. Her dress was white piqué, very simple, and Jeffrey wanted to tell her that he liked it, when she looked up at him and smiled, but there was no time. He watched the way she moved her hands. She was the best-looking woman in the room, but she was not trying to be—she had learned that she did not have to try. Buchanan Greene was lighting a cigarette for Mrs. Newcombe and Walter was talking to Madge.

"This must be an ideal place," he heard Walter saying, "for a rainy day."

"Jeffrey," Beckie said to him softly, "you're going to sit next to Mrs. Newcombe at dinner. I hope you don't mind."

"Mind?" Jeffrey said. "Why, no." He would not mind anything as soon as he had a drink.

"I knew you wouldn't," Beckie said, "and after dinner I want you to help me draw out Mr. Newcombe, and I think perhaps—Fred's going to try—perhaps Buchanan Greene will read us something."

Everyone was speaking in careful, measured tones as you always did before the cocktails, but it was different later. A glow of good fellowship began to fill the Rumpus Room.

"I was afraid Mr. Newcombe wouldn't mix," Beckie said, "but it's better now."

It was better now; all the voices were mixing loudly and Adam was bringing in sausages impaled on little toothpicks stuck in an apple, and contorted anchovies curled on crackers, and red caviar, and hot olives wrapped in bacon. Walter had picked up an olive.

"Le Touquet," he said to Madge, "have you really been to Le Touquet, Mrs. Wilson? Mrs. Newcombe and I went there for our honeymoon." Then his expression changed. He had placed the olive and the bacon in his mouth.

"Oh, dear," Madge said, "it's awfully hot."

Walter removed the olive.

"Excuse me, Mrs. Wilson," he said, "I have never seen one of those before."

"Why," Madge said, and she laughed, "I thought you'd seen everything." But nobody listened; everyone was talking.

"I'll have to speak to Fred," Beckie was saying. "If he takes another cocktail, he'll go to sleep after dinner."

The dining room upstairs had been enlarged from the old farm winter kitchen and Beckie had kept the general atmosphere carefully within the limits of what she called "old, farmy and kitcheny." In taking your place at the seventeenth-century trestle table, which Fred had found on Madison Avenue, you had to be careful not to stumble over spits and pots and candle molds and pestles and mortars and other ancient implements which had been collected on the old kitchen hearth. An old pine dresser, very old and very battered, was filled with pewter. Candles burned in pewter candlesticks and the central table decoration was a great mound of small multicolored gourds, all varnished and heaped on an enormous pewter platter. Around the platter and among the candles were ears of red and yellow corn, and a few small pumpkins to show that it was autumn. The chairs were simple wooden kitchen chairs which Fred and Beckie had been collecting over a period of years, constantly discarding one when they found a better one, until all of them now had a fine patina. Fred had once said that he hated to think how many pants seats had been worn out, and how many spines had been curved, giving those chairs their present luster.

The dining room might be plain and farmy, which was the way Beckie wanted it, but it was different with the food, because both she and Fred were members of the Wine and Food Society, and if you gave cooking and food a little thought, it paid enormous dividends. For just one thing there was the matter of salad. It made all the difference in the world if someone who was sensitive mixed the dressing, and somehow, even the greatest "treasure" you could ever get in the kitchen—Adam's wife, Cynthia, really was a "treasure," a rolypoly old darling who should be wearing a red bandanna and gold earrings—somehow the greatest "treasure" could not get the ingredients right. But Fred was marvelous with French dressing. He liked to tell that story about the Chinese servant who was able to give just a suspicion of garlic to his salads without putting garlic in them. And how had Wong done it? He had done it by eating the garlic himself and then blowing on the lettuce. Personally, Fred always rubbed the inside of the bowl with just a little garlic, but it was something you had to do yourself, because no servant knew when to stop, and you had to stop with garlic, and even so, husbands and wives had to promise both to eat the salad or not to touch it. Fred always mixed the salad at the end of the room on a hunting board, no matter how many there were for dinner. He needed exactly the right number of pepper mills, each containing a slightly different condiment, and a salt grinder, because common salt spoiled it. The lettuce leaves must be cold and crisp and dry, and none of that iceberg lettuce, either. The dressing was only half the battle. The main art of making salad consisted in *fatiguéing* it properly, as the French so picturesquely put it. It was not a matter of taking your wooden fork and spoon and torturing the mixed greens into a pulp. It was rather a problem of being sure that every leaf had its just proportion of the dressing on both sides.

Fred was there at the hunting board working at the salad already and when they sat down, Beckie tapped on a glass because she wanted everyone to know that the recipe for the cream of leek soup that they were going to have had come from a very old English cookbook, and she hoped that everyone would excuse her about the wild ducks. They were mallards which a client of Fred's had sent them from the Eastern Shore, but mallards or not, Beckie felt that ducks were ducks, not to be served raw, but cooked like any other ducks with bread stuffing and onions and applesauce.

They were all seated by the time Beckie had finished telling them about the ducks, and the soup was coming on. Jeffrey was seated between Mrs. Newcombe and Mrs. Sales.

"What's the matter, dear old playmate?" Mrs. Newcombe said to him. "Does the soup taste bad, old chap?"

"It isn't the soup," Jeffrey said. "You ought not to kill a duck and do anything like that to it." But Mrs. Newcombe was not interested.

"Not rahally," Mrs. Newcombe said, "not rahally, dear old chap."

"Where do you get the 'dear old chap' stuff?" Jeffrey said.

"From that rahally delightful poet," Mrs. Newcombe said; "he's a dear old chap, and whether he's a friend of yours or not, he gives me a pain in the—"

"Now, sweet," Jeffrey said, "now, sweet."

Mrs. Newcombe looked at him and smiled.

"Why hasn't Walter ever told me about you?" she asked. "How did you ever get in here, precious?"

"By accident, like you, I guess," Jeffrey said.

"What's the nice man doing over in the corner?" Mrs. Newcombe asked. "Why doesn't he eat his soup?"

"Now, sweet," Jeffrey said, "he's making you a nice salad."

He glanced across the table and saw that Madge was watching him.

"Not rahally," Mrs. Newcombe said. "Shiver my timbers, precious, not a salad, rahally."

"Now, sweet," Jeffrey said, "now, sweet."

"Jeff," Madge called across the table, "what are you two laughing about?"

Jeffrey pretended not to hear her, but he knew she would ask him about it later. He was relieved when Mrs. Sales turned to him. You knew that you would behave exactly as a guest should when you looked at Mrs. Sales. She looked the way a well-bred woman, a wife and mother, ought to look—clear brown eyes, dark hair with a silver threading of gray in it, not too much lipstick, not too much of anything—and not more than one old-fashioned.

"I just adore your son Jim," Mrs. Sales said.

It startled Jeffrey. He had never thought of Jim's confession seriously before, but there was something uncomfortably possessive in this stranger's manner. She seemed to imply that they both had a common interest, that they were both dear old people, the course of whose lives was completely finished and who now could live again in the lives of others. It made him very uncomfortable, and it fitted perfectly with the onion-stuffed wild ducks. He was sure that Mrs. Sales was going to refer to Jim and her daughter as "the young people."

"I hope Jim hasn't been making a nuisance of himself," Jeffrey said.

"Oh dear, no," Mrs. Sales answered, very quickly, "Dick and I both adore your Jim. Dick and I love young people. The house these days," and she looked at him with arch meaning, "is full of young people."

Jeffrey smiled mechanically.

"I've never met your daughter, Sally," Jeffrey said. "But I've heard Jim speak of her. I don't seem to meet many of his friends."

"I hope," Mrs. Sales said, "you haven't got the idea that Sally doesn't like to talk to older people. We must arrange to meet sometime—the old folks and the young people all together. I feel I know you very well already, Jim has talked so much about you."

The smile still lingered mechanically on Jeffrey's lips. He had never thought of Jim's mentioning him to anyone, and he wondered what Jim had said.

"You and he must have such a pleasant relationship," she told him. "He admires you so. That's why I feel I know you."

The balance of everything was shifting. Jeffrey had never thought that he would be grateful to his son for having said a kind word about him.

"Jim's a good boy," he said.

He began to feel like a sweet old codger, but there was no way to prevent it.

"You must be very proud of him," she said, "he's such a thoughtful boy. He's so helpful around the house."

Jeffrey could not believe that she was talking about his Jim. From childhood Jim had always faded out when there was anything to do around the house.

"How do you mean he's helpful?" he asked.

"In all sorts of ways," she answered. "When Dick was working on the rock garden on the lawn, Jim pitched right in and helped him, and he always helps Sally and me with the dishes on the maid's night out."

It meant of course that Jim loved her; it was exactly what you would do if you loved a girl. You would be useful with the dishes. The mention of the maid's night out indicated quite accurately their social position and their financial bracket. Jeffrey was very much ashamed that he had noticed it, but then, perhaps, that was the way it was when you suddenly became an old codger and thought of your children. Madge's father must have thought of him with much the same doubts and reservations.

"You must be very proud of him," Mrs. Sales said again. "Dick says he would have known he was your boy right away. Dick says he looks the way you did in France. Dick's told me so much about you."

It was embarrassing, that he still could not remember anyone in France named Dick Sales, in spite of that episode in Paris which had been mentioned on the lawn. It must have been one of those times on leave when faces and scenes shifted too fast. The idea lingered in his mind that someone who remembered him in uniform had thought that his son looked like him.

Beckie had risen and everyone was standing up.

"We're not going to leave the boys alone," she called. "We're all going together to the living room, and you can have your Armagnac in there and your cigars, too, if anybody wants them."

Jeffrey knew that Beckie hoped that no one would want them because Beckie always said that one cigar made the whole house stale the next morning, and, as Jeffrey looked around the table, he knew that he would be the only man who would take one, with the possible exception of Dick Sales, and Madge would shake her head at him when Fred offered him the box.

"Jeff," Beckie called, "oh, Jeff, do you mind if I whisper to you just a minute?"

She put her hand on his arm.

"Jeff," she whispered, "why didn't you or Madge tell me? It had to be Mr. Newcombe who told me that you and he came from the same little town."

"I never thought of it, I guess," Jeffrey said. "I haven't thought of Walter for quite a long while."

"I can't get over it," Beckie said, "it's like something in a novel, you and

Walter Newcombe. You'll get him started, won't you, Jeff, and I'll get everyone to listen."

There was no doubt that it was going to be what Beckie called a worthwhile evening.

In the living room they were all drawing chairs around the fireplace, and Fred was saying that just a little fire wouldn't do any harm, would it? He was explaining about the fireplace to Walter, saying he supposed everyone else had heard about it, and he did not want to bore anybody. First there had only been a hole for a stovepipe, and then a little fireplace behind it and believe it or not, when they were taking out the little fireplace . . .

"I guess they walled them up because they took too much wood," Walter said.

"Oh, Fred," Beckie called, "what do you think? Mr. Newcombe and Jeffrey both came from Bragg in Massachusetts, and Jeffrey's never told us."

Jeffrey could not understand why he felt awkward, or why coming from a place like Bragg should have made him or Walter any the more interesting. For some reason he thought that Madge looked embarrassed too.

"Just two barefoot boys from Wall Street," Jeffrey said; and then he added, "You have to come from somewhere."

"Mr. Newcombe has been away," Beckie said. "It's what Secretary Ickes called Wendell Willkie, Mr. Newcombe."

There was a moment of constraint. Adam was passing the brandy.

"Willkie's building up," Mr. Sales said, "he's building up all the time."

"Fred and I have talked it all over," Beckie said. "Haven't we, Fred, dear?"

"Yes, dear," Fred said. He was still working with the fire.

"We've made up our minds," Beckie said. "What we're going to do may seem a little queer, but it shows how strongly we feel, doesn't it, Fred dear?"

"Yes, dear," Fred said.

"Which will it be," Buchanan Greene asked, "Browder or Norman Thomas?"

"No, no," Beckie said, "don't be silly, Buchanan."

"Forgive it," Buchanan Greene answered, "it's only a poor poet's whimsey." But Beckie was standing very straight.

"Fred and I always think the same way at election time, don't we dear? We voted for Hoover in 1932. We voted for Landon in 1936. This year for the first time we're voting for Mr. Roosevelt, aren't we dear?"

"Yes, dear," Fred said.

"We're voting for Mr. Roosevelt," Beckie said, "because England wants us to have Mr. Roosevelt. That's the least we can do for England."

"Yes, dear," Fred said, "I suppose so."

"You don't suppose so, Fred," Beckie said, "you know so."

There was a moment's silence.

"Well, I suppose all you bright people will hate us," Mrs. Sales said, "but Dick and I are going to vote for Willkie. We think he can do more to keep us out of war."

"Keep us *out* of it?" Beckie began, and then she stopped and sat down by the coffee table.

There was a moment's uncomfortable tension in the room. There was a parrotlike sort of repetition in those women's voices. They were obeying their emotions and not reason, as everybody did. Jeffrey took a cigar when Fred offered it to him. "It comes from the Racquet Club," Fred said, "but I'm afraid it's a little dry, Jeff."

Jeffrey looked at the end of his cigar. Their voices had all risen again. Roosevelt had promised that none of our boys would be involved in a European war, hadn't he? He had said it again and again, and again, and Willkie had said the same thing again and again. They should have known that no one man could keep a country out of war, and no small group could get a country into war. You drifted into it on the tide of destiny; and now he had his social duty to perform, and there was no need to be artistic about it.

"Walter," Jeffrey said, "tell us, what's happening over there?"

The plain fact was, as everybody must have realized who gave it thought, that England would be whipped if we didn't help her; but Jeffrey knew that Walter wouldn't put it just that way. Walter stood in front of the fire with his hands still carefully tucked into the side pockets of his dinner coat.

"You mustn't think of me as knowing much," Walter said. "No one does in a situation that teems with imponderables."

That was the way it always was—no one knew much, but everyone was pathetically expecting something.

"Everyone always asks me," Walter said, "definite questions. But no answer can be definite, not on a broad world canvas obscured by the fog of war."

That was a new expression, and it covered everything, "the fog of war."

"To put it another way," Walter said, "it reminds me of a story about a Navvy by the East End docks in London in the blackout . . ."

Jeffrey only half listened to the adventures of the Navvy. He had heard about the doorman at the Savoy, and the man who used to wheel in the beef at Simpson's, and the little old woman who sold lucifers near Trafalgar Square. He wondered if all the people who must still be dining at Claridge's or the Savoy, or wherever it was they dined in London now, repeated those stories endlessly to each other with a sort of thankful wonder that those who had so little to lose or gain were standing with the rest of them. London had always seemed to him a city where poverty assumed a more sinister aspect than it did in any other city in the world, and yet where poverty was orderly and quiet. Everyone else was listening to the story of the Navvy, and like all those other anecdotes, it elicited applause and understanding laughter.

"That was beautiful," Beckie said, "I can see him as you tell it."

Then Buchanan Greene spoke, but Jeffrey found it hard to listen. Buchanan's words sounded like all the pages one read daily, words which had been squeezed dry of any particular meaning. He was saying something about the little people, and about our way of life.

"Naturally, I can't describe it all," Walter said, "but if you could see their faces you would see that it has the inevitable sweep of a Greek tragedy."

Walter put his hands firmly in his pockets, and swayed slightly backwards on his heels. It was obvious that Walter had used this phrase many times before. He paused and swayed from his heels to his toes, and then there was the sound of the front door opening.

"Just a minute," Beckie said, "I don't want to miss a word of it."

They were visitors whom she must have asked to come in after dinner. Men and women in evening clothes filed into the room, fresh from the autumn night, like the people who stumbled over your feet just as the first act was beginning. Walter could hear Fred and Beckie whispering to them in low undertones that they were just in time, that Mr. Newcombe was just beginning to tell them about the war. There were discreet scrapes of chairs and the sound of ice and glasses while Walter stood in front of the fire, self-conscious but obliging like a lecturer at a Women's Club.

"I hope you don't mind—" Beckie began.

"Oh, no," Walter said, "let me see, where was I?"

Mrs. Newcombe was the one who answered him.

"You were saying it was like a Greek tragedy."

"Oh, yes," Walter said, "thank you, sweet."

Jeffrey was reasonably sure that Walter had never read a Greek tragedy, but Walter was repeating the same endless sort of chant as a chorus from Euripides. He had no background of scholarship to help him and no knowledge of history or language. He was only telling what he saw, drawing conclusions from interviews and reading. It made Jeffrey wonder whether he himself could have done any better. Walter was speaking of the break-through in the Ardennes and the way the hinge of the line had broken, but he could not explain why it was not stopped. It reminded Jeffrey that Walter had never seen another war. His descriptions of bombings and of refugees all made this obvious. It was part of an old familiar story; everything had smashed, but there were units which had been magnificent. Now all the equipment was lost and the British Expeditionary Force was crowding the beaches of Dunkirk and the small craft were coming across the channel, taking out loads of soldiers. It was just what he had read, and Walter Newcombe added nothing new. It seemed to Jeffrey that this experience had conveyed nothing to Walter himself. It was like the words of "The Star-Spangled Banner" that told about the rockets' red glare and bombs bursting in air, but you could not see the rockets or hear the bombs.

Yet everyone was listening, and Jeffrey was sorry for himself and sorry for everybody there. It all had something to do with the Rumpus Room and with Fred's wine-colored velvet coat. He remembered what he had said to Madge—that they all were dead and didn't know it.

"And now," he heard Walter say, "I'll be awfully glad to answer any questions."

Then there was the usual silence and the usual question about what England could do next and about the bombing of the British Isles. Walter was saying something which he must also have read—that a military defeat could not conquer the spirit of a people; and then everyone was talking, and Fred was asking him if he would like a Scotch-and-soda.

"That was a great talk, wasn't it?" Fred said. "It's better than all the newspapers put together to hear someone who's been there."

"Yes," Jeffrey answered.

"It makes me feel as if I'd been there myself," Fred said.

Jeffrey wondered whether Fred meant it, or whether he only wanted to feel that way because it was the proper thing to say. He was thinking of the other war and of British officers with their belts and French officers in their horizon blue who had talked in the town hall at home. All the guests' voices now were raised in a futile sort of clamor; everyone was trying to express some idea of his own, although not a single idea had any value. Then there was a slight drop in the voices. There was a thumping, grating sound in the corner of the room where Fred had turned on the radio. He was saying that here was the eleven o'clock news, if anyone wanted it, and then Jeffrey heard a phrase which had already grown familiar.

"To get the news direct, we now take you to London."

"That will be Ed," he heard Walter say. "I wonder how Ed's doing."

It was a casual remark enough, and yet it seemed to Jeffrey that it was the first remark of Walter's that was not repeating what someone else had told him. The voice came across clearly, with a slight dramatic pause.

"This–is London."

Walter Newcombe nodded.

"Yes," he said, "that's Ed," and he stood there listening.

"It is two o'clock in the morning. The bombers are overhead again. They have been coming in fives and tens ever since midnight. It seems that they are flying higher, due, we hope, to more accurate antiaircraft fire. Just as I entered the studio, demolition bombs and incendiaries had fallen on a section of the city known to every American tourist. During the day, the air battle has continued . . ."

Jeffrey did not want to hear any more of it; he wanted to be out of that room and out of the house and by himself. He was acutely conscious of everyone sitting there, of the dinner coats and the evening dresses, of the fireplace with its crane and of the cobbler's bench, holding bottles and glasses, and of the overheated air, full of cigarette smoke and the faint, sticky fragrance of talcum. Nothing fitted with that simple statement that this was London. He walked slowly to the door which led to the little paneled hall filled with antique colored prints and walking sticks and canes that opened into seats, and golf bags.

"I return you now . . ."

He could still hear the voice. "I return you now . . ." It was as simple as "Now I lay me down to sleep." You could turn the speaker off the way you turned a water tap. He did not want to have any part in that scene any longer. He did not feel that he was any better than those other people, or more intelligent or more sensitive. It was simply that he did not belong with them at the moment. He did not seem to belong to anything. In leaving the room, he knew that he was trying to leave himself and a large part of his experience behind him, but it was not possible to turn the clock back, or possible to be younger. He could not even tell what he wanted to get away from unless it were a sort of insincerity, an insulation there which shut off all genuine expression. If you wanted to you could call it the way of life that everyone was leading—a way of life which had no more depth than a painting on a screen, but that was because you tried to get away from depth. You tried to live graciously and easily. You tried to get as far away as possible from fear or want or death.

12

I'll Wait for You by Moonlight

Jeffrey felt better when he had closed the front door behind him, but even then he could hear the measured words. "This—is London." They were artificial in themselves; the man who had spoken them must have consciously timed that pause for dramatic effect, just as an actor timed his lines. "This—is heaven. This—is war. This—is murder." It was an old trick which you could use in all sorts of ways. "This—is London." It had been London for just a moment. Jeffrey had been conscious of the planes and the antiaircraft, although there had not been a sound. He could feel his own utter insignificance and the imminence of danger all around him, although the night was clear October moonlight, beautiful, and very still. He could see the house behind him in that cold light. In spite of the warm glow from its windows, the mocking clarity of the moonlight made it look deserted as it certainly would be some time. It made it look as lonely as the houses along the Post Road which he had seen that afternoon. There was no kindliness or tolerance in that moonlight or in the shadows which the landscaped trees cast on the lawn. He knew why the goddess of the moon had been a frigid beauty in all the amorous mythology of Greece. There was something hostile in that moonlight, which raised a question in his mind.

"How in hell did I ever get here?"

The barn in the moonlight was black and white and it was much more motionless than it had been in the sunset. For some reason, it made him think of ghost stories that his brother Alf used to tell him when they were children. When he faced the blackness of the gaping open door, he remembered his grandfather's barn at night with its welcome restless stirrings of animals inside, but in here there was nothing. A sort of curiosity about its silence made him walk into the shadows, and then he heard footsteps on the gravel of the driveway, and someone called his name.

"Oh, Jeff." It was Marianna Miller. "Jeff. Where are you? I can't see." But he could see her white dress plainly enough in the moonlight.

"Didn't you hear me calling?" she asked, and he was certain that he had not. He had not heard a sound, but now that she was there the unbearable quality of his loneliness was broken.

"Why," he said, "Marianna," and then he added one of those obvious questions which had always annoyed him in play dialogue, "What brought you out here?"

He was smiling at her through the dark exactly as though she could see him, although she was only a white shape walking toward him through the shadows of the barn.

"Oh, Jeff," she said, and she gave a quick little laugh and rested her hand on his arm. That laugh of hers that came at exactly the right moment reminded him for a second of the theater, until she was closer to him, and then he put his arm around her and she clung to him in the dark.

"Marianna," he began, and then he forgot what he was going to say. It was never possible to explain impulses in the light of any sort of wisdom or experience. It must have been that voice from London more than her nearness. He had always been very careful in all the time he had known her to keep their relationship impersonal, and now she was in his arms and that other sort of friendship was entirely over.

"Oh, Jeff," she whispered, "darling, why didn't you ever do that before?"

"Why," he told her, "I don't exactly know." But, of course, he did know. He had never been as defenseless or unstable in all the times they had been together, and now she represented security and release. When he kissed her he forgot the voice saying "This is London."

"I'm a little sorry," he said, "but I hope you're not."

"Darling," she said, "don't be such a fool."

Still there was an element of regret because it was the end of a rational friendship which had always made him happy and the beginning of something else which he could see would lead to endless complications.

"Don't—" she said—"don't say you're sorry."

"Well," he began, "that's not exactly what I meant."

"Darling," she said, "we should have done this long ago."

He did not answer. It was too dark to see her face, but he could tell from her voice that her eyes would be half-closed and she would be smiling very faintly.

"It mixes everything up," he said, "that's all I mean."

"Darling," she said, "it had to happen to us tonight."

"Why tonight?" he asked.

"You and I," she answered. "We're the only ones alive here."

"What?" he said. It surprised him very much that her thoughts should have been so much like his.

"All those dreadful people," Marianna said, "in that room. You and I may not amount to much, but we're alive."

"Yes," he said. "Maybe you're right."

"I know I'm right," she said. "Oh God, Jeff, this—is London."

But he was still disturbed by the realization that they would never meet in quite the same way again, because he was more aware of consequences than she.

"Marianna," he said, "there isn't anything we can do about it."

"Oh, Jeff," she answered, "don't you know I've always loved you?"

"You shouldn't have," he said. "I'm not what you really want, dear. You've wasted a lot of time."

"Oh, Jeff," she said, "I wish–" and then she stopped, and he was very glad she had.

"So do I," he answered, "at the moment, but you know–"

There was no need to say any more, and it was better to leave it there in silence.

"Jeff," she said, "she–" And she stopped a second. "She's never been right for you, has she?"

"Madge?" he said. "Why, no one is exactly right for anyone else, not ever."

"I would be," she answered, "I'd make you–"

"Make me what?" he asked.

"I'd make you know how good you are. I'd make you write a play."

"Marianna," he said, "it's a little late for that." It hurt him when he said it, and he was glad that it was dark.

"Jeff," she said, "don't laugh."

"I'm not," he said; "it's kind of you, but just the same–"

"Don't," she said, "don't say it's kind."

"Not kind, exactly," he answered, "but this idea you have about me, it's a little corny, dear. You see, I'm only good for what I am. It's late to go on with something else."

It was no good blaming other people for anything that happened to you. You could only blame yourself.

"Jeff," she said, "you'll be going out to the Coast this spring, won't you?" And they seemed to have reached some sort of understanding without his knowing it or even being sure he wanted it.

"Yes," he said, "sometime around April."

"Well," she said, "I'll be there too."

She said it as though it settled everything and it made him more unsure of himself than he had been for a long while. He stood without speaking, and she sighed.

"I suppose we'd better go back now," she said.

He could hear the voice again: "This–is London." If it hadn't been for that, none of it would have happened.

"Yes," he said, "I suppose we'd better."

13

You Can't Blame Those Little People

The cool night air striking on the lower ground was causing a mist to rise, a mist that was solid and white and palpable in the moonlight, stretching like a high tide across the road, already partially concealing the walls and fences. Higgins Farm appeared even more unsubstantial than it had before. It gave Jeffrey the same sort of feeling that he sometimes experienced when he awoke at night in a strange room—that he might have been carried there without knowing it.

When they closed the front door behind them, he could see the naked exposure of the dark hand-hewn beams in the living room and the floral decoration on the oval hooked rug and the embers in the fire shining through the glasses on the cobbler's bench. Everyone was sitting silent in a circle around the fireplace, and at the sound of the front door everyone whispered "Hush."

He thought it was some sort of parlor game, until Beckie hurried toward them.

"Hush," Beckie whispered, "Buchanan is just in the middle of a poem."

"Oh," Jeffrey whispered back, "sorry."

Buchanan had evidently paused, disturbed by the interruption, and now he was looking at them with courteous reproach. He had no paper in his hand. He had been reciting from memory, because he was a poet. Jeffrey saw Madge frowning at him. Her eyes were asking him where on earth he had been, and why he had slammed the door. It reminded him of a Sunday, long ago, at home, when he had come running into the dining room because he was late for Sunday dinner only to find that the minister was there and was in the midst of saying grace.

"Sorry, Buchanan," Jeffrey whispered, "don't mind me," and everyone said "Hush," again.

"It's quite all right," Buchanan said. "It's my poem called 'The Cry of the Little People.'" And Buchanan laughed good-naturedly. "Don't listen to me pontificate, if you don't want to. Go romp on the lawn with Marianna."

"Go on," Jeffrey said. "I'm sorry, Buchanan." And he sat down on the floor. He felt his knees creak, but somehow you always sat on the floor when a poet was delivering a poem.

"Let me see," Buchanan said, "where was I?"

"We swink for you, naïvely, behind your grimy factory windows," Beckie said.

There was a pause. A cramp was seizing Jeffrey's right foot around the instep, but he did not venture to move. Buchanan had half-closed his eyes, and his voice was firm and clear, and actually his words were smooth and able, almost moving. The poem was about the little people whose small voices rose to reproach the privileged few who were living wrongly in the present. They were reproachful because they, the little people, and not their drivers, made this, our country. Through the lines of Buchanan Greene, the voices of fishermen and dirt farmers and lumberjacks and fallen women from the mining camps and a great many other people from other categories, including refugees, were rising in a reproaching, unanswerable chorus, principally in unrhymed iambic pentameter. Everyone else appeared to be listening to those bitter voices, but Jeffrey's mind strayed from the subject. He was thinking that everyone now wrote and talked about the Little People, and that the Little People were a new discovery in creative literature, and no doubt a wholesome one, but he wished that their discoverers would not invariably refer to them as Little People. It seemed to him that the Little People themselves would have every right to resent it, for the phrase, if you stopped to think of it, implied an intolerable sort of patronage. It was the way Beckie referred to the little grocer and the little cabinetmaker and the little village. It tacitly implied that you yourself were not quite as little, and actually no one, if you got to know him, was a little person. The phrase was snobbish and undemocratic, and yet it was used most frequently by mouthpieces of democracy.

"We have died for you," said Buchanan, "in the jade-green waters off the Georges Banks . . ."

It sounded well, but granting the necessity for poetic license it did not sound like the voice of a fisherman.

The lines revealed to Jeffrey that Buchanan Greene's acquaintance with the Little People, although he lived now by interpreting them, was purely academic. Buchanan Greene would not have known what to say to the Little People, and neither would most of the others who listened to him. All they knew, and all they would ever know, about Little People was what Buchanan Greene was telling them. It made Jeffrey wonder how he had ever got there on the floor, struggling with a cramp in his foot and listening. There was no doubt that Buchanan Greene was right—the Little People were correct in being very, very angry.

"And so, for this, too, we denounce you . . ."

There was no appreciable change in Buchanan's voice, no crescendo to indicate that his poem was ended. His voice simply faded into silence, though he still sat with half-closed eyes while everyone waited to hear some more strictures from the Little People, but none came. Someone moved uneasily, and now it was necessary to express one's feelings intelligently and appropriately because Buchanan Greene had given very freely of himself. It was necessary to convey the impression, not only to him, but to everyone, that his effort had meant something to you in particular, which you understood and were the better for. It was necessary not to speak for a moment. It would have been vulgar to hurry over to the shoemaker's bench and help yourself to a Scotch-and-soda or even to a little charged water. Even the resorting to that common sign of approbation, clapping of hands, would not have been quite in order. That must have been why everyone was silent. Someone sighed, and then Beckie sighed too, and shifted her position slightly on the fireside settle.

"Oh," she said, "oh, it's over." Her voice indicated incredulity that it could be over so quickly and at the same time she made you feel that she wanted it to go on forever, and that everyone else did, and now she was striving to get back into a workaday world through the magic that those words had wrought.

Jeffrey struggled to his feet and stamped softly upon the hooked rug. He could see Beckie looking at Fred meaningly. It was obvious that Fred had to say something.

"Buchanan," Fred said, "I think that's one of the best ones of yours I've ever heard. It's time we got more socially conscious. How about a drink?"

"Just a drop of Scotch," Buchanan said, "and plain water, please."

Then Walter Newcombe was speaking, in his capacity of man-of-letters. "That was a swell job, Mr. Greene," he said. "I enjoyed every minute of it." Mrs. Newcombe pulled his sleeve.

"Don't stop me, sweet," Walter said. "Mr. Greene knows what I mean. It was a swell job, Mr. Greene."

"Did you like it," Buchanan asked, "really?"

He asked it as though he were appealing to a superior judgment, but before Walter had time to speak again, they were all telling Buchanan how much they liked it and just what it had meant to each one of them and how much better it was than anything that MacLeish had done—not that it was in any way reminiscent of MacLeish.

Upstairs in Uncle Joel's room, Jeffrey removed his coat and hung it carefully over the back of one of the ladder-back chairs, but the chair was not made for such a purpose, and it tipped over. He picked up both the chair and the coat carefully, and found a hanger in the closet. Madge was sitting in front of the dressing table combing out her dark brown hair.

"Well?" Madge said.

It always ended up with him and Madge. After all those other people, they would always end up irrevocably alone.

"Well, what?" Jeffrey said.

Madge turned around on the little stool in front of the dressing table. "Don't say you didn't like it," Madge said.

"I didn't say I didn't like it," Jeffrey said. "What's happened to the luminal? I meant to bring some luminal."

"It's wherever they put it." Madge lowered her voice carefully. "Don't talk so loud. I can't *ever* tell when you're going to have a good time, not *ever*."

Jeffrey stood looking at the colored pictures of the tombstones.

"Neither can I," he said.

"Well, you must have had a good time when you ran off with your Miss Miller."

"I didn't run off with her," Jeffrey said. "I just met her out there."

"What did you talk about?"

"About you," Jeffrey said, "you—and London."

"I don't suppose she likes me." Madge picked up her comb again.

"No," Jeffrey said, "I don't suppose she does."

"Well, I'm glad she doesn't," Madge said, "as long as you like me better." Her eyes grew wider, and the vertical line on her forehead deepened. "You do like me, don't you Jeff?"

"Yes," he said, "I like you better."

"I suppose she thinks I cramp your style."

"Yes," Jeffrey said, "I suppose so."

"And you know I don't, don't you?"

"Yes," Jeffrey said, "I know you don't."

"You know we want the same things, basically."

"Yes," Jeffrey said, "basically."

"And if I try to live in any different way, if I try to simplify things, you're the first one to complain, you know you are."

"Yes," Jeffrey said. "Do you suppose they put that luminal in the bathroom, Madge?"

"Why," Madge asked, "didn't you ever tell me more about Walter Newcombe?"

Then she was talking about all the other people. She always loved parties and she was wondering what they were going to do tomorrow, and she was hoping that she could have a long talk with Beckie, and then she thought of something else.

"Jeff, did you think Dorothy Sales was intelligent?"

"She was all right," Jeff said.

"Jeff, you don't think it's serious about Jim, do you? She acted as though it were. Jeff, I do wish you'd listen to me. No one's ever heard of them. He's just someone that Fred met in some bank."

He knew that expression was elastic.

"Don't keep thinking Jim's going to get married," he said.

"But, Jeff, it's true. Beckie says no one knows them."

He stood looking at the pictures of the tombstones and at the wax flowers on the mantel.

"Jeff," she said, "I wish you'd ever talk to me. What are you thinking about?"

He did not answer.

"Jeff," she said, "you're worried about something. What is it? You've been worried all evening."

"Not worried, particularly," he answered, "but I'll tell you what I've been thinking. I've been thinking we're pretty close to the end of the world."

"The end of the world?" she repeated, and that line on her forehead grew deeper.

"The Post Road was the end of one world," he said, "and now we're at the end of another. You won't know this place when the war is over."

"I know," she answered, "that's what everybody says." But he knew she did not believe it, and again he was wondering how he had ever got there. It was the way it always had been when he passed from something he knew into something unfamiliar. The actual passage was always imperceptible. If there should be such a thing as survival after death, it might be like that—you would be somewhere else and wondering how you got there.

"Jeff," she asked him, "what *are* you thinking about?"

"Darling," he told her, "never mind." And then she was saying what she was always saying, that he never told her anything.

Jeffrey began pacing slowly back and forth across the room, first stepping upon a hooked rug that depicted a dog in front of a kennel, beneath which had been worked OUR FRIEND TRAY, and next upon a rug showing a cat playing with a ball, beneath which had been worked I LOVE LITTLE PUSSY, and next upon a rug with flowers and the single word WELCOME. He stepped carefully from one to another.

"Listen, Madge," he said, "don't keep asking me that. I'm thinking about the war."

He was thinking of those war novels. They had a sort of a pattern, even the best of them. A novel about the Civil War always started in the old plantation house, called Mary's Pride or Holly Bush. Someone was always playing a polka because little Mary Washington Archibault was going to marry one of the young Pringles, and Mary Washington's old mammy was leaning over the stairs, ivory teeth sparkling in polished ebony, and old Pompey (you might as well call him Pompey), who had started as Mary Archibault's grandfather's house nigger, was passing the juleps and perhaps a fruit cup for the ladies, when a door opened from somewhere and there was Mary Archibault's father, "Wild" Jim Archibault. His face was unusually grave. He had to announce that those damn Yankee shopkeepers were firing back from Sumter, and now the war was on.

Or take the World War, which people like Walter Newcombe were already calling World War I. The scene always opened at Chelmhurst Manor in Hants. They were out on the terrace with the fine Perpendicular Gothic façade of the old country house behind them, watching Reggie, the Oxford blue, play mixed doubles with the curate's second daughter against someone else, while the air and the sunlight were filled with young laughter. Then the door from the old priest's hole which now connected old Colonel Castlewood's study with the out-of-doors would open, and there was old Colonel Castlewood, his face unnaturally grave. The laughter stopped and the tennis stopped when they saw him. Hugh the footman put down his sandwiches. It had come at last, the old Colonel told them, and Hugh the footman said good-by to my lady, and went off to take his place in the Territorials.

Even Tolstoy could not get away from it. *War and Peace* began in a salon with a lot of trilingual Russians lapsing carelessly from Russian to French to English over their champagne. But then, you had to start somewhere. You had to pick a setting which showed the spirit of the time. If you wanted a setting for World War II, as Walter Newcombe was already calling it, perhaps Higgins Farm was as good a place as any. Perhaps it all meant something.

"Jeff," Madge was saying, "we're not in it, and there's nothing you can do about it."

There was nothing you could do about it, absolutely nothing, except to walk from the rug that had the dog on it to the one that had the cat to the one that had the flowers, and to wonder how you, or anyone else, had ever got where you were.

14

Those Ways We Took from Old Bragg High

Often when Jeffrey wondered how he had got where he was, his mind would go back to a morning at the square house on Lime Street in Bragg, Massachusetts. He was up in his room on the third story looking at himself in the wavy glass of the washstand mirror. He had borrowed his brother Alf's new safety razor and was shaving himself for the third time in his life. Jeffrey was distressed because the distortions of the mirror did his features an injustice. The top of his skull was cramped and he was certain that his nose and mouth appeared too large. When he had gone to the kitchen for some hot water, Tilly had asked him what he needed to be shaving for when he didn't have so much as a hair on him, and why was he wearing those white flannel pants—they looked like underdrawers! He was inclined to agree with Tilly that they were conspicuous, but Mr. Oakley, the High School superintendent, had suggested to Summers Harris, the president of the Class, that white flannel trousers, white shoes—not sneakers—a blue serge coat with a white handkerchief jutting from the breast pocket, and a high stiff Arrow collar, would be a suitable costume for the boys. The girls naturally would be dressed in white, and Mr. Judd, the proprietor of the Bon Marché Store, had given each girl a big bow hair-ribbon in the High School colors.

The door to Alf's room, next to his, was open and he could hear Alf singing. Alf always knew the latest song hits.

" 'I know a little chicken,' " Alf was singing. " 'She's the kind of a chicken for me.' "

It was a fine June morning. The sky and the elm trees and the spire of the Congregational Church with its rooster weathervane all seemed to have been washed clean by the shower the night before. He had seen that view often enough from his window, but now it looked brand-new, as new as he himself looked.

" 'Yes sir,' " Alf was singing, " 'she's the chicken for me.' "

Jeffrey had just finished washing his face with his knitted washcloth when

Alf came in. Alf was in his shirt sleeves and suspenders. Alf was whistling, and then he stopped.

"Well," Alf asked, "how did the razor go?"

It was very kind of Alf to ask. His tone was clean and new like the morning. It implied they were both men, discussing a subject which concerned men only. Alf looked wonderful, even in his shirt sleeves: snappy, with a dimpled cleft in his chin.

"It's got real balance to it," Alf told him. "No one can fool me on razors."

"That's right, it has got a mighty fine balance to it," Jeffrey said.

He was putting on his stiff collar. It was one of those high collars scarcely divided in front, and as he wrestled with the front stud, it gripped him about the larynx.

"Wait a minute," Alf asked, "where's your talcum powder?"

"Powder?" Jeffrey asked. "What for?" Alf was very kind that morning.

"You put it on after shaving," Alf said. "I'll get you some of mine."

"Gee, Alf," Jeffrey said, "it stinks. It stinks of violets."

"What the hell else should it smell like?" Alf said. "Read on the box, it's Violet Talcum Powder isn't it?"

"But, gosh, Alf," Jeffrey said, "if I go there smelling like that, some of the guys—"

"Some of the guys will what?" Alf asked.

"Some of the guys will start kidding," Jeffrey said.

"Say," Alf said, "look at me, does anybody kid me? Gentlemen use violet talcum powder, and you're a gentleman, aren't you?"

"The Old Man doesn't use it," Jeffrey said.

"The Old Man doesn't use it," Alf told him, "because he doesn't go around. Put it on your face, and now hold still and let me brush you off."

Alf dusted a handkerchief across Jeffrey's face and looked at him critically but kindly.

"You've got to be careful about little things like that," Alf said. "That's the way you get on. Where's your tie? I'll tie it for you."

Jeffrey showed him a blue tie with large white dots.

"No, no," Alf said, "you've got to have something with class to it. I'll lend you one of mine."

"Gee, Alf," Jeffrey said, "thanks a lot."

The tie was Paris green with diagonal white stripes. As Alf stood in front of him, knotting it, Alf began murmuring.

"'Who are you with tonight, tonight—Who is that peachy, dreamy, creamy vision of sweet delight?'"

"Gee, Alf," Jeffrey said, "where did you get that one?"

"Down at the picture house last Wednesday," Alf said. "A new vaudeville team . . . 'Two little chickens, chick, chick, chicken, you're the kind of a chicken for me . . .'"

"Gee, Alf," Jeffrey said, "you certainly know all the songs."

"I make a point of it," Alf said, "that's how I get along. There's always a glad hand in the crowd for someone who can sing."

Alf put on his coat, which was so tight at the waist that it made his shoulders as massive as a football player's. He pulled a box of Sweet Caporal cigarettes from his pocket.

"Well," he said, "just time for a drag at a butt before breakfast." He opened the box carefully. "Smoke up, kid!"

"Gee, Alf," Jeffrey said. "Thanks, but Aunt Martha would smell it on me."

"You can eat a clove," Alf said. "You've got to fix it so you don't act small-town."

"Thanks, Alf," Jeffrey said, "but I've got to read my speech today. Maybe I'd better not start smoking until I've read it."

But Alf's mind had moved forward already.

"Say," Alf said, "have you ever heard this one? . . .

"Don't look at me that way, Sonny, I'm not one of those small town
hicks,
But I love a little girlie who lives way out in the sticks.
Her dress, it is pure gingham, but her heart is tried and true,
She's a stylish stout and she won't walk out—with anybody else—and,
Sonny, this means *you!*"

Alf's voice grew more prosaic. "Say, kid, you can learn a lot from me."

"Gee, Alf," Jeffrey said, "I guess I can."

Alf was standing there, casual, magnificent, a man of the world.

"Anything you want to know about girls," Alf said, "or anything, just come around and ask me, man to man, kid. And I'll tell you my problems. I've got a problem now."

Alf had never been so kind.

"What?" Jeffrey asked. "What is it, Alf?"

"Hell," Alf said, "I don't mind telling you, Jeff, as man to man. I'm just a little short of berries."

"Berries?" Jeff repeated. Alf always had new words.

"Spondoolix," Alf said. "Dough; money, kid." He made a gesture with his thumb and forefinger, as though he were counting bills. "I've got to go out tonight, kid. Chicken feed for chickens—do you get the point? Do you get the point?—as Willie said when he put the tack in Teacher's chair. I've got a book all full of ones like that. I'll lend it to you, kid."

Jeffrey got the point.

"Gosh, Alf," he said, "I had to spend all of my Christmas money on these pants. Now maybe Ethel—"

"Listen, kid," Alf said, "you're graduating from High School today, aren't you? Well, you'll get a graduation present, won't you? The Old Man will give you five. And then there's Gramps. He'll slip you something. All I want is ten, see? 'I'll just telegraph my baby, she'll send ten or twenty, maybe, and I won't have to walk back home.'"

"Why, sure," Jeffrey said, "all right, Alf."

It was worth ten or twenty, maybe, to do Alf the slightest service. Alf patted his shoulder affectionately.

"That's the ticket, kid," he said. "The Wilson brothers stick together, don't they? Wilsons, that's all. Well, we've got to put on the old nosebag now. I've got to be going to the bank."

"Nosebag?" Jeffrey said.

Alf laughed.

"Well, well," he said. "What do horses eat out of? Wise up, kid."

He paused and they could hear Tilly shouting up the stairs.

"Boys," they could hear Tilly shouting, "breakfast, boys, is on the table."

Alf was looking at himself in the mirror.

" 'Is she your little sister, mister?' " Alf was singing. " 'Answer me, honor bright–' "

"Alf?" Jeff asked.

Alf turned away from the mirror. "Yeh?" he said.

"Alf, who are you going with, tonight?"

"None of your God-damn business, kid," Alf said.

When you were seventeen you still took most of the things around you for granted, and that was the way Jeffrey always felt about the house on Lime Street. He remembered as he ran downstairs, turning sharply into the front hall landing, that the house seemed to have a new luster that morning. It did not mean that the white paint in the second floor hall was not shabby, or that the steel engraving of General Washington's reception was not dusty, or that the tall clock on the landing was any more reliable; but everything seemed fresher. Afterwards he would think of things in that house and would wonder what had become of them–of the engraving and the tall clock, and of the horsehair sofa and the what-not in the parlor, and of the carving on the bannisters. Ethel had taken some of the furniture and Alf had sold what he could. Jeffrey had often tried to tell Madge and the children about the house but he could never make it as interesting to them as it was to him.

The front door was open that morning and a draft eddied through the hall from Lime Street out to the back garden, and the orioles and the robins were singing and all the leaves were out on the trumpet vine. The yellow and purple iris were blooming in the bed out back, but you only thought of those things later.

The round walnut table in the dining room had a checked cloth over it and there was a cage over the butter dish to keep out the flies, though it was too early for them. Tilly was bringing the oatmeal and Ethel was filling the pressed-glass water goblets. Aunt Martha was pouring the coffee. Aunt Martha had on her black silk dress with the high collar held up by strips of whalebone. Jeffrey's father was dressed in a blue serge suit that looked too tight for him. Ethel's hair was done in a pompadour with rats in it and was tied in back by a large bow, and she had on an embroidered waist with little holes in it. When Alf came into the dining room, he whistled at Ethel's shirtwaist.

"Peek-a-boo," he said.

"Oh, you shut up, Alf," Ethel said.

Alf made his fingers into imitation binoculars, and stared through them at Ethel's waist.

"Pa," Ethel said, "won't you make Alf stop it?"

Their father set down his coffee cup. When he looked up, everyone waited for what he was going to say. His forehead became creased with wrinkles and he wiped his heavy brown mustache slowly with his napkin.

"Martha," he asked, "what's the matter with her shirtwaist?"

"There's nothing the matter with it, Howland," Aunt Martha said, and she gave a little giggle, and then she sat up very straight.

The Old Man drank his coffee. He pulled a large silver watch from his waistcoat pocket and looked at it. "Time to be going to the bank, Alf," he said.

"Yes, sir," Alf said. "Are you coming to the office, Pa?"

"No," the Old Man answered, "I won't be going until after Jeffrey graduates."

"How about my seeing Jeff graduate?" Alf asked. "Ethel's going, isn't she?"

"You go to the bank, Alf," the Old Man said. Alf stood up.

"All right," he said, "all right. 'Everybody works but Father.' "

"What?" the Old Man asked.

" 'He sits around all day–' " Alf began to sing it–" 'Feet in front of the fire, passing the time away. Mother takes in washing, so does Sister Ann. Everybody works in our house but my Old Man'–and he drinks Peruna."

"Alf!" Ethel said, but she could not help laughing.

"Don't," the Old Man said. "It doesn't help to laugh at him." He was folding his napkin. "Jeff, stand up and let's see you."

Jeffrey stood up and pulled at his blue coat to straighten it. Aunt Martha's hair was stretched back so tightly from her forehead that her eyes were always unnaturally wide open, and now, as she watched him, she had that worried look which she always wore when she was looking to see if he had really washed his face. He could hear the pots and pans clattering in the kitchen sink.

"Tilly," the Old Man called. "Come in and look at him." And Tilly came in all hot and steamy, wiping her hands on a dish towel.

"God bless us, Mr. Wilson," said Tilly, "the white pants on him, and all."

There was something serious about it. Jeffrey could not have stood it if he had thought they were making fun of him. His father wiped his mustache and Ethel looked at him as though he were not her brother but more as though he were one of her girl friends' boy friends. A breath of warm air came in through the open window, and he could hear the birds singing.

"Jeff," Ethel said, "don't stick your stomach out. You look like Arthur Howard."

"Anyway," Jeffrey said, and he felt his color rising, "anyway, I don't look like Martin Howard. My ears don't stick out."

Ethel's face also grew flushed.

"You mind your own business," Ethel said. "You would be lucky if you looked as nice as Martin Howard."

"Ethel's sweet on Martin Howard," Jeffrey called. "She's sweet on Martin Howard."

"I am not," said Ethel. "You tell Jeff to stop it, Pa."

Ethel was fingering the small washed-gold watch which was pinned to her shirtwaist. "When we come to that," Ethel said, "a little bird told me—" and she gave her head a toss—"a little bird told me something about some-one named Louella."

Jeffrey felt himself growing beet-red.

"Who kissed you last night?" he said. "Martin Howard, Martin Howard. 'It's half-past kissing time and time to kiss again.'"

"That's enough," the Old Man said. "Never mind it now."

"Well, he's blushing," Ethel said, "look at Jeffie blush."

Aunt Martha stood up and her black silk dress rustled.

"Before you go, you'd better put some soap on your hairbrush, Jeffrey," she said. "Give your hair a good soaping, and maybe it won't stick up."

The Old Man's face was turned towards Jeffrey, but he did not seem to be looking at him.

"Have you got your speech with you, Jeff?" he asked.

"Yes, sir," Jeffrey said.

"All written out so you can read it and not stumble?"

"Yes, sir," Jeffrey said.

"Well, you'd better read it now, to be sure. We've never had a class salutatorian in the family."

"Pa," Jeffrey said, "don't make me read it in front of everybody."

The Old Man pushed back his chair and stood up.

"All right," he said. "You and I'll go into the back room and read it there. And Martha, tell me when Father comes and then we'll all walk over to the Hall. Come on, Jeff."

His father always sat in the back room in the evening. The table was littered with old magazines and lighted by a green-shaded gas lamp connected with a green rubber tube curving like a snake to the jet on the wall. There was a bookshelf along one wall with a fishing rod standing beside it, and over it hung a photograph of some men in their shirt sleeves beneath which was written, "*N. E. Insurance Agents' Clam Bake, 1905.*" Beside the picture was a framed diploma that certified that John Howland Wilson was a member in good standing of the Eagle Brigade of Pumper #2, Volunteer Fire Department. Above the fireplace was a large tinted photograph of Jeffrey's mother, who sat stiffly with her right hand resting on a pedestal table. On another wall there hung a large colored calendar, depicting a lusty man with snow on his head and shoulders entering the kitchen with an armful of wood for the stove. Beneath it was written, "*With the compliments of the season.* HOWLAND WILSON. REAL ESTATE—INSURANCE."

Jeffrey's father sat down on a golden-oak easy chair and pulled out his silver watch.

"We had better time it," he said, "but don't hurry, and remember what I told you. 'Mr. Oakley, members of the School Committee, Ladies and

Gentlemen.' You don't have to read that off the paper. Stand and bow, and then just take the paper out of your pocket. You've got lots of time. Now, go ahead. Mr. Oakley and the School Committee are over by the fireplace, and I am the Ladies and Gentlemen."

Jeffrey cleared his throat.

"Mr. Oakley, members of the School Committee, Ladies and Gentlemen." Jeffrey drew the paper from his pocket, just as he had practised before the mirror. "We, the graduating class of the Bragg High School, greet you. We have learned much. I hope we have learned more than we have forgotten."

"Wait there," his father said. "Give them time to laugh."

"When we step from this hall–" Jeffrey was remembering to speak slowly –"we will enter into a larger sphere of activity. We will assume new responsibilities. We wish to promise that we will remember what you have taught us. We wish to greet all those who are here today, and to thank our parents and our teachers and our School Committee and the taxpayers of this town for having made our education possible. I cannot express our gratitude more fittingly than by quoting the words of one of New England's most famous sons. Speaking of Dartmouth College, Daniel Webster said, 'It is a small college, yet there are those who love it.' That is the way we feel about Bragg High. But the smallness of a school does not concern its greatness. Abraham Lincoln learned his letters before a log fire . . ."

Jeffrey held the paper in front of him but he did not need to read from it because he knew it, word for word. He could see his father looking toward him, but not at him. In the room there was a stale odor of pipe and cigar smoke.

"Five minutes and forty-five seconds," his father said. "That's a nice speech, Jeff. It went all right." Then he stood up. There were voices in the hall. "Your grandfather's coming."

Jeffrey's grandfather and his Aunt Mary were standing in the hall. They had driven in from the farm in the buggy with the dapple-gray horse that was tied at the hitching post. His Aunt Mary was in black, like his Aunt Martha, and his grandfather had on his best black clothes. His hair was snow-white. His nose was thin and hooked, and his face was faintly pink. He was like the house–you took him entirely for granted. His hand was thin and cold when Jeffrey shook it.

"Well," he said, "how's the Wonder Boy?"

"Now, Pa," Aunt Martha said, "don't joke about him. Jeffrey's nervous."

"I'm not joking about him," his grandfather said. "What I need is a drink. What about it, Howland?"

"Father," Aunt Mary said, "not right in the morning! You can have a little something when we get home."

"At my age," the old man said, "I can have a little something right now. How about it, Howland?"

The parlor shades were drawn, so that it was cool and dusky. Jeffrey's grandfather and his father sat on the horsehair sofa, and Aunt Martha brought in a tray with a whisky bottle and two small glasses.

"You give me a good slug, Martha," his grandfather told her. He smacked his lips when he took the little glass. "Here's a toast for you. 'I hope you may all be hung, drawn and quartered—hung with the finest jewels, drawn in the handsomest carriages, and quartered in the most comfortable residence in the land.' Did you ever hear that one?"

"Father!" Aunt Mary said. "Don't give him any more, Howland."

Jeffrey stood in front of his grandfather.

"So you're feeling scared, are you?" his grandfather asked.

"I didn't say I was scared, sir," Jeffrey answered.

"If you'd been where I was at your age," the old man said, "by God, you'd have been scared."

"Father," Aunt Mary said, "don't start talking about the war."

She was referring to the Civil War, but it had never seemed possible to Jeffrey that his grandfather could have been in any war. Jeffrey's father looked at his watch again.

"We ought to be going, Father," he said, "if you want a seat up front."

The old man teetered unsteadily on his feet, and clung to Jeffrey's arm. "Easy now," he said, "don't shake me."

"Father," Aunt Mary said, "there was something you were going to tell Jeffrey."

"What—" his grandfather asked—"what was I going to tell him?"

"You were going to tell him how proud we are," Aunt Mary began.

"All right," his grandfather said, "I didn't say we weren't."

"And then," Aunt Mary said, "you were going to tell him something that's a surprise."

His grandfather's hand tightened on Jeffrey's arm.

"Your Aunt Mary," he said, "who can't ever keep her fingers out of other people's affairs, means I'm going to put you through Harvard College."

There was a silence in the dusky room, and Jeffrey knew that something had been offered him which he should deeply appreciate, but the thing was entirely intangible.

"You see," his Aunt Mary said, "it's your grandfather's graduation present to you, Jeff."

But Jeffrey was only wondering how keenly it would affect Alf later in the afternoon, because the gift appeared to involve no money.

"Jeff," his father said, "say 'Thank you' to your grandfather."

"Thank you, sir," Jeffrey said.

He was thinking about Alf's song—telegraphing your baby, who'd send ten or twenty maybe, so you wouldn't have to walk back home.

"You can pay back part by working summers," his grandfather said. "I've been to see Mr. Thompson at the carpet factory. He wants an office boy, and you can start in tomorrow."

"Oh, Pa," Aunt Martha said, "can't he have a week off?"

"If I'm paying for it," his grandfather said, "he can start in at the carpet factory tomorrow."

"Jeffrey," his father said, "say 'Thank you' to your grandfather."

"Thanks," Jeffrey said, "thanks a lot, Grandpa."

Jeffrey sometimes tried to recall what he had been like when he was Jim's age. Jim's environment was so dissimilar from his own that whenever Jeffrey began that familiar speech, "When I was your age . . ." it carried no possible conviction. There was only one thing of which he was sure. When he was Jim's age, life must have conveyed more; his thoughts surely must have been more vivid. When Jeffrey was salutatorian of his graduating class at the Bragg High School, he could not have been as completely callow as Jim.

The Town Hall was a boxlike brick building that stood on a patch of lawn behind a white fence. It had two doors in front and between the doors was a bulletin board with a voters' list and lost-and-found announcements. The boys and girls of the graduating class stood on a far corner of the lawn watching the audience move into the hall. The girls' faces were fresh and shining, because even a touch of rouge meant, then, that you were not a nice girl. The boys' necks looked high and stiff and their hair was plastered unnaturally to their skulls. The class exchanged glazed glances with Jeffrey when he joined the group. Even Summers Harris seemed nervously lost in his own thoughts, although he was known in town as "the King of Bragg High." Jimmy Ryan stood snapping his knuckles one by one. Milt Rolfe's wrists hung too far out of the sleeves of his blue serge coat. Mr. Oakley's bald head and pince-nez glasses glittered in the sun.

"You'll be toward the head of the line, Wilson," Mr. Oakley said, "and you're to walk with Christine Blair. Find Miss Blair, we'll be starting in a minute."

It was not difficult to find Christine Blair. Christine's nose looked pinched and she was biting her lips, but they were still thin and white. Christine was the Class Prophet and she was standing alone and whispering to herself.

"I had a dream the other night," she was whispering, "and I woke up in an awful fright. I saw the future drifting by, and my classmates of the Old Bragg High."

It was a great relief that Christine would be his partner, for it might have caused foolish talk if he had walked up the aisle with Louella Barnes; but he was conscious of Louella, although he only stole a glance at her. She was so pretty, with her yellow hair and her gold and purple bow, that he was afraid to look.

"Now, remember," Mr. Oakley was saying, "it's a fancy step—first one foot forward and then hesitate with the other, in time to the music. When you reach the stage, the girls go left and the boys right. And Ryan, spit out that gum."

Everyone looked at Jimmy Ryan but only with detachment because of the approaching crisis. Jeffrey felt in his inside pocket for his paper. The palms of his hands were clammy.

"I saw the future drifting by," Christine was whispering, "and my classmates of the Old Bragg High."

The classmates of the Bragg High were already walking dazedly but firmly up the Town Hall steps. A group of small boys stood by the entrance uttering soft catcalls and such personal remarks as Yoo hoo, Christine. Kiss me, Ella." But the classmates scarcely noticed these mild obscenities as they approached the ordeal before them.

There was a smell of clean linen and of ferns and the piano on the stage was playing. Jeffrey looked straight ahead of him, moving one foot and then the other. It was a strange dragging approach, half a walk and half a slide. He could see backs and heads and flowers on hats rising from the long wooden settles. He could see the School Committee and Mr. Peterson, the Congregational minister, already on the stage. Jeffrey's place was with them in the front row, and a printed program was resting on his chair. The first item was a prayer by Mr. Peterson, and then came the Class Song, composed by the Class Odist. Then he saw his own name. "SALUTATORY ADDRESS . . . JEFFREY WILSON." It was the first time he had ever seen his name in print; his hands felt very moist as he put them across his eyes while Mr. Peterson prayed. Mr. Peterson was asking God to guide the steps of these, the boys and girls from Bragg. He was imploring God, in measured tones, to help them lead upright lives, and Jeffrey hoped that it would last for a long while. Anything was desirable which would stave off his ordeal, but time was moving on inexorably. The class had risen with their programs and they were singing the Class Song.

"The way we take from Old Bragg High is narrow, steep and long . . ." His mouth felt dry and there was a tremor in his knees. The road through life from Old Bragg High had tribulations and difficulties, but the light of faith and their gratitude to Old Bragg High would lead them, onward and upward. The Class was sitting down.

"The Salutatory Address," he heard Mr. Oakley say. "Jeffrey Wilson."

At the sound of his name, unseen hands seemed to jerk Jeffrey out of his chair. He was met by a round of applause as he made his way to the center of the stage and came to a stop by a table that held the stack of diplomas and a large crockery jar full of pink petunias. The faces in front of him were blurred into one face and the applause was dying down, and nothing could put off the moment when he must speak unless he dropped down dead or ran away. He turned with a spasmodic swivel motion toward the elders in their chairs.

"Mr. Oakley," he said. He was aware of a quaver in his voice and he tried to steady it. "Members of the School Committee–Ladies and Gentlemen."

He reached slowly toward his breast pocket, but his fingers did not touch the paper. He snatched out his hand and felt in his side pockets, but the paper was not there. The faces in front of him faded to a mist as he thrust his hand for a second time into his inside pocket. The feeling of relief which surged through him when his fingers finally found it must have been shared by his audience, for he became aware of a faint sighing sound, of an uneasy shifting of feet.

"Stand up and take it easy," he could hear his father saying. "You have lots of time." But he only had a sense of the whole world's waiting while he unfolded the paper.

"We, the graduating class of the Bragg High School, greet you. We have learned much. I hope we have learned more than we have forgotten."

He wanted to remember to do it right, now that he was standing there. "Wait there," he heard his father saying. "Give them time to laugh."

He waited, but in front of him there was only dull expectancy. He waited for another moment until it became plain to him that neither he nor his audience was in any mood for literary merriment.

"When we step from this hall we will step into a larger sphere of activity."

Jeffrey could hear his voice continuing, and he looked up and swallowed.

"And, so, in behalf of the senior class of the Bragg High School, I take the liberty of paraphrasing a little of what the gladiators in ancient Rome used to say when they entered the Colosseum." Jeffrey swallowed again, and cleared his throat. "We, the senior class of Bragg High School, who are about to go out into the world, salute you." Jeffrey bowed like a seasick passenger. He was pale and he was shaken, but he was through with it. His knuckles holding the paper were white. He turned his back and retired quickly to his seat in the midst of the applause.

"And now the Class Prophecy," Mr. Oakley was saying.

Christine had one advantage; she did not have a pocket, and the prophecy was in her hand. The first words came in a whisper.

"I had a dream the other night, and I woke up in an awful fright. I saw the future drifting by, and my classmates of the Old Bragg High."

At first Jeffrey could not give the Prophecy his full attention, but gradually the dream of Christine impinged more clearly upon his consciousness. It seemed that a great deal had happened before Christine had awakened. By some odd piece of fortune, there had been revealed to her much of the public and not a little of the private lives of every member of the class as they appeared, of all things, in the distant future of nineteen hundred and thirty-three. Summers Harris was a soldier and a wonder to behold, and he had three lovely children with pompadours so bold. Jimmy Ryan's butcher shop was always neat and clean and Jimmy never would short-change you, because he wasn't mean. Jeffrey fidgeted in the chair.

"Jeff Wilson, that great orator, is known the world around.
The bands play, and they wave the flags, when Jeff Wilson comes to town.
Who helps him with his speeches I can very easily see,
Her first name has Lou and Ella in it, and her last begins with B."

At this moment Jeffrey would have welcomed death. He sat there wondering how he could take up life and go on. It was not so much a misery that concerned himself, for another shared in this libel. He could sense the humiliation which Louella Barnes must have felt to have her name publicly connected with his own. And there was her father on the stage, the chairman of the School Committee, and before they left that stage, they must meet head on—since Mr. Barnes himself was presenting the diplomas. He could never explain to Mr. Barnes that this libel was completely groundless—that he had always been afraid of girls, particularly of Louella, and that he had hardly exchanged a word with her during the entire High School course.

Mr. Barnes was standing up, a tall, pale man handing out the diplomas. The boys and girls were marching forward, and as Jeffrey moved toward the table, Mr. Barnes was holding out his hand.

"That was a fine talk you gave us," he said. "Congratulations."

The only explanation Jeffrey could give for it was that Mr. Barnes had not heard.

Then everyone was singing the National Anthem, and it was over. He was walking with the class toward the steps of the stage and he never knew how it happened, except that he could not have been looking, for suddenly he was face to face with Louella Barnes. At first he thought that Louella herself could not have heard the poem, because she smiled at him, and she had never looked so pretty.

"That was a lovely speech. You didn't act a bit afraid," she said. She was speaking as though nothing at all had happened. She was still smiling at him. "I didn't think much of Christine's poem, did you?"

"No," Jeffrey said, "not much."

"Some people are awfully silly, don't you think?" Louella said.

"Yes," Jeffrey said. "It was silly." And he smiled too. She was beyond the jibes and japes of ordinary people. She was too fine, too rare. She was what he had always thought her—unattainable, untouchable.

"Well, good-by," Louella said.

"Good-by," Jeffrey answered.

There was a finality in that last word. He would never sit in the same room with her again. He would never hear her recite French. He would never watch for her in the morning at the High School door. They were on the path of life, treading different paths, but she could not stop his loving her. That was the way he felt that summer about Louella Barnes.

15

Now You've Found Your Way

In the autumn of 1939 when he was in Boston helping at the try-out of a play which Jesse Fineman was producing, Jeffrey drove out to Bragg. He had not been there since his Aunt Martha's funeral, after which they had sold the house on Lime Street, for the simple reason that no one wanted it any more. It would have made more sense if he had gone to see his sister Ethel in West Springfield. Somehow it seemed easier to get to Chicago than to West Springfield, and when Jeffrey did get there, it was an effort and one which he did not believe Ethel liked any more than he did. Alf was the only subject they had in common, and you could not talk about Alf indefinitely. He drove out to Bragg because he wanted an excuse to get away from Jesse Fineman's suite at the Ritz, and away from the show business.

The suite at the Ritz had been filled with that sort of hysteria which was always present at the try-out of a play that was likely to be a flop. It was the moment when anyone connected with such a venture was sorry for himself and was hating everyone else. The doors of all the bedrooms were open and members of the cast were sitting on the beds, and Room Service was bringing up highballs and dry Martinis and milk and three-minute boiled eggs and black coffee and aspirin and all sorts of people kept coming in. Jesse Fineman had a headache and was drinking Bromo-Seltzer. Hazel Harris was in tears and the playwright had passed out on the bed in the next room. For some reason, Jeffrey began to think of Bragg. He thought of Bragg as something solid which might give him the same sort of perspective as a visit to the Art Museum or the tomb of the Unknown Soldier, or it may have had something to do with the phrase that was common then about "rededicating oneself." He knew that all sorts of memories would hurt him, but it hurt him more to stay at the Ritz.

He rented a Drive-Yourself car from a garage near Park Square and drove through Somerville. It was colder, much colder than it ever was in New York at that time of year. Even by the time he reached the Fellsway the trees looked barer than they ever did outside of New York, and there was a grimness in the lead color of the sky, and a damp chill in the air as though winter had come already. It was still light when he reached Bragg, a solemn, dull sort of light. The trees above the houses were black. Leaves had been piled around the cellar walls and there was a smell of wood smoke. The German gun which had been placed in front of the Town Hall after the last war looked as old as the Civil War Soldiers' monument. His own name was there with the others on the bronze plaque, between the doors of the Town Hall, commemorating the sons of Bragg who had answered their country's call in nineteen hundred and seventeen, but there was nothing else of him left in Bragg any more. In a way it did not seem decent for him to be there, because he was looking at it as some person from the city might who wanted to see the fine old houses. He did not want to drive through Lime Street, but he drove quite slowly through Center Street where the Barnes house stood.

There had never been much money in Bragg, but they used to talk of Center Street and "the Center Street crowd." The brick sidewalks were still there and the ornate fences in front of the houses. The Thompson house, which had belonged to the owners of the carpet mill, looked smaller to Jeffrey than it should have. The weeping birch trees in front of it had grown larger but they looked smaller too. The Barnes house itself looked smaller and he could see that it made an ugly interpolation on Center Street, having been built in the days when people had learned that you could do all sorts of things with turning lathes. Its shingles were cut in scallops and it still was painted yellow. There was the same iron fence and the same tar walk leading up to the front steps, and the same maple tree. There was a couch swing on the porch just where the other couch swing had been. Two boys about eleven or twelve, in blue jeans and sweaters, were chasing each other and shouting on the lawn. He remembered the tail ends of autumn afternoons when he was just their age, when you felt that there was nothing left to the day and that it might just as well be dark.

If he had wanted to, he could not have helped stopping. He could almost believe that the idea had been in the back of his mind all the time and that he had come to Bragg for just that purpose. He walked up the tarred walk, looking at the cracks in it, and as he approached the granite steps he had a spasm of innate guilt. There was a certain fine sort of justice to it that was better than the Victorianism of Locksley Hall, closer to a poem by Yeats. Nobody there preached down a daughter's heart with a little hoard of maxims. The porch made the familiar drumming sound as he stepped on it, and when he rang the bell there was Louella.

It was not fair, because he had been expecting to see her, but there was nothing except incomprehension on her face. She wore the look that a certain type of woman wears when a Fuller Brush man comes knocking at the door.

"Hello," he said, "don't you know me?" And then she knew him.

"Why, Jeff," she said, "Jeff Wilson." And then she added something which was hardly true about his not having changed at all.

The little parlor looked as it always had. He faced the same heavy brass fender and high andirons and the same varnished-oak mantelpiece with the beveled mirror and the same sofa with fringes hanging from it. If the old Brussels carpet had worn out, the new one looked just like it. There was even a newspaper lying on the carpet just as though Mr. Barnes had gone out so that the young people could have the parlor to themselves. Only he and Louella had changed. Her hair was darker, and she had put on weight, but she looked the way he knew she would, integrated and comfortable.

"I haven't seen you since the funeral," she was saying.

"What funeral?" He asked the question because he was thinking of something else.

"Your Aunt Martha's funeral," she said. "I was there."

"Oh, yes," Jeffrey said. "Yes, I remember."

"No, you don't," she said. "You didn't see me."

"That's right," he said, "I didn't." He was thinking that he had not seen her for well over twenty years.

"Are those boys yours out on the lawn, Louella?"

Yes, they were her boys, and he was thinking that they might have been his, and he supposed that she was thinking the same thing. It was getting dusk, and she lighted a lamp on the table. And then she was asking him to tell everything about himself and he told what you might tell anyone, but they never referred to what they must both have been thinking except once.

"It's funny, your stopping by," she said. "I still think about you, sometimes."

He wanted to change the subject, in spite of all that time.

"Louella," he asked, "are you the president of the Women's Club?"

"Yes," she said. "What of it?"

"Nothing," Jeffrey said, "I'm glad you are. Your mother was."

"We had a good program last year," Louella said, "and this year we're going to have a better one. How's Ethel?"

"Ethel?" Jeffrey said. "Oh, she's all right. You know they're living in West Springfield."

"Yes, I know," Louella said. "How's Alf?"

"Right now," Jeffrey said, "he's in California somewhere."

"California is a lovely state," Louella said. "Last year I was at the Federation Convention in Los Angeles."

"Yes," Jeffrey said, "there are lots of conventions in California."

"California is beautiful," Louella said. "But I wouldn't want to live where there's no change in climate. Have you read *The Grapes of Wrath?*"

"Yes," Jeffrey said.

"I read it first for the Public Library," Louella said, "and somehow it didn't appeal to me. Father wouldn't have had it in the house. Times keep changing, don't they?"

"Yes," Jeffrey said, "I wish they wouldn't change so fast."

"I like it," Louella said. "It keeps you alive. Well, here's Milt."

There was a footstep on the porch, and the front door was opening.

"Milt," Louella called, "guess who's here! It's Jeffrey Wilson."

Milt Rolfe looked heavier too. He said he had not seen Jeff for a dog's age.

"Did you stop at the drugstore the way I asked you?" Louella said.

"No," Milt said, "did you ask me?"

"This morning," Louella said, "I distinctly told you to stop at the drugstore."

"For what?" Milt asked.

"I can't say what I wanted you to get, now," Louella said, "but I did tell you to stop. Milt, come into the hall a minute. You'll excuse us just a minute, won't you, Jeffrey?"

Jeffrey could hear them whispering in the hall.

"Well, get in the car," he heard Louella whisper, "it's still open. Go down and get two more."

Then Louella and Milt came back.

"We're having a pick-up supper tonight," Louella said. "The real meal's in the middle of the day, but Milt and I would love it if you'd sit down with us and have chops."

"Yes," Milt said, "come on and stay, Jeff."

But the last thing he wanted was to stay. It was growing dark outside and he wanted to get away. He had simply grown out of it and the door had closed behind him.

"I wish I could," he said, "but I've got to be getting back."

"Now you've found your way, come again," Louella said.

But he knew that he would never come again, and she must have known it, too. Milt walked through the dusk with him to the car.

"Come again," Milt said, "now that you've found your way."

And that expression stayed with him, "Now you've found your way." It had a solemn sound because you never found your way. You fell into it, or someone kicked you into it, but you never found it. Those might have been his children on the lawn. He might have been working in some newspaper telegraph room. They might have been living on Lime Street and perhaps they might have been happy. When you came to think of it, Louella Barnes was responsible for everything. He would never have jumped into the war so fast, he would never have been where he was at all, if he had not run away from Louella Barnes. The answer had been written somewhere. If he had married Louella Barnes, he might have been one of the men who went with their wives to the Federation of Women's Clubs' convention at Los Angeles.

16

Just the Day for Tea

During all of his four years at Harvard Jeffrey went home for Saturday and Sunday because it was cheaper than stopping at the rooming house near Central Square where he stayed during the week. Besides his tuition, his grandfather gave him four hundred dollars annually for room and board, a limitation which practically prohibited any social activities, even if he had understood that they existed at college. When they asked him at home how he liked it there, he always said, of course, that he had a fine time, but even then he did not entirely believe it. He only realized later that he was one of those boys to whom others referred as grease-balls, or other less printable names. He was a part of that grim and underprivileged group that appeared in the Yard each morning with small leather bags containing books and papers. He was one of the boys who wore celluloid collars which you could wash off in your room, and who used the reading room in the Library as a resting place because there was no other place to go, and who ate a sandwich there for lunch, and to whom no one spoke unless it was absolutely necessary. He was one of those grease-balls who used to swallow and stammer and mispronounce long words, but he was more sorry for himself later than he had been then. It was hard for him even to understand his former attitude of patient unawareness, for later he could only be appalled by his utter immaturity, and his ignorance of other modes of living.

A professor might occasionally reveal a disturbing vista, might allude to student days at Heidelberg, or pass on to Jeffrey his contagious enthusiasm for a line of poetry or a historical personage, but Jeffrey never felt that he could fully share this knowledge. He thought humbly that this was due to his natural stupidity and only realized later that those men and those books seldom used his terms of expression or resorted to any illustrations with which he was familiar. It was the same with the students who would not speak to him after class was over. It was only later that he knew any of them and that was during discussions in advanced courses, when he had developed a certain ability in prose composition. He could only recall a few occasions when glimpses of this difference had been revealed to him, for he was too absorbed in his own struggles then to understand their meaning.

One morning, for instance, at a section meeting of a large elementary course, which he learned years later was known as a "necktie course," there were a hundred or so students waiting when the section man came in and laid his books and papers on the desk. The section man, young and handsome, dressed in tweeds, spoke in a weary voice.

"I suppose," he said, "that most of you, like me, were at the dance last night at the Plaza."

The Plaza and the dances were unknown to Jeffrey then.

"It may be," the section man went on, "although I hope for your sakes it is not the case, that a great many of you feel the way I do this morning. Anyone who was at the ball last night may leave now, and take a walk in the fresh air, or do anything else he may think proper—anyone who was at the ball."

The room was filled with applause and merry stamping, and two thirds of the students left the room while the section man watched them, smiling. Those who were left were the plain boys, the last pieces of candy in the box, and Jeffrey was among them. He still could remember their anxious serious features, their hunched shoulders and their shining elbows. The section man's glance passed slowly over them, and then he smiled.

"So you weren't at the ball last night," he said. "Well, we'll go on. We'll talk about something that does not require too much effort."

When you were young, of course you accepted the environment in which you lived and which was beyond your power to change. It sometimes seemed to Jeffrey that his father must have always accepted it, living incuriously just where he was, not successfully, but placidly. Occasionally in the evenings, when Jeffrey was back from college, his father would talk to him about getting ahead. It was only later that Jeffrey realized that the Old Man knew nothing much about this except in theory. When he was Jeffrey's age, he got a job in Mr. Wilkins' Real Estate and Insurance office, and when Mr. Wilkins died, he had gone right on with it from there. That was virtually all he ever told Jeffrey about himself, but sometimes he spoke of Jeffrey's mother. "She was a mighty pretty girl," he said once. "You can tell it from her picture." But that was about all he said. Perhaps he did not want to talk about her, or perhaps he thought that Jeffrey knew of her already.

"Everybody has a chance in this country," he said once. "If you work hard and are honest, you'll get where you want to get."

The town and home meant much more to Jeffrey than anything he learned at college. Later when he heard people talk of the democracy of the small town, he knew it was a half truth, because a small town was actually a complicated place, with social gradations which one accepted without being entirely aware of them. There were people who lived on Center Street whom his father spoke to with a special tone, such as the Thompsons and the Nestleroades and the Barneses. And then there were people like themselves and Dr. Adams and Mr. Pratt who ran the clothing store. And then there were people whom his father referred to as "scrubs," the workers in the carpet mills and the employees in the shoeshop and the people who did odd jobs.

When Jeffrey walked up Center Street, he always had an uneasy feeling. The houses there had striped awnings in the summertime and there were round flower beds on the lawns. They kept watering the lawns on Center Street with sprinklers that whirled around, and the Thompsons and the Nestleroades had automobiles. That was where Louella lived–on Center Street. Sometimes on Saturdays he would meet her downtown and he would always take off his hat quickly and smile. Sometimes he would see her at church on Sundays but he never thought of talking to her, and he never called on Louella until the spring of his last year at college.

He was taking a course on the English Novel that year and it was a hard course for him because it was necessary to read and read. First there was Samuel Richardson's *Clarissa*, and then *The Castle of Otranto* and *Roderick Random* and *Joseph Andrews*, dealing with phases of English life which were completely beyond the scope of his imagination. When they reached the Victorians, it was not much simpler for him. The people in *Middlemarch* or *David Copperfield* or *Vanity Fair* never could fit into his surroundings. It was grim work for him, always, acquiring an education against the narrow background of his own experience.

One Saturday close to the time for the final examination he went to the Bragg Public Library to borrow Meredith's *Diana of the Crossways*. Years later when he heard someone say that Meredith was a young man's writer, his mind went back to his efforts with *Diana of the Crossways* up in the hall bedroom where he lived in Cambridge during the week. When he tried to read *Diana* again he seemed to be back sitting on that iron bed of his that smelled faintly of kerosene, listening to the trolley cars on Massachusetts Avenue. He had that old feeling that he must finish it and remember it, that he must make notes on the physical appearance of all the characters because that was the sort of question which would be on the examination.

The public library was a brick building, like the Town Hall, but smaller. To the left was the reading and periodical room, to the right Miss Jacobs sat behind her desk with the catalogues in their golden-oak cases and with three lilacs in a vase in front of her. The room smelled of floor oil and of books arranged along the wall and in alcoves. *Diana of the Crossways* was there in the catalogue, and Miss Jacobs told him that he could find it himself over by the window.

"Well," Miss Jacobs said, "you're quite a stranger."

"Yes," Jeffrey said, "I'm just home Saturdays and Sundays."

"I see your father and your aunt," Miss Jacobs said. "They say they haven't heard from Alf."

"No," Jeffrey said, "Alf doesn't write much."

"Dear me," Miss Jacobs said, "how everybody flies away."

Then there was a footstep behind him and the light glinted on Miss Jacobs' glasses.

"Why, hello," Miss Jacobs said, "here's someone else who's quite a stranger."

Jeffrey stepped away from the desk, holding *Diana of the Crossways*. It was Louella Barnes.

Jeffrey sometimes wondered later what he would have been like if there had been anything in his youth to promote self-confidence or self-assurance—if he had ever owned a suit of clothes that had cost more than fifteen dollars, if he had gone to one of the preparatory schools or had played football, or if his father had owned a car which he had been allowed to drive. It was always a difficult and thankless game to stack the decks of the cards which had been dealt in the past, for there was no way of telling whether he would have been better or worse for it. But he was sure of one thing, he would not have felt that Louella Barnes was an unapproachable vision that afternoon. He would have possessed some standard for comparison. He would have placed her in a gallery of other girls whom he had met. It did not mean, of course, that he was entirely without experience. He had been on picnics with Alf and with girls Alf knew, but they were noisy and provocative and they smelled of musk and perfume. They were not nice girls like Louella Barnes. If he had known more, if he had "loosened up" as Alf often advised him, that vision of Louella in the library might not have been quite so compelling. As it was, no one living was ever like the Louella Barnes that he saw that afternoon.

She was standing by Miss Jacobs' desk, and the light of the window in the alcove just behind her put her face in the shadow, but it made a glow on her yellow hair, which was done up in a tight, uncompromising knot just below her little hat. She wore a gray tailored suit with the frills of a shirtwaist in front. Her lisle stockings looked almost like silk, and she wore low tan shoes with high heels. She was like Beatrix Castlewood walking down the stairs. All sorts of thoughts like that passed through Jeffrey's mind. It was the first time in his life that his academic studies had assumed any practical significance. She was like Botticelli's Spring, she was like Milton's pagan nymphs. . . .

He did not want to look at her for more than a brief instant. Instead he backed slowly away from Miss Jacobs' desk and gazed intently at two posters on the wall behind her. One was a British Tommy, saying that England expected every man to do his duty, and the other was of a French poilu saying "*On les aura*."

"Oh, Miss Jacobs," Louella said, "doesn't the library look nice?"

"That's sweet of you to say it," Miss Jacobs said. "We try to keep it nice."

Jeffrey was still staring at the posters, trying to detach himself from the group, wondering whether he should speak to her first, or whether she would speak to him.

"Why," Louella said, "if it isn't Jeffrey Wilson. Hello, Jeffrey."

She was holding out her hand to him. He forgot that he was holding *Diana of the Crossways* and when he tried to shift it over, it fell with a flop on the brown linoleum floor.

"Oh," he said, "hello, Louella." And then he stooped to pick it up. He felt the blood rushing to his face as he stooped and he knew that his coat was too tight behind and his trousers were binding. But Louella was still speaking.

"Father wants to know," Louella was saying, "if it's time for him yet to have *Letters from America.*"

Miss Jacobs opened a drawer in her desk and consulted a white sheet of paper.

"If Mr. Barnes wants it," Miss Jacobs answered, "we'll just forget that anyone's ahead of him if he brings it back on Monday."

"That's dear of you," Louella said, "thank you, Miss Jacobs."

"Besides," Miss Jacobs said, "there's no one else ahead on Center Street." She tapped a little bell on her desk.

"Walter," she called, "Walter!" Miss Jacobs' voice dropped to a kind and gentle murmur: "We have Walter Newcombe now. He's a West Ender who dusts books and tidies, when he's back from Dartmouth."

Miss Jacobs meant that the three of them standing at the desk, although they might not all come from Center Street, were certainly not West Enders.

"Oh." Louella also lowered her voice.

There was no time for an answer because the door at the end of the main room opened. Walter Newcombe was a gangly boy of seventeen, who obviously knew he was a West Ender. His hair was not brushed, and his nose was shining.

"Walter," Miss Jacobs said, "get *Letters from America,* please."

"Who wrote it, ma'am?" Walter asked.

"Rupert Brooke," Miss Jacobs told him, very gently indicating that West Enders never knew things like that. Jeffrey knew that he should be going, but if he left he would not hear Louella speak again.

"How does it feel to be a college girl?" Miss Jacobs asked.

Louella gave a deprecating laugh.

"College girls are just the same as other girls," she said. "At least, I feel the same, and this is my last year." And she looked at Jeffrey and smiled.

"A college boy and a college girl," Miss Jacobs said, "right together in the library at once. My, it's quite a day."

She did not seem to think of Walter as a college boy. Jeffrey knew that they were both expecting him to say something and he cleared his throat, but he was spared the effort, because Walter Newcombe was back.

"Give it to Miss Barnes, Walter," Miss Jacobs said. "I won't bother to stamp it, because I *know* you'll bring it back on Monday."

Anyone would have known who saw Louella smile.

"Thank you, Miss Jacobs, it's sweet of you," she said. "Well, good-by."

Jeffrey did not know exactly what to do, but there was no reason for him to stay because he also had his book.

"Well," he said, "it's time I was going. Good-by and thank you, Miss Jacobs."

He thought Louella would walk out first, but she waited for him, and they walked down the hall together. He lunged forward and opened the door for her.

"What's the book you're reading?" Louella asked.

"Just a tough old book," he said, "*Diana of the Crossways* by George Meredith."

"Oh," Louella said, and she nodded with knowing sympathy. "It must be the English Novel course. We have it too, at Smith."

"It's sort of hard to understand," Jeffrey said. "Well–"

He stopped, and Louella stopped, too. They had come to the end of the library path.

"It's just the right afternoon for iced tea, isn't it?" Louella said.

"What?" Jeffrey asked her.

"Iced tea," Louella said. "I've got some made. Wouldn't you like to have some on the porch?"

It took a moment to grasp that she was asking him to accompany her to her home to have iced tea, asking him to walk with her up Center Street and right to her front porch. His common sense told him that he ought to take it casually and so he framed his words carefully in his head before he spoke them.

"I wouldn't mind some iced tea at all," he said.

The new leaves of the maple trees on Center Street were all yellowish green, but he was not thinking of the leaves. He was thinking that his trousers were baggy. He was wondering what the people on Center Street would be saying when they saw him walking with Louella Barnes without a hat.

"May I carry your book for you?" he said.

"Oh, no," she answered, "it's very light." He did not want to snatch for it, but he knew that it would not look right unless he carried the book.

"I'm not as delicate as that," she said. "I'm not just a Dresden china affair." But she had handed him the book.

Her heels tapped sharply on the brick walk beneath the maple trees. She was almost as tall as he was, but not quite, and he wished that his trousers were pressed. He wanted her to see that she had made no mistake in asking him to walk home with her.

"It's funny," Louella said, "we haven't seen each other for a long while, have we? That is, not to talk to."

"It's because we've been away at college," Jeffrey said.

"Some men in your class," Louella said, "were at the Senior Prom this winter. I had a blind date with one of them."

He did not know what a blind date was, but he certainly did not want her to know that he did not know it.

"Did you?" he said. "Who was it?" He did not know whether you should have said "it" or "he" but it must have been all right.

"Dick Elwell," she said. "He comes from New York. Do you know him?"

"Elwell?" Jeffrey said, and he pretended to be groping through the endless list of his acquaintances. "Maybe I've met him, but I don't know him."

"Then there's Tommy Rogers," she said, "the one who plays hockey. He's in your class, isn't he?"

"Rogers," Jeffrey said. "It's a pretty big class at college. Rogers—maybe I've met him, but I don't know him."

"Then there was a boy named Ames," Louella said. "A red-headed boy with freckles who had a new way of dancing the Boston. I think his first name was Tom. He's in your class, too; do you know him?"

"Ames," Jeffrey said. "Let's see, Ames—It's a pretty big class. Did anybody come up there whose name begins with 'W'?"

"Why with 'W'?" Louella said.

"Well, you see, it's a pretty big class," Jeffrey said, "but all the 'W's' sit together. I know a good many men whose names begin with 'W.'"

"Williams," Louella said, "why then you must know Bert Williams."

"Williams," Jeffrey said, "there was a man named Williams in Phil I, but we didn't talk much."

Louella was right. It was just the day for iced tea. It had not struck him as being particularly hot, until he walked with Louella up Center Street, but after all, though he hardly knew anyone to speak to after four years in college, he was a college man. The iron fence of the Barnes lawn was in front of him. They were turning in the gate. They were walking up the tarred walk and the white lilacs by the yellow porch were all in bloom. The awnings were out above the downstairs windows. Jeffrey drew his shoulders back. After all he was a college man.

"In English 12," Jeffrey said, "there's a man named Winterstein. He's quite a writer. That's English 12, under Professor C. T. Copeland. We call him 'Copey.' Did you ever meet a man named Winterstein?"

"Winterstein," Louella said, "let me see. I seem to know the name, but I don't think I ever met him."

The porch was cool and shaded from the afternoon sun, with a slate-gray floor and a bilious yellow railing. There was not much effort at beauty on porches in those days—no colored rugs, no tables with plate glass tops—but Louella's porch remained in his mind ever afterward as a sort of metric standard. Ever afterward, he found himself supporting a fixed belief that no porch was in proper taste unless it had heavy dull-green rocking chairs, and a round wicker table painted black, and unless it had one of those Cape Cod hammocks made of khaki canvas with a purple denim cushion in each corner, suspended from the ceiling by galvanized iron chains. For years the Barnes porch was clear and solid in his mind. He dreamed of it once in the war—he saw the green rocking chairs and the white lilacs that half-concealed the street. He was standing there again with that same sensation of happiness and there was that same sound, the faint squeak of the Cape Cod hammock, swinging on its chains.

"I'll get the tea," Louella said.

"May I help you?" Jeffrey asked. It must have been the right thing to say, because she smiled, although she shook her head.

"Oh, no," Louella said. "I'll be only a minute. Just sit down and make yourself at home."

Jeffrey smoothed his coat and mopped his forehead and then folded his handkerchief carefully and put it in his breast pocket. A Cadillac car went by and then a Ford with a brass radiator and brass lamps, and then an ice wagon. He was trying to plan what to say to Louella next, telling himself that he must not laugh or talk too loudly, and that he must not shuffle his feet. Louella was gone for such a long while that he wondered whether she might not be sorry that she had asked him and whether she might not be waiting in the house, hoping that he would go away, but just as that thought came to him the front door opened and there was Louella, carrying a tray. She had taken off her tailored coat; and her shirtwaist had more frills and pleats on it than he had expected and her hair did not look so tight. On the tray she carried was a pitcher of real cut glass, and two tall goblets and a cut-glass sugar bowl, and also a large glass plate containing some thin sandwiches cut in hearts and circles with a little ring of parsley around them. From the top of the pitcher arose a green spray of mint leaves.

"There," Louella said, "sit down and make yourself at home."

Jeffrey could not take his eyes from the tray and the cut glass and, without intending, he must have looked at it too hard.

"I think it's nice to have things nice when you have iced tea, don't you?" Louella asked.

"Yes," Jeffrey said, "that's right."

He sat down in one of the rocking chairs and Louella sat down on the one beside him and crossed her ankles carefully and smoothed her gray skirt.

"I suppose you have to work pretty hard, now," Louella said, "with final exams coming. I do."

"If you do your work every day," Jeffrey said, "there's no reason to be afraid of examinations." He sipped his iced tea thoughtfully. "I'm not afraid of them."

He smiled when he said it, because he did not want to show off.

"I'm not either," Louella said, "but a lot of people are."

He was glad that they were both brave and not afraid of examinations, but now that they both had said so, the subject seemed to be completely exhausted. He leaned back in an effort to think of something else to say. He forgot it was a rocking chair. He had to raise his legs straight off the floor to right himself.

"They rock back pretty quickly, if you're not used to them," Louella said, and she laughed and Jeffrey laughed.

"Yes," Jeffrey said, and changed his center of gravity by hitching himself forward.

"Some men are so silly, aren't they?" Louella said, "and some girls, too."

It made him forget about the rocking chair.

"I like men who do things, and girls, too," Louella said, "I mean worth-while things."

He felt easier, even in the rocking chair, because it must have meant that she thought he was doing worth-while things.

"Have you read *The Winning of Barbara Worth?*" Louella asked.

"No," Jeffrey said, "I don't have much time. I only read what they hand me out to read."

"I'll lend it to you when you go," Louella said.

Jeffrey pulled his feet under him. The rocking chair pitched slightly forward. He put his hands on the arms to steady himself.

"Maybe I'd better be going now," he said.

"Oh, no," Louella said, "no, please."

Jeffrey leaned backward and again he forgot it was a rocking chair.

"I'll tell you what we'll do," Louella spoke quickly before he could answer. "We'll play the phonograph. We'll bring it out here, that is, if you like music, but I guess you'll have to help me."

Jeffrey wiped his feet on the jute mat by the front door and followed Louella into the hall. The phonograph was in the little sitting room, on the left. He saw the beveled mirror over the fireplace and a fan of white paper between the andirons. He had never seen white paper made into a fan like that. The phonograph was square and heavy, but even with the iced tea, there was room for it on the porch table.

"Here is 'Gems from The Pink Lady,'" Louella said. And they sat side by side in the rocking chairs.

There was no need to talk as the songs went on. He could sit relaxed, and occasionally he could look at her, as she listened. He could see her profile as she looked out toward Center Street. He could see the way her hair curled tightly over her ears, held in place by her hair net. She was the beautiful lady to whom he raised his eyes. He was the gay roué who was saying Not yet, he'd be single for six months more. The river was flowing on to the sea, and she was the girl from the Saskatchewan.

"It's lovely music," Louella said.

"Yes," he said, "it's fine."

There was a moment's silence, but he was not embarrassed by the silence. He was still by the banks of the Saskatchewan.

"Now, we'll play the 'Gems from The Quaker Girl,'" Louella said. "Here it is—"

As he sat there, he seemed to be dancing with Louella Barnes at the Senior Prom at Smith. His arm was around her waist. Her hand was resting on his shoulder. He forgot that he did not know how to dance.

"There're lots more," Louella said. "I'll play them when you come again."

Jeffrey hitched himself forward in the rocking chair.

"Maybe I'd better be going now," he said.

"No, no," Louella said, "it's early. Father isn't back yet."

It occurred to Jeffrey that it might be better if he left before Mr. Barnes appeared, but he sank back in his chair.

"We haven't talked about anything at all," Louella said. "What are you going to do when you're finished with college?"

It must have been the music, it could not have been the iced tea. It must have been some strain of romanticism within him which made him think of the impossible. He had only taken a drink once in his life, and that had been with Alf, but the music had the same effect, relaxing, blotting out all inhibition. The idea that his father wanted him to help out at the office selling real estate was repellent there on the Barnes porch. He thought of mentioning the Foreign Legion or the Lafayette Escadrille, but he was sure that she would think that he was showing off.

"I guess I'll be a newspaper man," he said.

He had never intended to be a newspaper man, and he did not know how one went about it, but now he knew he would have to do it, or he could never speak to Louella Barnes again.

"Oh, Jeffrey," she said, "why, I think that's wonderful."

He could see himself with a horrible clarity afterwards, seated there by the cut-glass pitcher and the cut-glass goblets, trying to reach beyond himself.

"Oh, Jeffrey," she said again, "I think that's wonderful. Do you know anyone who works on a newspaper?"

"No," Jeffrey said, "that is, not exactly."

"Well, I think it's wonderful," Louella said. "Here come Mother and Father now."

Jeffrey pushed himself out of the rocking chair. "I've got to be going now," he said. "Really."

"Oh, no," Louella said, and she put her hand on his arm. He could not believe it, but there it was. "Please wait. Father and Mother would love to see you."

He could see Mr. and Mrs. Barnes walking slowly up the tarred path. Mr. Barnes wore a straw hat and carried a rolled-up newspaper which meant that he must have come from the city on the 6:01 train. Mr. Barnes waved his paper when he saw Louella.

"Hello," he called, "hello, Chick."

Jeffrey felt that he ought not to have been there to have heard that term of endearment.

"Well, of all things," said Mrs. Barnes, "if it isn't Jeffrey Wilson."

"Well," Mr. Barnes said, "I'm glad to see you, Jeffrey. Are they working you hard at college?"

"And iced tea," Mrs. Barnes said, "and the best pitcher. It's a real party."

"Oh, Mother," Louella said, "you know the pitcher makes it nicer."

"I could do with some of that myself," Mr. Barnes said.

"I'll get you some in the kitchen, Harold," Mrs. Barnes told him, and she smiled at Jeffrey. "Are you coming, Harold?"

But Mr. Barnes lingered on the porch.

"Where's that brother of yours?" he asked. "Where's Alf?"

"He's down in New York, sir," Jeffrey said, "the last we heard of him."

Mr. Barnes laughed.

"Of course he is," he said. "This town couldn't hold a boy like Alf. Alf was quite a card."

"Yes sir," Jeffrey said, "we miss him."

"The girls must miss him," Mr. Barnes said. "Alf was quite a ladies' man."

"Father," Louella said, "what do you think—Jeffrey's going to be a newspaper man."

"Well, well," Mr. Barnes said, "are you? Now that's an interesting thing to do."

"Harold," Mrs. Barnes called from the house. "Can I talk to you a minute?" And Jeffrey and Louella were on the porch alone.

"I've got to be going, really," Jeffrey said.

"Oh, no, please don't," Louella told him. "I'll get you some more iced tea. Father and Mother don't like sitting on the porch. They like to sit inside."

"It's pretty near time for supper," Jeffrey said. "I've got to be going, really."

"Wait a minute," Louella said, "I'll get you *The Winning of Barbara Worth*, and next time you come, you can tell me how you like it." She looked at the empty cut-glass pitcher. "I'm afraid I didn't make enough iced tea."

"There was plenty of it," Jeffrey said. "Thank you very much."

"Good-by," Louella said, "and come back soon, now that you've found your way."

She was smiling at him when he held her hand. "Come as soon as you can," she said, "now that you've found your way."

17

We'll Show 'Em, Won't We, Jeff?

Once, it might have been a year before that afternoon upon the Barnes porch, Jeffrey had been intrigued by an advertisement which extolled the merits of a book on the power of will. It seemed that the author of this volume had stumbled accidentally upon a means of mobilizing a great reservoir of force and energy which hitherto had lain unutilized within the mind of everyone. This could be called forth by exercising the power of will. If you knew this secret, you, too, could dominate any situation. You had only to look at Napoleon Bonaparte and Andrew Carnegie. It appeared that both these men had been plagued by seemingly insuperable deficiencies until they had learned the Secret. The author of this volume himself admitted freely that he had been a pitiable mental case. He had lost job after job; he had been the constant butt of ridicule and had been tongue-tied at social gatherings, and then, one day, he too had hit upon the Secret. Today, the author of this book, whom Jeffrey had never heard mentioned as a prominent character, simply by exercising his mind for a few minutes each day had arisen from the ruck of the many to the pinnacle of the few, and there he stood, offering you, too, a helping hand. Out of the kindness of his heart, and not in any sense out of a desire for personal profit, since riches and fame now rained upon him automatically, he was offering his revelation to you, too. He had charted your way for you, step by step in simple, easy lessons which you could study yourself in your own room without making any noise. And here was the first lesson in putting your will to work. There was the coupon. All you had to do was to cut it out, and the postman would deliver the book at your door, and if you did not feel a mental upsurge at the end of ten days, you could send it back.

Jeffrey had clipped the coupon, largely out of shame because a year before that he had not bought a book about how to have big muscles. Yet, when the book arrived—and he still kept it hidden in his upper bureau drawer under his knitted muffler in case Tilly or his aunt should ask him about it—it had not been exactly what he had hoped, perhaps because he had not been up to it. Printed on absorbent and pulpy paper was a series of exercises for your will. When you had one perfectly, you could continue to the next. You first said to yourself—not aloud because you never had to say anything aloud—"I will to will. Attention." Then you stood for a moment focusing your eyes on every object in your room, blotting out all extraneous thought. Then you turned your back and, upon a clean sheet of paper, you wrote down all the objects, and then you checked the list. And then you said again to yourself: "I will to will. Attention." There were not many objects in Jeffrey's room on Lime Street except the bed and the hooked rug and the washstand and the bureau. He was able to accomplish the first lesson, but when he was finished with it he seemed to feel no stirrings of a new and unknown power. It was true that the book told him that he might be disappointed at first and exhorted him to continue with the next lesson, but somehow he never got to it, what with the pressure of his college work. He knew he was what the book called a "quitter," but he never did do the second lesson.

He had often suspected that he had been becozened into buying that book, but now as he walked down Center Street, he had a revelation of what the author meant. The clouds and mists of illusion were rolling back. His step was firmer, his eye was clearer; he was in tune with everything, just as the book had told him that he should be; but it was not the book that had done it. It was Louella Barnes who had raised him beyond himself, out of the ruck of ordinary men.

When Jeffrey walked home that afternoon, the stores and the church and the brick block where his father had his office assumed a new aspect. Their lights and shadows made them like a part of a modern interpretive canvas. The door in the brick block, wedged between the drygoods store and the jewelry shop and giving access to the business rooms above, was open as he walked past, and he could see the stairs that led up to the second floor where his father's office was; and he could see the iron signs tacked on the risers so that a client could learn all that Jeffrey's father had to offer as he walked up the stairs. "Wilson, Real Estate–Insurance. Wilson, Insurance, Fire and Life. Wilson, Farms and Dwellings." The sight of the stairs made him walk faster, and he discovered that he was saying to himself: "I will to will. Attention."

The house on Lime Street looked shabby in that new light, more gray than white because of its chipping paint. The broken palings of the front fence and the yard and the large elm all looked as though they belonged to someone else. Long afterwards he had the same sensation when he found himself unexpectedly in an apartment which he had once rented in New York. He possessed only the memory of himself as he had been when he was living there. The part of him that was actual, the part of him to which philosophers gave Greek names and definitions and which went on living and thinking, was gone. He had the same sense of inevitable motion utterly beyond one's controlling power that he experienced when a ship was leaving dock, when the gangplank was pulled back and the hawsers were coiling in, when the first perceptible motion came, when it was too late to go ashore.

His father and Aunt Martha sat already at the supper table. His father was cutting a piece of cold lamb and helping himself to potato salad and his Aunt Martha was stirring her tea.

"Hello, Jeff," his father said. "Where have you been?"

"I just stopped at the Barneses'," he told them. "I didn't realize it was so late."

"My, my," his father said, "that's a new place for you to stop."

"Now, Howland," Aunt Martha said. "I've always liked Louella. She's such a–" Aunt Martha paused, and Jeffrey found himself waiting with unexpected interest for her to finish. "She's such a homey girl."

The clumsiness of that description was appalling and he wanted her to leave it there.

"Mrs. Barnes keeps everything so nice," Aunt Martha said. "I was there at the Flower Committee tea."

Jeffrey could hear the conversation, but he heard it from a distance because he did not belong there any more.

"I got a letter from Alf today," his father said.

Aunt Martha stopped stirring her tea and she held the teaspoon over the cup.

"Well, you might have said so in the first place. What did Alf say?"

"Alf wanted twenty dollars."

"What's he working at?" his Aunt Martha asked.

"He didn't say," his father answered. "Martha, that Harris girl–the one the boys call 'Pinky'–she's left town. They tell me Alf used to go around with Pinky Harris quite a lot."

"Well, I don't see," Aunt Martha said, "when there are so many nice girls around, why a boy like Alf, that all the girls were always asking over, should see anything in a girl like Pinky Harris."

His father glanced around the table.

"It's kind of lonesome," he said, "without Alf and Ethel. It makes the house so quiet."

"Now, Howland," Aunt Martha said, "we've still got Jeff. Jeff isn't going anywhere. Jeff's what I call a 'home boy.'"

When his father smiled at him, it gave Jeffrey an unexpected spasm of pain. He knew his father liked him, although he never said much, and now he knew that his father liked him better than the lot. His father was proud of him; he could see it in the Old Man's face.

"Yes," his father said, "everyone keeps leaving town, but Jeff and I will keep things going. We'll show 'em, won't we, Jeff?"

18

Never Twice in a Lifetime

When Jeffrey took the train out to Woburn to call on Mr. Fernald who had been the telegraph editor a whole river of time seemed to sweep between them. It had been years and years since Jeffrey had left the paper and he was twenty pounds heavier and his suit, which had been made by a good tailor, had cost a hundred and fifty dollars. His attitude and methods of thought were so much altered that it was exceedingly difficult to project himself backwards. Mr. Fernald must have still thought of him as a boy, as his old boss began to tell him what he had looked like during his first weeks on the paper. They talked about it for quite a while because it made a bridge between them, and Jeffrey realized that Mr. Fernald's descriptions offered him the only objective picture he would ever have of himself at that stage of his career. Mr. Fernald said that he had hired him only because Elmer Gaines, who handled the domestic news, had been called out with the National Guard and had gone to the Texas border. Everyone had to move up and Mr. Grimes, the managing editor, had offered Mr. Fernald someone from the City Room, but Mr. Fernald had told Mr. Grimes that he would rather break in a mule than any reporter they would send him from there. Mr. Fernald said that he had been too damned busy with the war news to go out looking for anyone, and that was the reason he took Jeffrey when Jeffrey applied for a job. Actually, the last thing he wanted was a college boy and he had especially not wanted one who thought he was good at English. Mr. Fernald himself had not had the benefits of a college education and in his opinion, it didn't help newspaper men. College boys were fresh and knew too much, and the only people who were worse, in Mr. Fernald's opinion, were the graduates of these newfangled schools of journalism. He wanted to break his man in himself and not have some professor do it. He had hired Jeffrey because Jeffrey had looked scared and this made Mr. Fernald feel that it would be possible to break him in, and by God, Mr. Fernald had broken him in, and that was why Mr. Fernald had hired Walter Newcombe later—because Walter also looked scared.

"You were clumsy," Mr. Fernald said, "but you were all right."

Mr. Fernald looked at Jeffrey and rubbed his hand across his eyes. "It doesn't seem so long ago, either. God almighty, the whole show has speeded up. Here we're doing it again. Here we're at the start of another war."

They sat for a moment, looking backward. Mr. Fernald was smoking the same five-cent cigar he had always smoked. He narrowed his eyes and squinted through the smoke.

"Do you think we'll get into it this time?" Jeffrey asked him.

Mr. Fernald removed his cigar and looked at it.

"Don't be a God-damned fool," he said; "of course we will." He frowned at Jeffrey. He had lapsed back into the old pattern of the telegraph room and perhaps he felt that it was bad manners now to call Jeffrey a "God-damned fool."

"The boys will go just the way you did," he said. "Do you remember when you came in to say good-by? You weren't the same when you came back."

Mr. Fernald went on talking. He said it was a nice shop and a nice crowd. It might have been slow. There might have been a lot of dead wood, but everybody was friendly and no one tried to knife you in the back. They didn't make newspaper men or newspapers like that any more.

Jeffrey could hear the old sounds. He could almost see the old faces and Mr. Fernald made it all incredibly ancient because of the quaver of age that had crept into his nasal voice.

Mr. Fernald was right—they didn't make newspapers like that any more, and maybe it was just as well. Jeffrey's acquaintance with modern New York dailies housed in modern buildings made it difficult to realize that he had ever worked on such a paper. His own memory gave it a quality that was more like a steel engraving than a photograph, and perhaps the days before the last war were all like that. Despite all that he remembered to the contrary, those days had an orderly quiet quality. The office buildings on Milk and Congress and State Streets gave forth an impregnable feeling of confidence in the indestructibility of a definite order. The food in all the restaurants was better then. He was certain that the turkeys were fatter in the market district, that the fruits were rarer, that the flowers and vegetables were larger. Everything was in the hands of an older generation who must have felt that everything had been done and that there was nothing else to do. Mr. Fernald was chanting of an epoch which would never come back again, and once you were possessed with that certainty, you saw in it the essence of the Yale song which stated that bright college years were rife with pleasure and that they were the shortest, gladdest years in life. The old days on the paper seemed just like that.

Jeffrey could hear the sound of the linotype machines. He could feel the gentle tremor of the building when the presses began to move. There was that sweetish smell of ink on the freshly pulled proofs that you impaled on sharp hooks upon the wall. He could remember the stacks and stacks of clippings in the morgue, which Mr. Sawyer examined daily as he worked on the page for recent deaths. He could remember the smell of the stairs as you climbed to the telegraph room, and the crowd around the blackboards on the street reading the news about the shifts on the Western Front, but he could conjure up no recollection of what he must have been like himself.

"I must have been young for my age," he said.

"You were all right," Mr. Fernald said, "as soon as you got to taking a drink. I never had a better man do the war summary. You could make the pieces fit."

A perfectly good word has been worked to death in the last few years—the adjective "nostalgic." It has been applied to ladies' dresses, perfume, porch furniture, and even to saddle horses. Yet it is the only adjective which seems adequate to describe a certain wistful sort of feeling that a newspaper man has about the old shop and the old crowd, and even about a great many unpleasant individuals whom he may have encountered at City Hall and at Police Headquarters. The City Editor in those days might very well have been one of the worst stinkers on Newspaper Row, but as the years went on, one thought of him as a nostalgic stinker. His very persecutions, and his high-handed acts of injustice, grew monumental, given time, so that finally when one or two of the old crowd met together, they could all agree a little sadly that there never was such an old so-and-so as old So-and-so back there on the City Desk. They don't make so-and-so's like that any more.

Take almost any group of middle-aged gentlemen in the men's washroom of a Pullman car. When the talk wanders aimlessly on the affairs of the nation in the dark hours between Chicago and Kansas City, sooner or later someone unbuttons another button in his vest and glances at the black landscape out of the window and says:—

"I was a newspaper man once myself."

At such a time, a spirit of brotherhood pervades that smoky retreat, unless he says:—

"I was once in the newspaper game."

There is something wrong about almost anyone who has been in "the newspaper game." In some way he has surely been tried and found wanting. His experience has not enriched him as it has those who have been newspaper men once themselves.

It had been Mr. Fernald's custom in those days to run a lead of several hundred words under the war headlines, giving a picture of the general situation before the reader became involved with the actual dispatches. One day old Mr. Jenks, who customarily wrote this lead and sent it up to the composing room by five minutes of three so that it would catch the last edition, had gone out to lunch and had not come back. Jeffrey was too new then to realize that this sometimes happened to Mr. Jenks after payday. On these occasions, Jeffrey learned later, Mr. Jenks often became mellow and expansive, and when his mood was exactly right he would develop the desire to call upon the Governor at the State House. It was a harmless enough desire and one which could easily enough be prevented if anyone were watching, but this time it seemed that no one in the group that had gone out to lunch had watched Mr. Jenks, not even Mr. Fernald. In fact when Mr. Fernald returned from lunch to give the last directions for the page in the next to last edition, he was smoking a ten-cent instead of a five-cent cigar, and in finding his way to his swivel chair he stepped directly into a cuspidor.

"Every year," Mr. Fernald said, "there seem to be more spittoons in here. Every year there is more and more of everything, and that makes progress: more of everything."

Then Mr. Fernald sat down and asked if President Wilson's message to Congress were coming in, but he did not wait for the answer because he wanted to know where Mr. Jenks was, and when no one knew, Mr. Fernald became alarmed because he and Mr. Jenks had been right there having lunch. Then they began ringing from the composing room for the war lead, and Mr. Fernald began to swear and search through the copy for it, and Edgar, the office boy, told him that Mr. Jenks had not put it anywhere, because Mr. Jenks had not written it.

That was all there was to it—a slightly sordid affair, and anyone could see that Mr. Fernald was not quite in the right condition to do the lead himself. In fact, he had forgotten it already, and had fallen sound asleep.

That was all there was to it. Jeffrey picked up a piece of yellow copy paper and a pencil. He remembered that he started it, "The situation today on the Western Front . . ." and then, just in time, he recollected that it was a rule of the paper never to start a lead with "The."

Mr. Fernald had awakened and was beginning to sing "Where the River Shannon Flows." The melody interrupted Jeffrey's train of thought and he wished that Mr. Fernald would stop.

"Heavy fighting on the Somme sector," Jeffrey wrote, "and an artillery duel in the neighborhood of Lille stand out as the main action on the Western Front today."

Mr. Sims, the foreman of the composing room, was wearing a green eyeshade and was cutting copy into sections with a long pair of shears. The machines made such a noise that Jeffrey had to shout at him.

"There it is, sir," Jeffrey shouted.

"What?" Mr. Sims shouted.

"The war lead," Jeffrey shouted.

Mr. Sims took the first sheet and slashed it into three parts.

"What's going on?" he asked. "Is Fernald drunk again?"

Jeffrey remembered that Mr. Sims, in all the excitement of the closing pages, had time to smile at him as though they, as men, both understood the weakness of the world.

"Tell him next time," Mr. Sims shouted, "to save some of it for me."

Mr. Fernald had stopped singing when Jeffrey came downstairs.

"Where have you been," Mr. Fernald asked him, "to the toilet?"

"No, sir," Jeffrey said, "I wrote the war lead."

Mr. Fernald started and looked at the clock. The room was vibrating softly. The paper had gone to press.

"Well, laddie boy," he said, "laddie boy."

It was customary for Edgar to go downstairs and bring up the last edition and to pass a copy of the paper to everyone in the room. It was the first time that Jeffrey had ever seen words of his in print, and they were in the right column and on the front page in brevier. He would remember them until he died: "Heavy fighting on the Somme sector . . ."

Mr. Fernald folded his paper, pushed back his chair and reached for his hat. "All right," he said. "How about a drink?"

"What, sir?" Jeffrey asked him.

"I said," Mr. Fernald told him, "how about a drink?"

He knew it was not polite to refuse Mr. Fernald.

When Jeffrey reached the five o'clock train at the North Station, he still grasped the paper firmly. He also held a cigar which Mr. Fernald had given him. Although he did not mean to smoke it, he went into the smoking car. He had only taken one drink, although Mr. Fernald had offered him two, but he took two pieces of mint candy from his pocket, and chewed them carefully. He could feel no ill effects. His only sensation was one of relaxation after nervous exertion. The train was pulling out of the station. A man in the seat in front of him had unfolded his paper and was reading the very words which Jeffrey had written. Half the people on the train were reading them, little realizing that the man who had written the war lead made one of their number in the smoking car.

He kept hoping that Louella might be at home, and there she was, sitting in the Cape Cod hammock, looking fresh and rested, and she had on a new blue silk dress.

"Hello," Jeffrey said, "hello, Louella." He felt that he should give some reason for being there, but she spoke before he could give a reason.

"What happened to you yesterday?" Louella said. "I was looking for you."

"Well," Jeffrey said, "I thought I'd sort of be bothering you if I stopped in all the time."

"Why, silly," Louella said, "it doesn't bother me."

"I don't want you to get tired of me," Jeffrey said, "because I come around too much."

"Why, silly," Louella said, "sit down." And she patted the place beside her on the Cape Cod hammock.

"Oh, no," he said, "it's sort of crowded, isn't it?"

"Why, silly," Louella said, "there's room for three in the hammock. Last night Milt Rolfe and Summers Harris and I all sat in it."

"You ought to be careful doing things like that," Jeffrey said, "it might have broken down. I can only stay a minute."

He put the paper under his arm and gave his trousers a little pull so as not to spoil the crease in them and sat down beside Louella. There was a gentle swinging motion, hardly perceptible, but intoxicating. Louella, with her little brown shoes, was pushing the hammock softly back and forth.

"It's nicer," she said, "than the rocking chairs, isn't it?"

"Yes," Jeffrey said, "it doesn't throw you backwards."

Louella laughed.

"We were pretty busy today," Jeffrey said. "Have you seen the paper?"

Louella said she hadn't seen it, because it hadn't come yet, and Jeffrey took his own copy from beneath his arm and pointed to the right-hand column.

"The man who usually does it didn't come back from lunch," he said. "I wrote that."

She leaned closer toward him to see. Her shoulder touched his and then she drew away.

"Why Jeffrey Wilson," Louella said, "you didn't write all of that."

He felt a surge of disappointment. If he had written all the column she might have leaned longer against his shoulder.

"No," he said, "just that much."

"Oh," Louella said, "why, Jeffrey Wilson!"

"You can keep it," he said, "don't bother to read it now. It isn't anything, really." And then he wanted to change the subject. There was a piece of knitting between them on the hammock.

"What's that?" he asked. "Something you're making?" And then he thought it might have been something which Louella would not want to speak about, something that girls wore.

"Why," Louella said, "it's a washcloth. I knit them for Father and Mother, and I'll give this one to you."

Jeffrey swallowed, and for an instant he sat mute.

"But maybe your father needs it," he said.

"Oh, no," Louella said, "Father has lots and lots. Not that I don't think you're clean—" Louella giggled and Jeffrey laughed too. He had never lived through such a day as that. He had written a war lead in the paper, and Louella was going to give him a washcloth if he stopped to see her tomorrow—a durable article which he could keep always, which he could keep until he died.

19

And All the Heart Desires

In the afternoon the evening war communiqués would come over the A.P., and Mr. Jenks would get out his maps and Mr. Eldridge and Mr. Nichols would come in from the editorial rooms out front and all of them would chat agreeably and perhaps intelligently about the war. They had all read the critiques of Mr. Frank Simonds and other military experts and they had read the London *Times* and the Paris *Matin* and the *Spectator* and the *London Evening Post* and the *Chronicle*. They were also familiar with more permanent works on the art of war, so that their conversation was sprinkled with such expressions as "camouflage" and "aerial observation" and "no man's land" and "creeping barrages" and "box barrages" and "primary and secondary objectives." It was like being in a conference of generals when those elderly men were talking, dispassionately removed from actuality, striving to put order into a confusion that was a very long way off. They talked of the submarine blockade and of attacks without warning on our merchant shipping. The German soldiers were sheep being driven to slaughter, but at the same time they possessed barbarous vindictiveness. They cut the hands off little Belgian children and they had crucified British prisoners. It was Mr. Eldridge's opinion that they were inhuman swine. There was even a story that they had rendering plants in which they manufactured soap out of their own dead. There were lots of rumors which you could not set down in print. At such times Mr. Nichols wished fervently that we had a *man* in the White House and not a Presbyterian college professor. Even that smile of Woodrow Wilson's was anathema to Mr. Nichols. There was such a thing, Mr. Wilson had said, as being too proud to fight, which simply meant, according to Mr. Nichols, that we were afraid to fight. We were a soft nation of yellow-bellied cowards, particularly those people in the Middle West. They did not know, by God they didn't, that there was such a thing as national honor. They did not care if we were insulted and it was no wonder the Germans laughed at us in Berlin. After sinking the *Lusitania*, they knew we wouldn't fight. There had only been a cringing sort of note penned by William Jennings Bryan. We would go on playing the part of poltroons and cowards, making money out of war contracts until we had someone else besides a college professor in the White House. It was a good thing that election was coming, for there might be a few men left in the country who were not glad that Woodrow Wilson had kept us out of war. He wished that Theodore Roosevelt were in there; that man might interfere with business, but he was not afraid to fight. Mr. Nichols wished to heaven that he were ten or twenty years younger. He wished that he were Jeffrey Wilson's age and he would not be wearing out the seat of his pants in any office.

Those conversations never reached any conclusion. Nevertheless it began to be plain, and Jeffrey felt it vaguely, that those nations known as "the Allies," on the other side of an ocean which Jeffrey had never crossed, were not going to defeat the Germans by themselves. There was a dread which lay behind nearly everyone's thoughts and words—a mass emotion—and perhaps this was all that ever caused a war—a mass contagious thought shared by all the people, which the poets, the writers and the artists of the generation would never bring to full expression.

Later Jeffrey realized that he had been witnessing the phenomenon of a people drifting into war, and that it had been a collective impulse beyond the power of any group to stop. The formation of his own convictions was as imperceptible as the rotation of a planet. You were told on impeccable authority that the world made a complete revolution in space each day, which meant that half the time you must have been walking upside down, like a fly upon the ceiling; but there was nothing you could do about it—everyone else was walking upside down.

None of it impressed him much—the autumn election, the campaign speeches, the German note on unrestricted submarine warfare—none of these had anything to do with what had happened between him and Louella Barnes; and that itself, when he thought of it later, was something like the war, for it had the same inescapable quality.

Once that winter he had actually held Louella's hand. They had been sitting alone in the little parlor and Louella had made a plate of fudge. Jeffrey had been careful not to eat more than two pieces of it, but when he had told her that it was very good fudge, she must have thought that he was going to reach up to the little table and take a third piece because she laughed, and placed her hand over his to restrain him.

"Don't be such a greedy pig," Louella said, "and eat up all my fudge."

On thinking it over later, he knew that Louella must have regretted that playful gesture, because, without intending to in the least, he had taken advantage of it. She had put her hand over the back of his and somehow the next moment he was holding it and then all time seemed to stop. He could not even remember whether she had tried to draw her hand away. It lay there for a moment, and he believed that it was better to pass it over without mentioning it specifically.

"It's pretty late," he said, "I guess I'd better be going."

"You always think it's getting late," Louella said. "You're not mad, are you?"

"Why," he asked her, "why should I be mad?"

"Because you said you had to be going home."

He smiled at her, blankly, but he knew that she had forgiven him, and that they would say no more about it.

"Silly," Louella said, "open your mouth and shut your eyes, and I'll give you something to make you wise." It was infinitely sweet of her, but he knew that he must be more careful after that. It would not do to frighten a girl like Louella by trying to hold her hand.

Toward the end of March, when Jeffrey had stopped by on his way from the train, Louella asked him if he wouldn't come back after supper—that is if he didn't have something better to do. Her father and mother were going to a whist party at the Thompsons and she was going to be alone. It had pleased him very much, because lately he had been afraid that he was taking up too much of Louella's time. It must have meant that Mr. and Mrs. Barnes did not think that he was paying Louella too much attention.

There was a soggy blanket of snow over everything and it was raining.

"My," Louella said, when she opened the front door, "you haven't got a muffler on—you'll get your death of cold." And then when he was taking his overshoes off she told him to hurry and come in by the fire, and she asked him to help her pull the sofa near the fire so that she could see that he got thawed out. Louella said she was awfully glad that he had come because she knew it was silly, but it was spooky just sitting in the house all alone and hearing the rain on the windows. The rain sounded just like ghosts trying to get in, and she asked Jeffrey to sit still and not say anything. Jeffrey said it always was lonely in a house alone, and Louella said but now it was company—two made company and three made a crowd, but the ghosts knocking on the window didn't make a crowd, because she knew that Jeffrey would see that they didn't get in.

There was nothing in Louella's appearance to show that she was afraid of ghosts or spooks. She had on a new yellow silk dress that was very tight around her arms and shoulders, but the skirt was all yellow pleats and ruffles and the color went beautifully with her hair. When she asked Jeffrey what he was staring at, he said that he was looking at her dress and Louella said it was just a dress she had made from a pattern.

"I was just trying it on," she said, "and then I heard you coming. Mother doesn't like it," Louella said, "she thinks it's a little—too tight in front."

Jeffrey looked carefully at the fire.

"Down on the paper," Jeffrey said, "they think we're going to get into the war."

"Oh," Louella said, "men always talk about war."

She said she hated the Germans, but she did not want to think of Jeffrey going to the war.

"But I suppose you'll be dying to go," Louella said.

Jeffrey had not thought of it at all until she mentioned it, and then she asked him if he was sure he had not caught cold. They must have talked for some time, for all at once when he looked at the clock on the mantel, in front of the beveled mirror, it was half-past nine.

"Maybe I ought to go home," Jeffrey said, "it's getting sort of late."

"That's what you always say," Louella said. "I don't know why I like to have you here when you always say that."

"Well, I just meant—" Jeffrey began—"I just thought maybe you were tired."

"You mean you don't like being alone with me," Louella said.

And then her voice broke.

"You don't like me," Louella said, "I always knew you didn't."

Jeffrey could see himself, years afterwards, seated on that sofa with the golden oak of the Barnes mantelpiece in front of him. He could see himself edging furtively toward Louella Barnes. He could see himself extending his arm, gingerly, and putting it across her shoulders. He could remember Louella's sobbing, and the exact crinkling sound of that yellow dress. Whenever anyone said afterwards that Americans were bad lovers—and there was a time when serious thinkers were inclined to find that the answer for everything that was wrong in America—its brashness, its lack of good food, its inferior literary output and the frigidity of its women—whenever this assertion was advanced, Jeffrey would wince internally, and live that scene again. When he did, he would try to discover what had been wrong with it. He would wonder, with a lack of gallantry which he confined only to his thoughts, what might have happened if Louella had been more experienced. Often when he read passages on the beauty of young love, Jeffrey wondered if it did not rather possess a certain tragedy and a lack of fulfillment which the writer had conveniently forgotten. At any rate, that dated picture of Louella and himself on the sofa would tangle itself irrationally with all sorts of thoughts and moods.

"Louella," he said. "Louella, I—"

He always thought of it when he read love scenes, particularly the parts about kissing. He thought of it when he read about the couples kissing each other carefully, lingeringly, or thoughtfully, or hungrily. He thought of it when he read that their lips met or that her lips found his. Whatever he and Louella did, it did not fall into that category. He had visualized that moment for so long that when it happened it was all a hasty blank. Somehow, doubtless because Americans were not great lovers, the fire tongs and poker fell upon the hearth when he kissed Louella Barnes, but he was not conscious of the sound. He was only conscious that Louella's dress was pressed against his coat. Her eyes were tight shut, and he saw that there were little freckles on her cheeks, and there was an aura of the same violet talcum powder that Alf had loaned him. He did not know whether she pushed him from her gently, as those love passages had it, or whether it was he who released her reluctantly. He only knew that they were sitting side by side on the sofa and that Louella's face was flushed.

"Oh, Jeffrey," she said, "oh, Jeffrey."

His first impression was that it was irrevocable. He could see his past moving from him, and he had never realized how comfortable his past had been. He was bewildered because reality could never have equaled the embroidery of his imagination. The clock on the mantel ticked more loudly. The rug in front of the hearth was scuffed and turned in little folds and Jeffrey found himself bending down and straightening it.

"Jeffrey," Louella said, "do you think we ought to tell Father and Mother?"

"Why, I don't know," he answered, "why?"

"But we're engaged, aren't we?" Louella asked.

The inescapable fact of it gripped Jeffrey.

"Yes," he said, "I guess so."

"Well, aren't you glad?" Louella asked.

"Why, yes," Jeffrey said, "yes, Louella."

"Then you might act glad," Louella said.

Her voice had a sharpness that was unfamiliar to him, but he felt the justice of it. The least he could do was to act glad.

"I'm just getting used to it," he said. "I never thought—"

Louella's laugh interrupted him. He could see that she must have wanted it to happen.

"Maybe it would be nicer to have it a secret," Louella said, "just for a little while. Do you think it would be nicer?"

"Maybe it would, for a while," Jeffrey said.

"Oh, Jeffrey," Louella said. "I can't believe it, can you?"

He was already believing that perhaps it had not happened, even though he knew it had.

"Oh, dear," Louella said, "here come Mother and Father now."

He could hear their footsteps on the porch. He could hear Mr. Barnes stamping on the mat and then the front door closed.

"Why," Mrs. Barnes said, "hello, you two."

"Hello," Mr. Barnes said, "Jeffrey's been calling, has he?"

"Yes, sir," Jeffrey said, "is it still raining outside?"

"It's raining cats and dogs," Mr. Barnes said. "How cozy you two look in front of the fire."

"I guess I ought to be going now," Jeffrey said.

"Well, it's so nice you came over," Mrs. Barnes said. "Harold, will you come out here for a minute?"

"Why," Mr. Barnes said, "what's the matter now?"

"Harold," Mrs. Barnes said, "there's something I want to show you in the kitchen."

Back in the kitchen he could hear Mr. Barnes's voice.

"Don't keep telling me," he said, "I *am* leaving them alone."

But Jeffrey pretended not to hear it. He was pulling on his overshoes. He and Louella were alone in the front hall. Louella was helping him into his coat and telling him to button it tight around his neck. She was saying that she would see him tomorrow, and of course he would see her tomorrow, and he was wondering if Mr. and Mrs. Barnes could hear them.

"Well," Jeffrey said, "good night, Louella, I had a very nice time."

But he knew that something else was required of him. He bent down quickly and kissed Louella's cheek.

"Good night," Louella whispered, "dear."

He hoped that Mr. and Mrs. Barnes did not hear them. There was no doubt that they were engaged.

Jeffrey found himself walking very quickly and in the confusion of his thoughts he did not mind the rain. He wanted to feel that he was absolutely happy, but instead he had a feeling that was almost like relief that he was not there any longer. He had known that he would love Louella Barnes always. Yet, now that he had discovered that Louella Barnes loved him, instead of experiencing the acme of happiness, he wanted to get away. He told himself that he must be going mad, that decency and obligation and every proper instinct made any sort of escape impossible. He told himself it would be better the next time he saw her. He told himself that it was all because he was so surprised. He never realized, as he was walking away in the rain, that he was leaving Louella Barnes already, and with her leaving everything he had ever known.

20

Old Kaspar, and the Sun Was Low

One morning in the summer of 1935, when Jeffrey was not obliged to go to New York, and when there was nothing to do at all, he was reading the paper under a tree in front of the house in Connecticut. Madge had bought the place two years before with her own money, and Jeffrey had not approved particularly. He had told her that everyone was buying farms in Connecticut, especially in the neighborhood of Westport, and that now the whole country was being filled with all sorts of people who wanted to get away from the city. They were just like all the people that they were trying to get away from, except that in the country they had allowed their personalities to expand. Jeffrey had told her that she was only buying the place because her friend Beckie had bought one. It had not helped, either, when he had heard Madge saying to someone across the table, when they were out at dinner, that she had bought it so that they could have some place to live, come the Revolution.

Jeffrey could trace phases of this thought trend, "Come the Revolution," through most of his adult life. First there had been the Bolsheviki, a menace which had appeared on the horizon with the close of the war. Bolsheviki was a new word then, and the Bolsheviki were going to infiltrate into the United States; they were going to blow up everything, and they had started when they exploded that mysterious milk wagon in front of the Morgan offices on Wall Street. Then there came Russia's Five Year Plan, which was going to industrialize Russia in no time, and make all of Russia so comfortable that people over here would forget the advantages of a democratic system. Then came the depression and that was when they all began saying "Come the Revolution." Personally Jeffrey had been unable to perceive any signs of the Revolution, but a friend of his, Edward Mace, who had been a social worker in Chicago and who had written reports for various foundations which Jeffrey had never been able to read, had told Jeffrey that the New Deal had staved off violent revolution. Edward Mace agreed with Mr. Tugwell that it was necessary to make over the station but to allow the trains still to go in and out of it, a simile which indicated that Mr. Tugwell and a few others with the proper intellectual endowment hoped to repair a shaky economic system without tearing everything down. Edward Mace said that Rex was perfectly sound about this; and that was one thing about the New Dealers which annoyed Jeffrey—they were always calling each other by their first names, or what was worse, by nicknames, as though they were all members of a club or of an athletic team. Edward Mace, for instance, referred to the President as "the Skipper" and Mr. Roosevelt, not to be outdone, had stated that he was the quarterback who called the signals. This New Deal intimacy disturbed Jeffrey much more than the Revolution, which, according to Edward Mace, was going on right now, although people like Jeffrey did not know it because people like Jeffrey possessed no social sense.

Jeffrey thought of this as he sat beneath the tree, reading his morning paper. He had told Madge that it would be cheaper to go on renting a house for the summer, as they always had before, but Madge had said that she wanted something solid. If he did not want to pay for it, why, she would pay for it out of her own money which she had inherited from her father and mother. This was what always happened when Madge wanted something which he did not want. It was useless to explain to her that whenever she bought something with her own money, he was the one who maintained it. She had bought the house, and having bought it, the least he could do was to pay for the plumbing and the painting and for keeping up the grounds, which cost more than renting a summer house, any way you looked at it, any summer. Yet he could understand Madge's desire to own it. It was a place of their own where they could keep their own things without ever being compelled to move them, a place which they could furnish the way they wished with a separate room for each of the three children and a garden where the vegetables cost more to grow than they would have to buy in the chain store. In spite of everything, he was pleased, on that summer morning in 1935, that Madge had bought the house. He felt a sense of security that morning, and a sense of peace. The new couple, who were Finnish, gave an illusion that they might stay and the man, whose name was Frank, gave an illusion of being interested in waxing the floors. The woman, whose name he believed was Hulga, made good coffee, and there had been bacon and eggs for breakfast. There were sit-down strikes in France and there was unrest in Spain, but on the whole, the world seemed quiet.

That summer of 1935 was one of the few times in his life that Jeffrey had felt free to relax and turn around. He had bought a part interest in a play the previous winter which unexpectedly had netted him eighty thousand dollars, and he had income from other work which he had been doing. Even with the income tax it meant that he could relax that summer. He knew very well that buying a share in a play was like betting on a horse race, but now he was considering trying it again and Jesse Fineman had sent him a manuscript, which he proposed to read that afternoon. Meanwhile, Madge had taken the station wagon to do the shopping and she had taken Gwen and Jim somewhere to play tennis and swim. He was glad they were all gone; the house was quiet.

Just then the screen door slammed, and he looked up. It was his youngest son Charley, who was eight years old then, walking down the path, scuffing his shoes in the gravel.

"Hey," Charley said, "what's this?"

Jeffrey did not care what it was; he did not want to be disturbed. When he looked at Charley, he felt, as he often did, that he scarcely knew the little boy. Charley was wearing gray Oxford shorts, stockings which came up to his bare knees, and a blue jersey with white stripes. The whole costume made him look like Christopher Robin as he appeared in *The House at Pooh*

Corner, a book which Jeffrey wished had never been written, and which he knew that Madge had read to the children without telling him. As he looked at Charley, he could not believe that a son of his could be dressed like that, and all of Charley's mental processes were equally unfamiliar to him. Charley had gone to a progressive school, something unheard-of in Jeffrey's youth. At the age of eight, Charley could talk enthusiastically about the architecture of Indian wigwams, and about the care and diet of small rodents. He lived in an environment unknown to Jeffrey, made up of small workbenches and of water-color paints in rows of bottles, and electric questioners.

"Hey," Charley said again, "what's this?"

They did not teach spelling or manners to the pupils in progressive schools, but they did teach them to be natural and rude to their elders.

"What's what?" Jeffrey asked.

He endeavored to speak with interest, since one should exhibit no impatience with a child of eight. He did not want to antagonize Charley. He was only conscious that he did not know Charley well. It was different with Jim because he had been obliged at times to take care of Jim himself, but he had been busy ever since Charley was born, and Charley was his mother's boy. His clothes, his features and his voice made it a little like talking to a child who did not belong to him.

"This," Charley said, "what's this?"

He plumped the thing on Jeffrey's knees, so that it crumpled up the newspaper. Charley was used to expressing himself, and he was not afraid of grownups. He leaned against Jeffrey's knee, wriggling and snuffling.

"Where did you find it?" Jeffrey asked.

It was a flat canvas case with a web strap which looked as though it had been out in the weather. At first Jeffrey could not recall what the article was or whether it had ever belonged to him.

"Upstairs in the trunk room," Charley said, "hanging on a nail. Does it have guns in it?"

"Guns?" Jeffrey answered. "No, it hasn't."

Charley still leaned against his knee and shuffled his feet.

"What's it got in it?" Charley asked.

"Nothing," Jeffrey said, "and you should have left it where it was, and you shouldn't be in the trunk room anyway. Haven't you got the whole place to play in? It's just something I had in the war."

"What war?" Charley asked.

"What war?" Jeffrey repeated. "When we fought the Germans."

He supposed that he should have put his hand on the little fellow's head and should have told him all about the war and just what Daddy had done in it. If Madge had been there, Madge would have explained it, but Madge had gone to town.

"Listen, Charley," Jeffrey said, "suppose you go away and play somewhere. I want to read the paper."

"There isn't anywhere to play," Charley said.

"Not anywhere to play?" Jeffrey repeated. "There's the whole place, isn't there?" He searched his mind for something more specific. "There's a swing, isn't there? Why don't you go and swing in it?"

Charley didn't want to swing in it, because he didn't want to swing.

"Listen, Charley," Jeffrey said, "if you go away and play somewhere, I'll give you twenty-five cents."

But Charley did not want twenty-five cents.

"Then go into the kitchen and see Hulga, or whatever her name is," Jeffrey said, "and tell her to give you a cookie or a glass of milk. I want to read the paper."

But Charley did not want a glass of milk.

"Then don't talk to me," Jeffrey said. "I want to read the paper."

He picked up the *New York Times* and turned to the second page, aware of Charley standing beside him silently. Then he heard Charley kicking the gravel and then he heard him throwing stones and when he finally looked up, Charley had disappeared, but the satchel was where Charley had left it, on his lap.

Jeffrey could remember it well enough now. It had been designed by some house which had specialized in uniforms and officers' accessories as a receptacle for holding maps and papers. It was one of the articles on those interminable mimeographed lists which an officer was expected to have in his possession before he went overseas. It went with the collapsible rubber basin and the collapsible camp chair and the collapsible cot, and all those other articles which were usually left behind after a few weeks in France. Jeffrey had finally carried the map case in his bedding roll, not for maps as much as for letters. He had bought it at Abercrombie and Fitch on his one-day leave in New York before he sailed; he had done so in a fine wave of extravagance shortly after he had received his commission and his pilot's wings. He could even remember the map case on display behind the plate-glass window, and he could recall that he had looked at his own reflection in the window more closely than he had looked at the display. He had been wearing a garrison cap, which he never wore again, but from there his memory was a blank. He could not remember ever using the map case, or opening it, since the war was over.

Now when he pushed the rusty spring catch it was like examining the property of someone else. It was like prying into the intimate possessions of someone who had not come back, as one had been obliged to do often, in the Squadron. The papers, he saw, were growing a little yellow. Two stubs of pencils fell out and a small card with writing in purple ink in a foreign hand —Marie Bouchet, and the address was the Rue Jacob in Paris. He could not remember anyone named Marie, although he must have asked that unknown Marie for her address. He must have kept it hoping to renew his acquaintance, or the paper would not have been there. She must have been one of the girls you knew on those few promiscuous nights in Paris when you knew that your number was coming up sometime soon, and when you took any chance you could to forget it for a while. They had understood about the war; the

French had been kind to the Americans in those days. Then there was one of those battle maps showing the Verdun sector and the German lines as they had existed before the Argonne drive. He could see the peaceful curve of the Meuse River and the high land on the right bank and the triangles and squares of forests. There was also a part of another map showing the railroads and the depots at Conflans and he seemed to be looking down on them again in the glint of the autumn sun while the black puffs from the German archies were exploding in constantly changing compact patterns. Then there were some envelopes and some letter sheets marked "Soldiers' Mail," which included a half-finished note. Though the writing was his own he found himself reading it furtively like an unsympathetic stranger prying into another's past. It was a very bad letter, stilted, without eloquence, written with a pencil so hard that it had made grooves on the yellowish paper.

> Dear Mrs. Rhett:–
>
> I am another of Stan's friends, who writes to say that he shares in his own way your sense of loss. You have been told that he was shot down. I was with him; he was my observer. I tried to get him back. He died after we got in, from loss of blood. I did not know him very well before, but I got to know him on the way back, and I want to say you should be very proud of Stan. Wherever he is now, someone must have said, "Well done!" . . .

As he examined it, the whole tone was trite and immature; and it could not have satisfied him at the time. It was hard to write such letters, and he must have tried again.

He reached into the map case blindly for another envelope with his name and address and Squadron written on it and he recognized that writing too, although he had not seen it for years. It was a letter from Louella Barnes. When he read it now, it did not seem to be his business any more. It would have been more decent if he had never looked inside that map case.

> Dear Jeff:–
>
> When I went down to the post office this morning, looking for you know what, whom should I meet but your father and he had a letter from you "Somewhere in France." My letter did not come. I hope it comes tomorrow. I know you are very busy, Jeffrey dear, so I don't mind if your letters are short, and I know it is against the rules to tell much. They sound as if you were having a good time. You say you remember me, and I hope you do, but sometimes they sound a little bit as if you didn't, but then, perhaps I'm just a "silly" with you so far away "over there." You sound as if you are having a good time with all those other aviators. I am glad they are all college men. I don't remember that any whose names you mention were ever at a Smith prom. I keep wondering what that Minot Roberts must look like and Stanley Rhett, who you say is his best friend. They sound as if they were "swells." Captain Strike sounds very nice, but all of them sound a little "fast." I don't see how you can

keep getting into automobiles and going to Paris and places. I hope they do not make you "fast." I hope you think of me as often as I think of you, which is nearly all the time.

We have just had a big rally for the Liberty Loan and we have gasless Sundays. Who do you think I saw last week? Your brother, Alf! I almost ran into him when he came out of the barbershop. He is just a doughboy and he asked if I had heard from you lately and I said I had, which wasn't true, because I didn't want him to know I hadn't. Now Jeffrey, it makes me so proud of you "over there." It is as if I were fighting "over there" too. . . .

He knew that her last letter must be there too, for suddenly he recalled that some sort of superstition had prevented his destroying it even though he had not wished it to be among his effects if he did not come back. He found it there when he reached in the map case, a short letter, so carefully written that it was plain that Louella must have copied it, and recopied it:—

Dear Jeffrey:—

I know that this is not going to hurt you, it has been so long since you have written. I tried to pretend that I got letters whenever your father said he had heard from you. I tried and tried, so of course I know you've never cared the way I cared. I guess it must have started before you went away. I suppose I made you tired because I am too "homey," but I cared, I don't want to tell you how much.

I don't want to be cross about it, and I hope you won't be. Milt Rolfe wants to marry me, and I guess I'd better, don't you think? I'll wait to hear what you say, if you have anything to say, because we are still engaged, and I have your little ring. If you don't want to write, please don't, and I'll understand. Please don't be angry, please let's be friends. There's so much I can't forget. . . .

The letter still awakened in Jeffrey a vague feeling of both guilt and freedom. It had been the best way out of it, although the most cowardly, never to have answered. He stared for a while at the map case and the maps and letters, and a sensation came over him that was fierce, insistent, discordant, as he sat there comfortably under the tree. He was aware of his heart beating and of the vividness of the grass and of the brilliance of the sky. Something was telling him that he was alive, but that he did not have much time to be alive. He had never thought that a few unrelated objects in that map case could make him feel that way again. It was the way they all had felt—alive, and that they did not have much time. Fear had nothing to do with it, unless that sensation of living was related to fear. It used to come to him when he landed and climbed out of the plane. He was back again this once and he did not have much time. It was not fear as much as the thought that he would be cheated if he did not use his time. There might be years for some people instead of a question of days or hours or minutes. Although you did not admit it, you knew that some morning you would not come back. The new faces around the mess table would tell you. Once or twice a week the Squadron car would bring the latest replacements in from the railhead and everyone would be quite jolly.

"This is Bert Newell," Captain Strike would say—or "Bill Jones," or whatever the stranger's name might be; and everyone would smile and shake hands, and then go on playing bridge, or reading the illustrated magazines. Everyone would be amusing about the flight that morning, and someone would ask if you had seen him get that bastard, and then they all would laugh at small misfortunes. Fliers were apart from all the rest of the show, consecrated for a special purpose. They could hear the gunfire up ahead, but that was not their problem. When they were on leave, they liked to stick together and to hell with the infantry and artillery. The M.P.'s very seldom troubled them no matter what they did. The M.P.'s must have understood, and so did the colonels and the generals, that they did not have much time, and the ground mechanics and the mess orderlies all knew it.

The orders usually came through in the evening when everyone was sitting around the table, smoking and making jokes about how much they had eaten or about someone's physical peculiarities. The orderly would call Bill Strike, and he would go out to the telephone box and then there would be a little silence when he came back. Bill Strike would be wearing a faint anticipatory smile as though he had a secret to tell them, but wanted to tease them first. His eyes would rove over the faces at the table and then he would say, Well, there was going to be another job at four-thirty in the morning sharp, and So-and-so would lead it and So-and-so would go, and So-and-so, and they might as well look over the map. They were going to bomb the railroad yards at So-and-so and the rendezvous with the fighters would be over such and such a point at such and such a time. The Captain's eyes would move from face to face and he would go into a few technical and slangy details and then he would ask if everyone had got it straight. Then he would ask who wanted to play a rubber of bridge and someone would start the phonograph in the corner and someone else would be reminded of a story and everyone would be elaborately careless, particularly if the assignment sounded bad. Then someone would yawn deliberately and say he might as well be turning in if he had to be waked up at four and for God's sake not to wake him sooner, because he wanted to get his beauty sleep. Everyone was cool and ready to laugh, but not boisterously, and all the time throughout the room there was that atmosphere of feeling alive and the intense beauty of living.

If you were used to it, you did not sleep so badly, either. Sometimes you could hear the gunfire, but you hardly noticed. It seemed to Jeffrey that his dreams were always happy, if he dreamed. Then the orderly would shake him and tell him it was four o'clock, sir, and no one made much noise, so as not to disturb those who were not going. Then you would hear the motors warming up on the field. There was hot water to shave with, unless you wanted to put off shaving until later, and there was toast and coffee at the mess table. You could get your real breakfast later, and everyone was a little distrait, perhaps, but very thoughtful of everyone else, and there was talk about the weather and a conscious effort to be very sure that everyone had the sugar and the evaporated milk. If you were casual, you might suggest doing something that afternoon, but you seldom did. If you stopped to think of it, the coffee tasted very good, except that sometimes there was a bitter taste of bile in your mouth as you walked out of the shack across the dusky field. That feeling of not having much time was always gone for the moment. There was no time at all now, since you were face to face with something that was very close to zero. You might wonder why you were there, but there was a great deal else to think about—whether it would be worth while to take a pistol or a cake of chocolate or some chewing gum, whether you should have written a letter last night. Still, it was over quickly. It was all right when the motors were going. When you started moving, you did not give a damn, for there never had been anything like it again—the clouds and the road and the lines and all the world unrolling like a map.

It was only when you were back on the field, when you knew that all of the others would not come back, that the old realization was waiting for you. You were through with it for this time, but something was waiting to call your number, something as implacable, as unfathomable as the blueness of the sky. You could not go on with that sort of thing forever. You did not have much time.

It was possible to treat the disappearance and death of others not callously, but calmly, even if someone of whom you were very fond had gone. There was no particular impression of shock or of bereavement. You were only sorry for him because his time was up. There was no point in wondering what he might have become if he had lived through it, because it was best to dismiss the idea that anyone would live through it. In spite of any sort of hope, or any individual belief that you would never get it, common sense and the law of averages told you that you would. Your conceivable future stretched to a matter of weeks, and not much further, and yet this was something to which you could adjust yourself, because everyone was in the same box with you. That mutual impermanence built up a relationship which was hard to explain, if you had not experienced it. There was a universal courtesy and kindliness. You never cared what you had been before, since what there was in you that amounted to anything came out very quickly. Jeffrey had never known his capabilities and perhaps he never would have known them, until he faced that experience. As it was, he saw that he had a mental equipment as good as anybody's there. He was no longer shy, no longer impressed, because there was not much time.

When they came back and ordered coffee, they would look at each other inquiringly, like old friends who were surprised at the coincidence which had allowed them all to meet again. Jeffrey could remember how Minot Roberts would give his head a little shake when he finished his coffee. His hair was done in a crew cut. His eyes were dark and deep-set and his mouth was very firm, and he and Stan Rhett were always having a wonderful time. They had been made for that sort of thing, but they understood how important it was to live as long as they could. He could remember how Minot would pull out his gold cigarette case, and there was no doubt that it was solid gold and so were the backs of the military brushes in his toilet kit. Money was a detail then, because they did not have much time.

"All right," he heard Minot call, "let's go."

Those were the days when the Squadron car was ready, and Minot wore his broadcloth breeches which were not strictly regulation, and his whipcord tunic, and all their belts were polished.

"All right, boys, let's go." He could still hear Minot calling. When you only had two days' leave, you did not have much time.

"Montmartre . . . A suite at the Crillon . . . the Bois . . . the Dôme . . . Voisin . . . Foyot . . . Rue du Brais . . . Let's go." He could still hear Minot calling out the names. You had to see all you could.

"Come on," he could hear Minot calling to him on mornings after. "Take a pull of this." He could hear Stan Rhett splashing in the bathtub. Stan Rhett was always bathing.

"Take it down." He could still hear the urgency in Minot's voice, and Minot was handing him a tumbler of brandy. "It's ten o'clock. Let's go."

There was no use sleeping when you were on leave. You did not have the time. He could remember the Place de la Concorde and the bridges, the Left Bank and the shop windows, crisscrossed with paper in case of bombing, and all the girls smiling. He felt that old desire to see it all and drink it all.

The insistence of that past was drumming in Jeffrey's pulses—that old belief that he might never drink again or love again, that he must explore what there was to living because he did not have much time. He had not realized how far he had been carried away, until the past of which he had been thinking and the present seemed to draw together like the converging of light rays through a strong but eccentric lens. It was as though he were trying to read through someone else's glasses. He was under the tree with the map case on his knees. He was no longer young and misbehaving in Paris. The recollection was receding somewhere into the shadows in his mind where it had stayed for years and where it should have stayed. His son Charley had emerged from the side door and was walking toward him again, kicking at the blue gravel of the path. All the minor irritations of living were back again. If Charley went on kicking gravel onto the grass, it would dent the lawn mower and then the lawn mower would have to be carried in the station wagon downtown for an old man named Mr. Sykes to sharpen. . . . Somehow extreme old age and a bad disposition went with sharpening lawn mowers. If Charley kept on kicking the stones, he would ruin the toes of those shoes of his, known to the trade as "Moccashoes." It made Jeffrey think that someone always had a name for everything. Charley was eating a piece of bread and jam, and his face was dirty.

"Hey," Charley said, "when is Mums coming back?"

Jeffrey wished that Charley would not refer to his mother as "Mums," instead of "Ma" or "Mama." When he referred to her as "Mums," it made Charley incomprehensible again, a part of the new juvenile jingles to which

Jeffrey could not adjust himself, or like a picture in a department-store advertisement, which stated that the emporium had a corner for little tots and bigger tots.

"She'll be back in about half an hour," Jeffrey told him. He felt abused because Madge had told him distinctly that he need not do anything about Charley while she was away—that Charley could look out for himself—but Charley still stood there watching him, eating his bread and jam.

"Hey," Charley said.

"Yes," Jeffrey answered. "Yes, what is it?" Charley was looking at the map case; at first Jeffrey thought that Charley would want to play with it, but he did not.

"When you fought the Germans, did you hate the Germans?"

"What?" Jeffrey asked him, and Charley repeated the question. It was much too precocious a question for a boy of Charley's age to have asked. Jeffrey wondered how it had ever got into Charley's mind, and then he realized that, of course, it had come from the progressive school, where children now discussed such problems. He recalled that Charley had participated in a pageant there dealing with the fallacies of war and the beauties of peace. Jeffrey could see himself, before he answered, through his son's eyes as an incomprehensible and rather a grim human being. He realized that he had never asked himself that question. They had all been there in the Squadron for a definite purpose. There had been no rancor, but there had been instinct.

He lifted the map case from his knees, put the papers back, and snapped it shut.

"Take this back and hang it up where you found it," Jeffrey said, but Charley asked him another question.

"Did you ever kill a German?" Charley asked him.

Jeffrey frowned at Charley. Somehow it was like endeavoring to explain the principles of procreation; in order to answer Charley's question, it would be necessary to give a number of specious explanations.

"Yes," he said, "I did."

"What with?" Charley asked.

"What with?" Jeffrey repeated. "Never mind it, Charley."

Jeffrey moved uneasily in his chair. Charley's interrogation was impersonal and almost disinterested, but as lucid as some line from Wordsworth. He had never dreamed that Charley could put him in a position where he would be so completely uncomfortable.

"Did he make a noise?" Charley asked.

"What?" Jeffrey said. "Did who make a noise?"

"When you killed him," Charley asked again, "did he make a noise?"

Jeffrey pushed the map case at him.

"Never mind about it now," he said. "You take this back where you found it."

Charley took the map case, but he did not move away.

"Were you sorry?" Charley asked.

"What?" Jeffrey asked him.

"Sorry when you killed him?" Charley asked.

There was no use being impatient with a child.

"Put that thing away where you found it, Charley," Jeffrey said, "and don't come back here to disturb me. I'm busy."

Charley went away again. Jeffrey could see the striped back of his sweater as he moved slowly toward the house, still kicking at the gravel, but even when he was gone, something uncomfortable moved in Jeffrey's mind. If human beings were sorry enough, if such actions shocked them sufficiently, there would be no war, but all that it had meant to Jeffrey was the solution to a problem. In war, killing was the natural reflex of training, coupled with an instinct for survival.

Just the summer before—that was in 1934—he and Madge had taken a trip to Germany. Madge had gone there once to some watering place with her Fräulein as a little girl, and she always had wanted to see Germany again. Jeffrey had never been there. He had wanted to sail on a French or British ship as he always had when going abroad, but Madge had wanted to go on the *Bremen*. She had told him that the Germans were marvelous with ships. There were all sorts of things in the shop on the *Bremen*—beautiful cameras and fountain pens that always worked. It had been a fine ship, and they had sat at the Captain's table, but when they had stopped at Cherbourg, he had wanted to get off. Though he had been comfortable, he had not liked it. The stewards had all looked alike—clear skin, pale eyes, close-cropped hair—but then, English stewards, and French stewards, had always looked alike. They had been completely courteous, absolutely understanding. The Purser had explained to him carefully about travel-marks, which visitors could buy at a lower rate, but Jeffrey had never been able to get the system through his head.

The Captain had asked them to his quarters for cocktails—that sailor's duty foisted upon captains by steamship agents. The Captain's quarters had been carefully arranged, giving an impression of unnaturally elaborate hospitality. The Captain himself was as jolly as a cruise director, and so were the junior officers, all heavy, capable men. It was easy to see that they were all going through a perfunctory ceremony which had been ordered for every trip, but somehow Jeffrey could not be sorry for the Captain, as he was sometimes for unfortunate French and British commanders in similar circumstances. It was all done too well and too efficiently. He and the other passengers were being pushed through the party, whether they wanted it or not, yet Madge had said that the party and the officers were cunning. She had said it all showed the inherent lovable quality possessed by the Germans, like Christmas trees and Grimm's fairy tales. She had asked Jeffrey if he had not loved the way the Captain had laughed and said "*Ach*," but Jeffrey had not loved it. He had not loved it, either, when the Captain slapped him on the shoulder and asked him if he did not like a ship where there were so few Jews, and laughed again and said "*Ach*." Jeffrey had not liked it when the Captain said he would be comfortable in Germany; they were all one race together and they should be friends. He had not wished to seem hostile. The war had been over long ago, but he was not at ease. He felt that he should not have been there, and he had felt the same way when he had seen the German shore. Madge had asked him to look at the soldiers on the dock—they looked like toys. Nevertheless, the sight of them gave him a strange sensation. The trouble was that he could not get it into his mind that the war was over, now that he was in Germany.

Madge had said that he had simply made up his mind not to like Germany, that he acted with all those people as though there were still a war with Germany, when the war had been over for more than fifteen years. He could not understand the language—he did not wish to—and the people who spoke English, the waiters and the guides and concierges, would never speak frankly, though they told of the efficient beauties of their country. He felt they were not at ease with him and that they did not like him. When he had motored with Madge from Bremen through Hamburg to Berlin, he was impressed by the steely neatness of the countryside—trees growing just so on every hill, fields plowed in meticulous, even furrows. Nature was completely subjugated, too, in England and France, but not with such relentlessness. Jeffrey found himself being on the side of weeds and cutworms, wishing that he might observe some blight or other agricultural misfortune. The Teutonic faces seemed to him neither happy nor unhappy, the expressions ironed-out and masklike.

Although the sun was out and the weather settled, he could not like Berlin with its endless parks and statues. The restaurants were modernistic and garish and the public buildings dull. When he went to that museum which housed an entire marble temple brought from somewhere in Asia Minor, the women with their tightly knotted hair and the men with their bristly heads, walking conscientiously up and down the steps reading from their guidebooks, gave him a sense of indignant revulsion. He felt they had no right to possess such an antiquity, and yet he had never felt that way about the Elgin Marbles in the British Museum, a much more bare-faced piece of appropriation. It did no good to tell himself that he should not dislike those people because there had been a war, for there remained an ingrained instinct which he could not conquer. When they changed their money at the frontier and he eventually heard Italian voices, he knew that he never wanted to go to Germany again. He did not like the Germans, and that was all there was to it. He could try, but he could not like them because he had learned to hate them once.

Now that his mind was on Europe, he recalled an earlier visit which he and Madge had made. It must have been in the summer of 1926, that he and Madge had left the children and gone to France, and Madge had wanted to see the battlefields, so they had rented a car in Paris and had motored through Château-Thierry to Verdun. The country around Château-Thierry already looked as though nothing had ever happened to it. The red-tiled roofs were back on the houses and the farms had risen again out of their rubble. It was only on the heights around Verdun that any trace of the war was left. The soil of Dead Man's Hill and of Hill 302 had been so churned by shellfire that no one had tried to touch it or fill in the remains of caving trench systems and dank pools of stagnant rain water. The French Government was constructing the Voie Sacrée that year, and there was a hideous concrete shelter over the Trench of Bayonets, beneath which the bayonets of the dead still rose above the ground. Some laborers near by were still raking through the rubbish, resurrecting human bones for burial, placing those bones in heaps beside the road. Madge had walked beside him, speaking occasionally, in a voice which was only intelligently curious. At first this made him surprised and indignant—until he realized that she could not notice as much as he did. A young soldier, too young to have been in the war, took them through Fort Vaux and explained in a parrotlike way the methods of defense in the battle of Verdun. Madge had listened carefully, as she always did, because she always wanted to see everything and to get the most out of everything when she traveled, particularly out of churches and picture galleries. As far as he could see, Madge looked upon that ruined fort as another sort of church. He could almost imagine her looking for the nave and the apse. When they emerged from the fort and stood looking toward the north, Madge had spoken to the French soldier in her fluent and precise French—Madge was always good at languages.

"But the Boches," he remembered Madge saying, "will never come again."

He should never have taken her to such a place. He wished that Madge had not been so fluent and that she had not called them "Boches." He still remembered the soldier's answer. The boy had obviously been taken from some farm to do his military duty, and his uniform did not fit him. The sleeves of his tunic were too short, and the cloth looked shoddy. The blue spiral puttees were frayed. The boy had an unintelligent dish face with high cheekbones. He was *enrhumé* and not possessing a handkerchief, he occasionally wiped his nose on his sleeve. He did so while Madge spoke about the Boches.

"But yes, madame," he said, "they will certainly come again."

There was the sense that nothing had been settled, but Jeffrey was sure that Madge had not noticed it. Her eyes were on the meandering curve of the Meuse River. She was looking at the clustered little houses of the villages to the north—a pretty, peaceful picture in the sunlight.

"My husband," Madge said, "was an aviator of the American Army. He fought here for *La France*."

Jeffrey thought her remark completely uncalled for. The soldier did not give a continental whether or not Jeffrey had fought for *La France*. His nose was running and he was waiting for his tip, which he would necessarily have to turn over to his sergeant, who watched him sharply from a distance.

"Truly?" the soldier said, and rubbed his sleeve across his nose.

But Madge did not notice. She was getting the most out of an interesting visit.

"My husband's airplane," she said, "was shot down over there. Jeffrey, it was over there somewhere, wasn't it?"

"Truly?" the soldier said, and his eyes met Jeffrey's. The franc at the time was two cents, fifty to the dollar, and the soldier wanted his *pourboire*. The French no longer had that warm gratitude toward Americans which they had evinced in other days. When the war had been fought, that soldier had been wearing a black smock and marching with his books to some country school.

"Here," Jeffrey said in English, and gave him twenty francs. Ten francs would have been sufficient, but if he had given ten, the man would have told his squad that no Americans were generous, bloated with gold though they were, having sucked the very vitals of *La France*. Now that he had given twenty, the lad would doubtless say that Americans were wealthy fools, insulting France by treating their money like wrapping paper. It would be one thing or the other.

"Jeffrey," he heard Madge saying, "where was it that your plane was shot down?"

He wished to heaven that he had never brought her there. The soldier was giving him his thanks, and asking him if he could be of further service, and Jeffrey told him no. He did not want the soldier, he did not want Madge, he did not want to speak to anyone.

"Jeffrey," he heard her say again, "where was it?"

He had to control himself. That experience belonged to him and not to her. The day had been very hard, and he had seen enough of it.

"It's a little hard to point it out," he said. "It was away off, over there."

He waved his arm anywhere at all. He was trying to remember where it was himself. It was somewhere beyond the woods and the rolling hills. The footsteps and voices of some of his countrymen were sounding behind him. They had come by bus, shepherded by a courteous uniformed attendant, to see the battlefields. Doubtless they had been to the cemetery at Belleau Wood. He did not want to see them. He wanted to get away.

He had crashed—though he must have come out of his dive in time, so that it was not entirely a crash—somewhere up there beyond the scrubby squares of forest land on the heights to the south and west of a ruined town known as Brieulles-sur-Meuse. What had actually happened was guesswork. He believed that the motor was still going, although it had been acting badly. That was why he left formation and left for home before the Fokkers came. They had come out of the sun, seemingly out of nowhere, the way they often did. It was impossible to explain to anyone who had never been in air combat how difficult it was to be aware of an enemy when you were a small point eight thousand feet above the earth with all of space to watch. The first he saw of them was over his right shoulder when Stanley Rhett had shouted to him. Three of them were diving at his tail and he had pulled on the stick. There was nothing to do but dive as straight as he dared without losing his wings. He could hear Stan's guns going above the motor and all the other noise. It was a Brequet two-place day bomber. There were no self-sealing gas tanks, no metal wings, only yellow fabric, and there was no way of bailing out. He saw the bullets striking. His windshield smashed, and then it was covered with oil. Then the tracers must have hit the gas tank. The whole business was afire. They were for it—and they would be dead in a matter of seconds, but he was only thinking of flattening out from the dive. There was no time to experiment with the controls. When the plane began to burn, the Fokkers must have considered it over, because they did not bother to follow. He could see the terrain rising up to meet them through the smashed and spattered windshield. The ground, which seconds before had looked like a beautifully drawn staff map, was suddenly very near. The nearest town he saw was Brieulles. There was a bare brownish hill and woods and a stretch of whitish road, completely vacant. He even recalled identifying the road as one which led westward toward Cunel and Romagne. He must have loosened his belt and he must have flattened out, but he had probably drawn a blank because he had no recollection of jumping or being thrown. First he was in the air and then he was writhing on his left side on the grass, facing the burning plane that seemed to be rising to heaven in a pillar of smoke. He was choking and gasping for his breath, because the wind had been knocked out of him, and then he saw Stan Rhett crawling away from the side of the plane slowly on his hands and knees.

During those years after the war, Jeffrey had read much of the fiction connected with it. He had read *The Enormous Room* by E. E. Cummings, which at one time he had looked upon as an intellectual's artistic whimpering, and later had grown to admire. Then there was Dos Passos, and his three maladjusted soldiers. War was no place for sensitive, social-minded intellectuals. There was *Through the Wheat* by Thomas Boyd and *The Spanish Farm* and *No More Parades* and *Chevrons* and *A Farewell to Arms*. In the late Twenties and even the early Thirties, a lot of good writers had taken a crack at it; but in his opinion the net result of their efforts added up to almost nothing. They tried to give dramatic significance to something in which significance was utterly lacking. They tried to give an interpretation to something which actually offered nothing for an artist to interpret.

The trouble was that no one with an artistic sense could do anything about a war. Artists and scholars were utterly unnecessary in a war. There used to be loud complaints from bright boys who had shown exceptional ability in officers' training school that they were always kept behind as instructors or sent to Corps Headquarters. If you had any brains, they said, you were not wanted at the front, but then, perhaps the Army was right. There was such a thing as too much imagination, and a too highly developed critical sense. Jeffrey often thought that he would have been quite useless in the Artillery or the Infantry. If he had been there, he would have been like the rest of them—he would have tried to write about the war.

It surprised Jeffrey that no one was near the burning plane, because he knew that the lines were somewhere near Brieulles. There seemed to be no other sound except the roaring flames and he was sitting up alone in a sunny field, and Stan Rhett was crawling toward him. He remembered that Stan's face was streaked with oil, and his hair was singed and the sleeve of his coat was smoking.

"Hey," Stan said, "I got one of them. Did you see me?"

There was a hideous levity in the remark as though it were all a game. Jeffrey pulled himself up to his knees. He had thought that something would be broken, but he felt all right.

"I got one," Stan said again. They were alone in a field, but someone must have seen the plane. If they were behind the German lines it was time to get away.

"Can you walk?" he asked Stan. "We'd better get going."

"Hell, yes," Stan said. "I always walk."

There was a patch of woods about fifty yards away. They had fallen in a meadow of long brownish grass and Jeffrey could see that people had been there, although no one was there now. He could see a pot-shaped German helmet on the ground and an American web belt and a blanket. There had been fighting in the field, but he could not tell where the lines were. It would be better to get to the woods, for no one would think they had come out of the plane alive. He watched Stan draw his feet under him and stand up, but something gave way and he sat down.

"Jesus," Stan said, and he laughed. "Something isn't working."

It was exactly what Minot Roberts would have done—try to make a joke of it. It might have been a fine gesture, but it was not so funny then because blood was streaming down Stan's right leg. His breeches were sodden with it, and the grass was growing red.

"Get your arm around me," Jeffrey said.

When he heard aviators long afterwards discuss the war, Jeffrey realized that most of them had only observed a battlefield from the air. Most of them had never stood on the ground in an advanced position. Few of them had ever walked through the hideous terrain where there had been fighting. The sights and sounds of that place came up to hit him now almost the way the ground did when he had crashed. He had been through the war, without ever facing war's full implications except for that one day. Stan Rhett leaned his full weight on Jeffrey's shoulder, moving his legs with the vague mechanism of someone who is drunk, and Jeffrey staggered beneath his weight, drenched with perspiration, still fighting for his breath.

"Does it hurt you?" he asked Stan.

"No," he heard Stan say, and Stan laughed again. "I just feel like passing out." And then he added a moment later, "Let's call a taxi, Jeff."

Jeffrey wanted to get out of the sunlight. They were near a thicket of saplings, with some taller trees among them, the branches of which were twisted and broken, as though they had been struck by a high wind. He pushed his way through the saplings, looking for a cleared place—which was not hard to find, since the French were neat about their forests. He did not look around him, until he sat Stan down, with his back against a tree. Then he saw that three dead men were lying about ten feet in front of him, two in German field-gray, and one in olive-drab. He had never encountered the dead on a battlefield, and his reaction must have been the same as that of anyone who first saw war dead—the same instinctive spasm of fear that makes a horse shy and bolt away from death. He knew at once that they were not asleep. They lay sprawled as though a strong gust of wind had struck them. A number of others had been there, too, who had dropped things and had forgotten to pick them up, but it was no common sort of human forgetfulness. They were personal belongings which could only have been dropped because of panic or death.

The sunbeams cut through the leaves and branches of the trees, making uneven spots upon that disorder on the ground, and moving with the breeze, erratically centering on new objects. He never forgot the moving light first touching a regulation mess kit, which had burst open, then a roll of toilet paper festooned across the bushes, then a mess tin and a letter stamped into the earth, a muddy blanket, a hand grenade, a torn section of an olive-drab puttee, a rifle with a pair of socks near it, a canteen—a combination that was senseless and indecent; and the dead had collapsed in the same disorder. One lay with his head lower than his heels, with the rim of his helmet jammed against the bridge of his nose, and the mouth gaping. If there were wounds on the two Germans, he did not see them, and he did not care to look, but there was no doubt how the doughboy had died. A fragment of a high explosive shell had blown the top of his head clear off, just above the eyes, leaving all that was left of the head and face turned upward toward the trees. The blasted skull was like a cross section from a book of physiology, and for a moment, Jeffrey could not take his eyes from the spectacle, although there was too much which no living decent person was meant to look at. It was an effort to draw his glance away and to turn to Stanley Rhett, who leaned against the tree.

"Company," Stan said, "got company." His face was white, but he smiled at Jeffrey when Jeffrey knelt beside him and began pulling down his breeches. Jeffrey had read about administering to the wounded, but he had no vestige of practical experience. The right leg of Stan's breeches was full of blood, which spilled over the dead leaves when he pulled it down, and the sight made Jeffrey gasp and retch.

"Stuck pig," Stan said. "It's up there," and he moved his right hand vaguely. It was a bullet wound in the middle of the right thigh. Jeffrey picked up a web belt, and ripped open a First Aid packet. It was lucky it was there, for he had never thought of carrying one, but the gauze bandages and iodine could not stop the bleeding. He always thought later that he had done as well as he could, given the time and place. The first tourniquet which he made out of a piece of gauze and a stick broke and then he used a spiral puttee which was lying in the bushes. It was one of the larger arteries, and as he turned the blood kept spurting, but finally the stream died down.

"Boy," Stan said, "I'll give you a drink for that when we get home." His face was dead white and his voice was very faint.

"How are you feeling?" Jeffrey asked. "It's stopped now."

"Cold," Stan said, and Jeffrey laid him down and brought a blanket from one of the abandoned infantry packs to cover him. There was nothing else that he could think of doing, and so he walked carefully to the edge of the wood and looked through the thicket at the plane. The patch of wood had seemed still except for the breeze in the trees, but now far behind him he could hear artillery fire and the machine guns were rattling somewhere to his right. He knew that if they could move south, they might be safe; they had a chance of getting out if they stayed there until dark. The glass of his wrist watch was shattered and the mechanism must have stopped when he had fallen. The hands pointed to half-past seven, so that it must have still been early morning, and this surprised him, for he had thought it was late afternoon. He had lost all sense of time.

He could see the black smoke still billowing above the plane and he heard voices. He heard the voices before he saw the men. First he saw their helmets, streaked with yellow paint, above the crest of the yellow hill, and then he saw four German infantrymen walking carefully toward the plane, and glancing toward the woods. That lack of assurance made Jeffrey very sure that he was near the lines. He only found out later that he was in no man's land, and that the lines were very fluid. The men held their rifles ready as they approached the burning plane, and the sight of the rifles made Jeffrey move his hand to his side very slowly. He touched the holster of his forty-five regulation automatic which he had strapped over his leather flying coat that morning. He had not fired one since he left officers' school in the States, but now he drew it.

As the soldiers stood there examining the plane, Jeffrey heard a sound carefully described by war correspondents—something like a train of cars crossing a trestle bridge. He knew it was a shell before it struck. It landed in the field near the crest of the hill and burst in a wave of dirt and smoke. The four men by the plane threw themselves on their faces, then were up, running for the crest of the hill, and then were gone, but the shellfire continued. There was nothing erratic about the fire; the shells seemed to be groping blindly for something to destroy, moving methodically up the slope, and over the crest and out of sight. Someone told him later that it must have been artillery searching for machine-gun nests, and that he was lucky that the woods were not the target. Stan opened his eyes when Jeffrey touched him. It was necessary to lean close over him to hear what he said.

"What," Stan asked him, "God-damned sort of management is this?"

Jeffrey told him to keep still and asked him how he felt.

"Boy," Stan said, "how about a drink?"

As a matter of fact there was a full canteen on the doughboy's belt. When Jeffrey took it off, he felt completely familiar with everything. Reaction was setting in on him so that nothing upset him any longer. He did not give a damn about anything, except to get out of there. His mind and body felt filthy dirty, and he wanted to get out of there, but they had to wait for night.

All that he could remember were snatches of that day—odd moments spent crawling through the thickets and looking for a path. The burst of firing kept drumming in his ears, the rattle of machine guns, the sound of light artillery, but nothing stirred in the wood. He never forgot the smell of it, a combination of moldy leaves and of vanished human beings and the cordite fumes from the shelling, and the faint antiseptic odor of mustard gas. The shadows finally told him that it was late afternoon and that he had been asleep. Stan was beside him, ashy white, with his eyes closed, breathing slowly. It must have been the rustling in the bushes that awakened Jeffrey because he remembered the sound before he saw what caused it. Everything had been black until he opened his eyes, and then he saw a figure of a man not ten feet away. The shadows and the sunlight mottled his gray uniform. It was a German soldier, probably some confused straggler looking for his outfit.

It would have been different if the man had seen him first, but as it was, the face was turned sideways when Jeffrey opened his eyes. It gave him the opportunity to reach his holster and get the automatic out of it. His only thought was that the soldier must be kept quiet for reasons of safety, that there must be others where he came from, and that he must not get back to the others. The sound he made had caused the soldier to turn. The German's shoulders had been stooped forward as he pushed his way through the thicket, and he was holding his rifle ready. Jeffrey could see the face, wan, and drawn with fatigue and covered with a dusty stubble of blackish beard. He could see the lips draw back. He could hear the startled intake of breath and Jeffrey remembered speaking, without any thought that the other might not understand his language; and he even remembered that his voice had a thin, unpleasant treble.

"Drop that gun," he said.

Though the expression came to him naturally, it sounded melodramatic. Jeffrey wanted to get it down to common sense and reason; he always thought that if they could only have talked they could have reached some understanding, for they were two human beings. As it was there was no opportunity to consider either action or consequence. He was often ashamed, not for what he did, because that was a question of survival, but for the way he acted afterwards. When the muzzle of the rifle jerked in his direction, he did not know he had fired until he heard the shot. The impact of the bullet hurled the man backwards. He was on his back, kicking in the bushes, by the time Jeffrey was on his feet. Jeffrey could hear the other's breath coming in snoring gasps and the sound made him bend forward and retch. That was when he knew that Stan Rhett had seen it all, for he heard his voice.

"Bull's-eye," he heard Stan say and except for the firing to the right, which did not matter, they seemed to be surrounded by silence, like the silence of a deserted house.

Toward dusk, just as he was thinking they should be moving, Stan spoke and said that he thought that he was going. It took Jeffrey an appreciable time to comprehend that Stan was saying that he thought he was dying, and Jeffrey told him that he wasn't, that he had stopped bleeding, that he would take him in right now. He lifted Stan in his arms and got part of him across his shoulders and began walking through the trees to the south until he found one of those paths which were always cut through French forests.

Every few minutes he would have to rest and put Stan down. At such times he would ask how he was, and at first Stan said he was fine, but toward the end he did not talk. It was nearly dark when he met an infantry patrol. There were six of them. He remembered the bayonets and the flat tin hats.

"Leave him down, buddy," he heard someone say. "He's all right now." And then some stretcher-bearers must have come.

It should have been easier to walk with the load off his shoulders, but the ground moved so uncertainly that he stumbled and fell flat on his face, and then someone took his arm.

They took him to a small dugout which had been scooped from a cut in the side of the road, the command post of a battalion, where an infantry major sat on an ammunition box with a map in front of him. Jeffrey must have told who he was. He remembered answering questions and he remembered being given something hot to drink. A non-com from the patrol must have been with him too, because Jeffrey heard the enlisted man answer when the Major asked a question. It was difficult for him to keep his attention on the Major. The place was lighted by a single candle by the map and all objects would blur and then come into focus.

"What about the other one?" he heard the Major ask.

"Dead, sir." Jeffrey heard the voice behind his back. "Dead when the Lieutenant brought him in."

Everything was as black as though something had struck him in the head. He was always glad of it. There was nothing else he wanted to remember.

21

Careful How You Stir Them, George

Although it was only one o'clock, the afternoon papers were out, and Jeffrey bought one at Columbus Circle—not that there would be anything much except headlines. The British had made another bombing raid on Berlin. Churchill had appealed to the French people not to fight Britain. German planes had swarmed again in considerable force over the south and east coasts of England. Jeffrey dropped the paper into one of those cans with swinging tops. He wished that he could break himself of the habit of seeking for the latest news when most of it meant nothing, but he knew that he would keep on doing it, chiefly out of a fear that he would miss something colossal and unbelievable. It had been that way since the spring, and that uncertainty and shock of defeat had steadily grown worse. It was beyond imagining what was going to happen after the fall of France; he no longer could face the news objectively. He kept wondering if that month of October, 1940, were as clear in Europe as it was in New York, with the same full moon and the same high tides. With those tides and the autumn fog over the channel, conditions were correct for an invasion, and people who ought to know, if anyone knew anything, were saying that October was the invasion month. With clear weather in the daytime, the ceiling was infinity, and the moon was right for night bombing.

As he crossed toward the corner of 59th Street, he wondered whether everyone else shared his feeling of suspense, but he could see no sign. The crosstown traffic was waiting for the green lights, and the skyview windows of the taxicabs were open. When he passed the open door of a drugstore, he could see the lunch-hour crowd—the girls and boys from the office buildings, pressing against the soda counter, slipping on and off those revolving leather stools, eating pale sandwiches stuffed with lettuce and mayonnaise, and gulping double orange juices because they were rich with vitamins. There was that steamy smell which always permeated drugstores during the lunch hour, and the white coats of the counter boys were spattered with chocolate and butter and coffee. He could see the display of brightly packed confections by the cigar counter where you paid your check—Tootsie Rolls and Baby Ruths and Coconut Mounds and Crunchies and Chock-Full-o'-Nuts bars, or whatever the names of all those things might be. They were heaped up beside a display of electric razors and electric heating pads. For the first time, he rather liked the spectacle because it pushed the war out of his mind. It reminded him that it was time to buy a stick of shaving soap, but he could not walk around all day carrying it in his pocket.

It was already so late that he would have to take a taxicab and he decided to go east on 59th Street and find one at the Plaza. Jeffrey always liked the Plaza, if only because it was one of the few surviving buildings in New York which had been with him always. He thought of that song in the Twenties about the professional jazzer who played at the Plaza; and working out the words took his mind off the war. By the 59th Street entrance to the Park, General Sherman was all in gold with his gold angel walking at his horse's head, and the nude lady on top of the marble fountain was basking in the sun, and three Victorias with spavined horses stood in the sunlight, and the balloon men and the peanut men were out. He felt better seeing them, for they also pushed the war away. The windows of the Fifth Avenue busses were open and their green sides towered above the roofs of the motors. He saw the stores with the contorted figures of pale blond and brunette models disporting themselves in static groups, decked in the latest evening gowns. The models were physically undesirable, consumptive, hollow-chested wraiths, an effect which might have been deliberate so that one's attention could be wholly focused on the clothes. The driver of the taxicab he took was listening to his radio, which was discoursing on the mild benefits of a certain laxative. The driver gave a start, and the voice was cut off in the middle of a syllable.

"The Clinton Club," Jeffrey said.

It put him in a false position to give the name of the Clinton Club, since Jeffrey was not a member, but simply going there for lunch. In spite of the number of times he had been there, he was always acutely conscious of not being a member. Although he could tell himself as often as he liked that the Clinton Club was a dull and stuffy place and actually an object of fun, Jeffrey was always careful to arrive late so as to be sure that Minot Roberts would be there first. He did not want to sit in the little room off the main rotunda and have the doorman keep eyeing him through the half-opened door while he tried to read the London *Sphere*. No matter how emphatically Jeffrey told himself that it was complete foolishness, he could not escape the belief that the doorman was thinking that he was not quite the right type to be there. Yet the doorman was kind, benevolent and old, looking just as the doorman of the Clinton Club should look. Jeffrey squared his shoulders and walked into the little marble hall with the double marble staircase which led upward to the main rooms. He found himself taking off his gray felt hat, and then he wondered whether he should not have left it on until the boy from the coatroom had come to get it.

"Is Mr. Roberts in yet?" Jeffrey asked. "Mr. Roberts is expecting me for lunch."

He should not have said that Mr. Roberts was expecting him for lunch. It was in the nature of offering an excuse for being there at all, a betrayal of a fear that he might have been thrown out if Mr. Roberts were not expecting him for lunch. He should have simply asked whether Mr. Roberts was there yet, and should have kept his hat on, but the doorman was very gentle, very kind.

"Who is it, please, sir?" the doorman asked, and Jeffrey misunderstood him. He always did misunderstand the doorman of the Clinton Club.

"Mr. Roberts," Jeffrey said. "Mr. Minot Roberts. He's expecting me for lunch." And the doorman was still very gentle, very kind.

"Your name, please, sir," he said.

"Mr. Wilson," Jeffrey said, and then he found himself adding, although immediately afterwards he knew it was unnecessary, "Mr. Jeffrey Wilson," but the doorman was very kind. His every action was a deliberate effort at reassurance, a gentle, thoughtful endeavor to put Jeffrey at his ease.

"Oh, yes, Mr. Wilson," the doorman said, "Mr. Roberts is expecting you. He is in the Oak Room. Will you go right up?"

They never referred to the place where one drank in the Clinton Club as "the bar"—they called it the "Oak Room."

"Your hat, sir," the doorman said as Jeffrey started up the stairs.

"Oh," Jeffrey said, "excuse me." He had completely forgotten his hat. He might have gone up to the Oak Room still holding it, if the doorman had not been kind.

Instead of being heavy or pretentious or baroque, the Clinton Club had a slightly run-down atmosphere of solid tradition which reminded Jeffrey of a club off Piccadilly. Everyone in the Clinton Club felt able to pass the time of day with everyone else, since merely being there made it socially safe to do so, and as Jeffrey made his way toward the Oak Room, several members looked up at him, obviously expecting to see a friend, and to call a friendly greeting. It seemed to Jeffrey that when they saw him, although he knew it was his imagination, their glances betrayed puzzled incredulity, and they turned from him hastily back to their papers, except for one older member who called him "Bobby" by mistake and then apologized. The Oak Room was not garish like the Oak Room of a hotel or a chophouse. The paneling was decorous Jacobean, and the wooden chairs and tables looked as though they had come from a public room in an English Inn. The man behind the bar looked gray and benign, like the doorman, used to the vagaries of gentlemen. Two members were shaking poker dice in the corner, and Minot was at a table by himself. Minot looked as though the room had been made for him. He looked like a drawing in *Punch*. Minot wore his clothes carelessly, although they fitted him as smoothly as a Hollywood actor's. He had a way of lounging in the oak chair without having either his coat or waistcoat drift upward the way Jeffrey's always did. Jeffrey realized again that he could never be like Minot in this world or the next.

"Where the hell have you been?" Minot asked him. "My tongue's hanging out."

It would have sounded petulant and boorish if anyone else had said it, but Minot could give his voice just the proper lilt.

"I didn't want to sit in that stranger's room downstairs," Jeffrey told him. "That room is like the office of a nose and throat specialist. I wanted to be sure you were here first."

Minot laughed. "Fuzzy wouldn't have put you in there," he said. "He'd have let you come up here."

"Do you call the man at the door 'Fuzzy'?" Jeffrey asked.

"Why," Minot said, "everybody's always called him 'Fuzzy.' George." He waved his hand to the bartender, and the bartender moved forward, smiling at them informally but respectfully.

"Now, George," Minot said, "we want two Martinis, and Mr. Wilson is very particular about his Martinis. Do your best for us, will you George?"

If Jeffrey had made that speech to anyone, it would have sounded bustling, but when Minot made it, it sounded right.

"And, George," Minot said, "the special London gin, and my own vermouth. You still have a bottle, haven't you?"

"Yes, there's still a bottle, Mr. Roberts," George said.

When Minot smiled, Jeffrey felt like a member for a moment.

"We'll have to drive them the hell out of France," Minot said, "before we get some more vermouth."

Jeffrey did not have to answer, because one of the dice players called across the room.

"Drive who out of France?"

Everybody in the Clinton Club knew everybody else.

"Who do *you* think, Bunny?" Minot called. "This is Jeff Wilson. That's Bunny Rotch, and that's Sam Hughes."

Jeffrey was never sure what to do when he was introduced to anyone at the Clinton Club, whether he was supposed to spring from his chair and shake hands and say that he was pleased to meet them, or whether to nod and smile across the room. He nodded and smiled across the room.

"Hello," they said, and began shaking dice again, but they were not rude. It showed that he was a friend of Minot's, and that any friend of Minot's was a friend of theirs.

"Bunny Rotch," Minot said softly, "you know, from Westbury."

"Oh," Jeffrey said, "that Rotch."

A faint wrinkle appeared between Minot's eyes, and then he laughed.

"Jeff," he said, "you can always dish it out."

Jeffrey did not answer. He was watching George at the bar pouring the Martinis, not sloppily, like a commercial barkeeper, and not medically, like a chemist, but exactly as he should have poured them.

"It's funny," Minot said, "I always think of you as knowing everyone."

"Not around here, Minot," Jeffrey said.

Minot looked at him again and laughed.

"Don't make fun of us," he said, "we're just poor boys trying to get along." And then George brought the Martinis. He placed one before each of them, and stood waiting. Minot looked at his glass carefully before he picked it up.

"Right, Mr. Roberts?" George asked.

"That gin," Minot said, "is that the special gin?"

"Yes, Mr. Roberts," George said.

"It's a little pawkish," Minot said.

"What?" Jeffrey asked him.

"Pawkish," Minot said.

"Well," Jeffrey said, "it tastes all right to me."

"All right, George," Minot said, "Mr. Wilson likes it."

"God almighty," Jeffrey said. "Do you always do this, Minot?"

Minot finished his drink.

"Two more, George," he called, "and a little more vermouth. And just a little more careful how you stir them, George."

"God almighty," Jeffrey said.

"Where were you Sunday?" Minot asked. "I tried to get hold of you Sunday."

"We were out in Connecticut," Jeffrey said. "Out at Fred's and Beckie's."

"God!" Minot said. "What did you go there for?"

"Madge," Jeffrey said; "you know, Madge loves Fred and Beckie."

"Who else was there?" Minot asked.

"Some people named Sales. Fred met him in some bank."

Minot shook his head; clearly the name meant nothing.

"And then Walter Newcombe and his wife."

"You don't mean," Minot said, "Newcombe the correspondent? Why didn't you tell me? We could have had him around for lunch."

"I don't know," Jeffrey said, "whether you'd like him, Minot."

"How do you mean I wouldn't like him?" Minot asked. "What's his wife like?"

"I don't think you'd understand her," Jeffrey said.

"How do you mean I wouldn't understand her?" Minot asked. "You know damned well I can get on with anyone. These correspondents are always at dinners at the speakers' table. I know what they're like."

George brought the second cocktail.

"Right, Mr. Roberts?" George asked.

"It's better this time, George," Minot said. "I think the stirring did it. Thank you, George."

"Thank you," George said, "Mr. Roberts."

"All these newspaper men," Minot said, "are like anybody else who comes from a small town and gets ahead. You can tell them every time."

"Yes," Jeffrey said, "I guess you can."

Minot was not embarrassed, because he was too old a friend. His eyes, and his whole face, were kind.

"You were never like that," Minot said, "and if anybody says you were, he's a God-damned liar."

"Minot," Jeffrey said, "do you remember that afternoon when I first came to visit you? Madge and I drove past the station there last Saturday."

But Minot did not remember, and there was no reason why he should have.

"That time you asked me to visit you," Jeffrey said. "Well, I was just like that."

"No you weren't," Minot said. "Who else was there?"

"Where?" Jeffrey asked.

"For the week end," Minot said.

"Well, there was Buchanan Greene, the poet," Jeffrey said, "and then–" He glanced at the dice players in the corner, and then back at Minot– "Marianna Miller."

Minot set his glass down.

"Did Madge know she would be there?"

"Of course she knew," Jeffrey said.

"Well," Minot said, "how did she like it?"

Jeffrey was not as much offended by the question as he was by the simplicity of Minot's thoughts and reactions. It made him impatient, not so much with Minot, as with everyone like Minot. Those people lived according to a book of rules which they had learned by heart without ever stopping to analyze them.

"How do you mean?" Jeffrey asked him. "Why shouldn't Madge have liked it?" But of course he knew what Minot Roberts meant. Minot was a friend of his who knew according to his book of rules that friends could speak about such things.

"You know I'd go down the line for you any time," Minot said. "You know that, don't you?" And Jeffrey knew it. It was a part of the book of rules. The rules said that you were loyal to your friends.

"Jeff," Minot said, "I know you're always lunching with her. You don't misunderstand me, do you?"

"No," Jeffrey said. "I don't, Minot."

"Just having them both in the same place," Minot said.

That was what troubled Minot, because it was not in the book of rules. It was hardly necessary to read between the lines to understand what Minot was taking for granted. Minot did not mind his having an affair, because such a contingency was cared for in several paragraphs in the book of rules. He minded because there were also paragraphs laid down as to conduct when one found oneself in such a situation.

"You know," Jeffrey said slowly, and he found himself speaking patiently, "I've known Marianna for a long while, but you're wrong in your assumptions, Minot."

But he knew it would have done no good to explain everything candidly to Minot—to tell him that in spite of the week end he was not seriously contemplating such a thing. Minot would have approved of everything he said, for such an explanation was proper in the book of rules. No gentleman in the book of rules would have been expected to have made an admission. Besides, Marianna Miller was on the stage, and stage people did just one thing according to Minot's book of rules.

"Let's have another one," Minot said. "Oh, George. Front and center, George."

George entered into the spirit of the thing, not brashly or blatantly but with the kindly smile of one who loved the vagaries of members and who had been through a lot with them. George walked to the table and did a smart right face.

"George was in the old Second," Minot said. "Continue the exercise, George."

Jeffrey did not want another drink, but if he had refused one, Minot would have thought he was irritated, since under the circumstances, when friends touched on such a subject, a drink was called for in the book of rules. It meant that everything was over and that you were back to where you were before, that nothing more need be said about it. Yet it made him restless. He had never thought, until Minot mentioned it, that he and Marianna might be talked about.

"I'll tell you who's a guest here," Minot said. "Sir Thomas—Sir Thomas Leslie."

But Jeffrey had never heard the name.

"British Information Service," Minot said. "Just fresh from London. We gave him a party Sunday night. Tommy's quite a boy."

But Jeffrey was only half listening. They were always giving parties to the British—it was all a part of the British War Relief and Bundles for Britain. They were always making speeches about blood's being thicker than water. They were always reading letters from some cousin in the R.A.F. He knew why the Sir Thomases were over. They were over here to get everything they could, so that they could carry on, and Jeffrey wished that they would tell the truth instead of beating about the bush. They wanted America in the war, and they were right to want it. He wished they would say so flatly instead of asking for tools, so that they could do the job. They wanted America in the war because their backs were to the wall; he wished that he could be sure that America could save them. He wished that someone would tell him how it could be done instead of selling him enamel lions to attach to his lapel. It was going to take more than an enamel lion, and the British and everyone else were talking double talk. Roosevelt was saying that none of the boys would fight in a foreign war, saying it again and again, and asking if it were clear. It was not clear; but Mr. Willkie was saying it, too—that every possible aid must be given England, but we must not get into the war.

"I wish they'd tell the truth," Jeffrey heard himself saying.

Minot shrugged his shoulders slightly.

"That's too much to ask," he said. "We should have been in it last winter. If we'd been in it—"

It was an impossibility to have been in it, and Minot should have known. It was all like an old record turning again, whose strains he vaguely remembered—that propaganda of gallant rebuke, as though it were all our fault, as though we were slackers letting our blood brothers down while they were fighting the Hun. They should have known that no people went to war for anything like that except a few like Minot who followed the book of rules.

Jeffrey realized suddenly that he was not at home with Minot, or with any of those people. It was the same mood which had overtaken him there at Higgins Farm, when the voice had said, "This—is London." He was thinking of Marianna Miller, wondering what Minot had heard, and whether Madge could have said anything.

"Minot," he asked, "have you seen Madge lately?"

"Madge?" Minot said. "Well, let's see. Why, yes, yesterday. What was it? —something for the British War Relief."

It all tied up together.

Madge must have discussed Marianna Miller, and it gave Jeffrey a most indignant feeling. Madge might have thought that there was something in it because Madge knew the book of rules. All those people were alike, and no matter how he tried, he could not be like them.

"Jeff," Minot said, "you're not mad, are you?"

"No," Jeffrey said, "of course not. You couldn't make me mad."

"You know, I like you better than anyone I know."

There was nothing awkward in Minot's statement. Jeffrey could not have said such a thing to Minot or to anyone else, but it was utterly guileless, and natural when Minot said it. It drew them together in the warmth of a friendship which was both very old and extremely valuable. It made no difference to Jeffrey that he felt older and more cynical and more intelligent. All at once the friendship seemed indestructible.

Yet it was hard to keep his mind on what Minot was saying. All sorts of elements seemed to have combined into a sort of chaotic discontent, and even the dining room at the Clinton Club was part of it.

The dining room was Georgian—the chairs and the silver and the soft green paneling all very good, and used by people who understood them. The Sheraton sideboard against the north wall was a fine authentic piece. It was covered with a great mass of non-functional silver—cups, bowls, and urns, such as appear in clubs—but the silver was completely in place, like the few diners at the tables, and like the waiters. There was a watchful dignity in the room and a tacit assurance that there would be no mistake about forks or fingerbowls. It seemed to Jeffrey that he was the only one who was not completely at home, completely a part of it. He had ordered cold guinea hen and lyonnaise potatoes had come with it. When the waiter, whom Minot called Stephen, passed the potatoes, Jeffrey was aware that something was not quite right. When it was too late, Jeffrey saw that he should not have put the lyonnaise potatoes on the cold plate with the guinea hen. There was a warm plate just beside it, and, though Stephen had drawn the silver potato-dish back a hair, maneuvering it nearer the warm plate, Jeffrey had put the hot potatoes with the cold guinea hen. It was a small matter and there was no reason for him to try to convince Stephen, indirectly of course, that he had been aware of the hot plate and that he was simply eccentric and liked hot potatoes with the guinea hen. It showed that he did not belong there.

"How's Jim doing?" Minot asked.

"Jim?" Jeffrey repeated. He fumbled over the word, just as he had with the potatoes, before he understood that Minot was asking about his son. "Oh, Jim's all right. He's up there. Up in Lowell House."

"He ought to be in Eliot," Minot said. "Jeff, I wish I had a boy."

"How are the girls?" Jeffrey asked.

"I'll have them for Christmas," Minot said. "That's the way the agreement goes this year. Maybe we can all do something together. They're not too young for Jim now. Jeff, Jim's quite a boy."

"Yes," Jeffrey said. "Jim's all right."

"He looks the way you used to," Minot said. "I don't see Madge in him at all."

It was what Minot always said whenever he mentioned Jim.

"You and Jim always get on so well," Minot said.

"Well," Jeffrey answered, "I suppose I saw more of him than I ever did of the other kids. I always saw a lot of Jim."

"Is he still taking Military Science?" Minot asked.

Jeffrey found himself sitting up straighter. It was exactly as though someone behind him had tapped him softly on the shoulder.

"He said something about it," Jeffrey answered. "Something of the sort."

"You don't want him drafted as a private," Minot said.

"Oh, no," Jeffrey answered. "Not as a private. That would never do."

Minot put his fork down so gently that it made no sound against the plate.

"Once this election's out of the way, they'll enlarge the Army. Jeff, you know what I mean. It doesn't look well, waiting to be drafted."

"Maybe if you had a son," Jeffrey said, "you wouldn't be so anxious to get into this war."

"If I had a son," Minot answered, "I'd want him in it now."

"Would you?" Jeffrey asked him. "I wonder if you would. Jim's just twenty so he won't be drafted yet. I'd rather go myself."

Jeffrey knew by the way the wrinkles disappeared from Minot's forehead that he had said the right thing.

"God," Minot said, "who wouldn't?" and then he pushed back his chair. He was looking past Jeffrey toward the entrance of the dining room. "There's Sir Thomas now," he said. "Oh, Tommy!"

Jeffrey turned in his chair. Sir Thomas was pink and plumpish, middle-aged and a trifle bald, but his face was one of those which never change much from boyhood. From the way he paused, it was plain that Sir Thomas had met so many Americans lately that he was having difficulty keeping them all in his memory.

"Oh," Sir Thomas said, "hello there."

As Sir Thomas walked toward the table he radiated that curious combination of complete good nature mingled with faint surprise which Jeffrey had seen on the faces of other Englishmen.

"Sit down, Tommy," Minot said. "Won't you have your lunch here with us?"

Sir Thomas still seemed to be trying to put himself into the proper role, and to recall under what circumstances Minot could ever have called him "Tommy."

"Splendid," Sir Thomas said. "But aren't you nearly through?"

"We started early," Minot said. "We've got lots of time."

And now it was clear that Sir Thomas finally remembered everything.

"Oh yes, the dinner," Sir Thomas said. He glanced at Jeffrey and laughed gently. "You 'spooned' me—that's your word for it, isn't it? You spooned me out of the cab."

"Sir Thomas," Minot said. "This is Mr. Jeffrey Wilson. Sir Thomas Leslie."

"How do you do," Sir Thomas said. "I do hope I'm not 'butting in.'"

"Oh, no," Jeffrey said. "No, of course not."

"I don't want to be a 'table hopper,'" Sir Thomas said. "That's your word for it, isn't it?" He glanced at both of them merrily and unfolded his napkin.

Sir Thomas was an Englishman, and no matter how you tried to put it, there was no way of escaping what Sir Thomas thought of Americans. Sir Thomas, sitting there, was like one of those teachers who is the boys' "best friend," who can allow the boys to call him by his first name and still be a teacher, and even Minot must have been aware of it.

Sir Thomas was examining the luncheon card. He had taken a pair of spectacles from his pocket and placed them on his nose, while Stephen stood there waiting. Now he took his spectacles off and glanced first at Jeffrey and then at Minot.

"Three choices—" he said. "You chaps are very lucky."

"Yes," Minot said, "too damned lucky."

The talk moved on to London, but Jeffrey was not listening. He was thinking, as they sat there at the table, of their three utterly divergent origins. Sir Thomas had possessed everything that Minot Roberts had possessed, but for a longer time. Jeffrey was the only one of the three who had ever been a had-not.

All at once his life and experience seemed compressed between two wars, like books between two book-ends. He could see himself entering the Clinton Club, and everything that had happened there gave him one of those flashes of insight, so disturbing when one grows older. He was actually wondering if it might not have been better if he had never met Minot Roberts, if he had never gone to visit Minot when he came back from France.

He could see the station platform when he got off the train, early in the afternoon. He could even remember the bag he had carried, known as cowhide, which he found later consisted of a very thin layer of leather glued to cardboard. He could remember his sensation exactly, a deceptive feeling of being in masquerade.

Then he heard Minot call his name.

"Am I right or am I wrong?" he heard Minot say. "What do you think, Jeff?"

There was not even an opportunity to pretend that he had listened.

"I'm awfully sorry," he began, "I didn't hear. I'm just a grease-ball, Minot."

"Oh, God," Minot said, and he began to laugh.

"What's more," Jeffrey said, "I've always been a grease-ball."

It amused him particularly to see Sir Thomas's face, and the effort that Sir Thomas was making to grasp the context of a phrase with which he was not familiar, debating whether to let it pass and whether, if he did, he might not miss something colloquially significant.

"What are they?" Sir Thomas asked. "What are grease-balls?"

22

Where Everything Was Bright

Although Jeffrey's most violent ambitions and emotions had been fulfilled or frustrated in the years following the last war, that postwar decade now possessed the same elusive quality which he encountered in the pages of what the book trade termed "Costume fiction." Somehow it had actually become a historical epoch and sometimes he could think that he and all the rest of his contemporaries might just as well have been wearing satin breeches and cloaks and swords, and taking snuff and saying "Zounds!" It seemed as far removed from the present as that.

Jeffrey had saved six hundred dollars from his officer's pay and the bulk of the bills in his inside pocket made him feel richer than he had ever felt before. When he tried on the civilian clothes which he had left behind him, they fitted as badly as all the life which they had represented. They were too tight across the shoulders and too short in the sleeves, and so he had bought a new gray flannel suit in Boston. He bought it in a store on Boylston Street which he would not have thought of patronizing before the war. He had entered the store in his uniform, so the clerks had no way of judging him by his clothes. Later, he knew the suit he had purchased was not at all bad. He remembered standing before the mirror so that he could see himself from the front and side while the fitter marked the sleeves and the length of the trousers, and he had as hard a time recognizing himself as anyone else did who had been in uniform for two years. His face was tanned, and his hair was still very short as he had worn it in France. His eyes were grayish like the coat and at first the whole suit had felt loose, too light, and too easy. He stood straight in it, although there was no longer need for standing straight.

"How much does it cost?" he had asked the clerk.

When the man said that the price was fifty-eight dollars, Jeffrey was startled. He could see that he had made a mistake, going to a store on Boylston Street, but now that he was there, he had to buy it, and besides, he had six hundred dollars. What made it more difficult was that they expected him to buy other things. He bought a pair of low tan shoes which cost ten dollars and three pair of socks for a dollar and a half apiece, and three soft shirts at four dollars apiece, and two ties for two dollars each, and a brown felt hat for seven dollars. The total cost was appalling, but somehow he had to buy them, now that he was in the store.

"What about something dark," the clerk asked, "for afternoon?"

"No, thank you," Jeffrey said, "not today."

"How are you fixed for evening clothes?" the clerk asked.

The clerk was wearing rimless spectacles. Jeffrey had never thought about evening clothes.

"No, thanks," he said, "not today."

"How about a suitcase?" the clerk asked.

The clerk and the whole store were driving him into a corner, obviously taking him for someone else.

"I guess not, thanks," Jeffrey said, "not today."

Jeffrey bought the suitcase in a luggage store near Franklin Street where everything was marked down fifty per cent for the August sale. When he took the ten o'clock train at the South Station, he wore the gray suit and the brown hat and one of the soft shirts. Inside his suitcase were the other shirts, the socks, one clean suit of underwear and one pair of pajamas. When he stopped at the newsstand to buy a morning paper, a porter asked if he might carry his suitcase. It must have been the fifty-eight dollar suit, for no porter had ever asked him that before. All these details were trivial, but in some way they illustrated his state of mind, and that of his country, now that he was back. Everyone was very prosperous in those days. Everyone was spending too much money. It was hard when he saw the people hurrying past him to the trains to realize where he had been or what he had seen. Everyone was getting back to normalcy, as Mr. Harding was to say a little later. Everyone in America was forgetting about the war.

Jeffrey waited on the platform for a half an hour at Stamford for the local train. He did not mind because everything was still new to him. He watched the automobiles drive up, and the chauffeurs get out and the baggage trucks roll down the platform with the mail. He wondered where the automobiles were going—surely not to any of that part of Stamford which he saw from the platform. There seemed to be more of everything than he had ever remembered and the whole face of his country seemed transformed. When he took the local train and sat looking out of the window, there were no soldiers on the platforms and no Military Police. He pulled his suitcase from the rack above his head when the brakeman called the name of the station, and when he was standing on the platform in the sunlight, looking at the automobiles, he saw Minot Roberts. Minot was in tennis flannels, white buckskin shoes and a tweed coat. Each one must have felt for a moment that the other was a stranger.

"Hello, boy," Minot said, and then they shook hands. "Give me your bag, and let's get out of this."

"Oh, no," Jeffrey said. "I can carry it."

"Go to hell," Minot said. "Give me your bag," and they both grabbed for the yellow suitcase.

"God almighty," Minot said. "It's funny seeing you."

Minot had met him in a gray Cadillac phaeton with red leather seats, and Jeffrey even remembered the smell of the leather. He wished that it all had not reminded him of *David Copperfield* for he had never admired either the novel or the style of Charles Dickens. Once long afterwards Madge had spoken of it, when he tried to tell her about that week end.

"Why, darling," Madge had said, "it must have been like David Copperfield and Steerforth."

This had annoyed Jeffrey more than he had ever told her, though Madge had been annoyed when she said it. For one thing, he did not want Madge to think, or anyone else, that he had ever been like David Copperfield, whom he had always looked upon as an impossible, sniveling and conceited little fellow; besides he was always sure that Dickens had never known any people like the Steerforths, and had drawn them very badly.

They drove through the main street and out along the Post Road. The houses standing on their lawns behind their shrubbery kept growing larger, but Jeffrey had no definite impression of them, until the car turned between two granite gateposts and moved up a blue gravel drive toward a granite house with a large stable and greenhouses.

"Here it is," Minot said.

"You mean you live here?" Jeffrey asked—"God almighty," and somehow it made him laugh.

Jeffrey was always glad that he took it that way, and he never forgot that Minot took it that way, but then, there was no other way in which they could have taken it. When the car stopped, a man came running down the steps and took the bag.

"Up by my room, Burns," Minot said. "Come on, Jeff, Mother wants to meet you."

Mrs. Roberts was in the morning room, writing a letter at a high secretary desk. When they came in, a small griffon in a basket began to bark, and Minot picked the dog up and tucked it beneath his arm.

"Shut your ugly little face," he said. "Mother, here's Jeff Wilson."

Mrs. Roberts must have been beautiful when she was young. She was dressed in black. Her brown hair was growing gray, and she was smiling.

"I've been wondering what you'd look like," she said.

Jeffrey never understood why he was not afraid of her. He remembered the roses in the bowl on the table and the way the blinds were drawn so that shafts of light made a ladder across the carpet.

"It's very kind of you to have me here," he said.

"It isn't kind," Mrs. Roberts said, "we're proud to have you here."

In the second's silence that followed, Jeffrey felt his face grow red. He had never encountered anyone before who could make such an answer sound entirely kind and simple.

"That's it," Minot said, "you tell him, Ma," and Minot put the dog back in the basket.

"I've been wondering how you'd look," Mrs. Roberts said again. "Minot, where are you going this afternoon?"

"Tennis," Minot said, "over at the Hayeses'. How about a set of tennis, Jeff?"

Jeffrey glanced at Minot and back at Mrs. Roberts.

"I'd like to watch," he said.

"What?" Minot said. "You don't play tennis?"

"No," Jeffrey said, "I never had much time to learn, but I'd like to watch."

Even while he was speaking, he thought how beautiful Mrs. Roberts must have been when she was young. Later he sometimes suspected that the picture he had always kept of her in his mind was not accurate at all. He must have always believed—as a boy sometimes believes of an older woman—that she knew all about him. He had never wished to tell anyone else everything, but he wanted to tell her about Bragg and about Louella Barnes—about everything he thought.

"We'll be alone for dinner," she said, "but don't be late."

He often thought of all of the things that another woman would have said—that of course no one played tennis well, and that you had to learn sometime and that now was the time to learn, that there were sneakers and tennis clothes and racquets in the house, and that Minot would get them for him and that they must all hurry out now and have a good time. She did not say anything like that; she made him feel that he was all right the way he was, and she always made him feel that way.

"It's very kind of you to have me here," he said again.

His room was done in glazed chintz and the spread on the bed matched the curtains and the cushions on the window seat. There was a fireplace with brass andirons and a mahogany bureau with a shaving mirror. There was a table beside the bed with books on it and a thermos water jug and an eight-day clock in a leather case. There was an armchair by the window seat, and in back of it a door opened to a white-tiled bathroom. The man named

Burns had opened Jeffrey's suitcase, and he asked if there was any other baggage coming from the station.

"Mr. Wilson's just back from France," Minot said. "That's all now, Burns."

Jeffrey stood in the center of the room. It seemed necessary to make some sort of explanation for not having brought more clothes but he did not mind it as much as he should have, because he knew Minot Roberts.

"I'm sorry," he began, and then he stopped. He did not want to say that he had not known any better, and it would have been bad taste to say that he hadn't known what he was getting into.

"I can lend you anything you want," Minot said.

"Oh, no," he answered, "no, thanks."

He had never borrowed anything from Minot Roberts. He must have seen that it would spoil everything and that Minot would think the less of him; and also he must have had some sort of fear of losing his own identity, the primitive sort of apprehension which one experiences among strangers in a strange place. Jeffrey remembered how the chintz curtains in the window rustled, and the clean, waxy smell of the room and the faint scent of blue petunias in the little vase on the mantelpiece. No matter what clothes he was wearing, he wanted to be himself.

"I'll be ready in five minutes," Minot said. "Just sing out if you want anything. My room's right here."

Minot opened an adjoining door and left it open, and Jeffrey could hear him moving about in the next room, singing a catch of that song:—

"You're going to a happy land where everything is bright,
Where the hangouts grow on bushes and we stay out every night. . . ."

Jeffrey was still grimy from the daycoach. He took off his coat, laid it very carefully on the armchair and walked into the white bathroom. The tub was a huge piece of glazed porcelain set on a floor of octagonal white tiles. There was an elaborate shower fixture with a white curtain. The washstand stood on a solid pedestal, and there was a smell of scented soap. There were huge bath towels with monograms and smaller towels of different sizes. He had never seen so many towels.

"Jeff," he heard Minot call. "Are you all right?"

"Yes," he called back, "I'm all right."

Then that old pursuing thought came over him again as he picked up an embroidered washcloth. He wondered why he was there and how he had ever got there. He had never been so far away from anything familiar, even in the war. His mind went back to the Barneses' front porch that first time he had called on Louella, and he remembered how the rocking chair had tipped backwards and how he had kicked out his legs involuntarily to balance it. He was not the same person any longer, and the worst of it was, he could not tell how it had happened. Even his face in the mirror above the washstand looked as though it were a stranger's.

They drove over in the gray Cadillac with the red leather upholstery. It was a warm day in late August, and whereas at home at Bragg there was already a hint of autumn which was making the first swamp maples turn, it was still hot summer by the Sound. This may have been why Jeffrey always associated the place with that steaming hum of the tree locusts in the daytime and with the insistent clamor of katydids at night. He always pictured the water of the Sound as peacefully blue, beyond a warm golden light which fell on lawns and silver beeches, and on umbrella trees and weeping birches. He always heard the snipping of shears, squaring off a privet hedge, and voices and laughter from the lawns. He always connected Willow Road, where Madge had lived, with a clear hot summer's day and with just a faint breeze stirring from the water; so that often on a hot day when he heard the locusts on the trees, a great deal about Willow Road would come back to him again. He had seen it all, he had heard all the voices first in summer, and that was the way it stayed in his mind. Somewhere back among the pages of what was known as "youth's lexicon," that 1919 model Cadillac was running on tires which sometimes would last for as much as eight or ten thousand miles, and he was on the front seat with Minot Roberts.

"Here it is," Minot said. "The court's in back. It's better than the Club." There was no way of telling that he would know the Hayes place very well and that Mrs. Hayes would ask him to plant willow trees on it because he was so practical and that finally he would be the one who would see about selling that place and removing all the furniture. The house was one of those rambling structures, built with the grotesque effort at informality which was common in the early nineteen-hundreds, and all the landscape gardening was dated and too ornate, but it did not seem so then.

Minot Roberts parked the car at the edge of the turn-around at the front of the house and slammed the door and picked up his tennis racquet.

"They're all at the court," Minot said. "Come on."

When they walked across the lawn there was a smell of freshly mowed turf that was sweet and very warm. He could never understand why, as the voices came nearer, the idea of meeting strangers had not thrown him into a panic, except that he was still so far removed from anything he had known. There was so much of everything and everything seemed to be untouched by any of the things that worried most people.

They were playing mixed doubles on the clay court beyond a broad sweep of lawn. The backstops were covered with rambler roses. Some men and girls were seated watching, and a man in a white crew sweater clutching a handful of grass was chasing a girl in a short white dress along the terrace. The players had stopped their game, and everyone was laughing. The girl ran very fast, and she was laughing too, and it seemed to Jeffrey that they were too old to be making so much noise. It made him feel embarrassed, because the girl was pretty, although he never could tell what her looks had to do with it.

"Damn you," he heard her call, "please, Roger, damn you, not in my hair."

She was slender and very pretty, especially her legs, although Jeffrey realized that he should not have thought of them.

"Minot," she called. "Minot, he—"

It was the sort of byplay, indirectly connected with sex, that embarrassed Jeffrey then, and afterwards. He wished that people, if they wanted to do that sort of thing, would chase each other in private. When they saw that Jeffrey was a stranger, the girl and the man both stopped. The man named Roger had short, blond hair. His face was chubby and red from his exertions.

"She put grass down my neck," he said.

Perhaps the man knew he had made a fool of himself, but it would have been better to have passed over the explanation. The girl pushed a wisp of damp hair off her forehead. She was out of breath, and she had stopped laughing, but her lips were parted in a smile. She was smaller than Jeffrey had thought at first, and she stood very straight.

"This is Mr. Wilson," Minot said, "Miss Hayes."

"Oh, yes," Madge said, "hello." Then she wriggled her shoulders and clutched at the front of her dress.

"Something's come undone inside," she said. "I don't suppose you've got a pin."

She was looking up at him, smiling, and that memory always had a queer discordant note of triviality. He had no way of knowing that Madge's underwear was always coming loose and that she was always unnecessarily frank about it. He had no way of knowing that they would fall in love. Jeffrey supposed that all married people must have shared some such moment of their own, for he had heard many of them speak of something like it with a sort of faraway affection. "We met in the strangest way," they would say. "It was in front of the Information Desk at Grand Central." They met on boats, they met at hotels, or someone introduced them. After all, they had to meet somewhere. They must have remembered it so clearly because it was the one time that most human beings ever realized how greatly a fortuitous circumstance could change a life. All this was so obvious that it made him impatient when he heard them talk about it; but when it came to himself and Madge, it had the difference of being their private property. It stayed there, suspended in time. It was something mentioned in happiness and quarrels. It was always there, something they would always share in common. He had heard Madge wish to God that he had never come there that afternoon, and he had wished the same thing. He had heard her say how dreadful it would have been if he had never come, and he had said the same thing, too. No matter how he and Madge might feel, it was always there, and there was something a little sad in the knowledge that it was so irrevocable, and a sadness in the thought that they had both been so free, so young and so unwise, perhaps. They were always young in that picture in his mind.

Once when they were speaking of it with that queer sort of curiosity with which one speaks of such things, Jeffrey asked her what she had ever seen in him. It was an unfortunate time to ask the question for it was during one of those occasions when Madge saw nothing in him that was desirable.

"I don't know," she said, but she must have tried to live it all again. "You were different."

It was not any sort of answer, and he told her so.

"That gray suit," she said, "it looked like blotting paper." He knew that she was seeing it all again.

"It wasn't a bad suit at all," he said, "it cost me fifty-eight dollars."

"The trousers were too long," she said. "They wrinkled around your shoes, and your necktie didn't match."

"It wasn't meant to match," he said, but he knew that she could see it all, just as he often saw it.

"It was all a terrible mistake," she said.

"All right," Jeffrey said, "all right, if you say it was."

"Everyone always said it was," she answered, and then neither of them spoke for a while.

"You looked so alone," she said. "You looked so sure of yourself."

At first he thought she did not mean it. It showed how little she had understood him to have thought that he was sure of himself.

"Besides, you were very good-looking," she said. "You looked—I don't know. You had nice shoulders."

He tried to piece something together from her words, but they did not make much sense.

"Darling," she said, "if you hadn't liked me, you wouldn't have—looked the way you did."

"How did I look?" he asked.

"I don't know," she answered, "the way you did. Darling, what was it—"

She stopped, but he knew what she meant.

"It must have been your hair," he said. "I liked your hair. Your hair was coming down."

"Jeff," she said, "there must have been something else, there must have been—"

"There's no use analyzing everything," Jeffrey said, and then before she could stop him, he knew the answer, although it could not bear analysis. "There's no use going over it. We couldn't help it, Madge."

23

The Peach Crop's Always Fine

It was often difficult for Jeffrey to get his mind on any sort of work after lunching at the Clinton Club. In the last few months it had been particularly difficult to work, since whatever he turned his mind to seemed to have little connection with anything that was going on in the world. Whenever he tried to concentrate on something, his attention had a habit of focusing on something else—on the past, for instance, as it had that day. He was sure that it was not so much that he was growing older, as that time was moving so fast. New York was changing faster than he had ever known it, although it had always been a restless city; and what was more, there was a continual hint of more change to come.

When he left the Clinton Club that afternoon, the bank buildings on Fifth Avenue seemed only to give an illusion of solidity, although the architecture of banks was designed to indicate permanence. The Fifth Avenue Bank adhered doggedly to the old tradition, showing without fanfare, as Walter Newcombe would have put it, that it was the New York family bank, handling the solidest accounts over generations. Its exterior was consciously shabby, like Barclays or Brown, Shipley's in London. But the Bankers Trust was designed on a newer basis. The Bankers Trust with its plate-glass windows rose proudly toward the sky as impregnable as a superdreadnought. You could not doubt your money would be safe in such a building, all filled with bright vice presidents who knew everything about securities. Though those banks were as familiar to Jeffrey as his own face, the sidewalks in front of them and the crowds moving by them seemed shoddy, reminding him that Fifth Avenue in the Forties was not quite what it used to be.

The clock by the corner pointed to the hour of three, and Jesse Fineman had wanted to see him any time that afternoon in his office off Broadway. First he passed the restaurants on the cross street west and the windows of secondhand shops filled with bronze statuary and Arab pistols and all sorts of other articles which he could not imagine anyone's wanting to buy. Then there were the small hotels with marble fronts and with palm trees in the lobbies. Then there were the subway entrances where the Interborough and the B.M.T. entwined beneath the street, and then Times Square. Broadway was always shabby in the afternoon. The electric signs stood nakedly against the sky like the frames of elaborate fireworks displays. Although Times Square was crowded, it all seemed half-asleep. The picture houses and the drugstores and the newsstands never seemed to try in the afternoon.

Nothing Jeffrey saw had changed much from the way he first remembered it. There was the same cynicism, the same disregard for sobriety, the same combined efforts of millions of people to escape from what troubled them. It was all pathetic like every fallacy, but at least it was not new.

"Plenty of seats in just a minute," the men in the horizon-blue uniforms were saying. "The main picture will be over in three minutes. Seats now only in the mezzanine."

The police whistles were blowing, crowds were streaming solidly across the street. It was all more permanent than Fifth Avenue—timeless, too complicated to understand, but then, there was no reason to understand it.

The outer room of the new Fineman office looked as it always had at that particular time of year. There was the same crowd. Jeffrey could hear them speaking of him in respectful undertones as he walked to the desk, and the smile of the girl there was just the same as always.

"Hello, Sylvia," he said.

"Yes, Mr. Wilson," she said, "go right in."

It was not like the Clinton Club. Everyone knew who he was.

In the last few years, Jesse Fineman had paid attention to his office and a decorator had gone to work on it, making it into a suitable background for art and serious thought. The windows were framed with heavy velvet drapery. There was a single oil painting on the wall, a copy of a portrait of Edwin Booth with a museum light above it. There were a cellaret and a dressing room where Jesse could relax on a couch or change into evening clothes if he had to, and there were comfortable red leather chairs with chromium ash receivers beside them that seemed to sprout like mushrooms from the broadloom carpet. The desk behind which Jesse sat was also covered with red leather, and it was large enough so that one was conscious of its size when one walked around it to shake hands. It was bare except for a single manuscript, a thermos jug and a framed photograph of Jesse's wife. It was all new and in bad taste, but Jeffrey felt at home.

When Jeffrey came in, Jesse was talking to a girl with dark hair who was dressed in gray broadcloth, gray gloves, gray bag, gray stockings, gray suede shoes.

"Hello, Jeff," Jesse said. "This is Miss Ainsley. Miss Joan Ainsley."

Jeffrey did not know her, but then, he did not need to because the name fitted perfectly with everything else. She must have been one of those girls who had been working in some summer theater, and she would not have got in to see Jesse unless someone had given her a very special letter. She would be anxious to show that she was not just an ordinary girl like the other girls sitting outside. She would want to show that she was just like Katharine Hepburn, educated, intelligent, not like the girls outside. She would want to make it clear that she knew about golf and tennis and lived on Park Avenue, and just as soon as she spoke, Jeffrey knew that he was right. She shook hands with him nicely and smiled.

"Didn't I see you at Vassar, Mr. Wilson?" she said.

"Oh," Jeffrey said, "are you a Vassar graduate, Miss Ainsley?"

"Dad insisted on Vassar," she said, and she smiled affectionately at the thought of Dad.

"Well," Jeffrey said, "that's nice."

"Weren't you at the Experimental Theater," she said, "when we were doing 'The Infernal Machine'? The Cocteau thing—"

"No," Jeffrey said, "I wish I had been. Were you in it, Miss Ainsley?"

"I understudied for the Sphinx," she said, and she laughed to show that she knew it was silly.

"Jesse," Jeffrey said, "have you a cigarette?"

"Oh, Mr. Wilson," Miss Ainsley said, "here's one," and she opened her bag and drew out a small enamel cigarette case, "that is, if you don't mind the brand. Dad gets them from the Club."

Jesse put his elbows on the red leather desk, put the tips of his fingers together, and cleared his throat softly.

"Miss Ainsley has come with a letter for advice," he said. "I've been trying to tell her a little—" Jesse waved his thin hands gently—"a little about the theater. But—why should I go on when we have someone with us now who really knows theater? My dear, ask Mr. Wilson."

Jeffrey smiled. It had occurred to him that lately Jesse was always making curtain speeches.

"I'm just a play doctor," Jeffrey said, "not a real producer," and he looked at Jesse again. "But Mr. Fineman, although he is too modest to admit it, is what we might call 'the grand old man of the theater.'"

Jesse put the tips of his fingers together again.

"My dear," he said, "if you had known Mr. Wilson as long as I have, you would know that he has a puckish sort of humor. My dear, Mr. Wilson and I have stood shoulder to shoulder through good times and bad. No, Mr. Wilson is a very great artist, and I am a mere vessel."

Jeffrey was beginning to enjoy himself.

"My dear," Jeffrey said, "if you had known Mr. Fineman as long as I have known him, you would realize that modesty is a fault with him that is almost congenital. Mr. Fineman is such a great artist that he has become completely selfless."

"My dear," Mr. Fineman said, "it will be something for you to remember that you have seen Mr. Wilson at his witty best. Mr. Wilson is always full of fun. It is an inseparable part of his artistry."

Jeffrey was going to go on with it, but when he looked at Miss Ainsley, suddenly he felt sorry for her. She did not look much older than his daughter Gwen.

"All I want is a chance," she said. "All I want is a bit."

He wished that they would not always talk about "bits." It was the first word that girls like Miss Ainsley picked up. She was too thin. She did not have the manner or the charm. She made him think of Marianna Miller. Once Marianna had been like that, looking for a job, but if Marianna had heard him being silly, exchanging superlatives with Jesse Fineman, she would have fallen into the mood and she would have lived it for the moment. He saw Jesse move his hand to the button beneath his desk and a minute later his secretary opened the office door.

"It's Mr. Bush from Paramount," the secretary said, and Mr. Fineman immediately stood up.

"Oh," he said, "Mr. Bush from Paramount. I'll see him right away." And he walked around the desk.

"My dear," he said. "If there is anything I can do any time, just call on me again."

Jeffrey felt sorry for her, but there was no use being sorry. When the door closed, Jesse passed his hand across his forehead.

"God damn it," he said. "You don't think I'm ruthless, do you Jeff? Why don't they stay in college?"

"Mr. Bush from Paramount is new, isn't he?" Jeffrey said.

"Every week," Jesse said. "This week it is Mr. Bush from Paramount. It hurts their feelings if you don't change them every week. Can I help it? You don't think I'm ruthless, do you, Jeff?"

"No," Jeffrey said. "You're tender-hearted, actually."

Jesse looked hurt.

"Cynical," he said. "It's not kind to be cynical."

"I'm not," Jeffrey answered. "You've always been kind to me."

It reminded him that Madge always referred to Jesse as "that dreadful man" when Jesse and Mrs. Fineman came to dinner once a year, and that Madge always referred to the Finemans' apartment as "that dreadful place" when they dined with the Finemans once a year.

"Yes," Jesse Fineman said, and his face lighted up. He sighed and placed the palms of his hands carefully on the desk. "Except for you, I have no other friends."

"That's because you're a big bastard," Jeffrey said.

Jesse looked happy. He always did when Jeffrey called him names.

"Jeff," he said, "all we've been through together."

"Yes," Jeffrey answered, "we've been through a lot."

"Jeff," Jesse asked, "is everything all right with you?"

"How do you mean, all right?" Jeffrey asked.

"Jeff," Jesse Fineman said. "You know I like you better than anybody—like my own family, Jeff. You haven't been looking happy. Don't answer if you don't want to, but is there anything wrong domestically?"

"What?" Jeffrey asked.

"Domestically," Jesse repeated. "Is there anything wrong domestically?"

Jeffrey wondered exactly what it was that Jesse had noticed. It was like one of those advertisements discussing a personal malady of which even your best friends hesitate to warn you, for two of his best friends, completely removed from each other, within a few hours had both seen something in him of which Jeffrey was not aware. It was a little like standing on a carpet on a polished floor, and having it slip from under him while he made an undignified effort to keep his balance.

"If anything were wrong, I'd have told you," Jeffrey said. "I don't know what you're thinking about. Everything is fine at home."

There was a silence, and he heard Jesse sigh. He heard the traffic from Seventh Avenue and the murmur of voices from the outer office, while he sat with his hands clasped over his knee, looking at the brown carpet.

"Jeff," he heard Jesse say, "is it money?"

If it was not marriage, of course Jesse would think it was money, because marriage and money had always worried Jesse, and all at once Jeffrey knew that he would not mind talking to Jesse, because although he knew Jesse well, Jesse's life only touched a part of his life.

"It isn't money, Jesse," he said, "it's this damn war."

Then Jeffrey felt completely relaxed and anxious to go on with it, anxious to sort out all sorts of half-formed thoughts.

"Perhaps it bothers everyone," he said. "It's like a thunderstorm coming up when you're outdoors and you know you're going to get wet. You have that still sense all around you of something that's bound to happen. You drink it every morning with your coffee. Do you know what I mean?"

He did not look at Jesse. He did not know whether Jesse knew what he meant or not, but he was very glad that he had tried to put it into words.

"When you're young," Jeffrey said, "lots of other things are more serious, but when you're older, you wonder—whether anything you've done has ever been worth while. You can see it all about to go sour and you haven't any way to help it. It's not a pleasant feeling."

He stopped again. He was not thinking of Jesse as much as he was wishing that he could put it all more clearly.

"I keep wondering what's been the use," he said, "and exactly what I've been trying to do. I suppose I've been like everyone else, trying to build some sort of an umbrella, because I thought it would rain, and now I know that none of it's going to work."

He stopped again, still disturbed by his own vagueness. The whole thing sounded grossly material, and yet somehow it should not have been.

"You don't know what's going to happen," he said. "You buy the papers and you read the gossip columns. You ask people who ought to know. You listen to the 'Fireside Chats'—and that's a damn funny thing to call them—and you try and find out by his voice what he implies without saying it, and then you talk about it and hear what someone says who knows someone. *He* doesn't know what's going to happen, and you wish to God that something would happen and at the same time you hope it won't, but you know that something will, because it can't go on this way."

It sounded like an inartistic whine when it all came out in words.

"I don't like to be afraid," Jeffrey said. "I don't think I am afraid for myself. You see, I've been to one war, Jesse, but now there's Jim—and he's about military age."

Jesse Fineman's mouth looked thin, and the corners of his lips twitched. He pulled back his left sleeve and consulted a square gold wrist watch. The gesture made Jeffrey look at his own watch, and he found it was nearly five o'clock. Jesse poured himself a glass of water from the thermos and took a box of capsules from a drawer.

"Now Jeff," he said, "when you talk like that it goes straight to my stomach. Neither you nor I should be worried. That's what the doctor continually says to me. Why worry? He says I should think of some outside hobby, perhaps painting a picture or buying glass. Perhaps you and I should both learn how to play."

"Play what?" Jeffrey asked. "A musical instrument?"

"We both worry," Jesse said, "but as long as it is worry about a war, what can you do about it? Nothing. You have a fine wife and fine children, and as long as everything is all right domestically, there is always work. We have great responsibilities in these days, and we open in Boston on Monday, please don't forget."

"All right," Jeffrey said. "I'll go up with you on Monday, but there's no use rewriting it any more."

"I think what worries me," Jesse said, "is the complication of my own ideas. Sam says they're running through it again at seven o'clock. Suppose we go somewhere first for supper." Jesse filled his glass of water again and swallowed another capsule. "We could go to the Rockwell for just a bite to eat, and just talk pleasantly and forget about it before we see them run it off again."

"All right," Jeffrey said.

Jesse pulled at the front of his blue double-breasted coat, then he opened the door of his dressing room and looked at himself in the mirror and put on a broad-brimmed, black felt hat, and then he picked up a Malacca cane.

"There's just one thing," he said. "If you can possibly do it, Jeffrey, just as a favor, let us not speak again about the war."

"You mean it worries you, too?" Jeffrey asked.

"You wouldn't understand," Jesse said, and he stared ahead of him, as though he saw something that Jeffrey did not see. "Please, Jeffrey, not about the war."

Downstairs at the Rockwell was not what it had been once, because the face of the Rockwell had been lifted, like the faces of so many other New York hotels. At the Rockwell there had once been a grillroom in the basement, frequented by men only, combining the atmosphere of a chophouse and a German rathskeller. There had been a bar at one end, and shelves with steins of all sizes along the walls, a quiet place off Broadway where you could talk business—but now it was renovated. In the last few years there had been a good deal of advertising of what the management had called "downstairs at the Rockwell." "Meet me," little cards read, "downstairs at the Rockwell after dark." If you went downstairs at the Rockwell after dark, you would run a very good chance, according to the management, of rubbing elbows unexpectedly with celebrities, who, according to the management, looked upon the Rockwell, downstairs, as a second home. There was something that they liked—the management did not know what, unless it was the cuisine and the ample cocktail glasses and the general atmosphere of good-fellowship.

Downstairs at the Rockwell was air-conditioned now, and the walls had been brightened up with light plywood and the bar was intimate and continental with high stools all along it, so that no one needed to stand to have a drink. There was a table as you went in which always had some dead pheasants on it and pieces of Virginia ham and cheeses, guarded by a man with a chef's cap, named Louie. The tables had red-and-white-checked cloths and soft music was piped into the air from the ventilators. Also, ladies now came downstairs at the Rockwell. It was the cocktail hour and there were lots of girls and boys on the stools at the bar talking with animation. Jesse handed his hat and cane to the coatroom girl.

"Hello, Jenny, dear," he said.

"Good evening," she answered, "good evening, Mr. Fineman."

Jules, the headwaiter, saw Jesse right away.

"Good evening, Mr. Fineman, sir," Jules said. "How's the indigestion?"

You could see that it pleased Jesse to have Jules inquire because it meant that Jesse was a Celebrity.

"Just milk toast, tonight, Jules," Jesse said, "at a table in back where there's not too much noise."

It was impossible to find a table where there was not too much noise.

"Good evening, Mr. Wilson, sir," Jules said, "and how is Mr. Wilson?"

The music always made Jeffrey nervous because it came from everywhere at once and yet from nowhere. The refrain of "In the Good Old Summertime" was wafted through the room and some of the boys and girls at the bar were singing it.

"I like it here," Jesse said, "because I can just sit still and I don't have to think."

But Jeffrey knew that this was not the only reason why Jesse liked it. Jesse had a superstition about going to the old places when a play was opening, and besides he liked it because everyone knew him.

"It's Fineman," he heard someone say, "Fineman, the producer."

Jesse must have heard it too, and he frowned carefully.

"Jules," he said to the headwaiter, "remember, no publicity. I wish I could go some place where everyone doesn't know me."

"Then why do you come here?" Jeffrey asked him.

"I don't know," Jesse said, "habit, loyalty. I feel very strongly about loyalty."

"Since when has this come over you?" Jeffrey asked.

Jesse looked hurt.

"Don't ask it that way, Jeffrey," he said. "I want you to think about the first act. It may be the interpretation, but I'm still not satisfied with the timing. The timing is but very dreadful."

"If you use the word 'but' that way again," Jeffrey said, "I won't be able to stand it."

"I pick up the new words and phrases," Jesse answered. "I know it is but terrible."

Jeffrey did not answer. He was wondering what peculiar ability it was that Jesse possessed that others did not have. It had something to do with instinct, rather than education, an instinct that made him very sure of what people wanted, and with it was a strange sort of sensitiveness that was almost taste. Yet, at the same time Jeffrey could understand why Madge and everyone like her thought Jesse was terrible. Madge always said that Jesse had used him for years and clung to him when Jeffrey really knew that he would be better off without Jesse. It did no good to remind Madge that he had always worked with Jesse. Madge would tell him that there were other producers who were gentlemen, all of whom wanted to work with Jeffrey, and she would name them. She often said that he had outgrown Jesse Fineman long ago.

Jeffrey thought of it as Jesse began talking again about his indigestion. When he was a boy, a college boy, at the College of the City of New York, it seemed that Jesse always had a cast-iron stomach, and when Jesse had done publicity he still could eat but anything. It was the same when Jesse went into the Burns office. It was only when Mr. Burns made him a stage manager that Jesse began to think about his stomach. He first thought about it when the shows went on the road and the cast kept complaining to him about hotel accommodations. Then when the Old Man made him his assistant and he had to read plays, Jesse first began to notice that burning sensation. He thought when he got married to a nice girl and settled down his stomach would be better, but when he married Lottie Lacey, who was a singer from Alabama, Jesse's stomach not only had that burning sensation, but he had occasional cramps, and when Lottie went to Reno, Jesse had his appendix out, but it was just the same with his second marriage and his third marriage. It was the life he led, and that was what the doctors said, the emotional wear and tear and the nervous strain. They had X-rayed his gall bladder. They had made him stand in front of a fluoroscope and drink barium, which tasted like a bad malted-milk shake. There was nothing wrong with him, but still he had indigestion, and now since the fall of France it was getting very much worse. That was why he did not want Jeffrey to talk about the war.

"I'm not talking about the war," Jeffrey said.

"I did not say you were, Jeffrey," Jesse answered. "I'm merely asking you not to."

Everything that Madge had said was true, but still he liked Jesse Fineman, perhaps out of habit. The place where they were sitting, downstairs at the Rockwell, was but terrible. The play that Jesse had bought and was going to try in Boston was but terrible, and so was the music that kept echoing all around them. And yet, Jesse was the one who understood that gift of Jeffrey's long before he himself knew of it. Jesse had seen that Jeffrey knew how to take a play apart and put it together again, that he had a sense of dramatic construction. It was curious, since Jesse himself was completely lacking in that sense.

"Jeffrey," Jesse said, "I've been meaning to ask you—What do you hear from Alf?"

"I had a letter from him the other day," Jeffrey said. "Alf's in San Bernardino—San Bernardino, California."

"You should be ruthless with him," Jesse said. "Is he after money?"

Jeffrey did not answer.

"Has he got a job?" Jesse asked.

"Alf gets tired of them," Jeffrey said. "You know Alf."

"That's why I say you should be ruthless with him," Jesse said.

The music was flowing all around them. Now that Alf's name was mentioned, Jeffrey realized that he would not have been there now if it had not been for Alf. Jeffrey remembered the suit that Alf had worn, belted in the back, a plum-colored suit with a yellow foulard tie.

"He sold me my first car," Jesse said. "That was 1919—November 1919."

Jeffrey was listening to the music, a tune from "The Red Mill," so old that it was hardly decent to resurrect it. It had been old even before Jeffrey was grown up. . . . "In old New York, in old New York, the peach crop's always fine."

"I remember the date exactly," Jesse said again, and Jeffrey remembered too.

It was the month after Jeffrey had come to New York and had taken a job in the City Room, down on Newspaper Row. "In old New York, in old New York, the peach crop's always fine." Alf always took a song, no matter what it was, and worked the thing to death. It was early November 1919, just after Jeffrey had learned that he had received ten thousand dollars from his grandfather's estate. The estate had been divided between himself and Ethel, and Alf had been left out. "In old New York, in old New York, the peach crop's always fine."

"I wish to God," Jeffrey said, "they'd turn that music off."

"It's interesting," he heard Jesse say, "the effect. Now Jeffrey, in the first act, with the curtain. It's a thought—perhaps there should be music offstage."

"In old New York, in old New York, the peach crop's always fine." It was exactly what Alf had been singing that day when he called on Jeffrey at the City Room of the old sheet.

24

Well, Hardly That

The City Editor at that time was Lew Brown, for whom Jeffrey had always retained a great respect and liking. The boys in the City Room and the boys at Police Headquarters called Lew Brown a fish-eyed, stuck-up bastard, and they always said they weren't going to stay there sweating their hearts out for any son-of-a-bitch who talked like a college professor, but they were afraid of Lew Brown. There wasn't any loafing, and there wasn't any sitting around chewing the fat in Lew Brown's City Room. As far as anyone could tell, he never seemed to get around anywhere, but he knew the city inside out. Lew Brown was a Harvard man, which was something of a handicap, and he wore a Phi Beta Kappa key on his watchchain. He had been through Law School and he always said that law was a great foundation for newspaper work. When he finally got fired—they were hiring them and firing them very quickly in those days—he ran the Washington Bureau for another paper, and ended up, in the uncertain days of the Roosevelt administration when everybody sought avidly for news behind the news, as a syndicated columnist with an income of fifty thousand a year. He was a very able man.

He hired Jeffrey because Jeffrey was a Harvard man himself and back from the war with previous newspaper experience. He first sent Jeffrey to help Art Swasey on the waterfront and two weeks later he pulled Jeffrey back to the office to work on rewrite, which was not a bad idea, because Jeffrey wrote clean copy fast.

Jeffrey was doing rewrite at half-past six that evening when one of the copy boys told him that a guy was outside in the waiting room asking for him. Jeffrey could remember the yellow sheet of paper in his machine and the sounds of the other typewriters and the ringing of the telephones in the booths. The night shift was just beginning to come in and his job was very nearly over.

"He's a big guy," the copy boy said. "He says he's your brother."

The news surprised Jeffrey very much, for no one back at home had known where Alf was, when Jeffrey had been there last. Jeffrey had not seen Alf for so long that his ideas of what Alf was like had lost their definition. Although he was busy at the moment, he got up right away and walked to the uncomfortable cubicle that was known as "the waiting room." The waiting room was just off the elevators lighted by a single globe on the ceiling and without much ventilation. It was furnished as uncomfortably as possible, presumably to discourage anyone's waiting there. It was presided over by a sour unhappy girl with whom Alf was chatting when Jeffrey came in.

"Listen, loveliness," he heard Alf saying, "this is a hell of a dump for you and me to be in, loveliness."

The sour girl did not look so sour as Alf was speaking.

"Loveliness," Alf was saying, "put down that *True Love Story Magazine*. You don't need it. I'm here now. 'All I want is a little bit of love, just a little bit of love from you.'"

You could see that she was a nice girl, and not used to being addressed in such a manner, but still she did not wholly mind it.

For the first time in his life Jeffrey was able to look at Alf as though he were a stranger. He could see that Alf was noisy and that his clothes were in bad taste, and perhaps Alf experienced a similar feeling of unfamiliarity and was particularly boisterous because of it.

"Hi, kid," Alf said. "Well, by God, if it isn't the kid." He took Jeffrey by both shoulders and shook him. "This is my kid brother, loveliness. Mike and Ike, do we look alike?"

Jeffrey wished that Alf would not make so much noise, and he hoped that they did not look alike, but still, something made him laugh. "Don't mind him," Alf said. "He's slow, loveliness. Why didn't you look me up, kid? This is a hell of a note, making me come here."

"How could I?" Jeffrey asked. "I didn't know where you were."

Alf gave Jeffrey's shoulders another shake.

"It's the same old kid," Alf said. "God damn it, aren't you glad to see me?"

"Yes," Jeff said, "of course I'm glad."

"Well, act glad," Alf said. "I didn't put a tack in your pants, kid. Get your hat and let's get out of here."

"I'm sorry, Alf," Jeffrey said, "I'm busy, but I'll be through in twenty minutes."

"Twenty minutes," Alf shouted, "I park myself here for another twenty minutes? Listen kid, a man like me can't wear his pants off on these chairs."

But Jeffrey knew that Alf would wait, and he was back in twenty minutes.

"Alf," he asked, "where do you want to go? There's a little place to eat–"

Alf took him by the arm and pushed him toward the elevator.

"We don't eat in any little place," Alf said. "The car's downstairs. I've got a date uptown," and then in the elevator he began to sing, "In old New York, in old New York, the peach crop's always fine." The other people in the elevator stared at them, obviously thinking that Alf had been drinking.

"What car?" Jeffrey asked.

"My car," Alf answered. "She's a two-seater, and she's a pretty little job."

"Get out!" Jeffrey said. "You don't own a car!"

"Well," Alf answered, "it's mine for tonight. We're taking it to show a customer, and we're going to buy him dinner. Come on, kid."

A new Buick runabout was standing on Park Row, close to the roaring traffic over Brooklyn Bridge. In the present it would have been an incongruous awkward sight, but back there it was so shining and beautiful that people slowed their steps to look.

"It's not a bad can," Alf said. "Have you got a girl? You let me know and I'll buzz you over sometime. It knocks them for a row, kid. There's nothing like a car."

Madge and her family had moved to town by then and Jeffrey had been seeing too much of Madge, her family thought. Jeffrey had a brief sickening picture of Alf, with his purple coat that was belted in the back, taking him in that Buick to call on her, but in another way he was impressed by Alf.

It was a warm night for November with a gentle west breeze that made the air and the streets clean and fresh. Alf said that he could get everything there was out of this can, and it was quite a can. Alf slouched behind the wheel and pulled his hat over his eyes. They made a U turn, and passed the old Post Office and turned uptown on Broadway. Lower Broadway was a sleepy place at that hour, but farther on there were more and more lights and more traffic and more pedestrians, but they did not bother Alf. Jeffrey wished he did not feel the way he did about Alf, secretive and anxious that Alf should not know too much about him, but there had been no need to be anxious. Alf did the talking, all about himself. Alf had been everywhere. Alf could land on his feet anywhere. He had been over with the Rainbow Division, and to hell with that. He had been a clerk in a store and he had hopped a train to Los Angeles. He had picked oranges in California and he had sold copies of Dr. Eliot's Five Foot Shelf of Books, because he was a great salesman. Alf did not know why it was, but he could sell anything—books, cars, or anything—and it was easy, now that everyone had lots of money. They stopped for the traffic at Times Square, and then turned west.

"Where are we going, Alf?" Jeffrey asked.

He had been in New York for such a short time that the traffic and the electric signs around Times Square confused him, although he would not have admitted it. Alf stopped the car at the curb and a doorman in a bright blue coat ran toward them.

"You're a hell of a guy to work on a newspaper," Alf said. "Don't you know your way around? We're going downstairs at the Rockwell. Give the nice man four bits, kid. Brother, watch the car."

It was strange having the past mingle with the present downstairs at the

Rockwell. It was like the technique of a dramatic flash-back, fading lights, and twenty years earlier . . . and, in no time, there was the old Rockwell bar with its brass rail and the old beer steins and the dark oak tables and the grill in back where they did the steaks.

"Hey, buddy," Alf called to the headwaiter, "give us a table, bud." And Jeffrey wished that Alf would not call the headwaiter "bud." "We'll have a drink, but we won't order yet. If a gentleman asks for a Mr. Wilson, show him over here."

They sat opposite each other at a table in the corner.

"What's your snort, kid?" Alf asked.

"What's that?" Jeffrey asked.

"Jesus," Alf said, "can't you speak English, kid? Waiter, the kid can't speak English. Make it two side-cars, bud."

Jeffrey felt his face grow red.

"Make mine a dry Martini," he said, then he saw Alf stare at him, and he knew that Alf was sorry. The trouble was that their old relationship was gone, with nothing to take its place.

"Kid," Alf said, "you're kind of different, but I always knew that you'd be quite a kid." Then before Jeffrey could answer, he began humming again, " 'In old New York, in old New York, the peach crop's always fine.' "

"You're in the money," Alf said. "You're pretty lucky, kid."

Of course Jeffrey knew that Alf was referring to their grandfather's estate. He wanted to tell Alf that he thought it had not been fair, but Alf stopped him before he could start.

"Forget it," Alf said, "I suppose you've heard a lot about me, kid."

"What about you?" Jeffrey asked. Alf was looking at him, still smiling. "Old Nestleroade at the bank talked, didn't he?"

"I don't know what you're talking about," Jeffrey said.

Alf's expression changed, and he sighed.

"Well," he said, "forget it, kid," and then the drinks came, and whatever it had been that Alf wanted him to forget, Alf seemed to have forgotten himself. He stood up and waved his napkin.

"Hey, Jesse," he called, "come and get it, Jesse."

You could almost create that effect right now with lights and that tune from "The Red Mill." Jesse Fineman was walking toward them, downstairs at the Rockwell, and he looked much the same then as he did now. Perhaps his indigestion had always kept Jesse thin. Jesse had been wearing a blue double-breasted coat and a shirt with a blue-and-white-striped collar and even then he carried a cane.

"Your car's outside, Jesse," Alf said. "Right off the floor this morning, and believe you me, you won't regret it, Jesse, and this is my kid brother. Jeff, shake hands with Mr. Jesse Fineman. My brother's in the newspaper game."

Jeffrey wished that Alf would not talk so loudly, but Mr. Fineman did not appear to mind.

"I'm glad to meet you," Jesse Fineman said. "I was in the newspaper business once myself."

"Hey, bud," Alf called to the waiter. "Bring the minoo. Take a look at Mr. Fineman, kid. He's somebody for you to eat with."

"Oh, come now," Jesse Fineman said, "hardly that."

"You don't know who you're eating with," Alf said. "Jesse Fineman's in the theatrical game."

"Hardly that," Jesse Fineman said, "only in a small way."

Back in those days, Jesse could not have helped selling himself if he had tried. Alf was selling the car all through dinner, and Jesse was selling himself. Jesse was saying that he needed the car if he had to pass the week end with stage personalities. When you were dealing with stage personalities, Jesse said, it was necessary to do things right. If the Old Man sent him around to see George Arliss, for instance—good old George, a truly great actor and a grand man—and sometime he must tell them what he said to George and what George said to him at a party that Margaret Anglin had given (dear Margaret)—why, it would make all the difference if he could take George out for a ride. And Julia and Ina, they liked to have you ride up in a car when you went to see them—he meant Julia Sanderson and Ina Claire, of course; he just unconsciously referred to them by their first names. When he talked to Ina about a new vehicle, it would help to take Ina for a spin. And Walter Hampden liked motoring, and someday Jesse would tell them something perfectly killing about Walt that happened backstage at the Little Theater. Some night they must all go to the Little Theater. All he had to do was to ask for the house seats.

Later, Jeffrey knew that it was impossible for Jesse to have had more than a nodding acquaintance with any of these people, and that certainly Lee Shubert and Florenz Ziegfeld would not have known him if he had handed them their hats . . . but at the time, that monologue had the scintillating effect that Jesse intended.

It must have been in the middle of the dinner that Jeffrey made up his mind to speak about what he was writing. He was eating lobster, and Jesse Fineman was eating a mutton chop, and Jesse had been telling just how he had been a newspaper man once himself. Jeffrey supposed that he must have felt toward Jesse as one feels toward anyone who has the power to do a favor, and he knew that his voice sounded strained.

"I wonder if you would mind giving me a little advice, Mr. Fineman," Jeffrey said. His words seemed to make Jesse Fineman watchful and Jeffrey reached for his glass and took a quick swallow of water. "That is, if it wouldn't bother you. I have an idea for a play. I don't know how I got it, but I've worked on it in my spare time."

He stopped and tried to laugh. He could see Alf frowning at him because Alf was selling a car to Mr. Fineman and he did not want anything to interfere with it.

"Everybody on a newspaper is always writing something, I guess," Jeffrey said. "I guess you know that as well as I do. Well, I've written a sort of play."

Alf told him not to bother Mr. Fineman, and what was he doing, trying to write a play? But Jesse Fineman had been nice about it, not that he was in the least interested, but still, he was polite. Jesse drew a pigskin wallet from his pocket and produced a printed business card.

"We're rather crowded with scripts just now," he said, "but if you call sometime, I shall be glad to look it over personally."

"That's awfully kind of you," Jeffrey said. "I hope it isn't asking too much."

Jesse Fineman put his pocketbook away inside his double-breasted coat. "Hardly that," he said, "well, hardly that."

"Come on, Jesse," Alf said, "it's time for that spin in the Park. Hey, bud, bring the check. You'll excuse us, won't you Jeff? It's too crowded with three in the seat."

Jeffrey wondered why Alf had asked him there at all, but not for long. Alf too was reaching in his inside pocket and pulling out his wallet.

"Hell, what the hell?" Alf said. "Slip me something, will you, kid?"

"What?" Jeffrey asked.

"Anything you've got in your pants," Alf said. "You don't want Jesse here to pay for your dinner, do you?"

"No," Jeffrey said, "give me the check, Alf."

"That's the kid," Alf said. "Come on, Jesse, we'll leave the kid to pay it. 'That's the way the money goes. Pop, goes the weasel.' "

Jeffrey sat watching while Alf and Jesse Fineman walked out of downstairs at the Rockwell. All that time was filled with a strange golden glow. There was love in it and there was time for everything, plenty of time. He was young enough so that those days always possessed a sort of immortality. Jeffrey picked up the check and reached in his trouser pocket. The dinner check was very large—eight dollars and seventy-five cents. It was lucky that he carried money with him. It was lucky that he had ten dollars.

He supposed that something like that came to everyone in some way. Long afterwards when he read that play of his, it was sophomoric and mawkish; but back there it must have had a certain value, because they had thought it might be something for Ruth Chatterton, and they bought the option. He did not realize until later that entertainment money was very easy at that time.

All that was important was the way he felt and what it did for him. When he got the check and put it in the bank, he was not conscious of walking; there was only that golden glow . . . he could feel that same glow now. The Rockwell was plywood now and the lighting was indirect. He knew a lot more about financial dealings now, but there was Jesse Fineman sitting across the table and they were sitting not so far from where that older table had been, downstairs at the Rockwell.

"Jesse," Jeffrey said, "do you remember when you bought that option? Fifteen hundred dollars was an awful lot of money."

Jeffrey and Madge used to meet sometimes near the Library on Fifth Avenue, not that Madge cared what anybody thought any more than he did. Madge said that it was all too beautiful for anyone to spoil and she did not care what happened, and it was true. She did not care. He used to see her coming toward him when he waited near the steps by the Public Library, walking as straight as though she had been a soldier, her chin held in that queer high way, as soon as they saw each other they would hurry toward each other faster, and Madge would take his arm and press it tight to her side, and then they would walk along up Fifth Avenue in the dark. There always was that moment when she seemed a little strange, and he must have seemed that way to her. They must have both wondered sometimes what on earth they were doing there, but in a second this was over. She would have to get back in time for dinner, back where her winter house was on Murray Hill between Lexington and Park. There was never time enough to tell each other everything.

He could never remember exactly what they talked about, although it must have been intensely real to both of them. He supposed that the truth was that he had wanted something different from what he had, and that the same was true with her, and that each of them had represented in some vivid way a totally unformed wish of what the other wanted. It was the same sort of motivation that caused city girls on dude ranches to fall in love with cowboys, and vice versa, but he never could think of it quite in that way, or see himself as Madge must have seen him. Of course, he must have been gauche in a great many ways. He must have been like all the other thousands who came to New York from somewhere else and who were educated in what might be termed "the American Way" and who were totally oblivious of what politicians now term "the inequities." Nevertheless, he could not see himself as the sort of person whom Madge's mother had once referred to as "a mere adventurer." He could think of himself as a very decent sort of person trying to fit into a type of life which he could not understand. When two people were in love the way he and Madge were, nothing could make much sense and he was glad of it, because it would have spoiled the memory. He would never be such a fool again or so utterly inexperienced or so brave or so gentle. It was all too poignant for any sort of repetition.

Years later, when he was out in Hollywood working on a script for Paramount, he tried in vain to put those early impressions into words. The director was Hal Bliss who had a very good sense of pictorial drama, and Mae Jackson from the studio had written the script which he had been called from New York to rewrite. The electric fan was going and the Venetian blinds were drawn, and from the music department across the way he could hear the ceaseless tinkling of pianos.

"Good-by," someone was calling outside, "good-by, you lovely people."

It was obviously a new and charming phrase to the person saying it, because he called it out again.

"Good-by, you lovely people."

Hal Bliss was sweating through a salmon-colored sport shirt and all the doors were closed. Mae was in blue slacks, and she did not look well in slacks, but then, none of them cared how they looked.

"Now, let's see if we can get away from it and get on top of it," Hal said.

"It's where they fall in love. I want to get the feel of it, where they fall in love."

Hal made a grasping gesture at the air in front of him to show how he wanted to get the feel of it.

"Perhaps they don't meet cute enough," Mae said.

You could not get away from the studio jargon. "Meeting cute" meant roughly that our hero did something like stepping on a banana peel, losing his balance and sliding on his behind up to the girl, though of course there were infinite variations.

"No," Hal said, "I can't express it. I'm talking of reality."

It made Jeffrey think of the stages outside and of the experts manufacturing cobwebs and artificial dust, but Hal was right, they had to talk about reality.

"They might meet with a little conflict," Mae said, and she must have liked the idea, because she pulled at her slacks. "Suppose he says something—this is only very rough, of course—something that makes her think he's just a playboy, just Café Society, and that makes her mad and she says she only likes people who do something with their hands or brains, and he gets a little mad, too, so that he won't tell her that he's just that type. Then something happens, and she sees it, and then they come together."

Hal rubbed his sleeve across his face.

"Is that real?" Hal said. "I'm just asking. Is it real?"

"It's just the old corn again," Jeffrey said. "I don't think there's much conflict when people fall in love."

"My God," Hal said, "how do they do it, so you can see it in the pictures? Millions of people do it every day, but I ask you. *How* do they fall in love?"

"Well, how did you?" Mae said. "You boys ought to know."

"Now," Hal said, "don't leave yourself out of it. How about you, darling?"

"Yes," Mae answered, "yes, I ought to know."

It was a very curious conversation. They sat there like card players looking at the hands which had been dealt them by their private lives, thinking of things which they would never tell anyone, and no one said anything for a while. There was only the sound of the fan and the pianos from the music department.

"Good-by." It was the same actor outside, trying it again. "Good-by again, you lovely people."

"There isn't any trick about it," Jeffrey said, "you just meet and you fall in love."

No one answered. Jeffrey did not care what those other two were thinking. He was thinking about Madge, and they were in love again. He did not care what circumstances had brought them to it. They were in love again. . . .

He was waiting for her again in the downstairs parlor of that brownstone house between Lexington and Park. He was calling there, although she had told him it would be better if he didn't. He was standing waiting, not caring whether it was better or not, in one of those formal parlors which now had practically vanished along with the brownstone stoops of New York. Of course, the house was still standing and he had seen it the last time he had crossed through that street. Its windows were dull and dusty and litter was blown upon the steps, and it was for sale, like other Murray Hill houses which had been speakeasies in the late Twenties. That was the way it was now, but it was not the way he still saw it. It was December 1919, and the parlor smelled of soap and wax as a well-kept parlor should, and the electric lights were glowing in the chandelier. He was standing on the rose-colored Persian carpet, waiting. Then he heard Madge coming down the stairs in quick little jumps the way she used to run. He remembered the catch of her breath when she saw him.

"Darling," she whispered, "it's all right. No one's here." Then she was in his arms, and he heard her say, "Oh, darling." It was better in the house. Half the time they could only make believe they kissed each other when they met outside.

He was holding her close to him. There were no years, no children, no servants, no illnesses, no boredom of being too much together to spoil it. There was no predictable future, nothing but the present. They were in love again. There was nothing to stand between them, no quarrels over friends, no divergence of taste or of ambition. He was young again, not cautious, not careful, not afraid.

"Madge," he said, "you're beautiful."

"So are you," she said.

He knew he was not beautiful, but he knew what she meant. No one could change what they said or did; no one could take it away.

"Madge," he said, "that play."

"What play?" she asked.

It was like her, although of course he did not notice it at the time. She had wanted him for something else. She had never known that side of him.

"The play I wrote," he said, and then he told her what had happened. He told her he had sold the option. He did not know exactly what an option was and neither did she, in those days. He told her he had sold it for fifteen hundred dollars. She drew away from him, but she still held his hand. They did not look at each other, but he knew what they both were thinking.

"Jeff," she said, "I don't know much about it. Could you write one again?"

Of course, he did not know much about it, either. He had only written it in his spare time. If nothing more came of it, he could easily write another.

"All right," she said. "Now they can't say anything." Then before he could answer, she looked up at him quickly, the way she sometimes did, when he should have spoken.

"You want to, don't you, Jeff?"

"Yes," he said, "I want to."

"You can back out if you don't."

"No," he said, "I want to."

"It's funny," Madge said. "I don't care what they say. You'd better wait and we'll see them now. It's funny, I'm not afraid."

He remembered that she said it again. She always had a way of making things sound simple, even when she did not understand them. He could recall the exact note of her voice. It was not as much a question as begging him to share something which was too much for her alone.

"I like it, don't you like it, Jeff?"

25

He Had to Call on Jim

It was always a gamble what sort of audience you would get in Boston for the tryout of a play. Sometimes it would be made up of groups that had the mistaken idea that it was going to be musical comedy; sometimes the audience would consist of students, and sometimes of the subscribers to the Watch and Ward Society. Thus the tryout, the only purpose of which was to get the reaction of the average theater public, was apt to have no value. Nevertheless, Jeffrey was very glad that they were going to try this play in Boston because it meant that he could take the time to go out to Cambridge to see Jim. He and Jesse had come up on the club car of the one o'clock and they got to the suite at the Ritz about twenty minutes before six. The big sitting room was already filled with the sort of people who appeared at a time like that, and waiters already were coming up with the bowls of ice, and milk, and tomato juice and sandwiches. Bill Lucas, who was doing the publicity, was there and Jesse's secretary, Hazel, and of course the cast and the stage managers and the property people. There were some reporters, piling their overcoats on the floor beside the chairs and hurrying over to the table to help themselves to whisky. The press photographers were setting up lights in the corner, crawling about on their hands and knees looking under chairs and divans for electric outlets in the baseboards and asking people please not to trip over the extension cords and asking Miss Rogers, please, if she would not sit on the sofa and talk intimately with Mr. Jessup, please, and if Mr. Fineman would not lean over the sofa behind them, please, and say something amusing so that they could look up and smile, please, and they might all be looking at a magazine or something, please. And then who was it that wrote the play? Oh yes, Mr. Breakwater. If Mr. Breakwater would just sit on the sofa with Miss Rogers, sir, and just hold a piece of paper like Mr. Breakwater was telling Miss Rogers about some hot piece in the play, sir; and could Mr. Breakwater maybe pull down his coat a little in front, sir? And it was just a suggestion, sir, but since Mr. Breakwater was not wearing garters, could he lower his trouser leg over his right sock, please? And at the same time one of the feature writers wanted to see Mr. and Mrs. Breakwater for just a minute to ask them if they were not excited and not glad they had come to Boston.

It was all the same, like any number of similar times. Dick Breakwater's eyes had the glazed look of the eyes of other playwrights, but when Jeffrey saw him, he felt a slight twinge of jealousy. He wished that he had stuck to writing his own plays instead of discovering that he was one of the few people who could rewrite and adapt someone else's work. He felt as coldly professional as a house physician. He found himself wondering how temperamental Breakwater would be and what would be the best way to handle him when they sat alone, as they certainly would, in the small hours of the morning, taking parts of the Breakwater work to pieces, cutting lines and writing in new ones. Actually, Jeffrey was doubtful about the play as he had seen it. He still did not know whether it had enough in it to open in New York, and he was the one who would have to decide.

"Dick," he said, "how did they do this afternoon?"

It was only a question asked because he had to say something. A young playwright never knew how anybody did and Dick was saying that as far as he could see, they were horsing it. He had never liked Ruth Rogers and he wished that Jeffrey would speak to Ruth, and Marianna did not understand what he wanted, at all, although he had tried to make it as clear as he could without being rude. He did not know where Marianna was, just when it was very important to explain to her what he meant in the lines in the break-up scene—he knew that Miss Miller was a great artist, but he did want her to see what he meant, and then she could do what she wanted with it; but just when there was a chance to go over it with her she had gone away somewhere to tea. He did not think it was kind of Marianna. He thought the brutal truth was that Miss Miller did not like him personally. If Jeffrey would only talk to Miss Miller, Miss Miller might listen to him about the break-up scene, because he knew that he and Jeffrey felt the same way about it. It was just that piece where she put down the picture. She should not slam it down. She knew it was all over when she put down the picture, but there should be regret, a certain tenderness.

"And now if Mr. Fineman and Mr. Jessup will sit together on the sofa, please," the photographers said.

"Dick, dear," Mrs. Breakwater was saying. "Look at the orchids that Mr. Fineman sent me. Mr. Wilson, can't you get Dick to lie down?"

"Yes, Dick," Jeffrey said, "just keep your shirt on, Dick." Then he said that Dick Breakwater did not know what a good job he had done. He was too close to it to know. You had to butter everybody up and talk the strange double talk of the theater at a time like that, and it helped, even if no one believed it. But there was no reason for him to stay there indefinitely, building up uncertain egos and whistling in the dark, because his own work of surgery would not come till later. It was better to be out of that atmosphere and to maintain his perspective before he became emotionally involved and before he became deceived himself by that artificial optimism. He went farther down the hall to his own room facing Newbury Street and called up Jim at Lowell House in Cambridge. It was always hard for Jeffrey to remember that Jim and nearly everybody else had their own telephones in those houses, but then there was a great deal about Jim that was hard to remember.

"Hello," he heard Jim say, "is that you, Pops?"

"Listen," he said, "don't call me 'Pops.' "

"Do you want me to come in town?" Jim asked.

Jeffrey supposed that Jim would have liked the excitement just as much as he had liked it once, but the last thing he wanted was to see Jim with all that crowd.

"No," Jeffrey said. "Get me a chicken sandwich and a glass of milk. I'll have supper in your room."

"You mean you want to have a quiet little talk?" Jim said.

He could tell that Jim was disappointed, for every tone of Jim's voice was completely familiar to him.

"Well," Jim said, "okay."

"In about twenty minutes," Jeffrey said, and that was all.

When he put down the receiver, and when Jim's voice was gone, Jim seemed to have been more in his thoughts than actually speaking. He wondered whether this were so with other people's children, whether other people had them in their thoughts as he did, somewhere in the back of everything immediate. Jim had been away for years at school and college, and yet they had a sort of relationship that they could take up again, no matter where it was broken off.

Jeffrey was just picking up his overcoat and hat when someone knocked. It was Jessica, Marianna's colored maid, quite a character, like all theatrical maids.

"Mr. Jeffrey, Miss Marianna, she wants to see you." Jessica lowered her voice although there was no one in the corridor who could possibly hear. "She's been asking and asking for you. It seems like all day, Miss Marianna —she's been asking."

Marianna was lying on the couch in her sitting room. The bedroom door was open and the bed was covered with dresses.

"Darling," Marianna said, "thank God you've come. There's something you must promise me."

"What?" Jeffrey asked.

"Promise me I don't have to set eyes on Jesse Fineman before I go on. I can stand anything, if I just don't have to see Jesse, and promise me you'll stay and take me over yourself. Stay with me, Jeff, please."

Marianna was always like that before an opening, but now, familiar though her words were, they had a possessive note. It seemed to Jeffrey that they were lovers when she held out her hands to him. She was not only asking, she was taking it for granted that he would stay, and she spoke again before he had a chance to answer.

"Darling," she asked him, "what's the matter? You have your worried look."

"It's only the crowd," Jeffrey said, "I'm never used to them." And he smiled at her, while she lay there looking up at him.

"I always know when you're worried," she said, "it's in your eyes. It's in the corners of your mouth."

"It's like Jesse," Jeffrey answered, "just nervous indigestion, sweet."

"I like to know what you're thinking," she said. "I nearly always know."

"That's fine," Jeffrey said, "keep your mind on me. Don't think about yourself."

"I don't," she said, "when I see you, I never do. Don't look so worried. You're glad to see me, aren't you?"

"Yes," he answered, "awfully glad."

"Then sit down, and we'll have supper. Sit down, and don't let anybody in."

"I can't," Jeffrey answered, "I'll see you before the curtain. I've got to go out and see Jim."

Marianna sat up and leaned toward him.

"I wouldn't ordinarily," he said, "I've been thinking about Jim quite a lot. You see—it's this damned war."

"The war?" she repeated.

"Yes," he said, "the war."

"Darling," she said, "I know what you mean. Don't look so worried."

"I just want to see him," Jeffrey answered. "I don't see him very often."

"Of course, you have to go," she said. "There may not be much time."

"I didn't say that," he answered.

"No," she said, "I know you didn't."

She stopped. He was still surprised that she had guessed what he was thinking.

"You see, I love you, dear," she said.

* * *

Just by the steps that led to the revolving door on Arlington Street were two tables side by side with two pretty girls behind them. One was selling buttons for the British War Relief, and the other was selling handkerchiefs and cigarette cases for the Free French. He should have bought something as he went by, but he did not. It was a quarter past six already.

There had never been any places like Lowell House when Jeffrey had lived in Cambridge and yet all sorts of attitudes which he had outgrown remained. When he knocked on Jim's door, he could not entirely get away from an impression that he was calling on himself—so many of his wishes were there, and so much that he had left behind him.

Still he knew that Jim was not like him. He had never even lived in a room like Jim's. There were black wooden chairs in it with the Harvard seal upon their backs, a desk, a bookcase, and the rug that Madge had given him, and photographs on the wall of boys in rows, one row standing up and the other row sitting down in front. When he saw Jim again he saw a good deal of himself. It was what Minot Roberts had said. He had the same eyes and the same posture, but Jeffrey had never worn a tweed coat and gray slacks and those shoes that looked like slippers.

There were two other boys in the room to whom Jim introduced him. This is So-and-so, my father, and So-and-so, my father—Jeffrey did not listen to their names, when they called him "sir" and shook hands. He knew that he should say something to put them all at their ease, until he realized that they were more at ease than he was. He was pleased that they were there because it meant that Jim was not keeping his friends from him.

"Well," Jeffrey said, "it's comfortable up here," and the boys said, Yes, sir, the rooms were very nice; and then in a few minutes they said they must be going and that they were very glad to have met him, sir.

"Jim," he said. "I get on pretty well with most people, but I don't know what to say to boys."

"It's all right," Jim said, "they didn't expect you to say anything. It's all right, as long as you didn't pretend to be a boy yourself."

"I know," Jeffrey said, "I know what you mean."

"Besides," Jim said, "they wanted to see you. When I told them you were coming, they had plenty of time to go."

It was surprising how grateful and relieved it made him feel. Everything was just the way it always had been between himself and Jim.

"It's funny coming here," he said, "and seeing you the way you are, and thinking of the way I used to be."

"How's everything at home?" Jim asked. "How's Ma?"

"She's fine," Jeffrey said. "We spent the other week end at your Aunt Beckie's and your Uncle Fred's."

"You did, did you?" Jim said. "How did she ever get you there?"

Jeffrey laughed. It still amazed him that Jim was old enough to see things that way.

"Where did you get that coat?" Jeffrey asked. "You look like a golf professional."

Jim looked down at his coat. It had yellow stripes and woven leather buttons.

"It's quite a number," Jim said, "what's the matter with it?"

"It's too yellow," Jeffrey said. Never in his life would he have worn such a coat, but it looked all right on Jim.

"Don't come here and tear me to pieces," Jim said, "it isn't fair. Here's your milk and sandwich, or maybe you'd like a drink."

"You mean you keep liquor here?" Jeffrey asked, and then he supposed that everyone did and that Jim was old enough.

It was hard to see Jim in perspective, for Jim seemed to have grown up suddenly, without his knowing it, and Jeffrey still kept thinking of Jim in short trousers and of Jim when he used to take him on Sunday to see the animals in Central Park and to sail toy boats in the boat pond. He had seen more of Jim than he had of the other children because there had not been so much money when Jim was a little boy. He remembered Jim's nurses, and taking Jim to school, and now there Jim was with his hands in his pockets asking if he wanted a drink. It was confusing, thinking of him as entirely grown-up, but that was the way Jeffrey wanted to consider him—as someone who had tastes and ideas of his own and with a personality which one must respect. Jeffrey tried to see him as he might see someone whom he had just met, and he had very much the same glow of satisfaction which he experienced, very rarely, when he had written something he had liked.

"I didn't come here to pull you to pieces," he said. "I like to talk to people I like. I've always liked you."

He had never said so much before, and now he felt embarrassed and he knew that Jim did, too.

"I've always liked you, too," Jim said.

There was a confused silence, but it was not the sort of silence that he minded. They seemed to be saying in that silence all sorts of things that they probably never would say. When he looked at Jim, he felt a lump rising in his throat. He had never thought of him before as being so physically perfect, or so close to being beautiful, although he supposed he was not thinking of Jim as much as he was thinking of youth. There was that perfect co-ordination and that queer fearlessness. Then suddenly he wanted to skip it, because if he did not skip it, if he did not think of something else, he would make a fool of himself. He could not imagine what had put him in such a mood. He poured his milk from the little cardboard container into the glass.

"Oh, hell!" he said. "Well, it's great to be young."

"You think so?" Jim said. "Did you used to think so?"

"No," Jeffrey answered, "you only think so later."

"Listen," Jim said, "there's something I want to ask you."

Jeffrey wished that he did not instinctively assume a defensive, careful attitude when Jim wanted to ask him anything. His first thought was what it always was, that Jim was in some sort of trouble, probably about money.

"Well," Jeffrey said, "don't stand there. Go ahead and ask me."

"How old were you when you got married?" Jim asked.

Jeffrey put his hands carefully on the arms of the black wooden chair. "What makes you ask?" he said.

"Oh, nothing much," Jim said. "I was just wondering, that's all."

Jim was half sitting, half leaning against the desk, swinging one leg carelessly in front of him. Jeffrey remembered noticing Jim's heavy knitted sock.

"Jim," he said, "is it that girl? The one you told me about last spring? What's her name—Sally Sales?"

It was not fair. When you were old, you knew too much and you guessed too quickly. He saw Jim's expression of surprise and he saw it had been a secret which Jim had not intended to tell him.

"Don't tell Mother," Jim said. "I was just thinking. I know it's silly."

"That's all right," Jeffrey said, "I won't tell anyone."

It was pathetic that Jim knew it sounded silly. It stopped him from saying all sorts of things he might have. When Jeffrey looked at him, when he thought of all the rest of it, it was not silly.

"It's a pretty serious thing, getting married, Jim," he said.

It was not entirely what he had meant to say.

"I know," Jim said, "you don't have to tell me, but you can't help thinking, can you?"

"No," Jeffrey said, "of course you can't." He felt a certain respect for Jim, a furtive sort of sympathy.

"If you feel that way," he said, "she must be quite a girl. I'd like to see her, Jim."

"You'd like her," Jim said. His voice was suddenly warm and his words came faster. "Of course, I was just thinking. You're not laughing at me, are you?"

"No," Jeffrey said, "of course not."

"I'll tell you why I was thinking about it," Jim said. "Of course I couldn't do anything about it. I'm not as crazy as all that, but maybe we'll be in the war. I was just thinking if I got through it and we felt the same way we feel now—"

Jeffrey found himself sitting up straighter. Something seemed to be in the room, just behind him.

"There's a lot of talk around here about whether we ought to get in it or keep out of it," Jim said, "but it looks as though we won't have much to say about it. Of course, if we get into it, I want to do what you did. I don't want to wait to be drafted. I'm keeping on with Military Science."

"Yes," Jeffrey said, "I know, you told me you were going to."

"You like it, don't you?" Jim asked him. "What's the matter? I thought you'd like it."

"Yes," Jeffrey said, "I approve of it. I'd be doing it myself."

It was back with him, as though he were living it again, only Jim was living it now, and there was not much time. It filled him with a sort of panic. No Americans were going abroad . . . there would never be another Expeditionary Force. . . . He could remember all the phrases, but they had a hollow note.

"Just remember," Jeffrey said, "we're not in this show yet. Maybe it'll be all over without our being in it, I don't know." The words did not help it, and he knew that no reasoning would. "The main thing to remember is not to take this too seriously."

Then he found himself looking at Jim in the cool appraising way that he had looked at troops long ago, as though Jim were already in uniform and not his son. He was wondering whether Jim would make a good soldier, whether he was physically sound, whether he had too much imagination.

"I didn't know you'd take it this way," Jim said.

"I'm not taking it any way," Jeffrey answered.

"Why," Jim said, "the way you act, you'd think that I was dead."

"I'd just as soon you wouldn't say that," Jeffrey said. He did not know that his voice would sound so loud and he saw that Jim looked startled. He was not behaving in a way that Jim would understand. He looked at his watch.

"I've got to get back to town," he said. "If you want to have dinner tomorrow night, I'll take you to the show, but it's quite a mess, just now."

"I should think it would drive you nuts," Jim said. "It would drive me nuts."

"Well," Jeffrey answered, "it's one way to earn your living. Maybe I wouldn't be doing it, if it hadn't been for you."

That was true enough. If it had not been for Madge and for Jim and Gwen and Charley, he would not have been rewriting other people's plays.

"I've been a lot of trouble to you, I guess," Jim said. "I guess we all have."

Jeffrey smiled at him and held out his hand.

"Let it be a lesson to you. Don't get married young," he said. "Jim, have you got enough money?"

"It's near the end of the month. I could do with a little more," Jim said, "but I don't like to keep taking it out of you."

"That's all right," Jeffrey answered. Everything was better, the way it had always been. "Call for me in town tomorrow, and I'll write you out a check. And Jim—" He paused and cleared his throat. "I think it's nice about that girl. I'd like to see her."

"I'll tell her," Jim said. "She'd like to see you, too. Why don't you ask her out to lunch sometime?"

26

We Were Young Ourselves Once

It was seven o'clock in the morning—the most uncomfortable hour of the day to Jeffrey—when he walked up the ramp from the somnolent row of Pullmans into the lights of the Grand Central Station. The station seemed to be rising out of a sullen sort of slumber. New York was always closer to being asleep at seven in the morning than at any other time. The faces of the Pullman porters and of the gate guards and of the few travelers crossing the deserted expanse by the information booth all bore a look of resentment. They all seemed to be saying that it was too early for them or for anyone else to be up. It was too early for the clothing shops and the bookstores and for most of the magazine and paper booths to be open. Nearly all the ticket windows were closed and so was the newsreel theater and so was the refreshment stand near the entrance to the subway. Outside the station on Lexington Avenue the sun was out, but the street looked bleak because it was too early. The taxicabs had a living, drooping air of cab horses standing in a rank.

Jeffrey knew that he would have felt better if he had stopped for a cup of coffee, but he wanted to get back to familiar surroundings. He was tired after a number of nights in a hotel and he wanted to get home. The taxi traveled quickly across town along the nearly empty streets. He smoothed the newspaper he had purchased across his knee. In Greece the Italians had reached the Kalamis River, wherever that might be. It was announced that German planes during the blitz had damaged, among other buildings, the Bank of England, the Tate Gallery, and Westminster Abbey. Election Day was just around the corner, and the Democrats were saying that the Republicans had nothing to offer, that Willkie agreed with the Roosevelt foreign policy and with the New Deal's social gains, but was there any reason that he could do it better? All the front page of the paper confirmed the frustration which always surrounded Jeffrey at seven o'clock in the morning. At his apartment house the elevator boys and the doorman were not on duty. The rugs had been rolled up from the floor of the entrance hall, and competent, muscular men in overalls who did not fit with the chandeliers and mirrors were working sullenly with mops.

The air in the living room was heavy; he put down his bag carefully and took off his coat and listened to the ticking of the clock. The place was still asleep, as it had been hundreds of times before when he arrived in New York from a night train. Effie and Albert would be down soon, and so he sat down on the living room sofa and lighted a cigarette. He had never liked that living room or any of that apartment. It was too bare and too pretentious, and their furniture had never fitted in it properly. The whole place seemed to be waiting for them to move out and to go somewhere else, as one always did in New York; and now, that sense of impermanence disturbed him.

It made him think of all the places they had lived in up and down New York. There had been the ground floor of the house on West 10th Street, where they had lived first—two rooms and a kitchenette which somehow involved itself intimately with the bathroom. He could never get over the idea that the rent for it had been very high, but he had liked it in the village. He could never understand why Madge had wanted to get out of it before Jim was born. Madge had not liked it because it was Bohemian, and there were too many germs there for a baby. Madge's mother had wanted to give them a nurse and she had said that they must have a maid and that she would send them her old Sophie. Jeffrey had not wanted Sophie, because he had felt that it was very important not to have Madge's family give them things. He remembered that Madge had cried in the hospital when he told her that he did not want her mother to give them a nurse. Everyone had said that he must not upset Madge just two days after Jim was born, and that had meant that suddenly he had been obliged to pay for the nurse himself and a woman named Hattie had come in by the day. It had meant that all the expenses had doubled. Nevertheless, he was still sure that he had been right about it. He had wanted Jim to be his, not his mother-in-law's child, and they had rented a room on the second floor of West 10th Street for Jim and the nurse, a very melancholy woman who had disliked men. It had been very hard to pay the bills, and this had first started his doing work on collaboration at a fixed price on every job. Even so, it had been difficult to come out even. Madge could never have stood it if they had not been so much in love.

He could see now that it must have been very hard for a girl of Madge's "traditions," as Madge's mother used to call them. That was when Madge began to be afraid that they would be Bohemian. It was the year he had done some work on the play called "Rainy Afternoon," and he had been given a substantial percentage of the author's share, the first of such arrangements that he had ever made, and the first play that he had been involved with that was close to being a hit. Then Madge had wanted to rent a little house in Scarsdale because the country would be better for Jim. Jeffrey still could feel a quiver of dislike when he thought of all the rows of little houses where everyone called on everyone else—neither the country nor the city. The year that Gwen was born they moved back to New York and lived on a floor of a brownstone house on West 18th Street, but as Madge said, the neighborhood was not good for children. Then there was the apartment on the West Side near Central Park, where the rents were lower, but Madge said that her friends never came to see her, and that year Jeffrey had made twenty thousand dollars, so they moved to the East Side.

That was the way it went. He could think of his whole life in terms of apartments, of moving days, of doormen, of visits to antique shops when they had money, of nurses' days off, of restaurants on the maid's night out, of the entertaining Madge did for her friends, of the parties which he sometimes had to give, for Madge had understood that it was necessary occasionally to entertain those "business people." It was one apartment after another, and here he was in the last one, a duplex, the largest they had ever had.

In a way, it was the summing up of everything and what Madge had always wanted, large rooms with all the cheap furniture removed, as though there had never been any, and replaced by the kind of chairs and tables that were called "important pieces" in Madison Avenue shops. It was what Madge had wanted, and what she had always tried to get, and it was what he had wanted, too, and there it was. If it had not been for the war and the income tax, there would no longer have been much worry about money, because in his way Jeffrey was an important piece, too, like one of the Georgian armchairs by the fireplace, a piece with grace, with good finish, without anything new added, a piece that fetched a good price even when business was bad. There he was, hungry and tired, with the realization, which always came to him after a night on the train, that he was not properly washed and brushed. There he was, sitting in the living room, opening a silver cigarette box, furtively, as though it were not his, and actually it was not, because Madge had bought it with her own money.

When a shuffling sound in the dining room told him that Albert or Effie was downstairs, he walked to the petit-point bellpull and pushed the little button behind it. Ringing a bell at home had always seemed to him like ringing for the curtain, obliging him to assume a proper and dignified position. He lighted his cigarette carefully and picked up the newspaper and waited, sitting up a little straighter as he heard Albert cross the dining room.

"Good morning, Albert," he said.

Albert was in his alpaca house coat. Albert looked pained and surprised. "We did not know that Mr. Wilson was coming, sir," Albert said. It was something else that Albert had learned from a book of etiquette. "Mrs. Wilson was not expecting Mr. Wilson until tomorrow."

"Well," Jeffrey said, "Mr. Wilson expects some orange juice and coffee and scrambled eggs and bacon upstairs in his study in fifteen minutes. Mr. Wilson is very hungry and he has a headache. Mr. Wilson feels like hell."

He smiled at Albert to show that he was being amusing, but he saw that Albert did not appreciate his effort. In the hall, when Jeffrey started to pick up his suitcase, Albert darted forward.

"Permit me, please, sir," Albert said.

Upstairs by the master's bedroom, the hall was still asleep. Gwen's door was closed though it was time for her to be getting up to prepare herself for Miss Spence's School—but Gwen was too big now for him to wake her up. His study door was open and a few shafts of morning light were coming through the carefully drawn curtains, crossing his desk which was covered with letters. He put his suitcase on a chair. It was filled with soiled shirts and pajamas. He had begun to open it when he remembered that Albert would unpack for him. It was still early to wake up Madge, but suddenly he wanted to talk to someone. He wanted to be convinced that he was back at home.

The Venetian blinds in the bedroom were drawn, except at one window which was open. The open window made the room cool and noisy because of the stirrings of the morning from the streets outside. It was the restless combination of sounds to which he always awakened in New York, indefinably different from any night sounds or day sounds. He could almost hear the shuffle of hurrying feet already in the rising drone of elevated trains and cross-town busses, mingling with the whistles on the river. Though the sounds were too dull to disturb him, they fitted into the background of his thoughts, making him already a part of the city.

The master's bedroom was larger than any he and Madge had ever slept in. It was furnished with her chaise longue and her bow-front bureau and the Sheraton dressing table which he had given her and his own mahogany chest-on-chest with its heavy brasses and its mirror. Even with the twin beds and the new green carpet and the chairs and the still life above the mantelpiece, the room still required more furniture. It all made him think of something that was built for another age, when nothing was too good for anyone. Madge had selected the papering herself, gay blue birds of a species he did not know, birds and baskets of flowers. The curtains were bright yellow to make it gay and the blanket covers on the twin beds were yellow too, because the color was becoming to Madge.

Madge was sound asleep. He always envied her that ability to sleep in the morning. The book she had been reading, *Country Squire in the White House*, lay beside her bed where she had dropped it, and the blue leather traveling clock, which her mother had given her, years before, was ticking beside the lamp. Her Japanese kimono was carefully folded over a chair where Effie had placed it, and her silk mules were at the base of the chair, just so. She was lying on her side, her face half-circled by her bare arm, her lips half-parted, her dark hair around her on the pillow. She looked very young there asleep. Her cheek looked very smooth and round. Her lips had that determined curve which had once made him want to laugh. That little upward curve of Madge's nose was what made her still look young, that and the roundness of her chin. There she was and there he was and all at once he did not want to waken her, and so he stood there thinking of all the other rooms which he and Madge had slept in, of the cabin on the *Bremen*, of that stuffy room at Garland's, of the corner room at the Adlon in Berlin, of the suite with the balcony at the Crillon, of the room in the front at Shepheard's the time they had gone to Cairo. He remembered, for some reason, a German and his wife in Cairo.

"The pyramids," the German had said, once when they had all taken an *apéritif* together before dinner, "were built in three phases."

"But, Karlschen," his wife had said, "I thought the pyramids were built with four faces."

"No," the German had said, and he had grown angry, "phases, phases, not faces."

There was no reason why such an anecdote should have come to his mind as he stood there looking at Madge asleep. It made him feel very kindly toward her, for a thing like that made a little joke which only they two had in common. Those were the things that you remembered when you had forgotten so much else. He remembered that the Arab had wanted more money in the inside of the pyramid and that Madge had been frightened. He remembered riding on a camel as all tourists did in Cairo, and he remembered how silly he must have looked with the drivers all shouting at him, wanting him, of course, to pay more money.

Then Madge stirred and opened her eyes.

"Why, Jeff," she said, and then the little line on her forehead grew deeper and she looked a little older, now that she was awake. "I thought you were coming tomorrow."

"Yes," he said, "I should have telephoned."

"What are you laughing at?" she asked. "Do I look funny?"

"No," he said, "phases, phases, not faces."

Her forehead wrinkled again, and then she remembered.

"Why, Jeff," she said, "what ever made you think of that?"

"I don't know," he answered, and he bent down and kissed her.

"Close the window, will you dear?" she said. "Jeff, Effie and Albert are leaving."

"All right," Jeffrey said.

"Albert thinks you don't like him," Madge said. "I told him of course you did, but Effie says that Albert can't work for anyone who doesn't like him."

"What does he want me to do," Jeffrey asked, "kiss him?"

He was glad that Madge was awake, and the news that Albert and Effie were leaving seemed to draw them closer together.

"Jeff," she said, "get me that kimono, will you?" And he wrapped it around her shoulders and sat on the edge of the bed.

"Darling," Madge said, "how was everything?"

That was what she always asked him when he came back from anywhere.

"Everything?" he said. "Everything was about as usual."

"Well," Madge said, "tell me about everything."

"Well," Jeffrey said, "it was about the same. I'm glad you didn't come. You didn't miss much."

"Oh, Jeff," Madge said, "you never tell me anything. You used to tell me."

"No, I didn't," Jeffrey said. "You used to think I told you. Did the man come to fix the clock downstairs?"

"No," Madge said, "he didn't. I'll call him up this morning. Jeffrey, how was Dick Breakwater?"

It was hard to tell in detail how people were, and he was feeling tired.

"Just the way he always is," he said, "artistic."

"Was his wife there?"

"Yes," Jeffrey said.

"Was she attractive?"

"I don't know, Madge," Jeffrey said. "Jesse gave her some orchids."

"He sent some to me, too," Madge said.

"When Jesse is worried," Jeffrey told her, "he always sends out orchids."

"But, dear," Madge said, "how did it go? I wish you'd tell me."

"It didn't go," Jeffrey answered. "Jesse is taking it off."

"Oh, dear," Madge said. "Did you put any money in it?"

"No," Jeffrey said, "no, dear, I never put money in a Breakwater."

"Oh, dear," Madge said, "now you'll have to start on something else. How was Marianna Miller? It must be hard on Marianna, after taking it off and putting it on again and taking it off again."

"Marianna—" Jeffrey said—"oh, Marianna was all right."

He was quite sure that it was not his imagination which made him think that both her voice and his voice had changed. They had often discussed Marianna before as they discussed all those other acquaintances who moved in and out of their daily lives, but now something had set Marianna apart, and Jeffrey resented that change because there was absolutely no reason for it.

"Madge," he said, "I wish you wouldn't put such emphasis on Marianna."

"Why, Jeffrey," Madge answered, "I was just asking how she was."

"Well, I hope you haven't got the idea," Jeffrey said, "that Marianna—" and then he stopped. "There isn't anything to it, Madge."

"Why, darling," Madge answered, "did I ever say there was?"

"I know you don't like her," Jeffrey said, "but I can't help it if she has a part in something I'm working on."

"Jeffrey," Madge said, "don't be silly."

"I'm not," Jeffrey said, "I just don't want you to be."

Then he knew that the whole thing was ending up in nothing.

"Oh, Jeff," Madge said, "I'm awfully glad you're back. Of course, I've been having all the people here that you don't want to see and doing all the things that you don't want to do. I always think it's going to be fun, and it isn't. Did you miss me?"

"Yes," Jeffrey said, "I missed you."

"Did you see the living room?" Madge asked. "Did you notice?"

"Why, no," Jeffrey said, "what about it?"

"I had the secretary moved to the other side, the way you said you wanted it, and I had the piano turned around and that little upholsterer brought back the two chairs. They pep the whole place up."

He wished that she would not use the word "pep." Madge was never still, she was always moving things around.

"I didn't notice," Jeffrey said. "It's funny, I didn't."

"This is the nicest apartment we've ever had," Madge said. "You like it, don't you, Jeff?"

"Why, yes," Jeffrey said, "I like it."

"I wish you'd say whether you like things or not," Madge said. "You know I want things just the way you want them. I don't think we've ever had a place where the furniture and everything fit so well. You do like it, don't you, Jeff?"

"Yes," he answered, "I said I liked it."

"It all makes me feel so secure," Madge said. "Jeff, did you see Jim?"

It was a conversation that seemed to touch everything.

"What was he wearing?" Madge asked. "Did he look handsome? Did he look tired?" She was like every mother, reaching hopelessly toward the hidden life of a son who had left her.

"He looked very well," Jeffrey said. "Jim's all right."

"That's what you always say," Madge said. "Jeffrey, did he say anything about that girl? You know, the one he's been so crazy about, the one called Sally Sales."

Somehow her question made him careful, almost hostile—though Jim was just as much her son as his.

"Yes," he said, "he did, but that's Jim's business, Madge."

"Oh, dear," Madge said, "you don't think it's serious, do you?"

"Now, listen," Jeffrey said, "it doesn't do any good to worry about Jim."

"I'm not worrying," Madge said. "I don't know why you and Jim always think I do, but you can't see him the way a woman does. He's—well, Jim's very physically attractive. He's just the sort of boy that a girl might lose her head over. You saw the Saleses up at Fred's and Beckie's."

"Yes," Jeffrey said, "I know, I saw them."

"You saw what they were like," Madge said. "She really talked to me in the most take-it-for-granted way—as though they were engaged."

"Well," Jeffrey answered, "I don't know—suppose they are?"

"Oh, Jeff," Madge said, "I wish you wouldn't try to make a joke of it. You saw the Saleses and you know they don't amount to anything. Don't say that I'm being Freudian or jealous. I love Jim to have girls, but he's too young to have just one girl. It—it just simply isn't normal, and Jeffrey, you can tell from the Saleses what she must be like."

Jeffrey sat on the edge of the bed, looking at the wall. He could hear the dim noises of the city.

"Jeff," he heard Madge say, "I wish you'd talk to Jim. It's something a man can do much better than a woman; it's what a father's for. He'll listen to you, Jeff."

They were speaking lines which had been used again and again. They were not like individuals just then, but like types, the wife and husband, the father and mother, Mr. and Mrs. America. He knew exactly what Madge meant. When he had talked to Mrs. Sales, he had thought himself that Jim was too good for any such combination. He had thought of all the economic and social and intellectual complications. He seemed to have developed two personalities when he thought of Jim. Madge could not identify herself with Jim, as he could, or live life over in Jim again as he did.

"You know, we were pretty young ourselves," he said.

She brushed her hair back from her forehead and drew her silk kimono more closely over her shoulders.

"It wasn't the same thing at all," she answered, "you—you always looked older than Jim. Besides, you were almost twenty-four."

"Listen, Madge," he said, "if Jim is having a good time—"

"A good time," Madge repeated. Her voice had changed. "Jeffrey, you don't think he—" and her voice changed again—"he's—living with her?"

The polite phrase was always jarring. He could not see why Madge had leaped at the conclusion, and it was not fair to Jim.

"Listen, Madge," he said, "we don't know anything about it. Maybe she's a very nice girl. Jim has to start living his own life sometime, and it doesn't help to monkey with other people's lives. Just remember, Jim's grown-up."

"Darling," Madge said, "won't you please try to be sensible and not so emotional about it? No one Jim's age knows what he's doing. It's—it's simply biological."

Jeffrey stood up and walked to the window.

"I don't suppose," Jeffrey said, "you knew what you were doing?"

"No," Madge answered, "not very well. Did you?"

Jeffrey walked back across the room, and then he heard Madge laugh.

"Jeffrey," she said, "Jim has everything ahead of him. Everyone his age has."

"No," Jeffrey said, "not always." He saw Madge look up at him, startled. "I knew a good many people Jim's age who didn't."

"Why, Jeff," Madge began, and then she stopped as though they both had said something they should not have. "You don't think that we're going to get into the war now, do you?"

He drew a deep breath. It was the way it had been in Jim's room, as though something were just behind him.

"It doesn't do any good for you or me to think," he said.

"Jeff," she began. Then someone was knocking on the bedroom door. "Yes," Madge called, "what is it?"

That was the way it always was. When you were married and had children, you changed from one mood to another, passing, each day, through a gamut of moods. It was Gwen dressed ready for school.

"Oh," Gwen called, "oh, Daddy, darling."

Now he was a lovable, broken-down old gaffer again, and Gwen was kissing him, just as she knew a girl of sixteen should kiss a dear old father. "Daddy darling, your breakfast is ready in the study. You must be awfully hungry."

"Why, Jeff," Madge said. "Haven't you had breakfast, dear? I didn't mean to keep you talking."

"No, I haven't," Jeffrey answered. "I should have got a cup of coffee when I got off the train."

"But Jeff," Madge said, "why didn't you?"

He stood there looking at Gwen with her little brown hat and short skirt, his daughter, who thought he was a lovable old darling and of whom he did not know what to think, and at Madge with her new kimono with white storks on it. It occurred to him that the decorations were inappropriate. There had been too many storks.

"You see, I wanted to get home," he said.

He thought that Madge looked happy, and so did Gwen.

"Daddy," Gwen said, "you like us, don't you, Daddy?"

"God, yes," Jeffrey said. "I like you."

There they were, and there he was, tied together by that sort of accident that makes a family, tied inescapably, no matter what apartment they might live in, no matter whether the servants left, no matter whether everything split wide-open, but he was thinking about Jim. Jim might as well have been there. He wished they had not guessed that he was not entirely happy. . . .

27

The World of Tomorrow

At first Jeffrey told himself that he had always respected the privacy of other people and that he surely should respect his son's. Nevertheless, Jim had asked him to see Sally Sales. When he wrote the letter, all sorts of hesitations and trepidations emerged from his past. He seemed to be Jim's age or younger when he wrote it. In the first place he did not know whether to call her "Sally" or "Miss Sales," and there was no book of usage to help him.

> Dear Sally [he wrote]:
>
> I hope you'll excuse my calling you by your first name, but I think of you that way because Jim has told me so much about you.

Then he threw the letter away. He seemed to be building himself up into a character in a Barrie play, or worse still, becoming like the hero of a drama in which Ruth Chatterton once starred. He could almost hear Sally Sales saying, "Oh, I'm going to call you 'Daddy Long-Legs.'" The trouble was, he did not know what Sally Sales was like; all he could do was to picture her from his limited experience with girls he had known in his youth, or from the works of Scott Fitzgerald, from a few short stories in the *Saturday Evening Post*, and from his observation of his daughter Gwen who was younger. There was his niece, Ethel's child, in West Springfield—but he was sure that Sally would not be like her. Gloria wore glasses and her chin receded and her parents were saving money to send her to Wellesley College.

> Dear Sally [he wrote again]:
>
> Jim has told me so much about you that it seems strange to me that I have never seen you. I wish we could have lunch together someday, if you ever find yourself in town, only because any friend of Jim's is a friend of mine—no other reason.

He wanted to make it very definite that there was no other reason. There were any number of restaurants in New York, but each one had a certain quality. If he took her to Twenty-One, he would see people he knew who would ask him later who the little girl was. It was the sort of thing anyone would make a joke of, and later Madge would hear about it.

> I sometimes have lunch at the Echelon [he wrote], a little place on 56th Street on the right-hand side, between Fifth and Sixth Avenue, going from Fifth. I don't remember the number, but you'll see the name outside on a canopy. If you could let me know some day when you'll be in town, I'll meet you there. I suppose I might be wearing a carnation in my buttonhole, but I won't.

He crossed the last sentence out, because it sounded too cute, too much like "Daddy Long-Legs."

> You won't know what I look like, but if you ask any of the waiters for me, they'll point me out. They say I used to look just like Jim, but I don't believe that the resemblance would impress you. I do hope that you can arrange to come.
>
> Sincerely yours, . . .

He understood that he could not expect an answer immediately, but on the second day when none came he wondered whether there had been anything wrong with his letter; whether she had been frightened, or whether she had shown it to her parents, or what had happened. On the third day, when Madge was sorting out the mail at breakfast, he saw her holding a letter addressed to him. There was always something unconcealable about a young girl's handwriting, something conscientious, confident and sprawling.

"Why, Jeff," Madge said, "here's a letter from a little girl."

He wished that Madge would hand it to him and not keep examining it. He felt the way Jim must have felt when Madge looked at his letters.

"What makes you think so?" Jeffrey asked.

"I don't know," Madge answered. "You can always tell. They look like the letters Jim gets, not yours. Why Jeffrey, I think it's that Sales girl's writing."

It never occurred to him that of course she might know the writing, having seen it before on envelopes addressed to Jim.

"They all look alike," Jeffrey said. "It's probably an advertisement. They get debutantes to address them so you'll open them, you know."

When he opened it with Madge still watching him, he felt exactly as though Madge were his mother or his aunt, and that he had dropped a rung in the generations.

> Dear Mr. Wilson [he read]:
>
> It's simply grand of you to ask me to lunch and at the Echelon. If I don't hear from you, will Thursday at one be all right? I'll know what you look like and I'll adore having lunch, and thank you.
>
> Sincerely,
> SALLY SALES

"Is it an advertisement?" he heard Madge ask.

"Yes," he said, and he thought he was quite clever. "It's a restaurant. The Echelon restaurant."

There was one thing certain, he did not want Madge to know, and Madge had come very close to guessing.

When he examined the letter later, it did not tell him much about Sally Sales. The paper came from that place in Peru, Indiana, with her name on the top, "Sally Sales," and her address. He found himself examining it exactly as though he were Jim, trying to read between the lines to discover whether she was glad that he had asked or not. He imagined that any girl in those days "adored" to go to lunch and that it was "simply grand" to be asked. He wondered whether she had simply dashed off that note or had written it as many times as the one he had written her.

The one thing he wanted was to try to meet her without a sense of that gap in age, to try to talk to her naturally as he sometimes talked to Gwen—but what would there be to talk to her about? Nothing except Jim.

When he reached the Echelon, he had doubts as to whether he should have asked her there. The Echelon was one of those restaurants for people who understand the art of eating, one of those little places, self-consciously transplanted from France, with a tiny and uncomfortable lounge just off the coatroom where you could wait for your companion if you wanted, and then the main room, two steps down with red leather seats along the wall where you and your companion would sit side by side, tête-à-tête, or perhaps a little more than tête-à-tête. There was a little bit of a bar, made to look like a *bistro* with some slightly off-color Parisian illustrations and a great many tables on wheels so that salads and *crêpes Suzettes* could be prepared right under the noses of you and your companion. Jeffrey had entirely forgotten that the Echelon was so intimate.

When he arrived there were already a few companions at the tables. In one corner there was a redheaded girl, toying with her cocktail glass and talking softly to a man who was obviously not her husband although she looked as though she had one. There were also two corpulent French refugees speaking in their native tongue and two young men seated very close together, one of whom wore a bracelet. Jeffrey had never been so conscious before of the atmosphere of the Echelon. It had not seemed like that when he had last taken Marianna Miller there to lunch.

"Good day, Mr. Wilson," Jacques, the headwaiter, said; and then he added, because the Echelon was Continental, "*Bien bon jour, Monsieur Wilson, vous portez-vous bien, monsieur?*"

"I'm expecting someone," Jeffrey said, "I won't order yet."

"The corner table, then," Jacques said. "*Pssst.*"

Jacques's smiling mask changed for a second into a malignant threatening expression which shocked a waiter who was lounging near the bar into nervous action. A busboy also came running and all of them began pulling back the corner table. Jeffrey sat down cautiously on the red leather bench. Wherever you sat in the Echelon, your legs were curled around a table leg.

"Can't you move it a little sideways?" Jeffrey said.

"But certainly," Jacques said. "*Pssst.* . . . An *apéritif* while you are waiting, Mr. Wilson? A little cocktail?"

He sounded like one of those books describing a French scene where the French words were always repeated in English for the benefit of the ignorant reader.

"Dry sherry," Jeffrey said. "I'm expecting a—young lady."

He was curious about her, but at the same time, he wished that he had never attempted it. Even after the sherry he felt old. He was the man about town, the gentle, cynical roué who had tasted life. He kept looking across the room toward the little vestibule and the revolving door out front so that he saw her just as soon as she came in, and so did the other patrons. He saw the two Frenchmen look up with the hard, appraising glance that Frenchmen bestow on women. The redheaded girl and the man beside her looked with momentary curiosity, and then they must have thought it was a father taking his daughter to the matinée. At least Jeffrey hoped that was what they thought, for she was as young as that. Her complexion was very fresh and fair. Her mouth was a little large, with too much lipstick on it. Her hair was the color of pulled molasses candy, very fine with little crinkles in it. Her legs looked a trifle large and she walked with a slightly shambling gait. She was wearing a black-fur-trimmed coat, and her dress was green wool trimmed with the same black fur cut round at the neck. She was utterly indistinguishable from any other girl her age. He had forgotten that anybody could look so young.

For a moment Jeffrey struggled behind the table. It was always difficult to stand up in those places, where they pressed the edge of the table into the pit of your stomach. He had to push it out, and the glasses rattled.

"Hello," he said. "It's ever so nice of you to come."

Then she smiled. Her voice was high and unmusical.

"It's swell of you," she said, "to ask me, Mr. Wilson."

The waiter and the busboy were pulling out the table. He had not thought of her sitting on the bench right beside him. It was difficult to see her, turning sideways.

"Well," he said again, because he had to say something. "It's swell you *could* come."

Then he saw that she was nervous and frightened. They were pushing the table back, now that she was sitting down. They were handing them menus, written on huge pieces of paper in indistinguishable characters. "*Canapé*," "*Entrée*," "*Roti*." He saw her hand shake when she took the card, and he saw her swallow.

"Perhaps," Jeffrey said, "you'd like a drink."

He saw her glance at him, frightened, but trying to be as nice as she could.

"I shouldn't," she said, "but, yes, thank you. I'd like a little sherry."

Then she was looking helplessly at the lunch card.

"Never mind," Jeffrey said, "I'll read it. They fix it so you can't understand it. They like the chance to explain."

When he ordered the lunch, he was sure that he was not appearing well. He knew that he was more emphatic and more artificially gay than was absolutely necessary, behaving as he sometimes did with someone whom he did not know and wished to impress favorably. It was a part of a shyness which he had never entirely lost. Now that he had seen her, he did not know what to do next, any more than she did. It all reminded him of something, he could not remember exactly what, until he noticed the color of her hair again. All his shyness was a part of that past, some half-forgotten pattern of behavior. Just as the clear soup was coming on, he remembered—Louella Barnes.

Sally Sales looked just enough as Louella had looked once to set the train of habit stirring. Her hair, voice, the way she held her head—it was as though he were living through an encounter with Louella again, vicariously.

He had been wondering what on earth Jim saw in that little girl and why Jim liked that undeveloped sweetness. She had seemed so young, so devoid of poise, but now she assumed her own individuality. He could understand Jim better, now that he remembered, although it was disconcerting, eating fillet of sole with her there at the Echelon. She had been talking and he had not even been listening.

"But I liked the World of Tomorrow best," she said.

Jeffrey wished that she had been sitting across the table, so that he did not have to turn his head to see her. He did not know at first what she meant by "the World of Tomorrow."

"Everyone does," he said. "That is, when they're your age."

Then it came to him that she must have been talking about the World's Fair, which seemed as old as his own thoughts, gone like a dream, as though it had never existed, a sad, materialistic fantasy of peace and plenty, a sort of satire which should have had no place in the world of today or any other world. He thought of the Moscow subway and of the red workman holding up his star, and of the Japanese pavilion, with its silkworms, both slightly dubious monuments to international good will, and he thought of those other buildings around the Lagoon of Nations, glorifying nations which had already fallen, while that fantasy was going on—Czechoslovakia, Holland, Belgium, France.

"Did you see the Houses of Tomorrow?" he asked.

Yes, she had seen the houses, too, and the Kodak Building and the Telephone Building. It had been funny at the Telephone Building. It still made her laugh before she told about it. A boy in the booth on the stage had been talking to a girl in San Francisco.

"Herbert," the girl asked, "do you still love me?"

"Don't ask that, Myrtle," the boy had said, "there's five hundred people listening."

Then Sally's cheeks had a higher color. She glanced away from him and looked hard at her plate.

"I don't see why he minded," she said, "what difference did it make?"

It was the first thing she had said which gave him any idea of what she might be like.

"Did you see the Midget Village?" he asked, "and Bring Them Back Alive?"

She had seen them all, and the Panda and the Seminole Indians.

"But I liked the World of Tomorrow best," she said.

He looked at her again, wondering what she had seen in it, trying to discover some taste that they might possess in common. It was hard to find one because Sally Sales was the world of tomorrow, not even the world of today.

"I wonder—" he said—"did Jim take you to the Fair?"

"Yes." Her voice sounded startled. "Yes, didn't he tell you?"

"No," he said. "You see, Jim comes and goes. He never tells me much."

He was thinking of Jim and Sally Sales on one of those clear, hot August days perhaps, wandering over the crowded bridges with all the pennants waving, walking down those endless streets, stepping aside for the little cars whose horns caroled "The Sidewalks of New York," walking endlessly, walking in a dream. It was not for him, but it gave him vicarious pleasure. He could see Jim looking at it as he would have once, and he could imagine he was Jim sitting with Sally Sales in the dark, holding her hand and gazing down at the roads and streets and cities of the peaceable World of Tomorrow. And now he knew, and everyone must have known, that the world of tomorrow would never be like that, for it was gone, exactly like his world of yesterday.

"It must have been a nice place to take a girl," he said.

"Yes, it was," she answered. Her voice was softer, and she smiled.

"You remind me of a girl I used to know," he said.

He glanced up from his coffee and saw that she looked startled.

"Was she nice?" she asked. "I hope she was."

"Of course she was," he said. It was not the way he had intended to talk to her at all. "Her name was Louella—Louella Barnes."

He was walking up the tar path off Center Street again, not that it made any sense. He was sitting on that rocking chair again, looking at the iced-tea glasses. There was a magic in it which he had entirely forgotten. . . .

"Perhaps I should have married her," he said.

Then he came to himself abruptly. He was back in the Echelon again talking to a rather gauche little girl in a green dress with hair like molasses candy, with hands a little too large, with too much lipstick, and not enough powder on her nose.

"Oh, Billy," the young man with the bracelet was saying, "oh, Billy, say you *like* it, but you simply can't *adore* it."

Jeffrey frowned. He had never told anyone in the world that perhaps he should have married Louella Barnes. All at once he felt very warm, and kindly. He wished she had not spoken of the World of Tomorrow because he could not get tomorrow from his mind.

"I wonder—" he said, and he hesitated—he was never good at sentiment—"if you would mind if I asked you something."

She turned toward him enquiringly, and then looked frightened.

"It's none of my business," he said. "It's about Jim. I hope you'll be nice to Jim. I mean, let him be what he is. Don't turn him into something that you think he ought to be."

He saw her eyes grow wider.

"Mr. Wilson," she said, "you—you're awfully nice."

"Not really," Jeffrey said, "I'm only thinking about Jim."

Then he knew she liked him. He had wanted her to like him, but now it was disconcerting because he was still not sure whether or not he liked her.

"Mr. Wilson," she said, "I think you're swell."

He wished that she had not used the word "swell." There was nothing swell about him.

"It's been swell seeing you," he said. "Perhaps you'll come again and see me, now you've found the way."

28

Your Sister, Not Mine

There had been a time when a winter in New York had seemed utterly devoid of pattern, always containing an infinite promise of variety, which was difficult now for Jeffrey to visualize. He knew that this was the way Jim now felt about New York. Jim said everything was in New York. Jim said that he was happy, just standing in Grand Central Station, catching scraps of people's conversations. Jim said that he would not mind standing all day on Sixth Avenue where they had the joke shops and the Orange Drinks, just watching the crowds go by. Jim said he would not mind standing all day in Radio City, where the French and British shops and the travel offices were, and the evergreens at Christmas and the tulips in the spring and where the fountains in summer sprayed ceaselessly around Mr. Manship's golden boy and where exhibition fancy skaters salved their egos in the winter. If he grew tired of the skaters, Jim said he would not mind standing and staring up and up, watching the mass of building cut into the sky. It made him know what people wanted and what they thought. It taught him more about geology and astronomy and history than he had ever learned at school. Then, Jim said, there was Central Park and the pool with the sea lions—that was something you could always go to; and when you got tired of the sea lions, there were the Fifth Avenue busses and the Madison Avenue shops, and at night there was La Rue where you met everybody you knew, and if you were too broke for La Rue, there were places like Hamburger Heaven. Jim said there was everything in New York, everything. When he was in New York, Jim hated to take time out for sleeping. Jim could not understand why Jeffrey could not see it. He hoped when he was Jeffrey's age he would not be blasé about New York.

Jeffrey had seen it that way once, and still could up to a certain point. Sometimes in the dusk when all the taxis jammed the cross streets, starting, stopping, starting, he could feel a little of the old excitement, but again, sometimes, he would think that he had seen too much of it. When he had been Jim's age, he remembered how he had felt about books—Plutarch, *The Anatomy of Melancholy*, Balzac, Montaigne, Molière, the British poets, the Five Foot Shelf of Books which would turn you into a man of culture if you gave them fifteen minutes a day. Once when he saw a wall of books, he had been sure that he would read them all, someday. There had been nothing impossible in that assurance because he knew that he would have the time—someday—when he could get through with what he was doing. Now he knew he never would read them all. The realization did not make him exactly sad. He had simply grown sufficiently wise to know that there would eventually be an end to himself and everything around him. It was the same way about New York. He would never know it all and he was not young enough to think he would, and what was worse, he was so old that he knew New York did not have anything. There was not the clear cold winter's silence that he used to know when he was a boy; the snow did not belong there, and neither did the moon.

Nevertheless, he was so used to it that it always called him back. He was so used to it that he entered a winter there much as a horse might enter a stall. He could tell the seasons in New York without knowing that the trees were bare or that the snow was falling. First there was the summer when you kept away as much as you possibly could. Autumn in the city was that period of hope when everyone was coming back . . . the new cars and the new shop windows and the new plays and the Horse Show. Then you had the Christmas trees and the Santa Clauses on the street, and new ideas for Christmas presents (and did you remember to give a little something to the doorman, and the iceman, although there weren't many icemen now, and the postman, and the Club employees, and Miss Wynant, your secretary?) and the boys coming home for the holidays, and the wreath you put on the apartment door, and the elevator, all full of hemlock and holly so that you would not forget the elevator boys, and too much food, and Christmas parties and church at midnight. Madge always wanted to go to church at midnight.

Then before you got over Christmas there was New Year's with eggnog parties given by people who each knew some secret, indigestible way of making eggnogs. Then came first nights and dinner parties and it would not be polite unless you stayed until one in the morning. Then came February with dirty snow being sucked up from the streets, and window displays of skis and bathing suits and sun glasses, all mixed together. February was the time for cocktail parties. Madge used to say, "We'll go around to see So-and-so and have a cocktail." Jeffrey always felt tired in February with March and the income tax around the corner. First you paid out to Santa Claus, and then you paid the income tax. There had been the autumn, with a note of hope, then a strange hysterical sort of crisis, then a leveling off in January, and then wondering in February what it was all about. That was the time that everyone needed a stimulant, and then there were the cocktail parties.

All the mechanics of early 1941 were just what had motivated the previous years. Custom moved on doggedly, in spite of the war. It was February and he knew that Gwen would send him a valentine because Gwen still believed in valentines. It was February and he was suffering from a slight cold in the head, so he stayed in for the day to work in his study instead of the office where he usually did his work. It was February and the Greeks were beating the Italians; and General Wavell, too, was beating the Italians. There was an Italian general called Old Electric Whiskers and the Australians, known affectionately to newspaper readers as the "Aussies," romped through Tobruk, Derna, and Bengasi, singing those songs of theirs, "Roll Out the Barrel" and "We're Off to See the Wizard of Oz." The military experts were saying that at last something was clearly wrong with Hitler's timetable, and Jeffrey realized that there was something wrong with his timetable too.

It was eleven in the morning and he could see ice cakes on the river. The door of his room was closed and the telephone was shut off, but there were familiar sounds beyond the door. Joseph and Harriet, the new couple, seemed to be operating the vacuum cleaner and at the same time moving furniture, and from somewhere in the distance he could hear Madge's voice on the telephone. Madge could never understand why he did not want to work at home, because she always promised that everything would be quiet. No one would be allowed to disturb him and his study was much more comfortable than an office, and if he had an office, why did he need a study?

Actually, it was quiet enough that morning. It was only the sense of responsibility connected with those vague outer sounds which disturbed him. When he heard Madge on the telephone he wondered whether she was calling long distance, and talking for half an hour, as she sometimes did. When he heard the vacuum cleaner, he wondered how long since it had been oiled. An odor from the kitchen reminded him that there were usually queer things for lunch. He had read the morning paper very carefully and now there were a number of things he should do, but he had no desire to do them. Instead he began looking through the drawers of his desk which should have been cleaned out long ago, and he came upon a first draft of a play, jammed between some old checkbooks and some scenarios from Hollywood. The paper was worn and musty, because he had not looked at it for years, and now it filled him with a sensation of defeat. It was like those books he had always planned to read when he was young, something which he had meant to put his mind on when he had the time, something of his own which he had never discussed with anyone. He did not particularly want to read it now, but it occurred to him that if he went out to the Coast in April as he was planning, he might stay another two weeks alone and finish it. Yet, he wondered whether he ever would, for he knew enough about himself to know that he was afraid to finish it. His powers of analysis had grown so much greater than his creative enthusiasm that he would see its defects, and those defects would be too much a part of him to correct, as he might have done so easily with someone else's work. He put the manuscript on the desk in front of him. He was looking at the first lines when Madge knocked on the door.

Madge had on that gray flaring dress which she had bought in January and the diamond-and-sapphire clip which he had given her for Christmas.

"I just came in," Madge said, "to see if you were comfortable. Jeff, it's awfully nice to have you in the house."

Jeffrey smiled at her. It reminded him of the years when he had to work at home because he could not afford to work anywhere else. It reminded him of the times when he had talked with her about what he was doing. No matter how often he had asked her not to interrupt, she had never been able to leave him alone for long. She had always said she only wanted to know what he was doing. Now, Madge was just the same. She was looking about the room, mentally putting it back in order, as she always did.

"Jeff," she said, "it's stuffy in here. You ought to have more air."

"No, no," Jeffrey said, "it's all right."

"We're going to have an avocado salad for lunch," Madge said. "You like that, don't you?"

"Yes," Jeffrey said, "that's fine."

"Jeff," Madge said, "what's that?"

She had seen the manuscript on the desk.

"It's just something I tried to write once," Jeffrey said, "about five years ago."

"Well," Madge asked, "what is it?"

He wished that he did not think of things so often in terms of fiction or drama. All at once that draft of his had a spurious sort of significance. It was the Great Idea that would make him famous, and he was sharing it with his wife—but he knew it was not a great idea.

"It's the first draft of a play I started once," he said.

"Oh, Jeff," Madge said, "I hope you're going to try another play."

If he had not married Madge, if he had not done so much of what she wanted, he might have written plays of his own, and now she hoped he would.

"I've forgotten how to write one, Madge," he said, "I'm a play doctor, an adapter, I'm not a playwright. Besides, I can't afford it."

"Darling," Madge said, "don't be so silly."

"I'm not silly," Jeffrey said.

"Of course you are," Madge answered. "You don't have to think about money, Jeff. I'll tell you what we'll do."

"What?" Jeffrey asked.

"If you want to write it," Madge said, "you can start right now and I'll pay all the bills."

"No," he said, "I can't do that."

"Oh, Jeff—" she began.

"Madge," he answered, "don't."

But she still went on.

"Jeff," she said, "I wish you'd ever be frank about your work. I wish I could make you see."

"See what?" he asked.

There was a familiar note of insistence in her voice, as she tried to place herself into a part of his life where she did not belong.

"See what it means to me," she said. "I don't like to feel I've ever stopped you from writing what you want."

"You haven't," Jeff said. "It isn't your fault, Madge."

He did not look at her, but he knew that she was standing by the desk very straight and motionless.

"You never say so," she said, "but I know you think so sometimes. Jeff, I wish you'd tell me what you think."

He wished that he could tell her. It made him sorry for himself, but sorrier for her.

"You see," he said slowly, "we're only talking about a fallacy. If you're good enough, you do write what you want. I've never been good enough, that's all."

That was the trouble with being old—you knew too much about yourself, so much that it hurt; but it did not matter as long as you were not sorry for yourself, and he certainly did not want Madge to think that he was sorry.

"Oh, Jeff," she said, "that's just a pose. I know how intelligent and clever you are—everybody knows."

"No, I'm not," he said, "I'm not good enough."

"But Jeff," she said, "you've never tried to write what you want."

He wished that she would not go on with it, arousing old reproaches, old regrets; and that whole expression about writing what you want was the sort of thing they said at cocktail parties—what people like Madge said who could not possibly know anything about it. There was no way of her telling what he wanted to write; there was no way of his knowing himself.

"Oh," he said, "never mind it, Madge," and then he was sorry. He did not look at her, but he knew she was still standing straight and motionless. He knew she was unhappy, and he could not help it.

"I'll pay all the bills," Madge said, "and if you want to be so silly, why, you can pay me back."

Jeffrey moved uneasily.

"If you did that," he said, "you'd be taking away the only thing I've ever done. There wouldn't be any reason for anything. Madge, I can't do that."

Suddenly that capacity of his to pay the bills seemed to be everything there was between himself and Madge.

"There's the telephone," he said. He had heard the bell out in the hall and he was grateful for the interruption, and he pointed to the extension on his desk.

"If I take it, it's always for you," Madge said. "Hello," and then her expression changed and her smile grew more fixed. "Why, my dear," Madge spoke in the brittle, hearty way she did when she was surprised and wanted to make the best of something, "why, when did you get here and how long are you staying?"

As she listened to the answer, Jeffrey saw her look at him meaningly.

"Why, that's wonderful, dear," Madge said. "When can we see you? We're all dying to see you."

"Madge," Jeffrey asked, "who is it now?" Her voice was sweeter and still more cordial.

"Why, dear," she said, "it's so exciting, isn't it, just coming down suddenly. Now, let me think, we'll all be just crazy to see you and to hear everything. No, not this afternoon. Jeff and I have to go out this afternoon. Yes, he's very well and terribly busy. No, we're not as busy as that. Jeff will be crazy to see you. Why not supper, just the family? Wait, I'll ask Jeff—if you don't mind a pick-up supper. It's Thursday, you know."

"Madge," Jeffrey said, "who's coming to supper? *Who* is it?"

Madge put her hand carefully over the transmitter and lowered her voice. "It's Ethel," she said.

"Ethel?" Jeffrey repeated.

Madge frowned and shook her head, forming her words very carefully with her lips.

"Your *sister*, Ethel—and she's down here with—Gloria."

"What are they doing down here?" Jeffrey asked.

"She's on what she calls a 'spree,'" Madge said, "and they're staying at the Hotel Lexington. She's showing Gloria New York. You've got to do something about them. It's your sister and your niece. She isn't *my* sister."

"All right," Jeffrey said. "All right."

"Is it all right," Madge asked, "to have them up for supper? She's your sister, she isn't my sister."

"Ethel's all right," Jeffrey said, "even if she isn't your sister. You don't have to see her. You can go out."

"But, Jeff," Madge said, "I'd love to see her. I've always been nice to Ethel."

"I didn't say you hadn't been," Jeffrey said.

"Don't argue," Madge said, and her lips formed the words still more carefully, "and don't talk so loud. She's right on the telephone. Shall we have them for supper?"

"Yes," Jeffrey said, "God, yes. Have them for supper. Is Wilbur there with them too?"

Madge lifted the palm of her hand from the transmitter.

"Dear," she said, "it's wonderful. Jeff can't wait to see you. Gwen will be back from school, and we'll be just family. Darling, we're *crazy* to have you. Jeff would kill me if you didn't come. We may be a little latish, but Gwen will be here. Jeffrey and I have to go to a cocktail party. Jeff is simply furious, but we'll get away as soon as we can."

"What?" Jeffrey asked. "What cocktail party?"

"There," Madge said, "do you hear him? No, don't wear anything. No one's coming. Seven-thirty. We can't wait to see you."

Madge put down the telephone.

"Don't look that way, Jeff," she said; "she's your sister, not mine."

"Madge," Jeffrey asked her. "What cocktail party? I didn't know we had to go out this afternoon."

"You told me you wanted to go," Madge said. "Don't you remember? It's Ella and Sinclair Merriwell."

"My God," Jeffrey said, "I never said I'd go to one of those things."

"It's for Priscilla Jenks," Madge said, "a birthday party for her book. The Book-of-the-Month Club's taken it."

"Who is she?" Jeffrey said.

"You know who," Madge told him. "She's one of Sinclair's authors. Jenks, Priscilla Jenks. You met her at their eggnog party."

"Which eggnog party?" Jeffrey asked. "He's always giving parties."

"Darling," Madge said, "you know you like Sinclair, and I like him, too. He wants me to get you to write a book."

"It's his disease," Jeffrey said. "He wants everybody to write a book."

"After all," Madge said, "he developed Walter Newcombe."

"Well, I don't want him to develop me," Jeffrey said.

"But you'll go this afternoon, won't you?" Madge asked. "Sinclair called me up, and he wants you particularly. Jeffrey, please. You know what a good time we had at Happy Rocks."

"Sinclair always wants everyone particularly," Jeffrey said.

"But you know you like him," Madge said.

"All right," Jeffrey said, "I like him. I didn't say I didn't like him."

Everybody always liked Sinclair and it seemed sometimes that everybody was under obligation to Sinclair. Madge patted him on the back and placed her cheek beside his.

"Chin up, darling," Madge said, "and before you go, you'd better shave."

29

To the Publishers, God Bless Them

When Jeffrey first came to New York, he thought that publishers were simple people, perhaps because he did not know much about them, and it had seemed to him that there were only a few old-line houses which had published all the books—such as Scribner's and Harpers and Putnam's—all with a long and dignified tradition. Now the canvas was broader—there were lots of newer, brighter publishers, many of them excellent, who had stepped out of nowhere, like a hardy mountain folk descending on the fat burghers of the plains. When Sinclair Merriwell came down from Yale he started with one of those old houses as an editor and author's contact man, and he made up his mind, as soon as he began entertaining authors at the Yale Club, that he was going to be what he called "a bookman." Sinclair had worked hard, and even when he slept, he must have dreamed about being a bookman. Besides having persistence, Sinclair had a way with authors. He was familiar with all their works, even with their bad ones, and in some way Sinclair could make every author he saw, even if he saw a dozen in a day, feel that at last here was a publisher who understood him, who had real faith in his genius and his future, who sympathized with just what this particular author was trying perhaps unconsciously to do, who loved and delighted in what he was trying to do, and who knew implicitly that this particular author was not quite understood where he was and was not quite being presented to his public as he should be (although of course he was being published by a fine old house, all the members of which were grand fellows and personal friends of Sinclair's). When you came to think of it, it was not so difficult to make authors feel this way since nearly every author living knew very well that he was not being given a square deal and that the house which published him, as bookmen put it, had done absolutely nothing about promoting his last book, had hardly given him a line of advertising but had simply thrown the book out perfunctorily and let it sink or swim. Sinclair always understood very well just why these authors should feel this way about their publishers (although their publishers were grand fellows who did a perfectly swell job with certain authors).

But there was one thing that Sinclair wanted to make perfectly clear at the start—he never, never wanted for a moment to take an author away from another publisher. Sinclair was not that sort of person, even though there was a good deal of cutthroat competition in publishing, and a great many friends of his, swell people in other ways, occasionally did just this type of thing. He could tell you what they had done to authors of his own, in those hard days when he and Ella had first established the Grimpian Press. If an author wanted to leave him, well, he could, and God bless him, but it was surprising how many of them came back and said they were sorry. That was one of the rewards of being a bookman. Publishers who shanghaied other publishers' authors were not bookmen; and Sinclair wanted you to know that he was not that sort of fellow at all. He was glad to give his advice, as any friend might, but it was no part of his ethics to say anything destructive about any other house. He was frank to say that those houses had done a swell job for certain authors of theirs, certain authors—a much better job than he could have.

Take Hemingway, or Faulkner, or Steinbeck, just to pick a few names out of the hat at random, and he was not making a pun—he did not mean Random House. Their publishers had done a swell job for them, not that anyone couldn't have with Hemingway and Faulkner and Steinbeck. Actually he thought that their houses had done a better job for them than he could have, because they were more interested in Faulkner and Hemingway and Steinbeck than he would have been. Personally, just between us both, there was something about Hemingway and Faulkner and Steinbeck that left Sinclair just a little cold. He did not know why—no reason, and please don't think it was sour grapes on his part, just because he had not discovered Hemingway or Faulkner or Steinbeck. He did not know why it was that Hemingway and Faulkner and Steinbeck left him just a little cold. But that was the fun of being a bookman. Sinclair never wanted to work for and with an author whose work did not give him a warm, tingling little glow, did not ring a little sort of bell in his mind, whose pages he did not understand intimately and did not wish in a little way that he had written himself. He knew that this idea was a little out of the ordinary line and perhaps was not good for business, or was it? Sinclair was not entirely sure and really he did not care. He did not care because there was more than dollars and cents in being a bookman.

To put the whole thing in a nutshell, now that he and his author had finished their dessert, and their demitasses were on the table and Sinclair had signed the check (and had ticked it off to business expense, Grimpian House, tax exempt), he did not want an author on his list who did not give him that warm feeling of enthusiasm that would make Sinclair work for and with that author intimately. There was just one thing—and you could have a cigar, if you wanted one, Sinclair never smoked cigars, and some brandy too, though Sinclair never drank in the middle of the day—there was just one thought that Sinclair wanted to leave with you. He did not want to take any author away from any other house. On the other hand, if an author wanted to think it over and wanted to come to him and be one of the Grimpian crowd, that was another matter. That was the way Priscilla Jenks had come to him. She had just not been happy where she was, but he did think she was happy, really happy, at Grimpian, and all the cards were always on the table at Grimpian. And perhaps the best thing to do about this whole conversation (and it had been a lot of fun, just talking at random, and he didn't mean Random House) would be more or less to forget it, because it had been all a little off the record. But if you wanted to think it over, and if you had any ideas later, Sinclair would be awfully glad to hear them, and why not come out to Happy Rocks sometime? Ella would love to have you, just to ramble through the country and to talk about books. And Walt Newcombe might be there, or Priss Jenks, or someone from the *Saturday Review of Literature*—it never hurt to meet a critic, did it? Someone worth while was always around at Happy Rocks.

The publishing world was changing when Sinclair Merriwell got started on his own. Instead of Harpers, Scribner's and Macmillan, there began to be Presses with fine, comfortable names, and also Houses—The Viking Press, The Heritage Press, and even the Press of the Woolly Whale; and Random House, and Courtright House, and Halcyon House. When Sinclair broke away from what he called being a wage slave and a yes man in that old-line publishing company where he was first employed (taking with him a few authors whom he had begged not to leave a place where they were comfortably established but who had insisted, though he didn't know why), and when he had borrowed some money from some friends and had started his own enterprise, he did not know whether to call this new venture a press or a house. That was the year that Sinclair had married Ella Fredericks, who was doing a perfectly swell job in a literary agency, and to whom Sinclair always referred as "a perfectly swell gal." It was Ella who thought of the name, the Grimpian Press. Jeffrey had never known what it meant exactly, and had never heard of it except as a mire in *The Hound of the Baskervilles*, but after all, this made no difference. He always thought of it as a good, sound name that reminded him of fine, sound talk and the burning logs in a bookman's library and the sizzling, perhaps, of roasting apples. It was Ella who had made Happy Rocks what it was. It was Ella, too, who did most about the cocktail parties in their penthouse in New York on Central Park South, although Sinclair did a lot to help. They both understood how important it was to entertain if you were a bookman and a bookwoman. That was part of the fun of it, knowing interesting people, having open house for everyone.

Ella and Sinclair both thought it was only natural that authors, particularly their authors, should be interested in critics, and that the critics should know and like authors, particularly their authors. And both Ella and Sinclair were very hurt if they heard anyone say anything about making hay or log rolling, or anything like that. This was the last thing they ever had in mind when they brought interesting people together; besides, the idea of influencing a book critic—that is, a book critic who had any following at all—was perfectly absurd, wasn't it? Because a critic was meant to say frankly what he thought and felt about an author's work and that was what critics on our really fine book pages were for, wasn't it? And criticism was an art in itself. Just to prove it was an art, Sinclair had published the collected critical essays of Samuel Fullerton Breaks, and of course you had followed the reviews of Samuel Fullerton Breaks. It made no difference to Sinclair that this work sold only two hundred and fifty copies. He was not publishing the works of Samuel Breaks for money. He published the works of Samuel Breaks because, in his opinion (and all a bookman could do was to stick to his opinion), these essays were some of the finest pieces of expository prose since the time of Dryden, Addison and Steele, particularly the chapter about Priscilla Jenks and the future. You must be sure to read that chapter about Priscilla Jenks, and if you hadn't, Sinclair would send you a copy. It always made Sinclair and Ella, and it would have made any other good bookman, too, laugh to think that they or any other publishers could influence an honest book reviewer. That was not their idea when they asked critics to Happy Rocks or to their cocktail parties. Ella and Sinclair did not want anyone to think for a minute that they were doing business over gin and vermouth and *canapés*. They asked the critics because they liked them and some of their very best friends were critics and book page editors, not only in New York, but all over the country. That was the fun of being a bookman, and of keeping up with book fairs and book-and-author luncheons—you made so many friends.

Furthermore, you might not know it, but a great many literary critics were rather wistful, lonely people who wanted to write books themselves, and who really wanted secretly to get to know the authors about whom they wrote. Even if a critic like Lewis Gannett or Charley Poore or Clifton Fadiman had treated something you wrote unkindly, it did not mean that he would not like you personally, if he could ever meet you. If a critic didn't like an author's work, Ella and Sinclair believed that this was really because the critic did not understand what the author was basically trying to do. In their experience it was surprising how often this all changed when a critic and an author had a little talk in the company of a lot of other people of kindred interests, over a little sherry or gin and bitters or whatever it was that old Sam, whom Sinclair always had over from the Paxton Club on such occasions, might be passing. Now, certainly this was not hay making or log rolling or anything like that. They had always found that reviewers and authors, no matter how self-conscious and silly they might have been at first, always ended up by having a good time together, and if there was any trouble, Ella could make them have a good time, and that was what cocktail parties were for, wasn't it?

Furthermore, it was silly, really silly, when someone had written a really good book that might in the end be a great book, someday, not to give him a little encouragement to go on. It did not matter a fig, that was what Ella said, a fig, whether the Grimpian Press had mothered (or was it fathered?) that book or not. They were just as glad to give a party to an author from Scribner's or Harcourt Brace, or anywhere, if he had written a book that made Ella and Sinclair feel warm inside. When one of their authors, like Walter Newcombe or Priscilla Jenks, had done something that was definitely important, and had made a real creative contribution to our time, it was only fair to them to set a little social punctuation mark upon it. It was only a kindness to other people to let them meet and talk to authors like Walter Newcombe and Priscilla Jenks.

And Ella and Sinclair did not want to have those parties too booky either—they made a real study of their cocktail lists, so that they should represent a cross section of thoughtful, intelligent people who kept abreast of the new books. This did not mean only literary agents, or only their friends from publishing houses—and you'd be surprised how many of their very best friends came from rival publishing houses—or only buyers from book departments, or bookstore managers, or only authors or only critics. They liked to have artists, too, who were doing things in other media, such as painters and sculptors and composers. That was what they meant by not wanting to have their parties too booky or provincial, too printer's inksy-winksy, as Ella put it.

What they wanted, they told Jeffrey, was to have an invitation to their cocktail parties mean that you were someone interesting and worth while and to guarantee in return that you would meet interesting and worth-while people there. And that was the sort of cocktail party that they were giving for Priscilla Jenks. They wanted Jeffrey, not for what he did, but for what he was, and they hoped that Jeff could have a few minutes with Priss, because Sinclair had a perfectly crazy idea that this new novel of Priss's—the finest thing she had ever done—had the makings of a play somewhere inside it, and if it did, Sinclair—and so did Ella—knew that Jeff Wilson was the man to nose it out.

Madge had on her mink coat and her cheeks were pink from the cold air outside. The elevator was overcrowded and Jeffrey took off his hat and held it carefully against his chest. Everyone in the elevator was obviously going up to the Merriwells', except a fat lady with a small Cairn terrier, who got off at the fourth floor by ploughing a path through the interesting people. None of the occupants of the elevator spoke. They simply examined each other guardedly. Jeffrey felt Madge nudge him gently in the ribs. He was afraid she was going to whisper about some important figure in the elevator, but instead of whispering, she looked at Jeffrey meaningly and then at a tall man in the far corner. Jeffrey followed her glance. Madge looked at him more meaningly and her lips moved noiselessly. When the elevator door finally opened, the first impact was a wave of sound combined with an aroma of spilled alcohol and cigarette smoke, like every other cocktail party. From the living room down the hall, voices rose like the clamor in the Paris Bourse, but the arrangements went like clockwork because Ella and Sinclair understood cocktail parties. Almost the instant they were out of the elevator, a hatchet-faced woman took Jeffrey's coat and hat and another took Madge's mink coat and Madge told her please to be careful when she put it in the bedroom and not get it mixed up with somebody else's because that had happened once and Madge had never got her coat back, never.

"Jeffrey," Madge said, "that was Henry Bernstein."

"Who?" Jeffrey asked. Even in the hall he had to raise his voice.

"The man in the elevator," Madge said, "wasn't it Henry Bernstein?"

"No," Jeffrey said, "it wasn't, Madge."

"The other man," Madge asked, "who was he?"

"Which other man?" Jeffrey asked.

"The man with that faded blond woman in the silver fox," Madge said, "the one with gray hair and bushy eyebrows. I must have seen his picture somewhere."

"Oh, that man," Jeffrey said. "That was John L. Lewis, and the lady with the dog who got off on the fourth floor was a house detective."

"That isn't funny," Madge said. "I know I've seen him somewhere."

They began pushing their way into the living room. Jeffrey knew that when he had a drink he might feel a little better. Everyone was talking, everyone was having a wonderful time, and Jeffrey began to feel the way Madge must have about the faces. They all did look as though he had seen them somewhere, and as though they expected to be recognized and to be photographed suddenly—but yet, Jeffrey could not place any of them. He was right however, about the photograph. As he and Madge entered, a blinding flash of light made him jump. A sallow young man with a candid camera was weaving his way between two Filipinos in white coats who were passing trays covered with olives and elastic-looking red caviar on crackers. It reminded Jeffrey that Sinclair always liked to have candid photographs of those parties. He and Ella mounted them in books with the date and a little description of the occasion—And how could you tell? *Town and Country* or someone might like to use them—it was a way of helping *Town and Country*. And if they didn't, it was a lot of fun to look over them in the scrapbooks at Happy Rocks.

"Excuse me, sir," the young man with the camera said, "could I have your name, please, sir?"

"Yes," Jeffrey told him, "Secretary of the Navy Stimson."

The young man looked hurt, and Madge pulled at Jeffrey's arm.

"Jeff," she began, "that isn't funny." Then Madge began to laugh, and he liked everything better. "Suppose we come out in *Town and Country*," Madge said, "as Secretary and Mrs. Stimson of the Navy. Jeff, don't you know anybody? Don't you know anybody at all?"

"No," Jeffrey said, "the only thing to do is to get into the spirit of it."

Jeffrey had a feeling that everyone else at the party was like him, nobody in particular, waiting for the appearance of someone who counted.

"Oh," Madge said, "there's Ella."

Ella was standing in the center of the room with a stocky, dark man who wore a thin ribbon in his coat lapel. The man was looking filmily from right to left, and Ella was shouting at him above the voices. She was just what Sinclair had called her, "a perfectly swell gal," and Ella was a big gal, too, five feet ten and a half, and more than that with high heels—a big gal with yellow hair, in a blue dress, known technically as a cocktail dress, with a heavy necklace and a bracelet, known as costume jewelry.

"Oh, Madge," she said. "Oh, Jeff, you must see Priss. Priss is just dying to see you."

"Priss?" Jeffrey repeated.

Ella slapped his shoulder playfully.

"Don't be so vague, dear," Ella said. "Stop looking at everything through a lorgnette. Priscilla Jenks, or you can call her Miss Red Sky if you want to."

"Oh," Jeffrey said, "that's the name of the novel, is it?"

"Madge, don't let him be so vague," Ella said. "Captain Bouchet, this is one of the cleverest men in New York. This is Captain Bouchet of the French Army."

Jeffrey and the stocky foreigner looked each other over with polite disinterest. Jeffrey wondered whether Captain Bouchet also would write a volume about how he saw France fall.

"Captain Bouchet was saying this is just like France," Ella said—"France before it happened. He says that we just don't know—"

Just now everyone was saying that we were like France, that if we did not wake up, we would end just like France. It made no sense, because America was not like France any more than Jeffrey was like Captain Bouchet.

"Here comes Sam," Ella said, "Sam knows what we want."

It was Sam from the Paxton Club with a wine steward's chain around his neck.

"Ella," Jeffrey heard Madge say, "isn't Henry Bernstein here? I thought I saw him in the elevator."

Jeffrey swallowed his cocktail quickly and took another. He wished he were like Madge, able to keep his mind on a single idea.

"What's that?" Ella cried. "Did you say Henry Bernstein's here?"

"Over there," Madge said, "eating something."

"Oh," Ella said, "no, that isn't Henry. That's Swinnerton Brown. You know, who runs the shop called 'Books and Books.'"

"Oh," Madge said. "I thought he looked—"

"But Henry's coming if he possibly can," Ella said, "and so are Kip Fadiman and Lew Gannett, if they possibly can. It's a little businessy now, but it won't be in a few minutes."

Now that Jeffrey had finished one drink and was starting on another, he discovered that there were all sorts of people in the room whom he did know, whom he had seen year after year at cocktail parties. He saw George Stanhope, the literary agent, who handled Walter Newcombe whenever Sinclair Merriwell was not handling him, and Leander Brickett, of Brickett's Lectures, Inc., and some solitary dyspeptics who looked like unknown authors, and in the distance he saw Walter Newcombe and Mrs. Newcombe. One drink seemed to have made everyone there an old acquaintance. After a second he began moving confidently through the crowd. As soon as he had spoken to Sinclair Merriwell, it would be all right to leave, if he and Madge could find their coats. They could do it without saying good-by and Madge could call up Ella later and say there'd been such a crowd that they'd not been able to find her.

He did not know what had become of Madge. Jeffrey was first in one group and then another, without knowing how he got there. He was shaking hands with Sinclair Merriwell, who was full of fun, as a host should be on such an occasion, but at the same time, just a little serious, too, exactly as a host should be—in a blue double-breasted coat with white stripes and a handkerchief jutting out of his pocket just so, and a gardenia in his lapel—Ella always gave Sinclair a gardenia before a cocktail party.

"Jeff!" Sinclair called. "Come here to Papa. Here's Priss. I don't think you've ever met Priss, have you? Priscilla, this is Jeffrey Wilson who knows everything about plays."

Jeffrey felt a little sorry for Priscilla Jenks, since it wasn't her fault that she was there and probably she didn't want to be looked at. At any rate he hoped she did not want to be looked at, because it would have been better if she had not been. He never could understand why everyone wanted to see people who wrote books. In Jeffrey's experience, writers, particularly novelists and more particularly women novelists, were, as a rule, not physically attractive. For one thing, novelists, particularly women novelists, were not as young as they used to be; and usually they had a look that made him think that even when they were young they would not have been much to look at; and the trouble with most novelists, particularly women novelists, was that they never seemed to know that they were not as young as they used to be. He was afraid that was the trouble with Priscilla Jenks. Something about writing a novel always went to the heads of novelists, particularly women novelists. Yet, it was not altogether their fault, when publishers' advertisements said that they were the greatest artists of their time, filled with charm and humor and a subtle magnetic power. Naturally they thought they must be beautiful. That was why they so often dressed like High School girls at a graduation and wore orchids and strange fixed smiles, and Priscilla Jenks was doing just that right now.

"Sometime when there isn't so much noise," Sinclair said, "we must all get together about The Book. It's just a funny idea of mine that there's a play in it."

"I don't think a novel is ever basically a play," Priscilla Jenks said. "The conception of a novel and a play are so entirely different."

"Now that you mention it," Jeffrey said, "that's perfectly true, but I never thought of it in quite that way."

"Jeff," Sinclair said hastily, "we can't be serious about it now, Jeff."

"The novel," Miss Jenks said, "that is, the novel as I see it, is more of an eventless stream of time than drama. A novelist's problem is the creation of character through the medium of words, without having any thought for the purely visual. At least, that's the way I see it; so I'm sure I don't know whether The Book can make a play or not. Is that the way you see it, Mr. Wilson?"

"I suppose," Jeffrey said, "that's the way I've always seen it, but no one has ever posed that problem quite so clearly."

"Jeff," Sinclair said, "let's not talk about it now. Priscilla was in Greece in 1939. Have you ever been to Greece?"

"It isn't," Miss Jenks said, "that I haven't a great respect for the problem of the dramatist—the net result of either medium is the same, of course—a picture of life and of our time as I tried to show it in The Book, but the tools used by the dramatist have a different cutting edge and a different bevel."

"That's perfectly true," Jeffrey said. "Sinclair, I never thought of that, did you?"

"Jeff," Sinclair said, "let's not talk about it now. When Priscilla was in Greece she got to Thrace."

"There was one part of The Book," Miss Jenks said, "that I did think of in terms of a play—I shut my eyes before I wrote that part and thought of the page on the typewriter as a curtain. I made the characters as static as the characters on a stage at the rising of the curtain. I wonder if you can guess what part of The Book that was."

"Jeff," Sinclair said, "let's not talk about it now. Priscilla, here's someone who's talked about you until he's talked my right ear off. This is Swinnerton Brown who runs the shop called 'Books and Books.' "

Sinclair drew Jeff very gently to one side.

"God damn you," he said, "don't pull her leg."

Jeffrey laughed.

"Sinclair," he said, "no one here is going to do that," and then Sinclair began to laugh.

Jeffrey moved away to a little semicircle and talked with two men he knew whose names he could not remember and to a redheaded girl who kept singing some sort of a song about money and babies.

"They can't come over here," one man said. "It's a matter of logistics. How many ships could bring a hundred thousand men over here?"

"What about Brazil?" the other man said. "What's to keep them from the big bulge of Brazil?"

"You can't have babies," the girl said, "unless you have a definite cash reserve."

"Just how in hell, George," the first man said, "can they get to any bulge in this hemisphere across the Atlantic Ocean? You tell me how they can do it. I'm listening."

"God damn it," the other man said, "I am telling you."

"Well, God damn it, George," the first man said, "you tell me."

"What about Dakar?" the second man said. "Don't shut your eyes to facts. What about Dakar?"

"All right," the first man said, "you tell me. What about Dakar?"

"God damn it," the second man said, "I am telling you."

"What are you telling me?" the first man said.

"God damn it," the second man said, "if you close your ears to reason, George, I can't tell you. I'm telling you about Dakar."

"All right," the first man said. "You don't tell me anything I don't know already. You're hysterical, and you don't tell anything."

"My God," the other man said, "what's the use of trying, if you close your mind to it?"

"I'm not closing my mind to it," the first man said, "I'm just waiting for you to tell me. All right, go ahead and tell me."

"I am telling you," the other man said.

Jeffrey moved away. He suddenly realized that everyone except Priscilla Jenks, who was talking about her book, was talking about the war. He had listened, years ago, to the same phrases. No one wanted it, but there seemed to be a feeling that we ought to go to war.

"My, my," he heard someone say, "imagine seeing *you* here."

He turned and saw the white hair and the white jade cigarette holder of Mrs. Walter Newcombe.

"Why," Jeffrey said, "hello, sweet."

"Hi ho," Mrs. Newcombe said, "hi ho to you, and isn't this a lovely, lovely, God-damn' lovely, lovely party?"

"Now, sweet," Jeffrey said, "now, sweet."

"Walt's back from Egypt," Mrs. Newcombe said, "or wherever the hell it was Walt went, and now every afternoon we go to lovely, lovely parties, when Walt isn't talking to groups of lovely ladies. Hi ho to you. Hi ho."

"Now, sweet," Jeffrey said. "Where's Walter now?"

It had been a long time since he had seen Mrs. Newcombe or had thought of Walter.

"Where do you think he is, big boy?" Mrs. Newcombe said. "He's over in the corner now, talking about the God-damn' war, and we mustn't stop him, must we–talking about the God-damn' war?"

"Has he really been to Africa?" Jeffrey asked.

"Rahlly, rahlly," Mrs. Newcombe said. "Just think of it, all by himself. He's rahlly been to Africa. And he knows what we're fighting for, rahlly. We don't know it here, but he does, rahlly."

"Now," Jeffrey said, "now, sweet."

Mrs. Newcombe looked up at him.

"Sometime you ought to come up to the Waldorf Tower," she said. "And you and Walt and I ought to all get fried. I can't take this all the time, big boy, rahlly, and it isn't good for Walt."

There was that shine on Walter Newcombe's nose which Jeffrey remembered from the old telegraph room. Walter had a new suit of salt-and-pepper brown. His tie was working up from his waistcoat, but like Sinclair Merriwell, he had a handkerchief in his pocket just so, and he, too, was wearing a gardenia, which Ella must have given him.

"Not another drink, just now," Walter said, "and don't—please don't get me started on that."

Then he saw Mrs. Newcombe and Jeffrey and his eyes widened.

"Hello, sweet," he said, "hello, Jeff."

Walter spoke impersonally, not unkindly, but like someone engaged in a professional duty, and of course he was. Walter and all his colleagues were a little like the side-show barkers outside the tents at a county fair. They had to tell what was inside but they could not tell too much. They had to bring out the python and the man who chewed nails and the dog-faced boy, but only for just a moment, and then they had to whisk them back again because the big show was inside. Walter, and all the others who had come to grips with the realities of war, had to show that they knew everything, that they heard the low grindings of the mills of destiny, but that it was all there in their books, lucid and implicit, a lot more than they could tell right now.

"Hello, sweet," Walter said again, "hello, Jeff." It seemed to Jeffrey that there was a note of appeal in Walter's voice, as though he begged them privately not to spoil his pitch. Walter was gathering a crowd, and this was a little hard on Priscilla Jenks, since the occasion was a birthday party for The Book and not for Walter Newcombe. It occurred to Jeffrey that it was not quite fair of Walter, but then, perhaps Walter could not help it.

He simply stood with his hands in the pockets of that unattractive salt-and-pepper coat, with his thumbs jutting slightly upward, and swayed sideways with a pendulum motion from one foot to the other. Jeffrey felt the audience pressing about him. He was aware of muted breathings down his neck. Walter was speaking of Greece and Crete and of the African desert. You had to be on the desert to know the desert, and he had been very lucky. The Staff had sent him out in a staff car to see General Wavell. Archie was a simple fellow when you got to know him, and bookish. He and Archie had talked quietly about first editions, just as though men weren't dying in the desert. Imagine a man reading Byron as he flew across the Aegean—well, that was silent Archie for you . . . but Walter did not want to get started on that. He could not do better than sum the whole thing up in the words of a grubby little cockney tommy, whom he had met just outside the mine fields near Bardia, just one of countless other cockney tommies who were doing their bit out there. They had stopped and chatted for a moment—you had to be out there in the desert to understand the democracy of war, that great universal leveler—and this was what the tommy had said to Walter as he had rubbed the impalpable dust of the desert off his plain, sweating little face.

"We haven't given them 'arf, yet," the cockney had told Walter, "not a 'arf by a 'ole."

Well, there you had it in a nutshell, or in a thumbnail sketch, if you wanted to put it that way. They hadn't given them 'arf yet, and the 'ole was coming. You could see the portents in the making, looming vaguely. It astonished Walter that Americans here were so blind to it. The main thing to remember in the broader implications was that Hitler's timetable had been upset, and time was the essence for the gangster nations. It was true that Hitler was mobilizing the Balkans, but this very mobilization was upsetting Hitler's timetable. It was off the record, just among friends, but Walter's own impression, not that anyone's impression had the least validity, was that there would be a German drive on Greece, and Greece would be a different nut to crack from France and the Low Countries. Walter had seen the mountains of Greece—he wished that everyone here had seen them. It would be a different cup of tea when the Panzer divisions found themselves in those mountains, but Walter did not want to get started on that. He was not a military expert, he had just been out there trying to glean an impression and he might best round out his picture by telling of an encounter with a little Greek soldier, which had occurred shortly after Walter's car had been mired in a mountain pass, and Walter had been eating a can of peaches while waiting for someone to pull it out. You people sitting here would never realize what a can of peaches meant in a mountain pass in Greece. Walter was eating those peaches when a little Evzone soldier plodded by, a Greek Tommy Atkins. The man was a little fellow with an olive-tinted face, who looked tired, carrying his rifle, and he was wearing a ballet skirt as those Evzones did. (But don't laugh at those skirts, please.) When this little Evzone saw Walter, he said something in Greek, and Walter did not know Greek and Walter's interpreter had gone to the P.C. to get someone to pull the car out of the mud, but you did not have to know Greek to get along with Evzones. Walter handed him a peach and Walter wished that everyone there could have seen that Evzone's smile as he took that peach in his grimy hands and gobbled it like a squirrel.

The group around Walter laughed softly—but Walter said they would not have laughed if they had been there with the drumming of artillery fire down the road ahead. When he had finished his peach that man made a gesture, which rounded out the whole picture and put it in a nutshell. That man's white teeth had flashed in a shy smile and he had shoved his grimy fists in front of him, right under Walter's nose—thumbs up, and then he had walked up that mountain pass toward the gunfire. That was the spirit of everything that Walter had seen—thumbs up.

Jeffrey had heard it all before. It was the old war books, the ones he had read when he was young. It was *Over the Top*. It was *The First Hundred Thousand*, and *The Silence of Colonel Bramble*—He was sure that Walter's words were true, but nevertheless they had a spurious and meretricious note. No doubt Walter had seen the tommy and the Evzone, for every other correspondent also had, but Jeffrey knew that the picture which Walter gave of war and soldiers was distorted. It was not artistically fair to select such simplicity to illustrate something that was immense and tragic. If it were not sad, it would have been ridiculous. Jeffrey knew that war was not like that. He seemed to be standing alone again, back in that patch of woods where the dead lay in the bushes. He could feel the disorder and the nausea and the waste and the fear. When Walter Newcombe said "thumbs up," it was a silly travesty. It would have been better if people like Walter would stay at home where they belonged instead of trying to round out pictures in a nutshell.

Some of the listeners must have felt as Jeffrey did, but they all gave rapt attention to that tinseled, pathetic little story in a nutshell. He realized suddenly that wars were all the same and that he was living in history, and he wished to God that he were not. All at once, even Walter Newcombe had assumed a tragic shape, and Jeffrey knew that Walter Newcombe and his colleagues were the chorus of a tragedy too immense for exposition. All of them were a part of that chorus—all the Major George Fielding Eliots, the Raymond Gram Swings and Johannes Steels, the Gabriel Heatters, and the News and Views by John B. Hughes—chanting of an agony which would never fit into words.

"What's the matter, big boy?" he heard Mrs. Newcombe ask.

"Nothing," Jeffrey answered, "nothing, sweet."

"Take it easy, big boy," he heard Mrs. Newcombe say. "You don't like it, do you?"

"It's a picture," Jeffrey said, "a picture in a nutshell."

"Not rahlly," Mrs. Newcombe said, "not rahlly, Mr. Bones."

The group had broken up. The voices were rising again, joining the other voices in the room. They sounded like those of an audience leaving a very worth-while lecture, and Jeffrey knew that the party was what Sinclair Merriwell would call a party that had meat in it and one you would not forget. Any gaiety Jeffrey had felt previously was entirely gone. He was taking another cocktail, although he knew he had had enough of them.

"Buchanan Greene?" he heard someone say. "Yes, the tall one with the bald head and glasses—Buchanan Greene, the poet." And sure enough, Jeffrey was in another little group, and Buchanan Greene was talking to a middle-aged lady who kept nodding.

"That's what I meant to say," the middle-aged lady kept saying; "why couldn't I have said it? Why?"

And Buchanan Greene also was speaking of the war. It was not like other wars, Buchanan Greene was saying. This was a war of revolution, a war of absolutism against democracy. They were fighting our fight—they were fighting for our beliefs. It was for our writers to define those beliefs of ours, and why could they not define them?

Once more Jeffrey seemed to have heard it before. It was another part of that chorus chanting the chant of democracy. Buchanan Greene was saying democracy was not easy to define, for it was less of a fact than an essence.

"Why couldn't I say that?" the lady said. "Why couldn't I?"

"We all say it," Buchanan said, "again, and again, and again. Franklin Roosevelt says it, and the little man on the subway says it. It's in the shuffling of a thousand feet. It's in the motor horns."

"In the motor horns?" the lady said.

"It's Greene," Jeffrey heard someone say. "Buchanan Greene, the poet."

"It's everywhere implicit in our way of life," Buchanan Greene was saying. "It's the dust from the highway. It's the tractor, plowing out its furrow. It's the motor tire being pressed out in Akron. It's what we live for and what we die for. It's the little funeral winding to the graveyard."

Jeffrey moved away slowly. He felt cold sober, and he had heard that all before too. Buchanan Greene had written it for the radio, and he was simply reciting it all again—the First Voice, and the Second Voice—meaningless, but all the more tragic for its very lack of meaning. Walter, Buchanan Greene and the rest of them were trying to explain why people killed each other, and to endow hideousness with some sort of rational beauty. You always tried to in war, that is, if you weren't in the front line, and God knows, perhaps you tried it then.

The people in that room were another page of history. They were the polite people, the intelligentsia on the verge of crisis, drifting toward it with the sensitive awareness of intelligentsia but without the power to change their course one whit. They were the *salon* group in *War and Peace*, they were Thackeray's dancers before Waterloo; they were the dinner guests of Petronius in *Quo Vadis*. When Jeffrey thought of them in that light, it no longer mattered what they said. All the catchwords of the time, Fascist, Communist, Trotskyist, New Dealer, Conservative, Right Wing, Left Wing, Interventionist, Isolationist, Defeatist, Appeaser, Anglophile, America First, Defend America by Aiding the Allies, Lend-Lease, Lend Your Neighbor a Hose When His House Is Burning, Way of Life, the Yanks Aren't Coming, Keep America Out of War—all these smooth phrases failed to change the basic outline of the picture. They were the intelligentsia, drifting inevitably toward an unknown fact, and their awareness filled them with a dread which they did not admit. They made half-articulate the mass realization growing up about him that nothing would be the same again—no matter what might happen, nothing. They were in a barrel, going over Niagara Falls, and they could not help it, because they were a page of history. . . .

Jeffrey did not want to be on that page. He wanted to be himself again, managing as best he could in the limits of the social system he had known. He wanted to get out of there, and to find Madge, and to get his coat and hat, and to get into the elevator, and into the open air.

"Where are you going, big boy?" Mrs. Newcombe asked.

"It's time to be getting home," Jeffrey said. "I've got to find Madge. She's around somewhere."

"Well, hi ho to you, big boy," Mrs. Newcombe said. "It isn't getting you down, is it, rahlly, rahlly?"

"No," Jeffrey answered, and he laughed, "not rahlly."

"Well, hi ho to you," Mrs. Newcombe said again, "and thumbs up and V for Victory with your fingers. Three dots and a dash to you, and they say it with apples in the restaurants, and a dear, sweet kick to everybody; that puts it in a nutshell, rahlly."

He began seriously looking for Madge. It was later than he thought—and there was another of those phrases. The Filipinos were still passing cocktails.

More and more guests had flowed out of the big room of the penthouse into the dining room and the library and the bedrooms. Jeffrey could not find Madge, and it was later than he thought. All at once he was face to face with Marianna Miller. She was dressed very quietly, as though she were making an effort to be severe and plain and to show that she was not preoccupied with her looks.

"Why, hello," Jeffrey said.

His momentary surprise at meeting her made him forget everything else around him. He was completely himself again, just as he had wanted to be, with desires and wishes that were entirely his own property.

"Hello," she said, "are you going to take me home?"

"I wish I could," he said. "I've got to find Madge. She's around here somewhere."

"You're looking well," Marianna said.

"So are you," Jeffrey answered, "very well."

"Do you like my hat?" Marianna asked.

"Yes," Jeffrey said, "it's a nice hat."

Marianna smiled.

"I wondered if you'd like it when I bought it."

"I like you better without a hat," Jeffrey said. "Even a little hat covers up your hair."

Marianna smiled again.

"Well," she said, "good-by."

"Well," Jeffrey said, "good-by, Marianna."

"Jeff," Marianna said, "you're going out to the Coast?"

"Yes," he answered, "I've got to pay the bills."

"When?" she asked.

"I don't know just when," he answered. "The last of March or early in April, I think."

"I've rented a house on the beach," she said.

"Where," he asked her, "Malibu?"

It was time to be going, later than he thought.

"Call me up as soon as you get there," she said.

"Yes," he answered, "of course I will."

"You're sure?" she asked.

"Sure," he answered.

"Well," she said, "good-by, darling."

"Good-by," he said.

Then he saw Madge. Their glances met across the room and he knew she had been looking for him too, wondering where he was.

"Where have you been?" he asked her.

"I've been right here," she said. "I haven't seen you anywhere. Did you see Marianna Miller?"

"Yes," he said.

"She always looks so plain," Madge said, "doesn't she, in the afternoon?"

"Yes," Jeffrey said, "let's be going now."

"I've been looking for you everywhere," Madge said. "It's late. Did you forget that Ethel was coming?"

"Good God!" Jeffrey said. "Yes, I forgot about that."

"Well, it's your fault we're late," Madge said. "Don't say it's my fault. And she's your sister. She isn't my sister."

30

But When It Comes to Living

Once Jeffrey had hoped that his life would become simpler as time moved on. When the children were able to dress and undress themselves and when there were no more nurses around, he had believed that there would be less disorder at home, but it did not work that way. Each winter he would hope that he and Madge would not have to go to quite so many first nights or have quite so many obligations, but it never worked out that way. He knew too many different people, each connected with a different side of his life and all unconnected with each other. There was Jesse Fineman, and the theater. There were writers whom he knew, and entrepreneurs, like Sinclair Merriwell, and friends from the Air Corps, and old friends like Minot Roberts and friends of Madge's like Beckie and Fred, and then his own children and his children's friends, boys whom Jim knew and boys Charley's age and queer callow youths who were beginning to call on Gwen. It was like juggling balls and plates and knives to keep them all in their places and keep any continuity in his own life. He was obliged to shift his point of view so often that he was not sure he had any of his own. Sometimes he did not seem to belong to himself because he had seen too much and done too much. Madge used to say she did not mind variety because it kept her young, but after all, Madge had not seen as much of it as he had.

As Madge had said, Ethel was his sister, not hers. Madge did not have to drop one chain of relationships and pick up another when she saw Ethel—she did not have to go back to a half-forgotten life. It was hard to realize that Ethel was his sister, but she was, and not Madge's sister—coming out of nowhere, like a thought in the night. Now, without any real preparation for it, he was obliged to adjust himself. When he would have liked to sit quietly and read the paper, he was juggling balls and knives.

It was not half-past seven, it was nearly eight o'clock and Ethel and Gloria and his daughter Gwen would all have been waiting without any supper, wondering what had happened to him and Madge, and what was more, Ethel would notice his breath when he kissed her, and she would think that he was getting more and more like Alf.

"Hello," he called when they got home, "hello, are you there, Ethel?"

Her coat of worn black broadcloth trimmed with gray squirrel was there in the hall and her sensible, backwoodsy sort of hat, also trimmed with gray squirrel, was on top of it.

"Hello," he heard Ethel call, "hello, Jeffie." It was like the hall in Lime Street when she called him "Jeffie." He was Jeffie again and she was Ethel, his sister, not Madge's sister.

He always hoped whenever he saw Ethel that he did not look quite as old and settled as she did, but it was comforting to remember that, after all, Ethel was four years older than he. She wore a dark blue serge suit, which he imagined she must have cut herself from a Butterick pattern, because Ethel loved her electric sewing machine as much as she loved her washing machine that washed and dried everything in a twinkle, or her electric stove, or her electric mangle, or any of those other appliances which she and Wilbur had been buying on installments—and Wilbur could get them at special rates, because he was a salesman for General Electric. Ethel, seated in one of the armchairs, seemed to have let herself go more than Jeffrey remembered. She had a middle-aged spread; her hair was comfortably gray and she was wearing a cameo brooch which had belonged to their mother, and this made her look a little like a Grant Wood canvas. Beside the brooch was pinned an enamel American flag. Somehow the sight of Ethel made Jeffrey feel that it was absurd for him to try to be young and keep his figure; he became convinced that he and Madge must be like old people whom he used to know who insisted on going to dinner dances, instead of recognizing sensibly their infirmities.

"Hello, dear," Madge said, "we're awfully late, but you know the way Jeffrey is at cocktail parties."

Jeffrey watched them kiss each other. Whenever Madge saw Ethel she said something like that.

"He always says he's coming home," Madge said, "until he's had a drink or two, and then he stays and stays."

"Now, Madge," Jeffrey found himself saying, "I'm not as bad as all that."

"Don't scold him, Mother," Gwen said, "it's nice for Daddy to have a drink."

His niece, Gloria, was looking at him through her horn-rimmed spectacles and so was Ethel, in a fascinated way, as though they both were trying to measure the effect of alcohol upon his system.

"Well," Jeffrey said, "let's forgive and forget. Hello, Ethel." He bent down and kissed her cheek in a restrained manner and patted her on the shoulder.

"What's the American flag for?" he asked.

"It's for America," Ethel said, "America First."

"Oh," Jeffrey said, "have you got that up there?"

"Yes," Ethel said. "Now, don't make fun of West Springfield, Jeffie. We're just as American in West Springfield as you are, and perhaps a little more so."

"You must be starving," Madge said. "Jeffrey, take the girls and get the salad out of the icebox and be useful. The table's set in the dining room. Ethel, have you and Gloria been upstairs?"

"Yes"—he heard Ethel lower her voice—"thank you, Madge, dear."

"Well, well," Jeffrey said, "how's Gloria? How's Miss America?"

From the way Gloria glanced at him, and from the tittering sound she made, he was afraid Gloria thought that he was drunk.

"I'm fine, Uncle Jeff," she said.

"And you've never been to New York before, have you?" Jeffrey said. "How do you like New York?"

"It's fine," Gloria said.

"Now you're here," Jeffrey said, "we've got to be sure you see everything." He found it difficult to work out what a girl like Gloria ought to see in New York, but he wished to be clear about it so that neither Gloria nor her mother would think he had been drinking too much. "What do you think Gloria would like, Gwennie?"

Gwen uncrossed her legs and smoothed her skirt.

"I don't know, Daddy," she said. "There's so much."

He could see that she was not going to try to help him. There was no use pretending that Gwen and Gloria could get on together.

"Well," Jeffrey said, "there's the Aquarium."

"Daddy," Gwen said, "have you ever seen the Aquarium?"

Gloria turned in her chair and tittered.

"No," Jeffrey said, "not lately, but it's a fine place. There are penguins in the Aquarium, some of Admiral Byrd's. Well, there's the Aquarium, and then there's the Planetarium and the African Room in the Natural History Museum and the Art Museum. Well, you two girls go out in the kitchen and get the salad. Gwen can tell you all about what to see, Gloria."

"Yes," Madge said, "let the children work. Ethel, why didn't you tell us sooner you were coming? How long are you going to be here?"

"Just until Saturday afternoon," Ethel said. "Gloria and I are just here on a spree."

"Oh, dear," Madge said. "I know just the way you feel. It's so nice to get away from your own kitchen. I wish I could get away from mine."

Jeffrey stirred uneasily. Now that Gwen and Gloria had gone it was quieter. He wished that Madge had not said that about the kitchen, although Ethel smiled.

"I love my kitchen," Ethel said. "I'd rather do my own work than have someone do it for me. I wouldn't want any cook ruining my electric stove. I wish you could see it. It's a 1941."

"I know, they can do everything but talk," Madge said. "Jeff, what's the name of the stove we have in the country?"

"I don't know," Jeffrey said.

"Oh, yes you do," Madge said, "just try to think. You talked to the electric man about it."

"Jeffie always used to be in the kitchen," Ethel said. "He had to bring the coal in. Do you remember Tilly in Lime Street, Jeffie?"

"Oh, yes," Jeffrey said, "Tilly. You used to dry your stockings over the stove."

"Oh, Jeffie," Ethel said, "I don't see how you remember."

"It's easy," Jeffrey said. "You used to have big legs. We used to call you 'Piano Legs,' do you remember?"

"Jeff!" Madge said. "Don't mind him, Ethel." It was like juggling plates and knives again.

"Where's Wilbur?" Jeffrey asked her. "I hoped Wilbur was coming."

"Wilbur wished he could," Ethel said, "but just Gloria and I came, on a spree—well, not a spree, exactly. I've come down to a meeting of Chapter Chairmen of the America First Committee."

Jeffrey looked quickly at Madge.

"Let's not talk about the war," Jeffrey said.

Madge laughed, with a controlled inflection in her merriment. It was the way Madge laughed when she wanted to show that she could be very gracious, very gracious, even if other people weren't.

"Isn't that just like Jeff?" Madge said. "He's always afraid of any difference of opinion. You might think we were going to bite each other's heads off because we look at things differently."

"Madge," Jeff said, "do you think the girls know where the salad is?" Madge laughed again.

"Darling," she said, "we're all grown-up, really. I think it's fun, don't you, Ethel, when people have two opposing points of view, to compare them? If you could only stay here a little longer, I know you would see it the way we do. You'd know that England is fighting our fight, and that it's suicide for us not to help."

Jeffrey saw his sister fold her hands carefully on her lap.

"I know what you mean," she said. "It isn't that I don't love England. I've never had the chance to see foreign places as much as you and Jeffie have, and so they're not as dear to me, but I did go to England and to France too, and to Italy for six weeks when I was teaching at Springfield High. We went on a Colpitts teachers' tour."

"That must have been wonderful," Madge said, "but it must have been hard to get any impression. You move about so fast on a tour."

"I don't know," Ethel said, "it seems to me that I brought back a very good impression, and a store of memories too. I can still shut my eyes and see Westminster Abbey and Notre Dame Cathedral."

"Well," Jeffrey said, "I'm hungry. Let's see what the girls are doing."

"Oh, Jeff," Madge said, "relax, darling. There's no hurry about supper on the servants' night out."

He saw Ethel fold her hands and unfold them again.

"When we came back," Ethel said, "we were in the Tourist Class, but we were just as comfortable as could be, and there were a great many interesting, stimulating people—college boys and girls from Iowa, and college instructors, and a High School principal from Berkeley. I remember a poem one of the teachers recited. I know the way Jeffie is about poetry. He'll laugh and call it small-town, but it sums up—"

"Listen," Jeffrey said, "let's have supper. Let's not sum anything up."

"I'm not talking to you," Ethel said. "Madge and I are having a nice visit, and after all, you're not as clever as you think. I used to do your algebra for you once Jeffie, and I'm going to recite that poem."

"Don't mind Jeffrey, dear," Madge said.

"I know what Jeffie's going to say," Ethel said, "but just the same . . ." She drew a deep breath and half closed her eyes.

"Oh, London is a man's town, there's power in the air;
And Paris is a woman's town; with flowers in her hair;
And it's sweet to dream in Venice, and it's great to study Rome,
But when it comes to living, there is no place like home."

The silence when she finished was not amusing. There was something impressive about those lines as Ethel spoke them, because they expressed a belief. He thought of Ethel playing the melodeon at Lime Street, and of his father and his aunt singing hymns after Sunday supper. After all, Ethel was his sister.

"Why, of course," Madge said, but from her voice Jeffrey could tell what she was thinking. "That's the way I've always felt when I've got back. But Ethel, the only question is how to keep our homes, and our way of life."

"Come on," Jeffrey said, "I'll tell you a poem. 'Good food, good meat, good God, let's eat!'"

"Jeffie," Ethel said, "you stop!"

She spoke to him just as she would have back at Lime Street. He stopped, there was nothing more that he could do about it. He could see the dining room at home again and the bread board and the butter dish, covered with its netting frame to keep off the flies, and Ethel and her shirtwaist, with her gold-filled watch pinned upon it. He could feel a simplicity and a continuity that seemed more actual than any home of his that had come afterwards. Ethel's voice brought back to Jeffrey too a picture of her house in West Springfield with its brown-stained shingles and the two forsythia bushes by the front door. He could see the heavily upholstered suite in the parlor and the golden-oak chairs in her little dining room just off the kitchen and the radio that was part Gothic and part Jacobean and part Sheraton. He could see the *Ladies' Home Journal* and the *Country Gentleman* on the parlor table and the new *Encyclopædia Britannica* on its little glossy shelves that came free with the Encyclopaedia, and the tapestry carpet that was made to look like a Turkish rug. It was great to visit Venice, it was fine to study Rome, but when it came to living . . . He wondered whether Ethel were not a more solid citizen than he, and if her life had not been more useful. Then he heard the girls come back.

"Daddy, dear," Gwen was saying, "don't be cross. Supper's ready."

"I wish you could see," Madge said. "It isn't a matter of the Atlantic Ocean, dear. We're a part of the world and not a separate planet, and it doesn't have anything to do with the wave of the future."

"I'm only saying," Ethel answered, "we can't solve the age-old feuds of Europe—"

"Come on," Jeffrey said, "come on, don't fight."

"We're not fighting, dear," Madge said. "Why do you always call a friendly argument fighting? I was just telling Ethel—"

"Well, don't tell her," Jeffrey said, "come on."

Madge rested her hand on his arm as they walked into the dining room.

"Don't be so rude," Madge whispered. "She's your sister—she's not my sister."

"Damn it, Madge," Jeffrey whispered back, "don't say that again."

The dining room looked more pretentious than usual, as it always did on the couple's night out, and the table was set too elaborately. He saw Ethel looking at it and he knew that she was reducing the things there into dollars and cents, but there was no envy or malice in her. He was carving a cold chicken and everyone was passing plates.

"My," Ethel said, "I haven't asked about the children. How's Charley?"

"He's fine," Jeffrey said, "he's at school."

"Dear me," Ethel said, "I haven't seen him since he was five. I wish we were living nearer. How's Jim?"

"Jim," Jeffrey said, "oh, Jim's fine."

"Madge," Ethel said, "it gave me a start the last time I saw Jim. He looked just the way Jeffie used to, before he went to the war. Don't you think he looks like Jeffie?"

"I know people say so," Madge said, "but I've never been able to see it. He reminds me more of his grandfather—his forehead and around the eyes."

"Jeffie," Ethel said, "I never thought of that. I never saw Father in Jim."

It was like juggling balls and knives—balls and knives.

"I mean my father," Madge said. "Let me see, I don't believe you ever saw him."

"Oh yes I did," Ethel said, "at the wedding."

"How about some more chicken, Gloria?" Jeffrey asked. "Gwen, pass your cousin's plate and give Gloria some cocoa."

"No thank you, Uncle Jeff," Gloria said, "cocoa's fattening."

"We asked Jim to come up and take Gloria to the Harvest Ball," Ethel said. "He couldn't come. Boys are always busy in college."

"Let me see," Jeffrey said, "I think he told me about it. He was awfully sorry he couldn't do it. Be sure to ask him again."

"We'll ask him again," Ethel said, "if he'd really like to come."

"Of course he'd like to come," Jeffrey said.

"I'd like to see him," Ethel said, "beside that picture of you in uniform. Do you remember that picture, Jeffie?"

Madge glanced at him down the length of the waxed mahogany table through the soft light of the Georgian candlesticks. It was a glance of kindly but puzzled curiosity which he had observed whenever those days before they had known each other obtruded themselves into the conversation. She always said she loved to hear about them because they made her remember how much he had done for himself, and she said that it always gave her a new respect for him. Nevertheless, he was not entirely sure that she liked it.

"You had it taken at Halsey's—Mat Halsey with the shriveled arm who always did the High School groups," Ethel said. "You remember, Jeffie—over Martin's Hardware Store. Father made you have it taken."

"Yes," Jeffrey said, "I remember. I thought they were all thrown away. I burnt mine up."

"Oh, Jeff," Madge said, "you never told me. Why did you burn it up?"

"You should have kept it for the children," Ethel said, "so they could have seen you in uniform. You should have seen Jeffie, Madge. He kept looking at himself in store windows before he went away—Well, I have one of those pictures and someone else has too—can you guess who?—Louella Barnes."

"Oh," Jeffrey said, "she has one, has she?"

"She showed it to me," Ethel said. "She has it in her memory book."

"Oh," Madge said, looking at him, "poor Louella Barnes."

"She may have been slow for Jeffie," Ethel said, "but she isn't poor exactly."

Jeffrey glanced to his left where Gwen and Gloria were sitting. Gwen was looking at him with a puzzled look that was like her mother's, and in some way Gwen and Gloria seemed to personify Madge's difficulties with his past.

"Jeffie," Ethel asked, "have you heard from Alf?"

"No," Jeffrey said, "not for quite a while."

"You haven't seen his new wife, have you?"

"Why Jeff," Madge called across the table, "you never tell me anything. I never knew he was married again."

"They've got an orange grove," Jeffrey said, "near San Bernardino. She had it. He met her in Las Vegas."

The girls' faces had lighted up when Alf's name was mentioned.

"Uncle Alf knows a lot of songs," Gwen said.

"The last time Uncle Alf visited us," Gloria said, "he was drunk."

"Now, Gloria," Ethel said, "your Uncle Alf was only a little tired. Next thing you'll be saying that about your Uncle Jeffrey."

The table with its silver and its Wedgwood plates dissolved into the table at Lime Street. By some odd alchemy, Ethel had accomplished it simply by being there. There was the same dull, prosaic talk, meaningless and full of meaning, but Jeffrey could no longer fall back into its comfort. He seemed to be suspended between the personalities of Madge and Ethel.

He found himself staring into the candles and thinking of his conversation with Marianna Miller.

"Why, hello."

"Hello, are you going to take me home?"

"I wish I could. I've got to find Madge. She's around here somewhere."

"You're looking well."

"So are you, very well."

"Do you like my hat?"

"I like you better without a hat. . . ."

"Well, good-by."

"Well, good-by, Marianna."

But he did not want to say good-by to it. It belonged to him more completely than anything around him. It meant that he was still a person, and not a completed fact.

Then he heard the telephone. For an instant he thought that it might be Marianna calling—

"Gwen," Madge said.

Gwen pushed back her chair. He could hear the uncertain tapping of the high-heeled shoes which she had just begun to wear. The incessant ringing broke upon them rudely as it always did, snapping the thread of conversation although there was not much to snap.

"It's probably for her," Madge said.

"I suppose she's very popular with boys," Ethel said. "She looks like you, Madge."

But it was not for Gwen. Jeffrey heard her high heels clicking back.

"Daddy, dear," she called, "the telephone."

"Who is it?" Madge asked. "Couldn't you take the message?"

"Never mind, Madge," Jeffrey said, "that's all right."

"She ought to learn," Madge said. "Who is it, dear?"

"I asked who it was. It's Jim."

"Oh, dear," Madge said, and she sat up straighter, "did he say what he wanted?"

"Ma," Gwen answered, "you always think Jim's done something crazy. He just wants to talk to Daddy."

"All right," Jeffrey said, "all right. Never mind it, Gwen."

He put his napkin on the table. That was the way it always was in New York; he had to move from one contact to another. First it was Marianna Miller and Madge and his sister and Lime Street, and now he walked down the hall to the library, getting ready for something else.

"Hello," he called, "Jim. Hello, Jim."

The connection was bad, and Jim's voice was faint.

"I'm coming down to see you," Jim said. "It's something I can't tell you over the telephone."

"Can you hear me?" Jeffrey called back. He felt a sudden stab of anxiety mixed with anger. Jim had no right to do this. "What's the matter with you? Are you all right?"

"Yes, I'm all right," he heard Jim say. "Don't get mad. I'm just telling you I'm coming down tonight. I can't tell you why over the telephone."

"Wait a minute," Jeffrey called, and he tried to control the tautness in his voice. "Speak louder and just tell me what it is in general."

"I can't," Jim said, "it takes too long."

"Listen," Jeffrey said, "do what I tell you. Tell me what it is in general."

"Well, it's this way," Jim said. "The Captain in the Officers' Course . . ."

Jeffrey walked back slowly into the dining room. He tried to look composed and he even tried to smile. It was curious that he felt closer to his sister than he did to Madge at the moment. Somehow, he knew that Ethel was still fond of him and he did not mind her being there at all.

"It's all right," Jeffrey said, and something made him repeat it. "It's all right." But when he smiled at Madge, the muscles of his face felt tight.

"Jeff," Madge said.

He laughed, but the sound surprised him. "Don't worry," he said. "I talked him out of it."

"What?" Madge's voice was shriller. "Out of what?"

"It's all right," Jeffrey said again. "He wanted to enlist."

He sat down, still smiling, and took a drink of water, and no one spoke.

"He's taking a Military Science course, you know," he said to Ethel. "Artillery. I guess he's pretty good at it." He felt a little proud, just as though he had been good at it himself. "The West Pointer who gives the course called in two or three of them. They're looking for material for the School of Fire at Fort Sill."

"Fort Sill?" he heard Madge say. "Jeffrey, where's Fort Sill?" It annoyed him. Women could talk about the war, but they never knew anything about it.

"Fort Sill, Oklahoma," Jeffrey said, "the regular Army Artillery School. I know the way Jim feels, having that West Pointer recommend him."

"But Jeffrey," Madge said, "I can't see exactly what he's recommended for."

He did not mean to be impatient; it was his business and Jim's business, and he could look out for it better than a lot of other people, because he had been in the service once, himself. He knew what should or should not be done, so that there was no need for argument.

"As far as I can gather," he said, and he could sound intelligent about it, "the War Department is looking for officer material, and I suppose they've been inquiring through the colleges. That's all it was, Madge."

It had been a long while since he had been so proud of Jim.

"But what did Jim want to do?" Madge asked him.

He could not see why she was so slow, when she was usually quicker than he to grasp a fact.

"He wanted to leave college and enlist as a private in the Artillery," he said.

"But Jeffrey," Madge said, "why a private when you said he was going to be an officer?"

"No–no," he answered. He was speaking louder than he had thought. "A private with orders to attend the Officer Candidate School at Fort Sill."

Then he saw that the fact had struck her just as it had struck him–a son of hers in the Army–someone else's son, but not her son.

"Don't worry, Madge," Jeffrey said, "I told him to stay where he was and to keep his shirt on. He doesn't have to get into this thing yet."

"Of course he doesn't, Jeffie," Ethel said.

Ethel could see it through his eyes more clearly than Madge could. Madge was sitting up straight, and the wrinkles around her eyes were deeper.

"You haven't told us," she said. "Did he want to go?"

"Of course he did," he answered.

He saw her twist the corner of her napkin between her fingers.

"Then," she began, "don't you think—"

He had not expected it. He wondered whether it was due to a difference in temperament or whether it was because he had been to war himself. He was pleased that she took it that way, but he did not like it.

"No, Madge," he said, "I won't stop him if he wants to badly enough. But he's better off where he is now, trying to learn something, and maybe he hasn't got much time."

That last phrase of his tripped off his tongue and out of his thoughts inadvertently, and brought back to his mind another of those silly glib expressions that people were using then—that we were in the war already and we did not know it. He had been trying to push time away from Jim, and now they were back to where they were before the telephone had started ringing.

Ethel's glance was kindly, her age and her plainness were comforting. All at once he felt much better.

"Let's talk about what Gloria ought to see in New York," he said. "I remember the first time I saw New York. There's so much to see—you don't know where to start. Gloria, would you like to go behind the scenes in the theater?"

"Oh," Gloria said, "oh, Uncle Jeff."

He would not have dreamed of suggesting it, if Jim had not called up, but now he was glad to be kind to someone, and after all, it might be that Gloria and all of them did not have much time. He stood up and leaned over Gloria's chair.

"All right," he said, "come on, Gloria, and let's see what the town looks like at night—just you and me."

31

It Was Simpler for the Prince

It was very kind of Minot Roberts to ask Jeffrey to see his new hunter. The obvious truth that it was entirely out of his line made it even kinder. It meant that Minot liked his company, and in a sense depended on it.

"Someday you'll break your God-damn' neck," Jeffrey said.

Minot laughed. His teeth looked whiter and more even than usual because he was tanned from a fishing trip off the Florida keys.

"Someday," Minot answered, "maybe. When I do, I'll hold out my hand to you and say 'Kiss me, Wilson.'"

"What do you do it for?" Jeffrey asked.

He had often asked Minot the same question. He recognized that physical fear had its own consoling reaction, but he never could find the reaction sufficiently compensating. The best way he could explain that proclivity of Minot's was to think of it as a dark psychosis, connected in some way with the same craving for self-destruction which lurks, perhaps, in everyone.

"Because I've always done it," Minot said. "You used to do it once."

"I had to do it," Jeffrey said. He knew that Minot was referring to the Squadron in the war. "I don't like being scared to death."

Minot rested his hand on Jeffrey's knee.

"I'll tell you something," Minot said. "There's just a moment in it—it's like flying. You do everything you can. You get the pace, you steady him, and then there's nothing more you can do. You've shot the works, and there it is. That's the part that's worth waiting for. It's—well, it's worth waiting for."

"You sound like *Death in the Afternoon*," Jeffrey said.

Minot sat silently for a few seconds, and then he nodded.

"That boy Hemingway knows how to say it exactly right," he said. "What's the matter with it? Why be afraid of dying?"

"Reflex," Jeffrey said, "that's all."

"Well," Minot said, "there are worse things."

It was more than Minot usually said. It occurred to Jeffrey that ever since the last war, Minot had spent a good deal of his time and thought and money in not being afraid of dying, but Jeffrey could not develop that point of view. It seemed like a waste of time. Perhaps Jim would have understood Minot's motives better. Jim was at an age when you liked to demonstrate that you were not afraid of dying.

"You'll like him," Minot said, "when you see him, you'll know what I mean."

"Who?" Jeffrey asked.

"Who?" Minot repeated. "Bozeybones. He cost plenty. I was bidding against the Whitneys."

One thing Jeffrey could never understand was the selection of names for horses. "Powder Puff," or "Binkey," or "Nighty-night," or "Carmen."

"You'll like him," Minot said again. "He's got what it takes behind. When you're looking at a hunter, look at his rump."

"Why in God's name," Jeffrey asked, "do you call him 'Bozeybones'?"

"I didn't call him that," Minot answered. "Technically, he's Bozeybones II. He's sired by Bozeybones I."

"Never mind it, Minot," Jeffrey said.

"Valsky will be there," Minot said. "That's really why I wanted you to come. You'll like the Prince."

"I thought he was a Colonel," Jeffrey said.

"He's both of them," Minot said, "Colonel Prince Valsky."

Minot had often spoken of the Colonel. The Colonel had been in command of a cavalry regiment under the Czar. It was something, Minot often said, to get the Prince a little liquored-up in the evening and hear him tell about medieval life on the family estates on the Don. Then came the Revolution—not "come the Revolution" for the Prince—and the Prince fought with Denikin against the Reds, and somehow it sounded like a technical war game when Minot spoke of it. Then came the bust-up—not come the bust-up, for the Prince—and out he got, through the back door near Urga, with a few gold rubles and some of the Valsky diamond rings, and finally he appeared in that queer closed corporation of exiles, the White Russians, in New York. The Prince was a soldier who had seen a world turn upside down and, as Minot said, knew how to take it like a gentleman. Make no mistake, Minot said, Prince Valsky was a gentleman, and you could always tell one. Prince Valsky knew how to drink, and he could draw diagrams charting the course of a horse clearing an obstacle as accurately as he could chart the curve of a projectile. Prince Valsky was a disciple of the forward seat, a perch, as he put it, such that the rider's weight was right on the withers, allowing the animal's hindquarters necessary free play. Prince Valsky could ride anything, and when Prince Valsky was up, no matter what he was up on, he could make nothing seem like something. And what was more, don't forget it, he was a gentleman, an educated man of family from the Czar's Military Institute. What was more, Prince Valsky was a great teacher, patient and sensible, and he needed patience with the pupils who came to him who wanted to get into the right set by learning to ride. There had been a time when Prince Valsky was held back by his English. Once, when he was watching a middle-aged lady in the ring of his riding establishment, he could not think of the English expression for rising to the trot, and he had been obliged to say, "Soft sit, soft sit." But Valsky's English was good now. He had that Russian facility with languages, and he could teach anybody to ride. Minot said he ought to teach Jeffrey. If Jeffrey gave the Prince the chance, Jeffrey would love it.

"But I don't want Valsky to teach me," Jeffrey said.

Nevertheless, he liked to hear about Prince Valsky because the Prince was like a page in foreign literature.

The snow was melting fast, as it did in late March, and there was a faint touch of spring in the afternoon air. Minot's car had stopped uptown on the West Side in front of a building that looked like a storage warehouse. There was a green door in the center of a blank brick wall, with a discreet bronze plaque on which was lettered VALSKY.

Pierre had hopped out and had opened the door and was pulling the rug carefully from their knees.

"When you go out to the Coast," Minot said, "tell them about Valsky, Jeff. He's thinking of taking a trip out there."

The reception room had comfortable chairs and cigarette stands and sporting magazines, and a stout woman in black took their coats and hung them up carefully in a little cubbyhole.

"We've got the place to ourselves," Minot said. "It's a private hour."

A door opened and a smallish man with dark hair, dark eyes, and delicate, regular features was standing there, dressed like Minot in riding breeches with black shining boots.

"Ermak!" Minot said.

"My dear Minot," the other said. "Always on time, eh?" And he laughed about nothing, just the way Minot sometimes laughed.

"This is my old friend Jeffrey Wilson," Minot said, "Colonel Prince Valsky."

Jeffrey never knew exactly what to say to anyone like Colonel Prince Valsky.

"Minot's told me a lot about you," he said.

"He must not tell too much," the Prince said, and he laughed again, heartily, about nothing, "not too much, eh? We'll see him ride now, eh? Shall we go now?"

Minot was pulling on a pair of gloves and the little room that smelled of the stable seemed very still. Jeffrey's reading was always making him place ordinary incidents in fictional categories, and this was like the fencing school in the cloak-and-the-sword story—two gay young bucks from London, Corinthians, perhaps, dropping into the academy of an *émigré* to test their skill with the smallsword. But it was also close to Tolstoy—those stilted phrases of the Prince's, his courtesy, his good nature—and it was odd, coming upon it that winter at just that time.

"Well," the Prince said, "shall we go? Come with me into the ring. There is no one to bother. We shall see our dear friend fall off, eh?" And the Prince laughed again.

The ring was small and covered with tanbark, built on what might have been once the floor of a warehouse or a garage. It was lighted by dirty barred windows, partially opened, and some sparrows had entered and were flying among the beams and girders which supported the roof. On one side of the ring were some benches, somewhat like a circus box, with steps leading down into the ring itself. On the other side was a dusty mirror, arranged, presumably, so that riders might criticize their posture in the saddle. The ring was vacant except for a jumping standard. They stepped noiselessly down onto the soft tanbark, and when the Prince called out in a sharp staccato tone a door slid open, and with a slithering of hoofs a horse appeared, led by a small Russian with a fat, rosy, inexpressive face. He should have been wearing a blouse and a belt, and Cossack boots instead of overalls.

Jeffrey looked at the animal in the baffled way in which he always looked at horses. Whether it was bay or chestnut, Jeffrey did not know, but the horse looked unhappy, judging from the twitching of its nostrils and the quivering of its forelegs, and the impatient way it threw its head. The animal was bony—big-boned, Jeffrey supposed the technical term would have been, or raw-boned—and he could not understand why under the sun anyone had wanted it, but Minot and the Prince had the look that Jeffrey had seen before on the faces of "horse lovers"—the serious, enigmatic look of connoisseurs regarding a picture. The appearance of the hunter gave them some sort of secret aesthetic pleasure. Minot turned to Jeffrey and Jeffrey knew he was expected to say something.

"He's sort of big for this room, isn't he?" Jeffrey asked, and Minot laughed rudely.

"Did you hear that, Ermak?" Minot said, but the Prince only smiled politely.

"A small ring makes better training," he said, but his eyes were still on the horse. All his attention was focused on Minot as Minot walked forward and tested the saddle girth and began fussing with the stirrups. There was a slight argument about the bit, which Jeffrey could not understand, and then Minot was hopping in an awkward way, with one foot in a stirrup which was much too short for him, while the horse kept circling, snorting gently, with the man in overalls holding its head. When Minot was up in the saddle the man let go, and the horse began bouncing sideways. Minot's body conformed to all the eccentric motions, and the concentration on Minot's face showed that he was enjoying it, but to Jeffrey it all seemed a waste of everyone's time. He stood there in the center of the ring, beside the Prince, feeling uncomfortable and cold.

"Nice hands," the Prince said.

"What?" Jeffrey asked him.

For an instant the Prince's clear, dark eyes looked impatient.

"His hands upon the reins," he said. "The touch is very necessary for a rider. Nice hands."

"I'm sorry," Jeffrey said, "I don't know much about this."

They stood in the center of the ring while Minot walked the horse.

"He is a friend of yours?" the Prince asked.

Jeffrey could see no reason for the question, but then it was always hard to tell what a foreigner was thinking.

"Nice hands," the Prince said, "nice sit."

Jeffrey did not answer. There was no reason why Minot should not have nice hands and a nice sit, since he had given a great deal of attention to them.

"An old friend?" the Prince asked.

Considering everything, it seemed kind of the Prince to be interested.

"Ever since the last war," Jeffrey said.

The horse was trotting now, snorting and throwing its head. The Prince's voice was warmer. All Russians had a social sense, and now he and the Prince had something in common.

"Ah," the Prince said, "you were a soldier?"

"Aviation," Jeffrey said.

"Ah," the Prince said, and he laughed for no particular reason. "That was a war."

"Different from this one," Jeffrey said.

"Ah, no," the Prince answered. "All war is the same, I think. Just war."

"I suppose you know," Jeffrey said.

A part of Jeffrey's attention was upon Minot and that horse, now moving at a slow, collected gallop, and part on what the Prince was saying, and part on his own thoughts. The Prince had wrinkled his forehead in a polite, exaggerated interrogation.

"Perhaps you can tell me something, sir," he said. "With my people, war has seemed natural. With so many here, they do not seem to understand this. It seems to shock them very deeply."

"They're far away from it," Jeffrey said.

"Yes," the Prince said, "yes. It is amusing for me to think of."

"How do you mean, it's amusing?" Jeffrey asked.

"For me it is amusing," the Prince said, "to hear them talk. For me, I am lonely in this war. I can stand and look, because I do not care."

His detachment was tranquil and refreshing.

"I see what you mean," Jeffrey said.

There was the sound of thudding hoofbeats all around them.

"I can see the combinations," the Prince said, "and I wish that I might care."

"I don't know—" Jeffrey said—"I wish I didn't."

"No," the Prince said, "believe me, it is better to care."

They were silent for a moment, and then Jeffrey asked a question because the answer that the Prince might give to it could have some authority.

"Who's going to win?" he asked.

"I think," the Prince said, "no one will win. You see, I know about war very well, I think." Then he called to Minot. "He does better today."

"Yes," Minot called back, "he's all right."

Then Jeffrey asked another question and he was reluctant to ask it, because he was afraid that he would believe the answer. "Do you think we'll get into it?" he asked.

"Why, surely," the Prince said. "Our friend has nice hands."

The riding ring felt cold and the Prince seemed to be lost in thoughts of his own.

"If I might fight," he said, "I should like to fight the Japanese. I do not like those people very much." The Prince reached in his pocket and drew out an enameled cigarette case. "Please," he said. "People here are so disturbed by what is inevitable. I do not understand it."

"You're a fatalist, aren't you?" Jeffrey said.

The Prince laughed very heartily.

"My dear," he said, and it sounded like a literal translation from *War and Peace*, "I and all my people are, I am very glad to say. Shall we set the jump up now?"

"Yes," Minot called. "Put it up at three feet six. Let's go."

The Prince gave a sharp order and the man in overalls moved the jumping standards.

"That fellow," the Prince said, "was a soldier. Please."

The Prince lighted a match unhurriedly, and held it out to Jeffrey.

"Oh," Jeffrey said, "thank you," and he bent over the Prince's small, delicate hand to light his cigarette. For some reason it was comforting to stand by someone who could view the future without emotion.

"Our friend," the Prince said, "tells me you leave for Hollywood."

"Yes," Jeffrey said, "next week."

"I do not understand," the Prince said. "Most of them ride poorly in the films. I might teach them, do you think?"

"Do you mean," Jeffrey said, "you want to go to Hollywood?"

Of all the places the Prince might want to go, it seemed the least plausible.

"It has always been my dream to go there," the Prince said. "If you should see a chance for me, tell me please."

Jeffrey nodded. Suddenly the Prince had shrunk into a fallible little man, no longer to be taken seriously, slightly sad, perhaps amusing, like Jeffrey himself and like everyone else. His words had lost their value. He still wanted something; he still had something to lose and something to gain, like everyone else, and what was worse, the thing he wanted was exactly the same as the thing desired by some little girl behind a drugstore lunch counter.

The jumping standards were up just opposite them, and Minot walked the horse to the center of the ring, so close that Jeffrey could feel the warmth from the animal's sweating shoulder.

"What are you two talking about?" Minot asked.

"Philosophy, my dear," the Prince answered.

"Well," Minot said, "let's go."

He put the horse in a canter and went squarely at the jump. It looked effortless and easy.

"All right," Minot called, "put it up to four."

There was the same thudding of the hoofs. The Prince's eyes narrowed and he flicked the ash of his cigarette.

"He is very nice," the Prince said softly.

"Have you tried him over five?" Minot called.

"No," the Prince called back, "not five. The ring is small."

"All right," Minot called, "put it up to five."

Minot looked as young as he had looked years ago. His face was lighted by a sort of concentration that was entirely selfless.

"I thought so," Jeffrey said, "he wants to break his neck."

"Do you think?" the Prince asked, and he glanced at Jeffrey quickly and back to the jumping standard. "I do not think. I think it is he likes to live."

The Prince's face was like Minot's, absorbed and watchful.

"Very nice," the Prince said. "He is—very nice."

You could not tell whether he meant that Minot was a very nice horseman or a very nice man. You could not tell anything about the Prince. As the horse rounded the curve and approached the short stretch before the jump, Minot brought his crop down hard and Jeffrey watched his friend's face. Minot seemed to have recaptured something that Jeffrey never could. He was leaning forward. The horse reached with its neck toward the jump and Jeffrey could see the reins slither through Minot's fingers.

"Now," he heard the Prince say softly, "now," and then the Prince raised his voice. "Very nice," he called, "very nice."

His eyes were on the jump, watching the horse sail through the air. Then there was a bell-like sound, made from wood struck heavily, followed by a crash. The horse had landed, entangled somehow with the falling bar, stumbling, throwing Minot forward, half out of the saddle.

"The wrong lead," the Prince called, "was it not?" The horse stood trembling, and Minot slid from the saddle. Minot seemed to be considering the proper answer to the Prince's question. He turned back toward the fallen jumping standard and pulled a handkerchief from the pocket of his riding breeches and mopped the perspiration from his forehead.

"No, the lead was right," he said. "He wasn't going, that's all."

He turned and looked at the horse. "Maybe I didn't give him enough. Maybe I'm getting old."

"Oh, no," the Prince said, and he laughed. "No, no, not that."

Minot slapped his hands softly against the horse's neck and looked back at Jeffrey and the Prince. His face no longer looked young.

"I've seen it happen," Minot said. "You get too careful. You think too much." He smiled. "Maybe I should have died young."

The Prince laughed very heartily.

"Oh, no," he said, "not that. In this ring, five feet is very high."

Then Minot laughed.

"There you go," he said. "You wouldn't have put it that way, either—once." The Prince was silent and Jeffrey could hear the twittering of the sparrows on the iron girders over head.

"I was a very big fool," the Prince said, "once."

Then Jeffrey cleared his throat.

"All right," he said, "you're old, so what? You're both old enough to know better."

But Minot and Prince Valsky only looked at him as though he were speaking another language, and then Minot ran his hand carefully over the horse's forelegs.

"He isn't cut," he said. "Put it up again." He climbed back into the saddle and took off his coat and then he walked the horse to the little grandstand and tossed the coat over the railing.

"Old enough to know better," the Prince said to Jeffrey. "I do not like that saying. One should never know better."

Jeffrey did not answer.

"He wasn't going," Minot called across the ring. Minot walked the horse slowly toward the jump, halted in front of it and touched the bar with his hand, and turned the horse. The Prince reached in his pocket and drew out his enameled cigarette case.

"Please," he said.

"Oh," Jeffrey said, "thank you."

Minot had turned the horse back toward the jump.

"In war," the Prince said. "I say all war is the same in the end. I shall tell you why. Please."

He struck a match and Jeffrey leaned forward to light his cigarette.

"War is a matter of killing," the Prince said. "In this war, not enough have been killed. In this war, no one will win, unless more are killed. I ask you, how can it happen? There is not an opportunity."

"Yes," Jeffrey said, "I see what you mean."

"Now," the Prince said, "he will try again."

The Prince blew a cloud of cigarette smoke and stared through it at the jump. The ring was very still again. The whole procedure proved absolutely nothing, and yet Jeffrey felt very nervous, very tense.

"Mr. Wilson," the Prince said softly, "I shall tell you something."

An intensity in the Prince's dark eyes made it seem as though the Prince had touched him.

"I think it is what living is for, perhaps. I think, I am not sure."

Jeffrey's thoughts were pounding through his head with the gallop of the horse. The horse was rounding the turn and straightening into the stretch. He saw the white of Minot's shirt and heard the crack of Minot's riding crop, and suddenly he felt envious. Minot had everything he wanted, everything.

"Hi," the Prince called, "hi," and he slapped his hands together as though he could raise that horse into the air.

"Ah," the Prince called. "Bravo!" And he slapped Jeffrey's shoulder hard.

They had cleared the jump and when it was over the whole thing seemed simple. Minot was resting his weight in the saddle again, pulling the horse down gently to a stop.

"It was just the way he was going," Minot said. "Well, that's all."

The attendant was holding the horse's head and Minot walked quickly across the ring and reached for his coat.

"Well," Minot said, "it's getting late. Good-by, Ermak," and he shook hands with the Prince.

"Good-by," the Prince said, "it was very nice. Good-by, Mr. Wilson. If you should think, remember me at Hollywood."

Minot was singing beneath his breath:—

"I'm going to a happy land, where everything is bright,
Where highballs grow on bushes, and we stay out every night."

"What is that," the Prince asked, "that tune?"

Minot laughed. His face looked warm and gay.

"'Where highballs grow on bushes,'" he said, "'and we stay out every night.' Well, I'll be in next week, Ermak. Jeff, you'll come back to the apartment with me, won't you?"

They were in the reception room by then, and the woman in black was helping them with their coats.

"It has been a pleasure," the Prince said, "believe me, really."

"You're coming back with me, aren't you?" Minot asked him again.

"Yes," Jeffrey answered, "I want to talk to you about something."

The car was moving eastward to the Drive through Central Park. The afternoon was like so many other incidents which Jeffrey had experienced: time would smooth it the way water smoothed a rock, removing from it all the edges of individuality. He would not remember, because he had seen too much—too many people, too many faces, all of which were merged in the trivialities of every day. As Minot leaned back, Jeffrey envied him, not only his happiness, but the simplicity of his happiness. Minot could make everything he saw and did fit into definite standards, as though he had worked out some problem to his satisfaction when he was young, and had kept working it out again and again, without erasing or correcting the addition or adding new equations and proportions.

" 'I'm going to a happy land,' " Minot was humming, " 'where everything is bright, Where the highballs grow on bushes, and we stay out every night.' "

They were crossing Central Park. Jeffrey could see the bare trees and the melting snow, reflecting faintly the color of the sky in the late afternoon, but he knew Minot did not notice. Minot was thinking of the war.

He was like all those other people in the Contact Club, whose minds continually turned back to 1918; and the Prince had been thinking about the war—in a different way, but thinking of it, wanting it back again. They had not considered it as something that was over, and perhaps Jeffrey had been wrong, and they had been right. Perhaps it had never been over.

" 'I'm going to a happy land,' " Minot was humming.

"Minot," Jeffrey said, "if you'd just as soon, would you hum something else?"

32

He Didn't Have Much Time

Minot lived in an apartment on the upper part of Fifth Avenue, overlooking the Park, just where he should have lived. He had moved there, twelve years before, after his mother died, and it had never occurred to Jeffrey until that afternoon that all that part of Fifth Avenue could ever be out of date. He had never noticed before how dingy the baroque façades of the private houses had grown. He had never noticed how many of them were unoccupied, how many were for sale or to let. He remembered the Richard Harding Davis story of the big red touring car panting at the curb, waiting for our hero to descend in his dustcoat and goggles from the old family mansion on the Park. The Park had scarcely changed, except for the additions to the Art Museum, which had been too large before, and except for the monument to the 27th Division. But opposite, the houses and the apartments looked as dusty and as technically dated as the works of Davis or Chambers. Even Minot's apartment house, which had obviously always been kept in meticulous order, gave Jeffrey, that afternoon, the illusion of a perfectly preserved survival. It had as little to do with what was going on at present as Minot himself or the Prince or the horse or the five-foot jump, and yet neither Minot nor the apartment was very old. The building had actually been erected in 1915, and Jeffrey could never get it out of his head that 1915 was only yesterday. It always surprised him to realize how much taste had changed, and taste, he supposed, really represented a sort of human aspiration. The hall was Gothic. The floor, of course, was laid in black and white marble squares, slightly worn. The walls were decorated with excellent replicas of tapestry, or they might have been originals, as far as Jeffrey knew. The elevator was of gilded metal and black walnut with a green plush seat, and the little car and its white-haired attendant, who was wearing a livery not unlike a Prince Albert coat, seemed to Jeffrey to move upward with a tantalizing slowness, very unlike the elevators on Park Avenue.

The hall of Minot's apartment was dark oak with an Italian refectory table and a Venetian gilded mirror above it and a silver plate for calling cards. Minot's man—Minot always called him his man—must have come to the door as soon as he heard Minot's latchkey. He smiled at Jeffrey, because Jeffrey was Minot's friend.

"Make us a cocktail, will you William?" Minot said. "And light the fire. Where shall we sit, Jeff, in the parlor or the den?"

That was an anachronism, too. It went with the apartment house and that part of the Avenue, with Robert W. Chambers and Richard Harding Davis. You never called them "dens" any longer. They were "libraries" or "studies" now, not that he could ever think of Minot as seriously studying anything, and when Jeffrey thought of the leather-backed books which Minot never read, and of Minot's silver trophies on the mantelpiece, he did not want to go there.

"How about the parlor?" Jeffrey asked.

"All right," Minot said. "Wait for me there, will you, Jeff? Read the paper or get the six-o'clock news. I'll just take off these boots."

It always interested Jeffrey to observe how other people lived. Their tastes, and the possessions with which they surrounded themselves, often set a punctuation, sometimes amusing and sometimes sad, upon everything they had done. Until that afternoon he had always accepted the big room in Minot's apartment uncritically, but he thought of it analytically now, in spite of himself, and this seemed almost disloyal. When he and Madge had first come there to dinner, when the chandeliers were lighted and the logs in the Italian marble fireplace were burning, it had seemed to epitomize, more than any room he had ever seen, an impregnable sort of stability. Now it seemed silent, sensitive to his criticism. Those minutes before dusk were the least flattering time for any room, for everything had a weary look, and the curtains should have been drawn and the lights turned on in order to conceal a day that was dying. The room was crowded with pictures and furniture and bric-a-brac and Persian rugs which were a little too large for the floor space, all from Minot's mother's house, brought there after she had died. The Louis Seize chairs in blue damask had come from his mother's parlor. There was a bench covered with *petit point*, with Jacobean legs, standing just in front of the Renaissance lion-headed brass andirons, which were too large for the fireplace. The piano in the corner was covered with a silk Persian rug, and on top of the rug was a cluster of photographs of Minot's friends and family, each in a heavy silver frame.

There was one of Minot's father sitting at a desk and pictures of Minot's two daughters in white frilly dresses, and in one of the frames Jeffrey saw a picture of himself, heavily lighted and dramatized by a theatrical photographer, taken, he remembered, on the only occasion when Jesse Fineman had ever produced a play of his. There was a photograph, growing a little yellow, of Stanley Rhett in his leather coat and helmet. He was leaning against the wing of a biplane, smiling, and always young, because Stan was dead, smiling from the past that Minot still loved best. Across the corner in rather unformed letters were the words, "*Happy Landings–Stan.*" Then there was a picture of Captain Strike, their flight commander. "*Always, Minot–Bill.*" The photographs stared at Jeffrey from their frames in the unrelieving light. They had always seemed to him completely natural until that afternoon, but now they had become the sort of thing that guests would look at surreptitiously and speak of gently among themselves without asking impertinent questions.

In the silence of the room, Jeffrey could almost hear their voices: "The old man, Minot's father . . . Jeff Wilson, you know, the one who does something about plays–the one he met in the war who married Madge Hayes . . . Minot's little girls–living with their mother after the divorce . . . That one, Stan Rhett–you know, Bill Rhett's brother, killed in the war . . . Captain Somebody-or-other, someone he knew in the war." But Jeffrey had always been pleased that his picture was among them. It was a part of Minot's loyalty.

There were two Sèvres vases on the marble mantelpiece, so large that you knew that they had never been bought for it, and on the wall above the mantel was John Singer Sargent's portrait of Minot's mother. Jeffrey had always loved to see her there–she was so alive, so much the way he always remembered her. As he looked at her now, she seemed very glad to see him. All sorts of memories came to him of her kindness, and yet that afternoon, he had another thought. It might have been the skill of Sargent that made her appear to own that room and to give every object in it some fragment of her memory. Everything in that room had been hers. It had always seemed fitting and touching to Jeffrey that it had been so, until that afternoon, but now he understood how difficult it might have been for another woman to have come to that place and to have lived with a memory. There was no unity in that room, to which everything had been brought so obviously from somewhere else. It represented a taste belonging definitely to another generation. The room itself was an effort at survival. It was Minot's effort to cling to everything that he liked. It was Minot's lack of resilience and compromise. Jeffrey told himself that the room was all right because it was a part of his friend, but he wished that he had not suddenly seen it in a new perspective.

The radio, too, was like Minot in that it represented his self-indulgence and his ability to get anything he wanted. The box was covered with all sorts of dials for short wave and long wave which Jeffrey could not understand, and adjustments for every sort of kilocycle. It was one of those radios which could pick up Japan as easily as a local station, and he finally saw where to turn it on. The uncanniness of a strange voice breaking the silence was stranger that afternoon than usual.

"And now this ends Jo-Jo and Mu-Mu. They'll be back again with you tomorrow, same time, same station. In fifteen seconds it will be exactly six o'clock, Lovely Watch time. L-o-v-e-l-y . . . and spelling, too, compact daintiness. Lovely Watch time. And now, friends, in these late days of March, the danger month, do you feel run-down, a little headachy, without the old pep to put things over? There's an easy answer. Mu-Mu Tablets. They work in six easy ways. At your neighborhood druggist, and remember, the letters of these two words read backwards spell 'um-um,' and that's the way they taste. And now it is six o'clock, and the friendly voice of your friendly reporter brings to you the latest flashes off the wires of the world press."

It was not decent. Jeffrey wondered why he tolerated such an intrusion on his thoughts. If he turned it off, he would not hear the news. The makers of Mu-Mu, spelt backward meaning "um-um," and of Lovely Watch, were trading on anxiety, tramping over the blood of battlefields to get the sordid anticlimax of their message home. He knew he would not like the voice of the friendly reporter, either, a fluty, cheery voice, dealing with headlines which were a distortion of fact.

". . . and now—Berlin. . . . On his arrival in Berlin from Moscow, Japan's foreign minister, Matsuoka, said in a message to the German people, 'The Japanese nation is with you, in joy or sorrow.' And he went on to say that Japan, and I quote, 'will not lag behind you in fidelity, courage, and firm determination to arrange the world on the basis of the New Order.'"

It was not hard to form an idea of what was meant. After waiting patiently, balancing everything, the government of Japan was reaching the conclusion that Germany could not help but win the war. It was possible to consider it as another piece of devious, oriental straddling, but he knew he would not have thought so if he were a Japanese. He thought of Japanese he had known, mostly salesmen in oriental stores and houseboys. Once he and Madge had employed a Japanese, an unhappy little man.

"The little bastard," Jeffrey said, and he turned off the radio. Then he heard Minot's voice behind him.

"What's the news?" Minot asked. Minot was wearing a quilted smoking jacket and patent-leather pumps.

"Japan is going to get into the Axis," Jeffrey said.

"A damn good thing if she does," Minot answered. "Let 'em come on in. You ought to hear the boys in the navy. What we won't do to Japan!"

"If we're going to convoy," Jeffrey said, "we won't have much navy in the Pacific."

"We'll have enough," Minot said. "I'll tell you something. When I was coming North, I stopped in Washington, and I won't tell you who told me, but they're just waiting for the Japanese—I'll tell you something, Jeff, a war with Japan would be an air war and people with Mongoloid eyes can't focus the way we can. Everybody knows they can't fly."

Minot was like everyone else, busily repeating something which someone else had said, and Jeffrey listened, as others always listened, hopefully taking that piece of gossip and trying to add it to something else.

"Gosh," Minot said, "it's gloomy here. Why haven't you turned on the lights? Where's William? Let's light a fire."

It was not so much the light that made it gloomy as those obtruding thoughts from which you could never escape. There was that tremor of insecurity again. It looked stormy outside and Jeffrey could see lights across the Park through the windows. He had loved the sensation once of standing behind the dark panes and listening to the invisible rain beat against them and hearing the roar of thunder overhead. He had loved it, because he had felt dry and secure, but now it was like standing behind a window and knowing that the rain would smash through into the room before the storm was over, and that everything would be a sodden, irreparable mess.

"Yes," Jeffrey said, "it still gets dark early."

Then the lights were on, and the whole room looked better. William had entered, with two cocktails on a silver tray.

"Well," Minot said, "happy landings!"

William touched a match to the fire and there was a sudden illusion of serenity and ease. Jeffrey raised his glass. He found it easier to take a drink that winter than it had ever been before. You could take a cocktail, and you did not care so much.

"So you're going to Hollywood," Minot said. "What do they want you for?"

Jeffrey had a suspicion that Minot looked upon Hollywood as a gay adventure, a round of yachting parties and night clubs. Jeffrey might have talked until he was blue in the face without ever convincing anyone like Minot that the work was hard.

"It's a script," Jeffrey said. "Their regular writers are bogged down with it. I have a sort of reputation for pulling things together."

Minot sat comfortably, looking at the fire.

"You won't be mad if I say something?" Minot said.

"No," Jeffrey said, "of course not," but he knew exactly what it was that Minot was going to say.

"Jeff, why don't you write something of your own instead of doing potboiling for someone else?"

It sounded exactly like Madge. That was what they always called it, "potboiling." He could not understand why that hackneyed term had such appeal for an amateur. It indicated the same type of mind that referred to writing as "scribbling," and he hoped very much that Minot would not use that term, but Minot used it.

"I mean," Minot said, "if you're going to do scribbling, why don't you do your own scribbling?"

Jeffrey hesitated. He even contrived to smile.

"I can't afford it, Minot," he said. "You see, I've got to pay the bills, and it takes a good deal of money, with the new income taxes."

When he saw Minot smile, he knew that Minot was exactly as annoyed by this explanation as he had been by Minot's reference to scribbling.

"Jeff," Minot said, "Madge has plenty of money."

"I thought you'd say that," Jeffrey answered. "Maybe it's funny of me, but I like to run my own show, while I can."

Minot nodded, and Jeffrey knew Minot was thinking that it was quite correct, that one did not take money from women.

"I know what you mean," Minot said. "Jeff, I'll tell you what I'll do. I'll stake you. You wouldn't mind that, would you?" And Minot leaned forward impulsively. "Jeff, you're too damned good. You're too good to waste your time working for a bunch of Jews in Hollywood."

"They pay for what I give them," Jeffrey said.

"God damn it," Minot said, "why do you always think about money?"

"I suppose you think it's funny of me," Jeffrey said. "There's only one thing I've ever done, and I want to keep on doing it. I want to run my own show."

Minot was silent and Jeffrey could see that he was puzzled.

"Jeff," Minot asked, "are you afraid?"

Jeffrey raised his head sharply.

"Afraid of what?" he asked.

Minot was watching him intently. Minot's knees were crossed, and he was moving one ankle nervously, so that Jeffrey could see the light from the fire reflected on Minot's patent-leather pump.

"Afraid that anything you do won't be any good."

Jeffrey sat looking at the fire. He did not want to take it, but he had to take it.

"Yes," he said, "I suppose so, in a way. Maybe, Minot, it's pretty late to try."

"It's never too late," Minot said.

The problems of human beings could not be expressed in such simple terms, but Minot did not see that.

"I don't know," Jeffrey said. "I've lived with myself for quite a while. Maybe I'll try it sometime, but I can't right now."

"You ought not to go to Hollywood," Minot said, "and work for a bunch of Jews."

"Why Jews, particularly?" Jeffrey asked. "You'd be surprised. They're about the same as anyone else."

"You know what I mean," Minot said. "It's just a figure of speech."

"Well, I wouldn't use it," Jeffrey said. "It doesn't make any sense."

Somehow, even talking to one's friends in these days you came to racial issues that bordered on a party line. Somewhere in the background, the old phrases were dangling. He could almost hear Minot saying that Jews were all right if there were not too many of them and that he was just as broad-minded as Jeffrey and that he liked Jews as individuals.

"I'm not saying anything against them," Minot said. "You know more about them than I do."

"Well, let's leave it at that," Jeffrey said. "I've got to go out to Hollywood, Minot, and there is something I want to ask you."

Minot looked up from the fire.

"Go ahead and ask it, Jeff," he said. "Anything at all."

Then Jeffrey's irritation at Minot evaporated. It was true that he could ask him anything at all. If he hesitated, it was only because he himself could not fully understand what disturbed him. After all, it was only another trip to Hollywood—simply a matter of the Twentieth Century to Chicago and the Super Chief out in the afternoon—Kansas City, the plains and Albuquerque, the sagebrush and the desert.

"I'll be there for a month or six weeks," Jeffrey said. "It's hard to put a definite time on it, but it won't be long. Anyone can get me on the telephone in five minutes. I can take the Stratoliner and get back here overnight. I don't know why it seems so far away this time. I suppose it's because no one can tell exactly what's going to happen."

"How do you mean," Minot asked, "what do you think's going to happen?"

"Nothing," Jeffrey answered, "nothing, really. Well, I'll tell you, Minot. While I'm away, I wish you'd keep an eye on Jim. Maybe you could see him and talk to him. You know, he thinks a lot of you."

"Jim?" Minot asked. "What's the matter with Jim?"

"There's nothing the matter with him," Jeffrey answered, "nothing the matter at all. I don't know why it is, Minot, I feel a little differently about Jim from the way I do about the other kids. It may be because he's pretty well grown-up. You know, he's nearly twenty-one. I keep worrying about Jim."

"Listen," Minot said, "Jim's all right."

"I don't worry in the way you think," Jeffrey said. "I'll tell you something, Minot. Do you remember last spring, almost a year ago—the night of the Contact Club dinner—you gave Jim a fifty-dollar bill and told him to spend it all that night?"

"I know," Minot said. "I remember."

"Do you remember what you said to me afterward," Jeffrey asked, "when you were telling me why you did it? I suppose it's clearer with me than it is with you. You said he didn't have much time."

Minot looked up from the fire.

"I remember," he said, "I was a little tight."

"Maybe you were," Jeffrey said, "but maybe it's true."

Then Minot spoke suddenly.

"He isn't mixed up with some woman, is he?"

"Not the way you mean it," Jeffrey said. "But try to remember, Minot. There's always a girl in a boy's life, isn't there, when he's going on twenty-one? Well, Jim has a girl. I don't know whether it's serious or not."

"Who is she?" Minot asked.

"Well, as a matter of fact, she's a nice girl," Jeffrey said. "Her name is Sales—Sally Sales. She lives somewhere around Scarsdale."

"Sales," Minot said. "I've never heard of anyone named Sales. Do you know them?"

"I met them last autumn," Jeffrey said, "at Fred's and Beckie's. They're all right. Not particularly interesting, but they're all right."

"Does Madge know about it?" Minot asked. "Fred and Beckie know the darnedest people."

Jeffrey nodded.

"Oh, yes," he said, "of course she does."

"Well, what does Madge think?"

Jeffrey moved uneasily.

"Oh, you know what Madge would think—that it's too bad for anyone of Jim's age to be so intense. The little girl isn't good enough for Jim. She says the Saleses are suburban."

Minot nodded.

"Madge makes a lot of sense sometimes," he said. "Have you seen the little girl?"

All at once, Jeffrey realized that he had gone further than he had intended, that Jim had really grown up, that he was betraying a confidence of Jim's, but now it was too late to stop.

"Yes," he said, "I've seen her." He put his hands in his pockets and took them out again. "I asked her out to lunch."

"Did you tell that to Madge?" Minot asked.

Jeffrey stirred uneasily. He had wanted to tell Minot something and not to answer questions.

"No," he said, "because it's Jim's business, really." He stopped to control the irritation in his voice. "It's up to Jim to tell his mother what he wants. You know the way Madge worries."

"What's she like?" Minot asked.

"Well," Jeffrey said, "I can't really tell you, Minot. Have you ever noticed how all girls in their teens look alike?"

He had simply wanted to talk to Minot casually, and now Minot had reached in the pocket of his quilted smoking jacket and had taken out a pipe and a pigskin tobacco pouch.

"I can always think better," Minot said, "when I smoke a pipe. Jeff, did you ever try this mixture? A little man makes it down on Broad Street, to order."

"But I don't want you to think," Jeffrey said, "I just wanted to tell you."

But he knew that Minot wanted to think. Minot was turning him into the Distraught Father, whose son was sowing wild oats. Minot was tamping the tobacco into his pipe, like the Old Friend of the Family.

"You mean, you think this is serious?" Minot asked.

"I told you," Jeffrey answered. "I don't know. I've never thought of it that way."

"Well," Minot said, and he lighted his pipe. "I guess I've got this straight now."

"There isn't anything to get straight," Jeffrey said. "I was just telling you about Jim."

"Well, it's a good thing you have," Minot said. "It's clearer when you talk something out instead of keeping it to yourself. Anyone Jim's age can't know what he wants."

"I don't know," Jeffrey said; "why can't he?"

"Don't be soft about it," Minot said. "Jim can't know what he wants. We've got to break it up."

"No," Jeffrey said, and he knew that he should never have told Minot Roberts. "That's the whole point of it. I don't want to break it up."

"You don't?" Minot repeated.

"No," Jeffrey said, "I want Jim to do what he wants. I don't want to interfere with Jim."

"Now, wait a minute," Minot said. "You don't want Jim to do anything he'll be sorry for."

Jeffrey moved in his chair and looked up at the Sèvres vases that were too large for the mantelpiece.

"I don't think it matters so much—not right now," he said.

"My God," Minot said, "you don't think it matters?"

Minot and everything in the room seemed to surround him with cold incredulous reproof. Jeffrey sighed and shook his head.

"You ought to know what I mean," he said. "It doesn't matter, because he hasn't got much time." And then he found himself speaking more quickly. "It's the way things are going, Minot. I haven't any right to interfere, and Madge hasn't. No one has, if he hasn't got much time. I thought you'd agree, or I wouldn't have brought it up. All I want, when I'm away, is for you to tell Madge not to worry, if she speaks about it. And if Jim should speak to you about it be nice and don't give him advice. Try to think of it as though you were Jim."

He paused, and then he began again.

"Let him work it out for himself. It's true what I'm saying. It isn't fair to interfere."

Minot listened attentively, and then his expression brightened.

"I see, now," Minot said. "You mean he wants to live with her?" Minot stared at the bowl of his pipe and pressed the ashes gently with his finger. "I hear they do quite a lot of that nowadays."

"Do what?" Jeffrey asked.

"Live together," Minot said. "Maybe it's not such a bad idea."

"Minot," Jeffrey said, "never mind it. Either forget it, or be nice to Jim. Will you be nice to Jim?"

Then he saw that Minot was smiling. The curves about his mouth and the wrinkles in the corners of his eyes were kind and tolerant.

"Why, Jeff," he said, "of course I will. Don't worry about Jim and me."

Jeffrey drew a deep breath, and the tension which had been built up inside himself relaxed suddenly.

"And there's one thing more," he said. He stopped for a moment. "Jim's a little restless. He called me up not so long ago. He's taking Military Science. Last week the officer wanted three of them to go to the School of Fire at Fort Sill as enlisted students."

"By God," Minot said, "only three of them? You must be awfully pleased."

"I told him to wait," Jeffrey said, "and keep his shirt on."

Minot's lips puckered slightly. "You did?" he said. "By God I don't understand you, Jeff. First you want him to run his own life, and then you won't let him do what he wants. If he went to Sill, he'd forget about that girl."

Jeffrey felt his nerves grow taut again.

"We're not in this war, and he's not your son," he told him.

"Don't get so excited, Jeff," Minot answered.

"I'm not excited," Jeffrey said, "I'm just telling you." And then he paused, trying to speak carefully. "This is a bad time to have a son growing up. I don't think it's the same thing with daughters. You don't identify yourself with them as you do with a son. I don't see him much, but I think a lot of Jim. I'd like to have Jim have a happier life than mine. I suppose that's what every father wants—"

"Look here," Minot asked, "what's the matter with your life?"

"Never mind it now," Jeffrey answered, "I'm talking about Jim."

And then he made a final effort to express himself.

"Wait, Minot—think of it this way. People like you and me—we've pretty well seen the show, but Jim has no perspective or background. I have an idea he may need someone older to talk to, and he thinks a lot of you, Minot. Just keep an eye on him, but don't make up his mind for him. That's all I'm trying to say."

Jeffrey had seen a play years before, "The Return of Peter Grimm," in which a man appeared after he was dead and watched the living. Sitting there in that overdecorated room, he did not seem to belong to the present any more than that portrait of Minot's mother, and Minot did not, either.

"Of course, Jeff," Minot said.

"Thanks," Jeffrey said. "Well, that's about all. I'd better be going."

"Good-by, boy," he heard Minot say. "We had a swell afternoon, didn't we?"

The elevator was descending slowly and he stood looking at the back of the elevator man's white head and at the uniform that looked like a Prince Albert coat. The coat made him think of a period with which even he was too young to be familiar, of hansom cabs and of horses' hoofs on the Avenue, and Sherry's and Delmonico's and Jack's and Rector's. He had a sense of having done something wrong, of having said something wrong; without in the least knowing why, he wished that he had not talked to Minot Roberts about Jim.

33

Where the Initials Are Marked in Pencil

"Good evening, Mr. Wilson," the doorman said. "It's a pretty good day for March."

"Good evening," Jeffrey said. "Yes, it hasn't been a bad day."

The doorman's solid face was middle-aged, like his own. He pulled back the door with a flourish and closed it quickly to keep out the March wind.

"March is always a bad month," the doorman said, "but it's the beginning of spring."

It occurred to Jeffrey that he and the doorman had exchanged those same remarks for a long while without knowing much about each other. You gave him a Christmas present and now and then another present, but he maintained his private life inviolate. That impersonality was all a part of a complicated society. It was a defense against knowing too many human beings.

The apartment house seemed new and pleasant after his call on Minot Roberts. If it was out of date, at least it stood for the more recent days of 1929 when Washington statesmen were speaking of two cars in every garage and two chickens in every pot. It was a monument dating from the time when Mr. Fisher of Yale had announced that stocks had reached a permanent high level which they would maintain for years and years. The glory had not vanished yet, and this may have been why Madge said it made her feel secure. The doorman was secure; the elevator boy was young, sprightly, sober, and intelligent.

"Good evening, Mr. Wilson," the elevator boy said. "It's been a nice afternoon for March, hasn't it?"

"Yes," Jeffrey said, "not a bad afternoon."

"How's Mr. Jim, Mr. Wilson?" the elevator boy asked.

Jeffrey smiled. He remembered now that this was the boy who always asked for Jim. He wondered whether he asked just to be polite, or whether he liked Jim, and whether Jim had ever talked to him, and if he had, what they would have said.

"He's all right," Jeffrey said. "You don't see much of boys when they get to be Jim's age."

"He's busy at college, I guess," the elevator boy said.

"He's always glad to get down here," Jeffrey said.

"Yes, sir," the boy answered, and he laughed. "He certainly likes New York."

"Yes," Jeffrey said, and he laughed, too. "He certainly likes New York."

"Jeff," he heard Madge call, when he was taking off his overcoat, "where *have* you been?" A note of irritation in her voice made him realize that she had been waiting for him. The front hall had been picked up very neatly.

The chairs in the living room were all in the right positions. The shades were drawn and there was a bowl of daffodils on the piano. Madge was wearing her russet-brown dinner dress with gold trimmings.

"Jeff," Madge said, "hurry. You know they're always on time. And you know they always dress."

"Who?" Jeffrey asked. "I didn't know anyone was coming to dinner."

"Darling," Madge said, "Laura and Milton Cooke are coming. He wanted you to sign your powers of attorney before you go. Don't you remember?"

Of course, it all came back to Jeffrey's mind at once.

"I'm awfully sorry, Madge," he said, "I won't be a minute," and he began running up the stairs.

He had wanted to talk to Milton Cooke about investments, of course, before he went to the Coast, and for some reason, which he could never get clear in his mind, having everything right was a part of the background when one talked investments. There was a slight professional tenseness to everything, just as though the doctor were coming for a purely social visit, which demanded that you look fresh and healthy.

"Oh, Jeff," Madge said, and he stopped on the stairs. Madge had never lost the habit of calling him back just as he was leaving. "Jeff, you'll remember to ask him about who is to take the exemptions, won't you?"

"Madge," Jeffrey said, "I've told you—there's no use bothering about that when nobody in God's world knows what the income taxes will be next year."

"Well, Jeff," Madge said, "it won't do any harm. He'll know more about it than you do."

"I don't want to make a damned fool of myself asking him such a question," Jeffrey said.

"Well," Madge said, "just to please me, won't you ask him?"

He did not know why he should be sensitive about appearing financially foolish before Milton Cooke. After all, he did not have implicit confidence in Milton's judgment, and yet he depended upon Milton because Milton was in the Standard Bank and knew about such things. What was more, Madge always depended on Milton, because Milton was what she described as "a man of business." When Madge's father had died, she had started right away having Milton look after her things, because she had to have somebody, and Jeffrey was not a man of business. It was true that Milton had sold some of Madge's things, which had gone up later, and had reinvested the proceeds in South American bonds and in a German department store with branches in Berlin, Munich and Hamburg. It had not seemed to Jeffrey a wise choice at the time; but then, Milton had private sources of information. It was true that all the bonds defaulted, but as Milton said, that was water over the dam, and if you had distribution, you could cut losses. And Madge said it was water over the dam, too, and that no business man could always be right, always, and besides, Milton was "in touch."

When people from the Internal Revenue Bureau began to call upon Jeffrey, after he had paid his income tax, with all sorts of questions which he could not answer, Madge had said that Milton ought to look after his things too, because he was looking after her things. Besides, Milton was a friend—they had been in the same class at Harvard. Jeffrey had never known about this until Milton had told him one day, shortly after he began looking after Madge's things, and shortly after that, Milton had asked him to lunch at the Harvard Club at one of the tables where there were waiters and not self-service. Shortly after that, Milton had asked them to his apartment for a quiet little dinner, and while Madge and Laura, Milton's wife, talked in the other room, Milton had told Jeffrey what a headache everything was on Wall Street. There might have been a time, Milton said, when one man, with reasonable intelligence, could supervise his own savings, but now it was getting to be more and more of a science. Only the other day, Roger Newell—Jeffrey knew Rodge Newell, didn't he?—well, Rodge had come to him in an awful state, because his things were all mixed up; and the Statistical Department at the Bank had looked over Rodge's things, and then Milton had rechecked the suggestions. It changed Rodge's whole setup. He had been in a very dangerous position, but now he was sixty per cent liquid and this was the time to be sixty per cent liquid. Milton didn't care what Babson or what any other of those professional dopesters said, liquidity was the only safe position for the next six months, and Milton hoped that Jeffrey was liquid, and particularly not tied-up in chemicals. And speaking of liquidity, how about a highball? Then Jeffrey asked Milton what about du Pont, and Milton asked if Jeffrey owned any. When Jeffrey said he did, Milton said that it was typical. Anyone like Jeffrey, who didn't work downtown, would own du Pont—not that du Pont wasn't a fine stock with a real potential leverage. It depended on what else Jeffrey had on his list. Then Milton said that he didn't want to be personal, but why didn't Jeffrey let him see the list and let the Statistical Department go over it. The things he had should after all be co-ordinated with Madge's things—and after that, Milton began handling Jeffrey's things. Shortly before the fall of France, Jeffrey had suggested to Milton over the telephone that it might be well to sell some common stock, but Milton had said that now was the time to hold on with the big orders for heavy goods coming from France and England. When everything dropped Milton had said you should take the long view. It was a matter of holding on, and no time to be liquid.

"Jeff," he heard Madge calling, "Jeff, they're at the door."

"All right," he called, "I'll be right down."

"Well, hurry," Madge called back. "Don't keep them waiting." For some reason, he felt, too, that it was not right to keep Milton waiting.

Milton was bald and wore horn-rimmed glasses. He was in a dinner coat and Laura was in a dinner dress.

"I came in late," Jeffrey said, "I'm awfully sorry."

"Oh, no," Milton said, "you're not late. We're early," and Laura laughed.

"You know Milton," she said. "I call him my alarm clock. Milton's always on time."

Milton must have been on time for school when he was a little boy. He must have been on time at all his lectures later, on time when he worked in a bond house downtown, on time to his luncheons at the Harvard Club, on time for golf dates, and now he was on time to dinner, right there on the tick. Jeffrey wondered what Milton had gained by it. It made Jeffrey think of Milton as someone trying to deal with certainties when there were no certainties, trying to balance columns and averages when there were no averages. It would come out all right in the end, Milton always said. You had only to look at the curve of industrial activity. There had been wars before, but there had also been curves of industrial activity. Jeffrey often wondered whether Milton really believed it.

"It's such a lovely apartment," Laura said. "I'm awfully glad that Milton let you take it."

Madge laughed and looked at Jeffrey.

"If Milton says we can afford it, it must be all right," she said, and Laura laughed.

"Don't you love it," she said, "the way Milton always treats his people as though they were children? And the queerest thing about it is that Milton doesn't like children."

Milton stood with his hands clasped behind him, gazing out of the window at the lights on the river.

"They're complicated," he said. "You'd know if you ever set up a trust fund for children. If they die before their majority, where does it go then?"

"To the Government," Jeffrey said.

"Oh, no," Milton said, "it's not as bad as that."

Milton's expression was patient and serene, as though he had some secret information that the clouds were breaking somewhere.

"In certain brackets," he said, "perhaps; but for most people, hardly as bad as that. They're not going absolutely crazy in Washington. You see, some of them have some money themselves, some of them."

Jeffrey felt as he always did when he knew that he must talk to Milton about business after dinner. In a way, it was like preparing for a confessional, or for a minor operation, something which was personal, but would not really hurt. Milton with his pencil would probe into his affairs, discovering his carelessnesses and his extravagances, but they must not talk about business at dinner. They must find something else in common, and this was always hard, because Jeffrey's mind was always on what he was to say to Milton afterwards.

Milton was talking about the S.E.C., and about a scandal that had broken downtown, and Milton had known the man very well. No one had been as surprised as Milton. It was not so much the money that was involved, as the disloyalty. In times like these, one should be loyal to one's class. It had hurt morale badly downtown, but it was just as well to have it over and out in the open and not hanging fire.

Jeffrey sat listening, watching Joseph pour the sherry.

"Joseph," he said, "will you leave the brandy in the library—"

The dining room seemed like the place where you waited in the Bank before the grilles of the safe-deposit vault. Milton's voice was as suave and confident as the voice of the man to whom you showed your key and who guided you past the tiers of the safe-deposit boxes to the one that had your number. Then you went into a little cubbyhole and opened up the box, and all around you was the rustling of heavy paper and the soft snipping of scissors, busy with the coupons. It was a world that was unfamiliar to Jeffrey, it was a world of saving and estate building, where you tried to keep what you had and to make a little more.

"Laura, let's go into the living room," Madge said. "They can have coffee in the library and have their talk."

"We don't want to go, you know," Milton said. "But then, it won't take long."

"Jeff," Madge said, "you'll be sure to ask Milton about—that, won't you?"

Jeffrey often thought that the library was made for private talks, and for nothing else. Milton seemed to belong more to the library than he did, perhaps because much of Milton's life had been spent in quiet talks in libraries. Milton sat down near the desk, and Jeffrey closed the door, and Milton unsnapped his brief case.

"Here you are," he said, "the powers, in triplicate. We might as well sign them now and get it over with. Write where your initials are marked in pencil."

Milton laid the powers of attorney before Jeffrey, gently.

"Take my pen," he said. "It works pretty well." Milton always had a fountain pen that worked and he always said that it worked pretty well.

"Just in case anything comes up while you're in Hollywood—" Milton said —"not that anything will come up."

Milton was always sure that nothing would come up, but then, you never could tell. Milton seemed to have a dusty sort of immortality. He made Jeffrey feel that he might die, but that somehow Milton never would, since estates and investment lists must go on forever. Milton was reaching into the brief case again, his fingers moving adroitly through the papers.

"Here we are," Milton said, "here's the whole picture." Milton always referred to it as a picture. "You've got a good deal of cash on hand. We might invest a little. There's International Nickel."

"Don't you think we've been losing enough," Jeffrey said, "in International Nickel?"

"You never lose," Milton said, "when you're holding. Only when you sell. Now, let's look at the rest. Railroads, industrials; we're low on utilities, but it's just as well, considering what they're doing in Washington. Now, let's see, how much money do you think you'll make this year?"

"God knows," Jeffrey said. "Maybe none at all."

"That's what makes your picture interesting," Milton said. "You see, most of my clients don't make money. It's a question of a fixed income from securities."

"Yes," Jeffrey said, "I know."

"You haven't saved much, have you?" Milton said. "I wish that we could fix it so that you'd be a little more secure."

"There's no way to fix it," Jeffrey said. "I've never been secure."

"Have you ever thought," Milton said, "of saving and letting Madge spend her income? So you'll have something to fall back on—well—when you don't do so well in Hollywood."

Milton looked up, and the light was reflected from his glasses.

"No," Jeffrey said, "I don't want that."

"It would be nice," Milton said, "if you could leave something, have something to show for it all. Of course, the income tax is unfair on earned income, very unfair."

"Why should I want to leave anything?" Jeffrey asked. "Madge can leave it."

"I know," Milton said, "but it would be nice to have something to show. If you had a little backlog—"

"It's too late for a backlog," Jeffrey said. "Never mind it, Milton."

All he had wanted was to sign the powers of attorney. There might have been a time when he would have listened to Milton's advice, but now it sounded futile and as dry as dust.

"You see," Jeffrey said, "I don't see any good in worrying. There'll be inflation. The whole thing's going to go."

Milton nodded patiently, as though he had heard and heard the same remark. "There will always be money. There will always be estates," Milton said.

"What makes you think so?" Jeffrey asked.

"Because I believe in common sense," Milton said. "Eventual common sense. Let's look at it this way." Milton raised two fingers. "We will either get into this war, or we won't get into this war. Now, if we do get into this war—but we're not in it yet—we must act as though we weren't going to get in it until the times comes."

"Well," Jeffrey said, "do what you want to, Milton."

There was a moment's silence, a helpless sort of silence.

"You see, Milton, I've never had much money, excepting what I've made. I suppose that's why I don't mind so much."

Milton took off his glasses and looked at them and put them on again.

"I've thought about it," Jeffrey said, "but I don't see that there's much we can do, I really don't."

"You mean we ought to give up," Milton said. "You mean we shouldn't try? What do you think's going to happen?"

He looked disturbed, much more disturbed than Jeffrey. "We've got to keep on trying."

"All right," Jeffrey said, "you go and keep on trying."

"Look at it this way," Milton said. "You have your place in Connecticut. You'll want to leave it to your children. You like it there. You'd like to have your boy—what's his name—Jim—have it, wouldn't you?"

"Yes," Jeffrey said, "I'd like it, but he couldn't afford it. You know that."

"Well," Milton said, "perhaps, but we don't know yet. You would like to keep it for yourself, wouldn't you?"

"Yes," Jeffrey said, "but maybe I can't. I don't know."

Milton picked up his brandy glass and laughed softly.

"My God," he said, "you don't believe that anything is permanent tonight."

Jeffrey was facing the fact that nothing which Milton considered permanent was going to be permanent. The apartment was not permanent. He could see the books at auction somewhere with the Georgian chairs. He could see the whole thing going.

"Oh, well," he said, "I suppose there'll be something left."

"Of course there will," Milton said. "You leave it to me, Jeff. Where are those powers? Oh, there they are," and he snapped his brief case shut and looked at Jeffrey over his glasses.

"I hope you don't talk to Madge like this," he said.

"No," Jeffrey said, "of course I don't. Let's go in and see the girls."

The girls were sitting on the sofa by the fire. They looked up and smiled and moved a little, as women always did when men came in after dinner.

"Well, you weren't long," Madge said. "Have you got everything settled so soon?"

"Yes," Milton said, and he laughed. "There wasn't much to settle."

"Jeff's so careless," Madge said, "he always leaves things at loose ends. It's like having a medical check-up, isn't it? Now, I can get him packed tonight and get him off tomorrow."

Jeffrey smiled. "And if I die on the way," he said, "just call up Milton and open the tin box. Everything is there."

"Oh, Jeff," Madge said, and she looked startled, "Jeff, *please*, don't say things like that."

Madge never liked to joke about death. But then, that was what Milton was there for, because Madge knew that Milton, or someone like Milton, would live forever.

34

Dear Jim: . . .

Superficially, everything had been the same that winter as any other winter—too much the same, when it should not have been. There had been a limited national emergency, and then a national emergency, and hemispheric solidarity and lend-lease, and the Draft Act; and convoys meant shooting, and shooting meant war. With each step Jeffrey had expected something to change but nothing had, on the surface. You saw the same shops on the cross streets. You saw the same books in the bookstore windows, yet nothing should have been the same, and that was what disturbed him most. He was going out to the West Coast as he had every winter for a number of years, but it should not have been the same.

He had known for the past three weeks, ever since Hal Bliss had called him from Beverly Hills, that he would be going. Madge was used to it—she had not asked to go. He knew exactly what he was going to take and where he would stay—at the Bronxville in Beverly Hills, and Hal would let him have a car so that he could drive out to the studio. Jesse Fineman had arranged for his tickets, a compartment all the way. His bags had been brought up from the storeroom in the basement, and now they were open in the study—the heavy pigskin bag which he had bought in London, and the smaller suitcase for the train, the fitted suitcase which Madge had given him one Christmas and his brief case and the case for his portable typewriter. They were going with him, and he was leaving all the rest of it. He wished he could get the idea out of his mind that Madge and the apartment might not be there when he got back, though what might happen to them he could not remotely imagine. He tried to tell himself that it was a mood. He wished that he could get the idea out of his mind that he was saying good-by to something he would never see again, for of course he would see it all again. There had been talk of change for years and nothing could change so quickly.

"Darling," Madge said, "I wish I were going with you."

It was nice of her to say it. She had been out there with him once or twice, and she knew very well that it had not worked. The hours were too irregular. There never was a chance for them to do anything together, and as Madge said herself, it was all too queer—a lot of fun, but no one there was leading a real life, and Jeffrey supposed they weren't, according to her standards. She was simply being nice when she said she wanted to go—she did not really want to.

"But you know I can't, don't you?" Madge said. "I can't leave Gwen."

"No," Jeffrey said, "of course you can't."

"It's never the same when you're gone," Madge said. "There's never any point to anything, but Beckie will take care of me. I'll go to all sorts of things that you don't want to go to, and Jim'll be coming down. Jeff, have you heard from Jim?"

"No," Jeffrey said, "not lately."

"I wish he'd write more often," Madge said. "He's so careless about writing."

"It doesn't mean anything," Jeffrey told her. "He's got too much to do. Boys don't like to write."

"I know you think it's silly, my worrying," Madge said. "But Jeff, I think he's getting over it, about that girl."

Jeffrey had been looking into his empty pigskin suitcase. When Madge was with him, something always came up that mingled discordantly with humdrum detail. If they were making toast in the kitchen, for instance, when the couple was out, they would suddenly begin talking about the bills, or whether So-and-so was going to get divorced, and then before you thought of it, the toast was burning. He always hated to combat the inertia which came with packing. He was wondering what shoes he would take and where he would put them, so that they would not get mixed up with his shirts, and at the same time he was trying to make a list in his mind of everything he needed. And now Madge brought up Jim.

"What makes you think he's over it?" he asked.

Madge looked at him and looked away. The study was bright and sunny, almost too bright from the glare on the river, and he could see the roofs of the buildings downtown, shining wet from the melting snow. He could see plumes of steam rising above them.

"He's hardly mentioned her," Madge said. "When I brought her name up, he didn't even seem interested. You can tell, you know. Jeff, we mustn't stand here talking. You've got to pack. There isn't much more than an hour and don't throw things in at the last moment, the way you always do."

Then Jim was gone, and they were back at the business of packing again. He knew Madge so well that he knew exactly what she would say, and it must have been the same for her, but now that he was going away there was no sort of irritation in that sense of knowing her too well. Instead, there was value and charm in being so completely used to someone. He felt as if he were going away for a long time, as though he might never see her again, and he found himself anxious to remember how she looked, just standing there helping to pack his bags—not that her suggestions were ever necessary. Madge always said that he just threw clothes in and never folded them. He always replied that there was no need of fussing for days over something you could do in half an hour. He remembered the time they had hurried with their packing in Paris and the upper drawer of her wardrobe trunk had slipped out and she had sat laughing, with stockings and lace nightgowns all around her. She did not look much older now. Her chin had the same upward tilt—he had always thought her chin was beautiful—and she had the same reproving expression which she always wore when he was packing, as though he knew nothing whatsoever about it.

"It won't take long when I start," he said. "I just have to decide what I'm going to take."

He opened the door of his clothes closet and stared at his suits all pressed, all in a neat long row. Madge had always been very good about putting clothes in closets, sending coats to cleaners' and keeping out the moths. There they hung in an even row, his cutaway, his tails, his dinner coat, the tweed jacket he wore in the country, his gray flannels, his spring suits, his winter suits, all of them—too many of them—and down below on a little shelf, secure with their trees, were all his shoes—too many shoes. He would take his dinner coat and the gray flannels and one light summer suit, and then there would be the suit he was wearing. Then there would be the shirts . . .

"Jeff," Madge said, "why don't we call Joseph? Tell him what you want, and Joseph will put them in."

"He wraps everything in tissue paper," Jeffrey said.

"Darling," Madge said, "that's the way you ought to pack."

Then, for some reason, he felt a lump rise in his throat. It was just as though he were never going to be there again, as though he would never see that study again, as though he would never again wear those clothes which he was leaving behind him.

"I wish I didn't have to go," he said. "I wish I weren't going."

"Darling," Madge said, "we'll do all sorts of things when you get back. We'll be moving to the country and there'll be the garden and the seed catalogues. I'm going to start getting the house open when you're away, and I'm going to see that Mr. Gorman gets the seeds in right. Jeff, I wish we could get someone else beside Mr. Gorman."

That was another subject. You could never tell when it might come up. Madge had always felt the man in the country was a mistake.

"Never mind Gorman now," Jeffrey said, "I've got to pack."

"The apple blossoms will be coming out when you get home," Madge said, "and the children will all be back."

"Yes," Jeffrey said. "Well, I've got to pack."

He began doing exactly what Madge said he would, throwing everything quickly into the suitcase.

"Jeff," Madge said, "don't be in such a hurry. Fold them."

"They'll have to be pressed, anyway," Jeffrey said. "I'm in a hurry now."

"Jeff," Madge said, "did you put the money into the account?"

"Yes," Jeffrey answered, "and you've got the number of the Bronxville—I left it on the desk. You can get me any time."

"You'll call me when you get there, won't you?" Madge said. "And if you have time when you get to Chicago, you'll stop and see the Harkers, won't you?"

"I can't get to Lake Forest, Madge," Jeffrey said. "There won't be time."

"Well," Madge said, "try to see them. They always hear about it when you go through Chicago, and you never see them."

"Yes," Jeffrey said, "I'll try, but there isn't time to get to Lake Forest."

"And give my love to Hal Bliss," Madge said, "and don't go out to too many parties."

"There won't be any parties," Jeffrey said. "When I'm not at the studio, I'll be asleep."

"Darling," Madge said, "don't be so annoyed. I want you to see people so you can tell me all about it."

"I'm not annoyed," Jeffrey said. "I wish I weren't going."

"Darling," Madge said, "you do like everything, don't you?"

"Yes," Jeffrey said, and he did like it, now that he was going.

"Then try to think of things to tell me," Madge said.

"Yes," Jeffrey said, "and if you want anything, call up Minot."

"Yes," Madge said. "Now, think what you've forgotten. You must have forgotten something."

The bags were closed. It was half an hour before train time, but he knew that he might as well be going. He always hated to say good-by and then stand and talk.

"Don't bother to come down to the station," Jeffrey said.

"Why, dear," Madge said, "I'd love to."

"No," Jeffrey said, "that's silly. I like to think of you here. Kiss Gwen for me, will you? Good-by."

He held her in his arms for a moment.

"Good-by," Madge said. "I love you, dear."

He was out in the hallway by the elevator. Joseph had carried out the bags and Madge stood in the doorway.

"Darling," Madge said, "it won't be any fun while you're gone."

Jeffrey reached in his inside pocket and took out the envelope which held his ticket. In the Grand Central Station, people were moving hurriedly in all directions, or standing with their luggage by the Information counter waiting. Up in the gallery, workmen were taking down the snow display, which invited you to go to New England for the skiing, and were putting up a backdrop showing a fishing scene, because the railroads would take you there, where the big ones were biting—just ask your Passenger Agent. The railroads had grown very friendly in recent years. The conductors now said, "Thank you, sir," when they took your tickets; and instead of being enigmatic dyspeptics, they had turned into jovial old gentlemen who loved a good joke, just as much as you did. Why strain yourself at the wheel of a motor car, and risk the horrors of the highway when the railroads would take you there? The railroads were your home on wheels, and how you could sleep and rest and relax on the railroads! That was the new word of the day—"relax." He had seen it growing in fashion, like a snowball rolling downhill. Don't let taut nerves get the better of you, just sink down and relax. Relax in that seat with those magic inner springs. Relax with a cigarette or with a beer. It was the end of March, 1941—and they still told you to relax.

The porter stood waiting with the luggage.

"Car 287," Jeffrey said, "Compartment C. Wait a minute, I want to buy a paper."

The newsstand was piled high with newspapers and periodical literature. There were stacks of *Time* and *Newsweek* and *Life* and the *Reader's Digest* and *Look*, and there were new Pocket Books, for twenty-five cents, most of them showing pictures of corpses which had been stabbed in the library. There were toys for the kiddies, in case you had forgotten the kiddies, and cigarettes and Tootsie Rolls and Baby Ruths and Life Savers, in case you were taken with a spasm of hunger. Jeffrey bought two papers. It seemed this afternoon that Italian and German crews were busy disabling interned vessels. England was promising everything to the Greeks and Serbs and everyone else, and so was the United States, and all the advertisements told you to relax.

"Car 287," Jeffrey said again, "Compartment C."

The platform always looked the same, whether it was day or night. There was the usual musty smell which gave him, even as an experienced traveler, a faint sense of anticipation. They were telling you to buy the latest novel—nothing sold after the train left; and on his right was the Twentieth Century with the platform of the Observation Car emblazoned with its name. He could see the soft lights inside and all the chairs done in varied upholstery and the little tables and the attendant in his white coat, waiting to open the drinks as soon as the train was moving. He could see lounge cars, club cars, plain Pullmans and cars with rooms, all solid and magnificent and unbelievably material.

"Yes, sir, Compartment C," the porter said, and would he care for a little ice or White Rock or anything?—and Jeffrey asked him to put up the table. He wanted his typewriter—he wanted to write a letter—no White Rock, nothing else. When the door was closed, he took off his overcoat and hung it in the little clothes closet with his hat, and then he opened the typewriter case.

Jeffrey still could not shake off the feeling that he was saying good-by to something. In that compartment he was cut away from all ties and Madge and the apartment and all the details of it already seemed like something he had imagined long ago. There was nothing so lonely as traveling by yourself for any length of time. You were so completely with your own thoughts and your own identity. If there were such a thing as survival after death, he could think of moving over great distances entirely alone, with only his own integrity as a companion. And now the train was moving, first in the dark of the tunnel, and then in the waning light. They would pass the apartments around 125th Street where you could stare at the faces and at the domestic arrangements of the dwellers, and then would come the Hudson and the Palisades—and then Harmon where they changed the engines. He could tell where he was, almost without looking. He was looking instead at the keys of his typewriter which he could still manipulate with a newspaper man's awkward adequacy. He always thought of the City Room when he composed on a typewriter. There was the old absorption and the same compulsion to hurry, although now there was no hurry.

Dear Jim [he wrote]:—

Well, here I am on the Century again, and I wish you were with me because I don't like going out to the Coast alone, and I'm not good at picking up people in club cars, and when I do, they're not worth picking up. As far as Chicago, they're all selling something, and after that, they're Congressmen, or they talk about beef on the hoof or mining properties or what is slowing down the train, or else they are going out to the Coast, like me. Frankly, I wish I weren't going this time. I've been thinking about you quite a good deal and I wish I could have seen you before I left.

Jeffrey stopped and stared at the typewriter. He never had been good at letters.

I hope you're having a good time. I hope you're seeing a lot of things and doing a lot—that's what I want for you more than anything else. I hope everything is interesting you; I don't care much what it is, as long as it interests you.

I've heard a lot of people say they wouldn't miss living now for anything, and maybe they're right, but I wish you were my age, not yours.

If you were, you would realize that you had seen part of it all before, and that nothing is entirely new. I know it does no good to tell you that —you can't pass on experience, but I wish you would get through your mind that all this war talk and everything else is not as immediate as you think. Your mother says it does no good to worry about the war, and maybe she is right, but when I think of you, I do worry. It gave me quite a shock when you telephoned that time in February. I don't know why, exactly, except that I have seen it all before.

Jeffrey stopped. It was rambling, it was dull. He was never good at writing letters. He could see the Hudson, very cool and blue.

I wish you would look at it this way. This is a very large country and very strong. You feel it when you travel. You get a new sense of its power, but it moves slowly. It's a free country, and it has to talk and think.

Jeffrey stopped again. It sounded like one of those stage speeches which always slowed up a play, or like those bits on the radio, designed to make you conscious of something you knew without being told, and Jim knew about this, just as well as he did. If he were not careful, he would next try, as everybody did, to write a definition of democracy, but he could not help it. There was something that he wanted to say to Jim, if he could ever say it.

Personally, I think we're going to get into this war. If we had only got into it while France was there, we might have done a great deal, but I know that was impossible. Right now I hope we stay out until we see what we can do, but I think we're going in. I know it's hard for anyone like you. I want you to try to take it easy for a while. I don't want you to be in there until you have to be, and I know what I'm talking about—I wish you'd take my word for it. I've never liked the army very much. I'm not like Minot Roberts, and I don't believe you are, either. I know I don't put it very clearly. I think about you, that's all, but I want you to see what a normal life is, while you can. I want you to enjoy it while you can, and I'm afraid you haven't got much time.

Jeffrey stopped, and sat staring at the last phrase in type. It was what the whole letter was about, and he could not put it any better.

I don't want to tell you what to do about anything. It's hard not to, but I know it does no good to tell you. You've got to do what you want yourself, and not to worry about the way I or anyone else may feel. You know about it, better than I do. This is your show, and it isn't mine. But I do want you to have a good time, and I want to know if there's anything I can do to help you, and I mean anything, and I hope you won't be shy about it. Well, that's about all. If you feel like it, call me up at the Bronxville. The operator will get it for you, and reverse the charges.

With love . . .

It was the sort of letter that any father would write, but it was the best that he could do. If he tried to write it over, it would only be more careful, more rhetorical and literate, but it would say no more. And then he had a final thought.

> P.S.—I'm awfully glad I saw Sally Sales. When you see her, tell her so.

And that was that. He gave the envelope to the porter in the lounge car to mail, but he still could not get his mind off Jim. Jim's life and what Jim wanted belonged entirely to Jim, and he wished that other people understood. There was very little, under the circumstances, that one could plan or do for him. Something had taken it entirely out of Jeffrey's hands. Two years back there had been time for trial and error, but now Jim must work out what he wanted for himself.

Nothing was entirely new, and there was a time for everything. He could think of himself as a boy in Bragg, sitting with his father and his aunt in the Congregational Church—uncomfortable in his blue serge suit, listening with half his mind to the minister reading from the Scriptures. There was a time for everything, and nothing was wholly new.

> One generation passeth away, and another generation cometh: but the earth abideth forever.

It was from the book of Ecclesiastes, the saddest and yet the most beautiful of any in the Bible.

> To everything there is a season, and a time to every purpose under the heaven. . . . A time to weep, and a time to laugh: a time to mourn, and a time to dance: . . . A time to love, and a time to hate: a time of war, and a time of peace.

He was sitting in the white pew while the words moved over him, looking at the head of Louella Barnes. His youth seemed to mingle with Jim's youth. He was living it again, because Jim was living it. He was living it without its poignancy or its anguish. He could see its beauty again, and he wished that Jim would see that beauty, but one never did when one was young.

35

Mr. Mintz Was Very Tired

That futile wonder at how under the sun he had ever got there usually came to Jeffrey in Hollywood more strongly than anywhere else. It was especially compelling that first afternoon after he arrived, as he sat in the office of Mr. Mintz, the producer under whom Hal Bliss was working. It was related to the sensation that had come to him on the train and had stayed with him through Colorado and New Mexico and in the pitiless sunlight of Barstow—the sensation of being a disembodied spirit. He could see himself seated in a leather armchair in Mr. Mintz's office and at the same time he could see himself back in New York, the father of a family, meeting people whom Madge called "nice people." He wished that he did not have to keep moving into different worlds in order to earn his living.

Mr. Mintz was not troubled that way. Mr. Mintz had a lovely home in Beverly Hills which was pointed out by the sight-seeing busses, and Mr. Mintz stayed there all the time. He did not have to cope with anything else, and Hal Bliss was not troubled that way, either. Hal had a low, white bungalow in Palos Verdes where he stayed all the time, except when he went East in summer. Hal and Mr. Mintz were not always getting into different *galères*.

The office was very large and completely air-conditioned. The walls and ceilings and windows were soundproof. The furnishings were very, very restful and the motif was gray. The leather upholstery on the chairs was gray and so was the carpet and so was the telephone and the blotter on Mr. Mintz's desk, and so were the homespun curtains on the windows and so were the walls. There was a picture by Benton on one wall, because Mr. Mintz was collecting American artists.

They were all in Mr. Mintz's office and no one else could come in—but no one, because there were two secretaries in the outer office, a male secretary who did physical exercises with Mr. Mintz each morning and afternoon, and a female secretary who had been told to keep everyone out, but everyone. Hal Bliss was sitting with his coat on because the place was air-conditioned, and there were two writers there who had been working on the script whom Jeffrey had never seen before, both called from the writers' wing to sit in on the conference, and they, too, were wearing coats because the office was air-conditioned. One of them named Archie Willis had a pointed blond beard, and he wore a badly fitted bottle-blue coat. The other, whose name was Harold Soskin, looked very limp, with deep circles under his eyes because he had been up all night—but all night—trying to reconcile his version with Archie Willis' version. And there had to be some sort of version right away, for a shooting script, because Hal was already making tests. Mr. Mintz was lying on a gray leather couch with his eyes half-closed, because he was very tired. He could always think better lying down—it cleared his mind and he was very, very tired.

"Now," Mr. Mintz said, "that we're all here, perhaps we had better start at the beginning."

It was not fair to look at the whole scene objectively. It was like one of those gossip columns, but Jeffrey knew that in a few days he would consider it all completely natural. All the people in the room were specialists. It was a part of the system that too many people usually worked on a single picture, particularly on an "A" picture. Mr. Mintz was the producer and it had to be the way he wanted it—but it had to—because he would be responsible if it didn't make money; and it had to be the way Hal wanted it because he was a director with his own reputation to consider. It was not so important for the writers. You could always get more writers on it, but then you couldn't push writers around too much, either, because they had temperaments.

Now they were at the beginning, Mr. Mintz said, he would like Hal to talk about it quietly, just quietly, as though they were all coming to this fresh for the first time, and the room was silent while Hal Bliss marshaled his ideas. Mr. Mintz told him not to get excited, because he was very, very tired, and Mr. Mintz wanted everybody to listen but not to butt in with any new ideas, and he did want to say one thing, he was the producer but he knew that Hal was a great artist and that was why he wanted Hal to direct the picture. It was going to be a great picture, because it had everything—*but* everything.

Mr. Mintz closed his eyes, and Jeffrey sat listening. It was what he was being paid for. . . .

The whole thing, Hal Bliss said, happened this way. The studio wanted a war picture that would have real significance, something like "Escape," but something with more significance. While they had been searching around, a novel had come in from the Book Department. Hal had not read it, but the Book Department had. It was the title which had first excited Hal, and it was the same with Mr. Mintz. The title was "Good-by to All." It was true, as the Research Department had pointed out, that another book had appeared, Hal thought by an Englishman, called "Good-bye to All That," but it did not have the same pull as "Good-by to All." You could see what it suggested—good-by to the prewar world, good-by to all its social injustices—but when they started to work on it further, the title had no pull to it, and now the working title was "The Sun Shall Rise Again." The Nazis might try to kill a nation, but they could not kill its soul, and that was the theme of the picture. It was to show that democracy would rise again.

The story, as they had tried to block it out, Hal said, was a simple little story. It dealt with the adventures of a simple little person, who realized suddenly, through a series of circumstances, what freedom meant, who knew suddenly that freedom was worth dying for, and who in the end, when he realized it, would kiss the girl good-by and would go and fight for freedom. And the girl would understand it, too. They were just two plain kids—that was all the story was—going out to fight for freedom.

"But it has to be laid in America," Mr. Mintz said. "Every American kid in the sticks has to be those kids."

Hal waited until Mr. Mintz had finished. He said that Mr. Mintz was absolutely right, but it could not all be in America. There were not any Nazis stepping on Americans yet, and we weren't at war and you didn't want the isolationists to be against it. That was why the action—some of the action—was to be laid in Norway. Norwegians were blonds, and Marianna Miller was a blonde. You had to have blonds if it was to be a Miller picture.

"I didn't know she was making a picture," Jeffrey said.

"But that is the whole point of it," Mr. Mintz told him. "It is to be a Miller vehicle, but it must be laid in America."

"Norman," Hal Bliss said, "all that's important will be in America."

"Then why," Mr. Mintz asked, "do you mention Norway?"

"Norman," Hal said, "I thought we had that all clear."

"But it isn't clear to me," Mr. Mintz said. "I've never heard of Norway coming into it."

"Norman," Hal said, "I told you about Norway at lunch last week. The Nazis come to Norway. I read it to you. It's in a little fishing village. The Nazis come walking down the street—goose step. She's in the doorway in the little village. They see her brother, he's just back from fishing. They kill her brother."

"Her father," Archie Willis said.

"It doesn't make any difference, Arch," Hal said. "They're all up against the wall. The Mayor and the doctor and the fishermen, all in their boots. She stands there and sees it. We've tested it already. Norman, you've seen the tests."

Mr. Mintz opened his eyes and everyone watched him.

"I remember," Mr. Mintz said, "but why should it be Norway?" Mr. Mintz stirred on the couch. "They had fishermen in 'Captains Courageous' and that was in America."

"But Norman," Hal said, "after that she comes to America. A letter comes to St. Paul, Minnesota, and the Swedish ship comes into New York. She's standing on the deck, looking at the harbor."

"Who?" Mr. Mintz asked.

"Miller," Hal Bliss said, "Marianna Miller. She's on the boat."

"Hal," said Mr. Mintz, "there's a white tablet in my right-hand desk drawer. Would you give it to me with a glass of water?"

"Yes," Hal said. "Here it is, Norman." Mr. Mintz stirred on the couch again. "That's the whole trick to it, Norman, the letter is misdirected. It goes to Tyrone Power. I told you, he's just a playboy, Norman."

"Yes," Mr. Mintz said, "where is he?"

"In St. Paul," Hal said, "St. Paul, Minnesota."

Mr. Mintz stirred again.

"Mr. Wilson," Mr. Mintz said. "I don't understand it. Do you understand what they're talking about, Mr. Wilson?"

"I'm just beginning to get it," Jeffrey said. "I think it's going to be clear in a minute."

"But it's not clear to you now, is it, Mr. Wilson?" Mr. Mintz said.

"Well," Jeffrey said, "not entirely."

"That's all I'm getting at," Mr. Mintz said. "Did everyone hear what Mr. Wilson said? It isn't clear to him and it isn't clear to me. That's what Mr. Wilson is here for. It's got to be clear to him before he can make it clear."

Jeffrey looked at Hal Bliss. Hal was looking at the Benton landscape on the wall.

"Let's go right through with it from the beginning," Hal said. "We're only mixed up with the details. Arch, you tell the story."

Mr. Willis straightened himself and stroked his beard carefully.

"All right," he said, "if Hal will help me. Just interrupt me, Hal. Help me out with anything you want to," and Mr. Willis grasped his knees firmly and leaned forward.

"First, it's a little fishing village on a fiord," he said. "You pan from the little houses to the wharf. There's a shot of the sea gulls eating fish. The boats are coming in. The men in boots are pulling up the nets and fish. The camera pans to the main street of the village, and you see Selma Holm in the doorway with her hair down in the sunrise. She's looking at the wharf, waiting for the menfolk, and then she hears the planes, and then she hears the guns."

Mr. Mintz folded his hands across his chest and closed his eyes and Jeffrey felt his own body relax almost somnolently as the writer's voice went on. Whether he wanted to or not, he was becoming part of it. They all were working with unreality to produce reality. None of them had been to Norway, but the Research Department on the lot would know. If you looked at it objectively it was like a dozen other pictures he had seen, but it had illusion. He could see the story in terms of Marianna Miller, and when he did, he could feel some faint thread of emotion. He knew that she would do it well. If he had tried to write the thing himself, his sense of self-criticism would have made him see its garishness, but he could work on it.

The man with the beard was telling it rather well. It had all the tricks, and all the polish. It faded out with the rifle shots and Marianna Miller watching, wide-eyed. There was no novelty in it. What Jeffrey objected to was their effort to make it novel. The next sequence was the millionaire's home in St. Paul, Minnesota—the playboy, comical and whimsical, after a hard night of it, was in his dressing gown, trying to get down his orange juice—a playboy who did not understand democracy. Everything he did showed his obliviousness to suffering and to world events—his snobbish treatment of the servants, his selfish and ludicrous solicitude for his own comfort. Cleverly and resourcefully the artists were filling in the portrait, although none of its creators had seen such a character. It supplied a glimpse of a society about which the audience knew nothing, but it gave them the chance to live vicariously in that society. You could see that the playboy had good stuff in him—if someone would put him on the right track—and someone would. He was opening the morning mail, and there, sure enough, in a foreign, girlish hand was that misdirected letter to Cousin Hanson, from a girl who was coming to America, and would Cousin Hanson meet her and help her? Then you had that pretty little trick, the playboy, for a selfish whim, meeting the boat—the boy who did not understand democracy. Then love. He was ashamed of himself for that masquerade, but what could he do? He had to go on with that pretense which shamed him. He had to pretend to be her relative, whom she had never seen. New York, night clubs, dances, orchids, hotel suites, clothes for the refugee. He was very sorry. He tried to tell her, but she did not understand. He had to go on with it, and he loved her. Then, like a clap of thunder, in the night club, just when they were dancing to the Blue Danube, she saw A Face. There was no way of hiding her revulsion.

It was the face of the German Oberleutnant who had attempted to violate her in that little Norwegian Village, and there he was in New York, a German spy. In that flash of recognition, the German Oberleutnant knew that his jig was up, if the girl lived. That was when the playboy ceased to be a playboy and learned about democracy. . . .

Jeffrey sat giving it his full attention, because that was what he was there for, but he had heard it all before. It was like doing a trick with cards, always using the same cards. If it were cut down to stark simplicity, with all the scrollwork removed from it, it might become real. A part of his mind was cutting down the scenes already.

They were coming to the end of it—the scene in the hotel room where the Nazi spy was cornered, but defined his foul ideology, and the girl countered with her bright beliefs. Sure enough, she defined democracy, and the playboy was not a playboy any longer. He knew what democracy meant because he loved her and because he was an American, and he was going over there to settle things. He was taking the first boat over there because it was his fight as much as hers. And she would wait for him—they both knew that there were beliefs that you could try to kill but could never kill. In brief, the sun would rise tomorrow.

Mr. Mintz had opened his eyes. Everyone was looking at Jeffrey. It was up to him to say something, and he wished that he felt more in the mood for it.

"Well," he said, "that's quite a story."

He saw Mr. Mintz open his eyes wider, and then he knew why Mr. Mintz was there. He knew that somehow Mr. Mintz had sensed the same thing he had.

"Go on," Mr. Mintz said, "what else?"

"What do you want me to do with it?" Jeffrey asked.

Mr. Mintz pulled himself very suddenly up from the couch and sat up straight.

"Take that thing and do it over," Mr. Mintz said. "Pull the crap out of it."

There was dead silence in the soundproof room. Jeffrey was careful to look at no one except Mr. Mintz, and his heart warmed to the sudden coarse brutality of Mr. Mintz.

"Get something in it," Mr. Mintz said. "My God, I don't know what, but something." Mr. Mintz rose from the couch. "My God!" His voice was higher. "Is this life, or isn't it? People are starving and dying and we sit here and write this crap."

There was another muffled silence.

"Mr. Mintz," Jeffrey said, "how much crap do you want taken out?"

Mr. Mintz drew a deep breath. The spasm of pain had left his face. "All of it," Mr. Mintz said, "or nearly all of it. Do you hear what Mr. Wilson says? He says what I've been saying. Mr. Wilson says it's lousy."

"I didn't say that, Mr. Mintz," Jeffrey said. "I said it was quite a story."

36

You're in the Army Now

Jeffrey was not tied like other people in the writers' corridor by six-month contracts. He was not like Hal Bliss, unfitted for any other environment—he could take it or leave it alone. That was why he liked to see the place again. He was paid, but he was not like an employee paid for his time and worried sick about the renewal of a contract. He could think of himself as a workman: not an artist, but an artisan. He was contented with himself and glad he was there because he was doing what he was meant to do. He could see that he had a skill which was not genius but which nevertheless was a gift. If he had used that skill differently—if circumstances had allowed him—he might perhaps have been a playwright, standing on the same ground as Barry or Sherwood or Howard. As it was, he knew that he was better than the other writers who had sat in that office, more of a master of the trade or business, if you wanted to call it that, than they would ever be.

Jeffrey walked with Hal Bliss through the halls of the Administration Offices. They came out into the hot glare of the West Coast sun, and he blinked helplessly, and wished that he had worn his dark glasses. He could see the framework of the oil derricks, standing up like extended fingers from the brown hills in the distance. To the right, where there had been nothing but fields a year or two back, he could see clusters of white dwelling houses, each on its little lawn, each for sale for about six thousand dollars. Mechanics for the aviation plant and for the shipyards at Wilmington were moving in. Los Angeles and all the towns around it were boom towns now. All at once he wished that Jim were there, for Jim had never seen that side of his life. Jim would have seen it all as he had seen it once, and Jeffrey could have seen it through Jim's eyes simply by watching Jim. . . . It would have given him, in a measure, the same pleasure he had known when he had taken Jim to the circus as a little boy, that slightly melancholy pleasure which every parent must have felt. He would have taken Jim on the stages. There was no way of telling what they might be shooting, but if Hal went with them, they could go in anywhere. They could see them building up and tearing down farms, countrysides, drawing rooms, medieval palaces and South Sea islands. They could talk to the property men and the actors; and he could take Jim out at night to the drugstores and the Brown Derby and to the night clubs and the Mexican and Japanese quarters. Jim could see it all as he had seen it once. He wished that Jim were there.

"When Norman is tired," Hal Bliss said, "he can't ever get anything straight."

Jeffrey nodded, but he did not answer. Jim and the story were both running through his mind.

"Norman has a great respect for you," Hal Bliss said. "He told me so. He always has for anyone who's new."

Hal Bliss looked worried, but then, everyone was worried there. It was a palace and filled with palace revolutions.

"I'm working for you," Jeffrey said, "not Mintz. Don't worry, Hal."

Hal Bliss's face relaxed.

"This God-damn' place!" he said. "You know your way around."

"Yes," Jeffrey said, "I know my way around."

"Marianna's been asking for you," Hal Bliss said. "Elise is having her for dinner and the night. You'll come, won't you? Just us four."

"It's a pretty long way out," Jeffrey said.

"We'll stop at the hotel," Bliss said, "and get your bag. You can spend the night. There's lots of room."

Everything was easy. Everything was always easy there. They had a friendship which seemed to Jeffrey very agreeable, for there was no common ground except the story, no other relationship to bother them.

"Yes," he said, "I'd like to, but let's wait here a minute, first. Let's talk about the story."

"Let's talk about it in the car," Hal said, "it's getting late."

The chauffeur drove them across Wilshire Boulevard on the way to the Bronxville to pick up Jeffrey's bag, past the new real estate developments which seemed to Jeffrey to possess the impermanence of the sets on the indoor stages. There was no need for deep digging, since there was no frost to heave the foundations, and so the framing of those new communities rose up overnight. You did not need much heat in those houses, except to remove the fog and the damp in the rainy months. Trees and shrubs would grow like weeds in the benign climate, so that in a few months the bougainvillaeas and the oleander and the casuarina and the palm trees, if you wanted them, and everything else that you planted, looked as though they had been around your house for a long while. Beginning now, you could be sure of months of sunny, rainless days, but there was plenty of water for the gardens. He could see the date palms, and palmetto and royal palms and Italian cypress and traveler's palms, and avocado and monkey-puzzle trees, all mixed together in a confusion that made him curious about the point of view of the people who had planted them.

They passed the places where you could drive in for a light luncheon from a tray hooked to the door of your car, served by little girls called "car hops" dressed in the uniforms of sailors or cowgirls. They drove up the Avenue to the hotel and Jeffrey walked through the lobby past the gift shop and the oriental shop and the flower shop and the automobile livery. The manager, in a doeskin suit, was standing near the desk. The Topaz Cocktail Room was open, and he heard dance music.

An old man, also in a doeskin suit, and suffering from arthritis, like so many of the other guests, was complaining about the noise that the birds made in the early morning.

"Well, well, well, Mr. Wilson," the manager said. "So you're back again with us, are you? Hasn't it been a glorious afternoon?"

Everybody always said it. It was always a glorious afternoon. Anything that Mr. Wilson wanted, just come to see him—that was what he was there for, just anything at all.

"There are a number of telephone messages for you, sir," the clerk said when he handed Jeffrey his key, but Jeffrey said never mind them, now. He was spending the night with Mr. Bliss at Palos Verdes, but if any call came from New York, would they put it through to Mr. Bliss's house?

"Mr. Newcombe has been asking for you, sir. Mr. Newcombe, the author."

"Mr. Newcombe?" Jeffrey repeated. He had never thought of Walter Newcombe's turning up there. "Where's he staying?"

"He didn't say, sir," the clerk said, "but he said he would call again tomorrow; and a man who said he was your brother called."

"Well," Jeffrey said, "never mind it, now."

Then he was back in the car again, sitting beside Hal Bliss.

"You ought to live out here," Hal said.

"If I lived out here," Jeffrey answered, "I'd want to get back home."

"I know," Hal said. "But you get over it. After a while it gets you."

"I don't want it to get me," Jeffrey said.

"This place has got everything," Hal said. "Tell me something it hasn't got."

"That's it," Jeffrey said, "it's got everything."

It occurred to Jeffrey that the script, as he had heard it outlined, was very much like the boulevard along which they were driving. It had everything. Just tell him something it hadn't got. All it needed was a single idea and they discussed it during the entire drive to Palos Verdes.

"You mean, no one knows his country," Hal said. "Americans don't appreciate democracy."

"Never mind democracy," Jeffrey answered.

That was the tangent they were always going off on in those days. You could not make a picture about an academic concept. He wanted Hal to think of it in human terms. All you needed was to throw two characters together. You did not need misdirected letters or Nazi spies or a shooting gallery in Norway, or long speeches. All you needed were two characters and butter on the table, the town meeting, eggs for breakfast, the school bus, the church supper.

"You mean," he heard Hal say, "butter and not guns?"

He could see that Hal was trying to fit it into a formula, and it was not what he meant at all. The idea was all in the script, but you had to make it simple.

They were both sitting there pursuing a half-formed plot. He could see the sun setting in the ocean. He could see a cloud bank on the horizon, but he was not conscious of time or distance. He was doing what he liked best. The road was winding over the headland of Palos Verdes and he could see the Japanese in broad-brimmed straw hats working in their truck gardens.

"We're getting somewhere," Hal said. "We've got an idea, but we haven't got a story."

Jeffrey was not worried about the story, because it seemed to him to develop naturally and he was already thinking of it in scenes, and Bragg was mixed up in it, and his father and his life there as a boy.

"We'll talk about it with Marianna," Hal said. "I want to see if I see Marianna in it."

They were driving close to the edge of the cliffs, approaching Hal's house on a bluff overlooking the sea.

When the car stopped, Jeffrey realized that he had been seeing Marianna Miller in all those half-formed scenes. She came to the door with Hal's wife Elise. She was in a gingham dress with her hair brushed back and tied down hard with a ribbon.

"Jeff," she called, and she ran to the car, and he kissed her, as he always did, and then he kissed Elise, because it was the friendly thing to do.

"Hal's asked me out for the night," he said. Elise smiled at him. He did not know her very well. She was Hal's fourth wife, and all his wives were pretty.

"That's all right," Elise said, "I can stand it if you can."

"Marianna," Hal said. "Stand just that way, will you, again? Now move your head a little. Jeff's got quite a story."

"Story!" Elise said. "That's all it is out here—and when we're finished with one of them, there's always another God-damn' story."

"Well," Hal said, "it's better than having none at all."

The nice thing about Hal Bliss's house was its complete impersonality. There was no sense of obligation in it. Jeffrey felt that it could all be folded up and trucked away at any time and that neither Hal nor Elise would mind. Hal had said that it was just a whim and that maybe it would not work. Just after he had finished a picture, and, like Mr. Mintz, had been very tired, Hal and Elise had gone off in the roadster to motor just anywhere and they had parked on that bluff at Palos Verdes, looking out to sea. Hal was still feeling very tired, but as he sat there in the car, something made him feel at peace, something in the clear sweep of the breeze and the sound of the waves on the cliffs, and then he knew that he wanted to be away from it all where he could think, where he could feel the wind on his face and look at space and hear the murmur of the sea—and right where he and Elise were parked was just the place to do it.

Later he admitted that perhaps he had made a mistake in not asking Elise whether she wanted to get away from it all, too; because it seemed when they moved there that Elise hadn't. Elise said that it drove her nuts there, listening to the waves, and it drove her friends nuts. Admitted she had her own Cadillac and her own chauffeur, there wasn't anyone for her to see unless she drove about twenty-five miles. Hal realized that all this might be a little hard on a girl like Elise, but in the end, if it didn't work, if Elise didn't like La Cabaña Blanca, as the house and the servants' quarters and the garage and the gardener's house were called, why they could write it off and pull up stakes and try something else. In the meanwhile, it gave Hal a chance to turn around and think.

As Hal had said, when he had decided to get away from it all, he was very tired, much too tired to oversee building the house himself or furnishing it, and Elise could not help him because she did not know what he wanted, anyway. So, Hal got an architect whom he had met at the Desert Inn at Palm Springs who had built a good many ranchos for friends of Hal's who had also wanted to get away from it all; and then there were some boys in the Technical Department in the studio who could furnish anything. They had not told him a word about it until it was finished. The only thing the architect had asked him was whether he had wanted it "windswept" and Hal had said that windswept was exactly his idea, and that there had to be a tennis court and a swimming pool. He had not realized until later that it was usually too windy to play tennis, and they had been obliged to build a brick wall around the swimming pool later so he would not shake his teeth out shivering when he got out of the water. But there it was.

The living room was restful. Space was the theme of it, the architect had told Hal—wind and space; and if you did not close the windows at the right time, the wind would blow all the books and cigarette boxes right off the table in the living room, and all the flowers out of the vases; but still the living room was very large and restful. The man from the Technical Department had furnished it with modern woods and the chairs were so large that it was difficult to get out of them. There was a room with a draftsman's table and photographs of personalities where Hal could think. The dining room was a bit of old Spain, and there were three Japanese houseboys whose names Hal could not remember and neither could Elise, but they came when you called "Boy." They had not finished with it yet—perhaps they would never finish it, but upstairs there were bedrooms and any amount of plumbing and a balcony in front of each room where the occupant could sit and look out to sea, if there was not too much wind. Everything was there and if it wasn't, you could call "Boy." Jeffrey felt very happy because he had nothing to do with any of it. There was nothing there to bother—just Hal and Marianna and Elise.

Hal took off his coat and he told Jeffrey to take off his, and Elise said they had better put weights on them so they would not blow away.

"Well," Hal said, "let's go into the bar." Of course the house had a bar, like every proper house out there. You could either sit on little red stools and drink at the bar itself, or else, if the spirit moved you, you could slide up the whole back wall and there the bar would be, right in Hal's workroom. They all sat down and looked at the refrigerator and the shelves and glasses.

Hal pressed a button and they all waited.

"It doesn't work," Hal said. "Let's all yell together. One-two-three, *Boy!*"

A door at the side of the bar opened and there was a Japanese, but the gray in his hair showed that he was not a boy.

"I come," he said. "What to drink, please?" And then everybody told him what to drink.

"You makee chopchop," Hal said, "wikki, wikki, Boy." Hal unbuttoned his shirt collar and sighed.

"I learned that in China," he said. "Elise and I took an oriental cruise in '36. It's a great place, the Orient."

"It isn't a great place, the Orient," Elise said. "You had trouble with your intestines and an itch in your scalp and you were in the hospital in Peking."

"Peiping," Hal said. "A great place, Peiping."

"Don't try to say it the way they say it, dear," Elise said. "It was a dirty place with a lot of poor ginks pulling carts and eating curds in the street."

"Just the same," Hal said, "it was a great place, Peiping. It didn't drive me nuts like Tokyo."

"Shush, dear," Elise said. "Not in front of the boy. Maybe he likes Tokyo."

"Oh," Hal said, "he doesn't mind. He's an American boy. You're American, aren't you, Boy?"

"Oh, yes," the boy said. "Yes, sir."

"There," Hal said. "You see? I'll tell you something. They're wistful in Tokyo."

"What?" Jeffrey asked. "How do you mean, wistful?"

"Wistful," Hal said again. "They want to be like Americans. By God, you ought to see them try."

"Shush, dear," Elise said. "You don't want the boys to walk out on us, do you?"

"Oh, hell, Elise," Hal said. "These are all nice boys."

"Are you going to talk story?" Elise said.

"Yes," Hal said, "we're going to talk story. Nobody understands America."

"That's a big thought, isn't it?" Elise said. "So what? Suppose nobody understands America, so what?"

"When we get through with this," Hal said, "you, even you, will understand America."

"All right," Elise said, "so what?"

"She's a big help to me," Hal said. "She talks like Mintz. Do you know what Elise did before she came to Paramount? She was in the Miss America contest at Atlantic City. She ought to understand America."

"Listen, fat boy," Elise said, "I know more about it than you do, and more about it than—what's your first name, dear?"

"It's Jeffrey," Hal said. "You always call him Jeffrey."

"I always forget," Elise said.

Then Marianna touched his arm. She was smiling at him.

"Darling," she said, "are you glad you're here?"

"Yes," he said, "it's quite a change."

"I can always tell," Marianna said. "Elise, is there time for me to show Jeffrey the garden?"

"There isn't time for anything," Hal said, "and besides, we're going to talk story."

"Okay with me," Elise said. "If you're going to talk story, I'm going to bed with Amytal."

"I'll tell you one thing that you never went to bed with, honey," Hal said.

"What?" Elise asked. "Don't keep me waiting. What is it, fat boy?"

"With a good book," Hal said.

"There aren't any good books here," Elise said. "You never went to bed with a good book, either, unless it was a sleeping dictionary."

"Now honey bunch," Hal said. "Just be quiet. We're talking story."

There was nothing there to bother him. He did not have to worry about what Madge might think of Elise. She was just Hal's fourth wife, a very pretty girl, and when Hal told her to be quiet, she kept quiet. He was only there to talk story. It made the basis for a pleasant sort of friendship, temporary, but very genial, and they all were speaking a language that he knew. After dinner Marianna sat on the floor by the fireplace with her arms wrapped around her knees. Jeffrey sat near her and he kept looking at her while he was talking. She had interpreted so many characters that she could turn moods on and off, according to her wish, as any actress could. Now and then he could watch her with an amused sort of detachment, thinking of her stage career and of her as a motion picture property, as though he did not know her. Her nose, her forehead and her cheekbones were made for the camera. He remembered that the molding of her face had struck him the first time he had seen her. That had been at one of those theatrical parties somewhere in New York when she was studying at some school for dramatics, and that was quite a while ago. Her face was more mobile now, more sensitive because, like any actress, she was conscious of her beauty. He knew that she had studied the way she sat, clasping her knees with her thin hands, and once she turned to look at him, tilting her head back and giving her hair a quick toss. He knew her about as well as anyone, and yet there was no way of knowing what was attitude and what was not, because she did not know herself.

"Wait a minute," Hal said, "what about a highball?"

"Don't get yourself soused," Elise said.

Hal was sitting with a block of note paper across his knee. Elise was lying on the sofa smoking cigarettes and the wind was rattling the windows.

"Windswept," Elise said; "hear it? My God, it's getting late. You talk and talk and you don't get anywhere at all."

Jeffrey had no idea of the time, and time did not matter.

"You always get soused when you're on a story," Elise said. "It's going to be colossal. It's going to get the Oscar—and then you go to bed and come down with a head in the morning."

"It's all illusion, anyway," Hal said.

"It's all illusion, and so what?" Elise said.

"So you can get your bath salts," Hal said, "and have a mud pack on your puss, dearie, that's what it's for."

Jeffrey knew that in the morning when he tried to write the script its luster would be gone. He would begin to see the faults in it and the bareness of the mechanism. It would be like any other script when he began to write it. There would be that eternal tragedy, the difference between performance and creative conception. But now he was awake and alive with the stimulation of ideas.

"You feel what I mean," Jeffrey said, "in just a small way when you come back home from abroad. You've left things one way and when you're back, they're another. When I came back from the war—"

He saw Marianna tilt back her head to watch him. He saw Elise on the sofa throw away her cigarette, and he realized that they had all forgotten about the war.

"I had quite a time in the war," Jeffrey said, "but never mind it now. I was only talking about coming back. We were all jammed in the steerage, a lot of lieutenants in the steerage, coming back. Colonels and majors and generals and captains were in the First Class—a whole ship full of casual officers coming back, and those of us down in the hold were pretty sore. We were officers, and we'd seen a lot, maybe more than the generals in the First Class."

He could see them all crowded in the bow as they steamed into New York Harbor, the whole deck full of younger officers. He remembered the wonder that he felt when he reached New York and stepped through the barriers beyond the pier, and saw the streets and the automobiles and the well-fed faces. No one had looked at him—they had seen too many soldiers, and he was lost there in the city. He was unfamiliar with the land he had left, completely lost.

"We ought to get that for the girl," he said, "that sense of being lost, not a part of anything."

Then he saw Hal turn in his chair and look toward the hall and he saw one of the Japanese boys in a white coat.

"The telephone," the boy said, "for Mr. Wilson, from New York."

Jeffrey felt a twinge of conscience when he pulled himself out of the chair. It was retribution for having had too good a time. Now, something serious must have happened in New York, particularly when he considered the difference of time. His watch showed him that it was half-past twelve, and it would be later—half-past three in the morning—in New York.

"Take it in my workroom," Hal said. "You know, just across the hall."

There must have been an accident or he would not have been called at half-past three in the morning. Someone was ill, or someone was dead. Marianna was standing up, and her eyes showed him that she had seen what he was thinking.

"Thanks, Hal," he said, and then he made an inane remark. "I'm sorry."

He walked across the hall to Hal's workroom with the framed photographs of all the celebrities that Hal had ever met on the wall around him—celebrities dressed like cowboys, celebrities in bathing suits and shorts, celebrities candidly snapped in night clubs. The telephone was on the draftsman's table and when he looked at it, he had a faint feeling of nausea.

"Mr. Wilson?" The operator's voice was precise and impersonal. "New York is calling. Just a minute, please." He could hear the buzzing in the transmitter. "New York, we have your party, ready to talk. One moment, please. Mr. Wilson? Ready with New York."

He wished to God she would not talk so much, and then he heard a burst of dance music, and then Madge's voice as clear as though she were talking across the room.

"Hello, Jeff. Is that you, darling?"

"Yes," Jeffrey said. He was talking louder than was necessary as he always did on the telephone. "Yes, what is it, Madge?"

"Are you at a party? What time is it out there?"

"It's half-past twelve," Jeffrey said. "No, I'm not at a party. What is it, Madge?"

"We're at El Morocco."

"My God," Jeffrey said. "What's the matter?"

"Darling," Madge said, "there's nothing the matter. We're just at El Morocco, Minot and Jim and I. We wanted to tell you the news, that's all."

"What?" Jeffrey asked. "What news?"

"Don't shout so, darling," Madge said. "We all want to talk to you. We're just celebrating. We wish you were here."

Something seemed to clutch at Jeffrey's throat. Madge's voice had the tinny, unnatural gayety which it sometimes assumed when she was being brave.

"Celebrating," he repeated. "Has Jim—Celebrating what?"

"No," her answer came quickly, too quickly. "No, it isn't that."

"God!" Jeffrey whispered. "God!" But he controlled his voice. "Get hold of yourself, Madge. Tell me what's happened."

"Don't be so cross, dear," Madge said. "It's Jim's last night in New York."

"What?" Jeffrey said.

"Don't shout so, dear," Madge said. "Your voice goes right through my ears. Just wait a minute until I close the door. Just wait a minute. . . . Jeff, Jim's in the army."

"What?" Jeffrey said, but he had heard her perfectly.

"Jeff, I can't tell you over the telephone. Minot will call you tomorrow. Jeff, just listen." And then she spoke very slowly and carefully. "It was—serious—much—more serious—than we thought."

"What was?" Jeffrey asked.

"I can't tell you over the telephone," Madge said. "You know what I mean. What we were worrying about. Something—I found out the day you left. It was much more serious than we thought. She—she was completely losing her head about him."

"Who?" Jeffrey asked, but he knew who.

"You know who. Jeff, dear—" Her voice was low and strained. "Jim's waiting just outside. It's much better this way. Can you hear me, Jeff? Minot dropped everything and went up to see him. It was dear of Minot. Jeff, it'll take his mind off it. It's much better. Can you hear me? Are you there, Jeff?"

"Yes," Jeffrey answered, "yes, I'm here."

"He had that chance," Madge said. "It was still open—that chance at Fort Sill. Jeff, we really had to do something."

"Do what?" Jeffrey asked. "What happened? Were they—"

"It wasn't anything definite, dear," Madge said, "but it's much better the way it is. Minot told him he'd talked to you. Jim really wanted to enlist. Minot told him he was sure you wouldn't mind."

"Why didn't you tell me before he did it?" Jeffrey asked.

"Oh, Jeff," Madge said. "Don't sound that way. You weren't *here*. It was just much better for Jim to go away somewhere *quickly*. Wait, Minot wants to talk to you. Here he is."

"I don't want to talk to him," Jeffrey said.

"What?" Madge said.

"I said I didn't want to talk to him," Jeffrey said. "You can tell him so for me."

"Oh, Jeff," Madge said. "You don't know what you're saying. Minot—"

He interrupted her. He did not want to lose his temper.

"Madge," he said, "I don't think you've been fair. I think you waited to get me out of the way, but there's no use going on about it. I want to talk to Jim."

He realized that his hand was gripping the telephone so hard that his fingers hurt. He realized that he must not make a fool of himself, that it was no time to show resentment. He knew that they both had done what they thought was absolutely right, and perhaps they had been right, but Jim was his son, not Minot's. Jim was his business, not Minot's.

"Jeff," Madge said, "I wish you'd listen. If you were here—"

"I'm not there," Jeffrey said. "You should have let him alone."

"Darling," Madge said, "why should you be the only one who gives advice? You *never* let him alone."

"Never mind it now, Madge," he said. He did not want to hear her voice any longer.

"All right," Madge said, and she was speaking the way she did when she knew that everything would be all right if she wanted it to be. "Are you having a good time, dear?"

"What?" Jeffrey said, but he had heard her and it was exactly like her.

"Don't worry," Madge said. "Have a good time, dear, and think of it this way—It's something definite. At least we're doing something. Here's Jim, now."

She must have been opening the door of the telephone booth, for he could hear the dance music playing louder.

"Jim—" he heard her say—"here he is . . ." and then he heard her say something else, but the music made her words indistinct. Jeffrey could almost smell the close air of El Morocco. He could almost hear the talk and the clatter of the dishes and see the couples dancing. People never knew how badly they looked when they danced. A tune that had nothing to do with El Morocco was running through his mind, and he could hear the grim gayety of the bugles as they blew it. "You're in the army now—You're not behind the plow. You'll never get rich, you son-of-a-bitch—You're in the army now." He could feel his foot tapping the time of it on the floor as he waited to hear Jim's voice three thousand miles away.

"Hello, Pops," he heard Jim saying, "how's it going, Pops?"

"Close that door," Jeffrey called to him, "I don't want to hear the music."

Jim's voice sounded just as his own sounded once, not careful, not measured, but triumphant and not afraid of anything. It seemed to wash the care from his mind. He knew what Jim felt and thought, because he had felt the same things, once.

"Hello," Jim said. "Can you hear me now?"

Jim's voice seemed very near. Jim would be in his dinner coat with his hair in a short crew cut, and with his tie sliding a little off center. He would be smiling and he might even be a little tight, although Jim had never been bad that way. The sleeves of that coat were too short, Jeffrey remembered, but Jim would not need another now for a while.

"Yes," he said, "I hear you. You don't have to yell."

"Well," Jim said, "I'm in the army now."

"Yes," Jeffrey said, "your mother said you were."

"They're only sending three of us," Jim said. "That's all—just three."

"Well," Jeffrey said, "that's fine."

"You're not sore, are you?"

"No," Jeffrey said, "why should I be? I told you to do anything you wanted. Just remember that."

"Well," Jim said, "I guess I'm doing it."

"You ought not to guess," Jeffrey said. "You ought to know."

"All right," Jim said, "I know."

"As long as you think you do," Jeffrey said, and he cleared his throat. "A kid like you can't know. You can only think you know."

"Well," Jim said, "as long as you're not sore."

"I told you—" Jeffrey told him—"as long as you've done it, I think it's fine. When are you going?"

"Tomorrow. We're pulling out tomorrow morning."

The room where Jeffrey stood was very still. The expression was familiar. They always "pulled out" in the morning.

"Have you got everything?" Jeffrey asked.

"They don't want us to bring anything," Jim said. "We'll get it there."

Jeffrey remembered. You left everything behind, or almost everything. Jeffrey cleared his throat again.

"Jim," he said, "I wish I were going too." Suddenly he wished to God that he were going. He wished that he could see the barracks again and the streets.

"I'll write you," Jim said.

"Thanks," Jeffrey said, "be sure you do—and Jim?"

"Yes," Jim said.

He hesitated, for after all, it was Jim's business and not his, but still he had to ask.

"What about Sally? What does she think?"

"Sally? She thinks it's fine. Sally's quite a girl."

There was more that Jeffrey wanted to say, but there was no time for any of it.

"Well," he said, "I'm right with you, Jim."

"Yes," Jim said, "I know you are. I wish I could see you, I'll be seeing you."

"Yes," Jeffrey said, "you'll get leave when you get through there. Well, good-by."

"Wait a minute," Jim called, "wait a minute."

"Yes," Jeffrey said, "what is it?"

"I wish you'd see her sometimes."

"Yes," Jeffrey said, "of course I will."

"And that's between you and me," Jim said, "just you and me."

"Yes," Jeffrey said, "that's all right, Jim."

"I wish I could see you," Jim said. "Well, good-by."

"Good-by," Jeffrey said, and he cleared his throat again.

He had never been more conscious of silence than at the moment when he put down that telephone. There had been something that went beyond Jim and concerned himself. It might have been vanity, but he did not think it was vanity. All he could remember later was the silence. It was like having a door slammed in his face. He knew that his feelings toward Madge and Minot Roberts would never be quite the same again.

He could hear Madge's voice, a little breathless, a little strained, sounding as it always had when she wanted to manage something that he did not approve of, but which she knew was exactly right.

"There isn't any conclusion to jump at, dear," he could hear her say. "It is just much better if he's away somewhere."

He wanted to forget the sound of her voice. It had all that assurance of hers that was based on nothing.

Now it was a question of taking up where he had left off, of putting it behind him, and of going back to the other room. He pulled out his handkerchief and rubbed it hard across his forehead. The voices were back with him again, his own voice and Jim's.

"Well, I'm right with you, Jim."

"Yes," he heard Jim answering, "I know you are. I wish I could see you, but I'll be seeing you."

In the living room there was exactly that sort of silence which he had expected, the questioning silence of people who wanted to know but who could not very well ask. He was glad that Marianna was there, because there was no reason to put on a façade for Marianna, but it was different with Hal Bliss and Elise. It was necessary for him to say something, to put it all in a casual little capsule.

"Well, hello," he said, and he smiled exactly the way one should have at such a time. "It was the family at El Morocco, celebrating. Jim's just joined the army." And then he realized that the Blisses might not know who Jim was. "Jim's my son," he added, and he sat down and smiled again.

"My, my," Elise said, "you must have been married young."

"What?" Jeffrey said.

"You must have been married young," Elise said, "to have a son old enough to get in the army."

"Oh," Jeffrey said, "yes. He's old enough."

"Well, you don't look it, dear," Elise said, "it must have been an accident."

"No," Jeffrey said. "No. Not any more than anything else is."

"Was he drafted?" Hal asked.

"Oh," Jeffrey said, "drafted?" And he put his mind on it. He had to put the whole thing in a capsule. "No, he wasn't drafted. He was in college. They picked out three boys for the Officers' School at Sill." And he smiled again.

"Well," Hal said, "that's fine. All he'll do will be to go to South America or Trinidad or somewhere, or maybe the Philippines. That's fine."

"The Philippines?" Jeffrey said.

"Yes," Hal said, "we're sending quite a lot of troops out there. A great place, Manila. Those God-damned Japs won't get the Philippines."

"Does he look like you?" Elise asked.

"What?" Jeffrey said.

"I said," Elise asked, "does the kiddie look like you?"

"Oh," Jeffrey said, "well, yes. Some people think he does. Yes, I guess so. Something like me."

"Well, he must be cute," Elise said. "Marianna, don't you think he's cute too?"

"Who," Jeffrey asked, "me?"

"Yes," Elise said, "you. You're cute, having a son in the army."

"Would you like a drink?" Hal asked.

"What?" Jeffrey said. "Oh, yes, I'd like a drink."

"Well," Hal said. "There's the bottle. Pour it out. Pour a stiff one. It isn't every day this happens."

Jeffrey reached for the bottle carefully.

"Here," Marianna said. "I'll mix it for you, Jeff."

"Well," Hal said, "here's to him. I wish I had a kid in the army."

"No, you don't wish you had a kid in the army, either," Elise said. "You've got too many wives to have kids in the army, but it's cute."

When Marianna handed him the glass he sat staring at it for a moment, and then he drank it very quickly. He reached for the bottle again without exactly thinking. It made him feel better, but not happier. He forgot that drinking had never been a means of escape for him—it only intensified his mood.

"Who told you?" Marianna asked him. "Did Madge tell you?"

"Madge?" he said. "Oh yes. Yes, Madge told me."

"Did you know about it before?" Marianna asked.

"Oh," Jeffrey said. "Why, yes, of course. Well, not exactly."

"Was Madge upset?" Marianna asked.

"Upset?" Jeffrey repeated. He was glad that she was asking. "No, not exactly. I think she rather likes it. I was the one who didn't like it. It seemed a little needless, right now. It—Well, it rather surprised me. I didn't think Jim was going to do it, but—Oh well, they wanted him to do it."

He had said both too much and not enough. He stared at his glass again.

"I suppose they persuaded him," he said, "but I don't imagine it took much persuading. When you're that age, you're ready for something new." He stopped and smiled. "Well, it's getting pretty late, isn't it?"

"Yes," Hal said. "It's one o'clock. Come on, Elise."

Marianna was standing by the fireplace with her hands clasped behind her.

"I'm not sleepy," she said, "I'm going for a walk. Jeffrey, you're not sleepy either."

"What?" Jeffrey said. "No. Well, no. I'm not very sleepy."

"Well, I am," Elise said. "Never mind the lights. The boys will be around."

"Good night, Jeff," Hal said. "It's swell he's in the army. We'll talk to Mintz in the morning."

"Mintz?" Jeffrey said. "Oh, yes. Thanks for having me here, Hal. Good night."

"Good night," Elise said, and she patted his shoulder.

The way Hal and Elise spoke reminded him of something.

"I'll just get something to put around me," Marianna said. "I'll be right down."

"If you'd like to take the car—" Hal began.

"Oh, no," Jeffrey said. "No, thanks, Hal."

Then Jeffrey remembered. It was all like Louella and Mr. and Mrs. Barnes. He had the same self-conscious feeling he had once suffered, when he heard Marianna running upstairs to get something to put around her.

37

Don't Speak Any Lines

It was starlight outside. It was cool, but not cold. The first minutes outdoors gave Jeffrey the same sense of release which he used to feel on leaving a room where he had been struggling with a college examination. You thought and thought and you wrote the answers down in a blue copybook which was waiting for you on your desk with the printed examination form beside it; and when you had finished, you closed the book and gave it to the instructor in charge. If you finished early and walked down the aisle with that blue notebook, everyone in the room would stamp perfunctorily in time to your footsteps, because it was a custom. Outside, there was always relief and freedom because you had done all you could. Now Jeffrey had exactly the same sensation of being out with the answers all left behind him. He had done what he could in New York and now it did not matter what he did.

The wind was dying down. There was a damp, moist smell from the ocean, unlike the Atlantic. It came from the fog bank that he had seen at sunset. It might be misty in the morning, but now the sky was clear. They were standing on the lawn by the front door and the lights of the house were behind them. Marianna drew a deep breath of the fresh air, and reached up to fasten her light blue cloak more tightly. Over to the north, he could see the lights of the city against the sky, miles and miles of lights.

"It's a nice night," Jeffrey said.

"Yes," Marianna said, "let's go to the garden. The garden overlooks the sea."

"Did you ever read *Candide?*" Jeffrey asked.

"Yes," Marianna answered. "What about *Candide?*"

"The only way you can be happy," Jeffrey said, "is digging in the garden. You don't dig in your garden, do you?"

"No," Marianna answered. "Why?"

"I don't either," Jeffrey said. "I never have the time. People always talk about a garden and then pay a man to do it."

It was too dark to see more than the shape of the garden. He could see the outline of the hedges and the dark black of cypress trees.

"They have spotlights in the trees," Marianna said, "and in the swimming pool."

"Have they?" Jeffrey said. "Good God."

Marianna laughed.

"Darling," she said, "do you mind if I tell you something?"

"Please don't," Jeffrey said, "not right now."

"Darling," Marianna said, "it isn't that kind of thing. You're the only man I know who makes me feel completely natural. It's because you think of me as a person, that is, when we're not working."

"You never bother me," Jeffrey said, "when you're not speaking lines. Marianna, don't speak any lines tonight."

"I'm not," Marianna answered. "I never do when I'm with you."

"You can't tell," Jeffrey said, "you can't tell that."

"Let's sit by the swimming pool," Marianna said, "by the wall, out of the wind."

The swimming pool was exactly what he thought it would be. There was a lawn around it, and the high wall cut off the wind. He could see the water in the starlight, and the outlines of the dressing rooms which they called cabañas. He could see the shapes of reclining chairs on wheels and metal tables and folding umbrellas.

"Anything but going in swimming," Jeffrey said.

"No," Marianna said. "I only like it in the sun."

"Then what are we doing at the pool?" Jeffrey asked.

"It's out of the wind," Marianna said. She undid the clasp of her cloak and tossed it on the lawn, close to the white wall, and patted the side of the cloak that lay dark on the grass.

Jeffrey felt that he should have been wearing a pullover and slacks and shoes like Jim's with no laces in them, instead of his gray flannel business suit with a notebook and a billfold and a fountain pen in the pockets. He wished that he had been out there for a longer time and more adjusted to his surroundings, and he was very conscious of Marianna, but in a way which was not altogether comfortable. Her face as she leaned back on her elbows and looked up at the stars had a disturbing, unsettled quality.

He could recall all the roles he had ever seen her play. First she had been an ingénue in one of those boy-and-girl plays, something like Mr. Tarkington's "Seventeen," and that was quite a while ago. He remembered her in a drawing-room comedy, one of those English importations which were just lines, lines, lines. It had always seemed to him that there was nothing more sterile than an English drawing-room comedy, and yet the critics had said it was like the first fresh breath of spring at the end of a disappointing season. She had been in a Shaw play about marriage—he could not remember the exact one because so many of Mr. Shaw's plays dealt with marriage—and that was when the critics realized that she was a great actress, as critics always did if a girl could take on a Shaw play and get away with it. She had played Ibsen's "Lady from the Sea," and thank God, Jesse Fineman had not had her do "Ghosts" or "The Wild Duck." He could think of all the times that he and Marianna had gone over lines together. Although he was in no sense a director, he could always explain character to her, because for some queer reason they could both see it in the same way. When she was younger her taste had been as obvious as department store advertising, but now it was restrained. He had taught her not to be impressed by all the patter and he had taught her not to be spoiled. She seemed to welcome rather than resent the influence he had on her and it gave him a sense of possession when he thought of it. Now that he was sitting beside her on the grass he felt that she belonged to him, simply because he had done so much toward making her what she was.

"A penny," Marianna said.

"What?" Jeffrey asked.

"A penny," Marianna said again. "A penny for your thoughts."

The triteness of the expression hurt him.

"Don't use someone else's lines," he said. "Say it. Don't be fancy. I was thinking about you in that Shaw play. Do you remember how I taught you to sit down? That's the main thing about a Shaw play, isn't it? Everybody must sit down all the time."

He could not see her face clearly, but he knew that she was smiling.

"Yes," she said. "Not slop down, but do it slowly. I can do it now. Do you want to see me do it?"

"No," Jeffrey said, "you've learned it."

"Darling," Marianna asked, "what else are you thinking of?"

"I was thinking about Jim," he said. She did not answer. He was glad she did not answer.

"There's a girl," he said. "Madge is afraid he'll marry her. That's all."

She did not answer, and he spoke again. "There's nothing the matter with her. He likes her. She's a nice girl."

"You're angry," she said, "aren't you?"

"Yes," he said, "but never mind it now."

"Then don't think about it," she said. "Of course, it isn't Madge's fault."

"What isn't her fault?" Jeffrey asked.

"That she can't see things as you do, and that she tried to stop you from growing. She knows that you're too kind."

"Too kind?" Jeffrey repeated.

"You've never thought enough about yourself," Marianna said. "You mustn't always be thinking about other people."

"No one does," Jeffrey said, "not really. Only in terms of yourself."

"Jeff," she said, "please be happy. You were earlier. Please, I'm so happy."

"You can't make yourself, you know," Jeffrey said. "No one ought to try. It's silly to see everyone trying."

"Then don't think about it," Marianna said. "You're here and I'm here."

"You're here and I'm here, so what do we care." He wished that his mind did not keep running into jingles.

"I don't know," he said. "Maybe Jim's too young. You can't know exactly what you're doing when you're young."

"You're here and I'm here," Marianna said again. "Jeffrey, darling, all that matters of you is here. The rest of it doesn't matter."

"I got to thinking on the train," he said, "maybe there isn't as much of me—not as much of me left as there used to be."

It was not a consoling thought. There were Madge and the children and things he was used to, but none of it had any sense or value any longer.

"You don't know," Marianna said, "you can't know. You're better than you ever were. You're better all the time."

It was because she was younger. He could remember that same sort of faith in capability, that belief in an eventual happy ending.

"Thanks," he said, "it's nice that someone thinks so."

She leaned closer to him, and her face was clearer in the starlight. "Don't say it that way," she said. "There's everything here—everything."

Suddenly everything seemed completely natural. There was a simple way to get away from all the rest of it and he kissed her. It was not entirely desire, it was because he knew that something of the sort was inevitable. There had even been some sort of graceless, perfunctory idea of getting it over with, now that they were there. Yet it was entirely different when the time came. He had never thought that anything would be like that for him again. When his arms were around her, everything that he had lost and forgotten seemed to come back to him from all sorts of distant places.

"Darling," she said, "are you feeling better now?"

"Yes," he said, "much better," but he did not want to speak. He wanted to be silent, to deal with his own surprise that that sort of thing was not over with him long ago. What astonished him most was that he felt no qualm of disloyalty. Something in that talk with Madge seemed to him very final, leaving him free to do anything he wanted.

"Don't," he said to her, "don't speak a line."

"I don't want to talk at all," she said. "It's never happened to two people just this way, ever."

"No," he said, "not just this way."

It must have been what everyone had said. It was that sad human desire to keep individuality out of universal experience. Yet even so, he knew that he would always believe that nothing like that had happened in just that way before.

"You needed someone else," she said. "Don't worry, dear. It doesn't have to be for always, unless . . ."

"I'm not worried at all," he said.

There had been no one for a long while to whom he could tell everything and they must have talked for a long while about all sorts of things.

Some problem that he had been trying to reconcile seemed to be solved. He did not want to see Madge or any of it again.

"I brought a play out with me," he said. "When I'm finished with this script, I might stay on and work on it."

The truth was that he felt like someone else, someone he might have been if things had been different.

38

It's Time to Take the Clipper

When Jeffrey stopped at the Bronxville at half-past nine one morning some weeks later, to get his mail, the clerk looked up from arranging a bowl of white magnolia flowers, which, according to Jeffrey's observation of the clerk, was a very nice thing for him to be doing.

"You haven't been with us much for the last few days, Mr. Wilson," the clerk said.

It was an obvious, and, to Jeffrey, not a comforting remark. Although he kept his room there, he had not been at the Bronxville very much, and now it seemed necessary to offer the clerk some logical explanation, although the clerk and the Bronxville had no connection whatsoever with what he did or where he went. He wondered if it were because he was not used to that sort of thing that he felt it necessary to be logical with so many people. After all, there was no reason to think that anyone cared where he went or what he did.

Yet only yesterday, when he had been interviewed by Mary Pringle, who wrote one of those syndicated gossip columns on Hollywood, she had made a similar remark—that he was always too busy to talk to her at the studio and that he must be very gay, like every other writer, because he was never at the Bronxville. He had not wanted Miss Pringle to interview him, but the Publicity Department had asked for it, particularly since the word had been passed about that the new Miller script, when he had finished with it, was a real, terrific story, but terrific. He was not to say anything to Miss Pringle about the script except in the most general terms. That was why Jerry Small from the Publicity Department was right in the room with him when he was being interviewed by Miss Pringle, and all Jerry Small could say was that Mr. Wilson was top-flight, brought from New York at as high a figure as they had ever paid a writer, and that Mr. Wilson had batted out a terrific job for them—but terrific; and Miss Pringle could say it was a Miller vehicle if she wanted to, all Miller. All Mr. Wilson could do now, under orders from Mr. Mintz, was to answer questions about how he wrote, whether he wrote with a pen or on a typewriter, and whether he wrote regularly or when the spirit moved him, and whether he wrote in the morning or in the evening. If Miss Pringle wanted anything more, she must really ask for it from Mr. Mintz personally—but really.

That was when Miss Pringle asked Jeffrey about his wife and kiddies, and said that he must be very gay, because she had tried and tried and had never been able to contact him at the Bronxville. And now she saw why she couldn't contact him because Jeffrey looked so handsome. He was what she called a "writer heartbreak type" and was he breaking many hearts in Hollywood? Jeffrey had said that Miss Pringle ought to know how hospitable Hollywood friends were—always asking you out to spend the night at their cabañas and their ranchos, and besides, he had worked on the script a great deal with Mr. Bliss out at Palos Verdes. That was why he was not at the Bronxville as much as he wanted to be. Then Miss Pringle had said that a little bird, but it was a little bird that was off the record (and Mr. Wilson must have heard that she could be like a clam when she wanted to be, no matter what a feather in her hat the story might be personally)—Well, a little bird had told her that Mr. Wilson had been quite often at the lovely home of a certain Someone at Malibu Beach. And Jeffrey had said that of course he had, and if the little bird hadn't told Miss Pringle who it was, he could tell her. He had been working on the script with Miss Miller, since it was a Miller vehicle, and she could add, if she wanted to, that he had known Miss Miller for years and years. Miss Miller had great charm, but she also had a bad temper. Miss Pringle knew what actresses were like, and he had seen too many of them. Besides, he did not believe that emotion between people working on a picture was ever conducive to good work, and Miss Pringle could put that down, if she wanted to: No emotion and good work. He saw enough of stage and screen celebrities in working hours. He wanted to get back to New York and to his Connecticut farm, and that was that.

Yet now the clerk was making the same remark, that Mr. Wilson had not been with them at the Bronxville very much.

"Not as much as I'd like," Jeffrey said. "You see, I have a good many Hollywood friends and you know how hospitable everyone is in Hollywood."

"Yes," the clerk said, "indeed I know. Lady Gregson—she is with her Pekingese in Bungalow E—Lady Gregson was just saying to me this morning that she had never seen a place with so many delightful people."

"Yes," Jeffrey said, "and it's a delightful place."

"Oh Mr. Wilson, I forgot to remind you," the clerk said, "there is a friend of yours who has been inquiring for you. Mr. Walter Newcombe, the world correspondent. He said he wanted very much to see you."

Walter Newcombe's messages had completely slipped Jeffrey's mind and he hoped that other more important things had not also slipped it.

"Is he staying here?" Jeffrey asked.

The clerk said he was not staying there, though he wished that Mr. Newcombe might be with them. He was staying with Mrs. Newcombe at the Val Halla, rather too near the center of things to be as comfortable as they could have made Mr. and Mrs. Newcombe at the Bronxville. . . .

"Thank you," Jeffrey said. "I'm going down that way before I go to the studio. I'll stop in to see him." He disliked giving so many explanations, but it occurred to him that it might be just as well to see Walter. He did not want Walter to go back to New York saying that he was never at the Bronxville.

The Val Halla was on a side street off the boulevard and the city had grown up around it. It was near the filling stations and the drive-in luncheons and the drugstores and the open-air markets and the Motels where you could drive your car right under a shelter and walk into a room. It was noisy, as the clerk had said, and a great many people known as "fallen stars" lived in little apartments near it. The Val Halla, however, still had its large grounds and its date palms and its monkey puzzle trees and its roses. It was built, Jeffrey supposed, on lines inspired by one of the old Spanish missions—a main building where the guests ate and lounged and then lots and lots of cloisters with rooms opening right out upon lots and lots of miniature gardens, each with a little pool filled with lotus flowers. Hanging from the arches of the cloisters were lots and lots of birds in gay lacquer cages, known as "parakeets" when Jeffrey was younger, but now termed "lovebirds." Their conjugal quarrels and their reconciliations, all going on at once, formed an odd and slightly hysterical background. It was what the clerk had said, "a very delightful place, but a little noisy."

"Yes sir," the bellboy said, "Mr. and Mrs. Newcombe are in. They're directly at the end of cloister Number 3."

"Perhaps you'd better show me," Jeffrey said. "I don't know whether I can find cloister Number 3."

Then he began following the bellboy through the cloisters past bougainvillaeas, roses, snapdragons, and nasturtiums, past orange trees, grapefruit trees, fig trees, avocado trees, and monkey puzzle trees.

"That one," the bellboy said, "is called a 'monkey puzzle' tree because they say a monkey wouldn't know how to climb down it."

"Yes," Jeffrey said, "I know. You've got a lot of birds."

"Yes, sir," the bellboy said. "Lovebirds. This is Mr. Newcombe's room."

"Thank you," Jeffrey said.

"You bet," the bellboy said. Out there they always said "You bet."

There was one of those serving trays on wheels outside the Newcombes' door with empty coffee cups and eggshells and the remains of grapefruit in cups of ice with the green leaves that hotels use to dress up grapefruit. A battered wardrobe trunk and two new suitcases stood beside the tray.

"Is Mr. Newcombe moving out?" Jeffrey asked.

"Yes sir," the boy said. "They're checking out on us this morning. Mrs. Newcombe is going back East. Mr. Newcombe's taking the plane to Frisco to catch the China Clipper."

It was peculiar to hear the boy speak of it so casually, just as he might have said that Walter Newcombe was going to the races; but somehow it all fitted perfectly with the cloisters of Val Halla, and with the preposterous conglomeration of flowers and fruits and pools and clock-golf sets in the courtyards. If a Siamese elephant, white and sacred, should have appeared around the corner, Jeffrey thought he would have accepted it implicitly.

"Well," he said again to the bellboy, "thank you."

"You bet," the boy said.

The door to the Newcombes' apartment was heavily studded with hand-beaten nails. Before Jeffrey could knock, it opened suddenly and both of Walter Newcombe's hands appeared filled with empty White Rock and whisky bottles. Jeffrey could not see Walter at the moment—only Walter's clean, purple shirt sleeves with a handsome pair of gold cuff links and the bottles—but he could visualize Walter's position behind the door. Walter would be half crouching in his effort to shove the bottles outside, furtively.

"Hello, Walter," Jeffrey said.

Then he saw Walter's foot encased in a self-ventilating white buckskin shoe and a purple sock, as Walter pushed the door open.

"Who the hell is that?" he heard Mrs. Newcombe say.

"It's all right, sweet," Walter answered. "It's Jeffrey Wilson."

Walter stood there, blinking through his glasses at the morning glare of sunlight reflected from the whitewashed walls of the cloisters. Walter was in his shirt sleeves and in light tropical trousers supported by pink suspenders. The sunlight glittered from his glasses and from the shiny ridge of his nose. His forehead was peeling with sunburn.

"Well, well," Walter said, "hello, Jeff."

"Well, well," Jeffrey said, "hello, Walter."

"Well," Walter said. "It's a lovely morning, isn't it? Just wait till I set down these bottles. It's a little stirred-up inside. We're just getting ready to check."

"Well, I'm glad I caught you," Jeffrey told him. "Why not sit outside in the sun?"

Then he heard Mrs. Newcombe's voice.

"The hell we'll sit outside," Mrs. Newcombe called. "Get out of that damn sun before it fries your brains out. Whistle for some more White Rock, honey, and come in and close the door."

"Sweet," Walter Newcombe said, "we don't want any more White Rock if I'm going to hop the plane."

"Don't get your pronouns twisted," Mrs. Newcombe said, "*I* want more White Rock. Get inside here and close the door."

"All right," Walter said gently. "Excuse me, sweet," and then he lowered his voice and looked meaningly at Jeffrey. "Mildred's a little upset this morning. You know, ideas about the Clipper—ideas."

As Walter said, the room was a little stirred up as rooms were with morning rising combined with packing. The heavy casement windows were set in artificially thick whitewashed walls. It was one of those airy, simple, tasteful rooms with a bit of Spanish brass on a table and a piece of old fabric on the wall, a room made for light and air and sunshine. There were wicker chairs, and you could cover up the twin beds in the daytime and use them for couches, heaping them, presumably, with the multicolored sofa pillows which were now strewn about the matting-covered floor, mingled with pages of the *Los Angeles Times*, towels, and an occasional White Rock bottle. On one of the beds he saw a typewriter case and a brief case and a small, battered, cheap suitcase covered with old customs labels. Mrs. Newcombe was seated on the other bed and on the floor beside her was a tray on which was some cracked ice and a bottle of Scotch and Mrs. Newcombe's handbag. Mrs. Newcombe was carefully dressed in a white tailored suit and was holding her long cigarette holder.

"Well, well," she said to Jeffrey. "Whoops to you, big boy. Sit down and have a little drink."

The last thing Jeffrey wanted was to have a little drink.

"It's a little soon after breakfast," Jeffrey said.

"Walter," Mrs. Newcombe said, "give him a little drink. It isn't a little soon after breakfast today—yesterday, perhaps, and perhaps tomorrow, and excuse Walter if he doesn't join us. Liquids make him upchuck in the plane."

"Now, sweet," Walter said. "Jeffrey doesn't have to take anything in the morning if he doesn't want to. Don't be upset, sweet. The Clipper's just as safe as a church."

"And why is a church safe?" Mrs. Newcombe asked. "Pour him out a drink. Sit down, big boy. He's not leaving for an hour."

"The boy just told me," Jeffrey said, "that Walter was leaving for China. I didn't know."

"Well, you know now," Mrs. Newcombe said. "The wonder boy, the news ace. Look at him, he's off to China."

But Walter looked like a salesman about to take a Pullman. He was sitting on the other bed in his shirt sleeves, rustling through the papers in his brief case.

"It's just a swing around," Walter said. "I thought you'd seen it in the papers, Jeff. It's getting a little hot out there. The Japs—but don't get me started on that. I won't be more than two weeks, all told. It's just a matter of dropping in and seeing the 'Lissimo and Mei."

"Who?" Jeffrey asked.

Walter looked up from his brief case, but Mrs. Newcombe spoke first.

"Smarty pants, isn't he?" Mrs. Newcombe said. "It's Chiang Kai-shek and his Madam to you, dearie, but they're just palsy-walsies to Walt. Everybody with a name's a palsy-walsy."

"Jung Kuh-juh," Walter said. "That's the way you pronounce it, sweet. As a matter of fact, I feel very close to the 'Lissimo. The last time I saw him, he received me very informally."

"Well, put it in your God-damn' book," Mrs. Newcombe said. "Don't talk about it now. What are you looking for now?"

Walter was searching through the suitcase.

"Those nylon stockings," Walter said. "I just wanted to be sure I had them in for Mei."

"My God," Mrs. Newcombe said, "since when did you start in giving her stockings?"

"It's just a thought, sweet," Walter said.

"Perhaps if Walter's just leaving," Jeffrey began, "I'd better–"

"No," Mrs. Newcombe said, "sit down. You hadn't better."

It was one of those times when two people needed someone else. Walter was whistling gently as he arranged the clothing in his suitcase. Mrs. Newcombe was lighting another cigarette. Jeffrey had not thought of her as being in love with Walter before, but now he could see she loved him. He was glad to stay, for they seemed suddenly like old friends. They reminded him of home, of the voices of his boyhood. He was thinking of Walter Newcombe in his shirt sleeves in the library at Bragg carrying books. It was preposterous to think of him on his way to China.

"Well, well," Walter said, "it agrees with you here, doesn't it? Jeff, you're looking fine."

It made him self-conscious, because everyone had been saying lately that he was looking fine.

"Yes," he said, "I'm feeling fine. It must be the climate. I don't know."

"It's odd here, isn't it?" Walter said. "I'm glad to have seen it, and of course I've been on the inside, but I wouldn't like to live here."

"Yes," Jeffrey said, "it's an odd little world, Hollywood."

"Don't be so hotsy-totsy, big boy," Mrs. Newcombe said. "Don't you know Walt's having a big thought? Give him a chance to get it out before he hops the Clipper."

"Now, sweet," Walter said. "I know Jeff knows it here. They've been very sweet to Mildred and me in the studios. They make me feel important."

"Well, get it out of your head," Mrs. Newcombe said. "None of you little news bastards are important."

Walter looked up from his brief case. He was obviously checking up his passport and his tickets and his various cards of identity.

"Now, sweet," he said, "I didn't say I was important."

"All right," Mrs. Newcombe said. "Just be damn' sure you're not like the other little news bastards, and don't start thinking you're important. You know what you do for your living."

"Tell me," Jeffrey said. "I've always wondered what world correspondents do."

"Dearie," Mrs. Newcombe said, "pull yourself up out of the suitcase and give Jeffrey another drink. I'll tell you what they do, when they're sleeping alone."

"Now, sweet," Walter said, "don't be so upset about it, sweet."

"When they're sleeping alone they hop on Clippers," Mrs. Newcombe said, "and they get impressions. Poops! It seems to them . . . They sense the atmosphere, the romance, the glamour, the sheer stark horror, the sweet simplicity . . . Poops! . . . By great good fortune, through no fault of their own, they are your first correspondent who has arrived on the scene to give you a word picture of the ruins of Cracow . . . Poops."

"Crackov," Walter said, "you pronounce it Crackov, sweet."

"You shut up," Mrs. Newcombe said. "And when they're not doing that, they're giving hosiery to Chink ladies and telling Archie Wavell how to win the war, and Winnie Churchill how to win the war, and saying it's later than you think. Oh, God almighty, it's later than you think. There is only one road to freedom. . . . Norway, Sweden, Czechoslovakia, Turkey, Greece, China, Afghanistan, and where those guys heat their houses with camel dung. Wake up, America! It's later than you think. And what does it all add up to?"

"Now sweet," Walter said, "don't you think . . . ?"

"You tell us," Jeffrey said. "What does it all add up to?"

"Yes," Mrs. Newcombe said. "Yes, I'll tell you. It adds up to some little poop from the Podunk High School getting on a Clipper when he ought to be jerking sodas, and saying 'The time is now.' "

Walter pushed his glasses more firmly on his nose, looked up at the ceiling and snapped his fingers.

"He's got another thought," Mrs. Newcombe said. "Let him get it off. Don't choke him."

"Now, sweet," Walter said, "don't go on about it. I know I'm not important, and Jeff knows I'm not important. I'm just going out to China on the Clipper to buy shoes for Edwina and you, sweet, but don't get me started on that."

But Jeffrey knew that by some piece of luck which was not his fault at all Walter Newcombe was there to sing the dirge of destiny.

"But don't get me started on that," Walter said again. "We've had a lovely two weeks, and we've contacted some lovely people. I just took sweet here to relax before I hopped the Clipper. I mean, without fanfare, just to relax. Well, there hasn't been much fanfare, has there, sweet?"

"Oh, God!" Mrs. Newcombe said. "Get me the bottle-opener, Walt."

"Yes," Walter said, "coming up, sweet. We've been looking for you, Jeffrey. I've been calling again and again at the Bronxville, but you're never in."

"Why should he be in, if it's like this dump?" Mrs. Newcombe said. "Does he want to get the heebie jeebies? That tree's a monkey puzzle tree."

"Now, sweet," Walter said, "what tree?"

"Any God-damn' tree out here," Mrs. Newcombe said, "is a monkey puzzle tree, because it would puzzle a monkey to climb up it. Poops."

Walter looked at Jeffrey.

"Mildred's a little upset," he said. "I'm sorry we didn't contact you sooner so we could have gone on a party together. Sinny Merriwell said you were here. I've been talking book with Sinny. Twenty thousand dollars cash advance. I shook it out of him."

"Oh," Jeffrey said. "What's the book going to be about?"

"*Free China Snapshot,*" Walter said, "and a brush-up on Nehru and Gandhi. I kept looking for you at the Bronxville. My God, you were never there."

Again it seemed necessary to explain in detail why he was so seldom at the Bronxville.

"You see," Jeffrey said, "I have a good many friends in Hollywood, and you know how hospitable people out here are. Then, I'm doing a little work for myself—the first I have done for a long while. I've been working on a play."

Walter Newcombe's head turned quickly. There was a high light on his nose.

"That's funny," he said, "I've been working on a play myself—not physically, just turning it over in my mind."

"Well, don't tell us," Mrs. Newcombe said, "just don't tell us. You news boys think you can write anything—plays, sonnets, novels, anything. And why do you think you can write them?—Merely because you can go on Clippers."

But Walter was not listening.

"I'll make a note of it," he said. "Maybe we could collaborate on it, Jeff. I've been trying to say it in lectures, but it would go better in a play. If they could see it right there it might wake them up."

"That's it," Mrs. Newcombe said. "You tell us, honey. All you news boys want to wake up America."

"Sweet," Walter said, "something's got to wake up America."

"There he goes," Mrs. Newcombe said. "It's later than you think."

Walter was smoothing the collar of his purple silk shirt. His forehead was puckered, and he was looking at the floor.

"Sweet," he said. "It really *is* later than you think, you or anybody. You'll find it out someday. You'd know now if you'd been there. It isn't funny."

All the slapstick had left the room. Walter's shirt and Walter's ventilated buckskin shoes were lost in the utter conviction of someone who had seen something that Jeffrey had not.

"They're fighting our fight, really," Walter said. "If they lose it, we'll be fighting alone, really, and they will lose if we don't wake up."

It may have been Walter's nasal, unpractised voice that gave those phrases their vitality, and Walter's sudden earnestness which seemed to have arisen from nowhere. Walter did not go on. There was nothing but the silence of that disordered bedroom and the twitterings of the lovebirds outside in the cloisters.

"Walter," Jeffrey said. Walter turned toward him slowly without speaking. "Do you remember a year ago? You said you thought we were out of it."

Walter raised his hand from his brief case and then put it back again gently.

"A year ago?" he said. "Well, that was a year ago."

"All right," Jeffrey said, "what do you think we ought to do?"

He waited anxiously for Walter to answer, though the answer depended entirely on how an individual might feel.

"We'll be in this," Walter said. "We'll be in this before next year. We're in it now and we don't know it."

Jeffrey moved slowly as though a weight were on his shoulders.

"Yes," he said, "I know," and then the spell was broken and the room was just the way it had been at first. Walter blinked his eyes and closed his brief case.

"I'm sorry," he said, and he pushed back his cuff to look at his wrist watch. "I'm sorry you got me started on that. I'm sorry, sweet."

"Oh, nuts," Mrs. Newcombe said. "Nuts."

"You know," Walter said, "it's later than I thought," and he laughed. "The car ought to be here any minute now. Don't go out to the field with me, sweet. Let me see." Walter snapped his fingers. "Where's my overcoat?"

"Where you dropped it," Mrs. Newcombe said, "over in the corner. Have you got your aspirin? You know what you are without aspirin."

"Oh, yes," Walter said, "aspirin." He snapped his fingers again. "Don't go out to the airport. You never like the sun, sweet. We'll say good-by here and you stay with Jeffrey. You don't mind, Jeff, do you? Mildred likes you."

"Yes," Mrs. Newcombe said. "I'm funny that way. Honey, have you got your colored glasses?"

Walter put on a Palm Beach coat which was belted at the back.

"Yes," he said. "Yes, sweet, here they are. Maybe Jeffrey wouldn't mind helping you get on the train."

"Of course not," Jeffrey said.

Walter folded his overcoat and put it on the bed. Then he stood and snapped his fingers again.

"The bill's all paid," he said. "Leave something for the maid, won't you, sweet."

Then Jeffrey remembered the Newcombes' suite in the Waldorf Tower and remembered thinking that within five minutes Walter could leave it without leaving a trace, and here that sort of impermanence was just the same. They would be leaving that room and no one would know they had ever been in it. Those words of Walter's were brittle, and yet they had a mocking helpless sort of insistence, and they joined all that other torrent of distracted words—America First . . . the age-old quarrels of Europe . . . pulling their chestnuts out . . . Thumbs up . . . V for Victory . . . There'll always be an England . . . I tell you again and again and again, and I repeat . . . hemisphere defense . . . frontier on the Rhine . . . the hose for your neighbor when his house is burning . . . way of life . . . social gains . . . democracy . . . we don't have to discomboomerate ourselves . . . on hand

and on order . . . later than you think . . . blood, sweat and tears . . . fighting our fight . . . later than you think.

"I'll cable you from Hong Kong," Walter said. "I don't know about Chungking, but you'll hear from me from Calcutta, sweet."

"WELL AND HAPPY," Mrs. Newcombe said. "LOVE TO EDWINA. Nuts."

Walter snapped his fingers again.

"Don't forget Edwina's teeth," he said. "The band needs tightening, sweet."

"Keep your mind on your stomach," Mrs. Newcombe said.

"Sweet," Walter said. "I'll tell you something. When I get back—I've got an idea. We'll buy a little farm in Connecticut, where we can be quiet, sweet."

"That's a swell idea," Mrs. Newcombe said, "lovely, lovely, lovely."

There was a knock on the door. It was the same bellboy who had led Jeffrey through the cloisters.

"The car's here, Mr. Newcombe," the boy said.

"Yes," Walter answered, "coming right up. Just those three pieces on the bed. Thank you, sonny."

To Jeffrey the word "sonny" had a jarring note.

"You bet," the boy said.

When the suitcase and the brief case and the typewriter were gone, there seemed to be nothing left. Walter tossed his overcoat over his left arm and took his felt hat off the bureau.

"Well, Jeff," he said. "Good-by now." That was what you said in Bragg. "Good-by now, keep an eye on Mildred, will you?" and he lowered his voice. "She's a little bit upset. Well, I haven't got much time."

He looked at his watch as he said it, and then Walter put his arm around Mrs. Newcombe and slapped her twice on the back. Jeffrey felt he should not have been there, but there he was. Some sort of restraint, some sort of awkwardness and a clumsy effort at casualness gave the parting a peculiar pathos. It was like the partings at the hostess house at Camp Dix more than twenty years before. Something made Jeffrey's eyes smart, but he could not look away from them.

"No need of going to the airport, sweet," Walter said again. "Have a drink with Jeffrey. So long, sweet."

Mrs. Newcombe did not answer. To Jeffrey it had the awkward unfinished quality of an amateur theatrical. Walter would not know how to walk off, because amateurs never did. Walter stepped backwards and when he reached the door, he must have felt that something more was demanded because he raised his hand exactly like one of a group of shipwrecked sailors posing for a picture for the Associated Press.

"Well," Walter said, "toodle-oo." Mrs. Newcombe did not answer. He was gone, leaving a silence that shut out the sounds outside. Jeffrey knew that he should think of something suitable to say, but he could think of absolutely nothing. He could only think of the Pacific and the islands and a vast stretch of nothing where Walter would be. Mrs. Newcombe was standing looking at the door. All the lines in her face had deepened. She looked old and tired, and yet, strangely enough, he could see traces of childhood and girlhood on her face which he had never seen before.

"You know," Mrs. Newcombe said, and she stopped, still staring at the door. "You know, he's a brave little guy."

"Yes," Jeffrey said, and he stopped too. "Yes, he's brave."

And then Mrs. Newcombe began to cry.

39

By the Numbers

All that time in Hollywood had a quality which was more like wish-fulfillment than an actual succession of events. Jeffrey was living it, and he was very much alive, and yet so separated from past experience that he could not make it fit in anywhere. Marianna asked him why he should and there was no reason why he should. Still, he liked to tell her what it was like; he liked to tell her everything, because she always listened. Marianna was not like Madge, who had so many things to do that she could very seldom put her mind on what he said. Marianna had been working at the studio, but she was resting now. When she was not being massaged, or taking exercise, she always had time to listen.

He told her once that it was like being on an island somewhere, and that the boat had left him there and sailed away, and there would be no other boat for quite a while. He had no sense of time on that imaginary island with Marianna, and it was only on rare occasions, such as when he saw Walter Newcombe, that Jeffrey was aware of any urgency. He seemed to have left everything he knew behind him for a while and it surprised him sometimes that he had no conscious sense of guilt about it. He did not even have that feeling of wondering how he had got there—he was simply there.

"Darling," Marianna asked him, "are you happy?"

He wondered why it was that all the women he had ever known well asked him whether he was happy.

"Yes," he said, "I've never been so happy."

He only wished that happiness were more definite. He was sitting in Marianna's living room, which opened right out on the beach. It was like a curtain rising on the set of a play he had worked on once, a play somewhat like a Maugham piece or Noel Coward's "Point Valaine." He could almost see himself and Marianna being written into stage directions. He was seated to the left by a card table before a portable typewriter. He was dressed in slacks and beach shoes and one of those striped Norman sailor shirts that looked a little like the top of a bathing suit in the Nineties, but not entirely. On the Chinese-red carpet beside him were sheets of the last act of his play script. To the right, by the long windows that opened on the beach, Marianna was reclining on a Chinese wicker chaise longue. All the folds of her long blue silk beach coat looked prearranged, just as though the curtain were going up, and her gold hair, with those natural little waves in it, was all brushed and fluffy, just as Jessica, her maid, had left it, catching the light to its best advantage, and in back of her was the white sand of the beach and the horizon of the Pacific. The ocean was very still and blue, exactly like a backdrop. Outside on the terrace was the little round table where they had breakfasted in the sun with the chairs pushed back and the napkins and cups and glasses exactly as they had left them. The room itself had the precise quality of a stage set. The table with the magazines and the latest books, still in their dust wrappers, the chairs near the fireplace and the glass-top dining table in its little alcove near the pantry, all seemed to have been put there for effect. He could think of them as showing very clearly, as the curtain rose, that the room was Marianna's, not his own; and all that setting showed at once, if anyone should see it, that he and Marianna were not married, that their gay relationship was something else, and you could tell exactly what—not that it bothered him. It did not bother him at all. It must have been that he was so busy writing that play of his that he saw everything lately in terms of the theater.

"Darling," Marianna said, "kiss me."

He pushed back his chair and walked toward her. He felt her arms around him. He felt the pressure of her lips and he wished that it were all more credible.

"Don't look around, darling," she said, and she laughed. "Jessica's in the kitchen and Jessica doesn't count, and Wong's out doing the marketing."

He was not sure whether Jessica counted or not, but Marianna always said she did not, and Wong was the Chinese cook who always went home at night after he had done the dinner dishes.

"Now, try it again," Marianna said, "and throw yourself into it, like this."

"Was that better?" Jeffrey asked, and he began to laugh.

"Yes," she said, "much better. Darling, you look so young."

He did not feel old, but again he wished that everyone had not kept saying lately that he looked so young.

"I'll tell you something, dear," he said, and he felt conscious of himself again, a little like Walter Newcombe. "This is the first time I've ever done everything I've wanted to do, with no compulsion, nothing. It's what makes it seem a little—" He stopped, still bending over her.

"A little what?" she asked him.

"I don't know," he said, "not exactly—real."

She raised her hand and touched his head and her sleeve fell back from her arm. He had always thought that no one had arms and hands like hers.

"Dear," she said, "it's real."

He stared into her face without exactly seeing it, but he could have seen it with his eyes shut: the greenish-gray eyes, the high cheekbones, the sweep of the hair as it was brushed back from the temples, the tilt of the chin that was not too pointed but pronounced, and the curve of her lips that almost broke into a smile, but not quite. That picture of her would be with him until he died.

"I know," he said, "it's one of the realest things I've ever known. I didn't mean that exactly. I'll tell you what I mean."

It was amazing how free he felt to tell her everything he thought.

"I mean, it's a question of time," he said.

"Time?" she repeated.

"Yes," he said, "I know it sounds a little corny, dear," and he wished there were something else to call her besides "sweet" or "dear" or "darling." There was nothing more sadly limited, more infantile, than the vocabulary of love, and judging from the letters read in court everyone else had found it so. "It's just as though I'd taken a whole piece of time out from back somewhere, as though I were doing over what I should have done a long time ago. It's time out. That's what I mean."

"Time?" Marianna said softly. "Borrowed time?"

"No, no," he answered. "It isn't that I'm going to die—it isn't that. It's just time." Her eyes had a faraway look which told him that she was thinking of what he said, but that she did not exactly understand him, which was not surprising since he did not wholly understand himself.

"What I'm getting at," he said, "is, it's a little like being given a second chance, when you think that every chance for a second chance is over. But it isn't exactly that, either. It's more like being allowed to do something that you should have done quite a while ago. It's more like having a piece of time on your hands that you can't relate to any other time. I don't believe you've ever felt it."

"Don't say I'm too young," she said. "Women are much older than men. They always are."

"I wasn't saying that," he answered. "You've lived more consistently. You haven't so many ties—that may be one way to put it. I'm not like anything I ever was before. I don't mean that it isn't swell. I only mean it doesn't seem exactly real."

She was silent for a moment. He wondered whether he was seeking some sort of human justification for unfaithfulness to the marriage vow. He supposed that everyone in his position sought for some alleviation.

"Don't say that," she said. "It's real to me. Jeff, you're not saying you're sorry, are you?"

Jeffrey laughed. "Don't be silly, dear," he said. "It's the nicest thing I've ever known." He walked back to the table and looked at the typewriter and picked up a sheet of paper and put it down.

"You're good for me, you know," he said. "I'd never be finishing this, I'd never have touched it, if it weren't for you."

"Darling," she said, "is it going better now?"

"Yes," he said.

In the last few days the play had been going much better and he felt more familiar with the medium than he had ever been before. He felt very much like a commercial artist trying to paint a non-commercial picture. All sorts of tricks kept creeping in, artificialities of motivation, easy ways of drawing character derived from other media he knew, though he tried not to use the smart, shallow ruses with which he was most familiar. But lately, his work had been improving, particularly toward the end of the last act.

"Is the girl better?" Marianna asked.

"Yes," he said. "At least I think so. The third act's beginning to fit now—at least I think it is."

It was like a stage set again. There he was in his slacks and his Normandy shirt, a temperamental playwright racking his brains, lighting a straight-stemmed pipe. No doubt he was looking quizzical and interesting as he lighted his pipe. Marianna, with her head upon the pillows of the wicker chaise longue, looked exactly as she should have looked, affectionate and anxious and amused.

"Darling," Marianna said.

"What?" he answered.

"What's it about?"

"It's about a boy and a girl in a brownstone house in New York," he said.

"When are you going to read it to me?" she asked.

Marianna and the room were all in perfect focus. He was familiar with every intonation of her voice, and yet it was not as definite, for instance, as Madge's voice. He had to give it more attention and to consider more carefully what she said. She was there, and he was there, but she was not as actual as Madge who was not there. It had something to do with time.

"I've told you, dear," he said: "when I've finished with it. When it's all here."

"Won't you read some now?" she asked. "Darling, it might help you. You're not working now."

"No," he said, "not now."

"Why not?" she asked.

And then the artificiality was gone and he was surprised that he told her the truth.

"Dear, because I'm afraid," he said. "I don't like to be a coward, but I'm afraid."

"Why darling," she said, "what are you afraid of?"

The best thing about it all was that she was like his conscience in a way. He could tell her anything, and she always listened.

"You see," he said, "it's all I've got. It's all the justification—all that I can give you. If it isn't good—and I'll know and you'll know when I read it—there won't be any reason for you or me, or any of this at all. It will mean I haven't anything to offer you. It will all be over, dear. That's what I mean by time."

He had not put it clearly, but he knew she understood him. He had made himself entirely defenseless, but he did not mind.

"Darling," she answered, "you don't have to give me anything."

"Oh, yes I do," he said, "if I haven't anything to give—"

"Darling," she said, "I wish you'd read it now."

"No," he said, "not now."

"Darling," she said, "what did you mean, having a piece of time, and doing something which you should have done a while before?"

"I don't know exactly," he said, "that's the trouble, dear. You can see yourself in the mirror but your face is flat. You can hear your voice in your ears, but it's not the way it sounds to anybody else. I can see you and hear you. You can see me and hear me, but we can't see ourselves."

"That's why I love you," she said, "because you say things like that. Are you going to work any more?"

"No," he said, "not now," and he began pacing from the fireplace to the table and back again.

"What are you thinking about?" she asked.

"I was thinking about my brother Alf," he said. "He called on me, and I ought to look him up. He's at San Bernardino."

"What's he doing there?" Marianna asked.

He was glad to be talking about Alf and not about himself.

"Alf?" he said. "Why, Alf's married someone with an orange grove out at San Bernardino. You ought to see Alf."

"I'd like to," she said. "Let's go out and see him."

"You may not like him," he answered, "but I'd like to take you there."

"What are you laughing at?" she asked.

"It's funny," he told her, "thinking of you and Alf."

They rode to San Bernardino with the top down in the runabout he had rented. He wanted to drive his car and not her Packard. Marianna had a blue silk handkerchief knotted beneath her chin to keep her hair from blowing. She sat close to him, leaning lightly against his shoulder just as Madge did sometimes, and that proximity, nothing else, made him think of the ride he had taken with Madge down the Post Road, and then over the Merritt Parkway and out into Connecticut, less than a year before.

The houses by the Post Road had been old and tired, the sad remnants of another day, but here, until they reached the flat valley where San Bernardino lay, everything was new. They had passed through miles of small houses all set close together, built for the employees of one of the aircraft companies working on lend-lease aircraft, and on those thousands of planes which the President had ordered. He could see and hear the planes circling overhead. They were drab and camouflaged, but the sound of the motors was familiar and he wished he could try one out—but they would be too hot for him, those planes. He would have lost that co-ordination of hand and eye. You had to be young, very young, to handle them. The air was so clear that he could see the cloud-covered peaks to the east; those "stuffed clouds," as pilots called them. He could see the blue fields of lupine on the foothills, but already in early May the grass was growing brown, as it always did out there in summer. That atmosphere of drought on the Pacific Coast had always disturbed him. It was not his country and it never would be, no matter how long he remained there.

Its people had come from everywhere—from the Middle West, from New England, from upstate New York, from everywhere. They had come there with their savings to die in the sun, or else they had come to live again and to grow oranges. Most of the valley floor was very green from the square miles of orange groves. Everyone was growing oranges or lemons or grapefruit or tangerines or those new monstrosities called "tangelos," the juice of which was being dispensed from little booths all along the road, five cents a drink or all you could drink for ten cents. The air was redolent of orange blossoms, but Jeffrey had nothing whatsoever to do with it. It was not his country.

"Darling," Marianna said, "tell me some more about Alf. Tell me some more about Lime Street."

He had told her a great deal about Lime Street already, and she was not like Madge who only pretended to like to hear.

"Alf's always stayed just the way he always was," Jeffrey said. "When you've grown up with someone—did you ever think you can't change that proportion? It's always constant. He always calls me 'kid.' He'll show off when he sees you. It's like a Sennett Comedy a little—custard pies, a hearty laugh when there isn't anything to laugh about. It makes it a little sad. And then there's another thing about Alf."

"What?" she asked.

"Money," he said. "Alf never could learn about money. 'I'll just telegraph my baby, she'll send ten or twenty, maybe, and I won't have to walk back home.' "

Marianna was too young, and he himself was almost too young to have heard that song, but she was able to catch the mood of it. It went with the sound of the motor and with the sound of the tires on the road.

"Darling," Marianna said, "I'm your baby."

"Perhaps," he answered, "but I've never telegraphed to any baby, dear."

"Jeffrey," she said, "you love him, don't you?"

"I wouldn't say so, exactly," he answered. "He's really a big bastard, dear."

"Darling," she asked, "who's his baby, now?"

Marianna had never seemed so near to him. He dropped one hand from the wheel and raised her hand and kissed it. Somehow she belonged to him more than she ever had.

"I haven't seen this new baby," he said, and he was laughing. "I've had to cope with the other ones, but not this baby. This one—she's a widow. Alf met her playing numbers. Do you remember that song? How did it go? 'Give me a kiss by the numbers, one, two, three.' "

"That was in the last war, wasn't it?" she asked.

"Yes," he said, "the last war."

"I was ten in the last war," she said, "that was when we lived in Portland."

"Did you wear pigtails?" he asked.

"Yes," she said, "two pigtails."

Then he was telling her about Alf. This new wife, this time, Alf had told him, was the jack pot. You couldn't be wrong always. They had met right at one of those tables in the center of a drugstore at Las Vegas where you could play the number game or buy a thermos jug for the desert, or get a Coca-Cola. It was just the time of the Helldorado at Las Vegas, when they had the beard-growing contest and Gila Monsters in cages on street corners. It was all wide open at Las Vegas, not that everything wasn't always wide open there. Alf said that you ought to be there in Helldorado Week. The only thing that he had seen that gave him more of a laugh was the Poets' Round-up at Sante Fe. The poets' round-up, Alf said, was a sort of rodeo. The master of ceremonies was dressed like a cowboy and he would call out a poet's name and they would open the trap of the pen and out would come a poet and read a poem. They had poets, too, in Las Vegas—poets and pansies, everything, in Las Vegas, and they had the beard-growing contest during Helldorado Week. Alf had been growing one for the occasion and he was going to lead a burro in the parade and be dressed like a desert rat.

He was growing a beard right there in the drugstore when he met Agnes next to him at the number game, and he'd hit the jack pot this time. She wasn't so much to look at. She was a little on the fat side. She was a numerologist—that is, as Alf said, she could do anything with numbers, and when she asked him the date and year of his birth, she got out a piece of paper and worked out those numbers with the date and year of her own birth, and there you had it. She wasn't so much to look at, but she could do anything with numbers. She was lonely and you know why Alf was living in Nevada, and he was lonesome, too. He wanted to pick up the pieces and start all over again; and she was a real widow, not grass, and her husband had left her an orange grove at San Bedoo—that was what you called San Bernardino out there, in case you didn't know it—and the numbers showed that they had the same vibrations, right there in the drugstore at Las Vegas. And as Alf said, what did you know about that? There wasn't much else to know about it. They were married that night at Las Vegas, because it was down in the numbers. She wasn't much to look at, but he was tired of looks. Her name was Agnes, just plain Agnes, five letters and when you added them to Alf, it made eight, and Alf was settling down. It was a little cuckoo sometimes, having Agnes fry the eggs and do the coffee all by numbers, but she could do it if she liked. No one had understood Alf for a long while. He was getting fat himself and he was settling down.

Jeffrey could ad lib like that with Marianna. Nothing mattered that afternoon. He was thinking it was the way his life always should have been. They were passing through San Bernardino by then and Alf had told Jeffrey how to get to their place. You went to the end of the Main Street and to the left, then past a Giant Orange Drink Stand and then past Hawkins' Lemon Grove, and then past a roadside stand run by a man called a "rockologist," who sold mineral specimens he had brought from the hills—ROCKOLOGIST was written with rocks in front of the stand—and then the next gate on the left was Alf's. The name was "Rednow"—Wonder spelled backwards.

"Show me something that it hasn't got," Jeffrey said.

"What?" Marianna asked him.

"Nothing," Jeffrey answered, "nothing, dear."

40

Wonder Spelled Backwards

They were approaching the Giant Orange Drink Stand before Marianna spoke again. It was one of those huge plaster and composition spheres, painted like an orange, with a hole cut in it, from which projected a counter that was heaped with oranges and glasses, and bearing that familiar sign: "All you can drink—ten cents." The thought of stopping there and testing one's capacity with successive glasses of orange juice brought up an unpleasing gastronomic picture.

"Jeff," Marianna said, and her voice broke abruptly into his mood. There was a hesitation in it, and a studied carelessness that was reminiscent of Madge's voice. "You're not worried, are you?"

"Worried?" he answered. "About what, sweet?"

He supposed she meant that he was worried about explaining her to Alf, and that was nothing to bother about, but her voice went on, still carefully and hesitantly.

"About you and me and Madge."

Jeffrey felt his hands grip the steering wheel tighter. This was an impasse which he had tried to keep out of his mind and it had not been there much, but now it drained the joy out of him like liquid from a bottle. It was not the time or the place to bring it up, and he wondered whether all women were alike and whether they all chose instinctively to embark on difficult subjects at just the wrong time. It reminded him of the way Madge would bring up some problem in a taxicab just before they reached a friend's house for dinner. It was not the time and place. He did not want to think of it as a problem, and certainly not now.

"Why?" he said. "What makes you think I am?"

"I thought you were," Marianna said. "You must be. Darling, I keep wondering. Have you ever done anything like this before?"

His hands still gripped the steering wheel. He could not imagine why she had brought it up now, when he had to watch the side of the road for the shop of the rockologist. They were passing other roadside stands—"Orange Water Ice For Sale" . . . "Persian Kitties For Sale" . . . "Canary Birds For Sale" . . . just tell him something that wasn't here.

"No," he said, and it was true, but she must have known that he would say no. "Do you mean I've been too casual? I'm awfully sorry, dear. I'm—well, maybe I'm not the type. But you knew that, didn't you? You've known me long enough."

"No," she answered quickly, "of course—of course it isn't that—but you must be worried, dear, and I wish you'd tell me about it. You're—so enigmatic sometimes, and so reticent about some things."

Jeffrey stared straight ahead at the road. There were orange groves everywhere—just oranges with the mountains to the east. It sounded exactly like Madge when Madge said that he never told her anything.

"I wish you'd tell me, dear," Marianna said again, "please. I have a right to know, haven't I? How do you feel about Madge and you and me?"

"I wish you wouldn't bring it up now," Jeffrey said, "right in the middle of everything. We'll be at Alf's in just a minute."

"Then stop the car," Marianna said, "please, dear."

"Oh, God," Jeffrey said, and he stopped the car. "I don't see what we have to get into this now for."

"Darling," Marianna said, "I just want to know."

"Well, there'd be plenty of other times to know," Jeffrey said.

It was much warmer, now that he had stopped the car right beside an orange grove. He could feel the sun beating down on him and he could smell the orange blossoms. He could see the black smudge-pots under the trees, left there the previous winter in case of cold. It was not the time and the place to tell her, but he had to tell her. He had to sort it all out in his mind and separate it from the smell of the orange blossoms. A bee struck the windshield, and that was not peculiar. After all, you could not have oranges without bees.

"Oh, God," Jeffrey said, "all right, Marianna. Just wait a minute and don't say 'please.'"

"Don't be so rude," Marianna said.

"I didn't mean to be rude," Jeffrey said. "Just wait a minute and let me think. I guess this had been growing on me for quite a while. You see, Madge—well, Madge. Oh, hell."

He stopped and stared straight ahead at the road, but there was nothing on the road, just the sun and the orange trees. She was waiting for him to go on and he did not want to think about it. His hands relaxed on the steering wheel.

"I don't mean I'm not understood," he said, "but I suppose I do mean it. Everyone says that."

"You mean she doesn't give you what you want?" Marianna said.

"Dear," Jeffrey said, "are you telling me, or am I telling you?"

"Darling," Marianna said. "You're telling me. At least, I hope you are."

"Then let me tell it," Jeffrey said. "All those things are always a part of it, but it isn't the real reason. I suppose it's been building up, building up, for quite a while. Madge just sees things one way."

He stopped again and suddenly he wondered how he had ever got there, on the side of the road, telling things about Madge that he had never told to anyone.

"It's more that I haven't anything to give Madge," he said. "I suppose when two people get married each thinks he can change the other; it must have something to do with sex." It was hot and Jeffrey pulled out his handkerchief and mopped his forehead. "You see, Madge was brought up in a certain way. She thinks in terms of concrete possessions. She's wanted security—she's wanted children. Well, I've tried to give them to her. I've made quite a lot of money. She doesn't know about money. She only thinks that all nice people have it. She wants me to be like people she used to know. I've tried to be. Maybe I shouldn't have tried so hard. Well, I suppose this has been building up for quite a while. You just wake up suddenly—something hits you. There's been the war—I can't explain it, Marianna. There's just nothing I can give her."

He wished she would say something. He was aware that he had been talking for a long while and not saying much. He was simply saying what anyone would say who had strayed off the reservation.

"Oh, well," he said, "it's about Jim too, I suppose. The other kids have always looked on me as an abstraction, but there was always Jim. When Madge called up that night—I suppose something just hits someone suddenly, sometimes. It just seemed to me I was superfluous. It seemed to me I had a right to something else—and you were there."

It occurred to him that this was not entirely complimentary.

"I don't mean it would have been just anybody," he said, "I mean you're all the things I should have had if everything had been a little different, if I had known more about myself—but nothing you do is ever right, is it? I suppose it's a matter of self-expression, a matter of feeling I'm not dead yet. I'd just like to try something else. I'm not dead yet—" His voice trailed off, and he looked ahead at the road.

He felt her hand close over his, and he turned to look at her. He could see her blue scarf knotted under her chin. The color matched her soft, blue sweater. She was not looking at him, but ahead at the road.

"Darling," she said, "you're awfully sweet."

"No," he answered, "I feel like Alice in Wonderland. I wish you hadn't brought it up."

"Dear," she said, "you've found me, haven't you? It's going to be all right. Everything's going to be all right."

"Is it?" Jeffrey asked her. "Maybe—if the play's any good."

"Yes," she said, "of course it is."

Jeffrey knew very little about California, aside from a few hotels and the studios. The rest of it he had seen from the highway, or from his seat in the car when he had stopped at filling stations. Although he had been in California often, he had never turned off the road into any place like Rednow.

The bungalow looked frayed and seedy, somewhat like a disreputable unrepentant old man sitting on a curbstone whittling in the sun. It was of plain board construction, painted green and white once, that universal color of bungalows, but now the paint was peeling off so that it looked more gray than green and white. It had been built on posts quite high off the ground, and the posts at one end had begun to settle, so that the roof was sway-backed, and the stovepipe, which protruded from the ridgepole as a chimney, was canted at an acute angle. There was nothing in the way of shrubbery, only a stretch of sand and crab grass in front of it, decorated by a rusty bathtub and some assorted lengths of pipe. The only new thing there was a robin's-egg-blue coupé that stood in an airy shelter beneath a tree. The steps leading upward to the porch were sagging and the tread of the lower step was gone.

Alf was seated on the porch, and it was plain that he was not expecting visitors because his costume was so like the house that it resembled a sort of protective coloration. It came as a shock to Jeffrey, because Alf had been well-turned-out when he had called at the Bronxville the first week Jeffrey had arrived, but now Alf looked seedy and old. He was seated in an armchair, tilted back against the house, with his feet encased in frayed white sneakers. His dungarees were so tight about the waist that his stomach protruded and sagged over the piece of knotted clothesline which supported them. The rest of his costume was a simple sleeveless undershirt, yellowed by the dust, and a pair of nickel-rimmed glasses. Jeffrey had never thought of Alf's needing glasses, particularly to read the last Sunday's comic sheet that he was holding.

It was unfair to have come unannounced like that on Alf. It was almost like that scene in the Bible where the boys had encountered their father sleeping naked in the sun, for Alf and the plumbing on the lawn gave that same sense of indecent exposure. Alf peered through his glasses. They must have been reading glasses and not bifocals, because when he took them off, he saw Jeffrey right away.

"Whoops," Alf called. "Hello, kid. Who's your lady friend?" Jeffrey had stopped the car. Alf got out of his chair and walked carefully down the steps, seemingly testing the treads before trusting them with his full weight.

"Well, well," Alf said, "so it's the kid. 'Who are you with tonight?' Do you remember that one, kid?"

"What one?" Jeffrey asked, and he glanced sideways at Marianna. He could see as Marianna glanced at the house and Alf that she was obviously trying to throw herself into a part without knowing just where to throw herself. In spite of all he had tried to tell her, Alf must have been a shock to her.

"What one?" Alf said, and he patted his white hair. The gesture reminded Jeffrey that someone had once mistaken Alf for Paul V. McNutt, and since then Alf had always worn his hair that way. Alf was pulling himself together, slowly, but steadily.

" 'Who are you with tonight?' " Alf said. "This one—hold everything kid: 'Who is that peachy, dreamy, creamy vision of sweet delight? Is she your little sister, mister? Answer me, honor bright. Will you tell your wife in the morning, who you were with tonight?' That one, kid, get it?"

In spite of all the years, a certain reluctant admiration and awe returned when Jeffrey heard Alf.

"Alf's quite a card," he said to Marianna. "Quite a card. This is Miss Miller, Alf, Miss Marianna Miller."

"Oh-oh," Alf said. "Oh-oh, excuse me for living, Miss Miller."

"That's all right," Marianna said, and then she began to laugh.

"Oh-oh," Alf said. "Where have you been all my life, bright-eyes?"

"Alf," Jeffrey said, "just relax."

"Don't be so tense yourself, kid," Alf said, and he winked at Marianna.

"The kid's always been tense, but he's a pretty good kid. Welcome to the old plantation lovely lady, honey bee. And bless yore pretty soul, missy, never yo' all mind the pickaninnies and the houn' dogs, the little rascals. Just yo' light down and rest yo' pretty se'f on the veranda, missy, effen you-all doan' want to rest yo'self in yonder bathtub. An ol' Mose, mah body servant, will come a totin' out the juleps in jes' a jiffy, missy. Light down and bless yo' pretty se'f for coming to the ole plantation and laying eyes on the pore ole Colonel, so tired from the wo'."

Jeffrey could not help laughing, although he had heard it all before.

"Whah, honey," Marianna said, "Ah don't mind if Ah do."

Until she answered, Jeffrey had been afraid that she might think Alf was drunk, and Alf was not drunk.

"Atta baby," Alf said, and he patted Marianna's shoulder as he helped her from the car. "Don't mind me. Oh-oh. I know you're big-time, baby. Jes' you lean on the ole Colonel and never fret yore pretty head about the houn' dogs and pickaninnies, baby."

Then the screen door of the bungalow slammed and Alf glanced sideways quickly. A stout woman in a chintz Mother Hubbard was standing on the porch. Her gray hair was cut in a page bob with a straight bang over her forehead and Jeffrey thought that her eyes looked like the coal eyes in a snow man. She was wearing a heavy Navajo silver necklace and she was blinking in the sunlight. To Jeffrey she looked half like Ma in *The Grapes of Wrath*, and half like someone from a religious cult, and he was thinking again, just show him anything that California hadn't got–anything. It was his new sister-in-law, Agnes; he imagined that she must have struck him in much the same way that Alf had struck Marianna. He had tried incapably to picture her, and there she was.

"Wha', God bless me," Alf called, "if yonder ain't Missus Betsy herse'f, jes' up from seeing those no-'count niggers killin' hogs and hominy in the kitchen. Betsy, honey! Light down these steps. Throw a kiss to your brother Jeff. It's Agnes, Jeff, you ole rascal. Don't yo' know yo' sister when you see her?"

"Alf," Jeffrey said, "stop. It isn't funny," but he was laughing. The whole little group seemed to be seized with an unaccountable sort of hysteria. Jeffrey saw that his sister-in-law was doubled up with laughter.

"Oh, dear," Marianna said, "it's like Saroyan."

He could not blame Marianna for thinking so because Alf always struck strangers that way until the novelty wore off. Then, when they saw behind that façade, it was not like Saroyan, because you could not die laughing at Alf continually.

"Alf," Agnes was saying. "Stop it. No matter what, you always get a laugh out of Alf. Come and settle down on the porch and I'll get some Orange Crush."

"Oh, never mind," Jeffrey said. "Don't bother, we just dropped in."

And then they were up on the porch and Agnes took his hands in both of hers, and stared meaningly into his eyes.

"Alf's brother," she said, "Alf's baby brother."

Jeffrey found himself shifting from one foot to another.

"Jeffrey," she said, "J-e-f-f-r-e-y. Seven. I've tried before, but it doesn't spell anything backwards."

"Well," Jeffrey said, and he shifted his weight to his other foot, "maybe it's just as well."

She was still holding his hands in both of hers. He had never learned what to do on such occasions.

"Think of you coming here today," she said, "this particular day."

"Well," Jeffrey said, and he shifted his weight to his other foot. "It's awfully nice to be here."

He looked sideways at Alf who was retying the rope that held up his dungarees.

"Today, of all days," she said. "It's strange. Strange. You didn't think what day this was, did you?"

Jeffrey found himself looking through the screen door into a bare room furnished with a sagging couch and a sagging Morris chair and a kerosene heater, a floor strewn with newspapers and a table covered with unwashed dishes. His mind struggled aimlessly with her question.

"Why, no," he said, "no, I didn't think—I just thought I'd like to look in on Alf."

She shook her head slowly, smiling at him from a height of superior knowledge.

"It was more than that," she said. "Oh, much, much more than that."

"Was it?" Jeffrey asked. He made a feeble effort to draw his hand away, but she held it fast.

"It's the day," she said, "the date, the seventh of May. The seventh day. J-e-f-f-r-e-y. Seven. Seven is dangerous, but it's my favorite number."

"I know," Jeffrey said, "lucky seven."

"Not luck," she said, and she shook her head again. "Numbers never lie. Alf, did you hear? It's the seventh."

"Yes, honey," Alf said. "Wait, I'll get some chairs." Then she dropped his hand and turned to Marianna.

"This is a very wonderful day," she said. "This is very thrilling, to see Miss Miller here. What is your year and birthday, dear?"

"What?" Marianna asked, and Jeffrey felt that he had to say something.

"She's a numerologist, Marianna," Jeffrey said.

"Yes, dear," Agnes answered, "and numbers have a great deal to do with God."

Jeffrey grew increasingly restless, now that God had entered the conversation. He kept wondering what Alf could ever have seen in her, and how it could have happened.

"Oh," Marianna said quickly. "I see. I'm sorry. Why June 2d, 1908."

"Dearie," Alf's wife said. "Let's go into the house while I work it out. God is in the numbers."

For a few moments, Jeffrey found himself on the porch alone staring at the bathtub and at the car that had brought him there. He heard himself sigh, and he suddenly felt moist and limp, but there was no time to get any of it straight. Alf was returning to the porch carrying two golden-oak chairs with imitation-leather seats surrounded by brass tacks.

" 'Don't look at me that way, sonny–' " Alf was reciting the piece he had recited once long ago in Bragg–" 'I'm not one of those small-town hicks . . .' "

"I'm all right," Jeffrey said. "This is quite a place, Alf."

Alf looked at him from the corners of his eyes and kept on reciting.

" 'But I love a little girlie who lives 'way out in the sticks.' " His voice trailed off, and he looked sideways again at Jeffrey. "See that bathtub and that hopper out there, kid? I'm going to build a bathroom when I get the money for the pipes."

Jeffrey had known that it was coming. It was a repetition that seemed to grow more garish with time.

"How much do you need for pipes?" he asked.

Alf glanced at the plumbing and waited carefully before answering.

" 'Her dress, it is pure gingham,' " Alf recited, " 'but her heart is tried and true . . .' "

Jeffrey pulled his chair around so that he could face Alf more directly. He could hear one of those Diesel trucks roll by on the invisible highway behind the orange trees. There was a gray color in Alf's face. His jowls looked heavy. There was nothing bright and handsome to him any more, except that quick sideways look.

"How much are the pipes going to cost, Alf?" Jeffrey asked again.

The corners of Alf's lips twisted upward and then relaxed.

"How would it be," Alf asked slowly, "if they cost five hundred dollars, kid? Pipes with a silver lining. You know, kid."

Jeffrey did not answer at once and he saw Alf watching him rather anxiously.

"Just pipes," Alf said again. "Five hundred kissers. Five yards. It's like tipping me a quarter. Don't get mad, kid."

"I gave you five hundred," Jeffrey said, "for your last installment on this place."

Alf was looking at the sky.

" 'She's a stylish stout and she won't walk out–' "

"Stop being a panic," Jeffrey said. "I gave you five hundred to pay on the place, and I gave you five hundred in March."

"Kid," Alf said, "I wasn't asking. I was just suggesting. Don't get sore. Turn on the big smile, kid."

"What did you do with it?" Jeffrey asked. "You wanted orange crates and wages. Didn't you sell the oranges?"

"Didn't we sell the oranges?" Alf said. "Stick around a while, kid."

Jeffrey wished that Agnes and Marianna would come back, but he knew they would not. Agnes' knowledge of numbers must have included dollars and cents.

"I won't be bothering you forever," Alf said, and he turned and looked Jeffrey straight in the face.

"All right," Jeffrey said. "What are you going to blow it in on this time?"

Alf still looked at Jeffrey and the corners of his lips turned up again and relaxed again, and his eyes narrowed, as though he were laughing at some private joke.

"Look at me, kid," he said. "Did it ever occur to you as the hearse goes by–"

Jeffrey drew his feet under him. The sand beneath his soles grated on the boards of the porch.

"What in hell are you talking about?" he asked.

"Look at me, kid," Alf said. "The doctor checked me up in March. It's the old ticker. It won't be long now, kid."

Jeffrey did not answer, because the fact was as tangible as though he held it in his hand.

"Why didn't you tell me, Alf?" he asked. "What's the matter with your heart?"

The smile left Alf's face. Then he blinked and smiled again.

"Dun't esk," Alf said. "Dun't esk. God-damn' near everything. Thrombosis, kid."

Then there was nothing that Jeffrey could think of to answer. His brother Alf was going to die and that truth seemed to stand between them, intimate and terrible.

"Hell," Alf said, "don't take it that way, kid. Don't say anything. God damn it, shut your mouth."

He was grateful for Alf's words. They freed him from a sort of compulsion and left him only with the discovery that he was at the end of something which he had thought would last forever. Alf was going to end there in the orange grove under the arch of Rednow. Jeffrey cleared his throat.

"You never can tell about things like that, Alf," he said. "Listen, if you'll come to New York–"

"Atta boy!" Alf said. "Atta kid. But I'd like those five yards, baby. I haven't got much time."

Something inside Jeffrey turned cold.

"Yes," he said, "all right, Alf, and there's more if you want it." He saw Alf's face relax and Alf began to smile.

"'She won't walk out–'" Alf was reciting–"'with anybody else–and, sonny, this means you!'"

"Alf," Jeffrey said, "shut up."

"Don't take it that way, kid," Alf said. "There's just one other thing."

"What?" Jeffrey asked.

"Don't tell"–Alf's voice became low and insistent–"Agnes or anybody, kid. If you do, I'll bat your ears back."

"Alf–" Jeffrey began.

"Shut up," Alf said, "I've had a pretty good time, kid, a better time than you."

"Maybe," Jeffrey said, "I don't know."

"Listen, kid," Alf said, "why don't you get out? What do you do it for? Look at me. Six weeks in Las Vegas—"

Alf stopped. The screen door had slammed. Marianna and Agnes were back on the porch.

"It's all right, baby," Alf said. "We're all through with business." Alf got himself up to his feet. "Wait till I get that jug from under the bed. Hey, Jeff, have you ever heard this one? I bet you've never heard this one. You never hear anything, kid. You ought to stick around. 'Up to the lips, close to the gums. Look out, guts, for here she comes.' See? You've got to warn them."

"Alf," Agnes said. "You! I always get a laugh out of Alf," and then they were all silent as the screen door closed.

"Jeffrey," Agnes said, "come over here and talk to me. Don't you think he's looking well?"

"What?" Jeffrey said.

"Don't you think he's looking well?" she repeated.

"Alf," Jeffrey said. "Oh, yes, Alf. He's looking fine."

When they were driving back, Jeffrey had to pull the brim of his hat down low to shield his eyes from the glare of the sunset. The sun was turning the mountains gold and purple and little clouds had come from nowhere. He had never thought before of the setting of the sun as so inexorable. He was there in the car with Marianna. He was talking to her, but most of him was still involved with that secret between himself and Alf. It was a complete, accepted fact, like the sunset. Time, without any warning, was lopping off a piece of Jeffrey just as the wind snapped the branch from a tree. He was very glad that Marianna did not notice his preoccupation for she was recalling little pieces of the visit, smiling over them as you might over a box of souvenirs brought home from a trip abroad. She was asking whether he noticed this and that, and he was saying yes, that he had noticed.

"I thought you might like it," he said. "I'm glad you saw Alf."

Then he realized that he was speaking as though they had been to a sickroom to see someone whom they might not see again.

"He was sweet," she said. "He talked a lot about you while you and Agnes were working out *your* birth dates."

"Yes," Jeffrey said. "God is in the numbers." And now he could see a sad sort of truth in that pathetic groping effort to give order to the unknown.

"He talked about you and Madge," Marianna said.

"He doesn't know much about Madge and me," Jeffrey said.

"He knows more than you think," Marianna said. "He thinks about you the way I do. I told him—perhaps I shouldn't have—"

"You shouldn't have done that," Jeffrey said.

"Dear," she asked, "do you know what Alf said?"

But he did not want to know what Alf said.

"Wait," he said, "it's six o'clock. I want to get the news."

All he had to do was to press two buttons on the panel and the mellifluous voice of someone from a Hollywood studio was there. It was the news with the compliments of someone. It made him think of the radio in the room in the apartment which Madge had fixed up as a study. Whenever he was at home he always turned it on at six o'clock. That act in Greece was over, and he had always thought that the effort to hold Greece was a strategic mistake, but there were only three votes in Commons against Churchill's conduct of the war. We were building a two-ocean navy. The navy was taking over the Coast Guard . . . and then he was thinking about Jim. He had not heard a word from Jim, but then, Jim very seldom wrote. In New York, it would be nine o'clock in the evening. Gwen would be in her room doing her homework and perhaps Madge was out to dinner.

"Darling," Marianna said, "turn it off. That's all the news."

"Yes," Jeffrey said, and he pressed the button on the panel.

"Jeff." Marianna's voice was more insistent. "Do you know what Alf said?"

He was back in the car again. Whether he wanted to or not, he would have to learn what Alf had said.

"No," he answered, "what?"

He looked at her, but not for long because he had to watch the road. His eyes were back on the road again when she spoke. They were back among the aircraft buildings and the planes were still droning overhead.

"He thinks we ought to get married."

He wished that she had not brought it up. It was not the time or the place.

"Listen, dear," he said. "Let's not talk about it now. We'll know better about it when I've finished that play."

He was back with the play again. He had never realized how strongly it held him.

"It isn't an excuse," he said. "If I can write . . ."

41

Nothing Goes On Forever

There was something that Madge had never been able to understand, or Minot Roberts, either, or any people like them. When Jeffrey had tried to explain it to them, they would listen and say that of course they understood, but he always knew that they did not. After all, it was difficult to explain to anyone the vagaries of literary creation, and "creation" was a pompous, inaccurate name for it. He did not mean to offer his work as an excuse for eccentricity or laziness. He did not like to think that he was different from other people when he was writing. He did not want to ask for special consideration, he only wanted to explain why he was more vague at such times than he was ordinarily and why he was less patient with detail and why he seemed oblivious to the ordinary facts of life. You were living in two worlds when you were writing. You were trying, very unsuccessfully, to be omnipotent in the region of the imagination. You had delusions not so very unlike those of some man in an asylum who thought he was Napoleon Bonaparte. The main difference was that you never possessed the inmate's sublime conviction. If you had any modesty at all—a very bad thing for a writer—you lived in a little hell of your own uncertainty. Without any help, and out of thin air, you were obliged to create an imaginary world and to people it with what were known as "Characters." Jeffrey had often explained to Madge that you had to live two lives at once at such a time, to exist with ordinary people and at the same time to adjust yourself to the people of your imagination. They were with you all the time and you could not get away from them. They were there when you were talking to someone else. They were there when you read the newspaper or paid the bills, or went out to dinner. Madge always said that she understood, but there was no reason why she should have. He had often tried to tell her that this process was not agreeable. He simply wanted her to see why he was not good company in the weeks when he was working and why he sometimes did not seem interested in what was going on and why he liked to sit alone, doing nothing, when she thought he should be working. The thing had some of the elements of a nervous malady, except that you knew you would get over it eventually.

When he was there in California working on that play, he had those same distractions. He could remember the sun and the sea. He could remember Marianna, but it was all like something in the pages of the script. He had that old urge to get on with it, because he knew that there was always a moment at the end, very transient, but a moment of complete relief when everything was finished.

He wrote most of that play in Marianna's living room on a card table, but it might have been anywhere at all because the present was away, somewhere, just behind him. When it was finished, he knew the present would all come back—Madge and Jim and Marianna, everything would come back. It was like going to the dentist and taking gas. There was that same lapse into unconsciousness and all at once you were there again.

When Jeffrey finished the play it was very late in the evening and Marianna was reading. She had said she liked to be there when he was working and she did not disturb him. When he pulled the last sheet from the typewriter the sound was so loud that he was markedly aware of it. He could see the bridge lamp above the table and he could see Marianna with her book. He felt very tired, as he always did at such a time. There was the usual moment of pause and then he knew that he could think of something else—of anything. He would not have to sit in front of that typewriter any longer, he would not have to worry about it any longer, because the thing was finished.

"Well," he said, "that's that."

Marianna put down her book.

"You mean you're through for the night?" Marianna asked. "You should be—you look tired."

"No," he said, "I mean it's finished."

He was very glad that she was there, because she understood that sort of thing.

"The last part went very fast," she said.

"Yes," he answered, "as soon as I got hold of the beginning."

You had to have the beginning right, and the end would fit almost inevitably.

"It's queer," he said, "isn't it? No matter how much you've worked on these things, you can't be sure; but I think the first act is right."

That sense of relief was leaving him already. He was going over the first act again in his mind.

"I can tell you," Marianna said.

"Yes," he answered, "I know you can," and the knowledge made him feel doubtful. "That's why I've waited, so that I could read it all to you. You'll know whether it's lousy or not, you'll know better than anyone else."

"Why do you say that?" she asked.

"You'll know," he said. "We'll both know, and I want you to tell me the truth. Promise to tell me the truth."

"It's going to be all right, Jeff," she said, "of course it's going to be."

"Will you tell me the truth?" he asked her.

"I can't do that," she said, "because I'll think it's good, whether it is or not." And then she smiled at him, and he smiled back.

"Anyway," he said, "I'll know."

He looked at the pages on the table and picked them up and gathered them together.

"You see, I've got to know," he said. "If it isn't any good, I'll know I can't write a play. That's something."

"Jeff," she said, "everyone feels just the way you do—everyone. It's the reaction."

"Maybe it's too late," he said. "Maybe I've done too much else too long."

"Jeff," she said, "Jeff, don't say that."

"It's what I told you," he said. "It's like doing something that I should have quite a while ago. No matter what happens, I can't thank you enough for it. You know that."

"No matter what happens?" she repeated.

"I don't mean that exactly," he answered. And he repeated what he had said before. "It's like doing something that I should have done and there's been so much else."

There had been so much else without her—so many years, so many other people, so much of life, and the words seemed to stand between them. She must have known what he meant because suddenly there was a queer sort of suspense. It would have been better—he was always sure of it later—if he had spoken of it definitely.

"Jeff," she said.

"What?" he asked her.

"Do you want to read it now?"

"No," he said, "not now. Tomorrow morning."

He could tell himself that he was tired, but his anxiety to put it off came from something much deeper.

"Suppose," he said, "that we just think I've read it and that we both know it's good. Let's forget it. Let's think of it that way until tomorrow."

He could hear the waves on the beach. It was still all right to think of it that way because he had not read the play aloud and he could tell nothing about it himself until he had. He could still live for a little while in that world with Marianna which was so far away from everything and believe that it might be possible to stay in it, but he did not have much time. . . .

42

Author's Reading

It was a lovely morning, warm for May, but not too warm by the sea. But then, they always told you that the weather was never really hot in Southern California. It was largely one's imagination when one thought that it was warm. Jeffrey could imagine everyone in Los Angeles and its suburbs looking at the blue Pacific sky and saying it was a lovely morning. It was only ten o'clock, but the glare from the water and the white sand of the beach made it necessary to lower the Venetian blinds of Marianna's living room, and the voices of the early bathers beneath their sunshades on the beach and the cars on the highway in back of Marianna's house were like incidental sounds offstage. Breakfast had been cleared from the glass table and Wong and Jessica had driven to town to shop, leaving the whole house quiet just as he would have wanted it. The living room seemed to have been arranged deliberately for the reading of that play. There was no one in the room but Marianna on the wicker chaise longue near the window and Jeffrey himself seated near her in a wicker armchair that creaked gently whenever he moved. No one but Marianna, and yet Jeffrey felt as conscious of an audience as an actor must feel when he cannot see the theater through the footlights. He wished he could get it out of his mind that the reading of his play was dramatic in itself and represented a "turning point." Perhaps he was attaching undue importance to it all, but he felt certain that anything he might do in the future was peculiarly involved with it.

"Don't look so tense," Marianna said, and she laughed. "You're only reading it to me."

He was about to read the play to her but he was also about to read it to his conscience or to providence, or whatever it was that had allowed him the time to write it. He recalled that remark of Alf's wife—that God was in the numbers—and he would be reading that play to whatever ordered force there was that moved numbers and moved lives.

"Of course," he said, "it's a first draft, Marianna." And he was saying exactly what other people said who had read plays to him. "It's just for the general effect."

He realized that he was excusing himself already, trying to protect his ego, like everybody else.

"Go on with it," Marianna said, and she laughed again. "Settle down—curtain."

He cleared his throat.

"All right," he said, "curtain." And he raised the script and focused his eyes on it. "The curtain rises on a cold New England parlor in a small town in about the year 1910. The threadbare neatness of this room is what first impresses the audience. There is a fire laid in the fireplace, center, with a paper fan in front of it. On the mantel is a waxed flowerpiece, under glass. In front of the fireplace is a round woven rag rug—to the left, a horsehair sofa. A kerosene lamp stands on a Victorian table to the right. A Boston rocker is beside the table. The lamp has glass prisms around it. The globe is green and painted with pink roses. . . ."

He felt better, now that he was reading. He had always believed in giving an accurate description of a set and as he heard his voice he knew that he had not done it badly. He knew that those first few moments, just as the curtain rose, were very vital. Before a word was spoken they could indicate the whole spirit, the atmosphere, and as often as not, the theme, and he could see the set as he was reading. Curiously enough, he had not realized, while he was writing, how accurately he had been describing the parlor at Lime Street. Reading aloud something which one had written could give it values which one might not previously perceive.

As he grew more conscious of his own words, he could almost forget that Marianna was listening. He seemed to be alone there, listening to another voice reading what someone else had written. He was intensely interested in this other work, intensely anxious to see all that was best in it, and his critical faculties were very wide-awake.

"She enters from right," he read. "Her hair is done in that ugly pompadour of the period. It is tied in back by a large bow ribbon. She is wearing a brooch watch on her white shirtwaist. . . ."

The first awkward minutes of the act were over, that difficult business of setting the character and the mood, and with the succeeding minutes, his own mood was changing. He was thinking that he was caught there in a sort of justice of his own contriving. He was thinking that he knew too much. There was no way of stilling the analytical sense which he had developed from examining other people's work, and now that part of his mind was examining his own work remorselessly. It was an exquisite sort of retribution. He could see exactly what that other part of him, the submerged creative side of him, had been trying to do. The self-revelation of it was painful, but he had to face it. It was not that it was bad—he found himself wishing that it might have been frankly bad. Instead there was a veneer of accomplishment about it, a perfunctory sort of smartness, which made it worse. There was a veneer over the dialogue, a certain specious cleverness, but there was no conviction or emotion. The play he was reading had the plausibility and the coldness of a mechanical toy pirouetting on the sidewalk at Christmas time.

If it had been really bad he could have stood it—but he was too technically competent for that. His voice was running smoothly. He was reading rather well. He could feel himself unconsciously trying to add a value which it did not have.

Once when he had been with Madge at Monte Carlo he had watched a man at the tables, and Jeffrey was like that gambler, versed and wise in all the combinations. He was a gambler who was playing safe, who did not put his chips on a number, but continually straddled the columns and the odds and evens, who was losing always just a little and was never making much. There was no brilliance and no creative daring, and yet he knew that he had possessed both once. They had been there long ago, in the first things he had written, and now they were gone, he could not imagine where.

It must have been in the middle of the second act that he thought he could not go on, and he paused for a moment. He did not want to look at Marianna, but he heard her voice.

"Go on," she said, "don't stop."

He was reading again, but perhaps it would have been better to have left it there because it had nothing to do with his thoughts. All his life—at least all of his artistic life—floated before him and still Jeffrey kept on reading.

It was like running a race, simply to get through with it, but he was not aware that his voice showed it. He read the last page slowly and then he straightened the pages and put a clip on them. He did not want to look at her, but he had to.

"Well," he said, "that's that."

Marianna was sitting up straight. Her hands were clasped tight on her lap. She was a good actress, but he knew her too well, and he could read her eyes. There might have been a moment of some sort of hope, because of course no one could be sure of oneself, but in an instant he knew he was right. It made a lump rise in his throat, because she was so kind. He could see her trying, with all her loyalty and affection, to evade the truth.

"It's—" she began, and all her inflections were right and all her words—"it's swell, darling. It's awfully swell."

Perhaps ten years ago he might have done it. There was no way of telling, but it was too late now. He was smiling at her. He stood up and tossed the manuscript on the chair. His anxiety was gone because everything was gone. He was thinking that he could get the Chief that afternoon and change at Kansas City, if that was the place to change, for Fort Sill, because Jim was at Fort Sill. Ten years ago it might have been different, but it was too late now.

"Nuts," he said, "it's lousy."

She was an actress and she knew what he was thinking—she was very quick that way. She stood up very quickly as though someone had pulled her to her feet and her voice was almost harsh.

"No," she cried, "no, no. It isn't. It's swell. It's beautiful. It's wonderful." And then she was clinging to him and sobbing in his arms. "I loved it," she sobbed. "I loved it all. Please don't say it's lousy."

"Nuts," Jeffrey said, "it's lousy, dear."

43

You Can't Do with Them—or without Them

Madge had been telling Jeffrey for the last three years that he would have to do something about Mr. Gorman. If Jeffrey did not want to do anything else, at least he should have a frank talk with Mr. Gorman. Jeffrey had told Madge that she saw only what Mr. Gorman didn't do and didn't appreciate what Mr. Gorman did do, and Madge usually replied that there wasn't anything to appreciate because every year Mr. Gorman did less and less, and Jeffrey was always soft about it. There was the cow the year before last, but when Jeffrey had called in Mr. Gorman to go over the matter, he and Mr. Gorman had ended up by telling each other jokes. Then there was the time the pipes had burst in two bathrooms, and the repair bills had amounted to one hundred and eighty-five dollars. Mr. Gorman had explained to Jeffrey that the plumber who had installed the plumbing had cheated Jeffrey and had done something mysterious with the shut-off valves. Mr. Gorman had worked on those shut-off valves for hours and hours until he had thought he had them licked. Mr. Gorman felt as sick about it as Jeffrey did and he had told Jeffrey to come right down cellar and see the shut-off valves himself. But Jeffrey had been soft about it. Jeffrey had not gone down cellar to see the shut-off valves and Madge had said that Mr. Gorman had a reason for everything.

Last winter Mr. Gorman had not taken the screens off the windows or the porches, and Mr. Gorman had a reason for that, too. He said it got the screens loose, taking them on and off and the estate superintendent on the Haskell place, who was a personal friend of Mr. Gorman's, had told Mr. Gorman that Mr. Haskell never took his screens down and everything had gone much better. Then the cook said that Mr. Gorman never brought in vegetables and Mr. Gorman told Jeffrey that Mr. Wilson knew what women were like, didn't he? You couldn't do with them, and you couldn't do without them. Then there was the apple orchard on the hill. For two years Mr. Gorman had not been able to get it sprayed, but Mr. Gorman had taken that up, too, with the Haskells' estate superintendent. The Haskells' estate superintendent had read somewhere in a book that there was nothing better for an apple orchard than to let the bugs and caterpillars at it for a couple of years. This gave the trees resistance. Furthermore, it seemed that after the bugs and caterpillars had really got at it and were not expecting anything, why then you could spray them with a new type of poison which cost a dollar a gallon, but which was worth it, and you had them all cleaned-up for good. Mr. Haskell's estate superintendent had tried it and Mr. Haskell's apples were doing fine.

Then there was the matter of mulching the flower garden. Mr. Gorman was frank to say that he never got around to the flower garden as much as he would like to, because the women in the house were always hollering after him to fix that lock on the bathroom door, but Mr. Gorman loved flowers and Mr. Wilson knew he loved them. It was simply that there were two ways of thinking about flowers. Mr. Gorman felt they were stronger in the spring if they weren't coddled and cuddled in the winter. The ones that died in the winter wouldn't be worth anything in the spring if they'd lived, in spite of what Mrs. Wilson said. Those ladies at the Garden Club were just being worked on by seed and fertilizer salesmen. Mr. Wilson knew that you couldn't get on with women or get on without them.

Then that summer Mr. Gorman had let the front lawn go. He was danged if he had ever seen grass grow so fast, and he didn't want Mr. Wilson to think that it had got ahead of him, even if Mrs. Wilson thought so. He had let it get ahead of him because it did lawns good to be let go for one summer. The grass got rooted and you could make a real project of it in the spring. It was the same way with weeds and the paths out back and the driveway by the garage. That was what farming was: let the weeds take hold and then do a blitzkrieg on them. There wasn't any use just pecking at them. When you got good and ready, go at it, all at once.

Madge told Jeffrey that Mr. Gorman was doing less and less, but Mr. Gorman had a different story. Mr. Gorman said that all the time there were more and more things to do and he was busy as a one-armed paperhanger. When he got going at one thing, the next would come up and when the next came up, the women would holler to him from the house. He was working like a one-armed paperhanger and if Mr. Wilson wanted to have the place like Mr. Haskell's, why he could do it with five or six men under him, like Mr. Haskell's estate superintendent, but he knew that Mr. Wilson didn't want to have the place like Mr. Haskell's. Mr. Wilson wanted to rest there and not to worry. Mr. Gorman knew that Mr. Wilson didn't want a show place but a farm, like the farm where Mr. Gorman worked when he was a boy; and the main thing about farming was to take it easy and not let it get you down. If it weren't for the women, he and Mr. Wilson would have a good time on the place with husking bees and clambakes and barbecues and—oh-oh—hard cider.

Several times that summer Jeffrey had told Madge to let him handle Mr. Gorman, that Mr. Gorman was all right, but as the summer had gone on, Jeffrey began to believe, as he looked about the place, that there might be something in what Madge said; and finally Jeffrey had told Madge that he would have a talk with Mr. Gorman.

Then for several weeks he and Madge had talked about that talk he was going to have with Mr. Gorman. It seemed to Jeffrey that sometimes he was Mr. Gorman and sometimes Madge was. Madge had told him that he must be perfectly firm with Mr. Gorman and at the same time that he must not lose his temper. The thing to do, Madge said, was to call Mr. Gorman into the house just casually and then have a list of questions on a piece of paper which he could ask Mr. Gorman in a perfectly casual way. If Jeffrey did not want to do it, Madge would write out the list herself. What had happened about spraying the apple trees? Why was the cow dry during the few months the family was there? Why were there so few eggs when the hens were laying? Why was it there were never any vegetables in the garden? Why was it they seemed to use two hundred gallons of gasoline a month? Madge would write down all those questions and Jeffrey would simply ask them, and then Mr. Gorman would know that Jeffrey was not completely simple. Jeffrey had told Madge that this was not the right way to go about it. In the first place, Mr. Gorman would know very well that she had written out those questions. He knew Gorman, and he could handle Gorman. He would simply call Gorman in and tell him to sit down.

"And then you'll give him a cigarette," Madge said. "And then you'll go soft and you won't tell Mr. Gorman anything."

"I won't go soft," Jeffrey said. "It's hard to get a good man, Madge, and Gorman is a good man, and I can handle Gorman."

Jeffrey said that he had always handled Gorman. All he needed to do was to call Mr. Gorman in and say, Look here, Mr. Gorman, the place was a little run-down this year, and what was the matter? It was perfectly true that Mr. Gorman would have a good reason and Jeffrey would simply listen to the reason and then he would say something bitter, something about not being Mr. Haskell and that Mr. Gorman was not Mr. Haskell's estate superintendent.

"He puts on side," Madge said, "he calls himself your custodian."

"All right," Jeffrey said, "I'm going to talk to him. I'm going to handle this, Madge. Gorman's been pretty loyal. I don't believe he ever said he was my custodian."

"When he comes in," Madge said, "just be definite with him."

"Never mind," Jeffrey said. "Never mind. I can handle this. I can talk to Mr. Gorman."

Jeffrey had been out looking for Mr. Gorman. He had walked out to the rose garden. He had been to the building where Mr. Gorman kept the cow. He had been to the woodshed which they had repaired when they had bought the place, and he had been to the garage with the living quarters for the couple over it. He had also been to the tennis court which needed rolling badly, and he knew that he must speak to Mr. Gorman about it because Jim always liked to have friends around for tennis. He had seen Charley in the garage doing something with the Ford truck. He had never been able to understand why a child of his should like machinery. Charley was fourteen and he kept taking the truck to pieces. Charley was always engaged in activities which Jeffrey could not understand.

"What's the matter with it?" Jeffrey asked.

Charley looked up very brightly. Charley had on white flannels, and his school tie and his hands were covered with grease.

"I was just looking at the points," Charley said.

"Well, put on something else," Jeffrey said. "If you're going to mess around with the car. Put on overalls."

"It isn't messing around, looking at the points," Charley said. "I can be all washed up in just a minute."

Jeffrey did not want to argue with Charley because somehow all that summer Charley had always been right. Charley knew all about points and timing, and if Charley said he would not get dirty, he would not. There was no use arguing with Charley.

"Have you seen Mr. Gorman anywhere around?" Jeffrey asked him.

"No," Charley said, "I guess he's faded out."

"Where?" Jeffrey asked. "Where has he faded to?"

"I don't know," Charley said. "He always fades at three in the afternoon. Say, Dad, you ought to see what he's done to this distributor."

"What's he done to it?" Jeffrey asked.

Charley pointed to a piece of mechanism.

"You can see for yourself," Charley said. "He's completely bitched it, Dad."

Jeffrey felt a faint qualm of uneasiness. He had never been able to understand Charley and that summer he could understand him even less, now that Charley had begun talking to him as man to man, using Anglo-Saxon words which no boy of fourteen should have employed.

"Suppose you try to say that some nicer way," Jeffrey said.

Charley shrugged his shoulders. The boy was only fourteen, but he shrugged his shoulders.

"Frankly," Charley said, "there's no plainer way to say it. He's bitched it, Dad, but I can fix it. The instruction book's right here. Any moron can follow this instruction book."

"Why aren't you out at the Haskells' or somewhere?" Jeffrey asked.

As soon as he asked it, he realized that he was always asking Charley why he was not somewhere else. Charley shrugged his shoulders.

"Frankly," Charley said, "I've taken the afternoon off. This is going to pay me better."

"Oh," Jeffrey said, "you're going to be a little Tommy Edison, are you?"

"I mean," Charley said, "they'll need mechanics in the war."

"What war?" Jeffrey asked.

"Frankly," Charley said, "I've been thinking it over, Dad. It'll be a twelve years' war."

Ever since Charley was five he had been completely self-sufficient. There was nothing new about Charley, except that there was more of him every year. Charley's room was filled with leather-bound books which he brought home from school every Prize Day—the Current Events Prize, the History

Prize, the Pinkham Essay Prize, the Best Personal Project Prize, the Sawyer Prize for the Year's Best Personal Adjustment, the Rogers Memorial Prize for Oral Latin Translations. Charley was not fresh; he was simply very bright and adjusted to his environment. Charley was holding that part of the Ford truck. Jeffrey was the world of yesterday; Charley was the world of tomorrow. It was Shuffle Shoon and Amber Locks, sitting together building blocks, except that Jeffrey had never wanted to build blocks with Charley, intellectual or otherwise.

"Just get this into your head," Jeffrey said, "we're not in the war yet."

Charley's even features, which resembled rather more closely his mother's than his father's, assumed the patient look of a well-informed adolescent conversing with a poorly trained elder, who could not help his limited background.

"We're in the war now, Dad," Charley said, "and we don't know it. President Roosevelt has said what I mean—convoys mean shooting and shooting means war. They've already torpedoed the *Greer*." Charley shrugged his shoulders again. "That's war."

"And why do you think it's going to last for twelve years?" Jeffrey asked.

"I'll be glad to tell you," Charley said, "if you're interested and not just making conversation."

"Remember," Jeffrey said, "what I've told you. Manners, Charley, manners."

"Sorry," Charley said, and he made a helpless gesture with both hands.

"Careful," Jeffrey said, "don't get too big for your pants, Charley."

It gave Jeffrey a cruel sort of pleasure which was not paternal, but he knew, even when he was speaking, that he was not being fair. In all their encounters he always ended up by not being fair to Charley.

"I'm sorry, sir," Charley said. "I can't say anything more, can I? I said I was sorry."

"All right," Jeffrey said, "why do you think it's going to last for twelve years?"

"Well," Charley said, "I've been working on it quite a little lately. I don't suppose you were much in touch with the war in Hollywood."

"No," Jeffrey said, "I imagine not."

But his sarcasm was lost on Charley. Charley's glance was focused somewhere beyond Jeffrey and Charley was marshaling his facts, thinking on his feet, just as he had been taught to do when he had won the Judkins Prize for Extemporaneous Speaking.

"I've been making quite a study of the commentators, lately," Charley said.

"Oh," Jeffrey said, "you've been sampling opinion, have you?"

"I've been listening to Swing and Kaltenborn and Newcombe," Charley said, "and then of course there's *Time* and *Life* and *Newsweek* and *Berlin Diary*. That's not a bad book of Shirer's. Have you read it, Dad?"

"Yes," Jeffrey said, "I've read it, Charley."

"I'd like to have a talk with you about it sometime," Charley said. "But—I've got most of my ideas from Hanson Baldwin."

"What about Major George Fielding Eliot," Jeffrey asked, "and Fletcher

Pratt, and the General in *PM*? Have you followed those, too, Charley?"

"Yes," Charley answered. "We follow them all year in Current Events, but it doesn't seem to me that those men have quite the weight of Baldwin. Did you see his article in *Life* called 'Blueprint for Victory,' Dad?"

"Yes," Jeffrey said, "I came across it, Charley. Of course, I haven't put my mind on it as much as you have, but I thought Baldwin rather discounted the Russians."

"Yes," Charley said, and he nodded brightly. "Yes, a little. Perhaps his timetable may be a little off."

Jeffrey drew a deep breath.

"You'll have a lot of fun telling this to Jim," he said.

Then the picture changed. Charley was what he should have been, a little boy again, playing with the car, and his face had all the helplessness of a little boy when he faces grownups after studying hard and knowing all the answers. His eyes reflected all the injustices meted out to childhood.

"Jim," Charley said, "oh, nuts."

Then Jeffrey felt almost sorry for him. He knew again that he had not been fair to Charley.

"Listen, kid," Jeffrey said, and he wanted to pat Charley on the shoulder, but he knew that Charley would not have liked it.

"You go out and find Mr. Gorman, will you? Tell him I want to see him in the house."

"You mean right now?" Charley asked.

"Yes," Jeffrey said, "I mean right now."

"Are you going to fire him?" Charley asked, and his eyes had grown larger as he visualized the human drama.

"Who said I was going to fire him?" Jeffrey answered. And he knew he would lose what dignity he had left if he took it up with Charley. "You go and find Mr. Gorman and tell him I'm waiting in the house."

Then he remembered something that Jim had said about Charley a year ago. Jim had said that Charley was a wise little apple, an expression which was new to Jeffrey, but that was just what Charley was, a wise little apple.

The room where Jeffrey sat to wait for Mr. Gorman had been called his "office," largely because no one had ever thought of a proper name for it. When Madge had bought the house in Connecticut, he had told her that he had to have a room where he could be by himself, away from the children, where he could keep his desk and a few papers and books, and he had not wanted anything done with it in the way of decoration. That was why the walls were bare and why Madge had never put up any curtains. He had bought the furniture over the past few years himself—a tall green filing cabinet, a bookcase filled with plays and works on the theater, a flat desk with a swivel chair and two leather armchairs, which he had purchased at a country auction, and a tavern table, which he had bought in Maine. The broad pine floor boards had been waxed and he made a point of allowing the ashes to remain in the fireplace just as they always had in his father's fireplace on Lime Street.

He knew that the room was ugly and Madge had often said she did not see why he wanted a room like it, because he had good taste, but its bareness and ugliness had always consoled him. That room was the only place which was entirely his own and it represented no effort and no compromise. He could sit in it as long as he liked and no one disturbed him. Madge had been very thoughtful about not disturbing him, particularly that summer.

You entered the room from the back hall and there was also a door that opened out on the back lawn. It had been muggy and sultry all day, as days so often were in early September. He could hear the notes of the crickets on the lawn outside, but this was the only sign that another autumn was coming. Jeffrey looked at his wrist watch and saw that it was half-past three. It occurred to him that he had not been by himself that day or for a good many days before.

He and Madge had been going out a good deal lately to parties at Westport and Greenwich and Stamford and Long Island. They both must have had the same desire to see other people. He could not get it out of his head that they might not see their friends in quite that way again and that there might not be the same food and wine on the table, and he believed that everyone else must have had the same idea. A suspense had been in the air all summer and it was here now with the humming of the crickets. It aroused a desire for human companionship and familiar faces. There was a curious consolation in other people's confusion because the truth was that no one knew anything, although everyone tried to know. There was always someone who had been to Washington, who would say it was a madhouse and that all the new bureaus were clogged with red tape, and the army was using trucks instead of tanks, and the morale of the draft troops was very low; and they were chalking up a mystic sign on the barracks, O.H.I.O., which meant, in case you did not know it, "Over the Hill in October."

There was always someone who knew someone in the State Department or who knew someone who had seen the President or who had a friend who was back from England or the Orient. The news had ceased to be reliable so that everyone listened avidly for such bits of gossip, all of which added up to nothing. The only tangible fact seemed to be that, although it was September, the Russian armies were still fighting. There was still an unreality about the war. It seemed to Jeffrey that very few people that summer understood that war was a matter of killing. Everyone seemed to think that you could win a war by a few quick moves. He and everyone else were pathetically grasping for fact, and the only fact was death.

There was always someone who had been on a tour to Japan, or someone who knew someone in the navy. The Japanese would make no trouble unless it came to a matter of face. The Japanese were bogged down in China. They were a third-rate military power and now that we had cut off shipments of gasoline and oil, they knew that we meant business. We were drawing a ring around them, now that the Philippines and the East Indies were being reinforced, and there was always the British base at Singapore. Japanese air power was nonexistent and when it came to the Japanese Navy, someone always knew someone who had been talking with one of our Admirals. And the Admiral had said that the American fleet could meet the Japanese fleet any morning and it would all be over in time for lunch. Then there was the other story, the one about those blueprints of a battleship. The Japanese had negotiated with a British company for the building of a battleship and had stolen all the plans, but the British understood their Japanese, and you know what happened. When the battleship was launched in Yokohama, or wherever they did launch battleships, it was top-heavy and turned right over. That was Japan for you. They were funny little people.

Then the conversation would shift back to home. There would be no new automobiles next year, and no new washing machines or electric refrigerators or radios. If you were short of any of these things, you had better buy them quickly. The French vermouth was going.

There was only one thing that was obvious, and everyone must have seen it. They were living in a sort of peace which was no longer peace. There was no longer neutrality. There might not be a war, but it was time to be ready for war, the way the world was going, and nothing would ever be the same again. He could feel it in the house that afternoon. Outside there was a stillness in the air, as though it were about to rain. Through the open windows he could hear the birds and he could hear the couple quarreling in the kitchen. You could not run away. It was necessary, instead, to cultivate the illusion that there would be the same amount of money, the same cars in the garage, the same oil burner in the cellar and the same electric water system, and the same schools for the children, and there was still Mr. Gorman. Jeffrey had almost forgotten Mr. Gorman until he heard him knocking at the door.

Instead of wearing work pants and a khaki shirt or overalls, Mr. Gorman was wearing seersucker trousers and a blue shirt with the sleeves cut off like a tennis player's. Mr. Gorman's mustache was freshly trimmed, his face was very smooth, and his hair was newly cut and shaved in a fresh arc in the back so that there was a white space between the hair and the heavy tan on his neck. Mr. Gorman was holding a small bottle, and Mr. Gorman was smiling.

"It's a mean kind of day, isn't it?" Mr. Gorman said. "It makes you sweat like a horse."

"Where have you been?" Jeffrey asked. "I've been looking for you everywhere."

"Oh-oh," Mr. Gorman said, and he looked concerned. "Why didn't you tell me you were going to be looking for me, Mr. Wilson? I'd have been right here."

In a way it seemed as though Mr. Gorman were right. It would have been easier if Jeffrey had told him that morning that he would be looking for him that afternoon.

"Well, where were you?" Jeffrey asked.

Mr. Gorman shook his head and Jeffrey was aware of a heavy odor of hair tonic pervading the room.

"I told 'em in the kitchen," Mr. Gorman said, "or else, did I tell 'em? I don't remember. I've been working like a one-armed paperhanger, and maybe I forgot. I had to get downtown. It was the hose."

"What's the matter with the hose?" Jeffrey asked.

"Well, I thought we ought to lay in some," Mr. Gorman said. "So I just hopped in the station wagon and got us two hundred feet at Maxon's Store. It was lucky I did, too, Mr. Wilson. Hose is going to be as scarce as hen's teeth and that's something else I want to take up with you."

"What?" Jeffrey asked.

"It don't seem worth while bothering you about it," Mr. Gorman said, "and you know me. I always want to run this place without making any bother for Mr. Wilson because I know that you don't want to be bothered, but it just seems to me we ought to stock up a little. I was saying it to Maxon downtown and Maxon says it, too. Tom Maxon's quite a card, but he knows his business."

Mr. Gorman rubbed the back of his head.

"You got a haircut down there, didn't you?" Jeffrey asked.

"Oh-oh," Mr. Gorman said. "Yes, sir, I just snatched off a quick one at Tony's while they were getting out the hose. My God, Mr. Wilson, there's never time these days to get a haircut or anything. But what I say is, when you have a moment, you and I ought to go out to the barn and get together. We've got to make a project of it, and look at all the tools."

"What's the matter with the tools?" Jeffrey asked.

"I'll tell you," Mr. Gorman said. "Frankly, tools don't last the way they used to when we were kids, Mr. Wilson, and I give 'em wear. I'm not hard on them, you understand. I get more out of tools than anybody, but I give 'em wear and they don't stand up like they used to. Now the lawn mower, she's on the blink again, and that hand cultivator and the pruning shears. We just ought to stock up while there's anything to stock."

"Didn't we buy a lot of tools this spring?" Jeffrey asked.

"Sure," Mr. Gorman said. "Don't think I'm coming in here and begging you for tools. I'm only saying we ought to get some while there's anything to get. You can't keep this place the way you want it unless you get some tools. Now take the lawn. I'll tell you something. Mrs. Wilson was out this morning complaining about the lawn again. You know what women are, you can't do with them, and you can't do without them. Now I didn't want to say anything. You know me. Do your work and shut up, is what I say. I didn't talk back, but it's the lawn mower. It isn't me, but the mower and the bearings are acting up again."

"I thought it was a new mower," Jeffrey said. "Didn't I buy you a new one?"

"Oh-oh," Mr. Gorman said, "the new mower. Oh-oh. That was one on you that time, Mr. Wilson. Didn't I tell you about that mower?"

"I don't remember," Jeffrey answered, "what about it?"

"It isn't your fault, Mr. Wilson," Mr. Gorman said. "I always do what I'm told, don't I? You wanted a cheap mower, and we got it, didn't we? Well, at the time I thought maybe I was wrong, but I wasn't wrong." Mr.

Gorman laughed. "It's one on you, Mr. Wilson, that mower." Mr. Gorman lowered his voice to a whisper. "A bunch of junk. My God, just junk."

"It can't be junk," Jeffrey said, "it cost twenty-five dollars in June."

Mr. Gorman nodded.

"I know," he said, "I know. It isn't your fault, Mr. Wilson. You ought to get a good mower for that price. Anybody ought to, but they don't make them like they did when we were kids, Mr. Wilson. And it isn't I haven't worked on it. I've babied it. I've coddled it. I've been out here until eight in the evening taking her to pieces."

"Now wait a minute," Jeffrey said. He knew it was time to say something and it was very difficult to interrupt Mr. Gorman. "I've been wanting to have a talk with you." Jeffrey cleared his throat. "It just seems to me—perhaps I haven't been around as much as I should have, but it seems to me the whole place looks like hell."

Mr. Gorman uncrossed his knees and leaned forward.

"Well, now," he said gently, "in what way, Mr. Wilson?"

Jeffrey wished that he had the list which Madge had spoken of. Now that he was face to face with Mr. Gorman, there seemed more ways than he could specify.

"You ought to know," Jeffrey answered. "The lawn, the paths, the flower beds—they don't look right, Gorman. I suppose you've been pretty busy. I'm just asking you what the matter is."

Mr. Gorman nodded slowly.

"Mr. Wilson," he said, "may I ask you a question? Do I love this place, or don't I?"

Jeffrey looked at Mr. Gorman. There was personal hurt and earnestness and real sentiment on Mr. Gorman's face.

"I'll answer it for you," Mr. Gorman said. "A fellow can't help loving something he's sweated over, Mr. Wilson. He can't help loving the flowers he's planted. I love this place better than you do, Mr. Wilson. Now, let me ask you another question. Has Mrs. Wilson been saying this about the place?"

The moment Mr. Gorman mentioned Madge, Jeffrey realized that Mr. Gorman had overstepped himself, but under the spell of Mr. Gorman's personality he felt himself being pushed onto the defensive. Mr. Gorman had put his finger upon the crux of the difficulty, and Jeffrey knew that Mr. Gorman would keep his finger there.

"There's no reason to bring Mrs. Wilson into this," Jeffrey said. "It isn't only Mrs. Wilson. Anyone can see that things look run-down, Gorman."

Mr. Gorman was momentarily silent. He sat looking at Jeffrey with a new sort of understanding that was kind and companionable.

"Women," Mr. Gorman said, "these women."

"Never mind about women," Jeffrey said. "We aren't talking about women, Gorman."

Mr. Gorman nodded. His face grew more somber but he was very kind.

"Now you and I," Mr. Gorman said, "you and I know this place is as sound as a nut underneath, don't we, Mr. Wilson?"

"How do you mean it's as sound as a nut?" Jeffrey asked.

"You know," Mr. Gorman said, "and I know. It's the good stuff that goes into it underneath. It isn't the little doodabs that count. Not all-the-same thingumajigs that women see. It's what's down there under it." Mr. Gorman lowered his voice. "I'll tell you what I mean, Mr. Wilson. Frankly, I mean manure."

Jeffrey was unable to follow Mr. Gorman's train of thought, but he knew that everything that Mr. Gorman said was true, or that it would turn out to be when Mr. Gorman finished.

"I don't quite see what you're getting at, Gorman," Jeffrey said, but he knew he was going to see, and Mr. Gorman knew it.

Mr. Gorman was nodding slowly and smiling at him kindly.

"I'm coming at it hind side before, Mr. Wilson," he said, "but I'm getting up to it. What I mean is no woman understands manure, Mr. Wilson, and why should she? It isn't up to them to know it. Oh-oh, you can't get along with 'em and you can't get along without 'em."

"All right," Jeffrey said, "you said that."

"Now," Mr. Gorman said, "you're going to get my point, Mr. Wilson. There's no reason why you should have thought of it because I'm paid to do that thinking for you and you're busy and you come down here to rest, and I don't want to bother you. But when you put manure down on a place, good well-rotted manure like the kind we buy, Mr. Wilson, things grow, don't they? By jinks, they can't help growing—every kind of thing! Now that's why the place sometimes looks a little raggedy." Mr. Gorman's eyes widened and he pointed his finger slowly at Jeffrey. "It's because the soil is rich. The dressing is down there underneath."

Jeffrey did not answer. He was thinking that Mr. Gorman was a type, and he was not entirely amused by him.

"Every danged thing grows when you put down good dressing," Mr. Gorman said. "That's why the lawn keeps shooting up and why you can't keep it down with a twenty-five-dollar mower."

Jeffrey listened. Mr. Gorman was going on. It was why the paths got weedy. By jinks, you couldn't kind of help things getting away from you when there was good stuff underneath. And there was one example that Mr. Gorman wanted to bring up particularly and that was those young apple trees in the orchard on the hill. Mr. Gorman loved good apples, and Mr. Wilson loved them too because they made—oh-oh—hard cider. Now when you had good stuff around little apple trees they put on big soft juicy foliage and bugs and caterpillars knew good stuff. By jinks, you couldn't blame the bugs and caterpillars for knowing good stuff when they saw it and kind of settling in on that orchard on the hill more than they did on other people's orchards. Now Mr. Gorman didn't mind seeing them there. In fact, just between himself and Mr. Wilson it made him feel easier when there was a good crop of tent caterpillars. Now you couldn't have things both ways. If you had good ground everything would grow—weeds and bugs and everything. You couldn't have it both ways, and Mr. Wilson could see that. You could either starve the ground and not have so many weeds and just have everything mean and stringy, or else you could have it nice and rich and kind of let it get away from you. Mr. Wilson could see that.

Jeffrey could see it vaguely, and Mr. Gorman was going on. When you had everything going great guns, Mr. Gorman was saying, of course it kept a man busy, and Mr. Gorman didn't mind that. He didn't want to just be sitting around. All Mr. Gorman needed was a whole new deal, as you might say, on tools—and he didn't want to bother Jeffrey about it because Mr. Wilson had other things to think about. So how would it be if Mr. Wilson just forgot about it, and let Mr. Gorman go down to Maxon's and stock up while there was something to stock with?

He could smell the tonic on Mr. Gorman's hair. The country which had nurtured him and Mr. Gorman was so rich, so kindly and so powerful that it could afford to produce a type like Mr. Gorman, and there was nothing like him anywhere else in the world. There was no other place in the world where the sort of friendship which he felt for Mr. Gorman could develop. Mr. Gorman was as good as he was and he was as good as Mr. Gorman. Jeffrey could even understand that his faults were Mr. Gorman's faults. There was no other country in the world where one could shirk hard labor and still live and where one could deal in fallacies and feel that they were real. In many ways he was like Mr. Gorman and so was everyone else, soft and unconscious of inherent values—and now the world was changing. He wondered what people like Mr. Gorman would do about it. The answer to everything lay with Mr. Gorman.

"Well," Mr. Gorman said, "we've got that straight now, haven't we?"

"Yes," Jeffrey said, "you go down to Maxon's and get anything you need. I'm not criticizing you, Gorman. Just see if you can't get everything brushed up a little."

"Sure," Mr. Gorman said, "sure! Oh-oh, I forgot. I brought you something."

Mr. Gorman reached to the floor and picked up a small bottle.

"Applejack," Mr. Gorman said. "Oh-oh, don't ask me where I got it."

"Thanks," Jeffrey said, "why, thanks very much."

"Maybe we could try a little right now," Mr. Gorman said. "Nothing like a little smile at the end of the afternoon. You sit right there, Mr. Wilson. I'll go out and fetch some glasses."

Mr. Gorman was back with the glasses and Mr. Gorman was tilting up the bottle. He was saying you wouldn't know what was in it until it hit you.

"Smooth as cream," Mr. Gorman said.

It was not as smooth as cream and it tasted very badly.

"That's quite a drink," Jeffrey said. "Thanks ever so much."

"I'll bet you one thing," Mr. Gorman said, "I'll bet the picture stars don't have anything like that in Hollywood."

"No," Jeffrey said. "That's right. They don't."

"Someday," Mr. Gorman said, "I'll tell you what we'll do, Mr. Wilson, when things are kind of slack around here in the winter, I could motor you out just as easy as not to Hollywood."

"Yes," Jeffrey said, "you ought to see it. Maybe we'll do it, Gorman."

"Oh-oh," Mr. Gorman said, "oh-oh." And then his expression changed. They were friends again, old friends. "You must be feeling good today, Mr. Wilson. Say, I meant to ask you, when's Jim coming back?"

"He's coming tonight on the 7:02. He has a ten-day leave," Jeffrey said.

"Say," Mr. Gorman said, "I tell you what I'll do. I'll stay over and drive you in the station wagon. I'd kind of like to take a look at Jim myself."

"Why, thanks," Jeffrey said, "if it isn't any trouble."

"No trouble at all," Mr. Gorman said. "I kind of want to take a look at Jim in his uniform and all. You and me, we were soldiers, Mr. Wilson."

"Yes," Jeffrey said, "that's so."

"The old Seventy-seventh," Mr. Gorman said, "you ought to have been in the old Seventy-seventh. Mademoiselle from Armentières, *parlez-vous*— Well, we've got a soldier in the family. Say, Jim's quite a boy."

"Yes," Jeffrey said, "he's quite a boy."

"I'll tell you, Mr. Wilson," Mr. Gorman said, "Jim's just common like you and me. I bet at that camp they've been working him like a one-armed paperhanger. Let's have another little smile. Here's looking at Jim!"

"All right," Jeffrey said, "here's looking at Jim."

"This war," Mr. Gorman said, "I tell you how I look at it. Don't you worry about Jim. We're not going to get into this war."

"Well—" Jeffrey began, and then the door to the hall opened. It was Madge.

44

My Son as Much as Your Son

There was nothing to say about it, and nothing to do about it, because Madge had known he was going to have a talk with Mr. Gorman, and there he was having a drink with Mr. Gorman.

"Oh," Jeffrey said, "oh, hello, Madge."

Madge had just come in from bridge or lunch, judging from her dress, but he did not know how long she had been in the house because he had not heard the car. Jeffrey stood up and Mr. Gorman stood up.

"Well," Mr. Gorman said, "it's kind of a mean hot day, isn't it, Mrs. Wilson?"

Madge did not answer.

"We've just been going over everything," Jeffrey said. "We've been having quite a talk and everything's going to be a lot better, isn't it, Gorman?"

"It's going to be okay," Mr. Gorman said. "We've got it licked, Mrs. Wilson. You're going to be surprised."

Madge did not answer. At first her silence gave Jeffrey acute uneasiness, until he saw that it had a distrait quality. All at once he saw that Madge was not thinking about Mr. Gorman, that she had not even noticed the glasses, although he was very sure that she would notice them eventually. Her manner filled him partly with apprehension and partly with relief. Something else had happened in the house which had made Madge disturbed. Jeffrey's first thought was that the couple might be leaving, but Madge was usually competent and cheerful when couples left.

"Jeffrey," Madge said, "can I see you for a minute?"

It was always serious when Madge wanted to see him for a minute.

"Well," Mr. Gorman said, "I've got to be gitting. Don't give it another thought. I'll hop right to that right away, Mr. Wilson." Mr. Gorman opened the door to the lawn very quickly and closed it behind him softly and efficiently. It was clear that Mr. Gorman also knew that something had happened. It was not his funeral, and he was glad to be gitting.

Jeffrey was aware that Madge was trying to compose herself, as though she were making a gymnastic effort. For an instant he had a wild sense of guilt. He was thinking that sooner or later you had to pay for everything. He was thinking that it must be about California and Marianna Miller and he had often thought what he would tell Madge if the matter ever came up; but it was not the proper time and place there in his room at the end of the afternoon just when his mind had been concentrated on having a talk with Mr. Gorman, and then he had forgotten exactly what he was going to tell Madge about Marianna Miller.

Madge was still composing herself. He wished that Madge would not always try to be calm and a perfect lady when something serious happened.

"Jeffrey," Madge said, and then stopped.

"Yes," Jeffrey said, "Madge, what is it?"

"A telegram has just come from Jim," she said and she stopped.

If it wasn't one thing it was another. He had often wondered whether other people's lives were as complicated—and now he had to turn from what he thought it was to something else. It was like being hit from behind when he heard her speak.

"Jim?" he repeated. "What about Jim?"

Madge spoke very slowly. She was very calm and obviously wanted to consider every angle.

"Jeff," Madge said, "will you close the windows, dear? I don't want everyone in the world to hear what we're saying."

Jeffrey turned and closed the windows quickly with a sense of frustration and dread. At the same time he was thinking it was not fair of Madge not to tell it quickly.

"Go ahead, Madge," he said, "what about Jim?"

Madge looked about the room. He wished to heaven she would stop trying to compose herself.

"Jeff," Madge said, "he's bringing that girl."

She looked at him steadily, waiting for his reaction. When he did not answer, he saw her forehead wrinkle and Madge's voice, though very quiet, assumed a higher note.

"That girl, Jeffrey," Madge said, "that Sally Sales."

Jeffrey felt his shoulder muscles relax. He wanted to sigh but he did not. "Oh," he said.

The wrinkles on Madge's forehead grew deeper.

"Jeff," Madge said, "do you know anything about it?"

"What makes you ask that?" Jeffrey asked. "How should I know anything about it?"

"Then he never told anybody," Madge said. "At least I think he might have told one of us and not just sent a telegram."

Jeffrey put his hands in his pockets and took them out again.

"Madge," he said, "he probably just got the idea. He wanted to see us and see her too." He stopped and looked away from Madge and out of the window. "He's only got ten days' leave, you know."

It seemed perfectly clear to him and entirely beyond argument.

"Jeff," she said and her voice was sharper, "don't be such a fool!"

"Don't get so upset!" Jeffrey said. "There's nothing to be upset about. Why shouldn't he ask her here if he wants to?"

"Jeff," Madge said again, "can't you see what it *means*–sending a telegram –just bringing that girl here out of the blue?"

He saw what it meant but he did not want her to know it.

"I don't see that it means anything," he said.

"Oh, God!" Madge said. "Don't pretend you don't see. It means–Jeffrey, he's completely *lost his head about her*." She took a step toward him. "If we don't do something, Jeffrey–Do you think he's going to marry her?"

"Now, Madge," Jeffrey began. He did not know what he thought, but she did not wait for him to finish.

"Don't stand there and look so stupid!" Madge said. "He's your son, Jeffrey, just as much as mine. Jeffrey, dear–she's just an ordinary little girl from Montclair. She–"

"Not Montclair," Jeffrey said, "Scarsdale."

"All right," Madge said, "Scarsdale. Jeffrey, we can't let him ruin his life."

Jeffrey stood looking at her.

"Madge," he said, "we don't know anything, and besides, do you remember you and me? You're a great one to be talking, Madge."

But then perhaps no one really remembered, and women were relentless, much more so than men. If she did remember, he saw she did not want to then.

"Jeff," she said, "you keep saying that. It isn't the same thing at all. You can't just be complacent and superior. Why do I have to worry about it while you sit here and drink with the hired man?"

Jeffrey did not answer. He had known that the scene with Mr. Gorman would not be entirely lost on Madge. She was using it now and he knew she would use it again.

"Jeff," Madge said, and she took a step nearer. "Jeff–"

"Yes," Jeffrey said, "what is it, Madge?"

Madge lowered her voice almost to a whisper.

"Jeff," she said, "perhaps you can say something to Jim. I can't, but you could because you're a man. Perhaps if you just told Jim it would be all right to—live with her—" her face brightened and her voice was louder—"then he might get over it. Don't you think, Jeff—perhaps they're living with each other now?"

Madge's thoughts seemed brutal and unkind to him, though he had to admit that he had entertained the same idea himself. It simply seemed all right for him to think of it but not all right for Madge. Madge should have seen that you could not get over loving a girl simply by going to bed with her at odd moments. It was a fallacy which most nice people seemed to accept.

"You mean," Jeffrey asked, "you want me to suggest that to Jim?"

"Darling," Madge said, "can't you be realistic? Anything to get him over it."

For some reason he could not define, the whole thing was a kind of grim slur on decency, and Jim was not like that.

"Madge," he said, "I'll be damned if I'll do any such thing." And then he lost control of his voice. "You leave Jim alone, Madge. Don't you interfere with Jim."

He saw Madge bite her lip, but Madge was still composed. It was just as well that they had closed the doors and windows.

"Just remember," Madge said, "he's my son just as much as yours."

"And you remember what I told you," Jeffrey said. "You leave Jim alone!"

It had been years since he had been so angry at her—years. There was no way of explaining the mixture of his emotions at such a time.

"Don't shout so," Madge said. "Do you want all the servants to hear you?"

It was what always happened in a quarrel.

"I'm not shouting, Madge," Jeffrey said. "I'm simply trying to tell you. I mean it. You mustn't interfere with Jim. You got him into the army. Well, I'm here now."

There was another moment's silence and then Madge's voice changed.

"Don't lose your temper, Jeff," Madge said. "You don't know how silly you look—you really *do* when you lose your temper."

"You leave that boy alone," Jeffrey said.

"Jeff," Madge said, "don't shout at me!"

"I'm not shouting at you," Jeffrey said. "I can handle this."

He saw Madge shrug her shoulders and the gesture reminded him of Charley in the garage.

"I know," Madge said. "You manage everything so well, dear, just the way you manage Mr. Gorman."

"Damn it, Madge," Jeffrey said. "Never mind about Gorman."

"He isn't going to marry her," Madge said. And she bit her lower lip again.

"He can marry her if he wants to," Jeffrey said, and he wanted her to understand. He reached toward her and tried to take her hand but she drew away.

"Madge," he said, "I wish you'd look at it this way. We haven't any right to interfere with Jim. He hasn't got much time."

"What do you mean by that?" Madge asked. "Much time for what?"

Jeffrey put his hands in his pockets and leaned his shoulders against the wall.

"Much time to live," he said, "perhaps."

It gave him a profound sense of relief to be sharing that secret with her. He saw the anger die out of her eyes and she looked surprised. That was all—very much surprised.

"Why, Jeff," she began, "why darling, you don't really think—"

There was no way of her seeing. She had never been as he had been once, without much time.

"It might be, very well, you know," he said.

At any rate it was better. Simply saying it aloud and having her listen made it better.

"Darling," Madge said, "there's no need to be so upset and impulsive. You know he isn't old enough to know the sort of girl he wants and they have nothing to live on. Darling, I won't help them out."

It was amazing that she could not understand that nothing you said mattered, if you did not have much time. And even if you lived, the time afterwards was not time.

"Well, she's coming, isn't she?" Jeffrey said.

"Yes," Madge said, "of course she's coming."

"Then you mustn't act as though you were opposed to it, Madge," he was saying, "that would only make it worse. Just remember Jim only has ten days' leave. Be nice to her, Madge. Please be nice to her."

He heard Madge sigh.

"Of course I'll be nice to her," she said.

"Maybe you'll like her," Jeffrey said. "You've never seen her, have you?"

But he knew that Madge would never like her.

45

Well, Here We Are

Jeffrey was standing in front of the beach wagon which was parked beside other beach wagons and all the gay cars that were always at that drab, yellowish station beyond Danbury. He was conscious of looking down the track and listening for a whistle or for a humming sound on the rails which might indicate that the train from New York was coming. He was even looking at his watch and thinking that the 7:02 was nearly always late, but his mind was not on it. In his thoughts he was back there in Bragg in the last war.

He had been commissioned from the flying school in Texas and he himself had come home for a ten-day leave before he reported to New York for his orders. The memory was very vivid. His uniform was new, made by the post tailor in Texas so hastily that the tunic wrinkled at the shoulders, but still he was pleased with his uniform. He had not yet broken himself of occasionally touching the insignia which showed he was an aviator, or of glancing sideways at his shoulders to see that his gold bars were pinned on firmly—diaper pins they used to call them in the last war. The post tailor had made his breeches bulge in all the wrong places, as he found out later, but he did not know it then. He was wearing riding boots and spurs, and God alone knew why it was regulation for aviators to wear spurs, but there it was. He was wearing a garrison cap which was a little too tight and he must have looked so thin and gangling in that uniform that anybody could have seen what he was, a shave-tail just commissioned in the Officers' Reserve, but he had not been aware of any of this then. He thought he was like those pictures of officers he had seen in advertisements and he was coming home on leave. He was walking down the steps of the car a little carefully so that he would not trip on his spurs. He had had trouble with them once in New York and once in Boston, when he had found his heels locked together in an unexpected moment and had nearly lost his balance. He was not going to let anything like that happen when he got off the train at Bragg. He was carrying a canvas kit bag which the post tailor had sold him down in Texas. He was a commissioned officer and a gentleman who in ten days would be going to war. He was learning how to take salutes from enlisted men. On the way from New York a colonel in the dining car had referred to him as Mister and had asked him very nicely to take the chair opposite. He was in the army now and the President of the United States was placing special trust in his integrity and ability.

The season of the year and the time of day were the same. He remembered the way the shadows had fallen near the station in Bragg. He remembered the faces turned up toward him as he got off the train. Louella Barnes was waiting for him and he had taken off his garrison cap with his left hand, and he was still holding his kit bag with his right so that he could not touch her; and when he stepped forward there were those spurs again catching somehow together. He had stumbled slightly, but only very slightly.

"You have to wear spurs with riding boots," he had said. "It's regulation."

All that old emotion was back with Jeffrey, that sense of his own position and the callow pride he had taken in it, but he could excuse that pride. Not everyone had got his wings. He could remember his feeling of remoteness as he looked at Louella and at everything. He was back at home, but much of him was away from home already. When the train came in, it was all so vivid that it seemed to be he getting off that train, not Jim. Jeffrey did not move toward him. He simply stood there.

The uniform was different now, easier to wear. If it had been the last war he would have thought Jim was a British officer. The tunic was no longer choked about the neck. He saw the lapels with the crossed cannons, the black tie and the glistening belt, but when he saw the gold bars it seemed to be his uniform again. It was bulging also in the wrong places just as his own had once. The garrison cap was not at the right angle. Jim's hands projected a little too far from the sleeves. Jim's face looked thinner and harder. It made a lump rise in Jeffrey's throat. It was just as though he himself were getting off the train at Bragg. Jim had not seen him yet, and Jeffrey did not want him to for just a moment. Jim was turning and holding out his hand. He was helping a girl down very carefully because he was an officer and a gentleman. Jeffrey recognized Sally Sales but she might as well have been Louella Barnes.

There was no exact resemblance between her and that memory of Louella except the common awkward resemblance of youth. Louella must have thought for hours and hours about what she was going to wear and what she was going to say that day when he had come back home; and it was just as though it were happening again when he saw Sally Sales. Madge was right—Jim and Sally were too young to know about anything. Sally Sales, too, must have thought and thought about what she was going to wear, because she was too young to realize that Jim would never notice. She was dressed in a beige gabardine tailored suit and an organdy blouse and shoes with heels that were higher than any she had worn before. He could tell it from the careful way she stepped; and that whole costume was brand new, as new and guileless as Jim's uniform. Somehow it made Jeffrey smile and made his eyes smart when he saw them and he wondered whether he and Louella could have looked like that. As sure as fate they must have, long ago. Louella had worn a hat, of course, and Sally's head was bare, but when the sun was on Sally's smooth pageboy bob her hair was just the color of Louella's.

Sally saw him first, and when she did, the illusion was gone and he knew that he was old. She had that look that all young girls wore when they met him, but she was frightened too. He knew she had worried for hours and hours about that moment; she had wondered what she might say so that he would like her; and he knew that all those little rehearsals would not help her because they never helped anyone. He could see her now in her right perspective, a little girl somewhat too carefully dressed with too much powder on her nose and her lipstick too meticulously even. He knew that she must have applied it in those last leaden moments before the train came in. Now that he was speaking to her he felt shy and old.

"Well," he said, "hello, Sally."

Then he thought it would have been nicer if he had called her my dear or something a little warmer.

"Hello, Mr. Wilson," Sally said. "It's wonderful that you came to meet us."

He was sure it was not what she had meant to say and that she wished she had said something different.

"Well," Jeffrey said, "I'm awfully glad you're here, dear."

That was more than he had meant to say and he hoped that it did not sound too familiar. When he shook hands with Jim, his eyes kept smarting and for a moment he thought he was going to make a fool of himself right there in front of everyone.

"Hi, Pops," Jim said and Jim's voice was gay and careless and oblivious to so very much, just as his own voice had been once. "Hello, Mr. Gorman," Jim was saying. "How's it going, Mr. Gorman?"

"Busy as a one-armed paperhanger," Mr. Gorman said.

"Let's all three sit in back," Jim said. "Get in, Toots."

That was what he called her, Toots. Jeffrey sat between them in the station wagon and they drove past the liquor package shop and the stationery shop and the chain store and the drugstore and the bank, past the church and out into the country. He was very conscious of Jim and Sally Sales sitting close beside him.

"How have you been, Pops?" Jim asked. "Are you slap-happy?"

"Yes," Jeffrey said, "slap-happy," and he laughed, but the colloquialism disturbed him. He was suddenly tired of all the new words—"streamlined," "blitz," "three-point program," "blueprint." He would never have thought of calling a girl he loved "Toots."

"Where did you get that coat?" he asked.

"At Sill," Jim said. "Those tailors were buzzing around like flies when they gave out commissions."

"It doesn't fit you right," Jeffrey said, "not around the shoulders and chest."

"I know," Jim said. "Sally's noticed it too. There's something the matter with it."

"It gathers up too much in front," Sally said, "doesn't it, Mr. Wilson?" He wished there were something else that she might call him.

"Those tailors make everything too fast," Jeffrey said. "I want you to go in town and get one custom-made. Sally can come with us. We might drive in tomorrow."

He saw Jim glance at him. Jim still took his word for things and still valued his advice. He always could get on with Jim.

"That would be swell," Jim said.

"If you get a coat that fits right," Jeffrey said, "you won't have to keep worrying about yourself. He keeps looking in mirrors, doesn't he, Sally?"

"Yes," Sally said, and she laughed, "he's always sneaking up to mirrors."

"I know," Jeffrey said. "You should have seen the first uniform I bought. . . ."

He looked at the road and at the neat shaved curve of Mr. Gorman's neck. It was growing dusk and the rolling country was filled with shadow. The fields were still green, but the swamp maples were already turning red.

"Jim," Jeffrey asked, "how does it all look?"

"It looks fine," Jim said. "It is like seeing it after you've got out from somewhere."

"I wish you were staying longer," Jeffrey said. "I hope there's enough for you to do—you and Sally."

"Don't worry," Jim said. "There are lots of things to do."

There were all sorts of things that Jeffrey wanted to ask him but he could not ask them then.

"As long as you enjoy yourself," Jeffrey said, "as long as you have a good time." And he smiled at Sally Sales.

"Here's the house," Jim said.

"Oh," Sally said, "I love old houses."

The car stopped at the front door.

"Well," Jeffrey heard himself saying, "here we are!"

That was what you always said no matter where you were. The lights were burning in the windows. The front door had opened because of course they had heard the car and Jeffrey saw Charley with his white trousers and his school tie and Gwen in a short skirt and a canary-yellow sweater and Madge in a tea gown. He could not understand why Madge should have changed into a tea gown. He was wondering how much Jim might be aware of, as they all three walked up the steps, but then, perhaps Jim was not aware of anything. You felt that everybody liked you when you were Jim's age, and Jim was coming home.

"Hello, Mother," Jim called, and kissed his mother, and Madge clung to him for a moment.

"Dear," Madge said, "let me look at you." And she put her hands on Jim's shoulders and looked at him. "It's so funny, dear."

"What's so funny?" Jim asked.

"So funny," Madge said, and there was a catch in her voice, "and so perfect!"

"Jim," Charley said, "you've got your right-hand cannons upside down."

"Well, well," Jim said, "there's the wise little apple." And he smiled at Sally Sales. Jim must have told her about Charley and about the rest of them.

"Oh, Jim," Gwen called, "oh, Jim dear." And she threw her arms around him.

"Break," Jim said. "Come out of it, lovely." And he looked at Sally over Gwen's shoulder.

Sally was standing there alone as she had to while Jim was speaking to everyone. She was standing up straight, smiling nicely, and her lipstick was on very straight.

"Well," Jeffrey said again, "here we are, dear." He called her dear because he wanted her to feel at home. After all there was no reason why he should not have, but he knew that Madge had heard him.

"Mother," Jim said, "wait a minute. This is Sally—Sally Sales."

"Oh," Madge said, and she turned toward Sally. "Dear, I've heard so much about you."

Sally was still smiling. Her lipstick looked very straight.

"It's sweet of you to have me, Mrs. Wilson," she said, and then she stopped. Jeffrey knew that she had been thinking and planning and thinking what to say. "It's sweet of you when I came so suddenly."

"It was sweet of you to come so suddenly," Madge said. "We'll have supper in a few minutes now. Gwen, will you take Sally upstairs to the blue room? You don't mind my calling you Sally, do you, dear?"

Madge was looking at the gabardine tailored suit and at the page bob and at the organdy blouse and at the little bag that Sally was holding which just matched her shoes and at the heels that were too high for her. She was seeing everything at once.

"I'd love it," Sally said. "I'd love it if you would, Mrs. Wilson."

Something about it made Jeffrey wince. He had that awful helplessness of someone in a dream.

"Of course, Mother," he heard Jim say, "yes, of course call her Sally."

A cheerful drum-like voice from the end of the hall started with a roar and ended at a more moderate pitch.

". . . by the courtesy of Your Own Foot Shop. Remember, Your Own Foot Shop where your feet from the street meet a treat. . . ."

Jeffrey whirled on his heel at the sound.

"What the devil's that?" he asked.

It was the radio, of course, and Charley had turned it on.

"It's just the seven-thirty news, Dad," Charley said.

And then they all stood there involuntarily listening, all of them—Madge and Jim and Sally and Gwen—as though the voice had put a stop to all the small cares in the house. The radio made a breaking, crashing sound, although the evening was quite clear. It was Jeffrey's first intimation that a September thunderstorm might end that muggy day.

"Russian resistance continues all along the front with heavy fighting in the vicinity of Moscow. In the meanwhile, the R.A.F. has not been idle. Continuing their air offensive, large bomber formations streaked across the Channel into Western Germany, finding their targets with difficulty because of inclement weather."

Jeffrey raised his voice against the other voice.

"Turn that damn thing off," he shouted at Charley.

46

Conversation in the Small Hours

Before Jeffrey was fully awake his common sense told him that the sound that had awakened him was from one of those thunderstorms that sometimes swept up the valley. Nevertheless there was a familiar booming cadence like guns, and for just an instant when his eyes were closed and he was moving into consciousness, he might have been back where the Squadron slept beyond the flying field. The sound of the thunder was not alarming as much as it was insistent. When the guns had awakened him, their cadence would rise and fall like thunder. As Jeffrey listened a flash of lightning lit up the room where he and Madge were sleeping so that he knew he had been dreaming, but the mood of the dream was left with him.

He felt very definitely that he would not live forever, and then he was wide awake and listening to the rain outside. All at once he felt very weary, for his time had not been severed suddenly in one grand sweep, as it would have been had he died out there when he was young, and as Jim might die. Instead his time had been cut off bit by bit without his having noticed, painlessly but surely. There was the lack of resilience in his muscles and the grayness in his hair. They still said that he looked "so young," but that in itself meant that he could not be young. The years had been cut off one by one without his knowing where they had gone. There were all the things that he meant to do and which he knew he never would. There was that play which he wrote too late, and that was gone. There was Marianna Miller and that was gone—none of it would ever come back, and what there was in the present was not as important as the past.

"Jeff?" He heard Madge call quite softly to him. "Are you awake?"

"Yes," he said, "I'm awake."

"How long has it been storming?"

"I don't know," he said. "It woke me up."

"Do you think it's blowing in anywhere?"

"No," he said, "there isn't any wind. It isn't blowing in."

"Jeff," she said, "turn on the light."

"Why?" he asked. "It's all right. Go to sleep."

"Jeff," she asked, "what were you thinking about?"

"About my sins I guess," he said. "Go to sleep, Madge."

"No," she said. "Turn on the light."

He turned on the light on the bedroom table, and there he was and there she was, and all the present and all the years of their intimacy were back. Madge had propped herself up on her elbow and was looking at him across the space between their twin beds.

"Jeff," she said, "I don't see what he sees in her."

"What?" Jeffrey asked. "Who?"

Then he realized they were back exactly where they had been before they went to sleep. He heard Madge sigh.

"Jeff," Madge said, "you must have thought—you couldn't help thinking . . . she was very unattractive."

Then Jeffrey sighed. He wished that Madge did not feel it necessary to go over Sally Sales in the middle of the night.

"I don't know, Madge," Jeffrey said. "I told you I didn't know what I saw in her. All girls that age look alike. There isn't anything to see. When Gwen grows up she'll look like that. They all do."

"Gwen will *not!*" Madge said.

"All right," Jeffrey said, "all right, she won't look like that, unless she can't help it. They all wear the same clothes. They all do the same things. It's life."

"They don't all do the same things," Madge said. "Gwen is a lady, at least she ought to be."

"Gwen is an overmannered silly little girl," Jeffrey said.

"Jeff," Madge said, "why do you keep saying that again and again? I've told you and I've told you Gwen is simply going through a phase. All girls go through it and all girls get over it."

"Well, it's a hell of a phase," Jeffrey said. "I don't believe the Sales girl ever went through any phase like that. If I had to pick between the two of them to live on a desert island with, I'd pick Sales."

Madge laughed softly but not agreeably.

"What's the joke?" Jeffrey asked.

Madge laughed again softly but not agreeably.

"You," Madge said. "Dear, you're amazing sometimes."

"Oh," Jeffrey said, "am I?"

"Sometimes I think you know so much about people," Madge said, "and then you show your blind spot; but then only women can judge women."

"Darling," Jeffrey said, and he laughed too, "didn't someone say that before?"

"Darling," Madge said, "I'm not finding fault. I know you can't help it, because you do have a very queer taste in women. I don't mean vulgar exactly. I just mean queer. Now I know you like that Mrs. Newcombe. I do watch you sometimes, darling. I suppose it's because you've been in the theater so much, where everyone is overdressed and overemphasized and overemotional. There are all those theater people like Marianna Miller."

Jeffrey sat up straighter in bed.

"Madge," he said, "maybe I'd better go downstairs and see about the windows. It's a little windier now. It may be blowing in."

"I don't know why you always change the subject when I talk about Marianna," Madge said, "because I like her, Jeff. I really like her very much. I know how good she is professionally, but you know what I mean. There are all sorts of little things about her that you seem to miss."

"What," Jeffrey said. "What sort of things do I seem to miss?"

"All sorts of little things," Madge said. "And you're so sensitive and so perceptive sometimes. You're able to be so devastating about so many people. You tear poor Fred and Beckie apart, for instance, and yet you don't see any of those things in Marianna Miller."

"What things?" Jeffrey asked.

It was as though he had been awakened again by the sound of the thunder. Madge seemed to be talking unnecessarily about something which was over long ago.

"I like her, dear," Madge said. "I like her very much and she's very sweet in a great many ways, but I don't see why you've never seen that she's a little on the dull side. I suppose it's her looks that make you miss it. And she is pretty when you add her features all together and don't take them individually. I know she has a certain charm, and I love having her with company because she's so gay. But I don't see why you don't see that she's overemotional and a little vulgar."

"Vulgar?" Jeffrey asked. "Why is she vulgar?"

"Now don't be hurt, dear," Madge said. "Perhaps I shouldn't have said vulgar, but egotistical, and there are any number of other little things—"

"Go ahead," Jeffrey said, "what little things?"

Madge laughed again and this time her laugh was soft and happy.

"Darling," she said, "you'd find out in a day if you'd ever lived with her. There are all sorts of things that would drive you crazy and that's why I've never worried about Marianna—little small-town cosmetic-counter things—that Bellodgia, clouds and clouds of Bellodgia, and those billowy dresses and that bouncy little obvious way she has, and that sort of a night-club-hostess voice. Of course, you don't notice because all a man sees is her face. He wouldn't see that she doesn't wash behind the ears."

"My God," Jeffrey said, "Marianna washes all the time. . . . She washes and washes."

"Why, Jeffrey," Madge asked, "how do you know how much she washes?"

"Perhaps I just assume it," Jeffrey said. "Never mind it, Madge."

"I don't mind it," Madge said, and she laughed again. "I always feel perfectly safe when you're with Marianna, because I know you couldn't stand her for a day, but I didn't mean to be hard on Marianna. I just brought her up, just as an example, because—"

"Because what?" Jeffrey asked and he sat up straighter.

"Because it shows you're so oblivious in some ways. Now that little thing —what's her name? I keep forgetting it."

Madge puckered her forehead and smiled, seemingly amused by her own forgetfulness, but of course she knew her name.

"You mean Sally Sales?" Jeffrey asked. They were back again with Sally Sales. No matter how long he lived he still made curious and disturbing discoveries about himself. There in the middle of the night he seemed to be more involved with Sally Sales than he was with Marianna Miller, perhaps because of his earlier thought that Marianna Miller and all that he associated with her was gone for good, cut off by time, while Jim was still a part of him. He could see Jim helping Sally from the train and that light on her hair and that embarrassed understanding between them, and her loneliness in the hall.

"Of course," Madge said, "I don't know why I keep forgetting. Sally Sales. Jeff, didn't it occur to you, really, that she's a little common? That's what I can't understand in Jim, because I would have thought Jim would see it. He's always been very fastidious. You do admit, don't you, that she's common?"

"How do you mean?" Jeffrey asked, and he was anxious to know. He did not want Sally Sales to be common.

"Any woman would see," Madge said. "Of course, superficially she's rather pretty, and she has a pretty figure. I suppose you noticed her figure?"

"If she's all right superficially, what's wrong with her?" Jeffrey asked. "And I didn't notice her figure."

Madge sighed again and looked straight ahead of her at the shadows in the corner of the room, as though she were conjuring up Sally Sales and her pretty figure.

"Her ankles, Jeff," Madge said. "Didn't you notice her ankles?"

"Yes, I did," Jeffrey said. "She couldn't help it. She was wearing high-heeled shoes."

"Yes," Madge said. "Those dreadful little shoes and the bag that matched."

"No kid knows how to dress," Jeffrey said, "when she's as young as that."

"Her mother might have taught her," Madge said. "It shows where she came from."

"My God," Jeffrey said, "look what Gwen manages to buy when you let her in a store. No young girl knows how to dress."

"Darling," Madge said. "Gwen's years younger, and she's going through a phase, and suppose you let me worry about Gwen's clothes, and don't keep comparing her with Gwen."

"I only say," Jeffrey said, "that no young girl knows how to dress, and no boy does either. You've got to be older before you know how to wear clothes. Look at that uniform of Jim's."

"He was stunning in it," Madge said. "What's the matter with it?"

"Never mind," Jeffrey said. "I wish you wouldn't be so hard on her, Madge."

"I'm not, dear," Madge said. "I feel a little sorry for her really—but that hair-do and the lipstick—ugh, that lipstick!"

"Kids don't know about lipstick when they first try it out," Jeffrey said. "You didn't know about it. Ugh, your own lipstick!"

"Why, Jeff," Madge said, and she laughed, "why haven't you ever told me you didn't like it, dear?"

"Because I'm not a woman," Jeffrey said, "thank God; and what about Gwen's lipstick?"

"Jeffrey," Madge said, "please. Don't keep trotting out poor little Gwen, when she's going through a phase."

"All right," Jeffrey said, "maybe little Sales is going through a phase."

"I hope she is, dear," Madge said, "but I don't think she'll change much. She's a little old to change."

"Old?" Jeffrey repeated. "My God, Madge!"

"Not in terms of you and me, dear," Madge said, "but if you notice her eyes and forehead you'll see what I mean. Of course she's older than Jim—perhaps three or four years older."

"Well, she isn't," Jeffrey said. "She's just nineteen."

Madge laughed.

"Why darling," she said, "I didn't know you'd got so far with her. It didn't seem to me she said anything to anybody. When did she tell you? After dinner?"

"She didn't tell me," Jeffrey answered. "Jim told me."

"Jim?" Madge repeated. "Why don't you ever tell me anything, Jeff? I tried to talk to Jim about her and he was so self-conscious and elusive—What else did Jim tell you, Jeff?"

"Ask Jim," Jeffrey said. "He can tell you if he wants."

"Don't be so mysterious, dear," Madge said. "Please don't act as if Jim were grown-up and you were men sticking together."

"I'm only being fair," Jeffrey said. "She's his girl, she isn't mine. Go ahead. What else is wrong with her?"

Madge looked at him sharply and her forehead wrinkled.

"Jeff," she said, "you act as if she were your girl. You really do."

It startled Jeffrey, because she was right in a way.

"You're not jealous, are you?" he asked.

The wrinkles in her forehead deepened.

"Darling," she said, "I suppose you read that somewhere, the mother-son complex. I suppose I'm secretly in love myself with Jim and I don't know it. Jeff, you must have noticed her voice. You're so sensitive to voices. And the words she used. Everything was 'sweet, sweet, sweet.'"

"Listen, Madge," Jeffrey said. "Don't you know she was scared to death? Don't you see she's awfully young?"

"I wish you'd stop it, Jeff!" Madge said, and her voice had a wholly different note. "Don't keep saying she's young."

"Well, she is," Jeffrey said. "She's young."

"If you keep saying that," Madge said, "I'll scream! Do you or don't you want Jim to marry her?"

"Madge," Jeffrey said, "the storm's over now. Let's turn out the light and go to sleep." But she said it again.

"Do you," she asked, "or don't you want Jim to marry her?"

"My God," Jeffrey said, "I don't know. Let's turn out the light and go to sleep."

"You don't know?" Madge repeated, and her voice rose higher. "You don't know?"

"No," Jeffrey answered. "It just seems to me he's in love with her, awfully in love with her, and she's awfully in love with him. You and I don't know what may happen. We were awfully in love ourselves once, Madge." He was sorry for her because she was as much involved with it as he was and she too was identified with Jim. She too was living his life vicariously and passionately, and there was nothing you could do about it the way the world was going. The thunder was moving off eastward to the Sound but it still sounded like artillery. The air was fresher as it always was after rain.

"Oh, Jeff," she said.

He did not answer.

"Jeff, I wish you wouldn't keep acting as if Jim were going to die."

It made him answer very quickly.

"I never said that," he answered. "And don't you say it, either, Madge."

"You act that way," Madge said.

"Madge," Jeffrey said, "I'm tired. Let's go to sleep."

"Jeff," she began, "oh, Jeff, don't you see . . ."

There was enough light in the sky to show the outlines of the maple branches against the window. He could see the leaves moving softly because a light breeze was coming up. He was listening to her ideas and everything she said was true. It was absurd because they were so young. Their characters were not developed and they both might realize later that they had made a mistake. Then there was the matter of difference of background. She and Jeffrey had struggled with that difference—and how could Jim marry a girl if he could not support her? As soon as Jim saw her with some nice girls . . . Jeffrey lay there listening and staring at the dark.

"They've been in love quite a while," he said.

He lay there listening, staring at the dark. There were those verses from Ecclesiastes again. For everything there was a season, a time to love and a time to hate, a time to laugh and a time to weep, and a time to live. The way things were going, God knew there was not much time.

47

Just around the Corner

Jeffrey was old enough to know that nothing ever turned out quite the way one hoped, but he had looked forward for a long time to those ten days when Jim would be at home. He had thought of them ever since he had come to the country that June and he had not considered them entirely in terms of himself. He had thought of the whole family being together, and of getting back again to the family where he belonged. He was more conscious than he ever had been before that Madge and the children were all that mattered and all that he had left. Then, also, there were all those things that he wanted to say to Jim, now that Jim was grown-up, but for which there seemed to be no time now that Jim was back. Jeffrey felt as though he were only standing watching in a helpless sort of way, listening to the children's voices and to Jim's voice, and somehow he was not an essential part of it. Everything seemed to be going very well without him, almost as though he were not there.

Madge said, because Madge was conscious of it too, that Jim's infatuation for Sally Sales had spoiled it all, and sometimes Jeffrey agreed with her, but not entirely. He did not want to impose on Jim; he only wished that he were not standing looking while the time went by, because there were so many things he wanted to do with Jim which he thought Jim would like. He told himself that it was not Jim's fault, that Jim had no time for him.

He did not want Jim to feel any obligation toward him and he told himself so carefully every day. Yet when Jim got his orders in the middle of the week to report to a camp near Portland, Oregon, Jeffrey wished that they might have gone over Jim's plans together. Jeffrey could have told him a good deal about the West Coast and Oregon. He still felt that he knew camps and the army better than Jim did. There were things that might make you very unhappy in the army if you did not understand them. When you were young, for instance, all field officers seemed very old and as far removed from the realities of military life as a group of strange animals. When a young officer came in contact with his superiors he generally considered them overbearing and stupid and usually they were. Nevertheless, he wanted to tell Jim that this apparent stupidity and this West Point conceit, which every civilian officer hated, was apt to cloak a distinct combative ability when you got into a fight. He wanted Jim to realize that he must suspend judgment on majors and colonels and to realize that they were not as bad as you thought they were. He wanted to tell Jim a great many things that had happened in the A.E.F. in France which he had never told anyone, but which he thought might be useful if they got into war. He wanted to tell Jim to remember that everyone was afraid and not to be ashamed of it. He wanted Jim to realize that there were times to be careful and times not to be. He wanted to tell Jim about Stan Rhett that day they were shot down; and there never seemed to be an opportunity—never the time or the place. Madge or Charley was always there, or Sally Sales. There was never any time.

Jim came into that bare room of his two days before he was to leave. Jeffrey always remembered it as one of those rare moments which come when you least expect them. It was ten o'clock on a hot Monday morning and he was reading the *New York Times,* avidly skimming over each dispatch with the hope that he might come on something reassuring between the lines. He was reading one of those accounts of a bombing raid over Germany—"bad weather over the Channel but the clouds had cleared away over the target." Somehow the clouds in those dispatches always cleared away, and the bombs were dropped through a heavy fire of ack-ack—Archies, as they used to call them in the other war—and then there were a few terse lines from a pilot or an observer. "We hit them on the button this time. The fires were visible for thirty miles."

Then Jim knocked on the door.

"Are you busy?" Jim asked.

"No," Jeffrey said, "I'm not busy."

Jim stood leaning against the side of the half-open door, exactly as he had years before when he wanted to ask something.

"I haven't seen much of you," Jim said. "If you're not busy how about you and Sally and me taking a picnic and going somewhere?"

"Oh, no," Jeffrey said, "you and Sally had better go alone."

"No," Jim said. "No. Sally thought of it."

It was strange how tactless one could be when one was young. He would have given a great deal if Jim had thought of it instead. Somehow it did not seem fair to Madge, going off with Sally and Jim, but he knew that it was a chance he might never have again.

"All right," he said, "we'll take a bottle of wine."

It had been a long time since Jeffrey had even considered going on a picnic. The summer he and Madge were first married and owned their first car, they had bought a picnic basket with cups and plates and two thermos bottles which had cost sixty-five dollars, but somehow the picnic basket had not worked. Now it must have been given away long ago, or else it was in the attic somewhere with all those other forgotten objects of the past.

Jeffrey could remember a number of reasons why those picnics had been discontinued. Madge would say how nice it would be to go for a picnic, just she and Jeffrey and a book, and if Jeffrey did not want to read, Madge would read aloud as long as Jeffrey did not go to sleep. Then they would get the picnic basket, which was very heavy when it was filled with ice and sandwiches and milk and tea. Then they would get in the automobile—it was one of those four-cylinder Dodges, Jeffrey remembered, which seemed capable of lasting forever. They would get into the Dodge and the top would rattle and Madge was always distracted when it rattled, because it was her Dodge, not his Dodge. It was always a sunny morning like the present one, for picnics and the sun always went together. Jeffrey would begin to feel very hungry after motoring for a while, and he would say to Madge, "How about stopping here, or here, or here and eating?" But Madge would never want to stop here or here. Madge had a number of definite requirements for a picnic place. She always wanted it to be "cozy," which was a term which covered almost anything, and then it had to be near a brook without any cows. It was amazing when you looked how few brooks there were, and all of them had cows. Sometimes they would even get to the brook and then along would come the cows and they would have to close the basket up and go. Jeffrey had always told Madge that cows in pastures were harmless, but Madge always said there might be a bull. Jeffrey said you could always tell a bull by his general contours if nothing else, and Madge said she did not want to get near enough any cow to judge.

He and Madge would ride and ride looking for that brook and that "cozy" place, and Jeffrey was always dull about suggesting here and here. He did not seem to have the spirit of picnicking, and Madge did not want to stop there or there either. They could go a little farther and then they would find it, or just a little farther still, because they had all day. Finally a time would come when Jeffrey would say he had to eat and why not stop the car and eat in the car? And Madge would not eat in the car. They would stop over there, just around the corner, and when they stopped over there, there was no brook, nothing but paper cups which other people had left. There was never any place to sit, except hard rocks or soft moist sod, and Madge would ask him why he hadn't stopped back there—miles back where she had thought of stopping. And while they ate he would explain to Madge that she was the one who had told him to go on, and not stop there, and Madge would not remember that she had said any such thing. Madge would ask him why he wouldn't sit down and be comfortable and not stand up munching a sandwich and looking as though someone were going to come out of the farm on the hill and chase them. They had just crawled under the barbed-wire fence and of course the farmer wouldn't mind. Then Jeffrey would say that there wasn't anything to sit on, and besides he liked to eat standing up.

Then, as he stood there with his sandwich and one of those paper coffee cups that always burned his fingers, Jeffrey was always reminded of something else, which may have been why picnics never worked. Wherever they might be, all at once the field and the woods and even the cozy brook assumed a sinister aspect. Although he never said a thing about it to Madge, because it was absurd, there was always a quality for him in the sun and the stillness that reminded him of that field in France and that patch of woods where he and Stan Rhett had been shot down. He and Stan Rhett, always young, would seem to be there with Stan leaning heavily on his shoulder. It was absurd, but he would always feel the old watchful attitude and he would find himself staring around him carefully, and Madge would tell him to sit down, to please for heaven's sake sit down.

Jeffrey had not been on a picnic for years and years with Madge or with anyone. Even in California when Marianna had suggested one, he had told her no, that he was not good at picnics.

Yet, when Jim spoke of it that morning he was surprised to feel a sense of anticipation that included no thoughts of rocks or cows or hardship. His mind had gone further back to a time when he was younger even than Jim, to a time when there were family picnics at Bragg, when you hitched the horse to a tree and gave him a bag of oats and Jeffrey and Alf went swimming somewhere, while his father and his aunt and Ethel set out the things. You did not mind where you sat then, and his aunt had always said that food always tasted better outdoors, and it did taste better outdoors then. There was a fresh scent of flowers in the fields and a more subtle scent of leaves and that basking heat of summer. You were never tired. Your muscles were never stiff. You never needed a drink to make it bearable. That was the way he felt when Jim asked him to go. It was like being offered something that had belonged to him once and which had been lost for a long while.

Jim and Sally had planned the picnic before they had invited him, because the station wagon was out by the front door already with the picnic in the back seat and with Sally waiting to get in. They must have just been leaving when the idea struck them that they should ask him.

Sally was wearing a green pull-over sweater, the sleeves of which were pushed up. Madge was right; Sally did have a good figure and carried her head and shoulders very well. She had on a short flannel skirt and her legs were bare. Girls never wore stockings any more. She was wearing low-heeled sandals that showed her toes between the strips of braided leather.

She was smiling at him as though she were a pretty girl he was going to take somewhere—as though he and she were going somewhere alone.

"It's awfully nice you asked me," Jeffrey said. As soon as he spoke her expression changed and he was old and she was young. He saw her glance toward Jim, and Jeffrey wished he did not know so much because he knew exactly what was going through her mind. She was thinking that Jim should never have told him, that Jim had spoiled some of it.

"Jim almost thought of it," she said. It was exactly as though she owned Jim and yet as though they both owned him, and as though they both knew a great deal more about Jim than he knew about himself.

"Come on," Jim said, "let's go. I'm getting hungry."

It sounded like Jeffrey's own voice years back telling Madge—"Let's go."

"Jim," Sally said, "have you brought a book?" And she smiled at Jeffrey. "I always like to bring a book and Jim always forgets it."

"It doesn't matter," Jim said. "We never get to reading it."

"Jim," Sally said, but she laughed.

"We've been on a whale of a lot of picnics," Jim said, "last summer and the summer before, and we've never read a book yet."

Sally laughed again.

"We might," she said. "We ought to."

"We ought to, but we don't," Jim said, and then he looked at Jeffrey. "Sally's hell for picnics. I know why it is—she's never had to eat outdoors."

"You two get in the front seat," Jeffrey told them. "I'll sit in back with the lunch."

"Oh, no, don't," Sally said. "There's lots of room in front."

That was what girls always said when Jeffrey was young. It was always crowded but there was always room in front.

"Come on," Jim said, "let's go!"

Jeffrey felt very anxious to get away before anyone saw them from the house, before the telephone rang or before Madge came back from town, before anything could spoil it. The September sunlight was softer and yellower than August and nothing that he saw felt as if it belonged to the present.

" 'We're going to a happy land,' " Jim was singing, " 'where everything is bright, where the highballs grow on bushes and we stay out every night.' "

Jeffrey turned toward him very quickly.

"Now where did you learn that?" he asked.

"They sing it out in Sill," Jim said. "It's an old Air Corps song, I guess."

"Yes," Jeffrey said: " 'Where you never lift a finger, not even darn your socks, and little drops of Haig and Haig come trickling down the rocks.' "

"Let's eat," Jim said. "When do we eat?"

"When we find a nice place," Sally said. "We'll find one pretty soon."

"How about finding one now?" Jim said. "How about right here?"

"No," Sally said, "not here. There must be cows in there."

"Yes," Jeffrey said, "there must be cows, and besides there might be a bull."

"Sally's always looking for a nice place," Jim said, "and you can't tell what she means."

"Jim doesn't understand it," Sally said. "He just wants to stop anywhere beside the road."

"How about here?" Jim asked. "Here's a nice place."

"No," Sally said. "Let's go a little farther."

"You tell us, Sally," Jim asked, "what you mean by a nice place."

"I know," Jeffrey said. "There has to be a brook in it."

"Of course there has to be," Sally said.

"And pine trees and moss and rocks and ferns and hay and no papers," Jim said.

"You see, he'll never wait long enough," Sally said. "But I'm right about it. There has to be everything."

"My dear," Jeffrey said, "there has to be, but there never is—not ever."

"There's no harm in wanting there to be," Sally said.

"No," Jeffrey told her, "no harm at all."

"I just mean," Sally said, "it seems to me silly not to be happy when you have a chance, and you have a chance when you go on a picnic. That's what I mean."

"Listen, Toots," Jim said, "how can you be happy if you don't eat? How about stopping right here and eating in the car?"

"He always wants to eat in the car," Sally said. "Jim dear—"

Then she stopped.

"Go ahead and call him that," Jeffrey said, "if that's the way you feel about him."

"Jim dear," Sally said, "let's go on a little longer, just around the bend."

"There'll always be another bend," Jim said.

"No," Sally answered, "just this one."

"Promise?" Jim asked her.

"Yes," she answered, "promise."

"Boy," Jim said, "it looks as though we're going to eat! We're going to eat even if it's a junk yard."

Once during the next summer even in spite of the gas rationing Jeffrey took the station wagon by himself and tried to find the place. When he sat alone in the front seat he tried to think of Jim and Sally as being there with him. He tried to fit those trivial bits of conversation again to the landmarks as he passed them. No, not here; there were cows here. No, not there; it wasn't a pretty place. There had to be a brook and everything, and there was no harm in wanting everything.

"I want to eat," he could hear Jim say. "We've got to eat sometime, Toots."

Jeffrey knew the country very well. They had driven up the concrete road. He remembered the turn to the right on the tar road, and where the roads forked, and where they had taken the dirt road to the left. Ever since the last war Jeffrey had noticed terrain and hills and woods, and his mind sorted them out carefully whether he wanted it to or not, but when he tried that next summer, he could not find the place, certainly not for sure. There was a maddening similarity about those bends in the road, so that he could not recall the bend where Jim had said promise and Sally had said, yes, promise. He knew there was a brook and a barbed-wire fence, but he found two brooks and two bends and he could not tell which was the right one. It was gone like Jim and everything else, and perhaps he was glad that it was gone, for it could always be something to remember that belonged to the three of them and to no one else.

At any rate it was not a bad place. There was a brook, a rather wide brook with a sandy bottom, and Jeffrey remembered distinctly that there were trees growing near it, because he remembered the sun and shadows on the water. There was a bank where they sat looking at the water and a rock against which Jeffrey had leaned his back and it was not a bad rock either. Sally had gone in wading. She had left her sandals beside the rock.

"She always goes in wading," Jim said, "whenever she sees a brook, and she's that way whenever she's on the beach. Come on, Toots, we're hungry!"

"Yes," she called, "I'm coming."

"She always likes to set the things out," Jim said. "And she polices it afterwards. She's pretty good that way."

When Jeffrey heard the word, the war was back again and he stared up at the sky.

"Sometime," he said, "I'd like to talk to you about war, but never mind it now."

"No," Jim said quickly, "Sally, she—Well, never mind it now."

"It gives you a different point of view," Jeffrey said. "I've never lost it, quite."

"What point of view?" Jim asked.

Jeffrey still looked at the sky. It was very clear. There was not a cloud in it, not a sound in it, nothing.

"It won't be long now," Jeffrey said. "That's one way to put it."

Then he looked at Jim. He could not keep his eyes from Jim because Jim looked as though time could never touch him.

"How do you mean," Jim asked, "it won't be long now?"

"Boy," Jeffrey said, and he smiled because he knew something that Jim didn't. "Maybe you'll never know. I hope to God you won't."

Sally was on her knees taking out the picnic and laying it on the ground, and Jim was saying he didn't care how it looked if he could eat. When he reached for a sandwich, Sally slapped his wrist and Jim turned and kissed her quickly before she could guess what he was going to do.

"Jim!" Sally said.

"Don't say 'You stop,'" Jim said. "You had it coming to you."

It was completely unexpected, but they must have been doing that sort of thing for a long, long time, and it caused Jeffrey no embarrassment. It seemed quite all right that he was there.

They ate the sandwiches and drank the wine and coffee. He listened to Jim and Sally talking and Madge had been wrong about Sally. Her voice was not bad at all. It was a contented voice. He was not conscious of her actual words because he was thinking of one thing she had said—"silly not to be happy when you have a chance. . . ."

"I'm going to walk up the brook," she was saying to him. "I'm going to sit somewhere under a tree. You haven't had a chance to talk to Jim."

It was easy to see why Jim liked her.

"No," he said, "don't go away. There's something I want to talk to you and Jim about. I suppose it's none of my business. No one can mind his own business really. Maybe you'll find it out someday."

He stopped because he was afraid of being wheezy and portentous, and then he went on.

"It's a funny thing to say to you, but I think this is the last quiet summer we're going to have for quite a while. You two kids like each other quite a lot, don't you?" He waited and they did not answer, and he spoke louder. "Don't you?"

"Yes, sir," Jim said. "I'll say we do."

Jeffrey smiled. He always could get on with Jim.

"All right," he said. "This is a time when, if you love someone, you'd better love her."

It was not exactly what he had meant to say but now he had started, he spoke more quickly.

"I mean, if you kids want to get married, you'd better get married. It may not work, but—you haven't got much time. I mean a lot by that. I mean before you die you want to live. I'd do it before anybody tells you differently. I'd do it—right away."

"Right away?" Jim repeated after him.

"I don't mean that exactly," Jeffrey said, "but if you want to, this is between you and me. I'll do the talking afterwards and don't worry about money. . . . I have fifty thousand dollars in stocks and bonds, but you'd better think fast, both of you. You haven't got much time."

48

The Little Men

In his last letter to Sally, Jeffrey had mentioned that he would be at the Hotel Shoreham in Washington early in November with Jesse Fineman and the cast of the play which Jesse was preparing for Broadway. Jesse had been unusually worried about this particular play, and Jeffrey thought with reason. They had tried it out in Bridgeport; they had tried it out in Baltimore; and it was not ready yet. Jesse felt it had the intrinsic qualities but not what he called the "sweep," and that was why they were trying it in Washington for three nights. Jeffrey had never approved of it and he had told Jesse so. He had told Jesse that it was too much like the Sherwood play "There Shall Be No Night."

It was one of those plays the scene of which was laid in an occupied country of Europe. There was a family of happy folksy people with liberal leanings. There was a pretty girl with pigtails, and not much else, and a neurotic brother who wanted to be a composer—You knew he was a composer because he kept ticking a metronome at odd moments during each act—and a comfortable bourgeois father who ran some sort of a cannery, and a mother who fried things in the kitchen and kept bringing in plate after plate of them all through the acts, for the family to eat when they were emotionally disturbed. Then came the Nazis—stamp, stamp, *Heil Hitler!*—and talked of the New

Order. Then you saw each member of the family reacting to the New Order, and then the man from the Gestapo in his black leather coat who loved the girl with the pigtails. You can imagine what he did to the girl with the pigtails and what all the other Himmler employees did to the father when he came home from the cannery and to her brother when he dropped his metronome and tried to break down the door. It was what Jesse called a stark, ruthless work. They stepped all over that family in the second act, and continued stepping on them in the third act, and then shot them in the last five minutes—all except the girl with pigtails who would have been better, far better, dead. Yet through it all was that unconquerable spirit. You stepped on them but you could not conquer them. Jesse said it had the message, it had everything, and when Jeffrey said it was the same old pap Jesse was very hurt and asked Jeffrey if he was turning into a fascist or an isolationist, and whether he believed or did not believe in democracy. That was the trouble with everyone in November 1941. They could not discuss art or entertainment without bringing in long and indigestible words.

Jeffrey told Jesse that it did not matter whether he was pro-Semitic or anti-Semitic, or a Stalinist or a Trotskyist, or a Liberal or one of Mr. Pelley's Silver Shirts—it was a poor play and no one would want to sit through it, and Jesse could call him a fascist if he wanted.

Jesse said it showed that Jeffrey was fascist-minded though perhaps he might not know it. It was the nearest Jeffrey had ever come to quarreling with Jesse. But then that autumn everyone was close to quarreling. He told Jesse that he was tired of reading books and seeing plays in which everyone was stepped on. He would like to see a play for a change where some of those people who believed in democracy bashed a few Nazis over the head; and Jeffrey believed it might make a play if the family killed a few Nazis in the last act and escaped over the border with some of the mother's fried food. He and Jesse were scarcely speaking when they got to Bridgeport, but after Baltimore, Jesse said that perhaps Jeffrey was right. He asked him if he could change the last act, and that was why they were at the Shoreham.

Everyone in the world was in Washington that November—so many people that there were no tables in the restaurants, no rooms in the hotels, no seats in taxicabs. It had turned abruptly into the center of the world.

The lobby of the Shoreham was crowded like every other hotel lobby in Washington, so filled with people day and night that there was hardly time to clean the carpets. The air was heavy with constantly shifting humanity. Suitcases and brief cases were piled in front of the hotel desk. There were business men fighting for priorities and generals and colonels and admirals and midshipmen and members of the British Mission. It was no place to try out a play or to work on one.

When Jeffrey left his key at the desk, the clerk, whom he had known quite well in past years, handed him a letter with an Air Mail stamp and he saw that it was in Sally's handwriting. He opened it and read it by the desk without minding being jostled and without being disturbed by the voices.

I wish you could see the camp here [Sally wrote, and it was still that queer progressive-school printing] and our bungalow. It only has three rooms and when it rains the bedroom leaks. Jim is away at the range and won't be back until late tonight. It's very funny being an officer's wife and seeing regular army officers' wives who have moved around everywhere. Mrs. Sykes, that's Jim's C.O.'s wife you know, has asked me in to tea this afternoon. Yesterday at the hotel the colonel asked me who I was, and when I said I was Jim's wife he said that Jim was a good soldier. That means a lot, in case you don't know it, because those officers are very snotty, just the way you said they would be. When they say someone is a good soldier it means he really might have got by at the Point and that he ought to be wearing one of those rings. I'm awfully busy all the time and I must dash off now with Mrs. Jason—they're the ones who share the bungalow with us, you know. If Jim were here he would send you his love. Don't bother about his not writing. You know how Jim is about letters. He hardly ever wrote any to me. If you are going out to the Coast the way you say you are, the Jasons say they will move out somewhere and you can have their room if you come for Christmas, or else we can get a barracks bed and put it in the living room and we can all sort of be in together. Do come for Christmas. There isn't anything else I can tell you yet, at least I don't think so, but perhaps there will be at Christmas. We're awfully happy and I love you,

SALLY

He stood with his overcoat over his arm and his hat on the back of his head still looking at her letter and Jim and Sally were with him as he held it. The letter gave him a sort of vicarious pleasure for a moment and then the illusion faded and he was conscious of the crowds around him.

"Take them up to 717, boy," he heard someone saying, "and leave the key and keep the change. I'm not going up."

The voice fell on Jeffrey's ears, suave and familiar, and he looked up and saw Minot Roberts. There was no reason why Minot should not have been there because everyone in the world was in Washington that autumn. Minot was wearing a polo coat and holding a pair of pigskin gloves. Something in the way he held his head made him stand out among all the people in the lobby.

"Well, well," Minot said. "Are you doing it too?"

"Doing what?" Jeffrey asked.

"Going down to the Munitions Building," Minot said. "Lining up with all the other boys."

"Why the Munitions Building?" Jeffrey asked.

Minot put his arm through his.

"Come on," Minot said, "Air Corps headquarters, boy. The line is forming on the right. Come on. Let's go."

"Do you mean you're joining up?" Jeffrey asked.

Somehow the old pilots wanted to get into it again more than anybody else. Yet in a certain way it surprised Jeffrey to see Minot so oblivious to time. Minot was not as young as he had been once.

"Swinburne," Minot said, "you know Bill Swinburne. I've got a date with him at eleven-thirty. Have you been writing to Bill?"

"No," Jeffrey said, "not yet."

"Then what in hell are you doing here?" Minot said.

"Just a play," Jeffrey said. "Just the same old thing."

"Oh hell," Minot said, "you come down with me. It won't hurt you to see Bill. They're going to want us back."

"Why?" Jeffrey asked. "Why should they?"

Minot's eyes opened as if he had never asked himself the question.

"Of course they'll want us back," he said. "My God, look at Bill, and who is Bill? And he's right in there with the General all the time. The General can't leave him alone for a minute."

"Why can't he?" Jeffrey asked. "I could."

"Come on," Minot said. "Bill will fix us up."

"I'll go downtown with you," Jeffrey said, "but I'm not going any farther unless there's a war."

"Look around you," Minot said. "Isn't this a war already? Come on, let's go!"

"I'll go downtown with you," Jeffrey said, and he laughed. "I can't drop everything. I'm not in your position."

"You'll be sorry," Minot said.

He had not seen Minot so happy for a long while. Minot kept whistling while they waited for a cab outside.

"You'll be sorry, boy," Minot said. "God, I can't tell you what it does to you when you make up your mind. It may be Iceland; it may be Africa. Bill knows I know Africa."

"Just why," Jeffrey asked him, "should anyone be sending you to Africa?"

"Boom-boom," Minot said. "Boom-boom!" He was making a sound like African drums. "Well, maybe it's Honolulu, Yaaka-hula, Hikki-dula!"

Jeffrey wished that Minot would calm down. He had not seen him so gay in a long while. It gave him an uncomfortable illusion, which he had often felt before with Minot, that the war had never stopped. He did not speak for a while as they drove down Connecticut Avenue. Washington had never been finished, and sometimes he thought it never would be even if the United States lived as a nation for a thousand years. Washington seemed to Jeffrey that November morning like a replica of the nation it represented. There was the same widespread ambition, the pride and the complacency and the squalor all together; and Washington would never be finished. It would never be static like Paris or grimy like London or smug and ugly like Berlin. It would always be spreading out and building and changing as the nation changed. Jeffrey could see what was wrong with it. As they came nearer the Capitol he could see the portentous monstrosity of the Commerce and the Agriculture buildings. He could see the sterile marble imitations of the classic . . . but taken altogether, Washington made him proud.

"Minot," he said, "you've got a half hour yet; let's get out and walk."

"All right," Minot said. "Let's go."

There was no other city that gave Jeffrey a sense of ownership like Washington—not even New York where he had lived so long. He felt free to criticize every aspect of Washington because it belonged to him as it did to everyone else. He had been taxed enough to pay for quite a piece of it, particularly in the last few years. He felt perfectly free to think what he thought of all the buildings and of all the parks and circles and fountains.

"Jeff," Minot asked, "is Marianna Miller here?"

"No," Jeffrey said, "she isn't. I wish you'd get Marianna out of your head, Minot."

"I was just asking," Minot said, "that's all. How's Madge?"

"Madge is fine," Jeffrey said. "I thought of bringing her down but I'm pretty busy now."

"The hell you did," Minot said.

"The hell I didn't," Jeffrey answered.

"How's Jim?" Minot asked. "Have you heard from Jim?"

"I got a letter just now," Jeffrey answered, "back at the hotel. They're fine. Jim's all right."

Minot was walking briskly and he did not speak for a moment. They were near the State Department and Jeffrey looked at his watch. He was thinking that Minot would have to get another taxi to get to the Munitions Building.

"I don't understand it about Jim," Minot said. "I don't see what made him marry her."

"Well, he did," Jeffrey said.

"Well, it's tough," Minot answered. "I'm just telling you. I wouldn't tell anyone else."

"Maybe it is," Jeffrey answered. "You and I aren't Jim."

"That's right," Minot said. "Stand up for him."

"Of course I'll stand up for him."

Minot put his hand on Jeffrey's shoulder and it reminded Jeffrey that Minot was his oldest friend and his irritation died.

"Of course you will," Minot said. "You say you're not supporting them. They can't live on a lieutenant's pay—"

It was like Madge and it was like Minot. They always thought in terms of money because they had always had it.

"It's all right, Minot," Jeffrey said. "Sally had a little money."

"How much?" Minot asked.

"Not much," Jeffrey answered. "About fifty thousand dollars."

"Fifty thousand," Minot said. "That isn't much, but it's something."

"Yes," Jeffrey said and he laughed. "I know. You mean they literally haven't got a cent."

"Hello," Minot said, "something's going on."

They were near those steps to the State Department, that descended to a little court off the sidewalk. Jeffrey always remembered the gray granite façade and the lighter gray of the sky behind it and the darker gray of rain clouds.

A limousine had stopped at the curb and a few pedestrians had stopped; and then Jeffrey saw men with cameras by the steps. When the car door opened, he saw two little men. That was the way he always thought of them—incongruous and small. He was near enough to see their faces as they stepped out of the car and to see the brief case one of them was holding. They wore black coats and high silk hats, uncomfortable costumes which somehow seemed to have a rented look. The cameramen were gathering around them and they paused and took off their hats—two oldish, roundheaded parchment-faced little men, smiling into the flashlights.

"By God," Jeffrey heard Minot say, "it's the Japs!"

Jeffrey always thought of them all in black with the gray building in front of them. Their coats and hats reminded him for just a minute of undertakers at a country funeral. They were the two Japanese envoys of course, Nomura and Kurusu, on their way to call on the Secretary of State, to continue that interminable discussion the formal announcements of which filled the pages of the press.

"Mike and Ike," he heard Minot say softly, "they look alike."

But they did not look alike; the older man, Nomura, had gray hair and a broad face the lines of which were deepened by age. He was the old friend of America who was negotiating patiently to reconcile the interminable differences with Japan. The one with the glasses, whose smile was less weary, was Kurusu, who had flown across the Pacific with all those special messages. Kurusu, Jeffrey remembered, was the one who had even talked to the reporters in football slang, saying that he would try to carry the ball. He was carrying the brief case now. Their silk hats were on again. They were walking side by side across the court and up the State Department steps.

"Funny little bastards, aren't they?" he heard Minot saying. "They walk as if their breeches were full of tacks."

But Jeffrey did not think they were very funny. They were too small, too patient, and too plodding.

"God," Minot said, "I'd better take a cab. I've only got five minutes."

"You know," Jeffrey said, "I wish I were going with you now."

"Come on," Minot said.

"No," Jeffrey said, "not yet."

"All right," Minot said, "you'll be sorry. So long, boy."

49

The Time for all Good Men

Because he had traveled so much Jeffrey's impressions were apt to grow blurred and to run together into a filmy background of hotels and Pullman cars and theaters, and faces often turned up against the wrong background.

In the next few weeks, that November day in Washington began to fall into this quiet confusion, but it was all there waiting, clear and completely defined when he needed it. He imagined later that it would have been practically possible to yield and to call the murder of China an incident of expansion. It might have been expedient to argue that the United States as a nation had no vested interests in East Asia that were worth the shedding of a single drop of blood, and that the acquisition of the Philippines had been a jingoistic mistake and that Japan was a progressive nation and our best customer. It was simply a matter of throwing China overboard. Jeffrey's knowledge of world affairs was not profound, but he could see that. There only remained an element, hard to define, which ended by being simply decency and honor. In the last few weeks he had a growing conviction that all debate was coming down to that, and the final conclusion lay in the combined thought of millions of people which made up the conscience of his country. You could see by November that some clash was inevitable—not war, perhaps, but a break in diplomatic relations, and then something which resembled the situation in the Atlantic, a delay of weeks and months but not quite war.

It was the beginning of a dull Sunday afternoon. Gwen was in her room studying with the radio half on. Jeffrey could hear the sound of it through the upstairs hall, while he read an interview by Secretary Knox which dealt with the strength of the United States Navy. Madge was sitting on the sofa with some sewing, and was interrupting him, as she usually did, when he was reading.

"Jeff," she said, "have you seen the gas bill?"

"Yes," he said, "but never mind it now."

"I wonder whether Hugh and Jessie are going to stay," Madge said.

"Who?" Jeffrey asked, and then he realized that Madge was referring to the latest couple.

"I think they're going to wait until they get their Christmas present," Madge said, "and then they'll leave. I think it looks that way."

Jeffrey did not answer.

"Jeff," Madge said.

"What?" he asked.

"About Christmas?"

Jeffrey put down the paper.

"Do you really think you'll have to go out there?" Madge asked. "Why can't they come here?"

"Who?" Jeffrey asked. "Who, Madge?"

"Jim and—Sally," Madge said, and her voice changed slightly as it always did when she mentioned Sally's name. "I don't see why they can't come here."

"Madge," Jeffrey began, and he pulled his thoughts together. They had been over the subject several times, but Madge always came back to it. "If you want to go too, why, come ahead, but I've told you—"

And then he heard Gwen running down the stairs.

"Daddy," Gwen was calling, "Daddy!"

He remembered wishing that Gwen would not always be so intense. For the last two years, Gwen had made a scene out of every trivial incident, and Madge had kept telling him that it was just a phase.

"Sing it," Jeffrey said, "don't scream it, Gwen."

"Daddy," Gwen said, "the Japanese—" and she stopped to catch her breath, and that was how he heard it. At first, as he stood by the radio, he did not believe what was being said, and then he was filled with a furious anger and he wanted to give everything, everything.

"Well," he said, "it's the real show this time." And he seemed to be a part of it again. He had been a soldier once, and not such a bad soldier, either. He was not physically defective. His eyes and ears were not bad. He had put on some weight but his heart and blood pressure were normal and he knew quite a lot about war. He knew that he could never fly in combat but he knew what it meant from A to Z and he wished to God that he were there. He must have thought of all those things at once and then he thought of Jim. He did not want to talk to Madge or anyone. He wanted to talk to Jim. His idea was purely impulsive but his common sense told him that he could not reach Jim that day, not in an Army Camp, or across the continent. He wanted to do something, and there was nothing he could do, absolutely nothing.

"Madge," he said, "I think I'd better go."

It surprised him that she did not understand him.

"Don't go out now," Madge said, "stay here, darling."

"I mean to Washington," he said, "I mean—"

Jeffrey knew that the Air Corps and every other branch of the army would be swamped with applications, but if someone knew him, this someone might recommend him to someone else. When he tried to reach Minot Roberts, he found that Minot had already gone to Florida. Knowing Minot, he imagined that Minot would already be on some General Staff, and Jeffrey did not want to be on any Staff. He knew that he could not fly, but he thought that he might get on the ground with a combat group, and then he remembered Bill Swinburne, whom Minot had gone to see and whom the General could not leave alone for a single minute. They had been in the same Squadron in the last war, and Bill had been an observer, and not much of an observer either. However, Bill Swinburne had liked the army and had stayed in the Reserve instead of dropping the whole thing as nearly everyone else had after the Armistice. Except at the old Squadron Dinners when Bill was always pretty tight, Jeffrey had not seen Bill for years, but still, if you had been in the Squadron you could not let someone down hard who had been in it too. That was why of all the people Jeffrey knew in Washington he thought that Bill Swinburne would be the best—Colonel Swinburne, as he was now, Lieutenant Colonel Swinburne. That was why Jeffrey sent him a wire to the Munitions Building, Washington, asking if Bill could give him fifteen minutes if he should come down.

After waiting two days for an answer, Jeffrey decided to telephone him, person-to-person, and he sat for two hours, waiting. First the operator said that Colonel Swinburne was in conference and she would try again in twenty minutes. Then the operator said that Colonel Swinburne had left for the Hotel Mayflower, and should she try the Mayflower? And then she said that Colonel Swinburne was in a very important luncheon conference at the Mayflower and could not be disturbed, and should she try Colonel Swinburne's office in another half an hour? Then, when she tried Colonel Swinburne's office, the Colonel was talking on another line, but she would get him in fifteen minutes. Then, fifteen minutes later, the Colonel was talking on another line, but she was still trying to get the Colonel. Fifteen minutes later the Colonel had just stepped out of his office, and no one knew where he was or whether or not he would be back, and would Jeffrey like to talk to the man at the Colonel's desk? But Jeffrey said he wanted to talk to Colonel Swinburne, person-to-person, and the operator said she would keep on trying Colonel Swinburne. The next time the telephone rang the operator was more hopeful.

"We have Colonel Swinburne for you now," she said. "He'll be with you in just a minute." Jeffrey waited for just a minute, and then for just another minute, and then he could hear a conversation which he was not meant to hear. Someone was asking who it was who wanted to talk to Colonel Swinburne and the operator was saying it was Mr. Wilson from New York and then the question came, what did Mr. Wilson want to talk to Colonel Swinburne about?

"They want to know what you want to talk to him about, please," someone said.

"Tell him I'm Wilson, Jeff Wilson," Jeffrey said. "He knows who I am. Tell him I used to rank him in the army. Wilson."

"Yes," the operator said, "here he is right now," and then Jeffrey heard Bill Swinburne's voice.

"Jeff," he heard Bill Swinburne saying, "why didn't you say it was you? They told me someone wanted to speak to me named Pilson."

Jeffrey laughed mechanically.

"That's all right, Bill," he said. "I suppose you're awfully busy down there. I just wanted to know if I came down, could you see me?"

"Sure," Bill Swinburne said, "any time, Jeff, any time."

Jeffrey smiled. He had never liked Bill Swinburne as much as he did then.

"Tomorrow?" Jeffrey said. "Could I come tomorrow?"

There was a second's silence, but Bill Swinburne's voice was still cordial. "Any time," he said, "any time."

Jeffrey was in his study at half-past three in the afternoon when he put down the telephone. He had never felt as much connected with the room as he did just then. He had felt it was rather ornate, simply Madge's idea of what a man's room ought to be. He had never worked hard in it, or experienced in it any sense of deep elation or sorrow. It was a room where he left his clothes at night and where he and Madge had breakfast on the card table and read the papers in the morning.

His feeling toward it was different now that he had finished with the telephone. Through the window he could see the river and the roofs of the brownstone dwelling houses and the outlines of the tall buildings to the south touched with the dim lights and shadows of a December mist. He saw it all differently because he was leaving it, perhaps for good, and he realized it represented, in a way, a combination of his and Madge's life. It was in a way not what he wanted, but what she wanted, and it was better than he had thought now that he was leaving it.

It made him realize how hard Madge had tried, much harder than he, to maintain certain standards and ideals. It made him see that she had been more honest than he and more definite. It made him sorry for her and at the same time very fond of her, and there was a queer sort of remorse connected with his thoughts, for he could see his faults so very clearly. He could see how much he had taken for granted and how unkind he had often been and how critical in all the times when he had been involved in struggles with himself. Her side of it had never been so clear. Yet the worst of it was that he knew he was not deeply sorry to be leaving. He was going into a world again which he had left for years—a world away from women. It might have been what war was for, a solution to unsolvable problems.

Now that he had telephoned, he realized that he had not told Madge what he proposed to do. He had only mentioned his idea a few days ago when the news first came, and he was sure that Madge had discounted it. Even when the air alert had sounded over the city it seemed to Jeffrey that Madge had been totally oblivious to the implication. She kept discussing what they would do next week, and next month, and wondering whether they ought to move to the country early. She had even talked about going out to the Coast with him when he went there again to work on a picture.

He could hear her using the telephone downstairs, and he knew from her tone that she was talking about him with her best friend, Beckie, comparing husbands as she and Beckie had for so many years.

"Darling," he could hear Madge say, "there isn't anything queer about that. Jeffrey's just the same way too. He hasn't been able to keep his mind on a solitary thing, dear. He keeps walking up and down trying to fight the war. Yes, he acts that way—as though it were his fault. No dear, he says just that too, and it doesn't help to tell him he can't do anything about it. It only makes him furious, darling. No . . . no, I don't think he's doing anything like that. He may be thinking about it but he wouldn't without telling me, with all the children . . ."

Jeffrey walked to the stairs and looked down into the hall. He could see Madge sitting by the telephone beside the little table with the pad and pencil and the big Manhattan directory and all the suburban directories which no one ever used.

"Madge," he called, "I wish you'd stop. Could you come up here for a minute?"

But Madge only put her hand over the transmitter and called up to him.

"Yes, dear," she called, "it's Beckie. They want us to come over for a cocktail tomorrow afternoon, Fred and Beckie. You can come, can't you Jeff?"

"No," Jeffrey said, "I'm going to be away tomorrow."

Madge still held her hand over the transmitter.

"Jeff," she said, "please. Just for half an hour. Beckie—" and she shook her head again.

Jeffrey knew why Madge shook her head. She meant that Beckie thought he didn't like her and Fred. He could show that he did like Beckie and Fred by going over there for a cocktail tomorrow for just half an hour.

"Madge," he said, "I can't. If you'll come up here, I'll tell you."

"Yes, dear," he heard her saying, "that was Jeff. He was sending you his love, dear, and he's going to try to come if he possibly can. You know the way they are dear . . . just as cross as bears. Yes, I'll tell him Fred is too. They can get together in a corner."

"God damn it, Madge," Jeffrey called down the stairs. "I can't go, and I don't want to get together with Fred in any corner!"

"He's calling downstairs now," Madge said over the telephone. "He's going to come if he possibly can."

Then it was over and Madge was coming up the stairs.

"Jeff," Madge was saying, "I wish you wouldn't shout at me when I'm talking. I can't hear myself think."

"I know," Jeffrey said, "I'm sorry, Madge."

"You always say you're sorry," Madge said, "and then you keep on doing it."

"I'm sorry, Madge," Jeffrey said again, "but there's something I've got to tell you—right away." He saw the line between her eyebrows deepen, and he knew that she was listening. "I've just been talking to the Air Corps, the Air Corps in Washington."

He wished that she did not look as though she did not believe him. Her expression was just as it had been when she was telling Beckie that he was as cross as a bear.

"Oh," Madge said. "Is Minot back in Washington?"

He wished that he could understand why Madge thought it was perfectly just and right for Minot to be back in the army, and never considered it possible for him to be.

"No," Jeffrey said, "I've been talking to a friend of mine there, Madge. Colonel Swinburne, Bill Swinburne. Maybe you've heard me speak of him?"

"No," Madge said, "I've never heard you speak of him. Who is he?"

"He's very high up in the Air Corps," Jeffrey said. "He's asked me to come down to Washington. He wants to talk to me about joining the Air Corps."

It was not exactly true that Bill Swinburne had asked him to come down to Washington, but somehow it seemed right to put it that way to Madge. It still did not seem to dawn upon her that it could be real.

"Why, darling," Madge said, "why should they want you in the Air Corps? You're too old to fly."

"Listen, Madge," Jeffrey said. "There are lots of other things to do in the

Air Corps besides fly. There are ground jobs. There's intelligence, liaison, airfield defense. I'm good enough for that."

"Oh, Jeff," Madge said, "of course you are, but there are lots of others."

"There are not lots of others," he said. "Anyway, if they want me—"

He wished that he did not see so much of his life in scenes from plays or popular fiction. He was going to the war again. He was the old doctor in *Gone with the Wind* going to war. He was young Prince Andrey in *War and Peace*, going to the war.

"Darling," Madge said, "I know just how you feel. It must be awful not to be able to do anything when you were in the war before, but aren't you doing it because it's the easiest thing to do? Aren't you doing it because you'd like to get away? You are—" Her voice broke. "You'd like to get away. It's just as though you've always been waiting for it. It's just as though you didn't like any of us, as though—"

"Now that isn't so, Madge," Jeffrey said, but he knew it was partly so. "If I can go out there and get one crack at them . . . I can't stay here and . . ."

"And what?" Madge asked him. "And what?"

"If I can get out," Jeffrey said, "where I can hear a gun go off—" He had hated it once and now it seemed the most desirable thing in the world. He only hoped that Madge would not say the obvious thing—that he might be too old. "I don't mean to sit in Washington, and I can't sit here—"

"Sit where?" Madge said.

"In this damned study," Jeffrey said, "and look out of this damned window." He had not meant to say it. He had not meant to hurt her. "Madge," he told her, "I did not mean that exactly. It isn't that I don't like it, but God, Madge, don't you see?"

There was something left of him yet, something that was not gone.

50

Old Soldiers Never Die

Once in 1917 Jeffrey had passed through Washington, and now in December 1941, the city was much the same. It was a bleak morning with a stormy chill in the air and the station was crowded, just as it had been back in 1917, with swiftly moving people; and their faces looked as they had then, wholly concentrated on their own thoughts. It was hard to get a taxicab, and early as it was you had to wait to get a table in the hotel dining room.

While Jeffrey waited for his breakfast and waited for a reasonable time to call on Bill Swinburne, he tried again to recall what Bill Swinburne was like, now that Bill Swinburne had suddenly become more important to him than anyone in the world. Jeffrey wanted to say the right thing and do the right thing.

He kept looking at all the officers he saw, and a good many of them had the ribbons of the last war. If he were in uniform he could show up as well as a lot of them and perhaps better. He could wear two gold V's on his left sleeve for his twelve months overseas. He could wear the World War ribbon with three stars on it for three offensives, which was more than a lot of men in uniform could; and besides he could wear the ribbon of the Croix de Guerre if that were regulation still—not that the Croix de Guerre meant much because the French had always been passing them out to pilots, but still it was a ribbon that you got for fighting.

Jeffrey tried to remember about Bill Swinburne; he did not want solely to think of him as being always tight at the Squadron Reunion Dinners. Minot had mentioned Bill Swinburne now and then, since Minot was always loyal to everyone in the Squadron. There had been something about trying to get Bill Swinburne a job, and then another job, and that was all that Jeffrey could remember. But now he was going to the Munitions Building to see his old friend Bill Swinburne, who must have been a first-rate fellow.

The Navy Building and the Munitions Building on Constitution Avenue of course had never belonged there. They had been built as a result of an old emergency and here they were again in the midst of a new one. Officers and civilians were passing in and out and it seemed to Jeffrey that if he wore the uniform again, even the new coat that looked so British, he would not have forgotten how to hold himself. He had been reasonably careful about his figure. With a coat properly tailored about the shoulders he would not look badly and he would know what to do with his hands. Many of the officers seemed to be his age, majors or lieutenant colonels, and he supposed you had to have that rank if you reached his age, but they wore their uniforms like civilian clothes.

There were guards at the doors examining the passes and Jeffrey had no pass. He was taken to the long reception desk just below the stairs where a thin, tired-looking girl looked up at him from her memorandum pad.

"I wanted to see Colonel Swinburne," Jeffrey said.

"Have you an appointment with him?" she asked.

Jeffrey said he had an appointment, because he thought it would be better to say so, though it was not entirely true.

"Where is he?" she asked.

"Where is he?" Jeffrey repeated and he listened to the footsteps and voices in the corridors. "I don't know. He's in here somewhere."

"Swinburne?" the girl said. "How do you spell it?" Jeffrey spelt it and the girl picked up a mimeographed list and then she wrote down the number of a room.

"What do you want to see Colonel Swinburne for?" she asked, and Jeffrey smiled at her.

"I thought maybe I could get back in," he said. "If you could get him on the telephone and tell him I was here—"

She still looked tired. Her eyes looked older than his although she was much younger.

"You want to get back?" she said. "You mean in the army?"

"Yes," Jeffrey said. "There seems to be a lot of army here."

But she was in a hurry and other people were waiting. She asked his name and if he could identify himself.

"If you'll ask him to come down," he said, "he knows me. He'll come down."

She used the telephone and she said yes, he was coming down if Jeffrey would wait right by the desk, and Jeffrey stood there for fifteen minutes waiting. As he saw the people move back and forth his interest did not flag. They were mostly older officers but some of them were younger. The lieutenants were the best. He could see their pilots' wings and he stood staring at the sheer beauty of their youth. It made him remember that you had to be nearly physically and mentally perfect to get your wings. The features of those boys were completely familiar to him—the same eyes and the same set of the lips and the same arrogance that flying officers always had. They reminded Jeffrey of all the faces in the Squadron and it gave him a strange aesthetic pleasure to see them. Then he saw an officer, a lieutenant colonel, coming down the stairs and striding toward the desk. His hair was gray and close-cropped, his face looked sodden and heavy. He had a mustache that was streaked with gray.

"Where's that man?" he was asking the girl, and then Jeffrey spoke to him.

"Bill," he said. "Hello, Bill."

Bill Swinburne looked at him in the way in which acquaintances of their age always regarded each other, and his face broke into a quick mechanical smile.

"Why, Jeff!" he said. "Why, Jeffie!" And Jeffrey was sure he had never called him Jeffie back there in the Squadron. "Jeffie, you look just the same."

"So do you, Bill," Jeffrey said and he knew both were lying.

"Give him a badge," Bill Swinburne said, and the girl at the desk handed him a badge with a number on it.

"Come on, Jeffie," Bill Swinburne said. "Come up to the room. I'm sorry to keep you waiting but this is quite a war—quite a war."

They climbed a flight of stairs and began walking down a corridor.

"Keep on walking," Bill Swinburne said, and it seemed to Jeffrey that they walked for a long way before they came to Bill Swinburne's office. It was a small room with two desks, neither of which was occupied. Bill Swinburne sat down behind one of them and Jeffrey drew a chair up beside it.

"Well," Bill Swinburne said, "it's great to see you, Jeffie."

"It's great to see you, Bill," Jeffrey said.

Then for a second they sat looking at each other.

"I don't want to take up too much of your time, Bill," Jeffrey said, and then he was telling about himself as though he were a clerk applying for a job, and somehow his enthusiasm was dying.

"I know," he heard Bill Swinburne say, "I looked you up, Jeffie. You're in

Who's Who. I think we can work something. You've done a lot of scribbling, haven't you?"

Jeffrey looked at the bare office. It occurred to him that he was a better man than Bill Swinburne ever was, but Bill Swinburne ranked him now.

"Yes, quite a lot," Jeffrey answered.

"And the movies," Bill Swinburne said, "that puts you in a real category. The Chief's been interested in the movies."

"What have the movies got to do with it?" Jeffrey asked.

"Public relations, boy," Bill Swinburne said. "Of course, I can't promise you, but I think there's a spot for you in there. The Chief was talking about the movies yesterday. Wait a minute, Jeffie."

"What about Intelligence?" Jeffrey asked. "Isn't there something else?"

Bill Swinburne shook his head.

"Wait a minute, Jeffie," he said. "We can't all be in there batting, but maybe I've got a spot for you. Stay right there. Don't move."

Colonel Swinburne had opened an adjoining office door and closed it and Jeffrey sat there waiting. He could see what was coming—Public Relations, and the movies—and then Bill Swinburne opened the door again.

"Come on," he said. "Come on, Jeffie."

They crossed a room with a green carpet where two officers sat behind desks and Bill Swinburne opened another door. Then he was in a third room, larger than any of the others, with a map of the world on the wall, and there was a general behind another desk. Jeffrey could see the stars and the ribbons.

"This is a friend of mine, sir," Bill Swinburne said. "Mr. Wilson. He was a pilot in the old Squadron."

The General looked up at him and he was an old man too.

"Oh," he said, "the old Squadron? The one that was always bombing Conflans. Captain Strike—did you know Strike?"

"Yes, sir," Jeffrey said. "He was my captain."

"And you want to get back, do you?" the General asked.

"Yes, sir," Jeffrey said. "If I could get into the field."

He saw he had not said the right thing because the General's face hardened.

"You all want to get overseas, don't you?" the General said. "Well, so do I want to, but some of us have got to stay right here and we've got to build up public relations. The Colonel here says you're familiar with the movies."

"Yes, sir," Jeffrey said.

He stood—the General did not ask him to sit down—he simply stood there listening to the General talking. It would take time, the General was saying. If he would come in tomorrow and fill out an application and meet Colonel So-and-so, there was room in the Public Relations particularly for someone who had been overseas and who knew the spirit of the Air Corps.

Jeffrey knew there was no use talking back to a General. He could see that they were being kind to him—very kind. He could be in uniform again, but he could not get anywhere at all. Finally he and Bill Swinburne were passing through the room with the green carpet and back into the third room, and Bill Swinburne slapped him on the shoulder.

"It's in the bag," Bill said. "Come back again tomorrow."

But Jeffrey knew that he would not be back again tomorrow. He thought of the young officers he had seen downstairs and he knew that he was out of it. He might go back tomorrow, and like Bill Swinburne, pretend that he was in it, but somehow it was not his war any longer.

"Thanks, Bill," he said. "It's been swell seeing you."

"Yes," Bill answered, "it's been like old times, hasn't it?"

"Yes," Jeffrey answered, "like old times."

The only consolation that stayed with him as he walked out to the street was that he had tried, but what he had expected had been too much to ask.

He had a chair on the four o'clock to New York and time lay ahead of him. He would have to tell Madge in the evening and he did not like to face it, because he suddenly suspected that Madge had known it all along. There was nothing he could do but go to the hotel.

It was too early in the morning for a drink. He did not believe in drinking before noon, and in rare times when he had done so, he had never done it by himself; but now he knew he was going to do it.

The bar was just off the main entrance of the hotel and it had a welcome name emblazoned near its door: "Men's Bar"—and that in itself was funny. If you lived long enough a great many things were funny. Back in the last war it would have been obvious that any bar was a men's bar, and now well-conducted hotels had to label their barrooms as carefully as they labeled their retiring rooms—Gentlemen's Bars, and then that middle ground, the Cocktail Lounge, where the sexes could mingle. He had never been to a bar so early in the morning and he found himself moving toward it furtively. He even glanced around to be sure that no one noticed him particularly. There was a step leading up to the Men's Bar with an illuminated green sign thoughtfully placed upon it marked "Step up," and Jeffrey was about to step up when he saw that the bell captain was beside him.

"The bar doesn't open till twelve, sir," the bell captain said.

"What?" Jeffrey answered, and he tried to look incredulous and amused at such a regulation. "Not till twelve?"

He had an idea that everyone was watching him and he moved quickly away to buy a newspaper. Now that he was deprived of the solace he had been seeking, he could not remember ever having been so anxious for a drink. Nevertheless, although he knew he must wait till twelve, he was determined now that he would not be the first one in that barroom. He read the *Washington Post*, page after page, deliberately, until five minutes after twelve; then he waited five more minutes before he arose and returned to the Men's Bar. The doors were open now, and his foot was on the step again when he heard his name called. His first instinct was to leap away from the place, but it was too late to pretend that he was going anywhere else. He knew that that would make him look ridiculous. At any rate there was no time for anything. It was Beckie's husband, Fred, and he was the last person Jeffrey wanted to see because he knew that Madge would hear about it eventually.

Fred and Jeffrey maintained that odd relationship of being husbands of best friends, an accident which neither of them could help. Jeffrey had always put up with it and he supposed that Fred had too. Fred still had that handsome band-leader look that went with his particular time in Yale, and it still seemed to Jeffrey that Fred was trying to live in the pages of *This Side of Paradise*, and *The Beautiful and Damned*, and *The Great Gatsby*, when all the boys and girls were gay, oh so gay.

As Fred stood there in the Mayflower he looked a little gray and tired to Jeffrey, but very gay, as if he should be carrying a box of orchids with a gay white ribbon around it, on his way upstairs to someone's room, but Fred was not carrying anything.

"Hello, Jeff," Fred said. "Where are you going?"

It did not seem to Jeffrey that it was kind of Fred to ask, because it was quite obvious where he was going.

"I thought you and I were going to have a cocktail," Jeffrey said, "in New York."

"Oh, yes," Fred said, "the girls." He waved his hand airily like a band-leader when he said it. "I couldn't make it, Jeff, but then I heard you couldn't either."

"Oh," Jeffrey said, "were they on the telephone again?"

"My God," Fred said. "All through the night one or the other of them was on it. They were still on it at half-past seven when I left for the plane."

"Yes," Jeffrey said, "it's like a party line."

"That's right," Fred said. "Any time you lift up the receiver, they're on it."

Then the subject was exhausted, exactly the way subjects were through all the years when Jeffrey and Fred had been left alone together; you could not keep going on about the telephone. They were still at the entrance to the bar.

"I was just going in to have a drink," Jeffrey said. "Do you want a drink?"

Fred's expression was peculiar. He did not disapprove exactly because he could not and be a character in *The Beautiful and Damned*—and yet it was obvious that he did not want a drink.

"Well, not this morning, Jeff," Fred said, and it sounded as if he had often said it in just that way and that it was never just this morning, but any other morning. "You see, I've got a little business, but don't mind me. I'll watch you. Don't let me keep you. I'll watch you."

When Jeffrey entered the Men's Bar he was surprised to see how many of the patrons, like himself, must have been waiting for a drink. It was one of those modern bars with dim reddish lights, so dim that it was impossible to read a paper, so dim that it required almost a conscious effort to distinguish the potato chips from the cheese-encrusted popcorn. At high noon this faint religious glow gave everything, even the cold-sober bar boys, a dissipated aspect.

They sat down together on a bench before a small round table.

"A Scotch-and-soda," Jeffrey said to the bar boy, and then he thought again. "A double Scotch-and-soda."

"White Rock for me," Fred said, "just White Rock," and he smiled at Jeffrey apologetically. Their voices were low and furtive because of the lights.

"God damn it," Jeffrey said as he looked around, "it's a little like going to church, isn't it?"

"Yes," Fred said, "if you're mixing metaphors, I see what you mean. You know if I didn't have an appointment–" He hesitated. "You see, I heard the girls talking . . . I mean, you can't help overhearing when they get going. Well, I guess I'm down here for what you're down here for. That's all."

It sounded pleasant. It sounded honest.

"I'll tell you, Fred," Jeffrey said, "the woods are full of us."

But Fred was not listening to him. He was listening to his own ideas.

"I couldn't sit there," he said. "I've kept thinking, Jeff. I've always had a pretty damned good time, a pretty easy time. Well, I've got to pay it back somehow."

Fred's statement had an honest dignity even in the bar.

"Yes," Jeffrey said; "you're not the only one, Fred."

But Fred was not listening to him. Fred was going on.

"Of course, I haven't had the experience you've had, Jeff, but I was in the R.O.T.C. at Yale. I was pretty good. I was a sergeant in the R.O.T.C."

"I know," Jeffrey said. "A whole lot didn't get over, Fred."

It was another war and Jeffrey was not in it, but still he could feel a smug and completely superfluous sense of superiority. He could think of Fred going down to that bureau and telling someone of his experiences in the R.O.T.C., but Fred was going on.

"Of course," Fred said, "I don't want to be swell-headed, Jeffrey. I suppose anyone can get a desk job here, but I don't want that. I don't care about rank. I just want to get in there and take a sock at somebody. I'm not in a wheel-chair yet, and I don't give a damn if Beckie thinks so."

"Oh," Jeffrey said, "does Beckie think so?"

"My God, Jeff," Fred said, "what do women know about this sort of thing anyway? She didn't say so, but I sort of think she thinks so. Frankly, well, Beckie and I had a sort of a row all night. She's got the damnedest idea."

"What idea?" Jeffrey asked.

"She's got the damnedest idea," Fred said, "that I'm doing this for some sort of personal satisfaction–that it's just a sort of excuse to get away from her and home and the kids. I don't know what put it into her head, and it doesn't do any good to tell her that I'm not in a wheel-chair yet."

The idea was firmly in Fred's mind that he was not in a wheel-chair yet.

"Well, I know a man down there," Fred said. "I've never seen much of him, but he's quite a friend of mine–and I called him up and he asked me to come down. Did you ever hear of him? His name is Swinburne–Bill Swinburne."

Jeffrey set down his glass. He was thinking that they would walk out on you if you were to put an inartistic coincidence like that in a play.

"Yes," Jeffrey said, "I know him. I've been down there myself, just now."

It was pathetic to see Fred's face light up.

"And now you're celebrating," Fred said. "Gosh that's swell, Jeff!" and he held out his hand across the table.

"Not exactly," Jeffrey said. "You see, I'm going back home. But go ahead and try it," he said, "maybe you'll do better. You see—well, perhaps I'm silly —I used to be shot at, once. I know it's too much to ask—Well, I'm going back home."

It was dusk, almost dark, when the train passed through Wilmington and sped along the Delaware to Philadelphia. As Jeffrey sat staring out of the black window the sky was aglow with light. He could see the glare over factories in the distance and the floodlights of the shipyards and the rolling mills. He was thinking of the young men he had seen, and, God, they were beautiful, and they were the ones who would see the show. It was not fair, because he could have died more easily, having lived—but they would see the show. He was reminded of the older men during the last war—they had seemed very old, but they must have been about his own age. They were always saying the same thing and always selecting the most inopportune occasions on which to say it. They were always saying that if they were twenty years younger, why they would be there too, and how much they envied the boys their chance. Jeffrey could remember how often he had brushed those remarks aside as insincere and hypocritical. There was one thing he would not do. He would not say the same thing to anyone now. It was their war, not his war.

"Good evening, Mr. Wilson," the doorman said. "It's been kind of a mean day, hasn't it?"

"Yes," Jeffrey said. "It has been a kind of a mean day."

He was in the hall of his apartment just as though he had not been anywhere in particular, and when he was taking off his overcoat, he heard Madge calling from the living room.

"Oo-hoo?" Madge was calling. "Is that you, Jeff?"

She smiled at him and she kissed him, but she was waiting to hear his news. He knew he had to tell her, although he knew from her voice that she had guessed already.

"How was it," she asked, "down in Washington?" But he did not want to go into it then.

"I'm glad I went," he said, "but there wasn't much down there, Madge."

There was one thing about it. He could see she had been thinking that, in spite of everything, they might have taken him and sent him somewhere. Her face was alight with sheer relief that he was not going, and it made him feel better.

"Oh," she said, "poor darling!" And she kissed him again. He wished that she might have said something else.

"Dinner's waiting," she said. "Do you want a cocktail? You look tired, dear."

"No thanks," Jeffrey answered. "I've had quite a few already."

She held his hand.

"Oh," Madge said, "poor darling."

"For God's sake," Jeffrey said, "don't call me 'poor darling,'" and then he was sorry about it and he held her hand tighter. "I didn't mean exactly that," he told her. "You see when I saw the boys down there, I mean the young officers, there didn't seem to be much I could do right now. Madge, I'll tell you what–"

"What?" she asked.

"We'll call up Jim tonight. Somebody ought to see him, Madge. I ought to get out there for Christmas."

"Jeff," Madge said, "can't you do it later? You're running everywhere, lately."

"I can take a plane," Jeffrey said. "I'm not in a wheel-chair yet."

It was a question of mathematics again. If he were to call Jim at eight it would only be five out there. A young officer would not be in his quarters by five, particularly in wartime. It would be near the time for Retreat and though he had never seen the camp where Jim was, it would be like all those other camps, or forts, or whatever they called them now. There would be the same monotonous rows of barracks with their Battery streets and the Company streets. There would be the same dull hum of voices and the stamping of feet on the wooden floors, and the Companies, and the Batteries, coming out to form their ranks, in the evening light. The officers who would take Retreat would be moving out to their places, and there would be the commands and the Batteries would be present or accounted for, and the senior officer would take over. There would be parade rest and the bugles would be blowing, and their thin notes would fill the silence. Retreat, he had often thought, was the closest thing to prayer in war; and Jim would be at Retreat, but he might be in his quarters later, say at eight o'clock his time.

It was after eleven in the East when the operator said that the party was ready. Jeffrey and Madge were sitting in the upstairs study. He first thought he could get it all into three minutes but of course Madge would speak to him too. After all Jim was her son as much as his son. He had to say it all very quickly, and there was too much to say, for the time in which to say it. He always seemed to be talking to Jim across vast spaces, both of distance and of time. He was always trying to bridge those unbridgeable gaps, and as long as he lived, or Jim lived, he would always be trying. Jim would not care so much because he would never perceive those distances. He was too young. He was so young that he would think, no matter what might happen, that it would not be he–it could not be he–that he would live forever; and Jeffrey had thought that once.

"Hello," Jim was saying, and he sounded impatient, as though he had been on the line for a long while.

Usually the sound of Jim's voice brought Jim back as though he were right there, but it was different this time. In spite of the clearness of the connection, Jim was very far away.

"Hello," Jeffrey said, "Jim." He had to speak fast because there was not much time. "How's everything out there?"

"Fine." Jim's voice was louder. "Everything's fine. We're–" Jim seemed to hesitate. "We're pretty busy now. How's everything back home?"

"Fine," Jeffrey said. "Your mother's right here. She's going to speak to you in a minute. Jim, I'm calling about Christmas. I think I can make it. I've got reservations . . ."

There was a slight pause and Jeffrey was very conscious of the pause.

"I wouldn't try that," he heard Jim say. "It–Well, put it this way. Sally will be back East by Christmas."

It seemed to Jeffrey that his heart had stopped, that everything had stopped, but his own voice was measured. He knew there were things you could not say.

"Suppose I put it this way," he said slowly, "suppose I come tomorrow."

There was another pause and he knew that Jim was thinking.

"I don't think so," Jim said. Jim was being careful, but he knew exactly what Jim meant. "It wouldn't be worth your while."

It hurt Jeffrey at the moment and he could not hide his hurt.

"I think you might have told me, Jim," he said.

"There are some things you don't know until just about the last minute. You ought to know."

The time was running short and he was sitting there. There was nothing he could do–nothing he could say. He felt that his voice was choked and hoarse and he cleared his throat.

"If you get the chance–" he was speaking very slowly–"call me again, Jim. Will you do that, please?"

"Yes," Jim said, "if I get the chance. You know how it is, but it's fine out here. I wish to God that you were here."

Jeffrey cleared his throat again.

"Well, keep your shirt on," Jeffrey said, "and don't take any wooden money. Your mother wants to speak to you."

He handed Madge the receiver and nodded. He noticed the mark on it from the perspiration on his hand.

"Hello, darling," Madge was saying, but Jeffrey was not listening. He knew that Jim would not tell her and there was no need of telling Madge–no need to worry her because Jim was going overseas. Out there on the Pacific Coast, it would be the East Indies, or Australia, or Hawaii–he hoped to heaven it might only be Hawaii, but there was no way of telling.

"Darling," Madge was saying, "are you warm enough? Is it raining all the time?"

But Jeffrey was only half listening. Jim was going and he knew that feeling because he had gone out once. He had left from old Camp Merritt just across the river, with perhaps two hundred other casual officers; and that was a queer word when you thought of it–"casual." You never knew when it was coming. You were only told to have everything ready, not to leave, to be there waiting. They had been awakened at four in the morning, he remembered, and by daylight they walked in columns of twos along the road to Fort Lee where an old ferryboat was waiting. They were going and there was no way of going back. He had seen the buildings of New York, but they were not going there. They were as good as gone already. They were on the pier and he remembered the sound of the donkey engines. He remembered the lines of troops waiting with their duffel bags to go aboard and to take their places below. He remembered the side of the transport painted crazily in the camouflage that they did not use any more. He remembered the voices of the troops. They were on the pier but they were as good as gone already. Good-by Broadway, hello France. You were as good as gone already and no one ever knew. That was the way you went to war.

Then he was thinking about Madge. He must think of some excuse as to why he was not going out to the Coast after all. There was no need to tell her yet that Jim was going. It was something you did not shout all over town.

"Jeff," Madge was saying, "do you want to speak to him again?"

"No," Jeffrey said, "that's all right. There's no use talking to him any more."

"Well, dear," Madge was saying, "give my love to Sally, dear. I didn't say I was worried. I mean we miss you dreadfully."

Then Madge turned to Jeffrey and sighed.

"Jeff," she said, "he sounded awfully happy. He sounded as if he were really interested and having a good time."

"What?" Jeffrey said.

"He sounded as if he were having a good time," Madge said. "Didn't he sound that way to you?"

"Yes," Jeffrey said, "he did. He's having a swell time, Madge."

51

Forgive Us Our Debts

Some chain of circumstances, some familiar aspect connected with another time, made Jeffrey half remember something that next morning. It was one of those things that you would half remember and then lose before it assumed any concrete shape. It had something to do with his study, where he and Madge always had breakfast when they were in the city. The table was placed in front of a window which looked south over the chimneys and skylights of old brownstone houses. The sun was breaking through the December haze which so often obscured the city on those mornings. He could see the geometric bulk of apartment houses and the pointed top of the Chrysler Building and the shadowy forms of other buildings farther in the distance. The shifting light, caused by the sun breaking through the haze, changed the texture of all those buildings from minute to minute so that they seemed to have a life of their own.

The breakfast trays were on the table and the morning paper and the mail were with them. He could see Madge's orange juice and her Melba toast and her black coffee, which she always took without any cream or sugar. Madge was wearing her blue kimono with the white bamboo design on it. The thought that it was Japanese annoyed Jeffrey, but still it half reminded him of something. Jeffrey was wearing the Burgundy silk dressing gown which he always felt he had to wear because the children had once given it to him for Christmas and that also half reminded him of something.

He was back there in the study which he had thought yesterday he was going to leave for good, and he and Madge were having breakfast just as though the world were on its way in peace. He had never realized before that externals could be so stubborn or persistent, but this was not what disturbed him. He was disturbed because he could almost remember something which had happened when he and Madge had been having breakfast some other time, but he could not quite remember. He could remember the orange juice and the way the buildings had looked from the south window on another morning. It was like one of those interminable rehearsals where someone said, "All right. Take it up and run it through again." It was just as though he and Madge were repeating something. It could not have been very important, because he could not remember what it was they were repeating.

"Darling," Madge asked, "is that a letter from Alf?"

"What?" Jeffrey asked. He had been looking at the Currier and Ives prints and the books in the study.

"Is that a letter from Alf?" She was pointing to a letter beside his plate, and he looked down at it and picked it up. It was an Air Mail letter and the postmark was San Bernardino, California. When he opened it, it was just as if he were doing something over again, but he could not remember what.

"Yes," he said, "it's from Alf. He's back from the hospital again and he wants five hundred dollars."

"Oh," Madge said, "I hope he's better."

"He must be better for a while," Jeffrey said, "if he wants five hundred dollars." And then he thought of something else. "You ought to see that orange grove," he said. "It's called Rednow. That means Wonder spelled backwards. Alf was going to put in a bathroom."

But Madge's mind had moved away from it. She was seldom interested in anything she had not seen herself.

"Darling," Madge said, "did you sleep well? You look rested. You looked so tired last night after Washington."

"What?" Jeffrey asked her. He was thinking of all sorts of things and none of them came together.

"You looked so tired after Washington," Madge said.

"Yes," Jeffrey said, "yes. I guess I was pretty tired."

"Jeff," Madge said, "you mustn't let it worry you. You did everything you could." And she patted the back of his hand and he held hers for a moment.

"All right," he said, "it doesn't worry me."

Her voice came through his thoughts as though she were a long way off even when he held her hand. He was looking out of the window again at the buildings, watching the brightening sunlight. He was thinking of something that Jim had said once—it must have been quite a while ago—"New York has everything, there's everything in New York." And it sounded like a line in a song. Then suddenly he remembered exactly what it was that disturbed him. It had been another morning when they had been having breakfast, and everything about that morning came back. Madge was speaking, but he could not give her his full attention. She must have said something which he only half heard, because she spoke again.

"Darling," he heard her say, "what are you thinking about?"

All at once he was glad that she had asked him. It was much better to have her with him than to be alone. He saw that the line between her eyebrows had grown deeper.

"I was trying to remember something," he said, "and I just remembered it. We were having breakfast, Madge, and I was telling you a story. It wasn't so long ago, either. It was only a year ago last October but it seems like quite a while ago."

"A year ago last October?" Madge repeated. After all there was no reason why she should have followed his thoughts.

"Before the whole show started," Jeffrey said, and his mind was back there on that October morning. "You'd never have guessed that things would be like this. We were just sitting here and you were saying that I never told you anything."

"Well, that's true," Madge said, and she smiled. "You never do tell me anything, Jeff, dear, I wish you would. You're worried about something. Are you worried about Jim?"

"No," Jeffrey answered, "not Jim exactly." He had not been thinking of Jim, but now that his name was mentioned he began to think of him. He would have to tell her that Jim was going, but he did not want to tell her until he was sure, absolutely sure.

"I was just thinking," he went on, "we were having breakfast, and you said I never told you anything, and then I told you about a time when I was coming in on the train from Bragg; and a little man sat next to me with a purple shirt. He gave me a drink out of a bottle. Do you remember?"

The line between her eyebrows grew deeper.

"A little man?" she repeated. "What little man?"

"You said he was funny," Jeffrey said, "and I said he wasn't. I said he was sad."

"I said he was funny?" Madge repeated, but he saw she did not remember.

"It isn't anything," Jeffrey said, "not anything, really. It's just one of those things that come into your mind. Maybe I was wrong. Maybe he wasn't so sad."

"Darling," Madge said, "I wish you'd tell me what you're talking about."

"It isn't anything much," Jeffrey said again. "It was just that he said he could lick any So-and-so his weight in the world."

"Oh," Madge said, "yes, I remember. Why, darling, what ever made you think of that?"

Jeffrey did not answer for a moment because there was no way of telling her exactly why he had thought of it.

"You know, maybe it's a good idea," he said, and then he stopped.

"What?" Madge asked him. "What's a good idea?"

"Maybe it's a good idea," Jeffrey said, "even if you know you can't, to go on thinking that you can. Maybe that's what everybody ought to do."

But Madge was no longer interested. Her mind had moved back to the present.

"Darling," she said, "I'm awfully glad you're not going out there."

"Out where?" Jeffrey asked.

"Out there to see Jim."

"Oh," Jeffrey said, "yes, it's just as well."

"Darling," Madge said, "are you going to be in for lunch?"

"No," Jeffrey answered, "not today."

"Oh," Madge said, "where are you going?"

"I'm just going out," Jeffrey said, "to lick anyone my weight in the world. Jesse Fineman's got another play."

"Darling," Madge asked him, "what about that play of your own you were writing out there in California? You've never told me anything about it. You never tell me anything."

Jeffrey pushed back his chair and stood up.

"I know," he said, "it wasn't any good."

"But darling," Madge asked, "how can you possibly know? I wish you'd read it to me sometime."

Jeffrey walked over to her chair and bent down to kiss her.

"All right," he said, "sometime. But I can lick anyone my weight in the world."

Those words were back in his mind when he was in the front hall of the apartment putting on his hat and coat. That apartment had always seemed to him too large for their furniture, and now the hall seemed to stretch into new angles of ungainly space. The living room door was open and shafts of sunlight came through the windows, throwing bright squares on the carpets and on the Georgian chairs and on the sofa. Everything was in its proper place exactly as it should have been, but the room was completely empty. He could think of it as waiting for something, not for people to fill it, not for voices and laughter, but for something else. It was as ephemeral that morning as a well-planned stage set that was waiting for the stagehands and the vans to cart it all away. It conveyed no impression of permanence, nothing that Madge called security, perhaps because there had ceased to be security the way the world was going. It made him think for some reason of that trip that he and Madge had taken down the Post Road a little more than a year ago. He was thinking of those houses along the Post Road which no one wanted now, but which had been built to last almost forever. He was thinking of the house where Madge's Uncle Judson lived with its mansard roof and its golden oak hallway. There was no security there either. He was thinking of Fred and Beckie and of Higgins Farm in Connecticut. Nothing was meant to last forever, and now everything in the world which he had known, living and inanimate, seemed to have come to a momentary stop. Everything was waiting for the stagehands and the vans.

The elevator was decorated with laurel and hemlock and holly as it always was at Christmas time. The boy who ran the elevator was the one who liked Jim.

"It's a nice day, Mr. Wilson," the boy said, and he pulled at his white cotton gloves and smiled, "a little snappy outside, but it's a nice day."

"Yes," Jeffrey answered, "it's a fine day."

That boy would be in the army in a very little while, and nearly all the other employees in the building would be too, and they must have all been thinking of it. They must in their own ways have been thinking all the thoughts that he was thinking, but they gave no sign.

"Good morning, Mr. Wilson," the doorman said, and he would be going too. "Taxi, Mr. Wilson?"

"No, thanks," Jeffrey said, "I'll walk."

"Yes sir," the doorman said, "it's a fine morning for a walk."

You could not tell what anyone was thinking. The windows of the stores were full of Christmas decorations; the dogs were being aired; the trucks were rumbling up the avenue. There was a familiar background of sound that pulsed through the air like heartbeats. There was the smell of spruce from the Christmas trees on the sidewalks. There was the clatter of ash cans from a truck, on which was written the admonition about keeping the city clean, and the signs were still on the green busses: "Welcome to New York." It was astonishing to see everything move on as it had always moved—too much in the shops, too much traffic in the cross streets, too many people, too much of everything. But everyone must have known there would never be a day quite like that again. Everyone must have known that everything was changing. The trouble was you could not see it change.

It was not yet noon, but the first editions of the papers were already out. He could see the headlines on a newsstand, where there were too many papers, too many magazines.

"*Jap Fleet on the Run*," he read, and he knew it made no sense, after what he imagined must have happened at Pearl Harbor. It made no sense, but Jeffrey was only half thinking of it, because the sights and the sounds were only half intruding on his thoughts.

He was thinking of all sorts of things that were as disorganized as those sights and sounds. He was thinking of what was permanent, and he was thinking that very little was, except perhaps personal relationships, but even these kept changing. You clung to beliefs and people and yourself, but even these kept changing.

A girl with yellow hair and with one of those small hats which women were wearing then was walking half a block ahead of him, and her figure and the way she walked made him think of Marianna Miller, but it was not Marianna Miller. You knew someone, you loved and laughed, and then it was all different. Nothing in the world ever stayed quite the same. He had not thought of Marianna for some time, but now all sorts of things that he had said and she had said were running through his mind. For a minute or two these filled him with poignant regret, and made him very sad. There had been something which he had tried to capture, something she had offered freely, that was a part of a half-formed desire, he supposed, to be something he might have been. Jeffrey knew now that he would never attain that desire, but the memory of having tried made him feel very kindly toward Marianna. He was wondering again why it had all come to nothing, and why he had not been able to go on with it, but it all eluded analysis. She had given more than he had, he was quite sure, when he heard again the things that she had said and he had said, but there was no way of telling exactly. You could think of it as a matter of too little and too late, and that might be the better way to think of it, since the truth was you only had a certain amount to give. The truth was that he had given most of what he had away already, and he had tried to tell her that. Yet there were some things that you could not make anyone understand, because, perhaps, you never knew enough about yourself. For a moment as he walked across town Marianna Miller seemed to be walking there beside him, and then she was gone and Jim was there.

He had given more than he had ever thought he would to Jim, and more than Jim would ever know. Yet as he thought of Jim, he was already more of an abstraction than a person, simply a combination of Jeffrey Wilson's own thoughts and emotions. Now that Jim was gone there was nothing but a chain of memories left.

He had given, and now he knew that he had nothing more to give which Jim would need. There was no cause for regret, for this was exactly as it should have been. To Jeffrey Jim might always seem young, and often in need of help, but he knew that Jim had already received the independence which one really wanted for him. You grew fond of someone and then it all began to change. Perhaps the people you knew and those you were fondest of lived mainly in your mind. There was Jim, and then all sorts of other people whom he had known moved beside him in his thoughts. There were Minot Roberts and people in the old Squadron whom he thought he had forgotten. There were Alf and Jesse Fineman, and Walter Newcombe and Mrs. Newcombe. You saw them and you talked to them and then they went away. Then he was thinking of his father. He had not thought of his father for a long while. In that last war, Jeffrey was thinking, his father would have been his own age. He remembered his father's speaking of the Liberty Loans, the gasless Sundays, the meatless days—his father had lived the life that Jeffrey was living now.

They were all there with him, but there was nothing that was permanent until you thought of Madge. For some reason he was thinking of her as she had looked when he had first seen her there by the tennis court at her father's house, years and years ago when they had been so young. Something had happened to her dress, he remembered. She had wanted a pin for her dress. She had always wanted something from him. He had thought at one time that he had nothing left to give her, but now he knew that there was always something he could give, without desiring to, perhaps, but always something, although he never told her anything. She had never said so, and perhaps she never would, or perhaps she had when she had held his hand that morning. He could always give her something, and she was the only one.

He had reached Fifth Avenue by then, and the bulk of Radio City stood in front of him, and he remembered what Jim had said: that you could stay there all day long just looking at the people. He could see the great Christmas tree and the bare branches of the trees along the sidewalk, while he was standing waiting for the lights to change before he crossed the Avenue. You could stand there if you wanted just looking at the people, provided always that you did not feel too much alone. And now suddenly, in spite of the noise of the motors, in spite of all that sea of sound, he felt entirely alone. He was not pleased with anything he had been thinking, but there he was. He seemed to be standing still with time and everything else moving past him. It was twelve o'clock and the chimes were ringing. It was time for him to cross the Avenue, but he stood still. The chimes made him look at the cathedral and the people moving up and down the steps.

He had never particularly admired the architecture of Saint Patrick's. He had only been inside it once years before when he and Madge had stopped there for a moment to hear the midnight mass at Christmas. He remembered the candles and the incense and the painted, plaster figures, and the faint lights in the chapels. He wondered what made him go inside there again at noon when the sun was out. It may have been simple curiosity, or it may have been that idea of his that everyone must have been thinking what he was thinking, but above all he felt an impulse to be where it was quiet. It seemed to him that there had been too much travel, too much talk, too much noise for a long while, too much of everything. Inside Saint Patrick's he might be quiet for a few minutes, absolutely quiet.

He was not a Catholic or a member of any church. Nevertheless he had always been moved by church architecture, particularly the Early Gothic. Whenever he had been in Paris he had often walked alone to Notre Dame for no other reason than to stand and to allow his eyes to rove upward along the columns to the shadow of the arches. He had always thought that Chartres was the greatest cathedral of them all, and he hoped that nothing had happened to Chartres after the fall of France. Once he had been there with Madge and they had paid the sacristan a substantial sum so that they might enter the church alone by moonlight. That light, he remembered, had come through the stained glass very dimly, but there had been enough light so that the nave and the transept were not wholly dark. When he and Madge had stood alone there in the shadows, it had all been so still that the faintest motion you might make would have sounded very loud. She had held his hand,

and the best of it was that she had said nothing, not even in a whisper, because anything you might have said would have spoiled that ghostly peace. It was different when he entered Saint Patrick's, because of course there would never be another religious edifice like Chartres, nothing as naïvely great, nothing as grandly simple. The trouble when he entered Saint Patrick's was that he was thinking of too many things. That was what always seemed to happen to Jeffrey when he went to church. While he stood there with his eyes still dazzled from the sunlight of the street, he was thinking about Jim. He was thinking that he must tell Madge about him, that he should have told her hours before, and now that he was inside Saint Patrick's he was suddenly absolutely sure that Jim had gone. He was there alone, a stranger, standing awkwardly, looking at the candles on the high altar, listening to echoed footsteps and whispered prayers. It was not entirely for him because he was not of the Catholic faith. Some instinct, derived perhaps from his Protestant childhood at Bragg, made Jeffrey faintly suspicious of all the symbols; and yet, though his mind still dealt with his own thoughts, those thoughts were moving more slowly. There was something in that building which had also been in Chartres, and he remembered what it had been. There was no sense of time. Although the scent of incense and the burning wax from all the candles spoke of time, still time did not disturb him.

He had not prayed for a long while and he was not used to prayer, and he was quite sure that he had not come there to pray. Yet he found himself repeating the Lord's Prayer in his mind and he remembered how it had sounded spoken in unison on the occasions when he and Madge had attended an Episcopal service.

"Forgive us our trespasses, as we forgive those who trespass against us."

Those words, he remembered, were always sibilant and awkward when the congregation murmured them; but now, as they ran through his mind, they were solemn and beautiful, although they were not the words he had been brought up on when he was a boy in Bragg—"Forgive us our debts, as we forgive our debtors."

and the rest. Still it was that she had said nothing [illegible] anything [illegible]
It was different when he [illegible]
would never be another [illegible]
[illegible]
was that he was thinking of so many things that was what [illegible]
[illegible] when he went to [illegible]
[illegible] from the sunlight of the street [illegible]
[illegible] thinking [illegible]
[illegible]
[illegible]
[illegible] looking at the [illegible]
[illegible]
[illegible] of the Catholic faith. [illegible]
Protestant [illegible]
[illegible]
[illegible] more [illegible]
[illegible] in Chartres, and he remember [illegible]
was [illegible] of time. Although [illegible]
[illegible]

He had not prayed for [illegible]
[illegible] quite sure that he had not [illegible]
[illegible]
[illegible]
[illegible]

[illegible]
[illegible] these words [illegible]
[illegible]
[illegible]
[illegible]
[illegible]

POINT OF NO RETURN

To B. F. H.
with love

Contents

PART ONE

PART TWO

PART THREE

PART ONE

1

Thy Voice Is Heard thro' Rolling Drums

—ALFRED LORD TENNYSON

Charles Gray had not thought for a long time, consciously at least, about Clyde, Massachusetts, and he sometimes wondered later what caused him to do so one morning in mid-April, 1947. It was a mental accident that reminded him of certain passages on telepathy in *Man the Unknown,* the book by Alexis Carrel which everyone had been reading before the war. For a month Charles had read snatches of *Man the Unknown* each morning on the train, after finishing the headlines and the financial page of the *New York Times.* In fact he had done this while going through one of those self-improving phases that sometimes still overtook him—although he had begun to doubt, even before the war, that you could materially better your general cultural deficiencies by thirty minutes' reading every day. He would probably have done as well for himself by doing crossword puzzles or pondering on the financial difficulties of the New York, New Haven and Hartford, or by simply staring out of the window at Rye, Harrison and Mamaroneck. Still he had those hopeful moods occasionally. When he looked at the sets of Conrad and Kipling around the fireplace of the knotty pine library and at those newer books that Nancy kept buying and at the older ones of his father's that had come from Clyde, he could still feel that he, too, might become familiar with the world's great classics, provided he could get things sufficiently straightened out at home so that he could have a moment by himself without Nancy's coming in to take up some problem or without Bill's interrupting with his algebra. At least he had not yet lost his old desire to read, though Nancy said he had. He had read *Man the Unknown* all the way through, sometime around 1935, and now in 1947 he could still remember that it had something in it about telepathy.

In Charles's own experience when something was about to happen to you, particularly anything rather unpleasant, you always had a vague sort of a preview of what was coming. It was like those previews that flashed before you in the darkness of a motion picture theater—"*It's one way or the other, Clifton—Take it or leave it—Darling, I can't leave you, but I must—Don't fail to see next week the struggle between love and duty.*" At any rate, he did not feel the way he should have felt that morning. When Nancy waked him up, he had a slight headache—nothing that would not pass, however, when he had some coffee.

"Are you awake now?" Nancy asked.

"Yes," he answered, "naturally I'm awake. It's a terrible morning, isn't it?"

"If you'd only remember," Nancy said, "not to take anything to drink after dinner. I've learned it long ago and I don't see why you can't."

It always annoyed him when Nancy got on the subject of alcohol, because she invariably made it seem as though alcohol were a problem. She was always saying to people that she and Charles, when they were just quietly at home, enjoyed each other's company so much that they did not need a cocktail—which sounded well enough but was not strictly true, particularly when Nancy got started on the household bills.

"I hate sitting around with a lot of people," he said, "just talking after dinner. I can't take four hours of steady conversation after I've been talking all day."

"Now, darling," Nancy said, "who was it who wanted to go to the Cliffords'?"

"All right," Charles said, "who was it?"

"I told you," Nancy said, "that we didn't have to go to the Cliffords'. They had us in January and we had them and everything was square and now we'll have to have them again."

"Well, we don't have to have them right away," Charles said. "Let's try not to think about it now. She's the one who gets me down. You know, when I see the whole picture I can't help feeling sorry for Bradley Clifford."

"Everybody's always sorry for him," Nancy said. "I wish you'd start feeling sorry for yourself."

"I do," Charles said, "right at this moment."

"And I wish you'd feel sorry for me."

"I do," Charles said. "I do feel sorry for you and for everybody else who lives in this bedroom town and in fact for everyone else in the world. That's the way I feel at the moment."

"Darling," Nancy said, "don't be so broad-minded. You'll make me cry."

"Is Bill awake?" Charles asked.

"Yes," Nancy said. "He doesn't have your troubles."

"He doesn't have to stay up all night," Charles said. "Is he out of the bathroom?"

"Yes, dear," Nancy said. "There's no excuse for you to lie there. You'd better get up or there'll be the usual morning marathon."

"Is Evelyn up?" Charles asked.

"She's up and she's studying her geography," Nancy said. "And besides, she doesn't use your bathroom."

"All right," Charles said. "All right."

"And don't go to sleep again," Nancy said. "I have to go down and cope with the coffee."

"What?" Charles asked.

"You heard me," Nancy said. "You're always better when you have your coffee. Now don't go to sleep again."

"What's happened to Mary?" Charles asked.

"She went to spend the night with her sister in Harlem," Nancy said. "She won't be back until tomorrow afternoon."

"Are you sure she's coming back?" Charles asked.

"Oh, yes, she's coming back," Nancy said. "She's left everything in her room."

"All right," Charles said. "All right. Is it raining?"

"Yes," Nancy said. "It's raining hard, and the windshield wipers on the Buick hardly ever work."

"Well, that makes it swell," Charles said. "It's nice it's come to our attention."

"I thought that might wake you up," Nancy said. "You'd better wear your herringbone suit. It came back from the cleaners yesterday. I've put your ruptured duck on it."

She was, of course, referring to the gold emblem which had been issued to ex-soldiers and sailors by a grateful government, but there was no reason why she had to call it by its GI name, as though she had been in the service, too. Also there was no reason why she should keep inserting it in his buttonhole. The emblem placed him in a youthful category to which he did not belong. He was not sure how well it looked at the bank, either.

"Never mind it," Charles said. "I'm not running for any office." He checked himself because he knew exactly what she would say before she said it.

"Oh, yes, you are," she said, "and don't you keep forgetting it. You're right in there polishing apples."

"All right," he said, "I'm not forgetting." There was no way to forget, since most of his life had been spent polishing some apple or other. If you had to earn your living, life was a series of apples.

"And don't forget," and Nancy shook his shoulder, "to put two hundred into the housekeeping account. It's down to twenty dollars and I'm going to draw on it today."

"What," Charles asked, "again?"

"Yes," Nancy said, "again and again and again. I thought you'd like some cheerful news, darling."

"All right," Charles said. "It's a hell of a morning, isn't it?"

"And don't forget that herringbone," Nancy said, "and don't take that thing out of the buttonhole. No matter how well Roger Blakesley looks, he hasn't got a duck."

"No," Charles said, "that's right. He was too bright to get one."

"And remember we're going to the Burtons' Friday night," Nancy said. "Don't forget to tell Mr. Burton you're looking forward to it when you see him." Nancy was good at putting details into useful order.

When Charles was in the bathroom shaving he disassociated himself from the activities of the moment and though he had always heard people say that you had your best thoughts while shaving, all that he usually thought about at such a time was that he was in a hurry. Now that he looked in the plate-glass mirror in the baked-enamel medicine cabinet—the expensive cabinet that Nancy had induced the architect to install instead of a cheaper fixture—the brushless cream on his face, the battered safety razor he was holding, and in fact the entire bathroom gave him a transient feeling. He had been moving about in the last few years from one set of plumbing appliances to another, in Pullmans, hotels, in ships' heads and in Quonset huts, but he was still paying for this unfamiliar bathroom.

The house had been a thirty-thousand-dollar house before the war, not including extras and there had been a number of extras. It had been more than they could possibly afford, but then the house itself had never looked expensive. Nancy had wanted everything to be right and she had always dreamed about the right sort of bathroom. Those were the days when there was no shortage in materials and when there were all sorts of catalogues. You could have fixtures in colors and you could select from a dozen built-in showers. You could have it done in tile or any way you wanted—and then there were all those waterproof wallpapers. Charles had wanted the one with fishes but Nancy had wanted the one with sailboats and after all he was doing it for Nancy and the children.

He should have felt at home in that bathroom because the architect had drawn and redrawn it, and he and Nancy had quarreled over it twice; but now, although the building of the house and the bathroom and all those struggles with copper pipes and automatic gas heaters were a part of the comparatively recent past, the memories seemed as hazy as those of childhood. The whole house now seemed to belong to him only vaguely. It was the same way with the branches of the oak tree that he saw outside the window.

It was, as he had said, a hell of a morning. The sky was leaden and the air was full of the pervasive, persistent sort of rain of early spring. The water was soaking into the frostless ground and was dripping from the bare twigs of the oak tree, giving them a purplish silver tinge, and the buds on the branches were already swelling. He was thinking of the family bathroom in Clyde, Massachusetts, which everyone had used before his father had added others in 1928. He was thinking of its white walls, its varnished floor and its golden-oak-framed mirror—not a specially designed bathroom but one that had been installed in what must have been a small bedroom once at the end of the second-story hall. For a second this recollection had been so vivid that the tree and the rain had not seemed right. Trees and the rain were different in Clyde, particularly at that season in the year. April rain was colder in Clyde. It generally came with the east wind, so it would beat hard on the windows; and the house, in spite of the hot-air furnace, was always damp and chilly. There were more elms than oaks in Clyde, and in April there was hardly a hint of spring.

His herringbone suit had a slight benzine odor which showed it was just fresh from the cleaners. He had worn it very little though it was four years old and now it was tight in the waist and shoulders, but not too tight. It was not a bad-looking suit at all and in fact it made him look rather like one of those suburban husbands you often saw in advertising illustrations, a whimsically comical man who peeked naïvely out of the corners of his eyes at his jolly and amazed little wife who was making that new kind of beaten biscuits.

There were ten minutes left for breakfast and it was important to keep his mind on the immediate present, yet when he went downstairs that memory of Clyde hung over him in a curiously persistent way, almost like a guilty secret, not to be discussed. Clyde had always bored Nancy and he could not blame her much. Nancy had come from upstate New York and he seldom wanted to hear about her home town either.

"Darling," Nancy used to say, "we never saw each other in either of those places, and thank God we didn't."

She was absolutely right. Thank God they hadn't, or they might have misunderstood each other. He had first seen Nancy in a partner's outer office in a law firm downtown on Pine Street, the firm of Burrell, Jessup and Cockburn. He could remember the exact, uncompromising way that she sat behind her typewriter and the exact amount of attention she had given him, not a bit more than was necessary and that was not very much.

"Mr. Jessup's in conference and he won't be free for half an hour," Nancy had said. Nancy was always able to keep track of time as readily as a railroad conductor. That was the way he and Nancy had met and that was all there had been to their meeting.

"You needed a haircut," Nancy told him later, "but not very badly, and the way you held your brief case showed you weren't one of those bond boys, and you didn't have a handkerchief in your breast pocket."

"Well," he had told her later, "you didn't look so lovable either."

"Darling," Nancy said, "that's one of the nicest things you've ever told me. I spent a long time cultivating just that look."

When he came down to the dining room, Nancy was sitting in much the same posture, very straight in her bleached oak chair. Instead of a typewriter she was manipulating a toaster and an electric percolator, and there was a child on either side of her—their children.

"Don't trip over the extension cords," Nancy said. "Billy—"

His son Bill rose from the table and pulled out his chair for him, a respectful attention on which Nancy insisted and which always made Charles nervous.

"Well, well," Charles said. "Good morning, everybody. Hasn't the school bus come by yet?"

"It's not the school bus," his daughter Evelyn said. "It's the school car. Why do you always call it a bus?"

"It ought to be a bus," Charles said. "You kids ought to be going to a public school."

Nancy was looking at him critically as she always did before he went to town.

"You've forgotten your handkerchief," she said.

That idea of hers that every well-dressed man should have a corner of a handkerchief peeking from his breast pocket he often thought must have been a hangover from Nancy's earlier days, but then perhaps every woman had her own peculiar ideas about male dress.

"Now listen, Nance," he said, "never mind about the handkerchief." It surprised him that she let it pass.

"Evelyn, pass your father his coffee," she said.

"And don't look cute when you're doing it," Bill said.

"Mother," Evelyn said, "won't you tell Bill to stop that, please?"

"Yes," Nancy said. "Stop, Bill, and go out in the kitchen. Put the eggs in and watch the clock."

There was no necessity for listening carefully to the voices of Nancy and the children. He could go on with his orange juice, toast, and coffee as though the conversation were a background of words issuing from a radio. He had heard the program again and again.

"You've got to leave in five minutes," Nancy said. "The roads will be slippery."

Charles pulled his watch from his vest pocket, the one that Nancy had given him just before they were married, and glanced at it.

"And remember," Nancy said, "you'll have to go and get the Buick out. Something seems to be wrong with the automatic choke."

"Didn't you send it down to be fixed?" Charles asked.

"Yes," Nancy answered, "but you know what they're like at that service station. They just look at the carburetor and don't do anything. I wish you'd go to that new Acme place."

"Acme. I wonder what acme means exactly," Charles said.

"Why, Daddy," Evelyn said. "Don't you know what acme means? It means the top of everything."

It startled him to have Evelyn tell him something which he should have known himself and which, of course, he would have known if he had put his mind on it. The trouble was that he had not been back long enough for broken links of habit to be wholly mended, and everything at home still seemed to have sprung ready-made out of nowhere. There was something in Berkeley's theory of philosophy—as he had learned it at Dartmouth—that there was no proof that anything existed except in the radius of one's consciousness.

Before the war, Bill had been nine and Evelyn had been six, and now Evelyn was able to look up acme in the dictionary. He was in a ready-made dining room, though he had been responsible for its having been built in 1940. He and Nancy had bought the bleached chairs and table and sideboard and had agreed that the walls should be done in pickled pine because they had wanted it to look light and modern. The glazed chintz draperies still had their original luster and the begonias and ivy and geraniums in the bow window looked as though they had just come from the florist, because Nancy had made an intensive study of the care and feeding of household plants. There were no finger marks or smudges on the table or the chairs and the light carpet was just back from the cleaners without a smudge on it either. It was amazing how beautifully Nancy could keep a house with only one maid to help her.

"You'd better get the Buick now," Nancy said. "There's no use killing ourselves getting to the train."

The rain gave the blue gravel near the garage a metallic sheen. The water on the lightly whitened brick of the house—he believed it had been called Southern Brick—made the variegated color look like new plastic, and the leaves of the rhododendrons and the firs near the front door glistened like dark cold water.

The Buick started easily enough, though it was a 1940 car. It reminded him of a well-preserved old gentleman with an independent income, cared for by a valet, and he did not see how Nancy could have kept it looking so well considering all the bundles and the children it had carried.

"Move over," Nancy said. "I'll drive down."

She adjusted a little cushion against the small of her back and took the wheel. She had on one of those transparent, greenish rain capes over her greenish tweed suit. She pulled her gloves deliberately over her engagement and wedding rings, but then she had fixed it so there was plenty of time. She had always said that she was never going to have any man of hers get ulcers running for the train.

When they were out of the drive and safely through the gates marked Sycamore Park, he glanced at her profile. The rain had made her hair, where it showed at the edges of her green felt hat, moist and curly. They always seemed much more at peace when she took him to the station than at any other time and for some reason it was always the friendliest moment of the day. He and Nancy were alone together, undisturbed by all the rest of the world.

"You didn't forget your reports, did you?" Nancy asked.

"No," he said. "I've got them."

"Have you still got that headache? There's an aspirin in the glove compartment."

"It's all right," he said. "It's gone."

"Well, that's good," she said. "Darling?"

"What?" he asked.

"It's nice driving you to the train again. It's sort of like coming back to where we started."

He looked at her again. She was looking straight ahead of her, but she was smiling.

"Yes, I know what you mean," he said. "It's funny, when I came down there to breakfast this morning the whole place seemed ready-made."

"Ready-made?" she repeated.

"Yes," he said. "Just as though I'd never done anything about it."

"I know," she said. "I'm too efficient."

"That isn't what I mean," he said.

"It's all right," she answered, "as long as you don't mind."

He was never nervous when she was driving. She had a peculiar gift of being able to divide her concentration, which permitted her to drive and at the same time balance the household budget or quarrel artistically or give intelligent answers to the children's questions about God and the life hereafter. The casual way in which she spoke told him that she was thinking very carefully about what she was saying.

"I wish I could stop coaching from the sidelines, but I can't help it, can I?"

There was no use answering because of course she knew what he would say, but still he answered.

"Hell, no," he said. "Of course you can't."

"Someday you're going to say you don't like it. I'm afraid of that."

There were drawbacks, he was thinking, to knowing anyone too well, and yet there was no way to avoid this. There was no actual chance for decent concealment when you knew someone's voice as well as he did hers. It was all part of the relationship that was known as love, which was quite different from being in love because love had a larger and more embracing connotation. It was a shadowy sort of edifice built by habit, without any very good architecture, but still occasionally you could get enough impression of its form to wonder how it had been built.

"Darling," she was saying, and her voice broke briskly into his thoughts, "why don't you ask Burton what the score is? Aren't you tired of waiting?"

The question made him edgy because that phrase about the score was as out of place as her allusion to the ruptured duck. She might just as well have said, Why not go and ask Burton what's cooking, and he was very glad she hadn't. The car had stopped at the Post Road for the red light. They were almost at the station.

"That would be stupid," he said. "Naturally he knows I want to know."

"Well, can't we get it over with?"

"It will get over," Charles said. "Everything does."

"Well, if we just had the cards on the table," Nancy said. "If you just said to him—"

"Now don't tell me what to say to him," Charles said, "because I'm not going to say anything."

The light turned green and the car moved forward.

"Well, I hope Roger Blakesley likes it. Do you know what Molly told me yesterday?" Nancy asked.

Charles moved uneasily. They were going down the main street. A gift shop had opened there and also a new antique shop on the corner and he wondered why he had not noticed either of them before.

"She said Roger's so glad you're back and settled down."

"Well, that's swell," Charles said. He had observed that Roger Blakesley had lately been assuming the attitude that Charley had only just returned from the service and was still getting adjusted. He was very glad they were reaching the station. "If the officers and directors want him, they'll take him."

"And you'll have to resign," Nancy said.

"The next thing," Charles said, "you'll be asking me to think of the children." He began to laugh. "'Thy voice is heard thro' rolling drums, that beat to battle where he stands; thy face across his fancy comes, and gives the battle to his hands.' Alfred Lord Tennyson." They were stopping at the last light and the station was just ahead of them and there were still three minutes before eight-thirty. "This whole business sounds like Tennyson. It's exactly as contrived."

"All right, why is it so funny?" Nancy asked.

"I didn't say it was funny," Charles said. "I said it was contrived. The little woman kissing her husband good-by. Everything depends on this moment. He must get the big job or Junior can't go to boarding school. And what about the payments on the new car? Good-by, darling, and don't come back to me without being vice-president of the trust company. That's all I mean."

Nancy threw the car into gear.

"Don't say that," she said.

"Why not?" Charles asked.

"Don't say it," Nancy said, and her voice was louder, "because maybe you're right."

"Now wait a minute—" he began, but she did not let him finish.

"Because if you say that—" she said, "if you mean that—maybe it isn't much but it's all we have. Maybe it isn't much, but then maybe we aren't much and if you feel that way there won't be anything any more."

It was a discordant instant of revelation and it broke unpleasantly into the morning. He thought of Clyde again, and Clyde was suddenly more real to him than the car in front of the station. He was thinking of peaceful voices saying that you often had moments of doubt or disappointment, that you often wondered whether what you were doing was worth while. The solution was to continue doing the best you could and everything would turn out all right in the end.

"Now listen, Nance," he began, and then for some reason he felt as deeply moved as if he were saying good-by to her for good. "Let's not get so emotionally involved."

"Involved with what?" Nancy asked.

"With each other," he said. "Let's get some sense of proportion."

"Don't talk about proportion," Nancy said. "There isn't any time."

It was only one of those minor partings, but he was leaving her again. "If you're not taking the five-thirty," she said, "call me up. Good-by."

"Good-by," he said. "I'll make the five-thirty all right."

2

A Moment, While the Trumpets Blow

—ALFRED LORD TENNYSON

Shortly before the outbreak of the European war, Charles had begun taking the eight-thirty. This was a privilege that had raised him above the ruck of younger men and of shopworn older ones who had to take the eight-two. It indicated to everyone that his business life had finally permitted him a certain margin of leisure. It meant that he was no longer one of the salaried class who had to be at his desk at nine.

The eight-thirty train was designed for the executive aristocracy, and once Mr. Guthrie Mayhew, not one of the Mayhews who lived on South Street, not George Mayhew, but Guthrie Mayhew, who was president of the Hawthorn Hill Club and also president of Mayhew Brothers at 86 Broadway, had even spoken of getting an eight-thirty crowd together who would agree to occupy one of those club cars with wicker chairs and card tables and a porter, to be attached to the eight-thirty in the morning and again to the five-thirty in the afternoon. Mr. Mayhew was a public-spirited man who always enjoyed organizing small congenial groups. He had suggested the idea first to Tony Burton and they both had decided that they did not want it to be an old man's car. They wanted some of the younger fellows, too, who were coming along, and they wanted it informal. You could play bridge or gin rummy or pitch if you wanted, or else you could merely sit and read; but the hope was, if you got a congenial group aboard, both young and old, coming not from all walks of life, because there was only about one walk of life on the eight-thirty, but from different business atmospheres—brokers, lawyers, doctors, architects, civil engineers, and maybe even a writer or two from as far away as Westport, if you could get one—it was the hope that if you could get such a crowd together, you could have some good conversation going to and from the city.

You could have an interchange of ideas on all sorts of subjects, and goodness knows there was a lot to talk about in these days, a whale of a lot, Mr. Mayhew said. There was the New Deal, and Mr. Mayhew was broad-minded about the New Deal. He wanted some New Dealers aboard that car, if you could get them, who would stand right up on their hind legs and tell what the New Deal was about. That car would be a sort of open forum, Mr. Mayhew said. They might even find some newspaperman. They could talk about the Chinese war and about Hitler and Mussolini and the whole European mess. It ought to make the ride to New York a real occasion to which everyone could look forward, because there were a lot of interesting people going to New York if you only got to know them, and in Mr. Mayhew's experience about everything came down to just one thing—knowing and understanding people, and somehow you kept being shut away from people. That, roughly, was Mr. Mayhew's idea, but naturally it had evaporated after Pearl Harbor. Charles remembered Mr. Mayhew's idea vividly, if only because it had come up at the same time that Mr. Burton had suggested that Charles call him Tony.

Charles could still recall the glow he had felt on this occasion and the sudden moment of elation. Mr. Burton had been shy about it in a very nice way, as an older man is sometimes shy. Charles remembered that Mr. Burton had fidgeted with his onyx pen stand and that first Mr. Burton had called him "feller." It had all happened one evening when they had stayed late talking over the Catlin estate, which was one of the largest accounts in the trust department.

Mr. Burton had just made one of his favorite remarks, one which Charles had heard often before. It had happened, Mr. Burton had said, that when he was a sophomore at Yale he had studied Greek. He never knew just why he had hit on Greek, but the result showed that a concentration on any subject trained the mind.

"Now you'd think, wouldn't you," Mr. Burton said, "that the orders of Greek verbs would be a long way from banking. Well, I can only tell you that Greek verbs have taught me more about corporate figures than anything else I ever learned at Yale."

Though Charles had heard this before, he had been pleased that Mr. Burton had touched upon the subject of his Greek studies for it showed that everything was going smoothly.

"Yes, sir," Charles had said. "I'm just beginning to see that everything fits into banking somewhere."

"Everything," Mr. Burton had said. "Everything. You see banking basically is only knowing how to use extraneous knowledge. I like to think of banking as being not only the oldest but, well, the most basically human business that there is in the world, for it deals with all the most fundamental hopes and aspirations of human beings. In fact, I don't like, honestly I don't, to think of banking as a business or even as a profession. Banking—it may startle you a little that I say this, but I'm right, I know I'm right—banking, for a good banker, is an art. The last of the arts, perhaps, but the oldest of the professions."

Charles had heard Mr. Burton advance the idea several times before but he did not interrupt.

"Now you may remember," Mr. Burton had said, "that Mrs. Burton and I took a little trip in 1933. You hadn't been with us long then, but I don't believe that you or anyone else will forget how tense things were in 1933, and now and then I found I was getting a little taut, so when things eased up I decided to go away somewhere to get a sense of perspective. That was when Mrs. Burton and I went to Bagdad. You ought to go there sometime."

Charles could not imagine what had ever made Mr. Burton want to go to such a place, unless it had something to do with Burton's *Arabian Nights*, and he wondered also what connection it had with all the reports that lay on Mr. Burton's mahogany roll-top desk. Mr. Burton had placed his elbows on the desk, had linked his fingers together and was resting his narrow chin on them, and there had been nothing for Charles to do but listen.

Well, it appeared that it had been a very interesting trip to Bagdad. The cruise ship had stopped at Beirut and from there everyone who wanted to take the side trip, including Mr. and Mrs. Burton, had embarked on buses that were as comfortable as the Greyhound buses in America, and after a night in quite a nice French hotel in Damascus, where Mrs. Burton had bought from a real Arab the rare rug that was now in Mr. Burton's library, they had proceeded in these buses at dawn right across the desert. It had been hot, but there was plenty of ice water and the seats were comfortable. Toward evening the buses had stopped at a place called Rutba Wells right out in the middle of nowhere. It was a mud-walled fort like something in the story *Beau Geste*, except that, fortunately, it was run by the British and so was sanitary.

After a very good meal of soup and fried chicken, Mr. and Mrs. Burton had played a game of darts, that British game, right in that mud-walled fort; and then in the cool of the evening they had proceeded right across the desert to Bagdad, and there it was at dawn—a city on a muddy river, spanned by a bridge of boats. They had stopped at the Tigris Hotel, right on the river, large and not uncomfortable, though one strange thing about it was that the water from the bathtub came right out on the bathroom floor and then drained through a hole in the corner.

The first morning he and Mrs. Burton had gone to the museum to see the treasure from Ur, parts of which looked like something in a case at Cartier's. You got a lot out of travel if you kept your eyes open. There had been a man in the museum, a queer sort of British archaeologist, who showed him some mud bricks that were actually parts of an account book. When you got used to them, you could see how they balanced their figures; and on one brick, believe it or not, there was even an error in addition, preserved there through the centuries. This had meant a great deal to Mr. Burton. That clerical error in mud had given him an idea for one of the best speeches he had ever written, his speech before the American Bankers' Association in 1936 at the Waldorf-Astoria. Mr. Burton had opened a drawer and had pulled out a deckle-edged pamphlet.

"Take it home and read it if you have the time," he said. "I dashed it off rather hurriedly but it has a few ideas. It starts with that mistake in addition."

The pamphlet was entitled *The Ancient Art of Banking, by Anthony Burton, President, the Stuyvesant Bank, Delivered before the American Bankers' Association, May 1936.*

"Why, thanks very much, sir," Charles had said. "I certainly will read it." It was not the time to say that he had read the speech already or that for years he had made a point of reading all Mr. Burton's speeches.

"Look here, feller," Mr. Burton said, and he had blushed when he said "feller," "why not cut out this sir business? Why not just call me Tony?"

That was in 1941 but Charles still remembered his great joy and relief, with the relief uppermost, and that he could hardly wait to hear what Nancy would say.

"You know, Charles," Mr. Burton had continued, "Guthrie Mayhew and I have quite an idea. We're going to get hold of Tommy Mapes on the New Haven and see if he can't get us a special car on the eight-thirty. How about getting aboard? My idea is to call it the *Crackerbarrel*."

"Why, thanks," Charles had said. "I'd like to very much, Tony."

He had worked late that night and he could not remember what train he had taken home, but Nancy had been asleep when he got there.

"Nance," he said, "wake up. I've got something to tell you. Burton's asked me to call him Tony." And Nancy had sat bolt upright in her twin bed.

"Start at the beginning," Nancy had said. "Exactly how did it happen, and don't leave out anything."

They must have talked for a long while, there in the middle of the night. Nancy had known what it meant because she had worked downtown herself.

"Now wait," she had said. "Let's not get too excited. Who else calls him Tony?"

"I don't think anyone else does," Charles had told her, "except the officers, and old Jake when he speaks of him."

"Who's old Jake?" Nancy asked.

It surprised him that Nancy did not know, for she usually kept everything straight, but when he told her that old Jake was a day watchman in the vault who had been there when Mr. Burton had first started at the bank, Nancy had remembered.

"Darling, we ought to have a drink of something, shouldn't we?" she said, but it was pretty late for a drink. "Darling, I knew it would happen sometime. I'm pretty proud of you, Charley."

It was only a week later that they found out that Mr. Burton had also asked Roger Blakesley to call him Tony and they never could find out whom Mr. Burton had asked first.

Tony Burton always boarded the eight-thirty at Stamford and it occurred to Charles that it might be a good idea to walk through the cars and to sit by him if the seat beside him should be vacant. He had nothing particular to say to him, but it might be a good idea. He even went so far as to think of a suitable conversational subject and he decided on the action of the market. He knew it would be a risky subject, to be approached cautiously, because Tony Burton was always careful to say that he was not interested in stock-market gyrations. The Board was convinced, and Charles was too, that the general situation predicated a long-term rise and that the present slump was a temporary adjustment and not the beginning of a bear market, no matter what the statisticians might conclude, unless a drastic change appeared in the foreign situation.

The station was crowded and damp, but in spite of the crowd the atmosphere was restful. You had a feeling that the rush of commuters was nearly over for the day and that of the whole army that had marched to the city only the rear guard was left. The men in the station gave an impression of executive leisure, appearing as if they did not have to arrive anywhere at any particular time, but as if nothing of importance could happen until they did arrive. Their mail would be open and waiting and everything else would be waiting. In the meanwhile, they gathered about the radiator near the ticket windows, talking about the weather, and the waiting room was almost like a club where everyone was on a first-name basis.

As Charles moved to the newsstand to buy the *New York Times* he noticed that Mr. Mayhew was wearing a new gabardine raincoat. He nodded to Courtney Jeffers of the New York Life and to Rodney Bishop in the General

Foods sales department and to Bill Wardwell in Eckert and Stokes. Curiously enough, it was all more familiar than home because it was all a part of the city to which they all were going, something more important than any suburb, a part of life that was more genuine.

There was a sort of preoccupation today, almost a feeling of suspense. He had just bought the *New York Times* and had turned away from the newsstand when he saw that he was face to face with Roger Blakesley. Roger was wearing a blue, pin-striped suit, double-breasted and carefully pressed, in Brooks Brothers' most conservative tradition. His dark brown hat went very nicely with his cheviot overcoat. He was polishing his rimless glasses with a fresh handkerchief and his face, which had grown plumper and more rotund lately, was fresh and shining.

"Why, hello, Charley," Roger said.

"Hello," Charles answered, and then he went on because one had to say something. "Are you still using that electric razor, Roger?" It must have been the smoothness of Roger's cheeks that made him say it.

"Frankly, yes," Roger said. "My beard is just the thing for it, and besides" —he put on his glasses and laughed—"it makes me feel like a putting green." It was just the sort of thing that Roger would have said and his broadening smile showed he was pleased with it.

"Or a bowling green," Charles said.

"All right," Roger said, "a bowling green, as long as you don't cut it too fine. That was a swell party last night, wasn't it? I couldn't tear myself away."

"Neither could I," Charles answered, and they both smiled.

"Listen, Charley," Roger asked, "will you have any time on your hands today?"

"Not much," Charles said. "How about lunch?"

"I can't make it," Roger said. "I have a date with Tony at the University Club. After that Mapes is coming in, but we've got to check up on that Catlin thing sometime before we meet the attorneys."

There was a roaring sound outside and everyone was moving. The eight-thirty was coming in.

"We can go over it on the train if you want to," Charles said. "I've got the papers here."

Roger Blakesley patted his shoulder.

"Boy, I simply can't," he said, close to Charles's ear because of the roaring of the train. "Tony wants me. He's saving me a seat."

Charles raised his voice.

"There's a lot more to banking than you think, isn't there?" he said. "It's an art, isn't it?"

Roger laughed and linked his arm through Charles's.

"Charles," he said, "you're always subtle in the morning. Well, I'll see you in the studio."

"All right," Charles said. "Don't mix your colors wrong, Roger."

Roger had not heard him. He was already bounding up the steps of the third coach. Roger was always quick on his feet and this sort of thing had been going on long enough for Charles to understand its shades of meaning. He was reasonably sure that Tony Burton had not asked Roger to sit with him, and he was not even entirely sure that Tony Burton had asked Roger to lunch at the University Club, even though Tony Burton tried to lunch there when he could on Tuesdays.

Charles found a seat by a window and opened the *New York Times* to the financial page. There was nothing like competition. His mind had been working more alertly since he had met Roger Blakesley and everything assumed a new significance. They were both assistant vice-presidents in the trust department now, but they had both worked almost everywhere in the bank, except the vaults. Either could handle customers about as well as the other. They both were very bright boys, but he had never worried about Roger much until lately. There would have been no reason to do so now if Roger had gone to the war instead of using that period to make himself useful. The financial page was dull but Charles put his mind on it. Roger had a quick way of jumping at facts without examining them first. His own memory was far more retentive and reliable than Roger's and Tony Burton undoubtedly knew it. Charles knew more about the trust accounts than anyone in the bank, more about the limitations under the wills and about the lawyers and the specific family situations. His mind was working smoothly now that he was on the train.

When the train pulled into the lower level of the Grand Central Station, habit made Charles move instinctively, almost oblivious to his surroundings. Without consciously noticing the polished marble of the lower level or the starry vault of the concourse on the upper level, he was aware of the changing spaces, for habit had made him a proprietor of that station and all the streets around it. Habit made him move instantly to the broad stairs on the right and he ran up gently and easily, for no good reason except that he had always taken them at a run. On the upper level he turned sharp right again, walking past the parcel checkroom to the ramp on the left and past the heaps of newspapers by the doors and out to the corner of Forty-second Street and Vanderbilt Avenue.

Whenever he emerged from the station and set foot on Forty-second Street, he experienced in varying degrees a sense of coming home. Sometimes this feeling was one of deep gratitude and more often only one of boredom, but whenever he arrived there, all those other times he had reached Forty-second Street somehow added themselves together into an imponderable, indivisible sort of sum. His mind was adjusted to the traffic, to the drugstores and the haberdasheries, to the Lincoln Building and the Park Avenue ramp. He belonged to New York, and conversely New York belonged to him, if only because so much of his life and energy and thought had been spent within its limits.

It did not matter that he had not been born and raised there, because New York belonged almost exclusively to people who had come from other places. New York in the end was only a strange, indefinable combination of triumph, discouragement and memories. It did not matter what the weather was there, or the season of the year, or whether there was war or peace—he was always able to lose himself in the city's abstractions. The place was changing—new stores, new façades, new plastics—without his being able one jot to influence that change, but still the changing place belonged to him. The only institution in the neighborhood that had not been altered much was the Stuyvesant Bank, which had been given its name when Murchison Brothers had first started the business on lower Broadway in the early 1800's. It had moved uptown long since, but almost from the beginning of its history the Stuyvesant had been what it still was, a family bank.

It was essentially the same, Charles often thought, as it had been when he had first entered it with his father on a trip to New York when he was twelve years old. It was too late now to recall the circumstances which had caused that trip, but it must have been one of those times when some transaction in Boston had put his father temporarily in a genial and opulent mood or they never would have come to New York or stopped at the Hotel Belmont. Another sign that something must have gone exceptionally well was that his father had brought his cigar case, and what Charles could remember most clearly about the trip was the rich smell of heavy Havana tobacco. It was always a good sign when his father took his cigar case from the back of his upper bureau drawer. Charles remembered very clearly the oak woodwork in the downstairs room of the Belmont where they had breakfasted after driving in a taxicab from the Fall River Line pier. There was no need, his father had said, to bother taking the elevated or the subway. They had breakfasted on grapefruit with a red cherry in the center, oatmeal and cream, kippered herrings and scrambled eggs, and after consuming a pot of coffee his father had lighted a cigar.

"It's a great town, New York, when you get to know it," his father had said, "and everyone ought to get to know New York." It was pathetic, Charles sometimes thought, that desire of his father's to be a man of the world. It was not unlike Tony Burton's desire to be a great cosmopolitan, and their efforts achieved approximately the same measure of success. "Now straighten your tie. We're going to the bank to cash a check, and pull your stockings up."

It was God's truth, and not a very palatable one, that Charles wore black ribbed stockings and knickerbockers, purchased at Setchell's on Dock Street at Clyde. He was old enough to be painfully embarrassed at the way his stockings kept slipping down and he tried to change the subject.

"What bank?" he asked.

"Let's see," his father said, and he pulled a letter from his pocket. "The Stuyvesant Bank. It's just a few blocks from here."

Even in 1916, banks were beginning to be imposing, and Charles was disappointed when he first saw the Stuyvesant, for anyone could see that it was a bank in a former private dwelling, a big New York corner house of somewhat sooty brick and brownstone. A doorman in a black chauffeur's uniform stood on the sidewalk near what had been the front door, and once they were inside the impression of being in a house still remained, though all the ground floor had been remodeled to make room for the tellers' cages. One side was for ladies. Here in an open fireplace a little fire was burning, and near by was a desk behind which sat a white-haired gentleman whose duty it was to give the ladies advice and help, just as Mr. Cheseborough did now. There were the same mahogany roll-top desks by the windows, and other desks in the distance under electric lights. Charles could remember staring at the flight of stairs leading to the vaults in the old house cellar while the teller read his father's letter and asked his father whether he wanted it in fives or tens.

"That's a good bank," his father had said when they were out on the street again. "A family bank, without any funny business. It stood up through the panic of 'ninety-three."

That old house of the Stuyvesant was still an asset. It was still a family bank, whose doorman could greet depositors like the doorman of a club, and inside there was always a studied atmosphere of leisure. One had a reassuring suspicion, as one entered, that the Stuyvesant had handled the same family accounts for generations and that an effort had always been made to think of individuals as well as the size of their deposits. Superficially the Stuyvesant was more like Brown, Shipley, 123 Pall Mall, in London than like an American bank, and it paid to keep it that way.

Year after year there had been talk about a new building, not necessarily a modern one but something Colonial and bright like that brick effort of the Bank of Manhattan on Madison Avenue—but the directors had always in the end turned down such proposals. It paid to keep the Stuyvesant in that ugly old brownstone mansion with its floor plan about the way it had been when the Stuyvesant had first moved there. Though adjoining houses had been added and though its interior had been refinished and its exterior occasionally sandblasted and cleaned in the rough beauty-parlor treatment given to old houses, it paid to keep everything looking essentially the same. It paid to keep the open fire that burned real logs and to encourage tellers and investment counselors to be patient with confused old ladies and genial with arthritic old gentlemen. It paid to have a foreign department which could take great pains about letters of credit and perhaps advance allowances to depositors' grandchildren overextended while traveling on the Continent. It paid to have kindly tax experts seemingly willing to waste hours over minor problems of bewildered clients.

Other banks, larger ones, were constantly advertising their friendly services and pointing out the almost insoluble personal complications faced by anyone who owned property in this period of economic change and regulation, but the Stuyvesant seldom advertised. It was a matter of deeds rather than words at the Stuyvesant, and it paid. The wills of deceased depositors were proof enough that the Stuyvesant had been an institutional friend through life. The Stuyvesant had been named as executor and trustee in hundreds of wills. The employees of the Stuyvesant understood rich clients and knew all the pains and drawbacks of being rich, although they were not rich men themselves. They had to deal familiarly, almost jovially, but always scrupulously with large sums of money, while living usually on modest salaries.

If you were successful at the Stuyvesant you ended by developing a priestly, untouchable, ascetic attitude. You learned to think of your own financial life and your own problems as something apart from those other financial complications. If you did well enough to become an executive in the Stuyvesant, and this required a long time and an arduous apprenticeship, you found yourself solving the problems of individuals who had difficulty living within incomes approaching a hundred thousand dollars a year. You found yourself spending the working day discussing the investment of huge sums of money, only to get home yourself and to worry because the butcher's bill had risen some twenty dollars above the previous one. You had to debate the purchase or the sale of controls in business enterprises and then return home yourself to decide whether or not you could afford to buy a motor lawn mower, or a ready-made or a tailor-made suit. In time this gave you a split personality since you had to toss your own problems completely aside and never allow them to mingle in any way with those of clients and depositors when you reached your desk at the Stuyvesant. At your desk you had to be a friend and confidant, as professional as a doctor or a lawyer, ready and with an intelligent perspective for almost anything. Anthony Burton had once said that this attitude was one's responsibility toward society. Though personally Charles had never felt like a social worker, he felt this responsibility. He was already forgetting Nancy and the children, already assuming his business character, when he said good morning to Gus, the doorman on the sidewalk outside the Stuyvesant.

"Is it wet enough for you, Mr. Gray?" Gus asked.

"It has to rain sometime," Charles said. "Are you a grandfather yet?"

"No, not yet," Gus said, "but any minute now."

Then Charles said good morning to Joe inside the door. The bank was scrupulously neat and cleared for action. He could hear the click of the adding machines in back and he could see the new pens and blotters on the depositors' tables as he walked past the tellers behind their gilded wickets and turned to the right past the foreign department to the coatroom. When he had hung up his coat and hat, he looked at himself in the mirror. Though his herringbone suit was a little tight, it was adequate, and he automatically straightened the coat and adjusted his tie. His slightly freckled face was moist from the rain and his sandy hair, though it was carefully trimmed, needed brushing, so he went to the washroom. He had learned long ago that you did not neglect exterior details when you sat out near the vice-presidents' desks by the front window.

Though you seldom talked of salaries at the Stuyvesant, your social status was obvious from the position of your desk. Charles occupied one of the two flat mahogany desks that stood in a sort of no man's land between the roll-top desks of the officers and the smaller flat-tops of lesser executives and secretaries crowding the floor of the bank outside the cages. A green rug extended from the officers' desks, forming a neat and restricted zone that just included Charles's desk and the one beside it which was occupied by Roger Blakesley. Charles could see both their names, Mr. Blakesley and Mr. Gray, in silver letters, and he was pleased to see that he had got there first from the eight-thirty, a minute or two ahead of Roger and Mr. Burton and ahead of everyone else near the windows.

Mr. Burton's desk, which had the best light, was opened already and so was that of Mr. Stephen Merry, the oldest vice-president, and so were all the others except one. This was the desk of Arthur Slade, the youngest vice-president of the Stuyvesant, who had died in a plane accident when returning from the West Coast six months before. The closed desk still gave Charles a curious feeling of incompleteness and a mixed sense of personal gain and loss because he had been more friendly with Arthur Slade than with anyone else in the Stuyvesant—but then you had to die sometime. Once Arthur Slade had sat at Charles's own place but that was before Mr. Walter Harry, who had been president when Charles had first come to the bank, had died of an embolism and everyone had moved like players on bases—Burton to Harry, Merry to Burton, Slade to the vacant roll-top—and so on down to Charles himself. The Stuyvesant was decorously accustomed to accident and death and now it was moving time again and it was so plain where one of two persons might be moving next that it was embarrassing. Any observing depositor and certainly everyone employed in the bank, right up to the third floor, must have known that either Mr. Blakesley or Mr. Gray would move to Arthur Slade's desk by the window. Undoubtedly they were making side bets out in back as Charles used to himself when he had first come there from Boston. Undoubtedly the clerks and the secretaries and the watchmen had started some sort of pool.

Charles pulled back his mahogany chair and sat down, glancing coolly at all the desks in front of him. Miss Marble, his secretary, had already arranged his engagement pad and now she was standing beside him with his morning mail. She reminded him of Nancy as Nancy had looked when he had first known her—a front-office girl, an executive's private secretary, as neat as a trained nurse, whose private life, like his own, was temporarily erased. In spite of that crowded room, for a few hours he and Miss Marble would be almost alone, dependent on each other in a strange, impersonal, but also an intimate relationship. As soon as he said good morning to Miss Marble, his whole mind set itself into a brisk, efficient pattern.

"There's nothing on your calendar," Miss Marble said, "before the meeting, but Mrs. Whitaker has just called you."

"You mean she's called this morning already?" Charles asked.

"Well, not Mrs. Whitaker," Miss Marble said, and she smiled sympathetically. "Her companion called. Mrs. Whitaker's very anxious to speak with you."

"All right," Charles said. "Get her for me in five minutes," and he picked up the letters.

Then Roger Blakesley and Anthony Burton came in from the coatroom and Charles nodded at them and smiled. Roger walked to his own desk at once and Miss Fallon, his secretary, was there, but Anthony Burton stopped for a moment. As he did so, it seemed to Charles that the whole bank was watching them and Mr. Burton must have been aware of this too, but he was more used than Charles to being watched. He stood straight, white-headed and smiling, dressed in a pearl-gray double-breasted suit with an expansive, heavy, gray checked necktie. He had that air of measured deliberation which eventually always covered the features and the postures of bank officers and corporation lawyers. He was slender and athletic, almost young-looking considering that he was close to sixty-five, though Charles could never think of him as having been a young man. Charles always thought of him as unchanging, a measured, deliberate, constant quantity, like a Greek letter in a mathematical formula.

"I didn't see you on the train," Mr. Burton said.

Charles glanced at Roger Blakesley's desk. It was an opportunity but it was also a time to be careful.

"I didn't see you either," Charles said. "Mrs. Whitaker is after me."

It was better to do it that way. It did no harm to have him know about Mrs. Whitaker.

"Well, as long as she's after you and not me," Mr. Burton said. "We'll see you at dinner Friday, won't we?"

"You can count on it," Charles said. "Absolutely," and he laughed and Anthony Burton laughed.

"Yes," Mr. Burton said, "I suppose we can, Charley. How are Nancy and the children?"

"They're wonderful," Charles said. "They keep me out of trouble."

"Nancy's a great girl," Mr. Burton said. "You boys are getting together at eleven, aren't you? I'll be there."

He smiled and nodded and walked over to his desk in the corner.

Charles could not help but wonder whether Mr. Burton had weighed every word of that conversation as carefully as he had. For a second he wondered whether there might be some implication between the lines, but he could not think of any. It had simply been a bland routine conversation, friendly and nothing more. It could not very well have been anything else with Roger's desk right beside his own.

"Mrs. Whitaker's on the telephone now," Miss Marble said, and Charles picked up the desk telephone, speaking softly as one always did in the bank.

"Good morning, Mrs. Whitaker. This is Mr. Gray."

He could recognize a particular tone in her voice. It was the gracious, informal tone that she was in the habit of using when she wanted to make a pleasant impression on people who handled her affairs. It kept one at arm's length, though at the same time giving a pretty little picture of her capacities for universal understanding, democracy, and kindliness.

"Oh, Mr. Gray," he heard her say, "it's so nice to hear your voice."

It was difficult for Charles to respond properly to this remark because he was not at all glad to hear Mrs. Whitaker's and he had heard it a great deal lately, yet he had learned long ago never to be brief with a large depositor, particularly when the Chase, the Guaranty, and the National City were all making overtures for the Whitaker account.

"You sound well and happy, Mrs. Whitaker," Charles said.

Occasionally he was astonished at his own adaptability. He never sounded like himself when he spoke in those hushed tones at his desk. He sounded instead like a doctor or a diplomat, and now he was also a loyal friend of the Whitaker family, who could allow himself the least bit of jovial familiarity.

"Hewett and I are so dreadfully worried, Mr. Gray," Mrs. Whitaker said. "That's why it's so nice to hear your voice."

He could not tell whether it was a further act of graciousness or a lapse of memory that made her refer to Mr. Whitaker as Hewett and he could not recall that she had ever done such a thing before.

"Why, I'm sorry," Charles said. "What have you to be worried about?"

That was it. What did she have to be worried about?

"We have to sell something, Mr. Gray," Mrs. Whitaker said. "We have to sell something right away. We literally haven't got a cent of money."

At least he was able to smile since Mrs. Whitaker was not there and the strange thing about it was that her tone of desperation was completely genuine, as genuine as though she had to sell some piece of furniture to pay the grocer. One part of him could smile but another part was honestly sympathetic. This was one of the things that the bank had taught him.

"Oh," Charles said, and he was about to add that he was sorry, but he checked himself because he had learned that it made depositors angry if you became too actively sorry.

"And we simply don't know what to sell," Mrs. Whitaker said. "We've been going over it and over it."

"I know," Charles said. "It's always difficult to make up one's mind."

"We would like to sell something that has a loss to it," Mrs. Whitaker said, "but there literally isn't anything. Everything shows a profit. Why don't you ever leave us anything with losses?"

Charles drummed his fingers softly on the desk and raised his eyes to the baroque ceiling with its new indirect lighting. It was a wonderful conversation and he wished he could tell Nancy about it but he knew enough not to gossip about clients, particularly large clients.

"Well," he said, "I see what you mean, but the object usually is to show a profit. Most of our friends like it better that way. There are still advantages to having a profit rather than a loss."

"Are there?" asked Mrs. Whitaker. "I know it's so if you say so, but you've simply got to help us, Mr. Gray—anything you decide on—you will help us, won't you?"

"Of course I will," Charles said, and his voice was gently reassuring. "That's what I'm here for. Let me see, you have a number of short-term governments."

"I know. Mr. Whitaker doesn't want to sell those," Mrs. Whitaker said. "He refuses, absolutely."

"Oh," Charles said. "Why does he?"

"Because his father always said that you mustn't be a bear on the United States," Mrs. Whitaker said. "He says that we must back up the government no matter what it does. If we don't back up the government, where will we be? I believe that, don't you?"

"I wouldn't say it would be disloyal," Charles said. "Short-term governments are about the same as cash. That's the way they're generally used."

"Suppose we try to think of something else," Mrs. Whitaker said. "There must be something else."

"Yes," Charles said. "I'll tell you what I'll do. I'd better get a picture of the whole situation. If you're not well enough to come in yourself, I could send Mr. Joyce over to see you."

"I don't think Mr. Joyce has the experience, do you?" Mrs. Whitaker said. "I know he's a charming young man, but he is still rather immature and he's always so, well, so indefinite. And Mr. Thingamajig, what's his name? The one Mr. Burton turned me over to the last time I came in, when you were out. He was indefinite too, and besides I thought he was a little *chétif*."

"Whom do you mean?" Charles asked. "I can't exactly place him from your description."

"That round-faced, pussycat man with glasses," Mrs. Whitaker said. "The furtive, pussycat one."

"You don't mean Mr. Blakesley, do you?" Charles asked.

"That's it," said Mrs. Whitaker. "Mr. Blakesley."

Charles glanced across at Roger Blakesley, who was busy dictating.

"I know him pretty well," Charles said. "I wouldn't say he was a pussycat."

"It's a compliment to you, Mr. Gray," Mrs. Whitaker said, "that Hewett and I both want you to help us, and we simply have to find a hundred thousand dollars somewhere. It isn't asking too much for you to come over, is it?"

"No," Charles said. "It's rather hard for me to get away but I think I can arrange it."

"You see, we've decided after all to buy that ranch," Mrs. Whitaker said. "Albert's fallen in love with it, and I think Mr. Whitaker has too, a little. You'll come at five, won't you, when we can all be quiet at teatime, and tell us how unwise it is?"

"I suppose it depends on the ranch," Charles said. "Why, yes, I think I could arrange to come at five."

"But don't say it's too unwise," Mrs. Whitaker said. "You're so New England sometimes, Mr. Gray. Don't be too uncompromising, will you? Just say it's a little bit unwise."

"All right," Charles said. "At five. I'll remember. A little bit unwise."

"And Mr. Gray."

"Yes," Charles said.

"I adore New Englanders. Father came from Maine."

"Maine's chief export is character," Charles said.

"Do you know," Mrs. Whitaker said, "your voice sounds just like Father's when he was in a disapproving mood. You won't be too Olympian, too disapproving, will you?"

"Oh no," Charles said. "Only a little disapproving. I'll see you at five, Mrs. Whitaker."

Charles put down the telephone and rang for Miss Marble. He would have to call up Nancy and tell her he could not take the five-thirty train, but it was already ten-fifteen and Nancy would be at the chain store. Before he forgot, it would be well to tell Miss Marble.

Down there on the floor of the Stuyvesant you worked with the privacy of a goldfish. There might be certain sheltered corners in the neighborhood of the officers' desks, but there was no shelter at the edge of the green carpet where Charles and Roger Blakesley were stationed. They sat there in a kind of advanced bastion, barring the way to the higher executives, like a knight and a bishop on a chessboard, Charles sometimes thought, pieces expendable in a pinch, who had to pay for their own errors and for others' but who always must protect the rooks and the king and queen. Of course there was an outer ring of pawns in front. Individuals like Tom Joyce, his assistant, at his smaller desk well off the carpet, or Holland just behind him, or Miss Marble, were all protecting pawns. There was no physical railing to guard any of them from the customers.

Old Joe, who stood just inside the door, in a neat business suit instead of a uniform, was in the most exposed position, with duties roughly like those of a floorwalker in a department store. He was the one who helped with the counter checks and the deposit slips, who directed traffic and estimated the preliminary situation. It was he who decided that our Mr. Joyce or our Mr. Holland or, if it seemed justifiable, our Mr. Gray or Mr. Blakesley would be glad to help you.

Charles often wondered why this system of everyone's working in the open should exist. It might have been a part of the great tradition, stemming from the medieval days of the goldsmiths and the moneylenders, that all the workings of a bank should be as visible as the wheels and mainspring of a glass-enclosed French clock. It was perhaps a tradition that was deeply rooted in human suspicion regarding money and those who handled it. There must be positively no deception, everything open and aboveboard and nothing up the sleeve. If anyone had money in a bank, it seemed that he had an inalienable right to see the bankers sweating over it. Then, too, it established confidence to see a roomful of well-dressed, capable individuals sitting behind desks, reading, answering telephones, or moving in fixed orbits, according to their rank. You grew used to being an exhibit, of course, through time and training, and it was surprising how through sheer self-discipline you could avoid making mistakes of fact or even of judgment. You learned a lot about a certain kind of person there and certain facets of human nature.

Granted that the clientele of the Stuyvesant was well above the average and that a high balance must be maintained for a checking account, you still met fools and rascals, and you encountered fear and hopelessness and avarice. Sometimes it seemed to Charles that all human behaviorism was mixed in some way with money.

"That's all now, Miss Marble," he said, and he saw that Tom Joyce was coming over to his desk. It was his habit to come over in the morning to see if there was anything Charles wanted.

Charles must have looked much like Tom Joyce when he was twenty-six or -seven. Tom Joyce had come there fresh out of the Harvard Business School but had only worked at the Stuyvesant for about a year before he was drafted. He had returned there from Europe in 1946 as a captain of artillery to take his old place in the trust department about the time that Charles himself had returned, and now he was one of the bright young men, as Charles had been when he was twenty-six. New York had given Tom Joyce the same veneer and the bank had given him the same watchful manner. He made mental notes for future reference, he was careful, he was steady, he was giving his full attention to the business. He had so much promise that Charles would have liked to give him his place if he should be moved up. The only thing that interfered was age and lack of maturity. Tom Joyce was still too eager and impatient, as he had been once himself, too anxiously, openly competitive, without as yet the finished capacity for concealing his likes and dislikes. That was one trouble with being young and one that Charles was planning to point out when an opportunity arose.

"Good morning, Colonel," Tom Joyce said. It was a little joke between them that was wearing rather thin, and besides military experience did not help at the Stuyvesant.

That will do, Captain," Charles said. "Never mind the war."

"Don't you ever mind it?" Tom Joyce asked.

"I'm too busy to mind it this morning," Charles said, "but I'll tell you what. We'll talk about it if you'll come out some Sunday."

"That'd be swell," Tom said.

That was his trouble, overeagerness, but it was very pleasant to have anyone look at him as Tom Joyce did, pleasant and at the same time a little sad.

"It won't be as swell as all that," Charles said. "How do you like it here downstairs?"

"It's swell," Tom said.

It was a reflection of his own early enthusiasm, his own desire to sacrifice to get ahead, staring back at him over a gap of fifteen years.

"Banks are filled with nice boys, particularly up in front," Charles said. "We're all delightful fellows."

"There are quite a lot of bastards, too," Tom said.

Charles thought, before answering, that this was indiscreet as well as overeager.

"There are everywhere," he answered, "and sometimes it pays to be one."

"You're not one," Tom said.

"Thanks," Charles answered. It was not the conventional way to talk near the front desks of the Stuyvesant. "I'll tell you what I want right now, Tom. I want the Whitaker security list and I want everything on Smith Chemical. Tell them I'll be upstairs this afternoon to look things over."

"Yes, sir," Tom Joyce said. "I'll get them right away."

Nevertheless, he still lingered by the desk and his slowness made Charles look up at him sharply. Charles was about to ask what else he wanted but stopped when he saw the other's face and the guileless admiration in it. It was exactly the way he had looked at Arthur Slade in the old days.

"I've been thinking about Smith, too," Tom Joyce said. It was strange how easy it was to forget that subordinates could sometimes think. "The first quarter earnings were off again."

"Yes," Charles said.

"I met a friend of mine yesterday," Joyce went on. "He has a brother on the floor. He said—"

"Run along now," Charles said, "and never mind what friends' brothers on the floor say—never."

Sometime, he was thinking, he would have to have a talk with Joyce. He would have to make him see that the trust department was a great machine not governed by anyone's individual judgment but by the collective decisions of committees and boards. It might be possible to speak out in meeting and to influence the committee's decision, but that was all. When it came to trends, and the drop in Smith might indicate a trend, the conditions of industries and individual companies were being watched by a dozen subordinates. It was all very well to notice them but it was no use thinking you were a Napoleon running the trust department.

There was nothing more futile or more stultifying to sound investment judgment than being swayed by what other people said. It was one of the first things he had learned when he had started with E. P. Rush & Company in Boston and he had learned it again and again and perhaps he was still learning. The truth was that people who knew anything never said a word. The mere fact thay they were in a position to know guaranteed their silence. Personally, he had never obtained a word of useful information from them except by indirection. You had to work it out yourself. You had to read between facial lines and between the lines of all the financial reports, but in the end it all depended on yourself. There were certain rules, of course, but in these days even rules were flexible because they were influenced by personalities. If you were a good investment man, in the end you had to depend upon yourself. You had to have a sense of the whole financial balance coming from an accumulation of fact, and that accumulation developed as slowly as a stalagmite in a cave, drop by drop. He was thinking as he read the financial reports on the desk before him that they were all written by stupid little people and that no man in a high category would ever dare write one because there were always famines, the wind and the tide.

At any rate he had developed sufficient ability to concentrate so that he could block off the mechanical sounds and the sounds of voices and footsteps.

He was also able to break off from abstraction to immediacy. When he heard Joe speak to him, he was able to lay down his papers instantly and still to remember for future reference exactly where he left off.

"Mr. Gray," Joe said, "here's a gentleman to see you."

Joe had not said there was a gentleman who *wanted* to see him. There was no opportunity to ask who he was or what he wanted. The gentleman was right there.

3

The Business of America Is Business

—CALVIN COOLIDGE

Charles often wished that he was a back-slapping type like Roger Blakesley. Roger had a habit of cultivating acquaintance and contact as scientifically as a market gardener could start young tomatoes in flat boxes and tend them until they grew into vines. It was related to the extrovert, the Dale Carnegie practice of making everyone your friend and being a friend to everyone. Charles had never been good at using personal liking for business purposes, yet naturally he had developed some sort of technique since he was continually dealing with people.

Charles could see that the man whom Joe had brought to his desk was eight or nine years older than he, and this would place him in his early fifties. It was always hard for him to recall, when he met anyone of this age suddenly, whether he had ever known him before, because fifty is a period in life when time begins altering faces in all sorts of disagreeable and incongruous ways. Charles knew instantly that he was not a salesman and that he was not connected with any gainful occupation. Michael Cavanaugh, the bank detective, had once told Charles that he could always tell from one look whether a man had been in jail or not but he could not explain how he could tell this. Charles could not tell either why he knew his visitor was not a business man, except that his face was not smooth enough, his manner did not have that sort of breezy assurance, his clothes lacked uniformity. He had lumpy intellectual features, deep-set eyes and heavy, muscular hands. His shoulders were broad and his coat fitted badly. He was not in business, and at the same time Charles was certain that this man did not want to see him about money. His face with its rather untidy gray hair might have been that of a college professor or some minor employee from a Washington bureau or, finally and most probably, that of a crank, imbued and intoxicated with a social economic theory. You had to be very careful handling anyone like that. He gave Joe a quick questioning glance but there was no help in Joe's placid, pleased expression.

"Good morning," Charles said carefully.

The stranger answered in a nasal, twanging voice.

"Well," he said, "if it isn't Charley Gray."

Charles tried hastily to recall where or when or in what phase of his life they could have met. It might have been at Dartmouth. It might have been in Boston. It might have been somewhere in the war—they all looked different out of uniform.

"Charley," the stranger asked, "don't you remember me at all?"

It was one of those unpleasant moments that you could do nothing about and it was better not to try. This unknown from his past had an outdoors and at the same time an indoors appearance. His mouth was large. There was a patch of stubble at the left of his chin which he had missed in shaving.

"Come on," the stranger said. "I could tell you anywhere, Charles. The child is father of the man."

"Did I know you when I was a child?" Charles asked.

"No, you didn't," the other said. "You knew me when I was thirty-two. My God, Charley, I'm Malcolm Bryant."

Then, of course, he remembered. The deep eyes, the large mouth, the heavy hands—everything came together into sudden focus. He had been thinking of Clyde that morning and there in front of him was Malcolm Bryant, who, of course, had been locked untidily away in memory. It was not an entirely agreeable experience, for it illustrated how easily one could forget things that one once was certain could not possibly be forgotten.

He found himself shaking hands again with Malcolm Bryant and Malcolm was saying that he had dropped in to cash a government check and the cashier had asked him if anyone in the bank could identify him. Then he had looked across the room and there, by God, was Charles. At least the business of the check was useful because it placed everything on a routine basis. Charles initialed the check and gave it to Joe to cash and asked Malcolm Bryant to sit down in the visitor's chair beside him.

"How's Jessica?" Malcolm asked.

"I don't know," Charles said. "I haven't seen her for quite a while."

"What?" said Malcolm. "Didn't you marry Jessica?"

"No," Charles said. It seemed to him that the tellers were unreasonably slow.

"How's Clyde?" Malcolm asked.

"I don't know, Malcolm," Charles said, and, though it was the truth, the bareness of his answer made him feel uneasy.

"Aren't your family still living there?"

"My father's dead," Charles said. "My mother's living with Dorothea in Kansas City."

"Oh," said Malcolm, "so Dorothea's married."

"Yes," Charles said. "She married a man named Elbridge Sterne who was a metallurgist at Wright-Sherwin. He's in Kansas City now."

"Oh," said Malcolm. "Elbridge," and he must have remembered Elbridge Sterne. "What about the old house?"

"I guess it's still there," Charles said. "We sold it. I haven't been there for a very long time."

"A ghost town," Malcolm said. "A vital sort of ghost town. That's the way I described it in the introduction. Haven't you seen my book on Clyde?"

"No," Charles said.

"You've never seen it?" Malcolm said. "It's the best thing the foundation ever got out. I'll give you one."

"Why, thanks, Malcolm," Charles said.

"*Yankee Persepolis*," Malcolm said. "That's what I called Clyde—Persepolis."

Charles wished Joe would come back with the cash.

"Why Persepolis?" he asked.

"Where the Persians worshiped memories," Malcolm said. "I stopped off there in 'thirty-five on my way to India and looked in on the University of Chicago dig. I was studying some dog worshipers in India."

The dog worshipers made Charles more comfortable.

"So you're still on primitive man, are you?" Charles asked.

"Yes," Malcolm said, "but don't forget all man is primitive. You ought to know that. You're primitive."

"Yes," Charles said, "I suppose I am."

"And so is Clyde," said Malcolm. "Primitive, like any other social structure."

Charles glanced uneasily at Roger Blakesley's desk. Roger could not help but overhear the conversation.

"I don't know much about anthropology," Charles said, "except what I learned from you, but it always seems to me you people oversimplify."

"Man only has a few basic behavioristic patterns," Malcolm said, "that are constantly repeated with silly variations. You can't oversimplify. That's the beauty of it."

Charles laughed. Joe was moving toward them with Malcolm's money and Miss Marble had also appeared.

"It's eleven o'clock, Mr. Gray," Miss Marble said.

"Here is your wampum, Malcolm," Charles said. "You'd better count it."

"It's paper," Malcolm said. "It has less intrinsic value than shell money. It's symbolism. Where are you going?"

"I have to go to a meeting," Charles said.

"How about lunch?" Malcolm said. "Come on over to the Harvard Club."

Charles glanced meaningly at Miss Marble.

"Have I a luncheon engagement, Miss Marble?" he asked.

"Why, no," Miss Marble said. "Not today, Mr. Gray."

It was very obtuse of Miss Marble and now there was no reason for him not to have lunch with Malcolm Bryant.

"Well, thanks," Charles said, "if you don't mind lunching early. Can you make it twelve-thirty?"

"Meet me there at twelve-thirty," Malcolm said. "Good-by, Charles."

The depositors' room off the vaults had just been refinished and redecorated and Tony Burton had called the conference there because he wanted to see how everything looked. The vaults themselves, starting with the barred anteroom with its uniformed attendant at the gate, always reminded Charles of the prison scenes in films showing the brave wife on a visit to her erring husband at Sing Sing. There was an efficient smell of oil on all the glittering steelwork, and down the narrow, brightly lighted passages he had a glimpse of the safe-deposit boxes and the private cubicles where individuals could examine the contents of these boxes in an antiseptic seclusion almost as complete as the privacy of the Great Pyramid. Even the gentle sound of a ventilating system added to the impression of inexorable security.

The Stuyvesant was a small bank, but its vaults were completely modern, shock-proof, dust-proof, and time-proof, the acme of safety, the ultimate citadel of property and possession. Put your family jewels in the vault, leave your heirlooms for a modest sum, your priceless papers and mementos, your bond and stock certificates. The Stuyvesant would guard them, and if, for any reason, you did not wish to descend to the vaults yourself, walking the slightly slippery steel floors to your safe-deposit box, if you found it tiring clipping coupons and filling out all those troublesome federal forms, why not let the custodian service of the Stuyvesant do it for you? Why not leave such fatiguing details of ownership to the oversight of careful, conscientious experts? For a purely nominal sum the Stuyvesant would do it for you. Call today yourself and consult one of our officers.

Hugh Garrity, an old Second Division veteran of World War I, dressed now in a Confederate-gray uniform, was on duty at the gate, and Mr. William Poultney, who led clients to their boxes and put both clients and boxes into the private alcoves, was seated watchfully, like a Sing Sing warden but also like a kindly hotel clerk, at his desk behind the bars. Hugh Garrity, and Mr. Poultney too, both wore an air of lynxlike alertness, which was to be expected since the bank officers were making this unaccustomed use of the new room.

"Good morning, sir," Hugh said, and he saluted in that heavy, half-formal way common to all civilian guards. If he had been a dog, Charles thought, he would have slowly wagged his tail. Charles waved his hand to William Poultney and it occurred to him that William Poultney still owed him fifteen dollars, but it was not the time to mention it. Somehow there never did seem to be a suitable occasion for taking up this detail.

"William," Charles asked, "do you use an electric razor or a safety razor?"

William Poultney looked startled and passed his hand carefully over his smooth and rather heavy jowls.

"What's the matter?" he asked. "Don't I look shaved?"

"You look beautiful," Charles said. "I was just thinking of something else."

He was thinking of Roger Blakesley's electric razor, but Mr. Poultney still looked startled. It was seldom in order to joke in an eccentric way down there in the vaults. Besides, William Poultney had a thorough and conscientious mind and he approached every subject carefully.

"As a matter of fact, now you bring it up, I have this shaving problem licked," William said. "The truth of it is, the razor doesn't matter. It's the soap. I use a brushless cream. You just rub it on and there it is."

"Well, well," Charles said. "But you have to get it off later, don't you?"

Hugh Garrity smiled sourly.

"The whole secret is the lather," Hugh Garrity said. "Get a good heavy lather and swab it on your face with a big brush—" His face froze suddenly and he stiffened to attention and Charles saw William Poultney square his shoulders and he heard a light, quick step behind him. It was Mr. Anthony Burton, coming down for the conference.

"Hello," Tony Burton said. "What's the discussion?"

Tony Burton was smiling, but even so there was a faint atmosphere of constraint. After all, they were on their way to a conference.

"I don't know how the subject came up," Charles said. "We were talking about shaving and electric razors."

He was relieved to see Tony Burton smile and he remembered what Tony often said about the bank—that everyone in it was part of one big family.

"I wouldn't have one of those damned electric razors in the house," Mr. Burton said. "My wife gave me one for Christmas and it blew out half the fuses. Come on, Charles."

Charles had a vicious fleeting thought, which he immediately dismissed, that it might be appropriate to say that Roger Blakesley used an electric razor. It was one of those small matters that could possibly count for something, but as he weighed the question he was appalled at his own small-mindedness, and he followed Mr. Burton to the depositors' room without speaking.

That subterranean room, like most bank interiors, had formerly been decorated with dark paneled walls and indirect lighting, with an oval table, and chairs, until someone had hit upon the idea that the Stuyvesant was old enough to have a tradition and the room, in which large customers met with officers and attorneys, ought to have some of that tradition. Thus some interesting prints and pictures now adorned the walls, old prints of Broadway, the Seventh Regiment marching down Fifth Avenue in the Civil War, framed pieces of Continental currency, ancient lottery tickets, century-old advertising broadsides, and a shelf with the first account books of the Stuyvesant. The State Street Trust in Boston, Tony Burton used to say, went in for ship models and now they had so many it made him seasick. He did not want to go as far as this but at the same time it did not hurt to show that the Stuyvesant had a past.

The group had already gathered in the room with a past, although the material under discussion at this routine meeting was to deal essentially with the future. Stephen Merry was there, wearing his new oversize tortoise-shell glasses, and Roger Blakesley with his rimless glasses, and Alfred Brock from trust administration and Tom Joyce and two other men from the trust department. When the door was closed everything was friendly, because they were one big family.

"That was an awful rain last night," Steve Merry said. "Our cellar leaked again."

Then they all sat down and talked for a few moments about cellars and the difficulties of subsurface drainage and Tony Burton began to tell about his own cellar and heating plant until he checked himself and said they had better get to work.

Charles sat listening attentively with his eye on Roger Blakesley as Tony Burton took the meeting over. Since it was a routine conference, he knew most of the subject matter already—the general money situation, the holdings in new accounts, the stability of certain industries. Roger Blakesley, it seemed to Charles, was talking more than usual and trying almost too hard to contribute useful ideas. Charles could follow the discussion with no difficulty and at the same time think of Malcolm Bryant upstairs. He remembered, too, that he must have two hundred dollars transferred to the housekeeping account for Nancy, but his watchfulness never flagged. No matter how dull and how meaningless it was, you had to be very careful at a meeting. You had to remember the arguments and the way the minds had worked around the table. At any moment Tony Burton was apt to ask your opinion.

It was only after half an hour that anything came up of an unusual nature. It came so entirely out of the blue that he had to think carefully back to what had led up to it. Somehow the thread of the meeting and its purpose had been dropped and Tony Burton had embarked on an extraneous subject, and it was most unusual for Tony to stray from the agenda. Suddenly he had announced, out of a clear sky, that a new depositor, with whom Charles was not acquainted, was applying for a six months' loan of three hundred thousand dollars. He was a man named Godfrey W. Eaton who was the head of a substantial company manufacturing tiling. Roger Blakesley had seen him first and he had taken him to Stephen Merry and afterwards to Tony Burton. The bank had investigated Mr. Eaton through all the ordinary channels and now all his business life was down on a memorandum that sounded like the dossiers of a hundred other people whose names had come up at loan conferences.

Mr. Eaton was from the Middle West, where he had owned a number of small factories, and Mr. Eaton had obviously done well for himself because now he owned two apartment buildings free and clear, was a director of a chain of stores, and a part owner of a sugar refinery. He was obviously one of those adroit people who could move from one enterprise to another. The purpose of the loan was for additions to a tile plant. Part of the collateral was in government bonds and part in stocks. It surprised Charles that the officers had not given him the loan at once, particularly since it appeared that Mr. Eaton was a director of the Pacific Investors Trust and thus indirectly controlled several large accounts at the Stuyvesant which were not his own. If Mr. Eaton were disappointed personally, the disappointment might go much further, but recently Tony Burton and Stephen Merry had been exhibiting an unusual slowness in making decisions.

"I wonder why he didn't go to his own bank," Charles said, "not that it's any of my business."

Clearly Roger Blakesley was delighted by the question.

"Because I met him first, Charles," Roger said, "and I'm selling him on the personal service of small banks. I met him playing golf. I've seen quite a good deal of Godfrey Eaton. He's a friend of Sam Summerby—you know, Tony—Sam Summerby from Baltimore."

Perhaps it was Charles's imagination, perhaps he was becoming unduly sensitive, but it seemed to him that there was a slight rustle around the table. It seemed to him that everyone was watching them, and he realized that Roger had made a very good point. He knew that Roger was implying, without being obliged to say it, that he had brought in a very nice piece of business to the Stuyvesant, which was more than Charles had done lately. He was implying, without having to say it, that he brought in new business because he got around and sweetened contacts and played golf with people like Samuel Summerby, and everyone knew the Summerby Corporation. He was implying, without saying it, that it was too bad Charles played a very poor game of golf, and it seemed to Charles that he was called upon to give some sort of answer.

"Are you on a first-name basis with him, Roger?" he asked.

It was a small and sordid little contest. He was implying, without having to say it, that several times in the past Roger had been too prematurely friendly.

"Of course I am," Roger said. "I've known Godfrey Eaton for a year. Everybody at the club knows Godfrey."

"What club?" Tony Burton asked. "Where does Eaton play golf?"

"Why, the Seneca Club," Roger said. "I've got in the habit of playing there lately instead of at Oak Knoll. It's a sportier course."

Mr. Burton nodded and made a note on a memorandum pad. The meeting had turned into a club's committee on admissions.

"I rather liked him myself," Tony Burton said. "He's breezy, but he has an agreeable personality. But Charles has put his finger on it. Why should he come around to us?"

"Because he likes us," Roger said. "He told me he liked you very much personally."

"Why shouldn't he?" Stephen Merry asked. "I like Tony personally."

Roger Blakesley laughed.

"As a matter of fact, I do too," he said. "That's why the Stuyvesant is a great bank. Everybody likes Tony."

"I'd love Tony myself," Charles said, "if he'd lend me three hundred thousand dollars. That's the way it is. Love and money."

The officers laughed. Even the younger men around the table smiled, and Mr. Burton picked up a piece of paper. "He's putting up enough," he said. "There's only one security I question."

"What?" Roger Blakesley asked.

Mr. Burton frowned at the paper he was holding, and he looked very handsome there at the head of the table as everyone's eyes moved toward him.

"Here's an unlisted company from a place called Clyde, Massachusetts—a block of five thousand shares at twenty dollars a share."

That was how Clyde came into the conference room, suddenly, out of nowhere. It came because Tony Burton's mind had been on a loan when he should have been discussing trust business. It came like an unexpected gust of wind through an open window, except that there were no windows in the conference room—nothing but scientific air conditioning.

"I remember that five thousand shares," Roger Blakesley said, "but he has enough without it, hasn't he? We ought not to disappoint him. He's just the sort of person who in different ways controls a lot of business."

"The Nickerson Cordage Company, Clyde, Massachusetts," Mr. Burton read. "Five thousand shares. Now of course we don't want to disappoint Mr. Eaton, but has anyone here ever heard of the Nickerson Cordage Company? Wait a minute—" Tony's glance had turned toward Charles. "Clyde. Let's see. Charles, didn't you come from a place called Clyde?"

Mr. Burton had a good memory. As far as Charles could recall, he had only mentioned Clyde to him once and that was years ago when the Burtons were going to take a vacation trip to Maine. Mr. Burton had shown him a road map marked by the AAA and Charles had told him that Clyde was a pretty place, that he did not know about accommodations now but that he had once lived in Clyde.

"Yes, sir," Charles said. "I was born there but I haven't been there for quite a while."

"Well, what about the Nickerson Cordage Company?"

"They used to make rope," Charles said, "and twine and fish nets. They were near the Wright-Sherwin Company in Clyde." Charles cleared his throat. It did not seem appropriate to say any more, but Mr. Burton was still listening.

"They used to build a lot of sailing ships in Clyde," Charles said, "and they needed ropes for them."

He could see as he spoke the sheds of the Nickerson Cordage Company beside the river, a small and shabby plant, and he could remember the smell of tar and hemp that came from it. Mr. Burton was still looking at him and it seemed necessary to go on.

"I didn't know it was incorporated," Charles said. "It must have grown."

"If Godfrey Eaton has money in it, it must be good," Roger said. He spoke as an authority, as a golf partner and an intimate personal friend of Mr. Godfrey Eaton.

"Well, we'll leave this for now," Mr. Burton said. His voice was resonant and agreeable, but it seemed to Charles that it had changed slightly.

Charles relaxed in his leather-seated mahogany chair. It was peculiar that the name of Clyde should have cropped up at the table. Things happened all at once. You thought of a name or a face and then it would appear.

"I remember Clyde," Stephen Merry said. "The road to Bar Harbor used to go through it but it's by-passed now. It's a pretty little town, something like Wiscasset in Maine. Nice houses but not much of a hotel. Elm trees. I never knew you came from there, Charles."

"Well," Charles said, "that was quite a while ago."

Mr. Burton picked up another paper but it seemed to Charles that he was still disturbed about the Nickerson Cordage Company.

"Never mind it now," he said. "It's getting on towards lunch time."

Charles only half heard him. The mention of Clyde was taking his attention from the meeting. It was not that he was daydreaming, it was not that he was not listening carefully. He could see the faces about him very clearly and the papers on the table and the inevitable memorandum pads and newly sharpened pencils that were conventionally on every conference table, though you hardly ever used them except to draw squares and pictures if you did not smoke. It was only that he found himself wondering how he had ever got into that conference room and whether he really wanted to be there, and he wondered whether anyone else around that table had ever shared those thoughts. Certainly their faces did not show it, though they had all arrived there as he had, through some sort of accident, if only because banking was a dignified and fashionable pursuit and there wasn't much else but business when you finished college.

Charles glanced at his watch, not surreptitiously as one usually did at conferences but deliberately. It was ten minutes past twelve, and he was relieved because that situation with Roger was beginning to be difficult. They were both of them showing off before the bank officers like college boys running for manager of some team, although they were both assistant vice-presidents. They were doing it in a very nice way, and of course they both were justified, but he was glad when it was over. In five minutes everyone was standing up, looking almost carefree because there would be a breathing spell for lunch.

"I didn't know the Eaton thing was coming up this morning," Roger Blakesley said.

Probably, under the circumstances, it was right to hover around Tony Burton and to show eagerness and zeal, but at the same time it might be possible to go too far.

"Speaking of electric razors," Charles said, "there was a story in the war–" He had decided that he would bring up electric razors after all.

"What's that about electric razors?" Roger asked quickly.

"There was a story in the war," Charles said, "about someone who brought one to Port Moresby in New Guinea and there weren't any outlets at Moresby."

Charles was pleased to see that Tony Burton looked amused.

"Do you use one of those damned things, Roger?" Tony Burton asked.

"Of course," Roger said. "When you get the hang of one, you never want anything else."

"Don't you?" Tony Burton said. "Well, I wouldn't give one houseroom."

4

I Remember, I Remember, the House Where I Was Born

—THOMAS HOOD

There had been times in the past when Charles was embarrassed because he was not a Harvard or a Yale graduate as the New York banks he dealt with most were full of Harvard and Yale men, but in recent years he no longer felt any particular handicap. He had lunched at the Harvard Club often enough to find his own way to the checkroom and Malcolm Bryant had left word at the door that he would be at the bar.

Charles found Malcolm at once, standing beside a middle-aged man who wore a tweed coat and gray slacks. The sight of a tweed coat in the city made Charles slightly uneasy for it showed that Malcolm's friend, like Malcolm, belonged in some category where correct dress was not necessary. The tweed coat meant that he had just dropped in casually from the country and that he was a teacher or writer or something, and though it was a relief occasionally to meet personalities like this, still it was an effort in the middle of a crowded day to shift to them from people like Tony Burton and Roger Blakesley.

"Hello, Charley," Malcolm said. "This is Guy Lake. Mr. Gray, Mr. Lake."

Mr. Lake shook hands with Charles unsmilingly. His brown hair was closely cropped. His face was thin and studious.

"Malcolm says you're a banker," Mr. Lake said. "Malcolm says he picked you up somewhere at a desk. It's been quite a shock to Malcolm."

"It was quite a shock to me, too," Charles said. "I still haven't got over it." He smiled. At least he was able to deal with people. Experience had finally taught him to watch and wait and to find out what people were like.

"What'll you have to drink, Charley?" Malcolm asked.

At first Charles thought of saying that he would not have anything, but this would have been needlessly austere so he said that he would like a sherry.

"That's the boy, Charley," Malcolm said, and he waved one hand at Charles and put the other on Mr. Lake's shoulder. "You know when I was doing that job on *Yankee Persepolis*, Guy—"

"Yes," Mr. Lake said. "I know when you were doing it."

"Well, Charley was right there. That's where I met Charley."

"I know," Mr. Lake said. "You've been telling me."

Charles picked up his glass and wondered uneasily just what Malcolm had been telling him.

"That's right," Malcolm said. "I've been telling you—and he never read it. What do you think of that? It hurts me. It really hurts me."

"If it hurts you, you'd better take another drink," Mr. Lake said. "Alcohol kills pain."

"That's a very good idea, Guy," Malcolm said. "Two more bourbons and plain water. In fact it hurt me so much that I went right to the store and bought him a copy."

"What," said Mr. Lake, "is that thing still in print?"

"You're damned well right, it's still in print," Malcolm said. "Where's that book? I had it here."

"You left it at the other end of the bar, sir," the barman told him.

"Oh yes," Malcolm said. "Well, get it for me, will you?"

"Are you going to give it to him?" Mr. Lake asked. "You ought to make him buy it. It shows you're an amateur."

"He wouldn't buy it," Malcolm said. "Do you buy Guy's books, Charley?"

Charles smiled again.

"No," he said, "but I suppose I should."

There was nothing more difficult than standing at a bar with people who were a little tight and only being able to drink sherry. The barman had passed Malcolm an academic-looking volume in a plain dust wrapper with *Yankee Persepolis* printed on it—*A Social Study*—Malcolm Bryant.

"There you are," Malcolm said.

"Why, thanks, Malcolm," Charles said. "Thank you very much."

Malcolm put his hand back on Mr. Lake's shoulder.

"Charley's a nice boy, Guy," Malcolm said. "You see why I like him, don't you? He has that repressed quality."

"It's too bad you haven't got some of it yourself," Mr. Lake said.

"Oh, I wouldn't put it that way," Malcolm said. "It's healthier to be an extrovert—happier. Are you happy, Charley?"

"Frankly, no," Charles said. "Not at the moment, Malcolm."

Mr. Lake began to laugh.

"You'd feel happier if you had another drink," he said. "How about another drink?"

Charles was trying to remember what it was he had once liked in Malcolm and he thought it was largely that Malcolm had been an older man who had been very decent to him. There was still that gap in age as they stood there in front of the bar.

"How about lunch?" Charles asked. "I haven't got much time, Malcolm."

"Now that's what I was saying, Guy," Malcolm said. "It's control rather than introversion. It's control and environmental influence. We once went through an intense emotional experience together, something that must have shaken us both. Sex has a way of doing that. And now he asks about lunch. That's what I call control. Get me another bourbon and water."

"You'd better get lunch, Malcolm," Mr. Lake said. "I've got to be going now. I'm glad to have met you, Mr. Gray," and he shook hands and walked away.

Malcolm Bryant scowled and shook his head.

"He's a conceited bastard, isn't he?" he said.

"I didn't have a chance to find out," Charles said, and he knew he never would find out.

"Well, he's a conceited bastard," Malcolm said. "He's an ornithologist. We were on a trip once in the Orinoco."

"Oh," Charles said, "I remember. You used to talk about the Orinoco." He had been bored and ill at ease, but suddenly it all was different. "So you got to the Orinoco, did you?"

"Yes," Malcolm said. "I got there."

Up to that moment, it had been hard to remember much about Malcolm Bryant but now everything was beginning to be clearer. The mention of the Orinoco gave Charles a slightly guilty but at the same time a pleasant feeling. It brought him back to a time when he had been able to consider seriously regions like the Orinoco as places he might conceivably visit. He had never been able to understand Malcolm's interests or activities. He had only known him as an eccentric person, engaged in pursuits that demanded a queer accretion of knowledge.

Malcolm had always talked about foundations and fellowships and expeditions and surveys, and part of his life had sounded as dry as dust and part of it unintelligibly exotic. As they stood by the bar, he gave Charles an impression of being removed by virtue of his own brains and ability from all ordinary obligations. The fact that he was older brought back to Charles a familiar callow feeling, one partly of admiration and partly of envy, though envy was not exactly the right word. He had never envied Malcolm Bryant as much as he had mistrusted his influence. He was thinking again that people like Malcolm Bryant fitted into no reasonable category. They were pampered, preposterous creatures who lived an artificial life, who did not understand or want to be like other people.

"I guess you have to have a Ph.D. to go to places like that," Charles said. "You have to know about bugs or snakes or rubber, I suppose."

Malcolm was regarding him in his old friendly, detached way, as though he were examining a strange human specimen.

"Yes," Malcolm said. "It's better to have a Ph.D., but it's more important to think of a project. Then you sell that project to somebody and they give you the money and you go. That's why I'm going to New Guinea tomorrow."

"Oh," Charles said, "are you going to New Guinea?"

"Yes," Malcolm said, "for the Pacific Investigation Institute. They had to have an anthropologist. Walter Sykes was going—you know, Sykes at the Peabody, who did that work on the Micronesians. He's overrated, if you want my personal opinion, and he keeps harping on the Haynes method. His kidneys gave out last week and so they went around to the Birch Foundation and the Birch found me."

"Oh," Charles said. It was like groping in the dark in an unfamiliar room that was filled with odd odors and awkward pieces of furniture. "You mean you just pack up and go?"

"It isn't any problem," Malcolm said. "I have an assistant. He's doing all the work. The only thing that is going to be interesting is the circumcision rite. All the rest has been pretty well covered, but I hope to get in on that. You see, it's about the proper time of year." He stopped, as though he took it for granted that Charles understood everything he was saying.

"Oh," Charles said. "Do they like strangers to see things like that?"

Malcolm looked at his glass and set it back on the bar.

"It all depends on how you handle the head men," he said, "and head men are all about alike. Well, I suppose we ought to have some lunch. What is it, son?"

One of the club attendants had interrupted them. It was a telephone call for Mr. Bryant.

"Oh," Malcolm said. "I'm sorry, Charley. That will be about the penicillin. Just wait for me in the other room, will you? I won't be a minute."

Charles walked into the other room and sat down in a red leather chair. The snatches of talk he heard were reassuring and a part of his own language. No one, in this other room, was talking of head men or of circumcision, but about the weather and the news from Washington. Charles drew a deep breath and opened the book which Malcolm Bryant had given him. It was published, he saw, by a university press, but even university presses had bright accounts of their books' contents inside the dust wrapper.

"*Yankee Persepolis,*" Charles read, "appears as the final and considered summation of part of a study made some years ago of a typical New England town, its culture, and its social implications. This volume has been written by Malcolm Bryant, in general charge of the survey. Mr. Bryant, fresh from the study of the Zambesis of Central Africa, has applied, in broad principle, the methods of research which he developed and perfected there. The result of this, his concluding volume, is a brilliant and exhaustive case history which can serve as an adequate text . . ." Charles's attention had wavered. His eye traveled without reading down to the last paragraph. "Malcolm Bryant, though stemming from the Middle West, took his doctorate at Harvard University, is at present a Fellow of the Birch Foundation, and is widely recognized through his papers in scientific journals and as a lecturer."

That was all there was about Malcolm Bryant and it conveyed very little to Charles. The book, as he glanced at it, was written in an abstruse and awkward way, adding up to something that he could not possibly read continuously, though he knew the book was about Clyde. The first chapter was entitled "Yankee Persepolis, Its Geography and Population" and the second "Social Structure," with a number of charts and drawings which Charles could not understand. Turning the pages hastily, Charles could see the names of streets and neighborhoods and buildings, thin and inartistic parodies of real names. Johnson Street was called Mason Street, the North End was called Hill Town, Dock Street was called River Street, and so it went, down to the names of families. The Lovells were obviously called the Johnsons and the Thomases were called the Hopewells, in a chapter entitled "Family Sketches." It was not difficult to perceive, in spite of these clumsy concealments, that Clyde was Yankee Persepolis. It was like looking at Clyde through a distorted lens or seeing Clyde through rippling water, with small things assuming portentous shapes.

"For the purposes of distinction," Charles read, "it will be well arbitrarily to define the very definite and crystallized social strata of Yankee Persepolis as upper, middle, and lower. These will be subdivided into upper-upper, middle-upper, and lower-upper, and the same subdivisions will be used for middle and lower classes."

Charles turned to the middle of the book. Even that quick perusal brought him back to the time when Malcolm Bryant had been studying Yankee Persepolis. He could remember Malcolm's voice and Malcolm's alien figure on the main street, but it was curiously shocking to find that period preserved in print.

"Typical of a lower-upper family," Charles was reading, "are the Henry Smiths—father, mother, son and daughter. Like other lower-upper families, they dwell on a side street ('side streeters'), yet are received on Mason Street. Mr. Smith, with investment interests in Boston, whose father owned stock in the Pierce Mill, is a member of the Sibley Club, also the Country Club, but is not a member of the Fortnightly Reading Club, belonging only to its lower counterpart, the Thursday Club. Though a member, he has never been an officer of the Historical Society or a Library trustee. His wife, Mrs. Smith, was Miss Jones, a physician's daughter (middle-upper). She runs their home in the lower-upper manner, with the aid of one maid (middle-lower) coming in daily from outside. The son Tom, a likable young graduate of Dartmouth, works ambitiously in the office of the Pax Company and is thinking of leaving for a job in Boston. He and his sister Hannah are received by the upper-upper but are not members of the committee for the Winter Assembly. They are, however, in a position to move by marriage to middle-upper or possibly upper-upper status. There is even talk that in time Tom may be taken into the Fortnightly and he is on friendly terms with the daughter of Mr. Johnson (upper-upper) though there is little prospect of more than friendship. Hannah is occasionally squired by Arthur Hopewell (upper-upper) but here, too, the prospect of marriage both recognize as small. . . ."

Charles felt his face redden, because it was easy enough to read between the lines. It was his own family there in black and white, starkly indecent, without trimming or charity. He was Tom, that likable young graduate from Dartmouth. It was indecent and infuriating, but he still read further.

"Let us examine a typical day in the Smith family (lower-upper). The rising hour is seven. Tom starts the coal fire in the kitchen range. Mrs. Smith arises to prepare breakfast, the maid Martha Brud (middle-lower) not appearing until eight. Hannah does not assist at this function because of a parental effort, very marked in the lower-upper and continuing through the middle group, for social advancement, especially of the marriageable daughter. The distinction in this regard between son and daughter seems definitely marked."

There it was in black and white, devoid of tone and shading, but Charles could see the rest between the lines. He could remember Malcolm coming in to call and talking of the Orinoco River and even helping with the dishes and giving his father an Overland cigar. He might have called it pacifying the head man, and he must have rushed to his notebook before he could forget.

"The ancestral motif is as marked in this group as it is in the upper-upper. The same importance is attached to the preservation of the heirloom and the decoration of the grave. Thus over the mantel of the Smith parlor is jealously guarded a primitive oil painting of a sailing vessel captained by the Smiths' ancestor, Jacob Smith."

He could clearly recall Malcolm's interest in that picture and the satisfaction in his mother's voice as she had explained it to him. He himself owned the picture now and every word he read seemed to him a crude breach of hospitality. His eye was still on the page when he heard Malcolm Bryant's voice.

"All right, Charley," Malcolm was saying. "Let's go in and have some lunch." Malcolm was standing in front of him with his hands in the side pockets of his coat. "So you've been looking over the opus, have you?"

Charles stood up with the book under his arm and tried to look calmly placid, especially as he saw that Malcolm was regarding him with detached, scientific curiosity.

"Yes," Charles said, "I was just glancing through it. It's funny I never heard of it before."

"It's a professional sort of book," Malcolm said. "Everybody has to publish something."

"It's like all sociological books," Charles said. "It's a little over my head. It has a queer style."

"It isn't meant to have style," Malcolm said. "Scholars suspect anything with style."

"It has a lot of facts," Charles said, "but it doesn't sound much like Clyde."

They were already at the door of the long dining room and the clatter of dishes and voices were all about them so that Malcolm had to raise his voice.

"My God," Malcolm said. "It isn't meant to be Clyde. It's only meant to represent a characteristic social unit. Let's not wait on ourselves. Let's get a table at the end."

"All right," Charles said. "You're paying for it. I can't. I'm a likable Dartmouth boy."

Malcolm looked startled but he laughed.

"So you read that piece, did you?"

"I just glanced at it," Charles said. "There wasn't much time to go over it."

"It's funny—" Malcolm began, but he had no time to finish. The headwaiter was leading them to a table at the end of the room, and Charles was looking over the tables and faces of the diners because his training had taught him that it was worth while to recognize people. He smiled and waved his hand to a vice-president of the Guaranty Trust Company and he was back in his own life again—just out from the Stuyvesant for lunch with an unconventional acquaintance, an anthropologist who was going to New Guinea.

"You don't have to have the regular lunch," Malcolm said. "Order anything you like."

"Oh no," Charles answered. "The regular lunch is fine, thanks. I haven't got much time."

He unfolded his napkin and glanced out of the window at the traffic on Forty-fifth Street.

"That book—" Malcolm said, pointing at it—Charles had been carrying it and he had put it down on the table beside a small basket of rolls—"I thought everything was pretty well scrambled in that book, but you picked yourself out, didn't you?"

"Yes," Charles said. "The Smith family."

"I'm afraid it made you sore," Malcolm said. "Get it out of your head that it's personal."

Charles took a sip of water.

"I wouldn't say I was sore," he said, "but of course it's personal and I can't say that I like the idea."

"What idea?" Malcolm asked.

"The idea," Charles said, "of someone like you coming there and treating us like guinea pigs. As far as I can remember, we were pretty nice to you in Clyde."

"Now, listen, Charley," Malcolm answered. "A social survey hasn't anything to do with friendship. Besides, it was twenty years ago."

"That's right," Charles said. "It was quite a while ago."

"Just remember," Malcolm said, and he looked hurt, "it hasn't got anything to do with friendship, Charley. I wish you'd get it into your head that I liked a lot of people there. I liked you, for instance, God knows why."

"I used to like you, too," Charles said. "God knows why, and up to a certain point."

"What point?"

"Oh, never mind," Charles said, "but I'll tell you something—" And then he stopped.

"Go ahead. What is it, Charley?"

"A year or two after you went away, I tried to look you up in New York but you weren't there." He stopped again and fidgeted in his chair. "I thought you might get me on that trip you used to talk about, that one to South America." It was something he had never told anyone, although he had nearly told it once to his son, and now the only thing to do was to laugh about it, and he laughed. "You have a lot of queer ideas when you're that age."

"By God, I might have taken you," Malcolm said. "That would have been funny."

"Yes," Charles said, "it would have been," and he straightened his shoulders and took another sip of water. The sounds of the room came back, the voices and the gentle clatter of china. Malcolm had lighted a cigarette and was blowing smoke through his nose.

"You might at least," Charles said, "have put us in middle-upper instead of lower-upper."

Then they were silent for a minute, but it was not a constrained silence.

"Did you ever get married?" Charles asked. "You were always talking about marriage."

"Never mind it," Malcolm said. "Women always forget me when I go away. What happened about you and Jessica?"

"Never mind it now," Charles said.

"All right," Malcolm said, "what's happened to you since? I mean since I used to know you."

It was a blunt question but it offered opportunity, which came very seldom, of saying what you thought, to someone whom you would probably never see again.

"That's quite an order," Charles said. "Why do you want to know?" It was exactly as if a blank questionnaire had been thrust in front of him.

"Because I always liked you, Charley," Malcolm said, "and I'm interested in people, academically."

"That's it," Charles said. "Academically. But I don't believe you know very much about people. You know about custom and form and habit, but those are all results and not causes. I don't believe you know as much about people as I do."

"Now listen," Malcolm began, "I only asked you because I was genuinely curious. When you see someone whom you haven't seen for years—"

Charles interrupted him before he could finish and he was beginning to enjoy the conversation.

"Why don't you say what you really mean?" Charles asked. "You mean you want to fill in the end of a case history about likable Tom Smith from Dartmouth." He shrugged his shoulders. "You and that bird man in the bar were talking about it before I came in, weren't you? I don't mind. I rather like being a part of case history."

"That's true," Malcolm said. "I was telling him, Charley, you've got a damned tough mind."

"I have to have one," Charles said. "I've cultivated it, I suppose. There are a lot of tough minds in New York."

"Oh no," Malcolm said. "You haven't cultivated it. You've always had a tough mind, Charley, and a sensitive disposition. Clyde was full of minds like that."

"Never mind Clyde," Charles said. "Go ahead and ask me questions."

"All right," Malcolm said. "Never mind Clyde. What have you been doing, Charley?"

Charles looked at his plate. It was empty. He had finished the main course of the lunch without knowing what it was and now the waiter was taking away the plate.

"Well," he said, "I met someone in Boston once who asked me to look him up in New York. That was when I was working in E. P. Rush & Company. I got a job in the statistical department at the Stuyvesant and I did well enough so I held it through the depression. I married a girl who worked downtown in a law office. We have two children, and we've built a house in the suburbs that I'm still paying for, and now there's a vice-presidential vacancy. It rests between me and another man, who has a tough mind too. That's about all I've been doing."

Malcolm had lighted another cigarette, cupping his hands carefully around the match as though he were in a wind.

"I always said you were a nice boy, Charley."

"Thanks," Charles said. "Thank you, Malcolm."

"Of course you haven't filled in many details," Malcolm said. "For instance, do you love your wife?"

"I thought you'd ask that," Charles answered, "and the answer is yes. I love my wife. I love my home and my children."

"I thought you would. You're an essentially monogamous type." Malcolm Bryant sat there looking at him. "So you've been to the war." It was that discharge button that Nancy had put in his coat lapel.

"Yes," Charles said. "I'd forgotten about the button."

"I was in the war, too," Malcolm said. "In the OSS."

"As long as it wasn't the OWI," Charles said. "As a matter of fact, I saw the Orinoco." He paused a moment. "From the air."

"On your way to Africa?"

"Yes," Charles said. "It was one of those missions, before I was assigned to the Eighth. I was only good for staff work—the bank, you know."

"And now you're back don't you ever feel restless?"

"No," Charles said, "I'm not restless. I didn't like the army. Most civilians don't."

"Well, let's put it another way. Don't you ever get to wondering what everything's about?"

"Naturally, but what's the use in wondering? I'm doing the best I can."

"Let's put it still another way," Malcolm said. "Do you ever wonder whether everything is worth while?"

"It's a little hard to answer that one," Charles said. "I'm just Tom Smith from Dartmouth, trying to get along."

Malcolm must have known that he would not say any more, yet Charles had inadvertently told a good deal. He could almost see himself as Malcolm must have seen him, and this unexpected mental picture was close to his own impression of himself without the customary apologies and excuses.

"You're still thinking about that book of mine, aren't you?" Malcolm asked.

"Your categories and groupings bother me," Charles said. "I like individuals, not groupings. It doesn't make any difference where anyone comes from, it seems to me."

"Now look here, Charley," Malcolm said, "whether you like it or not, everybody's in a category."

"Yes," Charles answered, "but you're trying to put me in a category and keep out of one yourself. It isn't really fair. There weren't so many classes. Clyde's a pretty democratic place."

"I thought you said never mind Clyde," Malcolm told him. "Just remember that no matter what sort of system he lives under, man still stays the same."

"Do you mean to say that a political system doesn't change the mental habits of individuals?" Charles asked. "What about fascism? What about communism?"

"It doesn't matter," Malcolm answered. "All ideologies arise from instincts. You can't change instincts. Man is always the same."

It was getting to be one of those conversations that would never get anywhere and it was too heavy a one for lunch.

"Well, it's nice to know it," Charles said, "even though the left wing doesn't agree with you. It must be nice to sit there and be able to talk like God Almighty."

Malcolm pushed the end of his cigarette carefully into the ash tray.

"Charley, do you believe in God Almighty?"

"Yes," Charles said, "I think I do. It may be early habit. Yes, I do, since you ask me."

Malcolm leaned his elbows on the table and Charles saw that his coat fitted him very badly.

"Well, if you were to pin me down to it, so do I," he said.

It must have been the mention of God that made Charles think of time. He looked at his watch and it was a quarter after two.

"I've got to go," he said, and suddenly he realized that he had found out nothing, or almost nothing, about Malcolm Bryant.

"Don't go," Malcolm was saying. "We've only just begun to talk."

Charles pushed back his chair. "You've got to be taking off to New Guinea," he said.

They were both walking side by side between the tables and he was sorry that it was over.

"I wish you hadn't made me talk about myself all the time," he said.

They were out of the dining room and Charles had tossed his brass check on the coatroom counter when Malcolm put his hand on his arm.

"Charley," he said, "you've got a lot of guts."

"How do you mean, guts?" Charles asked.

"Saying what you do," Malcolm said, "doing what you do, takes guts. You're a very nice boy, Charley."

"I wish," Charles said, "you'd stop calling me a nice boy."

"Well, you are," Malcolm said, "and it takes guts to be your type, these days. Good-by, good luck, Charley."

"Put me down in Category E," Charles said. "Good luck, Malcolm, and thanks."

"Thanks for what?" Malcolm asked.

"Since you ask me, I don't exactly know," Charles said, "but thanks."

5

Everything Fits into Banking Somewhere

Though common sense told Charles that he should hurry, some other inner impulse made him walk with perverse slowness, as you did when you tried to hurry in a dream. The sun had finally broken through the clouds and the sky was almost entirely blue and when he reached Fifth Avenue he came to a stop. He saw the sunlight hit the wings of a plane that must have risen from La Guardia Field just a minute or so before, and in spite of the noise on the Avenue he could hear the drumming of the motors. The green lights were on and he watched the steady flow of the traffic as though the sight were new to him—yellow cabs, green-and-white cabs, and the new buses, so different from the old ones with the open tops. The sun was still high enough to shine through some plate-glass windows on a display of men's colored shirts—maroons, blues, salmon pinks and canary yellows. He still could not get used to colored shirts even though they were quite the thing now to wear at the country club on Sunday.

Everything was changing and Fifth Avenue was changing too, in spite of all the efforts of the Fifth Avenue Association; but then Fifth Avenue had always been in a state of flux, with old buildings coming down and new ones going up, the old ones crumbling into rubble and being poured into the wreckers' trucks. It was always changing, but the spirit of it was still as young, confident, and blatant as when Henry James had written of it long ago. It still conveyed the same message that it had when he had walked along it on that first visit with his father. The motion of it had the same strength and eagerness, so different from the more stately motion of Piccadilly and the Strand.

"On the Avenue, Fifth Avenue . . . you'll be the grandest lady in the Easter Parade." . . . He had gone with Nancy to that musical show and it must have been in the winter of 1934 when they still lived in a walk-up apartment on West Eighteenth Street. They had paid Mrs. Sweeney, whose husband was a policeman, a dollar to sit listening for the baby, and they had not been to the theater once that year or the year before. 'Thirty-four had been bad enough, though nothing to 'thirty-three. They had gone to dinner in a small French restaurant and had taken the bus up Fifth Avenue and had walked across to Broadway. When the chorus had sung that song about Fifth Avenue he had been holding Nancy's hand, just as he used to when he took her to the Capitol before they were married. . . . "You'll be the grandest lady in the Easter Parade." . . . He must have been deathly tired because he had dozed off in the darkness in the middle of it and she had dug her elbow in his ribs and he still remembered her whisper.

"Wake up. Don't waste your money sleeping."

It had been quite a while, in fact not since he had been upstairs at the Stuyvesant, since anyone had made a remark to him about staying out too long at lunch; and there was never the slightest criticism now that he was downstairs, at a desk near the front window. There was still the inner compulsion never to be late, but at the same time it was your privilege. Tardiness could be excused on the assumption that you were having a business lunch with a client. Nevertheless, Charles knew that Miss Marble and Joe had been wondering where he had been, and it did not help to see that Roger Blakesley was busy at his desk already. Charles repressed an instinct to hurry and hang up his hat and coat but instead he walked slowly past the desks and stopped where Miss Marble was typing and asked her if there was anything new.

"Nothing new," Miss Marble said. "I called up Mrs. Gray and told her you couldn't catch the five-thirty. She said to remember that you're going to the country club tonight."

"It isn't tonight, is it?" Charles asked.

"You didn't tell me to put it on the calendar," Miss Marble said, "but Mrs. Gray said to remind you."

"Well, call her again and tell her I'll meet her there," Charles said. "I'll get there as soon as I can, but I'll be late."

He stopped in front of the washroom mirror to see that his tie was straight. His short, sandy hair was in order and he looked competent and carefree. It was time to put the luncheon out of his mind. Malcolm had said that he was a nice boy, Charley, and he was not a nice boy any longer. He did not look the way he had at Clyde, though even there his mother had always said that he had the Gray high cheekbones and the Gray pointed chin. The roundness had gone out of his face. There were wrinkles at the corners of his eyes and his mouth was tighter but there was no gray in his hair. It was not the face that he used to have but it still looked young.

"Charley," he heard Malcolm Bryant saying, "it takes guts to be your type, these days. Good-by, good luck, Charley."

He was still not sure whether or not Malcolm Bryant had been laughing at him. Businessmen were not on the pinnacle they had once occupied. It was hard sometimes to tell the difference between strength of mind and habit.

The tellers' cages would close at three and already, as was usual in the afternoon, the pace was growing more leisurely. There were always new problems in the morning but these grew old by afternoon, fitting with still older problems into a symmetrical design so that you had a sense of everything running smoothly, a sense of teamwork, if you wanted to call it that, or what Mr. Burton called a meshing of the gears. You could think of the whole system of capital, of rates, discounts, markets and production, as running without interruption, like the traffic on the Avenue.

Charles had devised a system that permitted him to examine every trust account personally at least once a month, and now Miss Marble brought to his cleared desk the ones which he was to review that day. As he thanked her and settled himself in his chair, he glanced across at Roger Blakesley. Roger's desk was heaped with piles of papers. It was a habit of Roger's to shove a great many papers around in the afternoon, especially toward closing time.

"Hello there, Charley," Roger said. "Everything's backing up on me."

Charles knew this was not true but it gave the picture that Roger wanted, a picture of heavy and unremitting labor.

"You're back early," Charles said. "I thought you were going to have lunch with Tony."

"He canceled it," Roger said. "Something came up the last minute." Roger took off his glasses and polished them. When his glasses were off, his blinking eyes gave him a vacant, guileless look. "Are you going to the country club tonight?"

"Yes," Charles said, "but I'm afraid I'll be late."

"Who was that bird you went to lunch with?"

There was no privacy. Everyone heard everything, particularly Roger.

"A man I used to know," Charles said, and then some impulse made him explain it further. "He's an anthropologist."

"A what?"

Then Charles knew that it would have been better not to have mentioned it. It was just the sort of thing that Roger would remember.

"An anthropologist."

"He looked like a teacher in business school," Roger said. "One of those 'if you can't do, teach' boys."

As far as Charles could tell, everything in Roger's career had stemmed from his stay at the Harvard Graduate School of Business Administration, where business was the oldest of the arts but the newest of the professions. He had to admit that Roger used his academic background adroitly, extracting the last drop from it. Roger was always saying it was a great place, the Harvard Business School. When you studied under the Case system, you became aware of practicality and theories at the same time. It was a proving ground, the Harvard Business School, and it paid to keep up with it afterwards. If you were to ask Roger, but you did not have to ask him, this proving ground was directly accountable for the record he had made at the Guaranty before he had come to the Stuyvesant. He had been asked to come to the Stuyvesant and before accepting, of course, there had been certain reservations in his mind, but he had never regretted the step after taking it. There were fine fellows at the Stuyvesant, like Tony Burton and Steve Merry, and good boys like Charley Gray, fellows who always stuck together without getting out the old stiletto and inserting it between the shoulder blades.

Charles began on the first account. It was the Burrell School for Negroes in Tennessee, founded by the late Charles Burrell, the moneys for which were administered by Mr. Burrell's old bank, the Stuyvesant, in conjunction with Mr. Burrell's old law firm, Burrell, Jessup and Cockburn. Charles would have to meet with Mr. Cockburn the first of the week and the meetings were never agreeable. The trouble with institutional accounts of late had been that all institutions were screaming for more income, although they continued demanding a margin of absolute safety. Mr. Cockburn always wanted to lower the bond holdings and to increase the higher-yielding preferred list. That million-dollar fund had been beautifully invested. Even in the depression, income had held up well, and now the market was considerably above the book value.

Charles was in the middle of the security list when he realized that Miss Marble was waiting by his desk.

"It's twenty minutes to three," Miss Marble said. "Mr. Selig is coming in at a quarter of—the one who wants to open an account. I thought you'd like to see the credit department memorandum."

"Selig?" Charles repeated, and his mind darted swiftly away from the investments of the Burrell School.

"The matter that Mr. Burton asked you to take up," Miss Marble said. An anticipatory quiver in her voice showed that Miss Marble was interested. He had been asked yesterday to do that job and now he understood why Tony Burton was not yet back from lunch. He always seemed to be the one who was picked for unpleasant interviews.

"Thanks," he said, and he took the memorandum. "Does Joe know I'm to see him? You'd better check again with Joe."

His eyes traveled over the memorandum. He had learned to read office memoranda quickly and to pick the salient details out of the dull verbiage.

"Burt J. Selig," he read, "is part owner of the Teddy Club and the La Casita night club, owns real estate at . . . and also in Miami, was indicted for income-tax fraud but indictment was quashed . . ."

There was no use going any further because everything had been decided. It seemed to Charles that there was no reason for a personal interview and that the matter might have been settled as well by letter, except that Tony Burton had disapproved of anything as permanent as a letter. Charles's desk had just been cleared except for a pile of Moody reports when he saw Joe moving from the door accompanied by a thin, dark man who wore a bluish-purple overcoat and a lightweight gray felt hat. Except for the shimmering sheen of the overcoat and the violently brilliant polish of his shoes, Mr. Selig was quietly dressed. His tie was dark, like his suit; his face was tanned, probably by the Miami sun, into a smooth meerschaum color. When he took off his hat, as he did when he approached the desk, Charles saw that his forehead was high and that his close-cropped dark hair was receding from his temples. His eyebrows, which might have been trimmed, formed a straight, almost Grecian line. His eyes were gray, his jaw was heavy, but there was nothing heavy about his step.

"This is our Mr. Gray," Joe said. "He will take care of you."

Mr. Selig held out a carefully manicured hand.

"I'm happy to meet Mr. Gray," he said. "My name's Selig, Burt Selig."

"Yes, I know," Charles said. "Mr. Burton asked me to see you and I have all the details. Won't you sit down, Mr. Selig?"

He wondered for an instant where Malcolm Bryant would have placed Mr. Selig in his social scale, for Mr. Selig must have moved fast from group to group in combinations more complicated than any in Clyde or New Guinea. His voice had undertones of lost accents. His face had a look of things written on it that had been partially erased and of preparation for new writing. It was a face of a type that Charles did not know, but it was as marked and distinctive as a soldier's or a doctor's—positive, alert and confident.

"A nice little place you have here," Mr. Selig said. "Very nice."

"It's just a small bank," Charles answered.

"Yes," Mr. Selig said. "That's what draws me to it, Mr. Gray, particularly for Mrs. Selig. I know some lovely people banking here, some of my best friends. My friend Alf Fieldstone banks here. Do you know Alf?"

"Yes," Charles said, "I've met him."

"A very nice fellow, Alf," Mr. Selig said. "He likes La Casita. Have you been to La Casita, Mr. Gray?"

"I tried once," Charles answered, "but there was a long line waiting."

"Well, any time," Mr. Selig said, and smiled.

"Thanks," Charles said.

"Well," Mr. Selig said, "I suppose you've looked me over. I hope I've passed through the line-up by now."

He paused and smiled, but there was no need to give any answer.

"I'm used to being looked over," Mr. Selig said, "in my position."

"Well," Charles said, "anyone in business always gets looked over."

"Yes, that's right," Mr. Selig said. "How long have you been here, Mr. Gray?"

"Quite a while."

"I suppose it takes time to work up anywhere in a business like this. Nothing can move fast."

"That's right," Charles said, "it takes time."

"I wouldn't want any son of mine working in a bank," Mr. Selig said. "So little action."

"It all depends on temperament," Charles answered.

"Yes," Mr. Selig said. "Everybody has a different temperament. I ought to know."

The best way to hurry an interview was to wait, but he was sure that Mr. Selig ought to know.

"Well," Mr. Selig said, "what's the story? Do you want my account or don't you?"

Many people believed that banking was a matter of dull routine but whatever it might be to the boys in back, up front you could never count on monotony or even on a restful moment. It was necessary, as soon as Mr. Selig asked that question, to change from an investment consultant into a man of the world. It was necessary to remember that he was in a very responsible position, representing in his own person the prestige and dignity of the Stuyvesant and at the same time protecting the inviolate sanctity of its officers. Suddenly, with hardly any time to prepare, he had to change from book values to diplomacy and to draw smoothly on a store of conventional phrases, which were deceitful but which had to stick.

"Our officers have been over that question very carefully," Charles said, and the smoothness and the consoling tone of his voice reminded him of a hotel clerk saying nicely that there was no room for a certain guest. "We would value your account in a great many ways, Mr. Selig, but we really feel that you will be better off in another bank. You said yourself this is a small bank, and smallness has its difficulties." Charles smiled at Mr. Selig and felt still more like a hotel clerk. "I hope you'll understand, Mr. Selig, sorry as we are to turn away profitable business." Charles smiled again. "Mr. Burton asked me to tell you personally that this is a purely business decision."

Of course he was using Mr. Burton's name unofficially but still it had a soothing sound, even if it did not have the desired effect.

"So the answer is no, is it?" Mr. Selig asked.

"I'm afraid so," Charles said, "for the time being. We're very sorry."

Something made Charles sit up straighter and something made him feel that it would be unwise to shift his glance from Mr. Selig, for a film had seemed to drop over Mr. Selig's eyes. It was as though Mr. Selig had tried to suppress an impulse which he had been unable to conceal and for a second Charles had a sense of something close to physical danger.

"So I'm not a nice enough guy to play with you, is that it?" Mr. Selig said.

Charles spoke slowly and very carefully. You had to go on with the act and make no rash statements. You had to be glib and still say nothing.

"There's nothing personal intended," Charles said. "We often find the needs of some depositors are better filled by other banks."

"I'm not used to being given the run-around. Why didn't they say that the first time I came in?" Mr. Selig asked. He had not raised his voice but there was a difference in his accent.

"I'm sorry you put it that way," Charles said. "Mr. Burton was very impressed by your references. We never like to disappoint our friends, Mr. Selig."

"So you're fronting for the crowd, are you?" Mr. Selig asked.

"If you mean I'm out in front," Charles said, "I suppose I am. Mr. Burton asked me to attend to the matter, but of course if you're not satisfied—"

"How much do they pay you for doing it?" Mr. Selig asked. "Ten grand a year?"

Mr. Selig was looking at him curiously, in a way that reminded Charles of Malcolm Bryant.

"That hasn't anything to do with your account, has it?" Charles asked—but still, he was fronting for the crowd. He liked the expression "fronting for the crowd." Mr. Selig was looking at him with a new sort of interest.

"Guys like you fascinate me," Mr. Selig said. "I don't see why you do it, for that money."

"I suppose I think I'm underpaid," Charles said. "It's human nature."

Mr. Selig lowered his voice.

"How would you like twenty-five grand a year?"

"What for?" Charles asked.

"For what you're doing here," Mr. Selig said. "Fronting for the crowd."

It was something, after all it was something. At least it meant that he had not done his job badly.

"Thanks," Charles said. "I'm afraid I couldn't use it, but I appreciate your asking."

"You guys fascinate me," Mr. Selig said. "Money everywhere and you don't want money."

"Maybe we get too used to it," Charles said. "Maybe we get tired of seeing so much of it around."

"That's what fascinates me," Mr. Selig said. "All of it around, and you don't take it. Well, no hard feelings."

They both stood up and shook hands.

"Oh, no," Charles said. "Not at all. We're very sorry, Mr. Selig."

"It takes poise," Mr. Selig said. "I wouldn't have the poise."

"I wouldn't call it poise," Charles said. "I'd call it temperament and timidity. Good-by. We're sorry, Mr. Selig."

There was no flagging in the bank's activity, but Charles was conscious of a ripple of excitement, of curious glances from the cashiers' cages and the smaller desks. They were all like good little boys and girls who had witnessed one of their number having it out in the school yard with a naughty boy from the street. The adding machines were still clicking and whirring with the typewriters, the cashiers were still thumbing through their currency, but beneath it there was a flurry, a sense of the unusual. Mike Cavanaugh, the bank detective, was moving toward him, not hurriedly but quietly as though he were only making his afternoon rounds, and Roger Blakesley had turned in his swivel chair.

"How was he?" Mike Cavanaugh asked.

"He was a perfect gentleman," Charles said. "He asked me if I was fronting for the crowd."

Then Roger Blakesley asked whether Mr. Selig was mad, but Charles had no time to answer. Mike Cavanaugh had stiffened to attention and Charles saw that Mr. Burton had come in, still in his overcoat, just back from lunch.

"Has Selig called?" Tony Burton asked.

"He's just left," Charles told him.

"Well, I'm glad I missed him," Tony Burton said. "How did he take it?"

"His feelings were hurt," Charles said, "but then mine would have been. I wouldn't say he was angry at me personally."

"There aren't any complications, then?" Tony Burton asked.

"No," Charles said, "I don't think so."

"This sort of thing always worries me," Tony Burton said. He began to move away to the coatroom.

"Oh, Mr. Burton," Roger Blakesley said, and Mr. Selig and possible complications left Charles's mind. Roger sounded like a model student speaking in one of the classes at the Harvard Business School. He was being careful not to call the president by his first name right in the middle of the bank.

"Yes, Roger," Tony Burton said, benignly, like a kind teacher.

"Have you got time to see me for a minute?"

"Yes," Mr. Burton said. "If it's only for a minute."

Charles had rung for Miss Marble and Miss Marble was bringing back the trust folders. He was careful to show no undue anxiety but such a request of Roger's, at such a time, might have implications. Ordinarily, either he or Roger Blakesley, because of their position, would have risen and walked over to the president's roll-top desk without asking for any sort of appointment. That request of Roger's meant that he wanted to see Tony Burton privately and perhaps about something personal. It might even mean that Roger, like himself, was getting tired of waiting and that Roger was going to step over, as Charles had often dreamed of doing in the last few weeks, and ask right out about the vice-presidency. It was not like Roger, but it was possible—on the grounds that this sort of waiting was bad for general morale.

Mr. Burton had left his coat and was settling down at his desk and Roger Blakesley had risen.

Anxiety and self-inflicted suspense were useless and unprofitable, but there was nothing one could do. Charles was back in his personal world again, his little narrow world, and the trust accounts were facing him. It was time to be going through them, because it was after three o'clock, but something discordant moved him beyond the control of ingrained habit and system. Ordinarily his ability to concentrate enabled him to forget his own problems by plunging into a good page of figures on a balance sheet, but now he could not keep his attention on the trust accounts. His eyes were on a list of common stocks—American Can, American Cyanamid, American Tobacco B, American Telephone and Telegraph. Through wars and rumors of wars, in the midst of panic and depression, out of the maze of taxes and social change, through all the welter of a cracking tradition, American Tobacco B and American Tel and Tel stood, with occasional lapses, like the precepts of early life, like the granite peaks of a half-submerged continent, serene above a swirl of hostile seas. Other securities might go sour, but not Telephone and Tobacco—or not very sour. Still, though he was surrounded by those trusted symbols, his thoughts kept wandering off at tangents.

Roger Blakesley was over by the front windows, his chair pulled close to the president's desk, talking very earnestly. Charles could not forget what Nancy had said that morning—that he could go to Tony Burton and put his cards on the table. Even though he dismissed it as just the thing a woman would suggest, still Nancy had good judgment. She understood as well as he did the routine and jealousies and discipline of an office, and besides there was the question of personal dignity. It was humiliating, considering his position, to sit, day after day, waiting for Tony Burton to tell him what was on his mind, when he had probably made his choice already. It was humiliating to have one's life and a good part of one's future depend on one man's eccentricity, but that was the way it always was.

Charles had often thought that it was fortunate for Tony Burton that he seldom needed to make quick decisions. Tony Burton had told him himself that he liked to mull over problems and fuss with them, particularly problems of personnel, but he usually did what he decided in the first place, from sheer intuition and instinct tempered by training and experience. All his talk of mulling and weighing and balancing was vacillation, if you wanted to use a harsh word for it. There were also the qualms that always surrounded a definite negative. That probably was what was delaying Tony Burton—the certainty that no matter what he did someone would be hurt.

It would obviously have ruined everything if Charles had endeavored to end the suspense by talking it over with Tony Burton. It was against all convention and Tony would instantly have put him in his place, but still it was possible to consider such an impossible scene. He could even frame just what he would say.

"Listen, Tony," he would say, "let's face the facts. Maybe you're removed from office politics, but everybody here in the bank knows that you are considering proposing either Blakesley or me for this vice-presidency. Maybe you don't know, but you ought to, that they're making bets on it in the washroom. It isn't dignified. It isn't fair to Roger or me to keep us waiting. We're both of us making monkeys of ourselves running around and polishing apples. You know everything about me, Tony. I've been around here long enough. Of course, I was out in the war, but you approved my going, or you said you did, and I'm about the same as I ever was in spite of it. I know it's hard to step on somebody's face, but this thing has been going on for months, ever since Arthur was killed, and I'm tired of staying awake at night, and Nancy's getting tired, too. How about it, Tony?"

It was not a bad speech, either, even though it was out of his usual line and beyond the realms of discipline. In fact the words were so vivid in his mind that he seemed to be saying them right now at the far corner by the window, but of course he would never say them. He was at his desk and out of the corner of his eye he saw that Roger Blakesley was back again, leafing through a pile of papers with his left hand while he scribbled with his right on a memorandum pad. It may have been that Roger also had been dreaming of a talk with Tony. He could even make a savage, unkind parody of Roger's possible speech, which Roger would have called an "approach."

"Listen, Tony," Roger would have said (that is if he had said anything), "how about you and me doing a little mind reading? You've got one of the best poker faces I've ever seen. I love your inscrutability, but let's unscrute, shall we? That's a pretty good word, what? I always knew I should have been an English professor and not just a poor dumb bank boy. . . . Well, to get back to it, Tony. I know you're hot and bothered, and I don't want to bother you and I know old Charley doesn't. Why, Charley's the grandest guy I know. You and I don't want to hurt old Charley, especially after the war, and you don't want to hurt me, but you couldn't hurt me, Tony, the way I feel about you. It's just a little matter, Tony, and Charley and I can take it, though maybe Charley's more brittle than I am. I never take things hard, Tony. Let's help each other out and let's get an extra on the street . . ." That was the way Roger would do it, because Roger had the sales technique. If it made Charles impatient sometimes, he was broad-minded enough to know that a lot of people liked it.

The shades on the front door were drawn already, showing that the bank was closed to depositors, and there was the inevitable air of relaxation now that they were no longer on public display. Voices were louder. There was a snatch of laughter. People were assuming more comfortable positions and far in the back of the room, in that region where there was not so much to gain or lose, he saw some of the boys moving toward the washroom to smoke a cigarette. If he had wished to have that talk with Tony Burton, now would have been the time, but he still sat at his desk with the trust accounts in front of him. The tension was beginning to undermine his judgment and self-control but if they wanted to keep him waiting, he was not going to show that it bothered him. Just then his desk telephone rang with its specially contrived device to avoid undue noise. It was Miss Sumner, Tony Burton's secretary.

"Oh, Mr. Gray," Miss Sumner said. Her voice was sweet with the assured authority of being the dean of all secretaries, the repository of all secrets. "Mr. Burton wants to know if you can see him for a moment."

There were some reactions you could not control and in spite of himself his heart was beating faster. He deliberately finished the page of his report before he rose, and when he was on his feet he looked at Roger Blakesley.

"Yes, Sugar," Roger was saying over his own telephone, which meant that Roger was speaking to his wife. "I'll be there on the five-thirty, Sug. Yes, I'll pick up the prescription."

Roger's concentration on his conversation was not misleading. Charles was sure that Roger knew exactly why Tony Burton wanted to see him for a moment.

Tony Burton looked very fit, in spite of his white hair and his roll-top desk which both conspired to place him in another generation. For years Charles had accepted him as a model willingly, even though he realized that everyone else above a certain salary rating also used Tony Burton as a perfect sartorial example, and he was pretty sure that Tony himself was conscious of it. Charles never rebelled against this convention because Tony had everything one should expect to find in a president of a first-rate bank. It was amusing but not ridiculous to observe that all the minor executives in the Stuyvesant, as well as the more ambitious clerks, wore conservative double-breasted suits like Tony Burton's, at the same time allowing undue rigidity to break out into pin stripes and herringbones, just like Tony Burton's. They all visited the barber once a week. They all had taken up golf, whether they liked it or not, and most of them wore the same square type of wrist watch and the same stainless-steel strap. They had adopted Tony Burton's posture and his brisk, quick step and even the gently vibrant inflection of his voice. In fact once at one of those annual dinners for officers and junior executives when everyone said a few words and got off a few local jokes about the bank, Charles had brought the matter up when he had been called upon to speak.

Speaking was always an unpleasant ordeal with which he had finally learned to cope successfully largely from imitating Tony. He remembered standing up and waiting for silence, just as Tony waited, with the same faint smile and the same deliberate gaze.

"I should like to drink a toast," he had said, "not to our president but to everyone who tries to look like him. When I walk, I always walk like Tony, because Tony knows just how to walk; and when I talk, I always talk like Tony, because Tony knows just how to talk; and when I dress, I always dress like Tony, in a double-breasted suit. But no matter how I try, I cannot be like Tony. I can never make myself sufficiently astute."

It was the one time in the year, at that annual dinner, when you could let yourself go, within certain limits, and Tony Burton had loved it. He had stood up and waited for the laughter to die down and then he had spoken easily, with just the right pause and cadence. He had said that there were always little surprises at these dinners. He had never realized, for instance, that there could be a poet in the trust department, but poetry had its place. Poetry could teach lessons that transcended pedestrian prose.

"And I'm not too old to learn," Tony Burton had said, "and I'm humbly glad to learn. Sometimes on a starlit night I've wondered what my function was in the Stuyvesant. I'm very glad to know it is that of a clothing dummy. It's a patriotic duty. It's what they want us to be, in Washington."

That was back in 1941, but Tony Burton still had the same spring to his step, the same unlined, almost youthful face, and the same florid complexion; and he had the same three pictures on his desk, the first of Mrs. Burton in their garden, the second of their three girls standing in profile, like a flight of stairs, and the third of his sixty-foot schooner, the *Wanderlust* (the boat you were invited on once every summer), with Tony Burton in his yachting cap standing at the wheel. Time had marched on. All of the girls had come out and all were married, and the *Wanderlust* had been returned by the navy in deplorable condition, but Tony Burton had no superficial scars.

No matter how well Charles might know him, in that half-intimate, half-formal business relationship, he still had a slight feeling of diffidence and constraint. It was the same feeling that one had toward generals in wartime or perhaps toward anyone with power over one. There was always a vestige of a subservient desire to please and to be careful. You had to know how far to go, how long to laugh, and how to measure every speech.

Tony Burton looked up and smiled and waved his hand with the circular motion at the wrist that everyone had tried to imitate.

"Sit down, Charley," he said. "Have a cigarette and relax."

No matter how much you might pretend, it was no time for relaxing, and Tony Burton must have known it. It must have been a little hard for Tony, trying to be friends and always being faced by that line of demarcation. It might have been different, Charles was thinking, if he had inherited money of his own instead of being dependent on a job. It might have been different, even, if he had received some attractive offer lately, if he had known that there was something waiting for him elsewhere with the same salary, instead of knowing that times were tight and uncertain.

Everything was uncertain and there was nothing to do but to wait. He shook his head when Tony Burton offered him a club cigarette from his gold case. There was the unwritten rule of no smoking on the banking floor—even though Tony Burton suggested it be broken.

"What's on your mind, Tony?" he asked. There was nothing to do but wait, while Tony Burton laid his cigarette case on the desk in front of him. From where he sat Charles could read the engraving on its gold surface, done in script in three different specimens of girlish handwriting. "To America's most representative daddy, Gladys, Olivia, Babs."

"The girls gave it to me on Father's Day," Tony Burton said. "I didn't know I was a representative dad."

"I didn't know you were either," Charles answered, "but it must be nice to know."

There was nothing to do but wait, but it was clear already that they were not going to talk about the future or they would not have begun with the cigarette case. At the same time, it was also clear that Tony Burton did have something on his mind. Charles glanced at his cool and placid features, set in assured, easy lines etched by a career in which everything had always worked out right. From the very beginning Tony Burton could have had no doubts about anything. From the very beginning he must have known that he would end where he was sitting.

"I don't like being representative of anything," Tony Burton said.

"I don't see how you can help it very well," Charles said.

"How do you mean, I can't help it?" Tony Burton asked.

"Sitting where you are," Charles said, "you've got to represent. That's all I mean."

"Well, I was thinking the other day," Tony Burton said, "that you're pretty representative yourself."

"I hope I am, Tony," Charles answered. "I try to be, in business hours." He did not like the conversation because he did not know where it was leading, although he understood that this was all a part of Tony's technique.

"We ought to call this place the House of Representatives," Tony Burton said, "but it isn't a bad shop, is it?"

"No," Charles answered, "it isn't. I'm glad to be back in it, Tony," and Tony Burton smiled at him, almost as though they were friends.

"Well," Tony said, "speaking of representatives—" and he paused and Charles sat motionless. For a second he thought that he had been wrong and that they were coming to the point at last, but only for a second. "How did you represent things to Selig?"

"I told him he would be happier elsewhere," Charles said. "I told him there were too many complications."

"Why didn't you tell him that we'd have room for him in the quite near future?"

"Because he wouldn't have believed it," Charles said. "He had to know, not that he hadn't guessed already."

"Did he take it?"

"Yes," Charles said, "he took it."

Tony Burton leaned back and clasped his hands behind his head.

"He has a lot of good connections. That's the trouble with life these days. There's no pattern. You don't know where you're at any more. The girls keep going to La Casita. It's a damn funny world, isn't it? It's getting curiouser and curiouser."

"A man told me at lunch today," Charles said, "that no matter what the world is doing, man remains the same."

Tony Burton unclasped his hands from behind his head and placed them on the arms of his chair.

"Well, let's forget it, Charley. There's one other thing."

"Yes, sir," Charles said. He knew it was the other thing that Tony Burton wanted to talk about and he knew that informality was over. It was time to be a bright young man again and to call Tony Burton "sir."

"About that loan."

"Which loan, sir?" Charles asked.

"The one we were talking about this morning. That cordage company. You said you were born up there. What's the name of the place?"

"You mean Clyde?" Charles answered. He had never dreamed that Clyde would come into the conversation again, yet now that it had, it seemed inevitable. All day, from the moment he had arisen in the morning, Clyde had been behind everything.

"Yes," Tony Burton said, "that's it. Clyde. Somebody ought to see that company and it just occurred to me"—he raised his hand from the right arm of his chair and rotated it slowly from the wrist—"it just occurred to me if you've lived up there and know the background, you'd better go up for a day or two and look things over, just quietly. Talk to people. Find out from the bank. Nothing is secret about any business in a small town."

"No, sir," Charles said. "Everybody in Clyde knows about everything."

"Well, if you want to, take the midnight, or take the plane up to Boston tomorrow morning. Stay as long as you like and see if you can get some figures."

Charles nodded slowly. He did not want to speak for a moment. He was going up to Clyde and he could not help it. He was going back to where he had come from because Roger Blakesley had seen Mr. Burton for just a minute.

"I envy you getting away for a while," Tony Burton said. "You're looking a little tired, Charles."

"Do you want to come along?" Charles asked.

"I wish I could," Tony Burton said, and he laughed, "but I'm the representative dad."

Charles's thoughts were moving smoothly again. For an instant he thought of refusing. He even began to invent a possible excuse, but a refusal or excuse would have been as bad as going.

"Do you mind if I ask you a question, Tony?" he asked.

"Why, no, of course not, Charley," Tony Burton said.

"Did you think up this idea yourself?"

It was dangerous, impertinent, and out of order, but from the slight narrowing of Tony Burton's eyes and from a faint look of surprise, he knew that Tony Burton understood, and that was all he wanted.

"Why, no," Tony Burton said. "Now that you mention it, it wasn't entirely my idea."

At least Tony Burton understood, if he had not before, why Roger had suggested it. It was an opportunity to get Charles Gray away for a while, out of sight and out of mind in a crucial period. Charles had to admit that it was clever of Roger Blakesley.

"I suppose Roger ought to go," Tony Burton said. "It's his responsibility, but he doesn't know Clyde. How about riding back with me on the five-thirty?"

"I can't," Charles said. "The Whitakers want to see me at five. They're very short of money."

Tony Burton frowned. He was thinking, obviously, of dignity and convention.

"Why can't they come down here like other people?" he asked.

"Mrs. Whitaker hasn't been well," Charles said, "and so I thought—" He did not have to tell what he thought because Tony knew. They both knew the size of the Whitaker account.

"All right," Tony Burton said. "Let's see, you'll be back by Friday, won't you? Remember you're coming to dinner on Friday."

"I wouldn't miss it for the world," Charles said.

When their glances met, there was no doubt that Tony Burton knew what he meant. He smiled in a paternal way, far removed from any trouble of Charles's but still with sympathy.

"Well, relax and have a good time, Charley," he said, and he leaned forward and slapped Charles's knee.

"That's the second time," Charles said, "that you've told me to relax."

"Well, do it," Tony Burton said. He seemed to be speaking from a great distance, from Olympian heights of security which Charles would never reach; or he might have been speaking from the deck of the *Wanderlust*, with a wet sheet, a flowing tide, and sailors in white drilling pulling on the braces. He sounded like a doctor in his office, giving sound advice to a nervous patient.

"Go ahead and relax, Charley. I'll see you Friday," and then his voice had a note of kindly promise in it. "Just you and Nancy are coming, and you and I'll have a good long talk about the whole situation here on Friday."

6

We're Both Doing What We Do Very Well

The apartment building on Park Avenue where the Whitakers lived was one of those co-operative structures built in 1926 on an unstable foundation of high mortgages. Charles could recall as he walked under the green awning off the street through the travertine marble doorway into the travertine marble hall that the Whitakers' equity on the fifteenth floor of the house had cost them originally two hundred thousand dollars. He could also recall a later period when equities in nearly all co-operative apartments had dropped from nothing to a minus quantity, and when tenants had frantically endeavored to avoid their upkeep and mortgage charges by giving away their equities and even paying prospective tenants handsome bonuses for taking them off their hands. That was the period when people used to say the purchase of a co-operative apartment was like buying the hole in a doughnut.

This particular building, Charles remembered very well, had gone through the financial wringer in the year of 'thirty-three. There had been a time when its lawyers, agents, and even its uniformed attendants had worn the worried and courteous expressions that he had observed on the faces of all persons dealing with white elephants, but it was different now. It seemed to Charles that the hall attendant who ushered you to the elevator and who looked, even in his light blue uniform, something like Tony Burton wore an expression of unctuous triumph, and he was justified. God was in His heaven again. The building was solvent again. If you were in one of those brackets, with which Charles was academically familiar, it cost very little to live in a co-operative apartment now, when so much of the annual expense could be written off on the income tax as interest charges. On the whole the Whitakers had done very well because they had held on with faith in the ultimate victory of righteousness.

The hall attendant was looking now at Charles questioningly, particularly at his worn pigskin brief case. People, of course, who entered from the street with brief cases fell into a dubious professional category and were not always people whom tenants would welcome. No matter how beguiling their superficial appearance might be, a brief case always meant that such individuals were not calling on tenants for purely social purposes. They might be insurance agents or even a Fuller Brush man, or a server with a summons. Charles could understand and even sympathize with the doubt. He himself was like the attendant. He could feel the vague bond of fellowship that came of being an employee.

"Is Mrs. Whitaker expecting you?" the attendant asked. He might conceivably have asked the same question, Charles was thinking, but he certainly would have called him "sir" if it had not been for the brief case.

"Yes, I have an appointment with Mrs. Whitaker," Charles answered. "Call, if you like—Mr. Gray." If he had been carrying a small black bag, he might have been taken for a doctor and there would have been no question.

"Oh, no," the attendant said,—"if Mrs. Whitaker's expecting you. The elevator to the right."

"Yes," Charles said, "I know," and then it annoyed him that he had said he knew, because there was no reason for it except some subconscious one to make it clear that he had been to the Whitakers' before.

The street door opened. An elderly lady in a mink coat had entered. Her gray hair beneath her ineffective little hat had a fashionable bluish tinge. In front of her, pulling at a leash, was a toy poodle, cut to resemble an Airedale. Its fur was also bluish gray.

"Good afternoon, Mrs. Gorham," the attendant said. "It turned out to be a beautiful afternoon, after all, didn't it?"

"Yes, spring is almost here," Mrs. Gorham answered.

"Hello, Bobo," the attendant said, and he leaned forward eagerly to address the poodle. "How's it outside, Bobo?"

It was not clear whether or not Bobo had enjoyed it outside. He was pulling Mrs. Gorham also to the elevator at the right.

When Charles followed them into the small mahogany lift, neither Mrs. Gorham nor Bobo looked at him until he asked the elevator man for Mrs. Whitaker's apartment, please. Then when Mrs. Gorham saw his brief case she looked away and they rode in stony silence, both denizens of different worlds, both thrown together in that moving car against their wills.

Charles was very conscious of the fact that he belonged in a different world whenever he entered the Whitakers' apartment. When he handed the butler his hat and coat, he knew that he understood the whole place very well, academically but not practically. It was an environment in which he could move gracefully, without tipping things over, but one in which he would never live.

The hall was filled with all sorts of objects which he knew had come from the house on Fifth Avenue belonging to Mrs. Whitaker's father, that canny Yankee from Maine. The Isphahan runner in the hall, and the heavily gold-framed pictures on the walls of Corot-like landscapes and of Oriental ladies with guitars on Moorish roof-tops, all told their tale of an art collection acquired in the eighties and nineties when such things were an essential part of a businessman's background. Above the small refectory table that held a silver tray for visiting cards there was even a portrait of Cyrus J. Smedley, Mrs. Whitaker's father, still dominating those possessions. It was a three-quarters portrait of an elderly man in a high-lapelled dark business coat, a high waistcoat, and a large cravat. He had a lantern-jawed, wary look, and a sort of assurance that belonged to another generation. He was dyspeptic and dangerous looking, and Charles was always acutely aware of his presence. If the old man had been alive, he often thought, he would never have needed the services of the trust department of the Stuyvesant. His general taste in furniture might have been terrible, but it must have been impeccable in blue-chip securities. There must have been a time, Charles was also thinking, when Mr. Whitaker had been obliged to face Cyrus J. Smedley and to tell of his intentions, in a Victorian sort of way, and it made Charles feel sorry for Mr. Whitaker.

It was obviously going to be another family conference because the room at the end of the hall was set for it, a large room that looked small because of the piano and the Bouguereaus and Alma-Tademas on the wall, the Italian chairs, the overstuffed sofas, and the maze of silver-framed photographs on the tables. The family had all been waiting for him, although he was certain that he was there right on the dot of five. Mrs. Whitaker, in a dark tailored suit, was seated on a sofa in front of the fireplace, amazingly upright in spite of the sofa's yielding upholstery. She was obviously prepared for the interview because she was holding a tablet on her knee with questions written on it. She always wrote down questions. Mr. Whitaker was standing near the fireplace in a suit that was too tweedy for him, looking round and red and uncomfortable. Their son Albert, who had risen when Charles came in, looked more like his mother than his father. You could see that he had kept his figure by conscientious outdoor exercise, and he had kept his hair, too, though it was gray at the temples.

Albert's wife as usual looked very bored. Though she and Charles had never exchanged more than a word of greeting, it always surprised him how clearly she could tell him what she was thinking without saying a word, not that she cared whether he knew or not. She was telling him simply by perching on the edge of one of the Italian chairs that she was bored by having to be there, that she was too young, too pretty, too blond, to be there, that she hated the stuffy furniture and her family-in-law, and that she was bored by Albert, too. She was telling him that she wanted to get away somewhere and have a Martini, that she wanted to play a rubber of bridge or something, that only necessity had brought her to this place and that he mustn't think that she liked it, or that she liked him either. She knew just what he was, a tiresome man from the bank, called for one of those damned family conferences that Mother Whitaker was always having. She knew just where he belonged and there was no need for any introductions.

"I hope I'm not late," Charles said.

"Oh, no," said Mrs. Whitaker. "I know we can count on your never being late. Sit down here beside me, Mr. Gray, so we can read things together."

Charles sank down beside her on the sofa. He wished that he could sit upon it as straight as Mrs. Whitaker.

"Albert," Mrs. Whitaker said, "get Mr. Gray a little table."

"Oh, I don't need a table," Charles said. "There won't be anything to sign."

"You'll need it to put things on," Mrs. Whitaker said, "the things out of your brief case. It's always so reassuring to see you with a brief case. I can't imagine how you'd look without it."

"That's true," Charles said. "I don't believe you've ever seen me here without it."

"You'd look, well, almost naked without it," Mrs. Whitaker said. "I remember what Father always used to say."

"What did he use to say?" Albert asked.

"You were too young to remember Granddaddy well, dear," Mrs. Whitaker said. "I wish you could have seen him, Mr. Gray. Hewett, doesn't Mr. Gray remind you of Papa?"

"Well, not altogether, Ellie," Mr. Whitaker said.

"I don't mean altogether, Hewett. I mean partly. He has the same expression sometimes, when we're getting down to brass tacks, as Papa used to say. Papa always used to say when you do business with someone, be sure he does business."

"I understand what he meant," Charles said. "Shall we get down to brass tacks?" and he reached for the catch of his brief case where it lay across his knees.

"Hewett."

"Yes, Ellie," Mr. Whitaker said.

"Perhaps Mr. Gray would like a Scotch and soda."

"Oh, no, thank you," Charles said.

"Well, I'd like one," Albert said. "Come on, Dad. How about it, Dorothy?"

"Well," Dorothy said, and her voice was coldly sweet, "I might have one if Mother Whitaker doesn't mind."

"Of course I don't mind, darling," Mrs. Whitaker said. "Why on earth should I mind? Mr. Gray and I will have some tea when everything is over. Won't we, Mr. Gray?"

"Why, yes," Charles said. "That would be very nice." He saw Dorothy glance at him. She was telling him as plainly as though she had spoken for God's sake to get on with it, and he hoped that he was telling her when he glanced back at her that, for God's sake, he wanted to get on with it, that he didn't like sitting there any more than she did, that he was only present as she was because he had to be.

"Now," said Mrs. Whitaker, "let's begin at the beginning. Let's begin by having you scold us, Mr. Gray, because we all need a good scolding."

"About what, Mrs. Whitaker?" Charles asked.

"About the ranch," Mrs. Whitaker said. "I know how it must look with the world the way it is, but it's really for Albert's sinus. Albert and Dorothy are just back from Arizona. You can tell it by looking at them, can't you?"

Charles looked up at Dorothy and their glances met again.

"Albert," Dorothy said sweetly, "why don't you show him the photographs? That's what you brought them for, wasn't it?"

"Oh yes," Albert said. "If you have to be out there, you might as well have some sort of place and not stay at a hotel. We saw this one fifty miles out of Tucson. These are just snapshots but they'll give you an idea, and Dorothy's crazy about it. She needs some sort of place."

Curiously enough he could feel their uncertainty as Albert handed him the photographs and he knew that they were anxious for his approval. The photographs were mountain and desert views with low buildings of the Spanish hacienda type in the foreground, corrals, patios, galleries, a swimming pool. They represented an exotic life pattern which the Whitakers must have known was entirely out of his experience, but still they wanted him to approve.

"If you really want it," Charles said gently, "I don't know why you shouldn't have it. Is a hundred thousand the asking price? If you really want it, you'd better give me the agent's name."

"He does really want it," Mrs. Whitaker said. "If you could call up the agent it would be sweet of you, Mr. Gray. It would sound better than having Albert do it."

"Of course," Charles said, "you'll have to use a little capital, but I don't see why you shouldn't."

He was opening the brief case, taking out the folders and spreading them on the table. There was no earthly reason why they shouldn't, any more than there was any earthly reason why he should not have bought a three-dollar book if he had really wanted it, or an overcoat if he really needed it, but it hardly mattered as much to them as a new overcoat would have mattered to him. It was not a conventional way of looking at the problem and he wondered what they would have thought if he had presented it to them in this light.

"That's all that bothers me," Mrs. Whitaker said. "Papa always said never to touch capital. It always was his rule."

That was what clients like the Whitakers were always saying. No matter what capital might grow to, you must never touch your capital.

"Things are a little different now," Charles said, "with the tax rate the way it is in the higher brackets."

He saw that Dorothy was watching him. She was bored and telling him wordlessly to get on with it, but at the same time it looked as though she understood what he would have to go through. It would be necessary to discuss the tax structure again.

"But don't you think," Albert Whitaker was asking, "that there's going to be a twenty per cent reduction across the board?"

"They're talking about it, but I wouldn't count on it," Charles said.

"If they're going to reduce taxes," Albert said, "the only sensible, democratic way would be to reduce them across the board."

"I know," Charles said, "but I'm afraid that isn't the way a politician's mind works. But there's no reason why you shouldn't sell some of these short-term governments. They scarcely yield any income at all after taxes."

He was speaking quickly, easily, just as though their problems were his own, dealing in millions just as though they belonged to him. He explained painstakingly item after item on the list.

"You make everything seem so reasonable, Mr. Gray," Mrs. Whitaker said. "I really don't know what we'd do without you."

The Whitakers were as helpless as the soft Manchu descendants of the hardy Mongols who once sat in their moldering Peking palaces, surrounded by Chinese attendants and estate stewards, before they were overtaken by the Boxer rebellion. Somewhere along the way the Whitakers had lost their ability to cope with any present exigency. Their life had taken from them all the ordinary drives of ambition, hope and fear.

"You could always find someone else, Mrs. Whitaker," Charles said, "and he might be better."

"No," said Mr. Whitaker. "You're the only one who's ever seemed to make Mrs. Whitaker understand."

"I don't know why you say that," Mrs. Whitaker said. "I've always been taught to supervise my own affairs, and Mr. Gray knows it."

"Yes," Charles said. "I'm developing a great respect for your general judgment, Mrs. Whitaker."

"I do hope they appreciate you at the bank as much as we do," Mrs. Whitaker said.

"I hope they do, too," Charles answered, and he picked up some of the papers on the little table in front of him as a hint that he had been there for nearly an hour. He wanted very much to catch the six-thirty.

"Well," Albert said, "if everything's settled perhaps Dorothy and I had better be pushing off."

Dorothy rose from the edge of her chair, gracefully, without pushing herself from it.

"It stays light so long," she said, "that I keep forgetting what time it is," but Mrs. Whitaker had picked up the pad from her knee.

"I thought you told me that you didn't have any engagement until dinner, dear," Mrs. Whitaker said. "Now that Mr. Gray's here, I did have a few other questions, but if you want to run along—"

"Oh, no," Dorothy said. "We're really in no hurry."

She smiled at Charles—a ghost of a smile—and sat down again and folded her hands carefully in her lap. She did it brightly and cheerfully, without a hint of resignation, but Charles was sure he knew what she was thinking. Oh, God, she was thinking, here it goes again, the same damned questions.

Mrs. Whitaker's mind was always filled with unshaped, broad-gauge thoughts that mingled confusingly with little ones. There was still that matter of trying to settle a little more on Albert and of balancing the gift against inheritance taxes. She knew, as Charles had so often said, that these were really legal problems and she had nothing at all against Mr. Stone who handled them, but she did value Mr. Gray's opinion and her father had always said that two minds were better than one.

It seemed to her that the government, which she had always been taught was created to protect people and the things they owned, was making a deliberate effort to discourage people who had a little something. For some reason, no one seemed to appreciate any longer what people in her position were doing. What would charities do without people in her position, what would the government do without the taxes, what would business do without the money of people in her position? She knew that she had said all these things before, but she did wish that Charles would take a copy of Mr. Stone's last letter to read, and, when he had time, consult with Mr. Stone.

Then there was the question of the place on Long Island. With wages rising the way they were, she wondered if Charles would mind sometime looking over the books that Mr. Stone was keeping, because she knew, although it was not in his sphere, that he would have some suggestion for cutting down. Then she wanted to know what Charles really thought of the Atchison, Topeka and Santa Fe Railroad, and besides there were several other questions, but now tea was coming in and perhaps they had better put most of it over until another day, but while they were having tea she would like to look over the security list with Albert. It was high time that someone gave it attention beside herself because she was tired of having everyone expect her to do everything alone.

"Nothing's been changed since last time," Charles said.

"I know," she said, "but I would like to look at it with Albert for a minute if you wouldn't mind waiting, Mr. Gray. Why don't you take your tea and talk with Dorothy?"

Charles rose and picked up his teacup. Dorothy had moved to a window with her highball glass in her hand. She stood there straight and beautiful, smelling faintly of Chanel Five, looking out on Park Avenue, and she smiled cordially at Charles.

"I'm sorry it's taken so long," Charles said.

"Why don't you take a drink?" she said. "I would."

"Oh, no," Charles answered. "I don't believe you would."

"Well, maybe I wouldn't," she said, and she smiled again and glanced toward the sofa where Mr. Whitaker and Albert stood looking over Mrs. Whitaker's shoulder.

"I didn't know," he heard Mrs. Whitaker saying, "that we had so many shares in Homestake Mine."

Dorothy had turned toward him again. Her beautifully molded, made-up face and the wind-blown look to her hair had an impermeable sort of completeness. It made him nervous that there was so little wrong about her. There was nothing wrong about her delicate hands and her pointed red fingernails, nothing wrong about her silk print dress or her diamond clip or her straight, lithe figure or her nylon stockings, but still there was something baffling.

"What do you do," she asked, "when you aren't doing this?"

"I go home," Charles said. "It looks as though I'm going to be late tonight."

"You make me curious," she said. "You really do."

"Why?" Charles asked.

"You make me curious because I can't picture you as doing anything but what I see you doing."

"Well," Charles answered, "now you mention it, I've been thinking about the same thing about you."

Her lips curved in that same faint smile.

"That's because we're both doing what we do very well," she said, "but it takes a lot of trouble, doesn't it?"

"Well," Charles answered, "sometimes—yes."

"Do you ever wonder whether it's worth it?" she asked.

"Yes," Charles said, "occasionally. I suppose everyone does."

"That's the question," she said. "Is it worth it? I'm glad you're curious about me. I didn't know you were."

"I am," Charles said, "academically."

"You know," she said, "we ought to have a long talk sometime."

Charles squared his shoulders. He could not imagine how he had become involved in such a conversation and nothing would have been more unwise than having a long talk with Dorothy Whitaker sometime.

"I'm very glad you suggested it," Charles said. "It's an interesting idea."

"It would be a lot of fun." Her smile grew broader. "If we could sit in a bar some afternoon and get quietly tight and talk—"

Charles found that he was laughing. The beauty of it was that it was so impossible that there was nothing at all to worry about.

"You see," she said, "I'd find out what you used to be and how you got the way you are."

"It wouldn't be worth it," Charles said. "I've always been about the same."

"Oh, no," she said, "nobody ever is. We can't help working on ourselves."

He had a momentary picture of her working on herself, sitting before her mirror with her lipstick and her powder base, and brushing back her hair.

"Not on ourselves," he said. "Everyone works on us. Everyone wears us down."

"If you're tough enough," she said, "you don't have to be worn down."

Charles found himself laughing again.

"All right," he said, "what did you use to be?"

She shook her head slowly and her smile had gone.

"Nicer," she said, "quite a good deal nicer."

"Oh, Mr. Gray," Mrs. Whitaker was calling, "could you come over here for a minute?"

"Good-by," she said. "Good luck."

"I see you have a question mark in pencil after Smith Chemical," Mrs. Whitaker was saying.

7

Shadows of the Evening

The six-thirty from the upper level of the Grand Central was a good train, express to Port Chester and never crowded. Though it would get him home late for dinner, he welcomed the opportunity of riding on it because he could be reasonably sure of not having to talk to anyone and it gave him an opportunity to go over all the events of the day, the people he had seen, and what he had done well or badly. As the train moved out of the station into the dark beneath Park Avenue, Charles laid his brief case on the vacant seat beside him and took out the book, *Yankee Persepolis,* that Malcolm Bryant had given him. He laid it on top of his brief case and then looked at the headlines on the front page of the *New York World-Telegram.*

The headlines had the same disturbing quality as his personal thoughts for it seemed that nothing was in order that day with himself or with anything else. They were still arguing in Moscow over German reparations, which everyone must have known could never be collected. There were terrorist bombings in Palestine and the news was bad in Turkey and there were student riots in Cairo. It often seemed to him that Cairo students never had time to study. All that foreign world kept slopping over its borders like water spilling untidily out of a shaking dish.

He was thinking, for no good reason, of Shepheard's Hotel in Cairo as he had first seen it from the jeep that had brought him in from the army airfield in the desert. He remembered the beige façade and the robes and the red caps of the dragomans and the khaki shorts of the British and colonial officers crowding the terrace and their caps and tam-o'-shanters that somehow made them look like grown men pretending to be Boy Scouts at a children's party. It all made no particular sense, since neither he nor anyone at headquarters had ever found why he had been sent to Cairo. Then he thought of the field at Prestwick and of the uncompromising Scottish streets of Glasgow. Then he was thinking of the main street in Clyde, of the brick sidewalk and a display of elastic bandages and digestive powders in the windows of Walters's drugstore, and the tools and galvanized pails and hickory bushel baskets in front of Harrison's hardware store which was only a few doors further down the street, just before you came to Bates's grocery. There was no reason to think of Clyde and Shepheard's and of some dingy pub in Glasgow all at the same time, except that everything was closer together than it used to be.

He could hear the creaking, complaining sounds of the train and he was aware of the dim tunnel lights moving past the windows in an even sequence of light and dark that was punctuated now and then by a blue electric flash when some locomotive lost contact with the rail. Although his thoughts had no appreciable pattern, he knew that they were all symptoms of his own uncertainty.

The people he had seen that day and the things that he and they had said had no disturbing connotation in themselves. Taken separately, they were all elements that he might encounter in any working day. The trust conference, the interlude of lunch, the activities of Roger Blakesley, his words with Mr. Selig, his talk with Tony Burton and his conference with the Whitakers, were manifestations that he had encountered often in slightly different forms, yet taken all together they achieved a different stature. Even the question of competition, of his having been outmaneuvered, though he was keenly conscious of it, was not what disturbed him. There was something more in the sum of all of it that lay within himself.

For some reason Clyde kept coming into it, and for some reason he kept seeing events in terms of Clyde; and all the things he had done that day were like things he had done in Clyde, on a different projection and a wholly different scale. Actually he was not very different from what he had at one time been. But nicer. He remembered the word "nicer." The train was out of the tunnel, moving by the lighted tenements of uptown New York whose unshaded windows gave abrupt glimpses into other people's lives.

When he had stood by that other New York window watching Dorothy Whitaker's tapering fingers with their brightly polished red nails as she held her half-empty glass, he might again have been calling on Jessica Lovell at the Lovell house in Clyde. Granted that Jessica was a wholly different person, there was that same indirect involvement. It was true that if you weren't tough enough, contact with other people wore you down.

"Tickets," the conductor was saying. He had not noticed the conductor walking through the car. You had to have some sort of ticket for everything and it was generally one-way. Then he remembered that he had used up the last of his commutation ticket that morning.

"I'll have to pay you," Charles said. He could not remember when he had last forgotten a ticket. "How much is it to Clyde? . . . I'm sorry. I was thinking of something else."

Charles picked up the book from the top of the brief case and began to turn the pages.

"For the purposes of distinction," he was reading again, "it will be well arbitrarily to define the very definite and crystallized social strata of Yankee Persepolis as upper, middle, and lower. These will be subdivided into upper-upper, middle-upper, and lower-upper . . ."

Since he was late, he had to take a taxi. The taxi starter, who sorted the clientele, putting those who were going in the same general direction into the same cab, was standing at the far end of the platform, a lay figure silhouetted against the headlights of the cars.

"Sycamore Park," Charles said, and the starter called out his words above the rumbling of the train that was leaving.

"Sycamore Park. Anyone else going to Sycamore Park?"

The night air was fresher and it smelled of spring, and there was a vacancy of sound after the train had left. The train seemed to have carried away everything that Charles had been thinking. Everything connected with the city, Smith Chemical, Telephone, American Tobacco B, and short-term governments, was gone with the train. He was going home again, and no one else was going to Sycamore Park. He was returning to the basic reason for everything for which he had been working.

As he sat in the back seat of the taxicab he still thought about Clyde. They used to play hide-and-seek in the old back garden of the Meader yard in the spring, just when it was getting dusk—he and Melville Meader and Earl Wilkins and all the rest of the crowd along Spruce Street. There was a better chance of hiding, just when it was dusk. You could hide downstairs in the barn or back of the carriage shed or anywhere in the garden. There was always that indecision, that rushing about, until you heard "five hundred, coming, ready or not." Then you tried to sneak back without being seen. The best way was to dodge around the carriage house and then to the corner of the barn where you could watch the back porch, which was home, until everything was clear. There was always an uncertainty, a wondering whether you could make it, and then that dash for home. If you got there safely, all the other incidents were behind you. There was a triumphant, out-of-breath feeling, a momentary impression that nothing else mattered, when you called out "Home Free!"

Sycamore Park had been developed in 1938 on the forty-acre grounds of an old estate and the subdivision had been excellently managed by the local real estate firm of Merton and Pease. As Mr. Merton had said, it was a natural, and he had never understood why someone had not dreamed it up long ago—not too far from the shopping center and the trains, and yet in the neighborhood of other larger places. Every place had its own acre, and no house was to be constructed for a cost of less than thirty thousand dollars. It would have been wiser, perhaps, never to have gone there but to have bought a smaller place.

It would have been wiser, easier, and much safer. He had not at that time been moved up in the trust department and in 1939 all he had was twenty thousand dollars in savings, part of which was in paid-up life insurance. He could never analyze all the urges that made him lay everything on the line in order to live on a scale he could not immediately afford, discounting the possibilities of illness or accident and relying on possibilities of promotion. He only remembered having had an irrational idea that time was of the essence, that he would always stay on a certain business level if he did not take some sort of action, and Nancy, too, had shared that feeling.

The sight of the house at Sycamore Park still gave him qualms of uneasiness. Its whitened brick, its bow windows, still reminded him of what might have happened and of what he would have done if things had turned out differently. Those worries were all top-secret between Nancy and himself, to be shared with no one else. Yet, no matter what, that house was his and hers, a tangible achievement of the past and a sort of promissory note for the future.

When he had paid the driver and the car had driven off, he stood for a while at the end of the flagstone path that led to the green front door. The light from the ground-floor windows sharpened the outlines of the ell and roof, and his imagination enabled him to put the rest of it together in the dark—the yard, the lawn and trees, the garage and the flagstone terrace by the windows of the library. Now they were even talking at odd moments about selling and getting something larger, but nothing would ever be the same as that particular house. No other house of theirs would ever have the sleepless nights, the hours of argument, spent over it. There was too much of him connected with the house ever to view it objectively. He was thinking of the copper gutters and of the way the conductors drained over a part of the lawn. It would be necessary to have a dry well dug for the conductors; and then there was the broken latch on the garage door, and the oil burner needed a new lining of firebrick; and then there was the weather stripping around the living room windows, and there was something still wrong with the gas water heater. Then there was the mortgage. Then there was the part of the cellar that he was going to turn into a workshop for himself and Bill, now that you could buy lathes and drills again. Those were the species of thoughts that came over him as he stood there by the door, and they were a relief after everything else.

The hall, when Charles entered, seemed what the architect had called gracious and welcoming. At the left came the dining room; the living room was opposite, then the stairs, and the pine-paneled library at the end. Once he had thought this ground plan was entirely original until, to his amazement, he had found it repeated in all the other houses at Sycamore Park. The hall furniture was what made it undeniably their own hall, for the furniture, though Nancy had kept changing it, came from other incarnations, from apartments in New York, from the little house in Larchmont. The four rush-bottomed chairs they had bought once on a vacation trip and on which no one could sit were good antiques that never fitted well with the reproductions that Nancy had bought before she knew better. They still stood, with the gilt mirror and the console table, like parts of older civilizations, waiting to be absorbed into another way of life.

It was strange the way a family developed habits. For instance, no one seemed to use the living room much, although it was the largest and most comfortable room in the house. The children as usual were in the library listening to the radio—no longer learning parchesi and reading the *Wizard of Oz*. Instead they had progressed imperceptibly to the outer edge of childhood, a strange, transient region. Bill was sprawled on the sofa in a manner which he must have copied from some older boys. He was wearing a pullover sweater and his gray flannel trousers had worked halfway up to his knees, showing stretches of bare shin, and garterless knitted socks that wrinkled above those laceless moccasins that all the boys were wearing. His face seemed to have outgrown itself, like his body, so that his nose looked too big for his eyes, and he had a crew cut which was very unbecoming.

Evelyn sat sideways in an armchair. Instead of being nervous, petulant, and slender, as she had been when she was seven and eight, Evelyn was almost fat. He could imagine she would be pretty someday for she had Nancy's tranquil features and Nancy's chin and mouth, yet it was hard to believe that Nancy, when she was thirteen, could have looked like Evelyn, that Nancy could have worn a little girl's plaid dress or that Nancy's light brown braids had ever been so untidy.

When they saw him they both jumped up, clumsily yet with a puzzling sort of co-ordination. There had been a time when he had taken it for granted that they were fond of him, but now he found it very reassuring to realize that they were still glad to see him, even though their feelings toward each other were undergoing some adolescent change. Evelyn still kissed him like a little girl, winding her arms tight around his neck, but Bill simply stood there grinning at him, with his wrists dangling out of the sleeves of his sweater.

"Hello," Charles said. "How about turning that radio off?"

"It's going to be over in a minute, Daddy," Evelyn said, "and then there's going to be Eddy Duchin."

"Well, never mind Eddy Duchin," Charles said. "Turn it off. I'm tired."

Bill switched it off and there was a silence that was almost embarrassing to Charles. It was obviously incredible to both Bill and Evelyn that anyone could exist who could bear to miss Duchin.

"What's the matter?" Bill asked. "Don't you want to hear it, Pop?"

"Not right this minute," Charles answered, and he put his arm around Evelyn's shoulders. "You're getting to be a big girl, aren't you?"

"Don't," Evelyn said. "You tickle."

"Where's Mother?" Charles asked.

"She's gone to the club," Bill answered. "The Martins took her and she left the car. She said for you to go up there when you've had supper."

"Your supper's in the oven," Evelyn told him, "but I'll get it."

"Why do you have to go out?" Bill asked. "Why don't you just stay here?"

"Because he's on the committee," Evelyn said. "And don't forget to shave." She sounded just like Nancy.

"Don't worry," Charles answered. "I'll put on a black tie and everything."

"Mother laid your clothes out," Evelyn told him. "Daddy, why don't you use lotion?"

"What?" Charles asked.

"After-shaving lotion. Don't you want to be like other people?"

Charles started to laugh, but a desperate, tragic note in her voice stopped him.

"Do you really think that would help?" he asked, and she nodded without speaking.

"All right," Charles said, "I'll tell you what I'll do. If you really think so, I'll buy some of it tomorrow."

It must have been worrying her, because she smiled the triumphant smile of someone who has been through a considerable ordeal and who has been brave enough to speak frank thoughts.

"Oh, Daddy," she said, "you don't have to do it if you don't want to."

That expansive mood was still with Charles as he sat in the dining room eating warmed-over corned beef hash and string beans and drinking a cup of bitter, warmed-over coffee. Now that it was spring, he found himself saying, they would take the car some Saturday soon and drive away out in Connecticut for a picnic. It would be a cooking picnic, if they could find a place somewhere near a brook where they could light a fire. When he was their age, he was saying, they often went for picnics down on the beach and they always built a fire of driftwood because there was always a lot of dry wood on a beach. Bill was saying that he wished they had a sailboat, but Evelyn was saying that of course they couldn't afford a sailboat, and Charles said that perhaps they could sometime. Then Bill was saying that he had been with some of the boys to the airport that afternoon watching the Piper Cubs, and Charles said that maybe Bill could take flying lessons sometime, if he wanted, when he was seventeen or eighteen. This brought the conversation around to the war, and Charles was telling them again, as he had before, that he had not done anything much in the war and that a great many people in the Air Force were on the ground all the time, repairing the planes and briefing the crews who were going on missions. Then Bill was asking him if he had ever been on a mission, and Charles said that he had been, twice, but not doing anything, just there to see what it was like. He had never thought that their talk would end that way after beginning with shaving lotion.

"What was it like?" Bill asked.

Charles pushed his plate away. He would never be able to tell Bill what it was like, even if he wanted to. He was thinking that he had been about Bill's age after the last war and that he had always wondered what it had been like.

"It was cold . . ." he said. "If I'm going to the club, I've got to get dressed . . . It's all over anyway, Bill. All of it's all over."

He must have spoken sharply without having intended to because they were quiet when he stood up, but Bill followed him to the stairs.

"Do you mind if I come up with you?" he asked.

"No," Charles said, "of course not, as long as we talk about something else."

His brother Sam had been old enough to go to the last war.

While he was putting his studs in his shirt, he kept looking at Bill, who sat on the edge of the bed, and wondering whether he could ever have looked like Bill when he was fifteen. It did not seem possible that he could have ever been a gangling sight like Bill, so awkward or so immature.

"I don't want you sitting around wishing you'd been in that war," Charles said.

"Well, just the same, I do," Bill answered.

"It doesn't do any good to wish," Charles said. "I kept wishing I'd been to the first one and that's why I went to this one and it wasn't a very good idea."

"Why wasn't it a good idea?" Bill asked.

"It didn't help anything," Charles said.

"How do you mean," Bill asked, "it didn't help anything?"

"Never mind," Charles said. "It didn't. It was a luxury."

"A luxury?" Bill repeated.

The subject was not worth discussing. Bill was too young to understand him.

"When you do something that you don't have to do, it's generally a luxury," Charles said. "You've got a lot of other things to think about, Bill. I want you to go to college, and I want you to have more opportunities than I've had."

"What sort of opportunities?" Bill asked.

They were on ground where they could never meet.

"I want you to be able to see more things and do more things than I ever have," Charles said. "I'd like you to have some sort of profession, something you'll be proud and happy doing." He was pulling on his black trousers and it occurred to him that it was an undignified position from which to deliver a pontifical speech.

"Aren't you happy," Bill asked, "working in the bank?"

"Yes," Charles answered, "but that hasn't anything to do with you. What do you want more than anything else?"

"I want to go to Exeter," Bill said.

Charles did not answer. It was an anticlimax, but he could understand it. It was a disappointment, but he could understand it. It meant that Bill was like himself. When he was that age, he too had usually wanted something small and definite.

"Dad, is there any chance of sending me to Exeter?"

"Why, yes," Charles said, and he put on his coat. "I think so, Bill. I think there's a pretty good chance, if everything turns out all right. Do you know where the keys to the car are? I ought to be going now."

Not since he had left Clyde had Charles ever felt as identified with any community as he had since he had been asked to join the Oak Knoll Country Club. They were in a brave new world involving all sorts of things of which he had scarcely dreamed after they had moved to Sycamore Park. This cleavage between past and present, Charles realized, was a part of a chain reaction that started, of course, with one of those shake-ups in the bank. Charles had known that he had been doing well. He had known for a year or so, from the way Mr. Merry and Mr. Burton and particularly Mr. Slade had been giving him little jobs to do, that something was moving him out of the crowd of nonentities around him. He was aware also that Walter Gibbs in the trust department was growing restless. There had been a premonition of impending change, just like the present tension. One day Walter Gibbs had asked him out to lunch and had told him, confidentially, that he was going to move to the Bankers' Trust and that he was recommending Charles for his place. Charles was not surprised, because he had been a good assistant to Walter Gibbs, and he was glad to remember that he had been loyal to his chief, ever since the old days in the statistical department.

"Charley," Walter Gibbs had said, "a lot of people around here have been out to knife me. You could have and you never did, and I appreciate it, Charley."

He had known, of course, for some time that Walter Gibbs was not infallible, that he was fumbling more and more over his decisions and depending more and more on Charles's support, but Walter had taught him a lot.

"Slade keeps butting in," Walter had said, and then he went on to tell the old story which Charles had often heard of conflicting personalities and suspicions. Walter had felt that frankly he was more eligible for a vice-presidency than Slade, and the truth was he had never been the same after Arthur Slade had been selected.

"If they don't like you enough to move you up," Walter had said, "it's time to get out, Charley."

God only knew where Walter Gibbs was now. He was gone like others with whom you worked closely once and from whom you were separated. Walter Gibbs was gone with his little jokes and his bifocal glasses and the stooping shoulders that had given him a deceptively sloppy appearance. He was gone with his personality that would never have permitted him to be a vice-president of anything.

Charles was ready, not surprised, when Tony Burton, though of course he did not call him Tony then, had called him downstairs and had asked him if he knew what was coming, that he had been with them for quite a while and that they had all had an eye on him ever since he had done that analysis on chain stores. Even if you were prepared for such a change there was still an unforgettable afterglow, and an illuminating sense of unrealized potentiality. It was a time to be more careful than ever, to measure the new balance of power, and not to antagonize the crowd that you were leaving. One day, it seemed to Charles, though of course it was not one day, he was living in a two-family house in Larchmont that smelled of cauliflower in the evenings, stumbling over the children's roller-skates and tricycles, taking the eight-three in the morning, keeping the budget on a salary of six thousand a year. Then in a day, though of course it was not a day, they were building at Sycamore Park. The children were going to the Country Day School. They were seeing their old friends, but not so often. Instead they were spending Sundays with Arthur Slade. There was a maid to do the work. He was earning eleven thousand instead of six, and he was an executive with a future. New people were coming to call; all sorts of men he had hardly known were calling him Charley. It was a great crowd in Sycamore Park and he was asked to join the Oak Knoll Country Club. They were a great crowd in Sycamore Park.

It would have made quite a story—if it could have been written down—how all those families had come to Sycamore Park. They had all risen from a ferment of unidentifiable individuals whom you might see in any office. They had all once been clerks or salesmen or assistants, digits of what was known as the white-collar class. They had come from different parts of the country and yet they all had the same intellectual reactions because they had all been through much the same sorts of adventures on their way to Sycamore Park. They all bore the same calluses from the competitive struggle, and it was still too early for most of them to look back on that struggle with complacency. They were all in the position of being insecurely poised in Sycamore Park—high enough above the average to have gained the envy of those below them, and yet not high enough so that those above them might not easily push them down. It was still necessary to balance and sometimes even to push a little in Sycamore Park, and there was always the possibility that something might go wrong—for example, in the recession that everyone was saying was due to crop up in the next six or eight months. It was consoling to think that they were no longer in the group that would catch it first, or they would not have been at Sycamore Park—but then they were not so far above it. They were not quite indispensable. Their own turn might come if the recession were too deep. Then no more Sycamore Park, and no more dreams of leaving it for something bigger—only memories of having been there once. It was something to think about as you went over your checkbook on clear, cold winter nights, but it was nothing ever to discuss. It was never wise or lucky to envisage failure. It was better to turn on the phonograph—and someday you would get one that would change the records automatically. It was better to get out the ice cubes and have some friends in and to talk broad-mindedly about the misfortunes of others. It was better to go to the club on Tuesday evenings and to talk about something else—and that was where Charles Gray was going.

Charles was frank enough to admit that the Oak Knoll Club was not as good as the older country club at Hawthorn Hill. Charles's knowledge of people in the bank and his acquaintance with Hawthorn Hill clients had taught him that the Oak Knoll Club was intended for a definite sort of person, either one who could not afford the Hawthorn Hill dues or one who had not had the edges polished off. It was all very well to say that the Hawthorn Hill Club was meant for old men and older dowagers and that the Oak Knoll was a young man's club. That was what the Sycamore Park crowd always said, but any one of them would have dropped Oak Knoll like a hot potato if he had been asked to join Hawthorn Hill and could afford a share of stock. It was reassuring to Charles to recall that several members of Hawthorn Hill had spoken to him casually about joining it someday when he got around to it. Cliff Dunbarton, who kept his polo ponies and his hunters at the stable at Hawthorn Hill and who had come to Charles several times at the bank to ask him about investments, had once invited Charles and Nancy to the house for a drink, when he had met them walking on Sunday, and had said that any time Charles wanted to get into Hawthorn to let him know. Tony Burton himself, who was a member, had said only last year that it might be a good idea for Charles to think about getting into Hawthorn Hill, as long as Charles was a confidential advisor to so many of its members. It might even be a good thing for the bank to have him in there. When Charles had pointed out that he could not possibly afford the initiation fee or the purchase of the necessary share of stock, Tony Burton had said that there might be some way to wangle it, but it had either gone out of Tony's mind or there had not been any way, for the subject had not been brought up again.

Charles could not help wondering that night, as he drove between the stone gateposts of the Oak Knoll Club, whether Tony Burton had said the same thing to Roger Blakesley. Cliff Dunbarton certainly had not done so because it was clear from certain bitter remarks of Roger's about not having time to suck up to the Dunbartons that the Dunbartons had so far not bothered to know the Blakesleys. Charles had enjoyed assuring Roger that the Dunbartons weren't bad at all when you got to know them—not bad at all, only stand-offish.

It was true that in some sections of the town Oak Knoll was referred to as the "Monkey Cage," and now that Charles was a member of the House Committee he could see what was meant, but at the same time they all enjoyed themselves at Oak Knoll, and even some of the Hawthorn Hill crowd still kept their memberships. You did not have to worry so much about the furniture at Oak Knoll. If you wanted, you could drink a little more. You could be more relaxed, within reason—but not if you were a member of the House Committee. When Charles was hanging up his hat and coat in the men's coatroom, the first person he saw was Cliff Dunbarton, who looked more relaxed than usual.

"Why, hello," he said. "If it isn't Mr. Gray."

"That's right," Charles said. "The name's Gray," and he was tempted to add, "Fancy seeing you here," but he did not know Cliff Dunbarton well enough to be familiar and besides it was not up to him to belittle a party at Oak Knoll. Still they smiled at each other and he wished very much that he could be more like Cliff Dunbarton, happy wherever he was and not caring a damn about anything—but then, Cliff Dunbarton could afford it.

"Margie's away," Cliff Dunbarton said, and Charles realized that he must be referring to Mrs. Dunbarton. "She never can stand this place. Margie isn't what you'd call democratic, but this is quite a party."

"I wouldn't know," Charles said. "I just got here—but it must be if you say so."

"I've always kept my membership here," Cliff Dunbarton said, "out of community spirit. Frankly, Charley, there are some very amusing types and hurry-come-ups in this place. I've got to get around more. I'm having a wonderful time. How about having a drink, Charley?"

"I'd like to a little later, but not right now," Charles said. Obviously Cliff Dunbarton was quite tight or he would not have called him Charley.

"Have you got a pencil and a piece of paper?" Cliff Dunbarton went on. "There's a little number I was dancing with out there and I want to write her name down before I forget it."

Charles took a fountain pen from his inside pocket and tore a leaf from the back of his small black notebook.

"Where does she live?" he asked.

"She's a very nice little number," Cliff Dunbarton said. "Her name is Sherrill or Merrill or something, and I never would have met her if I hadn't come here. She lives in that new development. What is it? Something about a tree."

"Every new development is something about a tree," Charles said.

"Don't interrupt me. Let me concentrate." Cliff Dunbarton placed the notebook page against the wall and began writing slowly. "Bea Merrill. She asked me to call her Bea. I wish I knew what her husband's name was. She lives in that new, young-executive development. I remember the name now —Sycamore Park."

"That's right," Charles said. "She's Mrs. Tom Merrill."

"How do you know?"

"Because I live there," Charles said. "I live in Sycamore Park."

"By God," Cliff Dunbarton said, "that's right. Of course you do. You're the only person I've ever heard of who lives there."

"Except Bea," Charles said.

"Except Bea." Cliff Dunbarton began to laugh. "Well, thanks for the pen, Charley, and don't let the sycamores fall on you."

Perhaps Roger Blakesley was right, perhaps it was a waste of time to have anything to do with people like the Dunbartons, but it was pleasant to realize that he was the only person living in Sycamore Park whom Cliff Dunbarton had ever noticed. Yet though it was pleasant, he had a feeling of disloyalty. They were a great crowd in Sycamore Park, and he was on the House Committee of the Oak Knoll Club.

The Oak Knoll Club had been making one of its frequent drives for new members at just about the time the houses were being finished in Sycamore Park. A committee of good mixers had been formed for the purpose of the drive, known as the "Stir Up Committee," and its members had taken Saturday afternoon off and Sunday to go calling in a body on new Sycamore Park residents. Bill Forbush, the president of the club, who could play around any course in the eighties, and J. P. Swiss, who had once been an All-America tackle, and Walter Crumm, who had one of those one-man bands, which he played in his rumpus room, using his hands, feet, mouth, nose, and even his cranium, had dropped everything in order to get that committee going. Charles had only seen them in the distance, getting out of their station wagons at the eight-thirty, until they called on him.

He and Nancy were still hanging pictures in the new house and at first Charles had not been sure what they wanted, because a great many people he had never known before had been calling recently to see whether he needed insurance or to ask for contributions for Bundles for Britain, but when they trooped into the new pine-paneled library, they said their only purpose was to welcome Charles and Nancy into the community. Mr. Forbush said that his own son Rex was in the same class at the Country Day as Charles's boy Bill, and Mr. Swiss picked up a small plated-silver cup off the mantel, a trophy awarded to Charles for winning the quarter mile at Dartmouth; and they all talked about football and skiing, while Nancy was in the pantry getting something for them to drink. When Nancy had suggested this, Charles remembered that they all three had exchanged wordless glances and then Mr. Forbush had said that it would be a very good idea just to have a touch of something as long as it was the end of a long, hard Saturday afternoon. When Charles had gone out to help Nancy with the tray, he observed on his return that the three callers were pacing about the room, unobtrusively examining the furniture and exchanging low monosyllables, but when each had his glass everything was very cordial and there was an atmosphere of friendly confidence.

Charles had told them that he had given up track in his freshman year, that he had never been good enough for the varsity, and that he had never done much with golf. Mr. Forbush told Nancy that she ought to make that man of hers take it up. It would keep him from fussing around the house, and there was a fine professional at the Oak Knoll Club. Then Mr. Crumm asked why they didn't join the Oak Knoll Club. Nancy had looked a little startled, and Charles had said that they had never done much about clubs and right now the house and moving and getting settled had cost a good deal more than they had expected. Mr. Swiss had said that everything always did, but it was not the cost, it was the solid satisfaction that you got out of things that mattered. Regular exercise and fresh air and friends were what mattered. Now why didn't the Grays come around to Oak Knoll next Tuesday night and look the crowd over?

Then Mr. Forbush drew a deep breath. Seriously he didn't want to be a salesman, he said, and urge anything on the Grays, who looked as though they had minds of their own, particularly Mrs. Gray. They had really just come around to get to know the Grays and to welcome them into the community, but now they were all there, just friends together, he did want to say a few things about the Oak Knoll Club, because it was his special hobby, his baby. He remembered that when he and Mrs. Forbush first came to this town they came here cold, years ago, not knowing many people, and at first he didn't know whether he and Mrs. Forbush would fit in, particularly Mrs. Forbush. There were too many snooty people with too much money, all wrapped up in their own affairs, but then he found that there were a lot of regular human beings around, people who were busy, without too much money and without any side, and they were all in the Oak Knoll Club. Now they had heard of the Hawthorn Hill Club, hadn't they, where you had to wait for someone to die before you got in and where you had to mortgage your house to buy stock and pay initiation fees? Well, there were real human beings at Oak Knoll. It was just a simple building, made for people just like the Grays, one big old room with a few comfortable chairs, locker rooms with a few plain showers, a little bar and a kitchen where they tossed up simple meals, but a mighty nice eighteen-hole course and some good tennis courts, and they were raising money for a swimming pool. There was something for every member of the family there, and nobody complained about children having a good time. Everybody had a good time. Oak Knoll was a democratic club, for self-respecting people. The best friends he ever made, he made right there at Oak Knoll, boys like Swiss and Crumm and girls like Mrs. Swiss and Mrs. Crumm. They got up their own entertainments and made their own good times at Oak Knoll, and were they good times! You ought to hear Crumm and his one-man band and you ought to see Ma Epping do conjuring tricks. Did the Grays know any parlor tricks? Well, it didn't matter if they didn't. He didn't either, but the main thing was that the members made Oak Knoll and Oak Knoll didn't make the members.

Somehow once you started, you kept going to Oak Knoll, to the Tuesday dinner dances and the Saturday pick-up suppers, nothing elaborate, no lace parasols, not many chauffeurs in the parking lot, but somehow, he didn't know why, you got to think of it as a second home. What was it Daniel Webster said about Dartmouth? It's a small place, but we love it. Yet at the same time, he did not want the Grays to think for a minute that Oak Knoll welcomed all the rag, tag, and bobtail you always found in the suburbs. Actually, there was a pretty strict committee, who gave prospective members a good going over, but the Grays needn't worry their heads about formality, now that he and Swiss and Crumm had seen them and had sat with them in their gracious home. Well, he hadn't meant to run on so long about Oak Knoll. Someone should have stopped him. Yet seriously, why didn't they come and just look the crowd over at Oak Knoll? He would love personally to give them a card for two weeks. Come to think of it, he had a card right in his pocket and if anybody had a pen he would sign it now—and now they'd better all be going, but before they left how about making a date for the Tuesday night dinner dance at Oak Knoll? They would all personally guarantee that the Grays had a good time, and the Grays would meet all the crowd.

This had all happened before the war but war's aftermath had not changed the spirit of Oak Knoll. When Charles stepped out of the coatroom, though he felt tired, he knew he ought to dance, being a member of the House Committee. His ear for music was bad and, in spite of having gone once furtively for a course of lessons at the Arthur Murray studio, he had never developed an interesting technique, nor had he ever entirely mastered that basic Arthur Murray step, and he always had a feeling that he was back at his senior high school dance at Clyde or at a Dartmouth prom, both unwelcome memories. Nevertheless, he could see it was a good Tuesday night party, with a big enough crowd to make it more than break even financially. The tables had been cleared away from the big room and Sol Blatz and His Orchestra from Stamford were playing in one corner. The sight of Mr. Blatz, with his dark, waving hair and his languidly moving arm, reminded him that he must write Mr. Blatz a check.

The first girl he noticed was Bea Merrill, in the arms of Mr. Swiss. Mr. Swiss had put on weight in the last few years. His face was red and he was talking rapidly. Then he saw Cliff Dunbarton cut in on them. Then he saw Mr. Forbush dancing with Dotty Jack, the Jacks who had bought the stucco house, the one that had been hard to sell, near the entrance to Sycamore Park. Then he saw Nancy. She was dancing with Cyril Renard, who sold life insurance downtown. Cyril had been talking to him lately about a new endowment policy, and he hoped that Cyril would not bring the subject up again that night. He edged his way carefully across the floor and Nancy saw him and smiled. They looked as though they had been dancing for quite a while, and Cyril always wanted to change his partners quickly for business reasons.

"Hello, Cyril," Charles said. "I'm going to take Nancy off your hands."

"Don't put it that way," Cyril said. "Nancy and I were talking about you and education. Where's Bill going to college?"

Charles knew that Cyril was thinking of one of those educational policies which would both send the children to a proper school and you to a hospital if you needed it, and pay damages, too, if the dog bit the milkman.

"Charley, you and I ought to have a long talk sometime," Cyril said.

"All right," Charles answered. "Sometime, Cyril." He put his arm hastily around Nancy and began to dance.

"Thank God you've come. I've been dancing with him for ages," Nancy said, and then she gave him a little squeeze. "Is there any news?"

"Nothing much," Charles said. "I can't talk about it here, Nancy."

"There's that Dunbarton dancing with Bea Merrill."

"Yes, I see," Charles said. "Did he dance with you?"

"Yes, he danced with me. It was very gracious of him. He acts like someone in a settlement house."

"Oh, don't say that," Charles said. "Cliff's all right."

"Oh, you call him Cliff, do you?"

"Occasionally," Charles said. "There's no use being sensitive about people like Cliff."

"Well, as long as he doesn't feel he has to exercise seigniorial rights."

"What?" Charles asked.

"Oh, nothing. All those horsy people are highly sexed. What have you been doing all day?"

"I was stuck in the Whitakers' apartment."

"Oh," Nancy said, "the Whitakers. Did anything else happen?"

He knew he would have to tell her about Clyde and that he was going away tomorrow but he did not want to tell her then, to the sound of Mr. Blatz and the saxophone.

"Did you say anything to Tony Burton?"

"No," Charles said, "not exactly."

"How do you mean, not exactly?"

"What I say. Not exactly."

"Roger Blakesley's here tonight. Have you seen him?"

"No, but I've seen him all day."

"He looks exuberant."

"Oh," Charles said, "does he?"

"You look a little tired, darling."

"Well," Charles said, "I am tired."

"Did the children get you your supper?"

"Yes," Charles said. "Thanks for leaving the car. Whose table did you sit at?"

"Oh, the usual crowd," Nancy said. "They all missed you."

"Well, what's all this about Cliff Dunbarton?"

There was no time to answer. Someone had clapped him on the shoulder and they separated. It was Christopher DeMille, who lived two doors away from them and who wrote advertising copy.

"Hello, beautiful," Christopher said. "Are you two quarreling?"

"No," Nancy said. "We're having a second honeymoon."

"You ought to see Bess and me," Christopher said. "Bess and I always get fighting here on Tuesday nights. There's something in the atmosphere."

Charles moved away carefully over the dance floor. He could not imagine why anyone would think that he and Nancy had been quarreling.

8

We're All in the Same Boat—Eventually

Then Charles danced with Bea Merrill. Even though he did not enjoy dancing this was always something of an adventure—not that it was not expected of him and of other husbands, because of poor Tom Merrill. Charles had observed that everyone was beginning to refer to Bea's husband as "poor Tom," and this had no reference to his financial status because he was doing very well. Instead it must have arisen from the rumor that the Merrills were not getting on, and of course this was Bea's fault and not poor Tom's. Other wives were beginning to say that Bea was beginning to be talked *about* instead of simply *over*. You talked *over* couples, they said, like the Sellers and the Kendricks, wondering how they ever could get along together, or afford new cars on their incomes, but you talked *about* Bea, not that Bea was not a sweet, generous girl, but discontented, restless, and full of high spirits, even when Tom was always giving her everything she wanted, like a diamond clip at Christmas time.

It was even intimated by some of the men that Bea had what was known as hot pants, a vague condition that made wives check over afterwards whose husbands had danced with Bea on Tuesday nights—not that anyone was told not to dance with her as Bea was part of the crowd and no one wanted to hurt poor Tom. Besides, most of those stories about Bea, other wives said when they got together, were spiteful stories invented by jealous people, and certainly they were not jealous of poor Bea. Why should anyone be jealous of a kindhearted, restless little thing with a high voice who did not know what she wanted? It was true there was a story about Bea and a man, a house guest of the Kendricks', from New York, in poor Tom's coupé at the Labor Day dance, but no one was quite sure whether it had been Bea or that girl who had come from Old Lyme who looked like Bea. There was also the story about Bea diving into the swimming pool without a stitch on, not a stitch, but Bea herself had said that it had just been a hot summer night and she had just taken off her dress and nothing else—she was more covered than if she had worn a two-piece bathing suit. She hadn't even taken off her nylons. Still it was always an adventure, a slight step into the unknown, to dance with Bea. She was wearing a new black, sheathlike dress and the diamond clip that poor Tom had given her.

"Hello, darling," Bea said. "Have you read any good books lately?"

"I'm trying to read one called *Peace of Mind*," Charles said, "but I don't seem to be getting very far with it."

"My God," Bea said, "you're just like Tom. What do you need peace of mind for? Do you know what I've been thinking? I wish I were a Catholic. I wish that someone could tell me what to do."

"That's a great idea," Charles said, "but then you wouldn't do it."

"How do you know I wouldn't?" Bea asked, and then the music stopped. "Let's get out of here. Let's go outside."

This was not desirable because everyone always noticed who Bea's partner was when she left the dance floor. True, it was too cool outside to sit down and besides there were other couples on the terrace, but when Bea took his arm he knew that everyone was looking.

"Where's Tom tonight?" Charles asked.

"Where he usually is," Bea said. "In the office, working late, darling."

"I was late, too," Charles said.

"Yes," Bea said. "Well, here we are." Charles did not answer. It was obvious that they were out on the terrace.

"Darling, are you bored?" Bea asked.

"Why, no," Charles said, "of course I'm not."

"Well, I am."

"Never mind," Charles said, and he laughed. "In just a minute or two the music will be going around again."

"And it bores me to think of it," Bea said. "Everything goes around, right back to the same thing. Why can't you and I talk to each other like two sensible people? I don't mean about sex. You don't have that effect on me. To hell with sex."

Her voice had a rasping quality that could carry into out-of-the-way corners and tomorrow they would be saying that he and Bea Merrill had been talking about sex while poor Tom was working late.

"All right, Bea," he said, and he laughed. "Just remember I didn't bring it up."

Then Bea began to laugh.

"I don't have to remember. Darling, I don't suppose you've noticed, I don't suppose you've ever seen, the efforts I've made for years to make you bring it up."

That was why it was an adventure to dance with Bea Merrill. He could not very well help thinking of Bea Merrill in the coupé on Labor Day and of Bea Merrill in the pool.

"Why, Bea," he said, "don't give up. Please try again sometime."

"For years and years," Bea said. "You're completely unassailable, darling

—but then it wouldn't work anyway, would it? Our loving friends here surround us with chastity."

"What?" Charles said. "How do you mean, with chastity?"

"You know what I mean," Bea answered. Her voice carried perfectly and he noticed that couples around them had stopped to listen unobtrusively. "This is the chastest place I know, but that isn't what I'm talking about."

"Well, what are you talking about?" Charles asked.

"I'm talking about you and me. Do we really know each other? Answer me that—do we?"

It was one of those conversations to which Bea was growing addicted lately, and he wished that the music would start.

"Why, you and Tom and Nancy and I have seen quite a lot of each other," he said.

"But do we *know* each other? Does anybody around here really know anybody else? We all call each other by our first names, we're a big happy family doing parlor tricks, but do we know each other?—and I don't mean getting into bed with someone, either."

It seemed to Charles that there were no other voices on the terrace and that the waiting couples were drawing closer.

"Well, that would be a basis for acquaintance," Charles said. "At least, that's what I've always heard."

"Well, it isn't," Bea said, and she gave his arm an impatient tug. "I don't know Tom. I don't know Tom at all."

Charles began to feel very much like Tom.

"Listen, Bea," he said, "perhaps you're expecting too much, perhaps nobody does know anyone else so very well."

"But, darling," Bea said. "How well do you know Nancy? Didn't there use to be a time—"

The music started and Charles was very glad of it, and he was glad, too, that Cliff Dunbarton had seen them and was hurrying toward them.

"Have you two about finished?" Cliff asked.

"Why, yes," Charles said. "We were talking about knowing people, and chastity."

"Well, let's dance," Cliff said, "in a chaste way."

Charles watched them move toward the dance floor. It was true, what she had said, that they all knew a lot about each other yet very few of them really knew each other. He would have to dance at least once more. Considering everything, it would be advisable for business reasons to dance with Molly Blakesley. There were probably rumors already about himself and Roger and if he were not seen dancing with Molly someone would be bound to notice it. Still he did not want to, because there were things about Roger's wife that made him very nervous, not the same things at all that stirred him when he danced with Bea Merrill. There would be no brisk innuendoes about sex when he danced with Molly, no disturbing mental pictures.

Roger had wooed and won Molly in Cambridge, Massachusetts, while he was a student at the Harvard School of Business Administration. She was the daughter of a Harvard Business School professor, had gone to a Cambridge progressive school, and was finishing her junior year at Radcliffe, where she was specializing in social science, when Roger had met her at her father's house on Coolidge Hill Road. She had been interested in the New Deal in those days and was writing a thesis on the Tennessee Valley Authority, a preparation which did not help her at those parties at Oak Knoll. Charles had thought of her first only as a plump, earnest girl with glasses and once he had made a particular effort to be kind to her, but now kindness was no longer necessary. Instead it seemed to him that of late Molly was the one who was being kind to him. Molly had made what she herself would have called a beautiful adjustment. She had given up long ago going to Boston for her clothes, and Henri in New York looked after her hair, and she only wore her glasses now for reading. She specialized in Japanese iris and columbine in her little back garden at Sycamore Park, but she did not call them iris and columbine. To Molly they were *I. Kaempferi* and *Aquilegia.* Once after a visit to that garden, Charles had suggested to Nancy that she might do more with flowers herself—she had always been good with flowers—but Nancy had said there was no time for flowers with children. There was no doubt that children were hostages to fortune. The thought flitted across his mind as he saw Molly Blakesley dancing with Walter Crumm.

The trouble with dancing with Molly Blakesley was that since that situation had arisen at the bank they each knew too well what the other was thinking. He suspected that her dress must have come from Bergdorf's and must have cost at least a hundred and fifty dollars, which Roger could afford because the Blakesleys did not have children. He wished that he did not keep putting their lives into terms of dollars and cents and that he did not always seem to be going over expenses whenever he danced with Molly Blakesley. It was necessary to be careful with her, too. She had a way of remembering everything one said, accurately and usefully. She was a very good wife to Roger.

"Well, well, Charley," Walter Crumm said. "Who stole Bea away from you?"

"She said she was bored," Charles told him. "She said I was unassailable."

"Well, well," Walter said. "He didn't look unassailable, did he, Molly?"

"Oh, were you out there too?" Charles asked.

"We certainly were," Walter said, "but we won't tell Nancy, will we, Molly?"

It was all good clean fun, a part of the spirit of Oak Knoll, and you had to take it that way. Yet at the same time, Charles knew that Roger would hear of it, and it was the sort of thing that Roger might be able to use with Tony Burton—all in good clean fun.

"Poor Tom," Molly said. "But it was awfully funny, Charley. You didn't look like a banker."

"Perhaps Roger won't either," Charles said, "if Bea gets him out there."

"Roger wouldn't let Bea get him out there. You know how Roger can side-step." Molly laughed brightly.

"That must be the Harvard Business School training," Charles said, and he smiled back at Molly.

"Charley," Molly said, "seriously, do you know what Roger was saying the other night, when we were just alone in the kitchen having a drink of beer?"

It was a time to be careful, but Charles still smiled.

"We were talking about you and Nancy, and Roger was saying how fond everyone is of you at the bank, Roger particularly. You know how full he is of everything at the bank. And he was saying how wonderful it was that we were all such good friends and he hoped we always would stay friends, no matter what happens at the bank. You know what I mean. It's so embarrassing, isn't it?"

"It needn't be embarrassing," Charles said. "Roger and I are grown-up. We can handle anything that happens."

"You know," Molly spoke more quickly, "I think the war did you a lot of good, Charley. Roger thinks so, too."

Charles did not answer. It was kind of her to say it, but he wished that he was not always searching for hidden meanings when he listened to Molly Blakesley.

"I think it was pretty splendid of you," she was saying, "with a wife and two children, to give up everything and go to the war. Roger thinks so, too."

He could not bring himself to care what Roger thought.

"It was a sort of compulsion," he said. "It wasn't wise, and I wasn't much use when I got there."

"How lovely Nancy looks," Molly said. "She always looks lovely in the simplest dress. That's what Roger always says. How are the children, Charley?"

"Why, they're pretty well," Charles answered, "except they keep turning on the radio."

"Do you know what Roger said the other day? He's so sentimental, sometimes. He said he wished they'd call him Uncle Roger."

He was balancing Molly's kindness against the possibility that she had heard something which he had not heard about the bank and Owen Martin cut in before he could answer. Neighbors always had to dance with neighbors' wives.

"I'll see you later, Charley," Molly called. "Perhaps we can do something Sunday. Roger would love it if we could."

Now that Charles had danced with Molly Blakesley, he felt that he had done enough, but it was still too early to be seen going home, even though he wanted to go home very much. His imagination was aroused by Molly Blakesley. Certainly Roger had thought it a fine thing that he had gone to the war. If he had not gone, if he had stayed put, there would have been no doubt about anything in the bank.

Out in the passageway that led to the men's locker room, he glanced at the plaque which must have been placed there in the early days of the conflict—the club's honor roll of members and employees, carefully differentiated, who had gone, as the plaque said, to serve their country. There were more employees than members, and three gold stars against employees' names with only one in the members' list. That was the Wilkes boy, Joe Wilkes's son. Most of the other members had been overage. The plaque itself was in the shadows, a good place for it now that the war was over.

Nancy was always saying that it was a bad thing for him to drink after dinner and he had always found that alcohol only exaggerated malaise. Nevertheless, as long as he could not leave, he wanted to get away from the music. There were two bars in the club, the women's bar, with new chromium furnishings and red leather-topped stools—he could hear the loud chatter from it as he passed—and the men's bar behind the men's locker room, a Teutonic looking place which had been built before prohibition and before women needed bars of their own.

Charles opened the locker room door and walked along the wood grating past the rows of green steel lockers. He was going to the men's bar because, though it was open to all male members theoretically, it had a clannish atmosphere that discouraged certain members from entering. In fact, Charles had never entered it until Mr. Forbush, who was still president of Oak Knoll, had once asked him why he never joined the crowd there. You could either stand up at the bar, or carry your drink to one of the locker room benches if you'd been playing golf, or else sit at the single round table.

The individuals sitting at the table that night all were drawn together by the common guilty bond of having made an escape. They all knew implicitly that they should be dancing, and they weren't. They all half apologized for being there, and they were just going to stay for a minute. They were hot and their feet were tired. Bill Forbush, who was sitting at the table, always said at every dance that he was only going to stay for a minute. He only wanted to drop in to see that everyone was behaving, and Joe Swiss was there, just for a minute, too, and Walter Crumm must have come in there after his dance with Nancy. And so had Christopher DeMille, just for a minute, and Roger Blakesley was there, just to take the weight off his feet for a minute. When they saw Charles they all greeted him heartily, as though his appearance salved their consciences for being there, just for a minute. Slim, the barkeeper, who was leaning over the bar listening and occasionally taking part in the conversation, also seemed glad to see him.

"What's the matter, Charley," Bill Forbush called, "are your arches falling?"

"Sit down and take your weight off your feet, Charley."

"All right," Charles said, "I will, for just a minute."

"What did you do with Bea, Charley?" Christopher DeMille called.

He was already getting tired of hearing about Bea.

"She left me for a handsomer, richer man," Charles said.

"Who's handsomer?" Christopher asked. "You're handsomer than Dunbarton. Look at him. Isn't Charley handsomer than Dunbarton?"

"What were you and Bea talking about?" Roger Blakesley asked. "Investments, Charley?"

"Come on and tell us everything," Joe Swiss said. "The rumor is that you were talking about chastity."

Charles did not like to think he was growing angry. He preferred to think that only an academic question of taste made him feel alone and aloof from all the group. Their faces looked alike, stupid, overweight and middle-aged, but at the same time it was all good clean fun.

"Slim," he said, "give me a double Scotch, please."

Then he saw that Roger was drinking ginger ale. He remembered that Molly had said that Roger had learned *never* to drink after dinner.

"Charley," Mr. Forbush said, "have you got your name down for a new car?"

Charles said that he and Nancy were worrying along with the old Buick and that he felt it had better stuff in it than most of the new cars, and Joe Swiss said he was absolutely right. Mr. Swiss had a close, personal friend from Detroit who had told him a thing or two about those new cars, a thing or two that Chris DeMille and these other word artists never wrote into their advertisements. The truth was that a lot of stuff that was going into those new cars was junk, pure junk, and it was not all labor cost, though a lot of the trouble was sloppy labor. No one wanted to do a day's work any more, no matter what you paid him. Yet putting all that aside, look what was going into the new cars. All this rumor about plastics and new gadgets was turning out to be eyewash. Look at the paint jobs. Look at the so-called chromium finish that rusted overnight.

It was a conversation Charles had heard often before and everyone else must have heard it too, yet they all listened as if it were a new discovery. Charles himself sat listening without having to put his mind on it. Perhaps this was why so many people enjoyed these conversations. You knew what was coming next. It might be communism. It might be the advisability of pouring money down the European rat hole. At any rate, you did not have to think. All those ideas had worn comfortable grooves in your mind.

But then you had to buy a new car sometime, Mr. Forbush was saying, and what happened then? You went to a dealer, didn't you, and could you get a new car at the list price?—not any more than you could get a piece of porterhouse steak. They made you buy accessories, extra bumpers, radios, heaters. Everyone was listening in silent agreement. Mr. Forbush was having a hell of a time with that new car dealer. Somehow it was agreeable to hear the details of Mr. Forbush's suffering. It was a sort of universal cosmic grief and it was a long way from actual want—and in the end you did not really have to listen.

Charles found his mind moving off at a tangent. He saw Joe Swiss close his eyes and nod. He saw Chris DeMille making designs on the table with burned matches. They were all caught in a current that jostled them and interfered with normal existence. All anyone could do was to try to adjust his life within the limits of a constantly changing frame. That was the difficulty. Even the limits were continually changing.

The limits of happiness itself, Charles was thinking, were continually changing. You got somewhere and then you wanted to move somewhere else, to another, larger bar, to better, brighter company. Charles could still remember how pleased he had been when Mr. Forbush had asked him why he did not drop in sometimes and sit at the round table. It had meant that he had made good, that he was a part of a small group within a group. It had never occurred to him then that Mr. Forbush could be dull or Mr. Swiss either, or that they were older men whose thought processes had slowed until their minds ran in instinctive circles. He wondered if his own mind might be slowing also, because he did not give a continental damn what Mr. Forbush paid for a new car.

"Just wait, Bill," Christopher DeMille was saying. "There's a Ford in your future like the Ford in your past."

"I don't want a Ford," Mr. Forbush was saying. "I'm not talking about a Ford."

"It's only a figure of speech, Bill," Christopher was answering.

"You know," Roger Blakesley said, "in one way this talk is mighty interesting to me."

"In what way?" Christopher DeMille asked. "It doesn't interest Joe Swiss." Mr. Swiss was nodding, but he opened his eyes when his name was mentioned.

"It interests me," Roger said, "because it just goes to show we're in the same boat. No matter what happens, we're still in the same boat."

Charles moved uneasily in his hard oak armchair. Roger's voice was brisk and cheerful, full of sweet reason. Charles did not know why it should have annoyed him, except that it brought a disagreeable picture before him of himself and Roger in a small boat, each knowing that there was not room enough in it for two.

"You mean we've all got to pull together?" Charles asked.

"Now, Charley," Roger said, "don't be bitter. If we're not in a boat, where are we?"

"I don't know where we are," Charles said, "and neither does anybody else. But it doesn't do any good to oversimplify, Roger."

"What?" Mr. Swiss asked, and he woke up again. "How do you mean we don't know where we are?"

Charles saw from the way they were all watching him that he had introduced a new idea at an unpropitious time. He shifted his position again in his hard oak chair. He had not intended to get into an argument with Roger.

"I think we're in a pretty good boat," Roger said. "It rocks a little but it's the best boat in the world and I'm glad I'm aboard and I guess everyone else is."

From the way everyone else was listening, he was sure that they must have heard something about the bank. He could think of no other reason for their fascinated, strained attention.

"That's right," Charles said, "as long as we don't get tossed overboard. "Well, I've got to be getting along now. It's pretty late."

He stood up and smiled and said good night and walked away through the open door of the bar and over the worn boards of the dimly lighted locker room. As he left he was aware of a silence behind him. As far as he could recall, he had said nothing unusual, and yet something must have been wrong or they would have started talking. In some way he had been a disturbing element back in the bar. They were not speaking. They were waiting carefully until his footsteps died away; and what would they be saying then? He did not know, and it did no good to tell himself that he did not care. He had not made good with his group. They were all like strangers to him. He had not fitted in.

It was now late enough so that no one would say they were leaving early, and it was early enough so that no one would say the Grays were always up late at parties. It was, in fact, the right psychological moment for going home, and Nancy was waiting for him, because, as Nancy often said, she had been a working girl herself. It did not take Nancy half a minute to get her wraps on, and she was even waiting at the steps of the club when he drove there from the parking space, instead of allowing herself to be drawn into conversation like other people's wives.

"Move over. I'll drive," Nancy said.

All he had to do was to thank her and to feel pleased that she not only knew he was tired but cared about it. Probably she also knew that the combinations of his day had not turned out very well, but she would not ask questions. She would wait for him to tell her, because she knew he would, eventually—but then, what was there to tell? There was only a premonition. There was nothing to explain, because the disturbance was inside himself.

"These parties," he said, "sometimes they're good and sometimes they're bad. Did you have a good time, Nance?"

"Well, yes," she answered, "in a sort of long-term way."

"How do you mean, a long-term way?"

"You know," Nancy said. "It's what I've told you before. I like feeling we belong somewhere. You know it's what I've always wanted."

"Well, so do I," Charles said. "So does everyone."

Nancy knew every turn on the road home, and she took each turn as unconsciously as a taxi driver.

"It isn't the same for a man," she said. "He always belongs much more than a woman, up to a certain point. A woman just has to tag along. It's nice, when she likes tagging."

"What did you do all day?" Charles asked.

"You always ask that. You don't have to."

"I know I don't have to," Charles said. "I just want to know."

There was a slight pause before she answered.

"I've had a good day, but you wouldn't understand why. It's partly being a woman. I took the car to the Acme place and got the choke fixed. Do you notice the engine goes better?"

"That's right," Charles said. "I notice now."

"Then I went to the A & P and bought some corned beef. Then I left Bill's shoes at that place below the drugstore, that new Italian place."

"I wonder why Italians always like to repair shoes," Charles said.

"Then I left that book of yours at the lending library. Then I bought some soap. I still keep buying soap whenever I see it. Then I came back and did the breakfast dishes. Then the man came to fix the unit in the stove, and while he was doing it the men from Hanson's came to wax the floor in the living room. I had to be there to see that they put everything back right. Then I went upstairs and made the beds and counted the laundry. Then I went over and had lunch with Polly Martin and helped her run up some new curtains, because she's going to lend me her sewing machine. I don't know why Polly wants everything in chintz—curtains, dresses, everything. Then I came back and worked on the bills."

"How were they?"

"They were terrible. There were two mistakes again on the Thaxter bill, always plus mistakes, never minus. I called him up about it, and then Bill and I glued the back of your old chair in the hall, and then I read to Evelyn for a while."

"What did you read her?" Charles asked.

"You'd be surprised. I read her Plutarch. Then there was their supper, and the Martins called, and we all went over to the club. That's all. I knew it wouldn't sound like much if I tried to tell it, but it was a very nice day."

"I'm glad you liked it," Charles said, "but I don't see why."

They had passed through the gates of Sycamore Park, up the blue gravel of their own short drive, and the car had stopped.

"I'll tell you why," Nancy said. "Because I'm married to a damn nice man. That's the only possible reason I can think of. Now get out and open the garage door and don't jerk at it."

That door had never worked well in wet weather. Charles opened it carefully and stood holding it so that it would not swing to while Nancy drove the car inside, close to the garden tools, and shut off the lights. Then she was beside him in the dark.

"And now you can give me a kiss," she said.

9

A Fitting Place for the Enshrinement of Ancestral Relics

—MALCOLM BRYANT

Only the light at the top of the stairs was lighted, but the switch was just beside the door. There was a smell of fresh floor wax from the living room, and a moist smell in the dining room from Nancy's potted plants.

"Charley," Nancy said, "isn't it a lovely house?"

"Yes, it's a swell house," Charles said. Nancy had taken off her evening wrap and was straightening her hair by the mirror.

"I know it's got outs about it," Nancy said, "but don't forget one thing. You and I did this by ourselves, without any so-and-so to help us. I suppose you think it's a corny thing to say, but that's why it's a nice house."

Of course, the appearance of any house depended on one's state of mind, and now he was feeling more cheerful.

"And now come in and look at the living room floor," Nancy said. "Do you want a glass of milk before you go to bed?" The last thing he wanted was a glass of milk, but then Nancy had known that he had taken a drink after dinner.

The living room was always too neat for him ever to feel at home in it. The logs in the fireplace had a little paper fan beneath them, ready for a match, but the fire was too beautifully constructed for him to want to disturb the logs by lighting them, especially so late in the evening. Everything was dusted, every ornament on the tables was exactly where it should be. The picture of the ship above the mantelpiece, which had come from Clyde, had been cleaned and was bright with new varnish.

"I forgot to tell you," Nancy said, "it came back today from Jacobson's."

"They did a good job on it, didn't they?" Charles said, and he thought of that page in *Yankee Persepolis* about the lower-upper family. The picture had hung in a shabbier room in Clyde. Here it was stiffly formal, the central theme of a self-conscious decorative scheme.

"We ought to use this room more, shouldn't we?" Nancy said. "I wonder why we don't."

"That's easy," Charles said. "Because we're afraid of it."

"Well, let's not be afraid of it," Nancy said, and she lighted a cigarette. "Charley, take off your coat and sit down on the sofa." Nancy kicked off her slippers. "Don't say we're afraid of this room. I don't like it."

"Why not?" Charles asked.

"Because I don't like being afraid."

She looked as though she were startled by her last words. She had a blank, embarrassed, provoked expression and she caught herself up quickly before he had a chance to answer.

"I don't mean that I'm afraid of anything. I only mean I don't like the idea. You know what I mean."

Every word only made a top-heavy structure destined eventually for a clumsy fall. It was like the match game so popular before the war, that late evening pastime in which you laid a match over the mouth of the bottle and then your opponent laid one upon it, and so it went until there was a tower of matches rising in the air. The loser was the one who put on the last match and tipped it over. Nancy had put on the last match. The room was uncomfortable and strange in an entirely new way; and he seemed to see it, and Nancy too, through a lens that had suddenly come into focus. Charles found himself passing his hand over the stuff on the sofa, half aware of its softness and of its light color, which, Nancy had said, would show every spot, though admittedly it was just the right shade. Now that the truth was there, now that the thing was there in the living room—the thing of which neither of them had spoken—it was a relief, in a way.

"Nance," Charles said, "we didn't use to be afraid."

She was sitting opposite him on one of those small upholstered chairs, very straight, just the way she had been sitting the day he had first seen her.

"Oh, are you afraid too?" she asked, and though his instinct was already preparing him to answer that of course he was not, he found himself nodding slowly.

"Well, you might have told me," Nancy said.

"It's all relative, you know, Nance," he said.

"What's relative?" She spoke impatiently.

"The more you get, the more afraid you get. That's all I mean," Charles said. "Maybe fear's what makes the world go round."

"Not love?" Nancy said, and she tilted her head sideways. "I used to hear that it was love."

It reminded him of the first night he had taken Nancy anywhere, when they were both obviously trying to impress each other. There was the same atmosphere of suspense, the same effort to be at one's best, and the same intense consciousness of each other. It was almost like falling in love, an unfamiliar sensation now—but they were talking about fear.

"Of course," Charles said. "Everyone's afraid of something—afraid of living, afraid of dying. Maybe it's better than being afraid of losing money. That's what the boys are afraid of downtown. Do you know what I wish?"

"What?" Nancy asked.

He was filled with a childish desire to show off before Nancy. It was almost like falling in love.

"I wish we weren't always being pushed around. I'd like for once in my life to be able to tell someone to go to hell."

She was smiling at him as he had seen her smile at Bill when he asked for an impossible Christmas present.

"Darling," she said, "basically you have the most expensive tastes. You'd better just tell me to go to hell, if you want to, and let it go at that."

"All right," Charles said, "but it isn't the same thing, is it?"

"Maybe it isn't," Nancy said, "but I'm awfully glad we're afraid of the same thing. It's healthy to have things in common. I'm awfully glad we're in the same boat, darling."

"That's what Roger said tonight," he told her.

"What else did he say," Nancy asked, "and what did Molly say?"

"She said you looked lovely in the plainest frock," Charles said, "and Roger thinks so too, and he wants the children to call him Uncle Roger and she wants us all to do something together on Sunday, and Roger does too. Wait a minute, there's something else I've got to tell you. I'm taking the plane to Boston first thing in the morning. I'm going up to Clyde for a day or two on business for the bank."

He saw Nancy's lips tighten. Then he saw her grind the end of her cigarette carefully into an ash tray.

"How did Clyde get into it?" she asked.

"It's funny the way things happen," he began. "When I got up this morning it was raining, do you remember? I looked out of the window at the trees. They reminded me of Clyde. Spring's always late at Clyde. No one ever admits it. Every year they only say that it's a late spring. Have you ever found yourself thinking about a thing and then finding later that something was happening about it?"

He saw Nancy glance uneasily about the room, as though she were afraid that someone might be listening.

"When something bad happens," she said, "you keep going back and wondering how it started."

"I don't see why you always get edgy whenever I mention Clyde," he said.

"You know very well why," Nancy answered. "Clyde makes you difficult. It's a queer place full of ingrown people, and you say so yourself."

It always made him sensitive when she began criticizing Clyde, even when her points were well taken. He had never expected her to fit into Clyde. He had never asked her to, and he knew what she thought about it without her telling him.

"I can't help it if I was brought up there," he said, and it occurred to him that he might say something to Nancy about upstate New York and about Nancy's town with its gingerbread trimmings and its pseudo-Greek columns.

"Never mind," Nancy said. "You're always peculiar when you think about Clyde."

"Well, when I was at the bank," Charles began, "a man came in to see me and who do you think it was? I didn't recognize him at first. It was Malcolm Bryant."

"Oh," Nancy said. "You used to talk about him quite a lot once."

"That's the one," Charles said. "He wanted to marry Jessica Lovell once."

"Oh," Nancy said. "I always thought you were the one who wanted to marry Jessica Lovell." She said it in a very slow, disinterested way, as though Jessica Lovell bored her.

Charles spoke more loudly so that Nancy could not interrupt. "Then I went to the morning meeting, in the depositors' room downstairs by the vault . . ."

At last he was back where he wanted to be, telling her the details of that meeting and about the collateral on the loan and the stock in that company in Clyde. Then he told about Tony Burton's having called him later, and it was a relief to go into it fully. He never should have mentioned Jessica Lovell. Nancy was sitting up straight again, following every word.

"So you've got to go away for a day or two right now?" she asked. "At just this time?"

"Yes, it looks that way," Charles said.

"Why didn't you do anything about it? Why didn't you ask them to send someone else?" When it came to the bank, Nancy was always right there with him.

"I thought of it," he said, "but I think that anything I might have said would have made it worse. You'd have thought so too."

"If I'd been there, I'd have done something," Nancy said. "Something. Anything."

"No," Charles told her, "you just think so because you're here. If you'd been there, you'd have let it go. Besides"—he stopped and stared at the design on the Islamic rug—no animals, nothing but symbols—"I don't think it makes much difference. I think Tony Burton's about made up his mind which of us he wants."

Suddenly Nancy stood up.

"Then for God's sake why doesn't he tell you instead of letting us—letting us—" Her voice choked on the last words and she swallowed.

"Because perhaps he doesn't like to do it," Charles said. "Tony's quite a nice guy, as far as anyone like him can be nice. I think we'll get the news when we go there to dinner. He almost said so."

Nancy stood looking straight ahead of her. She did not answer, and Charles went on.

"Besides, maybe it's just as well for me to be away. Tony knows Roger worked it, at least I think he knows. Maybe Roger will try a little too much. Tony's rather bright sometimes."

Nancy still stood there and he noticed that her hands were clenched.

"If he picks out that damn fool he isn't bright."

"I only said," Charles told her, "that he's pretty bright sometimes."

Nancy was no longer staring in front of her at nothing. She was looking at him in a level, appraising way, putting herself in Tony Burton's place, balancing his faults against his assets, wondering whether he had the personality and the broad-gauge ability to occupy one of the front desks.

"Listen," Charles said, "it doesn't do any good trying to look like a statue on a courthouse."

"If you'd only get mad," Nancy said.

"You were just saying it's a luxury," Charles said. "There's no use getting mad at a system. We're part of a system where there's always someone waiting to kick you in the teeth in a nice way."

"It's a rotten system," Nancy said.

"Maybe it is," Charles answered. "A lot of people have been saying so lately." He looked up at her and smiled, but she did not answer.

"Of course if I hadn't been away at the war there wouldn't be anything to it."

"You never should have gone," Nancy said. "I told you so."

"Yes," Charles said. "Yes. I remember."

Nancy sighed and sat down again.

"Haven't you any idea at all," she asked, "which one of you he's going to take?"

Then Charles felt a slight twinge of anger. It had been a long time since he had seen himself so clearly—tied down by little things. They were a steady accumulation of little things, innocuous in themselves, like the ropes the Lilliputians used to pin down Gulliver—the ship picture, the Islamic rug, the wax on the floor, the mortgage, the insurance policy, tiny half-forgotten decisions, words suddenly spoken.

"Charley," Nancy asked, "what's the matter?"

"Nothing," Charles said.

"Charley, what'll you do if he takes Roger?"

"Nance," he said, "let's not think about it now," but of course both of them were thinking about it now. The irony of it was that after years of work one became specialized, used to the ways of just one organization, too old to start again in a new one. He had seen plenty of men his age looking for a job.

"Charley," Nancy said, "if you'd ever done something about investing for yourself instead of for other people—"

"Nance, you know very well," he answered, "you don't do much of that when you're working for a bank."

Nancy sighed and stood up again.

"Well," she said, "I guess we'd better go to bed."

Charles stood up too.

"You go ahead," he told her. "I'll be up in a few minutes. Good night, Nance."

After he had kissed her, she buried her head on his shoulder. She made no sound but he knew she was crying, and it always gave him a completely helpless feeling when she cried.

"Don't, Nance," he said. "The show isn't over."

"I'm sorry, Charley," Nancy said. "I'm all right now. You always hate having me cry, don't you?"

"Yes," Charles said. "Go on up to bed, Nance. I'll be up in just a minute."

"Are you sorry you married me?"

"No," Charles said, "of course not, Nancy."

"I suppose I sort of made you marry me."

"Why, Nance," Charles said, "I never noticed that you did."

"Are you sorry we had the children?"

"No, of course I'm not," Charles said.

"They were my idea more than yours. Are you sorry we bought the house?"

"Listen, Nance," Charles said, "it happened, like the children. Now go on up and go to sleep. I'll be up in just a minute."

"What are you going to do?" Nance asked. "Are you going to sit here and worry?"

"No, I'm not," he told her. "I'm not sleepy. I'm going to read for a little while."

"Because if you're going to worry, we might as well do it together."

"I'm going to read," Charles said. "I'm pretty well worried out tonight.

Good night, Nance"—and he kissed her again, and walked with her to the foot of the stairs. "I'll be sitting in the library."

"Don't be long," Nancy said. "I won't be able to get to sleep till you come up."

Yankee Persepolis—A Social Study was lying just where he had left it earlier in the evening on top of his brief case on the table in the hall. As Nancy went upstairs, he picked it up because it occurred to him that, considering his mood, something absolutely new was better to read than something he had read before.

All he could do was to recognize his present state of mind as a definite malady like a cold or a fever and tell himself that it would pass. He knew the symptoms well enough. First there was a period of general uneasiness about nothing in particular, and then a growing illusion of being hemmed in, followed by a desire to escape, and finally an indescribable sense of loneliness mingled with a sort of deep self-pity which he particularly hated. He wished he had not mentioned Jessica Lovell, as she was always a part of the shadows which surrounded him suddenly and swiftly when he was in that mood. The only thing to do was to tell himself to behave, that he would be better in a little while. It was also time to consider the dangers of inheritance, and to remember his father.

"Charley," he could hear his mother saying, "don't bother him. He's in one of his spells again."

Charles himself had never particularly noticed his father's "spells" until the summer of 1916 but they must have been chronic because his brother Sam had often spoken of them as though they had been going on a long time.

There was always a brittle atmosphere in the house on those occasions. His father was usually in his room with his books, on the second floor, and the door would be locked. His mother and Dorothea would be talking in whispers in the kitchen. There used to be a tradition that everyone should ignore those periods of dejection, and all the family did, except Sam when he was alive. Sam never had any patience with them.

"We all know what the Old Man was doing up in Boston," Sam had told him once, "and now he wants us to be sorry for him. He ought to have a good shoot in the tail."

Sam was the only one who said such things and Charles believed him and he still could not escape that old impression that Sam had been a great man, although Sam could have only been about seventeen at the time.

"You can always tell when it's coming," Sam used to say. "It goes in a circle. It starts as soon as he gets a check."

Their Aunt Mathilda Gray's estate was being settled in 1916 and whenever a parcel of her real estate was sold, John Gray would get a check in the mail from Mr. Blashfield, the executor. First he would open the letter and look at the check, and then he would go down to the bank and deposit it in his special account, and then for a while a pleasant wave of prosperity descended on the household. He would come home each evening with a copy of the *Boston Evening Transcript* and everyone would watch him as he sat in the parlor after supper reading the *Transcript*'s financial page. First he would only glance at it. Then in a few evenings he would read it when he thought no one was looking. Then he would read it openly. Everyone knew what John Gray was going to do, even if he did not know himself, and he probably did not know, because he had promised on his word of honor never to touch those things again. He would be highly indignant if his wife or his sister Jane attempted to bring up the subject. It was better not to stir him up. Perhaps a week later he would say that he was going to take a day off and go up to Boston. He hadn't seen Boston for a long while.

When he came back from the day in Boston, he was invariably exuberant. He usually returned with a box of candy and some magazines, and generally he smelled strongly of bay rum, showing that he had been to the barbershop at the Parker House. Then he would begin to discuss scholarly subjects, especially the London of Samuel Johnson. He loved to re-create a world of coaches and sedan chairs and smoke-filled coffeehouses. You could never say that John Gray was not industrious or erudite. He could quote pages of Boswell, fitting them aptly into every occasion. Charles still winced at the sight of a Boswell's *Johnson*, and yet when he finally saw London for himself he knew many aspects of the city very well because of certain evenings back in Clyde.

"The Old Man's off again," Sam used to say. "You can tell it as soon as he starts on Mrs. Thrale."

Still it was not always a bad time when the Old Man was off again. It was a cultivated household for a while, after John Gray got back from Boston. There was no doubt that he was a delightful man.

"Your father might have been anything," his mother used to say, "anything."

The next week he would take another day off and go to Boston. This time he would return with a box of cigars and with a few French novels. The cigars were a definite part of a pattern, because John Gray usually smoked a pipe if he smoked at all. That was why Charles always hated Havana cigar smoke. At this period John Gray's thoughts would turn to Honoré de Balzac, his sleepless nights and his strange, frustrated love. Someday they must all go to Paris. It was ridiculous for Malcolm Bryant to have placed them in the lower-upper class. He should have seen John Gray when his brown mustache, usually dejected and drooping, was clipped like a British colonel's and when he had a new suit from Dunne's.

"By God," Sam used to say, "now he's upstairs juggling figures," and John Gray could do it, too. Charles had never seen anyone who could make mathematics as logical and simple. "He must be doing pretty well. Why doesn't the damn fool ever stop?"

Of course he never stopped. There would always be the last trip in the cycle, when John Gray came home from Boston with nothing to say at all. There would be a discreet silence in the house. There was nothing in the world quite like those silences. . . .

The library where Charles was sitting gave him a sense of not belonging anywhere. His mouth felt dry and his forehead felt moist and he was terribly alone.

"Charley." It was Nancy calling softly from the top of the stairs so as not to wake the children. "Charley, aren't you coming up to bed?"

"Yes, in just a little while, Nance," he answered. "I'm not sleepy."

"Oh, Charley," she called back, "please come up. It's after one o'clock."

"In just a few minutes, Nance," he said, and he opened the book he was holding.

Malcolm Bryant and his father had taken to each other from the very beginning and when Malcolm began dropping in at Spruce Street in the evenings years previously, Charles's mother was delighted. It was so good for Father, she said, to talk with an intelligent young man who could share Father's interests. They were interests which were boring to Charles because of constant exposure to them. To Charles, Samuel Johnson was a rude, untidy old gentleman with an itch, who had made a number of rash and not very brilliant statements, set down by an assiduous toady named Boswell, a snob who sucked up to the nobility and who had nothing better to do than to run after the old gentleman with a notebook. Charles could see nothing whatsoever in Johnson's heavy-handed prose. It was as slow as cold molasses, but now as he ran through the pages of *Yankee Persepolis*, he began to understand why Malcolm had been a Johnson addict and he understood at last what Malcolm had seen in his father. Malcolm had been attracted to John Gray not as an individual but as a social entity, an odd piece which he was trying to fit into the social puzzle of Clyde which had produced and tolerated him.

All at once it occurred to Charles that he was doing right now what his father had often succeeded in doing so magnificently. He was trying to forget the present by immersing himself in something else, by striving to identify himself with someone else. Instead of Samuel Johnson, he was using Malcolm Bryant. He did not care about Malcolm's ideas or his social worker's patter in themselves, except insofar as they took him away from his own ideas. If he could only concentrate on Malcolm, if he could only give him the attention that he had learned to give to papers at the bank, he could forget the bank altogether, he could forget the conference room and the antiseptic, oily smell of the vault, and Roger Blakesley and Tony Burton. He could forget the scene in the locker room and the queer, disturbing conversation by the window in the Whitakers' apartment, when that girl had made him think of Jessica Lovell. He could forget the knotty pine walls of the library which were enclosing him in impersonal mediocrity. Please, God, his mind was saying, get me out of this. Please get me out of this.

He was examining a chapter heading, "The Concepts behind This Survey." The words were as heavy as Johnson's words, without any of their waxy Chippendale polish. Social scientists were usually involved writers, who continually tripped over a jargon of their own invention. He again remembered

Malcolm as the brain behind an agency of social spies, with an office force and card catalogues back in Boston.

Two of Malcolm's assistants, he remembered, had appeared one hot night at open house day on Johnson Street, a girl with dry brown hair and horn-rimmed spectacles, for whom he felt sorry because she was an outlander from the Middle West, and an undernourished man with an Adam's apple, who perspired beneath the armpits and only drank fruit punch. He never imagined that these two were a team of skillfully briefed probers who had been snooping innocuously through Clyde, standing away from it in a friendly way as though it were an ant hill, then worming their way deviously into the confidence of its inhabitants, sympathizing with frustrations, picking up gems of information, and rushing away secretively to an office to record those gems on charts of death and birth rates and of marriage incidence according to income groups. The investigative team operated according to scientific rules. They were directed to listen, when they buttonholed an individual, in a patient and friendly manner in order to discover the individual's approximate place in the society. They should only inject their own personalities in order to relieve fears or anxieties or to praise the interviewee. They should listen not only to what a person wanted to say but to what he did not say. All of this, according to Malcolm, demanded extreme flexibility. They must have done their work well, because Charles had seldom noticed it.

He remembered Malcolm Bryant and his team examining Clyde and occasionally descending to taste of its life, like minor gods and nymphs sporting with mortals. They were not interested in individuality, Malcolm was now explaining, but in social personality. It was clear now what Malcolm had been doing those evenings when he had called at Spruce Street and stayed for supper.

"Typical of a lower-upper family," Charles read again, "are the Henry Smiths—father, mother, son and daughter. Like other lower-upper families, they dwell on a side street ('side streeters'), yet are received on Mason Street. Mr. Smith, with investment interests in Boston . . ."

It was not fair to blame Malcolm, because it must have been confusing even for a god to know exactly what John Gray had been doing, but it was agreeable to remember that the god had fallen once.

"Charley." It was Nancy calling again from the top of the stairs. "Aren't you ever coming to bed?"

"All right," Charles called back. "I'll be up in just a minute, Nance, try to go to sleep."

"What are you doing down there?"

"I'm reading."

"Can't you read tomorrow?"

"I'll be up in just a minute," Charles said. "You'll wake the children up. Try to go to sleep."

His voice and Nancy's voice were only like the voices in a chorus. The interruption had not disturbed him.

"An upper-upper class family," he was reading as he spoke, "may be typified by the Johnsons, who live on the upper side of Mason Street in one of those fine, three-storied Federalist houses, capped by the delicate balustrade of the widow's or captain's walk."

Malcolm had let himself go at last. He was obviously describing the Lovells and their house on Johnson Street, studiously garbling the names, but as he had been writing, his memory of the Lovell house and of Mr. Laurence Lovell and Jessica must have blurred for an instant his concept of social personality.

"This gracious type of Federalist architecture is apparent here at its zenith. The gracious hallway of this mansion extends from front to rear, a fitting setting for the exquisite airy rising of its broad staircase . . ."

Yes, Malcolm Bryant for once had forgotten his social responsibility, now that he had turned from the Grays to the Lovells.

"A fitting place for the enshrinement of ancestral relics . . . a fitting frame for the rituals of the upper-upper class. . . . Mr. Johnson, a widower, suave and gracious, descendant of shipowners in the late eighteenth century, is a fitting head for the Johnson clan. Jacinth, his lovely only daughter, assisted by a maiden aunt, Miss Johnson, is eminently suited to give the family ritual an added charm. Her vivacity never quite conceals her seriousness or the impact of her social personality."

Yes, Malcolm Bryant had felt the impact of Jessica Lovell's social personality. He had forgotten that he was a social anthropologist, as he had penned those words. He had tried in a brief interval to be a poet in prose. He had contrived, within the limits of his talent, to express emotion and desire. He had called her Jacinth instead of calling her Mary or Molly or Miss X. In Malcolm's memory, Jessica was still there in the hallway, looking him straight in the eyes. She would never be Desdemona again and Malcolm would never be Othello, speaking of the habits of the Borneo head-hunters and the Zambesis or about that trip he would take someday to the Orinoco.

"In the rear of the house," Charles was reading, "on a gentle slope rises the hundred-and-fifty-year-old Johnson formal garden, a verdant shrine of ancestor worship in itself, crowned by a delicate latticed summerhouse known as a gazebo." Malcolm Bryant would never sit in that gazebo again, but then neither would Charles Gray.

Malcolm Bryant had shown without his knowing it that he had been impressed by austere beauty, a foreign interloper who could never have wholly grasped it. Through his own enthusiastic inadvertence, he had invoked a vision of Johnson Street—fantastic and beautiful on a dusky summer evening. Charles could see the broad uneven sidewalks of worn brick, pushed gently upwards by the roots of the elms. He could see the tall white fences with their urns and pineapples, and the houses rising behind them, disdainful of newer houses. He could see the cornices and the fanlights and the cupolas. The mere recollection of Johnson Street on a summer evening made this effort of Malcolm Bryant's a gross impertinence. It was still an impertinence when he thought of Spruce Street with its plainer picket fences, and of the moldering houses nearer the river inhabited by what Malcolm called the lower-lower class, the shanty Irish, not the lace-curtain Irish, and the Greeks and Poles. Malcolm Bryant and his team had seen them all and had checked them against their diagrams, but he and his team did not know Johnson Street or any other street in Clyde . . .

Yet, as he continued to turn the pages he could feel that his resentment was flagging, because momentarily, at any rate, time had dulled emotion, so that he could see the outlines of the Clyde of Malcolm Bryant, as he could never have seen them when he had lived in Clyde. He could see the passionless exactness of that scientific picture, stripped of sentiment's flattering lights and shades. The Clyde of Malcolm Bryant was a complex of instinctive forces and behavior. Its inhabitants moved into a pattern like bees in a hive, or like the Spartans under King Lycurgus. There was the individual's unknowing surrender to the group, the unthinking desire for order. He could see the Grays on Spruce Street and the Lovells on Johnson Street through Malcolm Bryant's eyes, and it was hard to believe that he ever could have lived in this arbitrary frame, illustrated by curves and diagrams, and now he was living in another. He could almost see the Stuyvesant Bank and that evening at Oak Knoll in a new revealing light—almost, but not entirely.

In spite of the years that had passed, in spite of all he had done and thought, he was still the likable Smith boy in the Bryant *Yankee Persepolis* striving to move on from the lower-upper, and still in mortal danger of dropping, of going down instead of up. He was still Charley Gray gazing wistfully at Johnson Street. . . .

"Charley." It was Nancy again. She was standing in the doorway in her quilted-silk wrapper. "It's two o'clock."

Her tone was definite, telling him that really this nonsense must stop, and he was very glad that she was there. He closed the book and pushed himself out of the leather armchair.

"All right," he said. "All right, Nance."

"Come on," Nancy said, "put out the light."

When he snapped off the light by the chair everything was pitch black for a second and then he saw her shadow against the dim light from the hall.

"The Martins will think we've been having a fight," Nancy said, "with a light on downstairs at two in the morning."

"All right, Nance," he said, and he put his arm around her and she raised her hand and touched his cheek.

"You shaved before the dance, didn't you? At least you won't need to shave again in the morning. If you're going to take that plane, I'll drive you to La Guardia."

"It's a pretty long way," Charles said.

"That's all right," Nancy said. "I'm going to miss you."

PART TWO

1

The Clyde of Alice Ruskin Lyte

Charles had never thought of Clyde as having proud traditions of its own—it had only been a place which one accepted naturally because one lived in it and knew nothing else—until his mother, one hot August afternoon, read a paper before the Clyde Historical Society entitled "The Clyde of Alice Ruskin Lyte." Charles's hair had been brushed and his sister Dorothea had seen to it personally that he wore a clean white shirt and a bow tie. He had left the house with Dorothea and his Aunt Jane at ten minutes before three o'clock. His mother had left earlier. He was told that he must be quiet and must not fidget and that perhaps he would not understand all about Mother's paper but it would be a nice thing for him to remember. Actually, he was struggling with a keen sense of personal embarrassment, arising from his knowledge that no one else of his age was going to this gathering and that he might be singled out as a mother's boy and a sissy. He felt better when he found that his father would meet them there. All the family was going to hear Mother read that paper, except Sam, who was away on a visit.

He did not understand Alice Ruskin Lyte's significance, though he had heard her name mentioned more and more frequently in the evenings after supper. It was only later that he knew that Alice Ruskin Lyte was a poetess who had lived and died in Clyde and that she had been a dear friend of his mother's Aunt Sally Marchby. These two had, in fact, both been teachers at the Bedlington Academy in Lawrence. It was called the Bedlington Female Academy then. It seemed that Miss Lyte had corresponded freely with his Great-aunt Sally Marchby, after Miss Lyte had left her position at the Academy to live at her estate on the river, called Lyte's Castle. Those packets of letters from Miss Lyte were now in his mother's possession and formed the basis of the paper.

Though Charles was not intelligently aware of these details, he had not missed the growing tension at home while the paper was being prepared. His mother had brought from the library a number of bound magazines in which Miss Lyte's verses had appeared, and also a small volume called *Stardust* by Alice Ruskin Lyte. Then he was told not to play catch with Jack Mason in the back yard because the noise disturbed his mother when she was writing. Then his mother began to worry about the paper. She did not know why she had ever said that she would do it. She never would have thought of doing it if Margaret Mason had not particularly asked her. She did not know a thing about writing.

"I wish you'd do it for me, John," she said. "You always write such nice papers."

"Now, Esther," Charles's father said, "if I were to do it, everyone would know."

"But they'll think so anyway," his mother said. "They'll know you helped me. You've got to help me."

"Esther, dear," his father said, "I wish you would try to be realistic. Let's grant that Miss Lyte was a dear friend of your Aunt Sally's. Let's go further and grant that she was a sweet old lady who never did anyone any harm intentionally except by writing jingles."

"Why didn't you tell me that you thought that in the first place," his mother asked, "and I wouldn't have said I'd do it? I wish I'd never promised, and now it's been announced."

"Poor Esther," his father said. "You'll get through with it. Your conscience will get you through."

"John, don't you think the idea's worth while?" she asked. "I mean—quoting from those letters?"

His father put his hands in his pockets and leaned against the parlor mantel. "This puts me in an embarrassing position," he answered. "I know your veneration for Miss Lyte and how your family have always felt about her. I have said she was a dear old lady. I can shut my eyes and see her now" —he made a gentle, expansive gesture as though he were conjuring up Miss Lyte—"sitting there under an oak tree, looking at the river that she no doubt loved, with that niece of hers. What's her name?"

"Priscilla," his mother said. "And don't make fun of Priscilla. She was always sweet with her."

"I'm not making fun," his father said. "I'm only thinking of the old lady's bright character. As a human being she was intriguing because, given an ego and the industry to drive a feeble talent to the limit, she contrived to make something out of nothing," and John Gray cupped his hands together and gazed at the nothing his hands were holding. "It all goes to show what can be done if only you have a deep belief in self. That's what I would say if I were writing the paper. Think of her as a determined, industrious human being with charming intentions, but don't quote a line of her poetry, Esther. It would be unfair to her memory. She wrote like the sweet singer of Michigan."

Charles heard Dorothea giggle, and Sam was smiling. The gentle, precise way in which his father spoke was what made it funny, and he could see that his mother was only pretending to be annoyed.

"But, John," she said, "they published her poems in *Harper's Magazine*."

"And in the *Youth's Companion*," his father said. "Don't forget that mentor of our childhood, Esther, the dear old *Youth's Companion*. I tried to earn a pony by selling subscriptions for it once. Charles ought to have a pony."

"You used to say I ought to have one," Sam said.

"Well, well," John Gray said. "The main thing is thinking about ponies,

Sam. Life is a series of ponies. I remember a story in the *Youth's Companion*, a Christmas story. A little boy wanted a Shetland pony more than anything else in the world. A little girl, a friend of his living in the big house on the hill, had one but his family was very poor, just like our family, Charles. His father, though he was hard working, was harassed by debts, just like your father, Charles, and Christmas was coming." John Gray spread out his arms. "Christmas was coming, and the shop windows were full of ponies."

"John," Esther Gray said, "what am I going to do about that paper?"

"Oh, yes, the paper." John Gray crossed the room to where she was sitting and put his hands on her shoulders. "We'll go through with it. We can't let the Historical Society down, can we? You and I will write that paper."

Everyone must have felt the same relief that Charles felt.

"John," his mother said, "are you going to be serious about it?"

John Gray laughed.

"You children go into the other room and close the door," he said, "and you read me what you've written, Esther."

Charles had already begun to mark off Dorothea's life into cycles identified with young men who appeared at the house, much as historians marked off eras by the names of monarchs. There was good reason for adopting this chronology because Dorothea's tastes, dress, and inclinations changed as her boy friends changed. At this time Frank Setchell was the most important figure in Dorothea's life. He was the eldest son of Mr. Setchell who owned Setchell's store, which sold ready-made clothing and haberdashery. Frank was hollow-chested, suffering from acne, and his appearance was never helped even by matching ties and socks.

Frank was going to take Dorothea to the beach that evening. She was to meet him at the corner of Meade Street because John Gray, whenever he saw Frank, asked him about his tie and always wanted to know whether he could get one like it, which was embarrassing to Frank and Dorothea. So Dorothea ran upstairs to get ready, and Sam went to the movies, leaving Charles to read *Guy Mannering* by the lamp on the dining room table, and it was difficult to read because he could hear his mother's and father's voices behind the closed door of the parlor. It seemed that whatever his mother had written was painful to John Gray.

"No, no, no," he could hear his father groan. "Oh, please, Esther, please."

"Can't you tell me what's wrong with it?" he could hear his mother ask. "It doesn't do any good to roar at me, John."

"I'm sorry," his father answered. "Go ahead and read it. I'll try to be quiet, Esther."

Then his mother's voice would go on half audibly, and then he could hear his father groan again.

"Oh, no, no. Why do you split infinitives? Why do you do it, why?"

"Because I thought it sounded better," his mother said. "How can I read if you roar at me, John?"

Then their voices died down again.

"John," he heard his mother say, "don't look as though you were swallowing castor oil."

"Go on," he heard his father say, "and don't start crying, Esther. Tears won't help it. Now don't interrupt me. Give me that paper."

Every evening for a week or so they all ate supper in strained silence and directly after supper the parlor door would close. His mother began to look pale and sleepless. She began to forget about the marketing, and when Dorothea broke the pressed-glass butter dish with the hen on top of it, she did not say a word—but finally the paper was finished. One evening after supper, his father rubbed his hands.

"Tonight Mother has a little surprise for us," he said. "Perhaps you've gathered that we've been working together. Come into the parlor and sit down and listen to Mother."

"John," his mother said, when Dorothea and Sam and Charles sat down in the parlor, "I feel so awfully silly."

"Of course you do," John Gray said, "and so do I. Now remember what I told you. I'm timing you. Stand up and look around, and don't keep looking at the pages. Look up at the audience and then find your place again."

"But I'll lose my place," his mother said.

"Not when you're used to it." John Gray set his watch on his knee. "We'll go over it and over it."

His mother looked red and hot and worried.

"Well, will everyone promise not to laugh?" she asked.

"It only makes it worse to talk, Esther," his father said.

"All right," his mother said. "Are you going to introduce me, John? Are you going to pretend to be Mr. Lovell?"

"I could if I wanted," his father answered, "but I don't want to be like Laurence Lovell, even in the realm of fantasy."

"Well, if you were more like Laurence Lovell—" his mother began.

"Don't get off the subject." His father tapped his watch with his forefinger. "I'm not like Laurence Lovell."

"Well," his mother began, and there was a silence. "Well." She looked at them over the top of her papers and began to read. "Every one of us here, I am sure, has seen a certain gray stone house with a mansard roof, known as Lyte's Castle. It does not in the least resemble a castle." She looked up. "I still don't see why you put that in, John. Everybody knows it."

"Everybody will know all the rest of it, too," John Gray said, "and it has to last for half an hour. Now you've spoiled it. Start all over."

"Every one of us here, I am sure, has seen a certain gray stone house with a mansard roof, known as Lyte's Castle. It does not in the least resemble a castle, but its name has been accepted through custom like so many names in Clyde and now no one would think of calling it anything else. No one would think, either, of calling its former chatelaine, known and revered by so many of us present, anything but a poetess, and the verse of Alice Ruskin Lyte, so much of which was penned within the gracious walls of Lyte's Castle, now stands to confirm our opinion of its writer."

His mother looked up again. "John, it doesn't mean what it says. It still doesn't."

"Esther, dear," his father said, "I've always loved your literal mind. It doesn't mean anything and yet it means everything, and you can go on from there. It's all you need to say about her until the very end. Now start it all over and don't interrupt again."

One thing was gained by all that preparation. All the Grays would always remember Alice Ruskin Lyte. Charles could see his mother standing straight and alone in the flowing dress of the period, looking like a full-length Sargent canvas. Her auburn hair was coiled and pinned together at the nape of her graceful neck. Her thin, eager face and her wide brown eyes were stamped with honest anxiety, because she wanted everyone to like her and that paper; and Charles could tell when the hard parts were coming from the way his mother swallowed and tossed up her delicate chin. John Gray must have enjoyed it all. Her words, the dress she wore, her pauses, and even the way she did her hair, were parts of his own creation.

It was one of those hot afternoons when the leaves on the trees were almost motionless and when everyone in Clyde hoped that a sudden east wind off the ocean might change the weather. One of the great beauties of summer in Clyde lay in that ever-present hope. The day might be stifling hot and suddenly the east wind, gratefully damp and cold and redolent of ocean salt, would make everything too cold—but in summer no one in Clyde ever believed this until faced by accomplished fact.

On his way to the Webster Grammar School, Charles always walked past the building of the Clyde Historical Society on Johnson Street, and he had often paused to admire the green brass cannon on the lawn, which had once been part of the battery of the Revolutionary War privateer *Eclipse*, built in Clyde and owned by Nathaniel Lovell, who had built the Lovell house. He had never been inside the building because when Charles had once tried to visit it, with his friend Jack Mason, Miss Hannah Smythe, the custodian, had told them that they had better run along. Little fingers had a way of getting into things, and little feet were always muddy. Nevertheless, he was already learning about Clyde, by listening to the words of elders. He already knew that the Historical Society had once been the Gow house, left to the Society by the will of old Mr. Francis Gow. He knew that the brick ell which had been added had been built by a contribution of Mr. Francis Stanley, who had come to Massachusetts to be the president of the Wright-Sherwin Company, and it was nice to have some money for an ell no matter where it came from. He also knew that the Historical Society was the repository of many valuable things left to it in wills and that it contained the collections of the Poseidon Society and the Captains' Club, passed on to the Historical Society when those organizations had closed their doors forever.

"Charley," his Aunt Jane said, when they reached the corner of Spruce and Johnson Street, "remember not to touch anything."

She reminded him not to touch anything again as they crossed Fanning

Street, where the iron horse fountain used to stand; and when they passed the Episcopal Church, with its carefully tended graveyard, Aunt Jane said she was glad she was a Unitarian.

"I hope your mother didn't eat much lunch, Dorothea," she said. "Your grandfather never liked to go to court on a full stomach."

"You mean she might vomit?" Charles asked.

"That'll be about enough from you, Charley," Aunt Jane said.

"My," Dorothea said, and she adjusted her butterfly bow, "isn't there an awful crowd. Poor Mother."

There was, indeed, an unusual number of people about the old Gow house, and it seemed that the history of Clyde's brave old days must have had a peculiar appeal for women, generally beyond the first bloom of youth. Only an occasional reluctant male was visible, except for three ministers, whose presence gave the gathering the appearance of a childless Sunday School picnic. As Charles, his aunt and Dorothea neared the tar path leading to the front door, these three members of the clergy were standing outside on the lawn, each surrounded by the loyal members of his congregation. Dr. Morton Berry, from the Smith Square Baptist Church, stood in the shade of a catalpa tree, fanning himself with his straw hat. The Episcopal clergyman, the Reverend Gerald Pond, looked better fed and more professional in his lightweight black suit and reversed collar. In fact, Charles had heard Aunt Jane say that if he wanted to look like an Irish priest, he would do better to be a Catholic. The group around him also exuded an air of prosperity. Miss Lovell stood near him with her niece Jessica, a thin little girl in a white party dress, white socks and patent leather shoes. Mrs. Stanley was there, too, and old Miss Sarah Hewitt in purple crackling silk, and Mrs. Thomas. Dr. Pond bowed and smiled placatingly and cordially when he saw Aunt Jane, but Aunt Jane only nodded curtly. Dr. Pond had made the mistake that spring of stopping Charles on his way to school and asking him whether he would not like to be a choir boy, and his Aunt Jane had not forgotten. Standing nearer the doorway, still lingering before entering and looking more like Puritans who had crossed the sea for faith, were the ladies of the Unitarian Women's Alliance, supporting their pastor, Mr. Henry Crewe, whose hair was not carefully trimmed and who looked like a pale ascetic compared to Dr. Pond.

"Well, this is a real occasion for you, Miss Gray," Mr. Crewe said to Aunt Jane. "Alice Ruskin Lyte. What a tempting subject for Mrs. Gray, and one I am sure she will handle beautifully."

"Well, we won't know till it's over," Aunt Jane said. "Charley, aren't you going to shake hands with Mr. Crewe?"

For some reason, some member of the family was always worrying for fear he would not shake hands with Mr. Crewe. He did not know why, because he always found himself trying to do it before he was told.

"How Charley's growing," someone said. "He has his mother's hair."

"And Charley won the fifty-yard dash at the picnic, didn't you, Charley?" Mr. Crewe said. "What did you do with the prize?"

"I ate it," Charles said. He was stricken, because his answer made everyone laugh, and he edged furtively away from the little group, while Aunt Jane began talking to Mr. Crewe about a candlelight service on the Isles of Shoals. Then, while no one was looking, he walked alone into the Historical Society.

The rooms were so crowded that he was allowed to wander unmolested from room to room and to encounter their confusion undisturbed. He did not realize until much later that it was a typical New England historical society, housing an odd assortment of things from garrets that combined to make an unscientific hodge-podge of the past. Yet its very disorder made so deep an impression on him that the unrelated, partially recognized objects in the hall and in the square rooms on either side occasionally appeared later in his dreams.

In the hall were two antique settles, three flintlock muskets, some powder horns and fire buckets, a blunderbuss, and a canvas done by a journeyman painter of an old gentleman in a wig. To the left was the room dedicated to the Captains' Club and the Poseidon Society and their collections from forgotten voyages. When he read *Java Head* some time later, he was strongly reminded of that room. Its walls were covered with paintings of ships, all bowling along under full sail, past lighthouses and Chinese pagodas, and between these pictures hung strange, rusted, rippling swords, and spears and clubs, a harpoon, and a few half models of the hulls of ships. He had seen most of those things before, in Mr. Burch's antique shop at the foot of Dock Street on Dock Square, but he had never seen so many of them at once. On a table in the center of the room, enclosed by a glass case, was an exquisite model of a ship, all carved in bone, with her standing rigging all intact. In another corner, on a black and gold lacquer table, was a miniature pagoda, with wind bells hanging from its eaves, and on still another table was a row of sextants.

Strangely enough, though the other rooms were becoming crowded, he was not conscious of people or of voices. The things there seemed to Charles to be wanting to return into the past, where they belonged. A soldier should have been wearing the moth-eaten Continental uniform that hung upon a clothing dummy. In another case, a bride should have worn the eighteenth-century wedding dress, and the Indian hatchet heads and gouges should have been back in a plowed field. They were all mixed together in those rooms—aboriginal arrowheads, muskets, candle molds, foot warmers, pine dressers, Chippendale sideboards, Lowestoft, pewter, and whales' teeth and four-poster beds. The elderly ladies of the Historical Society were drifting past them.

"That is a tooth extractor," one of them was saying.

"We have a better Chinese sewing box at home."

"We have some of that pink luster." It seemed that they all had something better or the same, and this made a visit to the Historical Society an occasion for personal triumph.

His Aunt Jane found him on the second floor, looking intently at a suit of Japanese samurai armor.

"Charley, where have you been?" she whispered, just as though they were in church. "We'll lose our place if we don't hurry." They moved downstairs, past more ship pictures, into the auditorium in the new brick wing. There was a buzz of voices in the auditorium and the slapping sound of folding wooden chairs, and the warm air smelt of cologne and talcum powder.

"We're sitting in front," Aunt Jane whispered. "There's your father. Move in beside your father."

John Gray was dressed in a gray flannel suit, and he raised his eyebrows slightly and patted the chair beside him.

"How would you like an ice cream soda—if you could get it, Charles?" he asked. He spoke in a needlessly loud tone and Charles was embarrassed. "Look at your mother." Then Charles saw that his mother was seated on a platform between Dr. Pond and Mr. Lovell. To Charles's way of thinking, Mr. Lovell was peculiarly dressed, in a blue coat and white flannel trousers and a soft shirt, and he especially noticed the mourning band on Mr. Lovell's sleeve—a sign, Charles knew, that Mrs. Lovell was dead. White flannels were still a novelty in Clyde, but they must have been correct if they were worn by Mr. Lovell. They made him look cool and aloof. His clean-shaven face was bronzed from the sun. He was smiling in a faint, embarrassed way and looking at his watch. Finally he put away his watch, rose, and walked over to a podium at the edge of the platform and glanced indecisively at a pitcher of ice water and two glasses on an antique candlestand. As Mr. Lovell stood up, the voices in the room died down, and he looked at the company in a tentative, agreeable way.

"If we are all here," he said, in a somewhat high but agreeable voice, "will the meeting come to order—not that this is one of our regular meetings but, rather, a delightful afternoon, or better still, an occasion." Mr. Lovell fumbled in the side pocket of his coat, drew out a small card, and stared at it. "We will begin, as is eminently fitting in this place, with a prayer from Dr. Pond."

As the clergyman rose, Mr. Lovell backed hastily from the podium as though he were afraid that he might be caught out of his chair before the prayer began, and Charles put his hand over his eyes.

"Oh, Heavenly Father," Dr. Pond began, "as we gather here among the relics of our forefathers and as our thoughts go back to the past of our town, we pray that our present may be as glorious as its past. We supplicate Thee to give us the courage of our fathers, who sailed the seven seas, and may our bread, too, return to us when it is cast upon Thy waters."

Charles heard his father cough gently. The prayer was long and Charles had lost the thread of it. There was a creaking of chairs and Mr. Lovell stepped forward again, groping in his pocket for the card.

"This, I think," Mr. Lovell said—"no, I don't think, I know—this is the twenty-seventh of our historical afternoons, and judging by the number present they are becoming increasingly successful. The other day"—he glanced at his card again—"I heard it said that New Englanders live too much in the past. It may be a bad habit, but whenever I come here, and I'm sure I wish we might all come here more often, I find it a rewarding habit. I think we are all better for realizing, as one must in a town like Clyde, that the present is a projection of the past, and I hope we will all grow increasingly to understand that this society is very much a part of Clyde, a piece of property to be shared equally by everyone who lives here. That is why I, and the other officers of this society, hope that you will all stay after our lecture for our tea party, supplied by our fellow member"—a frown creased his narrow, high forehead, and he glanced hastily at his card—"our fellow member Mrs. Jacob Plumm, so that we may all talk informally about Clyde as we have known it—and our future plans."

Charles heard his father cough again and he looked at his mother, who sat motionless in her armchair.

"Our speaker this afternoon"—Mr. Lovell paused and smiled—"is not an imported speaker. She is what we might call local talent"—he paused and smiled again—"not that I do not mean local talent is not very good talent. This building springs from local talent, from its fine cornices, carved by our shipwrights, down to the stone arrowheads, made by our first inhabitants. Now"—he cleared his throat gently—"I imagine that all of us here know the Grays. For generations a Gray has always appeared when he or she was needed. On the little monument by the First Landing Place, you will see the name of a Gray. A Gray was in the Civil War, and most of us here remember our late friend, Judge Vernon Gray. Now we have another Gray with us, Mrs. John Gray, whose aunt was a friend of Miss Alice Ruskin Lyte. She, too, answers our call in our time of need, and she will speak to us on"—he glanced again at his card—"'The Clyde of Alice Ruskin Lyte.' Mrs. . . . Gray."

His mother stood up, and Charles felt his heart beat faster.

"Every one of us here," she began, "I am sure, has seen a certain gray stone house with a mansard roof . . ."

Charles saw his father draw a handkerchief from his breast pocket and mop his forehead. She was reading it more quickly than she had at home and her words seemed breathless and frightened by the discreet silence they encountered. They seemed to flutter one after the other about the room, lighting in corners, hiding behind pictures. The pictures, like the motionless rows of people, seemed very used to words. The portraits, by journeyman painters, of men who looked uncomfortable in stiff coats and of women sitting in startled erectness, seemed to be following the discourse as carefully as the living people on the chairs, but the pictures of the square-rigged ships, with their owners' flags flying in long streamers, kept on sailing, involved in their own navigational problems, bending before their artistic breezes, their bows cutting furrows through even regiments of waves.

She was getting near the end of it now. She was coming to the part that had a poem in it . . . "As Longfellow, Miss Lyte's old friend, expressed it so beautifully once—'the beauty and mystery of the ships, and the magic of the sea.'" The ships in the Clyde Historical Society looked desiccated, devoid of mystery. There was nothing but a dry-as-dust accuracy in their realistic rigging and there was no magic in their painted seas—but now his mother's voice had stopped.

"Thank you," she said, and her voice sounded more natural. "Thank you very much for listening."

Then he heard the applause around him.

"Clap, Charley," his father said. "It's over."

"And I'm sure we are all most grateful to Mrs. Gray for a charming paper and a delightful afternoon." Mr. Lovell was calling above the rattling of the folding chairs, "And now shall we all adjourn to the Council Room for tea?"

Charles and his father walked to the edge of the platform.

"That was magnificent, Esther," John Gray said, "perfectly magnificent."

"It was," Mr. Lovell said. "It was a most interesting paper. Any time I want a good paper, I know where to go, John."

"And the introduction was even better," John Gray said. "It was superb. I ate up every word of it, Laurence. I don't believe you know my son Charles, do you?"

"Well, well," Mr. Lovell said, "I don't believe I do. And now we'd better get some tea."

"Let's go out on the lawn," his father said to Charles and his mother, "instead of getting in the crowd. Someone will bring us tea."

When they were standing on the lawn, just before the ladies came to tell his mother what a lovely paper it was, Charles heard her say to his father:

"You shouldn't have been so sarcastic, John."

"To you or to Laurence?" his father asked.

"John," his mother said, "you know what I mean, but perhaps he didn't notice. Here he comes. He's bringing us some tea."

"Oh, there you are," Mr. Lovell called. "I've been looking for you everywhere."

"Why, thanks, Laurence," John Gray said. "You keep that cup and stay with Esther. I'll get some."

"Why don't think of it, John," Mr. Lovell said. "It's a pleasure. Here."

"Well, thanks, Laurence," John Gray said. "It just goes to show I'm always right. I was just telling Esther if we came out here we'd get some tea."

The locusts in the elm trees were scraping out sad high notes which rose and fell in the still air, making a sound which Charles always associated with a hot summer afternoon in Clyde. More ladies, all holding teacups, were appearing on the lawn.

"Here they come," John Gray said. "Here's your public, Esther."

Then Charles saw Miss Lovell, and Jessica in her patent leather slippers and white socks, and Mr. Lovell saw them too.

"Why, Jessie darling," Mr. Lovell said, and he knelt on the grass and threw his arms around her. "How's my little girl?"

It did not seem right that Mr. Lovell should make such an abandoned gesture of affection right on the lawn of the Historical Society, and it made Charles feel sorry for Jessica because of what people might say. No one, however, seemed to feel it was in bad taste. Instead of being embarrassed, everyone stood watching the little scene with understanding sympathy.

"Isn't it sweet?" Charles heard someone say. "It's as pretty as a picture."

"Pa," Jessica said, "can't we go home now, please?"

"Yes," Mr. Lovell answered, "in just a few minutes, Jessie."

2

A Place for Everything

The way to learn about Clyde was to be brought up there. One learned who the Lovells were imperceptibly by a word here and there, and one grew up knowing that the Lovells could say what they wanted and do what they wanted and that they would always be right no matter what they said or did. One learned that there was a living plan in Clyde, without ever learning exactly what the plan was, for it kept growing as one grew, starting with Spruce Street and one's own back yard and spreading up to Johnson Street and down to Dock Street.

Everyone had a place in that plan and everyone instinctively seemed to know where he belonged. Its completeness reminded Charles of what his Aunt Jane said once when she was arranging the flat silver in the sideboard of her dining room—everything in its place and a place for everything. The Irish, for instance, had their place, and so had the French-Canadians and the new immigrants, like the Italians and the Poles, who naturally belonged close to the Wright-Sherwin factory and the shoeshops. There was a place for the North Enders, too. They lived in the North End and went to the North End Congregational Church and even if they lived in other parts of Clyde they were still North Enders.

The same sorts of people, he learned, usually lived in the same sections of Clyde; but you began to learn quite early, without ever knowing how, that certain people who lived on Johnson Street were not Johnson Street people, and hence, because you knew, their living on Johnson Street did not disturb the plan. For example, the Stanleys lived on Johnson Street. They had bought the old Holt house, and it was still called the Holt house though the Stanleys lived in it. Mr. Stanley, everyone knew, was richer than the Lovells or the Thomases or old Miss Sarah Hewitt. You could tell this from his new greenhouse and from the number of men who worked on the garden and the lawns; and Mr. Stanley had a Cadillac automobile, driven by old Arthur Stevens, who had worked for the Holts and whose brother was a clam digger. Yet the Stanleys' prosperity was without the same face value as that of others. They lived on Johnson Street but they did not belong there.

You came to understand that the Holts, who had sold their house to the Stanleys and had moved to the North End, still belonged on Johnson Street. Miss Sarah Hewitt's house needed painting and Mr. Fogarty, who worked for her and for the Lovells too, only gave her one day a week, but Miss Sarah Hewitt belonged on Johnson Street. The same was true with the Lovells. They had always been on Johnson Street. You understood that Mr. Lovell was not very rich but his money somehow had the dignity of age. You heard it spoken of as the Lovell money. He was a director of the Dock Street Savings Bank and a trustee of the West India Insurance Company, which were both partially founded on Lovell money. He was a trustee of the public library, also partially founded on Lovell money. You came to understand that Mr. Stanley could do more generous things because he was richer, and anyone who was richer could do these things of course, but his contribution did not have the same value as a Lovell or a Hewitt contribution. You seemed to know these things implicitly.

The same was true with Spruce Street. The Grays belonged on Spruce Street and so, too, did the Masons, who lived next door; but when Vincent Sullivan, who was in the contracting business and who had the contract for the addition to the Wright-Sherwin plant, bought the house on the corner of Spruce and Chestnut, he still did not belong on Spruce Street. Everyone knew that Mr. Sullivan's father had been the Lovells' gardener and that Mr. Sullivan had driven a truck for the Bronson Shoeshop until he had invested his father's savings in the old livery stable on South Street. You could not get away from your past in Clyde and few wanted to get away from it, perhaps because it was not worth trying.

There were no secrets in a town like Clyde and so, of course, everyone knew all about the Grays. Everyone knew that John Gray was harder to place than some people because he was different from other people, and Charles must have always been aware of that unspoken difference. No matter what his father did or said, he had a right to be different because he was the Judge's son. He had always been a wild boy and had given the Judge a hard time, but everyone knew Johnny Gray. They could remember the time when Johnny Gray had a fight with Martin Donovan and when he stole a trolley car out of the carbarn and drove it down to the beach with a lot of boys from high school. It had been hard for the Judge to clear that one up, but everyone knew Johnny Gray. He was not lazy, but he never stuck to anything. He and Laurence Lovell had started out in Harvard together and they might have been friends but he didn't even bother to go with the right people. Still, Miss Hewitt always had a kind word for him and so had the Thomases.

It was all right for Johnny Gray, though it would not have been for Virgil Mason or Melville Summers, to join the Pine Tree Fire Company and to help man the Pine Tree machine at firemen's musters and to play poker at the Pine Tree firehouse, because everyone understood that he was different.

He had been a wild boy but he was bright and he could have done anything he wanted if only he had put his mind on it. If only he had kept interested, he could have been a college professor or a lawyer. The trouble was, he was the only boy and the baby of the family and he had always been made too much of. Everything was too easy for Johnny Gray. He did not have to work hard, like other people, to get his learning. He could have gone through Harvard just as well as Laurence Lovell or Ralph Thomas. He was not a bad boy. He never got into a college-boy scrape, but he had not liked it there and after a year and a half the Judge had taken him out.

The Grays had always been solid people, not shipowners or warehouse owners like the old Johnson Street people, but solid people, and the Judge owned stock in the Crawford Mill. When Johnny Gray was tired of Harvard, it was natural for the Judge to put him in the mill and wait for him to settle down. It looked as if he would do it, too, when he began calling on Esther Marchby, old Dr. Marchby's daughter, and the Marchbys were good solid people, too. He was not getting on fast in the mill, but given time he would settle down. Yet perhaps the Judge himself was never sure. He had tied up Johnny Gray's share of the mill stock in trust when he died, though he let the girls own theirs outright. It was hard to fool the Judge.

Everyone knew who you were and what you were in Clyde and there was no need to guess. You always said kind things about everyone in the family and hastily dusted away discrepancies, but nothing was ever hidden because you could not help what other people said. Gossip always became in time a sort of mythology and lay before every inhabitant of Clyde like a long shadow on a summer afternoon. A word here, a word there, an embarrassed silence, a snatch of overheard conversation, an overelaborate explanation, an amusing anecdote—all those things finally could not help but make a picture. Everyone knew about John Gray, and so did Charles. Charles must have known when he was very young that John Gray was unstable, but he never could get to the bottom of this instability. When he tried to admire his father, even when he was a little boy, there was a gap somewhere, a total blank. The truth was, he often thought, that his father had been too busy with his own ideas, too involved with conflicting impulses, to have anything much left to give. John Gray was always too wrapped up in himself to have time for any of the children.

It was not the fashion in Clyde for parents to discuss each other before their children, but it was possible to hear bits of talk.

"It never does any good to nag John," he heard his Aunt Jane say once. "Father always said so."

"I never do nag at John," his mother answered. "I wouldn't dream of doing it."

"You mustn't ever let him see you're disappointed," his Aunt Jane said. "It's just as bad as nagging and it only makes him sullen."

"I'm not disappointed," his mother said. "I don't see why you say I am."

"Well, I never could have married anyone like John," his Aunt Jane said. "I couldn't have stood it."

"Well, I can stand it, Jane," his mother said, and she laughed in an exasperated way. "Maybe I like excitement, and you wait, John will do something someday. You wait, we'll all be surprised. I know he's planning to do something. Of course they don't understand him at the mill."

"What's he planning to do?" his Aunt Jane asked. "Whatever it is, don't encourage him."

"Why, I haven't any idea," his mother answered, and then she laughed again. "And if he never does do anything, Jane, I shan't mind. I love him just the way he is."

His father was the type of person whom women always loved. His mother was right, too, when Charles came to think of it later. John Gray finally did do something, and everyone was very much surprised.

Charles could at any rate start with a sense of having belonged somewhere. He had, at least, something from which he could revolt, and no one could very well revolt from anything as plastic as life in Sycamore Park. Bill would never see anyone like Miss Sarah Hewitt because Miss Sarahs simply did not exist in Sycamore Parks, or if they did they must have been pushed into corners where no one saw them. There never were elder statesmen, dominating the local scene. Active old ladies of eighty like Miss Sarah only seemed to flourish in towns like Clyde where climate, local biological selection, struggle for survival, and local respect rendered them indestructible. If personality were only strong enough, Clyde was the place for it. There would never be a base in Bill's background, Charles often thought, such as there had been in his own. The impermanence of a New York suburb with its shifting population of unrooted communities, with order that existed only on the surface, was as hard for a boy to grasp as it was for him to explain. He had been luckier than Bill in that in Clyde there had been so much to be accepted without argument.

One morning at about half past nine a few days after the meeting of the Historical Society, Mrs. Garrity, who was now Miss Sarah Hewitt's housekeeper and who had been in the Hewitt household ever since she had come to Clyde as a young girl from Ireland, pulled the glass knob of the front doorbell. The bell's tinkle in the front hall interrupted Dorothea's piano practice.

"You go, Charley," Dorothea said. "Someone's at the front door."

"Why don't you go?" Charles asked, and Dorothea tossed her head. "Because you're not doing anything. You never do do anything."

Charles had been on the point of doing something. He had just made up his mind to see what Jack Mason was doing and to persuade him to go over to the Meaders' and see what the Meaders were doing and to find out if they couldn't go somewhere and do something together.

"You're not doing anything either," Charles said. "You're just drumming on that old piano."

"You go to the door," said Dorothea, "or I'll tell Mother," and then before

Charles could move she began telling Mother. "Mother," she called, "Charley won't answer the doorbell. Should Charley or I answer the doorbell?"

Charles heard his mother's quick steps on the floor above them and he moved slowly into the front hall.

"You needn't start yelling," he called as he turned the brass knob of the front door. "I was going anyway."

Mrs. Garrity was standing on the doorstep, bareheaded, in her gingham dress but without her apron. She looked at him coolly but with kindness through her glasses.

"Young man, is your mother in?" she asked.

There was no need to answer. His mother was hurrying down the stairs.

"Why, good morning, Mrs. Garrity," she said.

She did not call her Ellen because only people who lived on Johnson Street would have dreamed of calling Mrs. Garrity Ellen.

"Good morning, Miss Esther," Mrs. Garrity said, and she stepped deliberately into the hall and glanced critically at the oblong mirror and at the steel engraving of Franklin at the court of Louis the Sixteenth and then at the colored print of the Clyde waterfront. "Miss Sarah sent me to wish you good morning." By calling his mother Miss Esther, Mrs. Garrity was obviously accepting her as a friend of Miss Sarah's—not just a calling acquaintance.

"I hope Miss Sarah is well, Mrs. Garrity," his mother said.

"Oh yes, she's well," Mrs. Garrity said, "and she wants to know if you would be at home this afternoon so that she might be dropping in for a cup of tea, Miss Esther, and to talk about the paper you've been reading."

"Why, tell her we'll be delighted," his mother answered in a new, bright voice. "Would she like to come at half past four?"

"Four," said Mrs. Garrity, "and she'll bring her own tea, and give her thin bread and butter only."

"We'd love to have her at four," his mother said, but Mrs. Garrity still stood in the doorway.

"I suppose you'll be getting Minnie Murphy in, Miss Esther."

"It isn't her day here," his mother said, "but yes, I'll see if I can get Mrs. Murphy."

"I'll tell her," Mrs. Garrity said. "Minnie will come if I tell her. Minnie knows how to do it. It would be best to get Minnie."

When the door closed, his mother looked worried.

"Oh, dear," she said. "Dorothea, stop playing the piano. Miss Sarah's coming to tea. Now let me see—Charles, I want you to go down to the mill and tell your father to be here at four o'clock, and then go and tell your Aunt Jane. Where's Sam?"

"He went fishing, off the breakwater," Charles said.

"Oh, dear," his mother said. "I suppose he'll come back all over fish. I think we'd better use the Canton tea set, don't you, Dorothea? Now run along, Charley. I wish we had more time."

Charles was the boy carrying the burning cross saying, Excelsior! Miss

Sarah is coming to tea. At the end of Spruce Street, he turned right, past Gow's wharf and the coal pocket and then past the gasworks and then past the mill houses where River Street children were playing hopscotch on the sidewalk. The tide was low and he could see the black mud flats with their still pools of water. A humming came from the long brick mill building, a busy but drowsy sound that made him understand why Mr. Felch, the watchman, was dozing in the gatehouse. The windows of the smaller office building were wide open and so was the door, but inside everything was hot. The clerks behind the railings were in their shirt sleeves. He could see Mr. Stafford in his large private office reading papers and only Mr. Stafford wore his coat. Far down the hall, beyond the accounting department, his father sat in his small room, running over a column of figures.

"Mother sent me," Charles said. "Miss Sarah's coming to tea at four o'clock."

"Well, well," his father said, "if it isn't one thing it's another. Run along and tell her I'll be there."

When he left the mill Charles turned up Gow Street, still carrying the burning cross. Beyond the small and shabby houses, Gow Street made a crooked turn, by French's grocery store, and then widened and changed for the better the nearer one came to Johnson Street. His Aunt Mathilda and his Aunt Jane lived in the square yellow house with the plain picket fence in front and a small stable and garden. It had belonged to his grandfather and it still had his grandfather's name on the silver plate on the dark door. He opened the door without knocking but he closed it carefully because his Aunt Mathilda was sick upstairs, and he walked softly down the hall into the dining room which was dusky and cool because the wooden shutters were drawn.

"Where's Aunt Jane?" he called into the kitchen to Mary Callahan, who was sitting at the table peeling potatoes.

"Where would she be," Mary Callahan said, "except upstairs reading with Miss Mathilda? But don't go stamping on the stairs."

Even if he had stamped, the stair carpet with its heavily padded treads would have deadened the sound. In the upstairs hall everything was as dusky and cool as the dining room, with everything in its place and a place for everything. The brasses on the highboy shone in the faint light. Miss Trask, his Aunt Mathilda's practical nurse, was sewing in the hall bedroom, and further down the hall, in the square corner room, he could hear his Aunt Jane reading poetry. She was reading it with pleasure because she loved declamation.

"*Shoal!*" he heard her saying. "*'Ware shoal!* Not I!"

His Aunt Mathilda was sitting in a Boston rocker and Aunt Jane sat stiffly in a straight-backed chair.

"Why, Charley dear, where did you come from?" his Aunt Mathilda asked.

Aunt Jane closed her book.

"Charles, I wish you wouldn't creep around," she said.

"You told him not to make any noise," Aunt Mathilda said. "I heard you, Jane. Come here and kiss me, Charley."

He kissed her timidly because he knew that his Aunt Mathilda was very ill.

"He doesn't have to creep around," his Aunt Jane said. "What is it, Charles?"—and then he gave the message again. Miss Sarah was coming to tea at four o'clock.

"Oh, dear," Aunt Mathilda said, and her thin white hands moved restlessly over her dressing gown. "Is she coming here?"

"Of course she isn't, Mathilda," Aunt Jane told her. "She's going there, to John's house, and I'd better go to help Esther. You know how things are there, Mathilda."

"Charley, dear," Aunt Mathilda said, "I think your mother had better get Minnie Murphy in. Tell her that I said so and we'll send Mary Callahan over to help."

It was not the question of food, he remembered his mother saying, it was the desire to have everything look right that made her nervous. She was not going to have Miss Sarah Hewitt leave the house and tell the Lovells and Thomases and other people that Esther Gray had started as a careless, flighty girl and had not improved. When she had become engaged to John Gray, she knew very well that Miss Sarah had said that it was a mistake and a pity, that Esther was not the right wife for John Gray because she was absent-minded; and Charles's mother did not want to have Miss Sarah saying this again. She had never liked to sit behind a tea tray, pouring hot water into cups and then pouring it into what was called a slop basin—a horrid term, a slop basin. She had to admit that she did not understand tea. She wished that Jane would pour but Jane said that it was Esther's house. The main thing was to have the parlor and the hall picked up and to get rid of John's canes and umbrellas and the boys' fishing rods and John's and the boys' hats—and John's books should be taken upstairs and not left in piles upon the floor.

Charles had never seen the hall and parlor look so neat. Mrs. Murphy and Mary Callahan had washed the woodwork with soap and water. They had beaten the braided hall rug and the two parlor Persian carpets. They had washed the mirror; they had polished the Benares brass tray in the hall and the andirons and the fender in the parlor fireplace and the candlesticks on the mantelpiece, and the two Staffordshire dogs had been washed. The picture of the brig *Comet*, which had been sailed around Cape Horn by Charles's great-grandfather, had been taken down and Aunt Jane herself had wiped off the canvas. Cleanliness had transformed the parlor. Shine and polish made everything look almost new, and this was true also with the family.

They were all there except Sam, who was still on the breakwater. Aunt Jane wore her plum-colored silk dress, with a cameo brooch. His mother wore her best afternoon gown, with old lace on it. Dorothea wore her embroidered shirtwaist and her new skirt and her hair was done in her Sunday way. Although it was a hot afternoon, John Gray had put on his blue serge suit and stiff collar, and Charles was again in a clean white shirt and a bow tie. A cloth of Italian lace was placed over the tea table that stood in front of the Victorian horsehair sofa, and the Canton tea set was already on it. A fresh antimacassar had been pinned on the wing chair, partially concealing its soiled upholstery, and a candlestand had been placed beside it.

"Oh, dear," John Gray said. "Oh, dear me."

"Don't say, oh dear," Charles's mother snapped. "You haven't done any of the work. What time is it?"

She did not need to ask because she could see by the banjo clock, but John Gray took out his watch.

"The clock is two minutes slow," he said. "It's exactly three minutes before four. She'll be here in exactly three minutes. It's amazing how rejuvenating this is. Don't you feel young, Jane?"

"No, I don't," Aunt Jane said, "and I hope you're going to act your age."

"That's exactly it," John Gray answered. "I am. It's an intimation of immortality."

"I wish you wouldn't chatter, John," Esther Gray said. "I don't see why you like to talk when you're nervous. I don't."

John Gray sat down in one of the stiff ladder-backed chairs and folded his hands.

"I'm too young to be nervous," he said. "I've been washed behind the ears, like Charles. I'm as young as Charles, and Charles and Dorothea aren't born. They're back in the land of the unborn children, and Esther is Dr. Marchby's little girl and Jane is in pinafores."

It was difficult, sometimes, to understand his father. It gave Charles a very queer feeling when his father said he had not been born. When his father waved his hand slowly, as he did so often when he spoke, Charles could almost believe that he and Dorothea had been rendered invisible.

"I wish you wouldn't be so confusing, John," his mother said. "No one understands you and there isn't time to try."

John Gray sighed.

"That's true. No one understands me." A church bell was beginning to strike four. The church clocks in Clyde had never been synchronized, any more than the religions they represented. Another bell was striking. "That's the Baptist bell," John Gray said. "You'll notice it's always behind the Congregationalist. Now, Dorothea." Dorothea looked at him doubtfully. "You and Charles are going to have a remarkable experience. Try to think of yourself as moving backward. I envy you. I wish I hadn't been born."

"Well, you are born," Aunt Jane said, "and here she is."

The bell in the hall was tinkling and his father and mother hurried out while the rest of them waited and Charles could hear their voices in the hall.

"Charley," Dorothea whispered, "your shirt is coming out." She seized him quickly, as though he were much younger.

"Let me alone," he whispered, and he was stuffing his shirt beneath his waistband when Miss Sarah Hewitt entered.

Charles had seen her often, but now she looked strange to him because his father had fixed it so that nothing seemed quite real. She looked as cool as though it were not a hot day. She looked so old that no weather could disturb her. Her brown dress of stiff silk rustled like autumn leaves, and the sound gave the artificial flowers on her small hat an incongruous, waxlike appearance. Her lips were set in an amused, determined line. Her hair was streaked with gray. Her eyes looked old and faded. There was a tremor in her thin, blue-veined hands that made the beaded reticule she was holding shake, but still she had a deliberate, airy way of walking. Her voice, too, had a quaver in it, but it retained a plaintive, musical note like an echo of a younger voice.

"Jane, dear, how do you do?" she said. "And these are the dear children, aren't they, Esther? I thought there were three. Isn't there an older boy?"

"Sam isn't here, Miss Sarah," John Gray said. "We had no way of reaching Sam. He's gone fishing."

"You needn't speak quite so loudly, Johnny," Miss Sarah said. "Fishing—and he should love the sea, shouldn't he? What are the other children's names? I've forgotten. There have been so many names . . . Dorothea, after her grandmother, of course. And Charles. Now who was Charles? Oh, I remember. Charles who went to the war. Where was it he was killed?"

"Fredericksburg, Miss Sarah," John Gray said. "Uncle Charles died at Fredericksburg. Won't you sit down? Try the wing chair."

"If you'll give me your hand, please, Johnny," Miss Sarah said. "Thank you. It was Burnside's fault, of course. There was a service, wasn't there—in the Unitarian Church, but then you wouldn't know. Esther, that paper at the Society was very good. I never knew you could write so well. It made me see her again. Dear Alice Lyte. And Laurence was so pleased with it. You know how particular Laurence is—a perfectionist like dear Nathaniel." She spoke with a conviction that was conjuring up the unseen, and the quick and the dead were moving about the parlor, mingling democratically together. "Dear, kind Nathaniel—but Laurence is more Lovell than Hewitt. I wish the children would move their chairs so that I can see them. So this is little Charles. He looks like Vernon. Do you know that your grandfather stole pears from the garden once, Charles? I didn't tell, but Father saw Vernon from the window. Did Vernon ever tell you, John?"

"Why, no," John Gray answered. "Father never told me that."

"We've all been friends for so many years," Miss Sarah said, "such friends, in such different ways, but do you know what's just happened? I mustn't forget to tell you."

"No, what's happened?" Aunt Jane asked.

"The Rose of Sharon bush is blooming again. The pink one. I saw it from my window, but it's not nearly as old as the lilacs. Grandfather brought the cuttings back from England."

"They're the most beautiful lilacs in Clyde," Charles's mother said. "I always stop to peek at them through the fence."

Miss Sarah had forgotten about the lilacs. Her expression had brightened, her glance had turned toward the mantelpiece.

"Why, there she is," she said. Everyone looked puzzled and John Gray cleared his throat.

"Who?" he asked gently. "Who, Miss Sarah?"

"I forgot you had a picture of the *Comet*, too," Miss Sarah said, "not that you haven't a perfect right to have one"—and then they realized that she was referring to the oil painting of the brig above the mantelpiece. "Grandfather always said that Captain Tom was his best captain," Miss Sarah said. "He always spoke so highly of him. Now he would be the children's great-grandfather, wouldn't he? And he had such bad rheumatism. You would never have thought he'd been before the mast. Grandfather always said so. Susan and I were brought downstairs to meet him. Grandfather wanted us to see what one of his captains looked like. Johnny, do you remember Captain Tom?"

"Why, no," John Gray said. "He was dead long before I arrived, Miss Sarah. He married after he was fifty."

"It's hard," Miss Sarah said, "to remember everything, but I did especially want to mention Captain Tom. There are more ship captains' families left than shipowners', aren't there, but then of course there were more ship captains, and the owners have moved away."

"Yes," his father said. "Things are quieter along the river now."

"It was the fire," Miss Sarah said. "Grandfather always used to say that nothing was the same after the fire."

"You don't mean the fire of 1820," Aunt Jane asked, "when the waterfront burned down?"

"My dear," Miss Sarah said, "what other fire has there ever been? I can almost remember it—almost. There was so much talk of it when I was a little girl that I was afraid of candles. It started in the Higgins boat yard, a careless Negro boy with turpentine. The poor Holts never recovered from it. The sparks blew up to Johnson Street. We have the buckets that we used in the barn, the Pine Tree fire buckets."

"Have you really?" John Gray said. "I didn't know that."

"It always made me afraid of Negroes," Miss Sarah said, "even before the war. If it hadn't been for the fire those new people, the Stanleys, would never be in the Holt house. Nothing has been quite the same."

"Charles," his mother said, "will you please go out and ask Mrs. Murphy for some hot water?"

Mrs. Murphy herself was a creaky old woman with snow-white hair and a round, florid face. She was talking to Mary Callahan in the kitchen.

"Sure those were the days," Mrs. Murphy was saying. "Sure the Lovells had six horses."

"Six horses?" Mrs. Callahan said. "What would they do with them?"

"Six horses or ten horses," Mrs. Murphy said. "The Lord knows how many, and my own husband was the coachman, God rest his soul. What is it, young man?"

"More hot water, please," Charles said.

"Now see the manners of him," Mrs. Murphy said. "He has the manners of anyone on Johnson Street."

"And why shouldn't he have the manners, I want to know?" Mary Callahan asked. "The Grays are as good as all your people on Johnson Street."

When he returned from his errand in the kitchen, Miss Sarah was sipping her tea, and her cup shook but nothing spilled.

"It's been a lovely tea party," she said. "What else was it I was going to say? I'm sure there was something else. I told you, didn't I, about the cemetery?"

"Why, no, you didn't, Miss Sarah," his mother said.

"Well, it doesn't matter at the moment. I remember what I wanted to say. That paper at the Historical Society—it reminded me so of dear Alice Lyte. She was such friends with the Marchby girls. Do you remember the colored woman?"

"What colored woman?" his mother asked.

"The one who was passing through to Canada before the war. She sewed a whole dress for Alice before they rowed her across the river, a whole dress in two days. She was very light colored. John?"

"Yes, Miss Sarah," his father said.

"I'm sorry that things didn't go so well at Harvard. It was such a disappointment to Vernon."

"So he told me," John Gray said. "I've been trying to do better since, Miss Sarah."

"And I know you will," Miss Sarah said. "You'll get hold of yourself in time. Let me see, there's something else I wanted to say. Oh, yes, do you know what's happened? The Rose of Sharon bush is blooming again, the pink one. And now I really must be going."

"Oh, please don't go," his mother said.

"No, dear, I must be going, if you'll give me your hand. It's been such a nice tea party. One should move out of one's orbit sometimes."

"May I walk back with you, Miss Sarah?" John Gray asked.

"Oh, no, Johnny," she said. "I can make my way quite well alone, if you'll see me to the door."

There was a silence after the front door had closed. The house was returning to its norm, but slowly, very slowly.

"Oh, dear me," John Gray said. "It was more nautical than I thought it would be, wasn't it?"

"I don't see why she came," Aunt Jane said.

"*Noblesse oblige,*" his father said. "She was calling on the Captain's family."

"She's failing," Aunt Jane said. "She isn't what she used to be."

Charles's father stood up and moved about the room restlessly, but there were still echoes of Miss Sarah's voice.

"Nothing's the way it used to be," he said. "Charley, did you ever have a telescope?"

"I don't see why you ask him that, just out of the blue," his mother said.

"Because my father gave me one," John Gray said, "a telescope or a spyglass. It's gone but it's around somewhere if I could only turn the clock back. It's back there in my mind, brand-new." Then Charles saw that he was smiling at him. The shadows were going from the room.

"I'm going to get you a telescope, Charley. Every boy ought to have one."

Charles did not want a telescope and it was just as well, because his father never kept those promises. Miss Sarah Hewitt was gone and the tea party was over.

3

Few Things Are Impossible to Diligence and Skill

—SAMUEL JOHNSON

Malcolm Bryant, who had come to Clyde as a complete stranger with a scientific preoccupation and only his boyhood in a small Midwestern town as a basis for comparison, had called Clyde a ghost town, as though it were like an abandoned Colorado mining settlement. It was true that Clyde had not changed much since the sailing days, because its harbor was now useless for heavy shipping. It had no water power as the mill towns further up the river had and it had little to attract summer tourists. It was a place to be born in and a place to leave, but it was not a ghost town.

There was a curtain, translucent but not transparent, between the present and the past. When you were young you did not bother in the least about it because there was too much present, and thus you accepted the older people and you accepted their deaths very easily, because you were so occupied with living. They disappeared behind that translucent curtain, which moved forward a little every year to cover up the year before. Charles knew, for instance, that Aunt Mathilda was going to die and when she did everyone said it was a mercy and so much easier for her poor sister Jane. She was gone and life went on, and she was hard to remember. Dorothea was too worried about Frank Setchell to remember much, and Sam was too occupied with problems of revolt, and Charles still had too much to learn.

He had to learn the new steps at dancing school and new jokes from the Meader boys and *The Bells* by Edgar Allan Poe for the declamation contest in the seventh grade. He had to learn why certain people thought the Catholic Church was a political menace, and what was difficult about the Irish, and why the boys on Johnson Street, the Thomases and the Stanleys, went away to boarding school when he and his friends did not. He had to learn why couples sat in back of the courthouse at night. He had to learn why Washington Irving's *Sketch Book* was worth reading, and he had to learn the dates and facts in the school history of the United States. Besides he had to follow Sam around when Sam would let him, and when Sam would not he had to talk things over with Jack Mason. It was hard to understand why Sam should have been discontented because Sam could come and go as he wanted, he was on the high school football team, and May Mason, who was the prettiest girl at high school, liked him better than anyone else.

One's ideas about everything underwent perpetual change while one was growing up, such as ideas of God and immortality and of wealth and poverty, and even one's family was not a constant quantity. You knew them better than anyone else, but suddenly something would happen and they were not the people you had thought they were. This experience was like seeing the back of a house for the first time when you had always been familiar with its front. You knew the lawn and the front windows, but in back were the clothes yard, the garbage pail, the woodshed, and the weedy garden. Nevertheless, it was still the same house. That was the way it was with the family, Charles used to think. Sometimes they turned their fronts to you and sometimes they turned their backs.

That was the way it was with Sam and his father and with Dorothea and all the rest of them. The scene that Charles remembered most clearly, the one that changed his ideas about them most, must have occurred when he was twelve and when Sam was seventeen. Dorothea must have been having supper with Olive Haskell, who was her best friend then, because he could not remember her being there at Spruce Street. It was obviously some months after his Aunt Mathilda's death, but the scene was unique and too vital to be confused with this or that.

His father had been in Boston all that day and Charles had been aware for some time that certain things happened, or were apt to happen, when his father went to Boston. Since his father had taken him with him to Boston several times, Charles could imagine his father stepping off the train, walking past the panting locomotive into the old North Station and through the dingy waiting room out to that street with the elevated railway overhead into a sea of sound and faces.

"I'll take you again sometime, Charley," his father used to say.

He was almost always too busy, but it was only fair to admit that those occasions on which his father had taken him to Boston must have represented a definite sacrifice, for they were antiseptic, useful and educational, consisting of a trip to the art museum or to the Old North Church, or a visit to the statue of the man who first used ether or to the brass letters on the sidewalk at the scene of the Boston Massacre. His father was conversant with all these conventional spectacles but Charles suspected, always, that when John Gray was alone he must have done other things.

"You're too young to understand what I have to do here, Charley," was all he ever said. "I have a few investments that I have to look out for on Congress Street. It's a very good thing to go to Boston or New York occasionally. I don't want you to pin me down to it, but sometime you and I will certainly go down to New York—sometime when everything is going right." It was only fair to remember, too, that John Gray did take him to New York, after Aunt Mathilda died.

It was a summer afternoon again and except for Mrs. Murphy in the kitchen no one else was in the house. Charles was reading *The House of the Seven Gables* in the parlor and had reached the eloquent passage where old Judge Pyncheon was sitting motionless in his chair. He heard the front door slam and then the sound of his father whistling in the hall. When his father entered the parlor, he was carrying a copy of the *Boston Evening Transcript* and the *Boston News Bureau* and the latest *Atlantic Monthly*, a box of cigars, and a pound box of candy.

"Well, well," he said. "Where's Mother?"

"She's out," Charles said. "I think she's at the Women's Club."

"Well, well," his father said. "So you're reading *The House of the Seven Gables*. Whoever thought it was a children's book was a very innocent person. Have you a knife in your pocket, Charley? That's right. A boy should always have a knife, to whittle things and carve his name. I think I'll open this cigar box." He sat down in the wing chair and lighted a cigar and the smell of the cigar smoke mingled with his words. "I think it's time, Charley, or about time, that we had a talk about your education. Hawthorne, Emerson, Thoreau, Whittier, Longfellow, James Russell Lowell, not to mention Irving and Harriet Beecher Stowe–they all have a place in the cosmos but it would be nice for you to know that there are other, better writers. These are only a twig on a great tree, but don't quote me as saying so, Charley." He smiled, leaned back in the wing chair, and blew a puff of cigar smoke at the ceiling. "I'm afraid you're having a wretched education–not that I'm against our public school system but it is a school of life, not letters. I wonder how it would be if you went to Groton next year? You'd be old enough to enter the first or second form. I wish I had gone to Groton."

There was no need for Charles to answer and he knew that his father did not want to be interrupted.

"I suppose Sam should have gone to Groton, but then the opportunity didn't exist for Sam. Well, suppose you did go to Groton, then a year at Harvard–I'd like you to meet Kittredge–and perhaps a year at Oxford." He flipped the ash from his cigar into the empty fireplace. "I wish we could all go abroad, but it's difficult with the war, even with Wilson keeping us out of it." He paused and looked at the smoke cloud above him. "If we can't go abroad, it might be a good idea for you to see a little of this country. We might take a trip in a week or two–Chicago, the Great Lakes, the Rocky Mountains, San Francisco." He paused again but his thoughts were moving in a swift, agreeable stream. "China. I don't see why it wouldn't be possible to consider a little trip to China. You've never read Huc and Gabet, have you? Or Lafcadio Hearn?"

He stood up and began pacing about the room waving his cigar in broad arcs, not caring where the ashes fell. His freshly cut hair, the aura of bay rum and cigar smoke, his closely clipped mustache, made his face the face of a world traveler, unburdened by inadequate finance or by provincialism. It was unreal. Charles's common sense told him it was unreal.

"Have you read *Rasselas*, Charley? 'Few things are impossible to diligence and skill.' Now the next time I'm in Boston, I'll stop in at the American Express." Then they heard the front door open. "That must be your mother. Hello, Esther."

"John," his mother asked, "did you have a good day in Boston?" Charles always remembered her expression, both pleased and doubtful. "I wish you wouldn't drop those ashes on the floor."

"Oh," John Gray said, "I'm sorry. You know, Esther, I was thinking, coming back on the train, that it's time we got away from the heat. How would it be if we went for two weeks to Poland Spring?"

"You know how it would be," his mother said. "What would they say at the mill?"

Groton school and China were gone, but Poland Spring was there.

"Never mind the mill," John Gray said. "We could go there and sit quietly and drink Poland water. Rocking chairs, soft music, a little golf."

"But I can't play golf," his mother said, "and you can't play it very well."

"That's just it," John Gray said, and his mind had moved from Poland Spring. "There isn't a golf course here, but there's the Shore Club."

"But we don't belong to it," his mother said, "and if we did, it's twelve miles away."

"We ought to belong to it," John Gray said, "and we ought to have a car. Nothing expensive, Esther, but what would you say if we bought a small car? Then we could drive to the Shore Club. It's about time Sam saw some different people, and Dorothea, too—instead of Frank Setchell and his socks."

"And learn how to play golf?"

"And why shouldn't we play golf?" John Gray answered. "Sam ought to learn a few skills before he goes to Dartmouth. It's nice of Jane to do this for us, but I don't know why she insists on Dartmouth."

"Well, as long as Jane's doing it," his mother said.

John Gray stared at the end of his cigar.

"Dartmouth," he said. "It is, sirs, a small college, and yet there are those who love it. His marks are bad enough and he likes football, but if he can't get into Harvard or Yale, why not Amherst or Brown?"

"I'd better help Mrs. Murphy set the table," his mother said.

John Gray began to laugh.

"All right," he said, "we can talk about the Shore Club later. Dear me, I'd better get washed."

After his father left the room, his mother still lingered in the parlor and her hesitation was novel and disturbing. She looked at the open parlor door and smiled. She looked younger and prettier than she usually did when she came home from a meeting of the Women's Club.

"Charley," she said, and she lowered her voice as though they were discussing something secret, "did he promise you anything?"

"No," Charles answered, "he didn't exactly promise anything."

She moved nearer to him and touched the back of his head gently. "What were you talking about?"

"About a lot of things," Charles said. "School, and I guess about China."

"Oh dear," his mother said. "Did he get as far as China?" She did not want him to answer and she had something else to say. "Charley, we both love him very much, don't we?"

There seemed to be no reason for her question, since Charles had always believed that loving one's parents very much was an accepted principle, like asking God to bless them in one's evening prayers. She touched his head again and her voice was slower and softer.

"I want to tell you something about him, dear, something I think you're old enough to understand." She stopped and he could still feel her fingers stroking the back of his head very gently. "You mustn't feel hurt when he promises you something and then forgets. When he makes a promise and doesn't keep it, it means that he wants us to have the things that he wants us to have. Do you see what I mean?"

"Yes," Charles said, "I guess I see."

It was the first time that his mother had ever spoken to him in that way about John Gray or had ever admitted that in any way his father was different from other people. It was not a bad apology, either, for John Gray. Yet there was one thing that Charles could not understand then or later. Why should anyone promise something unless the means were there for making that promise good? That was the weakness behind it all, the insidious, deceptive plank which destroyed all the rest of the structure.

"You see we've got to believe in him," his mother said. "It would hurt him so if we didn't." John Gray was always escaping from hurts, he was expert at it. "My, it's getting late. I'd better set the table."

"Do you want me to help you?" Charles asked.

"Oh, no," she said, and she rumpled his hair. "Your fingers are all thumbs, Charley. And here's Sam. Sam always knows when it's mealtime."

Sam had attained his full growth when he was seventeen and he already had the build of an athlete. Instead of working that summer, Sam had been playing ball in the Twilight League, on a team made up of employees from Wright-Sherwin and boys who hung around the news store. He had barely passed his college board examinations and Charles had heard his father say that at least Sam might have done a few hours of daily reading instead of fishing or taking girls to the movies or lining out flies. Yet when Sam came in that evening before supper he was like a younger and slightly larger replica of John Gray. He had the same swinging walk, the same quick smile, the same sharply defined features and the same brown hair, though there was more of it and it was not as carefully brushed. He had his mother's brown eyes but Charles was the one who had inherited her auburn hair. Sam had his father's neatness, too. His suit was not well pressed, his tie was knotted carelessly, his soft shirt was rumpled, his low tan shoes were scuffed, but still in some way he looked neat.

"Why, Sam," Esther Gray said, "where have you been?"

"Oh," Sam said, "just wandering around, over at the Masons'."

"Oh. Seeing May?"

"That's right," Sam said. "I wouldn't be seeing Jackie or Old Man Mason, would I?"

"Well, I think that's very nice," Esther Gray said.

"What's there for supper?" Sam asked. "Fish?"

"Cold roast beef," Esther Gray said, "and we have ice cream." Then she left for the dining room.

Sam sat down slowly in the wing chair, raised his left ankle over his right knee and began tying his shoe.

"Hi, kid," he said.

"Hi," Charles answered.

"What you reading?"

"*The House of the Seven Gables*," Charles answered.

Sam let his foot drop limply to the floor.

"That's about those old women," he said. "You're always boning up on books, aren't you, just like the Old Man?"

"I can read if I want to," Charles said.

"Sure you can if you want to," Sam answered, "but where does it get you? Look at the Old Man." Sam yawned and pointed at the ceiling. "Up there reading Boswell. Is the Old Man back from Boston yet?"

"Yes, he's upstairs," Charles said.

"How's he acting?"

"What?" Charles asked.

"How's he acting? Is he happy or is he sad? Is he sorry or is he glad?"

"He's happy, I guess," Charles answered.

"Oh, he's happy, is he?" Sam said. "Well."

"Well, what?" Charles asked.

"Well, nothing," Sam answered. "Listen, kid, you ought not to be sitting here alone pounding books. Get around and know people."

"I'm not snooty," Charles said.

"Well, that's fine." Sam leaned down and retied his other shoe. "There are a lot of snooty people in this town and there are a lot of guys here driving dumpcarts and clamming who are just as good as anybody else and nobody's going to tell me different."

"Who's been telling you?" Charles asked.

"Never mind who's been telling me. I stick by my friends."

"Has May Mason been telling you?"

"Listen, kid," Sam said, "there are lots of other girls around besides May Mason."

"Did you and she have a fight?" Charles asked.

"Who said May Mason and I had a fight?" Sam asked. "Did Jackie tell you that?"

"You just act mad about something," Charles said. "That's why I asked you."

"Well, it would be nice," Sam said, "if you and Jackie Mason didn't hang around and listen so much. I'm not mad. I'm feeling fine. And the next time you go over to the Masons' and you see May, tell her if she wants someone in lace drawers it's all right with me."

"So you did have a fight with her," Charles said.

Sam pushed himself out of his chair.

"Listen, kid," he said, "don't knock yourself out talking. That's all everybody does around here, talk, talk, talk. You shoot off your yap and then Dorothea and then the Old Man—everybody except me."

"What do you think you're doing now?" Charles asked.

"Listen, kid," Sam said, "you think you're funny as hell, don't you? I'm not going to sit around here all my life. I might go up to Canada."

"What would you do in Canada?" Charles asked.

"I'll tell you what I'll do," Sam said. "I'll join the Canadian Army and go overseas. You don't know there's a war, do you?"

Everyone knew there was a war in Europe and that Pancho Villa had been making trouble in Texas, but Charles knew that Sam was only angry about something May Mason had said.

"You're not old enough."

Sam laughed airily.

"That's the boy, kid," he said. "Go on and talk. It's catching"—but neither of them went on because they heard their father on the stairs.

"Hello, Sammy," John Gray said, and then he raised his voice. "Esther," he called, "is supper nearly ready?"

Supper would be ready now in just a minute.

"What are you two boys talking about?" John Gray asked.

"Nothing much," Sam answered. "Just talking."

"It seemed to me that I heard your voices raised in some sort of altercation. There's nothing more futile than shouting in an argument, Sam. It betrays a lack of intellectual resource."

"All right," Sam said, "maybe I haven't got any intellectual resource."

"That's the awkward thing about being seventeen," John Gray said. "Now when I was seventeen—well, I suppose I was like you. Well, it doesn't seem possible, Sammy, but I suppose I was."

Charles saw Sam's face grow red.

"I was madly in love when I was seventeen," John Gray went on, "and that may have made me worry about my personal appearance. Now, Sam, that suit you're wearing—it's time we began thinking about your clothes. I'll have to take you in to Boston, Sammy, and get you something new."

"When?" Sam asked.

"When?" John Gray repeated, and he raised his eyebrows. "Oh, almost any time. We've got to get you looking right for college, Sammy. I don't know exactly what the well-dressed young man wears at Dartmouth but we ought to be able to inquire."

"What's the matter with Dartmouth?" Sam asked.

"Nothing," John Gray answered. "It is, sirs, a small college, yet there are those who love it"—and then Charles heard his mother calling. Supper was on the table.

Charles wanted to say something that would break the sense of strain around him. He wished that his father would understand that Sam was hurt about something and that it was no time to make fun of him or to call him Sammy; but his father was in no mood, then, to notice anything but his own swiftly running thoughts. Sam sat down quietly at the table and every now and then Charles stole a glance at his face. Sam was looking stolidly at his plate.

John Gray was talking about the Poland Spring House again. He was saying that everyone was getting too much in a rut, and that was the trouble with Clyde. At the same time, his mind was back again on what had happened to him when he was seventeen. They used to have two horses then, he was saying, and one of them was a dappled gray named Skip. It was a pity they had no horses now, but it was about time he bought the boys a boat.

"Well, why don't you get one?" Sam said. "Joe Stevens's catboat is for sale."

"Is it?" John Gray asked. "I didn't know it was, but then I don't see as much of the Stevens boys as you do, Sammy. How much do they want for it?"

"I don't know," Sam said. "Around three hundred dollars."

"Well, Sammy," John Gray said, "you might go around and look at her and if she looks all right find what they're asking."

"You mean you'll buy her?" Sam asked.

"I don't see why I shouldn't," John Gray said. "We'll let Sammy negotiate it for us. It's about time Sammy learned a little about business."

"John," Esther Gray said, "three hundred dollars is a lot of money. Let's get the house painted first. Don't you think we ought to, John?"

The boat was safe at its moorings, and now the house was there.

"I'll have a little more cocoa, Esther," John Gray said. "I wish you'd tell Mrs. Murphy the cocoa's very good tonight. I don't know whether it's worth while painting the house. We ought to have a larger house—further back from the street, like the Weaver place, or something further out in the country. Do you know, I heard the other day that Lyte's Castle is for sale."

"Oh, John," Esther Gray said, and she laughed. "For mercy's sake, not Lyte's Castle. Why, it takes two men to take care of the garden and the lawns."

"Now, Esther," John Gray said. "Those things have a way of looking out for themselves. Dorothea needs a place to see the boys, and Sammy will be bringing friends from college, and Charley ought to have a pony. He ought to learn how to ride."

"Oh, John," Esther Gray said, and she laughed again, "let's try not to think of everything at once."

Then Charles heard Sam make a choking sound.

"What's the matter, Sammy?" John Gray asked.

"Nothing," Sam said. "I was just thinking about the pony."

"What about the pony?"

Sam looked carefully at his plate but his voice was hoarser.

"Nothing, except it's the same old pony I was going to get."

"Sam," his mother said. "Sam."

No one spoke for a moment. The rhythm of the talk was broken. They could hear Mrs. Murphy clattering the dishes in the kitchen and the rattle of a wagon and the clap of a horse's hoofs on Spruce Street. John Gray was looking thoughtfully at Sam, and something made Charles sit taut and motionless.

"I know," John Gray said slowly. "I'm sorry about that, Sammy."

Sam looked slowly up from his plate.

"If you're sorry," he said, "why do you go on with it?"

"Sam," Esther Gray said sharply. "Sam."

It was all new to Charles, new and unforgettable. Sam was not the person he thought he was, and neither was his father, as they sat there gazing at each other.

"Just exactly what do you mean," John Gray asked, "by going on with it?" Charles wished that nothing that was going on had happened and Sam must have wished it too, because he hesitated before he answered.

"The same old guff," Sam said. "That's all."

"I think it might be just as well," his father spoke very carefully, "if you were to leave the table, Sam."

In the silence that followed, Sam pushed back his chair and rose. "Sure I'll leave the table," Sam said.

"Sam," his mother called, "come back here and apologize to your father."

"Oh, never mind," John Gray said. "Leave him alone, Esther," and before he had finished speaking the front door slammed.

They were all intensely embarrassed. There was nothing left but the family responsibility for smoothing things over, for pretending that nothing had happened.

"Charley, do you know whether Sam is troubled about anything?" his mother asked. "I wonder whether he's been having some trouble with May Mason. Charles, will you go out and get the ice cream?" But before Charles could move, his father spoke.

"Esther," he said, "I think if it's all the same to you I'll go upstairs and read awhile. It's been a fine supper, but Charley will eat my ice cream for me, won't you, Charley?" and he clapped Charles on the shoulder.

"Oh, John," his mother began. "Sam didn't mean—"

"Oh, never mind it, Esther," John Gray said, and he rose and walked to her end of the table and bent down and kissed her. "There are some things I want to figure out upstairs and I can do it better without ice cream."

She followed him to the foot of the stairs.

"John," she called, "we might go sometime and look at Lyte's Castle."

Then he heard his father laugh.

"Well, perhaps not Lyte's Castle, Esther," he answered. "Let's trim it down a little. Perhaps Sammy was right about Lyte's Castle."

The house on Spruce Street was one of those two-and-a-half-story oblong dwellings which Charles came later to associate with New England seaport towns. It was plainer than anything on Johnson Street, but with the same architectural plan—the hallway running from front to back, the staircase with its landing, the spacious rooms on the second story and the lower-studded, smaller rooms above, hot in summer, cold in winter. Charles and Sam slept on the top floor, because there was not room for everyone downstairs, and the boys could do what they wanted with the rooms up there. They could use the spool beds and the old pine bureaus with the drawers that stuck. They could keep all their possessions upstairs, instead of leaving them in the rest of the house. They could pin pictures on the walls and arrange things in any way they wanted, but they had to make their own beds and look after the rooms themselves; and it was not such a bad idea, provided you had a sense of order.

When Charles went to bed that night, the moon was rising and the moon was large and yellow, almost full. He had been careful to move his bed so that the moonlight would not strike his face because Mrs. Murphy had told him that moonlight on your face when you slept made you crazy, but from the shadow where he lay he could see the rest of the room, looking not the least as it did in daylight but indefinite and larger, as though there were no walls. This must have been why, when he awoke suddenly, he had the unpleasant sensation of not knowing where he was until he saw the windows and the trees outside. Then he saw a shadow which did not belong there near his bed and he heard Sam's voice.

"Charley, I didn't mean to wake you up."

"What is it?" Charles asked. "Is anything the matter?"

"I just looked in," Sam said, and he sat down on the edge of the bed. His voice was the only thing that was like him. The rest of him was shadow.

"What time is it?" Charles asked, and the bed creaked under Sam's weight.

"I don't know. After eleven o'clock."

"Where've you been?" Charles asked.

"Out, around," Sam said. "Walking around, thinking."

Neither of them spoke for a while and Charles knew that Sam did not want to be alone.

"If he hadn't shot his mush off," Sam said, "I wouldn't have shot off mine."

Again there was an interlude of wretched silence and Charles could hear the elm leaves rustle.

"I don't like him," Sam said. "By God, I don't like him."

Sam's voice sounded unreal and unpleasant in the moonlight.

"What's he ever done for us?" Sam said. "Not a goddam thing."

It was very unpleasant in the moonlight and it was very unsettling to Charles because he had a deep respect for Sam's judgment.

"It's always the same damn thing," Sam said. "First he shoots off his mush and then he ends by walking around his room like a squirrel, and it's never his fault when he's licked." Again the room was filled with an uneasy, awful silence. "Whenever he gets his hands on money, he goes up to Boston and loses it."

Charles did not know that Sam was discussing the eccentricities of a profit system or that it was his own first contact with a segment of living that he was later to know so well.

"How does he lose it?" he asked.

"You wouldn't understand it," Sam said. "Never mind how he does. You wouldn't understand."

There were a great many things about life that Charles did not understand but he could start with the assumption that his father was a highly intelligent man and that he must have known perfectly what the odds were. There was something which prevented men like him from stopping, something beyond the realms of ordinary reason.

"Listen, kid," Sam said, "if you ever get to doing what he does, if you don't take a hitch in your pants and behave like other people, I'll beat the pants right off you."

Sam still sat there and Charles could see his shadow as he leaned on his elbows with his chin in his hands.

"Charley."

"Yes," Charles said.

"If you're over at the Masons' tomorrow and you should happen to see May, I wish you'd give her this." He was holding out a folded piece of paper.

"Why don't you give it to her yourself?" Charles asked.

"You give it to her," Sam said. "That's a good kid, Charley." Then Sam was gone and Charles lay staring at the moonlight, still wondering why his father acted as he did in Boston.

Once Charles did ask him why—long afterwards, the year when Charles had left Wright-Sherwin in Clyde to work in the Boston investment house of E. P. Rush & Company.

"Now don't preach to me, Charley," his father had said. "I'm not going to stand any of your damn sanctimonious lectures."

Charles said he was not preaching, he was only asking why he never stopped when he had a profit.

"There you go preaching," John Gray said again. "All right, I'll tell you why—because I want everything or nothing."

If you kept on wanting everything or nothing long enough, particularly if you became too anxious for it, perhaps you always ended with nothing.

4

Don't Let Anyone Tell You, My Young Friends, That There Is Any Such Thing as Luck . . .

Charles always thought of the Masons when things went wrong at home. In periods of bitterness and frustration he found himself wishing that Mr. Virgil Mason were his father and that the Grays could be happy like the Masons, living in a well-painted house with everything in order, even if Mr. Virgil Mason was not as bright as his father and never read much or talked about books. Mr. Mason's father had owned the drugstore on Lyford Street and had once compounded a toothache remedy which had sold well locally. Mr. Mason himself was in the insurance business in Boston and when he came home in the evening he liked to work in his small vegetable garden when there was light enough, a form of relaxation that John Gray hated. In the winter he liked to make things down cellar or do odd jobs around the house which were never done in the Gray house next door. Mr. Mason could make beautiful toy boats or little windmills and he liked having children around. Mrs. Mason, Charles realized, long before he was interested in such things, must once have been as pretty as May, but she was too stout now and did not worry any longer about her looks.

"Anyway," he heard her say once, "I caught Virgil."

His own mother was much prettier but he was sure she was not as happy as Mrs. Mason. At any rate, he always had a good time at the Masons'. May was pretty but she was not stuck-up about it and she did not correct him the way Dorothea did, and Jack was his best friend.

Charles could never discover why Jack was discontented, too. He used to think that Mr. Mason was the best sort of father one could imagine, but Jackie said once, in one of those long and confidential talks they used to have, that he wished his father were more like Charles's father.

"I don't see what's the matter with him," Charles had said; but Jack had said there was plenty the matter with him. He was always in his shirt sleeves doing work that other people should do for him. On Sunday he would be hammering and sawing and tinkering outdoors where people could see him when they went to church. His father ought to go to church more often and not work on Sunday, even if it was only the Unitarian Church.

"But my father never goes," Charles had told him; but Jack had said that all the rest of Charles's family did, even if it was only the Unitarian Church and not the Episcopalian.

"Besides," Jackie had said, "my father never wants to do anything but sit around the house. He doesn't know the right people, and almost everybody likes your father."

Charles agreed with Jackie Mason that they were both going to be very different from their fathers. They were going to make more money when they grew up, and they weren't going to live on Spruce Street. Yet Charles could never understand why Jack worried because his grandfather had been a druggist and why he was always complaining about the Mason house and the furniture. He was always reading magazine articles about successful men. It didn't matter where you started—even if your grandfather had been a druggist —it was a question of working hard, Jack said, and of meeting the right people. Jack had won the composition prize in the seventh grade by writing a composition on the boyhood of Andrew Carnegie, and his mind was always on success. For example, he was deeply interested in the career of Mr. Sullivan, who had bought the house across the street, because Mr. Sullivan had started out as a laboring man and now he was in the contracting business, making a lot of money.

"The only thing wrong," Jack said, "is that he doesn't know the right people."

It was Saturday afternoon when Charles went over to the Mason house with Sam's note in his pocket, and he opened the front door without knocking because he was Jack's best friend, Mrs. Mason had said, and he could go out and come in any time he wanted. When he was in the hall, he heard Mr. and Mrs. Mason talking in the front parlor.

"It's the way he is," Mr. Mason was saying, "and it's none of my business, Margaret. There's no use arguing when it's the way he is."

"It's so hard on poor Esther," he heard Mrs. Mason say just before he reached the parlor doorway.

Mrs. Mason was darning a pair of Jack's stockings and Mr. Mason was in his shirt sleeves, sitting in front of a table covered with newspapers, mending a Canton china plate. His glasses had slipped down to the end of his nose and his heavy reddish face shone with perspiration and he held the broken pieces of china very carefully. It was remarkable that his heavy hands could do such delicate things.

"Oh," Mrs. Mason said, and she looked startled. "Why, hello, Charley."

"Hello," Charles said. "Is May anywhere around?"

"My, my," Mr. Mason said, "aren't you pretty young to be looking around for May?" and he smiled and pushed his glasses back to the bridge of his nose.

"Why, May's in the back room practicing, dear," Mrs. Mason said, and then Charles could hear the notes of the Masons' old upright piano, "and Jack's out in the shed splitting kindling, and there's some lemonade in the kitchen."

That was the way it always was at the Masons', lemonade, and everyone was happy. As he moved toward the back room, he heard May playing a waltz from *The Pink Lady*, not well, but he could recognize it, and he wished that Dorothea would ever play anything on the piano that he could understand. May's yellow hair was gathered up in a knot and she was wearing what Charles knew was her third-best dress, but still she looked very pretty. It might have been a perishable, Dresden china prettiness, but Charles was not aware of such things then. He never forgot May, sitting straight on the piano stool, her hands pounding the keys conscientiously. He remembered the curve of her white neck and though her head was turned away from him, he already had an impression of her blue eyes and her red, half-parted lips.

"Why, Charley," she said, "I didn't know you were there. You sneaked in like an Indian."

"I was making a lot of noise," Charles said, "but you were making more."

"It isn't nice to call it noise," May said. "I wish I played as well as Dorothea."

"You play better," Charles said. "I like it a whole lot better."

"Oh, Charley, you know I don't," May said, and she laughed. "I don't do anything very well. Where's Sam?"

"I don't know," Charles said, "but he wanted me to give you this," and he pulled the note out of his pocket.

"Oh," May said, and she snatched it out of his hand and tore open the envelope, and then she put her hand on his arm. "Don't go away, Charley. Please stay here while I read it."

As she read it, with her head turned away from him, he felt the warm grasp of her fingers on his arm and he wished she were his sister. Standing there beside her, so close that her shoulder touched his, he could have read the note if he had wanted, but he never knew what Sam had written. He only knew that May was crying. She had dropped the note. She had drawn him toward her as she still sat there on the piano stool. Her head was pressed against him and she was crying. He was still very shy with girls, particularly with girls of May's age, and besides he was madly in love with Miss Jenks, who had been his teacher in the seventh grade.

"May," he said, "don't cry."

"Oh, Charley," May said, "I'm just crying because I'm so happy. Tell Sam," she held him closer, "tell Sam it's all right."

He was relieved when May found her handkerchief and wiped her eyes.

"I guess I'd better go and see Jackie," he said.

"All right," May said, "but bend your head down," and before he knew what she was going to do, her arms were around his neck and she had kissed him.

"Charley," she said, "you didn't mind it, did you?" He had no idea what Sam had written or why any note of Sam's should have made May Mason cry.

Out in the woodshed, Jackie was splitting kindlings in a languid way. When he saw Charles he dropped his ax and sat down on the chopping block.

"I don't know why an American boy has to split kindlings," Jack said.

"Oh, go on and split them," Charles told him. "Didn't Henry Ford split them?"

"I'll bet Henry Ford had a machine to do it," Jack said. "There ought to be a machine."

"Go on," Charles said. "Didn't Andrew Carnegie split them?"

"No," Jack said, "he had peat or something. He lived in Scotland."

"Well, hurry up and finish," Charles said, "and let's go over to Meaders'."

Jack pushed himself up slowly from the chopping block and pushed his hair from his forehead. He needed a haircut. He had yellow hair with a wave in it like May's.

"Are you going to the Lovells' party?" he asked.

Charles did not understand the question, until Jack explained. It seemed that Jessicia Lovell was having a birthday party and Jack had been invited that morning and the Meaders were going.

"I thought everyone was asked," Jack said.

"Well, I'm not," Charles answered.

"Well, that's funny," Jack said. "I don't see why they asked me and not you."

Clearly Jackie was pleased that he had been asked and Charles not, but Charles was not worried in the least, in those days, about the Lovells or about Andrew Carnegie or about meeting the right people. He was still thinking of May Mason and Sam and he felt proud and pleased. He knew she was Sam's girl, and he always thought of her afterwards as Sam's girl. She was still Sam's girl when she finally married Jeffrey Meader. It was a secret which they always held in common. He knew and she knew that she would have married Sam if Sam had lived.

Memory had an erratic way of leaving some things clear and others blank. Those were the figures, the reference points, of his childhood. Somehow other people and things that he thought he would always remember were laid away in the partially open, dusty drawer of forgetfulness, but not those figures. There was a time when he had been out in a rowboat with the Meaders and the boat had been swamped in a squall and they had nearly been drowned in the river. He had once fought with a boy in grammar school whose name was Slavin and it must have been of great immediate importance and a full dress affair for it took place on Cedar Hill beyond the water tank, where one customarily went for serious fighting. No events like these, however, carried into the present as did the changing figures of those few people nearest him, his father, his mother, his Aunt Jane, Dorothea, and the Masons, and of them all Sam was by far the clearest, because he was a finished memory, distinct and beyond future alteration.

He always associated Sam with the end of childhood. When the music of World War I played, Sam was always there. It was a long way to Tipperary, and while you had a lucifer to light your fag, smile, boys, that's the style, I didn't raise my boy to be a soldier to shoot some other mother's boy. Sam always came back with those tunes, still not in uniform, but Sam had enlisted in the National Guard and was waiting to be called.

Sam was sitting in the City Hall auditorium where Charles's class at the Webster Grammar School was undergoing its graduation exercises. Pack up your troubles in your old kit bag, smile, boys, that's the style. This must have been at the end of Sam's first year at Dartmouth. At any rate, he could still sometimes see Sam, in a suit he must have bought at Hanover—John Gray or someone must have done something about his clothes—winking at him from the audience, twisting the whole left side of his face, as Charles sat on the platform in the second row, behind the girls.

Martin J. Gifford, who was going to run that fall for the state legislature, was delivering the speech customarily made to a Clyde graduating class. It was a speech containing all the doctrines on which Charles Gray and his comtemporaries had been brought up and which so many of them tried in vain to reconcile with what they experienced later.

Martin J. Gifford was speaking in tender tones, in keeping with the tender age of his audience, but his discourse was keyed, too, to the mores of their parents, relatives and friends.

"Luck," Mr. Gifford was saying, in a quavering voice, "is a word that makes me laugh. Don't let anyone tell you, my young friends, that there is any such thing as luck. Do you think that you are here today, on the threshold of higher education, because of luck? No!"

At that moment Sam caught his eye and winked again. The faces of Dorothea, his mother, and Aunt Jane were blurred, but not Sam's.

"No, no," Mr. Gifford was saying. "You are here because of the sacrifices of your parents and the work of every citizen and the very fine achievements of the wonderful ladies and gentlemen on your school committee, your teachers, and of your great mayor, my dear old friend, Francis X. Flynn."

He did not intone the name of Clyde's great mayor but ended it in a shout, and then he waited for the fluttering of applause.

"And what made it possible for them to give you these advantages and to make their sacrifices and their dreams for you come true?" Mr. Gifford was asking. "Was it accident? Was it luck? No! I'll tell you what made it possible." And he walked to the edge of the platform before he told them. "It was possible because you live in the greatest country in the world, in the United States of America, where all men, I thank God, are free and equal, living in the frame of freedom, life, liberty and the pursuit of happiness, where each of us can look the other in the eye and say, 'I am as free as you are; no matter how rich you may be, I have the same chance as you, because this great land of ours is the land of freedom.'"

Mr. Gifford mopped his forehead before he went on with the credo of Clyde.

"Oh, no—there is no such thing as luck, my dear young friends, not for American boys and girls. As you sit here, not so far from entering the contest for life's prizes, you are all starting even because this is America, no matter what may be your religion or race or bank account. There is no grease for palms in America. The only grease is elbow grease. Look at our greatest men, born on small farms in small houses, boys without a cent to their names. Did they get there by luck? Oh, no. They got there by making the most of opportunities which are open, thank God, to every American boy and girl."

This credo was all a part of the air one breathed in Clyde. Later, if it did not jibe with experience, you still believed. If you heard it often enough, it became an implicit, indestructible foundation for future conduct. Even when Sam had winked at him, Charles was sure that Sam believed.

Charles was still sure that Sam believed when they were out on the sidewalk afterwards and when Sam clapped him on the shoulder. It was wonderful to be there with his older brother, who was in a fraternity at Dartmouth and who had been the captain of the football team at Clyde. It was wonderful to be walking down the street with Sam, where everyone could see.

"It was the same old bushwa, kid," Sam said. "He certainly could fork it out"—but Charles was sure that Sam believed.

The words of that speech were a tide that had carried him out of his childhood and there was no logical reason for associating them with his brother Sam but his memory always did. Johnny, get your gun on the run, we won't forget the memory of brave Lafayette, the Yanks are coming over there, you've got to get up in the morning. A long, long trail was winding to the land of my dreams, and how could you keep them down on the farm after they'd seen Paree. Sam had seen Paree one night, but there was no problem of keeping Sam down on the farm. He was going but he was not gone yet. Before the Twenty-sixth Division sailed, he had walked the streets of Clyde on leave from Framingham, in a uniform that was too tight around the neck. He had taken Charles with him to Winton & Low's jewelry store and he had bought a ring for May. It was getting close to autumn then, the year when Charles would enter high school. That was the year when he was first called Master Gray, and he was already madly in love with a girl named Doris Wormser, whose father was a foreman at Wright-Sherwin and who later married Willie Woodbury, when he got the farm machinery agency. Charles's head was already even with Sam's shoulder when they went in to Winton & Low's.

"She isn't going to wear it yet," Sam had said, "but she can tie it around her neck."

It seemed like a very good idea. Sometime he might buy a ring for Doris Wormser to wear around her neck.

"Let me know how May's getting on, sometimes, will you?" Sam had said.

He was getting almost old enough to be a friend of Sam's, right there at the end. That was almost the last of Sam, but he was always back with Charles whenever anyone played those tunes.

5

The Youth Replies, I Can

—RALPH WALDO EMERSON

Charles was through Dartmouth and he was working at Wright-Sherwin before he began to realize that no human problems are unique. He must always, though he only half knew it, have shared his father's discontent with what he had. He was very sure that success and happiness were the same thing, when he was twenty-three, and yet he could already see that different people had different ideas of success. It was a subject which he and Jack Mason discussed very often, for Jack had gone to work in Wright-Sherwin too, after he had graduated from Amherst. Naturally, they each would bring up personal examples, and this was the beauty of living in a place like Clyde, where the lives and careers of everyone were known to everyone else. Charles, who only knew Mr. Lovell academically then, did not consider Mr. Lovell a successful person, but Jackie said he was the most successful man in Clyde. Mr. Lovell knew the right people, not only in Clyde but along the North Shore and in Boston, and that was what success meant; but Charles said Mr. Lovell could not run Wright-Sherwin.

"That's exactly what I mean," Jack said. "He doesn't have to. He has everything that running Wright-Sherwin could give him."

There was a blind spot, Charles realized later, in everyone's line of reasoning. He could see that living on Johnson Street was not the end of everything and his nebulous ambitions were already larger than Jack Mason's. If you wanted to pick a successful man in Clyde, you could take Old Man Stanley, who ran Wright-Sherwin. He knew all the right people, too, because it was worth their while to know him. He was a director of the Clyde Fund, a trustee of the Old Ground Cemetery, a director of the Dock Street Savings Bank and a director of the West India Insurance Company without ever having belonged in Clyde originally. He was in everything because of his ability and not because he lived on Johnson Street. He had taken over Wright-Sherwin when it was nothing but an unsuccessful brass foundry and now it made parts for the best precision instruments in the country.

Then, if you wanted, you could go on to Mr. Thomas, who was president of the Dock Street Savings Bank. He belonged in Clyde; his father had been head of the bank before him, but Mr. Thomas knew his business besides living on Johnson Street. The Dock Street Bank might be in a queer-looking building, but it was as sound as any in Massachusetts—or you could take Mr. Sullivan, who ran his contracting business and owned shares in a dozen small enterprises—or Mr. Levine, whose father had owned Levine's drygoods store and who suddenly had bought the shoeshop. Mr. Levine and Mr. Sullivan did not know the right people except in a business way, but it seemed to Charles that they had done pretty well in spite of what Jack Mason said.

From this gallery of Clyde's great men, Charles could turn to his own father, who, by contrast, was an habitual failure, though actually there were many like him in Clyde who were much worse off. If John Gray did not know when to stop when he started, at least he had his own ideas of when not to start, and there was no use starting, he wanted Charles to understand, unless you had some capital. In the summer of 1916 and the next winter, when he had inherited his share of Aunt Mathilda's estate, he would have succeeded if Hugh Blashfield had not doled out the money by degrees, a thousand dollars at a time. He could never feel afterwards that Hugh Blashfield had been a friend of his, not that he wanted to mention this to anyone but Charles. If Hugh Blashfield had let him have the whole twenty-five thousand dollars as he had asked, instead of handing it out to him in little driblets, the whole story might have been different, because you had to have capital. He had tried it once with the five thousand that was left him out of trust at the time of the Judge's death and he had tried it again with the thirty thousand which had come to the family from Dr. Marchby, but this was something that Charles only learned later from his mother. Then he had tried it a third time with Aunt Mathilda's legacy. If Hugh Blashfield had not tried to stop it, it would have been a different story, but Hugh Blashfield had no imagination. Hugh was nothing but a small-town lawyer.

John Gray's appearance had changed very little since his reversals of 1916. His hair was shot with gray and so was his mustache, but he had retained his posture and he had not put on weight. He could still read without glasses and he still had the appealing smile of a younger man. As Aunt Jane used to say, John had matured beautifully, and Charles had even heard his Uncle Gerald Marchby admit it once, on one of those rare occasions when he and Aunt Ruth Marchby came to call. It meant a good deal when the Doctor, for Uncle Gerald was a doctor too, like Charles's maternal grandfather, had a kind word of any sort to say about his brother-in-law. He said he did not know what John had done to keep so young.

John Gray answered that if he looked young it was because he had not worried for years. He had no financial problems. Gerald and Hugh Blashfield, not to mention Esther and Jane, would not allow him to have them. He was referring, of course, to an agreement he had made at the end of 1917 to let Gerald and Hugh Blashfield pay the bills out of the proceeds of the Judge's trust. He had no financial worries, and Jane had paid for Charles's education, such as it was—he could never understand why Jane had wanted first Sam and then Charles to go to Dartmouth. He did not have to worry about the children. Charles was in Wright-Sherwin making twenty-five dollars a week, a miserable sum, even for a graduate of Dartmouth (a small place but he loved it), and Dorothea, who never could seem to find anyone suitable for a husband, although she had tried, was comfortably established in the public library, and she still had someone keeping company with her. It was Elbridge Sterne now, who had come from Kansas City and was doing something about metallurgy in Wright-Sherwin. No, he had no financial worries, and besides, he had no vices. He smoked very little and he hardly ever drank, except for an occasional glass of port in his bookroom upstairs, and he always walked to the mill, where he did not have to worry either. He could do the accounting with his eyes shut. If anybody worried about the mill, it ought to be Gerald and Hugh Blashfield. He had suggested that they sell the family's holdings, as cotton mills in New England were on the downgrade, but that was their responsibility since they were trustees for the Judge's estate. It was their blood pressure that ought to rise, not his.

Besides, he did not gamble. He was pained to see that Gerald and Ruth looked surprised but it was true, *he did not gamble*. He had attempted some investments occasionally in Boston, of a speculative nature, on the rare occasions when he had been allowed a little capital, but that was all over, now that Gerald and Hugh saw to it that he had no cash but pocket money. He did not mean to say that they were not generous. What they gave him, together with that wretched pittance that Stafford paid him for keeping the mill's accounts, would have been enough to have allowed him to do something at the race track, but there was one thing that they would all admit, Esther, Jane, and Ruth and Gerald, and Gerald could remove his gall bladder tomorrow morning if it wasn't true. He had never done anything with races. He had never approved of them and he hated the uncertainty of horse racing, and he did not like games of chance, dice, numbers or cards. He had never played them except for a little friendly poker down at the Pine Tree firehouse. He did not gamble. What was it Thomas Fuller said? "A man gets no thanks for what he loseth at play." Of course Edmund Burke took a wider view. What was it he said in his speech in the House of Commons? "Gaming is a principle inherent in human nature. It belongs to us all." Yet David Garrick put it another way. What was it David Garrick said? Oh, yes. "Shake off the shackles of this tyrant vice; Hear other calls than those of cards and dice." That would be a very good thing for Gerald to remember when he played auction at the Whist Club, but personally it did not apply to him.

He could not understand why certain people, particularly on Johnson Street, looked on him as a black sheep just because he had attempted to make a few speculative investments. He was faithful to his wife, and that was more than could be said of certain individuals on Johnson Street and on other streets in Clyde—but the trouble with Clyde was that Clyde never forgot. It remembered the indiscretions of youth as though they were yesterday and if you made one mistake in Clyde it did for you.

He still had a spring to his step when he walked down the street and he had what was commonly known as a cheery word for everyone. He and all the other John Grays Charles knew later were impulsively generous, always ready with a dollar when the hat was passed round, always ready to buy a tag, any sort of tag, on tag days. John Gray was the sort of man who would always stop when a child was crying in the street. When anyone was ill, he would always be the first to call. The people at the mill all loved him. He was the one they called on, when they were in trouble, to intercede with Judge Fanning at the police court or with Alf Jason, the truant officer, or with Miss Nickson, the visiting nurse. John Gray was exactly the sort of person who would give you the shirt off his back, impulsively and generously, if you needed his shirt.

It was true, as it sometimes occurred to Charles, that most people who said this about John Gray were not shirtless, and it was unfair to think that John Gray and people like him were tolerant and kindly because they were never sure when they would need such coin themselves.

Yet it was also true, as John Gray said so often, that no one forgot in Clyde, particularly about money. Everyone knew that John Gray had run through money, thousands and thousands of dollars of it. Everyone knew that Mrs. Gray and Dorothea would not have been able to afford even a part-time maid or a cleaning woman and that Charles could not have gone to college if Miss Jane had not helped out. If you were in the family you were always conscious of this, and though his father always treated those matters lightly when he mentioned them, John Gray was bitterly ashamed of his failures; but Esther Gray always understood his sensitivity, and Dorothea and Aunt Jane, and if the subject of poverty came up in the family it was always slurred over with great speed.

Charles first fully understood this family feeling from observing that his father was not put on the committee of the Clyde Fund after Mr. Finch had died. At this time Charles had been working for more than a year at Wright-Sherwin. He had recently been moved into the accounting department under Mr. Richard Howell, one of those assiduous slaves of detail so useful in any office. The man whose place Charles had filled, and an older man, too, had been fired by Mr. Howell, who used to say that things were either right or wrong and that there was no excuse for not doing them right. When things were done right he accepted them without a word but he always blew up when there was a mistake. Charles had been checking over an inventory that afternoon and he felt tired and uncertain.

It was a dull September day and the wind was so high that he thought it was blowing up for a storm. He was wondering what he would do if he were fired from Wright-Sherwin. It was the first time that his future had depended on the whim of a single critical stranger. As he walked into the wind down River Street and into the square at Dock Street, he hoped that for once the family would not ask him how he was getting on with Mr. Howell. This was a question which his father invariably asked each evening. John Gray, it seemed, had been to Sunday School with Dickie Howell, who had been in charge of passing out the hymnbooks, and now Dickie Howell passed the contribution box. It all went to show, John Gray had said, what happened if you were consistent. Dickie had married a girl in the Sunday School class named Myrtle Snyder, who had a thin jaw and a button nose like Dickie's. They lived in the North End and you could see Dickie clipping his privet hedge every Saturday afternoon. He had the straightest hedge in Clyde. Details like these were always interesting to John Gray, but they had nothing to do with Charles's difficulties.

"It must be a beautiful relationship," John Gray said, "yours and Dickie Howell's."

"Can't you tell me what he's like?" Charles asked.

John Gray only said that it did not matter what he was like. He said it was the old master and man relationship. He only said it was fascinating that Charles was working for Dickie Howell, and that it was a small world and a just world.

"I used to kick Dickie Howell's shins at Sunday School," John Gray said. "I never dreamed that he would be kicking yours, Charley."

Dorothea and his mother were in the parlor when he got home, reading the *Clyde Herald*, which Tommy Stevens always threw on the front porch from his bicycle at five o'clock.

"I think it would be just as well not to speak of it at all," his mother was saying to Dorothea, who was darning one of her best silk stockings.

"Well, here's Charley," Dorothea said. "Ask him. He knows everything."

"I know how you got a hole in it," Charles said.

"How?" Dorothea asked.

"Running after Elbridge Sterne."

"Well, I'd rather run after Elbridge," Dorothea said, "than trot around after Mr. Howell."

"I wish you children wouldn't always bicker," Esther Gray said. "Charley, the Clyde Fund didn't take your father."

The Clyde Fund was one of those generous bequests which so many New England citizens have left for the benefit of towns in which they lived. It had started with a bequest of five thousand dollars in 1820 by a Mr. Clarence Fanning, the principal to be held for a term of years at compound interest and then the income to be expended on shade trees and on other street improvements, under the direction of five representative citizens, to be named by the Dock Street Savings Bank. The trustees met three times a year, in the Dock Street Savings Bank directors' room, and Charles's grandfather, the Judge, had been one of the first trustees.

"Why should they have taken him?" Charles asked.

"Oh, Charley," his mother said, "don't say that."

"That's just the sort of thing Charley would say about Father," Dorothea said.

"Well," Charles said, "you might as well mention it, because he'll find out."

Just at that moment John Gray came in from his work at the mill.

"Well, well," he said, "the wind's getting into the northeast. How's Dickie Howell, Charley?"

"Don't tease him, John," Esther Gray said.

"Now, Esther," John Gray said, "Charley and I have our own brand of humor, acrid, but it's humor. Well, so you're all reading the *Clyde Herald*."

"John." Charles's mother smiled brightly. "You didn't tell us that the Pine Trees were going to another muster."

"Are they?" John Gray answered. "I didn't see that, but I saw about the Clyde Fund. Don't look disappointed, Esther. I'm hardly the type. What would I do in a savings bank talking about shade trees?"

Supper was the time in the day when the family was always drawn closest together and Charles's pleasantest memories, as well as memories of quarrels and crises, all began with the supper table at Spruce Street. The old sliding shutters were always drawn across the dining room windows and for light there were four candles in brass candlesticks and a hanging oil lamp above the table, a strange and ugly Victorian contraption which let itself up and down on pulleys. There was a halo of light above the round dark walnut table but the fireplace with its mantel and paneling over it and the white dado of the dining room were always in shadow. The same willowware pot of boiled cracked cocoa always stood by his mother's place. He had once told Nancy about that cocoa, which used to steep on the back of the stove for days, and out of curiosity Nancy had looked for some in New York but she could never find it. It only seemed to exist at Mr. Beardsley's grocery shop at Clyde. There was always a loaf of bread and a knife and a breadboard by Dorothea's place and a covered Sandwich glass butter dish at John Gray's end of the table. The napkins were neatly rolled in silver rings, each with its owner's initial. (Sam's ring was still in the Empire sideboard.) The chairs around the table were of the painted, Hitchcock type, and all these furnishings were so closely associated with the family that each thing in the room had an almost living relationship to each other thing.

Even if they were gossiping over the most humdrum events of the day at supper, John Gray was always entertaining. He began that evening by touching lightly on the Clyde Fund. The Fund, he said, had a definite effect on the mental processes of all its trustees and being a trustee was a great responsibility. Should the income be spent to sprinkle Johnson Street in the summer or should it be spent for public hitching posts on Dock Street? It was still to dawn, he said, on a Clyde Fund trustee that it was more important to regulate motor traffic. Or should the money be spent in erecting a suitable drinking fountain for horses at the southwest corner of Dock and Johnson Streets to balance the Hewitt Memorial Fountain on the northwest corner, and, if so, how high should the fountain be? These were problems, John Gray said, that needed Clyde's best minds, and how could the birds be kept from the head of George Washington near the courthouse without discouraging the birds? He was sorry, very sorry, that he could not be there to help.

Then his mind moved on. The Dock Street Bank had closed its mortgage on the old Bingham house. Surely Charles must have noticed it, the square brick house that he passed every day on his way to Wright-Sherwin. Its fence was gone and its window sashes were rotted but it had a perfect doorway. Tony Leveroni, who worked at the mill, lived there, and John Gray had been in to see him when his boy was sick. The Leveronis lived in the old ballroom but their stove and sink and washtubs could not spoil it. It was one of the stateliest rooms he had ever seen. The molding was as light as lace. It was a privilege to sit with Tony Leveroni and look at the carved medallion below the mantel. If the Clyde trustees wanted to do anything they should buy that house and restore it, and then he shrugged his shoulders.

Usually after supper he went upstairs alone to his room to read and it surprised Charles that evening when he asked him to come up too.

"That is, if you have time, Charley," John Gray said, "or have you a round of engagements?"

The room where his father spent his evenings was almost square with two deep windows with window seats and, on either side of the fireplace, arches and two other windows. A battered sofa stood in front of the fireplace and a table behind it held a student lamp and the books and papers in which John Gray was currently interested. Two ugly Morris chairs by the sofa had come from the Marchbys and some older Windsor chairs had been sent over by

Aunt Jane from the Judge's house, and the painted pine floor was partly covered with a worn Oriental carpet. The bookcases were filled with brown leather volumes from the Judge's library and others which John Gray had purchased. Among these were, of course, the works of Samuel Johnson and all sorts of other volumes of the period, all with elaborate dedications to their patrons. Tacitus, an early translation of the seventeenth century, stood beside Burton's *Anatomy of Melancholy*, and Boccaccio, with a broken back, leaned against Fuller's *Worthies*. The bookcases were far from adequate. Books stood in heaps on top of them and in piles on the floor near the table, like the broken columns of a ruined temple.

The room was never neat, because John Gray did not like to have the women dust it. He said he knew where every book was until people began to move them. Women never went with books. They did not understand why he did not want his print of London Bridge dusted, or why he liked the Landseer engraving of sad-eyed dogs. It might not be a good picture but he liked it, and he liked to have his shotguns leaning in the corner under one of the arches by the fireplace, and he liked to have his brass-bound box of old decanters on the floor, and the sea chest that had belonged to his grandfather, the Captain, cater-corner on the far side of the room, and he did not care whether the tall clock there kept time or not. He knew to the half minute how much time it lost during the week.

As Charles followed his father up the stairs, he could hear the clock ticking and then it made an asthmatic sound and struck the hour of three though it was half past seven o'clock. He could also hear the wind outside and a sharp spatter on the windows, showing that a northeaster was starting.

"You stand here by the door, Charley," John Gray said, "until I light the lamp. I don't want you tipping over books." There was a pungent smell of moldering leather and old wood and stale tobacco smoke as John Gray moved into the dusky room.

"Close the door, Charley," he said. "It's always better in here with the door closed." He had lighted the student lamp and had replaced the chimney and now he was turning up the wick and putting back the green glass shade. "Sit down in that Morris chair. That's right. Did I ever tell you that's the chair your Grandfather Marchby died in?"

"No," Charles said, "I don't think you ever did."

John Gray smiled and walked over to the fireplace and stood looking down at him.

"Well, don't look worried, Charley," he said. "He couldn't help it. There are a great many things we can't help, Charley, or do you think we can?"

"I don't suppose we can help dying, it that's what you mean," Charles said, and he was uneasy as always when he was alone with his father.

"You're at an age, I suppose, when you feel you can help anything by power of will," John Gray said. "How would you like a glass of port?"

"Why, thanks," Charles said, "if you want one."

"Open the decanter box, Charley, and hand me the right-hand bottle, filled with a purplish-red liquid, and take out two glasses. It's Jewish sacramental wine." His father was drawing a small tavern table in front of the sofa. "That's it. Moe Levine told me where to get it."

His father took the stopper from the decanter and filled two antique wineglasses. Nothing in his manner indicated that the occasion was in the least unusual, but Charles could not help wondering what he wanted. It was not a part of family custom to be sitting in his father's room. If his father wanted to talk he always came downstairs to the parlor.

"I suppose you've done a little drinking at Dartmouth," his father said. "But I'd have known it if liquor had ever passed your lips around here, Charley, above one fluid ounce," and he laughed and sat down on the sofa. "There would have been whisperings on the Rialto." His father raised his glass. "Try it, Charley, it won't hurt you."

The sacramental wine was heavy and unpleasantly sweet and its taste added to Charles's uneasiness. He felt, as he often did, that his father was laughing at him, and he was never sure whether the laughter was entirely friendly.

His father had half turned his head toward the window. "Listen to the rain," he said. " 'Neither coat nor cloak will hold out against rain upon rain.' Do you know who said that, Charley?"

"No, sir, I'm afraid I don't," Charles answered.

"Oh, dear," his father said. "Thomas Fuller said it in his *Gnomologia*, and I don't suppose you know what gnomologia is, either." He leaned forward and refilled his glass. "This is horrible wine. I wish you cared more about the polite adornments of the mind, Charley. 'Rain upon rain.' I've been through a lot of rains. Keep out of the rain, Charley." He smiled at Charles and seemed to expect him to make some reply, but when Charles talked with his father nothing ever seemed to be on a firm foundation.

"What does gnomologia mean?" Charles asked.

"Oh, dear," his father said, "didn't they tell you at Dartmouth?"

"I don't see why you keep picking on Dartmouth," Charles said. "It's a pretty good school."

His father raised his heavy, dark eyebrows. "I can't say it hasn't developed your mind," he said. "It seems to me that you have a retentive mind, neither receptive nor curiosity seeking, but retentive. Roughly gnomologia means a collection of sayings or proverbs. The word is obsolete."

"Then I don't suppose it will do any good to know it," Charles answered.

"That's an interesting way to put it," John Gray said slowly. "I suppose you mean that all knowledge should be useful, because someone has told you that knowledge is power."

"Well, I don't see any use in learning a lot of things that don't do you any good." He stopped and he felt annoyed at himself and his father. It did not help when John Gray laughed.

"Why, of course," he said. "Naturally, Charley. I'm not criticizing you for a single minute. You're only saying that you want to get on or get ahead. It's a very common objective around here."

John Gray leaned more comfortably back against the corner of the sofa.

Perhaps it was the room or the rain on the windows or the sacramental wine or his uneasy annoyance that made Charles say what he said next.

"Didn't you ever want to get on?" he asked. The question was too personal and his father was no longer comfortable.

"Why, yes, Charley," he said. "Yes, I've wanted to get on, but I suppose you think it was a silly way, the way I tried, and I don't blame you. You'd be following a convention."

"Well, I don't know much about it," Charles said.

"Do you remember what Jonathan Swift said?" his father continued. "'Ambition often puts men upon doing the meanest offices: so climbing is performed in the same posture with creeping.'" Suddenly John Gray laughed and stood up. "I've never liked creeping. I suppose I could have crept and if I had I might be on the Clyde Fund."

He said it without much emphasis and for the first time Charles felt sorry about it. He wanted to say something, to tell him it did not matter, but he could think of no way in which to say it which did not sound stupid or gauche. He picked up his glass nervously between his fingers.

"Well, we weren't talking about that anyway," he said.

His father stood with his head tilted to one side, listening to the hissing rhythm of the rain against the window. The wind had risen in sharp gusts so that the rain splashed against the panes in wavelike surges, as though someone from outside were throwing it with a dipper. Something was making John Gray restless and he took a short turn around the room before he spoke again, moving as though he did not need to see any of the objects in it.

"I'm hardly in a position to give you any sound advice, Charley," he said suddenly. "'Advice, as it always gives a temporary appearance of superiority, can never be very grateful.'" From the sonorous tone of his voice, Charles knew that he was quoting again. He wished his father would not keep leaning on other people's thoughts. He was wondering whose words had been resurrected now, probably Samuel Johnson's. Yes, it was Samuel Johnson.

"And yet," John Gray was saying, "Johnson himself spent most of his time giving unsolicited advice." He paused and stared at the floor. "Now this subject of your getting on interests me. Of course, I know why you want to. You want to because I obviously haven't."

It was much better, Charles was thinking, not to answer. Instead of answering he found himself pouring another glass of that sticky wine.

"But I would like you to know, Charley," and he noticed that his father was speaking with an artificial, constrained sort of lightness, "that I've made what I consider several intelligent and rather vigorous efforts to get on, considering the handicaps, and without creeping, always without creeping—but I couldn't beat the system. The system is not fluid, and it's very hard to beat."

"What system?" Charles asked.

"Why, the system under which we live," John Gray said. "The order. There's always some sort of order."

He was speaking more rapidly and confidently and suddenly Charles understood that he was cutting the cloth to fit his faults, as everyone did at some time or other.

"There's always the bundle of hay out ahead, for any ass who wants to get on," John Gray was saying, "and They make it look like a very pleasant bundle."

"Who are 'They'?" Charles asked.

"That's an intelligent question," John Gray answered. "They are the people who own the hay. They are the people who run the system, and They have to toss out a little hay now and then to make the system work; and the curious thing about it is that They don't realize in the least that They are running the system. They are only acting through a series of rather blind instincts and that's about all there is to anything, Charley, instinct. They'll tell you there's plenty of hay for anyone who can get it, but the main thing, Charley, is that They don't really want you to get it. It might be some of Their hay."

Charles could follow his father's metaphor and he could tell from the bright look on John Gray's face that he was delighted with it himself. Voltaire had the same brilliant bitterness, the same cynicism, and a similar painful undercurrent of truth—and John Gray was still speaking.

"You can get so far by effort, Charley. You will find you can obtain a little hay but if you reach for more you'll get a sharp rap on the muzzle. I'm being very wise this evening, Charley, and I know I'm right because I've tried to get some of that hay. Don't worry. It's all over now. I won't try again. All I want now is to keep out of the rain and to manufacture a suitable waterproof. I'm tired of the system, Charley. I'm delighted to give up."

John Gray sighed and sat down again on the sofa. What he had said was the apologia of John Gray, an alibi, a distorted story of the talents and of labor in the vineyard—and now he was finishing his apologia.

"If I were you," he was saying, "I wouldn't try too hard for the hay. You might be disappointed, Charley."

It sounded like *Candide* and Charles was thinking that if everyone followed John Gray's philosophy nothing would happen anywhere and yet he could think of no reasonable ground for argument.

"Well," he said, "if you call it hay it seems to me that you've had a lot more hay than most people and more than I'll ever have."

That was where it ended. He did not think that he was speaking out of resentment until he saw the light leave his father's face.

"That's a detail, Charley," John Gray said, "and it doesn't alter the general picture."

"Maybe it doesn't for you," Charles said, "but it does for all the rest of us."

John Gray was silent for a moment. The talk was gone and the quotations with it. He picked up his empty glass and stared at it and put it back on the table.

"Don't be so hard on me, Charley," he said. "I told you I wasn't going to do it again. It's like liquor, I can take it or leave it alone, and besides"—he looked apologetic but at the same time he looked as though a cheerful thought had struck him—"it was a wretchedly small amount of hay."

6

The Readers of the Boston Evening Transcript *Sway in the Wind Like a Field of Ripe Corn*

—T. S. ELIOT

Somehow, after their talk that evening, Charles and his father had arrived at a basis for friendship which prevented either of them from offending the other, though it was a little like the friendship between two lawyers who had argued in court and dined together afterwards. There was always something in their association that was like the mercury from a broken thermometer dividing and rolling about with the bits never really coming together. It was diverting when his father spoke about hay to remind him that there was still a little hay, in the shape of the mill stock left in trust under Uncle Gerald and Mr. Blashfield. They would not be able to live on Spruce Street if it were not for that hay.

"But it's getting moldy," John Gray said. "Mill stocks aren't what they used to be."

"But it's just as well it's in trust, isn't it?" Charles asked him. Somehow after that evening he could be as frank as that, and John Gray even seemed to enjoy it.

"But it ought not to be handled in Clyde, Charley," John Gray said, "not by a small-minded lawyer in a small-minded town."

If Clyde was a small-minded town, why had he stayed in Clyde? Had he not ever wanted to get out of it? Charles asked him, but he could never get a direct answer.

"The idea used to occur to me," John Gray said, "but where else could I have gone? Perhaps I was afraid. I'm aware of my deficiencies, Charley."

Being aware of his deficiencies, Charles sometimes thought, was a part of his stock in trade.

"I'll bet if you got your hands on some more money," Charles said, "you'd try it all over again."

His father was amazed, and not hurt at all.

"You know I never bet, Charley," he answered, "and it isn't so. I'm completely, magnificently aware of my deficiencies. I've learned my little lesson, Charley, and that's all over now." A part of his cloak was a garment of quiet puritanism, like so many other cloaks in Clyde. He was not an unregenerate figure of revolt with dangerous ideas. He voted a straight Republican ticket like everyone else in Clyde.

Dorothea was sure that he had learned his little lesson. As long as Charles could remember, Dorothea had been sure of everything. She had been sure that she would be a great concert pianist. She had been sure, when she had been sewing Butterick patterns, that she could be a successful dress designer;

and now she was sure that she could tell Elbridge Sterne ways to advance himself at Wright-Sherwin. It may have been that sureness which had driven the other young men away, but Dorothea never admitted it. She was sure that Father was never going to do that again. She wished that Charles would not joke with him about it. No one had ever dreamed of speaking of it until Charles had and it was highly disrespectful. Charles ought to see that it hurt Mother to talk about bundles of hay.

His mother, too, was sure that Father would never do it again, but she did not think it was disrespectful to treat things as a joke as long as Father did not mind. It showed, she said, that Father was very fond of Charles. If he had not paid as much attention to Charles as he might have, one should remember that he had been so upset about Sam. Father always felt things very deeply. The main thing was to be kind and remember that he was a very remarkable person, quite different from other people. You could not judge him by other standards. For instance, when he joked with Charles about Wright-Sherwin he was really very proud of Charles. Father was beginning to depend on him just as she was and he was their only boy. They were all very proud of Charles, even Dorothea.

Aunt Jane was sure about it, too. Once she had harbored doubts but recently she had been sure that John had turned the corner. It was a little late, perhaps, but he had turned it. After all, he was only fifty-five and Michelangelo was still painting when he was ninety. She had deep faith in John Gray. She knew that he had been the spoiled baby of the family, twelve years younger than she and fourteen years younger than Mathilda—but at least he did not have what she called the Gray heart. The Judge had suffered with it and so had Mathilda and now she had it too. Yet, when his aunt spoke of the Gray heart, she always ended by treating it as a proud inheritance.

Charles could gather that the Grays did not have the past glories of certain other families in Clyde. They had only been country people, on the farm upriver, before the embargo of 1811, but they did have the Gray heart and it carried you off quickly when you had it. Gerald Marchby had told her so. Gerald's deafness was growing but he could hear her heart. It was because of the Gray heart and because he was deeply fond of her that Charles stopped to call on his aunt nearly every afternoon after leaving the office at Wright-Sherwin. Dr. Marchby had prescribed sherry for her, the only way you could get sherry in prohibition days, and she had arranged to obtain two quarts a week, one for her and one for Charles, because Charley ought to have something in return for coming to see her and the Judge had always liked sherry.

Those calls at the Judge's house on Gow Street were difficult to distinguish one from another, except for one on an afternoon not long after that talk with his father. There was a chill in the air in spite of the sunlight and the yellow elm leaves were beginning to drop on the sidewalks. When Charles opened the front door, his aunt was seated in her favorite bannister-back armchair in the Judge's study. Mary Callahan had already brought in the tea and the sherry decanter and had lighted a lump of cannel coal in the grate. His Aunt Jane had on her spectacles and was reading from a piece of foolscap written in the Spencerian penmanship which she had learned long ago at the female academy. Charles knew at once it was one of those lists of personal effects she was always making. For the last two years she had been arranging for their distribution but the arrangements were never final. She wanted everyone to have something and she did not want any friend of hers to be out of sorts when she was dead.

"I told Mary to light the fire to take the chill off," Aunt Jane said. "Charley, I'm going to give Mary the Sheffield teapot and a thousand dollars."

There was no use trying to deflect her from this subject because she liked it, and he had learned it was best to fall in with her mood.

"I thought you were going to let her have the tray," Charles told her.

"I know," she answered, "but I asked her this morning. She thinks Dorothea ought to have the tray."

Of course, she had asked Mary Callahan. Mary had told him only the other day that she was going simply crazy being asked about every stick and plate in the house and being told about the Gray heart. In Mary's opinion, it was stuff and nonsense. Miss Jane, in Mary's opinion, was just as spry as ever she was, up and down stairs and all over the place, emptying out trunks and bureaus, her heart and all. In Mary's opinion Miss Jane was only being contrary to draw attention to herself, and Miss Jane had always been contrary.

Though his aunt's demise was a grim subject, Charles had grown used to it and somehow it was not as grim as it sounded in the Judge's study. He had never seen his grandfather but Charles could feel his presence in the room his grandfather had remodeled in the most unfortunate decorative period of the eighties. He could feel the Judge's precision and his love of order in the golden-oak bookcases and the shining brass about the black marble fireplace. He could feel that nothing was entirely gone, least of all his aunt, sitting as straight as she ever had, in the room's most uncomfortable chair.

Her mood usually changed for the better when she took her sherry. She always drank it in delicate sips and she always coughed.

"It's just as well I never touched it until now," she said. "Charley, I hear you're doing very well."

"Where did you hear that?" Charles asked.

"At the Women's Alliance."

"Where?"

"You heard me," Aunt Jane said, "and it's about time that someone in the family was successful. I think John would have got on if he had gone to Dartmouth instead of Harvard. Charley, do you think Dorothea's going to marry that factory man she brought in here, the one who squints?"

"Who?" Charles asked. "Elbridge Sterne?"

"Yes. He knows all about brass. He kept looking at the andirons. Is Dorothea going to marry him or isn't she?"

"I don't know," Charles said. "She's never taken it up with me. She'll probably get discouraged with him. You know—after a certain time she always gets discouraged."

"She's only particular like me," Aunt Jane said. "Esther thinks she's going to marry him."

"Mother always thinks she's going to marry someone," Charles told her.

"If she does," Aunt Jane said, "she can have the tea tray and the dining room chairs besides the five thousand dollars."

The cannel coal snapped viciously and a piece of it fell on the carpet. Charles rose hastily and kicked it back on the hearth.

"Charley," Aunt Jane said, "you look exactly like the Judge. Did I tell you I'm leaving you five thousand dollars?"

"Yes," Charles said, "you did tell me."

"Well, you might at least say thank you," Aunt Jane said.

"But I have thanked you," Charles told her, "and I've told you you ought not to do it after sending me through college."

"Well, I'm going to," Aunt Jane said, "and Esther's going to have ten thousand and the Queen Anne mirror and my bureau. It's time Esther had something. That's twenty thousand, isn't it? Charley, how do you think your father seems?"

"Why, Father's all right, I guess," Charles said.

The door opened and Mary Callahan came in with a glass and a bottle of pills. It was six o'clock.

"Thank you, Mary," Aunt Jane said, and she looked hard at her back and did not speak until the door closed softly. "Do you think she stands outside and listens, Charley?"

"No, Aunt Jane," he said, "I don't really think she does."

"Well, I don't want her to hear this," Aunt Jane said. "Charley, I've been thinking about your father. You don't know him as well as I do. I'm worried about his self-respect."

"His self-respect?" Charles repeated.

"Yes," Aunt Jane said, "and I'm not going to leave the rest to him in trust. It will hurt his self-respect."

The cannel coal snapped again with a sound that was like a punctuation mark. Charles had heard about the furniture and the silver and the rugs and about a bequest to the Unitarian Church, but she had never told him this before.

"I think it's a mistake, Aunt Jane," Charles said.

"I'm not asking your opinion," she answered, but of course she was asking his opinion. "I don't want to have anyone unhappy after I'm gone."

He felt sorry for her because he knew that she only half believed what she was saying, but it did not seem possible to discuss the subject, when he was still so young that his loyalties were confused.

"Charley," she asked, "aren't you going to say something?"

"No," Charles said. "There isn't any more to say if that's the way you want it."

She reached toward him and put her hand over his. "We have to trust him. He's your father, Charley," and then there was a quaver in her voice. "Charley, I'm so proud of you. Now turn on the lights. Isn't it nice to have electric lights?"

Until he pressed the switch by the door, he had almost thought that his aunt was dead already, but when the ceiling light was on in the old gas chandelier the brillance of the room erased all that talk of death.

"Well," she said, "that's settled. Charley, I wish you saw more girls."

"Why, you're my only girl," Charles said, and he laughed.

"I wish you saw some nice girls," his Aunt Jane said again. "Why don't you ever see Jessica Lovell?"

"Jessica Lovell?" Charles repeated. "Why, I hardly know her."

His aunt should have known he belonged in a different group from Jessica Lovell and that groups hardly ever mingled in Clyde.

When Charles arrived home after his talk with Aunt Jane on death and testaments, Dorothea was playing the phonograph. The family were sitting in the second-best parlor and Elbridge Sterne was with them, in an inconspicuous pepper-and-salt suit and a stiff collar. He had asked Dorothea if she would go to the movies that evening and if he could take her somewhere to supper, and Dorothea had asked him to come home to supper because there was no place to eat in Clyde, unless you wanted a sandwich and a soda at the Sweet Shoppe or a meal in a booth that smelled of fried clams in that restaurant of Nicky Demetrios's on Dock Street. A log fire was burning, which showed that Elbridge must have lugged the wood in from the shed outdoors, because Charles had not brought any in and his father disliked doing it. His father, he saw, was reading a newspaper by the big table lamp, not the *Clyde Herald* but the *Boston Evening Transcript*, and his mother was darning a sock. She had thrust her darning egg well up into the toe and she was bending over her work with an intent and puzzled look. She always said that she hated sewing.

"Hello, Charley," Elbridge said. "You weren't in my part of the shop today, were you?"

Elbridge was exhibiting the classic desire, shared by all Dorothea's other callers, to be agreeable to the younger brother. When Charles shook hands with Elbridge he had the younger brother's conventional feeling of amusement and slight contempt for anyone so weak as to put himself in the situation of calling on Dorothea, and Dorothea was looking at him suspiciously, as though she were still afraid he would blurt out some crude remark or play some practical joke on her and Elbridge Sterne. Elbridge in many ways looked like a shipwrecked sailor among strange natives. His voice was heavy and Midwestern, and he had not lost the hopeful breeziness of more open spaces.

"That's right," Charles said, "I was in the office all day."

"Well, come out into the plant sometime and meet some of the fellows," Elbridge said. "That's a fine crowd of fellows in Shed Two."

"Elbridge could show you a lot about the plant," Dorothea said, "if you'd only let him."

"Who said I don't want to let him?" Charles asked. "But I'm not supposed to leave the office and be wandering around."

"Well, as long as you know everything about everything," Dorothea said.

His mother looked up from her darning.

"I wish you two would stop arguing for just a minute," she said. "It can't be very interesting for Elbridge. How do you think Aunt Jane seemed, dear?" —and Charles said he thought she seemed very well.

"Was she still talking about the furniture?" Dorothea asked.

"Yes," Charles answered, "most of the time."

"That reminds me," Elbridge said, "I dropped into Burch's antique shop and I saw a desk there. It's got a sort of a curved front. I was thinking of buying it for a Christmas present for Mother. I wish you'd look at it, Dorothea, and tell me if it's any good."

There was a pleasant rustling sound and Charles saw that his father had lowered his newspaper.

"From my experience, Elbridge," he said, "I conclude that most attractive fronts should curve."

Then they all saw that the *Boston Evening Transcript* was open at the page of transactions on the New York Stock Exchange.

"The market's still going up, isn't it, Mr. Gray?" Elbridge said.

John Gray smiled faintly and his glance met Charles's for a moment and then he looked away.

"I suppose it is," he answered, "but I only buy the *Transcript* for the Notes and Queries. Do you ever read them, Elbridge?"

"Why, no, Mr. Gray," Elbridge said.

"You really ought to," John Gray said. "Sometimes you encounter the most unworldly queries—and then there's the genealogical column, and the department called the Churchman Afield. That's a fine active name, isn't it? It always makes me think of clergymen running about in riding boots blowing horns. Esther, dear, is supper nearly ready?"

Yes, supper was nearly ready, but his father had not been reading the Notes and Queries. Charles knew it when he continued speaking.

"That phonograph," he said. Dorothea had risen to put on another record. "It's about time, isn't it, that we changed it for a radio? I know what you're going to say, Dorothea. I know the house isn't wired for electricity but it ought to be. We ought to keep in touch with the times. Your Aunt Jane has had her house wired. Esther, we ought to get a radio for Jane."

Charles saw his mother close her sewing basket and she also must have known what John Gray had been reading.

"John," she asked, "have you been to see Gerald?"

"Gerald?" John Gray's forehead wrinkled. "Oh, yes. I had a nice talk with Gerald."

"What did he say about Jane?"

She must have forgotten that Elbridge Sterne was there.

"He said Jane's heart is doing very well," John Gray said. "He says we're all worrying too much about Jane." He stopped and began folding the paper carefully, as though he hoped the noise might distract everyone.

Charles saw Dorothea glance up quickly and uncertainly and his own eyes met Dorothea's for an instant. Dorothea also knew what John Gray had been reading. In spite of what had been said at Gow Street that afternoon about trusting, Charles knew that nothing could change.

"What do you think of this holding company Electric Bond and Share, Mr. Gray?" Elbridge asked. "The way the market's going, I don't see any use in keeping money in the bank."

John Gray had rolled the paper into a neat and careful cylinder.

"Elbridge, I really wouldn't monkey with anything like that," he said. His speech sounded elaborate and self-conscious and he went on with an unnatural haste. "Oh, by the way, Charley."

"Yes, Father?" Charles said quickly.

"There's going to be a muster tomorrow afternoon," and he must have noticed the blank look on Charles's face. "A muster, a firemen's muster. The Pine Trees will be there and there will be eight hand tubs and two hundred dollars in cash prizes. Why don't you watch me make a spectacle of myself, Charley? It's Saturday." The tension in the room had eased. His father had tossed the paper on the floor. "They don't have firemen's musters in Kansas City, do they, Elbridge?"

"Exactly what is the purpose of a firemen's muster, Mr. Gray?" Elbridge asked him.

It often seemed to Charles that Elbridge knew nothing about anything except the composition of brass, but John Gray was very patient.

"The purpose of a muster, Elbridge," he said, "aside from social relaxation, is to see which of these antiquated fire engines can squirt the longest stream of water from its tank—an athletic contest, Elbridge. You should come with Dorothea and see us, and, Charley, I want you particularly."

"I don't know whether I can get away in time, Father," Charles said.

"Charley," his mother said, "if your father wants you to, of course you can."

Charles could not understand why that homely conversation should have depressed him or why its humdrum quality should have made it so indelible. It had been as dull and quiet as everything in Clyde, and yet, when he was in his room that night, the words kept running back and forth in his mind and details kept cropping up with the words. He was again shaking hands with Elbridge Sterne, listening to Elbridge's anxious conversation, and again his mother was darning the sock and again he saw her half-startled look. He saw his father folding and rolling the *Boston Evening Transcript*—oh, no, he was not following the transactions of the financial page—he was only searching for Notes and Queries.

The door of Charles's bedroom was closed but it could not shut out those thoughts and every object in the room helped to give them emphasis. The framed picture of Sam in his uniform, standing on his bureau, was a part of them, and so was the silver cup he had won at freshman track in college and so were the books he had purchased, standing in the mission bookcase that he had brought from Hanover. The casual volumes from Everyman's Library, his copy of *Lord Jim,* his books on economics, his Channing's *History of the United States,* his Shakespeare, his *Oxford Book of English Verse,* and even the volumes of accounting and salesmanship—all of them were a part of what he was thinking.

At least everything in his room was neat, not like his father's room. When he hung his coat on the hanger in the narrow closet beside his extra suit and his evening clothes, it was a relief to see that his black pumps and his other shoes were in a straight and even row and that his blue suit of pajamas and his dressing gown were hanging tidily above them covering the illustrated list of morning physical exercises tacked inside the closet door. The Bible his mother had given him and a volume of Emerson's *Essays* lay on the candle-stand beside his narrow spool bed. He could see all those objects suddenly as belonging to someone else and he could read the character of the person who owned them almost as though it had nothing to do with himself. It was a small, cold, narrow room, but at least it was not like his father's. When he thought of it afterwards, he knew it was a priggish room, an accurate reflection of early attitudes, but still it had shown something of which he was never ashamed. No bedroom of his was ever quite like it afterwards, never as simple, never as serene.

He had yet to buy T. S. Eliot's poems, and Adam from the Sistine Chapel was not yet hanging on the wall, and Pliny's doves in white marble sitting on the edge of their little yellow fountain were not yet on his bureau in front of Sam's picture, between two wood-backed military brushes. Jessica Lovell had not given them to him yet. There was no trace of Jessica in that room, no hint of lightness or humor, no sign at all of love.

7

When We Ran with the Old Machine

"Charley," Jessica said to him once, "it was all so funny, wasn't it? You being there, and me, when we neither of us wanted to be there at all"—they were talking, of course, about the firemen's muster and it always seemed curious that neither of them had wanted to go there at all—"and if it had been anywhere else we'd have both been different. Do you remember the fife-and-drum corps?"

Of course Charles remembered.

"And your father in that red shirt," Jessica said, "standing on top of the machine?"

Naturally Charles remembered his father, in his helmet and his red shirt with "Pine Tree" written on the front in white letters, in his blue trousers and his belt with its ornate brass buckle. For years Charles had been deeply embarrassed whenever his father had appeared in that make-believe fireman suit. To Jessica Lovell it was only another Currier and Ives print, an amusing rustic scene, while he was close enough to it to feel that his father's standing on the tub and giving orders had an indecorous, discordant quality. Jack Mason's father, for instance, would not have dreamed of being in the Pine Trees, but his father enjoyed the organization and persisted in speaking of it on unsuitable occasions.

"I don't see why Father likes it," Charles said.

"Because he has a good time," Jessica told him. "He was having a wonderful time."

Charles never could understand the release of being dressed in an absurd costume and of pretending, even briefly, that he was not himself.

"And we had a good time too," Jessica said. "We had a wonderful time."

Still it was an impossible sort of time. He had not drunk hard cider in the Stevens barn and yet he had behaved as though he had.

"Charley, why did you get into that wrestling match?"

"You know why," Charles said.

"I know, but tell me why."

"Because you wanted me to. You shouldn't have been there in that crowd."

"But I was," Jessica said. "It couldn't have happened anywhere else, could it? It was all—" but she did not finish what she was saying . . .

Luncheon that Saturday afternoon had consisted only of a little cold meat and cracked cocoa and his father ate it hurriedly. He might not have been elected to the Clyde Fund but he had been elected captain of the Pine Trees, in a very close election, with Wesley Adams, the undertaker, running against him. As John Gray ate his cold meat he kept glancing critically at Charles and finally he told Charles that he had better put on some older clothes, that his business suit might get wet. He was really saying in a nice way, Charles knew, that Charles would look out of place if he came there all dressed up and in a white collar.

His mother was not going to the muster. If John had to pretend he was a fireman, she often said, he could go to those things alone. She had to draw the line somewhere. When Charles started upstairs to change his clothes, he heard them discussing the time-worn subject.

"I know, Esther," he heard his father saying. "It's a weakness of mine and I appreciate your indulging me, but you miss a lot. It's always quite a sight."

"I suppose it is," his mother said, "if it's a sight to see tipsy men pretending they're boys, running around bellowing at each other, squirting water."

Charles was wearing his gray flannel trousers, his old sneakers and his old tweed coat when he and John Gray walked out of the front yard and down Spruce Street. It was all very well to tell himself that everyone condoned his father's eccentricity, but nothing could reconcile Charles to the way his father's whole manner changed whenever he wore that red shirt and helmet. They turned him into a River Streeter. His father's voice had already assumed a nasal tone and he walked with a slight swagger that reminded Charles of members of the American Legion gathering for the Decoration Day parade. His father was glancing anxiously at the clear sky to gauge the breeze as it blew off occasional yellowing leaves from the elm trees.

"The wind's certainly calming down," he said. Charles noticed that he said "calming" in a flat way that was more River Street than Spruce Street. "I don't want any downdraft blowing the spray sideways before it hits the paper."

On one occasion some years ago, his father said, when he was pumping with the Pine Trees, right out on the old training field where the tubs were going to pump today, a puff of wind caught the spray and though the Pine Trees had never pumped a longer stream, that puff blew it sideways and the Eureka tub from Salem beat them. It was a fluke, because the Eureka tub was never as good as the old Pine Tree. Its stroke was too short.

It was going to be a small muster this afternoon but the Eurekas would be there and the Excelsiors from Smith's Common, and the Nonpareils were bringing their machine down from north of Kittery. They were already at the training field, and so was the old Blairtown pumper. There would be eight machines, and they had better hurry because the Pine Trees always pulled the old machine themselves. They didn't depend on a truck like the Lions and they ended up in a run, with the bell going.

As his father walked he continued worrying about the weather and the wind, as he always did on muster days. He had been to the training field already to see where the stand for the tubs would be placed. He and Wesley Adams had selected the spots for the tall bamboo flagpoles. The elms on the edge of the training field made a tricky downdraft, a draft that you had to watch on those wind flags before you gave the boys at the brakes the signal to turn it on and let her go. They had watched the long strips of paper being laid in the roped-off enclosure on which the stream from the hose would fall. He hoped that the crowd would not get too near the paper. That summer they had lost to the Haviland Protectors at the July muster because, he suspected, Haviland backers spat upon the paper, thus making the furthest drops appear to have come from the Protectors' hose.

Then he discussed the strengths and weaknesses of the hand engine that the Pine Trees owned—the old Pine Tree tub. Charles knew she was a beautiful machine, made by Button in 1878. He knew, or at least he had been told, that the Button machines were better than the Borgs or the Lyles. The tub had a new coat of paint and a new pressure gauge and the ropes for pulling her had been stitched with clean white canvas. Everyone always recognized the Pine Tree tub right away at musters.

The Pine Tree firehouse was the same shed which had sheltered the machine when Clyde actually relied on volunteers and hand pumps to put out fires. It stood on the water side of River Street in a vacant, weedy lot, not far from the gas tank and the coal pocket and the mill. Behind it was a good view of the old wharves and warehouses of Clyde. It was a shabby building outside but the Pine Trees had fixed it inside into a pretty comfortable clubhouse. A "salamander" stove warmed up the shed nicely in winter and there were tables and benches for cards and checkers and a big sandbox. The most striking feature of the firehouse was the rows of buckets hung on pegs along the walls, the decorated fire buckets which pre-Revolutionary Clyde firemen had once kept handy in their houses, with the dates and names of their former owners painted on them. The old shed was an amazing survival, but Charles had always accepted its history automatically because Clyde was full of other survivals. He was only wondering why the Pine Trees still enjoyed being Pine Trees and persisted in being Pine Trees when their usefulness was over.

There was a big crowd waiting outside the firehouse, old Pine Trees and young Pine Trees drifting in and out through the open doors and eddying about the weedy lot. Mr. Elmer Swasey, who must have been over eighty, was standing with his helmet tilted back on his head and his white beard cascading over his red shirt. He had led a useless, unregenerate life, but he had run with the Pine Trees in his youth and he was still a Pine Tree. Mr. Wesley Adams was there too, in his red shirt, and so were the fathers of a lot of boys Charles had known in high school, town tradesmen and mill foremen, and many of his former schoolmates were there with them. There was Earl Wilkins. They had played football together on the high school team and Earl was now a helper for Mr. Wesley Adams. There were Johnny Leveroni and young Vincent Sullivan and Andrew Garvin, and any number of little boys ran yelling around the legs of their elders, and the Pine Tree fife-and-drum corps was already beginning to play "The Gang's All Here."

His father was an integrated part of the Pine Trees but Charles was an outsider who had come to look on and who had no real part in the ceremony.

"Hi, Earl," he said, trying to get in the spirit of it. "Hi, Johnny." And they all said, "Hi, Charley. How's it going, Charley?" but they all knew he was not one of them. He belonged on Spruce Street, not on River Street. Charles was an outsider but somehow, by some strange alchemy, his father had bridged the gap.

"All right," John Gray was calling. "Now wait a minute." The fife-and-drum corps had stopped and his voice had filled the space of silence. "We're going to roll her out in a minute. This is going to look right, by God. And don't forget what happened at Smith's Common." Charles did not know but all the Pine Trees did. "We don't want anybody winded before he pumps. Now we all know there's a barrel of hard cider down cellar in Stevens's barn and you get into the cellar by the back way. Now, if the Excelsiors or the Lions want it give it to 'em, but no one on the Pine Tree brakes gets it till it's over. All right, boys, bring her out."

The tub clattered out into the sunshine, an antiquated hand-pumping mechanism with its long pump bars, called brakes, its brass and its bright red wheels and its name painted on the center bar, *Pine Tree, Clyde*—a beautiful, shiny, obsolete thing. The fife-and-drum corps started playing "The

Gang's All Here" again and the procession moved down River Street. Heads appeared in the windows and the mill whistle blew.

The training field was conditioned to musters of firemen and others. It had been the training ground for the militia in the Revolutionary War. The company sent by Clyde to the Civil War had performed its first drill there. For a hundred and fifty years, the elms on the edge of the field had cast their shadows over similar gatherings and over the South End ball games. Some of Clyde's oldest houses bordered the field, making a Colonial group not noticed by anyone in Clyde but eliciting the enthusiasm of strangers, who often turned their cars off the main highway and down Training Street to see their low sloping roofs and small-paned windows. Those windows so often shattered by baseballs now looked upon the crowded green and the roped-off area over which the hoses would play and the flag-draped booths from which chances were sold on useful articles, or which dispensed balloons, hot dogs, popcorn and tonic. It was always tonic, not soft drinks, in Clyde, but there was also a hint in the actions of certain citizens that something stronger was available.

The crowd had lined Training Street and covered the field as the hand tubs marched past, but Charles had dropped from the procession as soon as the Pine Trees reached Training Street and finally he found himself, when the pumping contest started, by the old tubs at the far end of the field. This was the more disorderly end where the pumping teams were congregating to await their turns on the tub stand, far back from the hose nozzle and the paper where most of the crowd had gathered. This was the spot where there was always quiet drinking and where the fife-and-drum corps played to encourage the pumpers and where individuals performed small, competitive feats of strength. The Excelsior machine was on the stand; the Excelsiors had lined the pump bars and their captain stood holding a handkerchief in his upraised hand, watching the wind flag and waiting for his assistant to tell him the pressure. As Charles watched the captain's arm drop, the pumpers moved into unified action, creakingly and slowly, and the fifes and drums began playing "Stars and Stripes Forever." It was hard for the captain to make himself heard above the squealing of the fifes.

At this moment Charles heard a girl somewhere behind him humming "Stars and Stripes Forever." Established custom made it unusual for many girls, or at least many nice girls, to be at that corner of the field, where it was necessary to shout crude Anglo-Saxon exhortations as the pumpers increased the beat.

"Come on, you bastards," the pump captain called.

At this exact moment Charles turned to see who the girl behind him was and he was very much surprised to find it was Jessica Lovell.

"Hello," she said. "I was wondering when you'd speak to me."

She was as tall as he was. She was dressed in a gray tweed suit tailored so that it seemed to add to her height. A tight red felt hat was pushed over her soft black hair and she was smiling at him, not in the cool way that she had smiled on other occasions when she had met him, but as though she were glad to see him.

"Oh, hello," Charles said. "They're really working now."

He could not think of anything else to say. Though he had always thought of her as Jessica Lovell, he could not very well call her Jessica and yet it would have sounded silly to call her Miss Lovell. "The Excelsior has a good pump team, at least that's what they say."

"I suppose you know all about this," she said. "Your father's in the Pine Trees, isn't he?"

It was not surprising she should have known, since everyone in Clyde knew his father.

"Yes," he said, "my father's crazy about the Pine Trees."

"Well, it must be fun," she said.

"He thinks it is," Charles answered, and then there was silence and it was just as though they had not spoken at all. He was thinking that she should not have been in that corner of the field, and then it occurred to him that she did not have to bother. Everyone knew who she was. She was Jessica Lovell.

"You haven't seen a queer sort of a man around, have you?" she asked.

Charles laughed and looked at the crowd. The Excelsiors were mopping their brows and panting after their first try.

"There are lots of them around here."

"But not like this one." Her voice had a confidential note, as though they were old friends. "He's been studying the head-hunters from Borneo. He was at the house for lunch. He's here to make a survey."

The captain of the Excelsiors was exhorting his pumpers and the crowd was helping.

"What sort of a survey?" Charles asked.

She gave her head a quick, impatient shake.

"Why, I don't know," she said. "Some sort of social survey. He wanted to see this thing and now he's gone away and left me."

"Do you want me to help you find him?" Charles asked.

"No," she said. "I'd rather stay here and let him find us, that is if it's all the same to you, Charley."

He was startled when she called him by his first name, but then nearly everyone in Clyde referred to him as Charley Gray.

"What are they going to do now?" she asked.

"They're going to pump again," he said. "They have three tries."

"It's nice to be here with an expert," she said. "Let's go over there and listen to the music."

The music had stopped. The fifes and drums had gathered in a sunny spot on the edge of the road opposite the Stevens barn.

"I wouldn't go over there," Charles said. There was always a tough crowd around the Stevens barn, but then everyone knew she was Jessica Lovell. She was moving over toward the tough crowd before she answered.

"Come on," she said. "I've never been to one of these things before."

Obviously no one would as much as whistle at her. It was only a question of convention and he was surprised that she did not realize it. Of course, she could join the fifes and drums and all the visiting firemen lounging on the edge of the road if she wanted, but she might have noticed that there were no other girls there. She should have understood that being there would cramp everyone's style.

Loud voices trailed off into whispers, the fife-and-drum corps, who had been to the Stevens barn cellar, gazed at both of them in a way that made Charles shift from one foot to another, but the lull did not last, because they had all been drinking cider. As soon as they saw that Jessica had not made a mistake and that she enjoyed being there, the red-shirted firemen and all the hangers-on reminded Charles of small boys showing off before a friendly adult. They were stealing timid glances at her, and Charles could only smile, like a guide who was taking a tourist to a corner of some foreign carnival.

"Aren't they going to play again?" Jessica asked.

Of course, the fifes and drums heard her and they were delighted to show how well they could play. They began playing "School days, school days, dear old golden rule days," and then with hardly a pause they began playing "Marching Through Georgia." Someone touched a cigarette to a balloon and it exploded in a very humorous way.

"You see, they've all been at the hard cider," Charles said.

"What hard cider?"

"In the barn over there. In the barn cellar."

In the warmth of the cider and group companionship, he and Jessica were beginning to be forgotten. There was a tightening circle around the fifes and drums. A heavy, florid young man, with short yellow hair that looked as if it had been cut by the old bowl method, shoved inside the circle. Someone tripped him and he fell down and it was just the thing that everybody needed to make the gathering a success. The young man took off his frayed coat sweater and began asking who had done it, while the fifes and drums played "School Days" again and a chorus began bellowing, "You wrote on my slate, I love you, Joe, when we were a couple of kids."

"Who is he?" Jessica Lovell asked. She had to lean close to him before he could hear her. "The one who got tripped up."

"He's a North Ender," Charles answered. There were always jokes about the unregenerate qualities of North Enders. It seemed unnecessary to tell her that he was Hughie Willis and that almost every Saturday Hughie Willis got into trouble.

A Smith's Common fireman pushed Hughie and one thing led to another. They were not fighting, they were wrestling. They were rolling over and over on the grass, and when the fireman's shoulders touched the ground everyone was delighted that Hughie had got the Smith's Common fireman down.

"Who else wants a try?" Hughie shouted. "Where the hell are all the wrasslers?"

"He's pretty good, isn't he?" Charles said, and he had some childish desire to impress Jessica Lovell. "I'd like to take him on myself."

He could certainly have had no serious intention of doing it. He could only have meant to explain to Jessica that he had gone out for wrestling at Dartmouth.

"Why don't you?" Jessica Lovell asked.

"Because it would be silly," he said.

"Then why did you say it?"

"I just said it," he answered.

"Oh," Jessica said, "you just said it."

He looked straight at her and she looked back, and she was telling him without words that she knew he would not do it.

"I don't suppose you think I would," he said.

"No," she answered, "of course you wouldn't."

"All right," he said. "All right."

So many things were always in a balance and so often before you knew it, it was too late to stop. When he was in the open space he wished to heaven it were not too late, but while he was wishing he was taking off his coat.

"What do you know?" somebody was saying. "It's Charley Gray"—and they were already taking sides, yelling for him and for Hughie Willis. He wished he were not there, but there was no time for wishing. Hughie was reaching for him as he dropped his coat. They were swaying together, holding each other's arms, when Hughie lunged for the back of his neck and Charles sprang forward into the old cross-buttock hold and it was good luck and nothing else that Hughie was off balance. It was simply the application of force at just the right moment that made Hughie fall. It was over so quickly that Charles was not out of breath. He was getting into his coat before Hughie could start to say it was not fair, but the Pine Trees were going to pump and no one was interested in wrestling any longer. The crowd was moving back to the hand tubs when he reached Jessica Lovell and by then reaction was setting in.

"Well," he said, "do you want to watch the Pine Trees?"

"Why, yes," she said, "I'd love to. Your tie's all on one side."

"Oh," Charles said. "Thanks. I hadn't noticed."

"I don't know why we've hardly ever seen each other before," she said. "It's queer, isn't it?" And it did seem queer, as they walked across the grass.

"Would you like some cold root beer?" Charles asked.

"No. Would you?"

"Not very much," and they both laughed.

"Oh," she said, "that's your father, isn't it, on top of the machine?"—and Charles saw his father, holding up a white handkerchief.

"Yes," Charles said, "that's Father."

"It's awfully funny," she said.

"What is?" Charles asked.

"Oh, everything," she said. "Oh dear, here he comes."

"Who?" Charles asked.

"That man." An angular-looking stranger was coming toward them.

"Jessica," he said quickly, "can I come to see you sometime?"

Jessica began to laugh.

"What are you laughing at?" he asked.

"It sounds so funny," she said. "Wait a minute. Can you drive a car?"

"No," Charles said. "We haven't got a car."

"Well, I can," she said. "We'll go driving tomorrow. Come around at three o'clock. Oh, hello, Mr. Bryant. What happened to you?"

Jessica Lovell was speaking to the stranger, an untidily dressed man in his middle thirties, with a bony face and deep-set eyes.

"This is Mr. Gray," Jessica was saying, "Mr. Bryant."

It seemed to Charles that Mr. Bryant looked like a teacher or a college professor. He had the stooping posture and the studious look, but his face was tanned and something in his manner was not entirely like that of a professor. It was sharper and more inquisitive.

"I'm glad to meet you, Mr. Gray," he said, and his speech reminded Charles of Elbridge Sterne's. "Do you live here in Clyde?"

"Yes," Charles said, "I live here."

"Well, that's fine," Mr. Bryant said. "Let me see now, you must be one of the Grays on Spruce Street."

"Yes," Charles said, "we live on Spruce Street."

"I'm still trying to orient myself," Mr. Bryant said. "It's a little hard to get the general structure straight. I suppose Miss Lovell's been telling you about me."

"Why, no," Charles said, "not much."

"Well, you see we're considering doing a little job on this town," Mr. Bryant said. "My God, it's a wonderful town, a beautiful, static, organized community."

Charles looked questioningly at Jessica Lovell. He could not understand what Mr. Bryant meant and he wondered if she did.

"Mr. Bryant is doing a survey," Jessica said. "I told you. Some sort of a social survey, and he's just back from Borneo."

"That's right," Mr. Bryant said, "just back from a call on the head-hunters."

The fifes and drums began to play again and the Pine Trees were putting their backs in it to beat the Eurekas. "Hail, Hail, the Gang's All Here," the fifes and drums were playing.

"What are they like?" Charles asked.

"What are they like?" Mr. Bryant said. "They're people, just like you and me. All men are basically alike. What's your first name, Mr. Gray?"

"It's Charles," Jessica told him. "Charley Gray."

"Well, why don't we all get on a first-name basis?" Mr. Bryant asked. "I'm Malcolm, and you're Charley and Jessica. God, this is a wonderful town."

"Charley and Jessica are awfully glad you like it," Jessica said. "Aren't we, Charley?"

"And, my God, this thing"—Malcolm Bryant waved his arm in a gesture that embraced the training field—"this beautiful, tribal ritual. It's like the

Maori war dance. I'm just beginning to get it straight. It doesn't include the whole tribe, does it?"

"Jessica and Charley don't know what you're talking about," Jessica said.

"I mean it's a folk custom," Malcolm Bryant said. "Of course, you think of it as a thing called a firemen's muster, but obviously, deep down inside, it's the survival of a tribal rite. But the whole community isn't in it, not all the classes. I mean your father wouldn't be in it, Jessica. It's more of a folk custom."

"Charles's father is," Jessica said. "He's right up there now on the machine."

"My God." Mr. Bryant turned around. The Pine Trees were pumping again. "That's interesting. Now let me get this straight. You're a college man, aren't you, Charley?"

"How did you know?" Charles asked.

"Because it's my business to know social groups." Malcolm Bryant rubbed his hands together. "Look at Jessica. She has Smith written all over her."

"Vassar," Jessica said, "not Smith."

"Is your father a college man, Charley?"

"He went to Harvard for a while," Charles said.

"And there he is up there," Malcolm Bryant said. "Now, that's very interesting. Up there and out of his group. It's going to take me quite a while to get this structure straight."

"It's four o'clock," Jessica said. "I'd better be going home. Are you coming back to the house, Mr. Bryant?"

"Well, if it's just the same to you," Malcolm Bryant said, "I'd better stay right here. Somebody says there's going to be a raffling off and I'm just beginning to get a picture of the cliques. You don't mind, do you, Jessica?"

"No," Jessica said, "I don't mind. Charley can take me home. He understands the cliques."

"My God," Malcolm Bryant said, "this is a wonderful town, and I certainly want to meet your father, Charley."

"Well, have a good time," Jessica said. "These head-hunters are going home. It's time to lock up the virgins. Come on, Charley."

8

Not That I'm Not Very Glad You Found Him

It was four and Charles had left the Pine Tree clubhouse at one o'clock but the gap of time seemed much greater when Jessica Lovell and he turned off Training Street to Johnson Street. They had left the hose players and the balloons and the sounds of the crowd on the training field, but Charles Gray had left more than this behind him. He had left a part of his gaucheness and shyness and some of the bewilderments of youth. He had stepped across a boundary into another land. He had reached one of those turning points, those unperceived corners, which everyone rounds at some time or other without knowing that there has been a corner—but he was not conscious of any of this. His thoughts were moving to that refrain of Malcolm Bryant's. By God, it was a wonderful town.

All of Johnson Street looked on them kindly as he and Jessica Lovell walked along it. No earlier memories of the sunsets across the river, gilding Clyde's white church spires, no memories of the waves on the beach by the river mouth, could compare with his present receptiveness. The chilly autumn air and the clear northern sunlight and the color of the turning leaves gave all of Johnson Street a friendly brilliance, and the Federalist façades of its houses behind their delicate white fences were no longer austere or untouchable. He was a part owner of all of Clyde that afternoon, of Johnson Street and the side streets, of the courthouse and the elms and maples, of Dock Street with its shops, of River Street by the river. He was like his father, able to move anywhere and to understand anyone in Clyde. By God, it was a wonderful town.

Jessica was talking about Malcolm Bryant. He had just appeared in the house one day with a letter from someone. He was working for some kind of foundation, like the Rockefeller or the Carnegie. Something, she could not tell what, had made her father like him. It must have been because he liked foundations and societies. Then when he had heard that Malcolm Bryant was doing a survey which might be published in some sort of book, he seemed to feel that Malcolm Bryant was his personal responsibility.

"You see," Jessica said, "Father feels he's the world's greatest living authority on Clyde."

"My father's an authority, too," Charles told her.

"Does he keep going on about it?" Jessica asked.

Yes, Charles said, he kept going on about it.

"Well, you and I don't have to, do we?" Jessica said.

They were at an age, of course, when they could condone kindly the errors of their elders. She was wondering what it was that made people in Clyde, especially as they got older, talk more and more about the place, as though it were the most remarkable town in the world. As Jessica wondered, she would occasionally turn her head toward him, giving him appraising little glances as though she hoped that he agreed with her. She was wondering whether he had noticed that living in Clyde made people different from other people. Whenever she was back from Westover or later from Vassar College, she was always very conscious of this. She always thought that people in Clyde were like bees in a beehive, concentrated on their own errands without knowing there were any other beehives. She wondered if Charles knew what she meant, and strangely enough Charles had never thought that anyone else had been bothered by those ideas, but then he had been away himself a good deal. She knew he had been, Jessica was saying. He wasn't all tied up, well, by invisible strings. He did not have any of the prejudices or any of the queer little, well, hesitations. Had he ever noticed that living in Clyde was like walking through spiderwebs without any spiders? There were always those invisible strings, getting around you, brushing across your face—and strangely enough Charles knew exactly what she meant.

There was a boy, she said, who knew Charles and who came to call on her sometimes and he was always all covered with spiderwebs. He never could be natural for a single minute and he made her feel, too, all spiderwebby. Charles knew whom she meant. His name was Jackie Mason. At least she always called him Jackie to herself.

"Now he's always worried," Jessica said, "because his grandfather was a druggist. That's one of his spiderwebs." If he had not kept alluding to it, she would not have given it a thought but now it worried her, too. "I'm sure," she said, "he reads the book of etiquette."

He wanted to do the right thing, Charles told her. It was wonderful that she did not put him in the same category with Jackie but with her on an emancipated plane.

"People ought to do the right things naturally," she said, "without reading them in books."

And this, too, was what he had often thought.

She could see how Clyde must look to an outsider, she said, because she was partly an outsider herself, and so was he, since they had both been away to college. She only hoped that Malcolm Bryant did not think that she and Charles were like the rest of the natives—and she was afraid he did.

"Did you notice the way he looked at us?" she asked. "It made me feel as though you and I were on a microscopic slide."

Charles laughed, and then they both were laughing. He was sure that he was not like Jackie Mason.

"I suppose there's something eccentric about every family," she said. "I suppose"—she hesitated and then looked at him as though she were telling him a secret—"I suppose some people think Father's a little eccentric."

"Well," Charles said, "so's mine, I guess."

He had never dreamed of saying such a thing to anyone before, but Jessica Lovell's mind was on her father—not his father.

"Of course," she was saying, "Father's the dearest person in the world. I love him because he's so shy."

Charles had never met Mr. Lovell, except long ago at the Historical Society, but he had seen him often enough, walking down Dock Street to the bank or to the post office. He had never struck Charles as being shy. Jessica must have been preparing him for an inevitable meeting, but he was not concerned with it then.

"Do you know what I think sometimes?" Jessica was saying. "When anyone comes to see me, I think Father's a little jealous, not that he really knows he is."

Charles had been so absorbed by the conversation that the dwellings on Johnson Street had passed by him in a pleasant blur—until he saw the pineapples on the wooden fence before the Lovells' house and the border of autumn chrysanthemums. The gate stood open and a brick path lay before them, leading to the Corinthian portico of the Lovells' front door, and he saw old Mr. Fogarty slowly and rheumatically raking leaves on the front lawn.

"Well," he said, "I'll come around tomorrow if you haven't got anything better to do."

"Aren't you coming in now?" she asked.

"I guess I'd better not," Charles said. "It's getting pretty late."

"Why, it isn't late at all. It's just time for tea."

He heard the leaves scrape noisily together under Mr. Fogarty's rake.

"I look pretty shabby," he said, "to go anywhere for tea." As a matter of fact, those old clothes of his were exactly the ones he should have worn, because his tweed coat and baggy flannel trousers showed that he did not consider calling on the Lovells a great occasion.

When they were in the hall, Jessica closed the front door noisily behind her and it made a cheerful, booming sound that echoed along the length of the hall and up the broad, airy staircase. She had pulled off her red felt hat and tossed it on a Chippendale chair and now she stood before the dusky glass of a great gold hall mirror, giving her head a quick impatient shake and pushing her soft wavy dark hair from her forehead. He could see his own reflection as he stood behind her and their glances met in the dark glass.

"We look like the portraits, don't we?" she said. "That's the trouble with this mirror."

He saw two portraits in the hall, dimly lighted by the arched window at the head of the staircase and by the fanlights above the front and back hall doors. It was true. The gold frame of the mirror was almost like the portraits' frames and for a moment they were both as still as portraits before he followed her down the hall.

Jessica was leading him, as Charles learned later, to what the Lovells called the wallpaper room. "This room," he read later in one of the many architectural accounts of Clyde, "is a triumph of Federalist interior. The windows set in deep paneled reveals are fitted prettily with mahogany window seats. The dado is a wide, clear board of pine. The baseboard is high, contrasting nicely with the door architraves, descending plinthless to the floor. It is as though the room were consciously built to house its greatest treasure, a magnificent wallpaper from France, showing, through the eyes of a French artist, a romantic interpretation of European merchants visiting a Chinese waterfront. The ships, the pagodas, the pavilions, blend most happily with the mantel and the few pieces of Chinese Chippendale which fit in the room as if they, too, were built for it." Charles read this later but he was only conscious then of the spaciousness the paper gave the room and of the dancing fire beneath the Chippendale mantel and of Jessica's aunt, Miss Lovell, who looked like his own Aunt Jane as she sat on a Hepplewhite sofa behind a low mahogany tea table, working on a panel of embroidery.

"This is Charley Gray," Jessica said. "I've brought him in to tea. You know Charley Gray, don't you, Aunt Georgianna?"

Miss Lovell inserted her needle in her embroidery and laid it down beside her and looked up at Charles. Her eyes, which were dark like Jessica's, gave her thin, pale face an expression of suspicious watchfulness.

"I don't know Charles," she said, "but of course I know all about him," and she held out her hand.

"Aunt Georgianna knows about everybody," Jessica said.

"Ring the bell, Jessica," Miss Lovell told her. "It's time for tea. You look as though you'd been walking."

"Well, not exactly walking," Jessica said. "We were at the firemen's muster."

"Oh, yes," Miss Lovell said. "What became of Mr. Bryant, Jessica? Did you get tired of him?"

"No," Jessica said, "he got tired of me. He's down there still."

"I'm sure I'd have been tired of him if I'd been you," Miss Lovell said. "His voice goes right through my ears. How is your Aunt Jane, Charles? Did I ever tell you, Jessica, that Jane and I went to the academy together? We used to call her Lady Jane Gray."

"Aunt Jane's pretty well, thank you," Charles said.

"All we can be at our age is pretty well," Miss Lovell said. "Jessica, I do wish you'd do something to your hair so it doesn't blow."

The tea on a silver tray was being carried in by Mrs. Daniel Martin, an old friend of Mary Callahan's, whom Charles had often seen in his own aunt's kitchen, but Mrs. Martin looked unfamiliar to him now in a black dress and a white apron. In another day everyone on Johnson Street would know who had been to the Lovells' that afternoon.

"Hannah," Miss Lovell said to Mrs. Martin, "will you please tell Mr. Lovell that tea is ready? How do you like your tea, Charles?"

"Oh," Charles said, "why any way at all, thank you, Miss Lovell."

Charles heard a footstep behind him and he turned to see Mr. Lovell, holding a folded newspaper.

"Well, well," Mr. Lovell said, "I didn't know we were going to have company."

"You know Charley Gray, don't you, Father?" Jessica asked him.

"Of course I know Charley Gray, Jessie," Mr. Lovell said, "or *of* Charley Gray. Where on earth did you find him, Jessie? Not that I'm not very glad you found him."

Then Jessica was explaining again that she had found him at the firemen's muster.

"This is quite a coincidence," Mr. Lovell said. "Only a day or two ago I heard Francis Stanley say that you are at Wright-Sherwin. Thank you, Georgianna," and he took his cup of tea.

Charles could not see why Jessica had said that her father was shy. He looked very much as he had there at the Historical Society. His voice had the same high but agreeably resonant ring. He had the same careless way of standing, even when he held his teacup. The lines in his face were deeper and his hair was grayer, but that was all. He did not look shy at all, as he stood in the wallpaper room, raising his teacup to his thin, straight lips and glancing at Charles over the edge of it.

"That was not a happy remark of mine when I asked where Jessica found you," he said. "I'm delighted to have a Gray in the house. Now let's see. You went to Dartmouth, didn't you? How's your father, Charles?"

"He's out on the training field with the Pine Trees," Charles told him.

"When we were boys he was always running to fires. Jessica, what became of your other friend?"

And Jessica told again where Malcolm Bryant was.

"Well, he'll be back for supper, won't he?" Mr. Lovell said. "We always call it supper in Clyde, don't we, Charles? But Jessie likes to call it dinner."

"Charley," Jessica said, "have you ever seen the garden?"

Charles shook his head. He said he had never seen the garden but he would like to see it.

"What do you want to show him the garden for?" Mr. Lovell said. "It's October."

"There's still the boxwood," Jessica said, "and the chrysanthemums."

"Well," Mr. Lovell said. "Well. I'll say good-by to you now, Charles, in case I don't see you again, and give your father my regards."

The wallpaper room was silent as Charles and Jessica walked down the hall together but before they reached the back hall door Charles heard Mr. Lovell's voice.

"Well," Mr. Lovell was saying. "Well."

"Come on, Charley," Jessica said quickly, and they stepped outside onto a long path bordered with boxwood. The formal garden of the Lovells so often described in Garden Club lectures lay before them, rising gradually to the top of a gentle slope, with its box borders casting long shadows across the gravel paths in the setting sun.

"You know," Jessica said, "I really think Father likes you."

"I don't see why you think so," Charles told her.

"Because he talked so much," Jessica said, "and you didn't do anything wrong."

He wondered exactly what she meant. They were following the path up to a summerhouse on top of the rise, past the terraced flower beds where everything was cut down ready for the winter. At any rate, nothing in the Lovell house had made him uneasy and perhaps that was what she had meant when she said he had done nothing wrong. Perhaps she had meant that he had been neither impressed nor disturbed by her aunt or father and that they had not seemed to him in any way extraordinary. He was even thinking that there was nothing so extraordinary about Jessica, either. He could still see her as she was, before whatever drew them together became too strong for him to see her in any true perspective. She was not strikingly beautiful. She was too tall and her chin and nose were both a little too long and her eyebrows were too black and heavy, but those defects were vanishing already as she walked beside him up the path. The open fire had made her cheeks glow and her eyes were bright and her lips, which were rather like her father's, were relaxed. Once they reached the summerhouse, it was cool and almost chilly in the shadows.

"Well," she said, "there's the garden."

They stood leaning on the summerhouse railing, gazing at the garden, which had been laid out by a French *émigré* more than a century before, and back at the house with its high-arched windows and its balustrade and cupola.

"You can see the harbor from the cupola," she said, and then she said it was strange to think of staying at home with no more college and nothing to do but just be there.

"I don't know what I'm going to do," she said, and Charles was telling her that there were all sorts of things to do in Clyde.

"Well," she said, "I'm awfully glad you think so." She had been moving her fingers idly, making little patterns on the summerhouse railing.

"Oh dear, here he comes. God, this is a wonderful town." Malcolm Bryant was coming toward them up the path.

"Jessica," Charles said, "you won't forget about tomorrow, will you?"

"No," she said, "of course I won't," and her hand touched his. "Good-by, Charley."

9

All the World's a Stage

—SHAKESPEARE

Charles knew there would be talk, because gossip always eddied through Clyde like smoke from the burning piles of autumn leaves, and it also usually assumed fantastic shapes. It was only to be expected that everyone would know by Monday of his encounter with Hughie Willis, but instead of looking on it critically people seemed in general to approve of his action. His father, when he mentioned it, appeared to be amused and only said that he must have had quite a time that afternoon at the muster. His mother, of course, was not amused. She had heard, both from Mrs. Mason and from Mrs. Gow, that Charles had got into a fight with a North Ender, and she could not understand why Charles had done such a thing, and it did no good to tell her and Dorothea that it was not a fight, because they could not understand the difference. Charles's main fear had been that someone would say that he and Hughie Willis had been fighting over Jessica, but he concluded that this was absurd.

As a matter of fact, his encounter with Hughie Willis did him no harm at all. Groups of his old school friends began calling to him in Dock Square with a new sort of familiarity. In fact there was a warmth about everything which made him imagine that people were saying that Charley Gray was not stuck-up because he had been to college. He had taken off his coat and pitched right into Hughie Willis. At Wright-Sherwin on Monday morning, it seemed to him that the girls in the accounting department smiled at him more brightly and nobody there appeared to disapprove, except possibly Mr. Howell who told him that it was Monday morning and time for fun was over, but even Mr. Howell was interested.

"That Willis was always a bad boy," Mr. Howell said. "When he was a kid, he was always putting cannon crackers in my hedge."

It even seemed to Charles that Mr. Stanley looked at him in a different way, when Charles met him in the hall.

"Good morning, Charley," Mr. Stanley said. "How are you feeling this morning?" Mr. Stanley had never asked him before how he was feeling and it seemed to Charles that Mr. Stanley was examining his face for possible contusions—but even Mr. Stanley's manner was not disapproving.

Of course, Jackie Mason knew all about it. All morning Jack kept looking at him across the room, trying to catch his eye, and when they met at the water cooler around eleven o'clock Jackie immediately brought up the subject.

"Charley, you ought not to do that sort of thing," he said.

"What sort of thing?" Charles asked.

"You know as well as I do, Charley, that someone always sees what you do around here—and wasn't it true that Jessica Lovell was there?" Jack Mason looked worried and his anxiety was friendly. "What I mean, Charley, is that a girl like Jessica Lovell won't forget a thing like that. It simply means she'll never have anything to do with you. What are you laughing at?"

"She never had anything to do with me anyway," Charles said.

"But she might have," Jack said. "She's going to be here all the time now and you've simply lost your chance of ever seeing anything of Jessica Lovell."

Those remarks of Jack Mason's came as a great relief because they showed that perhaps after all everyone in Clyde did not know everything immediately, but someone would have seen Jessica's new Dodge phaeton, with its top down, as it crossed the intersection of Dock and Johnson streets on Sunday afternoon. There was no way of escaping facts in Clyde, and, indeed, he did not care much what anyone would say. He only felt concerned that the offices at Wright-Sherwin where he was earning his twenty-five dollars a week already seemed smaller since the firemen's muster and he was already beginning to realize that it would take years for him to get anywhere in Wright-Sherwin—years and years.

Before long it began to be recognized, of course, that he was seeing a good deal of Jessica Lovell, but on the whole it was an acceptable fact. The Grays did not live on Johnson Street as the Thomases or the Stanleys did, but his father was the son of old Judge Gray and had married Dr. Marchby's daughter and so it was not markedly unusual for Charles Gray to go around with Jessica Lovell.

"Going around" was the expression which was used in Clyde when a boy and girl saw a good deal of each other. It was not the same as the more vulgar expression "going with" or "keeping company" which was employed when speaking of River Street couples and which had a more definite connotation. It was not even the same as saying that Charles was "attentive" to Jessica Lovell, which was more serious. His relationship in those months might have been better expressed as one of being "seen around" with Jessica Lovell, which was not even quite as strong as "going around" with her.

Since Jessica was fourteen she had spent her summers in Maine and had been away to school at Westover and then at Vassar College, so that now she was really back in Clyde for the first time in years, and Mr. Lovell had told several people that he wanted very much to have Jessica "show herself" in Clyde. It was exactly, she told Charles once, as though her father wanted her to go trotting up and down Johnson Street every afternoon, but of course he really meant that she should take part in Clyde activities, such as attending the Harvest Supper at the Boat Club and the Boat Club monthly dance and Pound Day at the Episcopal Church.

Her father had also told her that he did not want her to act as though she were just at home poised for flight to somewhere else. He wanted Jessica to show herself, and if she had to show herself obviously she had to be seen. She was seen with Charles but she was also seen with Hewitt Thomas, when Hewitt was not busy somewhere else. She was occasionally seen with Lester Gow, who was studying at the Harvard Law School, and now and then with Jackie Mason. She was even seen once or twice with Melville Meader, but if Mr. Lovell discouraged this everyone could understand why. The Meader boys were nice boys but Mr. Meader's father had been in the grocery business and Mr. Meader, though he was in real estate, often worked, himself, with the plumbers and carpenters, improving the buildings he owned. Besides, Jessica Lovell also had young men from Boston as guests sometimes for the week end. Thus if she was seen with Charles it did not mean that they were going around together.

When Jessica joined the Clyde Players that winter, it was natural for Charles to take her home because the other members of the theater group were married, except Jackie Mason who was the property man and who had to stay after the others. There was no reason for anyone to know that Charles had joined the Clyde Players only because Jessica had asked him to. Everyone believed that Charles enjoyed amateur theatricals.

It must have been an evening early in December when Jessica called Charles up, something which she did very seldom in those days. His Aunt Jane had been ill for two weeks with the grippe and his mother had gone to Gow Street to see how she was doing. When the telephone in the hall rang, his father was reading Boswell by the fire and Dorothea and Elbridge Sterne were playing backgammon and Charles was looking over a catalogue of surveying instruments which he had brought home from the office. Everyone stopped to count since it was a party line.

"Go and answer it, Charley," Dorothea said.

"It will only be for you," Charles told her. "It always is."

"I don't know why it should be," Dorothea said, "at this time of night."

The telephone was under the stairs in front of a line of coat hooks and it was necessary to bend one's head when one took the receiver off the hook.

"Is that you, Charley?" It was Jessica's voice. "You haven't gone to bed yet, have you?"

"Why, no," Charley answered. "It's only nine o'clock," and he heard Jessica laugh.

"Everybody's gone here except Father, and he's asleep in the library. Charley, would you mind coming over for a few minutes? I won't keep you any time at all."

It was only a step to Johnson Street. It was the most natural thing in the world, he was telling himself, for Jessica suddenly to ask him to come to see her at nine o'clock. He only thought of it as peculiar when he came back into the parlor with his overcoat to say he was going out.

"But why are you going out?" Dorothea asked. "Who called you up? Was it Jackie Mason?"

"It was Jessica Lovell," Charles said. "She just wants me to come over for a few minutes."

"Now?" Dorothea said. "At nine o'clock? I didn't know that you knew Jessica Lovell as well as that."

"I don't see why it shows that I know her very well," he answered.

"Oh, doesn't it?" Dorothea said, and she and Elbridge smiled at each other and his father looked up from Boswell's *Life of Johnson.*

"Now that I think of it," he said, "Jessica has been gracious to me lately. She stopped me in the street and asked me about fire engines. Her looks have improved, too. Her chin is still a little long and her eyebrows are too heavy, but she's improved."

When Charles walked up Spruce Street, the clear coldness of the December night air reminded him of new dark ice on a pond, just frozen thick enough to bear one's weight. His pulses danced with a strange elation, not because Jessica Lovell had called him up, certainly not because of that, but because of the beauty of the evening and the nearness of the stars. He seemed to have Clyde entirely to himself. The house lights were already going out on Spruce Street. It was absurd, he was thinking, for Dorothea to have made any comments when Jessica had called him up. It only showed that he and Jessica Lovell were not bowed down by small stupidities.

Jessica must have been waiting for him because she opened the front door herself and his idea that it was natural to be dropping in there at nine o'clock was contradicted by the soft tones of her voice and by the gentle way she closed the door.

"We'll have to sit in the wallpaper room," she said, as Charles was taking off his overcoat. "The library's the only comfortable place but Father's asleep in it. There's a little room upstairs—" She sighed. Of course they could not go to a little room upstairs. "We'll have to sit and look at the Chinese junks."

She asked Charles to put a new log on the dying embers of the fire and then she curled up on a corner of the Hepplewhite sofa. She was wearing a very simple, purplish woolen dress that fell just below her knees. She gave it a careless pull over her silk stockings and then she pushed her dark hair away from her forehead with both hands. His father may have been right in his remarks about Jessica. Her eyebrows were too heavy and her chin was too long and so were her legs, but she looked very well in the wall-paper room. She had none of the self-consciousness of other girls he knew, no fear that her hair looked untidy and she made no fluttering efforts to conceal her knees.

"Charley," she began, "the most awful thing has happened. I've got to join the Clyde Players. Father says I have to," and she let her hands drop helplessly on her lap.

"Oh," Charles said, "has Mrs. Smythe Leigh been to see you?"

"She just went away," Jessica said. "Who is she, Charley?"

It showed how little Jessica really knew about Clyde that she had never heard anything about Mrs. Smythe Leigh.

"She's pretty energetic," Charles told her. "She likes art and she's one of those people who like to run things."

"Charley, give me a cigarette," and she pointed to a box on the table. "Light it for me, will you?" He leaned close to her as he lighted her cigarette, and she pointed at the table where the cigarette box had stood. "Look at that thing, Charley, look at it."

"What thing?" Charles asked.

"That thing," she repeated. "That play. Tell me, how did she ever find it, Charley?"

She was pointing to a small volume covered with yellow paper and Charles picked it up. It was entitled *Lord Bottomly Decides, a Farce-Comedy*.

"Did she leave it here?" Charles asked.

"Of course she left it here," Jessica said.

"Well," Charles said, "it's just one of her ideas," and then he told Jessica about Mrs. Smythe Leigh.

Mrs. Smythe Leigh had come to Clyde about ten years before and she lived on Gow Street and was very active in women's organizations. Mrs. Smythe Leigh—she did not like being called plain Mrs. Leigh—had organized the Women's Club pageant in 1920 and she coached in dramatics at the high school and she sometimes even hinted that she had been on the stage herself. She had also organized the Clyde Players, and there were a number of people who liked that sort of thing. Dr. Bush, who was the osteopath, liked it, and so did Mr. and Mrs. Knowles, and there were always a few people who liked to paint scenery. It was not strange at all that Mrs. Smythe Leigh had asked Jessica to take part in a play. She was always asking everybody. All that you had to do was to say that you could not do it and then she would ask someone else.

"But Father says I ought to do it," Jessica said. "I know it's silly, but things like that make me sick."

She was serious about it—the whole idea really frightened her. She was saying that once she had tried to be in a play at school and that she had begun walking in her sleep. She had tried again at Vassar and she had been taken ill.

"Look at me, Charley," she said. "I'm all arms and legs and I trip all over myself and it's such a God-awful play."

It was one of those plays that started with a monologue by the engaging British hero. He was in a most frightful fix. His aunt, Lady Ponsonby, had made him her heir but just this morning she said she would cut him off with a shilling if he did not marry a hideous girl whom she deemed a suitable match instead of allowing him to marry lovely Lucy Clive, the curate's daughter, whom he loved to distraction. He was in a terrible fix.

"Father's making such a point of it and look at me, Charley," Jessica said. "Do I look like lovely Lucy Clive?"

She was wretchedly unhappy, curled up there on the corner of the sofa, and no consolation, only austere disapproval, came from the wallpaper room.

"Why don't you tell him you really don't want to?" Charles asked.

"Oh, Charley," she answered, "I can't do that. I simply can't."

"Why can't you?" he asked. "Why not just tell him how you feel?"

She passed the back of her hand across her forehead and she looked as though she were about to cry.

"Oh, Charley," she said, "nobody understands about Father and me. I can't."

Charles could only sit there baffled. He wanted to touch her hair softly and tell her that it was all right. He wanted to put his arm around her and draw her close to him, but the idea still seemed preposterous.

"Jessica," he said, "it isn't going to be as bad as all that."

"I don't know what you'll think of me," she said. "I haven't any right to ask you, but if I have to be in this thing, will you be in it too?"

He could still view it all aloofly. He had never until that moment thought that Jessica Lovell might need him for anything.

"All right," Charles said, "if you want me to, Jessica."

Then she smoothed her dress carefully over her knees and her voice had changed. She was Jessica Lovell again, back in the wallpaper room.

"Thanks ever so much," she said, and suddenly everything was completely settled, and he was saying that it was about time to be getting back home. He rose and put the paper-covered play back on the table.

"I wish you didn't have to go," Jessica answered.

When he was in the front hall, getting into his overcoat, he could hear the tall clock ticking on the landing; and when he saw Jessica glance behind her, toward the closed door of Mr. Lovell's library, his call suddenly became a clandestine meeting. Her voice had dropped almost to a whisper and he was sure that she was very anxious to have him on the other side of the great front door, walking down the path. When he put his hand on the heavy bronze latch and turned to say good night, she pulled his hand away.

"Let me do it," she whispered. "Don't wake up Father," and she opened the front door very gently. It was clear to him that she did not want Mr. Lovell to know that she had asked him to be in the Clyde Players.

When he arrived at Gow Street a few nights later for what Mrs. Smythe Leigh called a preliminary get-together of the group, Charles knew by the number of hats and coats in the hall that he was late. He had hardly seen Mrs. Smythe Leigh since his senior class in high school had done *Officer 666* and then Charles had only helped take in tickets. Now Mrs. Smythe Leigh squeezed his hand, holding it tight in both of hers. She was wearing a flowing gown of green velvet and on her right wrist was a Navajo bracelet.

"Why, Charley Gray," she said. "I hardly dared think that you would join us. Come right into the living room. Everybody's here."

The scene in Mrs. Smythe Leigh's living room, Charles sometimes thought afterwards, was one which must have repeated itself continuously in other places. Mrs. Smythe Leigh's living room was an intellectual fortress and it stood for the larger world. As Mrs. Smythe Leigh told him later, there was no reason to get in a rut because one lived in Clyde. Clyde was a dear, poky place, full of dear people, but one could always open one's windows to the world. One could bring something new to Clyde, and this was what she always tried to do . . . a few reproductions of modern pictures, a bit of Chinese brocade, a few records of Kreisler and Caruso, and the *American Mercury* and the *New Republic* and of course *Harper's* and the *Atlantic*, and the *New Statesman* and *L'Illustration*. All one had to do was open one's windows to the outer world—and the surprising thing was the number of congenial spirits who gathered if you did it. Sometimes, frankly, she had thought of giving up the Clyde Players. There was always the inertia, but the old guard, Dr. Bush and Katie Rowell, always rallied around her and would not *let* her give up. Once you had the smell of grease paint in your nostrils, you could never get away from it, and there was always that joy of getting out of oneself by interpreting character on the stage. Charles was a newcomer, but someday he might be the old guard, too.

The newcomers and the old guard were all seated in the living room. There were not enough chairs so some were seated on the floor.

"This is Charley Gray," Mrs. Smythe Leigh said, "but then of course everybody knows everybody"—and of course everybody did, in a certain way.

"And of course," Mrs. Smythe Leigh said, "you know Jessica Lovell?"

She obviously asked the question because she was not quite sure. Jessica was sitting on a piano stool and her face had the same strained, self-conscious look of all the other faces, but she smiled at Charles in a friendly, distant way.

"You'll have to sit on the floor, Charley Gray," Mrs. Smythe Leigh said. "It's your punishment for being late," and everyone laughed politely. "And now I'm going to begin by giving my usual little talk. It's an orientation talk. Some of us know it already but perhaps it won't hurt to hear it again."

When the first meeting was over and Charles took Jessica home, this was something everyone understood, including Mr. Lovell. In fact, when Jessica asked him in, Mr. Lovell seemed pleased to see him. As they stood in the front hall, they could hear voices from the library and Jessica put her hand on his arm.

"Wait," she whispered. "Let's see who it is." Then she recognized the Midwestern voice, that sounded almost foreign at the Lovells'.

"It's Malcolm Bryant," she whispered. "He always keeps dropping in," and she gave her head an exasperated shake. It occurred to Charles that he had heard other people saying lately that Mr. Bryant kept dropping in on them unexpectedly, and he should have known better since no one ever made sudden descents on anyone in Clyde. By this time, everyone in Clyde knew who Malcolm Bryant was. He was the professor who was writing some sort of book and he had rented two rooms from old Mrs. Mooney in Fanning Street, where he stayed when he wasn't in Boston and Cambridge, and he had his meals at Mrs. Bronson's boardinghouse. It was time he knew better than to be dropping in suddenly on people.

"Oh dear," Jessica whispered, "Father's telling him about the family again," and they stood for a minute side by side listening.

"I'd like to get this straight, Mr. Lovell," they could hear Malcolm Bryant saying. "It's a way of life that has just the continuity I'm looking for. Now when was it that your great-grandfather lived on River Street?"

"That was before he built the house here," they could hear Mr. Lovell saying. "Of course, River Street was different then. Johnson Street was hardly opened. My great-great-grandfather, Ezra Lovell, built and improved the house on River Street, before the Revolutionary War. The land ran down to the river, approximately where the gas company is now. There's nothing left but one of the old warehouses. Webley's blacksmith shop is in it now, and of course the wharf is gone."

"Oh dear," Jessica whispered. "Why does he want to know about it?"

"Ezra Lovell was in the coastal trade," Mr. Lovell was saying. "It was an old gambrel-roofed house, torn down after my grandfather sold the property. The countinghouse was in the ell, and then there were the slave quarters."

"What?" Malcolm Bryant asked. "Did they have slaves?"

"Only in a small way, I think," Mr. Lovell answered. "I came across a paper just the other day with Ezra Lovell's signature liberating a Negro he owned named Pomp, but that was before the Revolution."

The Lovell library was a large, paneled room, with mahogany bookshelves all around it, designed by the order of Nathaniel Lovell. The same gold-tooled sets of books must have always been on the shelves, and now, though age was making their backs shaky, Charles could imagine that many of them had never been read. A celestial and a terrestrial globe stood on either side of the fireplace and above the books were more Lovell portraits and two pictures of Lovell ships and also the well-known engraving of the Clyde waterfront. There was a comfortable sofa in the library, as Jessica said, the only comfortable sofa in the house, and there were some reasonably modern leather armchairs. Mr. Lovell was seated in one of these with a stack of papers on the floor beside him, and Malcolm Bryant was seated opposite him with a notebook on his knee.

"Hello, Jessie," Mr. Lovell said, and he held out both his hands to her and Malcolm Bryant stood up. "Back so soon? Why, hello, Charles."

Mr. Lovell gave him a questioning look, as though he could not understand his sudden appearance.

"Charley took me home," she said. "Charley's in the Players."

She gave a little exasperated laugh as though she were telling her father that there was no reason for her to explain everything.

"Why, of course, Jessie," Mr. Lovell said. "I'm delighted Charles is in the Players. I told you you'd find friends there. You know Mr. Malcolm Bryant, don't you, Charles? Jessie, why don't you bring us some milk and a little cake, or some crackers and cheese?"

"Oh, not for me, thanks," Malcolm Bryant said. "Please don't bother."

"No, please don't bother," Charles said. "I've got to be going home."

It seemed to him that Mr. Lovell looked relieved, although he said that it would be no trouble at all and that Jessica would love to get them something.

"Then how about a cigar?" Mr. Lovell asked. "Will you smoke a cigar, Charles?"

"Oh, no, thank you, sir," Charles said.

"You know Charles can tell you a good deal about Clyde, Mr. Bryant," Mr. Lovell said. "Charles is born and brought up a Clyde boy, aren't you, Charles? More of a Clyde boy than Jessica is a Clyde girl, I'm afraid. How were the Players, Jessica?"

"They were terrible," Jessica said. "I told you they would be terrible."

"Now let's see," Malcolm Bryant said, "I must have missed the Clyde Players. Where do they fit in?"

"Fit in?" Mr. Lovell repeated.

"I mean in the general picture."

"Don't you ever get tired of asking questions?" Jessica asked.

"Now, Jessie," Mr. Lovell said, "Mr. Bryant is here to ask questions. I should say that the Clyde Players is an ordinary community effort. Jessica is in it, and she should be, and Charles is in it. Why did you join the group, Charles?"

"Because he must be weak-minded," Jessica said quickly.

Malcolm Bryant was leaning back in his comfortable leather chair with his hands laced in back of his head. He was the outsider, enjoying that little scene and evaluating it, while his deep-set eyes kept shifting from Jessica to Charles and back to Mr. Lovell.

"And then there's Dr. Bush, the osteopath," Mr. Lovell said. "I believe he's very active in it. That shows it's a cross section—Jessica and then an osteopath. I had a stiff shoulder once and I got Bush in and he fixed it, just by pulling."

"Down in Borneo," Malcolm Bryant said, "I had a stiff neck once and I was treated by a tribal doctor. He killed a bird and put it on my neck, after cutting it open with an obsidian knife. There was an interesting ritual connected with it."

"Did it help your neck?" Mr. Lovell asked.

"I don't really remember." Malcolm Bryant was smiling at Jessica. "But I have some pictures of it. I'd love to show them to you sometime. Charley Schwartz, one of my assistants, took the pictures. He's at Johns Hopkins now. Men are about the same everywhere." Malcolm Bryant smiled again at Jessica. "Well, I mustn't keep you up too late. I always have a lot to think about after an evening here."

"I wish I knew what you thought," Jessica said.

Malcolm Bryant rose and Charles stood up too. It was time to be going.

"Grateful thoughts," Malcolm Bryant said. "This has been a really challenging evening."

"Good night," Mr. Lovell said, "and good night, Charles. It's good news you're in the play. We all have to take part in things, don't we, and I'm glad there's someone to take Jessica home."

Charles understood what Mr. Lovell meant—that it was better for him to take her home than for Dr. Bush. As long as they were both in the Players, engaged in a common community effort, there was no reason why he should not be seen with Jessica, no reason at all. In fact Charles could imagine later what Mr. Lovell must have said to Jessica.

"Jessie," he must have said, "I think it's very nice that Charles Gray is in the Players, and it's very nice if you see something of Charles Gray, as long as you don't take him too seriously, Jessie. You'll remember, won't you, that a young man like Charles Gray has no prospects, or hardly any."

Perhaps he spoke differently later, for there was a time, just for a little while, when he may have thought that Charles did have prospects—when John Gray bought a Cadillac car and when the market was going up.

By the time Charles and Malcolm Bryant left the Lovells' house that evening, the other houses on Johnson Street were dark except for an occasional light in their upper windows.

"By God," Malcolm Bryant said, "this is a wonderful town. It all fits together without a blur in the pattern. By God, I was lucky to discover it. How well do you know the Lovells, Charley?" It was an impertinent question and Charles felt annoyed.

"Not very well," he answered.

"Oh, I thought you did," Malcolm Bryant said. "You seem to be great friends with Jessica."

Charles caught his breath in astonishment, and then he was angry.

"Suppose you mind your own business," he said, and he stopped walking and stood facing Malcolm Bryant. Malcolm Bryant had stopped too. They were only two dark shadows standing face to face on Johnson Street, but all at once Malcolm Bryant's voice was placating and soothing.

"That's just the right thing for you to say," he said. "I had it coming to me. I'm sorry."

"All right," Charles said.

Charles could not understand why his resentment was ebbing but there was a disarming quality in Malcolm Bryant's voice.

"It was rotten investigative technique," Malcolm Bryant was saying. "If one of my team had done that, I'd have fired him. I just forgot myself. Don't get mad, Charley. It wasn't a personal question. I was just thinking about your groups, and the Lovells aren't quite in your group—are they?"

"No," Charles said, "I don't suppose they are."

"Now, Charley." Malcolm Bryant put a hand on his shoulder. "This is scientific—none of it is personal. Look at me as a father confessor—just an old man you can talk to. It won't go any further. You're not mad any more, are you?"

"No," Charles said, "that's all right. Good night."

Malcolm Bryant held out his hand and patted his shoulder again.

"Well, that's fine," he said. "We'll be seeing a lot of each other, Charley. My God, this is a wonderful town."

Malcolm Bryant walked whistling down the street of the wonderful town and Charles walked home, but Malcolm Bryant's hasty words were still running through his mind. He had never encountered anyone like Malcolm Bryant and he could not tell whether they were friends or not, but then perhaps a man like Malcolm Bryant never could be friends with anyone. Sometimes he was not sure that Malcolm Bryant had the same capacity for likes or dislikes that other people had. He was always thinking of everyone from a viewpoint which he called mass instinct. It was Charles's first contact with pedantries.

10

The Procedural Pattern

The Confessional Club, the men's club to which Charles's father belonged, met at the Grays' home that year in January. Annually each member of the Confessional Club entertained all the other members for supper and for the evening. Charles remembered the occasion especially, because Malcolm Bryant had been invited.

He had not known that his father knew Malcolm Bryant until a week before the meeting and already the house was in a turmoil, because John Gray always wanted to entertain the club properly. Until it was his turn to receive them, he was apt to make fun of the members of the Confessional Club and the club itself, although Charles was sure that he was proud to be in it. He used to say that the Confessional Club was only another of those blatant, self-conscious groups that had always cluttered up Clyde with preposterous, useless discussions. He used to say that those evening clubs were just like boys' clubs except that they were formed by men and that no one had anything to say in Clyde that was worth listening to for half an hour—yet people in Clyde always had wanted to gather around and listen to dull papers.

It showed a lack of personal resource, John Gray always said, and women, too, as well as men, were infected by the germ. No one ever really learned anything from these intellectual outpourings, but everyone wished to try to be improved, during the long winter months. The Women's Club continually met to hear lectures on French fans or on Mount Vesuvius, and the ladies of the Garden Club were always gathering to learn about cutworms or means of eradicating poison ivy. The Knights of Columbus kept listening to travelogues, the Rotary Club would hang on the words of someone who told about sewage disposal. The only organization, John Gray said, that had never wanted to be improved was the Pine Tree Association of Veteran Firemen.

Think of the geysers of words, John Gray used to say, that were spouted forth each winter in Clyde. Every two weeks the Monday Club had met, since 1787, and the Thursday Club had met every two weeks since it had broken away from the Monday Club before the Civil War. He could not imagine, he said, why he had ever joined the Confessional Club, unless because of local contagion. Why had the Confessional Club ever started? It had started thirty years ago because of hurt feelings and merely because there were certain people who were not included in the Monday Club and the Thursday Club; and now two more groups of men who could not get into these three clubs had formed other clubs, and they all met every two weeks in winter and some member always read a paper.

Think of the papers, John Gray said, to which he had been compelled to listen in the Confessional Club alone. Fortunately most of them went in one ear and out the other, but there were details in some which had an adhesive quality that awakened him at night and gave him nervous indigestion. There was the gallstone, for instance, which was removed from the interior of Samuel Pepys, the subject of a paper by Gerald Marchby. Gerald had read it ten years ago but it was very fresh in John Gray's memory. Then there was "The Story of the Mammoth," a paper which had been read by Willard Godfrey. The juvenile quality of this paper had caused John Gray to consult reference books in the public library and to discover that the whole thing had been cribbed from a children's encyclopedia. He might also mention that scholarly work entitled "Certain Old Teaspoons" written by Mr. Norton Swing, a retired official of the Wright-Sherwin Company. This was a double-header, because you not only had to hear about the certain old teaspoons but you had to examine them afterwards one by one. He could go further. If he wanted, he could describe that hour-and-a-half long paper by Hugh Blashfield entitled "Certain Personages in Bench and Bar of Massachusetts," but he was not even going to think of it. He would never even consider the hours of common suffering in the Confessional Club except with the belief that they may have drawn its members together into a sort of perverse bond of friendship.

Nevertheless, whenever it was John Gray's turn to entertain the Confessional Club, he appeared to forget the bitter things he had previously said. He wanted to have as good food as anyone else. The members could wait on themselves, but he wanted tables arranged on which they could eat comfortably and he always provided cocktails made by mixing medical alcohol procured from Gerald Marchby with distilled water and juniper. The main thing was to be sure that the members all had enough cocktails so they could endure the paper but not so many cocktails that they would become noisy or fall asleep during the paper's progress.

"Now, Esther," he said, "I'm not at all sure that you and Dorothea and Mary Callahan can do everything in the kitchen."

"Don't start worrying already, John," she told him. "Jane isn't well enough to let Mary come over, but all sorts of people like to come in and help. They like to sit at the top of the stairs, you know, and listen."

This was exactly what John Gray meant, he told them, when he said everyone wanted to be improved in Clyde.

"And don't forget to get the Wedgwood plates and the silver from Jane," he said, "and glasses. Plenty of glasses."

There was no reason to worry about it. Everyone in the house understood about the Confessional Club.

"And you can come, of course, Charles," John Gray said. "Someday you may be in the club yourself, if you don't get gallstones first. It's something to live for."

Then Dorothea asked if he was not going to ask Elbridge Sterne, and John Gray said that it would be unwise to ask Elbridge Sterne, that he might never come to the house again.

"But I am asking that professor," he said, "the one who's writing the book. He says he knows you, Charles."

"The one who says, 'My God, this is a wonderful town'?" Charles asked.

"Yes, that's the one," John Gray said. "I took him over to the Pine Trees. He kept talking about the aborigines in Borneo, and then we went to see the cemetery."

"Why did he want to see the cemetery?"

"We were talking about the cult of the dead," John Gray said. "He has some interesting ideas, but I'm afraid he has the unselective curiosity that goes with a closed mind. I don't know why people who know too much already are the only ones who keep trying to learn more."

Malcolm Bryant arrived at Spruce Street early. John Gray was still arranging cocktail glasses and struggling with the top of the large shaker he had borrowed from Dr. Marchby. Malcolm stood by the open fire examining the room and stealing glances into the dining room, where everything was on the table except the hot dishes.

John Gray poured the contents of a bottle into the cocktail shaker and gave it a few brisk shakes.

"Try some of this, will you," he said, "and tell me how it tastes?"

"There should either be liquor at a social function," Malcolm Bryant said, "or a few men beating drums. You'd be surprised–good drumming has nearly the same effect. Now a year or two ago I happened to be out with the Ojibways in the lake region of Ontario. I went out with Clarence Spinner from the Sykes Foundation. I don't suppose you've read his papers on the Ojibways. He has the gift of tongues, but he exaggerates."

Charles could see his father straighten up alertly. He always liked something new.

"It was a very unspoiled tribe," Malcolm Bryant went on. "Beautiful birch-bark wigwams and very fine canoes. They were completely out of liquor, but one evening they began beating a drum—four or five delightful old gentlemen around a big drum, beating with a quick syncopation that was more subtle than the African, I think, and singing a soft falsetto chorus. Just after sundown all of us began dancing in a circle, men, women, and children, quite slowly. Thank you, Charley." Malcolm Bryant held out his glass and Charles poured him another cocktail but he held it absent-mindedly without drinking it. "There was a compulsion in that drumming, a mass, hysterical compulsion. By God, it was a wonderful group. I've seen the same thing in Africa but not as well expressed. Oh yes, it was a beautiful exhibition. That drumming made you forget who you were. We danced until two in the morning. We all loved each other at two in the morning."

"Really," John Gray said, "it must have been a delightful party. I wish you'd brought a drum."

The paper that evening was read by Mr. Virgil Mason and Charles knew from Jackie that Mr. Mason had been working on it for weeks. It was entitled "Old Streetcar Lines in Clyde." Mr. Mason read it haltingly after supper, perspiring freely. He dealt with the river line that used to run up Johnson Street and with the Dock Street line that used to go to the beach. Instead of listening attentively, Charles found himself glancing at Malcolm Bryant, wondering what he might be thinking as he sat with his heavy hands clasped about his right knee staring fixedly at a corner of the room.

When the paper was over Dr. Marchby announced the reading time. It had taken Mr. Mason exactly twenty-seven and a half minutes to finish the paper and John Gray said it was a delightful paper. All of them there remembered when the first electric cars had come to Clyde and most of them remembered the horsecar lines that had preceded them. Then John Gray spoke of various motormen and conductors, dealing with their eccentricities. Mr. Blashfield, who followed him, said it was a delightful paper, too, but he was sure that Moses Wilkins had never been a motorman on the old Beach line, but on the other hand Dr. Marchby was sure that he had been, and when Mr. Crewe said he was sure he had not been, everyone said that Mr. Crewe had not been in Clyde long enough to remember. The argument became more heated as other motormen were discussed, but every member had said his say by ten-fifteen and it was time to be going home.

"Charley," Malcolm Bryant said, after he had thanked Mr. Mason for letting him hear the paper and after he had thanked John Gray for allowing him to be there, "why don't you walk back with me? It's still pretty early."

Actually Charles was glad to be asked and he could see that his father was glad that Malcolm Bryant had asked him, for obviously his father wanted very much to know what Malcolm Bryant might say about the Confessional Club.

There had been a heavy snowfall two days before and Charles could remember the walls of snow on either side of the cleared path, as they walked up Dock Street, and the penetrating chill that came from the ground. Though they spoke very little on the way Charles did not mind the silence.

"I'm trying to get it straight in my mind," Malcolm Bryant said after Charles asked him what he thought of the evening.

"I don't see what there is to get straight," Charles said. "There were just a lot of old men there, talking about streetcars."

"Don't interrupt me, Charley. There's a great deal for me to get straight. It was a wonderful occasion, a very wonderful occasion."

"Why was it wonderful?"

"Don't interrupt me, Charley. You're wonderful and none of you know what you're living in. By God, this is a wonderful town. Its crystallization is nearly perfect."

They passed the dark façade of the public library, and the barred windows of the Dock Street Bank with its single night light burning, before Malcolm Bryant spoke again.

"These male groups are always the same," he said. "They are simply the projection of the old men's council. They have the same taboos and the same drawing-together habits. Now out there with the head-hunters there were three councils. They all discussed their tribal exploits, just like the streetcars, exactly like the streetcars."

"I don't see how the head-hunters in Borneo have anything to do with the Confessional Club," Charles said.

"They have everything to do with it," Malcolm Bryant told him, "but you're too involved with this locale to understand. Actually I wish I could take time off someday to belong to a social group. It's just one thing after another with me, the Zambesis in those beehive huts in Africa—the elongated skull Zambesis, not the Pygmy offshoot—and then the head-hunters, and then this job, and next the upper Orinoco, that is if I can get old Smythe in the Foundation sold on the idea of sending me to the Orinoco. It's just one damn thing after another."

"Are you really going to the Orinoco?" Charles asked him.

"Oh, I suppose so," Malcolm Bryant said. "There's been very little first-class work in the area. There's a rumor that they have a very interesting way of getting rid of old people there, but not a line of documented investigation. These damned explorers are all exhibitionists. Thank God, I'm not an explorer." Malcolm Bryant was walking more rapidly. "Now the women were hidden tonight, weren't they? It's a characteristic pattern, that hiding of the women."

"What women?" Charles asked.

"It's the same with the Sicilian peasants," Malcolm Bryant said. "I mean your women."

"My women?"

"Your mother and your sister." Malcolm Bryant was speaking patiently. "I saw them flitting about but they didn't dare to show their faces, Charley, not before the old men's council, and they ate in the women's hut. It's always the same thing."

"It wasn't a hut," Charles said, and he laughed. "They were eating in the kitchen. Where else would they eat?"

"Nowhere else," Malcolm Bryant said. "It was absolutely perfect. Now don't interrupt me, Charley."

They did not speak again until they came to the rooms that Malcolm Bryant had rented on Fanning Street and then Malcolm Bryant only repeated himself.

"I wish I could give it up and be in a group," he said.

He had rented a bedroom and a sitting room on the second floor of Mrs. Mooney's house. The rooms were plainly furnished and Malcolm Bryant had done little to improve them. He had only brought in a draftsman's trestle table and two battered army lock trunks. When he turned on the light Charles saw that a blueprint map of Clyde, marked with colored crayons, was tacked on the drafting table and that there was a large pile of yellow paper beside the blueprint.

"Just a few notes," Malcolm Bryant said as he took off his overcoat and dropped it in a corner of the room. "All the real work is in the Boston office."

Malcolm opened a tobacco jar, filled a pipe and lighted it. Then he took off his jacket and unbuttoned his vest and began pacing up and down the room while Charles sat down in a rickety rocking chair and watched him.

"You know, I'm just beginning to get this town straight," he said. "I'm just beginning to get a pattern. That's the first thing you have to do on a job like this, create a procedural pattern, and once you get it everything fits into it."

"I don't exactly know what you're talking about," Charles said.

"Of course you don't," Malcolm Bryant answered. "There are only a very few people who can understand what I'm talking about."

"Then why did you ask me up here?" Charles asked.

"Because you interest me, Charley." Malcolm Bryant put his hands in his pockets. "You're in tune to the beating of the drums."

Charles leaned back in the creaking rocker. He had a picture of himself and everyone else in Clyde dancing to a tune that Malcolm Bryant was playing.

"All right," Charles said, "what is your procedural pattern?" He was not as much interested in the idea as he was in Malcolm Bryant himself, and Malcolm went on slowly, patiently, from the platform of his erudition.

"I am managing to get this whole town into a grouping," he said, "and to separate the cliques and classes. It's a wonderful town because its structural cleavages are so distinct and undisturbed and so unconsciously accepted. You see, it goes this way"—Malcolm Bryant raised his hand and began counting on his fingers: "there are three distinct social groups, the upper class, the middle class and the lower class, but each of these can be divided into thirds—the upper-upper, the middle-upper, and the lower-upper; the same way with the middle class—the upper-middle, the middle-middle, and the lower-middle; and the same way with the lower class—the same three categories. Everyone in Clyde falls into one of them. That's the procedural pattern."

"Well, I don't see why it's so remarkable. I could have told you that myself," Charles said, and then Malcolm Bryant became a kindly instructor in a lecture hall.

"Of course it doesn't seem remarkable to you, because you're integrated in the group. Look at yourself, Charley—not that you can possibly see. You have a suitable education, you understand your taboos and your rituals, you're working happily under an almost immobile system, and the beauty of it is you're perfectly happy."

The assumption that he was happy annoyed Charles.

"How do you know I am?" he asked.

"Of course you are," Malcolm Bryant said. "You've got to be. You have the greatest happiness vouchsafed any human being, you're an integrated, contented part of a group. You don't know how I envy you. You see—I'm personally not contented, Charley."

"Why aren't you?" Charles asked him. "You can go anywhere you want and you must like what you're doing."

"That's the trouble," Malcolm Bryant said. "I'm tired of moving. By God, I might settle down and do a little quiet writing and give up this Orinoco thing. Don't try to move away, Charley. Don't break out of your group."

Charles had not been sure of Malcolm Bryant's seriousness before, but now he was obviously saying that he was lonely and that he wanted friends. Charles heard the bell of the Baptist Church striking.

"Well," Charles said, "I guess I'd better be going. It's getting pretty late," and it occurred to him that this was what he was always saying in Clyde.

Malcolm had pushed himself from the table and was standing up again in his shirt sleeves and open vest and he looked uncertain.

"Wait a minute, Charley," he said. "There's something I want to say to you. As a human being, not as a social entity . . . frankly, just how interested are you in Jessica Lovell?"

Charles felt his back stiffen and his face grow red. The question was impertinent and a cold wave of caution descended on him.

"I don't know how much I am," he said, and his voice sounded hoarse and awkward. "I've told you that I don't really know Jessica Lovell very well."

"You don't?" Malcolm Bryant repeated, and he pulled his hands out of his pockets. "Well, that's fine. It makes everything easier. This is a sort of hard thing for me to say, but I believe in being honest, Charley. I've had the damnedest thing happen to me. Let's put it down squarely as a biological fact. Frankly, I've fallen in love with Jessica Lovell."

Malcolm looked at Charles questioningly as though he wanted Charles's opinion of the biological fact and for a moment Charles's mind was as vacant as his face must have been. It did not seem possible to him that Malcolm

Bryant could have said such a thing and yet he had heard the words distinctly, and now Malcolm Bryant was going on more rapidly.

"I don't know how in hell it ever happened and I may say it comes at a damned inconvenient time and I'm afraid any sort of adjustment is going to interfere with my work, but there it is, and I thought I ought to tell you, Charley."

Charles's mind was still a blank and the palms of his hands felt moist.

"Why did you think you ought to tell me?" he asked, and Malcolm moved his feet restively on the carpet.

"Because I thought it was the honest thing to do. I know it sounds silly, and of course you're in no position to marry her. You're just a kid, but I thought you had a right to know."

It sounded silly and yet at the same time Charles, in spite of a hollow feeling in the pit of his stomach, realized that not everyone would have been so honest.

"Who ever said I wanted to marry her?" he asked. "I've never thought of marrying her."

It was true. He had never thought until that moment of marrying Jessica Lovell and now his mind was running on tribal customs and beating drums. The worried look had gone from Malcolm's face.

"Well, that's fine," he said. "Of course, I haven't much to offer her but there's some talk about something in the museum at Harvard or there might be a permanent fellowship on the Sykes Foundation. I could give up that Orinoco thing. You know, I think I might make her quite happy."

Charles found himself standing up without ever remembering that he had risen from the rocking chair. He knew that he was smiling because his face felt stiff and contorted.

"Of course, she may throw you down."

"Oh, yes," Malcolm Bryant said, "she may."

"And of course"—his voice sounded louder—"I'll go on seeing her if I want to. Well, good night."

11

And You End with a Barrel of Money

It did not definitely dawn on Charles until the spring of 1928 that he was in love with Jessica Lovell. Then suddenly he was so much in love that nothing else seemed to matter and everything seemed possible. When all the reticences of caution or barriers of common sense, or whatever you cared to call them, broke, it was plain that this situation must have been developing for a long while without either of them having consciously perceived it. The slow growth of such an involvement, he sometimes thought later, made it something that left a deeper scar than any sudden flowering of passion. Yet it was possible that he would never have fallen in love with Jessica or she with him if it had not been for the irritating stimulus of Malcolm Bryant.

Malcolm was dedicating his life to the study of social relationships but when it came to the people around him, he displayed the unskillful ignorance of most dwellers in academic ivory towers. On the one hand he was a dispassionate analyst, a synthetic recording angel, employed by a learned institution to classify the inhabitants of Clyde according to their incomes and their prejudices; on the other, he was an absent-minded professor who had been shielded from many ordinary drives of living. As soon as Malcolm Bryant had confessed his interest in Jessica—because it was an honest thing to do—every day or so he would drop in to call at Spruce Street or ask Charles up to his rooms at Mrs. Mooney's.

It was easy for Charles to converse with Malcolm Bryant because he was always more like a doctor or a lawyer than a friend. Charles found himself telling about Sam and how he had been killed in the war, and about Jackie Mason's worries about his grandfather's drugstore, and about his Aunt Jane and the Gray heart. He was no longer annoyed when Malcolm asked him questions. He was glad to tell about himself in return for learning more about Malcolm and before long Charles was familiar with Malcolm's complete dossier.

It seemed that some wealthy individual or some university or some institution had always supported Malcolm. Thus, although Malcolm worked hard for the support, he had never been obliged, except when he had sold papers while he was a high school student in Kansas, to earn his living like other people. Instead, someone was always paying his expenses to places barely mentioned in school geography. He was always getting a Guggenheim grant or doing a piece of work for a museum or an institute. Ever since his father, a Kansas farmer, had sent him to the state university, Malcolm had consistently been receiving scholarships. His father, plus a scholarship, had helped him get an A.M. at Wisconsin, and other scholarships, plus instructing jobs, had helped him to his Ph.D. at Harvard. Then he had gone with a museum expedition to Polynesia and had written his paper on the knotting of fish nets, which tended to support certain theories on Polynesian migrations—a paper which gave Malcolm the beginning of his reputation. It seemed that social anthropology was not as crowded a field as it might have been. At least there were not so many brilliant social anthropologists who could get along with academic groups. As far as Charles could gather, besides having the requisite academic background it was also necessary to be assiduous and polite to the right people to achieve true anthropological success. Malcolm said that he had always been able to get on with heads of museums—it was a gift.

"Besides," Malcolm said, "I get on with primitive people. Put me anywhere and I can make friends with them."

Besides, Malcolm said, he was a good lecturer and he was good at raising money. They always liked him around when a money raiser was needed, even though he might be forgotten when they were passing around honorary degrees.

"Put me anywhere where there's money," Malcolm said, "and I can dramatize myself," and this was important, Malcolm said, if you wanted to get anywhere. He could tell good after-dinner stories about curare and shrunken heads in the Oriente, and besides, Malcolm said, he knew how to organize an expedition.

Charles was never tired of hearing about Malcolm's expeditions, though he sometimes thought if he were a rich man he would not finance one, and when he once told Malcolm so, Malcolm told him he was not the type. Malcolm said that most people who financed expeditions were frustrated and only wished to project their egos.

Charles preferred having Malcolm talk of his academic ambitions to listening to his ideas on love, but Malcolm frequently brought up the subject. As a rule, he said, he was too busy to think about love and he never approved of women on expeditions. Wives inevitably interfered with progress, and the women who did go along were a type it was hard to fall in love with. There was a time in central Africa when he had met the daughter of a British medical missionary, but it might be just as well to skip that; and once, when he was with the Persian nomads in Luristan, there was an archaeologist named Alvira Small, who wore shorts. He had always intended to look up Alvira in California sometime. There was also a girl in Kansas, but that was a long while ago. On the whole, women interfered with work, and there was seldom time to fall in love when you were always writing a report or getting organized for a trip. He could not understand why this had hit him all of a sudden, up there at the Lovells'.

"It happened late one afternoon in the wallpaper room," Malcolm said. "She was standing by the fireplace. Abruptly it came over me."

It was the room's fault, Malcolm said, that beautiful, frigid, restrained room, and then her lips and the way she narrowed her eyes when she smiled.

"And her figure," Malcolm said.

Until that moment Malcolm had never been conscious of her figure, and Charles hoped he would leave it at that, but Malcolm did not. She was wearing a silk dress that was too long and badly cut and suddenly something reminded him of "The Road to Mandalay."

"I don't know why the devil that dress made me think of an erotic dance in Burma," Malcolm said. "It was the damnedest thing to think of in that restrained and sterile room."

Charles wished that Malcolm would not go on with it, but Malcolm went right on.

"You know," Malcolm said, "her figure's Balinesque. I don't know where she got it. I don't usually mentally undress women."

That wasn't all, either, Malcolm said. She was so lonely, so unfulfilled, in front of that fireplace, so hopeless in that ugly dress. It all made him feel his own loneliness and that nothing he had done had amounted to anything and that until then he had never lived.

He had tried for several weeks, he said, to get Jessica out of his mind. He told himself that he did not like the Lovells. Mr. Lovell was frankly a desiccated stuffed shirt with an absurd approach to everything and Miss Lovell was a perfect tribal type, except that there were few virgins in primitive societies. He had tried, but he could not get Jessica out of his mind. He supposed it was love. He had once read half of Freud's *Interpretation of Dreams* in the South Atlantic, but he had lost the book when he came down with malaria in Kenya. He had learned enough, however, to realize that Jessica's father was in love with her. He wanted to do something about Jessica. He wanted to save her. He supposed that this was love. The only thing to do, he supposed, was to tell her frankly how he felt, but he never could find an opportunity. She did not seem interested in what he was doing, and she never wanted to talk about herself. It never should have happened and it was destroying his perspective, but he supposed that it was love.

It was embarrassing for Charles to listen but at the same time it gave him a perverse satisfaction. He was relieved to discover that when he saw Jessica at the Players she talked about herself very often and frequently asked him what he had been doing lately. It was wonderful when she told him once that his necktie did not match his suit and nothing was more wonderful than when she told him once that she wished Malcolm Bryant would not always keep popping in and out of the house. She wished he would stop telling her about Africa and Borneo and would stop comparing everyone in Clyde to the head-hunters. Charles was very much relieved when she said she liked to be with someone of her own age for a change. There began to be something new about Jessica every time he saw her. He did not know enough that winter to suppose that it was love.

Charles met Jessica Lovell in the Dock Street Savings Bank unexpectedly one Saturday morning near the middle of April. He had asked Mr. Howell at Wright-Sherwin for permission to go there before the bank closed in order to cash his pay check and deposit a part of it, and Mr. Howell had told him that it would be all right if he would hurry.

Malcolm would probably have called the regular visits of citizens to the Dock Street Bank a ritual, similar to a primitive temple offering, and Charles would not have disagreed with him. At birth his Aunt Jane had presented him with a five-dollar deposit in a savings book, entered in beautiful Spencerian writing, and this was the beginning of his financial biography. Charles had been taught, not by his father but by the women in the family, that regular, persistent saving was essential for successful living.

Among his earliest memories was one of those little scenes so dear to bankers. His mother had led him up the steps of the Dock Street Bank, holding a small coin receptacle, supplied by the bank, in the shape of a barrel, upon which was written the slogan, "Put in a coin and you'll soon have a barrel of money." Though he was scarcely tall enough to see over the dark walnut counter, he could remember being propelled gently forward by his mother and placing his barrel of money and his savings book in the hands of Mr. Gregg, the cashier, and watching Mr. Gregg open the barrel with a little key. Mr. Gregg always made some wise remark about thrift as he counted the nickels, dimes and pennies and he used to say that this was the way to make It grow but the slow growth of It was sometimes discouraging to Charles, even when he was conversant with the wonders of compound interest. He had learned what would happen if you left a small sum in the Dock Street Bank a hundred years undisturbed, in the care of its kindly officers. Every year you got four cents on a dollar and the four cents, too, would begin making money too if you left it long enough, but a hundred years was a long time. Mr. Gregg explained that the start was the slowest part of it but wait until Charles had a thousand dollars, then he would have forty dollars a year and think what a boy could do with forty dollars.

Now when Charles was twenty-four, his account had risen to a hundred and fifty dollars and the pages of his savings book told their own story of general self-denial and occasional indulgence. More through habit than through any faith in accumulating a large sum he was back again at the Dock Street Bank on that Saturday in April.

Mr. Gregg, now a frail, elderly man, was still behind the broad counter. There was still the old reassuring smell of oil and ink and ledgers, and still the same small pyramid of coin barrels that would give you a barrel of money. There were still the same rustle of paper and clink of coinage, and Mr. Thomas, also older, was still visible in the distance at his black walnut roll-top desk beyond the rows of bookkeepers; and beyond Mr. Thomas yawned the open doors of the Dock Street Savings Bank safe, an up-to-date addition, with its time lock and tumblers glittering in the light that came from the tall windows. Everyone in the space behind the counter seemed to move in his own stream of time, impervious to anything except geologic change.

Outside on Dock Street the pallid April sun had been dodging in and out behind low, wind-blown clouds. The trees were still bare and front yards and lawns were as brown and sodden as they had been when the winter's snow first melted. It was a gusty morning and the air had a reluctant touch of winter, but inside the bank there was a uniform climate. Charles had cashed his check and had just given Mr. Gregg five dollars and his deposit book when Jessica Lovell came in, and when Mr. Gregg saw her, he pushed his spectacles more securely on his nose.

"Good morning, Miss Lovell," Mr. Gregg said. "I'll be with you in just a moment, and it *is* a good morning, isn't it?"

Jessica, too, was holding her savings book. Her cheeks were red and fresh from the April wind and she was wearing a short coat of gray wombat, a sensible, inexpensive fur, and one of her tight felt hats was pulled down close over her unruly hair.

"Hello, Charley," she said, and she spoke in the low, serious tone which one always used in the Dock Street Bank. "Don't go. I'll be through with this in a minute. It's my Wright-Sherwin dividend. Father likes to have me bring it in myself."

She was entirely at home, friendly and confiding, as she should have been, in the Dock Street Bank. Her voice, though it was low, carried pleasantly through the banking room and Mr. Thomas when he heard it rose from his roll-top desk and walked to the counter.

"Good morning, Jessie," he said. "Are you getting on all right?"

"Oh, yes, thanks, Cousin Ralph," she said. She was just endorsing a check, and Mr. Thomas nodded pleasantly to Charles and asked if his Aunt Jane were feeling better.

"Tell her not to overdo," Mr. Thomas said. "We all forget we're growing older."

Jessica snapped her bag shut and thanked Mr. Gregg and Charles held the door open for her.

"It's like church, isn't it?" she said as they walked together down the steps. "I always want to whisper in there. Where are you going, Charley?"

He told her he was going back to the office.

"But it's Saturday," Jessica said. "What are you doing this afternoon? Suppose we go for a drive?"

She asked the question as though she were sure he would have nothing else to do and he understood, when she asked him where they would meet, that it would be better to have it seem like an accidental meeting.

"How about the courthouse at half-past two?" she said. "It's so much easier."

It was much easier than meeting at the Lovells' front door and going through explanations because there would be nothing underlined or portentous about it.

When Charles arrived in front of the courthouse at half-past two and while he stood with the wind whipping at his coat, watching the cars go by, the realization that there was a secret element to the meeting scarcely dawned upon him, because it was all connected with the Dock Street Bank. The bank had become a symbol of the way he felt about Jessica Lovell, a symbol of integrity and of serious intention. When he saw Jessica's black Dodge phaeton glide around the curve of Johnson Street, he actually considered it a delightful sort of accident. It seemed like an accident, too, that Jessica should see him and slow down and wave her hand.

"Why, hello," Jessica said. "What are you doing here? Can't I give you a lift?"

"I was just walking around," Charles said.

"Well, get in if you're going my way," Jessica said.

"Are you sure it won't be too much trouble?" Charles asked.

"Oh, no." Jessica shook her head slowly. "Not a bit of trouble."

Neither of them laughed until the Dodge was moving again and then they both laughed at once and though they each must have known most of what the other was thinking, they never explained their thoughts and actions of that afternoon. The sun kept trying to come out from behind the scudding clouds and it was still like winter as they drove through town, but when they were on the edge of town the sun was brighter and the brown fields seemed warmer. Where the roads forked at the small common where the Civil War monument stood, the Union soldier, too, with his visor cap and overcoat, standing on his pedestal flanked by pyramids of cannon balls, looked almost warm. Jessica turned to the right at the common and they crossed the river at the third bridge and drove over the hilly road that led to Walton Spring. There were farms on either side of them, old houses with their outbuildings attached, each with its apple orchard, its pastures and its hayfields. Charles was aware of stone walls and of weathered barns and piles of wood in woodsheds, but he noticed nothing in detail. He and Jessica were talking as though they had not seen each other for a long while and when they were silent they still seemed to be talking.

She was wearing the same gray suit and the same red hat that she had worn at the firemen's muster and though her eyes were on the road she would glance at him now and then in a quick, amused way. She asked what he had been doing since she had seen him last, and she was thankful that the winter was over. It was the longest winter she had ever spent. Granted she had been to New York and she had been in Boston quite often for the symphony, still it had been a long winter. It had been a long winter for Charles, too, though he had been working. He could tell her a good deal about brass and precision instruments, but he was not going to tell her.

"No," Jessica said, "don't. Let's not talk about anything constructive. I'm tired of being constructive."

The land around them also seemed tired of being constructive. The frost was seeping out from it, leaving it moist and weary. The further they went, the further they were away from anything that was constructive.

"I'm tired of sitting around and being nice, too," Jessica said. "I wonder how nice anyone is, really."

"Everyone has to pretend," Charles said.

"That's the trouble," Jessica said, "and so you never know what anyone is really like."

He never could remember how Malcolm Bryant's name came up but it must have been Jessica who spoke of him first because he never would have. She was saying that Malcolm Bryant was always dropping in and giving travel talks about central African beads and life in beehive huts. She never could keep her mind on what he was saying, and she always felt as though she were sitting in a lecture hall.

"But he's pretty interesting sometimes," Charles said. "He's been around a lot."

"Everybody acts as though I ought to like him," Jessica said. "Charley, did you really think I liked him?"

It was the most beautiful question that anyone had ever asked him. They were crossing a culvert, over a piece of swampy land, and there was a row of old willows on either side of the road.

"Did you really?" she asked again, and then before he could answer she slowed down the car and asked him what that singing noise was.

"It's the peepers," he said, "the frogs"; and the high notes of the singing frogs rose all around them.

"Sam used to take me out to catch them," he said, "but they were pretty hard to catch."

If you came near where they were they always stopped their singing, but if you stood still long enough you could see them, sometimes. They blew their throats up like balloons. You had to wait a long while, absolutely still, before they began to sing again.

"Sam could make the best willow whistles," he said.

This was just the time for whistles, now that the sap was running in the willows and the twigs were growing yellow. You could always tell by looking at the willows when spring was coming.

"Can you make a whistle?" she asked—but he was not good at making whistles. He never had been good at doing things with his hands. He never could carve boats or do any of those things in the *American Boy's Handy Book*.

Once long ago, she said, one spring in Clyde, she had gone out picking wildflowers in a place called the High Woods. She always remembered them coming through the dead leaves and she had always wanted to go again but somehow there had never been a chance.

"Do you suppose there are any flowers yet?" she asked him.

It was just the time of year when you thought of such things, whether you cared for flowers or not. He told her that the grape hyacinths were out by the front door at Spruce Street and this meant that there might be hepaticas in the woods—not liverwort, he hated the name "liverwort." It had been a cold, late spring, but still there might be hepaticas on a southeast slope. They would be pushing up through the leaves. He liked hepaticas, he said, better than any other flower, because they were the earliest.

The road was winding up into the hills again. They were not far from Walton Spring and he was thinking that it sounded innocent and artificial, talking so much about frogs and telling her that he liked hepaticas.

"I don't know why it always sounds flat when you talk about flowers," he said.

"No, it doesn't," she said. "It sounds all right to me," and she slowed down the car again. "Do you suppose there are any in those woods?"

She had stopped the car and she pointed to the woods on a hill above a pasture, and when he said there might be, that he didn't know, she said they might walk up and see. There were bars in a gap in the stone wall and he pulled the bars down carefully so that she could step over them. They walked quickly up the rocky, grassy slope and he held up a strand of barbed-wire fence so that she could crawl under. There was a stand of oak and hickory on top of the hill and when their feet rustled through the dead, sodden leaves there was a musty smell, half of winter and half of spring, but there was not a single hepatica.

The buds on the branches above them were as tight as though it were still winter, because oaks were suspicious trees, never coming out until they were sure it was spring. There was not a sign of life in those woods, not even a trace of green, except for some rock ferns growing in a crevice of a granite ledge. Nevertheless, they kept on walking. If she started to climb a hill, she said, she always liked to get to the top and they might as well get there. The hill was higher than it looked and when they reached the crest and turned around they could see a wide expanse of country below them through the bare branches of the trees. They could see the curve of the river and the third bridge in the hazy distance and further off to the left the roofs of Clyde, a long narrow town on its bank. Afterwards whenever he saw journeyman paintings, he always thought of himself and Jessica standing on that hill, looking at the toylike town.

They were both a little out of breath, both looking into the distance down the hill, and they both must have turned toward each other at the same moment. He stared straight at her and she had a grave, startled look and her brown eyes were opened very wide.

"Oh," she said, in a dry, matter-of-fact sort of voice, and then the next moment they were in each other's arms.

"Oh," she said again, and he kissed her and they clung to each other, their eyes closed, not speaking. When she turned her head away and let it rest a second on his shoulder he dropped his arms, but suddenly she pulled him close to her again and they stood side by side, looking into the half-defined distance.

"Well," she said, "there's Clyde." It was just as though nothing had happened.

"Yes," he answered, "there it is."

"I didn't know we could see so much from here." She was not looking at him.

"It's because the leaves aren't out," he told her.

The sun had broken through the clouds again, the slanting sun of late afternoon. It was just as though nothing had happened when Jessica and he walked down the hill, as though they had never stood locked in each other's arms and had never kissed, except that she put her arm through his while they were still in the woods.

"It's always harder walking downhill," she said, but she drew her arm away when they were out in the open pasture.

"I always like juniper in a pasture," she said. "Listen. You can hear the frogs," and they stood for a moment listening, with their shadows long on the brown turf. They walked across the pasture without speaking. It was almost as though it had never happened, but not quite.

When they were in the car, she pulled a gold compact from her pocket, opened it, stared at herself intently in its little mirror, put a dab of powder on her nose, and snapped the compact shut. Then she pulled down her hat.

"I wish my hair didn't always blow," she said.

"I like it when it blows," he told her. It was almost as though it had never happened, but he never would have said such a thing before they walked up the hill.

"Do you?" she said. "Well, I'm glad somebody does."

The truth was that so much had happened that it was better not to talk about it. It was better to sit quietly as they were driving home, conscious only that they were near each other.

"Charley," she asked finally, "have you ever been abroad?"

Once he had thought of working his way abroad on a cattle ship, while he was in college. Some of the boys in his fraternity had talked of it, but he had never done anything more than talk. It was different with her. She had been to England and France with her father last summer and before that she had been with some of the girls from school on a tour arranged by one of the teachers, one of those queer school girl tours when you walked in a small procession through the cathedrals and the galleries. They had gone to Rome and to Florence.

"I brought back Pliny's doves," she said. "Everyone seems to buy Pliny's doves."

As soon as you got home it all seemed a long way off in the distance. It was hard to believe that you'd ever been to Florence. It was like coming home after a dance that year her father had made her come out in Boston. She used to come down from Vassar in her coming-out year and stay at her Aunt Rachel's on Marlborough Street. She was always doing things, she told him, that she did not want to do particularly.

"I wish," she said, "we didn't always have to do things. Charley, tell me what you have to do."

He told her that he would have to go to Wright-Sherwin on Monday morning. He began to tell her about the office and about Mr. Howell, but when he started he had a desperate feeling of everything closing around him because they were back in Clyde again and Clyde was as orderly as the houses on Johnson Street, everything in its place and a place for everything.

"I might as well get out here," he said, when they came near the courthouse.

"Well, all right," she said, "I suppose it's better."

Everything was in its place and there was a place for everything.

"Thanks ever so much," Charles said when the car stopped. "I had a wonderful time."

"So did I," she said, and then she smiled. "I loved every minute of it."

"Did you?" Charles asked.

"Yes," she answered, "every minute of it. If it's a good day, let's do it again next Saturday."

"Why, that would be fine," he said.

She waved her hand to him when he took off his hat, and when the Dodge rounded the curve on Johnson Street he wondered what she would tell them at home of how she had spent the afternoon.

12

In the Spring a Livelier Iris . . .

—ALFRED LORD TENNYSON

Charles could occasionally see himself through the perspective of elapsed time. His mind still worked in much the same way as that of the Charles Gray who must have existed that spring in Clyde. He still had a desire to accept what was around him and to develop according to established rules. Not even in those days, he realized, did he wish to change the rules, although he could see their unfairness. He had never been a revolutionary, he had never possessed the reformer's urge, but still that spring he could perceive in himself undercurrents of discontent. He was acutely conscious of his own deficiencies and of his inexperience, but it was a healthy sort of discontent and at least he knew what he lacked and what he wanted. He wanted, of course, to be more like Jessica Lovell. He studied, that spring, as well as one could in the Clyde library, the Italian primitives and Del Sarto and Da Vinci. He read the autobiography of Cellini. He learned the difference between Gothic and baroque architecture and he read Hare's *Walks in Rome* and *Florence*. It was probably Jessica Lovell who stopped him from being a small-town boy, Jessica Lovell and possibly Malcolm Bryant. He never attempted to conceal his cultural deficiencies from Malcolm Bryant. In fact he must have felt instinctively that Malcolm presented intellectual opportunity.

"Listen," Malcolm said, one evening in May, "why are you always picking my brains about Europe? You wouldn't like it if you got there. You want to learn to cultivate contentment, Charley. It's a wonderful thing, contentment. Look at me."

"Why are you contented?" Charles asked.

"I'll tell you," Malcolm said. "If you want a frank answer, I think I'm doing better with Jessica. I used to have the idea that she didn't like to have me around, but now all of a sudden she really does."

There was a maddeningly inartistic lack of reticence in Malcolm's discussion of Jessica. He could not understand, Malcolm often said, what there was about her that attracted him in such a blind, irrational manner. Sometimes he could see very clearly that he was on the verge of making a fool of himself. It was a problem, he admitted, of his own emotional instability aggravated by the forces of biological selection. Did the things he seemed to see in Jessica exist in fact or were they manufactured out of his own imagination? Love was a biological disease, Malcolm said, and once you contracted it you could never be sure of facts. This was hard for anyone who believed in the empirical approach.

He liked to think, quite frankly, that he was a trained, scientific observer

—and quite frankly he was a very good one. His training showed him what was wrong with the Lovells—wealth and tribal ritual had a limiting effect that ended in atrophy. He had never previously been in a position to observe such ritual, aside from the South Sea taboos, and the Lovells were what he termed *kapu ali'i*, meaning that ritual removed them completely from reality. They lived in a world of antiquities and were actuated by ancestor worship and cultism of the dead. He could see this with painful clarity, only to forget it whenever he saw Jessica. It was emotion triumphing over reason. And what would he do with Jessica Lovell if he ever got her? It would have been amusing to tell Malcolm Bryant that he need not bother to worry, but of course Charles never did and actually he could agree in principle with many of the things that Malcolm Bryant said.

Charles, too, could see that the Lovells were shut off from most of the rest of Clyde by their own elaborations, but this was not strange because Clyde had made them what they were. Furthermore, he could see that though Jessica Lovell was touchable she was still unattainable, because they had different positions in the plan of Clyde. Though their clandestine meetings that spring had occurred in fact, they still held elements of the unreal and consequently their moments together were the more vivid. He also knew that this situation was bound to change eventually and that the reticences between them would have to break.

This happened on a warm day in May when the trees were all a soft green. They had driven along the Spring Road again to the same pasture and they had left the car and had walked up the same hill. They had spoken much as they had before as they walked across the pasture, shyly and uncertainly as though neither of them could be sure of what would happen when they reached the woods.

"It's been such a late spring, hasn't it?" Jessica said. "I was afraid it was going to rain today."

"So was I," Charles said.

"But if it had, we could have driven in the rain."

"Yes," he said, "of course we could have driven in the rain."

That meaningless conversation carried them across the pasture and into the woods.

"I like that coat of yours," she said. "It's old but it looks nice." It was the old tweed coat, he remembered, that he had worn at the firemen's muster. "You always look so nice, so self-possessed."

"So do you," he said. "You always do."

It did not seem possible that the same thing might happen again that had now happened several times before. It did not seem possible that he had ever touched her, because she was unattainable.

"I'm getting pretty good at walking up this hill," she said.

"Yes," he said, "but it's good exercise"—and then the same thing happened, the same impossible thing.

"Darling," she whispered, when he held her in his arms, "darling," and then he told her that he loved her. He could not have said it if she had not spoken first.

"Yes," she said, "I know."

It was still too immense to talk about intelligently, but suddenly it was fact, now that they had put it into words.

"Oh, Charley," she said, "what are we going to do?"

"I don't know," he said, "but I don't mind right now."

"I always wondered what would happen if we said it," she said. "Do you still love me?"

"Yes," he said.

"Darling," she said, "everybody's going to find out."

"Yes," he said, "I suppose they will."

"I wish they'd let us alone." She stopped and rested her head on his shoulder. "Charley," she asked him, "are you happy?"

Yes, he had never been so happy.

"It's so different," she said, "from the first time."

"It's because we said it."

"Well, let's not think about anything else."

"What else?" he asked.

"Oh, everything. What we're going to do next. All those silly things."

"Everything's going to be all right," he said, but all sorts of things that should not have mattered were already gathering around them when they walked back down the hill.

"I don't think Father will mind so much," she said, "if he gets to know it gradually and not all at once."

"You mean your father won't like it," he said. "I don't suppose he will."

"I wish he could just see more of you without its disturbing him. You're not cross, are you, Charley?"

"No," Charles said, "I'm not cross."

"Charley, don't look so unhappy." She took his arm and pressed it tight against her. "If we had only met each other somewhere else. Do you see what I mean?"

She was saying, of course, that everything would have been all right if he had only lived on Johnson Street. She was saying, without saying it, that everything would have been all right if the Grays had been better off or even if he had not been a Clyde boy, and it made him angry. It might have been better if his name had been Marchby, but at the same time he was Judge Gray's grandson. He was thinking that if Jessica had been Priscilla Meader or one of the Latham girls everything would have been all right.

"Oh, Charley," she was saying. "Charley, please."

He had forgotten until she spoke that she was still close beside him.

"Oh, Charley, I don't care what anyone's going to say."

"If you think I'm as bad as all that," he began, "why did you ever have anything to do with me?"

"Oh, Charley," she said, and they stood there in the pasture and she began to cry. It made him feel hopeless and desperate but there was nothing he could do about it. "I only said I didn't care."

"Then don't say it again," he said.

They stood there without speaking, and Jessica Lovell was still crying.

"Lend me your handkerchief," she said. "I haven't got a handkerchief."

"All right," Charles said. "Just stop crying, Jessica. It's going to be all right," and then something made him laugh.

"What are you laughing at?" she asked.

He was laughing, he told her, because it might have been Jackie Mason and what would she have done then, or it might have been one of the Meader boys, he was saying, or it might have been a North Ender. She should not have been allowed to wander around so much.

"You see what happens," he told her.

It was then that the idea came to him that changed so much of his life. It came to him suddenly, but perhaps it had been back of his mind for a long while.

"Jessica," he said, "I guess I'd better make some money."

He was thinking of Mr. Howell, who had been all his life at Wright-Sherwin and now was almost ready to retire, but Jessica still thought of Mr. Lovell.

"He'll like you, darling," she said, "if he only gets used to you little by little." She did not say how Mr. Lovell would get used to him little by little but she stopped the car about a half mile from the third bridge. "Aren't you going to kiss me again," she asked, "before we get into Clyde?"

When Charles arrived at Spruce Street, his mother was in the dining room in her oldest gingham apron polishing the flat silver. Charles wished he had never heard Malcolm speak of women in Clyde going through various phases of household ritual. The spoons and forks had come from the Marchby family. They had been the wedding silver of his Great-grandfather Marchby, and now his mother referred to them as "the Marchby Silver." The spoons were plain and very thin, each with a Spencerian M faintly engraved upon it. The forks were equally plain and their tines were worn and rounded from nearly a century of family use, but for his mother, and for Dorothea too, they had a spiritual value that made them rare and beautiful. They were The Marchby Silver. His mother was bending over the spoons now, handling each one gently, rubbing it lovingly with a soft cloth. Her hands were gray from dried silver polish and drops of it had fallen on her apron.

"Hello, dear," she said. "Where have you been all afternoon?" He remembered telling Dorothea that he was going to mow the lawn on Saturday and Dorothea had an uncanny ability for getting to the bottom of everything, but his mother only asked him curiously, not sharply or attentively.

"Oh," Charles said, "I've been for a walk in the country. Where's Father?"

His father was upstairs working on the paper which he was to read at the next meeting of the Confessional Club.

"He always puts it off," his mother said, "and now I suppose he'll have to work all night and all day Sunday. He wants coffee for supper instead of cocoa."

"Do you want me to help you?" Charles asked.

"No," she said. "I love to do the silver. Run along, dear." Children were always told to run along. It was just as though he were ten and could run along to the back yard and look for Jackie Mason.

Though he knew his father disliked being interrupted when he was writing a paper for the Confessional Club, Charles went upstairs to see him. John Gray had pulled up the leaf of the table that stood behind the dilapidated sofa and he had pushed off the books which usually stood on it. He was sitting in shirt sleeves and suspenders, writing with a pencil on sheets of yellow paper.

"Well, well," he said, "what's the matter? Are you lonely, Charley?"

His dropping in was so unusual that Charles realized how seldom there had been anything he had wanted from his father.

"Oh, no," Charles said. "It's just a question about something I'm thinking of doing."

His father tilted back in his chair and stroked his closely clipped mustache.

"In my experience," John Gray said "—not that my experience isn't almost completely without validity—it's usually a great deal better to think of doing something than to do it. Sit down on one of the Windsor chairs. They're uncomfortable and you'll have to leave soon. Now take this paper for this confounded Confessional Club. It was much better thinking about it. It's the action that's painful. Do you know how many tug boats there used to be in Clyde in the year 1902?"

"No," Charles said, "why should I?"

"Not the slightest reason," John Gray said. "But actually there used to be four tugboats tied up between the Nickerson Cordage Company and the old coal pocket in the year 1902, and their names were"—John Gray folded his hands behind his head and looked up at the ceiling—"the *Lizzie K. Simpkins,* named, I think, after the wife of Captain Simpkins who ran her, although he was living with another lady at the time, the *H. M. Boadley,* the *Indian Chief,* and the *Neptune.* Well, they're all gone now and the coal barges and the lumber schooners they used to tow are gone and I don't suppose you remember any of them."

"No," Charles said, "I don't remember."

"I don't know why it is," John Gray sighed, "I really don't know why, you and your generation care nothing about the river. When I was your age I was on it all the time in my catboat, and if I wasn't in my catboat I was in my canoe. I knew every rock in the river."

"I never had the chance," Charles said. "You were always going to buy a catboat and teach me to sail and you never did."

"That's true. I was," John Gray said. "Why didn't you ask me more often?"

"I asked you and asked you," Charles told him, "but you never got around to it."

"Well," John Gray said, "the river isn't what it was. It's better to sit on the shores and weep." He sighed and stared up at the ceiling. "Now downstairs your mother is polishing the Marchby spoons, while I sit up here blowing the dust from the pages of my lexicon of youth."

"Are you writing about tugboats?" Charles asked.

"No, no," John Gray said. "About the river, and the fish, and the boys who used to swim in it, and the golden plover, and, frankly, it's too good for the Confessional Club. Frankly, I'm too good for it too, Charles. I'm a little depressed this afternoon—and now you'd better not interrupt me any longer. Just run along and close the door behind you without stumbling over the books. I want to sit beside the river and weep."

"But I wanted to ask you a question," Charles said.

John Gray pushed his chair forward until its front legs came in contact with the floor.

"I was thinking of getting a job somewhere in Boston. I don't believe I'm going to get anywhere if I stay at Wright-Sherwin, not for years and years."

"You mean, Charley," John Gray asked softly, "that there isn't enough hay in the bundle?"

"The truth is," Charles said, "I'd like a chance to make some money."

John Gray said nothing for a moment.

"Why, Charley," he said, "you couldn't be thinking of a brokerage office or a bond house, could you?"

"As a matter of fact," Charles began, "I was just thinking that if you know anyone—if you wouldn't mind speaking to someone—"

"Why, Charley," his father said, and Charles had never seen him look so pleased, "I never thought our minds could ever work in the same way. It's about time you realized you can't get anywhere without money. It's queer that so few people ever see it clearly. It's the sophistries that catch them, the opiates."

The words had an ugly, materialistic sound and it was not fair to bring his thoughts of Jessica and all the ideas that were confusing him down to such unattractive terms.

"I didn't mean that money's everything," he said.

John Gray's forehead wrinkled and he shook his head slowly.

"Oh dear," he said softly. "Oh dear me, of course it isn't, but this is what always happens if you fall back on maxims. That was the trouble with Marcus Aurelius. He meditated in maxims. Naturally, money isn't everything, but money, it seems to me, helps most situations. Perhaps you can look down on it when you have it, but let's admit it does help, Charley, and let's try not to live by maxims."

There was no doubt that it helped but he hated to admit that it did. He did not want to have his mind work like his father's and he was fighting against the thought that it ever might.

"I don't want to get anything for nothing," he said. "If I make any money, I want to earn it."

John Gray sighed and shook his head again.

"Oh dear, there we go again," he said. "Those maxims. I don't blame you,

Charley, but do you think anyone who's accumulated a large sum of money has ever actually earned it? I doubt it, in the literal sense. It's so much easier when one faces facts, but then all life is largely based on an avoidance of fact, and I admit I try to avoid them. I try to turn them and twist them. Everybody does. I suppose you're implying that I have occasionally tried to get something for nothing." John Gray raised his eyebrows and waited for Charles to answer.

"I was just saying that I don't see how I can get ahead at Wright-Sherwin." Charles was speaking more loudly than he had intended, almost impatiently. "I was just asking you if I couldn't get something to do in Boston, and I don't know much about Marcus Aurelius."

He rose from his Windsor chair but his father was looking at him in a level, disconcerting way.

"Do you mind if I ask you a question, Charley? How did this idea ever get into your head?"

Charles looked straight at his father and tried to speak casually. "It just came over me."

"It couldn't have anything to do with Jessica Lovell, could it?"

"How did you know?" Charles asked. "Yes, it does have something to do with her."

"And you're in love with her?"

"Yes," Charles said.

John Gray pushed his chair back from the table.

"Well now, this really does me a lot of good. I wonder what Laurence Lovell will say," he said. "You and I have certainly got to do something about this, Charley. We had certainly better go up to Boston on Monday."

"Not Monday," Charles said. "I'd better tell them I'm through at Wright-Sherwin on Monday, but I guess they'll let me take the day off Tuesday."

"Do you want to do that before you get another job? I never thought you'd do a thing like that, Charley."

"I'll find something else," Charles said.

He was through with Wright-Sherwin but he had no way of knowing that the whole course of his life was changing, and his father's too—what was left of it. He had no way of knowing that they were both moving for good out of that dusty room.

"Charley," John Gray said, and put his hand on his shoulder. "If you want her, I'll see you get her, Charley." John Gray walked to the sofa and picked up his coat. "And now I think I'll go downtown and get the *Transcript*. It ought to be in now."

"Charley?" He heard his mother's voice calling from the hall downstairs. "Where are you?"

John Gray opened the door.

"It's that Mr. Bryant, Charley. He wants you on the telephone."

Malcolm wanted him to come over at eight o'clock that night.

"Tonight," Charles said. "Let's see." He disliked using the telephone as an offensive or defensive weapon.

"I wish you'd come as a special favor," Malcolm said. "I want you to meet the team."

"What team?"

"My team, of course." Malcolm's voice sounded sharper. "My investigatory team. They're starting in on Clyde on Monday. We're just talking over the field and I'd like to show them one firsthand exhibit." Suddenly Malcolm's voice was placating and exuding charm. "You don't mind co-operating, do you, Charley? Now don't argue over the telephone but come on over at eight o'clock and meet the team."

It was a relief that Malcolm did not want to talk about Jessica Lovell, such a relief that he was glad to go, and besides he was curious to see Malcolm in his own environment.

There were eight or ten people in Malcolm's room that night who all looked somewhat like Malcolm. Their faces were sharp with eager perspicacity and at the same time complacent with hidden knowledge. It was the peculiar look, of course, of the professional investigator which, he often thought later, was worn by people trained to interfere in other people's business, whether they were social workers, bank examiners or income tax examiners.

Malcolm Bryant's team sat on the couch and on Malcolm's trunk and on chairs which must have been brought from Mrs. Mooney's kitchen. Malcolm himself was perched on the drawing table with two glass gallon jugs of sacramental wine beside him and all the members of the team were holding cups and glasses.

"Well, here he is," Malcolm said. "Thanks for coming, Charley. This is Charley Gray, everybody, and I think Charley will be as much of a help to you tonight as he's been to me. This is Evangeline Scroll. Evangeline's back from Yucatán. And here's Bill Horsley. You've heard me talk about Bill."

As Malcolm mentioned the names of the team he waved his arm at each one but Charles did not remember them distinctly because he was not trained to associate names and faces then. Malcolm and all the rest of them, he imagined, were trying to put their subject at ease, but he could see them anxiously making mental notes of his skull, of his tweed coat and his flannel trousers. They made him feel as a Polynesian on an atoll must have felt when he suddenly encountered a boatload of strangers from a whaling ship. He remembered what Malcolm had said, that it was hard to fall in love with girls who were anthropologists, and he agreed with Malcolm as he gazed at Evangeline Scroll, fresh from Yucatán.

"Sit down in the rocking chair," Malcolm said, "where everyone can see you, and have a drink," and Malcolm raised his voice. "Now, my idea is for you and me to talk as though no one else were here. It's a new method, but you don't mind it, do you Charley?" Malcolm smiled at him ingratiatingly and Charles sipped his glass of sacramental wine.

"No," he said, "I guess I don't mind it."

Everyone laughed in a way which indicated that they had all been waiting for something to laugh at. It only showed again that Malcolm had a lot of good ideas but did not understand people.

"Let's think of Clyde," Malcolm said, "as a big aquarium, and, by God, it's a wonderful aquarium, and I scooped you out and put you in a globe to show the team."

"I hope the team likes it," Charles said, and again everyone laughed.

"Now, Charley, here, lives on Spruce Street. Spruce Street runs into Johnson Street and yet Charley is not a side streeter, in the broader sense of the term. He has an upward and downward mobility that is very interesting. He is able to touch, without belonging to, the cliques on Johnson Street, and yet at the same time he can move downward. His societal mobility is emphasized because he was brought up in the Clyde public school system. He has rubbed shoulders with all the groupings. He may not have the middle class mobility but he has mobility, the downward trend of which has been checked somewhat by a college education. The first time I laid eyes on him I knew he was a beautifully conditioned type."

Malcolm Bryant paused and Charles sat there staring blankly at the team.

"I think Mr. Gray is a very nice type," Miss Scroll said. "Don't let Malc disturb you, Mr. Gray."

Charles's face flushed and he looked around him uneasily. "Well," he said, "what do you want me to do for you—sing a song?"

"Nothing," Malcolm said. "That's the beauty of it, Charley. I just want the team to see you react. You're being a great help, Charley."

"Give him another drink," Miss Scroll said. "I think Charley's wonderful. You don't mind if I call you Charley, do you, Mr. Gray?"

"No," Charles said, "not if it makes you feel any better."

They laughed again in the same hearty, mirthless way, and their curiosity was too impersonal to be unpleasant. He was a Greek letter in a quadratic equation representing Clyde. He could even forget Jessica Lovell and his other problems as he sat there, because he was a part of Clyde. They were strangers invading his town and all at once he was anxious to have them understand it. It may have been the second glass of wine he drank that made him want to speak.

"All right," he said, "I'll tell you something about Clyde. I'm pretty tired of all this talk about classes and about Johnson Street and Spruce Street. It doesn't matter. Nobody thinks about classes because everyone in Clyde knows he's as good as everyone else. This is a free country and Clyde's a free town."

He was surprised at himself for having said so much. His words were like those of that grammar school commencement speaker.

"Listen to him," he heard Malcolm say. "You see he has great mobility."

He did not care what Malcolm Bryant said. He could see all of Clyde in one piece. Johnson Street, Spruce Street, Dock Street, River Street, the North End, the South End. You could pull it apart and classify it, as these preposterous strangers would try to do, but all of it fitted together and it fitted beautifully and there was no reason to disturb it. Everything was in its place and there was a place for everything.

"You ought to be here," he said, "for Decoration Day. It's coming pretty soon. And for the Fourth of July. That's when you'll see what I mean. Everyone's as good as everyone else."

"You see," Malcolm said. "The feast days—the mingling of the classes."

"But it isn't the classes," Charles said. "Everybody knows everybody else."

"There you are," Malcolm said. "It's beautiful conditioning. But you wouldn't marry a North Ender, would you, Charley?"

His thoughts went back to high school and Doris Wormser. She was surprisingly clear in his memory. He could see her as she walked in ahead of him in the assembly room in high school.

"No, not at the moment," he said.

"You see what I mean," Malcolm said. "By God, this is a wonderful town."

That evening in Malcolm's room was a most peculiar ending for a peculiar day. Charles had never thought of himself as convertible into diagrams and geometric curves and a mass of static, regimented fact. What was the social position of the Grays—in Clyde in the eighteenth century? In the nineteenth century? How often did he go to church? Were there cliques in the Clyde High School, and to what extent did the cliques mingle? A part of the survey, and a very important part, would cover the lives of the minority and racial groups that had found lodgment, as Malcolm put it, in the growth of that predominantly Anglo-Saxon community. Did Charles know any who had worked their way into the upper-middle? What about the politically-minded Irish-Catholic group? Did the French-Canadians exhibit adaptive capacities?

As time went on and as they continued drinking sacramental wine, the team itself began dividing into groups and cliques, arguing about charts and graphs and questionnaires and methods of cataloguing. None of them was thinking of him as a person, except possibly Evangeline Scroll, who asked him to sit next her on the couch. She was a thin girl, with straight, short hair and horn-rimmed spectacles. As they talked, her knee inadvertently kept touching his. Once when he saw Malcolm Bryant looking at them curiously, he was quite sure that Evangeline Scroll was not thinking of him wholly in a scientific way but he could not keep his mind on her, he had too much to think about.

"Do you go around much in Clyde?" she asked.

"No, I'm pretty busy. I don't go around much," Charles told her.

"Aren't you in a crowd?"

"What sort of a crowd?" Charles asked.

"Weenie roasts, or dances. That sort of thing," Evangeline said. "You know. I wish you'd introduce me to your crowd."

The last thing he wanted to do was to introduce Evangeline Scroll to anyone and he was glad when Malcolm Bryant interrupted them.

"Come on, Charley," Malcolm said. "Bill Horsley wants to ask you a question. This isn't a time for sexual selection."

"Now, Malc," Evangeline said, "you told me he was mobile."

That was the word, mobility, an awkward word. He could move either up or down, and when he thought of Jessica he could see that she could move nowhere at all. She must remain exactly where she was. If things had been slightly different, if he had not gone to college, it might have been Doris Wormser, and now the thought made him shudder. It was dangerous to have mobility, but at the same time if he had not possessed mobility nothing that had happened that afternoon would have happened.

It was after eleven when he left but it was a beautiful night and he did not want to go home at once. Nearly all of Clyde was sound asleep. There was a faint smell of lilacs in the air, although the lilacs were not in bloom. They always bloomed on Decoration Day. There was also a scent of new leaves and grass and a touch of salt from the sea. Spring in Clyde, the soft darkness of that starlit night, and the halo of the street lights with the May flies fluttering about them, were things that Malcolm Bryant and his team would never put in their cross-reference catalogues. There were still a few couples on the benches on the green by the courthouse and now and then a car would whirl by it, going you could not guess where. The last show at the movies was over. The last soda fountain had closed, but there were still lights in the pool parlor at Dock Square and there were lights in the firehouse. Its doors were open and a few men were sitting by the engine. Peter Murphy, who was on the police night shift, was standing in front of the darkened news store, staring up Dock Street.

"Hello, Mr. Murphy," Charles said. "It's a nice night, isn't it?"

"Why, hello, Charley," Mr. Murphy said. "What are you doing up this time of night? Are you in love?"

It was a beautiful night and he did not want to go to bed. Down on River Street, he could see the harbor lights and the light from the stars on the calm black water. The Wright-Sherwin plant was a grim black shadow on River Street, with the street light shining on its blind brick façade. A radio was blaring and a dog was barking, but when he walked up Dock Street and turned left to Johnson Street there was no sound except his own footsteps on the brick sidewalk. Johnson Street was sleeping in the starlight. The trees made black patches on the Lovells' lawn which hardly could be called shadows, but the fence and the house itself looked very white indeed, as he stood there for a minute looking at them. The night light was burning in his Aunt Jane's room on Gow Street. He had never felt the unity of Clyde as he felt it then. It all belonged to him that night, because he was in love with Jessica Lovell.

13

How About It, Charley?

The Wright-Sherwin Company was the oldest of the three or four small industries that furnished work for the inhabitants of Clyde and nearly everyone knew its history and origins, simply because they had always heard about them. Ezra Wright, who in 1795 had started a small brass-and-iron foundry on the river, must have been one of those ingenious artisans who could turn their hand to anything. He invented a new type of blacksmith bellows. He made certain improvements, too, on the Franklin stove, and for a time he made clocks and andirons, which were still in existence, but his main interest was in metals, especially brass. Then a newcomer to Clyde named Samuel Sherwin had purchased the company and had obtained valuable contracts during the Civil War, and it kept going in a modest way down through the turn of the century. In 1912 Mr. Francis Stanley, a modern entrepreneur more concerned with business methods and salesmanship than invention, came to Clyde and acquired the property, and he obtained several large subcontracts in World War I for the manufacture of precision instruments.

Thus Wright-Sherwin was a tidy, aggressive little company when Charles Gray worked there, with complicated inventories and a plant that was thoroughly new. Mr. Francis Stanley, though he made a good thing of it, had not drained the profits but had plowed most of them back into brick and mortar and modern machine tools. He hated to raise wages, but he was willing to pay generously when necessary for metallurgical designers and a sales-manager—and whatever one thought of Mr. Stanley, more than five hundred people were employed at Wright-Sherwin that Monday morning in May 1928 when Charles left Wright-Sherwin forever.

The plant always opened at eight and Charles could hear a pleasant humming sound when he walked up the granite steps of the administrative building. The clock on the wall opposite a cadaverous looking portrait of Ezra Wright showed that it was twenty minutes before nine and Daisy Glover, who ran the telephone switchboard, smiled at him and checked off his name when he pushed open the little gate that led to the offices. Typewriters were clattering in the sales and promotion departments and the safe in the accounting department was already open, and he noticed a smell of freshly scrubbed linoleum in the passageway between the ground-glass partitions.

The desks of the accounting department occupied a large room, the rear windows of which looked over the foundry roofs to the blue water of the river. By the time Charles opened the door of the little closet where he hung his coat, Jackie Mason had arrived and nearly all the girls as well. Though they were always called girls, they were all middle-aged except Lottie Barnes, the secretary, who had been a classmate of Charles's and had taken the business course at high school. On the other hand, Miss Rosa Follen, who handled the petty cash and all the data that came to the office, and Miss Winona Pearson had been school friends of Charles's mother before Esther Gray had gone to the Academy. Charles said good morning to them all in a gentle tone because Mr. Howell always kept the door of his small office open.

"Good morning, Jack," Charles said, and he pulled back the chair of his own desk across the aisle from Jackie Mason.

"Hello, Charley," Jackie said. "Where were you yesterday? I thought you were going over to the Meaders'." Jackie Mason had been checking up on him lately and he wondered whether Jackie knew how much he had been seeing of Jessica. He even wondered why he had never spoken to Jack about Jessica, because technically Jack was still his best friend though for a long while he had not seen much of him. When Charles saw his yellow hair still moist from its careful morning brushing and his sedulously knotted tie with its unduly brilliant colors, he was so conscious of Jackie's limitations that he had a guilty feeling. They were growing away from each other and it was not Jackie's fault. Charles knew it was he who had changed in the last six months and not Jackie Mason. Jackie was a small-town boy. It was the first time Charles had used such a term about anyone, even in his thoughts, and it was ridiculous since he was a small-town boy himself, but there was something too aggressively brown about Jackie's suit, something about his manner that made Charles know all at once that they could never talk unreservedly again. Still he should have told Jackie on Sunday that he was going to leave Wright-Sherwin.

Charles opened the drawer of his desk and took out the inventory figures which he had been transferring to the Boston account book on Saturday morning. It seemed like a year ago that he had started checking the final list in Shed Three against receipts.

"I had to mow the lawn," Charles said. "I couldn't get over to the Meaders'."

"What are you doing Decoration Day?" Jackie asked. "The crowd is going down to the beach."

Jackie meant, of course, that Jeffrey and Melville and Priscilla Meader and Sally Bolton and Olive Rowell and all the rest of them were going for a picnic on the beach.

"I don't know," Charles said. "I will if I can make it."

"You'd better come along," Jackie said. "Don't be a stranger." It was what the old crowd always said if you did not see enough of them. They had started saying it when he went to Dartmouth.

He should have told Jackie on Sunday that he was going to leave Wright-Sherwin, but actually, there was still time to change his mind about leaving. He had never before faced the fact that by saying a few words security could be irretrievably ended. He would be leaving Jackie Mason and the old crowd forever when he left Wright-Sherwin. He would see them but he would not be a part of them.

"Let's have lunch at the dog wagon," Jackie said. He was referring to the new luncheon place across the street where the Wright-Sherwin office ate if they did not go home. He could tell Jackie then that he was going to leave Wright-Sherwin—but nothing would amount to anything until he had done what he had to do.

It was impossible to keep his mind on the inventory figures. Charles twisted in his swivel chair so that he could see Mr. Howell's room behind him. Mr. Howell was at his desk, unlocking the red leather general ledger, that contained all Wright-Sherwin's financial secrets. He had already put on his black alpaca coat and his green eyeshade, relics from bookkeeping days at

Wright-Sherwin before Mr. Stanley had bought the company. Charles drew a deep breath, rose from his chair and walked down the aisle, even though he knew Mr. Howell did not like to be disturbed early in the morning.

Mr. Howell pushed up his eyeshade when he saw Charles and the green shade made Mr. Howell's gray hair rise in an untidy wave.

"Do you mind if I close the door, sir, for a minute?" Charles asked.

Mr. Howell straightened his bent shoulders and his pale lips tightened. If anyone closed the door it indicated, of course, that there would be some sort of trouble.

"What's happened now?" Mr. Howell said. "Don't just stand there looking at me."

Charles just stood there because there was not an extra chair in Mr. Howell's office. If other people wanted to see Mr. Howell, they sent for him, and so there was no need for a chair.

"I just wanted to tell you," Charles said, "that I want to leave, sir."

Mr. Howell took off his steel-rimmed reading glasses.

"What's the matter?" he asked. "After I've been losing my patience teaching you and you're just getting to be useful you want to leave? Don't you like your job?"

"Yes, sir, I like it all right," Charles said.

"Then, by godfrey," Mr. Howell said, "why don't you use your head? You're in the best place in Clyde and you're doing all right. Why do you want to leave?"

"Because I don't think there's much future here, sir," Charles said.

"Don't you?" Mr. Howell said. "What do you know about a future if you haven't got a past? How do you mean there isn't any future in Wright-Sherwin? Look at me. I've been here for forty years. I've got a house of my own and money in the bank."

"Yes, sir," Charles said.

"And how did I get it? By sticking to one job and not changing. That's the way to get ahead. You want to get ahead, don't you?"

Charles had never thought that Mr. Howell would be sorry to have him go. Mr. Howell had never said a word to him about his work unless it was incorrect and each day he had made some acid remark about penmanship.

"I'm leaving because I want to get on."

Mr. Howell closed his general ledger carefully.

"What in hades," he said, "do you think I've been training you for? Do you think I'll live forever?"

Mr. Howell took his long-view spectacles from his waistcoat pocket and snapped open the case. It was a tremendous statement, because it was the same as saying that he was offering everything he cared for most. It was the same as saying that Charles could be the head of the accounting department someday. The unvarnished simplicity of it was what made it pathetic. Charles could see himself, his hair thinner, growing older, sitting at Mr. Howell's desk unlocking the red control ledger.

"I'm glad if you think I've done all right."

"I didn't say you've done all right," Mr. Howell said. "I said you might do all right. Now get out of here. It's nine-fifteen."

"It isn't as though I were leaving you without anyone," Charles said. "There's Jack Mason and he's just as good as I am. I'd like to leave in two weeks, and if it's all right I'd like tomorrow off."

"Oh," Mr. Howell said, "so you don't believe what I've been telling you, do you?"

"I didn't say I didn't believe you," Charles began again, but he had to make it clear that he was going to leave.

When he was back at his desk he thought of himself for the first time as a possible asset or a piece of human material that could be sold at a price and it gave him a feeling of confidence. Mr. Howell emerged from his office a minute or two later and walked down the aisle between the desks and there was a quiver of excitement because it was obvious that Charles had done something to disturb him. When Charles heard that Mr. Stanley wanted to see him, he knew that he really must have been spoken of as a possible new head for the accounting department someday, but he also knew that nothing short of unforeseen accident would ever take him out of the accounting department if he was useful there.

Charles had only faced Mr. Stanley once in a brief interview when he had applied for work at Wright-Sherwin although they always had exchanged greetings when they met outside the office; but even this superficial acquaintance was enough to show Charles that Mr. Stanley carried on his shoulders the cloak of a larger world. Unlike most other Clyde businessmen, he attended out-of-town conventions and once or twice a year took trips about the country calling personally on his customers. Mr. Stanley was stout, bald, and wore rimless glasses. He had a plump face, hard and yet jovial, which was always to remind Charles of the photographs of successful executives which appeared on the *New York Times* financial page above the announcement of a large company's change in management. As he sat in his comfortable corner office, behind his leather-topped desk, surrounded by prints of sailing ships, Mr. Stanley looked deceptively approachable. He smiled and waved his hand at Charles as though they were old friends and, in the same gesture, waved to a green leather armchair beside his desk.

"Sit down. Take your weight off your feet, Charley," he said. "Will you have a cigarette? It's all right. You can smoke in here and I won't tell anyone," and he pushed forward a silver cigarette box.

"No, thank you, sir," Charles said. Something told him that it was not a good idea to accept anything from Mr. Stanley then, even a cigarette, and it was a habit to which Charles always adhered later. He never liked that easy, disarming business of taking a cigarette and looking for a match. If you refused when you were asked to smoke, it always put a burden on the other person. Instead he sat down, neither too stiffly nor too casually, and waited for Mr. Stanley.

"You get a great view from this room, don't you?" Mr. Stanley said, and he waved his hand to a long window with a view of the river and the harbor mouth. "I had that window especially cut for it."

Charles wondered why Mr. Stanley should take the time to offer him a cigarette and show him the river, which he knew as well as Mr. Stanley did, but Mr. Stanley was going on.

"When I'm down in New York, up in one of those tall buildings overlooking the Hudson, I like to tell my friends about our river here. When they ask me why I bury myself in a little one-horse town like Clyde, I tell them they ought to see our river; and that isn't all I tell them. I tell them there's no place like Clyde for contentment. I tell them they ought to see my house, or your father's house on Spruce Street, Charley. They don't have houses like those in Rye, New York, or Short Hills, New Jersey. They don't know what houses are or what living is. They forget that money doesn't buy everything." Mr. Stanley shook his head sadly. "They don't know what it means to be in a town with—" Mr. Stanley waved his hand, groping for a word—"with a Yankee historical tradition. They don't know what a good snowstorm means or looks like. They don't know what it means to be in a business a hundred years old and going strong, with men in the works who are there because they like what they're doing and wouldn't do anything else if you paid them maybe a little more than I can. They don't understand pride of craftsmanship or pride in a community. The longer you live here, the more you know that there's nothing like a small town for happiness. Maybe we don't make millionaires here, but what of it? This is a wonderful town."

Charles was obviously not expected to answer. He was wondering whether Mr. Stanley had picked up the wonderful-town phrase from Malcolm or whether everybody who came to Clyde and settled there thought that it was a wonderful town, and Mr. Stanley was going on.

"If I were young and had to start all over again, I'd want to live in a place like Clyde and never get out of it. I can talk all night when I get started on Clyde, but then we know it, don't we, Charley?"

"Yes, sir, I guess we do," Charles said. He thought that Mr. Stanley looked at him sharply. He almost thought that Mr. Stanley guessed what he was thinking—that Mr. Stanley was an outsider who did not belong in Clyde.

"We ought to get together and talk about this again sometime," Mr. Stanley said. "I've been meaning to tell my boy Norman to ask you up to the house sometime. Well, we'll make a point of it now it's getting on to summer and things are easing up. By the way, what's all this that Dickie Howell's been in here telling me about you, Charley?"

Mr. Stanley smiled, picked up a silver letter opener from his desk, and stared straight at Charles. It was obvious that Mr. Stanley wanted him to stay.

"What's he been telling?" Charles asked. Even then he had the right instincts. It was always better to let the other person talk when possible.

Mr. Stanley laughed indulgently.

"You've got Dickie Howell all upset. You don't want to do that, Charley.

There's no one more valuable to this plant than old Dick. You and I mustn't stir him up."

"I'm sorry if I stirred him up," Charles said. Mr. Stanley smiled and shook his head.

"All this talk about your leaving us. You're not leaving us, are you, Charley?"

"Yes, sir," Charles said. "I told Mr. Howell I was."

"Well," Mr. Stanley said, and he laughed but Charles saw that Mr. Stanley still watched him carefully. Then he stopped laughing but he still smiled and tapped the letter opener softly on the desk. "We've got to have a little talk about this, Charley. Maybe you think I don't watch you boys when you come in here. Well, I do. That's my business. We have to have young blood here. Now Dickie Howell—this is between you and me—Dickie isn't as young as he used to be. He needs someone to take the weight off his shoulders. We need a new system here and something besides Boston ledgers." Mr. Stanley laughed again. "Now I've been turning over an idea in my mind. I'd like to send you to a school of accountancy for six months, Charley."

Mr. Stanley stopped but Charles did not answer. Mr. Stanley hitched himself forward in his chair and lowered his voice.

"Confidentially, Dick Howell and I have been talking about this. How would you like to head the accounting department of Wright-Sherwin in about two years? How do you think that sounds?"

It was necessary, Charles knew, to pretend that he was thinking.

"It's very kind of you, sir," Charles said.

"Kind of me?" Mr. Stanley looked grave and shook his head definitely. "I'm never kind when I do business. My job is picking people, and maybe I know more about you than you think, Charley. You've got a good mind and you keep your mouth shut. I've never seen you when you haven't been working. How about it, Charley?"

It was time to say no, but he did not want to say no in the wrong way.

"Thank you, but I'd rather not," Charles said.

"Why not?" Mr. Stanley had laid down the letter opener and sat motionless. It was better to answer frankly.

"If I got the accounting department, I'd always stay there," Charles said. "I don't think I'd be useful anywhere else."

"Wouldn't you want to stay there?" Mr. Stanley's voice was gentle but it had changed.

"No, sir," Charles said. "I'd like to get higher in the business than that someday."

"Let's see." Mr. Stanley picked up a small sheet of paper. "You're getting twenty-five dollars a week. How would you like it if I gave you fifty?"

"No, thank you, sir," Charles said. He would have been delighted a little while ago at such an offer. If it had not been for Jessica Lovell, he might have stayed in Wright-Sherwin.

"You're pretty ambitious, aren't you?" Mr. Stanley said.

"Yes, sir, I suppose I am," Charles answered.

"It doesn't pay to be too ambitious. There's much more to life than money. Fifty dollars here is the same as a hundred and fifty in New York. Money isn't everything. Have you got any other reason, Charley? Any personal reason?"

Mr. Stanley watched him intently and smiled in a warm, engaging way. If Mr. Stanley had heard so much about him, he wondered if he had heard about Jessica Lovell.

"Yes, sir," Charles said, "but I can't very well discuss it."

Mr. Stanley was silent for a moment. Then he straightened his heavy shoulders and cleared his throat and Charles knew that the interview was over.

"Well, we'll be sorry to lose you," Mr. Stanley said. "What are you going to do?"

"I think I'll go to Boston," Charles said, and he rose.

"Well, we'll be sorry to lose you," Mr. Stanley said. "If you change your mind come around and see me."

Sometimes Charles considered that interview a model of its kind. Neither Mr. Stanley nor he had said too much but they had said enough. He often wondered whether he had learned more of Mr. Stanley than Mr. Stanley had of him. He often wondered whether Mr. Stanley had thought of offering him anything more, but this was hardly possible because he was too young. He often wondered whether he would have stayed if he had known Mr. Stanley better.

14

The Gambling Known as Business Looks with Austere Disfavor upon the Business Known as Gambling

—AMBROSE BIERCE

Charles had often heard his father speak at length on the old days of downtown Boston. Those were the days, he used to say, when Boston's alleys all led to dignified bars and secluded restaurants which served the best food in the world. In those days, Boston had a respect for the male, particularly in the State Street district, and Boston was a comfortable, civilized town. Woodrow Wilson and the income tax had begun to send it downhill, John Gray used to say, and the World War and prohibition had done the rest. The old places were closing, like the New England House, with its fat dog and its gray African parrot in the upstairs dining room. The bars with their free lunches had vanished. The old oyster houses around the market were not what they used to be, now that there was no ale. You could still get tripe at the Parker House, but no Parker House punch in the spring. To put it another way, Boston was becoming contaminated by New York and the rest of

America. It was, John Gray hated to say it, losing its fine isolation and its proud provincialism. Even the shoes of Boston women were not as sensible as they used to be.

John Gray repeated all this to Charles on that Tuesday morning in 1928 but Charles was too concerned with the future to bother with the past. The narrow sidewalks of Washington Street and the old State House, the Old South Church, Milk Street, and Congress Street seemed to Charles completely modern that morning. He could only accept Boston in a contemporary way, as one accepted everything when one was twenty-four. He never dreamed that the time would come when he, too, would speak of the old Boston he had known in the bond department of E. P. Rush & Company, the old pre-depression Boston of marble corridors and black walnut woodwork, of leisurely elevators moving upward through their shafts like giant spiders on webs of looped cables, the Boston of trustees and real estate trusts and well-trained barbers who came to clip the gray hair of trustees and lawyers as they sat in their offices gazing at the tombs in the Old Granary Burying Ground or into the dingy streets off Post Office Square.

"Dear, dear," John Gray said. "There used to be a time when everything was static here. I hate this sense of change."

He was always cheerful when he was back in Boston after a longish absence. He was wearing his best tailored suit, which he very seldom wore in Clyde, and his newest brown felt hat.

"It makes me feel old and even sordid to be taking a son of mine down here, but I suppose we have to start sometime."

As they turned left on Congress Street he began to whistle a snatch of an old waltz.

"Did you say this place is on Congress Street?" Charles asked.

"Yes," John Gray answered. "Congress Street, and on a third floor. Old E. P., the father of the present Mr. Rush, Charles, said an upstairs office stopped the riffraff from dropping in."

"Don't you think," Charles said, "if you're going to introduce me to Mr. Rush you'd better tell me a little more about him?"

"I'm not introducing you to E. P. Rush," John Gray said. "E. P. Rush is dead and perhaps it's just as well because I'm afraid he didn't approve of me. It's his son—not E. P. Rush—whom I met during my brief sojourn at Harvard University. We played poker and did other things together."

"I know, you've told me that"—his father was in one of his most exasperating moods that morning—"but you haven't told me what he's like."

"It doesn't matter," John Gray said, "because he'll probably make a different impression on you from any he has made on me. I wonder how the market's opening."

E. P. Rush & Company occupied half of the third floor of a building on Congress Street. It was a curiously planned office which seemed to have grown like a living organism, producing small clusters of desks and typewriters, throwing out new railed enclosures and rearing new counters and pieces of grillwork and acquiring, as an afterthought, a few leather armchairs and cuspidors grouped in front of a board on which were listed in abbreviations some but not all of the stocks on the New York Exchange. Two tickers near the board stamped quotations upon reels of tape which poured into tall wicker baskets. The exchange had not opened yet so the tickers were almost silent. The bookkeepers were already at work and the young men in the bond department were reading prospectuses and making their morning telephone calls. Charles did not know then that the studied, dusty carelessness of E. P. Rush & Company was an effect deliberately cultivated to create a sound atmosphere.

This impression of casualness was also reflected in the clothing of the young men in the outer office. They wore soft shirts and their clothes were not aggressively pressed. They slouched easily in their swivel chairs, and yet they were always ready to come courteously to attention. The secretaries, who were still called stenographers at E. P. Rush & Company, were gathered in a small paddock of their own, and they, too, fitted perfectly with the spirit, most of them approaching middle age, none of them endowed with disturbing beauty.

Behind this outer office, which smelled of creosote and paper and stale cigar smoke, was a railing guarding the ground-glass doors of the partners' rooms. A switchboard operator, a plump, cheerful looking girl, guarded the railing gate. John Gray, with Charles following him, walked across the room and bowed to her and she said that Mr. Gray was quite a stranger lately.

"Yes," John Gray said, "lately, but my thoughts are often here, Miss Swift. Is Mr. Rush in yet?"

"Oh, yes," Miss Swift said. "He's just reading the papers. I know he'll be glad to see you."

Mr. Rush sat at a shabby roll-top desk working on a crossword puzzle by the light from a single unwashed window. Mr. Rush was wearing a blue serge suit, which was shiny at the knees and elbows. The morning mail, opened and in a neat pile on the desk before him, was weighted down by an Indian hatchet head. In the corner behind him, like a leafless tree, stood a mahogany hatrack on which hung Mr. Rush's leghorn hat. The lenses of his horn-rimmed spectacles gave his light blue eyes a surprised look which did not fit with his mouth.

"Hello," he said. "Where did you drop from?"

"Don't let me interrupt your train of thought, Moulton," John Gray answered. "This is my son Charles."

"He looks the way you used to," Mr. Rush said.

"But he isn't like me," John Gray said. "Charley wants to get on."

"What class were you in?" Mr. Rush asked Charles.

John Gray sighed and spoke before Charles could answer.

"My sister Jane wanted him to go to Dartmouth. Don't hold it against him, Moulton. It's a small place but we love it."

"Does he want a job?" Mr. Rush said.

"Why, Moulton," John Gray answered, "why do you think we're here?"

Mr. Rush pulled a thick gold watch from his waistcoat pocket.

"It's five minutes after ten," he said. "Why don't you go out and see the opening, Johnny?"

After John Gray had left, Mr. Rush looked at Charles for a moment without speaking.

"Your father is a remarkable man," Mr. Rush said.

"Yes, sir," Charles said, "I suppose he is."

Mr. Rush stood up.

"Well, I suppose I'd better introduce you to Mr. Stoker. He runs our bond department."

They walked down the partners' row to Mr. Stoker's office. Mr. Stoker was younger, a barrel-chested man who looked like a football coach. In fact Charles learned later that Lawrence Stoker had once been a line coach for Harvard.

"Lawrence," Mr. Rush said, "this is Charles Gray. He comes from Dartmouth but I'd like you to find something for him to do."

It astonished Charles that Mr. Rush had not asked him a single question, but later when he knew the office better he approved of that method. Mr. Rush had known who he was and had passed on his personal appearance and this was about all that was necessary. As in Victorian England younger sons once rushed to join the Church and the army, so in those days on America's eastern seaboard they crowded into reputable investment houses. There were so many nice young men in those days that they were expendable material. Their energy and resilience could be used to the limit until almost inevitable disillusion made it evaporate. Not one in twenty of these young men, Charles heard Mr. Rush say later, ever developed a permanent value. They entered the Boston offices, in the late twenties, only to disappear eventually no one knew where. It was not the policy of Rush & Company to expend much time on their education. It was a matter of sink or swim, and there were always lots more waiting.

That was how he started with E. P. Rush & Company and though he sometimes wondered what would have happened to him if he had gone to sea or into publishing or if a little later he had gone with Malcolm Bryant to the Orinoco, he found the order and the relentless flow of forces at E. P. Rush & Company satisfying and congenial. Besides, as his father had said, he wanted to get on. He wanted to wear the right clothes and do the right things. He wanted to do well as quickly as he could, because he was in love with Jessica Lovell.

He had been a very nice boy, that day when he went up to Boston, devoid of disillusion, indoctrinated in all the right creeds. He had believed everything that Mr. Stoker told him. He was entering the finest investment house in Boston, a firm whose backing meant that any issue in which it participated was as sound as a nut. Everybody who worked for E. P. Rush was hand-picked. It was like being in a club to be in Mr. Stoker's crowd. Everyone had a chance to earn his letter. E. P. Rush & Company was a gentlemen's firm, with gentlemen's ethics. There was money enough in the firm to build an office that would look like an Italian palace, but E. P. Rush did not want the type of customer who was attracted by upholstery. Its partners were broad-gauge public-spirited men who were there not for window dressing but because they understood the investment business and were personally interested in most of the companies whose securities they handled. In fact it was all one big happy family and now Charles was in the family. Charles already realized that it might be just as well if he did not talk much about Dartmouth.

When Charles returned to Clyde at six o'clock, his manner was already changing. He was in the old-line house of E. P. Rush & Company and someday he would be a partner. The prospect was a long way off but already its charm was working. If he had not been in E. P. Rush he would not have called up Jessica Lovell that evening after supper. As a matter of fact, he might not have telephoned her if the family had not been so pleased.

"The funny thing about it was," his father said, "that I've never known Moulton Rush very well, Esther. It was Charles who did it. Moulton just took one look at him."

Charles saw his mother take one look at him too, a proud, possessive look.

"I don't see how Charles ever got in it," Dorothea said.

"Through accident, Dorothea," Charles told her. "They weren't thinking what they were doing."

"Well, see you stay in it," Dorothea said. "At least they must think he's honest, Mother," but she said it kindly. She even said it as though she were proud of him.

"I think I'll go over to see Jessica," he said. He was fully aware, from the pause at the supper table, that this was the same as announcing to the family, as it was said in Clyde, that he was attentive to Jessica Lovell.

"Why, Charley," his mother said, "I think that would be very nice, but don't stay too late."

Of course they were all listening when he went into the hall to telephone —but then he was in E. P. Rush & Company.

"Why, Charley," Jessica said over the telephone. "Of course I'm not doing anything. We'd love to see you." He was disturbed by the coolness of her voice until he remembered that the Lovells' telephone, too, was in the hall.

It was eight o'clock though it was still light and all of Johnson Street was bathed in a misty, mysterious afterglow that gave the Lovells' house a remote look, but a sense of never having been there before vanished when Jessica opened the front door herself. Her silk afternoon dress was a grayish-green color very much like the color of the new leaves in the fading light. The hall in back of her was dark and the light from the open door of the wallpaper room made it hard to see her face. She clasped his hand very tightly, and her own hand felt cold.

"I've been wondering where you've been," she said. "We're all in the wallpaper room." He walked slowly in behind her and shook hands with Miss Lovell and Mr. Lovell.

"We've been reading *Jane Eyre*," Miss Lovell said. "That is, I've been reading it. Do you like *Jane Eyre*, Charles?"

"How do you do, Charles?" Mr. Lovell said, getting up from the sofa.

"Please don't get up, sir," Charles said. "I didn't mean to interrupt you."

"It's just as well you did," Mr. Lovell said. "*Jane Eyre* is the most improbable book I know and, at the same time, the truest."

Charles wished he could remember more about the Brontë sisters.

"How's your Aunt Jane, Charles?" Miss Lovell asked.

"I'm afraid she hasn't been so well lately," Charles answered.

"Let me see"—Mr. Lovell was speaking—"I don't think I've set eyes on you, Charles, since the Players were finished. How is everything going at Wright-Sherwin?"

"I'm leaving there at the end of next week, sir." Charles tried to speak as though he were speaking about the Brontë sisters.

"Oh," Mr. Lovell said, "I'm sorry. Was anything the matter?"

"No, nothing was the matter," Charles answered. "Next week I'm starting work in Boston at E. P. Rush & Company."

A change had come over Mr. Lovell. He was looking at Charles for the first time as though he were not a Clyde boy who had come to call.

"Why, Charles," he said, "how did you ever get into E. P. Rush?"

"Father knows Mr. Rush," Charles said.

"I didn't know John knew Mr. Rush."

"Yes," Charles said, "he knows him."

Mr. Lovell still looked at Charles as though he had heard something incredible.

"Why, that's splendid," he said. "Well, well. Congratulations."

Charles wanted to look again at Jessica but he restrained himself, and then Miss Lovell spoke quickly.

"Charley, I'm awfully glad for you," she said. He always liked Miss Lovell after that.

"E. P. Rush & Company." Mr. Lovell was speaking again. "Well, well, well. If you hear of anything interesting in the way of securities, Charles, be sure you let me know."

"Jessica," Miss Lovell said, "why don't you show Charles the tulips in the garden? It's still light enough."

"It's getting damp tonight," Mr. Lovell said. "Jessica's the only girl I have and I don't want her catching cold. Well, just walk around the garden, Jessica, and then come back."

When they were opening the door at the end of the hall, Charles could still hear Miss Lovell's voice.

"Laurence," he heard her say, "try not to be so ridiculous."

The tulips made a beautiful show in the beds on the lower terrace and above them on the second terrace the peonies were just ready to bloom. Though there was no strong scent of flowers, the air was filled with that strange repressed vigor of a New England spring.

"I can't stay out long," Jessica said. "You understand, don't you, dear?"

She was walking quickly up the gravel path, climbing up the steps to the third terrace. "Father hates seeing me grow up. He always has." She sounded as though she were talking to an imaginary person, much as Charles in his thoughts had often spoken to her. "I wish I weren't the only thing he had."

Her coat was over her shoulders with its sleeves hanging loose, for she had not bothered to put her arms through it before she left the house. Her bare head and the loose sleeves and the way she talked made him think of Jane Eyre, hurrying away from something in the house, afraid that it might follow her or afraid that it might call her back.

The third terrace, a level, close-cropped lawn called the bowling green, was shut off from all the rest of the garden by a high, carefully clipped spruce hedge and she seemed uncertain that he was beside her until they were in that dusky green enclosure.

"Oh, darling," she whispered, "I've missed you so," and her coat slipped off her shoulders. She said she had missed him until she could not believe any of it.

"I've missed you, too," he said. "We've got to see each other, Jessica." It did not seem possible that they could be making love in that formal garden.

"Yes," she said, "we've got to. Everything's going to be all right, isn't it?"

"Of course," he said. "Everything's all right."

"Darling," she said, "I love you so that everything goes to pieces."

He kissed her without answering.

"I'm so proud of you," she said. "You're so honest and you never are afraid, are you?"

"What's there to be afraid of?" Charles asked.

"Oh," she said, and she turned her head away, "of something happening to spoil it all. I keep waking up in the night and thinking something's happened." She shook her head very quickly. "Darling, wasn't Aunt Georgianna sweet? She wanted us to see the tulips."

"Have you told her anything?" Charles asked. She shook her head quickly.

"Not exactly. I've talked about you. I have to talk about you, dear, and there's no one else."

"Have you told your father anything?"

"Of course not," she said. "That's a silly question. Darling, you can see, can't you? It's got to come over him by degrees. We'd better be going back now."

"Yes," Charles said, "I suppose we had," and he wrapped her coat around her.

"And now you're in Boston we can see each other there sometimes, too. Darling, everything's so wonderful. I've got to forget it's so wonderful." She seemed to be forgetting already as they walked back. "Look how black the box border looks. None of it was winterkilled."

She only said one thing more before they reached the house. She said it just as she put her hand on the heavy brass latch of the outside door.

"We've got to keep believing."

Nothing else mattered if you could keep believing, and nothing was left if you stopped.

Charles never considered that his or Jessica's manner, aside from all appearances, might indicate the probability of what had happened in the garden because they took great pains to walk into the room decorously, far apart and entirely unconcerned with each other.

"Hello," Mr. Lovell said. "So you're back."

"You were right," Jessica said, and she bent down and kissed his high forehead. "It was very cold out there. You're always right."

"Charles," Miss Lovell said, "would you mind getting my knitting? It's on the table."

"Patrick's doing pretty well with the garden," Mr. Lovell said. "None of the box border was winterkilled."

"I suppose it's pretty far north for box, sir," Charles said, and Mr. Lovell gave him a searching look.

"Virginia's the place for box, Virginia and England. Were you ever in Virginia, Charles?"

"No, sir," Charles said.

"You must go someday . . . Jessie"—Mr. Lovell smiled at her—"I've just been thinking you and I might go abroad again this summer."

"This summer?" Jessica repeated.

"I was just speaking of it to Aunt Georgianna," Mr. Lovell said. "Why, don't you like the idea, Jessica?"

There was nothing for Charles to do but to listen. Jessica sat with her hands carefully folded.

"I thought you wanted me to get used to Clyde," she said, "and now I'm getting used to it you want to go away."

"Now, Jessie"—Mr. Lovell laughed—"Clyde's always an easy place to come back to and don't look so upset. We couldn't possibly leave till toward the end of June. I'll want to go to Class Day and there are all sorts of odds and ends I have to attend to. I think it would do us a lot of good to get a change."

"But you were just saying yesterday—" Jessica began, and she stopped.

"When we get back, Charles may be a partner at E. P. Rush, but I'm afraid it's dull for you, Charles, our talking over plans," Mr. Lovell said.

It was clearly time to be leaving, but he did not want it to look as though he were hurrying away.

"I hope you have a good trip, sir," he said.

"Don't go, Charles." Mr. Lovell smiled at him, but Charles knew when it was time to go. He said good night to Miss Lovell and shook Mr. Lovell's hand.

"Good night, Jessica," he said.

"Oh, Charley," she said, quite loudly, when his hand touched hers, "don't forget tomorrow night," and she turned away from him before she dropped his hand. "Charles is going to take me to the movies tomorrow night."

He certainly had not asked her, but she said it so convincingly that he almost thought he had.

"Why," Mr. Lovell said, "that's very nice of Charles to take you," and his words rang with complete conviction. "Good night, Charles, and come in any time."

"Yes," Miss Lovell said, "any time. Good night."

He must have been thinking more of the way he had behaved than of anything else in the first few minutes after he left. He hoped he had shown no surprise or resentment; he even found himself admiring the way in which Mr. Lovell, with his flat, agreeably modulated voice, had contrived to show him that he had stepped into a region where he did not belong, gently, delicately, and yet in a way you could not possibly mistake. What lay between him and Jessica was now an incontrovertible fact or it would not have occurred to Mr. Lovell that it might be nice to take her abroad that summer.

He had never asked her to the moving pictures and perhaps everyone had known it. Nothing had been as wonderful as the moment when Jessica had said, still holding his hand, "Don't forget tomorrow night," for she might as well have said that she cared for him no matter what anyone thought. She might as well have stood beside him and have said that she would see him any time she pleased and that no one could prevent it. Perhaps Jessica actually did say so, after she had brushed her lips against his cheek in the dark front hall and had closed the door behind him.

When he returned to Spruce Street, his father was sitting alone downstairs openly reading the financial page of the *Boston Transcript*.

"How was it at the Lovells', Charles?" he asked.

"It was all right," Charles said.

"I suppose they were all sitting in that room with the wallpaper," John Gray said. "How did Jessica look?"

"She had on a grayish-green dress," Charles said, and he went on because he had to tell someone. "Miss Lovell was reading *Jane Eyre* aloud."

"Oh dear me," John Gray said, "the Brontës. Did you all read aloud?"

"No," Charles said. "Miss Lovell asked whether Jessica and I wouldn't like to go out into the garden and see the tulips."

"Oh my," John Gray said, "what did Laurence say?"

"He said it was getting cold outside."

"Well, well. How long were you in the garden?"

"Not long. Jessica thought we ought to get back."

"Well, well," John Gray said. "What happened when you got back?"

"Mr. Lovell said it had just come into his mind that he and Jessica might go abroad this summer."

John Gray smiled and passed his hand over the back of his head.

"There's nothing like a small town, Charley. Of course, everyone is going to guess why the Lovells went abroad."

Charles felt his face grow deep red, and his father leaned forward and put his hand gently on his knee before he could answer.

"I never did like Laurence Lovell, Charley." The intensity of his dislike must have had its roots deep in some past of which Charles knew nothing.

"Charley," John Gray continued, "this is a very small town, smaller than a smaller town, and someday you'll see what I mean."

15

Laugh, Clown, Laugh

"You're always on time, aren't you," Jessica said when he called for her the next evening in time for the late show. "Do I look all right for the movies?"

Naturally he told her that she did though it was obvious that she would not have been wearing a semi-evening dress and a short, dark velvet cloak if she had gone often to the movies in Clyde.

"I suppose you know that everyone will see us there," he said.

She moved closer to him before she answered and put her arm through his.

"I want everyone to see us," she said, and her hand was trembling. "You don't mind, do you?"

Of course, he said, he did not mind who saw them.

"It's been a dreadful day," she said. "It isn't anything Father says. It's the way he looks. You might think I was going to run away with you because you're taking me to the movies—but he's really trying to be sweet. It isn't you, you know, it's me. Do you know what he said at supper?"

Charles wished that he did not have the helpless feeling of an innocent bystander.

"No," he answered, "what did he say?"

"He said to be sure to ask you in when you took me home. He didn't want me to catch cold walking around outside. Oh, darling." He heard her catch her breath. "It has to be all right. As long as he sees there's nothing he can do."

They had turned down Dock Street and they were passing the Dock Street Bank.

"Do you remember the bank?" he asked her. "You had on your red hat." It had only been that spring.

Two years before, the only moving picture house in Clyde had been called the Acme Theater. It had been built in the days when there had been vaudeville acts and illustrated songs between the pictures. It had been renovated at about the same time the new soda fountain and the uncomfortable little booths had been installed in Walters's Drugstore, around the corner from it on Dock Street. The Acme Theater was called the Savoy now and was equipped with new soft seats and Romanesque decorations and an electrically lit marquee which cast a harsh halo of bright light on the sidewalk. Lon Chaney in *Laugh, Clown, Laugh,* was on that night, and the customers for the late show were already entering, while the new manager, Mr. Dupree, who was soon to sell it to a theater chain, stood by the ticket booth watching an out-of-town blonde making change.

Though it was now the Savoy and not the Acme, and though its lights were brighter, the whole scene reminded Charles of high school days when he used to take Doris Wormser to the same late show. The faces were different but there were the same crowds of adolescent boys and girls. They must all have been in grammar school when Charles had taken Doris there. There were all sorts of familiar faces, too, faces of older people and old schoolmates. First he saw Earl Wilkins, who had been tackle when he had been left end on the high school team, and Earl was with Lizzie Jenkins, one of the Wright-Sherwin girls.

"Hi, Earl," he said.

"Hi, Charley," Earl answered, and looked at him as if he had not seen him for a long while.

Then he saw Doris Wormser with Willie Woodbury, who was working in the Clyde Grain and Implement Company. Both Charles and Doris must have looked startled, but they called out to each other, and then he saw Melville Meader and Jackie Mason and Priscilla Meader.

"There's Jackie Mason," Jessica said.

He did not want it to seem unusual for him to be there with Jessica Lovell. He told himself that it was perfectly natural for him to be taking Jessica to *Laugh, Clown, Laugh,* and that it was only his imagination that made him feel that everyone was staring at them. At the same time, there was no reason why they should not have stared, because he would have been equally surprised to see a friend of his with Jessica in her velvet cape. It was a relief when he was in the dark theater, holding Jessica's hand, until he saw that Priscilla Meader was beside him and then he dropped her hand hastily.

"I thought you never went to the movies any more, Charley," Priscilla said.

"I don't often," Charles answered. "You know Jessica Lovell, don't you Priscilla?" It would have been much better if he had not asked, since it indicated that perhaps Priscilla did not know her.

"Oh, yes," Priscilla said, and there was no need for Jessica's having been quite so cordial. There was a cloying effort at politeness as they both leaned across him to talk during the short comedy.

"I haven't seen you for a long while," Jessica said.

"It was when the gardens were open, wasn't it?" Priscilla said. "I don't see how you ever got Charley to the movies."

"I had to ask him. He wouldn't have thought of it," Jessica said.

Tomorrow everyone would know that he had taken her to the movies and that she had asked him.

"How about going to Walters's after the show?" Charles asked. "How about it, Jack?" If he was going around with Jessica Lovell, they might as well go around to Walters's.

Everyone always went around to Walters's for ice cream after the pictures but Jessica looked foreign there in her velvet cape. They had divided decorously, like changing partners at a dance, so Charles looked across one of the little booths at Jessica sitting beside Jackie Mason. They were all speaking above the giggles and whistles of the high school crowd.

"This place is dreadfully crowded, isn't it?" Priscilla said. "But at the same time, I can't count how often I've been here. Can you, Charley? Do you remember Saturday nights at high school?" She beamed across the table. "You ought to have been with our crowd at high school, Jessica. You don't mind my calling you Jessica, do you?"

"I don't see what else you could call me," Jessica answered.

Jackie Mason was looking at his ice cream. It was a strawberry nut sundae and Priscilla was speaking again.

"We've seen each other around enough to be on a first-name basis, I guess. You honestly ought to have been with us at high school, Jessica. We used to have more fun. Gosh, it seems like a long time ago. Jackie, didn't we have fun?"

Jackie Mason looked up hastily from his plate.

"It was quite a long while ago, wasn't it?" Jackie said, and he smiled feebly.

"Everybody sort of drifts apart, don't they?" Priscilla said. "It doesn't seem like we could ever have been like all those kids over by the fountain. I don't think we ever behaved like those kids."

"They're just having a good time," Jessica said. "I wish I had gone to high school. Charley, have you any cigarettes?"

"Here, let me," said Jackie Mason.

"Look, Jackie's got a silver case," Priscilla said. "Who gave you the silver case, Jackie?"

"The family," Jack Mason said. "Just the family."

"Oh," Priscilla said, "it wasn't you-know-who? We had more fun in high school. We all paired off. There was Jackie and you-know-who—"

"There's Earl Wilkins over there now," Charles said.

"Oh, Earl," Priscilla said. "Just because Earl used to take me to the movies . . . What about you and Doris Wormser, Charley?"

Charles laughed. He had almost forgotten Jessica. He was back with the old crowd again.

"What about you and Wilkins in the physics laboratory?" he said, and then he remembered Jessica. "You ought to have been in high school, Jessica. If you'd been there, I wouldn't have worried about Doris Wormser."

"He never did worry about her much and I ought to know," Jackie Mason said.

"You don't want to believe him," Priscilla said. "Jackie's always sticking up for Charley. I'm just being funny. I never meant it was anything serious at all. Why, Charley and I played post office. Do you want a letter, Charley?"

Charles wondered what it would have been like if Jessica had been there, playing tag in the Meaders' back yard. He felt almost sorry for her because he knew she had missed a lot although he had moved a long way from it himself.

"I wish Priscilla hadn't talked so much," Jackie murmured, after they had paid the check at the cigar counter. "I'm afraid she gave a wrong impression." Jackie always worried about impressions. Priscilla and Jessica were waiting for them on the sidewalk.

"There's nobody like Charley," he heard Priscilla saying. "I've always been crazy about Charley, Jessica."

When he and Jessica were walking up Dock Street, he remembered thinking that he must not apologize for any of it—that she was the one who had asked to go.

"Priscilla Meader," she said, and obviously she had no previous recollection of Priscilla Meader at all. "Is her father the one who has the real estate and insurance office?"

"Yes," Charles answered, "that's the one."

Then they were silent again.

"I wish I'd been to high school," she said. "I wouldn't feel so far away and I wouldn't have worn this damn dress."

Charles at this time did not understand that there was a purpose behind many social gestures. As long as Mr. Lovell had especially asked that Jessica invite him in afterwards, Charles believed that Mr. Lovell might end by liking him after all. As early as a year later, however, Charles was able to appreciate Mr. Lovell's motives.

It happened that Mr. Rush had called Charles into his office to explain some details concerning the bond issue of the King Wassoit Textile Company to a trustee named Mr. Garvin, but when Charles entered they were talking, in that informal way they did in Boston, about their children and especially about Mr. Rush's daughter Ruth, whom Charles had never met but whose picture in riding clothes stood on Mr. Rush's desk.

"She met him somewhere," Mr. Rush was saying. "I never saw him until she brought him out to Brookline for Sunday dinner. God knows where girls pick up men nowadays."

"It's a phase that girls go through," Mr. Garvin said. "You've got to put up with it. Just don't let her see you don't like him, Moulton. That's the worst mistake you can make, you know."

"Yes," Mr. Rush answered, "that's what Alice and everyone keep saying."

"Let it run its course," Mr. Garvin said. "They're always crazy to do some damn fool thing that you don't approve of and as soon as you approve of it they forget it. Have him around to the house. Give him your whiskey and cigars."

"They all smoke cigarettes," Mr. Rush said.

"Just let her see you like him," Mr. Garvin said, "and she'll be tired of him in two weeks."

"But I don't like him."

"Well, don't tell Ruthie so."

Charles never knew what had happened to that boy of whom Ruth Rush had been fond but he understood then why Mr. Lovell had told Jessica to be sure to bring him home that night and why Mr. Lovell had asked him to drop in sometimes in the evening, in those few short weeks before he took Jessica abroad. It was, of course, before John Gray was at leisure and began taking the eight-two regularly to Boston and before the Grays bought the Cadillac and finally joined the Shore Club.

Everything had seemed possible that evening. Those minutes at Walters's drugstore had a reassuring quality that carried even into the wallpaper room. Charles no longer worried about the creases in his trousers when he sat beside Jessica on the sofa. The Chinese junks and the pagodas on the wall and the studied elegance of that English furniture had a homelike, welcoming quality, as though it were natural and proper for him to be there with Jessica. They talked for a while about those arid days when they had hardly known each other. He told her about Earl Wilkins and about the Thanksgiving Day football game with Smith's Common High. He asked her whether she remembered Sam. Jessica was the only person with whom he ever talked freely about Sam, except of course with May Mason. He must have told her about Sam's going to the war and that he still could not believe that Sam was dead. He surely must have told her what he had said to Mr. Howell and Mr. Stanley at Wright-Sherwin, because it was possible to tell her everything or almost everything. He must have laid his whole life, such as it was, before Jessica Lovell in a magnificent, prodigal gesture and Jessica did the same.

There was nothing more lonely than being an only child, Jessica said, particularly in a place like Clyde. She always knew she belonged there without any sense of belonging, if you could understand what she meant. If she had been a boy she would have belonged more to it, because she could have moved about. She could have gone everywhere, as Charles had. Her father had often said that he would have sent her to school in Clyde, at least for a year or two, if she had been a boy, because the Lovells belonged to Clyde and they had always played a part in it. His own father, Grandfather Lovell, had sent him to school there for two or three years and he valued that experience more than any other. He was always saying that it had taught him to get on with all sorts of people, though Jessica had never seen this side of him. He often said that he was disturbed at how the school system had changed. It was run now by politicians and so many foreigners had entered Clyde that there was not the background of good Yankee stock in the schools that he had known. He had never wanted Jessica to learn the habits of some girls, particularly foreign girls, at grammar school. Though girls from nice families went there, from all sorts of solid, self-respecting Yankee families, they usually ended by speaking ungrammatically in high, nasal voices.

It was not that he was snobbish in the least. If her mother had lived, instead of dying so suddenly when Jessica was six, her father might not have wanted her to be so perfect. As it was, there had been a governess for her until she went to school in Boston and she never belonged anywhere at all. She used to watch the children, sometimes, going along Johnson Street to school. She used to see them at her birthday parties. (She was sure she did not know why Charles had never been asked to her birthdays, because Jackie Mason had been.) They used to play together sometimes but she never really knew them and no one, or hardly anyone, in Boston knew about Clyde. Her father always brought her home for week ends when she was at school in Boston. He never wanted to be away from her too long, after her mother died. He had always given up so much for her. It was the same way at Westover and Vassar. He was often at Poughkeepsie for week ends and they were always together at vacation time.

"I sound like Emily Dickinson," she said.

She did not mean that she had not seen other men but there had always been something, something. It was just as though she had been asleep, or almost asleep, until that day at the firemen's muster.

"I don't know why it happened then," she said. "I don't see why you liked me."

"I guess it was your red hat and your hair," he told her. "I don't exactly know how it was. You seemed to be looking for someone and there wasn't anybody else there but me."

"I wasn't looking for you," she said. "I was looking for Malcolm Bryant."

"No, you weren't," he said. "You were really looking for me. It couldn't have been anyone else, and you couldn't have been anyone else. And there's another thing."

"What other thing?"

He found himself staring at the molding of the room, thinking of the time it had taken to saw and chisel its intricate design. There was just the faintest irregularity, something a machine could never duplicate.

"It wouldn't have happened if we'd known each other too well." And then he thought of Malcolm Bryant and he began to laugh.

"What are you laughing about?" she asked.

"About that chart of Malcolm Bryant's," he said. "It wouldn't have happened if we had both been upper-uppers. You'd have seen too much of me and we wouldn't have had anything to wonder about."

They were sitting together on the sofa so close that her hair brushed his cheek, but she moved closer to him.

"Darling," she said, "you don't really think that way about me, do you? It's so damned silly. You don't really?"

"Not right now," he said, "or I wouldn't have told you."

"Darling," she whispered, "don't let anyone ever put us on a chart"; and then she drew away from him because Mr. Lovell was calling from the top of the stairs.

"Oh, Jessie."

At least they did not spring guiltily apart; her hand was still on his shoulder when she answered.

"Yes, Father."

"Is Charles there?"

"Yes, Father."

Her hand dropped noiselessly from his shoulder and rested on his hand.

"You'll excuse me for not coming down, won't you, Charles?" Mr. Lovell called. "What was the name of the picture you went to see?"

"It was *Laugh, Clown, Laugh,*" Charles called back.

"Well, Jessie," Mr. Lovell said, "when Charles goes, don't forget to put out the lights."

There was no need to read the news notes in the *Clyde Herald* to find out what had happened to anyone in Clyde. The news notes dealt with engagement showers, illnesses, and the trips of citizens to visit close relatives, but the more vital matters never appeared on the printed page. These were retailed by word of mouth with bewildering speed, edited and exaggerated, cut and lengthened. This interest in other people's business was unmalicious in Clyde compared with what went on in any large office, for people in Clyde usually wanted to know about each other simply because there was human consolation in others' misfortunes, and at worst a mild envy in others' small successes, Charles had only told Jack Mason the whole story of his interviews with Mr. Howell and Mr. Stanley because Jack was his best friend and also because he wanted Jack to know that they were looking for someone to run the accounting department eventually. Jack had declared that he would say nothing about it, and Charles was sure that Jack had not, because they were friends and because Jack wanted a chance at that job himself; but in two days people were stopping Charles on the street to say they had heard he had left Wright-Sherwin and that it was fine that he had such a nice job in Boston.

Still, no one except Jackie Mason ever brought up with Charles his trip with Jessica to the movies. Actually all that Jackie ever said was that if *he* had invited Jessica Lovell to the movies he would certainly not have taken her to Walters's drugstore afterwards. He would have been afraid that she would have thought it was cheap of him or that he was trying to show her off. It would have been better to have taken her to the Sweet Shoppe on Dock Street. It was quieter at the Sweet Shoppe and the booths were more comfortable.

"You ought to think about those things," Jackie said, "when you take someone like Jessica Lovell anywhere. Somebody around here always sees everything you do."

He wanted to ask Jackie what someone had seen him do, but he did not want to talk about Jessica.

"I don't care what anybody sees," he said.

"But you ought to care," Jackie told him, and he looked very worried. "Now I never asked Jessica to the movies myself, Charley. I thought of it, but I knew how it would have looked. You know, I've been to call on Jessica sometimes, and you know what people began to say."

"What did they say?" Charles asked.

"Oh"—a faint touch of color came into Jackie's face—"you know. How is it up there? That sort of thing. Of course, it isn't the same with you, Charley, as it is with me. They wouldn't say just that about you, but you know how people talk."

All he had to do was to ask another question to learn what they were saying and it might have been better if he had, but the worries of Jack Mason were too like an exaggeration of some of his own worries for him to be comfortable with them. Besides, he had other things to worry about that May.

His Uncle Gerald Marchby had said as recently as the beginning of May that there was no reason to be concerned about his Aunt Jane. Dr. Marchby had been practicing medicine in Clyde for years, as his father had before him and as his son Jerry, who was now in the Harvard Medical School, might very well do after him, and Dr. Marchby had seen a lot of people live and die. There was no reason to feel that his uncle was wrong when he said that the Gray heart was only a cardiac condition common in older people and not serious in itself. At some time or other, he had entered the sickroom of nearly every house in Clyde, carrying his black bag with him and dealing imperturbably with shocking sights and sounds. That experience had given him the patient, inscrutable look which sets doctors apart from other people. There was no way to tell how much Gerald Marchby knew. You had to put your trust in inscrutability, but Charles as a layman could see that his Aunt Jane was not as well as she had been six months before. Still, Gerald Marchby only said not to worry, that Jane was in fair physical condition, that it was good for her to lose a little weight, and that everyone looked peaked after a hard winter. She liked attention, that was all. If she talked about making her will, so did a lot of other people after they reached a certain age. If she wanted her bed moved downstairs into the parlor and it made her feel easier, why let her. You only had to remember that people acted in certain ways when they got to be a certain age. They loved medicine and they loved attention.

Yet in spite of this reassurance when Charles called on her the Sunday before he started to work at E. P. Rush & Company he was disturbed by the thinness of her hands and by her general frailty.

"Charley," she said, as soon as he had kissed her, "are you going to remember those letters in the right-hand drawer of the desk or had I better burn them now?"

Of late she had often brought up the subject of letters and once he had asked her what was in them and she had told him they were just old letters. She wanted them burned because she did not want parts of herself drifting around after she was gone. She wanted to go, when she was gone, and not have the family prying into everything.

"Why, no, Aunt Jane," he said, "I wouldn't burn them now," and then she began again about the silver.

"I wish I could get the silver settled once and for all. I had Mary bring it in here this morning and here's the list." It seemed to him that her hand shook more than usual when she picked up the list. "I can't ever seem to get it settled because everything keeps changing."

"Why don't you just leave it?" Charles said. "Everything can't be exactly right."

"I don't know why everything shouldn't be," she answered. "Everything used to be. Now, Charley, come closer." He moved his chair next to hers and took her hand. "Now, tell me once and for all, is Dorothea going to marry that Elbridge Sterne or isn't she?"

"I guess she is, but you know Dorothea, she never talks," Charles said.

"I don't see why she can't make up her mind," she said. "Do you want that teapot, Charley?"

"Dorothea ought to have it," Charles said, "even if she doesn't marry Elbridge Sterne."

"You can have it if you want it, and Dorothea can have the spoons."

"Don't worry about it," Charles said. "Dorothea's used to the idea of getting the teapot."

She sighed and put down the silver list.

"It's a Burt teapot. . . . Charles." She was sitting very straight in her stiff-backed chair with her head half turned toward him. "Are you attentive to Jessica Lovell or aren't you?"

The word "attentive" as she spoke it had a delicate, half archaic sound.

"Yes," he said, "I suppose I'm attentive."

"Well," she said, "I'm glad that someone tells me something. . . . Charles?"

"Yes," he said.

"It isn't anything to be excited about. I'm not excited at all. I hope she is a nice girl, but there's no reason to be excited. Charles." And she picked up the silver list from the table.

"Aunt Jane," he said, "don't bother about the silver."

"I'm not bothering about anything," she answered. "I wish you'd go to the kitchen and call Mary. She never brings my medicine on time. And then you can read to me if you want to."

"All right," Charles said. "What do you want me to read?"

"Why, anything," she answered, "as long as it's reading."

She might have asked so many questions but that was all she ever said and somehow it gave him a warm and pleasant feeling. She said again before he left:

"You might have told me without my asking . . . but I'm not excited at all."

16

Shake Off the Shackles of This Tyrant Vice

—GARRICK

What was it that he saw and thought in those last years of the twenties? He must have been oblivious then to nearly everything outside himself, and Clyde had become a background which he had no time to examine. There was no sense of leisure in his recollections, not a single memory of a careless day swimming with the Meaders, no helping Earl Wilkins take his automobile apart, no long dusky evenings talking with Jackie Mason. These and all the other diversions that once made up a Clyde summer were lost to him for good. Everything was still around him in certain fixed positions, but there was no time for content or discontent, because he was too busy living to think of much except immediacy. Everything was just around the corner when once everything had been ahead of him and he had no way of knowing that this would continue to be so. He was already beginning to say to himself that he would not always be so busy, that sooner or later there would be an opportunity to do a few things he wanted to do.

Obviously he must have tried too hard, but at least he was not a prig because he did not have time for priggishness. He was already becoming externally a type which he was to know too well, but at least he always knew it was a type. It was just as well that Jessica was abroad. If she had been in Clyde that summer, he could never have concentrated so fully on E. P. Rush & Company—and what he had learned there was still valuable. The way one earned one's living had little to do with love and all the things one hoped for that were just around the corner. It was better never to take the office home with you. The people one knew in a business way might mingle sometimes with that other life, like oil and vinegar, but they never really mixed. There could be mutual respect and liking and loyalty, but it was safer never to let these merge into friendship if you wanted to get on downtown.

On his way home in the train Charles often reread Jessica's letters. She was in London, darling, and she wished he were there in large, scrawling strokes. She was in Paris, darling, looking over the Place de la Concorde, and she had bought an old book for him and she wished that he were there. She was in the *châteaux* country, darling, and in Rome, darling. She could not wait to get home, but they were staying a little longer. They were coming back in September—no, in October. Truthfully, there was not much time to remember Jessica, but she was safe around the corner. There was so much else without Jessica that he sometimes wondered how things would have turned out if she had come home later than she did.

His Aunt Jane had died suddenly in her sleep that summer. The Crawford

Mill, where his father had worked so long, had folded up, and John Gray was going into Boston every day when October came around. The house had been painted and equipped with electric lights and there were cigars in the parlor. Dorothea was definitely engaged to Elbridge Sterne. In August Charles had been moved into a new department at E. P. Rush designed to give investment advice to clients and to compete with the investment counsel services which were becoming popular.

Mr. Blashfield had nearly settled the details of his aunt's estate. The furnishings at Gow Street had been sold or divided. He and his father were wearing mourning bands, although his Aunt Jane had especially asked them not to. The legacies had been paid, and John Gray was the residuary legatee. His aunt had died less than a week after hearing the news that the mill was closing, but no one could say that the news had upset her. She had spoken of it, Charles remembered, one of the last times he had seen her.

"It's just as well I sold my shares," she said. "John always said it would happen."

It was, of course, what his father had been saying for years. He would have sold out his mill stock long ago if it had not been held in trust, and he had asked Hugh Blashfield again and again to sell it—but John Gray had not lost his temper when the mill went into receivership.

"There isn't anything to say, Hugh," was all he said. "Dorothea's getting married and Charles is working and I suppose Jane can give Esther and me a small allowance, but you might admit that I was right."

It was not fair or just to pry into his father's thoughts when his sister died. There was always something indecent about thoughts at such a time, because they were too much like the cool, bland passages of a Victorian novel, but at least there was no hypocrisy in the way his father took the news. He said that Jane always did the right thing at the right time, but his voice broke when he said it.

"I'll look after the funeral," he said. "I'm always good about funerals, Esther, and I don't mind undertakers," but his voice broke again. "Do you remember what Jane was always saying? She doesn't want any artificial grass around the grave."

She had wanted "Sunset and evening star" and she did not want gladiolas if she died in summer.

Charles wished that she had not discussed her will and arrangements so often for somehow all that discussion made him more conscious of her now that she was gone than he had been when she was living. She still seemed to have duties to perform before she could step back decorously into the past, and she still seemed to be watching to see whether everything was being done the way she had wanted it.

He was sure that she had been there at Gow Street when he had gone with Dorothea to the house to look over the furniture. Everything was still in its place, arranged by Mary Callahan exactly as Miss Jane had wanted it, and Mary herself was crying in the kitchen. He had the lists with him, but he hated to think of tagging things with other people's names, he hated to touch anything. He was sure that she was there, telling him not to be silly but to burn those letters as she had told him and to destroy those other things of hers that no one else would care about—the pincushion and the sachets in her bureau that her sister Mathilda had made for her one Christmas when they were little girls, and the boat that Johnny had once whittled for her, and her dolls in the attic. She had always said that she did not want parts of herself drifting around after she was gone.

"Don't just stand here," Dorothea said, and she spoke more loudly when he did not answer. "Aren't you going to say something?"

"Let's not start arguing," he said. "She never liked it when we argued."

"We're not arguing," Dorothea said. "What's the matter with you, Charley?"

"Nothing," he said. "Can't I just stand here for a minute?"

"We'd better start with the dining room," Dorothea said, "and leave the study till the end."

The Judge's portrait was looking down at them in the study and Aunt Jane's pills were on a candlestand by her chair.

"Don't be so fussy, Charley," he remembered Dorothea's saying. "You're beginning to act just like her."

And so was Dorothea. She was handling the silver so as not to leave marks on it. She was putting everything she touched back exactly in its place.

The illusion of her presence was even stronger when the family had gathered in Mr. Blashfield's office. His aunt had worked very hard over that will. If the dead ever could return this would, of course, have been the time when she would have insisted on a visit.

Mr. Blashfield had stood on the formality of reading every word of the will instead of simply telling what was in it, as John Gray had suggested. John Gray had said that wills, especially the ones that Hugh Blashfield drew, were becoming constantly duller and correspondingly incomprehensible. He would have enjoyed hearing it if Jane had written it, but if Hugh was going to insist on reading his original composition, they would all come to the office. He could not stand one of those conventional tableaux with the family lawyer sitting in the parlor.

Although John Gray must have known everything that was in the will, he kept looking at his watch to see what time it was; and when Dorothea suggested that Elbridge Sterne go with the family, he said that Elbridge had been at the grave and that was about enough for Elbridge, considering they weren't married yet.

"Only the four of us are going," he said, "and there's no reason to make a procession of it. Esther, it's five minutes before ten. You and I will go first, and, Charles, you take Dorothea along at ten o'clock."

"What do you mean by Charles's *taking* me?" Dorothea asked.

"I mean that Charles will accompany you," John Gray said, "to 76 Dock Street and upstairs to the first floor. You will turn to the right and open the door marked Hugh Blashfield, Counselor at Law. You're not married to Elbridge Sterne yet."

"There's no reason why you should be horrid about Elbridge," Dorothea said. "You're always making fun of Elbridge."

"Is it making fun of Elbridge," John Gray asked, "to say you're not married to him yet? I'm not even thinking about Elbridge." He pulled out his watch again.

Even if they did not go all four together, everyone who saw them must have known why they were going to the brick building at Number 76.

Number 76 Dock Street was a dingy Romanesque building which must have been constructed in the nineties. Its ground floor was occupied by Setchell's Toggery Shop and by Stevens's hardware store, divided by a flight of stairs that led to the upper floor. Charles nodded to the Toggery Shop, with its window display of ties and summer suiting.

"Do you think Frank Setchell still loves you?" he asked.

"Oh, shut up," Dorothea said, and he could almost believe that Aunt Jane was telling him not to tease Dorothea. She was tired and nervous. Engagements always upset a girl.

The names of the tenants of 76 Dock Street were painted on the wall at the head of the stairs large enough to be easily red in the ill-lighted hall, and pointing fingers were painted after them so that the directory looked like a signboard at a crossroads. If you turned to the left you could visit Dr. J. I. Brush, Dentist, and the whole hall had that sinister odor characteristic of dental parlors; or if you went further to the left you could visit E. C. Meader, Real Estate and Insurance, or further still, the Minnie Persepolis School of Dancing. To the right was Estelle's Beauty Shop and then the office of Hugh Blashfield, Counselor at Law.

Lawyers in Clyde, like the local doctors and dentists, all had their individual public ratings. Hugh Blashfield did work for Johnson Street, such as searching titles and other odd jobs for which it was not necessary to retain someone from Boston. Even if you did not live on Johnson Street but wished to draw a will, Hugh Blashfield was the one to do it, and besides he was the one who handled trust accounts which were not large enough to go to Boston, and who assisted Boston counsel in routine work for Wright-Sherwin and the banks. He was a sensible, reliable family lawyer, to whom you could safely tell family troubles which were not too bizarre or extreme, but he was no good at all on his feet in front of a jury. If you wanted any fighting done or if you were really in a scrape, it was better to keep away from Lawyer Blashfield, as he was called when he was safely out of earshot. The man to see was Martin X. Garrity. Mart was the one who might fix it out of court or if it got into court you could depend on Mart to see you safely through. On the other hand, Counselor Cooker was the one to handle a dignified damage suit, and the senior of them all, Judge Morby, could represent you in arguments before the probate court. There was a lawyer for each contingency, and each of them knew his place.

Katie Rowell, who had been with Hugh Blashfield for twenty years, was alone in the outer office. Her faded yellowish hair and her freckled nose looked like her golden-oak desk and the yellow shades and the yellow painted woodwork. Both the doors of the tall safe in front of her were open and she kept staring fixedly at the black japanned boxes inside it as though she were afraid that one of them might disappear if she shifted her glance. Charles had seen her at rehearsals of the Clyde Players last winter but Katie, when she greeted them, appeared to have forgotten this and to have forgotten, too, that she and Dorothea were in the same study club, because business came first during business hours.

"Hello, Miss Rowell," Charles said. "Have you been doing much acting lately?"

"No," Katie answered. "Not enough were interested in a summer group. Mr. Blashfield is expecting you and you can step right inside."

In Mr. Blashfield's office, his law books, his diploma and his engraving of the Clyde waterfront all had a confidential veneer which indicated that nothing that might be said would go farther than the room and that plenty had been said in it. Mr. Blashfield was seated in a golden-oak chair at the head of a long table with Charles's parents on either side of him. He was holding the will, a blue-bound document, informally but respectfully in his left hand. When he saw Dorothea and Charles he pushed back his chair noisily on the battleship linoleum and stood up and patted his double-breasted suit into place as though he were going to address a meeting.

"I don't believe I've had an opportunity to congratulate you on your happy news, Dorothea," he said. "Elbridge Sterne is such a fine young man, and how is everything going in Boston, Charley?"

There was an odd moment of hesitation as they all gathered around the table. Though he obviously wanted to read the will and though they all wished to hear it, at the same time it did not seem correct to be too precipitate.

"That last paper of yours at the Confessional Club was first-rate, John," Mr. Blashfield said. "I think it is one of your best."

"Why, thank you, Hugh," John Gray answered.

"A good reminiscent paper is a whole lot better than something cribbed from the *Encyclopædia Britannica*," Mr. Blashfield went on. "I suppose we all have a weakness for reminiscence, especially as we grow older. Now before we start I should like to say, aside from anything professional, how touched I am that Miss Jane wanted me to carry out her wishes. I remember her so well when we were boys, John, though of course we were younger."

"Yes," John Gray said, "we were, but I think Jane would like you to get on with it. She would tell you so if she were here."

Mr. Blashfield smiled in a kindly way to show that he remembered the definiteness of Miss Jane and Charles found himself looking at the empty chair at the other end of the table.

"Well, I suppose she would," Mr. Blashfield said, and he opened the blue-covered document. "Stop me if there are any questions . . ."

"I, Jane Gray, of Clyde, Massachusetts, in the County of–" His quiet voice was the only sound in the room. It was like the reading of a Clerk of the Court, which was probably what Mr. Blashfield intended. It was dull, as John Gray said it would be, but anyone could understand it—two thousand dollars to Mary Callahan, ten thousand dollars to Esther Gray, five thousand to Dorothea and five thousand to himself, and the remainder to John Gray.

Charles was thinking of the power of money and the respectful way one always spoke of it when sums above a certain amount were mentioned. It could arouse jealousy and dislike and all sorts of other small unpleasant thoughts. It was only decent to have gratitude, but the will, as Mr. Blashfield read it, had no human quality. It was Mr. Blashfield, not his aunt, who had been speaking. It was only Mr. Blashfield's pedantic interpretation of all her worries, consolidated into rotund legal phrases. Charles straightened himself in his chair and looked across the table at his father. He was disturbed by his father's expression. It was one of deep, almost indecent relief.

"Good old Jane," he said.

"It's a simple will," Mr. Blashfield answered. "Now if you have any questions—" Charles saw his father lean forward.

"Just one question, Hugh," he said. "I am right, am I, in understanding the remainder is left to me without any strings attached?"

Charles found himself gripping the arms of his chair nervously. He saw his mother's head turn sharply, and Mr. Blashfield's pale, rather dull face had a stiffer look as he glanced up from the paper.

"Yes, that's right, John," he said. "Miss Jane wanted it that way"—he cleared his throat—"though I advised her differently."

"I suppose you did," John Gray answered. "Good old Jane. Can you give me some idea of the amount?"

Mr. Blashfield cleared his throat again.

"I called on Mr. Thomas yesterday. After the legacies, debits and taxes, I should say approximately seventy-five thousand dollars, at the present market." He mentioned the sum diffidently, trying to hedge it around with words.

"Well, well," John Gray said. "I didn't know Ralph had done as well as that. When can I expect to get any of this, Hugh? Perhaps you know the Gray family is short of cash. The mill, you know."

"As soon as it goes through probate, John," Mr. Blashfield answered.

"That may take a year," John Gray said, "but I suppose I could raise a slight loan?"

Charles felt a faint shiver run up his spine. He hated the sound of his father's voice. It was his first close experience with such a sum of money. It was small compared with sums in customers' accounts at Rush & Company, but it had a peculiar value because they were all involved. It was something to be guarded and not to be spoken of with levity. It was nothing on which one should raise a slight loan.

"Why, yes," Hugh Blashfield said, "I suppose I can advance you something, John—or the bank can. I'll speak to Ralph Thomas."

"I shall want a very substantial sum," John Gray said.

"Oh, John," his mother said suddenly, "please don't try to borrow anything."

"Now, Esther," John Gray began. "Now, Esther," and Hugh Blashfield cleared his throat again.

"I know I'm not the one to talk, John," he said, "but don't you think—"

His father shook his head.

"I know, Hugh," he answered, "but I've done quite a lot of thinking myself, for quite a term of years. If you could arrange for me to have something this afternoon, I should appreciate it very much, and we can discuss then methods of paying me the balance." He paused and lowered his voice. "Remember, Hugh, I always wanted to sell that mill stock."

Charles felt himself sitting rigidly, still gripping the arms of his chair. John Gray looked at his watch.

"I think we've covered everything for the moment," he said. "I'll be in again this afternoon, Hugh. I'm always glad to hear your ideas, and thank you very much."

He must have forgotten that they should not look like a delegation because they all walked down the stairs of 76 Dock Street in a body and out into the hot summer sunlight.

"It was so sweet of Jane," Esther Gray was saying to Dorothea. "I'm glad she told me first and I'm glad I thanked her."

"Well, well," John Gray said. "These wills. I wish the lawyers could write testaments in verse like François Villon."

"Father," Charles said, "there's something I'd like to talk to you about when we get home."

It was absolutely necessary to take up the subject of that money. The money which had been left them was a product of self-denial and steady planning, something which had been saved and earned, something to be treated with decent respect.

"That is, if you don't mind," he said.

It was a hot summer's day and through the open windows of his father's room he could hear the drowsy sound of a lawn mower in the Sullivans' yard and the patient plodding of a draft horse and the rattle of one of the Mullins Company ice wagons on Spruce Street. The room, with its untidy collection of books and unrelated objects, was like his father's mind. John Gray was already moving about, searching for something in much the same way he ransacked his memory for an apt and comfortable quotation.

"Now wait a minute," he said. "Where the devil is it? Oh, here it is." He had found the case and the decanters of his port wine under a pile of newspapers. It was obviously an occasion for him.

"I know it's early in the day," he said, "but I think I'll have a glass of port. It's sweet and sticky but I need some sort of mild stimulant to get over Hugh Blashfield. Will you join me, Charley?"

"No, thanks," Charles answered, "only don't let me stop you," but John Gray was absorbed in his own ideas.

"All right," he said, "I don't blame you, Charley. Of course, Hugh Blashfield and all of this"—he waved his hand in a vague, expansive way—"doesn't have the same effect on you as it has on me. Going to a lawyer is like going to a doctor. No matter how well or how long you know them personally, they always put you at a disadvantage because of their specialized knowledge. I'd rather have a good, dry chat with a clergyman. He may know about God and sin, but God and sin are a sort of public domain and no one knows definitely about them. But a lawyer always knows about law and a doctor knows exactly where your spleen is and there's nothing whatsoever that one can do about them except sit respectfully and listen. Now I know all about Hugh Blashfield personally."

It was obvious that he was annoyed by Hugh Blashfield and that it would be impossible to divert him from the subject.

"I couldn't help thinking as I sat there this morning that Hugh Blashfield was a painfully small-minded man. I must have told him twenty times to sell that mill stock. He's plodding and rudimentary, without a single broad, long thought. I used to help him with his Latin and his algebra, and he always has trouble with women. I know all his frailties, and yet there he was, reading my sister's will. There's something queer about a lawyer in his office, but never mind it," and then a taste of the sacramental wine distracted his attention. "You know, I think it might be a good idea if we bought some Scotch whiskey. Mel Stevens keeps running it in. I don't know why I shouldn't go around and see Mel this afternoon—we ought to have electric lights, and we really ought to have a car, Charley. I don't know why we shouldn't have a car now."

He paused and in the silence Charles could hear the lawn mower.

"Father," he began, and John Gray sighed.

"Oh, yes," he said. "You wanted to ask me about something, didn't you?"

Charles cleared his throat, but even so his voice was hoarse.

"Father," he said again, "what are you going to do with Aunt Jane's money? Are you going to play the market with it?"

His father looked watchful. It was bluntly stated, but it was an issue, and his father had always been skillful in avoiding issues.

"How about a cigar, Charley?" he asked. "Let me see. There must be some around somewhere. If there aren't, I'll have to go down to the news store, but they haven't got Havanas."

"Father," Charles said, "are you or aren't you?"

John Gray finally faced the issue, and as he did so a film of cloud passed across his sun.

"It's rather like the old question of whether you have stopped beating your wife, isn't it?" he asked. "Everybody who makes an investment plays the market. I suppose I might tell you it's none of your business. I'm tempted to, but I won't."

There was another silence, a long, unpleasant silence.

"I don't like to talk to you this way," Charles said, and his father nodded and his voice was warm and kind again.

"I know you don't," he said. "That's all right."

"You know it's everybody's business," Charles began. "I don't care about myself, but what about Mother and Dorothea?"

He saw his father's face flush and then he saw him fold his hands. "Well, go ahead and tell me why I shouldn't. Do the best you can."

Charles could only say what anyone would have said. The market was like a wild river, that year, breaking through all the dams of prudence and common sense. Prices of common stocks had already discounted all conceivable earnings in any foreseeable future. The market might still go up, but it was already dangerous. It was time to invest in sound bonds, preferably governments. There was bound to be a break. It was only a question of when.

"You put it very clearly, Charley," John Gray said. "Do you know what I begin to think? You may be a good investment man someday. You're dead right, but it's all a matter of self-restraint. I know when to stop—but you don't believe that, do you?" He was going to be careful. He was watching the market, and he knew the market. He was going to get in and out.

Charles did not answer. There was no use saying aloud that he did not believe him.

"Let's leave it this way. You can watch me, and I'll be careful, Charley."

When it came to money, everyone always promised to be careful. In fact, it often seemed to Charles that most of his subsequent life had been spent in a series of timid, hedging precautions, in balancing probable gains and losses in order to keep sums of money intact. The probity, the reliability and the sobriety that such a task demanded were to make his own life dull and careful. Except for a few brief moments, he was to face no danger or uncalculated risk. He was to measure his merriment and hedge on his tragedies. He was to water down elation and mitigate disaster, and to be at the right place at the right time, and to say the right thing with the right emphasis. Yet whenever he thought of himself as a dull, deluded opportunist, compared with other people, he always remembered the intensity of his own feelings when his father had been speaking. There had been a hideous sense of inevitable disaster, and no possible way to stop it.

There was no point in pleading, because his father was growing angry, and Charles could hear their voices, each rising against the other.

"All right, Charley," his father said. "I understand you perfectly and you needn't shout. How are you going to get anywhere if you never take a chance? What is life but a chance, Charley? After all, what is seventy-five thousand dollars? Do you expect me to live on the income, at four per cent?" He shrugged his shoulders. He opened his hands and closed them. Did Charles really want his mother to live on three thousand dollars a year? And what was it Samuel Johnson said?

"A man who both spends and saves money is the happiest man, because he has both enjoyments."

That was what he was going to do, both spend and save. As soon as he made a profit, and any fool could make a profit in this bull market, he would put the original sum in a bank, he swore he would, and he would go on with the rest. And what was that quotation in Thomas Fuller's

Gnomologia about its being better to have a hen tomorrow than an egg today?

"A hen," John Gray said. "You can't stop me, Charley. It's the first chance I've ever had, the first real chance, to beat the system."

It was not worth while trying to stop him, now that he was talking about the system.

"When is Jessica coming back, in October? All right, we'll have a Cadillac by October. Don't look as though I were hurting you, Charley. I'm going to spend and save and it's perfectly possible."

There was no use in being angry, there was no use in being hurt.

"There was always that pony," Charles said.

"Oh, yes," John Gray said. "I'd forgotten about the pony. Well, he's growing now, Charley. I've given this a great deal of thought, but it might be just as well if you didn't mention this to your mother."

"Don't worry, I won't," Charles said.

"Come to think of it," John Gray said, "I might as well go up to Boston tomorrow, and, Charley, I wonder whether you would do something for me now, that is if you don't mind? Would you mind going downtown and seeing if the *New York Times* has come in yet and would you please stop at Southern's and buy me a small account book? I'm the one who's going to do the worrying, Charley."

Then, just before Charles reached the door, his father called him back. He had settled himself comfortably in his Morris chair, with one knee crossed over the other, and everything he had said seemed to have been erased already. The magnificence of his thoughts made him look like a New York customer of E. P. Rush & Company. He looked richer than Mr. Thomas at the bank and more distinguished than Mr. Laurence Lovell.

"Charles," he said, "I've just thought of another quotation, which won't ever appear in a gnomologia. You'll like this one. 'Everybody's doing it now.'"

Charles must have known that morning that his aunt's legacy was as good as gone. There was no use going to anyone for advice and it was pointless to tell his mother and Dorothea what he knew. He walked out of the front door and stared for a long while at Spruce Street, at the elms with their leaves drooping in the summer heat, and at the heat waves shimmering on the shingles of the Masons' roof. While he stood there at the front yard gate, he conceived a fear and contempt for certain aspects of finance, but it was a respectful contempt. He was afraid of money and he never lost that fear, and it was not a bad attitude, either, if you had to deal with investments—caution and contempt held together by respect. He was thinking of his mother and Dorothea in the house. He was trying, for the first time in his life, to cut a loss. He was thinking of the five thousand dollars his aunt had left him, an immense sum in one way and so insignificant in another, and someone had to do something. At least he was sure that he knew when to stop.

That was his only reason for playing the stock market that next year, a desperate and feeble reason. Circumstances forced him and he did it without satisfaction, as though he were engaged in a secret vice. It was interesting, sometimes, to imagine what would have happened to his mother and indirectly to Dorothea if he had not, or if he had not known when to stop, but it was hardly worth the time. Nothing could have altered what happened in Clyde, though he did not know it then.

17

If You Can Dream—and Not Make Dreams Your Master . . .

—RUDYARD KIPLING

Nearly everyone in Rush & Company was in the market and it may have been just as well that he was in it too, for it afforded a common ground on which to meet all those others who had come there to learn what was called finance. It was an era of apprenticeship, when most people preferred to pick up their knowledge by firsthand experience, backed only, perhaps, by a course in Economics I at Harvard. Finance still had the aura of a gentleman's profession, particularly in Boston. All those young men in Rush & Company, whom Charles knew and whose manners he studied so carefully once, were there because gentlemen handled the broader aspects of money. They did not count it or set it down in figures as the tellers did and the bookkeepers, who, whatever their abilities, could only by the most outside accident rise out of these departments to compete with the young men in the open spaces. In military terms, these latter were the officer class, who might be partners and bank officers some day.

They were a class not trained to realities and they were not, he often thought, well fitted to cope with the depression. The early thirties made gaps in their ranks, as though they had been hit by round shot and canister, and he still knew the crippled casualties of those days, the limpers, the spiritually legless and the armless. The truth was that finance, using that inclusive term for partners, bond salesmen, and bank presidents, was not entirely a gentleman's game, though it demanded as a rule the code of ethics and morality associated with a gentleman. However, all the temptations and spiritual stresses and strains which came later with the depression were negligible when Charles worked in E. P. Rush & Company with what Lawrence Stoker, the head of the bond department, called the Team.

Football men and crew men were somehow the most desirable material at E. P. Rush & Company and it seemed to Charles that all of the team came from what were known as final clubs at Harvard. He only learned these facts gradually but later he realized that they were important in a business way and he faced them without rancor. He had nothing in common with the team, except the market and the routine of the office, but he was sufficiently one of them so that he might listen when they talked to each other and about each other. His position on the team reminded him of the story of the man who maintained that the Harvard crew was democratic because after three years everyone in the boat spoke to him except number seven.

They were nice—the boys on the team at E. P. Rush—and they seemed to accept cheerfully the fact that he had to be more ambitious and brighter than the rest of them, much as Charles himself had accepted the same thing with a Chinese or a Japanese student in a college class. They even seemed pleased that he was getting on. There was none of that sense of competition and knifing in the back that he was to know later. They were nice boys and they began calling him by his first name—after a decent period.

Although he looked like most of the team, he knew that he would always stand out from them, and it had been just as well, even in E. P. Rush. He was not too different from the rest to have that difference disturbing, but he was different enough sometimes to be noticed. If he had not been a little apart, Arthur Slade would never have noticed him that time when Mr. Slade came on some errand from New York, and he told Charles so long afterwards.

"I saw you right away," he said, "and I said to myself, how did he ever get in here? But I said it in a very nice way. I wondered if you could be a Yale man, but that could not have been possible in E. P. Rush. It explained everything when you said you came from Dartmouth."

* * *

There was every reason to remember his first meeting with Arthur Slade, for had it not occurred he might never have gone to New York. Certainly he would never have been given his chance in the Stuyvesant Bank at the time when banks were firing instead of hiring. There would have been no Nancy, no children, no house in Sycamore Park. Instead, he might have stayed on in Rush & Company and married some girl in the Newtons, perhaps, and have been living now in one of those tapestry-brick Colonials, forgotten by people like E. P. Rush partners after business hours. Finally he would have been like all those other useful Boston wheel horses who knew the business like the palms of their hands and came through in a pinch and who disappeared daily behind a curtain of suburban life. He would have been Charley Gray, an agreeable and reliable person, whom you could trust to do anything. Mr. Rush would have invited him to his lunch club now and then, but never in the world would he have become a member. It would have been a pity that he did not have quite the background or connections to have made him partnership material. There was every reason why he should have remembered every detail of his meeting with Arthur Slade.

Charles's desk was about midway in the center of the open office and one September morning when he was reading market letters he heard Mr. Rush speaking, but he did not look up.

"It will only be what you've seen already," Mr. Rush was saying. He had brought a stranger with him to the investment advisory department.

"Oh, Gray," Mr. Rush called. "Mr. Slade wants to see everything we have on—" and he gave the name of that foreign stock which later was to make so many people poorer. "Gray will get you everything, and you can read it here if you want to."

"Yes, sir," Charles said, and he hurried to the files for the folders.

"I think there are a few rather frank office notes on it," Mr. Rush said. "Go ahead and read them, but don't quote us."

Mr. Rush walked away, leaving the stranger from New York. Mr. Slade must have come in from New York on the "Owl" but he did not show it. He was, of course, an imitation of Tony Burton, like everyone else in the Stuyvesant Bank. His dark hair, appropriately gray at the temples, was closely clipped, like Tony Burton's. His dark gray flannel suit had the style of Tony Burton's tailor. His face had Tony Burton's authoritative alertness. His whole appearance was like that song parody which Charles wrote later about walking and talking and dressing like Tony Burton. The Stuyvesant Bank was printed on Arthur Slade, indelibly, magnificently, an imprint distinguishable from anything in Boston.

"Wouldn't you like to use my desk, sir?" Charles asked.

"Oh no," the stranger said. "Go on with what you're doing," and he sat beside the desk reading, while Charles went back to the market letters. Mr. Slade did not speak again for three quarters of an hour.

"Dear me," he said, when he had finished, and Charles saw he was holding a memorandum in Mr. Rush's handwriting, "you certainly have a personalized investment service."

"Yes, sir," Charles answered.

"Well," Mr. Slade said, "I'm much obliged to you. You'd better put that away and lock it up." He was smiling and Charles did not like the suggestion because it somehow seemed to reflect on Rush & Company.

"You know I was told to show it to you," Charles said.

"I know you were," Mr. Slade answered, "but I hope you won't leave it around."

"We don't leave things around here much," Charles said, and he sat up straighter because he was a member of the team.

"It's about time for lunch, isn't it?" Mr. Slade said. "How about your coming over with me to the Parker House?"

Arthur Slade must have been curious about Rush & Company, because he asked a good many questions, Charles remembered, and Charles answered them as he should have, politely and loyally. When Arthur Slade asked him about himself, he told him that he lived at Clyde, and Mr. Slade had never heard of Clyde.

"I suppose you're in this market like everyone else," Arthur Slade said.

"Yes," Charles answered. "It's all a question of when to stop, isn't it?"

He said that the market did not interest him as it did his father, and he began talking to Arthur Slade about his father, a safe subject because Arthur

Slade would never meet him. Perhaps he spoke with the clumsy confidence of anyone his age, but whenever he thought of that lunch at the Parker House, he was never entirely sure that he had been clumsy. There was no reason to show himself in any sort of light or to strive to make a good impression, and besides he did not feel like a callow young man from Rush & Company.

"There's no such thing as unbiased advice from an investment house that markets securities," Arthur Slade had said. "It's a little like selling patent medicine that can be used externally and internally, for baldness, dandruff, muscular pains, and stomach-ache. Now in this investment advisory thing of yours, doesn't Rush recommend its own securities? Of course it does. It can't help it. All bond houses recommend Telephone and Tobacco B and General Electric and some railroad bonds and then they slip something of their own into the package."

It was true, of course, but Charles was loyal to Rush & Company.

"If you believe in what you're selling," he said, "why shouldn't you recommend it?"

"Now, it's different in a bank trust department. We haven't got anything to sell." Arthur Slade took a thin gold cigarette case from his pocket and opened it and laid it on the table.

"Don't you ever get stuck with anything in a bank?" Charles asked.

"Not usually," Arthur Slade said, and he smiled. "Not in our bank. Did you ever think of working in a bank?"

Charles shook his head. "No, I've got too much else to think about where I am."

It never crossed his mind that Arthur Slade might be offering him a job. As he looked about that solid, conventional room, the face of Arthur Slade stood out from all the other faces and Charles wished that he could ever manage to be like him. There was irony in the recollection, but a pleasant sort of irony for there at the Parker House it was like seeing himself mirrored in the future. He was not so far now from being like Arthur Slade, though without his money and without his game of tennis and without his place on Long Island, but he, too, could dress and talk like Tony Burton. Perhaps you always picked a hero when you were in your twenties, and Arthur Slade was the best trust officer he had ever known. Yet back there at the Parker House, Arthur Slade was still an impeccable stranger from New York, whom he would never see again, and lunch was nearly over, like all those other workday luncheons which he was to know so well later. It was time to get back to Rush & Company. No one liked it if you stayed too long for lunch.

"Some people think that banking's dull," Arthur Slade was saying, "but I've never found it dull. It's a matter of perspective. There's only one trouble about it." He stopped and lit a cigarette. "You get pressed from the bottom and the top. Something always hems you in."

As Arthur Slade was speaking, Charles saw his father walking toward them between the tables, with his hair and his mustache freshly clipped, and Charles's attention wandered.

"Oh," he said, "there's my father."

"Where?" Mr. Slade asked, but his father was already at the table and they both stood up. John Gray smelled pleasantly of bay rum and he was smoking a cigar. He remembered Arthur Slade's smile as they shook hands and he had that fear one always had about one's parents—that his father might say something startling or out of place.

"Won't you sit down and have coffee with us?" Mr. Slade asked.

"That's very kind of you," John Gray answered, "but I'd better be getting back to work. Perhaps I'll see you on the five-twenty, Charley."

John Gray smiled and nodded and walked away. He had said nothing significant, but Charles was always glad that Arthur Slade had met his father.

"He looks happy," Arthur Slade said.

"Yes," Charles answered. "Father is usually happy."

"It's curious how few people are," Arthur Slade said. "Have you ever thought of working in New York?"

Charles grew familiar enough with those luncheons later. It had been his duty, especially just before the war, to look for promising material and to size up individuals as candidates for minor executive positions in the Stuyvesant Bank, just as Arthur Slade must have been doing then. The technique was always the same. The Stuyvesant at its executive level was very much like an exclusive club, requiring of a candidate certain definite standards for admission. You watched his hands as he held his knife and fork, the expression of his eyes when your glances met. As you listened to the inflections of his voice, you tried to think of his possible behavior under the strain of exasperation or temptation. Discretion, loyalty and trustworthiness were, of course, among those standards, but there were others less susceptible of definition, such as his attitude toward money. He could not have the businessman's greed or anxiety for profit if he was to be in the crowd. He could not covet money, but at the same time he must respect it in an impersonal way, as an astronomer might think of light-years in interstellar space. It was hard to tell, even after long acquaintance, whether someone would fit into the Stuyvesant, but the method of selection was always the same.

"Have you ever thought," Arthur Slade had asked him, "of working in New York?"

Later Charles knew the technique perfectly, because afterward he had been in the position of both the watcher and the watched. In later years, just before and just after the war, he was used to being asked to lunch by someone from the City or the Chase or some other bank, and there was always that aimless conversation about how busy one was, what one did on Sunday, the Securities and Exchange Commission, anything at all. Then, if everything went well, just at the end of lunch there was always that question. Had he ever thought of moving over to some larger bank like the Chase, or whatever bank it might be, where there was a real future? Frankly, without mentioning names, a lot of the crowd had been talking him over. He was just the material that they wanted. Of course, if he was happy where he was, think no more about it, but at the same time, this was a real chance and it was not offered to everyone. They were not advertising in the papers; they wanted a particular man named Charley Gray and, if he wanted, he could write his ticket. He had better think it over.

He was used to those offers and they always made him happy and he always knew what to say. The Stuyvesant was a small bank, but he was used to it. He knew the office politics. He wouldn't know his way around anywhere else, and of course they wanted him because he was not available. You always wanted someone who was doing well and who was loyal to his crowd.

Had he ever thought of working in New York? He must have told more about himself to Arthur Slade than he could remember and perhaps that glimpse of his father had rounded the impression—but there was no appeal at all in the idea of going to New York.

"No, I haven't thought of it," he said. "I like it pretty well where I am, but thanks ever so much for the lunch. I've had a very good time."

"Well," he remembered that Arthur Slade answered, "if you should be in New York, stop and look me up. Just tell Joe inside the door you want to see me."

His father was keeping a seat for him in the smoking car of the five-twenty. He had evidently been shopping after the market had closed because there were a few carefully wrapped packages on the rack above his head.

"I happened to see two silver gravy boats in an antique shop," he said. "Your mother has always wanted a pair, and then I saw a small radio. Who was that Mr. Slade you were having luncheon with, Charley?"

"He came to see Mr. Rush about something," Charles said. "He comes from New York."

"Of course he comes from New York. Anyone can see he does. You know, if things would quiet down a little, Charles, and if you could get away for a day or two, we ought to go down to New York. There's nothing like the night boat—a good dinner and a quiet sleep and there you are. He was a banker, wasn't he?"

"How did you know that?" Charles asked.

"Because they're as easy to tell as clergymen. They have a slightly antiseptic, sanctimonious look, and yet they don't look like lawyers."

"How did things work out today, Father?" Charles asked.

John Gray tilted his hat away from his forehead.

"Oh," he said, "everything went very well."

The smoking car of the five-twenty was an old car with uncomfortable seats and painfully creaking woodwork, and its worn wheels made it sway on the rails with a rhythm of its own. Three million share days and the Parker House and especially Arthur Slade had nothing to do with the stale tobacco smoke and the pitch players and the elderly brakeman who was always watching the card games.

"If we only had a good car and a chauffeur," his father said, "I don't see why he couldn't drive us back to Clyde in good weather."

"We haven't got a car or chauffeur," Charles said.

"I didn't say we had," his father said. "I was just saying we might get one.

Charley, you're looking rather tired." His father was looking at him not impersonally, as he did so often, but in a kindly, interested way. "If I were you I wouldn't push too hard."

"How do you mean?" Charles asked.

"It doesn't pay. It isn't worth it," his father said. "You can't beat the system that way, Charley." Sooner or later John Gray's mind was always back there.

"You can't beat it your way either," Charles said. "I hope you're being careful."

His father laughed and slapped him on the knee.

"As careful as a banker," he said. "I'm as sound as Electric Bond and Share."

It was strange to think how little seemed unusual in those days, perhaps because nothing seems peculiar in any present. Lindbergh had flown the Atlantic. Human flies were scaling the exteriors of office buildings. Flagpole sitters were perched on their poles like Simeon Stylites, and marathon dancers were fainting in the clinches. They were all phenomena which one could accept. Nothing was ever very peculiar at the moment when it happened.

Charles was not particularly surprised, for instance, at an extraordinary episode that occurred one Sunday at church, shortly after he had met Arthur Slade; or if he was surprised at least it was appropriate to the contemporary scene. For years he had gone to the Unitarian Church with his mother and Dorothea. It was a habit of childhood, something which was expected of him and a part of Sunday, but his father seldom went with them. His father always said that church was a very good thing and that he approved of it entirely. He would have been glad to go to church if it had not been for Mr. Crewe. It might be all right for Esther and Dorothea and for Charles to listen to Mr. Crewe, but it always gave him an unholy reaction. He did not want to have Mr. Crewe telling him how to be good in a Unitarian way. He was not at all sure that Mr. Crewe knew much about goodness, because Mr. Crewe did not know anything about badness. He was not able to visualize the powers of evil.

Besides, he used to say, what was Unitarianism? He was in no position, not for a minute, to embark on a theological discussion or to criticize the tenets of a religion embraced by Emerson, Channing, and Samuel McChord Crothers. As a religion it was an obvious and enlightened outgrowth of the New England Congregationalist faith which had attracted his ancestors to these shores. He was willing to admit, too, that his own father had been a Unitarian and so had the Marchbys. He had been to Sunday School himself in the room behind the organ loft, and he had been married in the church. He realized also that a belief in the brotherhood of man and in the general progress of mankind, onward and upward forever, was a stabilizing influence, good for him and for everybody else, particularly for the children. He would have been glad to consider this mild dogma every Sunday and even listen to the asthmatic sound of the organ and to swelter with cold feet beside the hot-air stove in winter if it had not been necessary to have Mr. Crewe tell him about it. He simply could not follow Mr. Crewe's train of thought and instead of trying to follow it he found himself thinking instead of all sorts of things that had nothing to do with church or the possibilities of immortality. The best thing about Unitarianism was that there was no compulsion about attending its services—none at least for him. When it came to Charles and Dorothea it was different. If their mother wanted them to go to church, they had better go.

When John Gray came down to breakfast that Sunday morning, he was wearing a new double-breasted suit.

"I think it looks rather well, don't you, Esther?" he said. "Why are you looking at me in that critical way, Charles? Is there anything wrong with it?"

There was nothing wrong with it except that its impeccable newness and the careful tailoring of the coat gave his father the disconcertingly streamlined appearance of a figure in a fashion plate.

"Why, John," Esther Gray said, "you didn't tell me you'd bought a new suit. You look as though you'd stepped out of something."

"It's a surprise," John Gray said. "A new leaf, Esther."

"You're not going to church with us, are you?" Dorothea asked.

"I don't see why I shouldn't," John Gray answered. "It's been in the back of my mind." He sat down and stirred his coffee slowly. "It just occurred to me that a morning in church might do me good. You never can tell till you try."

"But, John," Esther Gray began, and her forehead wrinkled. "Why did it come over you this morning?"

"I'm sure I don't know why, Esther," John Gray said. "It must be some sort of compulsion."

"John," she asked, "why are you going?"

Charles could understand his mother's uneasiness. There was something unstable and bizarre about the morning.

"I'm sure I don't know," his father said again. "Let's say I have a new sense of spiritual responsibility this morning that demands direct action. After all, why shouldn't I go to church? I do believe in the institution, Esther."

It would have been like any other Sunday if John Gray had not been with them. The church was a hundred years old, a beautiful church, and its white woodwork with the delicate moldings, consciously devoid of all clerical richness, gave a sense of repressed peace and of serene plainness that must have been a part of an older, Puritanical tradition. The bell was ringing but Charles was more conscious of its vibrations than of its sound, which only accentuated the stillness and the cool, white light that came through the tall, plain windows. There were not more than fifty persons in the box pews, distributed unevenly, with large areas of unoccupied space between them. The church had been built for a larger congregation but its very vacancy added to his general sense of peace. He found himself thinking, as he had as a boy, of invisible presences in the vacant gallery and in the empty pews.

The past and the present always seemed to meet when the bell was ringing.

A spareness and a graceful restraint in all its detail, which reflected the old, deliberate attempt of its builders to eradicate any hint of papacy, gave the building its own peculiar sense of freedom and gave to Charles a feeling of personal loneliness that somehow was not disturbing. He always seemed to be drawn inside himself in those first silent moments, and his mother and Dorothea and his father were like strangers to him, cloaked in a sudden aloofness. The Meaders, three pews in front, and the Masons, to the right, and Mr. and Mrs. Howell, just below the tall white pulpit with its double winding stairs, did not look like weekday people. Though they were together, they were all alone with their thoughts. Mr. Crewe had climbed the stairs to the pulpit and now he stood, a small figure, high above them.

"Let us unite in singing," he was saying in his reedy voice, and the service began, an unadorned, rational service which had little beauty except in its plainness and which relied on little else to bring conviction.

"When two or three are gathered together," Mr. Crewe was saying, and Charles glanced at his father, still incredulous that he was there. Later he heard his father repeating the Lord's Prayer, in a voice which seemed to him unduly loud, and when they came to the responsive reading he was conscious again of his father's voice, more deliberate than the other voices, not to be hastened by others' haste. He saw Dorothea glance up nervously from her book. His father was enjoying the words of the Psalms for their own sake and he clearly did not care how rapidly others might slur over them. In church, as everywhere else, he was unwilling to conform and this did not disturb him in the least. He was reading the Psalm the way he wished it read and not the way the Masons or the Meaders or anyone else cared to read it.

"The lines are fallen unto me in pleasant places; yea, I have a goodly heritage."

His father spoke the last words, serenely and unabashed, long after everyone else had finished, and Charles knew that everyone there would speak of it later.

"Dear me," Charles heard him whisper as they sat down, "how they mumble."

When it was time for the offering, the organ in the loft played wheezily while Mr. Howell, Mr. Meader and Mr. Blashfield walked to the table in front of the pulpit. Each of them picked up a wooden contribution box, holding it gingerly by its long handle, and each walked down the aisle with self-conscious precision, their shoes and the boards beneath them both creaking. There was the usual furtive rustling sound above the music. His mother and Dorothea were opening their purses and he saw his father draw a wallet from inside his new double-breasted coat. It was a pigskin billfold, aggressively new, and his father flipped it open carelessly. Mr. Blashfield, conscientious and perspiring slightly, halted at the pew and pushed the box impersonally in their direction. Then Charles saw Mr. Blashfield's back stiffen. His father had taken a bill from his wallet and had dropped it in the contribution box. It was a hundred-dollar gold treasury note. Then he leaned back, gazing upward at the American flag and the service flag which hung suspended from the balcony. Mr. Blashfield paused uncertainly before he took the box away and at the same time Charles heard his mother draw a sharp, indignant breath. In a little while, perhaps even before the sermon was over, everyone would know about the hundred-dollar bill.

Outside the church, in the September sunlight, everyone spoke to everyone else agreeably.

"Well, John," Mr. Blashfield said, just as though he had not passed the contribution box, "it's nice to see you in church."

"I suppose I should go more often," he heard his father answer. "I really suppose I should."

"John," he heard his mother say, "we'll have to be going now or dinner will be late." She did not speak about the hundred-dollar bill until they were on Dock Street. "If you wanted to do that," she said, "at least you might have put it in an envelope."

"I know, Esther," John Gray answered, "I know. It was vulgar ostentation. I apologize to everybody. I'm sorry."

"You're not sorry," she answered, "because it's why you came."

"That's true," John Gray said. "Of course, that's perfectly true. I've always wanted to do that, Esther, ever since I was a little boy. I know it's childish of me, but I don't suppose I am sorry."

Everyone must have wanted to do that at some time. Charles could, of course, deplore many sides of his father, but usually his memories ended with a faint, reluctant admiration. His father had never tried too hard. He had never grown measured and tired by trying. He must have had a very good time in those months and this might have been worth the rest, and when the good time was over he paid for it in his own way. It was not a way that Charles could respect. It was all a gesture of supreme egotism, a futile, deplorable sort of selfishness, but vaguely Charles could understand it.

Most of Charles's life was dedicated to being as unlike his father as possible and yet he could not lose all sympathy because John Gray must have been a very sympathetic person. He had to be or no one would have tolerated him. Those dreams of his were like a boy's dreams. That desire of his for getting something for nothing and for beating what he called the system was shockingly immature, and yet immaturity lay often at the root of desire.

Whenever Charles heard the expression "wish fulfillment," he always thought of that bill in the contribution box and also of the expression on his father's face after luncheon that Sunday. The doorbell rang before the dishes had been cleared away and he remembered his mother's dismayed look. It was early for Sunday callers and people very seldom dropped in in Clyde, but his father must have been expecting the interruption because he pushed back his chair at once.

"I'll go, Esther," he said, and then they heard him calling. "Esther, Dorothea, Charley, will you come out here for a minute?"

There must have been a new note in his voice. At any rate, it was all like a dream, the Great American Dream. They were all gathered in the doorway staring out at Spruce Street and beyond the fence stood a long maroon phaeton shining in the sun and Mr. Robert Sweet, the Cadillac agent, was standing beside it.

"How about taking a ride this afternoon?" John Gray asked. "Robert will drive us, won't you, Robert?"

They must have all guessed before he told them that he had bought the car.

"Don't worry, Esther," he said. "We really needed a car."

Somehow it was inevitable, somehow the Great American Dream was not tawdry.

"Get in, Esther," John Gray said, "and we'll all go for a ride. Take us along Johnson Street, Robert."

"John," his mother said, "it's too big. Why didn't you get a little one? You know what everyone will say."

"Yes," John Gray answered, "of course I know. That's exactly why I bought it, Esther. I don't want a little one. A heavy car holds the road. What's the matter, don't you like it, Charley?"

At the moment, the car fitted in with nothing. It was simply there, glittering and preposterous, at the curb in Spruce Street, like the bill in the contribution box.

"I don't know," he said, and his father laughed, and Charles never forgot what his father said next.

"You'll learn to like it. You'll be surprised how fast you'll learn, and we'd better start in learning now."

It was remarkable how quickly one could adapt oneself to change. It must have been that same evening that his father told him that he was almost two hundred and fifty thousand dollars ahead of the game. That was the way he put it, as they sat upstairs.

"There's no reason to tell the women yet, Charles," he said. "It would only make them difficult and I'm not through just yet."

The sum that his father had mentioned was as implausible as the Cadillac. It only had an academic meaning.

"Isn't that enough?" he asked.

"Now you let me do the worrying, Charley," John Gray said. "The market will be going up after election, and I'll know when to stop"—but of course he did not know when to stop because wish-fulfillment people never did.

"Now," John Gray went on, "just remember, any time you want some money, Charley. There are a lot of things I want to do, but just ask me any time."

It was like the pony all over again. Of course, Charles should have asked him for a large sum but he never did. Instead he talked about a trust fund for his mother and Dorothea.

"We'll attend to that later," John Gray said. "There are a lot of things we've got to do"—but of course he never did any of those things.

18

When I Was One-and-Twenty, I Heard a Wise Man Say

—A. E. HOUSMAN

Charles must have conceded, at least in a measure, that his father had some pretty good ideas, for even in Clyde they were beginning to buy common stocks that autumn. Mr. Thomas, everyone knew, had begun, in a cautious way, and the word came from Wright-Sherwin that Mr. Stanley was doing the same thing in a more dashing way; and if these men, who knew all about business, were doing it, it was all right for everyone else. His Uncle Gerald Marchby had bought some General Electric, with results which were growing happier all the time. Hugh Blashfield, they were saying, had bought some Electric Bond and Share for himself, and Mr. Sullivan had said that United Gas Improvement was a good thing, and Mr. Levine, everyone knew, had subscribed to a market service which sent him the name of its favorite stock every week by wire. Mr. Walters, at the drugstore, had bought just a little McKesson and Robbins, because he was in the drug business. If everyone else was doing it, it was silly to leave your savings in the bank and miss cashing in on an era of prosperity. Even Jackie Mason had bought some International Telephone and in three weeks had made a hundred and fifty dollars. Everyone knew, or thought he knew, how much everyone else was making, and of course the figures became exaggerated, as everything did in Clyde.

It seemed that John Gray must have had a hidden talent and that he had been waiting for just this time. He might not have done so well previously but he had obviously learned from old mistakes and now he owned a Cadillac and the Grays had joined the Shore Club and there weren't many people from Clyde in the Shore Club. Somehow, somewhere, Johnny Gray had developed a head for business and he was getting rich and even Mr. Thomas had asked him about the market when they had been waiting for the morning train. Johnny Gray was doing so well that he did not have to go into Boston every day. Everyone knew, because he said so himself, that he could often do as well by sitting at home and calling up his broker, and everyone knew that he had a telephone of his own upstairs in his study for just that purpose.

He knew so much about the market that he still had time to enjoy himself. He still played poker at the Pine Trees and he had bought the Pine Trees a new pool table and he had even had the building painted at his own expense. He still had time to find out when anyone was hard up or sick or needed a little financial help. It was too bad that other people weren't more like him. Though Johnny Gray was getting rich, he still was just the same and he would stop and give anyone a lift in his Cadillac car, just as though it were not a Cadillac. He did not have to squeeze nickels because he knew there were more where they came from. He wanted everyone to share that pleasure denied to most, of easy-come and easy-go, and you had to respect anyone like Johnny Gray. That was what they must have been saying in Clyde.

Charles, too, had bought his own small list of stocks with the money his aunt had left him but he never had his father's flair or his father's careless courage. He only possessed a good capacity for reasoning. He did not have the temperament and his conscience always hurt him because he was sure you could not get anything for nothing. Once or twice, he remembered, he asked his father for advice and it was good advice, too, for a time when the market was running wild.

"Don't be too anxious," he remembered that his father told him. "Play it high, wide and handsome"; but he never had the temperament, and this may have been why he knew enough to stop in time. At least he was able to get out and stay out and he was never proud of any part of it and he never wanted to speak about it later.

Nevertheless, he must have learned a great deal. When Jessica and Mr. Lovell came back to Clyde in the middle of October and when Charles had bought Radio and Celanese on margin, he was not the same person he had been that spring. Jessica had called him after supper on the day they had arrived and had asked him to come over, and his father had suggested that he take the Cadillac for the evening, but his common sense had told him that it would need too much explanation if he were to drive up to the Lovells' in a Cadillac. He was wearing a new suit of herringbone worsted, a brownish-gray English cloth with a faint pinkish thread running through it, the sort of suit that looked very well at Rush & Company, and he was not a Clyde boy calling at Johnson Street.

The lights from Johnson Street shone dimly on the façade of the Lovell house and the railing of its widow's walk and its cupola possessed an airy, half-substantial quality, but it seemed to Charles that the house exhibited a pompous, fussy quality which he had never observed before. It was old and brittle and supported by a charitable sort of pretense, and to appreciate it fully you had to accept certain manners and traditions which no longer possessed validity. When he met Jessica in the front hall she did not look the way he thought she would though he was not sure how he had expected her to look. He was not exactly disappointed, but it seemed to him that her tweed skirt, her low-heeled shoes and her light brown camel's-hair sweater were too much like the country. She had not acquired as much veneer by taking that trip abroad as he had by staying at home.

"Why, Charley," she said, and they stood for a second or two looking at each other uncertainly. He had an unexpected feeling of constraint until he took her hand and then when she grasped his hand very tightly the constraint was gone and everything was just as it had been.

"I was so frightened," she said later, when they had a chance to talk. "I was afraid you didn't love me any more."

There had been an instant, just before he touched her hand, when everything must have been ready to fall one way or the other, a moment of concealment, a queer blind pause when everything was in balance. If Mr. Lovell had been there in the hall with her, denying them those few moments together, it might have been worth his while to have taken her abroad, but now it might have been better for Mr. Lovell if Jessica had stayed in Clyde.

He knew that Mr. Lovell and Miss Georgianna were waiting for them. Although he did not hear a sound, he was sure that they were in the wallpaper room listening.

"I loved your letters," Jessica said softly.

"I loved yours," he answered.

"Well," she said, "come on. Father's dying to see you," and the corners of her eyes wrinkled as she smiled.

Miss Georgianna looked nervous as she sat in a corner of the sofa. Mr. Lovell stood by the fireplace and their glances met before either of them spoke. Then he looked hastily at Jessica.

"Good evening, Charles," Miss Georgianna said. "I've just been telling them how thoughtful you've been, coming so often to call while I was here alone."

"Hello, Charles," Mr. Lovell said. "You look as though the summer had done you good."

"Well," Charles answered, "it's been quite a summer."

"I was sorry to hear of your aunt's death. I hope your father got my letter. He didn't answer it."

"He spoke of getting it," Charles said. "I didn't know he hadn't answered it. My father's been pretty busy, with one thing and another."

"There's no reason why he should have written and perhaps his letter never caught up with us. I think we gave Brown, Shipley too many forwarding addresses. It's better to let all letters stay at 123 Pall Mall, London. It's a perfect address, isn't it? 123 Pall Mall, London."

"Yes, sir," Charles said. "It's easy to remember. I suppose Brown, Shipley must have thought of that."

"I don't believe they ever did," Jessica said. "It was probably ordained."

Mr. Lovell turned his back to the fire and clasped his hands behind him. "It's good to be home again," he said. "One of the beauties of going away is getting back, the feeling that everything's been waiting. Sit down for a minute or two, Charles. What's the news? I don't suppose there's any chance of our friend Al Smith's winning the election?"

"The betting's against him," Charles said.

"I imagined so." Mr. Lovell smiled. "And the market's still going up, isn't it? I'll have to go into Boston tomorrow and see if my list of things is up to date."

He was the one who had changed, not Mr. Lovell. He knew that Mr. Lovell disapproved of him but he was no longer disturbed by his disapproval. He could see that Mr. Lovell was typical of certain customers of E. P. Rush. Banks, lawyers and trustees were especially made for people like Mr. Lovell, and Charles's attitude was already what it would always be toward Mr. Lovell's type, courteous and watchful but devoid of real respect.

"It's better not to try to do anything with the market, sir," he said. "All the trustees are moving very slowly."

He was older than Mr. Lovell already and infinitely wiser than Mr. Lovell but he knew enough not to show it unduly.

"They always do, don't they?" Mr. Lovell said, and he laughed. "March Associates take care of my things—the details. In the last analysis I like to rely on my own judgment and I don't think I've done so badly, either, by and large, have I, Georgianna?"

"No, you haven't," Miss Lovell said. "You have very good judgment, Laurence."

"I think I have a little of my grandfather's business instinct," Mr. Lovell said, "an instinct for survival," and he laughed again. "I'm still feeling the motion of the ship. It was rough the last day out. An unexpected squall, the captain said. Well, we've had a long, hard day. I thought that customs inspector was slow and disagreeable, didn't you, Jessica?"

"He was cross because you put down everything," Jessica said, "instead of just saying souvenirs."

"I only obeyed the instructions, Jessica. Well, I think we ought to get a good night's sleep. You should, especially, Jessie. There's always a letdown after an ocean crossing. You've been very nervous all today."

"I wasn't nervous," Jessica said. "I was just anxious to get home. I'm not tired at all."

"It's been very nice to have had a glimpse of Charles," Mr. Lovell said, "but I have an idea that Charles will keep and I know that Charles will understand."

"Oh, yes," Charles said. "That's all right, Mr. Lovell."

"Oh, well," Jessica said, "all right. What are you doing tomorrow, Charles? I'll be rested tomorrow."

"Tomorrow isn't a holiday," Mr. Lovell said. "Charles will be in Boston."

"I know," Jessica said, "but he'll be back in the evening. Let's do something tomorrow evening, Charles."

"Now, Jessie," Mr. Lovell began, and stopped.

There was a brief, heavy sort of silence in the wallpaper room and Charles was aware of everything that caused it.

"Would you like to go out to dinner, Jessica?" Charles said. "We could motor somewhere."

"Now, Jessica," Mr. Lovell said, "I don't want you driving the Dodge at night and Charles hasn't got a car. Have you, Charles?"

"No," Charles answered, "but my father will let me take his."

"Oh," Mr. Lovell said, "has your father bought a car? What sort of a car?"

"A Cadillac," Charles said. He had hoped not to have to mention it but he could not help enjoying the silence that followed. "We might have dinner at the Shore Club, Jessica."

"The Shore Club?" Mr. Lovell looked startled. "You're not a member, are you, Charles?"

"No, but my father is."

Mr. Lovell did not ask in words how John Gray happened to be a member of the Shore Club but the question was written on his face.

"My father knows a good many people," Charles said, and he hoped that he spoke politely.

"Why, I'd love to go," Jessica said.

"The dining room will be cold," Mr. Lovell said. "No one ever goes there for dinner in the autumn if he can help it."

But Mr. Lovell could do nothing.

"We can start early," Charles said to Jessica. "If it's all right, I'll call at half past six."

"I'll wear something warm, Father, and remember what we decided." Jessica's voice was sharper. For a second there was another blank silence.

"Well, well." Mr. Lovell sounded as though a valuable piece of bric-a-brac had been broken. It was all right. It did not matter, at least not before company. "I feel quite out of touch with things. Quite a lot must have been going on since we've been away."

"Not so much," Charles answered. "Everything's about the same."

The differences were only superficial. Everything between them was basically the same except that everything was better than it had been. When Jessica Lovell sat beside him on the front seat of the Cadillac, wrapped in her new polo coat from London, the lights on Johnson Street did not matter. It was a starlit October night and the headlights cut sharply into the coolness in front of them. There was that old smell of burning leaves and toward the end of Johnson Street there were wisps of autumn mist.

"There's no month as beautiful as October," Jessica said.

"It's the best month there is."

They spoke as though they were strangers because they were still on Johnson Street.

"Let's drive around the training field first," she said.

They were silent as they drove around it, but they both must have known they would stop awhile when they were back on the main road, where the houses ended.

Beyond the Royall farm on the main road there was nothing but the black of wind-swept fields and she moved closer to him as he brought the car to a stop. It was like the hill again, that spring. They were clinging to each other and they did not speak for a long while.

"Darling," she said, "aren't you going to say anything?"

"I don't need to say anything," he told her.

"I know. Darling, I've missed you so." That was when she said she had been afraid last night, just for a moment when she first saw him in the hall, that he did not love her any more.

"There's nothing to be afraid of," he said.

"No, I know there isn't," she said, "not any more, but we mustn't ever let ourselves get away from each other again. If you see me getting away, you'll tell me, won't you? And I'll tell you." She was thinking of the way things had been, before she had gone abroad, and now there was not the same sort of gap between them.

"I suppose we'd better go on," she said. "I wish we didn't always have to be going somewhere or saying good-by."

When he started the car again she was still close beside him with her head on his shoulder and with her arm through his as he held the wheel. There was so much to say that it was hard to know where to start. She had missed him every minute, she was saying. She had never been so wretched or unhappy as when they had sailed away and he had been on her mind every minute, or almost every minute. It was no fun seeing all those places alone if you were in love. She had never known how much she loved him. All those places had a sterile sort of blackness which she could not describe.

"It was awfully hard on Father, but he was awfully sweet," she said. "He kept trying so hard not to notice when I couldn't keep my mind on anything."

He did not answer her directly. They were in the car and they were going away from Clyde and he wished that they were going away for good right now, alone together, but he did not tell her that. There were all sorts of other things he wanted to tell her about what he had been doing and what he had been thinking. He had to tell her all about Rush & Company and about why he liked what he was doing there.

"If you want to get on there, you have to see things in a special way," he said, "and I'm trying to find the way."

If she could understand what he was trying to do, everything else he had to explain would be much easier. He had to tell about John Gray and it seemed very necessary that she should see his father as he did, what was wrong and what was right with him. He had never told anyone so much about his father and he had never spoken so many of his thoughts.

"Of course, I don't know much about him myself," he began. "We don't speak the same language, or at least we use different dictionaries. The same words don't mean the same thing."

Then he told her about the system and the ass and the bundle of hay and how his father was going to beat the system. The only trouble was that he did not seem to know when he had beaten it enough. People like him never knew. It was like walking outdoors into the sunlight being able to say those things to someone without being too careful how you said them.

"He thinks I'm the ass following the bundle of hay," he said, and then he laughed. "He doesn't care much about work. Sometimes I think everybody works but Father."

Of course his father was making a lot of money, money on paper, and he kept trying to persuade his father to get some of it off of paper, but sometimes when he was with his father he felt as though he were the tail of a kite, he said. Had she ever flown a kite? He and Sam used to fly them. If you did not put enough tail on to balance it, then the kite would begin darting from side to side and finally it would come crashing.

"Of course, when you're the tail of a kite," he said, "you've got to follow it. That's why we're in this car. We're both tied to the kite."

"It's nice, being tied to something."

She had always been tied to something, she said, and she supposed a girl always was, but all of this was new.

Yes, all of it was new and it would always stay so in memory. The car, he supposed, if he were to see it now would look antiquated and clumsy, and the dress she wore that night would be ludicrous if he could see it now, but the Cadillac, her dress, and everything they said always would be new and they always would be young, in memory, riding through an October night.

He was the tail of the kite and he was gambling as hard as his father, he told her. He had no right to criticize.

"You see," he said, "someone's got to beat the system. You're my system," and she laughed and her arm tightened through his.

"Darling," she said, "you don't have to beat me, and besides, I'm not much to beat."

He knew then that he would ask Jessica Lovell to marry him. The idea of its being possible was like the Cadillac. It was there, but it might not be there permanently. It might, and yet it might not, be illusion. It was just as his father had said—it was surprising how quickly you got used to things—even to impermanence.

The Shore Club, in spite of its name, was two or three miles inland from the water. It was old, for a country club. Its wooden verandas were pock-marked by the hobnails of more than a generation of golfing shoes. Its walls were decorated with mementos of great bygone events and with comical English prints of riders being tossed by their mounts into ponds and hedges. Antiquated drivers and tennis rackets, all suitably labeled, were hung upon the walls, together with whips, a few hunting horns, and the puckered, sad masks of foxes, for there were still a few foxes on the Shore, carefully watched by the owners of the estates on which they took refuge. The tables were decorated by large silver cups and bowls won by club teams and of such a cumbersome size, perhaps, that no one wanted to take them home and so left them where they properly belonged, at the Shore Club. All these objects gave the whole place an atmosphere of violent out-of-door activity, so it did not seem right to be there unless one had reached a state of suitable physical exhaustion.

The members must have been resting at home that evening because the club, when Charles and Jessica arrived there, was empty, and their footsteps echoed in a reproachful sort of silence. A fire was burning in the main room and the chimney must have still been cold for the room was drafty and smoky. They stood there for a moment uncertainly and then Jessica began to giggle.

"I guess nobody's here," she said. "It's like something in *The Green Fairy Book* or *The Purple Fairy Book*, isn't it?" The log snapped sullenly in the fireplace.

"What do I do now?" he asked her.

"Why, you ring the bell for Clarkson."

"Who's Clarkson?"

"I don't know," Jessica said, "except he's always been here."

Clarkson was the club steward and Charles supposed he should have known it, but then Jessica was used to the Shore Club and he had only been there once before.

"Where's the bell?" he asked.

"I'll ring it," Jessica said. "That's the way you can tell a college girl. They always ring bells when they're with a man."

Clarkson was a thin, elderly man, who of course knew Jessica and who accepted Charles when he explained who he was. It even seemed to Charles that Clarkson looked at him approvingly, as though Clarkson understood that he was on the team at E. P. Rush & Company. It was strange how quickly everything was changing. If they wanted, Clarkson said, he could set a table for them in front of the fire, and if they wanted something before dinner there was something in Mr. Gray's locker. He was sorry it was so lonely tonight, but then perhaps they did not mind. They could have a Martini cocktail, if they wanted.

"Oh," Charles said, "I didn't know my father had a locker."

Though he did not need the drink–he seldom did in those days–it was just as well to have one, but even without the cocktail, even with the smoking fireplace and the cold air about their ankles, the room would have been warm and friendly simply because Jessica and he were alone in it.

"I never knew what this place was good for until now," she said. "I wish we could do this all the time."

Then she told him it was the first time she had not been afraid of the Shore Club. She had been there for golf lessons and she had been there for dances but she had always felt uneasy because she did not live on the Shore.

"I know what the trouble was," she said. "I never had anyone who belonged to me–and you don't mind it at all. I never thought of your being able to get on everywhere. What are you laughing at?"

"Malcolm Bryant once said I had mobility," he told her. "I do feel awfully mobile. I guess Father and I both have it."

"You were mobile at the firemen's muster," she said. "Do you remember?"

There was so much to remember that belonged only to them. Did he remember, she asked at dinner, that Saturday morning at the Dock Street Bank? Did she remember the frogs and the swamp, he was asking, and she asked if he remembered the hepaticas. They had never found a single hepatica.

"We'll find some next spring," he told her.

"It was like playing hide-and-seek, wasn't it?" she said–"always pretending to hide what we thought about each other and yet not wanting to hide it, and now we don't have to hide anything any more."

It was not exactly so, because no one would ever tell anyone else everything, but there was the illusion that there was no concealment. When you were in love, all the cards seemed to lie face upwards on the table.

After dinner, they walked out to the parking place where they had left the car. It was the only car there and they did not drive away for a long while.

"I never thought I'd be in just this place under just these circumstances," she said.

"It's probably happened before," he told her, "but then I wouldn't know."

"Darling," she said, "I'm so happy. I'm not sorry about any of it, except one thing, just one thing."

"What one thing?"

He was not thinking attentively of what she was saying, because they had said so many other things, the things perhaps one always said when one was in a parked car when one was in love.

"It's Father," she said. "Poor Father. You like him, don't you, darling?"

There were still things it was better to conceal. She had raised her head from his shoulder. She was looking at him, trying to see his face through the dark.

"I'm afraid he doesn't like me much," he said, "but I don't blame him. Why should he?"

"He does." It hurt him because she was no longer happy and he wished that Mr. Lovell had not come into it. "He likes you as much as he can anyone who likes me, don't you see?"

"Yes," he said, "I guess I see."

"It's my problem anyway," she said. "You don't have to mind as long as you understand the way he feels. It's just waiting until he gets used to it." She was always saying to wait until he got used to it. "I wish I weren't torn in two pieces whenever I see you both together . . . Darling?"

"Yes," he said.

"He really does like you. At least, he tries to like you. He always says nice things about you, or at least he tries to. I've got to love you both at once. That's all I mean."

It was a time when nothing was a problem. When one talked of cold facts at such a time, they were like the roseate clouds of a summer sunrise, drifting like gilded islands across one's thoughts. If they were so large that they temporarily obscured the sun, you knew that the sun would burn through them. There had to be a happy ending, or you could not be in love.

He put his foot on the starter of the Cadillac and at the same time he switched on the lights. The sound of the motor was strong and reassuring. He did not speak as he backed the car and started it down the drive because he still had to give the gears his full attention. The car moved deliberately and slowly until it was in second, and then it was in high and the crunching of the gravel beneath the wheels was louder than the sound of the motor.

"Jessica," he said, "will you marry me? I wish you would."

"Why, Charley," she said, and there was a catch in her voice. "What made you think of that just now?"

Johnson Street and Spruce Street and all of Clyde seemed to be around him as he had proposed to Jessica Lovell.

"Why, I've been thinking about it all the time," he said.

"Well, so have I," and there was that catch in her voice again. "Oh, Charley, of course I will."

He felt the blood rush to his cheeks. He could never have described everything he felt but relief must have been a part of it, deep relief that the waiting was over. It had been bound to happen and it was over and now they could go on from there, anywhere they wanted, he and Jessica Lovell.

"But we can't get married right away."

"No," he said, "not right away."

"We wouldn't have anything to live on, would we? That's what Father keeps saying."

"No," he said, "not now, but we will have by spring."

At least he had offered her everything once. He told her that he was only making thirty dollars a week at Rush & Company but he would get a raise on the first of the year. He might be getting fifty dollars a week by spring. Besides, there was the five thousand dollars his aunt had left him, and now it was twenty thousand. He would not be afraid to marry her now, if she were not afraid, but he hoped to have fifty thousand by spring and if he did he would stop. The income from fifty thousand dollars, safely invested at five per cent, would be twenty-five hundred dollars, and if he were making fifty dollars a week that would be five thousand dollars a year. The prospect had a desperate quality, but with Jessica there listening he could believe in it implicitly.

"And Father will give me an allowance," she said.

"He doesn't have to," Charles told her. "I can take care of you, Jessica."

He could take care of her, now that his thoughts were moving on. He knew that he was doing well in Rush & Company. He might be a partner some day. He could see life stretching out before him like the dark road beneath the headlights.

"Of course, it won't be much to start with," he said, "and we don't have to live in Clyde." He must have known even then that they should get away from Clyde. Everything he was saying would be truer if they were somewhere else.

"Of course we have to live in Clyde," she said. "All our families are there."

They were already talking as though everything were settled.

"Charley," she said, "you like children, don't you? We'll have the nicest children, two boys and two girls. No, three girls"; and then she laughed. "And we can buy one of those little houses by the river, and we can do it over . . . Why, we're talking as if it had already happened."

When she said it, the house of cards fell down and for a moment he could see every fallacy of its flimsy structure.

"Well," he said, "it's got to happen. Jessica, please go on and keep believing."

"Of course I'll keep believing, but, darling," and there was a doubtful sound in her voice, "we'd better not tell anyone—and certainly not Father yet. He might stop me from believing."

By the time Charles had left the Cadillac in Rowell's Garage, the lights were out in the house on Spruce Street except in the front hall and in his father's room at the head of the stairs. The door to the upstairs room was half open and he could see his father sitting in front of his table adding a column of figures beneath the light of his old student lamp which had recently been wired for electricity. The sofa had been reupholstered in green velvet and there were glazed chintz curtains around the windows and a new green carpet, but no one had touched the books. Though the room was swept now and freshly painted, it was still like his father's mind, full of odds and ends for which he had never found a place.

"Oh, there you are, Charley," his father said. "You didn't smash the car, did you?"

"No, sir," Charles said, "nothing happened to the car."

"How was Clarkson—and the Shore Club? Did you see Clarkson?"

"Yes, sir," Charles said.

"You know, I rather like Clarkson. I'd like to have someone like him looking out for me. I'm tired of carrying my own clothes down to Dock Street to be pressed."

John Gray leaned back in his chair and pushed away his papers and opened the mahogany humidor which he had recently purchased.

"We really ought to have a man here to pass us things. We ought to have a couple to look after us, a nice woman who's a good cook and her husband. What we really need is two Filipinos, but I'm afraid your mother wouldn't like them. Perhaps we'd better look for a French couple and have some French cooking and a little wine at dinner. There's no reason to have these old Irishwomen in by the day. Mary Callahan when she comes in is more like my nurse than a maid. We'll have to find a couple."

His cigar cutter made a sharp incisive sound, and he struck a match.

"The devil of it is, we'll need another bathroom if we have a couple. We need more bathrooms at any rate. We can put two of them up on the third floor, one for the couple and one for you, and I suppose Dorothea ought to have one, too, but then she's going to marry Elbridge. Still, we could use it for a guest bathroom, couldn't we?—but then if you get married there will be another vacant bathroom. Well, we'll get three new bathrooms. I'll get Sid Stevens in here to measure them up tomorrow. There's always plenty of room for them in an old house. Now, how did my mind get on plumbing?"

"You were talking about a couple," Charles said.

"Oh, yes. I wonder how many bathrooms the Lovells have."

"I don't know," Charles said.

As he had told Jessica, if you were the tail of a kite you had to follow the kite. His father was glancing again at the papers on which he had been working.

"I always wonder why I'm doing so well, Charley, until I remember this is the first time I've had any real working capital," he said, and he puffed on his cigar and blew a cloud of that heavy, permeating smoke of expensive Havana tobacco. Charles would always associate cigar smoke with brokerage accounts and working capital. "You see, I'm pretty well up in the system now. Just between you and me—don't tell the women yet, it will only make them nervous—as of today there's three hundred and fifty thousand in the kitty."

"I don't like being out at sea in a canoe with just one paddle," Charles said. "When will you have enough, Father?"

John Gray's thoughts must have been winging happily over broader fields and it must have annoyed him to be brought up short.

"Dear me," he said. "There we are again. Don't you know, Charley, that once you're up in the system you have leverage? They'll find it hard to shake me down."

"Who are They?" Charles asked.

His father picked up a pencil and tapped it on the paper.

"I'm damned if I know who, but somebody's running this show."

"It isn't somebody," Charles said, "it's everybody. Why don't you call your system a common state of mind?"

Later he was to read the debates and the dogma of economists and weigh the theories of the orthodox against those of the disciples of John Maynard Keynes. Those people with their set conventions always reminded him more of theologians than philosophers. They were the high priests of materialism, constantly trying to establish their creeds and trying to give unbreakable definitions to acquisitive forces, and yet in the end it was nothing more or less than what he had said that night at Spruce Street.

"Maybe you're right," his father said. "Maybe it is a state of mind, but states of mind change, don't they? You know—I'm going to say something that may relieve you, Charley. I've been seriously thinking that there's an end to everything—you can't carry a good thing too far, can you? You know, I really think that perhaps I ought to make a limit. I think I'll stop all this and cash in—when I have a million dollars." It was the ultimate end, the mathematical symbol for security and happiness. "Well . . . good night, Charley."

19

"*Give Crowns and Pounds and Guineas, but Not Your Heart Away*"

—A. E. HOUSMAN

There was once good thing about Clyde. People there might know everything about you but they still had respect for individual privacy. No one, except his immediate family, ever asked Charles directly about Jessica Lovell. If you lived in a place like Clyde, you were keenly conscious of public approval or disapproval. Though Charles was too busy most of the time that winter to go around much, as the expression went, he still realized that he was a figure of interest. At the railroad station or when he went to the post office or to the news store or to Walters's drugstore, he could perceive an atmosphere of veiled expectancy. Jackie Mason, he thought, was always waiting for him to say something and he seemed hurt when Charles did not allude to his private affairs. The girls he knew had grown sedulously impersonal, as though he were no longer a part of any of their plans. They would smile at him brightly and say, "Why, hello, Charley. You're quite a stranger these days"; and friends of his, like Earl Wilkins and the Meaders, would say, "Hi, Charley. How's everything going, Charley?"

It was what one always said, but when they asked the question it seemed to him that other people would turn and look and listen for his answer. Everyone, of course, must have been talking about the Grays that winter, including Mr. and Mrs. Meader and the Masons and all the family's particular friends. They would all say when they met him, "Why, Charley, we haven't seen you for a long while. I suppose they're keeping you busy in Boston"—but they were not thinking about Boston. They were thinking of what was keeping him busy in Clyde. They were saying, in private, that he was "attentive" to Jessica Lovell and his own friends must have been saying that he was "crazy about" Jessica Lovell and down on River Street they were probably saying that Charley Gray was "going with" Jessica Lovell.

Everyone was watching the Lovells, too, and someone must have heard the Thomases and the Stanleys and other people on Johnson Street say that Mr. Lovell did not like it. He wanted Jessica to do better. After all, she had come out in Boston and the Lovells were always down on the Shore, but then he could not do much about it if Jessica liked Charley Gray. The Grays were doing very well. They had a couple working for them and a Cadillac and the house on Spruce Street had been redecorated and they had put in three new bathrooms and Wallace Brooks, who had done the painting for them, had said that the interior decorator himself had come from Boston to hang the drapes, and Mary Callahan, who now did the cleaning, said that Esther Gray had bought the loveliest new china and new sheets and blankets and candlewick bedspreads, and that Elbridge Sterne did look plain beside Miss Dorothea in her new dresses and her fur coat. The Grays were doing very well. Besides, Charley was getting on well, too, in Boston. Mr. Stanley had said that he had the makings of a businessman and that he wished he had him back in Wright-Sherwin. There was nothing that Mr. Lovell could do about it, and Jessica might have done worse.

This was what everyone must have been saying and Charles did not mind whatever repercussions he sensed of it because he was almost sure it was all said in a kindly, friendly way. Those rumors about himself and Jessica Lovell gave everyone a vicarious sort of satisfaction for it looked as though Jessica might marry a Clyde boy who did not live on Johnson Street and Mr. Lovell, in spite of all his talk about the Lovells and Clyde, thought the Lovells were too good for Clyde.

No one could say anything definite. The Grays had not been asked to the Lovells' for a meal and Laurence Lovell and Miss Georgianna had not been to call on the Grays, but then Clyde was never a hospitable place. However, when his mother finally asked her, Jessica Lovell did go to supper at Spruce Street, in spite of implications, and there was nothing Mr. Lovell could have done to prevent it.

Charles had somehow been reluctant to talk things over with his mother because he had felt that she knew enough of what was happening without his having to explain it. She knew that he and Jessica were always calling each other up and she knew how often he went to see her, and she had seen the marble Pliny doves on his bureau and the photograph of Adam from the Sistine Chapel and later a pair of silver-backed military brushes. He had told his mother immediately when she asked about the brushes that Jessica had given them to him and his mother had said they were perfectly lovely brushes and that Jessica had very good taste. A curious sort of pride had prevented his saying anything more to anyone until it could be more definite, but one December evening when he came home from Rush & Company, his mother and Dorothea were waiting in the parlor and something in their expressions told him that they were waiting for him particularly.

"Where's Father?" he asked, because his father had not gone into Boston.

"Just where he always is—upstairs reading the papers," Dorothea said.

"You can see him later, dear," his mother said. "Why don't you just sit down and talk to us?"

"Is anything the matter?" Charles asked. His mother and Dorothea exchanged a meaning glance.

"I don't know why you're so nervous lately, dear. Why should anything be the matter? Dorothea and I just like to visit, now that we don't have to get supper. It's awfully queer to sit here in the afternoon and have Axel and Hulda doing everything. Did Axel press your other suit nicely, Charley?"

"Yes," Charles said. "Axel's all right."

"I can't get used to having a man in the house in the daytime," his mother said, "and Dorothea was just saying Axel's lazy. He makes Hulda do his work and he sits in his room all afternoon reading *True Love Stories*."

"*True Love Stories?*" Charles repeated.

"Yes," Dorothea said. "There are such things as true love stories, in case you haven't realized it."

"Well," Charles said, "you ought to know. Where's Elbridge?"

"You ought to know, too, and never mind about Elbridge."

"Charley"—his mother smiled at him very sweetly—"Dorothea and I have just thought of something that we think might be nice. Don't you think now that we have the couple, Charley, it might be nice to ask Jessica Lovell for supper on Saturday?" The expectant way they watched him explained the uneasiness he had felt the moment he entered the parlor.

"I don't see any particular reason for it," he said. "Why should you suddenly ask her to supper?"

"But she's never been inside the house, dear, after all this time."

"After all what time?" Charles asked.

"Oh, Charley," his mother said, and she looked hurt.

"We know about these things better than you," Dorothea said. "It looks queer not having her. Don't you know that everybody's talking?"

"If anybody so much as looks at a girl around here," Charles said, "everybody starts talking."

"Now, really, Charley," Dorothea said, "have you only just been looking at Jessica Lovell?"

Charles felt his face grow beet-red.

"Oh, Charley"—his mother still looked hurt—"don't you see it looks as though you were ashamed of us? You're not ashamed, are you, Charley?"

"I didn't say I was ashamed of anyone," Charles said. "I just don't see any reason to underline things."

"Charley, dear," his mother said, "there's nothing to be so upset about. We all think she's a very nice girl and we're all very happy about it."

"I'm not upset about anything at all, Mother," Charles began. "I only think—"

"Then don't you think, dear"—she was speaking in a soothing tone she had used when he was much younger—"that it would be nice to have her for supper on Saturday night, just so we could all see each other? I'd love to ask her myself."

Charles shrugged his shoulders.

"Oh, all right," he said, "if you have to have her, if you all want to look at her, why go ahead and ask her." He did not mean to sound ungracious but he hated to think how it would be, with the family knowing everything and yet not saying anything.

As a matter of fact, it was not nearly as bad as it might have been. Everyone tried to behave as though it were the most natural thing in the world for Jessica Lovell to come to supper. The new silver candlesticks and a new Canton china dinner set were on the table—his father loved Canton china—but there was no reason for Jessica to have thought that a special effort was being made. In fact, it was almost like a family meal—just the family, Esther Gray had told Jessica over the telephone, just a family supper.

The worst of it was waiting for Jessica. Elbridge Sterne was there, just to even out things, as Dorothea said, and everyone gathered in the front parlor, which looked very well with its fresh curtains and with the new furniture from Gow Street. Everyone tried to talk about ordinary things, but his mother and Dorothea, in their dresses from Hollander's in Boston, kept moving about straightening ornaments or going out to the dining room to take a last look at the table. Elbridge Sterne was kind to him, almost like an elder brother. His father had a bland, noncommittal look.

"I'm sure Jessica won't mind if Axel brings in the cocktails," John Gray said, and then he went into the hall and called loudly. "Oh, Axel." He always loved to call to Axel, and Axel and Hulda were always saying what a fine gentleman Mr. Gray was. John Gray seated himself on one of the Martha Washington chairs from Gow Street and examined complacently his new shoes which had been made to order in London.

"I've just been rereading Ignatius Donnelly's *Atlantis*," he said. "Have you ever read it, Elbridge?"

"No," Elbridge answered. "What's Atlantis?"

"Oh, dear me," John Gray said. "That's another hiatus in a Kansas education, Elbridge. I know they only teach useful things in Kansas and Atlantis is perfectly useless—a mythological concept based on a geological fact. A body of land somewhere near the mouth of the Mediterranean actually did sink beneath the sea in the tertiary epoch and the rumor is that it was the cradle of civilization with beautiful cities and palaces, a dream world, perhaps the basis for the universal flood legend. Oh, here come the cocktails. Thank you, Axel."

"Now, Father," Dorothea said, "there's no reason to give us a free lecture. Why should Elbridge know anything about Atlantis?"

"I don't see why I shouldn't give one while we're waiting, Dorothea," John Gray said, "and it's very good for Elbridge, and Charles too. Ignatius Donnelly, though brilliant, is doubtless inaccurate, but think of Atlantis, the cradle of beauty and wisdom, and then a slight quiver of the earth's crust and then in comes the sea. Only the Azores are left, according to Mr. Donnelly. You know, I don't see why we shouldn't go to the Azores sometime. They have wild canaries in the Azores."

The doorbell rang.

"It must be Jessica," John Gray said. "You'd better let her in, Charley."

Her cheeks were glowing from the cold and she spoke a little breathlessly, saying she hoped she was not late. She must have been hoping, too, that she did not look nervous and that everyone would like her. She wore a new green dress, and he wished she had not walked into the parlor as though she were going to a formal dinner, but actually everything went very well. At first, Charles had a sinking feeling, but when she stood beside him in the parlor he suddenly felt proud and happy and glad that she had come.

"Would you like a Martini, Jessica?" John Gray said. "We were just talking about Atlantis."

"Oh," Jessica said, "the book about the lost continent?"

"Yes, Jessica," John Gray said. "I always keep it beside the *Origin of Species* and *The Voyage of the Beagle.* Atlantis is really a state of mind. Everybody is always on his own Atlantis sometime. We must learn to jump when the earth shakes. I suppose Charley talks to you about states of mind."

Jessica shook her head, the way she did when her hair blew across her forehead.

"I wish he would talk about Atlantis instead," she answered.

"Well," John Gray said, "here's to Atlantis, Jessica."

It was just as though he had said, Here's to Jessica and Charles. Everyone knew that they belonged to each other, as they stood side by side in the parlor.

"What is it, Axel?" his mother said. Axel was standing silent in the doorway to the dining room. She never could get entirely used to Axel's announcing supper.

It was something he would always remember, the dining room and everyone around the table. There was an irony to his father's having mentioned Atlantis, for the waves were to flow over all of that era and it was buried long ago, fathoms deep—but echoes of it were still with him, like the church bell that rang beneath the sea.

"Your father and I don't see as much of each other as we ought to, Jessica," his father said, as he carved the leg of lamb, "but we know each other very well. Did he ever tell you that we studied together for our entrance examinations before we went to Harvard? I was a very bad boy. I didn't last there long."

Then he was telling what things had been like in those days and about his sisters and the Judge.

"Esther, do you remember the first time I ever called on you? I'd just been excused from Harvard."

"I don't know why you should think of that now," Esther Gray said.

"It just passed through my mind," John Gray said. "If I hadn't come to call, if I hadn't quoted Shakespeare—" He stopped and looked at the carving knife. "Do you know what I wish?" He stopped, but no one answered. "I wish Sam were here."

It must have been years since his father had mentioned Sam and it was strange that he should have spoken of him with Jessica there.

"Charley has told me about him," she said. "Do you remember that time you told me about making whistles, Charley?"

"Yes," Charles said. "I never could make one, could I?"

"When did you two try to make whistles?" Dorothea asked, and Jessica laughed.

"Oh, that was a long time ago," she said. "Well, it was only last April, but it seems like a long time ago."

When he walked home with her, she said she loved the family. She loved his mother; she was so pretty and she seemed to be so happy. The whole place was so alive, she said, and she liked the way he and Dorothea kept arguing, without ever really getting angry. He would never know, she said, how lonely it was to be an only child. She liked Elbridge Sterne, too, though he had not said much.

"No one says much," Charles told her, "when Father starts talking."

"I hope he likes me," Jessica said. "Charley, do you think he does?"

"Didn't you see him showing off?" he said. "Of course he likes you."

"Darling," she said, "it seemed so, well, so ominous when I was standing ringing the bell, and now I'm awfully glad. I feel just the way I ought to feel," and then she sighed.

The wind was waving the bare branches of the elms in front of the Lovell house. Though it was late in December there was no snow on the ground yet, but the air felt like snow.

"Father's got to get used to it," she said, but it seemed to make no difference then whether Mr. Lovell was used to it or not. Jessica had gone to Spruce Street and though the Lovells did not ask Charles to dinner, Miss Lovell, a week later, asked his mother and Dorothea to tea.

Memories of that winter in Clyde had little or none of the continuity of his recollections of former winters. There was not the usual sensation of endlessness or the interminable waiting between the melting of the snow and spring. December and January were considered possible in Clyde but as long as Charles could remember he had heard people say each winter, as though it were a new thought, that February and March were the worst months in the year. He had always felt this monotony in his school days and in his days at Wright-Sherwin, but those early weeks of 1929 possessed a staccato quality which he had never experienced before or since. They had the rhythm and the irregularity of dots and dashes in a telegraphic code—a dot for the fenced-off desks at Rush & Company, another dot for the board room and for Mr. Rush taking off his arctics, a dash for hurried, furtive luncheons with Jessica when she came to Boston, a break in the cadence and two quick dots for Spruce Street.

Early in January, John Gray had said that he could see no earthly reason why they should congeal slowly in Clyde if it was not necessary. February and March were the hardest months and at least they could get away for a week or two. He could put things in shape and leave them for that long. Winter in Clyde did something to people's faces, particularly to women's. Charles could stay, he had to since he was following his bundle of hay at Rush & Company. Axel and Hulda could look after him, but his mother needed a rest and so did Dorothea.

By the middle of the month he was reading the travel folders, usually aloud, and the rich, glowing texture of their language kept setting his mind off on cruises of its own. They would sail to the Caribbean on one of those ships which was your hotel while you were in port, and it had better be an English ship because the English knew how to do things properly and English crews did not rush to the boats first when there was an accident. They stood at attention and sang "Nearer, My God, to Thee"—not that any ship would sink, not on a voyage of enchantment to the dreamlike Windward and Leeward Islands, to dark Haiti with its brooding citadel, to Yucatán with its Mayan ruins, to Cartagena, a topaz in a setting of old Spain, or to quaint, neat, varicolored Curaçao, a bit of old Holland, adrift, but charmingly, on a turquoise sea. What ho, for the Spanish Main, with its memories of pirates and buccaneers, its century-old frowning ramparts and cathedrals, its islets like emeralds surrounded by reefs of purple coral. Esther needed a change and so did Dorothea. They all needed to get out of themselves, and there was no reason why they shouldn't, for a week or two.

Another year, when things were quieter, they could take a longer trip—the Riviera, Monte Carlo. Even though he did not gamble himself, he had always wanted to watch those improvidents at Monte Carlo and there was no reason why he shouldn't. Egypt, up the Nile, India, the Taj, Japan, China, islands of the Pacific, Hawaii—they could do it, another year. In fact, there was no reason why they should stay in Clyde in the winter at all. Eventually they could get a house at Pinehurst or Sea Island or Palm Beach. Palm Beach might be best, because he could drop in at Bradley's and watch other people lose their money.

There were other dots and dashes that winter—a dot for the New Year's dance at the Shore Club—it was Jessica who suggested the New Year's dance—another dash for a call at Johnson Street when Mr. Lovell was away and when Miss Georgianna went up to bed and left them alone; but one of the longest dashes of all, of course, was his triumph at Rush & Company.

In England there was the New Year's Honors List and that custom of granting favors and distinctions applied also to American business. First, at E. P. Rush, there were the Christmas bonuses, a carefully prorated largesse expected of financial houses at the end of a good year and primarily intended for the clerical force, the boys and girls behind the grating, and not for the team. The raises at New Year's, however, had a different, more permanent value, not to be discussed as openly as bonus money.

Charles was not surprised when Mr. Rush sent for him on the afternoon of January second. First they talked about the weather, and then Mr. Rush shifted the papers on his desk and looked embarrassed. He always had a hard time with personnel relationships. The partners, he said, had all been having a talk about everybody, a routine, end-of-the-year talk, and they had all agreed that Charles was getting to be part of the family, and he hoped that Charles liked the family. He did not want to encourage Charles too much, Mr. Rush said, but it was beginning to be plain that there was an eventual future for him in E. P. Rush and he wanted Charles to feel happy and contented so that the good work could go on, particularly the investment advisory work. Of course, he said, Rush & Company was not noted for paying large salaries, but Rush & Company looked after its own. It was a two-way loyalty. Employees were loyal to the firm, and the firm to the employees. He had not been with them long, but Mr. Rush was willing to forget length of service. As of the first of the year—Mr. Rush looked wretchedly embarrassed and drew circles on his memorandum pad—Charles's salary would be sixty dollars a week, a pretty large salary considering his age and experience, and Mr. Rush hoped that Charles would be happy about it.

There was never again in his life anything else exactly like that moment. He had been vaguely thinking of a possible fifty dollars and secretly he had felt it was a presumptuous hope although Mr. Stanley had offered him as much. For a second he struggled with a dizzy sort of incredulity and then instinctively he knew that he should not show it.

"Thank you very much, sir," he said. "I'm very much obliged."

"That's all right," Mr. Rush said. "Well, that's all now."

At the moment, he would gladly have died for Mr. Rush, that simple man who always wore a last year's hat and had his suits turned by his tailor to avoid buying new ones. As of that moment he was making three thousand dollars a year. It was possible, barely possible, that he could marry Jessica Lovell on three thousand dollars a year.

He must have still been riding on the wave of that elation when he met Malcolm Bryant in a snowstorm one night after a call on Jessica. It was another of the dots and dashes of that winter, extraneous, because Malcolm was already like a shore line that he was leaving far behind. Yet the memory of Malcolm always formed a part of the design of that winter, a reminder of the things he had missed and of the way things might have been if he had done this or that.

Jessica had told him that she really thought her father was getting used to it. He had recently fallen into the habit of sitting in the library with the door open when Charles came to call instead of sitting in the wallpaper room and joining in the conversation, and this may have proved that he was getting used to it. It even was possible to sit together on the sofa, though it was better always to talk brightly, without any gaps of silence, or Mr. Lovell would grow restless. Charles had said good night to her at ten and they had not lingered in the hall except long enough for him to buckle his overshoes, but it did not matter because she would be with her aunt in Boston over the week end and they were going to spend Saturday afternoon together and go to the theater on Saturday night.

It had started snowing at eight o'clock and now the wind was rising and the small, hard snowflakes eddied and swirled with it and beat against his face. Since it was early he decided to walk down Dock Street before he went home, just to see the storm. The snow made a hissing sound, gentle but very persistent as the wind drove it against the brick walls of the public library. He was just passing beneath the light by the Dock Street Bank and by the blank, dark windows of the notions store when he saw a figure coming toward him, head down, moving noiselessly against the wind. He slowed his steps to see who it was, as one always did in Clyde, and it was Malcolm Bryant.

"Hello, Charley," Malcolm said. "Come on back with me. I haven't seen you for a long while." Malcolm had not been to call at Spruce Street for months. "I've been up in Cambridge," he went on, "getting all the material whipped into shape. We ought to be cleaned up here by March or April. God, this is a hell of a town."

"You always used to like it," Charles said.

"I know . . . I must have been crazy," Malcolm said. "At least it's warm where you get anopheles mosquitoes. Well, how has everything been going with you, Charley?" There was a vague note in Malcolm's voice. "Are you still with that stock-and-bond job in Boston?" He had once been a collected specimen of Malcolm's and perhaps he was somewhere in a card file now but obviously Malcolm's interests had moved on and so had his. "I'm damned if I know why you do it," Malcolm went on. "Where have you been? Calling on Jessica?"

"Yes," Charles said.

"My God," Malcolm said. "I suppose I have a mercurial disposition. When I first see a thing, I love it, and then when I get it worked out I'm ready to move on—but I've done quite a job here, if I do say so, and it ought to get me an honorary degree somewhere if anyone has any sense. God, the prejudices you run into, the small minds, but I'm not a prima donna. Thank God, I'm not a prima donna." Charles never felt at home with Malcolm Bryant's weakness for frank personal revelation, but obviously something had happened. Obviously Malcolm was disturbed. "And I'm not a politician, either, and I'm not interested in publication. After all, my job is field work. I don't know what ever put it in my mind to ask for the G. Price Fellowship."

"What's the G. Price Fellowship?" Charles asked.

"It's one of those stupid lecture fellowships." Malcolm laughed airily. "Well, if they don't want me, they don't have to have me. Frankly, Harvard's a damn provincial place and I should have known it. Thank God, I'm not a time server or a prima donna."

When they reached his rooms at Mrs. Mooney's, Malcolm switched on the light above his drawing board. The room had a crowded, restive appearance. His locker trunk and bedding roll, always closed before in neat readiness for departure from Clyde, were both opened. A rubber poncho and a mosquito net were draped across the couch and a collapsible rubber basin, a desert water bag and a pair of binoculars lay on top of them. All sorts of things had emerged from the tray of the locker trunk, small articles distributed in neat rows and piles on the floor like lead soldiers taken from a box—flashlights, medicines, camera film, and a great many other things that experience had taught the traveler were essential for a long journey.

"I'm just checking up on everything." Malcolm waved at the locker and bedding roll as he wriggled out of his snowy overcoat and dropped it on the floor. "There won't be many stores along the Orinoco."

He reached under the couch and drew out a whiskey bottle and told Charles to wait while he got a pitcher of water from the bathroom. As Charles stood there alone, he felt his own restiveness growing. In some ways Malcolm Bryant must have had a wonderful life and its design was right there in front of him, drawn with sheath knives, fishhooks, and mosquito netting. There was no need for careful, long-term planning in that life, because someone else did all the planning for him. Someone else supplied the money and the steamship tickets. If he did not like it where he was, Malcolm could move on, always supported by some learned foundation. He could go and he could return to tell his tales in his own strange, scientific jargon. He was returning now with the florid hot-water pitcher from a Victorian chamber set.

"There isn't any ice," Malcolm said, "but if you want it cold just open the window and scoop in some snow."

He leaned over the drawing board, poured a tumbler a third full of whiskey, and pushed it toward Charles. It was much more than Charles would have thought of consuming, yet Malcolm Bryant was escaping from Clyde and from whatever else it was that bothered him, and Charles felt, with the aid of that glass of whiskey, that he too could escape vicariously. He did not know from exactly what he wished to escape, but curious uncontrolled desires were pulling at him.

"I'm sorry you're going away, Malcolm," Charles said.

"Are you?" Malcolm's deep-set eyes had a kindly look. "That's nice of you to say so, Charley. You're a nice kid, Charley." Malcolm had tossed off his glass and was pouring himself another drink. "This whole thing is going to have repercussions, it's going to make a noise."

"What whole thing?" Charles asked.

"This whole survey and its ultimate conclusion." Malcolm waved his arm vaguely. "You see, I've been able to prove something."

"What have you proved?" Charles asked.

Malcolm pulled a pipe and a tobacco pouch from his pocket. He reminded Charles, as he filled his pipe, of a detective, explaining to an appreciative audience, in the last chapter of a mystery story, just how he caught the criminal.

"It's a little hard to clarify for a layman," Malcolm said, "but it can't help but get recognition when I get time to get it into print. Not that I want recognition. I'm against the whole theory of honorary degrees—but let me put it in one-syllable words. Man is essentially the same, whether he's in G-strings or plus fours, and I ought to know. After all, what is man?"

There was no need to answer the question. Malcolm Bryant was standing up. He was on the lecture platform, preparing to address a wider audience, fortifying himself first with a few swallows from his glass.

"What is man? Nothing but a very recent evolutionary form of mammal with a surprisingly adaptive brain. He tries to cloak himself with dignity. He's a self-conscious, worrying mammal, but he is only a small link in the chain of life. And what is life?"

Charles found himself groping cautiously through the maze of Malcolm's verbiage and he was thinking that Malcolm in his way sounded like a market letter, which also endeavored to prove something.

"What is our planetary system? Only a insignificant unit in a galaxy among other galaxies. There must be other planets, millions of them, billions of them, supporting life. What is man? To hell with him. Why should I worry?"

"But you are worrying," Charles said.

"Now when I get to the Orinoco—" He had dismissed the planetary system.

His gaze had traveled to the mosquito netting and the bedding roll. "Charley, how would you like to get away from all this and come with me to the Orinoco?"

"That would be fine," Charles told him, "but I don't see quite how I can work it now." He was using that placating tone one customarily employed in dealing with a drunk, and perhaps Malcolm recognized it.

"What are you going to do if you don't, Charley?" he asked.

"I guess I'll just have to try to get along," Charles said, "in my planetary system."

He did not like the way he sounded. He sounded like an old man or like a schoolbook, smug and reasonable. He was thinking of Jessica Lovell and Rush & Company, of a house and children of his own, of Jessica meeting him when he came home. If one could go beyond those thoughts at least those wishes were universal, but their ultimate purpose evaded him just then.

"The biological urge," Malcolm was saying. "I suppose you realize you're a victim of the urge."

"Yes," Charles said, "I suppose so."

"Oh, my God," Malcolm said. "Excuse me, Charley."

His meaning was perfectly clear. Malcolm was asking what a pedestrian life amounted to, a material plodding through the years—but then there was always Jessica Lovell, and there was nothing plodding about Charles's life. Then he thought of Malcolm's life—as much as he knew of it. It seemed to be spread out on the floor, between the foot locker and the bedding roll.

"Malcolm," he asked, "what will you do when you're through with the Orinoco?"

"Oh, hell," Malcolm said, and he stared at the floor for a moment and then he rubbed the back of his head. "You sound like the *Saturday Evening Post*, Charley. Don't bother me any longer. I'm not conditioned to environment. I'm not societal and I can't take punishment. I'm drunk and I guess I'd better go to bed, but there's one thing I'll say for you. You're a damned good type and you've got a lot of guts."

Charles was shaking hands with him. It was one of those aimless conversations, questions and no answers, but he had always liked Malcolm Bryant and somehow he felt that this might very well be his last talk with him.

He knew when he was outside in the storm again that he had been drinking too much whiskey and that he would have a headache in the morning, and yet it had been worth it. With every step he took on Fanning Street, he seemed to be leaving something further and further behind, some possibility, but something of what he was leaving must have been with him always or he would not have dropped everything years later, he would not have left Nancy and the children and the Stuyvesant Bank and have gone to the war when he was overage—and not the type.

20

No Time for Jubilation

—MR. LAURENCE LOVELL

Later, during long evenings in New York in which he used reading as a means of self-forgetfulness, Charles read a book on the Orinoco which he had borrowed from the public library but there was nothing in its pages resembling what he had hoped to find. Later still, he had seen a part of that country from the window of a C-54 on his way to Cairo, where he had been ordered during the war for no reason he could ever discover. From the height of eight or nine thousand feet he had looked down on the closely packed, tufted tops of trees, silvery gray like the olive, or angry green like a squally ocean, depending on how the clouds and the rainstorms happened to be passing over them. In the midst of this endless, regularly billowing carpet of treetops, he had seen winding stretches of muddy water, tributaries to the Orinoco or the Amazon, no one had told him which.

Malcolm Bryant had asked him, though perhaps he had not been serious, to go away from Clyde up a tropical river. He was young enough to be stirred by this invitation, but he knew the idea was preposterous. At that time in his life, he had no real desire to escape from what lay around him. If one wished to put it obviously, Clyde and E. P. Rush & Company made his Orinoco, and what lay between him and Jessica Lovell was as new and fascinating a country as any on a map. There was no premonition of failure, no sense of doubt. Everything grew consistently better as the days grew longer. There were no Cadillacs in the Orinoco, no Boston theaters, no walks like that one across the pasture, no spring sunsets above the river, and no savage chiefs more difficult to placate with beads and bangles than Mr. Laurence Lovell. There was no need to go to the Orinoco.

All the elements of his life were moving as they should that spring and he did not have the sense to pray that eventual compensation should be light. He knew that luck had entered into it, but also his own perspective and a maturing, instinctive judgment had achieved a result which he knew was above the average. He had wanted something and he had set out as intelligently as he could to get it and he was ending by getting it.

First there had been that raise at E. P. Rush & Company, which was something due entirely to his own efforts and there was no luck about that; then there was his brokerage account, starting with the five thousand dollars he had received from his aunt. Like other members of the team, he had done his trading through E. P. Rush, since it would have been disloyal and deceitful to have placed his business elsewhere. Also, he had had the good sense to speak to Mr. Rush about it personally. Mr. Rush told Charles he would probably lose it all, but if he did it would be a lesson to him. It was not his business what Charles might do with his money, but it was his business when employees used office time worrying about their own affairs and standing around the ticker and looking at the board. Charles was careful never to use the office time. He only watched the quotations during the lunch hour. It was his own judgment that put him into Radio and a few other equities that were being purchased without any regard to earnings but because of future prospects. The future was boundless that spring, in the light of mass hysteria.

Charles did not believe in this future. He was sure that buying power would not continue with inflated credit and he sold out in May, during one lunch hour, just as he had told Jessica he would, in the midst of a rising market. His account with E. P. Rush, less commissions, showed a balance of fifty thousand dollars. He had started on a shoestring, he had pyramided, he had been cognizant of every risk, and he had increased his money tenfold. He had not believed in what he was doing and he had hated every minute of it, but at least he had known when to stop.

He felt almost weak with relief that noon in May. In his way he had beaten the system, as he had told Jessica he would. Ever afterwards when he saw Radio among the stock quotations he always winced and saw himself standing on an unsubstantial pyramid already beginning to topple. Now that the profit was no longer on paper, he wanted it absolutely safe. He did not even like the risk of five per cent—it was ironical to think they used to call it five per cent and safety then. He bought Government 4's, and when they were delivered he rented a box for them in the State Street Trust Company and then he did something he had never done while he was in Rush & Company. Though he had always disliked the way certain members of the team chatted indiscriminately over the telephone, he had called Jessica from his extension during the noon hour and had told her.

He could walk now with Jessica anywhere in Clyde without pretending that they had just happened to meet. When he called on her he would no longer imply that he just happened to call because he had nothing else to do. They would not have to talk furtively about meetings in Boston, nor would they have to think that they were seeing too much of each other in public, considering everything. There was no reason for any of this any longer.

There was no reason, either, why he should have felt grim in his triumph, except that he instinctively never wanted to be too happy when things were going right. He went straight upstairs before supper and put on his blue suit, though it was heavy and though it was a warm May day. When he saw his face in the mirror, as he brushed his hair very carefully with the military brushes that Jessica had given him, he was surprised that his face did not look older after everything he had been through; instead it still looked young and there was the cowlick in his hair which Jessica always spoke about and there were the usual freckles on his nose.

"Charley," his mother said at supper, "has anything gone wrong in Boston?"

"No," he said. "Why do you ask?"

"You look so stern and efficient, dear," his mother said.

His father, at the head of the table, asked Axel for a bottle of Moselle wine that he had just brought home.

"Look at Charley," Dorothea said. "Why are you all dressed up?"

"Are you going to see Jessica tonight, dear?" his mother asked.

"Yes," Charles said, "I've been thinking of it."

Then he noticed that his father was looking at his new blue suit with a sudden, lively interest.

"Would you like the car?" he asked. "You could go to Rowell's and get it. We won't need it tonight."

When he met Jessica that evening, he was Jason back with the Golden Fleece, and at one and the same time, he was the small-town boy who had made good and the embarrassed young man who would have to speak to Her father. He was also the gilded youth of the Jazz Age, in his high-powered car, and Jessica, bareheaded, in her print dress, was a part of the age too, and so was the spring evening.

"Charley," she said, "don't drive so fast," but he knew that she did not really mind it.

They drove down Johnson Street to the main road and then over the causeway to the beach, because she said she would like to see the ocean, and they stopped where the road ended, just between the sand dunes. It was still too early for the small houses along the beach to be occupied so they were all alone, looking at the sea that grew continually darker in the twilight. When they were not speaking, there was no sound except the somnolent pounding of the surf and the bell on the buoy at the mouth of the river, tolling with the rhythm of the waves.

He could not help thinking that it was a queer place to be mixing love with bookkeeping, to be so conscious of the sea and of Jessica in his arms and at the same time to be talking about the Radio Corporation of America. He remembered that he told her that he was tired of hiding in corners with her, and she had said that she had liked it in the corners.

"But then, you know," he said, "everybody knows we're hiding."

"But I like to pretend," she said. "I like to think it's all just our secret. I don't know what it will be like when it isn't."

"It will be better," he told her, "much better."

"We've been so awfully happy the way it was," she said. "It's all going to be 'Is it wise? And how much will everything cost?' We never had to think about any of that before."

"But you don't mind thinking about it, do you?" he asked her. "I hope you don't mind, Jessica."

"Oh, darling, of course I don't really," she said, "it's just—"

"Just what?" he asked.

She was silent for a moment, looking at the dark sea.

"I know the way you feel," he said. "Everything seems to be happening all at once but you mustn't let it worry you, as long as you still love me. You do still love me, don't you?" It was only a rhetorical question.

"Oh, darling," she said, "of course I do. It's only—only that I used to think we couldn't be married for years and years and now it's so queer to have it happen. I don't mean I don't like the idea," and she laughed. "I'm crazy about it, really, darling, but so much else goes with it."

"Jessica." He stopped. He wished he did not sound so portentous. "I suppose I ought to speak to your father. We can't go on like this."

It had not occurred to him until then how necessary this was or how unendurable any further waiting would be.

"Oh, Charley." He heard her draw a sharp, quick breath. "We don't have to tell him just yet."

"We'll have to do it sometime," he said. "We'd better do it now."

"Oh, darling," Jessica said. "Suppose he—" Her voice trailed off into a wretched silence but it was too dark to see her face. "Charley, why are you starting the car?"

"Because I'm going to take you back," he said.

"Charley, you're not going to speak to him tonight?"

"I'm going to get it over with."

"Oh, Charley, I wish you'd let me talk to him first. It's—it's going to hurt him," she said.

He was thinking of himself, of course, and not of her, and for some reason the idea that it might hurt Mr. Lovell came close to making him angry. At any rate, it eliminated all feelings of diffidence.

"I don't know what you think is the matter with me," he told her. "I'm not as bad as all that. You must have known I'd have to see him sometime."

Of course he was really telling her without saying it that he lived on Spruce Street and not Johnson Street and that there had been ample opportunity for her to have faced those facts. It was something he could not say, but though Jessica was crying it was not a quarrel.

"It's not what's the matter with you, dear," she sobbed. "It's what's the matter with me."

"There's nothing the matter with you," he said. "It's going to be all right, Jessica."

It was not a quarrel, and he was stronger than she was once his mind was made up. It was one of those rare moments when he was not impressed by Jessica, and at least she had stopped crying.

"I wish you'd let me talk to him first," she said. "You don't understand him, Charley."

"No, I'll have to do it, Jessica," he said.

"Well, at least I've got to be there with you, and if he says anything don't be cross or I won't be able to bear it."

She did not seem to be beside him in the car. He was planning what he would say to Mr. Lovell and it did not do much good to plan. Experience was seldom present when you needed it, and it was always too late when you had gained experience.

"Back so early?" Miss Lovell called to them from the wallpaper room when they entered the front hall, and Mr. Lovell in the library said the same thing.

"Back so early?"

Mr. Lovell folded his newspaper carefully.

"Why are you closing the door, Jessica? I like the draft. It's a warm evening."

Mr. Lovell was sitting in one of the heavy leather armchairs, leaning backward comfortably, but he had dropped his newspaper when the door closed. Somehow Charles was not able to introduce the subject gracefully. Standing in front of the empty fireplace, he did not see the books or the ship pictures, but only Mr. Lovell's thin and rather handsome face and Mr. Lovell's hands gripping the arms of his chair.

"Mr. Lovell," he said, "I want to marry Jessica."

After all, it could not have been news to Mr. Lovell that he wanted to marry Jessica, yet suddenly Mr. Lovell looked deathly ill and raised a trembling hand to his forehead.

"Jessie," he said, "would you mind getting me a glass of water, please?"

"Oh, Father," Jessica began, and she ran to him across the room.

"It's all right, Jessie," Mr. Lovell said, and he smiled at her. "Just a glass of water."

Charles heard the door close as Jessica left the room and for a second neither he nor Mr. Lovell spoke.

"I'm sorry you feel this way about it, sir," Charles said, "but I thought I ought to tell you."

Mr. Lovell pushed himself forward and spoke in a steadier voice, as though he were rallying from the shock.

"Of course you should tell me, Charles, but someday, perhaps, if you have an only daughter who is everything in the world to you, perhaps you'll know a little of how I feel. I have to apologize, Charles. It's no reflection on you at all." He sighed, but before he could go on Jessica was back with a tumbler of water.

"Thank you, Jessie dear," Mr. Lovell said. "Sit down, Jessie. Sit down, Charles. We'll have to talk this over, won't we?" He took a sip of water and placed the glass carefully on the candlestand beside his chair. "I've just told Charles I'm very glad he told me."

"Father," Jessica said, "are you sure you feel all right? We don't have to talk about it any more."

"I feel splendidly now," Mr. Lovell said. "It had nothing to do with Charles, who did absolutely the right thing." Mr. Lovell smiled wearily. "Now don't interrupt Charles and me, Jessie. If there ever is a time to be frank, I suppose this is it. I hope you won't mind, Charles," and Mr. Lovell smiled again.

"No, sir," Charles said. "Of course not."

"I want to say first," Mr. Lovell began, "that I know what you're going through. I remember when I had to see Jessica's grandfather—even though everyone expected it. Jessica, as long as you're here why don't you get Charles a cigarette?"

"I don't care for one, thanks, sir," Charles said.

"Well," Mr. Lovell said, and his voice reminded Charles of that day years ago at the Historical Society. He was marshaling his thoughts, preparing to make a graceful speech. "I've naturally known for some time, Charles, that you and Jessica were interested in each other, but I never believed it would quite come to this. Naturally, I've always known that Jessica would marry someday and I've always hoped—well, of course I'm prejudiced. This is no reflection on you, Charles. I know how well you've done and I can see your romantic side, through Jessica's eyes, and I can see how Jessica must seem to you. At least you and I have that in common. You and I love Jessie, each in our own way."

He stopped again and took a sip of water, like a speaker on a platform.

"You young fellows, Charles," Mr. Lovell went on, and his voice was mild and playful, "always think we old dodos don't see things from your point of view, but I do know Jessie, perhaps a little better than you do. Now you say you want to marry Jessie. How long have you wanted to marry her?"

"For quite a while," Charles said. "I guess for about a year now."

"And a year is quite a while," Mr. Lovell said gently, "when one is—how old are you now, Charles?"

"Twenty-five, sir," Charles said.

"Well, well," Mr. Lovell said. "You've done very well, and I respect you for it, Charles, but we must both think of Jessie."

"Yes, sir," Charles answered.

"Now don't interrupt us, Jessie," Mr. Lovell said. "To me Jessie is one thing, Charles, and to you undoubtedly quite another. You mustn't blame me for wanting Jessie to have everything she's been used to. She wouldn't be the same in another setting. Now we'll have to think what you can do for Jessie, Charles. I know you're doing well at Rush & Company but how much are you earning there? You don't mind my asking, do you?"

"No, sir," Charles said. "Sixty dollars a week."

"Well, well," Mr. Lovell said. "That's splendid, but you can see, Charles, that a girl like Jessie—"

"Yes," Charles said, "I know."

Mr. Lovell looked at him triumphantly but kindly.

"Now, Charles," he said, "you know that wouldn't be enough for Jessie. It's hardly a time to talk about marrying Jessie, really, is it? Let's leave it the way you began. You want to marry Jessica. Let's leave it there."

"I have fifty thousand dollars besides that," Charles said, "in government bonds."

It sounded strangely primitive, as though he were buying Jessica, and Mr. Lovell suddenly looked blank. There was no longer any kindliness in his glance.

"Well," Mr. Lovell said, "well. Did your father give it to you?"

"No, sir," Charles said.

"Did you make it on the market, Charles?"

"Yes, sir," Charles said.

"I can't say I like that," Mr. Lovell said.

"I don't either," Charles answered, "but I wanted to marry Jessica."

"Money is one thing," Mr. Lovell said, "and stock-market money is another."

"There may be a difference," Charles said, "but as long as you don't lose it, it's money."

"It's not the same," Mr. Lovell said, "as inherited money."

Charles did not feel impatient. It was a pathetic intellectual quibble. "Everybody has to start sometime," Charles said. "I suppose your family did once, Mr. Lovell."

"Father," Jessica said, "it really doesn't make any difference, does it?"

"Jessie"—there was a new edge on Mr. Lovell's voice—"please be quiet."

"Unless you have some other reason, sir . . . ?" Charles began. Mr. Lovell sat quietly without answering.

"Father," Jessica said, "we had to tell you, didn't we?"

"Oh, be quiet, Jessica," Mr. Lovell said. "If I had thought there was any chance of this happening . . . If things have gone this far, I suppose—" Mr. Lovell pushed himself slowly out of his chair. "I can't say that I like this, Charles. I don't like being presented with an accomplished fact."

"Oh, Father," Jessica said, "you sound as if Charley and I—Father, please!"

"I'm sure I don't know how I sound," Mr. Lovell said, "but I expected a rational discussion and instead it's an accomplished fact. Very well, you can be engaged, but I don't want any public announcement until we get to know each other better. And now I'm feeling very tired. Good night, Charles. Good night, Jessie, dear."

"Oh, Father," Jessica said, and she threw her arms around him. "You know you'll get used to it in time."

It was hard to place events in order after all that time. They kept standing out irrationally by themselves, like sentences removed from the context of a carefully written page, but it was only a short time after this conversation that Jessica had shown him all through the Lovell house. It was a Saturday afternoon and Mr. Lovell must have been away playing golf at the Shore Club, as he usually did on Saturdays, and Miss Lovell had been out paying calls on Johnson Street. It was one of those days in Clyde when you wished the furnace were still going but felt it self-indulgent to have a fire in the cellar because it was after the first of May. The house was a little damp and the dampness brought out those smells one always associated with old Clyde houses, the scent of old leather, old carpets and of dust that could never entirely be swept away.

"It's awfully funny," Jessica said. "I don't believe you've ever seen the house. I don't believe you've ever been upstairs."

It struck him as strange, too, knowing Jessica so well, that he had only seen the front hall, with the portraits and the dusky mirror, and the little parlor with the Aubusson carpet which had been made for it in France, and the wallpaper room and the dining room with its highly waxed English table.

"You know all the rest of me," she said, "and the house is a part of me."

They walked up the broad staircase hand in hand to the landing and from there, where the stairs divided, to the upper hall, lighted by its two beautiful arched windows. The tall clock, which he had heard tick and strike the hour but which he had never seen, was standing near the landing and its ticking only emphasized the cool silence. The bedrooms were just as they should have been, each with its four-poster and its canopy, each with its bureau or its highboy. Jessica's room was the smallest, next to Mr. Lovell's large front room. She had slept in it as long as she could remember and her father's feelings were always hurt when she wanted to move the furniture because her mother had arranged the room herself, even down to the china dogs on the mantel above the little fireplace. Its windows, each with a window seat, looked over the formal garden where the tulips were already pushing up through the black earth of the box-bordered bed.

It was an enormous house, much too large for the Lovells now. No one occupied the third floor any longer, but all the rooms were still furnished as they had been when there were more Lovells. Finally there was the storeroom, containing generations of trunks and hatboxes. A narrow flight of unpainted pine stairs, redolent of pitch and dried by hundreds of summers, led upwards from the storeroom to the cupola. The cupola, enclosed by arched windows with old, uneven panes of glass, rose above the slate roof and above the elaborate railing of the widow's walk and looked across the town to the river.

As he stood there holding Jessica's hand, a little out of breath because they had hurried up the stairs, it seemed to him that they had traveled a long way together and that together they had reached a height where nothing could touch them. The leaves of the elms were still that soft, yellowish green and the trees rose plumelike above the roofs and the yards of the other houses. It was a dull day, because of the east wind, and the river had a leaden color and the sea was misty.

"There's your house," she said.

He could see the line of Spruce Street beneath them and he could see a corner of the house through the trees.

"There's the Meaders' yard," he said, and then they were in each other's arms. They were above everything and all alone.

"I like it here," he told her. "You and I are all that matter here."

They did not stay long because it was cold and drafty and they never went there again; yet whenever he thought of that spring and summer when he was engaged to Jessica and ever afterwards when he smelled seasoned pine, he was there in the cupola again, above the new leaves of the elms with Jessica, safe from what Mr. Lovell thought and safe from what other people were thinking and saying. They should have run away and got married, but neither of them could have thought seriously of such a thing. There seemed to be so much time that summer and everything seemed settled, and so it was, until the autumn, and so it should have been and might have been.

Mr. Lovell said that night in the library that it was still a tentative matter and that no one should be told except immediate members of the family. He supposed that Charles should tell his mother, his father, and his sister, but there was no reason to tell the Marchbys yet. He did not want any family jubilation, because there was no immediate reason for it. It was an ordeal for him, because Jessica was his only daughter and all he had in the world. He would face the ordeal, but at least he could expect reasonable consideration. There would be no engagement teas, no rounds of calling, and no other jubilation until matters were more definitely resolved than they were at present. Marriage, in case Charles did not know it, and Jessie too, was a serious matter. When two people were infatuated—he knew it was a graceless word, but one which he really thought described the situation—they could not be said to know each other or the complications of each other's backgrounds. Any engagement was a severe emotional strain and this whole affair's coming so suddenly was more of a strain on him than it was on Charles. He had not asked for it or expected it, but now they must share this period of strain together as best they could. They must bear and forbear and it was no time for jubilation.

Nevertheless, it seemed to Charles that there was an undercurrent of illicit jubilation. When he and Jessica had told Miss Georgianna, after Mr. Lovell had gone to bed that evening, she did not need a glass of water. Instead, she kissed Jessica and then Charles, and she told Charles that he must call her Aunt Georgianna now. She sounded like his own Aunt Jane when she told Jessica that she could have the silver tea set.

"And what did Laurence say when you told him?" she asked.

"It was dreadful," Jessica said, "but he was awfully sweet. Wasn't he sweet about it, Charley?"

But Miss Lovell said of course he was not sweet about it. That would be more than could be expected of him.

"You'll have to learn to put up with him, Charley. You'll get used to him in time. And now you'd better run along home. Jessica must be tired."

Jessica did look pale and tired, but she told him in the hall that she was very happy. She never knew that she had loved him so much. It was dreadful knowing what the two people she loved most in the world must have been going through.

"I feel just as though I had been cut in two, darling," she said, "and now I'm growing together again. Everything will be better now. You wait and see. Father didn't hurt your feelings, did he?"

There was a strange egocentric quality about being in love that created an acute perception but clouded any rational judgment. He was profoundly touched that she had been able to see that he might have been hurt. She was the gentlest, kindest, most understanding person in the world.

"He can't hurt me," he said, "as long as you understand."

"Oh, darling," she whispered, "I do understand. More than you think, so much more than you think."

It was past the family's bedtime when he left the car at Rowell's Garage, but even so they were all still sitting in the parlor. He knew at once from the quick, alert way they all turned toward him that they had been waiting for him.

"Charley dear," his mother said, "aren't you going to tell us what happened?"

"Charley," his father asked, before there was any time to answer, "did you see Laurence Lovell?"

"Yes," Charles said, "I saw him."

"Charley." His mother looked hurt. "Aren't you going to tell us what he said?"

All at once he was very glad they were all there waiting, because they were on his side and they would be no matter what.

"All right," he said. "I'm engaged to Jessica, but I'm only to tell you. It isn't to be announced yet."

It sounded as dry as dust when he told it but he never forgot how happy they looked. Dorothea hugged him, a very unusual thing for her to do, and his mother began to cry, but it was only, she said, because she was so happy, and his father shook hands with him.

"Oh, dear me," he said, "I wish I'd seen Laurence Lovell."

"Charley"—Dorothea hugged him again—"tell us what he said."

Suddenly he was very glad to tell them everything.

"I don't think he liked it much," he began. "First he asked Jessica to get him a glass of water."

"Oh, dear me," John Gray said. "A glass of water."

"I don't think he thought it was serious at first," Charles went on, "until we began talking about money."

He had never told them about his brokerage account and they were asking him why he had been so secretive and he found it hard to explain. He could only say there were some things he did not like to talk about, but there it was. He and Jessica were engaged, although it was not to be announced.

"And I don't want anyone to do anything about it," he said. "I don't want anyone to tell anybody."

"I can't quite fit this all together," his father said, "but it seems to me that Laurence Lovell was mildly insulting, Charley."

"I told you he didn't like it," Charles answered.

"And that's one part of it that I don't like," John Gray said. "I think I'd better go and see Laurence Lovell myself tomorrow."

It was the last thing that Charles had expected or wanted and it was utterly uncalled-for but he was not able to dissuade him.

"Can't you leave him alone?" Charles asked. "What did he ever do to you, Father?"

John Gray smiled and stared straight at the wall in front of him.

"That's just it," he said. "He never did do anything."

"Now, Charley," his mother said, "of course your father must have a talk with Mr. Lovell if you and Jessica are engaged and I think it would be very nice if we asked Mr. Lovell and Miss Georgianna here to dinner. Don't you, John?"

"No, Esther," John Gray said. "I don't think it's necessary to ask Laurence Lovell to dinner."

His father was playing poker at the Pine Trees when Charles got back from Boston the next evening. It was the Pine Tree get-together night, an annual occasion on which they all met at the firehouse and ate steamed clams and hamburgers, so Charles did not see his father until later. His mother and Dorothea both told him that his father had been to see Mr. Lovell that morning but when he came home he had been very busy telephoning Boston—something to do with some sort of auxiliary schooner—and that he had not mentioned Mr. Lovell and they had not wanted to ask him.

Mr. Lovell, however, had spoken of it himself when Charles had gone to see Jessica after supper.

"Your father dropped in this morning, Charles," Mr. Lovell said.

"I told him I wished he wouldn't," Charles said.

"There was no reason at all, under the circumstances, why he shouldn't have," Mr. Lovell said. "We had a very pleasant talk—largely about financial matters."

"I'm glad it was pleasant, sir," Charles said, but he could not very well ask Mr. Lovell what financial matters had been discussed.

His father never told him either. He was in his room upstairs later, reading *The Anatomy of Melancholy*, and he called to Charles to say good night.

"Oh, there you are, Charley," he said. "I had a little talk with Laurence Lovell this morning."

"What did you talk about?" Charles asked.

"Oh, this and that—financial matters. Do you know what I think, Charley?"

"What?" Charles asked.

"I think I'll get out of this market. I haven't been sleeping well lately. I had to go to Gerald's last week to get some pills. The market's getting on my nerves." He closed *The Anatomy of Melancholy* and placed it on the table. "I don't see why I shouldn't live on my money like the Lovells, for a while, and let someone else worry."

"You're not serious, are you?" Charles said.

"I don't see why you never believe me, Charley," John Gray answered. "I've never liked doing the same thing all the time. There's too much else going on. Dorothea's getting married in June and you're engaged. I've been using my mind too much. Now what I really need is a little sea air. Look at this, Charley."

He picked up a photograph from the table. It was a picture of a schooner.

"It's the *Zaza*. It's a damned funny name, isn't it? People who own yachts and horses never have much imagination. The *Zaza*. Sixty-five feet overall. Three in the crew. You'll like the captain, Charley. He says garlic cures indigestion, but he bunks forward with the crew. She'll be in the river tomorrow."

"You mean to say you've bought that thing?" Charles asked.

"I wish you wouldn't jump at conclusions," his father said. "I know my place, Charley. That's what I told Laurence Lovell this morning. I've just chartered her for a month. I need some relaxation."

"I wish you'd have some sense of proportion," Charles said.

It must have been a part of Clyde folklore still—his father and that schooner-yacht called the *Zaza*—but at least he only had her for a month.

"Father," he asked, "did you do this because you were going to talk with Mr. Lovell?"

His father did not answer him specifically.

"That's a very sensible question, Charley. I won't say yes and I won't say no. I admit it has its juvenile side." His father was enjoying every minute of it. He was having a wonderful time. "I'm sorry if it embarrasses you, Charley," he said, "but aren't you glad I'm getting out of the market?"

"If you're out, you won't stay out," Charles said. "You can't."

"I don't know why you're so sure of everything," his father answered. "I might stay out."

He was still holding the photograph of that schooner-yacht, a ridiculous plaything with its full white billowing sails. Everything had gone too far, Charles was thinking. Nothing could end in defiance of the laws of gravity.

"I wish I could believe it," he said.

He was thinking of what Sam had said long ago, that it was all a lot of guff. His father had assumed his old look of composed displeasure.

"That's not very complimentary, Charley," he said.

"Why don't you set up a trust fund for Mother?" Charles asked. "Then I'd be very complimentary, Father."

He had asked the same question again and again lately and his father's reaction was always exactly the same. "How many times have I told you," he asked, "that I agree with you? Of course, I'm going to do it, but Hugh Blashfield isn't going to handle it and there isn't any hurry. Don't be so worried, Charley."

Charles never liked to think about that schooner in the river and he only went aboard her once or twice. He told Jessica that he was ashamed of it and that he wished his father would keep her at Marblehead and not in the river. He always had a feeling that he ought to apologize to everyone and explain, but he could not very well explain that the boat was symbolic and a gesture, and after all no one seemed to be as upset about this as he was. Jessica was only amused and said it was just like his father and that it was nice he had something to play with. Dorothea said that of course it was silly and ridiculously extravagant, but then he was only going to have it for a month and it probably did not cost much more than that winter cruise to the Caribbean. His mother was more definite, because she always accepted everything that John Gray did. If he had earned the money—that was the way she put it because she always thought of money as being earned—there was no reason why he should not use it. There were all sorts of other, bigger yachts everywhere and it was not as though he were not sharing it with everybody. He was taking everyone he knew for a sail and there was no reason why he should not have some pleasure himself for once. He had worked so hard for years at the mill and no one had appreciated him and now that he was a success, as she always knew he would be, it was not fair to be so critical. He deserved to have a good time and she wished that Charles could see what a very remarkable man he was. She wished that Charles understood him as well as Dorothea.

"Charley," she said, "you're getting as fussy as Jackie Mason."

21

A Formal Announcement Will Be Necessary

A haze of unreality surrounded that summer and this may have been the reason why Charles found himself seeking Jackie Mason's company again. Jackie was still what he had always been—a constant quantity. When Charles told Jackie Mason that he hated to think what everyone was saying about his father's spending and extravagance, Jackie was reassuring.

"Of course," he said, "there's a certain amount of talk, but I wouldn't take it too seriously. You see, your father has a certain position, Charley, and if you have a position no one talks so much." Jackie frowned and patted his yellow hair carefully. He was always worried for fear his hair would not stay in place. "Now if Mr. Sullivan or Mr. Levine put a hundred-dollar bill in the contribution box, it would be different. It would be different with my father, or me too, Charley, because, well, my grandfather was a druggist and your grandfather was a judge. That gives position, and if you have it you can be more eccentric, Charley. It's the same way with you. You have more position than I have. Let's admit it."

Jackie Mason was looking at him wistfully, as though their positions were far apart already and as though he felt privileged that they were still friends. Charles wanted to tell Jackie to stop, that they were just the same as they ever were, that they had lived next door to each other and had known each other all their lives, but before he could speak Jackie was going on.

"You can really go anywhere now," Jackie said. "It must be nice to be so secure."

"But I'm not secure," Charles told him. "Don't you see, with Father nothing is secure?" But Jackie shook his head.

"That isn't so, Charley," he answered. "Really it isn't. I used to think you were hurting your position when you left Wright-Sherwin, but you knew what you were doing."

"I wonder if anyone really knows why he does anything," Charles said.

"Now, Charley," Jackie said, "we know each other well enough to be frank. I know you don't tell me everything, you don't have to." It was true. You never had to tell much in Clyde. "You can get anywhere you want." Jackie Mason sighed. "You'll be a director of the bank someday, and there's no reason why you shouldn't be a trustee of the public library." Jackie was always loyal. He was loyal to the end. "It doesn't even make any difference if Dorothea marries Elbridge Sterne, and furthermore, don't you see,

Charley—" and Jackie stopped as though he were going to say something indiscreet.

"Go ahead," Charles told him. "What don't I see?"

"Don't you see that Mr. Lovell can't do anything about it, in spite of his position?"

Jackie had lowered his voice when he mentioned Mr. Lovell's name. They had been standing in the dusk talking in the Masons' yard as they had ever since they were children, and Jackie looked half-apprehensively toward Johnson Street. It was as close as he ever came to mentioning what everybody knew, that Mr. Lovell could do nothing but accept what lay between Charles and Jessica. Mr. Lovell could do nothing about the accomplished fact. Mr. Lovell himself was a part of Clyde.

If there were anything in the theory that the past remained intact, he and Jessica Lovell must still have been somewhere, with the other ghosts of Clyde. Perhaps all of that summer might have returned to him again and again if he had stayed in Clyde. If he had never seen Jessica Lovell again except in the distance, he would have seen the shadows of Jessica and himself around every corner and on every country road. If he had walked down Dock Street, he and Jessica might still have been standing in front of the window of Stowell's furniture store, talking of living room curtains. She had wanted green monk's cloth curtains. Down at the foot of Gow Street, they might still have been gazing at the For Sale sign on the Pritchard house, for old Miss Pritchard had died that summer. It was in bad condition, but they could have fixed it up if they had bought it. If he had gone to the beach in the moonlight, he and Jessica would have been there with their picnic supper. Their two shadows would have been everywhere, because they had been everywhere in Clyde together. By God, it was a wonderful town.

They would have been talking still about the things they were going to do. There would have been the same surprise that they liked so many of the same things. They had been so very, very practical. Jessica was going to learn how to keep a budget and he was going to learn how to work in the garden. They were going to read together in the evening. They both loved to read aloud. At last it was possible to talk of all those practical things. She could buy him neckties now and she could go with him to Boston in the morning, if she wanted, and of course they were going to have a car, a Ford or a Dodge, perhaps—but they only looked at cars in Boston, because their engagement was not announced.

He could buy her a gold bracelet now and a moonstone pin, but not a ring because their engagement was not announced. They could not very well look at rings in Marston's Jewelry Shop but they could look at them in Boston and if anyone who knew them should happen to see them it would not matter much because they were engaged, although it was not announced. They could even go to Jessica's aunt's summer place at Cohasset for the night, because the family knew they were engaged. There were all sorts of things that they could do and say that summer. It was strange how few of them he could remember. It must have been because he had pushed them so relentlessly aside. That summer was now covered up by so much that was more actual—that summer and all of Clyde.

The summer and those shadows of himself and Jessica, and Clyde too, were like the Atlantis upon which his father had discoursed that night when Jessica came to supper. Elbridge Sterne had not known about Atlantis, but that was natural. Elbridge was an excellent metallurgical chemist, so excellent that a few months later a larger company from Kansas City had sent for him. He was too good for Wright-Sherwin and anyway it was a chance to get back home. Elbridge did not care about lands beneath the sea or sunken shoals that jutted above the water when the tide was very low.

Dorothea and Elbridge Sterne were married in the Unitarian Church that June. May Mason, who had married Jeffrey Meader and who already had two children, was matron of honor, though she said she was too old—still, she was not as old as Dorothea—and Elbridge had asked Charles to be best man, instead of his brother, who came on with Elbridge's mother from Kansas City. Dorothea had wanted Jessica to be a bridesmaid but they had not asked her in the end—because it had not been announced.

Nevertheless, the Lovells did come to the church, probably because Mr. Lovell had thought it would be more conspicuous had he stayed away. All that made the Lovells conspicuous was that they were placed up in front, just behind the Marchbys, and everybody saw them during their long walk up the aisle. If Charles had known of this arrangement he might have been able to stop it, but he only knew when he walked out with Elbridge from the minister's room under the pulpit stairs.

It was a very large wedding and John Gray wanted everyone to be in silk hats and cutaways and he would have been very glad to have paid for the clothes himself. He was hurt when Dorothea did not want this. He only had one daughter, he said, and he wanted it to be a good wedding, but instead the ushers wore blue coats and white flannels and the bridesmaids were dressed in pastel organdy.

"The bride," the *Clyde Herald* said, "wearing her mother's wedding veil, a family heirloom, was exquisitely gowned in a white satin dress from Bendel's, the well-known New York dress house . . . the flower girls were the Misses Edwina and Malvina Meader, daughters of Mrs. Meader, the matron of honor . . . the gifts to the bridesmaids were exquisite gold compact boxes and to each of the ushers was given a gold cigarette case . . . the music for the reception was furnished by the fife-and-drum corps of the Pine Tree Veteran Fire Company . . . refreshments and a buffet luncheon for the numerous guests at the Gray residence on Spruce Street were supplied by the J. E. Crowell Catering Company from Boston . . . the bride and groom left for the wedding trip in a Duesenberg convertible automobile—a gift of the bride's father."

His father had not succeeded with the cutaways but at least he had insisted on buying the compacts and cigarette cases and he had persuaded Dorothea to accept a foreign car instead of a check because he had always wanted a Duesenberg himself.

His future in the Duesenberg convertible disturbed Elbridge more than the crowd in the church as he waited with Charles beneath the pulpit stairs. Charles had always thought of Elbridge as being literal and phlegmatic, but instead he was perspiring freely.

"I don't know why we have to drive that thing," he said, "after all the rest of this."

It gave Charles a fraternal feeling when Elbridge spoke about "that thing." They were both creatures of circumstance, being moved without their own volition, there beneath the pulpit stairs. "Charley, it doesn't tie in with anything else."

"That's right," Charles said. "It doesn't really."

"Do you remember"—Elbridge mopped his forehead—"when I used to come to Spruce Street and Dorothea and I dried the dishes after supper?" Elbridge mopped his forehead again.

"I know, Elbridge," Charles said. "I know."

"We're like a lot of kids playing," Elbridge said, and he put his hand on Charles's arm. "It doesn't make sense." Charles often wondered what they would have done if Elbridge had not married Dorothea.

The reception was so large that there were tables in both their own and the Masons' yards. The fife-and-drum corps made too much noise and all the people he had known all his life seemed like actors in a play, crowded simultaneously onto the stage and half forgetting their parts. The Meaders, the Masons, the technicians from Wright-Sherwin, Mr. and Mrs. Howell, the Thomases, the Stanleys, the Lovells, the Sullivans, the Levines and the Walterses were there and so was everyone else. John Gray had insisted on inviting everyone and everyone had come, and no doubt they must still be asking each other if they remembered Johnny Gray before the crash and that wedding of Dorothea's; and Charley Gray and Jessica Lovell standing on the lawn and city waiters pouring champagne right where everyone could see from Spruce Street. When he had it he could spend it. It made Clyde look like a seafaring town again. That was quite a party, they must still be saying, quite a party, and did they remember the speech that Johnny Gray gave? It was too bad, they must be saying, too bad about the Grays, too bad about Charley and Jessica, but then he was a banker now, holding an important position in New York. It was too bad, they must still be saying, that the Grays had moved away. Easy come and easy go. Charley Gray was a nice boy, and Esther Gray was a Marchby and the Marchbys were good people. It was too bad that the Grays were gone.

Of course, Charles had the Lovells on his mind and it would have looked peculiar if he had not seen that Miss Lovell was comfortable and that Mr. Lovell had ginger ale when he refused champagne, but he had to be at the bride's table, too, and he could not be in two places at once and it annoyed him when Jackie Mason said, "Charley, I think you ought to be seen with the Lovells." He was going to be seen with the Lovells, but they could not have been at the bride's table. The fife-and-drum corps was playing "Put on Your Old Gray Bonnet" because they were running out of tunes. Miss Lovell was in rust-colored silk, with a parasol. Jessica was in green organdy. She always loved green, and she was wearing his moonstone pin.

"Well, Charles," Mr. Lovell said, "this is quite a day for all of you, isn't it, and quite a day for Clyde. This is really a most original wedding party."

It was unnecessary for him to have been quite so amused and tolerant—it was a time to be loyal to the family.

"I hope you're enjoying it, sir," Charles said.

"Of course, I'm enjoying it." Mr. Lovell smiled. "Especially the fife-and-drum corps."

"You know how father is about the Pine Trees," Charles said.

"Yes, indeed, I know," Mr. Lovell answered.

A minute later Charles was standing alone with Jessica and they were each holding a glass of champagne. At least it seemed to him that they were alone, in spite of the crowd on the lawn.

"You're not angry with Father, are you?" she was asking. "He's never nice in crowds."

"Angry?" and he laughed at her. "I'm glad you wore the pin."

"It's a lovely party. Dorothea looks so sweet and your mother is so darling. I love your father. He's so happy. He's so young."

"Look at poor Elbridge," Charles said. "I wish it weren't so noisy."

"He's wanted to marry her for a long time, hasn't he?"

"It took them a long while to make up their minds," Charles said.

Jessica smiled at him over the rim of her glass.

"I'm awfully glad we've made up ours. Where's Father?"

"Over there, talking to Mrs. Thomas."

"He always tries to talk to everybody. He's really awfully sweet. Charley, I really think he's getting used to it."

"To you and me?"

"I keep saying 'It,' don't I? You and me, everything."

The fife-and-drum corps had started again. The corps was not used to champagne and the drums were off beat.

"Charley," she asked, "does all this make you think of something?"

"What?" he asked.

"Why, the firemen's muster. . . . Charley, what'll we do tonight? Let's go somewhere and be alone."

It was wonderful to think that such a thing was possible.

The reception was growing more and more like a firemen's muster. The Pine Trees and the hand tub, with its brasswork shining in the sun, had suddenly appeared on Spruce Street. It was a surprise thought up by the Pine Trees and the Pine Trees were going to follow the bride and groom when they went away. Earl Wilkins and some of the boys had thought it up all of a sudden, perhaps because John Gray had sent six cases of champagne down to the firehouse. He would never forget Elbridge Sterne's stricken look. It was something that could only have happened in Clyde.

Later on other bright June days when the weather was cool, Charles would think of himself and Jessica standing there in the crowded Spruce Street yard, alone and not alone, and he could always recall those obvious words they both had said. Somehow everything they meant to each other, their beginning and their ending, was explained in that brief conversation. It was one of the glittering fragments of the summer and it was indestructible. The truth, of course, was that she had never grown used to it any more than Mr. Lovell. There was no reason why she should have, because she could not love them both at once, but she did not know this then and neither did he.

It was strange in the light of the present to recall that a period existed in his life's span when the only clouds on the horizon were the roseate prophecies of an even more roseate future. You could call it a fool's paradise or a debauch or all the other hard words the economic experts and the planners called that summer later, but Charles was never sure that most of them at the time had not been fooled by it even though all the sinister symptoms which everyone recognized later were already apparent. The low-pressure areas and the storms were already assembling behind the pellucid sky. There were inequities and there were greed and social blindness. It was a hectic, materialistic, egocentric world, along the lines of boom and bust, but it sometimes seemed to him, though he seldom said it, that no prophet had succeeded in making a securer society—not Mr. Roosevelt or his Brain Trust, or Hitler or Mussolini, or Hirohito in Japan, or Stalin, or even Mr. Attlee. This was a reactionary thought but his profession was investment which in the purest sense was only an endeavor to cut the cloth according to the situations which radicals and liberals created.

There were no wars or rumors of war that summer. Instead there was a sense of peace and almost of good will. There were no threatening, saber-rattling ogres and few confusions of thought. It was ironical to remember that the cost of government and general taxation were considered too high, and of course there were the gang wars and prohibition, but it was quite a world that summer. There was going to be enough for everyone, a standard of living that would grow always higher, a general advance in science and culture. The country was only dimly becoming aware of its resources and potentialities. Business and enlightened competition would take care of any contingency. It was a great place, the United States, and a great world, that summer.

You could not help but catch some of that contagion. There was freedom from want and freedom from fear for a little while that summer. He and Jessica were going to get married and live happily ever after, and perhaps even Mr. Lovell began to believe this.

It honestly did seem to Charles that Mr. Lovell was really trying to get used to him, but Jessica and Miss Georgianna were trying so hard to get them used to each other that they may have tried too hard. Miss Georgianna was always asking Laurence if he would mind entertaining Charles for a few minutes while she and Jessica went upstairs to look for something; and Jessica, if she and Charles were going out somewhere, was always saying that it would take her a few minutes to get ready but that Father would love to see him.

"Darling," Jessica said once, "what were you and Father talking about when I was upstairs?"

They had just been talking, he told her, and Mr. Lovell had said it was too bad—it was a great pity—that he had not gone to Harvard.

"He didn't mean it the way you think," Jessica said. "You mustn't be hurt about it."

"Why should it hurt me?" Charles asked. "It's a common point of view in certain groups. Mr. Rush said the same thing to me yesterday."

"What did you say to Father when he said it?"

"There wasn't much to say," Charles answered. "I just said that there are a lot of schools besides Harvard."

"You didn't call it a school, did you?"

"I don't remember," Charles said. "I think I called it a school."

"Darling"—she sounded bright and determined—"Father wouldn't have said that if he weren't interested in you. He really is. He's beginning to quote some of the things you say."

"I suppose he is," Charles said, "and I'm interested in him. I guess we both have to be."

"What did you talk about after that?" Jessica asked.

"About painting the house," Charles told her. "He had some estimates."

"Why, darling," Jessica said, "why didn't you tell me that first? If he told you how much it's going to cost it means you're almost in the family." She shook her head and pushed her hair back from her forehead. "It's awfully funny . . ."

"What's so funny?" Charles asked.

"If it weren't for me," Jessica said, "if it weren't for Clyde, why you're just the person he would like. He's always talking about people who make their own way, and he'd be doing nice things for you and giving you advice and he'd be just the way he was with Malcolm Bryant and you'd be having a good time together."

"I wish you wouldn't worry about us," Charles said. "We're getting along all right. I understand the way he feels. Honestly, I don't blame him. He just feels disappointed."

"Darling," Jessica said, "how many times must I tell you that he's getting over it. Every day, every minute, he's getting over it. His point of view hasn't got anything to do with you. You're just a general subject. Charley, he's trying so hard and you've got to try. I can't bear it, I simply can't, if you don't like each other."

It was that pressure. He sometimes found himself being almost sympathetic with Mr. Lovell, but he knew they would not have liked each other even had they met in a casual way. Both of them had tried yet neither of them knew the art of placation. Neither of them was the agreeable person, bearing gifts and little favors, and both of them were proud. Yet there always was that pressure. They were always circling about each other, seeking for some common ground, and the only common ground was Clyde, not the town of the present but the town of the past, and even in that past the Lovells had been shipowners and the Grays had been ships' captains—the Lovells had made money out of shipping while the Grays had only worried along. Yet both of them had tried.

The time had come when Mr. Lovell had to face the inevitable fact that there could not be an indefinite *status quo*. It must have been in late August, because Charles could remember the singing of the crickets. He was sitting with Jessica in the summerhouse in the garden, because Jessica had said that Mr. Lovell had recently asked her why they were always leaving the house to go somewhere when they could have the house and the garden all to themselves. It had been sweet of him. He had asked Jessica why Charles did not feel more at home. It did not look well, he said, always going somewhere else.

They often loved to sit without talking, and they were not talking when Mr. Lovell called to them from the house.

"Oh, Jessica, are you and Charles out there?"

"Yes, Father," Jessica answered. "Don't you want to come out with us?"

"No, Jessie," Mr. Lovell said, "but I wonder whether you and Charles would mind coming in. I'd like to speak to you both for a minute."

Mr. Lovell led the way to the library, which meant that he had something serious to say. Though Charles was gradually beginning to discover that Mr. Lovell had never read and probably never would read many of the old leather-bound English editions on the shelves, Mr. Lovell seemed to draw from the physical presence of Fielding, Sterne and George Eliot, Maria Edgeworth, the British poets and all the rest of them, a vicarious and genuinely deceptive erudition. Perhaps they all gave him an assurance which he may have lacked in other places. Perhaps they afforded him the background for being the person he wanted to be but never could be—the man of cultivated taste and tradition, who, through fortunate circumstances, had ample leisure in which to gratify those tastes. He did not possess, Charles was beginning to learn, the energy, the persistence, or the curiosity ever to become what he thought he was, but then few people like him ever did, outside of the novels of Jane Austen, and besides Charles admitted that he was overcritical of Mr. Lovell. As he stood with the books behind him Charles had an idea that Mr. Lovell must have been rehearsing what he was going to say while they were sitting in the summerhouse.

"Jessie, dear, I wish you'd sit down, and you too, Charles," Mr. Lovell said. "You're so used to my habits, aren't you, Jessie, that you won't mind my standing up? Jessie dear, the time has come—I did hope it wouldn't come so soon—to talk seriously about you and Charles."

"Oh, Father," Jessica said, "has anyone said anything?"

Mr. Lovell seemed surprised that Jessica should have guessed. He nodded and cleared his throat again and raised his voice.

"Yesterday afternoon I happened to run into Francis Stanley on Dock Street when I was on my way to the library meeting and he asked me, out of a clear sky"—Mr. Lovell lowered his voice—"if I were to be congratulated. Of course, I've always known Francis Stanley—I've always known the Stanleys were not real friends of ours, in spite of the amenities—but there you are."

"But Father," Jessica said, and she laughed feebly, "I don't see anything so bad in that. It's just the way Mr. Stanley always says everything."

"I suppose it is," Mr. Lovell said. "I know Francis Stanley very well, Jessica, and I've never been impressed by him or the Stanley money. He's a good businessman, but there are other things besides business, Charles. Now don't" —Mr. Lovell raised his hand "—don't interrupt me, Jessie. Let me make my point. It does show where we have drifted. If Francis Stanley felt himself free, and he did feel himself free, to ask me such a question even jokingly, it shows what other people must be saying. I don't mind about myself, Jessie, but I can't have your name becoming a byword."

Mr. Lovell paused and seemed to be looking back over what he had said. "Now this is every bit as embarrassing and as difficult for me as it is for you, more so because this involves my daughter, my only daughter. I can see by your expression, Charles, that you think I'm overemphasizing this, but perhaps your friends and family have a different view. I'm sure I don't know."

As always he was facing the situation honestly and fairly.

"In the first place, Charles—and I must address this to you rather than to Jessica, because I have never thought that any of this, well, this imbroglio, was ever primarily your fault, Jessie dear. It is the man who takes the initiative—well, in the first place, I feel in justice to myself—and I do think I have to be considered—that I should say frankly and without malice that none of this is my fault, any more than it was yours, Jessie dear. If I had been consulted in time, we would not have this problem. Instead, I had to condone it, because it was an accomplished fact. I had hoped if you were thrown together you both might have seen some of the things that are so painfully obvious to me . . . but no. This is where we've drifted." Mr. Lovell's face had reddened. He pulled a fresh white handkerchief from his breast pocket and blew his nose.

"Father dear," Jessica said, and her voice broke a little, "I've told you and I've told you you won't lose me. Charles doesn't want to take me away from you. Don't be so unhappy, dear. It makes us all so miserable, just when we all ought to be so happy. Don't you see?"

"I know, Jessie darling," Mr. Lovell said softly, "and I'm sorry if I've said too much. I'm trying to face the situation and it can't go on the way it is much longer." Mr. Lovell blew his nose again. "There's only one thing to do. Jessie, if you feel by the middle of, well, November as you feel now, I'm afraid a formal announcement will be necessary, a tea or something. This will have to be clarified somehow."

Mr. Lovell had a stricken expression. He folded his handkerchief and put it carefully back in his pocket.

"Father dear," Jessica said, "you're awfully sweet," and she threw her arms around him. It made Charles feel like an intruder when Mr. Lovell kissed Jessica's forehead gravely and softly.

"I'm glad if you're happy, dear," Mr. Lovell said, "and, Charles, I'm glad we've had this talk. Shall you and I shake hands?" It was hard to be elated in the face of Mr. Lovell's deep sorrow but he honestly tried to put himself in Mr. Lovell's position when he shook hands.

"And now, Jessie," Mr. Lovell said, "why don't you take Charles out to the garden again? I'd like to be alone, just for a little while."

Jessica closed the door softly and tenderly behind her, leaving Mr. Lovell standing on the hearthrug, resigned, head bent, alone with no company but his shattered dreams. If it seemed to Charles overtheatrical, it was not his place to say so. Instead he owed it to Jessica to show a decent, measured sympathy.

"Darling," Jessica whispered, "it's so hard for him. I wish he didn't love me so much," and then she began to cry.

"Don't, Jessica," he said, and he put his arm around her and gave her his handkerchief.

"I wish everything wouldn't hurt him so," she sobbed. "I wish he had ten children and every one of them a girl . . . Charley, he wasn't nice to you at all."

"He can't help it," Charles said. "I don't mind as long as you love me, Jessica."

"Darling, if I didn't I couldn't stand it," she said. "Do you still love me?"

"Of course I do," he said.

"In spite of everything?"

"All the more."

"That's why it's so terrible," she said.

"I don't see why you say it's terrible," he told her.

"I don't know why I did either. I didn't mean it," she said. "And, Charley, it won't be so long till November, will it?"

It would not be long. The goldenrod was out and they could hear the crickets and soon it would be time for the asters, the small white ones and the large purple ones. There was nothing but security, now that she had stopped crying. If their engagement was announced in the middle of November it would not be a long engagement. That was what Jessica was saying. There would be no reason for it. As soon as their engagement was announced they could buy the Pritchard house. They could start doing everything they were talking about. They could really start doing it now—almost.

22

That Gale I Well Remember . . .

—OLIVER WENDELL HOLMES

During all of his later business experience, many otherwise reasonable people kept resurrecting the details of the crash of 1929. They discussed it, apparently, for the same reason that old ladies enjoyed describing surgical operations and sessions with their dentists. There was a snob value in boasting of old pain. Instead of wishing to forget, they kept struggling to remember. The older men would talk about Black Friday in the nineties and the more technical panic of 1907 as though all these debacles were just alike and sanctimonious members of the Securities and Exchange Commission who had had nothing to do with that market would discuss the immoralities of the moneychangers in the temple and cast sharp aspersions on entrenched greed. There were even people, who should have known better, who seemed to be imbued with the fixed idea that the crash of 1929 caused the depression. They could no longer see it as a symptom or as an extreme example of mass hysteria. Only unattractively strong individuals should have been allowed to dabble in that market.

Most people never seemed to see what Charles saw in the crash—a sordidly ugly exhibition of the basest of human fears. They had forgotten the desperation that made cowards and thieves out of previously respectable people, and the fear evolved from greed which had no decency or dignity. Instead, they always harked back to the spectacular—the confusion, the lights in downtown New York burning night after night while clerks were struggling to balance the brokerage accounts; and sooner or later they always asked Charles where he had been working then and whether he too had been long on the market on that particular day in October. He had learned long ago to answer accurately, with only part of the truth. He always said that he had been in Boston with E. P. Rush & Company and nothing much had happened to him. He had made some money out of the market the year before and had put it into government bonds. His mother was living on the income derived from her late husband's estate. His mother was living next door to his sister Dorothea in Kansas City. His sister had married a man, a metallurgical chemist, who had a very good job in Kansas City.

He never told the whole truth to anyone, except to Nancy and to Arthur Slade, and Arthur Slade may have told some of it to Tony Burton at the Stuyvesant Bank but Charles was never sure. Naturally his mother and Dorothea and Elbridge Sterne knew part of the truth, and Jessica Lovell knew some of it. There were some things which were better not told, and there was no use digging up what was so completely finished. His own illusions and everything he had planned had crashed in that common crash, but then millions of lives and plans had been crashing ever since. It did no good to imagine what he might have done to have prevented it. Actually he could have done nothing. Everything was what Mr. Lovell would have called an accomplished fact before Charles had been permitted to face it. He was always glad he did not have to blame himself, at least not very much.

When the drop occurred in September, that minor break which nearly everyone considered a normal readjustment considering the market's phenomenally unbroken rise, he had seen it for what it was—the first rumblings of a landslide, an ominous shift of stress and strain that would never strike a balance until the whole structure broke. He knew this was the beginning of a greater break even before Mr. Rush, after a partners' meeting, called him in to help compose a letter advising customers of Rush & Company to sell their holdings of common stocks. While he was waiting for the letter to be typed, Charles wandered over to the row of leather armchairs before the tickers and the board. Although Rush & Company was essentially an investment and not a brokerage office a large group was there, as there had been all that summer. He was just looking at the last quotation for Telephone when he heard his father call him and saw his father standing near the tickers with his hands in his pockets and with his felt hat pushed back from his forehead.

He was surprised to see his father because John Gray had never done his trading at Rush & Company. He had always said he liked a bigger office and a bigger board and besides Moulton Rush was always disapproving.

"I've been feeling a little lonely, Charley," his father said. "I thought I would drop into the cloisters here. There's an atmosphere bordering on hysteria down the street. I'm seeking conservatism. There doesn't seem to be a rally yet, does there?"

"No, not yet," Charles said. "I thought you were staying at home on the side lines."

"I thought I was until I telephoned," his father answered, "and then I got Will Stevens to drive me in, just to see the show. Is the ticker much behind?"

"I don't know," Charles said. "I've only been here for a minute." He was not a customers' man and he had given up all interest in the mechanics of the market.

"Well, well." John Gray took his hands out of his pockets. "I think I'll see whether Moulton's busy. Willie can drive us back home if you'll be at Post Office Square around five o'clock."

"Father," Charles began.

"Don't say it," his father said. "Don't say it. We'll talk about it driving home." He walked away between the rows of chairs toward the ground-glass doors of the partners' offices.

Mr. Rush's door was open, as it usually was in the late afternoon, so Charles did not knock when he brought in the draft of the form letter half an hour later. Mr. Rush was using the bottom drawer of his roll-top desk as a footrest and he sat tilted back in his swivel chair. John Gray was still there with him.

"All right, Johnny," Mr. Rush was saying. "I only know what I think. If you're out, stay out. Go home and read Boswell."

"And three days from now it will be up again," his father said. "Do you want to bet me, Moulton?"—and then Charles gave Mr. Rush the draft of the letter.

He never told anyone but Nancy what happened that afternoon and he only told her about it at the time of the bank closing, in 1933. She awoke at two in the morning and found him staring at the floor without any idea what time it was, and he had to tell her why to prevent her from worrying. He had been thinking about his father and about that afternoon at Rush & Company and about the ride home in the Cadillac.

It had been hard to talk because the top was down and Willie Stevens began to drive over fifty once they were out of the traffic. John Gray had always loved fast driving and it had seemed as if they were hurtling through space. It was easier to tell Nancy than he thought it would be. She knew all about the Grays and she had formed her own opinion of Clyde, although she had never seen it. Besides she knew all about places like Rush & Company. She felt exactly as he did about board rooms and she shared his own ideas about getting on in the polite free-for-all of downtown offices.

"Pull up your socks and forget it," Nancy said. "You couldn't have done a single thing about it. It had to happen and you know it."

She sometimes told him to pull up his socks when she argued with him and it was partly affectionate and partly malicious. She was usually so austere and correctly cynical that it was always as surprising as though Psyche in the White Rock advertisements had said "Damn."

"It might have made some impression if I'd got mad at him," he told her, "but it was hard to get mad at him. He could always rise above everything."

"It wouldn't have made any difference," Nancy said. "You couldn't have done anything, not with all your piety and all your wit. Those boys are all just the same."

"You didn't know Father," Charles told her. "He had a lot of charm and he could shed things, consequences and everything."

"I wish you'd listen to me," Nancy said. "I didn't know him, but they're all alike. They have a congenital and insidious charm. They have to, to get away with what they do, and they don't want to be reformed. I know, because I tried to reform one once. You couldn't have done anything about it."

"When did you try to reform one?" Charles asked.

"When I was younger," Nancy said, "before you came along. Didn't I ever tell you?"

Actually she had said the same thing about John Gray that Moulton Rush had said that September afternoon.

After John Gray left, Mr. Rush went over the typed pages very carefully. He disliked market letters and he did not want anything from Rush & Company to sound like one and neither did he want to hedge behind provisos. He wanted a letter that said something and then stopped, but when they were finished Mr. Rush asked Charles to wait a minute.

"It's none of my business," Mr. Rush said, "but I'm worried about your father." The springs of Mr. Rush's swivel chair creaked. "He's intelligent, but I can't do anything with him. They're all alike, you see, the whole lot of them." He nodded toward the open door. "There are five or six of them in the board room now. They're all alike."

The Cadillac was parked in Post Office Square in a space where there was supposed to be no parking, because his father had learned that the traffic officer on duty there was interested in common stocks.

"Thank you, Tom," his father said to the policeman, "and don't forget what I told you. This is my son Charles."

"Pleased to meet you," the policeman said. "Just leave the Caddy here any time, Mr. Gray."

"Tom is very reasonable," his father said as they drove off, "but I wish he wouldn't call it a Caddy."

He leaned back on the red leather cushions and half closed his eyes. He had perfect confidence in Willie Stevens's driving and looked with relaxed trust at Willie's clean-shaven neck. Willie was wearing his best clothes but he refused to wear any sort of uniform and John Gray had sympathized with him. It was hard talking with the top down but also it was difficult for Willie to hear much of their conversation. His father had enjoyed his talk with Moulton Rush. He had always liked Moulton. He had a very human streak considering his type.

"He's a Puritan," John Gray said, "and I have more catholic tastes, but then I'm glad I'm not a Catholic."

"You're not really anything, are you?" Charles said.

"I have religious prejudices," John Gray said, "and I read a chapter from the Bible nearly every night."

"But you only read it for the English," Charles said.

"Charley"—his father pulled his hat down hard, because it was windy with the top down—"why do you imply that I'm a pagan?"

"I don't know what you are," Charles said. "You're too complicated, Father."

"I know. I have a lot of ideas, too many ideas." John Gray took his cigar case from his pocket and put it back again. It was too windy to smoke in the rear seat of the Cadillac.

They had reached the open road and Willie Stevens was driving faster. They did not speak for a while and his father closed his eyes.

"Father," Charles said, "haven't you done enough about beating the system?"

"Now, Charley." John Gray looked hurt. "Let's not spoil this drive."

"All right," Charles said, "but what about that trust fund?"

"I'll attend to it next week," his father said. "Now drop it. I really don't know why I like you, Charley."

Charles did not drop it although he had to speak so loudly in the car that his voice became hoarse and dry. What was the earthly use in taking any risks, he was asking, when his father had everything, enough, too much of everything? The market was shaky. Anyone could see there would be a break. It was egotism, it was childish, it made no sense. If he had set up that trust fund and then he wanted to be a fool, he could go ahead and lose the rest of it. Charles said all that was on his mind for once. It was utterly selfish, he was saying. His father might for once grasp the idea that everyone was involved. It was not as though he had earned the money to start with. He was losing his head because of a streak of luck. He had said himself he was not sleeping well. What was the use in going on with it if he did not need any more? There would be only one end to it.

His father folded his hands when Charles had finished and was silent for almost a minute before he answered.

"You've always said all that, without saying it, Charley," he said. "This must be unpleasant for you. I'm very sorry, but we can't help how we're made, can we? I suppose I'd better tell you the truth. I like what I'm doing, and what under the sun would I do if I stopped?"

Then his whole face brightened. It was what Charles had said to Nancy later. His father could always shed things.

"You're quite right about the trust fund, too, Charley. I'll attend to it right away. You remember that ten thousand dollars of your mother's and that five of Dorothea's? Well, they wanted me to do a little something with it. I thought perhaps I'd better not tell you, but I've done something, quite a lot, and it really is time I saw about that trust fund."

He undoubtedly was planning to attend to it. The papers were even drawn, as Charles found later, for a fund of a hundred and fifty thousand dollars. The papers were all there upstairs in his room, but his father had never signed them. It was one of those details to be taken up when he had the time.

The day when the market first broke in October must have started for everyone the way it did for Charles, as a part of the ordinary routine of living. He remembered reading later, in a brochure published by a banking house: "In years to come the 1929 crash will doubtless be remembered merely as a summer thundershower." When this was written prosperity was still just around the corner and happy days like those old happy ones would be here again if you were not a bear on the United States. When the storm did break, in a cloudless sky, work went on that first day without much interruption in conservative offices like Rush & Company. It was only when the drop went on the next day and the next and when the tickers lagged further and further behind the trading that Charles began to observe that all the faces in the office were stamped with an expression that began to erase individuality.

Jessica had come to Boston on the morning of the break and they were to have had lunch together but he had called her up at her aunt's house to say that, although it had nothing to do with his own department, he felt he had better stay at the office on general principles. Yet at home for the first day or so he could not notice any change and there seemed to be no more connection between home and E. P. Rush & Company than there ever had been. Back in Clyde he could forget the crowd around the board and those sickly individual attempts at indifference and composure.

That first evening before supper, his father said it would be nice if Axel were to mix some Martini cocktails because it had been quite a day in Boston and Dorothea and Elbridge were coming to dinner. Elbridge had something particular to tell them and he hoped that Elbridge had not been monkeying with the market. It was impossible to read anything on his father's face but as soon as they had a moment alone together Charles asked him if everything was all right, and his father looked very cheerful.

"I wish you wouldn't try to look like a doctor," he said, "and I wish you wouldn't think of me as a widow or an orphan. Hasn't everybody been expecting this? Of course I'm all right."

He was like all the rest of them. They were already beginning to say that they had seen it coming, but Charles felt deeply relieved. His father drank two Martinis, which was unusual for him, but he did not speak again about the market. Instead they talked about the announcement of the engagement in November and who would be coming to the tea. Miss Lovell had called that morning to go over plans for the tea.

When Dorothea and Elbridge arrived, John Gray was describing the next paper he was going to write for the Confessional Club. It would be about the South Sea Bubble, starting with Charles Lamb, and he was going to put it in one-syllable words so that it would not be over the heads of his audience.

"And, Elbridge," he said, "please don't ask me what the South Sea Bubble was, because it's nearly time for supper."

"Elbridge doesn't care anything about a bubble," Dorothea said. "He wants to tell you our news."

Elbridge fidgeted in his chair and asked for another cocktail.

"I don't know how you'll take it," he began, "but Dorothea thinks we ought to do it."

He liked Clyde, Elbridge said. He had always thought he was going to stay on in Clyde in Wright-Sherwin.

"But Charley knows how things are there," he said. "You get in a rut at Wright-Sherwin." Maybe he had been getting into a rut. Maybe he was more ambitious now that he was a married man. You had to think about the future. Perhaps they might have children.

"Oh, Dorothea," Esther Gray said, "I really think you might have told me."

"Axel," John Gray called. "I think we might have some more cocktails, Axel. Well, well. This is quite a day."

"Mother," Dorothea said, "I wish you wouldn't jump at things. Elbridge only said that we *might* have children."

Confidentially, Elbridge said, he had received an offer, quite a big offer, from a concern in Kansas City to be the head of their research department. It did not mean that he did not like Clyde.

"Well," John Gray said, "I'm sorry we can't start knitting garments, but maybe you're right, Elbridge. I never got very far here myself."

They discussed Elbridge and Dorothea and Kansas City all through supper and just before they left the table John Gray said that he had always wanted to go down the Mississippi—ever since he had read *Huckleberry Finn*. There was that musical play *Show Boat*. He wished that showboats were still running. There was no reason at all why they should not all charter a yacht next summer and go down the Mississippi. When Charles left to call on Jessica, his father was still talking about the Mississippi.

No one at the Lovell's discussed the break in the market for a moment.

If the engagement was to be announced in November, Mr. Lovell could not put off certain mechanics and formalities. As long as they were going through with it, and it seemed as though they must, it was a time for everyone to stand together. Jessica would have to have a new photograph taken. Also, an announcement must appear in the Saturday edition of the *Boston Evening Transcript*, and Mr. Lovell had been engaged all day in preparing it.

"Mr. Laurence Lovell," the announcement began, "of Clyde, Massachusetts, announces the engagement of his daughter Jessica to Mr. Charles Gray, also of Clyde, Massachusetts." Mr. Lovell's face had a set, determined expression as he read on and he sighed resignedly when he finished.

"I wish I could think of more to say about you, Charles," he said, "but I did mention your grandfather and I did say that you come of an old Clyde family. And now, Jessie, I hope you and Charles will go over this carefully. I've given my day to it. At least you can give half an hour."

The next afternoon Charles left Rush & Company for an hour to go with Jessica to look at engagement rings and whenever he saw a diamond in a platinum setting from then on he thought of the faces and the tickers. You could no longer tell what you might get for a common stock when you sold it. Quotations had no meaning because the ticker was so far behind. Yet there was not a flurry at home that evening. His father's one interest seemed to be Jessica's engagement ring. Charles did not want too large a stone, but John Gray wanted it large enough. All through supper he discussed the theory of diamond cutting, and after supper he suggested that they all read aloud. He was reading from *The Three Musketeers* about the Duke of Buckingham and Richelieu when Charles left to call on Jessica.

The third day was terrible but it was reassuring that his father had not bothered to go to town. He said there was no use going until things cleared up, and of course he was quite right. He did not want to answer any questions, he said. He would be glad to go over details with Charles when everything was brushed up and in order again. Short covering would cause an automatic rise —no matter what happened later. He was more interested in his new velvet smoking jacket of a deep Burgundy color which had come by mail that morning than in the news, and he wore his jacket to supper.

"Why, John," his mother said when she saw it, "you never told me about it."

"I still like to surprise you, dear," John Gray told her. "You always look so pretty when you're surprised. I hope you won't mind if I ask Axel for cocktails, and I've asked for champagne at supper."

"I don't see why it should be a party," his mother said. "It's just an ordinary supper."

"Charley looks tired," John Gray said. "You don't want to take these things too hard, Charley. Everything goes up and down." Charles felt deathly tired that night but his father did not seem tired at all.

"John, dear," his mother said, "I'm so glad you got all through with everything before this happened. Do you know what he's been doing all day, Charley? He's been at the library reading about the South Sea Bubble.

"You know, Esther," John Gray said, "I think perhaps we made a mistake not going abroad this summer instead of chartering the schooner. It's funny neither you nor I have been abroad, but there's always next summer. We can stay at Claridge's in London and I really don't see why we shouldn't take the Cadillac with us, and perhaps Charley and Jessica can meet us over there and we can go over to France. That reminds me—I haven't bought Jessica an engagement present, Charley. . . . Do you think she would like pearls?"

Charles was always up by seven in the morning in order to be in time for the eight-three train and the family usually had breakfast together at twenty minutes past seven. His father always said that he never could sleep late, because of those years at the mill. His mother was already at the table and the coffee was there too, in the new silver coffeepot, when Charles came down next morning.

"Charles, dear," his mother said, "I wonder whether you would mind going up and knocking on your father's door. He always likes to be with us at breakfast."

"If he's asleep," Charles said, "perhaps he'd like to sleep."

"No," his mother said. "You know he always likes to be down for breakfast."

There was no sort of warning or premonition. The sunlight had begun to creep through the fanlight above the front door. As Charles walked upstairs he heard the sound of a horse's hoofs and the rattle of wheels on Spruce Street. It would be the ice company. The ice company still used horses.

For years his father had slept in the small room to the right of the stairs, because he liked to go to bed when he pleased without disturbing anyone. Charles remembered the freshly painted panels and the brass latch of the old thin door. The latch was brightly polished, because Axel liked to polish brass. When he knocked, the ice wagon was still rumbling down Spruce Street.

"Father," he said, "are you awake?"

There was no sound on the other side of the door and he opened it instead of knocking again. The window was open and a cool breeze was blowing the new chintz curtains. His father was lying on his narrow spool bed. The bed had come from Gow Street and he had especially liked its hard mattress. His Bible was on the bedside table and beside the Bible was the bottle of sleeping pills which his brother-in-law had given him. There was nothing to explain the spasm of fear which shook Charles except his father's utter stillness. He was out in the hall again, closing the bedroom door very softly, before he faced the full realization that his father was dead.

A moment later he was in his father's study and he had closed the door behind him before he had consciously thought what to do next. His actions were automatic but at least they were correct. He could never admire himself for anything he did that day or the days following. He was only conscious of certain things he had to do and when he saw his father's private telephone he must have given the operator his Uncle Gerald Marchby's number from instinct rather than reason. It was still early and his uncle would be at home.

He told him to come to Spruce Street as soon as he could, to open the door without ringing, and that he would be waiting in the hall.

Instinct again rather than reason told him that his mother had better not be in the house when Dr. Marchby called, that it was better for him and his uncle to be alone for a few minutes. There was that dreamlike feeling of hurrying without being able to hurry, but he called up the Masons' house and asked for Mrs. Mason. He wanted her to call up his mother and to think of some reason to ask her to come over and to please keep her there for a while. He must have said that something serious had happened and that he would tell her later. He may have said that his father had died suddenly, or that his father was very unwell. He was never sure. Then he walked downstairs to the dining room.

"Here's your coffee, dear," his mother said, "and Axel will bring you your eggs right away. Was he asleep?"

Yes, he must have answered, he was asleep.

He remembered the taste of the coffee. He wanted to drink it in a gulp but instead he drank it slowly. He must have said something else, but he could not remember what. He had not finished the coffee when the telephone rang, and his mother said not to bother, that she would answer it.

"It's Margaret Mason," she said. "I'm sure I don't know what she wants so early in the morning."

"She probably wants to talk," he heard himself saying, "but it is early, isn't it?"

He was waiting in the hall when his Uncle Gerald came. He was not aware of any lapse of time. He remembered his uncle's heavy, stooping figure and his baggy trousers.

"Father's dead," he said.

"All right," his uncle answered, "let's go up."

Charles followed his uncle up the stairs but not into the room. He waited on the landing until his uncle called to him. Again he was aware of no lapse of time. He only knew that he had done the best he could and that the rest of it was up to his uncle.

"Charley, you can come in now," his uncle said. His uncle was standing by the bed holding his black bag and the pill bottle on the table was gone.

"He died in his sleep," his uncle said. "It was a heart attack. The Gray heart, Charley."

"Yes, sir," Charles said.

"Are you feeling all right?"

"Yes, sir," Charles said.

"Where's your mother?"

"She's over at the Masons'."

"Does she know?"

"Not yet," Charles said.

"How did she get over there?"

His voice was hoarse when he answered.

"I asked Mrs. Mason to ask her."

Their glances met and neither of them spoke for a moment.

"I'm glad you thought of that," his uncle said. "I'll go and tell her. I guess you'd better call up Hugh Blashfield, Charley."

"Yes," Charles said. "I guess I'd better, Uncle Gerald."

A time like that was a period of inevitable selflessness. Certain things which had to be done were cropping up successively and he was the only one who could possibly have done them. There was no time for deep subjective feeling. In all the rest of his days in Clyde, there was no time to think of himself and Jessica Lovell until the very end, no time to analyze his feelings about his father. It was only when he left Clyde that all the things he repressed and controlled came over him in dark, disorderly waves, and he could handle those moods by then, because he was away from Clyde. He was like someone who stood on the stern of a ship—by then—watching a vanishing cloudy shore line. Dreadful, half-believable things had occurred ashore. Those things had marked him, but now he was moving on, leaving the ruins of them behind.

It was possible at length to begin deliberately forgetting a great deal of what had happened there, not all but a great deal. It was better to make a clean break and to leave regrets behind, and feelings of hidden guilt, and thoughts of how one might have said and done things differently. There was not much he had consciously avoided. He had not run away from anything. There was nothing left to run away from except memory by the time he had left Clyde, and of course he had taken unavoidable elements of it with him. Yet even so his memory of that time was singularly devoid of pain. Something in that morning seemed to have killed desire or some capacity for feeling and he had been shaken by deep emotion only once or twice. His self-control was with him through all of it, perhaps because it was starkly obvious what everyone would say and do after his father's death.

Neither Charles nor his uncle ever spoke again of that moment when they had stood at the head of the bed inside his father's room; and as far as he knew no one ever heard anything about it. No one ever heard, but certain people must have guessed. At least he was sure that his mother and Dorothea had never learned the truth. His father had died of a heart attack, brought on by strain and worry, and perhaps it was just as well. He never liked to think of his father trying to face what was left.

A note came from Jessica that same morning. It was delivered by old Mr. Fogarty, who still sometimes did a little work in the Lovells' garden, and Charles could still remember the heavy blue paper.

"Charles, dear, I feel so sick and sorry for what you must be going through, and please come and see me, dear, as soon as you feel you can."

He telephoned her himself that afternoon and told her the family needed him and he knew she would understand. His mother and Dorothea were not seeing anyone just yet.

The doorbell was beginning to ring. He never forgot the sound of the doorbell. He never forgot the hours in that room of his father's with Mr. Blashfield and Elbridge Sterne, the closed door, the opening of drawers, and the stacks of papers. There was no way of keeping Elbridge out of it and he was glad he had not gone through with it alone with Mr. Blashfield.

When he called up Boston, he said he would come in at once with his father's lawyer, but even before they left, they had some idea of the figures and realized that the fewer people who knew, the better. They might already be saying that John Gray had left his affairs in a mess.

"Charley," Elbridge said, "I don't see why he did it."

"He couldn't help it." That answer explained everything, but excused nothing. "And no one must ever know."

"I don't see how you're going to stop it," Elbridge said. He was hopelessly at sea. Elbridge may have known all about brasses and bronzes but he always was confused when he had to separate liabilities from assets.

Of course, there was one way to stop a part of that inevitable talk. He could put his own government bonds into the assets. He would have to tell Hugh Blashfield and he would have to tell the Lovells and Elbridge would know, but there was no reason why it should go any further. There was no reason why his mother and Dorothea need ever hear of it. He could never give himself much credit for his decision, because it was the best way out and it was something he owed to the family.

"I'll get along all right, Elbridge," he heard himself saying. "Mother will have to have something and we can get her to put it into a trust."

All he wanted, all he could do, was to have everything look as well as possible. His father had said that he was being conservative and careful and he had expressed that conservatism by protecting himself with what he considered a ridiculously large margin. When he had been sold out at the market the previous day the account had come close to breaking even. It was even possible that it might be slightly in the black when the final figuring was completed, but even so there was almost nothing left.

Mr. Crewe had come to call. Charles could still see himself sometimes talking to Mr. Crewe in that upstairs room of his father's, which already was losing its character. Though it was a parochial duty, Charles was sure that Mr. Crewe was conscious of inadequacy. He could not draw upon ritual or upon *The Book of Common Prayer* and he must have known that John Gray had never liked his sermons. He said he had come to call, not to discuss the details of the service, because they could talk of that later. He had come as a friend, in the hope that he might be of some help in an hour of deep bereavement, and he looked very helpless when he said it, a thin, pale little man, struggling with abstract periods.

"I feel deeply for your mother and sister and you too, Charles," he said. "I wish there were something I could say which would bring comfort. Do you remember that '*in my Father's house are many mansions: if it were not so, I would have told you*'?"

Charles remembered. The word "mansion" always made him think of lawns and a driveway and of a white-pillared portico. His father would love to dwell in such a mansion. Mr. Crewe's glance had moved to the papers on the table and to the private telephone and Charles was sure that he wished to express the hope that his father had left his affairs in order.

"I knew him for a long while," Mr. Crewe said. "I've always admired the richness of his mind. We always depended on his spirit at the Confessional Club to lift us over hard places. You would be touched to know how many people have spoken of him to me today, many different sorts of people. There is a broad sense of loss, the loss of a generous friend."

"Yes," Charles said. "Everyone always liked Father."

"And memory continues much longer than life," Mr. Crewe said, "so very much longer. He is living still in memory. Your father was very proud of you, although he never expressed it in a conventional way, perhaps."

"I hope he was," Charles said. "No, Father was never conventional."

"At a time like this," Mr. Crewe said, and he glanced at Charles and then stared at the floor, "one feels, doesn't one, very keenly the presence of an outside power, of a guiding spirit, of–of God. I'm sure you feel it, Charles."

Mr. Crewe was doing the best he could, because it was his duty, and Charles felt anxious to help him.

"I know what you mean," he said, "but right now I don't seem to feel much of anything. I only know it's there."

Mr. Crewe coughed.

"A great deal has been said and written about the efficacy of prayer," he said. "I sometimes feel we speak too little of it. I think it might help us both if we prayed, that is if you don't mind."

"No, sir," Charles said. "It's very kind of you to think of it, Mr. Crewe. You're being very kind."

He had not anticipated Mr. Crewe's suggestion. It was a very awkward moment when Mr. Crewe left his chair, one of the old Windsor chairs, and sank abruptly to his knees upon the new green carpet. It was awkward, yet there was something that was beyond grotesqueness. For once that day everything was simple.

"I think we will both feel better for it," Mr. Crewe said before he began, and they shook hands when the prayer was over.

"Thank you very much, Charles," Mr. Crewe said, "and please remember that I'm always here to help."

He called on Jessica that night, just for a few minutes, because he did not want to leave his mother or Dorothea too long. When he reached Johnson Street it was late and he was glad that Mr. Lovell had retired. Somehow all the day was still with him and there was still so much to do that he felt strangely impersonal when he kissed her. It was what he had said to Mr. Crewe–that it was hard to feel anything, but he hoped that he said the things he had to say properly. She knew, of course, how he had felt about his father but he hoped that she did not think that he sounded cold and practical. He might have put off until later telling her about adding his bonds to his father's estate but it seemed to him that she should know right away.

"You see, don't you?" he remembered saying. "It's the only thing to do."

"Oh, Charley dear, of course it is," she said, and they did not speak for a while. They sat there in the wallpaper room, holding hands.

"You and I can get on," he said. "We can be married just the same."

"Darling," she said, "of course we can. I'll never marry anyone but you."

"I'm awfully glad you're with me," he said. "I don't know what I'd do without you."

"Of course I'm with you, dear," she said. "I'll always be with you."

"You see why I don't want anyone to know," he said, "but I suppose you ought to tell your father."

They kissed again in the front hall before he opened the door, and it never occurred to him—there was no possible way he could have told—that he would only see Jessica Lovell once again.

His mother and Dorothea were in the parlor when he reached home and Elbridge Sterne was with them and his mother said it was time they faced things. She could not stay in Spruce Street alone. There were too many memories in Spruce Street, and she could not go on alone in Clyde.

"Charley," she said, as she said so often afterwards, "why didn't he ever tell us he wasn't well—but it was just like him, wasn't it? He never wanted any of us to worry."

Then for some reason she asked him if he remembered that paper she had read long ago at the Historical Society about Alice Ruskin Lyte. Charles was only a little boy then but he must remember. Did he remember those evenings they worked over it together? John had been so patient and he always had loved words so, and Sam was alive. She could not live in Spruce Street any longer and Dorothea and Elbridge wanted her to go with them to Kansas City.

He had never thought of Clyde without his mother. It was only later that he was glad she felt as she had. It was better that she had left before the Cadillac and the house and the furniture were sold. It was better that she had gone to Kansas City instead of living on in Clyde. If she had stayed, he would have had to stay himself and that would scarcely have been possible with Jessica still there.

23

I Think That Frankness Has Been the Basis of Our Previous Relationship

—MR. LAURENCE LOVELL

Once, as a step in that long process of advancement at the Stuyvesant Bank, Arthur Slade had asked Charles if he could arrange to come out for the week end to his summer place on the beach at Wainscott, Long Island. Everyone knew that there were going to be some changes in the trust department and this obviously was the reason for the invitation. It was a week end in the summer of 1937 and Charles had said he would be glad to go if things were all right at home in Larchmont.

Arthur Slade had met Nancy but it was too early even to consider whether Nancy would be a help or a detriment as the wife of an officer at the Stuyvesant. It was only a question of the trust department upstairs. He had told Charles that they would love to have his wife too, but Charles had refused for Nancy because obviously there was no place to leave the children.

"I hate to ask you without her," Arthur Slade said, "but I hope you can manage to come yourself. I feel like sitting on the beach and talking."

Nancy understood perfectly what the invitation meant.

"He wants to see how you use your knife and fork and whether you're housebroken," she said. "They don't care whether I chew gum or not yet, but if you go and behave yourself, around next year they'll begin to care."

Nancy helped him pack his suitcase. She pressed his dinner coat. She brushed his tweed jacket. She made him take both white flannels and gray slacks, and his new crepe-soled shoes and the pullover sweater that went with his tweed jacket and four soft shirts and four assorted ties. She checked and double-checked everything in the suitcase.

"Don't let them get you into any games," she said. "You're rotten at golf and tennis, but play bridge if you want to. You're not bad at bridge."

"I wish you were going," Charles said. "It isn't fair to leave you."

"It's life," Nancy told him. "Drink two cocktails before dinner and don't drink anything afterwards unless you have to, and you'd better take a good book along. Take *Mathematics for the Million*. It will show them that you think."

He knew that Arthur Slade wanted to see how he would act on Long Island but he had not been self-conscious. He was devoted to Arthur Slade and he knew that Arthur liked him. When Arthur Slade had asked him if he would like to play golf, Charles told him he had better not. He had once taken a few lessons from a professional at the Shore Club north of Boston but he had never been good at golf. He had always worked too hard—no time for golf and no time for any bad habits either. He was not much at athletics. He had played a little football once. He had gone out for track at Dartmouth and he had been on the wrestling team, but that was all quite a while ago.

On Saturday evening there was a buffet supper, ten or a dozen people, a lawyer and his wife and some men from downtown who reminded him of Rush & Company. There were two tables of bridge afterwards and he played at a table with Elsie Slade and a couple named Murchison and when the rubber was over Elsie Slade sat with him on the steps of the piazza. They drank ginger ale, because, he told her, Nancy had warned him not to drink anything after dinner unless he had to. He told her about Nancy and about life in Larchmont, where they had moved because of the children instead of staying in town, and Elsie Slade talked about her two boys who were away at camp and she called him Charley because she felt she knew him very well. Arthur had said so much about him.

Obviously Arthur Slade had asked her to talk to him—certainly he wanted her reaction—but Charles did not mind in the least. In fact he found it surprisingly easy to talk about himself. Once, she said, Arthur had told her that he had met his father for just a second, in Boston at the Parker House.

"Oh, yes," he said, "I remember. Father was a big-time operator then."

He found himself speaking of it lightly, aware that it fitted well with the evening party and the cottage on the dunes and the cool air from the ocean. He told her about the Cadillac and the Shore Club and the *Zaza*.

"It was quite an adjustment for me," he said. "You see, I was a small-town boy. I'm still basically small-town."

Then Arthur Slade came out of the dark, manifestly to see how they were getting on. He sat on the steps beside them for a moment and asked Charles if he wouldn't like some Scotch.

"Don't ask him," Elsie said. "Nancy doesn't like him to drink after dinner."

Elsie Slade must have liked him or she would not have referred to Nancy by her first name, never having met her. He said he would like a thin drink of Scotch after all, as long as it was Saturday night, but it was not because of this, it was because he felt she was genuinely interested, that he told Elsie Slade about Clyde. It sounded like an amusing place, as he described it that evening.

She said that she had always lived in New York, except in the summer; her family had always spent their summers on Long Island, right here in Wainscott. She had met Arthur at a debutante party and here they were, still in Wainscott. It was a small-town life in itself, she said, but of course in a different way; and then she asked him the inevitable question. Why had he ever left Clyde? It sounded like a wonderful place.

He took a swallow of his thin drink of Scotch. Those days were so far away that he could see their amusing side, at least he could that evening sitting on the steps by the beach.

"It's a small-town story," he said. "It's the difference between Spruce Street and Johnson Street. I should have remembered we were Spruce Streeters. Both Father and I should have remembered."

He had never told Arthur Slade about Jessica Lovell but he did not in the least mind telling Elsie Slade that night. They had first really become acquainted, he told her, at a firemen's muster. She had never even heard of a firemen's muster so he told her about his father and the Pine Trees. It was the difference between Spruce Street and Johnson Street. They used to meet surreptitiously by the courthouse and go riding in her car—and then he had left Wright-Sherwin and gone to work in Rush & Company.

"Her father never did approve of it," he said, "but then why should he? He was always trying to break it up, and he did, when my father died. It was a strain for her, you see, divided loyalty, Spruce Street, Johnson Street. She couldn't go on with it. Her father took her away to forget."

He took another swallow of his whiskey. It was just what he had called it, a small-town story. All one had to do was change its emphasis to make it humorous.

"And what did you do?" Elsie Slade asked.

"Why, I left too," he said. "I was hurt, but it made me ambitious."

"Are you still ambitious?" she asked.

This made him laugh. He had never realized until then how little Jessica and the struggle for Jessica meant to him any longer.

"Of course I am," he said, "or I wouldn't be here now, Mrs. Slade."

"Aren't you going to call me Elsie?" she asked.

This made him laugh again. It was wonderful to be so wholly free from Clyde and he was thinking of Nancy and the suitcase and the four neckties and the crepe-soled shoes.

"No," he said, "not yet, but I love to have you call me Charley. Please don't stop. And I'd love to call you Elsie someday, when I'm a little further ahead at the bank, but not right now. You see, I know the difference between Spruce and Johnson streets."

Then Arthur Slade was back again.

"Arthur," Elsie Slade was saying, "Charley won't call me Elsie, but he'd love to sometime later. He's made a very favorable impression on me, Arthur, and you must be sure to get him to tell you the difference between Johnson Street and Spruce Street."

* * *

The Lovells were at the funeral but they sat in the back of the church, not near the family, and Charles had no opportunity to speak to them afterwards. After the service at the grave at the old North Cemetery, Jessica sent him another note by Mr. Fogarty. Her father was going away to New York for a few days, she told him, and he especially wanted her to go with him and she really felt she should. They would be back on Monday or Tuesday. She would call him the minute they were back and she would be thinking of him all the time.

He wished that he might have seen her before she left and he was as much surprised as one could be at such a time that she had not asked him to stop at Johnson Street instead of sending a note, but it was a very sensible thing for her to go away. There would have been no chance for them to be alone together. He was much too busy putting things in order.

Elbridge Sterne had left Wright-Sherwin and the sooner they could all move to Kansas City the better, now that they had definitely made up their minds. Still there were all those final farewells and repeated explanations. His mother could not be expected to leave immediately. She could not cut the ties all at once, but Elbridge's job in Kansas City could not wait indefinitely. It was as though she were leaving the house to go on a visit and always returning for some odd object she had forgotten.

In the end Charles was the one who had to make the decisions. They confronted him in every waking moment and they plagued him through the nights. He never realized until later how tired he must have been though it was not a physical weariness. Mrs. Mason and all his mother's friends kept telling him they did not know what his mother and Dorothea would have done without him, and his mother and Dorothea were always saying the same thing. He was the head of the family and in every detail he had to represent the family. Besides Mr. Blashfield and a lawyer from Boston, who were always giving him papers to sign and wanting to see him for half an hour, there were all sorts of extraneous questions. There was the stone in the North Cemetery, what furniture his mother and Dorothea wanted to take to Kansas City and what was to be done with the rest. What was to be done about the Cadillac, and what about the couple and the bills and the donation his father had promised to give the hospital? His mother was so relieved that he had left enough so that she could have her independence. She wanted to give a little of it to the library as a John Gray Memorial Fund. The books that would be purchased from it could have a note in them saying that they were bought by the John Gray Memorial Fund, and the library could have all his books, except the ones Charles wanted.

He was tired of seeing people. They were continually calling at Spruce Street and whenever he was not talking to Mr. Blashfield his mother was sending word for him to come downstairs and meet them. She had never known how many friends they had and how kind they all could be. Everyone had been to call except the Lovells, but then Jessica and Mr. Lovell were out of town.

He was tired of seeing people. They were always seeking a private word with him in the house, and they stopped him on the street whenever he went outdoors. They were very kind but they seemed to be saying something they had learned by rote—and he suspected that they were covertly scrutinizing him, seeking from him an answer to a question they did not care to ask. Yes, it was very sudden, he would reply. Yes, his father had been very well, but the crash had been too great a shock. At any rate there was no sign of financial embarrassment for anyone to see. The bills were being paid and twice he deliberately had Willie Stevens drive him in the Cadillac to Boston, and there was the John Gray Fund at the library. He was glad that his mother had thought of it. By the time the Lovells were back, he had been through so much that Mr. Lovell was only another problem—at least he always hoped that he had given Mr. Lovell that impression.

Charles and his mother and Dorothea and Elbridge were in the parlor discussing everything in an aimless way, saying the same things over and over—it was like a clock running down from lack of winding—when Axel had knocked on the door and had said that Mr. Lovell wished to speak to Mr. Charles on the telephone. Axel, in his black alpaca coat, was a false note in the house. He had never really belonged in it, but he had done very well. No doubt he wanted a good reference and was hoping for a financial present.

"Do you mean Miss Lovell?" Charles asked.

No, it was Mr. Lovell, and the telephone was still in the hall below the stairs.

"Good evening, Charles," Mr. Lovell said.

"Good evening, Mr. Lovell," Charles answered. "When did you and Jessica get back?"

"This afternoon," Mr. Lovell said. "I wonder if you would mind coming over for a little while, Charles—that is if you're not too busy."

Of course he was not too busy and he had thought that Jessica would surely be at the door to meet him but instead Mr. Lovell opened it himself. The house was very still, but he was used lately to portentous stilted silence.

"Good evening, Charles," Mr. Lovell said. "Shall we go into the library? There's a fire there."

"Where's Jessica?" Charles asked.

"Upstairs," Mr. Lovell said, "but she'll be down in a few minutes. Charles, I haven't had the opportunity to tell you how sorry I am for you and for everything."

Mr. Lovell seemed relieved as he always did when he reached the reassurance of his library.

"Have a comfortable chair, Charles," he said. "Take my chair, over by the lamp."

Charles did not sit down, as Mr. Lovell asked him, because as soon as they were in the library he had some premonition of what Mr. Lovell was about to say and he could feel some force within himself gathering to meet an immediate shock.

"Don't you really want to sit down, Charles?" Mr. Lovell said.

"No, thank you," he answered. "I've been sitting down all day."

"I don't exactly know how to begin," Mr. Lovell said, and it occurred to Charles that Mr. Lovell usually did not know how to begin, "but I think that frankness has been the basis of our"—he paused, groping for a word—"our previous relationship, don't you?"

"You've been frank, sir," Charles said. "Maybe I should have been franker myself." He was always glad that he said it in just that way.

"Now, Charles," Mr. Lovell went on. "Nothing that I have to say, please believe me, reflects on you personally. You have behaved magnificently. Everyone is saying so. Everyone has more than sympathy for you. They have respect."

It was a handsome speech. He must have been thinking of it and thinking of it, and now he was waiting for some adequate and grateful reaction, and Charles was always satisfied with what he answered.

"Perhaps you'd better tell me what you have on your mind, Mr. Lovell," he said. He would never have spoken in such a way if it had not been for what he had been through.

"Now, Charles," Mr. Lovell said, "I want to be kind, but I wish I did not have to be cruel to be kind." Mr. Lovell sighed. He was having a very unpleasant time, but then this was true of both of them.

"Jessica told me what you have done, Charles, toward settling your father's affairs. It was what a generous and dutiful son should have done, and I respect you for it, but, Charles, there's a change, an unavoidable change, in the whole situation, and I am not referring to its financial aspects. I wish I didn't have to be so frank." Mr. Lovell cleared his throat. "I don't mean there's anything verging on, well, scandal, but there's a shadow, Charles. In a way, there will always be a shadow of doubt as to whether something was not concealed."

Charles did not answer. He never would be able to allay that doubt. There was always a shadow but it never would have been as deep if the Lovells had stood behind him.

"I've thought this over carefully, Charles. I've been over it thoroughly with Jessica," Mr. Lovell was saying. "We've been most unhappy. It's an impossible situation, Charles. We must end it. It can't go on."

He had been ready for it but he was thinking that Jessica should have been the one to tell him, not Mr. Lovell.

"Jessica," he began, and his voice was hoarse and he hated to have Mr. Lovell see him so upset. "Does Jessica want it this way?"

"Jessica's very unhappy," Mr. Lovell said, "but I wouldn't have spoken to you if she did not want it this way. It's only fair for her to tell you so herself, fair for both of us. If you'll wait a moment I'll get Jessica."

He must have stood alone in the library for a minute or two but he was not conscious of any period of waiting until he saw Jessica in the open doorway with Mr. Lovell just behind her.

"Oh, Charley," she said. "Charley." Her voice shook him because she seemed to be crying out to him as though she were hurt.

"Don't cry, Jessie dear—" Mr. Lovell had his arm around her—"it's only fair to tell Charles how you feel yourself."

He had told her not to cry but she was crying.

"Oh, Charley," she said, "I'm so ashamed of myself. I'm not fit to marry anyone."

"Now, Jessie," Mr. Lovell said very gently. "Just control yourself for a minute and tell Charles and then it will be over, Jessie dear."

He seemed to have been waiting for a very long time before she spoke.

"Charley, darling," she said, "I can't go on. I can't marry you with both of you feeling the way you do."

Of course, it was the final truth and it had hung between them all the time. She was almost asking for forgiveness, and she was hurt as much as he was. He wanted to tell her not to cry, he wanted to quiet her with her head on his shoulder. He wanted to tell her not to bother to explain, but she was still speaking through her sobs.

"I'm so, so torn, Charley," she was saying. Though her father's arm was still around her, she was talking as though he were not there at all. "You see, don't you, that he's given up everything for me. I have to do what he thinks best." He wished that she would stop and her tears did stop her for a moment.

"Now, Jessie," Mr. Lovell said, "it's all right. It's all over, Jessie dear"; but it was not quite all over.

"Oh, Charley," Jessica sobbed, "it doesn't mean I don't love you. I do still love you."

It was long ago, but nothing that had happened since had ever put it in clear perspective. There was too much of him and Jessica in those next few seconds; they were always vibrant and alive with their own peculiar triumph and their pain, and, for just a moment, he believed she always would still love him. It was like that time that spring when they had spoken the words that had made everything different. Nothing else mattered, not Mr. Lovell or Johnson Street or Spruce Street or the shadow of John Gray's death. It was himself and Jessica, and that was all, and never mind the rest.

"Jessica," he said, "I love you too, and that's all there is to it, isn't it?" Although he did not expect an immediate answer, he waited and he did not go on until he was conscious of the silence. "Jessica . . . do you remember what you said one night . . . if I saw this happening to you . . . you wanted me to tell you?" At least this was what he always thought he said, but words had no great value as they stood there facing each other.

"Charley," she said. "Oh, Charley."

She called his name across the space that divided them and he always remembered the happiness and the relief in her voice. She pushed herself away from Mr. Lovell, gently but definitely, and moved toward him. He was always sure that if they had so much as touched each other they would never have left each other, and he was always sure that Mr. Lovell, and Jessica too, knew this as well. As she stretched out her arms to reach him he had a glimpse of Mr. Lovell's face, startled and stricken, and their hands never touched because Mr. Lovell made a gasping, strangled sound and Jessica turned when she heard it.

"Oh," Mr. Lovell said. "Oh." His face was alarmingly white. He took two wavering steps and slumped brokenly into a chair and covered his face with his hands. Jessica fell on her knees and put her arms around him.

"Father," she asked, "oh, Father, what is it?" and Mr. Lovell straightened himself and reached unsteadily for her hand.

"It's nothing, Jessie dear," he said. "I'll be all right in just a minute, my darling. I'm sorry to make such an undignified exhibition of myself. If you want it this way, my dearest, please forget about me, please."

Mr. Lovell's voice was gentle and controlled and he looked over Jessica's shoulder at Charles.

"Please forgive me, Charles, and please, my dearest dear," he said again, "don't think about me if you want it this way."

Then Jessica, still kneeling by Mr. Lovell's chair, looked up at Charles too and her voice was shaken with tears.

"Oh, Charley, I can't . . . Don't you see I can't? . . . I can't bear it any more."

It was natural and yet it was unnatural. To Charles there was something faintly repellent in that conjugal scene. The memory of it was always mingled with old reflexes of pain. They used to say in Clyde that a cat had nine lives and that a snake would live till sundown, but all at once Charles did not want to go on with that scene. As long as he lived he did not ever want to see Jessica or Mr. Lovell again.

"That's all right, Jessica," he said. "Please don't cry." There should have been something more for him to say, some sort of farewell speech, but he could not think of any. "Well, I'd better be going now."

This was what he had always said in the old days, when he first came to call on Jessica, and now he never even wanted to see the Lovell house again. He knew at last that Jessica could never be separated from it and in some vague way he wanted her to be sorry and to show her how wrong she was. He had no desire to stay in Clyde any longer, and perhaps the main reason why he went to New York was because he wanted Jessica to be sorry.

There were, of course, other reasons, all combining into an urge or drive the force of which he could not combat. The shadow of Clyde must have always lain behind his subsequent actions. He would never have had such a strong desire to get ahead or to make the necessary sacrifices if it had not been for his father and the Lovells. There was a negative force, a combined revelation and above all humiliation that needed to be surmounted. He must have always been seeking to assuage the pain that those few last weeks in Clyde gave him.

* * *

"It was all very good for you," Nancy said once. "It's made you into a very nice guy. Maybe it's made you too nice."

He told her this was not so. In many ways he was self-centered and perhaps they had both tried too hard to get ahead, though Nancy did not think so.

"You see, I'm like the Old Man," he said. "I'm just trying to beat the system in a different way."

"Everybody's trying to beat some sort of system," Nancy said, "but most people don't know it. It's nice that you and I know it and that we don't fool ourselves. It makes everything all right."

She had always loved that effort to beat the system because she possessed a quality of combativeness. She liked what they did together, she told him once, because there was no one to help them. It was always the two of them against the world.

"We'll show them," she used to whisper to him sometimes in the night.

She never had to explain whom she meant by "them" or what it was they were going to show. It was always himself and Nancy against the world and against all the systems in it, against Tony Burton and the Stuyvesant Bank and American Tel & Tel, against the furnace and the doctors and the bills. It was always himself and Nancy striving for security, and they never needed anyone to help. It was always himself and Nancy, striving within the limits of free enterprise if you wanted to put it that way.

"You see, I was looking for a man," she told him once. "That's what every girl is looking for and don't let anyone tell you differently. I suppose I might have married old Jessup if you hadn't come along." She was referring, of course, to Mr. Clive Jessup in the firm of Burrell, Jessup and Cockburn where she had been working when Charles went downtown that time on his errand from the bank.

"Well, you'd have beaten the system, Nance," he said, "and you could have had a box at the opera."

"Being a kept woman doesn't beat any system," Nancy told him. She always said what she thought.

Her father ran a real estate and insurance business up there in New York State and it was a relief that Nancy did not like her family much. It meant that they could always speak the same language. She had moved away from there as soon as she could, because she had wanted to go to college. She had gone to Barnard for two years and then to the Katharine Gibbs secretarial school because her family were always telling her about the sacrifice they were making. She was not going to go back home ever if she could help it. When he went up there with her just before they were married, he was reminded of his brother Sam and May Mason.

"You know," he told her once, "you're really a Spruce Street girl."

"I wish to God," Nancy said, "you'd get over thinking about Spruce Street."

But she really was a Spruce Street girl. It was always himself and Nancy against the world.

24

One Big, Happy Family

Charles came to New York early in January in 1930. He had taken the midnight from Boston and he had checked his suitcase in the parcel room at the Grand Central Station, the one beneath the stairs that led to Vanderbilt Avenue. He had eaten breakfast in the restaurant on the lower level, not at the counter but at a table, staying there as long as he decently could, reading the *New York Times*. He knew almost nothing about New York but he did not feel either lonely or confused. He felt that he was in a new country.

Outside the station, the streetcars and the traffic were already running in a steady stream under the ramp at Pershing Square. The shops on Forty-second Street, the drugstores, the optical stores and haberdasheries, were already opening for the day. When he reached Fifth Avenue the lions in front of the Public Library looked white and cold and those old buses with the seats on top were moving in lines on the Avenue, but New York was sleepy still. New York had the appearance of having been up very late, and everyone on the streets had a patient, complaining look of having been routed too early out of bed. As he walked up the Avenue the city seemed to him as impersonal as it always did later and he loved that impersonality. Now that he had left his bag at the parcel room there was nothing to tie him. The tides of the city moved past him and he was part of the tide. His own problems and his own personality merged with it.

The Stuyvesant Bank would not be open for two hours, so he walked up

Fifth Avenue to the Eighties, then down Park Avenue and then along Madison. Looking in the shop windows there was like carelessly turning the pages in a book while waiting somewhere. The depression had not fully gripped New York as yet. There was still a sort of shining plenty. Soon the sun began to break through the morning cloudiness and a fresh cold wind blew through the cross streets.

His impression of the Stuyvesant Bank was not very different from all his later impressions except that the details had more depth and breadth than they ever had again—the converted brownstone front, the illusion of leisure, the small fire near the front door burning in the open grate. There was none of the untidiness of E. P. Rush & Company. Everything was spick-and-span in a polite, aggressive way, as offices were in New York. It all had something of the present, amply able to compete with new trends but the more confident because of an established, dignified past.

Gus, the doorman, looked younger then but he already presented the appearance of a trusted chauffeur in a wealthy but dignified family, as well he might. Until a few years before, Gus had driven the black limousine of Mr. Mortimer Waldron, one of the largest clients of the bank, and at Mr. Waldron's death the bank had administered Gus as it had the rest of the Waldron estate. As the vanguard of the Stuyvesant service, he felt responsible for anyone who turned from the sidewalk to the bank's front door.

"Morning, sir," Gus said.

He was the first person who had said good morning to Charles in New York City and it had not been wholly necessary and this was undoubtedly the reason that Charles went to the hospital every few days to see Gus after Gus had slipped once on the icy sidewalk and had broken his hip while hurrying to open a car door for a depositor. The gesture had not hurt Charles because Tony Burton called at the hospital himself, and so had nearly everyone else, after Tony Burton went, but Charles had gone there first. He had never thought of any favorable impression it might make. He had gone because Gus had said good morning to him that first morning.

Joe was there, too, and Joe, too, looked younger. It was not long before that he had left the detective division of the police force, but Joe fitted there already. He was already part policeman, part greeter, and part club doorman.

"Are you looking for someone?" Joe did not call him sir but it was a polite, interested question. Joe was already classifying him and Joe never made a mistake, or hardly ever.

The gilded tellers' cages and the high tables with the pens and blotters and deposit slips only looked like additional ornaments in a large comfortable room. He saw the roll-top desks of the officers by the front windows and then the green carpet with the two large flat-top desks upon it and next the other smaller desks grouped more closely together on the uncarpeted floor. He saw the small marble staircase that descended unobtrusively to the vaults, and he saw Mr. Cheseborough at his inconspicuous desk in the comfortable nook near the open fire, ready to help old ladies with their checks and to lead them to the ladies' tellers. He saw all the Stuyvesant Bank just as he always saw it later.

"I wonder if I could see Mr. Arthur Slade," he said, "if he's not too busy."

He always remembered that Joe did not tell him to wait, or that he would see whether or not Mr. Slade would see him. Instead he walked with Charles across the room toward the edge of the green carpet. Arthur Slade was seated behind one of those two assistant vice-president desks, firmly on the green carpet—at the same desk which now belonged to Charles himself.

"I don't know whether you remember me or not," Charles said, but Arthur Slade remembered him.

When Arthur Slade asked him if he would like to walk around upstairs and see the trust and the tax and the statistical departments, nothing had been said about his working at the Stuyvesant. Charles was already experienced enough to know that it was wise not to be too eager. When Arthur Slade introduced him to Walter Gibbs, who was one of the key men in the statistical department at the time, and then excused himself because there was something he had to attend to downstairs, still nothing definite had been said.

The statistical department occupied what had once been the rear bedroom on the second floor of the brownstone house, with more desks in the dressing room and more in the hall. It was a compliment, though he did not know it, to be left in the statistical department talking to Walter Gibbs, but even when Arthur Slade returned and took him back downstairs and introduced him to Mr. Burton and Mr. Merry nothing was said directly. The whole problem of personnel was handled in a rather haphazard manner in those days, except in the statistical department. Arthur Slade must have vouched for him because the conversations were all general and no one asked him anything definite about his previous experience. An hour must have elapsed before Charles said he must not take any more of Mr. Slade's time and thanked him for showing him around. It was only then that Arthur Slade asked him whether he would like to try it in the statistical department.

"You can't tell," Arthur Slade said. "It might be worth trying. How much were you getting at Rush & Company?"

Of course they could not pay him what he had been getting at Rush & Company but there was a future in the statistical department. You were a part of the family. It was like E. P. Rush & Company again—one big happy family, as though all families were necessarily happy.

Yet the Stuyvesant may have been more like a family than many other business organizations. There were the same jealousies, the same incompetent poor relations, the same feuds. There was also a sort of loyalty, as much as there could be loyalty to as cool and grim an institution as a bank—but the Stuyvesant Bank was a force beyond the control of any individual or group. The president and officers might fix the rules and policies under the general advice of the directors' board but those rules and policies themselves had a way of changing in a manner no individual could anticipate. They were swayed by practices and theories of other vanished personalities, by economic laws of loan and interest that stretched into the hazy past of the goldsmith guilds in the Middle Ages.

The Stuyvesant was the aggregate of the character of many individuals, who merged a part of their personal strivings and ambitions into a common effort. It was like a head of living coral rising above the surf, a small outcropping of a greater reef. He only knew that in the end it was stronger than any one person. In the end, no matter what the rewards might be, a part of one's life remained built into that complicated structure. They were all asses following their bundles of hay, the clerks, the tellers, the department heads, the vice-presidents, the president and the directors, and Gus himself standing on the Avenue. They were all on an assembly line, but you could not blame the line. It was too cumbersome, too inhumanly human for anyone to blame. At least he and Nancy knew they were part of the blueprint. They would never have met if it had not been for the Stuyvesant Bank, not that the bank knew or cared. They would never have had the children. They would never have built the house at Sycamore Park.

They must have both been thinking of this one spring before the war just after they had moved to Sycamore Park. It was a Saturday afternoon and Charles was mowing the lawn. His son Bill was raking up the short grass in little piles and Nancy was sitting under a tree sewing and Evelyn was reading *The Purple Fairy Book*. He had just reached a difficult place near the recently planted rhododendron bushes when Nancy called him, and when the whirring sound of the mower stopped her voice sounded unusually distinct.

"Charley."

"Yes," he said, "what is it?"

"Why was it they sent you down there?"

"Down where?" he asked.

"Down to Pine Street. Down to Burrell, Jessup and Cockburn."

He stared at her blankly before he understood what she had in mind. "It had something to do with that fund," he said, "that Burrell School fund and the trust report. It was the Burrell estate, wasn't it? I don't exactly remember."

Nancy dropped the shirt she was mending.

"It's funny," she said. "I can't remember either."

They both must have been thinking that there would have been no lawn mowing or shirt mending or mortgage or Evelyn or Bill, they would never even have known each other, if it had not been for that trip downtown. It could not have been an important errand because he was new in the bank and yet they had not sent one of the regular messengers.

"It's funny," Nancy said again, "we can't remember."

That evening after supper when Nancy was upstairs hearing the children say their prayers, Charles did remember some of it by thinking but not trying too hard to think.

Charles had been like a mountain climber clinging to a precarious foothold up there in the statistical department. As there were no extra desks he had been stationed at a table in the corner of that converted bedroom, and one day Arthur Slade had come up from downstairs, which was unusual. He would not have noticed what Arthur Slade said to Mr. Gibbs if he had not felt at the time very dependent on Arthur Slade. Arthur Slade was a little like a commissioned officer that morning, entering the orderly room to speak to the sergeant major.

"Oh, Walter," he said to Mr. Gibbs, "where's the analysis?" Charles was beginning to realize already that Walter Gibbs had lapses and moments of forgetfulness.

"I've just finished checking it," Walter Gibbs said. "I was just going to send it down. I didn't know you wanted it in a hurry."

"Where is it?" Arthur Slade asked. "Those lawyers are meeting us tomorrow. It should have been in the mail last night. That's all right, it's my fault. I should have told you." It was probably not his fault because he never slipped up on things but Arthur Slade was always careful never to blame anyone when it was not necessary.

"Jessup's just been telephoning," Arthur Slade said. "It ought to be given to him personally. Is there anyone here you could send down to Pine Street?"

"Why, yes," Walter Gibbs said, "there's Gray."

All law offices, particularly in New York, Charles often thought, had a self-conscious atmosphere, which was very much like their stationery. Their pictures and chairs and tables and the personnel of the outer offices were all selected to create an air of erudition, security and ponderous judicial calm. The boy who greeted Burrell, Jessup and Cockburn visitors noted Charles's name and that of the partner he wished to see on a memorandum pad. Then he rose slowly and walked down a corridor, leaving Charles seated by a round mahogany table with his brief case on his knees gazing at a steel engraving of Chief Justice Marshall. Charles found himself thinking of all the other people who must have sat in that waiting room, rearranging their thoughts. He felt as if he were in the hands of Burrell, Jessup and Cockburn and that he must tell the truth and nothing but the truth. The office boy came back and led the way down a corridor to the partners' offices.

"You can go right in," the boy said.

It was obviously Mr. Jessup's office because his name was on the door, Clive W. Jessup, but when Charles opened the door he was in another outer office, lighted by a single window that looked across a few low roofs to the blank wall of a tall building. There was a new leather couch and a stiff armchair and a Burgundy-red carpet and behind a mahogany secretary's desk Nancy was sitting typing a letter.

Charles stood watching her because she did not look up when he came in. Her eyes were on her open shorthand book. Her fingers moved over the typewriter keys easily, almost contemptuously. She wore a plain silk shirtwaist. Her light brown hair was done up in a knot. Her lips were pressed in an even line and her whole face looked cool and aloof. Her skin was as clear as her white silk waist but there was a faint natural touch of color in her cheeks. There was no lipstick. Nancy never used it in business hours.

She did not look up until she had finished the paragraph she was typing and then she looked straight at him, but she did not smile. Her eyes were greenish-gray and they were wide, almost too wide, apart.

"Do you want to see Mr. Jessup," she asked, "or do you want to leave something for him?"

"I'm from the Stuyvesant Bank," Charles said, and that was the first thing he ever said to Nancy. "They sent me over with some papers. I'm supposed to hand them to Mr. Jessup."

"You're supposed to," Nancy repeated, and she sounded as though she were faintly amused but there was no way of telling. "What are they about?"

"They didn't tell me," Charles said. "They don't tell me much up there."

"Well, Mr. Jessup's busy now," Nancy said. "You can leave them with me and I'll see that he gets them."

"I'm afraid I'd better wait," Charles said.

"Haven't you got anything else to do back at that bank?" Nancy asked. "I'll see he gets them. I'm pretty good at handing people papers."

"So am I," Charles said, and he smiled.

"Mr. Jessup's in conference," Nancy said, "and he won't be free for half an hour."

"I'm supposed to give them to him personally," Charles said.

"What are you in that bank, a messenger?" Nancy asked.

"No," Charles said. "I'm in the statistical department."

"Have you been there long?"

"Of course I haven't," Charles said, "or they wouldn't be sending me on errands. This is the first important job that's been offered me."

Then she smiled. It was the first time he ever saw her smile.

"Well," she said, "take off your overcoat and sit down, if you want to waste your time."

She was much further along than he was then. She was Mr. Jessup's executive secretary and she was being paid forty-five dollars a week and they could never have been married if she had not kept that job.

"If I bother you waiting here," Charles said, "I can wait outside."

"You don't bother me," Nancy said. "This is my last letter."

He never bothered her, she always said, right from the beginning, and most men did. There were a great many maladjusted junior partners in that office.

"You didn't seem to have me on your mind," she told him once. "We just sat there and talked. And sex didn't seem to enter into it, but I suppose it did. It was all perfectly natural. God knows why it was so natural"—but then everything always was with him and Nancy.

[illegible]

[illegible]

[illegible] asked. [illegible]

[illegible]

[illegible]

[illegible]

[illegible]

[illegible]

[illegible]

[illegible]

PART THREE

Please Continue [illegible]

The cart on the subsidiary line [illegible] appreciating the branch for them [illegible] or the uses in roadbed, you could [illegible] that was especially as it was [illegible] as the train passed through the [illegible] Then came the hollow rumble [illegible] [illegible] the low [illegible] the short tunnel [illegible] [illegible] now often [illegible] [illegible] the year and [illegible] [illegible] always wanted [illegible] [illegible] he always added [illegible] [illegible] was never heard [illegible] [illegible]

[illegible] the three [illegible] Roger Bla[illegible] [illegible] expression [illegible] [illegible] part of [illegible] [illegible] of Rush [illegible] [illegible] a working [illegible] [illegible] Besides, he was [illegible] [illegible] knowledge [illegible] [illegible] as it did [illegible] [illegible] only recently [illegible] [illegible] Boston [illegible] [illegible] considered himself [illegible] [illegible] those quaint stor[illegible] [illegible] and even [illegible] [illegible]

[illegible] Charles that [illegible] [illegible] got back he [illegible] [illegible] at the First Nation[illegible] [illegible] Rush & Company [illegible] [illegible] had been talking [illegible] [illegible] the Old Colony [illegible]

1

Please Leave No Articles

The cars on the subsidiary line that led to Clyde were always antiquated, relegated to the branch for their final tour of duty. As they rocked and rattled on the uneven roadbed, you could tell from the sounds exactly where the train was, especially as it was approaching Clyde. There was a stifled roar as the train passed through the cut that came just before Brainard's Crossing. Then came the hollow rumble of the trestle that spanned Whiting's Creek. After the train crossed the low farmlands just outside of Clyde there came the louder roar of the short tunnel and with it an instant of darkness, always startling no matter how often one had experienced it, and the brakeman's voice mingled with the roar and the darkness.

"Clyde," he always shouted. "Clyde"; and if it was the three-thirty train out of Boston he always added, "Please leave no articles in the car," an admonition that was never heard, as far as Charles could remember, on any other train.

Charles had taken the three-thirty because he had stopped for a while in Boston to do what Roger Blakesley would have called sweetening certain contacts. It was an expression which especially revolted him, but he recognized it as an essential part of business to drop in, now that he was in Boston, on a few old graduates of Rush & Company and on other acquaintances. He always did so on his rare visits there because you never could tell when it might help to have a working relationship with someone on State or Congress or Milk Street. Besides he was the only executive in the Stuyvesant with much of a firsthand knowledge of Boston. When any Boston problem came up at the Stuyvesant, as it did occasionally, Charles was always called in to help with it. It was only recently that Roger Blakesley, too, had been making himself helpful with Boston problems, and in the last few months Roger seemed to have considered himself something of an authority, going so far as to tell a few of those quaint stories about Boston trustees that always went so well in New York and even giving the impression of knowing the subjects of those anecdotes.

It occurred to Charles that in his talk with Tony Burton and Stephen Merry when he got back he might say casually that he had dropped in on Tommy Sage at the First National, that they had known each other since those days at Rush & Company, and that some of the boys at the Boston Safe Deposit had been talking about United Fruit and that he had asked Bill Jenkins at the Old Colony about United Shoe. Bill was an old Rush &

Company graduate who was a director. It would be possible to make these allusions without any undue emphasis. As a matter of fact, his hours in Boston had been very useful in a business way.

When he stopped by at Rush & Company, old Lawrence Stoker had been surprisingly glad to see him and had asked him to lunch at the Union Club. Everybody had been glad to see him and everybody had regarded him in that polite, embarrassed way that they often reserved for old friends who had done well in New York and who must therefore be very prosperous. As always there was a suspicion about prosperity that came too easily.

It would not hurt at all to tell Tony Burton about his lunch at the Union Club with Mr. Stoker. The invitation in itself made Charles realize the long distance he had traveled since the old days. Though Mr. Stoker called him Charley and he still called Mr. Stoker mister, they were almost on an equal basis because of the Stuyvesant Bank. He was both an assistant vice-president of the Stuyvesant and a bright graduate back on the college campus. They had old-fashioned cocktails, and this in itself showed that Lawrence Stoker felt that the occasion demanded a special effort. There was a warm, mellow glow about their meeting and they spoke first of old times at Rush & Company and then edged gradually into the present.

"You boys who go away to New York," Lawrence Stoker said, and he looked across the table at Charles as though he were someone who had lived for a long while in a foreign country, "you go and you never want to come back." Charles believed that Mr. Stoker's words had a tentative, suggestive note. "Of course, we can't offer you enough to get you back. You boys get used to high living in New York."

"And low thinking," Charles said, and he laughed. He wondered how much Mr. Stoker thought he was earning. Obviously, Mr. Stoker was judging from appearances, as they always did in Boston.

"Of course," Mr. Stoker said, "money doesn't go as far in New York as it does here."

"It doesn't go far anywhere if you have a wife and two children," Charles said.

"Two? I didn't know you had two, Charley," Mr. Stoker said. "I thought you only had a boy. That boy must be growing up."

"Yes," Charles said, "Bill's getting to be a big boy now."

"Where's he going to school?" That was a question they always asked in Boston.

"He's going to one of those suburban country day schools now," Charles said, "but he wants to go to Exeter."

"It doesn't matter so much where he goes if you're going to send him to Dartmouth," Mr. Stoker said. "I hope you're not going to send that boy to Dartmouth."

You were always placed in Boston by your beginnings and Mr. Stoker had never forgotten that Charles had gone to Dartmouth.

"But you never acted like a Dartmouth man," Mr. Stoker said. "Moulton always said so. He always said he shouldn't have let you go."

If he had stayed there would have been nothing much for him at Rush & Company and both of them must have known it, but it was very reassuring to be there at lunch with Mr. Stoker toying with the impossible.

"You wouldn't have wanted me, you know," Charles said. "I couldn't have been a partner."

"I wouldn't say that," Mr. Stoker said. "The war would have made a difference."

His having gone to the war would have been a gesture that could have erased the educational stigma. It would have been almost as good as having been on a Harvard team.

"Three boys from the office were killed," Mr. Stoker said.

"I was just on an air strip," Charles said. "I should have stayed at the bank."

"Well," Mr. Stoker said, "it wouldn't have hurt you one damn bit at Rush & Company. It's too bad about Arthur Slade. Are they going to move you up?"

He had not thought that Mr. Stoker knew enough about him to connect him with Arthur Slade. He sounded as though he were asking Charles if there had been an injury on the football field and if the coach were going to call him from the bench.

"Of course I hope so," Charles said. "You never can tell what's going to happen, can you?" Sitting with Mr. Stoker in the Union Club looking at the bare trees of Boston Common, it was pleasant to conjecture that he might actually become a vice-president of the Stuyvesant Bank.

"Mr. Stoker," he said, "have you ever heard of anything over-the-counter called the Nickerson Cordage Company? They sent me up here to ask about it. The company's in Clyde. I'm going to take the three-thirty train down there. It's funny, isn't it, to be going back to Clyde." He wished he had not said it was funny going back to Clyde . . .

"Clyde," the brakeman was calling. "Clyde. Kindly leave no articles in the car."

He had been looking out of the window. He had seen the sodden April brown of the fields. He had seen the muddy banks and the low tide of Whiting's Creek. He had put on his overcoat and had pulled his suitcase from the rack above him. In a way it was just as though he were coming back from Boston after a day at E. P. Rush & Company and yet he was startled when the name was called. Even when he saw the drab station and the platform and the baggage trucks and the river and the old houses and the lunch-room across the street from the station, he could only half believe he was in Clyde again. It was all so entirely unchanged. It seemed only to have been waiting for him through a long hard winter instead of for almost twenty years.

He had always been as sure as one could be of anything that someday he would return to Clyde. It was an assurance based on a sense of dramatic fitness and a suspicion, that must always have been in the back of his mind, that something there needed to be finished and that he must finish it some day. For years he had not avoided thinking of it. He often spoke of Clyde to Nancy and rather enjoyed it, and Bill and Evelyn often asked him to tell stories about the Webster Grammar School and the Meaders and the Masons and old Miss Sarah Hewitt and Grandmama and Aunt Dorothea and his older brother, Sam. He had never brought them to Clyde but at least they knew its folklore. It never hurt him to tell about it. He even told Evelyn about Jessica Lovell, a little girl with filmy dresses and patent leather shoes who lived in a fantastic house with a widow's walk and a cupola and who played in a garden with box-bordered edges and flower beds stamped out in amusing shapes like cookies out of dough. He felt no pain any longer. He was completely free of Clyde. It was deep beneath the waters of experience.

His thoughts of returning to Clyde had usually been in the form of fantasies. His stay in Clyde was always brief, in these fantasies. He might be motoring north with Nancy during his summer vacation from the bank on their way to spend a few days together in Maine. They would be driving up from Boston in a new convertible with red leather seats and curiously enough the car would always be a Cadillac and he would say to Nancy, as though the idea had struck him suddenly:

"Let's turn off Route 1 and drive through Clyde."

Nancy would be wearing a new tailored broadcloth suit, the color of which was never definite, and Nancy would say:

"Why not, if we're going past it?"

They would drive down Johnson Street very slowly and they would never once get out of the car in that fantasy, but he would actually stop the car in front of the Lovell house and they would sit there commenting on it, as strangers often did who motored through Clyde.

"That's where she lived," he would say. "It's perfect Federalist architecture, but it's sterile, isn't it?" And she would say:

"Sterile as a test tube. Maybe she's in there now." And he would say:

"Possibly, but it isn't as bad as those Currier and Ives temples in upstate New York." And Nancy would say:

"You're the one who said it was sterile. All right, I've seen it. Check"—and she would tap the road map with her finger. She always loved to read the road map—"We can't stay here all day if we're going to spend the night at Poland Spring. What else is there to see?" And he would say:

"Well, there's the Webster Grammar School and the courthouse and the cemetery." And she would say:

"Let's skip the courthouse and the cemetery."

Then he would start the car and they would go down Dock Street and up Spruce Street so that she could see where he had lived and she would say when she saw the house:

"What, haven't they got a bronze plaque on it?"—and if there was time he would show her the Judge's house on Gow Street, and she would say:

"Yes, dear. Light a cigarette for me, will you? I know why you're so peculiar now. I'll tell you what you can do. You can give them a tower someday with chimes in it. What's the best way back to Route 1?"

Then they would be leaving. He would toss away his cigarette and pull down his Panama hat. Somehow in this fantasy he always thought of himself in a Panama hat.

When he was in England he had often daydreamed his way through another fantasy. In this one he would find himself traveling on Route 1 in an army car with the Air Corps insignia on the door. He would be alone in the back seat, just home from overseas, and a technical sergeant would be driving, and he would say, just on the spur of the moment:

"Turn right at the next crossroad, Sergeant. I want to go through Clyde," and when they reached the corner of Dock and Johnson streets he would say:

"Drive ahead, Sergeant, and I'll tell you when to stop. I want to get out for a minute. I haven't been here for quite a while."

The army car would stop in front of Walters's Drugstore and he would get out and stand on the sidewalk and light a cigarette. No one would speak to him but there would be a group of three or four people a few yards away whom he had known once but whom he could not remember. He would glance toward them in pleasant half-recognition. Then he would toss away his cigarette and turn back to the waiting car, and he would hear someone say in a low voice:

"Isn't that Charley Gray—and isn't he a lieutenant colonel?"

He would give no sign of having heard.

"All right, Sergeant," he would say, "let's go," and the army car would be moving down Dock Street.

It was strange, in spite of those occasional rehearsals, that he was not prepared at all for what he saw when he got off the train. He must have thought of Clyde in terms of climax instead of anticlimax, but instead Clyde was like the churchyard in Gray's "Elegy." When the train moved away from the station it was like the lowing herd winding o'er the lea.

He was standing on the platform holding his suitcase, an outlander now, a stranger, but at the same time nothing was strange to him at all. There was the same smell of coal smoke from the train, the same damp in the air, the same chill of frost in the ground and the same dull, forbidding April sky that he had known. It had been raining and the roofs were wet and the wind made tiny ripples in the puddles in the street and the clouds still hung sullenly over the town. It was going to rain again. The cars were parked about the station in the old disorderly way and a single car was waiting for passengers in the taxi space but everyone was walking home. The driver, a gangling boy of about seventeen, reminded Charles of Earl Wilkins but of course he was not Earl because he was too young to be.

"Taxi, sir?" he asked, and his voice sounded like Earl's.

It never occurred to Charles until he heard the driver's voice that he would not be walking home to Spruce Street, now that he was off the train. He had been thinking of himself and Clyde without ever planning what he would do when he arrived there. Now he did not know where to go and he did not want to go anywhere. He wanted to be alone but he could not stand there holding the suitcase.

"Taxi, sir," the driver called again. The taxis at the station had always called strangers sir.

His cousin Jerry and his Aunt Ruth Marchby were in Clyde, as far as he knew, through his mother's letters from Kansas City. They might be hurt if he did not stay with them but it seemed abrupt and almost rude to appear unexpectedly when he should have telephoned that morning from Boston. No one ever dropped in suddenly on anyone in Clyde.

"Yes. Just a minute," he said.

There were the Masons. He knew they still lived on Spruce Street, also from his mother's letters, and the Masons, too, might be hurt if he did not stay with them, but Mr. and Mrs. Mason would be very old and it might be upsetting to them.

"I guess I've got to go somewhere," he said, and he found himself staring at the driver again. "Are you any relation to Earl Wilkins?"—and the driver said that he was Earl Wilkins's son.

"Let's see," he said. "I haven't been here for quite a while. Is the Clyde Hotel still running?"

In all his years in Clyde he had hardly been inside the Clyde Hotel. It was where drummers stayed and visitors who came to do business with Wright-Sherwin and the mills.

"You mean the inn," Earl Wilkins's son said. "They call it the Clyde Inn now."

"Tell your father," Charles began, and he felt self-conscious and unsure of himself, "tell him Charley Gray was asking for him. We used to go to school together." He had never thought that he would have to introduce himself in Clyde. "I guess you'd better take my suitcase and take it up to the hotel, I mean the inn. Tell them at the inn I'll be along in a little while. I think I'll walk around." He took a dollar out of his pocket though he felt awkward about tipping Earl Wilkins's son. "Just take the bag and keep the change."

"Thanks," Earl's son said. "Thanks a lot."

"And don't forget to tell your father Charley Gray was asking for him."

"I'll tell him all right," Earl's son said, "and thanks a lot." At least he no longer called him sir.

It was not at all like those stories he had read of persons returning to the scenes of their childhood. He was not Rip van Winkle after a twenty-year sleep. He was simply back in Clyde on an earlier train than usual.

There were a few places that he did not want to see—the part of Johnson Street where the Lovell home stood, the Judge's house on Gow Street, and Spruce Street; so he walked up Fillmore Street from the station, not along Chestnut, as he would have if he had been going to Dock Street and then home. First there were the shabby rooming houses near the station, where the workers in the shoeshops and Wright-Sherwin lived, and then came the larger houses as Fillmore approached the northern end of Johnson Street, but he was not thinking of the street. The wind and the dampness of the air were so characteristic of reluctant spring that he might have been waiting in front of the courthouse again for Jessica to come by, just by accident, in her Dodge car. It was too late for snowdrops already but in a flower bed with a southern exposure blue grape hyacinths and a few crocuses might be blooming, flaming orange, white and blue. He saw none and he did not look for them but he was as certain that they would be there as that there would be robins in the budding branches of the lilacs. The willow branches would be turning yellow and on some wooded slope beneath fallen oak leaves there might even be hepaticas. Spring was like autumn, except that everything was coming to life instead of dying. In the country the peeper frogs would be singing in the puddles that could not yet soak through the sodden, frosty ground. Clyde, unhindered by its ghosts, was approaching its annual resurrection.

The Episcopal Church, with the flat tombs in its small churchyard, was on the corner of Fillmore and Johnson streets. He did not look up at its steeple and its cross but he remembered that his Aunt Jane always said as she passed it that she was glad she was a Unitarian. She had said so on the hot summer's day when he had walked past it with her and Dorothea on their way to the Historical Society to hear his mother read her paper. He was walking in the same direction now and soon the Historical Society was in front of him, behind its cast-iron fence on its moist brown lawn, but there were no groups of people waiting for a meeting. "Clyde Historical Society," a new sign by the old brass cannon read. "Open weekdays, 2 P.M. to 5 P.M., except Saturdays." It was a quarter before five.

A bell clanged when he opened the front door, like an old shop bell. There was the same disorder in the hall, the same two antique settles he remembered, and the flintlock muskets, the fire buckets and the blunderbuss. The light in the hall was gray but somehow strong, because the days were growing longer.

The custodian of the Historical Society, he remembered, had always been Miss Smythe, but it was a Miss Smythe of the present who appeared to answer the bell. She had the same grim, watchful expression—she was just the age Miss Smythe had been—and she wore a shabby buttoned sweater because the place was cold. She was looking at him with Miss Smythe's lack of welcome and he would not have been surprised if she had told him to run along as Miss Smythe had when he and Jackie Mason had called there once.

"We close at five o'clock," she said.

"Yes," Charles said, "I know. I just wanted to look around for a few minutes."

"There won't be time to see much before five o'clock," she said.

"Yes," Charles said again. "I just wanted to look around." He was simply another of the objects in that indiscriminate mixture of things in the Historical Society which all belonged somewhere else and to some other age.

"The admission is twenty-five cents," the custodian was saying. "The South Sea ornaments and the ship models are in the room to the left and there are collections upstairs, too, but we close at five o'clock."

The white bone ship still stood in the center of the room to the left. The

Chinese pagoda with its wind bells and the sextants were still on the tables and the ship pictures were still on the walls, still plowing under full sail through their conventional canvas seas. The chairs were in rows in the assembly room, facing the same stage on which his mother had stood, and he could almost hear his mother's voice. He could still remember the opening of that paper.

"Every one of us here, I am sure, has seen a certain gray stone house with a mansard roof . . . As Longfellow, Miss Lyte's old friend, expressed it so beautifully once—'the beauty and mystery of the ships, and the magic of the sea.'"

Nothing was ever entirely over.

"I'm sure we are all most grateful to Mrs. Gray for a charming paper and a delightful afternoon," he could hear Mr. Lovell saying.

Nothing was ever entirely over, but he still wondered why anyone should have brought a suit of samurai armor from Japan and why it should be resting upstairs now in the Historical Society, meaninglessly and yet with some hidden meaning.

Before he left he walked to the lawn in back where tea had been served that summer afternoon. He knew the exact place where he had stood with his mother and father and he remembered exactly where Mr. Lovell had knelt on the grass and had thrown his arms around Jessica. He could almost hear the locusts in the elm trees.

"Pa," Jessica was saying, and he could see her lacy white dress and her white socks and her patent leather slippers, "can't we go home now, please?"

The clock in the Episcopal Church was striking and then he heard the other bells. He remembered the deeper timbre of the Baptist Church and the almost nasal ring of the Unitarian bell. It was five o'clock and the Historical Society closed at exactly five.

2

Home Free

It was still too early in the season for raking up front yards and too early for ball-playing by the courthouse. Though the stores on Dock Street were open until six, everyone was hurrying home without lingering on the corners. There were a good many people on Dock Street but for some time Charles recognized no one, though they all had types of features he remembered, and the whole appearance of the street was just the same. The Dock Street Bank had its old grim, evening look. There was a display of seeds and gardening tools in the hardware store, a promise for the future that did not apply to the present. The North End bus was moving up the street and a few mud-spattered cars were following it. There was the same slow sound of traffic that he had always known, and the gentle, splashing sound of overshoes upon the wet brick sidewalks. All of Clyde was going home to supper.

It was just the time in the evening when everyone used to gather in the Meaders' back yard. The light was much the same as Charles remembered it. The shadows would be deeper downstairs in the barn and behind the carriage shed and you could run and hide behind the cordwood or behind the pung in the corner of the barn while the voice of whoever might be It counted five hundred by fives. You would hide where you could watch Home, which was the Meaders' back porch, or else you would sneak around the carriage house and wait until the coast was clear. There was always that uncertain moment for deciding whether to risk everything and run or whether to wait longer and risk being seen. Then there was that dash across the yard and the sharp, triumphant moment when you touched the steps of the Meaders' back porch first and shouted, "Home Free!"

In a way, Charles thought, Dock Street was like the Meaders' yard, now that he was walking down it. He was back at the start of everything, among the hidden reasons for everything, but he was not yet home. He saw the window display in Walters's Drugstore that had always been created for April, pyramids of bottles containing assorted spring tonics—Beef, Iron and Wine, Sulphur and Molasses, and also remedies that were guaranteed to break up a cold in twenty-four hours, all connected together by paper streamers which led to a colored cardboard cross section of the human nose and throat.

Beyond the bottles he could see the soda fountain and the booths, all newer than they had been but in exactly the same position. He could see a boy, wearing a Clyde High School sweater, and a girl, with a scarf tied over her head and wearing a green-and-white mackinaw, standing by the fountain. He should have known who they were, but of course he did not. He had stopped in front of Walters's Drugstore without realizing that he had stopped.

A woman was walking toward him holding a bag of groceries and it seemed to him that he should have known her, too, though there was nothing distinctive about her except that her face belonged to Clyde. He remembered thinking that she was too old to be wearing one of those silk scarves tied over her head and that it was not becoming. The scarf was too bright for her gray coat and its worn fur collar and for her blue mittens. Suddenly Charles recognized her—when the light from the drugstore window struck her face, making it look less worn and tired. They had been to Walters's Drugstore together. They had stood by the fountain just as that boy and girl were standing now, and he had often worn a maroon sweater with "CHS" lettered on it. It was Doris Wormser. Her yellow hair was darker, there were deep lines on her face, but it was Doris Wormser, and she recognized him, too, at almost the same moment.

"Why, Charley Gray," she said, and her voice was high and nasal, although he remembered that it had sounded delightfully musical once.

"Why, hello, Doris," he said.

"Well, of all the people I didn't expect to see," Doris Wormser said. "It's the funniest thing. I can't believe it, Charley."

"Well, I can't either. How about a soda, Doris?"

"Oh, no," she said, "I couldn't. I've got to go home and get supper on," and then she laughed. "But it's funny, right in front of the drugstore. You look like everything's agreed with you. You look just the same."

"So do you," he said. "Exactly the same."

"Oh, you go on, Charley," Doris Wormser said. Her voice rose as it did when he used to tell her in high school that she was awfully pretty. "You wait till I tell Willie."

Then he remembered that Doris Wormser had married Willie Woodbury.

"How's Willie?" he asked her.

"He still has the farm machinery agency. Let him know if you want to buy a tractor," Doris said. "We've got three children now, all boys. We're living in the old Adams house. You know, on River Street."

"Oh, yes," he said, and he was glad that she took it for granted that he knew. "I'd like to come and see Willie and the boys."

She smiled at him and held out her left hand because she had the bag of groceries in her right.

"I wish you would," she said, "if you get time, Charley," but she obviously could not ask him then because she had to get supper on and there was a place for everything in Clyde and everything was in its place.

"I've only got two children," he said. "A boy and a girl."

"Yes," she said, "I know. I always knew you'd get ahead, Charley."

He knew what she was saying. She was saying that their lives were entirely separate and that everything was in its place in Clyde, but she was saying it without bitterness or rebuke.

"If you get time, come down and see us," she said, but at the same time she was saying that she would understand if he did not. Just because they had been to high school together was no reason why he should go down to River Street. She was saying it without saying it and of course he understood. "But it's funny, isn't it, right in front of the drugstore, just as though we were meeting for the picture show."

She looked away from him up Dock Street and he knew what she was thinking. She was thinking that people would be wondering to whom she was talking so long in front of Walters's Drugstore. She was thinking that everyone would have noticed that she had met Charley Gray, not that it mattered any longer, not that it had ever mattered.

"Well," she said, "I've got to be getting on. It's been nice seeing you."

"Tell Willie he's lucky," Charles said.

"Oh, you go on," Doris Wormser said. "Good-by now, Charley."

In Charles's recollection, the Clyde Inn had been a dingy hotel that one passed thoughtlessly on one's way to the public library. He remembered that strangers sat on its porch in summer, their chairs tilted back, their feet on the railing, staring in a bored way at Dock Street and already abysmally convinced that Clyde had no recreational possibilities. There had been no service during prohibition for transporting liquor to a lonely drummer's room and there were certainly no merry girls on call for an informal evening party, because the hotel was right on Dock Street and everyone would have known about it. It had always been a place where one took a compulsory one night's rest and ate a mediocre meal and passed on to somewhere else.

That was the way it was when Charles had lived in Clyde but things were different now. The hotel had been transformed into one of those jolly little taverns, a delightful place for a weary motorist to drop in for the night. Everything had been done to bring back its Georgian lines and its new porch was solid and substantial, behind a thick grouping of evergreen shrubs. Its doorway and blinds were painted Colonial smoky gray and there was a pretty sign with a stagecoach and also the approving stamp of the American Automobile Association and the Lodging-for-a-Night Association.

"The Clyde Inn," the sign read, and beneath it in smaller letters, "The Fife and Drum Taproom, A Murgatroyd Hotel."

Each detail contrived to give a gentle hint that the Clyde Inn was a suitable place for a sophisticated, urban visitor compelled to stay in a provincial town. It was a Murgatroyd Hotel, and the inference was that Mr. Murgatroyd knew how to make you comfortable with a foam-rubber or an innerspring mattress and a private bath. Then, too, there was the Fife and Drum Taproom. It was disturbing to enter the Clyde Inn after his meeting with Doris Wormser. Its bright upholstered chairs and the mushroom-like ash receptacles that could not tip over did not belong to Clyde. Neither did the clerk behind the informal, semi-Colonial desk. He was not a Clyde native, he was trained by the Murgatroyd chain.

"We've been waiting for you, Mr. Gray," the clerk said. You could tell it was a piece of the Murgatroyd thoughtfulness that made that nice young man immediately catch his name and realize that he came from a larger world. "We were afraid you might have lost yourself somewhere," and he laughed in a way that indicated that one could hardly lose oneself in Clyde.

"Oh, no, I was just walking around," Charles said.

"Well, we're glad you didn't get lost," the clerk said, and he laughed again, "because you're only our fifth guest today. Things are slow this time of year, but you ought to see us in summer. How long are you staying with us, Mr. Gray?"

"Just overnight, I'm afraid," Charles said.

"I suppose you're making business calls," the clerk said. It was a natural question. Obviously he was not a tourist or he would not have been stopping there in April.

"Yes, a few calls," Charles said. "I'm just passing through."

"Mr. Jaeckel's here, calling on Wright-Sherwin," the clerk said. "He's from the Henderson-Wilckes Pump Company, the New York office. Perhaps you're acquainted with Mr. Jaeckel."

"No," Charles said, "I don't know him but I know the company."

The clerk did not belong to Clyde and plainly he was lonely.

"We have some nice little industries here in Clyde," the clerk said. "There's the shoe business. Clyde's an old shoe town. We have some nice ship pictures in the taproom. Mr. Murgatroyd collected them personally. We still build boats here, runabouts and cabin cruisers, and then there's Wright-Sherwin, brass precision instruments."

"Yes," Charles said, "I've heard about Wright-Sherwin."

"It's a fine company," the clerk said, "but that isn't all there is to Clyde. I wish you could see us in summer."

"Ought I to see you in summer?" Charles asked.

"You really ought to, Mr. Gray," the clerk said. "There's a lot to do in Clyde in summer."

"Is there?" Charles asked. "What is there to do?" He was interrupted by a distant strain of music and he recognized the tune. "Have you got a juke box here?"

"Yes," the clerk answered. "In the Fife and Drum Room. You have to have something these days," and he laughed apologetically. "Some of the local boys and girls come to the Fife and Drum Room for beer in the afternoons but they don't disturb anyone. You were asking what there is to do in Clyde? It isn't fair to Clyde to see it in April. I know how I felt when I came here a year ago myself, right from the Stars and Bars at Atlanta. Did you ever stop at the Stars and Bars, Mr. Gray?"

"No," Charles said. "I never stopped in Atlanta."

"Well, it's quite a shock to come from there to here," the clerk said. "I didn't think I was going to be able to stand it. I didn't realize the charm this place has, or the quaintness. It doesn't quite come through in April."

He was right, it did not quite come through in April.

The clerk reached beneath his counter and produced a small, narrow booklet. It was entitled *Stop Awhile in Clyde.*

"Take it with you, Mr. Gray," he said, "and read it when you have time. Clyde is really a lovely, unspoiled place. There are some very fine old homes here and beautiful gardens. There are several homes here owned by the Society for the Preservation of New England Antiquities, and then there's Johnson Street—I don't know whether your walk took you along there. Authorities say it is the most beautiful street in America—of its kind, of course."

The clerk paused and Charles looked at the title of the booklet in his hand, trying to imagine what Clyde would seem like if he had not lived there.

"You really ought to take five or ten minutes in the morning and walk up Johnson Street and especially you ought to see the old Lovell house, even if it isn't open to the public. It's in the Federalist style and there's a description of it here in the book. I'll mark it for you and I'll mark it on the map."

"Thanks very much. That's very kind of you," Charles said.

"It's just an unspoiled Yankee town, Mr. Gray," the clerk went on, "and the natives are friendly. Peculiar and ingrown, some of them, but friendly. And then there are plenty of recreational facilities."

"What sort of recreational facilities?" Charles asked.

There was an inviting pause before the clerk described them.

"There's a fine bathing beach and boating on the river and deep-sea fishing. We have a native here, Captain Willie Stevens, who knows where the big ones are, and there's another native, Captain Earl Wilkins."

"Are they both captains?" Charles asked.

The clerk laughed sympathetically.

"Well, you know how natives are. We call them captains here at the inn anyway . . . And then we're in easy motoring distance of some of the sportiest golf courses in America and we can issue cards to most of them right here at the desk to guests—most guests."

But he was tired of hearing about Clyde and he put the booklet in his pocket.

"Well," he said, "it sounds like a wonderful town."

"It is a wonderful town," the clerk said, "if you get the spirit of it, a wonderful town with lovely people, although most of them don't seem to come here much except for the Rotary Club luncheons. They all seem to like to eat at home and they're pretty tight with money, Yankee types. Well, the dining room opens at six-thirty and the Fife and Drum Room's open now, and if there's anything I can do for you just let me know, Mr. Gray."

"Thanks," Charles said. "Thanks very much. Can you tell me where the telephone is?"

"There's a booth down the hall to the left, on the way to the dining room," the clerk said, "but if you want to make a call from your own room, I can put you through on the switchboard."

"Thanks," Charles said, "the booth's all right."

It was time to face the situation. It was time to find who was alive and who was dead and in the course of it he knew he would have to hear about the Lovells. At least he knew from his mother's letters that the Masons were all alive. He wanted to call them and tell them he was here. He could not bear the thought of being alone with the juke box or alone at a table in the dining room.

When he put his five cents in the telephone coin box and gave the number, he kept the narrow booth open for air. He was sure that he had found the correct number—Virgil Mason, Spruce Street—and he remembered that it was their old number, 693. He could hear the ring at the other end of the line, not the steady, automatic signal of the city. There was an interminable wait and a long, dull silence between the rings but he was sure the Masons would be at home, unless there was a Unitarian supper, because it was six o'clock by then.

As he sat crouched in that narrow booth he tried to picture what was going on in the Mason house at Spruce Street. Mrs. Mason might be out in the kitchen doing something about supper, but certainly Mr. Mason would be in the parlor. Jackie might be upstairs in his room fixing himself for supper. Jackie never thought it looked well to get careless at home. Charles remembered that his mother had written not long ago that Jackie was still at Wright-Sherwin and a great comfort to his mother. He began jiggling the hook.

"Operator," he said, "will you ring them again, please?"

"What number are you calling?" the operator asked.

"The same number you're ringing, I hope," he said. "The number is 693."

"I'm ringing 693." The operator's voice sounded exactly like Doris Wormser's.

"Yes," I know," Charles said, "but would you ring it again, please?"

There was a silence and a very long and vicious ring on the other end of the line. He and the operator were both annoyed by then. His struggle with the telephone was as frustrating as both that walk down Dock Street among the unfamiliar faces and the Clyde Inn under the Murgatroyd management.

Then someone was answering and he closed the door of the booth very quickly although he could not imagine why he should be so anxious for privacy.

"Hello," he said, and he tried to sound bright and cheerful. "Is this Mr. Mason's house?"

"No, it isn't," a woman's voice answered. "What number did you want?"

"I wanted 693," Charles said.

"Well, you have the wrong number." The voice was acid and triumphant. "This is 603."

"Oh," Charles said, "I'm sorry," and he began jiggling the hook again.

"Operator," he said, and he had a strange feeling of defeat and hopelessness, a feeling that he would not get anywhere in Clyde and that nothing would come out right. "You gave me the wrong number. You gave me 603. I asked for 693."

"Oh," the operator said, "well I'll try them again."

"Don't," Charles said, "don't try them again, Operator. Try 693."

He was extraordinarily grateful when he heard Mrs. Mason's voice. Enclosed in that telephone booth, he had felt like a disembodied spirit, speaking through a medium, but at last he had got through to earth from the spirit world. He was as far away as that. New York, the bank, and Nancy and the children, and life, all lay between him and the Masons' house on Spruce Street.

"This is Charley, Mrs. Mason," he said. "Charley Gray."

She asked him where he was and where he had come from, and he could hear her calling, "Virgil, it's Charley Gray on the telephone."

He said that he was staying at the inn and Mrs. Mason told him to come right over—there was plenty of supper and Jackie was at home. He had hoped that she would ask him but he had known enough not to invite himself. You never dropped in suddenly on anyone in Clyde.

It was a little like looking through a box of old photographs when he reached Spruce Street, almost but not quite. It was nearly dark but some of the long spring twilight was left in the sky and the easterly breeze was dropping. He would not have been surprised in the least if he had seen himself running through the dark toward Gow Street to tell his Aunt Jane that Miss Sarah Hewitt was coming to tea or if he had seen his father walking up from the mill on River Street or if he had heard his mother calling. Nothing on Spruce Street hurt him as he thought it would, yet he did not want to look at the family's house. Nevertheless, he had to stop and turn toward it deliberately and when he did so, it was still their house, though plainer than he had thought it would be behind its uncompromising fence. The house looked as shabby as it had when he was growing up, just as it was meant to look. Some other family lived there now, with other boys and girls, perhaps, all with their own problems, but he could feel no resentment toward its present dwellers, whoever they might be, and he could still think of it as Our House. The yard was untidy again and it looked as though children had been playing in it. He reached and touched the white wooden fence, damp and cold from the rain, and then he turned his head away.

The Masons' house looked neater, as it always had, because Mr. Mason was good about doing things around the house. There was the porch, with its thin turned columns and its jigsaw decorations, and all that was new was an electric light with a milky globe fixed on the ceiling of the porch. There was the same bell in the center of the front door, a bell with a handle that you turned to make it ring, and it gave out the same sound that it had when he and Jackie used to play with it.

Jackie Mason opened the door and for a second each of them looked involuntarily but not impertinently to see what had happened to the other. Jackie was wearing a blue double-breasted suit with a fraternal button. His hair was faded but it was still yellow and it still had a natural wave, though it was thinner and receding from his temples. His face was heavier, but his eyes still had their old worried look.

"Why, Charley," he said, "I'd have known you anywhere."

"Hello, Jackie," Charles said, and then something told him that Jack Mason no longer liked to be called Jackie. "I'm awfully glad to see you," and for a moment it all was the way things used to be. They had been best friends once and they still were friends, without having anything in common.

"Come in," Jack said, "and give me your hat and coat. The old hooks are still under the stairs. I wish you'd let us know instead of going to the hotel, I mean the inn, but of course I understand exactly why you did it. If you'd stayed with us the Marchbys might not have understood, and it's quite an inn, isn't it? I go there Tuesdays to Rotary."

"I didn't know you were in the Rotary," Charles said, and Jackie looked worried.

"I can't say I'm a conscientious Rotarian, but the crowd down at Wright-Sherwin all sort of felt that there should be more Wright-Sherwin representation. Seeing you is going to be a thrill for Mother and Father. They're right in the parlor, Charley"—but Mr. and Mrs. Mason were no longer in the parlor. They were already crowding into the hall. Mr. Mason was in his shirt sleeves, as he always was before supper.

"Charley, dear," Mrs. Mason said, and she kissed him. "You haven't changed at all . . . except you look more like Sam. Virgil, I think at least you might put on your coat for Charley."

"Charley's used to it," Mr. Mason said. "Charley isn't company. I want to show him what I'm making," and they all went into the parlor.

The center table of the parlor was exactly as Charles remembered it, covered with something that Mr. Mason was making. It was now a model stagecoach. The pieces were sawed out but you had to smooth them down and put them together from the diagram.

"Now look at this damn thing," Mr. Mason said. "It says the front axle should go here and when you try to fit it there isn't room. I bet I'm the only person who ever got as far as trying to fit in the axle."

"May and Jeffrey are coming over right after supper," Mrs. Mason said. "It will be just like old times. Sit down, dear, and I'll see what's happening in the kitchen. We have Lucy Slavin working for us."

"Lucy Slavin?" Charles repeated.

"You know, dear," Mrs. Mason said. "She's Mary Callahan's niece—and you must go and see Mary tomorrow."

Jackie Mason cleared his throat.

"There are all sorts of people Charley ought to see tomorrow. Would you care for an old-fashioned cocktail, Charley?"

"Why, Jack," Mrs. Mason said, "I'm afraid we haven't anything in the house."

Jackie Mason cleared his throat again.

"It's locked in the sideboard, Mother," he said. "There was some left over, you know, from the time when Mr. Lovell and Jessica were here to dinner. There's quite a lot left over."

There was a short, sharp silence and Jackie Mason seemed startled by it. He cleared his throat again and his face looked redder.

"There's so much for all of us to catch up with," Mrs. Mason said, "but we have all night. You must tell us your news, Charley, and I'll tell you our news, and Jack will tell you his news, that is if it is news."

"Life has just been going on," Jackie said. "I'll go and fix those old-fashioneds," and he went out into the kitchen.

"Nothing's been the same," Mrs. Mason said. "I still keep thinking that the Grays are there next door—but Esther keeps writing me the news and I write her the news and she sent us some pictures you sent her, Charley, of Nancy and the children and that lovely home of yours. We're all so proud the way you're getting on—the president of a bank—" Charles found himself laughing nervously.

"Mother exaggerates things," he said. "She's showing off to you. I'm not the president of any bank. I'm just one of those boys who are trying to be and an awful lot of us are trying."

"We know you will be, dear," Mrs. Mason said. "Shall I tell about Jackie, Virgil? Or shall I let Jackie tell Charles?"

"I don't know what you want to tell him," Mr. Mason said, "but you might as well if you want to, Margaret."

Charles found himself sitting up straighter.

"Jackie's the head of the accounting department at Wright-Sherwin," Mrs.

Mason said. "They had a new man from out of town after Mr. Howell died but he didn't get on with Norman Stanley. Jack gets on beautifully with Norman Stanley."

"Well," Charles said, "that's wonderful. That's more than I could have done—get on with Norman Stanley."

Then Jackie was back with a tray and three old-fashioned cocktails.

"Father," he said, "would you mind moving some of the stagecoach so I can put this down on a corner of the table?"

"Put it on another table," Mr. Mason said. "If anything moves here, the whole thing will go."

"Jackie," Mrs. Mason said, "I've just been telling Charley your news."

"Now, Mother," Jackie Mason began, "I especially asked you—"

"Not *that* news, dear," Mrs. Mason said. "The other news, that you're the head of the accounting department at Wright-Sherwin."

"Oh," Jackie Mason said, and he looked relieved. "It isn't much, Charley, but the company's bigger than it was when you were there."

"I think it's wonderful, Jackie," Charles said, but of course it was not wonderful. Jack Mason was made to be the head of an accounting department someday in a small-town factory.

"You'll have to come down tomorrow and see the boys," Jackie said, as he handed him his cocktail. "I hope I haven't put too much bitters in it."

"And there's another piece of news," Mrs. Mason said. "Jackie's in the Shore Club now."

"It isn't anything," Jackie said, and he looked worried again. "It isn't what it used to be, since the war. It's a good place to take customers now and then. Well, here's looking at you, Charley."

"Yes," Mr. Mason said, "here's looking at you. Here's to the old days, Charley."

3

Second Man in Rome

When they sat down to supper Charles felt almost as if he were back at home in the family dining room on Spruce Street. Mrs. Mason was not unlike his mother as she sat behind the cocoa cups, and it was the same cracked cocoa they were drinking, clear and bittersweet. It was hard to get now, Mrs. Mason said, and they had done without it during the war, but Mr. Mason had found some in Boston recently. Mr. Mason was going to write a paper about cocoa for the Confessional Club.

"It's a funny thing to be writing about with the world the way it is," Mr. Mason said, "but it might just as well be cocoa as communism." Surprisingly enough there was quite a lot about cocoa and chocolate in the public library and it would start right with Cortez and the Aztecs. Their ruler, Montezuma, drank cocoa, and he ate small babies, too, that were cooked in a kind of chafing dish.

"Now, Virgil," Mrs. Mason said, "you're not going to put that in about the babies, are you?"

He could almost hear his father and mother speaking.

The room had almost the same proportions as the old Gray dining room. There were the same plain chairs, a pressed-glass butter dish, and a breadboard with its loaf of homemade bread. The wooden shutters had been drawn and now they shut out a distracted world. His father, Charles was thinking, would have loved to discuss Aztecs eating babies. He could see his mother's incredulous but patient look and Dorothea's expression of horror and his father's delighted smile, and if Elbridge Sterne had been there of course he would never have heard anything about Montezuma or Aztecs either. It was hard to realize that his father was not there, when Mr. and Mrs. Mason began talking about him.

"He was always saying he was going to beat the system," Mr. Mason said.

"Yes," Charles said, "I remember."

"Well," Mr. Mason said, "maybe he did beat the system, in his own particular way."

"Yes, perhaps he did," Charles said, and he saw that Jackie looked nervous, "but he never did get me that pony," and they all laughed just as though his father were not dead. He seemed to be with them in the dining room, pleased that they were speaking of him.

"Perhaps Charley would rather we talked about something else," Jackie Mason said.

"Oh no," Charles said, "I don't mind at all."

"Of course he doesn't, Jackie," Mrs. Mason said, "and, Charley dear, you know what people used to say about John Gray's running through money —people who didn't know him as well as we did?"

"Yes," Charles said, and he found himself smiling, "but then Father never cared."

"Well, no one has ever been able to say that he didn't leave his wife and daughter comfortable. He didn't mind about himself but he always thought of other people."

"Yes," Charles said, and he found himself sitting up straighter and speaking more carefully. All the Masons were looking at him and he took a sip of water. "Yes, I know what you mean."

"We're all so proud of him," Mrs. Mason said, "and then there was that fund for the library."

He could not get away from the idea that his father was there with them, and if he were, Charles knew that he would have been very much amused.

"I don't believe you've ever seen the bookplate for the John Gray Fund," Jackie Mason said. "The library trustees had one designed especially. By the way, I was made a trustee last year." He mentioned the news casually and modestly but Charles had not forgotten its value.

"Jackie's in everything these days," Mr. Mason said. "Why, he's even a director of the Dock Street Bank."

Jackie looked worried. He folded his napkin carefully.

"Charley will get wrong ideas about me," he said, and he laughed. "What's a local savings bank to Charley?"

For a moment it all was a little like one of his daydreams of coming back to Clyde. As he sat there with his herringbone suit still neatly pressed, he must have looked to them much as Arthur Slade had once looked to him, the aura of a city bank still about him, polite and measured, with all his edges smoothed.

"Charley, dear," Mrs. Mason said, "tell us where you live and what you do. Tell us about everything."

He folded his napkin, forgetting that he was a guest. They were all waiting for him to speak. He was a rich and glittering visitor from a strange and foreign land.

"Well," he said, "I'm in the trust department in the bank and that keeps me pretty busy. I don't ever seem to have much time to see Nancy and the children, but perhaps I will get time if everything turns out right. Nancy's an awfully nice girl."

It seemed very necessary to say that Nancy was a nice girl.

"We've always wondered," Mrs. Mason said, "why William wasn't named after his grandfather."

"Nancy named him," Charles answered. "I wanted to name him Sam." He stopped and for a second it seemed as though Sam were with them too. "But Nancy said let's make a clean break of it and call him Bill. Well, we live in a place called Sycamore Park . . ." He found himself speaking more quickly, more easily. He was laying out his whole life on the dining room table, just as though he were dealing from a deck of cards, and it sounded rather well.

"There's a good country day school for the children, but I want Bill to go to boarding school next year. And then there's a good country club; and then there are, well, my business associates. Nancy and I have a lot to keep us busy."

"We have a picture of the house," Mrs. Mason said. "It looks so new and lovely with your car standing in front of it on the driveway."

"Of course, there was that gap while I was away."

"You mean at the war?" Jackie Mason said.

All at once his going to the war was an action which he wanted to explain and justify. The Masons were almost the only people who could have understood all his reasoning.

"I shouldn't have gone," he said, "at my age and with a wife and two children. It's the sort of thing that doesn't help you in a business way. Nancy didn't like it and I don't blame her much." He was not sure himself why he had gone to the war but he was almost sure. "Sam went, and you know I always thought a lot of Sam. And then—well, maybe I was tired of beating the system." He laughed, but only because he felt it would be a good idea to laugh. "When I got there it was just the bank all over again with a different set of rules."

He had dealt the cards of his little game and they were in order on the table.

"Well," Mr. Mason began, "I think it was a mighty fine thing," but he did not finish because the doorbell rang.

"That's May and Jeffrey," Mrs. Mason said. "I guess they thought we'd be finished supper."

"Charley," Jackie Mason said, "would you care for a cigarette? Or would you rather have a cigar? They're right in the sideboard."

"No, thanks," Charles said. "Just a cigarette."

May and Jeffrey Meader came into the dining room and everyone was standing up and the room seemed very crowded, with those who were there and those who were not. The moment he saw May Mason he thought of the summer afternoon when May had been sitting alone in the back room trying to play "The Pink Lady" on the old upright piano and he had brought her that note from Sam; and he knew that May, stoutish, middle-aged and gray-headed, remembered, too.

"Charley," she said, "I guess I've got to kiss you." He could tell from the way she spoke that it was an impulsive break from what she had planned to do or say. "You look like Sam."

"I've thought of you a lot, May," he said. It had a brittle, banal sound and he wished he could have thought of something better. "I'm awfully glad if you think I look like Sam." It was a very public, awkward moment, because everyone was listening.

Jeffrey Meader was pudgy, with horn-rimmed spectacles, and almost bald. He looked like someone in a small real estate and insurance office, but then this was exactly the way he should have looked.

"Why, Charley looks like a good prospect," he said. "Hi, Charley."

"Hi, Jeffrey," Charles said.

"And here's Edwina," May went on, as though she had not heard Jeffrey. "You remember Edwina, don't you? She was Dorothea's flower girl." May's daughter was standing in the doorway, looking just as May had once looked except that her blond hair was cut in a page boy bob instead of being long and tied up in a knot, and she, too, must have been the prettiest girl in her class at high school.

"Why, I'd know Edwina anywhere," he said. "She hasn't changed at all."

"Malvina's married," May said. "She's living in Brockton and as long as we're just the family I'll tell you Malvina's news. What do you think—she's expecting, Charley."

"May means Malvina's going to have a baby," Jackie said. "I wish you wouldn't put it that way, May. It sounds local."

"All right, all right," Jeffrey Meader said. "No matter how it sounds May's going to be a grandmother any time now and that sounds pretty funny, doesn't it?"

"Now you're here," May said, "how long are you going to be here, Charley?"

He was a visitor again, that successful visitor from the city who had left them long ago, and his voice sounded polite and assured when he answered.

"Only over tomorrow, I'm afraid. I'll have to be taking the midnight from Boston tomorrow. I'm sorry I can't stay longer but perhaps some other time—"

"There are certain people that Charley ought to see before he goes back," Jackie said, "and there'll be talk if he doesn't. I'll make a list and go over it with Charley."

They all trooped back to the parlor, now that supper was finished, and when Charles took part in the conversation it was like speaking a language which he had known well a long time before and which he could still speak, although he was unfamiliar with the latest idioms and his tenses might occasionally be confused. In his absence Clyde, aloof and indestructible, had been drifting through a turbulent sea, but Clyde was made for trouble. Nothing could entirely alter its values. Everyone still knew his place and there was a place for everyone.

Charles had forgotten that everyone went to bed early in Clyde until he saw Mr. Mason yawn and then he said he would have to be getting back to the hotel, he meant the inn, and that he had had a wonderful time; and they all said it was like old times, seeing him, and they would see him again tomorrow.

"I'll go back to the inn with you," Jackie said.

"Oh, no," Charles told him, "don't bother, Jack. You'd be surprised. I know my way."

"Why," Jackie Mason said. "I'd really like to, Charley. You and I have a lot to talk about and there won't be time tomorrow."

Charles had begun to speak that forgotten language of Clyde so fluently that he and Jack Mason seemed to have picked up something which they had both dropped years before; when they began walking up Spruce Street, there was that old realization of having been friends, and it was still completely usable. There was a persistent quality in Jackie Mason's loyalty and he knew that Jackie admired him for the same reasons he previously had, and he liked Jackie, too, with the same old reservations. Their friendship was on a different footing from other, later friendships. It was deeper, it was unavoidable, and he felt very grateful for it. He seldom gave way to impulse. His training was all against it, but almost without thinking he slapped Jackie softly on the back.

"Well, Jackie," he said, "here we are on Spruce Street," and he knew that Jack was pleased.

They were walking toward Johnson Street and the houses were growing larger and more imposing. He did not want to see Johnson Street but if he had to he was glad that Jack Mason was with him.

"I guess it's going to rain," Jackie said. "We've had a lot of rain lately. It's nice to see you again, Charley."

"The same here," Charles said, and they walked for a while without speaking, now that each had said what he had meant to say.

"The old place hasn't changed much," Jackie said. "It's still about the same. Charley, I wish you'd never gone away."

It was not what Charles would have wished and he thought of what might have happened if he had stayed in Clyde. They had turned right at the corner of Spruce and Johnson streets and there was the Hewitt house, all dark, and the Lovell house diagonally across from it. He made a deliberate effort not to look at it, though common sense and his knowledge of human relationships told him that he could not blame the Lovell house or Johnson Street for what had happened to him and Jessica. Still he did not want to see it.

"I couldn't have stayed," he said, and it was a great relief that he had not a single doubt about it.

"Of course, it might have been a little difficult at first—" Jackie Mason hesitated—"but nothing would have affected your position. For instance, take the library," but he did not go on about the library.

It was very natural to be walking down Johnson Street with Jack Mason talking about position. Jackie did not mention that his grandfather had been a druggist but it was still on Jackie's mind.

"Or take the bank," Jackie said. "You would have been in just the right position, the first time there was a vacancy on the board."

If he had stayed in Clyde, he might certainly have been a director of the Dock Street Bank. He might even have been president of it if he had done the right things at the right time.

"Well, never mind it," he answered. "You're the one who's got position now."

"Oh, I haven't done anything much," Jackie Mason said, "except in a small-town way."

A sad note in Jackie's voice made Charles realize that Jackie wanted him to be impressed with everything he had done, and, after all, he was a trustee of the public library and a director of the bank. He had gone a long, long way.

Charles had to answer properly and he could not sound patronizing.

"Everything you do depends on where you are," he said. "Do you remember what Julius Caesar said"—he was like his own father, groping for an apt quotation—"about preferring to be the first man in Ostia to the second man in Rome? I'm sure it wasn't Ostia but let's call it Ostia." He could not see Jack Mason's face in the dark but he was sure that he had said the right thing, neither too little nor too much.

"That's awfully nice of you to say that, Charley," Jackie said.

"It isn't nice," Charles said quickly, "it's the truth," and he thought of something else, because it was an occasion when one could say anything. "What is that line in the Declaration of Independence—or is it the Constitution? 'Life, liberty, and the pursuit of happiness.' Well, I suppose everybody's pursuing happiness, and you usually lose your liberty when you do, and the best part of your life. Maybe that's what everything's about. Maybe. I don't know."

They had turned down Dock Street and it was a radical statement to have made in front of the Dock Street Bank and it had no reference to anything except that he was thinking of Jackie Mason and also of himself.

"I know what you mean," Jackie said. "You mustn't try to crowd your luck." It was not what he had meant but he was glad that Jack had misunderstood him.

"Maybe I am crowding my luck a little but everything does seem to be coming my way all of a sudden." Jackie stopped and sighed. "But it's taken a lot of time, a lot of time. Maybe it's just that somebody has to take hold and I seem to be elected . . . let's see, did I tell you I was in the Tuesday Club?"

"Why, no," Charles said, "you didn't. That certainly is something, Jack."

"It isn't anything really," Jackie said. "Everybody's dying pretty fast, but it's funny, isn't it, being in the Tuesday Club with Mr. Stanley and Mr. Lovell and everybody? I thought you'd be amused."

"It isn't so funny," Charles said. "You have what it takes, that's all."

They had crossed the street and they were in front of the Clyde Inn before Jackie spoke again.

"Don't think I look on myself as the first man in Ostia. I'm a long way from it—er—Charley, do you mind if I come up to your room with you? There's something else I want to tell you." Jackie looked worried again. "Something I hope you won't mind."

"Of course I won't mind," Charles said. "What is it, Jack?"

"I'll get it off my chest in just a minute," Jackie said, "but I can't tell it in front of everybody."

There was no one to tell it in front of at the inn except the clerk, who still sat behind the desk and who looked surprised to see them enter the place together.

"Oh, hello, Edgar," Jackie said. "Mr. Gray wants his room key. I hope you've given Mr. Gray a good room."

"Good evening, Mr. Mason," the inn clerk said. "I didn't know you were acquainted with Mr. Gray."

"It would have made all the difference, wouldn't it?" Jackie said, and he laughed. "I'll tell you what you can do for me, Edgar. Just get me a bottle of rye, the kind I bought for Mr. Jaeckel, and put it on my bill. You like rye, don't you, Charley?"

Charles said that it did not matter, he did not care for anything particularly, and Jackie may have been sorry for his impulse, because he was careful to conceal the bottle beneath his overcoat as they walked upstairs.

"Life, liberty, and the pursuit of happiness," he said. "I'm afraid Edgar was a little surprised. I don't do this sort of thing very often except in a business way, but seriously, it does mean a lot to the town having an inn like this, and this isn't a bad room, is it? I'm glad you have a quiet one that opens on the back."

Charles's room had a country, chintzy look, and was furnished in yellow Colonial maple, with an imitation spool bed and a bedside table with a telephone on it, a writing table, one small upholstered chair and one straight chair. The room was stifling hot. He had forgotten that the heat was on, and when he opened the window he found himself looking over the old back gardens toward the houses along Fanning Street.

"Yes, it's going to be quiet here," Charles said.

Jackie had put the bottle of rye on the writing table.

"Here, let me pour the drinks," he said. "This is my party, Charley. There ought to be some glasses in the bathroom. Dear me, I should have ordered up some ice."

"Oh, never mind the ice," Charles said.

It was rather like the war, sitting in an unfamiliar room with a bottle of rye whiskey and tepid water. It was not at all like Clyde.

"Well, now we're here," Charles said, "what is it you want to tell me, Jack?"

Jackie cleared his throat and his worried look returned.

"Well," he said, "all right," and he cleared his throat again. "Charley, I think I ought to talk to you about Jessica Lovell."

Charles knew, of course, that he could not erase his memory of Jessica Lovell and that at some time while he was in Clyde he would have to meet the past face to face, but so far he had heard nothing except that talk about cocktails and the remaining ingredients which had been left at the Masons' when Jessica and Mr. Lovell had been entertained. He was seated on the stiff chair by the writing table and he was conscious of many little things, of a draft on the back of his neck from the open window, of a soft hiss from the valve of the radiator. He had leaned forward as though he wanted to hear better and now he leaned back because he did not like that display of eagerness. Still the palms of his hands were moist and the room felt very stuffy. Mentioning Jessica was like opening a box filled with things you would never use again but which could not be thrown away.

"I'm glad you brought up Jessica," he said. There was nothing revealing in his voice. It had just the right note of friendly interest—exactly as he wished it. "I've been meaning to ask about her. How is Jessica?"

"Oh, she's very well," Jackie said. "Very well and busy. She has that same interest in things, but then you know Jessica."

"I don't know her now," Charles said, and he smiled agreeably at Jackie and everything he said was just as he wanted it. "I've been pretty busy, too."

"I know how you feel," Jackie said. "I don't want to bring up any painful memories."

"Oh, my God," Charles said. Jackie's manner made him impatient. "Don't call them painful memories, Jackie. They're too old."

"I'm awfully glad you take it this way," Jackie said, "but of course I know how you must feel."

"No, you don't," Charles said, "because I don't feel anything," and he smiled. He was saying just what he wanted to say. "I hope Jessica's well and happy and I'm glad we didn't get married because it wouldn't have worked

—and that's all there is to it, except I always supposed she'd find someone else. Why didn't she ever marry?"

Jackie looked at him reproachfully as though he had not assumed the serious attitude the circumstances demanded.

"She just never did, Charley," he said, and his voice was reproachful, too.

Charles rubbed his hands softly on his knees and he had an absurd notion that Jackie Mason was blaming him for Jessica's being unmarried. It was like those stories of old Clyde spinsters keeping a night light always burning in the spare-room window for lovers who had disappeared at sea.

"Well, I don't see why she didn't," he said, "unless it was her father again."

"No," Jackie said, and he sighed. It seemed to Charles an elaborate, overdramatized sigh. "I don't think it was entirely that."

Charles did not answer. Instead he stared at the yellow maple bed with its bright chintz cover. The conversation was reminiscent of a weeping willow above a suitably inscribed tombstone in an old memorial print.

"I think she always hoped that you'd come back sometime."

He could see that Jackie Mason believed it and he almost believed it too, because at one time she must have thought of him often—but it was not the way things were. There were no lights nowadays burning in lonely windows. The room was very hot and there was still that draft on the back of his neck.

"Maybe she did for a year or two," Charles said. "She knew I'd married, didn't she?"

"Yes," Jackie said. "Jessica's a wonderful girl. She's always wanted you to be happy, Charley. She's always wanted to hear about you."

"Well," Charles said, "I think I'll have another drink."

When Charles went into the bathroom to fill his glass with tap water he glanced at himself in the mirror above the washbasin, as he did usually at the bank. His tie was straight, his soft collar was smooth. He looked as he should have, like someone from New York, and suddenly he realized as sure as fate that he could have come back to Clyde, he could have married Jessica Lovell. Her father could not have stopped them, nothing could have stopped them if he had come back, but until this moment the idea had never crossed his mind. He walked out of the bathroom holding his glass and sat down again in the uncomfortable chair.

"Well," he said, "I never did come back."

He never would have. He would have been too proud.

"I thought I ought to tell you, Charley," Jackie said. "I thought you ought to know." He still could not understand why Jackie thought he ought to know except that Jackie had always found it hard to keep things to himself.

"Did Jessica tell you this?" he asked. "It doesn't sound like Jessica"—and for a moment he had a proprietary feeling, as though Jessica still belonged to him.

"Well, you see—" Jackie Mason looked too large for the small upholstered chair in which he sat. His face looked moist and he pulled out a neat handkerchief from his breast pocket. "It's awfully hot in here, isn't it, but it will cool off given time. . . . You see, Jessica had to talk to someone and I suppose I was elected—just because I knew you. She still talks a lot about you, Charley. Jessica was in love with you for years. She really was."

"I wonder if I could have another of your cigarettes?" Charles asked. He did not want to consider Jessica Lovell's having been in love with him for years.

"Oh, excuse me," Jackie said, and he snapped open his silver cigarette case. "You know, there's something about women—" his face was redder—"I think that women seem to stay in love longer than men, once they fall in love."

"Maybe they do," Charles said. "It's possible."

It was possible but not probable. Jessica Lovell, as Jackie Mason saw her, was an unreal character. Girls did not stay in love indefinitely unless there was some outside compulsion. He was glad that he was able to tell himself that this was so.

"You see"—Jackie was still speaking—"I thought you ought to know this so that you won't misunderstand Jessica."

"My God, Jackie," Charles said, "I don't misunderstand Jessica. It's all over and, I told you, I'm glad I didn't marry her and that's all there is to it"; but Jackie was going on.

"I'm glad you take it this way, Charley. You see, I've been seeing a lot of Jessica." He laughed deprecatingly. "I guess Mr. Lovell thought I was pretty harmless, but things can't help changing and that's what I want to tell you. I want to tell you that Jessica and I are engaged and are going to be married in June."

Somehow Charles had thought of everything else but not of that. He was reconciled to Jackie's being a library trustee, a director of the bank, a member of the Tuesday Club, but he had never thought of his marrying Jessica Lovell. He could not think that he resented it or that it was jealousy he felt, or envy. He was mainly disturbed because of something in the whole picture that was malformed, something that should not have been. He was thinking of what Jessica used to say about Jackie Mason, but as Jackie said, things changed if you saw someone long enough—and it had taken a long, long time. It was all as dry as dust, almost repellent, and for once he did not say the proper thing.

"Why, Jackie," he said, "it looks as though you have everything," and he heard Jackie's nervous laugh.

"Oh, I wouldn't put it that way," Jackie said, "and I know that Jessica and I are a little old to take this step, but then we've known each other so long."

The radiator hissed again and Charles still did not know how he felt.

"I wish you'd tell me," he asked, "how Mr. Lovell took it."

"Well, I was a little surprised," Jackie said. "He didn't seem to mind. It's funny, when I had my talk with him, he kept calling me Charles. Of course, his mind isn't what it was before he was ill last winter, but he's really a grand old gentleman, and we'll all be living there together. He couldn't live without Jessica."

At last Charles said the right thing. He said he thought it was splendid and he knew they would be happy.

"I'm awfully glad you think so, Charley," Jackie Mason said, "and now there's one thing more. I hope you'll call on Jessica tomorrow. She knows you're here, you know."

Charles picked up his glass and was surprised to find it empty. He set it carefully back on the writing table and rose.

"No," he said. "No, I don't think so, Jack. It—" His voice was unexpectedly hoarse. "It wouldn't help anything."

"But, Charley"—Jackie looked deeply hurt—"I wish you'd think of Jessica. Everyone will know you didn't see her."

It was that old phrase again, everyone would know, but it was something he could not do, something he would not do, even though everyone would know.

"I can't," he said, and his voice was still hoarse. "I suppose I ought to, but I can't . . . I'm sorry, Jackie."

No matter what Jackie Mason said, he would not go to the Lovells'. Jackie Mason was still his friend and Jackie was always loyal, but he did not have to see Jessica or Mr. Lovell or the Lovell house again.

"Why, Charley," he said, "if you really feel that way . . . But just think it over and we'll talk about it again tomorrow."

"All right," Charles said.

"And now I'd better be going. It's getting awfully late."

"Wait a minute," Charles said, and his mind was back to where it should have been. "Just a minute before you go, Jackie. There's something I've been meaning to ask you. What do you know about the Nickerson Cordage Company?"

His voice at last sounded the way it should have through all that conversation.

For a minute or two after Jackie Mason closed the door and after the sound of footfalls disappeared, Charles Gray had the illusion that he was in a hotel room somewhere else and that Jackie Mason had appeared unsubstantially and that their conversation had been still another fantasy. Although the place had the impersonality peculiar to any hotel room and though the presence of people who had occupied it could be erased from it as one wiped chalk off the surface of a blackboard, the imprint of Jack Mason's posterior was still visible upon the cushion of the small upholstered chair. The bottle of rye was gone, because he had insisted that Jack Mason take it back with him, under his overcoat if necessary, but the two bathroom glasses were on the table—his own empty and the other only faintly colored and still three quarters full, showing that Jackie Mason very seldom did that sort of thing.

Charles took his thin gold watch from his waistcoat pocket, the unnecessarily expensive watch that Nancy had given him just before they were married. Nancy had never liked wrist watches in an office because, without meaning to, you always glanced at them. It was very late for Clyde, almost half past eleven o'clock. He picked up the two glasses automatically and walked into the bathroom, where he rinsed them out carefully, but rinsing glasses could not change his frame of mind. He could not get his thoughts away from Jack Mason and the career of Jack Mason. A sense of emptiness and futility hung darkly over him. It was late, but he wanted to call up Nancy. He had never wanted so much to speak to anyone and he felt better already when he had given the number at Sycamore Park.

"Ring me when you get it, will you, please?" he said.

Then he walked to the single window and opened it wider and stood breathing the cool night air. There was the sound of a train in the distance. It would be the eleven-thirty going north to Portland. The timetable had not changed. It was a dark, cloudy night but the sky was lighter than the earth and he could see the blurred shapes of the elms and the houses on Fanning Street. The town was asleep but it was still alive and as full of blind instinct as a beehive. Malcolm Bryant had perceived this once and he had tried clumsily to translate it into the pages of *Yankee Persepolis*, so named because the Persians had worshiped memories there.

He thought again of Jackie Mason, beset by this instinct and wanting to get on according to the rules, and he had seen the result that night, a preordained and sterile ending. The worst of it was that it partially reminded him of his own career. He had been living carefully according to other rules. Someday he might be a vice-president of the Stuyvesant Bank in New York City, and Jackie Mason was engaged to Jessica Lovell. He wished that the night were not so dark. He wished that everything were not so deathly still. There was not even a sigh of wind in the branches of the trees.

The sharp ring of the telephone broke into those thoughts and he was relieved to hear the low and sleepy sound of Nancy's voice.

"What are you doing? Where are you?" she asked.

"I'm here in the hotel in Clyde," he said, and it sounded like the beginning of a letter—Clyde Inn, Clyde, Massachusetts. "Did I wake you up?"

"Yes, you did," Nancy said. "Never mind it. Are you all right?"

Nancy always hated wasting money talking aimlessly on the long distance and he disliked it too, but nothing could have made him stop talking.

"I'm fine," he said. "Are you all right? Are the children all right?"

"There's no perceptible change," Nancy said. "Molly Blakesley came to call."

"Oh," he said. "What did Molly Blakesley want?"

"She didn't want anything, damn her."

"Molly's all right," he said. "What else has happened?"

"Well, Bill cut his lip. A baseball hit him. And that man you called to see about the roof, he never came."

"Well, never mind," Charles said. "How about the Buick?"

"Why do you want to know about the Buick?"

"I don't know," Charles said. "I'm just feeling lonely for you and the Buick."

"It's a nice association of ideas," Nancy said. "How lonely are you?"

"Very lonely," he answered. "There are too many ghosts up here."

"Well, when are you getting back?"

"The midnight tomorrow," he said.

"What about that company?"

"I'm attending to it tomorrow."

"Well, what have you been doing?"

"Just talking," he said. "I had supper at the Masons'."

"Oh," she said. "The Masons—those people who lived next door?"

"Yes, they're the ones," he answered.

"Well, what about that Lovell girl?" He knew that Nancy would ask about the Lovell girl. "Have you seen her yet?"

"No," he said. "She's going to marry Jackie Mason. What do you think of that?"

"You mean the boy next door is marrying the girl in the big house?" Nancy said. "I've never seen him, so how should I know what to think?" It was wonderful to hear the indifference in Nancy's voice. "Now wait a minute. Is that why you're lonely?"

"No," he said, "it isn't. I wish you were here."

"Well, I'm glad you do," Nancy said. "Now listen, we're not getting anywhere and we've been talking more than three minutes. Come home as early as you can on Friday, and don't worry about anything."

"About what?" he asked her.

"You know what . . . the bank . . . And Charley, I didn't really mean what I said—about its not being much but its being the only thing we had. It was a silly thing to say."

"Just a second." At least he was no longer thinking about Clyde. "Have you heard anything?"

"No," she answered, "I didn't mean it that way, darling. Don't sit alone there worrying. I'll see you on Friday. Good night, dear."

He set down the telephone and stood up, conscious of a new sound which he had not noticed while they had been talking. It was the rushing sound of rain. It was pouring rain outside.

The rain had a finality that reminded him of the mechanical whir of the curtain in a theater falling inexorably upon the last line of a play. Random, undisciplined thoughts were with him again and there were voices in the persistent beating of the rain as clear as though they had been real. His mind was wandering off in aimless reminiscence as it had just the night before in his knotty-pine library at Sycamore Park. For no good reason, he was thinking of the time he had sat on the stage in the Clyde City Hall for the graduation exercises of his class at grammar school. He remembered exactly how his stiff collar had chafed the left side of his neck and Jackie Mason had been beside him, in a stiff collar, too. Jackie's hair was slicked smooth with soap but soap could never straighten the wave in it. They sat bemused in the second row behind the fluffy dresses and the big bow hair ribbons of the girls, while Mr. Martin J. Gifford, who was going to run that fall for the state legislature, was addressing the graduating class. His voice came back with the rain.

"Don't let anyone tell you, my young friends, that there is any such thing as luck . . . no, no . . . The wonderful ladies and gentlemen on your school committee, your teachers . . . your great mayor, my dear old friend Francis X. Flynn . . . The greatest country of the world . . . the United States of America, where all men, I thank God, are free and equal, living in the frame of freedom, life, liberty and the pursuit of happiness . . . Each of us can look the other in the eye and say, 'I am as free as you are . . . I have the same chance as you.'"

The voice was in the patter of the rain, mingling with other voices, and Charles could hear his father's voice beside it.

"The system, Charley. You have to beat the system."

The sound of the rain was growing louder. It was tapping out its own refrain on the sodden earth and on the sidewalks and on the roofs of Clyde—life, liberty and the pursuit of happiness.

It was true—the harder you pursued happiness, the less liberty you had, and perhaps if you pursued it hard enough, it might ruin you. His father had died pursuing it. No one had told the school children that freedom of choice was limited. He could see himself hurrying, always hurrying, and he would be hurrying again tomorrow, back to Nancy and the children and back to taking care of other people's money. It was not what he had dreamed of, there in Clyde, but if he had to start all over again he would not have acted differently. He would not have stayed at Wright-Sherwin. Inevitably he would have gone to Boston in that pursuit of happiness and he and Jessica Lovell would have pursued it for a little while together, but he would have used the same judgment and he would have made the same mistakes.

"But there is no such thing as luck," he heard Mr. Martin J. Gifford saying, "not for American boys or girls," and he remembered what Sam had said.

"It was the same old bushwa, kid," and so it was, but in a certain sense Martin J. Gifford was nearly right. It was not due to luck that Martin J. Gifford had been there to address the boys and girls.

The drumming of the rain was slackening, changing to the gentle, persistent sound of steady April rain, and again he was acutely conscious of the weather. Weather was a part of living again as it used to be long ago and he remembered how he had once hoped for northeast storms, wild enough and heavy enough to make the sirens blow in the morning, signaling no school. The brooks, already swollen, would spill over parts of their banks by morning, and the tufted grass on the swamp would be covered near the bridge on the road to Walton Spring. The peeper frogs would be singing their thin, plaintive song there in the morning. Jessica had not known what it was when she had heard it on the road that day . . .

4

I Suppose She'll Wear a Long Dress

Charles might have reserved a bedroom on the midnight back from Boston. It would not have been out of line and it would have been sensible, because he had not slept well that night in Clyde. The cost would not have exceeded that of a hotel room and no one would have dreamed of questioning the expenditure, but he was always very careful about expense accounts. His training in handling other people's affairs had made him absurdly meticulous in spending money that was not his own. He had taken a lower berth in what might have been the same grim and antiquated car that he had boarded at Boston when he left Clyde for good in 1930. He checked his suitcase in the morning at the Vanderbilt Avenue checkroom, just as he had checked his suitcase when he had arrived from Clyde that other time. There was the same sleepy emptiness in the Grand Central Station. He was in New York again following a familiar procedural pattern.

It was a quarter before eight when Charles arrived at the bank, too early for anyone to be there except Martin, the night watchman, and his assistant, Francis. Martin opened the side door carefully and spoke softly, like the sexton of a church.

"Good morning, Mr. Gray," Martin said, and his hand was on the emergency button, just where it should have been. "You're pretty early, aren't you?"

"Hello, Martin," Charles said. "I'm just down from Boston."

"How is the weather up there?" Martin asked.

"Rainy," Charles said.

"Is that so?" Martin said. "It rained here yesterday but it was fine last night."

"It certainly is quiet here," Charles said.

"It's spooky until you get used to it," Martin said. "You always keep waiting for an alarm to go off." There was no reason why Martin should not have been used to it. He had been in charge at night for over fifteen years.

The banking floor was very still and all the curtains were drawn over the windows so that the light reminded him of a bedroom in the morning. The officers' desks beside the windows all had their tops closed tight and his own desk and Roger Blakesley's stood side by side on the edge of the green carpet, impersonal and bare. Charles laid down his brief case and took off his overcoat.

"Well, it's nice to be back," he said. "I feel as though I've been away for quite a while."

He opened his brief case and pulled out his notes. The yellow scratch pad and the pencils were in his upper right-hand drawer and Miss Marble always saw that his pencils were sharp. He began to write his memorandum to Mr. Burton in clear, very legible handwriting. He could thank Miss Jenks, his teacher in the seventh grade, for that readable script, and once he had tried very hard to please Miss Jenks.

Another day was starting. First the bookkeepers and the tellers appeared, laughing and talking until their voices were lost behind all the preparatory sounds in the cages. He was conscious that the room around him was filling up but he kept persistently on with his writing. If he could get his memorandum finished before he was interrupted the whole day would run more smoothly and on schedule. He did not realize how late it was until he felt a hand on his shoulder. It was Roger Blakesley, with his rimless glasses, still in his overcoat, carrying his brief case. All the desks were occupied and Miss Marble was there. It was almost half past nine.

"Well, well," Roger said. "Did you blow in on the midnight?"

It was exactly the way Roger would have put it, "blowing in."

"Hello, Roger," Charles said. "That's right. On the midnight."

"Well, it's nice you're back, fella," Roger said. "How are things up north?"

"Fine," Charles said. "It was a nice trip, Roger."

Roger's grasp on his shoulder relaxed and they smiled at each other, like old friends, aware that they were being watched.

"Well, everything's just the same here," Roger said, "the same old rat race," and he lowered his voice. "Damn it, I wish they'd get this thing settled, Charley. It's getting on my nerves."

It was the first time either of them had mentioned the Thing to the other.

"So do I," Charles said. "It's on my nerves too, Roger."

"Anyway," Roger said, "it's nice to see you back, fella."

It was no time to look at Roger too sharply. He could only wonder whether anything had happened while he was away to make the Thing get on Roger's nerves.

The three-two local for home was a slow train, stopping at nearly every point along the line. Charles could tell where he was by counting the stops, and instead of looking out of the window he read the *World Telegram* and the Kiplinger *Washington Letter* and *Time* magazine. It was a beautiful, bright, sunny afternoon, not a reluctant New England April afternoon but more like mid-May. When he stepped off the train the station platform gave off a warm, tarry smell and the air was cool but languid. The waters of Long Island Sound in the distance had a blue that was almost like the blue of summer. It was suburban New York weather and so warm that he did not need an overcoat.

When he saw the Buick he knew that Miss Marble must have called Nancy or that Nancy had called Miss Marble at the bank. At any rate, she was there waiting for him and Bill and Evelyn were with her.

"Why, Nance," he said, "I didn't expect to see you all here."

This was not exactly true, because he had half expected them, and the best of it was they looked just as they had when he had left them, Nancy in her greenish tweed suit, Evelyn with her braids and her low-heeled shoes and Bill in his gray long trousers and his coat that was too short in the sleeves. It was time to take Bill into town and buy him a new suit. Perhaps they could all go to town and have lunch at Longchamps and see some sort of show, if there was anything on the New York stage that the children ought to see. It had been a long while since they had been to town together. All sorts of other plans came to mind as he saw them but there was no opportunity to sort out those plans because they were all so glad to see him.

"I called up Marble," Nancy said. "She said you were going to take the three-two."

"Here," Bill said, "let me carry that for you," and he took his suitcase.

"Hello, Evvie," he said. "Do you know what I did in Boston? I bought a bottle of that after-shaving lotion."

"Evelyn, get in back with Bill," Nancy said, and then she held his hand for a moment as they walked to the car. "I've got to pick up my dress at the cleaners'. That's all we have to do."

"What dress?" he asked.

"The almost new one," she said, "with flowers on it, for tonight."

"Oh, yes," he said. "Tonight," but there was a long while until evening. He felt pleasantly tired and he could not be worried about that dinner at the Burtons'.

"It's funny," he said. "I feel as if I'd been across the ocean. The climate's different here."

"I know," Nancy said. "It must be very difficult to pick up all the threads, but don't try too hard . . . just give yourself time."

"It isn't so hard," he said, and he laughed.

"It's nice to know it," Nancy said. "The first thing for you to do is to get to know the children all over again. I can come later and more gradually. We all may be a little shy with each other at first but we can all adjust together."

The grass was beginning to turn green and forsythia was out already and there were tomato plants and forget-me-nots in baskets in front of the hardware store.

"Mother," Evelyn said from the back seat, "I don't know what you're talking about. Daddy's only been away two days."

"Oh, put on another record," Bill told her. "Don't you know when Mother's being funny?"

"Don't try to put your feet into the front seat, Bill," Charles said, "and don't sit on the back of your spine. They won't approve of it when you go to Exeter."

He had not intended to mention Exeter. He did not want to talk about anything in particular. He felt relaxed and tired, but pleasantly tired.

"We ought to buy some garden hose," he said. "I wonder whether they have any decent hose this year."

"Oh, never mind it now," Nancy said. "Let's just go on home and maybe you and Bill had better rake the lawn, or perhaps we might just sit around and do nothing for a while. I'd rather like to do nothing." She glanced at him quickly. "How did it all look when you got back?"

"Oh," he said, "the general situation?"

"Yes," she said, "that God-damned situation."

"Now, Nancy," he said. "The children."

"It's all right," Nancy said. "The children know I swear sometimes," but of course neither of them could speak fully of the general situation in front of the children.

"It looks about the same," Charles said. "I only saw Tony Burton for a minute. He came in late and he was busy but he said he was looking forward to tonight, that he had something on his mind."

"Is that the way he put it, looking forward?"

It was awkward, talking in that veiled way in front of the children. "Nance," he said, "there isn't anything more I can do. Let's try to forget it, shall we?"

"Just as long as it gets over," she said, "one way or another. You haven't forgotten about that payment on the mortgage, have you?"

He could understand this association of ideas. They were turning into the gateway of Sycamore Park and he could see the whitewashed brick of their house already.

"No, I haven't," he said. "Can you name one time when I've forgotten about the mortgage?" The lawn had never looked so green and the house had never looked so well. "Do you know what I think?" He raised his voice because he did not like to think of Bill and Evelyn in the back seat trying to piece their words together as children always did. "I think it's about time Bill and Evvie learned to sail." The idea must have come to him both from thinking of the products of the Nickerson Cordage Company and from that glimpse of the Sound from the station platform.

"Learned to sail?" Nancy repeated.

"I don't see why not," he said. "Here we live right near the water and we've never had a boat. I don't see why we shouldn't—an eighteen-foot knockabout or something"—and then he checked himself before he said any more. He sounded exactly as his father had and even the words were almost the same.

"Do you really mean that about a sailboat?" he heard Bill asking.

"I don't know why not," he said. "We'll have to think about it, Bill." The car had stopped and Bill and Evelyn were on the graveled driveway.

He and Bill and Evelyn were still talking about that hypothetical sailboat when Nancy opened the side door and called him. The idea of the boat kept interfering with other things he was thinking and while they raked oak leaves from under the rhododendrons, everything he thought was also mingled with the persistent rustling and crackling of the leaves. It was a sound like the lapping of small waves.

He had put on sneakers, and a pair of khaki trousers from one of his old uniforms, and a white shirt with a frayed collar which Nancy had saved for him for working around the place. It would be torn up for cleaning rags after he had used it once or twice. He and Evelyn raked and Bill packed the leaves into a bushel basket and carried them to a shady place by the side of the garage where they were going to make a compost heap. He had never made one but Nancy had been talking about compost heaps for a long while and this year they would start one. The Martins had a compost heap, Evelyn was saying, and it was wet and soggy and it smelled, but it was meant to be wet and soggy, he told her, and when she asked him what they would do with it after it was made he told Evelyn to ask her mother, who knew about those things. Evelyn was getting old enough so that she ought to learn something about gardening. Lots of people liked it and it was good exercise, and it made no difference that he did not know much about it. He had always been too busy, but when he was Evelyn's age he had always cleaned up the back yard.

"Did Aunt Dorothea use to clean it up too?" Evelyn asked.

Yes, her Aunt Dorothea did sometimes, when he did not do it well enough. Her Aunt Dorothea always liked to have things picked up.

"You know," he said, while he raked the leaves, "we might all go up to Clyde this summer. I've always been thinking of taking you there. We really ought to get around to it. I don't see why we shouldn't just take the Buick and drive up there, if I can get some time off. It might be a new Buick. I've got my name down for one."

"Never mind about the Buick," Bill said. "Let's talk about the boat."

"If we went up to Clyde," he said, "we might go on to the White Mountains. I've never seen Mount Washington."

Some of his senior class at high school, he was thinking, had taken a trip to Mount Washington once, with Mr. Flanders, the physics teacher, but it had been one of those times when there was not much money and he had not gone with them.

"Never mind about Mount Washington," Bill said. "Let's talk about the boat."

"All right," he said. "It won't do any harm to talk about it."

"If we got it, where would we keep it?"

"Don't spill all those leaves," he said. "We could moor it somewhere. My father was always talking about getting us a boat and a pony but he never did and maybe I won't either."

"Well," Bill said, "we could get a magazine and look at pictures."

Yes, they could look at pictures, and perhaps no one believed entirely in the boat. But then Evelyn was saying that Mr. Swiss had one, with an auxiliary engine. But then he was not Mr. Swiss and he did not want to be Mr. Swiss.

"You see," he said, "you can't be anything very different from what you are."

They were all still talking but his attention was wandering. He was thinking about security, a popular word still, even when nothing was secure. The foundation of everything was shaky and yet there were always plans on top of those shaking foundations, pathetic plans, important only to an individual.

Nothing was certain. Yet he felt contented and at peace doing nothing but raking leaves on the lawn, he and his two children.

"Now, listen," he said, "let's stop all this about a sailboat. We'll probably never have one. I don't know what we'd do with one if we had it."

"You said it wouldn't do any harm to talk about it," Bill said.

"It doesn't matter what you talk about or think about," he said, "as long as you know what's real, and it's pretty hard to learn what's real and what isn't. A lot of people never learn." He rubbed the sleeve of his frayed shirt across his forehead. "This is a pretty tough world, Bill."

Bill and Evelyn looked at him with that half-astonished, half-bored expression that always came over children when grownups spoke of the hardness of the world. He could see that they did not believe him and it was just as well. No matter what might happen, all he could do was give them an illusion of security.

"Why don't you go in and get a baseball and a mitt, Bill?" he asked. "I'd sort of like to toss a ball around."

It was an effort to escape. It reminded him of his father reading *Candide* aloud—the part about digging in one's garden.

"Why is it such a tough world?" Bill asked. "You're doing pretty well, aren't you?"

"Well," he said, "there's always room for improvement."

Then Nancy opened the side door and called him.

"Charley," she called, "you'd better come in now if we're going to get there on time." They always got everywhere on time, they both felt the same way about punctuality, but for the moment he had completely forgotten about the dinner with Tony Burton.

Upstairs in their room Nancy pulled at the zipper of her housecoat and looked critically at the long flowered silk dress spread out on the bed, fresh from the cleaners.

"I suppose she'll wear a long dress," she said.

She was referring, of course, to Mrs. Anthony Burton, and Nancy had the same watchful, determinedly pleasant expression that she always assumed on those semiannual occasions when the Burtons asked them out to Roger's Point, near Stamford. It was quite different from the expression she assumed when they went to the Merrys' or when they had dined with the Slades.

"Nance," he said, and he put his arm around her.

"Don't kiss me," she said. "You'll muss my hair and I've got on lipstick."

"All right," he said. "All right."

"I put your studs in for you," she said. "It's your new shirt. I've laid out everything."

"Well, don't sound like an undertaker," he said.

"I don't sound like anything," she said, "but I wish you'd hurry, Charley."

Everything was laid out, as she said it was, on the fresh candlewick spread of his twin bed.

"I don't see why I should wear a stiff shirt," he said.

"Because you're going to the Burtons', that's why," Nancy said. "He never wears a soft shirt, Charley."

"You mean he expects it of me?" he said. Everyone always dressed like Tony Burton.

It was a small matter and he could not understand why he should have given it another thought but he had pulled open his second bureau drawer. Nancy had her flowered dress over her head but she heard the sound.

"Charley, what are you doing?" Nancy asked. "Everything's laid out."

No matter what she said, he was going to wear a soft shirt to the Burtons'.

There was no problem about the children's supper because Mary was back from Harlem and she would get it. The Buick was by the front door, where they had left it after the trip from the station.

"I'll drive," Nancy said.

"Let me drive over," Charles said. "I'd like the kids to remember that their father can drive a car."

Bill and Evelyn were standing at the end of the walk. The rhododendrons by the front door were budding and there were small soft dots of yellowish green on the tips of the yews. It was seven o'clock, the right time to be leaving for the Burtons', with a little leeway in case there should be heavy traffic on the Post Road. He stepped on the self-starter and the engine still sounded smooth and quiet. It was still a good car and it showed how long you could keep a car if you took care of it. People might not be changing cars every other year as they had before the war and this might affect motor stocks if Ford and Chrysler and General Motors ever caught up on their production.

"Good-by," he called. "We'll be back early, I guess."

"Wait a minute," Nancy said. "Evelyn, will you please water the begonias in the dining room, and, Bill, be sure to close the windows if it rains. Mary always forgets."

"Is that all?" Charles asked.

"Yes," Nancy said, "that's all," and she opened her white bead bag to be sure she had not forgotten her lipstick, her compact, and a clean handkerchief.

They were alone and there was a change in tempo because there was always a slight façade, a different set of manners, when they were with the children. Now they would have to talk about facts, plain contemporary facts. They were on that twisting road with all the driveways. Obviously they were each waiting for the other to speak and neither could wait too long or else the other might think there was a sense of strain.

"Well, tell me about everything," Nancy said.

What he wanted to say to her might have been possible in their room just before she had told him not to kiss her because of lipstick and her hair but it was not possible in the car on their way to the Post Road. Though there was a proper time for everything, opportunities were very rare when he could appropriately say what he really thought without its sounding simple and banal. She was asking him to tell her everything. It was a set speech, like a phrase in a book of etiquette. He wished to God he could tell her everything. At that moment, for example, he wanted to tell her that he loved her. He wanted to tell her that she and the children were all that mattered and that he had wanted to tell her so when he had called her up from Clyde, but it was not the time or place.

"Charley," she said, "don't drive so fast."

"All right," he said. "Nance, we've been through a lot together, haven't we? One damn thing after another."

"I always have that feeling after you've been driving for a while," she said. "Aren't you going to tell me about everything?"

"Well," he said, "it was queer going back to Clyde. It was quite an experience." He paused. They were coming to the intersection with the Post Road.

"You don't have to slow down," Nancy said. "The light's turning green."

"Well," he said, "anyway Jackie Mason's got everything," and he turned left on the Post Road.

"Who?" she asked. She was evidently thinking of something else and there was no reason why she should not have been because she had nothing to do with Clyde. Nevertheless, it was exasperating when she asked him who.

"Jackie Mason," he said. "You know, Jackie Mason."

"Oh, yes," she said. "Of course. Well, what about him?"

He was passing an oil truck on the Post Road. On the rear of it was a sign in chalk, "If you can read this, you're too damn close." He could not look at her but he knew she was looking at him and he could tell from the effort in her voice that she was trying to enter into the spirit of what he was trying to tell her.

"Well," he said, "there isn't much more except that he's got everything. He's a director of the Dock Street Savings Bank, and he's a trustee of the public library and he's in the Tuesday Club and he's going to marry Jessica Lovell, but I told you that, didn't I?"

"Well," Nancy said, "you could have done that too. I always told you so."

"Well," he said, "I'm glad I didn't." He took his right hand from the wheel and put it over hers.

"Darling," she said, "I wish you'd look where you're going."

"All right," he said, "I'm looking," and he took his hand away. "But at the same time he hasn't got anything, that's what I'm trying to say."

"Who hasn't got anything?" Nancy asked. She could not keep her mind on anything he was trying to say.

"Jackie Mason," he said. "I was telling you, Jackie Mason."

"Well, to hell with Jackie Mason," Nancy said. "There isn't any reason to shout. He hasn't made a touchdown. Besides, I thought you said he had everything."

"All right," he said. "Never mind it, Nancy."

It was well after seven o'clock and cars on the road were switching on their lights. She moved closer to him and she patted his hand as he held the wheel.

"I'm sorry, Charley," she said. "I just can't concentrate. Let's stop trying to talk as though we weren't both thinking about the same thing."

"Yes," he said, "I know." In just a minute they would have to slow down for Stamford, then right, then left at the first stoplight, and then a right turn at the underpass about a mile beyond.

"Charley"—her voice was sharper—"what's the matter?"

There must have been something in his voice, but then they knew each other too well for either of them to conceal anything.

"Oh, God," he said, "I wish everything weren't so contrived."

They were right back where they had been that morning when she had taken him to the station.

"Contrived?" she repeated. "How do you mean, contrived?"

"I mean what I say." He had not intended to sound so bitter. "I mean it's all so superficial. The bank president and the big job, and what will happen to Junior, and whether a boiled shirt will help. The values of it are childish. It hasn't any values at all."

"I know." Her voice was softer. "You've said it before."

"Nance," he said, "I wish you wouldn't be so tense. This isn't as important as all that."

"Charley." She sounded steady and controlled, a great deal too controlled. "Don't say it. I can't stand it if you say it."

"Don't say what? What do you think I'm going to say?" he asked.

"Don't say—" her voice became harsh and strident—"don't say we have each other. We *have* got each other but I don't want to hear it and you're just getting ready to say that, aren't you? It's been in your mind all afternoon. I knew it when you were out there on the lawn being sweet to the children. Say it later but don't say it now."

"Nance," he said, and his own voice was edgy, "I've done everything I can. Let's change the subject."

"You're acting licked already," she said. "I hate it when you act that way."

"All right," he said, "maybe I'm licked, and maybe I don't give a damn."

"I suppose you're going to say I've always been pushing you because I want us to get on," she said.

"I wish you'd stop telling me what I'm going to say," he answered.

They were through the underpass and now that they were approaching the Sound the places were growing older and larger. Houses with mansard roofs and newer Colonials were standing on broad lawns.

"You shouldn't have gone to that damned war."

It seemed to him that he was driving too fast and he glanced at the speedometer but the speed was only thirty miles an hour.

"Yes, you told me so at the time," he said. "You were right, but at least—"

"At least what?"

"I don't know," he said. "Let's not talk about it now."

"Can't we talk about anything?"

"No," he said, "let's not talk about anything."

It had been a long while since his nerves had been so on edge but even so they were almost at Roger's Point. He could see where the public road ended at a wooden booth where a watchman stood to exclude unwanted visitors. It was like entering a military installation when you went to dinner with the Burtons.

"I don't see what they see in him. Any fool ought to know you're ten times as good as he is."

"Who?" he asked.

"Blakesley. I wish you'd listen to me. Blakesley."

"Oh, yes. Well, Roger's pretty quick on his feet," he said.

"Charley, if—" She stopped and started again. "If . . . what are you going to do?"

He did not answer. He felt as though everything were hanging on a few threads and as though anything might break them. They were passing walls of dressed granite and carefully raked driveways. He and Nancy did not belong there. They were like intruders in a larger world.

"Haven't you even thought what you're going to do?"

"My God," he said, "I'm sick of thinking."

The threads had broken and he saw that she was crying. It was the worst possible time for this to have happened, just as they were approaching the private road to Roger's Point. He stopped the car.

"It isn't fair," she sobbed. "It isn't fair."

"Never mind, Nance," he said, and he put his arm around her. "We've got lots of time and it doesn't matter if we're late."

She was already opening her beaded bag.

"I'm all right now," she said. "I didn't mean to let you down."

"You haven't let me down," he said.

"I'm all right now," she said. "Start up the car. This wouldn't have happened if I'd been driving. Don't look at me, don't say anything, and to hell with everybody."

5

Fate Gave, What Chance Shall Not Control . . .

—MATTHEW ARNOLD

It was good business to learn unobtrusively all one could about one's superiors and through his years at the Stuyvesant Bank Charles had collected a considerable amount of information about Mr. Anthony Burton and his background. He had picked this up gradually, a little here and there from occasional remarks that Mr. Burton had made when there was general conversation, and more from Arthur Slade. In the course of time, Charles had been able to sift fact from gossip and to make his own evaluations, until now, if necessary, he could have written from memory a biographical character sketch of Tony Burton, and he could have filled in any gaps from his own firsthand observations of Tony Burton's habits. He knew that Tony Burton was both typical and exceptional—a rich man's son with inherited ability and with ambition that had somehow not been dulled by his having always been presented with what he had wanted. Though Charles knew that he would always observe Tony Burton from a distance, it was fascinating to speculate upon his drives and problems.

His life and Tony Burton's were actually two complete and separate circles, touching at just one point, and they were circles that would never coincide. Though they each could make certain ideas comprehensible to the other, the very words they used had different meanings for each of them. Security, work, worry, future, position, and society, capital and government, all had diverging meanings. Charles could understand the Burton meanings and could interpret them efficiently and accurately, but only in an objective, not in an emotional, way, in the same manner he might have interpreted the meanings of a Russian commissar or a Chinese mandarin. He could admire aspects of Tony Burton, he could even like him, but they could only understand each other theoretically.

When Tony Burton said, for instance, as he was recently fond of saying, that the neighborhood where he lived on Roger's Point was running down, it was not what Charles would have meant if he had made the statement. Tony Burton did not mean that any place on Roger's Point was growing shabby or that crude parvenus had pushed in on Roger's Point. He only meant that several places during the war had changed hands rather suddenly —nothing along the shore, of course, but in back. He did not mean that the new owners of these places were financially unstable or made noises when they ate their food. He only meant that one of the owners was the president of an advertising agency and that another controlled the stock of a depilatory preparation. Though these people were agreeable and wanted to do better, their having been allowed to buy into Roger's Point indicated that the general morale was running low. It would not have happened, for instance, when Mr. Burton, Senior, was alive. That was all he meant.

This did not sound serious to Charles, but it was to Tony Burton and Charles could understand it, intellectually. What was more, Tony Burton must have known he understood it, for he discussed the situation quite frankly with Charles, just as though Charles owned property on Roger's Point—not on the inside but on the water side. Yet they both obviously knew that Charles could never afford to live there. A backlog of inherited wealth was required to live there, unless one made a killing on the stock market or invented a laxative or a depilatory. There was no way of telling what might happen to Roger's Point. Anyone might live there in time, and Tony Burton could laugh ironically about it, and Charles, too, could laugh, sympathetically and intellectually, without ever fully savoring the suffering behind Tony Burton's mirth.

Tony Burton's father, Sanford Burton, had bought all of Roger's Point in 1886, when there were no houses there, and he had built the Burton house in 1888. He had already formed the brokerage firm of Burton and Fall, and the Point had been a profitable real estate investment. It had not been difficult to sell off parts of it around the turn of the century to the proper sort of person. Simpkins, a director of U. S. Steel, had bought the cove, and the Marshalls, the Erie Railroad Marshalls, had bought the place next, and the Crawfords, the Appellate Justice Crawfords, were there also. Charles could remember most of the owners' names. It was good business to know them as many of them had accounts at the Stuyvesant Bank. In fact Charles knew the names as well as did the watchman at the beginning of the private road.

"I'm going to Mr. Anthony Burton's," he said, and he could even employ the proper tone, intellectually. "Mr. Burton is expecting me for dinner."

"You needn't have told him all the family history," Nancy said. "Why didn't you tell him you're forty-three years old and show him our wedding certificate?" She was telling him indirectly that she was feeling better, that she was all right now.

"Oh, my God," she said, "here it is, and they've put on the lights."

She was referring to lights in the trees along the drive, a recent innovation of Tony Burton's, inspired by a winter's visit at the place of a friend of his in Fort Lauderdale, Florida. If they could have lights in coconut palms, Tony Burton said, there was no reason for not having them in the copper beeches at Roger's Point, but those new lights did not go so well with the house. Lampposts and gaslight would have fitted the whole scene better. The building had been designed by Richardson, the Romanesque architect—another fact that Charles had learned and filed away. It was too dark to see the detail of the slate roof, the brick walls and the arched doors and windows trimmed with old red sandstone, but its vague outline still looked indestructible. The light beneath the brick and sandstone porte-cochere shone on the iron and glass front door and on the potted hothouse azaleas in rows beside the steps.

The doors had swung open already and Jeffreys, the Burton butler, had stepped outside—but not as far down as the lower step—and was saying good evening.

"You go in, Nancy," Charles said. "I'd better put the car somewhere."

"There's no need to move it, Mr. Gray," Tony Burton's butler said. He was wearing a dinner coat with a stiff shirt. "There's no one else this evening."

"Oh," Charles said, "if you're sure it's all right." He had never been able to speak even an intellectual language with Tony Burton's butler. "It's a beautiful evening, isn't it?"

"Yes, sir," Tony Burton's butler said. "It's balmy for this time of year," and then Charles saw that a maid was behind him, relieving Nancy of her cloak.

It was impossible to forget Tony Burton's house once you had been inside it. In summer or winter the air in the hall was balmy like the evening and fragrant with the scent of hothouse flowers. It was a huge oak-paneled hall, with a double staircase and a gallery and a Romanesque fireplace. For a second he and Nancy stood in the shaded light of the hall almost indecisively. There was an especial feeling of timidity when one went there, a furtive sense of not belonging. Yet in another way he was perfectly at ease for at those semiannual dinners Tony Burton had always made them feel most welcome. Besides, each summer there was always that all-day party for everyone at the bank, with three-legged races and potato races and pingpong and bridge for the wives. Mrs. Burton, too, always made the bank wives feel comfortable. The bright light from the open parlor door shone across the dusky hall and Tony Burton was already in the oblong of light, a white carnation in the lapel of his dinner coat, holding out both hands, one for Nancy and one for him.

"Home is the sailor, home from sea," Tony Burton said, "and the hunter home from the hill. I wish you wouldn't always surprise me, Nancy my dear. Why are you more beautiful every time I see you, or do I just forget?"

"It might be that you just forget, mightn't it?" Nancy asked.

Tony Burton laughed. He had a delightful laugh.

"We've really got to do something about seeing each other more often," he said. "It's been too long, much too long. Why don't you come to work some morning instead of Charley? I'm getting pretty sick of seeing Charles around." He laughed again and slapped Charles on the back and they walked behind Nancy into the drawing room.

Charles knew all about Tony Burton's drawing room, too, both from Tony Burton and from Arthur Slade. Mrs. Burton and the girls, before the girls had been married, had made Tony Burton do it entirely over. The enormous Persian carpet had come from the Anderson Gallery and so had the two Waterford chandeliers. Charles remembered them very well because Tony Burton had sent him to the auction to bid them in on one of the first occasions that Tony had ever paid any attention to him, and this did not seem so long ago. He also remembered the huge canvas of a mass of square-rigged ships—the British fleet at anchor. Mrs. Burton was always buying new things for the living room and besides Tony always loved boats. The cup he had won in one of the Bermuda races was standing on the concert grand piano. You could roll up the carpet and clear out all the furniture. It had been a great place for dancing before the girls had married.

"Althea," Tony Burton said, "I told you Nancy Gray would be wearing a long dress."

"Oh, my dear," Mrs. Burton said, "I should have called you up. Tony's getting so absent-minded lately. He spoke of it as supper. There should be set rules for short and long. Now just the other evening at the Drexels' the same thing happened to me. I thought it was dinner and it was supper. But the men thought this up. We didn't, did we?"

"Charles should have told me," Nancy said. "Why didn't you tell me it was supper, Charley?"

"It's always some man's fault, isn't it, Charley?" Tony Burton said.

"That's one of the truest things you ever said, sweetheart," Mrs. Burton said. "Everything that happens to a woman is always some man's fault."

"Jeffreys can bring us almost anything," Tony Burton said, "from sherry and a biscuit to Scotch on the rocks, but Charley and I will stick to dry Martinis, won't we, Charley? What will you have, Nancy my dear?"

"A Martini," Nancy said, "and if I don't like it I can blame it on the men."

"But not on Tony," Mrs. Burton said. "Blame it on Jeffreys. Tony mixes terrible Martinis. Don't you think so, Mr. Gray, or have you ever tried one of his Martinis?"

It was characteristic of that relationship and perfectly suitable that Mrs. Burton should call him Mr. Gray. It meant that he was a business friend of Tony Burton's, or associate might have been a better word, who had come to supper on business with his little wife. She knew how to put Tony's business friends and associates at their ease, but there were certain limits and certain degrees of rank. They were not on a first-name basis yet and he was just as glad of it. It would have embarrassed him acutely, it would have seemed like a breach of etiquette, if he were to call Mrs. Burton Althea. He knew his place and they could meet on common ground by his calling Mr. Burton Tony and by Mrs. Burton's referring to Nancy as "my dear."

"I'm not in a position to say what I think of Tony's cocktails," Charles said, "except that Tony is always right."

"You all lick his boots so," Mrs. Burton said. "That's why he's so impossible when he comes home. Sherry, please, Jeffreys. Is Mr. Gray impossible when he comes home, my dear?"

"Usually," Nancy said. "Normally impossible."

"I wonder what they do at the bank," Mrs. Burton said. "I have a few vague ideas. That blond secretary of Tony's . . . we can compare notes after dinner." The oil of small talk soothed the troubled waters, if there were troubled waters. Mrs. Tony Burton was putting Nancy at her ease. It was necessary business entertaining, household duty, and one of these suppers that must have helped in some vague way.

Everything moved so smoothly that when Charles tried to discover anything revealing in Mrs. Burton's voice or attitude, he could hit upon absolutely nothing. He could discover no new flicker of interest or no new warmth. She was simply being as nice as she could possibly be to one of the younger men whom Tony had to have around sometimes and to the little thing the younger man had married. She had even dressed thoughtfully for the occasion in an oldish gown, with no jewelry except a simple strand of pearls, yet you could not say that she was dressing down to Nancy. Charles remembered Arthur Slade's saying that she was a good ten years younger than Tony, that she was one of the Philadelphia Brines, and Charles knew from the size of the Brine estate, which the bank was handling, that, like Tony Burton, she had always been free from want. He could tell it from the tilt of her head, from her confident happy mouth, and even from the tint of her hair. There was a single lock of gray in it and perhaps all of it should have been gray but he could not be quite sure.

"I love that little house of yours, my dear," she was saying, and he could see Nancy smiling at her with elaborate enthusiasm. "That whitewashed brick, and everything so compactly arranged. It must be a comfort to live in it instead of in a great barn, but Tony insists on the ancestral mansion."

"The only good thing about a small house," Nancy said, "is when the maid leaves."

"We've been marvelously lucky," Mrs. Burton said. "Ours keep staying on with us, I'm sure I don't know why."

Jeffreys, the butler, was passing round pieces of toast with cream cheese and recumbent anchovies on them, and a maid followed Jeffreys carrying an icy bowl of celery, raw carrots and olives.

"I hear that raw carrots are good for the eyesight," Charles said to Tony Burton.

"That's one of those new ideas," Tony said. He looked bright and alert as he always did before dinner. "It's on a par with the one about alcohol being good for hardening of the arteries. Have you heard the new one about Truman?"

Tony Burton always enjoyed those stories. Formerly it had been Franklin D. Roosevelt, though Tony was hardly what you would call a Roosevelt-hater, and now it was Truman.

"I don't know," Charles said. "I've heard a good many new ones lately." He had almost called Tony Burton sir but he had checked himself in time.

"I know just what you mean, my dear," he heard Mrs. Burton saying. "These country day schools are never quite right. Now when the girls were growing up—"

"Always remember it might have been Wallace," he said to Tony Burton. Everything considered, Tony was surprisingly tolerant about politics and politicians. To him politics was like the weather. You could make occasional forecasts but you could not control it.

"I'd like to know what those playboys are going to try next," he said. "And that's a good name for them, playboys. Did you ever read the Van Bibber stories by Richard Harding Davis?"

"The Van Bibber stories?" Charles repeated. "I'm afraid I must have missed them."

"Well," Tony Burton said, "they belonged to my flight more than your flight, Charley." This must once have been a shooting term, Charles thought, used when one foregathered in a gunroom after a hard day on the moors. "They typified a certain era—the period when I was a playboy myself. There used to be a fashionable character, believe it or not—the gay blade about town, the white tie, the silk hat, we won't get home until morning. He's an extinct type now, of course, a product of a different social scene. Dick Davis hit him off rather well in the Van Bibber stories. Dick Davis was quite a playboy himself. I used to try to model my conduct after his, in a small way. Here comes Jeffreys. How about another cocktail?"

"Oh, no, I don't think so, thanks," Charles said. He did not want to refuse too quickly or too eagerly, and of course Tony Burton must have known that when urged he would take another.

"It won't hurt you to relax and tomorrow's Saturday and I'm going to have another."

"Well, thanks," Charles said, "if you are. They're very good cocktails."

He wished that he could relax as Tony Burton suggested, instead of trying to read a meaning into every simple action. Tony Burton would never have taken a second Martini if they were going to talk of anything seriously after dinner. It meant that everything was settled in one way or another.

"Now, Henry Wallace," Tony Burton was saying, "and all the rest of the New Deal crowd are the playboy type. They have the same power and the same privileges expressed in different terms. They're all Van Bibbers."

Tony smiled at him triumphantly but it was hard for Charles to discuss the subject intelligently, not being familiar with the works of Richard Harding Davis.

"It's an interesting thought," he said, "but it might be that you're oversimplifying."

Tony Burton looked at him in a fixed, cool way that made Charles think that perhaps he had said too much. It was necessary not to forget just who he was and what he was. It was necessary to assume a convivial attitude and yet not too convivial, to be familiar and yet not overfamiliar.

"Sometimes you have a cryptic quality, Charley," Tony Burton said. "I never seem to know lately whether you're laughing at me or not. Sometimes you're an enigma."

"Well," Charles answered, "sometimes you're an enigma to me."

When he heard Tony Burton laugh he knew that he had been familiar but not too familiar.

"Oh, Jeffreys," Tony Burton said. "How about another one, Charley?"

"No, thanks," Charles said.

"Definitely not?"

"Definitely," Charles said. "You might start talking about books and authors again and I want to understand everything you say tonight."

It might have been too familiar but at least he had made a point. He waited smiling, watching Tony Burton, and he put his glass back on Tony Burton's butler's tray. He was thinking of what he had said to young Mrs. Whitaker in the apartment on Park Avenue when she had offered him a drink. He had told her that he did not think she would take one if she were in his place and she had said they were both very good for what they were. He watched Tony Burton and smiled an innocent friendly smile. He and Tony Burton were both very good for what they were. They had both been trained in the Stuyvesant Bank and they had the same veneer and discipline. He had come a long way from Clyde.

"Tony," Mrs. Burton called, "if you can stop talking business with poor Mr. Gray we might all go in to dinner."

"Now, Althea," Tony Burton said, "Charley and I have a lot of other things to talk about. I wish you would get it out of your head that I always talk business with the boys."

The dining room with its heavy oak chairs, and an English leather screen placed before the pantry door, and its ornate Tiffany silver upon the massive sideboard, was also a long way from Clyde. The table, set for four, beneath another Waterford chandelier, looked too small for the room but imposingly beautiful with its Venetian tablecloth, its water and wine glasses and its bowl of tulips. He was glad there were only four of them because the conversation would be general and he would not have to talk to Mrs. Burton. He saw Nancy glance at him quickly as he sat down and he smiled at her. It was better to let the Burtons start the conversation. It was better not to say what a beautiful tablecloth it was or to speak about the tulips. It was better to make no remark about the surroundings that would show how little one was used to them, but there was no reason to worry, because Mrs. Burton was already speaking.

It was so nice, she was saying, to have them drop in like this instead of coming to a large dinner. Eight was the limit for general conversation and four was better than eight, and she was thinking, just the other day, about the first time she had ever heard about Mr. Gray—from poor Arthur Slade. She did not think she had seen Mr. Gray since that accident. It was tragic and so unnecessary. They had both been so fond of poor Arthur, but then she knew that Mr. Gray knew all about flying. The conversation was moving very pleasantly. It was not necessary to think carefully of what he was saying, now that they all were talking. Tony Burton was asking Nancy about the children, as though he knew them very well, and while they talked the plates were changing. There were soup and guinea hen and then a salad and then dessert. He was glad that it was not a long or complicated dinner. There was no obvious sense of strain but all the while he felt that Tony Burton was watching him.

"I wish," Tony Burton said, "there weren't so many words, or it may be because I'm getting old that they confuse me more than they used to. Somehow they keep having more shades of meaning. Now even with Charles and me it's difficult. I say a word and he says a word and we can look it up in the dictionary, but it doesn't mean the same thing to either of us and it would mean something a little different to Nancy and it would be a little different even to Althea. I don't suppose this is a very new thought of mine, but it's a thought."

"I can't imagine what you're talking about, Tony," Mrs. Burton said.

"But Charley knows," Tony Burton said, "don't you, Charley? We all may be worrying about the same thing but we worry about it in different ways."

It was startling to find that Tony Burton was thinking during dinner exactly what he had been thinking earlier.

"Yes," he said, "I know just what you mean."

He saw that Nancy looked startled too and he saw Tony Burton glance at her and then look back at him triumphantly.

"I wish we could all get together," Tony Burton said, "and we might do something with the world, but of course we never can get together. That's the exasperating thing about it."

"Really," Mrs. Burton said, "I don't know what you're talking about, Tony."

Charles himself could not gather what this was leading up to, but as he watched Tony Burton he could see that Tony's face was set in the expression he always wore when he was about to say a few graceful words before a group of people.

"Perhaps I'm being cryptic now," he said, "but all I'm saying is that I wish we might all be friends. I really hope we can be, in spite of anything that may happen in the future, and the future isn't as clear as it used to be. That's all I'm trying to say. And now if you girls will excuse us, I'm going to take Charley into the library. Charley and I want to have a little talk tonight but we'll be back as soon as we can."

Mrs. Burton stood up and as Charles rose he felt a slight wave of nausea. He could only put one interpretation on that hope for friendship. He guessed the final answer to their little talk already. He felt the back of his chair biting into the palm of his hand but he still had to say the right thing.

"Why, of course," he said, "we'll always be friends, Tony." He said it automatically but he knew that they never had been and they never would be friends. They might wish it but it would never work for either of them, no matter what might happen.

"Don't stay too long and get too interested," Mrs. Burton said. "I don't see why Tony can't ever get through his business in New York."

Charles was no longer thinking clearly as he walked with Tony Burton from the dining room. What he desired most was to behave in such a way that no one would have the satisfaction of seeing how deeply he was hurt. That desire was partly discipline and partly human instinct for concealment. His own reaction was what shocked him most because he had believed that he was prepared for bad news and that he would not consider bad news as complete a disaster as was indicated by the sinking feeling in the pit of his stomach. Yet after that first moment the shock was giving way to relief. He suddenly felt free and a weight was lifted from him. There was no reason for him to try any longer, not the slightest reason. He did not know what he would say or do in that final interview but there was nothing more that he could expect from Tony Burton. He would never have to be obsequious and careful again. He would never have to go through anything like that dinner. If Tony wished that they could still be friends, this meant at least that Tony liked him personally, but that was inconsequential. There was no room for personal likes in a corporation.

It was not far from the dining room to the smaller room where men customarily gathered. They both walked across that gloomy hall without speaking and space had lost its significance. He was actually walking also over the road of his career, a feeble little human track like the progress of a sea creature in sand. It stretched all the way from the day on the stage at the City Hall to the accounting department in Wright-Sherwin, to Johnson Street, to

Rush & Company, to the day his father died, to New York, to the day h met Nancy downtown, and now the track was ending in that walk across th hall. There would never be the same hay in the bundle again. The ass would never have to walk after it so assiduously. He might still be useful, but in a business way his career was as good as over. He had gone as far as he would go.

It was amazing that his thoughts could move so far afield in such a short space of time. He was like a defeated general withdrawing to a prepared position. He could sell the house at Sycamore Park. Suburban real estate was still high. They could move to a smaller place. There would be funds enough to educate Bill, and there was that trust fund of his mother's which would revert to him eventually. He would never have his present reputation but he would have the commercial value of an educated wheel horse, if he knew his place. He would never have to try so hard again.

"It's over," he said to himself as he walked across the hall. "Thank God, it's over." It was the first time he had felt really free since the moment he had met Jessica at the firemen's muster.

Tony Burton's room had always reminded him of the corner of a men's club. It was filled with the mementos of the travels of Tony Burton, gathered on that trip to Bagdad and on two world cruises. There was a gilded Chinese Buddha on the mantel above the arched fireplace, and a Chinese ancestral portrait and other things, but Charles was no longer obliged to be interested in them. He seated himself in a comfortable armchair without waiting to see if it was Mr. Burton's chair or not. He no longer had to bother.

"Sugar and cream, sir?" Mr. Burton's butler asked.

"Just coffee, thank you," Charles said.

"And brandy, sir?"

"No, thanks," Charles said. "No brandy."

"Try it, Charley," Tony Burton said. "It's some of my father's brandy. There isn't much like it left."

Tony Burton was still standing up. He should have waited until Tony sat down but he no longer had to try so hard.

"Nancy always says I shouldn't drink after dinner," he said, "but all right if you're going to have some, Tony."

"Why not break down all the way and have a cigar?" Tony Burton said.

"Why, thanks," he answered. "I'd like one."

"Now that I think of it, I've never seen you smoke a cigar, Charley."

"I don't often," Charles said, "but I'd rather like one tonight."

Tony Burton was still standing and again he wore the look he customarily assumed when he prepared to say a few graceful yet pointed words.

"Close the door, please, Jeffreys, when you go out," Tony Burton said.

It was like a meeting in the bank directors' room when someone who came in with papers was told to close the door when he left. Charles leaned back comfortably in his chair. It was up to Tony Burton and he did not have to try. He was thinking of other talks in other libraries, the Judge's library at Gow Street and that hypocritical library of Mr. Lovell's and his own library at Sycamore Park. Thank God, it was all over, but he still had a detached,

...of curiosity. He was waiting to see how Tony would handle ... Tony was sometimes slow and fumbling with decisions but ...ade up his mind he carried them through cleanly.

... friendship in business—" Tony Burton said. "It's always bothered ...ney shouldn't be mixed together." He must still have been thinking of ... speech in the dining room.

"They don't mix together," Charles said. "Don't try to make them, Tony." It was the first time he had ever spoken to Tony Burton exactly as an equal and it was a great relief. He flicked off the ash of his cigar and picked up his brandy glass and waited.

"And yet they must mix," Tony Burton said. "None of us can help it, Charley. If you see somebody every day, if you have any human instincts at all, you get interested in him. You're bound to like him, or things about him. I like everybody at the bank. They're like members of my family. Now take Blakesley. What do you think of Blakesley, Charley?"

It was not a fair question and there was no reason to give a fair answer and besides it did not matter what he thought of Roger Blakesley.

"What do you want me to think?" he asked, and he was glad to see that Tony did not like the answer.

"It isn't what I want." Tony Burton gave his head an exasperated shake. "You and I are alone here, and you don't have to be so damned careful. There's no necessity for it any more. I want your opinion of him. Do you like him or don't you?"

"All right," Charles said, "as long as it doesn't matter any more, Tony. He's conscientious, energetic, and well-trained, but I don't like him much. Why should I?"

"I rather like him," Tony Burton said. "He's been on my conscience lately. He's been so damned anxious, so damned much on his toes. He's always in there trying."

"I don't know what else you could expect," Charles said, and he was almost amused, now that there was nothing to gain or lose. "I've been trying pretty hard myself."

He had never realized that it could be such a delightful moment, to sit sipping Tony Burton's brandy, entirely free, entirely without thought control.

"Not in the same way, Charley." Tony Burton shook his head again. "You're subtler. You've developed, you've matured. You don't fidget mentally—not in the same way, Charley."

"Thanks," Charles said, "but I wouldn't say that I've been very subtle, Tony."

Tony Burton shook his head impatiently as though he were being diverted from his train of thought.

"Of course I'm out of touch with things, being where I am," he said, "but I've been getting an idea lately . . . and maybe I'm entirely wrong. I wish you'd tell me, Charley. You're more in touch with the office than I am and you're in a position to know Blakesley. . . . It seems to me that he has some idea that we're considering him for Arthur Slade's place. Do you know anything about this, Charley?"

"My God," Charles said. "My God"; and he had a hysterical desire to laugh and then he found that he was laughing. "What did you think that Roger was considering?"

"I didn't give it much thought until about ten days ago," Tony Burton said. "I'm glad if it amuses you. It doesn't amuse me. When anyone gets ideas like that it's a problem what to do with him later. You never thought that any of us were considering Blakesley seriously, did you? He was useful while you were away but he is not the right material. Of course, there had to be a decent interval after Arthur died but it never occurred to me that you'd have any doubts about it. Your name's coming up before the directors on Monday. Now what do you think we'd better do about Blakesley?"

Suddenly Charles felt dull and very tired.

"You'd better tell him something, Tony," he said, "instead of teasing him to death."

"I suppose I'll have to on Monday. I don't suppose I can put it off on anyone else," Tony Burton said. "I should have discouraged him long ago. I'm sorry about the whole thing but perhaps he had better resign."

It was like the time at Dartmouth when he had won the half mile at freshman track. He felt dull and very tired.

"That was all I meant in the dining room." Tony Burton shook his head again. "Now that we'll be working together more closely, Charley, I hope that we'll always be friends."

Tony's voice seemed to come from a long way off. There was a weight on Charles again, the same old weight, and it was heavier after that brief moment of freedom. In spite of all those years, in spite of all his striving, it was remarkable how little pleasure he took in final fulfillment. He was a vice-president of the Stuyvesant Bank. It was what he had dreamed of long ago and yet it was not the true texture of early dreams. The whole thing was contrived, as he had said to Nancy, an inevitable result, a strangely hollow climax. It had obviously been written in the stars, bound to happen, and he could not have changed a line of it, being what he was, and Nancy would be pleased, but it was not what he had dreamed.

"Well, Tony," he said, "I guess that means I can send Junior to Exeter," and Tony Burton was asking why Exeter? He would not send any boy of his to Exeter.

They were on a different basis already, now that he was a vice-president. Automatically, his thoughts were running along new lines, well-trained, mechanically perfect thoughts, estimating a new situation. There would be no trouble with the directors. There were only five vice-presidents at the Stuyvesant, all of the others older than he, most of them close to the retirement age, like Tony Burton himself. For a moment he thought of Mr. Laurence Lovell on Johnson Street but Mr. Lovell would not have understood, or Jessica either, how far he had gone or what it meant to be a vice-president of the Stuyvesant Bank. Nancy would understand. Nancy had more ambi-

…an he had for himself. Nancy would be very proud. They …e house at Sycamore Park and get a larger place. They would … the Oak Knoll Club. And then there was the sailboat. It had …ensations but it was not what he had dreamed.

…veek from Saturday there'll be a little dinner. It's customary," Tony …on said. "You'd better be ready to make a few remarks."

'All right," Charles said, "if it's customary."

"And now we'd better go back and see what the girls are doing, unless you have something else on your mind."

"Oh, no, Tony," he answered, "I don't think there's anything else."

They would have to turn in the old Buick as soon as he could get a new one. There were a great many things to think about but they could wait till morning.

Nancy and Mrs. Burton were sitting together on a sofa in the living room and he thought they both looked relieved to see the men come back.

"Well," Mrs. Burton said, "I hope you two have settled the affairs of the world. You look as though you have, and poor Mr. Gray looks tired."

He saw Nancy look at him and Nancy looked tired too. He wanted very much to tell her the news but it would have sounded blatant. Then Tony Burton must have noticed that there was a sense of strain.

"I don't see why you keep on calling Charley Mr. Gray," he said, "when Charley's in the family—or at least he will be on Monday," and then he must have felt that he should explain the situation further because he turned to Nancy. "I don't suppose this comes as any great surprise. Why should it? It's hardly talking out of school. Charley's name is going before the directors on Monday, but I've spoken to them already. There won't be any trouble."

If it meant more to Nancy than it did to him, it made everything all the better, and he was very much impressed at the way she took it. She looked as though she had known all the time that he would be the new vice-president, that nothing else could possibly have happened. She was fitting into her new position more than adequately.

"I can't say I'm surprised," she said, "but it's nice to know definitely . . . Tony."

A minute before she would never have dreamed of calling him Tony, but it sounded very well.

"As long as we're all in the family," Tony Burton went on, "I was just telling Charley that I've been worried about Blakesley lately. Do you suppose he really may have thought that he was being considered?"

"Now that you mention it," Nancy said, "I think perhaps he did—a little."